FORTY THOUSAND QUOTATIONS

PROSE AND POETICAL

Choice extracts on History, Science, Philosophy,
Religion, Literature, etc. Selected from
the standard authors of ancient
and modern times, classified
according to subject.

COMPILED BY

CHARLES NOEL DOUGLAS

NEW YORK
GEORGE SULLY AND COMPANY

INTRODUCTION

The mission of this work is to supply a universal need, which is felt by the multitude of busy men and women of to-day, who, while eager to be initiated into the society of the great masters of literature, find it impossible to devote the time necessary to such studies as would accomplish that result. One to whom books are as strangers has not yet learned to live. He is a solitary, though he dwell amid a vast population. On the other hand, he to whom books are as friends possesses a Key to the Garden of Delights, where the purest pleasures are open for his entertainment, and where he has for his companions the master minds of all the ages.

Coleridge, writing nearly a century ago, asked: "Why are not more gems from our great authors scattered over the country? Great books are not in everybody's reach; and though it is better to know them thoroughly than to know them only here and there, yet it is a good work to give a little to those who have neither the time nor the means to get more."

In *Forty Thousand Quotations*, the busy man of affairs, the teacher and preacher. the public speaker, lawyer and writer, the man or woman who desires to make a creditable figure in conversation, correspondence or debate, in fact, the reader and student of either sex and any age, may turn at will to the choicest and most striking passages of the illustrious authors, orators and thinkers of all time, from the classic age to the present day. It will open, as with a magic key, the gateways of literature, and the realm of books will no longer be a *terra incognita*, since here are to be found the literary treasures of the ripest scholarship and the finest culture the world has ever known.

In making a collection of such magnitude, and from so many diverse sources, care has been exercised to render the indices, classification and general arrangement so simple that they can be mastered at a glance. One thousand four hundred topics are treated, covering almost the entire range of thought and emotion.

Famous classic, medieval and modern writers have contributed their quota. Here we have the loftiest strains of the poets, the highest flights of the orators, the keenest logic of the essayists, the strongest situations of the dramatists, the brightest *bons mots* of the humorists. Here are the flashes of genius that have stirred the souls of men, the famous epigrams, maxims, aphorisms, adages, similes and other utterances that have excited the world's admiration or amusement. A noted author once remarked that a dozen lines from a writer's works, familiar to the people after twenty years, constituted literary immortality. This volume is a Pantheon of Immortals in splendid array—rank upon rank of the novelists, poets, orators, philosophers, wits, sages, historians, scientists, statesmen, represented by utterances wherewith they have inspired and delighted men and women of every age.

There are many ways in which a work of this character can be made of great value to the reader and student, whatever may be his or her vocation in life. Take the best thoughts on the topic selected; read them; write them down; repeat them; make them your own, and they will become a part of your life and an influence on your career. You will find unconsciously that your mental horizon will be widened, your address enriched, and even your letters will acquire a polish which would be unattainable through other means. The art of apt quotation, happy simile, and pleasing witticism, is within your reach. Grace and power in writing and speaking do not consist in the employment of commonplace phrase and adjective, but come by studying the best models, and so also do the flexibility, range of expression and felicitous illustration which hold the ear, while they carry force and conviction to the mind.

George Eliot calls such a collection as this "The flowers of all books," and never was description more felicitous. Joubert, writing on the same subject, said "The coin of wisdom is its great thoughts, its eloquent flights, its proverbs and pithy sentences." That coin, struck at the mint of genius, is here in abundant measure.

This new and revised edition of *Forty Thousand Quotations* was first published as *Forty Thousand Sublime and Beautiful Thoughts*.

A

Ability

Ability is of little account without opportunity. — Napoleon I.

Ability is a poor man's wealth.—Matthew Wren.

Ability in a man is knowledge which emanates from divine light.—Zoroaster.

Ability involves responsibility. Power to its last particle is duty.—Maclaren.

The winds and waves are always on the side of the ablest navigators.—Gibbon.

Consider well what your strength is equal to, and what exceeds your ability.—Horace.

Ability wins us the esteem of the true men ; luck that of the people.—La Rochefoucauld.

Exigencies create the necessary ability to meet and to conquer them.—Wendell Phillips.

An able man shows his spirit by gentle words and resolute actions.—Chesterfield.

Every person is responsible for all the good within the scope of his abilities, and for no more.—Gail Hamilton.

The art of using moderate abilities to advantage wins praise, and often acquires more reputation than actual brilliancy.—La Rochefoucauld.

As we advance in life we learn the limits of our abilities.—Froude.

The wicked are always surprised to find ability in the good.—Vauvenargues.

Men, like bullets, go farthest when they are smoothest.—Jean Paul Richter.

I pride myself in recognizing and upholding ability in every party and wherever I meet it.—Beaconsfield.

To become an able man in any profession, there are three things necessary,—nature, study, and practice.—Aristotle.

We judge ourselves by what we feel capable of doing, while others judge us by what we have already done.—Longfellow.

You are a devil at everything, and there is no kind of thing in the 'versal world but what you can turn your hand to.—Cervantes.

Who does the best his circumstance allows, Does well, acts nobly ; angels could no more.—Young.

Men who undertake considerable things, even in a regular way, ought to give us ground to presume ability.—Burke.

The measure of capacity is the measure of sphere to either man or woman.—Elizabeth Oakes Smith.

The possession of great powers no doubt carries with it a contempt for mere external show.—James A. Garfield.

Natural ability can almost compensate for the want of every kind of cultivation; but no cultivation of the mind can make up for the want of natural ability.—Schopenhauer.

> Read my little fable:
> He that runs may read.
> Most can raise the flowers now,
> For all have got the seed.
> —Tennyson.

To the very last, he [Napoleon] had a kind of idea; that, namely, of *la carriere ouverte aux talent*—the tools to him that can handle them.— Sir Walter Scott.

No man is without some quality, by the due application of which he might deserve well of the world; and whoever he be that has but little in his power should be in haste to do that little, lest he be confounded with him that can do nothing.—Dr. Johnson.

> He could raise scruples dark and nice,
> And after solve 'em in a trice;
> As if Divinity had catch'd
> The itch, on purpose to be scratch'd.
> —Butler.

> There's in him stuff that puts him to these ends;
> For being not propped up by ancestry whose grace
> Chalks successors their way; nor called upon
> For high feats done to the crown; neither allied
> To eminent assistants; but, spider-like,
> Out of his self-drawing web, he gives us note;
> The force of his own merit makes his way;
> A gift that heaven gives for him, which buys
> A place next to a king. —Shakespeare.

Absence

Conspicuous by his absence.—Tacitus.

> Absence makes the heart grow fonder;
> Isle of Beauty, fare thee well!
> —T. H. Bayley.

Judicious absence is a weapon.— Charles Reade.

Thinking of thee, still thee, till thought grew pain.—Moore.

I dote on his very absence.—Shakespeare.

Absence is all love's crime.—Beaumont and Fletcher.

It is absence that tries fidelity.— Mrs. J. Hunter.

The absent feel and fear every ill.— Cervantes.

Achilles absent, was Achilles still.— Homer.

I believe absence is a great element of charm.—Beaconsfield.

Short absence quickens love; long absence kills it.—Mirabeau.

> In the hope to meet
> Shortly again, and make our absence sweet.
> —Ben Jonson.

Authors and lovers always suffer some infatuation, from which only absence can set them free.—Dr. Johnson.

Where'er I roam, whatever realms to see, my heart, untravelled, fondly turns to thee.—Goldsmith.

> There's little pleasure in the house
> When our gudeman's awa.
> —W. J. Mickle.

> Ever absent, ever near;
> Still I see thee, still I hear;
> Yet I cannot reach thee, dear!
> —Francis Kazinczy.

'Tis sweet to know there is an eye will mark our coming, and look brighter when we come.—Byron.

> Wives in their husbands' absences grow subtler,
> And daughters sometimes run off with the butler. —Byron.

> Thou art gone from my gaze like a beautiful dream,
> And I seek thee in vain by the meadow and stream. —George Linley.

> The joys of meeting pay the pangs of absence,
> Else who could bear it? —Rowe.

As contraries are known by contraries, so is the delight of presence best

known by the torments of absence.—
Alcibiades.

All days are nights to see till I see thee,
And nights bright days when dreams do
  show thee me.   —Shakespeare.

Condemned whole years in absence to deplore,
And image charms he must behold no more.
    —Pope.

Your absence of mind we have borne,
till your presence of body came to be
called in question by it.—Charles
Lamb.

'Tis said that absence conquers love;
  But oh! believe it not.
I've tried, alas! its power to prove,
  But thou art not forgot.
    —Frederick W. Thomas.

Days of absence, sad and dreary;
  Clothed in sorrow's dark array,—
Days of absence, I am weary;
  She I love is far away.
    —Rousseau.

I have this while with leaden thoughts
  been press'd;
But I shall, in a more continuate time,
Strike off this score of absence.
    —Shakespeare.

Oft in the tranquil hour of night
  When stars illume the sky,
I gaze upon each orb of light,
  And wish that thou wert by.
    —George Linley.

Ye flowers that droop forsaken by the
  spring;
Ye birds that left by summer cease to sing;
Yet trees that fade when autumn heats remove,
Say, is not absence death to those who
  love?   —Pope.

Where'er I roam, whatever realms to see,
My heart untravelled, fondly turns to thee;
Still to my brother turns, with ceaseless
  pain,
And drags at each remove a lengthening
  chain.   —Goldsmith.

How like a winter hath my absence been
  From thee, the pleasure of the fleeting
  year!
What freezings have I felt, what dark days
  seen!
What old December's bareness everywhere.

Not to understand a treasure's worth
till time has stole away the slighted
good, is cause of half the poverty we

feel, and makes the world the wilderness it is.—Cowper.

O thou who dost inhabit in my breast,
Leave not the mansion so long tenantless;
Lest growing ruinous the building fall,
And leave no memory of what it was.
    —Shakespeare.

What shall I do with all the days and hours
  That must be counted ere I see thy face?
How shall I charm the interval that lowers
  Between this time and that sweet time
    of grace?
    —Frances Anne Kemble.

In my Lucia's absence
Life hangs upon me, and becomes a burden;
I am ten times undone, while hope, and
  fear,
And grief, and rage and love rise up at
  once,
And with variety of pain distract me.
    —Addison.

What! keep a week away? seven days and
  nights?
Eight score hours? and lovers' absent hours,
More tedious than the dial eight score
  times?
O weary reckoning!   —Shakespeare.

Absence extinguishes small passions
and increases great ones, as the wind
will blow out a candle and blow in a
fire.—La Rochefoucauld.

With what a deep devotedness of woe
I wept thy absence—o'er and o'er again
Thinking of thee, still thee, till thought
  grew pain,
And memory, like a drop that, night and
  day,
Falls cold and ceaseless, wore my heart
  away!   —Moore.

Since you have waned from us,
  Fairest of women!
I am a darkened cage
  Songs cannot hymn in.
My songs have followed you,
  Like birds the summer;
Ah! bring them back to me,
  Swiftly, dear comer!
    Seraphim,
  Her to hymn,
  Might leave their portals;
  And at my feet learn
  The harping of mortals!
    —Francis Thompson.

Absent

Absent in body, but present in spirit.
—St. Paul.

Absolution

No man taketh away sins (which
the law, though holy, just and good,

could not take away), but He in whom there is no sin.—Bede.

It appertaineth to the true God alone to be able to loose men from their sins.—St. Cyril.

He alone can remit sins who is appointed our Master by the Father of all; He only is able to discern obedience from disobedience.—St. Clement of Alexandria.

Neither angel, nor archangel, nor yet even the Lord Himself (who alone can say "I am with you"), can, when we have sinned, release us, unless we bring repentance with us.—St. Ambrose.

It is not the ambassador, it is not the messenger, but the Lord Himself that saveth His people. The Lord remaineth alone, for no man can be partner with God in forgiving sins; this office belongs solely to Christ, who taketh away the sins of the world.—St. Ambrose.

Abstinence

Abstinence is approved of God.—Chaucer.

Abstinence is the surety of temperance.—Plato.

Too much is a vanity; enough is a feast.—Quarles.

Abstinence is the great strengthener and clearer of reason.—South.

Abstinence is many times very helpful to the end of religion.—Tillotson.

Abstaining is favorable both to the head and the pocket.—Horace Greeley.

Abstaining so as really to enjoy, is the epicurism, the very perfection, of reason.—Rousseau.

The more a man denies himself, the more shall he obtain from God.—Horace.

By forbearing to do what may innocently be done, we may add hourly new vigor to resolution.—Dr. Johnson.

Abstinence is as easy to me as temperance would be difficult.—Samuel Johnson.

Abstinence is whereby a man refraineth from anything which he may lawfully take.—Elyot.

Against diseases here the strongest fence Is the defensive virtue, abstinence.
—Herrick.

To set the mind above the appetites is the end of abstinence, which one of the Fathers observes to be, not a virtue, but the groundwork of a virtue.—Johnson.

A rich man cannot enjoy a sound mind nor a sound body without exercise and abstinence; and yet these are truly the worst ingredients of poverty.—Lord Kames.

His life is parallel'd
E'en with the stroke and line of his great justice;
He doth with holy abstinence subdue
That in himself which he spurs on his power
To qualify in others. —Shakespeare.

We read of a fountain in Arabia upon whose basin is inscribed, "Drink, and away;" but how delicious is that hasty draught, and how long and brightly the thought of its transient refreshment dwells in the memory.—Tuckerman.

Never add artificial heat to thy body by wine or spice until thou findest that time hath decayed thy natural heat.—Sir Walter Raleigh.

Abstract

Brief abstract and record of tedious days.—Shakespeare.

They are the abstracts, and brief chronicles of the time.—Shakespeare.

Absurdity

Absurdity refutes itself.—Bartholin.

Do not sanction an absurdity.—Mme. de Genlis.

The greater absurdities are, the

more strongly they evince the falsity of that supposition from whence they flow.—Atterbury.

Absurdities die of self-strangulation. —Haliburton.

Every absurdity has a champion to defend it.—Goldsmith.

Absurdities are great or small in proportion to custom or insuetude.— Landor.

Of all the authorities to which men can be called to submit, the wisdom of our ancestors is the most whimsically absurd.—Jeremy Taylor.

Abundance

In abundance prepare for scarcity. —Mencius.

Abundance changes the value of things.—Terence.

Abundance without discretion is plain penury.—Matteo Gribaldi.

Not what we have, but what we enjoy, constitutes our abundance.—J. Petit-Senn.

For out of the abundance of the heart the mouth speaketh.—Matthew, chap. xii., 34.

Great abundance of riches cannot be gathered and kept by any man without sin.—Erasmus.

Abundance consists not alone in material possession, but in an uncovetous spirit.—Selden.

If I have enough for myself and family, I am steward only for myself; if I have more, I am but a steward of that abundance for others.—George Herbert.

Abuse

Abuse is the weapon of the vulgar. —Goodrich.

It is better a man should be abused than forgotten.—Dr. Johnson.

The weak resort of cowardice.—Colton.

The bitter clamour of two eager tongues.—Shakespeare.

It is the wit, the policy, of sin to hate those men whom we have abused. —Sir W. Davenant.

A calumnious abuse, too often repeated, becomes so familiar to the ear as to lose its effect.

There is a time when the hoary head of inveterate abuse will neither draw reverence nor obtain protection.— Burke.

Abuse is often of service. There is nothing so dangerous to an author as silence. His name, like a shuttlecock, must be beat backward and forward, or it falls to the ground.—Johnson.

Nor aught so good but strained from that fair use,
Revolts from true birth stumbling on abuse, —Shakespeare.

There are more people abusive to others than lie open to abuse themselves; but the humor goes round, and he that laughs at me to-day will have somebody to laugh at him to-morrow. —Seneca.

I never yet heard man or woman much abused, that I was not inclined to think the better of them; and to transfer any suspicion or dislike to the person who appeared to take delight in pointing out the defects of a fellow-creature.—Jane Porter.

Remember that it is not he who gives abuse or blows who affronts, but the view we take of these things as insulting. When, therefore, any one provokes you, be assured that it is your own opinion which provokes you. —Epictetus.

It has been shrewdly said, that when men abuse us we should suspect ourselves, and when they praise us, them. It is a rare instance of virtue to despise censure which we do not deserve; and still more rare to despise praise which we do.—Colton.

Acacia

Light-leaved acacias, by the door,
  Stood up in balmy air,
Clusters of blossomed moonlight bore,
  And breathed a perfume rare.
    —George MacDonald.

Our rocks are rough, but smiling there
Th' acacia waves her yellow hair,
Lonely and sweet, nor loved the less
For flow'ring in a wilderness.
    —Moore.

A great acacia, with its slender trunk
And overpoise of multitudinous leaves,
(In which a hundred fields might spill their dew
And intense verdure, yet find room enough)
Stood reconciling all the place with green.
    —E. B. Browning.

The slender acacia would not shake
One long milk-bloom on the tree;
The white lake-blossom fell into the lake
As the pimpernel dozed on the lea;
But the rose was awake all night for your sake,
  Knowing your promise to me;
The lilies and roses were all awake,
  They sighed for the dawn and thee.
    —Tennyson.

Pluck the acacia's golden balls,
And mark where the red pomegranate falls.
    —Julia C. R. Dorr.

Accent

Accent is the soul of language: it gives to it feeling and truth.—Rousseau.

Accent and emphasis are the pith of reading; punctuation is but secondary.—Disraeli.

Accidents

The accident of an accident.—Lord Thurlow.

Chapter of accidents.—Burke.

Moving accidents by flood and field.—Othello.

By many a happy accident.—Thomas Middleton.

There is no such thing as accident; it is fate misnamed.—Napoleon I.

Nothing with God can be accidental.—Longfellow.

What men call accident is God's own part.—Bailey.

Promptly improve your accidents.—Napoleon I.

Nothing under the sun is accident.—Lessing.

Accident is simply unforeseen order.—Novalis.

The Orientals have another word for accident; it is "kismet,"—fate.—Macaulay.

The just season of doing things must be nicked, and all accidents improved.—L'Estrange.

The chapter of accidents is the longest chapter in the book.—Attributed to John Wilkes.

To what happy accident is it that we owe so unexpected a visit?—Goldsmith.

Our wanton accidents take root, and grow
To vaunt themselves God's laws.
    —Charles Kingsley.

Sometimes there are accidents in our lives the skillful extrication from which demands a little folly.—La Rochefoucauld.

There are no accidents so unfortunate from which skillful men will not draw some advantage, nor so fortunate that foolish men will not turn them to their hurt.—La Rochefoucauld.

Accommodated

That is, when a man is, as they say, accommodated: or where a man is—being—whereby—he may be thought to be accommodated, which is an excellent thing.—Shakespeare.

Accountability

Moral conduct includes every thing in which men are active and for which they are accountable. They are active in their desires, their affections, their designs, their intentions, and in every

thing they say and do of choice; and
for all these things they are accountable to God.—Emmons.

When illusions are over, when the
distractions of sense, the vagaries of
fancy, and the tumults of passion have
dissolved even before the body is cold,
which once they so thronged and agitated, the soul merges into intellect,
intellect into conscience, conscience
into the unbroken, awful solitude of
its own personal accountability; and
though the inhabitants of the universe
were within the spirit's ken, this personal accountability is as strictly
alone and unshared, as if no being
were throughout immensity but the
spirit and its God.—Henry Giles.

Accusation

Give me good proofs of what you have al-
    leged:
'Tis not enough to say—in such a bush
There lies a thief—in such a cave a beast;
But you must show him to me ere I shoot,
Else I may kill one of my straggling sheep.
                    —Shakespeare.

To vouch this is no proof
Without more certain and more overt tests
Than these thin habits and poor likelihoods
Of modern seeming do prefer against him.
                    —Shakespeare.

Aces

On the four aces doom'd to roll.—
Churchill.

We gentlemen, whose chariots roll
only upon the four aces, are apt to
have a wheel out of order.—Sir John
Vanbrugh.

Aches

Up start as many aches in his bones,
as there are ouches in his skin.—
George Chapman.

Can by their pangs and aches find
All turns and changes of the wind.
                    —Butler.

If thou neglect'st, or dost unwillingly
What I command, I'll rack thee with old
    cramps;
Fill all thy bones with aches; make thee
    roar
That beasts shall tremble at thy din.
                    —Shakespeare.

Acknowledgments

What makes false reckoning, as regards gratitude, is that the pride of

the giver and the receiver cannot agree
as to the value of the benefit.—La
Rochefoucauld.

Acquaintances

Make few acquaintances.—Rothschild.

Acquaintance softens prejudice.—
Æsop.

Slight acquaintance breeds distrust.
—Viera.

A long novitiate of acquaintance
should precede the vows of friendship.
—Bolingbroke.

It is good discretion not to make too
much of any man at the first; because
one cannot hold out that proportion.—
Bacon.

Should auld acquaintance be forgot,
  And never brought to min'?
Should auld acquaintance be forgot,
  And days o' auld lang syne?
                    —Burns.

If a man does not make new acquaintances, as he advances through
life, he will soon find himself left alone.
A man should keep his friendship in
constant repair.—Johnson.

Make the most of the day, by determining to spend it on two sorts of acquaintances only—those by whom
something may be got, and those from
whom something may be learned.—
Colton.

There is a wide difference between
general acquaintance and companionship. You may salute a man and exchange compliments with him daily,
yet know nothing of his character, his
inmost tastes and feelings.—Wm. Matthews.

Acquirements

That good sense which nature affords us is preferable to most of the
knowledge that we can acquire.—
Comines.

We shall at all times chance upon
men of recondite acquirements, but
whose qualifications, from the incom-
municative and inactive habits of their

owners, are as utterly useless to others as though the possessors had them not.—Colton.

That which we acquire with the most difficulty we retain the longest; as those who have earned a fortune are usually more careful of it than those who have inherited one.—Colton.

Acting

All the world's a stage.—Shakespeare.

All the world practices the art of acting.—Petronius Arbiter.

Come, sit down, every mother's son, and rehearse your parts. —Shakespeare.

Lo, where the Stage, the poor, degraded Stage,
Holds its warped mirror to a gaping age!
—Charles Sprague.

Who teach the mind its proper face to scan,
And hold the faithful mirror up to man.
—Robert Lloyd.

The play's the thing
Wherein I'll catch the conscience of the king. —Shakespeare.

A fool cannot be an actor, though an actor may act a fool's part.—Sophocles.

The part was aptly fitted and naturally performed.—Shakespeare.

An actor should take lessons from a painter and a sculptor.—Goethe.

Where they do agree on the stage, then unanimity is wonderful.—Sheridan.

They wear the livery of other men's fortunes; their very thoughts are not their own.—Hazlitt.

The concealment of art by the actor is as great a mark of genius as it is in the painter.—François Delsarte.

Let those that play your clowns speak no more than is set down for them.—Shakespeare.

To see Kean act was like reading Shakespeare by flashes of lightning.—Coleridge.

Let gorgeous Tragedy, in sceptred pall, come sweeping by.—Milton.

Comedians are not actors; they are only imitators of actors.—Zimmerman.

On the stage he was natural, simple, affecting,
'Twas only that when he was off, he was acting. —Goldsmith.

The world's a theatre, the earth a stage,
Which God and Nature do with actors fill.
—Thomas Heywood.

The drama's laws, the drama's patrons give.
For we that live to please, must please to live. —Samuel Johnson.

And what the actor could effect,
The scholar could presage.
—Thomas Campbell.

Even kings but play; and when their part is done, some other, worse or better, mounts the throne.—Dryden.

See, how these rascals use me! They will not let my play run; and yet they steal my thunder.—John Dennis.

To-day kings, to-morrow beggars, it is only when they are themselves that they are nothing.—Hazlitt.

The most difficult character in comedy is that of the fool, and he must be no simpleton that plays that part. —Cervantes.

God is the author, men are only the players. These grand pieces which are played upon earth have been composed in heaven.—Balzac.

A long, exact, and serious comedy;
In every scene some moral let it teach,
And, if it can, at once both please and preach. —Pope.

The play bill which is said to have announced the tragedy of Hamlet, the character of the Prince of Denmark being left out.—Scott.

The stage is a supplement to the pulpit, where virtue, according to Plato's sublime idea, moves our love and affection when made visible to the eye. —Disraeli.

In really good acting we should be able to believe that what we hear and see is of our own imagining; it should seem to us as a charming dream.— Joubert.

I can counterfeit the deep tragedian;
Speak and look back, and pry on every side,
Tremble and start at wagging of a straw,
Intending deep suspicion. —Shakespeare.

Is it not a noble farce wherein kings, republics, and emperors have for so many ages played their parts, and to which the vast universe serves for a theatre?—Montaigne.

Everybody has his own theatre, in which he is manager, actor, prompter, playwright, sceneshifter, boxkeeper, doorkeeper, all in one, and audience into the bargain.—J. C. and A. W. Hare.

As in a theatre, the eyes of men,
After a well-grac'd actor leaves the stage,
Are idly bent on him that enters next,
Thinking his prattle to be tedious.
—Shakespeare.

In other things the knowing artist may
Judge better than the people; but a play,
(Made for delight, and for no other use)
If you approve it not, has no excuse.
—Edmund Waller.

I have seen no men in life loving their profession so much as painters, except, perhaps, actors, who, when not engaged themselves, always go to the play.—Thackeray.

It is their province to make the public weep and smile, tremble and resent, and to light all the passions of the human breast in their enthusiastic audiences.—G. A. Sala.

Who rant by note, and through the gamut rage; in songs and airs express their martial fire; combat in trills, and in a fugue expire.—Addison.

Notwithstanding all that Rousseau has advanced so very ingeniously upon plays and players, their profession is, like that of a painter, one of the imi-

tative arts, whose means are pleasure, and whose end is virtue.—Shenstone.

Johnson told Garrick that he and his profession were mutually indebted to each other. "Your profession," said the doctor, "has made you rich; and you have made your profession respectable."—Colton.

It is with some violence to the imagination that we conceive of an actor belonging to the relations of private life, so closely do we identify these persons in our mind with the characters which they assume upon the stage. —Lamb.

The actor is in the capacity of a steward to every living muse, and of an executor to every departed one: the poet digs up the ore; he sifts it from the dross, refines and purifies it for the mint; the actor sets the stamp upon it, and makes it current in the world.—Cumberland.

Few men of any modern nation have a proper sense of an æsthetical whole: they praise and blame by parts; they are charmed by passages. And who has greater reason to rejoice in this than actors, since the stage is ever but a patched and piecemeal matter?— Goethe.

Players, sir! I look upon them as no better than creatures set upon tables and joint-stools to make faces and produce laughter, like dancing dogs.— But, sir, you will allow that some players are better than others?—Yes, sir; as some dogs dance better than others.—Dr. Johnson.

Remember that you are but an actor, acting whatever part the Master has ordained. It may be short or it may be long. If he wishes you to represent a poor man, do so heartily; if a cripple, or a magistrate, or a private man, in each case act your part with honor. —Epictetus.

Victor Hugo makes one of his heroines—an actress—say, "My art endows me with a searching eye, a knowledge of the soul and the soul's workings;

and, spite of all your skill, I read you to the depths." This is a truth more or less powerful, as one is more or less gifted by the good God.—Charlotte Cushman.

And, like a strutting player, whose conceit
Lies in his hamstring, and doth think it rich
To hear the wooden dialogue and sound
'Twixt his stretch'd footing and the scaf-
foldage —Shakespeare.

Is it not monstrous that this player here,
But in a fiction, in a dream of passion,
Could force his soul so to his own conceit
That from her working all his visage
wann'd. —Shakespeare.

A play there is, my lord, some ten words
long,
Which is as brief as I have known a play;
But by ten words, my lord, it is too long,
Which makes it tedious. —Shakespeare.

There is one way by which a strolling player may be ever secure of success; that is, in our theatrical way of
expressing it, to make a great deal of
the character. To speak and act as in
common life is not playing, nor is it
what people come to see; natural
speaking, like sweet wine, runs glibly
over the palate, and scarcely leaves
any taste behind it; but being high in
a part resembles vinegar, which grates
upon the taste, and one feels it while
he is drinking.—Goldsmith.

What's Hecuba to him, or he to Hecuba,
That he should weep for her? What would
he do,
Had he the motive and the cue for passion
That I have? He would drown the stage
with tears. —Shakespeare.

To wake the soul by tender strokes of art,
To raise the genius, and to mend the heart;
To make mankind, in conscious virtue bold,
Live o'er each scene, and be what they be-
hold—
For this the tragic Muse first trod the stage.
—Pope.

It's very hard! Oh, Dick, my boy,
It's very hard one can't enjoy
A little private spouting;
But sure as Lear or Hamlet lives,
Up comes our master, Bounce! and gives
The tragic Muse a routing.
—Hood.

Good, my lord, will you see the players well bestowed? Do you hear, let
them be well used; for they are the
abstract and brief chronicles of the
time: after your death you were better
have a bad epitaph than their ill report while you live.—Shakespeare.

I have heard
That guilty creatures sitting at a play,
Have, by the very cunning of the scene,
Been struck so to the soul that presently
They have proclaim'd their malefactions;
For murder, though it have no tongue, will
speak
With most miraculous organ.
—Shakespeare.

O, there be players that I have seen
play, and heard others praise, and that
highly, not to speak it profanely, that,
neither having the accent of Christians
nor the gait of Christian, pagan, nor
man, have so strutted and bellowed
that I have thought some of nature's
journeymen had made men and not
made them well, they imitated humanity so abominably.—Shakespeare.

The play is done; the curtain drops,
Slow falling to the prompter's bell:
A moment yet the actor stops,
And looks around, to say farewell.
It is an irksome word and task:
And, when he's laughed and said his
say,
He shows, as he removes the mask,
A face that's anything but gay.
—Thackeray.

Like hungry guests, a sitting audience looks:
Plays are like suppers; poets are the cooks.
The founder's you: the table is this place:
The carvers we: the prologue is the grace.
Each act, a course, each scene, a different
dish,
Though we're in Lent, I doubt you're still
for flesh.
Satire's the sauce, high-season'd, sharp and
rough.
Kind masks and beaux, I hope you're pep-
per-proof?
Wit is the wine; but 'tis so scarce the true
Poets, like vintners, balderdash and brew.
Your surly scenes, where rant and blood-
shed join,
Are butcher's meat, a battle's a sirloin:
Your scenes of love, so flowing, soft and
chaste,
Are water-gruel without salt or taste.
—George Farquhar.

I think I love and reverence all arts
equally, only putting my own just
above the others; because in it I recognize the union and culmination of
my own. To me it seems as if when

God conceived the world, that was Poetry; He formed it, and that was Sculpture; He colored it, and that was Painting; He peopled it with living beings, and that was the grand, divine, eternal Drama.—Charlotte Cushman.

Speak the speech, I pray you, as I pronounced it to you, trippingly on the tongue; but if you mouth it, as many of your players do, I had as lief the town-crier spoke my lines. Nor do not saw the air too much with your hand, thus, but use all gently; for in the very torrent, tempest, and, as I may say, the whirlwind of passion, you must acquire and beget a temperance that may give it smoothness.—Shakespeare.

Action

Let us do or die.—Campbell.

Push on,—keep moving.—Thomas Morton.

There is only one proof of ability,—action.—Marie Ebner-Eschenbach.

To the valiant actions speak alone.—Smollett.

Action, so to speak, is the genius of nature.—Blair.

We cannot all do all things.—Virgil.

The food of hope is meditative action.—Bulwer-Lytton.

Strong reasons make strong actions.—Shakespeare.

Time is short; your obligations are infinite.—Massillon.

Put his shoulder to the wheel.—Burton.

A bold onset is half the battle.—Garibaldi.

The act of God injures no one.—Juvenal.

Be great in act, as you have been in thought.—Shakespeare.

What the Puritans gave the world was not thought, but action.—Wendell Phillips.

And all may do what has by man been done.—Young.

Awake, arise, or be forever fall'n!—Milton.

Gentle in method, resolute in action.—From the Latin.

It is well to think well: it is divine to act well.—Horace Mann.

It is better to wear out than to rust out.—Bishop Cumberland.

Do well and right, and let the world sink.—Herbert.

It is praiseworthy even to attempt a great action.—La Rochefoucauld.

Do not do what is already done.—Terence.

Heaven ne'er helps the men who will not act.—Sophocles.

The thing done avails, and not what is said about it.—Emerson.

The Lord is a God of knowledge, and by Him actions are weighed.—I Samuel ii. 3

Never do an act of which you doubt the justice or propriety.—Latin.

Our actions are our own; their consequences belong to Heaven.—Francis.

Only the actions of the just
Smell sweet and blossom in the dust.
—James Shirley.

How much easier do we find it to commend a good action than to imitate it.—Anon.

Of every noble action the intent
Is to give worth reward—vice punishment
—Beaumont and Fletcher.

I profess not talking: only this,
Let each man do his best.
—Shakespeare.

The end of man is an action, and

not a thought, though it were the noblest.—Carlyle.

Activity is the presence of function, —character is the record of function. —Greenough.

The flighty purpose never is o'ertook unless the deed go with it.—Shakespeare.

All power appears only in transition. Permanent power is stuff.—Novalis.

Remember that in all miseries lamenting becomes fools, and action, wise folk.—Sir P. Sidney.

Our acts make or mar us,—we are the children of our own deeds.—Victor Hugo.

A stirring dwarf we do allowance give before a sleeping giant.—Shakespeare.

The only true method of action in this world is to be in it, but not of it. —Madame Swetchine.

Our actions are like the terminations of verses, which we rhyme as we please.—Rochefoucauld.

Speak out in acts; the time for words has passed, and deeds alone suffice.—Whittier.

When we cannot act as we wish, we must act as we can.—Terrence.

To be active is the primary vocation of man.—Goethe.

Our actions must clothe us with an immortality loathsome or glorious.— Colton.

Be slow in considering, but resolute in action.—Bias.

Nothing is more terrible than to see ignorance in action.—Goethe.

'T is human actions paint the chart of time.—Montgomery.

Men do less than they ought unless they do all that they can.—Carlyle.

Action is the parent of results; dormancy, the brooding mother of discontent.—Miss Mulock.

Action is happiness here; and without action there can be no heaven.— Voss.

The life of action is nobler than the life of thought.—Miss Mulock.

Living requires but little life; doing requires much.—Joubert.

The best way to keep good acts in memory is to refresh them with new. —Cato.

Action is eloquence, and the eyes of the ignorant are more learned than their ears.—Shakespeare.

The manly part is to do with might and main what you can do.—Emerson.

Active natures are rarely melancholy. Activity and melancholy are incompatible.—Bovee.

Our acts, our angels are, or good or ill,
Our fatal shadows that walk by us still.
—John Fletcher.

So much one man can do,
That does both act and know.
—Andrew Marvell.

Think that day lost whose (low) descending Sun
Views from thy hand no noble action done.
—Jacob Bobart.

A great mind is a good sailor, as a great heart is.—Emerson.

For good or evil must in our actions meet;
Wicked is not much worse than indiscreet.
—Donne.

How my achievements mock me!
I will go meet them.
—Shakespeare.

Not always actions show the man; we find
Who does a kindness is not therefore kind.
—Pope.

Action is transitory, a step, a blow,
The motion of a muscle—this way or that.
—Wordsworth.

Action may not always bring happiness; but there is no happiness without action.—Beaconsfield.

So smile the Heavens upon this holy act
That after hours with sorrow chide us not!
—Shakespeare.

He is at no end of his actions blest
Whose ends will make him greatest and not
best. —George Chapman.

If it were done, when 'tis done, then 'twere
well
It were done quickly. —Shakespeare.

Celerity is never more admired than by the negligent.—Shakespeare.

Act well at the moment, and you have performed a good action to all eternity.—Lavater.

Attempt the end, and never stand to
doubt;
Nothing's so hard but search will find it out.
—Herrick.

That action which appears most conducive to the happiness and virtue of mankind.—Frances Hutcheson.

When desperate ills demand a speedy cure,
Distrust is cowardice, and prudence folly.
—Samuel Johnson.

Attack is the reaction; I never think I have hit hard unless it rebounds.—Sam'l Johnson.

I have always thought the actions of men the best interpreters of their thoughts.—Locke.

Deliberate with caution, but act with decision; and yield with graciousness, or oppose with firmness.—Colton.

The firefly only shines when on the wing; so is it with the mind; when once we rest, we darken.—Bailey.

Men's actions to futurity appear but as the events to which they are conjoined do give them consequence.—Joanna Baillie.

It is vain to expect any advantage from our profession of the truth, if we be not sincerely just and honest in our actions.—Archbishop Sharpe.

Thought and theory must precede all action that moves to salutary purposes. Yet action is nobler in itself than either thought or theory.—Wordsworth.

Hast thou not Greek enough to understand thus much: the end of man is an action and not a thought, though it were of the noblest.—Carlyle.

Toil, feel, think, hope. A man is sure to dream enough before he dies without making arrangements for the purpose.—Sterling.

Action is the highest perfection and drawing forth of the utmost power, vigor, and activity of man's nature.—South.

Advise well before you begin, and when you have maturely considered, then act with promptitude.—Sallust.

With devotion's visage,
And pious action, we do sugar o'er
The devil himself. —Shakespeare.

Idlers cannot even find time to be idle, or the industrious to be at leisure. We must always be doing or suffering.—Zimmermann.

We must not stint
Our necessary actions, in the fear
To cope malicious censurers.
—Shakespeare.

Those graceful acts,
Those thousand decencies that daily flow
From all her words and actions.
—Milton.

Our grand business undoubtedly is, not to see what lies dimly at a distance, but to do what lies clearly at hand.—Carlyle.

Prodigious actions may as well be done
By weaver's issue, as by prince's son.
—Dryden.

Theirs not to make reply,
Theirs not to reason why,
Theirs but to do and die.
—Tennyson.

Although men flatter themselves with their great actions, they are not so often the result of a great design as of chance.—La Rochefoucauld.

Every man feels instinctively that all the beautiful sentiments in the world weigh less than a single lovely action.—Lowell.

What is there that you enter upon so favorably as not to repent of the undertaking and the accomplishment of your wish?—Juvenal.

For strong souls
Live like fire-hearted suns; to spend their strength
In furthest striving action.
—George Eliot.

All our actions take
Their hues from the complexion of the heart,
As landscapes their variety from light.
—W. T. Bacon.

Statesman, yet friend to truth! of soul sincere,
In action faithful, and in honour clear;
Who broke no promise, served no private end.
—Pope.

How slow the time to the warm soul, that, in the very instant it forms, would execute a great design!—Thomson.

We should often be ashamed of our very best actions, if the world only saw the motives which caused them.—La Rochefoucauld.

A contemplative life has more the appearance of a life of piety than any other; but it is the Divine plan to bring faith into activity and exercise.—Cecil.

I have lived to know that the secret of happiness is never to allow your energies to stagnate.—Adam Clarke.

Life is a short day; but it is a working-day. Activity may lead to evil; but inactivity cannot be led to good.—Hannah More.

Man is an animal that cannot long be left in safety without occupation; the growth of his fallow nature is apt to run into weeds.—Hillard.

When our souls shall leave this dwelling, the glory of one fair and virtuous action is above all the 'scutch-eons on our tomb, or silken banners over us.—J. Shirley.

Suit the action to the word, the word to the action, with this special observance, that you o'erstep not the modesty of nature.—Shakespeare.

This world is but the vestibule of an immortal life. Every action of our lives touches on some chord that will vibrate in eternity.—Chapin.

There is no secret of the heart which our actions do not disclose.—Molière.

There is no action so slight or so mean but it may be done to a great purpose, and ennobled thereby.—Ruskin.

Deeds always overbalance; and downright practice speaks more plainly than the fairest profession.—South.

No two things differ more than hurry and despatch. Hurry is the mark of a weak mind; despatch of a strong one.—Colton.

Press on! for in the grave there is no work and no device. Press on! while yet you may.—N. P. Willis.

Let thy mind still be bent, still plotting, where,
And when, and how thy business may be done,
Slackness breeds worms; but the sure traveller,
Though he alights sometimes, still goeth on.
—Herbert.

Let us then be up and doing,
With a heart for any fate;
Still achieving, still pursuing,
Learn to labor and to wait.
—Longfellow.

Remember you have not a sinew whose law of strength is not action; you have not a faculty of body, mind, or soul whose law of improvement is not energy.—E. B. Hall.

There is no action of man in this life which is not the beginning of so long a chain of consequences, as that no human providence is high enough to give us a prospect to the end.—Thomas of Malmesbury.

To live is not merely to breathe: it is to act; it is to make use of our organs, senses, faculties,—of all those parts of ourselves which give us the feeling of existence.—Rousseau.

The life of man is made up of action and endurance; and life is fruitful in the ratio in which it is laid out in noble action or in patient perseverance.—H. P. Liddon.

Those who labor to make human actions harmonize, find great difficulty in piecing them together; for, in general, they contradict each other.—Montaigne.

It is hard to personate and act a part long; for where Truth is not at the bottom, Nature will always be endeavoring to return, and will peep out and betray herself one time or other.—Tillotson.

Man, being essentially active, must find in activity his joy, as well as his beauty and glory; and labor, like everything else that is good, is its own reward.—Whipple.

Judge not of actions by their mere effect;
Dive to the centre, and the cause detect;
Great deeds from meanest springs may take their course,
And smallest virtues from a mighty source.
     —Pope.

Let's take the instant by the forward top; for we are old, and on our quickest decrees, the inaudible and noiseless foot of time steals, ere we can effect them.—Shakespeare.

That low man seeks a little thing to do,
Sees it and does it;
This high man, with a great thing to pursue,
Dies ere he knows it.
     —Robert Browning.

Rightness expresses of actions, what straightness does of lines; and there can no more be two kinds of right action than there can be two kinds of straight line.—Herbert Spencer.

I do not say the mind gets informed by action, bodily action; but it does get earnestness and strength by it, and that nameless something that gives a man the mastership of his faculties.—Mountford.

Unselfish and noble acts are the most radiant epochs in the biography of souls. When wrought in earliest youth, they lie in the memory of age like the coral islands, green and sunny, amidst the melancholy waste of ocean.—Rev. Dr. Thomas.

It is not to taste sweet things, but to do noble and true things, and vindicate himself under God's heaven as a God-made man, that the poorest son of Adam dimly longs. Show him the way of doing that, the dullest daydrudge kindles into a hero.—Carlyle.

It is good policy to strike while the iron is hot; it is still better to adopt Cromwell's procedure, and make the iron hot by striking. The master-spirit who can rule the storm is great, but he is much greater who can both raise and rule it.—E. L. Magoon.

Do not be afraid because the community teems with excitement. Silence and death are dreadful. The rush of life, the vigor of earnest men, the conflict of realities, invigorate, cleanse, and establish the truth.—Beecher.

All the means of action—the shapeless masses, the materials—lie everywhere about us; what we need is the celestial fire to change the flint into transparent crystal, bright and clear.—Longfellow.

Let us, if we must have great actions, make our own so. All action is of infinite elasticity, and the least admits of being inflated with celestial air, until it eclipses the sun and moon.—Emerson.

What a man knows should find its expression in what he does. The value of superior knowledge is chiefly in that it leads to a performing manhood.—Bovee.

Actions rare and sudden do commonly proceed from fierce necessity, or else from some oblique design, which is ashamed to show itself in the public road.—Sir W. Davenant.

With a double vigilance should we watch our actions, when we reflect that good and bad ones are never childless, and that in both cases the offspring goes beyond the parent,—every good begetting a better, every bad a worse.—Chatfield.

You had that action and counteraction which in the natural and in the political world, from the reciprocal struggle of discordant powers, draws out the harmony of the universe.—Edmund Burke.

Every event that a man would master must be mounted on the run, and no man ever caught the reins of a thought except as it galloped by him. —Holmes.

Indolence is a delightful but distressing state; we must be doing something to be happy. Action is no less necessary than thought to the instinctive tendencies of the human frame.—Hazlitt.

Better that we should err in action than wholly refuse to perform. The storm is so much better than the calm, as it declares the presence of a living principle. Stagnation is something worse than death. It is corruption also.—Simms.

To do an evil action is base; to do a good action, without incurring danger, is common enough; but it is the part of a good man to do great and noble deeds, though he risks everything.—Plutarch.

Action hangs, as it were, "dissolved" in speech, in thoughts whereof speech is the shadow; and precipitates itself therefrom. The kind of speech in a man betokens the kind of action you will get from him.—Carlyle.

If you think you can temper yourself into manliness by sitting there over your books, it is the very silliest fancy that ever tempted a young man to his ruin. You cannot dream yourself into a character: you must hammer and forge yourself one.—Froude.

The activity of the young is like that of rail cars in motion,—they tear along with noise and turmoil, and leave peace behind them. The quietest nooks, invaded by them, lose their quietude as they pass, and recover it only on their departure. Time's best gift to us is serenity.—Bovee.

"There is nothing so terrible as activity without insight," says Goethe "I would open every one of Argus' hundred eyes before I used one of Briareus' hundred hands," says Lord Bacon. "Look before you leap," says John Smith, all over the world.—Whipple.

Allowing the performance of an honorable action to be attended with labor, the labor is soon over, but the honor is immortal; whereas, should even pleasure wait on the commission of what is dishonorable, the pleasure is soon gone, but the dishonor is eternal.—John Stewart.

A slender acquaintance with the world must convince every man that actions, not words, are the true criterion of the attachment of friends; and that the most liberal professions of good-will are very far from being the surest marks of it.—George Washington.

Man is born for action; he ought to do something. Work, at each step, awakens a sleeping force and roots out error. Who does nothing, knows nothing. Rise! to work! If thy knowledge is real, employ it; wrestle with nature; test the strength of thy theories; see if they will support the trial; act!—Aloysius.

Not alone to know, but to act according to thy knowledge, is thy destination,—proclaims the voice of my inmost soul. Not for indolent contemplation and study of thyself, nor for brooding over emotions of piety,—no, for action was existence given thee; thy actions, and thy actions alone. determine thy worth.—Fichte.

Act! the wise are known by their actions; fame and immortality are ever their attendants. Mark with deeds the vanishing traces of swift-rolling time. Let us make happy the circle around us,—be useful as much as we may. For that fills up with soft rapture, that dissolves the dark clouds of the day!—Salis.

Words are good, but there is something better. The best is not to be explained by words. The spirit in which we act is the chief matter. Action can only be understood and represented by the spirit. No one knows what he is doing while he is acting rightly, but of what is wrong we are always conscious.—Goethe.

Newton's great generalization, which he called the "third law of motion," was that "Action and reaction are always equal to each other;" and that law has been one of the most pregnant of all truths about the mystery of force,—one of the brightest windows through which modern eyes have looked into the world of Nature.—Phillips Brooks.

Wouldst thou know the lawfulness of the action which thou desirest to undertake, let thy devotion recommend it to Divine blessing: if it be lawful, thou shalt perceive thy heart encouraged by thy prayer; if unlawful, thou shalt find thy prayer discouraged by thy heart. That action is not warrantable which either blushes to beg a blessing, or, having succeeded, dares not present a thanksgiving.—Quarles.

The only things in which we can be said to have any property are our actions. Our thoughts may be bad, yet produce no poison; they may be good, yet produce no fruit. Our riches may be taken away by misfortune, our reputation by malice, our spirits by calamity, our health by disease, our friends by death. But our actions must follow us beyond the grave; with respect to them alone, we cannot say that we shall carry nothing with us when we die, neither that we shall go naked out of the world.—Colton.

There are three sorts of actions: those that are good, those that are bad, and those that are doubtful; and we ought to be most cautious of those that are doubtful; for we are in most danger of these doubtful actions, because they do not alarm us; and yet they insensibly lead to greater transgressions, just as the shades of twilight gradually reconcile us to darkness.—A. Reed.

Not enjoyment, and not sorrow,
　Is our destined end or way;
But to act, that each to-morrow
　Finds us farther than to-day.
　　　*　　*　　*　　*
Trust no Future, howe'er pleasant!
Let the dead Past bury its dead!
Act, act, in the living Present!
Heart within, and God o'erhead!
　　　　　—Longfellow.

There is no word or action but may be taken with two hands,—either with the right hand of charitable construction, or the sinister interpretation of malice and suspicion; and all things do succeed as they are taken. To construe an evil action well is but a pleasing and profitable deceit to myself; but to misconstrue a good thing is a treble wrong,—to myself, the action, and the author.—Bishop Hall.

Acuteness

　　The keen spirit
Seizes the prompt occasion—makes the thought
Start into instant action, and at once
Plans and performs, resolves and executes.
　　　　　—Hannah More.

Adam

Adam, the goodliest man of men since born
His sons, the fairest of her daughters Eve.
　　　　　—Milton.

Adaptation

To wade in marshes and sea margins is the destiny of certain birds, and they are so accurately made for this that they are imprisoned in those places. Each animal out of its habitat would starve. To the physician, each man, each woman, is an amplification of one organ. A soldier, a locksmith, a bank-clerk, and a dancer could not exchange functions. And thus we are victims of adaptation.—Emerson.

Address

Address makes opportunities; the want of it gives them.—Bovee.

Brahmā once asked of Force, "Who is stronger than thou?" She replied, "Address."—Victor Hugo.

Give a boy address and accomplishments, and you give him the mastery of palaces and fortunes where he goes. He has not the trouble of earning or owning them; they solicit him to enter and possess.—Emerson.

A man who knows the world will not only make the most of everything he does know, but of many things that he does not know; and will gain more credit by his adroit mode of hiding his ignorance than the pedant by his awkward attempt to exhibit his erudition.—Colton.

There is a certain artificial polish, a commonplace vivacity acquired by perpetually mingling in the beau monde, which, in the commerce of the world, supplies the place of natural suavity and good-humor, but is purchased at the expense of all original and sterling traits of character.—Washington Irving.

Adieu

I take a long, last, lingering view;
Adieu! my native land, adieu!
—Logan.

Adieu, adieu! my native shore
Fades o'er the waters blue.
—Byron.

Admiration

Fools admire, but men of sense approve.—Pope.

Distance is a great promoter of admiration!—Diderot.

Few men are admired by their servants.—Montaigne.

Admiration is the basis of ignorance.—Balthasar Gracian.

Season your admiration for awhile.—Shakespeare.

Admiration and familiarity are strangers.—George Sand.

We live by admiration, hope, and love.—Wordsworth.

For her own person, it beggared all description.—Shakespeare.

Admiration begins where acquaintance ceases.—Dr. Johnson.

None knew thee but to love thee, nor named thee but to praise.—Fitz-Greene Halleck.

Admiration is a youthful fancy which scarcely ever survives to mature years.—H. W. Shaw.

All things are admired either because they are new or because they are great.—Bacon.

We always love those who admire us, and we do not always love those whom we admire.—La Rochefoucauld.

The king himself has follow'd her,
When she has walk'd before.
—Goldsmith.

There is a long and wearisome step between admiration and imitation.—Richter.

Those who are formed to win general admiration are seldom calculated to bestow individual happiness.—Lady Blessington.

When we view elevated ideas of Nature, the result of that view is admiration, which is always the cause of pleasure.—Dryden.

Amid the most mercenary ages it is but a secondary sort of admiration that is bestowed upon magnificence.—Shenstone.

That which astonishes, astonishes once; but whatever is admirable becomes more and more admired.—Joubert.

No nobler feeling than this of admiration for one higher than himself dwells in the breast of man.—Carlyle.

Not to be lost in idle admiration is the only sure means of making and of preserving happiness.—Horace.

Admiration is a forced tribute; and to extort it from mankind, envious and ignorant as they are, they must be taken unawares.—James Northcote.

The beauty that addresses itself to the eyes is only the spell of the moment: the eye of the body is not always that of the soul.—George Sand.

Admiration must be continued by that novelty which first produces it; and how much soever is given, there must always be reason to imagine that more remains.—Johnson.

To cultivate sympathy you must be among living creatures, and thinking about them; and to cultivate admiration, you must be among beautiful things and looking at them.—Ruskin.

It may be laid down as a general rule, that no woman who hath any great pretensions to admiration is ever well pleased in a company where she perceives herself to fill only the second place.—Fielding.

The love of admiration leads to fraud, much more than the love of commendation; but, on the other hand, the latter is much more likely to spoil our good actions by the substitution of an inferior motive.—Bishop Whately.

It is better in some respects to be admired by those with whom you live, than to be loved by them; and this not on account of any gratification of vanity, but because admiration is so much more tolerant than love.—Arthur Helps.

Admiration is a very short-lived passion, that immediately decays upon growing familiar with its object, unless it be still fed with such discoveries, and kept alive by a new perpetual succession of miracles rising up to its view.—Addison.

There is a wide difference between admiration and love. The sublime, which is the cause of the former, always dwells on great objects and terrible; the latter on small ones and pleasing; we submit to what we admire, but we love what submits to us: in one case we are forced, in the other we are flattered, into compliance.—Burke.

Admonition

It must descend, as the dew, upon the tender herb, or like melting flakes of snow; the softer it falls, the longer it dwells upon, and the deeper it sinks into the mind.—Seed.

Adoption

Faith unites us to Christ, and acquiesces in the redemption purchased by Him as the meritorious cause of our adoption.—Fisher's Catechism.

'Tis often seen
Adoption strives with nature; and choice breeds
A native slip to us from foreign lands.
—Shakespeare.

Adoption is an act of God's free grace, whereby we are received into the number, and have a right to all the privileges of the sons of God.—Westminster Catechism.

We need a spirit of adoption to take us out of the foundling hospital of the world, and to put us into the celestial family.—G. D. Boardman.

Adore

Adored through fear, strong only to destroy.
—Cowper.

We bear it calmly, though a ponderous woe,
And still adore the hand that gives the blow.
—Pomfret.

Led like a victim, to my death I'll go,
And, dying, bless the hand that gave the blow.
—Dryden.

Adorn

She came adorned hither like sweet May.
—Shakespeare.

Th' adorning thee with so much art
Is but a barbarous skill;
'Tis like the poisoning of a dart,
Too apt before to kill. —Cowley.

A poet, naturalist and historian, who scarcely left any style of writing untouched and touched nothing that he did not adorn.—Dr. Johnson.

Advent

The night is far spent, the day is at hand.—Bible.

Be ye therefore ready also: for the Son of man cometh at an hour when ye think not.—Bible.

I die in the faith of the speedy accomplishment of those glorious things which are spoken concerning the city of God and of the kingdom of Christ. "Amen. Even so, Lord Jesus! Come quickly."—Increase Mather.

What, then, is meant by the coming of the Lord Jesus? In answering it, the heart and mind must be exercised. First of all, the King of Zion is sometimes spoken of as coming in His grace, in His spirit, not in a visible way. He had promised "to come" to all believers in spirit to comfort them. —John Hall, D.D.

Great God, what do I see and hear!
  The end of things created!
The Judge of mankind doth appear
  On clouds of glory seated!
The trumpet sounds; the graves restore
The dead which they contained before;
  Prepare, my soul, to meet Him!
          —Martin Luther.

It is a very remarkable fact, that God's prophecies respecting the Advent of His Son seem to have spread athwart the whole habitable globe, and in the shape of traditional echoes to have been dispersed over all the world. The great promise of a Messiah, which was the grand truth that the Jew clung to in his most desperate fortunes, found itself translated into heathen tongues, and accepted even by heathen men.— French.

If I were but sure that I should live to see the coming of the Lord, it would be the joyfulest tidings in the world. O that I might see His kingdom come! It is the characteristic of His saints to love His appearing, and to look for that blessed hope. "The Spirit and the bride say, Come.' "Even so, come, Lord Jesus."—Richard Baxter.

There is a time appointed in the history of our world, when that very Jesus who appeared on earth, "a man of sorrows and acquainted with grief," shall reappear with all the circumstances of majesty and power, "King of kings and Lord of lords." We are led to expect a day when Christ shall find a home in the remotest hearts and families, and the earth in all its circumference be covered with the knowledge and the power of the Lord.—II. Melville, D.D.

But though that great day is far away, the heart asserts, and truly, that when there is deepest night over nations and the world and men, a day of the Lord is at hand; that a dawn is coming—not the last day nor the final dawn, but the uprising of Christ in light, deliverance, knowledge and love. The belief is born not only out of our natural hatred of evil and suffering and the desire to be free, but out of actual experience.

Earth, thou grain of sand on the shore of the Universe of God; thou Bethlehem, amongst the princely cities of the heavens; thou art, and remainest, the Loved One amongst ten thousand suns and worlds, the Chosen of God! Thee will He again visit, and then thou wilt prepare a throne for Him, as thou gavest Him a manger cradle; in His radiant glory wilt thou rejoice, as thou didst once drink His blood and tears, and mourn His death! On thee has the Lord a great work to complete.—Pressel.

There is an account come of the arrival of King George II. and a great rejoicing for it in Edinburgh. I see the fires and illuminations of that city reflected on the skies. O, how will the heavens reflect and shine with illuminations, when the King of kings, and Lord of lords, shall erect His tribunal in the clouds, and come in His own glory, and His Father's glory, and in the glory of the holy angels! O, what a heartsome day will that be! When Christ, who is our life, shall appear, then shall we appear with Him in glory. We shall then lift up our heads with joy, because it shall be a time of refreshing from the presence of the Lord.—Ebenezer Erskine.

The last words of the pious Henry Holmes, of Boston, were, "Lord Jesus, come quickly." In their primary sense, as referring to Christ's personal and glorious advent, these words have often dropped from the lips and pens of earnest believers. In a somewhat desponding mood, Martin Luther broke out, "May the Lord Jesus come at once! Let Him cut the whole matter short with the Day of Judgment; for there 'is no amendment to be expected." The martyr Ridley wrote: "The world, without doubt—this I do believe, and therefore say it—draws toward an end. Let us with John, the servant of God, cry in our hearts unto our Savior, Christ, 'Come, Lord Jesus, come.'"—Dr. A. C. Thompson.

No man rightly desires Christ's coming, but he that hath assurance of benefit at His coming. To him the day of Christ is as the day of harvest to the husbandman; as the day of deliverance to the prisoner; as the day of coronation to the king; the day of wedlock to the bride; a day of triumph and exultation, a day of freedom and consolation, a day of rest and satisfaction. To him the Lord Jesus is all sweetness, as wine to the palate, and ointment to the nostrils, saith Solomon; honey to the mouth, saith St. Bernard; music in the ear, and a jubilee in the heart. Get assurance of Christ's coming, as a ransomer to redeem you, as a conqueror to subdue all your enemies under you, as a friend to comfort you, as a bridegroom to marry you, and then shall you with boldness and confidence, with joy and gladness, with vehement and holy longings, say, "Come, Lord Jesus." —Grosse.

Adventure

Some bold adventurers disdain
The limits of their little reign,
And unknown regions dare descry.
                    —Gray.

* * * and now expecting
Each hour their great adventurer, from the
    search
Of foreign worlds.   —Milton.

Adversary

Oh that mine adversary had written a book.—Job.

And do as adversaries do in law:
Strive mightily, but eat and drink as
    friends.   —Shakespeare.

Adversity

He that has no cross deserves no crown.—Quarles.

Adversity is the first path to truth. —Byron.

Remember to be calm in adversity. —Horace.

Adversity's sweet milk, philosophy.

There is healing in the bitter cup. —Southey.

There is no education like adversity.—Beaconsfield.

Adversity reminds men of religion. —Livy.

Whom the Lord loveth He chasteneth.—Hebrews.

The fire of my adversity has purged the mass of my acquaintance.—Bolingbroke.

Afflictions are but conductors to immortal life and glory.—Aughey.

Brave men ought not to be cast down by adversity.—Silius Italicus.

Adversity makes men, and prosperity makes monsters.—Victor Hugo.

If thou faint in the day of adversity, thy strength is small.—Proverbs.

Adversity borrows its sharpest sting from our impatience.—Bishop Horne.

In adversity and difficulties arm yourself with firmness and fortitude. —From the Latin.

Great men rejoice in adversity just as brave soldiers triumph in war.— Seneca.

God's corrections are our instructions; His lashes our lessons, and His scourges our schoolmasters.—Aughey.

As adversity leads us to think properly of our state, it is most beneficial to us.—Johnson.

It is not affliction itself, but affliction rightly borne, that does us good.—Aughey.

God brings men into deep waters, not to drown them, but to cleanse them.—Aughey.

God strikes not as an enemy, to destroy; but as a father, to correct.—Aughey.

He that has never known adversity is but half acquainted with others or himself.—Aughey.

In the adversity of our best friends we often find something which does not displease us.—Rochefoucauld.

Little minds are tamed and subdued by misfortunes; but great minds rise above them.—Washington Irving.

Adversity, which makes us indulgent to others, renders them severe towards us.—J. Petit-Senn.

The Good are better made by Ill,
As odors crushed are sweeter still.
—Sam'l Rogers.

Then know, that I have little wealth to lose;
A man I am cross'd with adversity.
—Shakespeare.

'Tis good for men to love their present pains
Upon example; so the spirit is eased.
—Shakespeare.

In this wild world the fondest and the best
Are the most tried, most troubled and distress'd.
—Crabbe.

In all cases of heart-ache, the application of another man's disappointment draws out the pain and allays the irritation.—Lytton.

Heaven oft in mercy smites, even when the blow severest is.—Joanna Baillie.

Know how sublime a thing it is to suffer and be strong.—Longfellow.

Much dearer be the things which come through hard distress.—Spenser.

Prosperity is no just scale; adversity is the only balance to weigh friends.—Plutarch.

Through danger safety comes—through trouble rest.—John Marston.

In the wounds our sufferings plough immortal love sows sovereign seed.—Massey.

Half the ills we hoard within our hearts are ills because we hoard them.—Barry Cornwall.

A noble heart, like the sun, showeth its greatest countenance in its lowest estate.—Sir P. Sidney.

Let me embrace these sour adversities, for wise men say it is the wisest course.—Shakespeare.

He that has never known adversity is but half acquainted with others, or with himself.—Colton.

Clouds are the veil behind which the face of day coquettishly hides itself, to enhance its beauty.—Richter.

Prosperity is a great teacher; adversity is a greater. Possession pampers the mind; privation trains and strengthens it.—Hazlitt.

The winter's frost must rend the burr of the nut before the fruit is seen. So adversity tempers the human heart, to discover its real worth.—Balzac.

The most affluent may be stripped of all, and find his worldly comforts, like so many withered leaves, dropping from him.—Sterne.

Those who have suffered much are like those who know many languages; they have learned to understand and be understood by all.—Madame Swetchine.

Adversity is the trial of principle. Without it a man hardly knows whether he is honest or not.—Fielding.

Mr. Bettenham said that virtuous men were like some herbs and spices, that give not out their sweet smell till they be broken or crushed.—Bacon.

On every thorn delightful wisdom grows;
In every rill a sweet instruction flows.
—Dr. Young.

Heaven is not always angry when he strikes,
But most chastises those whom most he likes. —Pomfret.

In the day of prosperity we have many refuges to resort to; in the day of adversity only one.—Horatius Bonar.

Constant success shows us but one side of the world; adversity brings out the reverse of the picture.—Colton.

Adversity has the effect of eliciting talents, which, in prosperous circumstances, would have lain dormant.—Horace.

It is easy in adversity to despise death; he has real fortitude who dares to live and be wretched.—Martial.

When reduced by adversity, a man forgets the lofty tone and supercilious language of prosperity.

It is noble and so regarded both among nations and individuals to keep faith in adversity.—Silius Italicus.

Adversity is sometimes hard upon a man; but for one man who can stand prosperity, there are a hundred that will stand adversity.—Carlyle.

As every mercy is a drop obtained from the ocean of God's goodness, so every affliction is a drachm weighed out in the wisdom of God's providence.—Aughey.

Adversity tries men, and virtue strives for glory through adverse circumstances, undeterred by hard obstacles.—Silius Italicus.

The brightest crowns that are worn in heaven have been tried and smelted and polished and glorified through the furnace of tribulation.—Chapin.

As the ant does not wend her way to empty barns, so few friends will be found to haunt the place of departed wealth.

Adversity, sage useful guest,
Severe instructor, but the best,
It is from thee alone we know
Justly to value things below.
—Somerville.

Sweet are the uses of adversity;
Which, like the toad, ugly and venomous,
Wears yet a precious jewel in his head.
—Shakespeare.

His overthrow heap'd happiness upon him;
For then, and not till then, he felt himself,
And found the blessedness of being little.
—Shakespeare.

The firmest friendships have been formed in mutual adversity, as iron is most strongly welded by the fiercest fire.

Thou tamer of the human breast,
Whose iron scourge and tort'ring hour
The bad affright, afflict the best! —Gray.

Love is maintain'd by wealth: when all is spent,
Adversity then breeds the discontent.
—Herrick.

Remember that there is nothing stable in human affairs; therefore avoid undue elation in prosperity, or undue depression in adversity.—Isocrates.

By adversity are wrought the greatest works of admiration, and all the fair examples of renown, out of distress and misery are grown.—Daniel.

Affliction is the wholesome soil of virtue, where patience, honor, sweet humanity, calm fortitude, take root and strongly flourish.—Mallet.

In adversity be spirited and firm, and with equal prudence lessen your sail when filled with a too fortunate gale of prosperity.—Horace.

Affliction is the good man's shining scene; prosperity conceals his brightest rays; as night to stars, woe lustre gives to man.—Young.

Genuine morality is preserved only in the school of adversity, and a state of continuous prosperity may easily prove a quicksand to virtue.—Schiller.

Adversity has ever been considered as the state in which a man most easily becomes acquainted with himself, particularly being free from flatterers.—Johnson.

Prosperity is too apt to prevent us from examining our conduct, but as adversity leads us to think properly of our state, it is most beneficial to us.—Johnson.

It is often better to have a great deal of harm happen to one than a little; a great deal may rouse you to remove what a little will only accustom you to endure.—Greville.

Our dependence upon God ought to be so entire and absolute that we should never think it necessary, in any kind of distress, to have recourse to human consolations.—Thomas à Kempis.

God kills thy comforts from no other design but to kill thy corruptions; wants are ordained to kill wantonness, poverty is appointed to kill pride, reproaches are permitted to destroy ambition.—John Flavel.

There is strength deep-bedded in our hearts, of which we reck but little till the shafts of heaven have pierced its fragile dwelling. Must not earth be rent before her gems are found?—Mrs. Hemans.

He that can heroically endure adversity will bear prosperity with equal greatness of soul; for the mind that cannot be dejected by the former is not likely to be transported with the latter.—Fielding.

The truly great and good, in affliction, bear a countenance more princely than they are wont; for it is the temper of the highest hearts, like the palm-tree, to strive most upwards when it is most burdened.—Sir P. Sidney.

Men think God is destroying them

because he is tuning them. The violinist screws up the key till the tense cord sounds the concert pitch; but it is not to break it, but to use it tunefully, that he stretches the string upon the musical rack.—Beecher.

Prosperity is the blessing of the Old Testament, adversity is the blessing of the New, which carrieth the greater benediction, and the clearer revelation of God's favor.—Bacon.

Such a house broke!
So noble a master fallen! All gone and not
One friend to take his fortune by the arm
And go along with him.　—Shakespeare.

Adversity, if for no other reason, is of benefit, since it is sure to bring a season of sober reflection. Men see clearer at such time. Storms purify the atmosphere.—Beecher.

Aromatic plants bestow
No spicy fragrance while they grow;
But crush'd or trodden to the ground,
Diffuse their balmy sweets around.
　　　　　—Goldsmith.

When Providence, for secret ends,
Corroding cares, or sharp affliction, sends:
We must conclude it best it should be so,
And not desponding or impatient grow.
　　　　　—Pomfret.

A wretched soul, bruis'd with adversity.
We bid be quiet when we hear it cry;
But were we burden'd with like weight of pain,
As much, or more, we should ourselves complain.　—Shakespeare.

All is well as long as the sun shines and the fair breath of heaven gently wafts us to our own purpose; but if you will try the excellency and feel the work of faith, place the man in a persecution.—Jeremy Taylor.

Bold adversity
Cries out for noble York and Somerset,
To beat assailing death from his weak legions.
And whiles the honorable captain there
Drops bloody sweat from his war-wearied limbs.　—Shakespeare.

If adversity hath killed his thousands, prosperity hath killed his ten thousands; therefore adversity is to be preferred. The one deceives, the other instructs; the one miserably happy, the other happily miserable.—Burton.

Times of great calamity and confusion have ever been productive of the greatest minds. The purest ore is produced from the hottest furnace, and the brightest thunderbolt is elicited from the darkest storm.—Colton.

As the flint contains the spark, unknown to itself, which the steel alone can awaken to life, so adversity often reveals to us hidden gems, which prosperity or negligence would forever have hidden.—H. W. Shaw.

Adversity is a medicine which people are rather fond of recommending indiscriminately as a panacea for their neighbors. Like other medicines, it only agrees with certain constitutions. There are nerves which it braces, and nerves which it utterly shatters.—Justin McCarthy.

The gods in bounty work up storms about us, that give mankind occasion to exert their hidden strength, and throw out into practice virtues that shun the day, and lie concealed in the smooth seasons and the calms of life.—Addison.

One month in the school of affliction will teach thee more than the great precepts of Aristotle in seven years; for thou canst never judge rightly of human affairs, unless thou hast first felt the blows, and found out the deceits of fortune.—Fuller.

The willow which bends to the tempest often escapes better than the oak, which resists it; and so, in great calamities, it sometimes happens that light and frivolous spirits recover their elasticity and presence of mind sooner than those of a loftier character.—Walter Scott.

There are minerals called hydrophanous, which are not transparent till they are immersed in water, when they become so; as the hydrophane, a variety of opal. So it is with many a Christian. Till the floods of adversity have been poured over him, his char-

acter appears marred and clouded by selfishness and worldly influences. But trials clear away the obscurity, and give distinctness and beauty to his piety.—Professor Hitchcock.

The lessons of adversity are often the most benignant when they seem the most severe. The depression of vanity sometimes ennobles the feeling. The mind which does not wholly sink under misfortune rises above it more lofty than before, and is strengthened by affliction.—Chenevix.

And these vicissitudes come best in youth;
For when they happen at a riper age,
People are apt to blame the Fates, forsooth,
And wonder Providence is not more sage.
Adversity is the first path to truth:
He who hath proved war, storm or wom-
an's rage,
Whether his winters be eighteen or eighty,
Has won the experience which is deem'd so
weighty.
        —Byron.

The wisdom of God appears in afflictions. By these He separates the sin which He hates, from the son whom He loves. By these thorns He keeps him from breaking over into Satan's pleasant pastures, which would fatten him indeed, but only to the slaughter.—Aughey.

Present suffering is not enjoyable, but life would be worth little without it. The difference between iron and steel is fire, but steel is worth all it costs. Iron ore may think itself senselessly tortured in the furnace, but when the watch-spring looks back, it knows better. David enjoyed pain and trouble no more than we do, but the time came when he admitted that they had been good for him. Though the aspect of suffering is hard, the prospect is hopeful, and the retrospect will start a song, if we are "the called according to his purpose," in suffering.—Maltbie Babcock.

Advertisements

The great art in writing advertisements is the finding out a proper method to catch the reader's eye; without, a good thing may pass over unobserved, or be lost among commissions of bankrupt.—Addison.

The advertisements in a newspaper are more full of knowledge in respect to what is going on in a State or community than the editorial columns are. —Henry Ward Beecher.

Advice

The worst men often give the best advice.—Bailey.

Necessity is the only successful adviser.—Charles Reade.

Agreeable advice is seldom useful advice.—Massillon.

We ask advice, but we mean approbation.—Colton.

Good counsels observed are chains to grace.—Fuller.

Good counsel has no price.—Mazzini.

Many receive advice, only the wise profit by it.—Publius Syrus.

Men give away nothing so liberally as their advice.—Rochefoucauld.

We give advice, but we do not inspire conduct.—La Rochefoucauld.

Do not take a blind guide nor a bad adviser.

Bad advice is often most fatal to the adviser.—Flaccus.

A fop sometimes gives important advice.—Boileau.

Hazard not your wealth on a poor man's advice.—Manuel Conde Lucanor.

Whatever advice you give, be short. —Horace.

One can advise comfortably from a safe port.—Schiller.

Superfluous advice is not retained by the full mind.—Horace.

We give advice by the bucket, but take it by the grain.—W. R. Alger.

It is not advice, but approval, which we crave.—Boufflers.

The greatest trust between man and man is the trust of giving counsel.— Bacon.

He who was taught only by himself had a fool for a master.—Ben Jonson.

We all, when we are well, give good advice to the sick.—Terence.

To attempt to advise conceited people is like whistling against the wind. —Hood.

If you would convince a person of his mistake, accost him not when he is ruffled.—Dr. Watts.

Downright admonition, as a rule, is too blunt for the recipient.—Beecher.

I do not like giving advice: it is incurring an unnecessary responsibility.—Beaconsfield.

Advice is like kissing: it costs nothing and is a pleasant thing to do.— H. W. Shaw.

Before giving advice we must have secured its acceptance, or, rather, have made it desired.—Amiel.

Any one can give advice, such as it is, but only a wise man knows how to profit by it.—Colton.

When a wise man gives thee better counsel, give me mine again.—Shakespeare.

Begin nothing without considering what the end may be.—Lady M. W. Montague.

Advice is seldom welcome. Those who need it most like it least.—Johnson.

He who can take advice is sometimes superior to him who can give it.—Von Knebel.

Advice is seldom welcome; and those who want it the most always like it the least.—Chesterfield.

Even the ablest pilots are willing to receive advice from passengers in tempestuous weather.—Cicero.

Know when to speak, for many times it brings
Danger to give the best advice to kings.
—Herrick.

Do not give to thy friends the most agreeable counsels, but the most advantageous.—Tuckerman.

How is it that even castaways can give such good advice?—Ninon de Lenclos.

Admonish your friends privately, but praise them openly.—Publius Syrus.

The greatest trust between man and man is the trust of giving counsel.—Bacon.

Wait for the season when to cast good counsels upon subsiding passion.—Shakespeare.

Mishaps are mastered by advice discreet, and counsel mitigates the greatest smart.—Spenser.

Let no man value at a little price a virtuous woman's counsel.—George Chapman.

The pride of men will not often suffer reason to have any scope until it can be no longer of service.—Burke.

Let no man presume to give advice to others that has not first given good counsel to himself.—Seneca.

How is it possible to expect that mankind will take advice when they will not so much as take warning.—Swift.

Those who give bad advice to the prudent, both lose their pains and are laughed to scorn.—Phædrus.

Every man, however wise, requires the advice of some sagacious friend in the affairs of life.—Plautus.

Harsh counsels have no effect; they are like hammers which are always repulsed by the anvil.—Helvetius.

He had only one vanity; he thought he could give advice better than any other person.—Samuel L. Clemens.

And may you better reck the rede,
Than ever did th' adviser. —Burns.

'Twas good advice, and meant,
"My son, be good."
—George Crabbe.

Bosom up my counsel,
You'll find it wholesome.
—Shakespeare.

Be niggards of advice on no pretense;
For the worst avarice is that of sense.
—Pope.

For women with a mischief to their kind,
Pervert with bad advice our better mind.
—Dryden.

Here comes a man of comfort, whose advice
Hath often still'd my brawling discontent.
—Shakespeare.

It is always safe to learn even from our enemies, seldom safe to instruct even our friends.—Colton.

Advice is like snow: the softer it falls, the longer it dwells upon, and the deeper it sinks into, the mind.—Coleridge.

I pray thee cease thy counsel,
Which falls into mine ears as profitless
As water in a sieve. —Shakespeare.

Who will ever give counsel, if the counsel be judged by the event, and if it be not found wise, shall therefore be thought wicked?—Sir P. Sidney.

Remember this: they that will not be counselled cannot be helped. If you do not hear Reason, she will rap your knuckles.—Franklin.

There is nearly as much ability requisite to know how to profit by good advice as to know how to act for one's self.—Rochefoucauld.

It has been well observed that few are better qualified to give others advice than those who have taken the least of it themselves.—Goldsmith.

Counsel and conversation is a good second education, that improves all the virtue and corrects all the vice of the former, and of nature itself.—Clarendon.

Let no man value at a little price
A virtuous woman's counsel; her wing'd spirit
Is feather'd oftentimes with heavenly words.   —George Chapman.

In order to convince it is necessary to speak with spirit and wit; to advise, it must come from the heart.—D'Aguesseau.

When we feel a strong desire to thrust our advice upon others, it is usually because we suspect their weakness; but we ought rather to suspect our own.—Colton.

Ah, gentle dames! it gars me greet,
To think how mony counsels sweet,
How mony lengthened, sage advices,
The husband frae the wife despises.
              —Burns.

Direct not him, whose way himself will choose;
'Tis breath thou lack'st, and that breath wilt thou lose.   —Shakespeare.

I forget whether advice be among the lost things which Ariosto says are to be found in the moon: that and time ought to have been there.—Swift.

She had a good opinion of advice,
Like all who give and eke receive it gratis,
For which small thanks are still the market price,
Even when the article at highest rate is.
              —Shakespeare.

Advice, as it always gives a temporary appearance of superiority, can never be very grateful, even when it is most necessary or most judicious; but, for the same reason, every one is eager to instruct his neighbors.—Johnson.

He who calls in the aid of an equal understanding doubles his own; and he who profits by a superior understanding raises his powers to a level with the height of the superior understanding he unites with.—Burke.

Vanity is so frequently the apparent motive of advice, that we, for the most part, summon our powers to oppose it without any very accurate inquiry whether it is right.—Dr. Johnson.

There is nothing of which men are more liberal than their good advice, be their stock of it ever so small; because it seems to carry in it an intimation of their own influence, importance, or worth.—Young.

He that gives good advice builds with one hand; he that gives good counsel and example builds with the other; but he that gives good admonition and bad example builds with one hand and pulls down with the other.—Bacon.

No man is so foolish but he may give another good counsel sometimes, and no man so wise but he may easily err, if he takes no other counsel than his own. He that was taught only by himself had a fool for a master.—Ben Jonson.

A man takes contradiction and advice much more easily than people think, only he will not bear it when violently given, even though it be well founded. Hearts are flowers; they remain open to the softly falling dew, but shut up in the violent downpour of rain.—Richter.

There is as much difference between the counsel that a friend giveth and that a man giveth himself, as there is between the counsel of a friend and of a flatterer; for there is no such flatterer as a man's self, and there is no such remedy against flattery of a man's self as the liberty of a friend.—Bacon.

No one was ever the better for advice: in general, what we called giving advice was properly taking an occasion to show our own wisdom at finother's expense; and to receive advice was little better than tamely to afford another the occasion of raising himself a character from our defects.—Lord Shaftesbury.

If to do were as easy as to know what were good to do, chapels had been churches, and poor men's cottages, princes' palaces. It is a good divine that follows his own instructions: I can easier teach twenty what were good to be done, than be one of the twenty to follow mine own teaching.—Shakespeare.

Love all, trust a few,
Do wrong to none; be able for thine enemy
Rather in power than use; and keep thy friend
Under thine own life's key; be checked for silence,
But never taxed for speech.
　　　　　　　—Shakespeare.

It was the maxim, I think, of Alphonsus of Aragon, that dead counsellors are safest. The grave puts an end to flattery and artifice, and the information we receive from books is pure from interest, fear, and ambition. Dead counsellors are likewise most instructive, because they are heard with patience and with reverence.—Johnson.

Give thy thoughts no tongue,
Nor any unproportioned thought his act.
Be thou familiar, but by no means vulgar.
The friends thou hast, and their adoption tried,
Grapple them to thy soul with hooks of steel;
But do not dull thy palm with entertainment
Of each new-hatched, unfledged comrade.
Beware
Of entrance to a quarrel; but, being in,
Bear it that the opposer may beware of thee;
Give every man thine ear, but few thy voice.
Take each man's censure, but reserve thy judgment.
Costly thy habit as thy purse can buy,
But not expressed in fancy; rich, not gaudy;
For the apparel oft proclaims the man.
Neither a borrower nor a lender be,
For loan oft loses both itself and friend;
And borrowing dulls the edge of husbandry.
This above all: To thine own self be true;
And it must follow, as the night the day,
Thou canst not then be false to any man.
　　　　　　　—Shakespeare.

It would truly be a fine thing if men suffered themselves to be guided by reason, that they should acquiesce in the true remonstrances addressed to them by the writings of the learned and the advice of friends. But the greater part are so disposed that the words which enter by one ear do incontinently go out of the other, and begin again by following the custom. The best teacher one can have is necessity.—Francois la None.

I lay very little stress either upon asking or giving advice. Generally speaking, they who ask advice know what they wish to do, and remain firm to their intentions. A man may allow himself to be enlightened on various points, even upon matters of expediency and duty; but, after all, he must determine his course of action for himself.—Wilhelm von Humboldt.

Advice is offensive, not because it lays us open to unexpected regret, or convicts us of any fault which has escaped our notice, but because it shows us that we are known to others as well as ourselves; and the officious monitor is persecuted with hatred, not because his accusation is false, but because he assumes the superiority which we are not willing to grant him, and has dared to detect what we desire to conceal.—Johnson

Affectation

Affectation is the product of falsehood.—Carlyle.

There is a pleasure in affecting affectation.—Lamb.

Die of a rose in aromatic pain.—Pope.

Affectation hides three times as many virtues as charity does sins.—Horace Mann.

Affectation is a greater enemy to the face than the small-pox.—St. Evremond.

All affectation is the vain and ridiculous attempt of poverty to appear rich.—Lavater.

Affectation is as necessary to the mind as dress is to the body.—Hazlitt.

Great affectation and great absence of it are at first sight very similar.—Whately.

On the rich quilt sinks with becoming woe,
Wrapt in a gown, for sickness and for show.
            —Pope.

We are never so ridiculous from the habits we have as from those we affect to have.—La Rochefoucauld.

There affectation, with a sickly mien,
Shows in her cheek the roses of eighteen.
            —Pope.

By giving sixty-five's pale wither'd mien,
The blooming roses of sixteen.—Wolcot.

All affectation; 'tis my perfect scorn;
Object of my implacable disgust.—Cowper.

Affectation discovers sooner what one is than it makes known what one would fain appear to be.—Stanislaus.

Affectation is the wisdom of fools, and the folly of many a comparatively wise man.

'T is too much proved that with devotion's visage and pious action we do sugar o'er the devil himself.—Shakespeare.

Hearts may be attracted by assumed qualities, but the affections are only to be fixed by those that are real.—De Moy.

Affectation endeavors to correct natural defects, and has always the laudable aim of pleasing, though it always misses it.—Locke.

It is remarkable that great affectation and great absence of it (unconsciousness) are at first sight very similar; they are both apt to produce singularity.—Bishop Whately.

Affectation is certain deformity; by forming themselves on fantastic models, the young begin with being ridiculous, and often end in being vicious.—Blair.

Great vices are the proper objects of our detestation, smaller faults of our

pity, but affectation appears to be the only true source of the ridiculous.—Fielding.

Affectation in any part of our carriage is lighting up a candle to see our defects, and never fails to make us taken notice of, either as wanting sense or sincerity.—Locke.

Avoid all affectation and singularity. What is according to nature is best, and what is contrary to it is always distasteful. Nothing is graceful that is not our own.—Jeremy Collier.

In all the professions every one affects a particular look and exterior, in order to appear what he wishes to be thought; so that it may be said the world is made up of appearances.—Rochefoucauld.

Affectation is an awkward and forced Imitation of what should be genuine and easy, wanting the Beauty that accompanies what is natural.—Locke.

Among the numerous stratagems by which pride endeavors to recommend folly to regard, there is scarcely one that meets with less success than affectation, or a perpetual disguise of the real character by fictitious appearances.—Johnson.

Paltry affectation, strained allusions, and disgusting finery are easily attained by those who choose to wear them; they are but too frequently the badges of ignorance or of stupidity, whenever it would endeavor to please.—Goldsmith.

Affectation naturally counterfeits those excellences which are placed at the greatest distance from possibility of attainment, because, knowing our own defects, we eagerly endeavor to supply them with artificial excellence.—Johnson.

When Cicero consulted the oracle at Delphos, concerning what course of studies he should pursue, the answer was, "Follow Nature." If every one would do this, affectation would be almost unknown.—J. Beaumont.

Almost every man wastes part of his life in attempts to display qualities which he does not possess, and to gain applause which he cannot keep; so that scarcely can two persons meet but one is offended or diverted by the ostentation of the other.—Dr. Johnson.

There is a false gravity that is a very ill symptom; and it may be said that as rivers, which run very slowly, have always the most mud at the bottom, so a solid stiffness in the constant course of a man's life is a sign of a thick bed of mud at the bottom of his brain.—Saville.

Affectation is to be always distinguished from hypocrisy, as being the art of counterfeiting those qualities, which we might with innocence and safety, be known to want. Hypocrisy is the necessary burden of villany; affectation part of the chosen trappings of folly.—Johnson.

Affectation proceeds from one of these two causes,—vanity or hypocrisy; for as vanity puts us on affecting false characters, in order to purchase applause; so hypocrisy sets us on an endeavor to avoid censure, by concealing our vices under an appearance of their opposite virtues.—Fielding.

I will not call vanity and affectation twins, because, more properly, vanity is the mother, and affectation is the darling daughter. Vanity is the sin, and affectation is the punishment; the first may be called the root of self-love, the other the fruit. Vanity is never at its full growth till it spreadeth into affectation, and then it is complete.—Sir H. Saville.

Affection

Set your affection on things above, not on things on the earth.—Colossians, chap. iii.

No decking sets forth anything so much as affection.—Sir P. Sidney.

Entire affection hateth nicer hands.—Spencer.

Affection is the broadest basis of good in life.—George Eliot.

A loving heart is the truest wisdom.—Dickens.

Loving souls are like paupers. They live on what is given them.—Madame Swetchine.

Alas! our young affections run to waste, Or water but the desert.—Byron.

One touch of nature makes the whole world kin.—Shakespeare.

It is sweet to feel by what fine-spun threads our affections are drawn together.—Sterne.

Our happiness in this world depends on the affections we are enabled to inspire.—Duchesse de Praslin.

How cling we to a thing our hearts have nursed.—Mrs. C. H. W. Esling.

I have given suck, and know how tender it is to love the babe that milks me.—Shakespeare.

It is comparatively easy to leave a mistress, but very hard to be left by one.—Thackeray.

No affections and a great brain,—these are the men to command the world.—Beaconsfield.

Affection, mistress of passion, sways it to the mood of what it likes or loathes.—Shakespeare.

Such affection and unbroken faith as temper life's worst bitterness.—Shelley.

Dear as the light that visits these sad eyes; Dear as the ruddy drops that warm my heart.   —Gray.

Affection is a coal that must be cool'd; Else, suffer'd, it will set the heart on fire.—Shakespeare.

Of all earthly music, that which reaches the farthest into heaven is the beating of a loving heart.—Beecher.

O you much partial gods! why gave ye men affections, and not power to govern them?—Ludovic Barry.

Love is strong in its passion; affection is powerful in its gentleness.—Michelet.

Of all the tyrants the world affords, our own affections are the fiercest lords.—Earl of Sterling.

If there is anything that keeps the mind open to angel visits, and repels the ministry of ill, it is human love.—Willis.

Our sweetest experiences of affection are meant to be suggestions of that realm which is the home of the heart.—Beecher.

The affections are immortal! they are the sympathies which unite the ceaseless generations.—Bulwer-Lytton.

There are moments of mingled sorrow and tenderness, which hallow the caresses of affection.—Washington Irving.

Affections injured by tyranny, or rigor of compulsion, like tempest-threatened trees, unfirmly rooted, never spring to timely growth.—John Ford.

The poor wren, the most diminutive of birds, will fight, her young ones in her nest, against the owl.—Shakespeare.

The affection of young ladies is of as rapid growth as Jack's beanstalk, and reaches up to the sky in a night.—Thackeray.

The affections are the children of ignorance; when the horizon of our experience expands, and models multiply, love and admiration imperceptibly vanish.—Beaconsfield.

There comes a time when the souls of human beings, women more even than men, begin to faint for the atmosphere of the affections they are made to breathe.—Holmes.

There are few mortals so insensible that their affections cannot be gained by mildness, their confidence by sincerity, their hatred by scorn or neglect.—Zimmermann.

Even children follow'd with endearing wile,
And pluck'd his gown, to share the good
man's smile.   —Goldsmith.

Generous as brave,
Affection, kindness, and the sweet officer
Of love and duty, were to him as needful
As his daily bread.   —Rogers.

If the deepest and best affections which God has given us sometimes brood over the heart like doves of peace,—they sometimes suck out our life-blood like vampires.—Mrs. Jameson.

Universal love is a glove without fingers, which fits all hands alike, and none closely; but true affection is like a glove with fingers, which fits one hand only, and sits close to that one.—Richter.

There is so little to redeem the dry mass of follies and errors from which the materials of this life are composed that anything to love or to reverence becomes, as it were, the Sabbath for the mind.—Bulwer-Lytton.

The objects that we have known in better days are the main props that sustain the weight of our affections, and give us strength to await our future lot.—Wm. Hazlitt.

Hearts may be attracted by assumed qualities, but the affections are only to be fixed by those that are real.—De Moy.

I may not to the world impart
The secret of its power,
But treasured in my inmost heart
I keep my faded flower.
          —Ellen C. Howarth.

The heart will commonly govern the head, and it is certain that any strong passion, set the wrong way, will soon infatuate even the wisest of men; therefore the first part of wisdom is to watch the affections.—Dr. Waterland.

Affection is a garden, and without it there would not be a verdant spot on the surface of the globe.

Fathers alone a father's heart can know
What secret tides of still enjoyment flow
When brothers love, but if their hate suc-
  ceeds,
They wage the war, but 'tis the father
  bleeds.   —Young.

Who have not saved some trifling thing
  More prized than jewels rare,
A faded flower, a broken ring, .
  A tress of golden hair.
       —Ellen C. Howarth.

Caresses, expressions of one sort or another, are necessary to the life of the affections as leaves are to the life of a tree. If they are wholly re-strained love will die at the roots.—Hawthorne.

How often a new affection makes a new man! The sordid, cowering soul turns heroic. The frivolous girl becomes the steadfast martyr of patience and ministration, transfigured by deathless love. The career of bounding impulses turns into an anthem of sacred deeds.—Chapin.

How sacred, how beautiful, is the feeling of affection in pure and guile-less bosoms! The proud may sneer at it, the fashionable may call it fable, the selfish and dissipated may affect to despise it; but the holy passion is surely of heaven, and is made evil by the corruptions of those whom it was sent to bless and to preserve.—Mor-daunt.

A solitary blessing few can find,
Our joys with those we love are inter-
  twined,
And he whose wakeful tenderness removes
The obstructing thorn that wounds the
  breast he loves,
Smooths not another's rugged path alone,
But scatters roses to adorn his own.

Let the foundation of thy affection be virtue, then make the building as rich and as glorious as thou canst; if the foundation be beauty or wealth, and the building virtue, the foundation is too weak for the building, and it will fall: happy is he, the palace of whose affection is founded upon virtue,

walled with riches, glazed with beauty, and roofed with honor.—Quarles.

Talk not of wasted affection, affection never
  was wasted;
If it enrich not the heart of another, its
  waters, returning
Back to their springs, like the rain, shall
  fill them full of refreshment;
That which the fountain sends forth returns again to the fountain.
       —Longfellow.

Why doth Fate, that often bestows thousands of souls on a conqueror or tyrant, to be the sport of his passions, so often deny to the tenderest and most feeling hearts one kindred one on which to lavish their affections? Why is it that Love must so often sigh in vain for an object, and Hate never?—Richter.

Affliction

Affliction is but the shadow of God's wing.—George Macdonald.

Man is born unto trouble, as the sparks fly upward.—Job v. 7.

Afflictions clarify the soul.—Quarles.

Calamity is man's true touchstone.—Fletcher.

'T is a physic that is bitter to sweet end.—Shakespeare.

Sanctified afflictions are spiritual promotions.—Matthew Henry.

There is healing in the bitter cup.—Southey.

I am a feather for each wind that blows.—Shakespeare.

Afflictions are but as a dark entry into our Father's house.—Thomas Brooks.

Night brings out stars as sorrow shows us truths.—P. J. Bailey.

What region of the earth is not full of our calamities?—Virgil.

It is the best thing for a stricken heart to be helping others.—A. H. K.

We only see clearly when we have reached the depths of woe.—Ouida.

He who tenders doubtful safety to those in trouble refuses it.—Seneca.

The afflictions to which we are accustomed, do not disturb us.—Claudianus.

Distress is virtue's opportunity: we only live to teach us how to die.—Southern.

Affliction, like the iron-smith, shapes as it smites.—Bovee.

In time of affliction, a vow; in the time of prosperity, an increase of wickedness.—Hebrew Proverb.

Heaven gives us friends to bless the present scene;
Resumes them, to prepare us for the next.
—Young.

The Lord gets his best soldiers out of the highlands of affliction.—Spurgeon.

Corn is cleaned with wind, and the soul with chastening.—George Herbert.

Affliction's sons are brothers in distress;
A brother to relieve, how exquisite the bliss! —Burns.

Affliction is not sent in vain—
From that good God who chastens whom He loves! —Southey.

Heaven is not always angry when he strikes,
But most chastises those whom most he likes. —Pomfret.

If you would not have affliction visit you twice, listen at once to what it teaches.—Burgh.

Patience cannot remove, but it can always dignify and alleviate, misfortune.—Laurence Sterne.

As threshing separates the corn from the chaff, so does affliction purify virtue.—Bacon.

With the wind of tribulation God separates in the floor of the soul, the chaff from the corn.—Molinos.

Oft the cloud that wraps the present hour serves but to brighten all our future days.—Wm. Browne.

Affliction is enamor'd of thy parts,
And thou art wedded to calamity.
—Shakespeare.

It is from the remembrance of joys we have lost that the arrows of affliction are pointed.—Mackenzie.

We bleed, we tremble, we forget, we smile—
The mind turns fool, before the cheek is dry. —Young.

When sorrows come, they come not single spies, but in battalions.—Shakespeare.

How blunt are all the arrows of thy quiver in comparison with those of guilt!—Blair.

What seem to us but dim funereal tapers may be heaven's distant lamps.—Longfellow.

The good are better made by ill, as odors crushed are sweeter still!—Rogers.

Amid my list of blessings infinite stands this the foremost, "That my heart has bled."—Young.

Thy pleasure points the shaft, and bends the bow;
The cluster blasts, or bids it brightly glow.
—Dr. Young.

Affliction is a school of virtue: it corrects levity, and interrupts the confidence of sinning.—Atterbury.

The loss of a beloved connection awakens an interest in heaven before unfelt.—Bovee.

The eternal stars shine out as soon as it is dark enough.—Carlyle.

Affliction is the school in which great virtues are acquired, in which great characters are formed.—Hannah More.

As sure as God ever puts His children into the furnace, He will be in the furnace with them.—C. H. Spurgeon.

We should be more anxious that our afflictions should benefit us than that they should be speedily removed from us.—Robert Hall.

Christ leads me through no darker rooms Than He went through before.
—Richard Baxter.

Grace will ever speak for itself and be fruitful in well-doing; the sanctified cross is a fruitful tree.—Rutherford.

Affliction of itself does not sanctify any body, but the reverse. I believe in sanctified afflictions, but not in sanctifying afflictions.—C. H. Spurgeon.

Extraordinary afflictions are not always the punishment of extraordinary sins, but sometimes the trial of extraordinary graces.—Matthew Henry.

Affliction is the wholesome soul of virtue;
Where patience, honor, sweet humanity,
Calm fortitude, take root, and strongly
    flourish.   —Mallet and Thomson.

Believe me, the gods spare the afflicted, and do not always oppress those who are unfortunate.—Ovid.

God afflicts with the mind of a father, and kills for no other purpose but that he may raise again.—South.

God sometimes washes the eyes of His children with tears in order that they may read aright His providence and His commandments.—T. L. Cuyler.

Alas by some degree of woe,
  We every bliss must gain;
The heart can ne'er a transport know,
  That never feels a pain.
          —Lord Lyttleton.

Most of the grand truths of God have to be learned by trouble; they must be burned into us by the hot iron of affliction, otherwise we shall not truly receive them.—C. H. Spurgeon.

Thou art never at any time nearer to God than when under tribulation; which He permits for the purification and beautifying of thy soul.—Miguel Molinos.

Afflictions clarify the soul,
And like hard masters, give more hard directions,
Tutoring the non-age of uncurbed affections.
          —Quarles.

With every anguish of our earthly part the spirit's sight grows clearer; this was meant when Jesus touched the blind man's lids with clay.—Lowell.

The cup which my Saviour giveth me, can it be anything but a cup of salvation?—Alexander Maclaren.

Affliction is the good man's shining scene;
Prosperity conceals his brightest ray,
As night to stars, woe lustre gives to man.
          —Young.

The very afflictions of our earthly pilgrimage are presages of our future glory, as shadows indicate the sun.—Richter.

Perfumes, the more they are chafed, the more they render their pleasant scents; and so affliction expresseth virtue fully.—John Webster.

The furnace of affliction refines us from earthly drossiness, and softens us for the impression of God's own stamp.—Bayle.

Incessant falls teach men to reform, and distress rouses their strength. Life springs from calamity, and death from ease.—Mencius.

Nothing can occur beyond the strength of faith to sustain, or, transcending the resources of religion, to relieve.—Binney.

It is the crushed grape that gives out the blood-red wine: it is the suffering soul that breathes the sweetest melodies.—Gail Hamilton.

The mind which does not wholly sink under misfortune rises above it more lofty than before, and is strengthened by affliction.—Richard Chenevix.

Affliction is a sort of moral gymnasium in which the disciples of Christ are trained to robust exercise, hardy exertion, and severe conflict.—Hannah More.

> Henceforth I'll bear
> Affliction till it do cry out itself,
> Enough, enough, and die.
> —Shakespeare.

Thou art a soul in bliss; but I am bound
Upon a wheel of fire; that mine own tears
Do scald like molten lead.—Shakespeare.

With silence only as their benediction,
God's angels come
Where in the shadow of a great affliction,
The soul sits dumb!   —Whittier.

Every man deems that he has precisely the trials and temptations which are the hardest of all for him to bear; but they are so, because they are the very ones he needs.—Richter.

And this is the course of Nature: there is nothing like suffering to enlighten the giddy brain, widen the narrow mind, improve the trivial heart.—Charles Reade.

If aught can teach us aught, Affliction's looks,
  Making us pry into ourselves so near,
Teach us to know ourselves, beyond all books,
  Or all the learnèd schools that ever were.
        —John Davies.

Aromatic plants bestow
No spicy fragrance where they grow;
But crushed and trodden to the ground,
Diffuse their balmy sweets around.
        —Goldsmith.

God is now spoiling us of what would otherwise have spoiled us. When God makes the world too hot for His people to hold, they will let it go.—T. Powell.

When Providence for secret ends,
Corroding cares, or sharp affliction, sends;
We must conclude it best it should be so,
And not despondent or impatient grow.
        —Pomfret.

Are afflictions aught
But mercies in disguise? th' alternate cup,
Medicinal though bitter, and prepar'd
By love's own hand for salutary ends.
        —Mallet.

The great, in affliction, bear a coun-

tenance more princely than they are wont; for it is the temper of the highest heart, like the palm-tree, to strive most upward when it is most burdened. —Sir P. Sidney.

Affliction appears to be the guide to reflection; the teacher of humility; the parent of repentance; the nurse of faith; the strengthener of patience, and the promoter of charity.

The truest help we can render an afflicted man is not to take his burden from him, but to call out his best energy, that he may be able to bear the burden.—Phillips Brooks.

No man ever stated his griefs as lightly as he might. For it is only the finite that has wrought and suffered; the infinite lies stretched in smiling repose.—Emerson.

Afflictions are the medicine of the mind. If they are not toothsome, let it suffice that they are wholesome. It is not required in physic that it should please, but heal.—Bishop Henshaw.

No chastening for the present seemeth to be joyous, but grievous: nevertheless afterward it yieldeth the peaceable fruit of righteousness unto them which are exercised thereby.—Hebrews xii. 11.

There will be no Christian but what will have a Gethsemane, but every praying Christian will find that there is no Gethsemane without its angel!— Rev. T. Binney.

Now let us thank th' eternal power, convinc'd
That heaven but tries our virtue by affliction;
That oft the cloud which wraps the present hour,
Serves but to brighten all our future days!
        —John Brown.

Every man will have his own criterion in forming his judgment of others. I depend very much on the effect of affliction. I consider how a man comes out of the furnace; gold will lie for a month in the furnace without losing a grain.—Richard Cecil.

Human character is never found "to enter into its glory," except through the ordeal of affliction. Its force cannot come forth without the offer of resistance, nor can the grandeur of its free will declare itself, except in the battle of fierce temptation.—James Martineau.

What He tells thee in the darkness,
  Weary watcher for the day,
Grateful lip and heart should utter
  When the shadows flee away.
          —F. R. Havergal.

The damps of autumn sink into the leaves and prepare them for the necessity of their fall; and thus insensibly are we, as years close around us, detached from our tenacity of life by the gentle pressure of recorded sorrow.—W. S. Landor.

However bitter the cup we have to drink, we are sure it contains nothing unnecessary or unkind; and we should take it from His hand with as much meekness as we accept of eternal life with thankfulness.—William Goodell.

Tears and sorrows and losses are a part of what must be experienced in this present state of life: some for our manifest good, and all, therefore, it is trusted, for our good concealed;—for our final and greatest good.—Leigh Hunt.

It is a great thing, when our Gethsemane hours come, when the cup of bitterness is pressed to our lips, and when we pray that it may pass away, to feel that it is not fate, that it is not necessity, but divine love for good ends working upon us.—Chapin.

Fairer and more fruitful in spring the vine becomes from the skilful pruning of the husbandman; less pure had been the gums which the odorous balsam gives if it had not been cut by the knife of the Arabian shepherd.—Metastasio.

That which thou dost not understand when thou readest, thou shalt understand in the day of thy visitation; for many secrets of religion are not perceived till they be felt, and are not felt but in the day of a great calamity.—Jeremy Taylor.

As they lay copper in aquafortis before they begin to engrave it, so the Lord usually prepares us by the searching, softening discipline of affliction for making a deep, lasting impression of himself upon our hearts.—J. T. Nottidge.

The bread of bitterness is the food on which men grow to their fullest stature; the waters of bitterness are the debatable ford through which they reach the shores of wisdom; the ashes boldly grasped and eaten without faltering are the price that must be paid for the golden fruit of knowledge.—Ouida.

Afflictions sent by Providence melt the constancy of the noble-minded, but confirm the obduracy of the vile. The same furnace that hardens clay liquefies gold; and in the strong manifestations of divine power Pharaoh found his punishment, but David his pardon.—Colton.

Be still, sad heart, and cease repining,
Behind the clouds the sun is shining;
Thy fate is the common fate of all;
Into each life some rain must fall,—
Some days must be dark and dreary.
          —Longfellow.

God washes the eyes by tears until they can behold the invisible land where tears shall come no more. O love! O affliction! ye are the guides that show us the way through the great airy space where our loved ones walked; and, as hounds easily follow the scent before the dew be risen, so God teaches us, while yet our sorrow is wet, to follow on and find our dear ones in heaven.—Beecher.

As the most generous vine, if it is not pruned, runs out into many superfluous stems, and grows at last weak and fruitless; so doth the best man, if he be not cut short of his desires and pruned with afflictions. If it be painful to bleed, it is worse to wither. Let me be pruned, that I may grow, rather than be cut up to burn.—Bishop Hall.

In a great affliction there is no light either in the stars or in the sun; for when the inward light is fed with fragrant oil; there can be no darkness though the sun should go out. But when, like a sacred lamp in the temple, the inward light is quenched, there is no light outwardly, though a thousand suns should preside in the heavens.—Beecher.

The cloud which appeared to the prophet Ezekiel carried with it winds and storms, but it was environed with a golden circle, to teach us that the storms of afflictions, which happen to God's children, are encompassed with brightness and smiling felicity.—N. Caussin.

Had it pleased Heaven
To try me with affliction; had he rain'd
All kinds of sores and shames on my bare
    head;
Steep'd me in poverty to the very lips;
Given to captivity me and my utmost hopes;
I should have found in some place of my
    soul
A drop of patience. —Shakespeare.

There is an elasticity in the human mind, capable of bearing much, but which will not show itself until a certain weight of affliction be put upon it; its powers may be compared to those vehicles whose springs are so contrived that they get on smoothly enough when loaded, but jolt confoundedly when they have nothing to bear.—Colton.

In thy silent wishing, thy voiceless, unuttered prayer, let the desire be not cherished that afflictions may not visit thee; for well has it been said, "Such prayers never seem to have wings. I am willing to be purified through sorrow, and to accept it meekly as a blessing. I see that all the clouds are angels' faces, and their voices speak harmoniously of the everlasting chime."—Mrs. L. M. Child.

The truth is, when we are under any affliction we are generally troubled with a malicious kind of melancholy; we only dwell and pore upon the sad and dark occurrences of Providence, but never take notice of the more be-nign and bright ones. Our way in this world is like a walk under a row of trees, checkered with light and shade; and because we cannot all along walk in the sunshine, we therefore perversely fix only upon the darker passages, and so lose all the comfort of our comforts. We are like froward children who, if you take one of their playthings from them, throw away all the rest in spite.—Bishop Hopkins.

Oh, when we are journeying through the murky night and the dark woods of affliction and sorrow, it is something to find here and there a spray broken, or a leafy stem bent down with the tread of His foot and the brush of His hand as He passed; and to remember that the path He trod He has hallowed, and thus to find lingering fragrance and hidden strength in the remembrance of Him as "in all points tempted like as we are," bearing grief for us, bearing grief with us, bearing grief like us.—Alexander Maclaren.

Affront

Am I to set my life upon a throw,
Because a bear is rude and surly? No—
A moral, sensible, and well-bred man,
Will not affront me, and no other can.
                            —Cowper.

After

After me the deluge.—Madame de Pompadour.

After the war, aid.—Greek Proverb.

After death the doctor.—English Proverb.

When I am dead, may earth be mingled with fire! Ay, said Nero, and while I am living, too.—From a Greek Tragedian.

Age

Good old age.—Genesis xv. 15.

Slow, consuming age.—Gray.

Crabbed age and youth cannot live together.—Shakespeare.

Few people know how to be old.—La Rochefoucauld.

Age either transfigures or petrifies.—Marie Ebner-Eschenbach.

It is difficult to grow old gracefully. —Madame de Staël.

Begin to patch up thine old body for heaven.—Shakespeare.

The clock of his age had struck fifty-eight.—Cellini.

An old man is twice a child.—Shakespeare.

When the age is in, the wit is out.—Shakespeare.

Mellowed by the stealing hours of time.—Shakespeare.

No wise man ever wished to be younger.—Swift.

Old age is an incurable disease.—Seneca.

The evening of life brings with it its lamps.—Joubert.

'T is the sunset of life gives us mystical lore.—Campbell.

Age is suspicious, but is not itself often suspected.—Zimmermann.

Nor age so eat up my invention.—Shakespeare.

Men shut their doors against a setting sun.—Shakespeare.

O good gray head which all men knew.—Tennyson.

Age and want sit smiling at the gate.—Pope.

Thyself no more deceive, thy youth hath fled.—Petrarch.

The silver livery of advised age.—Shakespeare.

They say women and music should never be dated.—Goldsmith.

The Grecian ladies counted their age from their marriage, not their birth.—Homer.

As I approach a second childhood, I endeavor to enter into the pleasures of it.—Lady Montagu.

Age * * * is is a matter. of feeling, not of years.—George William Curtis.

Stronger by weakness, wiser men become,
As they draw near to their eternal home.
                    —Edmund Waller,

His cheek the map of days outworn.—Shakespeare.

Time's chariot-wheels make their carriage-road in the fairest face.—Rochefoucauld.

Age too, shines out, and garrulous recounts the feats of youth.—Thomson.

Have a care lest the wrinkles in the face extend to the heart.—Marguerite de Valois.

White hairs are the crests of foam which cover the sea after the tempest. —Elizabeth, Queen of Roumania.

What makes old age so sad is, not that our joys, but that our hopes, cease.—Richter.

Old age is a tyrant, which forbids the pleasures of youth on pain of death—Rochefoucauld.

We are to seek wisdom and understanding only in the length of days.—Robert Hall.

The silver-leaved birch retains in its old age a soft bark; there are some such men.—Auerbach.

Some smack of age in you, some relish of the saltness of time.—Shakespeare.

Your date is better in your pie and your porridge than in your cheek.—Shakespeare.

The defects of the mind, like those of the face, grow worse as we grow old.—Rochefoucauld.

Every man desires to live long; but no man would be old.—Swift.

His hair just grizzled as in a green old age.—Dryden.

Years steal fire from the mind as vigor from the limb.—Byron.

Years do not make sages; they only make old men.—Madame Swetchine.

As the evening twilight fades away, the sky is filled with stars, invisible by day.—Longfellow.

The enthusiasm of old men is singularly like that of infancy.—Gerard de Nerval.

As we grow old we become more foolish and more wise.—Rochefoucauld.

Nature, as it grows again toward earth, is fashioned for the journey, dull and heavy.—Shakespeare.

We do not count a man's years until he has nothing else to count.—Emerson.

As you are old and reverend, you should be wise.—Ibid.

An old age serene and bright, and lovely as a Lapland night, shall lead thee to thy grave.—Wordsworth.

A youthful age is desirable, but aged youth is troublesome and grievous.—Chilo.

How many persons fancy they have experience simply because they have grown old!—Stanislaus.

For my own part, I had rather be old only a short time than be old before I really am so.—Cicero.

As we advance in life the circle of our pains enlarges, while that of our pleasures contracts.—Madame Swetchine.

We see time's furrows on another's brow; how few themselves, in that just mirror, see!—Young.

What folly can be ranker? Like

our shadows, our wishes lengthen as our sun declines.—Young.

Cautious age suspects the flattering form, and only credits what experience tells.—Johnson.

At twenty years of age, the will reigns; at thirty, the wit; and at forty, the judgment.—Grattan.

To the old, long life and treasure;
To the young, all health and pleasure.
—Ben Jonson.

The best is yet to be,
The last of life, for which the first was made.
—Browning.

I love everything that's old,—old friends, old times, old manners, old books, old wine.—Goldsmith.

Forty is the old age of youth; fifty is the youth of old age.—Victor Hugo.

To be happy, we must be true to nature, and carry our age along with us.—Hazlitt.

Men, like peaches and pears, grow sweet a little while before they begin to decay.—Holmes.

Age, that lessens the enjoyment of life, increases our desire of living.—Goldsmith.

When men once reach their autumn, sickly joys fall off apace, as yellow leaves from trees.—Young.

You see me here,—a poor old man,
As full of grief as age; wretched in both!
—Shakespeare.

Thou shalt go to thy fathers in peace, thou shalt be buried in a good old age.—Genesis.

Youth changes its tastes by the warmth of its blood; age retains its tastes by habit.—La Rochefoucauld.

Age is rarely despised but when it is contemptible.—Johnson.

As you are old and reverend, you should be wise.—Shakespeare.

Age bears away with it all things, even the powers of the mind.—Virgil.

Care keeps his watch in every old man's eye.—Shakespeare.

These are the effects of doting age, —vain doubts and idle cares and over-caution.—Dryden.

Borne on the swift, tho' silent wings of time, Old age comes on apace, to ravage all the clime.   —Beattie.

Childhood itself is scarcely more lovely than a cheerful, kindly, sun-shiny old age.—Mrs. L. M. Child.

A healthy old fellow, who is not a fool, is the happiest creature living.—Steele.

Whatever poet, orator, or sage May say of it, old age is still old age.
                    —Longfellow.

Old wood best to burn, old wine to drink, old friends to trust, and old authors to read.—Bacon.

Youth is a blunder; Manhood a struggle; Old Age a regret.—Disraeli (Earl Beaconsfield).

Why will you break the Sabbath of my days? Now sick alike of envy and of praise.
                    —Pope.

Superfluity comes sooner by white hairs, but competency lives longer.—Shakespeare.

Age is a tyrant, who forbids, at the penalty of life, all the pleasures of youth.—La Rochefoucauld.

A time there is when like a thrice-told tale long-rifled life of sweets can yield no more.—Young.

Age makes us not childish, as some say; it finds us still true children.—Goethe.

Thirst of power and of riches now bear sway, The passion and infirmity of age.
                    —Frowde.

Age is frequently beautiful, wisdom

appearing like an aftermath.—Beaconsfield.

Old age has deformities enough of its own; do not add to it the deformity of vice.—Cato.

Boys must not have th' ambitious care of men, Nor men the weak anxieties of age.
                    —Horace.

Gray hairs seem to my fancy like the light of a soft moon, silvering over the evening of life.—Richter.

The sunshine fails, the shadows grow more dreary, And I am near to fall, infirm and weary.
                    —Longfellow.

The most dangerous weakness of old people who have been amiable is to forget they are no longer so.—Rochefoucauld.

What should we speak of When we are old as you? When we shall hear The rain and wind beat dark December.
                    —Shakespeare.

When he's forsaken, Wither'd and shaken, What can an old man do but die?
                    —Hood.

Beauty and ugliness disappear equally under the wrinkles of age; one is lost in them; the other hidden.—J. Petit-Senn.

There is nothing more disgraceful than that an old man should have nothing to produce as a proof that he has lived long except his years.—Seneca.

Nature is full of freaks, and now puts an old head on young shoulders, and then a young heart beating under fourscore winters.—Emerson.

And the bright faces of my young companions Are wrinkled like my own, or are no more.
                    —Longfellow.

Tell me what you find better, or more honorable than age. Is not wisdom entailed upon it? Take the pre-eminence of it in everything; in an old friend, in old wine, in an old pedigree. —Shakerly Marmion.

Most long lives resemble those threads of gossamer, the nearest approach to nothing unmeaningly prolonged, scarce visible pathways of some worm from his cradle to his grave.—Lowell.

Time has laid his hand upon my heart gently, not smiting it; but as a harper lays his open palm upon his harp, to deaden its vibrations.—Longfellow.

The tendency of old age, say the physiologists, is to form bone. It is as rare as it is pleasant, to meet with an old man whose opinions are not ossified.—J. F. Boyse.

There are three classes into which all the women past seventy years of age, that ever I knew, were to be divided : 1. That dear old soul; 2. That old woman; 3. That old witch.—Coleridge.

O sir, you are old; nature in you stands on the very verge of her confine; you should be ruled and led by some discretion, that discerns your fate better than you yourself.—Shakespeare.

Last scene of all, that ends this strange, eventful history, is second childishness, and mere oblivion; sans teeth, sans eyes, sans taste, sans everything.—Shakespeare.

'Tis the sunset of life gives us mystical lore,
And coming events cast their shadows before.
        —Campbell.

Thou shalt come to thy **grave in a** full age, like a shock of corn cometh in his season.—Job v. 26.

I feel I am growing old for want of somebody to tell me that I am looking as young as ever. Charming falsehood! There is a vast deal of vital air in loving words.—Landor.

The heart never grows better by age;

I fear rather worse; always harder. A young liar will be an old one; and a young knave will only be a greater knave as he grows older.—Chesterfield.

On his bold visage middle age
Had slightly press'd its signet sage.
        —Scott.

        At your age,
The hey-day in the blood is tame, it's humble,
And waits upon the judgment.
        —Shakespeare.

We hope to grow old and we dread old age; that is to say, we love life and we flee from death.—La Bruyère.

The tree that bears no fruit deserves no name; the man of wisdom is the man of years.—Young.

We must not take the faults of our youth into our old age; for old age brings with it its own defects.—Goethe.

It is only necessary to grow old to become more indulgent. I see no fault committed that I have not committed myself.—Goethe.

Set is the sun of my years;
And over a few poor ashes,
   I sit in my darkness and tears.
        —Gerald Massey.

        And his big manly voice,
Turning again toward childish treble, pipes
And whistles in his sound.
        —Shakespeare.

How far the gulf-stream of our youth May flow into the Arctic region of our lives, Where little else than life itself survives.
        —Longfellow.

Some one has said of a fine and honorable old age, that it was the childhood of immortality.—Pindar.

When a noble life has prepared old age, it is not the decline that it reveals, but the first days of immortality.—Madame de Staël.

The easiest thing for our friends to discover in us, and the hardest thing for us to discover in ourselves, is that we are growing old.—H. W. Shaw.

There is nothing against which an old man should be so much upon his guard as putting himself to nurse.—Dr. Johnson.

In an aged man appears ripeness of wisdom: it is the oldest sandal-tree which emits the most fragrance.—Sataka.

Old men's lives are lengthened shadows; their evening sun falls coldly on the earth, but the shadows all point to the morning.—Richter.

Age and youth look upon life from the opposite ends of the telescope; it is exceedingly long,—it is exceedingly short.—Beecher.

Old age was naturally more honored in times when people could not know much more than what they had seen.—Joubert.

Only when the sap is dried up, only when age comes on, does the sun shine in vain for man and for the tree.—Bulwer-Lytton.

Age is not all decay; it is the ripening, the swelling, of the fresh life within, that withers and bursts the husk.—George MacDonald.

The Disappointment of Manhood succeeds to the delusion of Youth; let us hope that the heritage of Old Age is not Despair.—Disraeli.

For we are old, and on our quick'st decrees
The inaudible and noiseless foot of Time
Steals ere we can effect them.
—Shakespeare.

That which is usually called dotage is not the weak point of all old men, but only of such as are distinguished by their levity.—Cicero.

Next to the very young, I suppose the very old are the most selfish. Alas! the heart hardens as the blood ceases to run.—Thackeray.

An aged Christian, with the snow of time on his head, may remind us that those points of earth are whitest which are nearest heaven.—Chapin.

If wrinkles must be written upon our brows, let them not be written upon the heart. The spirit should not grow old.—James A. Garfield.

In age to wish for youth is full as vain
As for a youth to turn a child again.
—Denham.

The surest sign of age is loneliness. While one finds company in himself and his pursuits, he cannot be old, whatever his years may be.—Alcott.

Old age takes from the man of intellect no qualities save those that are useless to wisdom.—Joubert.

Thus pleasures fade away;
Youth, talents, beauty, thus decay,
And leave us dark, forlorn, and gray.
—Scott.

Superfluous lags the veteran on the stage,
Till pitying Nature signs the last release,
And bids afflicted worth retire to peace.
—Samuel Johnson.

* * * Years steal
Fire from the mind, as vigor from the limb;
And life's enchanted cup but sparkles near
    the brim.   —Byron.

Each departed friend is a magnet that attracts us to the next world, and the old man lives among graves.—Richter.

Up to forty a woman has only forty springs in her heart. After that age she has only forty winters.—Arsène Houssaye.

When men grow virtuous in their old age, they are merely making a sacrifice to God of the devil's leavings.—Swift.

We grizzle every day. I see no need of it. Whilst we converse with what is above us, we do not grow old, but grow young.—Emerson.

Down his neck his reverend lockes
    In comelye curles did wave;
And on his aged temples grewe
    The blossomes of the grave.
—Old Ballad.

Depend upon it, a man never experiences such pleasure or grief after fourteen years as he does before, unless in some cases, in his first lovemaking, when the sensation is new to him.—Charles Kingsley.

To resist with success the frigidity of old age, one must combine the body, the mind, and the heart; to keep these in parallel vigor, one must exercise, study, and love.—Bonstetten.

As sailing into port is a happier thing than the voyage, so is age happier than youth; that is, when the voyage from youth is made with Christ at the helm.—Rev. J. Pulsford.

Thus fares it still in our decay,
And yet the wiser mind
Mourns less for what age takes away
Than what it leaves behind.
—Wordsworth.

The vine produces more grapes when it is young, but better grapes for wine when it is old, because its juices are more perfectly concocted.—Bacon.

My days are in the yellow leaf;
The flowers and fruits of love are gone;
The worm, the canker, and the grief
Are mine alone!   —Byron.

Natures that have much heat, and great and violent desires and perturbations, are not ripe for action till they have passed the meridian of their years.—Bacon.

Backward, flow backward, O tide of the
  years!
I am so weary of toil and of tears,—
Toil without recompense, tears all in vain—
Take them and give me my childhood again!
—Elizabeth Akers Allen.

The vices of old age have the stiffness of it, too; and as it is the unfittest time to learn in, so the unfitness of it to unlearn will be found much greater.—South.

I am much beholden to old age, which has increased my eagerness for conversation in proportion as it has lessened my appetites of hunger and thirst.—Tully.

Throughout the whole vegetable, sensible, and rational world, whatever makes progress towards maturity, as soon as it has passed that point, begins to verge towards decay.—Blair.

He who would pass the declining years of his life with honor and comfort, should when young, consider that he may one day become old, and remember, when he is old, that he has once been young.—Addison.

Age imprints more wrinkles in the mind, than it does in the face, and souls are never, or very rarely seen, that in growing old do not smell sour and musty. Man moves all together, both towards his perfection and decay.
—Montaigne.

So life's year begins and closes;
Days, though short'ning, still can shine;
What though youth gave love and roses,
Age still leaves us friends and wine.
—Moore.

Though now this grained face of mine be
  hid
In sap-consuming winter's drizzled snow,
And all the conduits of my blood froze up,
Yet hath my night of life some memory.
—Shakespeare.

For age is opportunity no less
Than youth itself, though in another dress,
And as the evening twilight fades away
The sky is filled with stars, invisible by day.
—Longfellow.

Though sinking in decrepit age, he prematurely falls whose memory records no benefit conferred on him by man. They only have lived long who have lived virtuously.—Sheridan.

Old age is never honored among us, but only indulged, as childhood is; and old men lose one of the most precious rights of man,—that of being judged by their peers.—Goethe.

Remote from cities liv'd a Swain,
Unvex'd with all the cares of gain;
His head was silver'd o'er with age,
And long experience made him sage.
—Gay.

Our life much resembles wine: when there is only a little remaining, it becomes vinegar; for all the ills of human nature crowd to old age as if it were a workshop.—Antiphanes.

Life grows darker as we go on, till only one pure light is left shining on it; and that is faith. Old age, like solitude and sorrow, has its revelations.—Madame Swetchine.

O, roses for the flush of youth,
And laurel for the perfect prime;
But pluck an ivy branch for me
Grown old before my time.
—Christina G. Rossetti.

Thus aged men, full loth and slow,
The vanities of life forego,
And count their youthful follies o'er,
Till memory lends her light no more.
—Scott.

Venerable men! you have come down to us from a former generation. Heaven has bounteously lengthened out your lives, that you might behold this joyous day.—Daniel Webster.

There cannot live a more unhappy creature than an ill-natured old man, who is neither capable of receiving pleasures nor sensible of doing them to others.—Sir W. Temple.

The mental powers acquire their full robustness when the cheek loses its ruddy hue, and the limbs their elastic step; and pale thought sits on manly brows, and the watchman, as he walks his rounds, sees the student's lamp burning far into the silent night.—Dr. Guthrie.

The damps of autumn sink into the leaves and prepare them for the necessity of their fall; and thus insensibly are we, as years close round us, detached from our tenacity of life by the gentle pressure of recorded sorrows.—Landor.

Like a morning dream, life becomes more and more bright the longer we live, and the reason of everything appears more clear. What has puzzled us before seems less mysterious, and the crooked paths look straighter as we approach the end.—Richter.

A comfortable old age is the reward of a well-spent youth; therefore instead of its introducing dismal and melancholy prospects of decay, it should give us hopes of eternal youth in a better world.—Palmer.

Age and sufferings had already marked out the first incisions for death, so that he required but little effort to cut her down; for it is with men as with trees, they are notched long before felling, that their life-sap may flow out.—Richter.

Old age is a lease nature only signs as a particular favor, and it may be, to one only in the space of two or three ages; and then with a pass to boot, to carry him through all the traverses and difficulties she has strewed in the way of his long career.—Montaigne.

What is it to grow old?
Is it to lose the glory of the form,
The lustre of the eye?
Is it for Beauty to forego her wreath?
Yes; but not this alone.
—Matthew Arnold.

Winter, which strips the leaves from around us, makes us see the distant regions they formerly concealed; so does old age rob us of our enjoyments, only to enlarge the prospect of eternity before us.—Richter.

We should provide for our age, in order that our age may have no urgent wants of this world to absorb it from the meditation of the next. It is awful to see the lean hands of dotage making a coffer of the grave!—Bulwer-Lytton.

Alike all ages; dames of ancient days
Have led their children thro' the mirthful
    maze.
And the gay grandsire, skill'd in gestic lore,
Has frisk'd beneath the burthen of three-
    score.
—Goldsmith.

Fate seem'd to wind him up for fourscore
    years;
Yet freshly ran he on ten winters more;
Till like a clock worn out with eating time,
The wheels of weary life at last stood still.
—Dryden.

One's age should be tranquil, as one's childhood should be playful; hard work, at either extremity of human existence, seems to me out of place; the morning and the evening should be alike cool and peaceful; at midday the sun may burn, and men may labor under it.—Dr. Arnold.

O blest retirement! friend to life's decline—
Retreats from care, that never must be mine
How blest is he who crowns, in shades like these,
A youth of labour with an age of ease;
                                    —Goldsmith.

I think that to have known one good old man—one man, who, through the chances and mischances of a long life, has carried his heart in his hand, like a palm-branch, waving all discords into peace—helps our faith in God, in ourselves, and in each other more than many sermons.—G. W. Curtis.

I venerate old age; and I love not the man who can look without emotion upon the sunset of life, when the dusk of evening begins to gather over the watery eye, and the shadows of twilight grow broader and deeper upon the understanding.—Longfellow.

Come forth, old man,—thy daughter's side
Is now the fitting place for thee:
When time has quell'd the oak's bold pride,
The youthful tendril yet may hide.
The ruins of the parent tree, —Scott.

So may'st thou live, till like ripe fruit thou drop
Into thy mother's lap, or be with ease
Gather'd, not harshly pluck'd, for death mature.   —Milton.

Learn to live well, or fairly make your will;
You've play'd, and lov'd, and ate, and drank your fill;
Walk sober off, before a sprightlier age
Comes titt'ring on, and shoves you from the stage.   —Pope.

What is the worst of woes that wait on age?
What stamps the wrinkle deeper on the brow?
To view each loved one blotted from life's page,
And be alone on earth as I am now.
                                    —Byron.

Vanity in an old man is charming. It is a proof of an open nature. Eighty winters have not frozen him up, or taught him concealments. In a young person it is simply allowable; we do not expect him to be above it.—Bovee.

The smile upon the old man's lip, like the last rays of the setting sun, pierces the heart with a sweet and sad emotion. There is still a ray, there is still a smile; but they may be the last.—Madame Swetchine.

Is it that Nature, attentive to the preservation of mankind, increases our wishes to live, while she lessens our enjoyments, and as she robs the senses of every pleasure, equips imagination in the spoil?—Goldsmith.

If the memory is more flexible in childhood, it is more tenacious in mature age; if childhood has sometimes the memory of words, old age has that of things, which impress themselves according to the clearness of the conception of the thought which we wish to retain.—De Bonstetten.

An age that melts with unperceived decay,
And glides in modest innocence away;
Whose peaceful Day benevolence endears,
Whose Night congratulating conscience cheers;
The general favourite as the general friend:
Such age there is, and who shall wish its end?   —Dr. Johnson.

True wisdom, indeed, springs from the wide brain which is fed from the deep heart; and it is only when age warms its withering conceptions at the memory of its youthful fire, when it makes experience serve aspiration, and knowledge illumine the difficult paths through which thoughts thread their way into facts,—it is only then that age becomes broadly and nobly wise.—Whipple.

Age, when it does not harden the heart and sour the temper, naturally returns to the milky disposition of infancy. Time has the same effect upon the mind as on the face. The predominant passion, the strongest feature, becomes more conspicuous from the others retiring.—Lady Montagu.

Some persons resemble certain trees, such as the nut, which flowers in February and ripens its fruit in September; or the juniper and the arbutus; which take a whole year or more to perfect their fruit; and others, the cherry, which takes between two and three months.—Whately.

Old age brings us to know the value of the blessings which we have enjoyed, and it brings us also to a very thankful perception of those which yet remain. Is a man advanced in life? The ease of a single day, the rest of a single night, are gifts which may be subjects of gratitude to God.—Paley.

Old age is not one of the beauties of creation, but it is one of its harmonies. The law of contrasts is one of the laws of beauty. Under the conditions of our climate, shadow gives light its worth; sternness enhances mildness; solemnity, splendor. Varying proportions of size support and subserve one another.—Madame Swetchine.

Remember that some of the brightest drops in the chalice of life may still remain for us in old age. The last draught which a kind Providence gives us to drink, though near the bottom of the cup, may, as is said of the draught of the Roman of old, have at the very bottom, instead of dregs, most costly pearls.—W. A. Newman.

Behold where age's wretched victim lies,
See his head trembling, and his half clos'd
    eyes,
Frequent for breath his panting bosom
    heaves;
To broken sleep his remnant sense he gives,
And only by his pains, awaking, finds he
    lives.   —Prior.

The course of my long life hath reached at
    last,
In fragile bark o'er a tempestuous sea,
The common harbor, where must rendered
    be,
Account of all the actions of the past.
    —Longfellow.

Weak withering age no rigid law forbids,
With frugal nectar, smooth and slow with
    balm,
The sapless habit daily to bedew,
And give the hesitating wheels of life
Gliblier to play.   —John Armstrong.

Old age likes to dwell in the recollections of the past, and, mistaking the speedy march of years, often is inclined to take the prudence of the winter time for a fit wisdom of midsummer days. Manhood is bent to the passing cares of the passing moment, and holds so closely to his eyes the sheet of "to-day," that it screens the "to-morrow" from his sight.—Kossuth.

There is a quiet repose and steadiness about the happiness of age, if the life has been well spent. Its feebleness is not painful. The nervous system has lost its acuteness. But, in mature years we feel that a burn, a scald, a cut, is more tolerable than it was in the sensitive period of youth.—Hazlitt.

Me let the tender office long engage
To rock the cradle of reposing age;
With lenient arts extend a mother's breath,
Make languor smile, and smooth the bed of
    death;
Explore the thought, explain the asking eye!
And keep awhile one parent from the sky.
    —Pope.

Old age is courteous—no one more:
For time after time he knocks at the door,
But nobody says, "Walk in, sir, pray!"
Yet turns he not from the door away,
But lifts the latch, and enters with speed,
And then they cry, "A cool one, indeed."
    —Goethe.

I'm growing fonder of my staff;
I'm growing dimmer in the eyes;
I'm growing fainter in my laugh;
I'm growing deeper in my sighs;
I'm growing careless of my dress;
I'm growing frugal of my gold;
I'm growing wise; I'm growing,—yes,—
I'm growing old.   —Saxe.

The careful cold hath nipt my rugged rind,
    And in my face deep furrows eld hath
      plight;
My head bespren with hoary frost I find,
    And by mine eye the crow his claw doth
      bright;
Delight is laid abed, and pleasure past;
    No sun now shines, clouds have all over-
      cast.   —Spenser.

Can man be so age-stricken that no faintest sunshine of his youth may revisit him once a year? It is impossible. The moss on our time-worn mansion brightens into beauty; the good old pastor, who once dwelt here, renewed his prime and regained his boyhood in the genial breeze of his ninetieth spring. Alas for the worn and heavy soul, if, whether in youth or age, it has outlived its privilege of springtime sprightliness!—Hawthorne.

Old age doth in sharp pains abound;
  We are belabored by the gout,
Our blindness is a dark profound,
  Our deafness each one laughs about.
Then reason's light with falling ray
  Doth but a trembling flicker cast.
Honor to age, ye children pay!
Alas! my fifty years are past!
                    —Beranger.

My way of life
Is fallen into the sear, the yellow leaf
And that which should accompany old age,
As honor, love, obedience, troops of friends,
I must not look to have; but, in their stead,
Curses not loud, but deep, mouth-honor,
    breath,
Which the poor heart would fain deny, and
    dare not.   —Shakespeare.

His silver hairs
Will purchase us a good opinion,
And buy men's voices to commend our
    deeds;
It shall be said his judgment rul'd our
    hands;
Our youths and wildness shall no whit ap-
    pear,
But all be buried in his gravity.
                    —Shakespeare.

These old fellows have
Their ingratitude in them hereditary;
Their blood is caked, 'tis cold, it seldom
    flows;
'Tis lack of kindly warmth, they are not
    kind,
And nature, as it grows toward earth,
Is fashion'd for the journey—dull and
    heavy.   —Shakespeare.

. It is noticeable how intuitively in age we go back with strange fondness to all that is fresh in the earliest dawn of youth. If we never cared for little children before, we delight to see them roll in the grass over which we hobble on crutches. The grandsire turns wearily from his middle-aged, care-worn son, to listen with infant laugh to the prattle of an infant grandchild. It is the old who plant young trees; it is the old who are most saddened by the autumn, and feel most delight in the returning spring.—Bulwer-Lytton.

Agree

Agreeing to differ.—Ovid.

The character in conversation which commonly passes for agreeable is made up of civility and falsehood.—Swift.

Nature never says one thing, Wisdom another.—Juvenal.

Agreement exists in disagreement.—Lucan.

If you wish to appear agreeable in society you must consent to be taught many things which you know already.—Lavater.

Most arts require long study and application; but the most useful art of all, that of pleasing, requires only the desire.—Chesterfield.

We may say of agreeableness, as distinct from beauty, that it consists in a symmetry of which we know not the rules, and a secret conformity of the features to each other, and to the air and complexion of the person.—Rochefoucauld.

The art of being agreeable frequently miscarries through the ambition which accompanies it. Wit, learning, wisdom,—what can more effectually conduce to the profit and delight of society? Yet I am sensible that a man may be too invariably wise, learned, or witty to be agreeable; and I take the reason of this to be, that pleasure cannot be bestowed by the simple and unmixed exertion of any one faculty or accomplishment.—Cumberland.

Nature has left every man a capacity of being agreeable, though not of shining in company; and there are a hundred men sufficiently qualified for both who, by a very few faults, that they might correct in half an hour, are not so much as tolerable.—Swift.

Agriculture

The farmers are the founders of civilization.—Daniel Webster.

The divine chemistry works in the subsoil.—Hawthorne.

Time spent in the cultivation of the fields passes very pleasantly.—Ovid.

He who owns the soil, owns up to the sky.—Juvenal.

Here Ceres' gifts in waving prospect stand,
And nodding tempt the joyful reaper's hand.
—Pope.

Command large fields, but cultivate small ones.—Virgil.

A field becomes exhausted by constant tillage.—Ovid.

He that sows his grain upon marble will have many a hungry belly before his harvest.—Arbuthnot.

Earth is here so kind, that just tickle her with a hoe and she laughs with a harvest.—Douglas Jerrold.

Methinks I have a great desire to a bottle of hay: good hay, sweet hay, hath no fellow.—Shakespeare.

In ancient times, the sacred plough employed the kings, and awful fathers of mankind.—Thomson.

Praise a large domain, cultivate a small state.—Virgil.

Smoothly and lightly the golden seed by the furrow is covered.—Goethe.

Agriculture engenders good sense, and good sense of an excellent kind.—Joubert.

The life of the husbandman,—a life fed by the bounty of earth and sweetened by the airs of heaven.—Douglas Jerrold.

When weary reapers quit the sultry field,
And, crown'd with corn, their thanks to
Ceres yield. —Pope.

And the maize-field grew and ripened,
Till it stood in all the splendor
Of its garments green and yellow.
—Longfellow.

An agricultural life is one eminently calculated for human happiness and human virtue.—Josiah Quincy.

The first farmer was the first man, and all historic nobility rests on possession and use of land.—Emerson.

Let the farmer forevermore be honored in his calling; for they who labor in the earth are the chosen people of God.—Thomas Jefferson.

He who would look with contempt upon the farmer's pursuit is not worthy the name of a man.—Beecher.

The sun, which ripens the corn and fills the succulent herb with nutriment, also pencils with beauty the violet and the rose.—J. C. Abbott.

The frost is God's plough, which He drives through every inch of ground in the world, opening each clod, and pulverizing the whole.—Fuller.

If we estimate dignity by immediate usefulness, agriculture is undoubtedly the first and noblest science.—Dr. Johnson.

The cattle are grazing,
Their heads never raising:
There are forty feeding like one!
—Wordsworth.

Adam, well may we labor, still to dress
This garden, still to tend plant, herb, and
flower. —Milton.

Where grows?—where grows it not? If
vain our toil,
We ought to blame the culture, not the
soil. —Pope.

Trade increases the wealth and glory of a country; but its real strength and stamina are to be looked for among the cultivators of the land.—Lord Chatham.

Heap high the farmer's wintry hoard!
Heap high the golden corn!
No richer gift has Autumn poured
From out her lavish horn!
—Whittier.

But let the good old corn adorn
The hills our fathers trod;
Still let us, for His golden corn,
Send up our thanks to God!
—Whittier.

The first three men in the world were a gardener, a ploughman, and a grazier; and if any man object that the second of these was a murderer, I desire he would consider that as soon as he was so, he quitted our profession and turned builder.—Cowley.

"Agriculture, for an honorable and high-minded man," says Xenophon, "is the best of all occupations and arts by which men procure the means of living."—Alcott.

God Almighty first planted a garden; and indeed it is the purest of human pleasures: it is the greatest refreshment to the spirits of man.—Bacon.

Ye rigid ploughmen! bear in mind
 Your labor is for future hours.
Advance! spare not! nor look behind!
 Plough deep and straight with all your
 Powers! —Richard Hengist Horne.

Agriculture is the noblest of all alchemy; for it turns earth, and even manure, into gold, conferring upon its cultivator the additional reward of health.—Chatfield.

Oft did the harvest to their sickle yield:
 Their furrow oft the stubborn glebe has
 broke:
How jocund did they drive their team
 a-field!
 How bow'd the woods beneath their
 sturdy stroke! —Gray.

Look up! the wide extended plain
Is billowy with its ripened grain,
And on the summer winds are rolled
Its waves of emerald and gold.
 —Wm. Henry Burleigh.

In the age of acorns, antecedent to Ceres and the royal ploughman Triptolemus, a single barley-corn had been of more value to mankind than all the diamonds that glowed in the mines of India.—H. Brooke.

Our rural ancestors, with little blest,
Patient of labor when the end was rest,
Indulg'd the day that hous'd their annual
 grain,
With feasts, and off'rings, and a thankful
 strain. —Pope.

And he gave it for his opinion, that whoever could make two ears of corn, or two blades of grass, to grow upon a spot of ground where only one grew before, would deserve better of mankind, and do more essential service to

his country, than the whole race of politicians put together.—Swift.

It is not known where he that invented the plough was born nor where he died; yet he has effected more for the happiness of the world ,than the whole race of heroes and of conquerors who have drenched it with tears and manured it with blood, and whose birth, parentage, and education have been handed down to us with a precision precisely proportionate to the mischief they have done.—Colton.

E'en in mid-harvest, while the jocund swain
Pluck'd from the brittle stalk the golden
 grain,
Oft have I seen the war of winds contend,
And prone on earth th' infuriate storm de-
 scend,
Waste far and wide, and by the roots
 uptorn,
The heavy harvest sweep through ether
 borne,
As the light straw and rapid stubble fly
In dark'ning whirlwinds round the wintry
 sky. —Virgil.

In ancient times, the sacred Plough em-
 ploy'd
The Kings and awful Fathers of mankind:
And some, with whom compared your in-
 sect-tribes
Are but the beings of a summer's day,
Have held the Scale of Empire, ruled the
 Storm
Of mighty War; then, with victorious hand,
Disdaining little delicacies, seized
The Plough, and, greatly independent,
 scorned
All the vile stores corruption can bestow.
 —Thomson.

In a moral point of view, the life of the agriculturist is the most pure and holy of any class of men; pure, because it is the most healthful, and vice can hardly find time to contaminate it; and holy, because it brings the Deity perpetually before his view, giving him thereby the most exalted notions of supreme power, and the most fascinating and endearing view of moral benignity.—Lord John Russell.

Alchemy

I have always looked upon alchemy in natural philosophy to be like enthusiasm in divinity, and to have troubled the world much to the same purpose.—Sir W. Temple.

It is an art without art, which has its beginning in falsehood, its middle in toil, and its end in poverty.—From the Latin.

If by fire
Of sooty coal th' empiric alchymist
Can turn, or holds it possible to turn,
Metals of drossest ore to perfect gold.
—Milton.

The glorious sun
Stays in his course and plays the alchemist,
Turning with splendor of his precious eye
The meager cloddy earth to glittering gold.
—Shakespeare.

Alchemy may be compared to the man who told his sons he had left them gold buried somewhere in his vineyard; where they by digging found no gold, but by turning up the mould, about the roots of their vines, procured a plentiful vintage. So the search and endeavors to make gold have brought many useful inventions and instructive experiments to light.—Bacon.

Alienation, Evils of

Nothing presents a more mournful aspect than a family divided by anger and animosity. Unhappily, however, this is not a very rare occurrence. We even behold at times, brothers themselves so indifferent towards each other, so wanting in affection, or even in a state of such hostility among themselves that they appear as if they had been cherished by the same fond heart only to be divided by their tastes and manner of thinking. Often they are less obliging to one another than they are to persons whom they know not.—Zachokke.

Allegory

Allegory dwells in a transparent palace.—Le Mierre.

A man conversing in earnest, if he watch his intellectual processes, will find that a material image, more or less luminous, arises in his mind, contemporaneous with every thought, which furnishes the vestment of the thought. Hence, good writing and brilliant discourse are perpetual allegories.—Emerson.

Allegories, when well chosen, are like so many tracks of light in a discourse, that make everything about them clear and beautiful.—Addison.

Almond

With a bee in every bell,
Almond bloom, we greet thee well.
—Edwin Arnold.

Blossom of the almond trees,
April's gift to April's bees.
—Edwin Arnold.

White as the blossoms which the almond tree,
Above its bald and leafless branches bears.
—Margaret J. Preston.

Like to an almond tree ymounted hye
On top of greene Selinis all alone,
With blossoms brave bedecked daintily;
Whose tender locks do tremble every one,
At everie little breath, that under heaven is blowne.
—Spenser.

Almond blossom, sent to teach us
That the spring days soon will reach us.
—Edwin Arnold.

Alms

Charity is the perfection and ornament of religion.—Addison.

Where there is plenty, charity is a duty, not a courtesy.—Feltham.

We may cover a multitude of sins with the white robe of charity.—Beecher.

Are we not to pity and supply the poor, though they have no relation to us? No relation? That cannot be. The Gospel styles them all our brethren.—Thomas Sprat.

Those good men who take such pleasure in relieving the miserable for Christ's sake, would not have been less forward to minister unto Christ Himself.—Atterbury.

Shall we repine at a little misplaced charity, we who could no way foresee the effect, when an all-knowing, all-wise Being showers down every day His benefits on the unthankful and undeserving?—Atterbury.

Alone

It is not good that man should be alone.—Genesis ii. 18.

They are never alone that are accompanied with noble thoughts.—Sir Philip Sidney.

The time never lies heavy upon him; it is impossible for him to be alone.—Addison.

When musing on companions gone,
We doubly feel ourselves alone.
—Scott.

Alone!—that worn-out word,
So idly spoken, and so coldly heard;
Yet all that poets sing, and grief hath known,
Of hopes laid waste, knells in that word—
Alone. —Lytton.

Amaranth

Bid amaranthus all his beauty shed,
And daffodillies fill their cups with tears,
To strew the laureate hearse where Lycid lies. —Milton.

Nosegays! leave them for the waking,
Throw them earthward where they grew
Dim are such, beside the breaking
Amaranths he looks unto.
Folded eyes see brighter colors than the open ever do. —E. B. Browning.

Amaranths such as crown the maids
That wander through Zamara's shades.
—Moore.

Immortal amaranth, a flower which once
In Paradise, fast by the Tree of Life,
Began to bloom, but soon for Man's offence,
To heav'n remov'd, where first it grew, there grows,
And flow'rs aloft shading the fount of life.
—Milton.

Ambassador

An ambassador is an honest man sent to lie abroad for the commonwealth.—Sir H. Wotton.

Ambition

Ambition is the mind's immodesty.—Davenant.

Ambition's cradle oftenest is its grave.—Longfellow.

By that sin angels fell.—Shakespeare.

The glorious frailty of the noble mind.—Hoole.

The noblest spirit is most strongly attracted by the love of glory.—Cicero.

Ambition has no rest!—Bulwer-Lytton.

Men would be angels, angels would be gods.—Pope.

The path of glory leads but to the grave.—Gray.

Ambition, like a torrent, never looks back.—Ben Jonson.

Vaulting ambition, which overleaps itself.—Shakespeare.

Ambition is not a vice of little people.—Montaigne.

I charge thee, fling away ambition:
By that sin fell the angels.
—Shakespeare.

No man is born without ambitious worldly desires.—Carlyle.

All may have, if they dare try, a glorious life or grave.—Herbert.

Ambition is like love, impatient both of delays and rivals.—Denham.

Though ambition in itself is a vice, yet it is often the parent of virtues.—Quintilian.

If you wish to reach the highest, begin at the lowest.—Syrus.

Fatal ambition! say what wondrous charms Delude mankind to toil for thee in arms?
—Rowe.

Ambition is but the evil shadow of aspiration.—George Macdonald.

You have greatly ventured, but all must do so who would greatly win.—Byron.

When once ambition has passed its natural limits, its progress is boundless.—Seneca.

Nothing is too high for the daring of mortals: we storm heaven itself in our folly.—Horace.

Ambition is like hunger; it obeys no law but its appetite.—H. W. Shaw.

He who surpasses or subdues mankind must look down on the hate of those below.—Byron.

The highest and most lofty trees have the most reason to dread the thunder.—Rollin.

Ambition hath one heel nail'd in hell,
Though she stretch her fingers to touch the
heavens. —Lilly.

They that stand high, have many blasts to
shake them;
And if they fall, they dash themselves to
pieces. —Shakespeare.

Ambition breaks the ties of blood, and forgets the obligations of gratitude.—Sir W. Scott.

Think not ambition wise, because 't is brave.—Sir W. Davenant.

Too low they build who build beneath the stars.—Young.

What is ambition but desire of greatness?
And what is greatness but extent of power?
—Higgons.

Beware ambition; heaven is not reached with pride, but with submission.—Middleton.

Who soars too near the sun, with golden wings, melts them.—Shakespeare.

How like a mounting devil in the heart
Rules the unreined ambition!
—Willis.

Take away ambition and vanity, and where will be your heroes and patriots?—Seneca.

It is the constant fault and inseparable ill quality of ambition never to look behind it.—Seneca.

Ah! curst ambition! to thy lures we owe
All the great ills that mortals bear below.
—Teckell.

Blood only serves to wash Ambition's hands.—Byron.

Remarkable places are like the summits of rocks; eagles and reptiles only can get there.—Madame Necker.

Ambition hath but two steps; the lowest, blood; the highest, envy.—Lilly.

We frequently pass from love to ambition, but one seldom returns from ambition to love.—Rochefoucauld.

————there is a fire and motion of the soul,
But once kindled, quenchless evermore.
—Byron.

Most people would succeed in small things if they were not troubled with great ambitions.—Longfellow.

Proud-crested fiend, the world's worst foe, ambition.—Bloomfield.

Ambition thinks no face so beautiful as that which looks from under a crown.—Sir P. Sidney.

Ambition is the germ from which all growth of nobleness proceeds.—T. D. English.

It is by attempting to reach the top at a single leap that so much misery is produced in the world.—Cobbett.

Ambition often puts men upon doing the meanest offices; so climbing is performed in the same posture with creeping.—Swift.

The tallest trees are most in the power of the winds, and ambitious men of the blasts of fortune.—William Penn.

One may easily enough guard against ambition till five-and-twenty. It is not ambition's day.—Shenstone.

Ambition, like love, can abide no lingering; and ever urgeth on his own successes, hating nothing but what may stop them.—Sir P. Sidney.

Neither love nor ambition, as it has often been shown, can brook a division of its empire in the heart.—Bovee.

It is observed by Cicero, that men of the greatest and most shining parts are most actuated by ambition.—Addison.

The cheat ambition, eager to espouse

dominion, courts it with a lying show, and shines in borrowed pomp to serve a turn.—Jeffrey.

The ambitious deceive themselves when they propose an end to their ambition; for that end, when attained, becomes a means.—Rochefoucauld.

Ambition is an idol, on whose wings great minds are carried only to extreme,—to be sublimely great, or to be nothing.—Southern.

What is ambition? It is a glorious cheat! Angels of light walk not so dazzlingly the sapphire walls of heaven.—Willis.

Our natures are like oil; compound us with anything,
Yet will we strive to swim to the top.
—Beaumont and Fletcher.

Ambition is a lust that's never quenched,
Grows more inflamed, and madder by enjoyment.
—Otway.

Ambition has but one reward for all:
A little power, a little transient fame,
A grave to rest in, and a fading name!
—William Winter.

Uncurbed ambition, unresisting sloth,
And base dependence, are the fiends accurst.
—Mason.

Ambition sufficiently plagues her proselytes, by keeping themselves always in show, like the statue of a public place.—Montaigne.

In the world there are only two ways of raising one's self, either by one's own industry or by the weakness of others.—Bruyère.

Unruly ambition is deaf, not only to the advice of friends, but to the counsels and monitions of reason itself.—L'Estrange.

To wish is of little account; to succeed you must earnestly desire; and this desire must shorten thy sleep.—Ovid.

When you are aspiring to the highest place, it is honorable to reach the second or even the third rank.—Cicero.

The object of ambition, unlike that of love, never being wholly possessed, ambition is the more durable passion of the two.—Bulwer-Lytton.

Ambition is an idol, on whose wings
Great minds are carried only to extreme;
To be sublimely great or to be nothing.
—Southey.

For my part, I had rather be the first man among these fellows than the second man in Rome.—Cæsar.

Dream after dream ensues,
And still they dream that they shall still succeed,
And still are disappointed.   —Cowper.

A slave has but one master; the ambitious man has as many masters as there are persons whose aid may contribute to the advancement of his fortune.—Bruyère.

Like dogs in a wheel, birds in a cage, or squirrels in a chain, ambitious men still climb and climb, with great labor, and incessant anxiety, but never reach the top.—Burton.

Be always displeased at what thou art, if thou desire to attain to what thou art not; for where thou hast pleased thyself, there thou abidest.—Quarles.

Every one has before his eyes an end which he pursues till death; but for many that end is a feather which they blow before them in the air.—Nicoll.

Ambition is a rebel both to the soul and reason, and enforces all laws, all conscience; treads upon religion, and offers violence to nature's self.—Ben Jonson.

But what will not ambition and revenge
Descend to? who aspires must down as low
As high he soar'd, obnoxious first or last
To basest things.   —Milton.

There is a native baseness in the ambition which seeks beyond its desert, that never shows more conspicuously than when, no matter how, it temporarily gains its object.—Simms.

The modesty of certain ambitious persons consists in becoming great without making too much noise; it may be said that they advance in the world on tiptoe.—Voltaire.

Wisdom is corrupted by ambition, even when the quality of the ambition is intellectual. For ambition, even of this quality, is but a form of self-love. —Henry Taylor.

I begin where most people end, with a full conviction of the emptiness of all sorts of ambition, and the unsatisfactory nature of all human pleasures. —Pope.

Ambition's like a circle on the water,
Which never ceases to enlarge itself,
'Till by broad spreading it disperse to
    nought.   —Shakespeare.

                    Talents angel-bright,
If wanting worth are shining instruments
In false ambition's hand, to finish faults
Illustrious, and give infamy renown.
                              —Young.

We should be careful to deserve a good reputation by doing well; and when that care is once taken, not to be over anxious about the success.— Rochester.

O cursed ambition, thou devouring bird,
How dost thou from the field of honesty
Pick every grain of profit or delight,
And mock the reaper's toil!   —Havard

All my ambition is, I own,
To profit and to please unknown;
Like streams supplied from springs below,
Which scatter blessings as they go.
                        —Dr. Cotton.

If love and ambition should be in equal balance, and come to jostle with equal force, I make no doubt but that the last would win the prize.—Montaigne.

Where ambition can be so happy as to cover its enterprises even to the person himself, under the appearance of principle, it is the most incurable and inflexible of all human passions.— Hume.

Most natures are insolvent; cannot satisfy their own wants, have an am-

bition out of all proportion to their practical force, and so do lean and beg day and night continually.—Emerson.

Ambition! deadly tyrant! inexorable master! what alarms, what anxious hours, what agonies of heart, are the sure portion of thy gaudy slaves?— Mallet.

A hop and skip shall raise the son of a cobbler, well underlaid with pieces, to the government of a prince, till overmuch ambitious cutting wears him to his last.—Nabbes.

It is not for man to rest in absolute contentment. He is born to hopes and aspirations, as the sparks fly upward, unless he has brutified his nature, and quenched the spirit of immortality, which is his portion.—Southey.

Ambition makes the same mistake concerning power that avarice makes concerning wealth. She begins by accumulating power as a mean to happiness, and she finishes by continuing to accumulate it as an end.—Colton.

Moderation cannot have the credit of combating and subduing ambition,— they are never found together. Moderation is the languor and indolence of the soul, as ambition is its activity and ardor.—Rochefoucauld.

Ambition is but avarice on stilts, and masked. God sometimes sends a famine, sometimes a pestilence, and sometimes a hero, for the chastisement of mankind; none of them surely for our admiration.—Landor.

Who knows but He, whose hand the light-
    ning forms,
Who heaves old ocean, and who wings the
    storms,
Pours fierce ambition in a Cæsar's mind.
                              —Pope.

Dreams, indeed, are ambition; for the very substance of the ambitious is merely the shadow of a dream. And I hold ambition of so airy and light a quality, that it is but a shadow's shadow.—Shakespeare.

Ambition is like choler, which is a

humor that maketh men active, earnest, full of alacrity, and stirring, if it be not stopped, but if it be stopped, and cannot have its way, it becometh fiery, and thereby malign and venomous.—Bacon.

We should reflect that whatever tempts the pride and vanity of ambitious persons is not so big as the smallest star which we see scattered in disorder and unregarded on the pavement of heaven.—Jeremy Taylor.

Ambition is a spirit in the world
That causes all the ebbs and flows of nations,
Keeps mankind sweet by action; without that,
The world would be a filthy, settled mud.
—Crown.

Aspiring to nothing but humility, the wise man will make it the height of his ambition to be unambitious. As he cannot effect all that he wishes, he will only wish for that which he can effect.—Chatfield.

Ambition is to the mind what the cap is to the falcon; it blinds us first, and then compels us to tower, by reason of our blindness. But alas! when we are at the summit of a vain ambition, we are also at the depth of misery.—Colton.

Ill-weaved ambition, how much art thou shrunk! when that this body did contain a spirit, a kingdom for it was too small a bound; but now, two paces of the vilest earth is room enough.—Shakespeare.

When ambitious men find an open passage, they are rather busy than dangerous; and if well watched in their proceedings, they will catch themselves in their own snare, and prepare a way for their own destruction.—Quarles.

If not for that of conscience, yet at least for ambition's sake, let us reject ambition, let us disdain that thirst of honor and renown, so low and mendicant, that it makes us beg it of all sorts of people.—Montaigne.

Nothing can be more destructive to ambition, and the passion for conquest, than the true system of astronomy. What a poor thing is even the whole globe in comparison of the infinite extent of nature!—Fontenelle.

Don Quixote thought he could have made beautiful bird-cages and toothpicks if his brain had not been so full of ideas of chivalry. Most people would succeed in small things if they were not troubled with great ambitions.—Longfellow.

Be not with honor's gilded baits beguil'd,
  Nor think ambition wise, because 'tis brave;
For though we like it, as a forward child,
  'Tis so unsound, her cradle is the grave.
—Davenant.

Ambition's monstrous stomach does increase
By eating, and it fears to starve, unless
It still may feed, and all it sees devour;
Ambition is not tir'd with toil nor cloy'd
  with power.
—Davenant.

Oh, sons of earth! attempt ye still to rise,
By mountains pil'd on mountains to the skies?
Heav'n still with laughter the vain toil surveys,
And buries madmen in the heaps they raise.
—Pope.

Ambition is a gilded misery, a secret poison, a hidden plague, the engineer of deceit, the mother of hypocrisy, the parent of envy, the original of vices, the moth of holiness, the blinder of hearts, turning medicines into maladies, and remedies into diseases.—Thomas Brooks.

Hard, withering toil only can achieve a name; and long days and months and years must be passed in the chase of that bubble, reputation, which, when once grasped, breaks in your eager clutch into a hundred lesser bubbles, that soar above you still.—Mitchell.

Ambition is frequently the only refuge which life has left to the denied or mortified affections. We chide at the grasping eye, the daring wing, the soul that seems to thirst for sovereignty only, and know not that the flight of this ambitious bird has been from a bosom or home that is filled with ashes.—Simms.

We must distinguish between felicity and prosperity; for prosperity leads often to ambition, and ambition to disappointment; the course is then over, the wheel turns round but once, while the reaction of goodness and happiness is perpetual.—Landor.

What's all the gaudy glitter of a crown?
What but the glaring meteor of ambition,
That leads the wretch benighted in his errors,
Points to the gulf and shines upon destruction.   —Brooke.

Ambition is torment enough for an enemy; for it affords as much discontentment in enjoying as in want, making men like poisoned rats, which, when they have tasted of their bane, cannot rest till they drink, and then can much less rest till they die.—Bishop Hall.

Ambition becomes displeasing when it is once satiated; there is a reaction; and as our spirit, till our last sigh, is always aiming toward some object, it falls back on itself, having nothing else on which to rest; and having reached the summit, it longs to descend.—Corneille.

To be ambitious of true honor, of the true glory and perfection of our natures, is the very principle and incentive of virtue; but to be ambitious of titles, of place, of ceremonial respects and civil pageantry, is as vain and little as the things are which we court.—Sir. P. Sidney.

Lowliness is young ambition's ladder,
Whereto the climber-upward turns his face;
And when he once obtains the upmost round,
He then unto the ladder turns his back,
Looks in the clouds, scorning the base degrees
By which he did ascend.   —Shakespeare.

Lives there the man with soul so dead as to disown the wish to merit the people's applause, and having uttered words worthy to be kept by cedar oil to latest times, to leave behind him rhymes that dread neither herrings nor frankincense.—Persius.

A noble man compares and estimates himself by an idea which is higher than himself, and a mean man by one which is lower than himself. The one produces aspiration; the other, ambition. Ambition is the way in which a vulgar man aspires.—Beecher.

Ambition, that high and glorious passion, which makes such havoc among the sons of men, arises from a proud desire of honor and distinction; and when the splendid trappings in which it is usually caparisoned are removed, will be found to consist of the mean materials of envy, pride, and covetousness.—Burton.

It is the nature of ambition to make men liars and cheats, and hide the truth in their breasts, and show, like jugglers, another thing in their mouths; to cut all friendships and enmities to the measure of their interest, and to make a good countenance without the help of a good will.—Sallust.

If at great things thou would'st arrive,
Get riches first, get wealth, and treasure heap,
Not difficult, if thou hearken to me;
Riches are mine, fortune is in my hand,
They whom I favor thrive in wealth amain,
While virtue, valor, wisdom, sit in want.
                —Milton.

The man who seeks one thing in life, and but one,
May hope to achieve it before life be done;
But he who seeks all things, wherever he goes,
Only reaps from the hopes which around him he sows
A harvest of barren regrets.
                —Owen Meredith.

Man was ·mark'd
A friend in his creation to himself,
And may, with fit ambition, conceive
The greatest blessings, and the highest honors
Appointed for him, if he can achieve them
The right and noble way.   —Massinger.

If we look abroad upon the great multitude of mankind, and endeavor to trace out the principles of action in every individual, it will, I think, seem highly probable that ambition runs through the whole species, and that every man, in proportion to the vigor of his complexion, is more or less actuated by it.—Thomas Hughes.

Those that were up themselves, kept others
   low;
Those that were low themselves, held others
   hard;
He suffered them to ryse or greater grow;
But every one did strive his fellow down to
   throw.   —Spenser.

I am as one
Who doth attempt some lofty mountain's
   height,
And having gained what to the upcast eye
The summit's point appear'd, astonish'd sees
Its cloudy top, majestic and enlarged,
Towering aloft, as distant as before.
      —Joanna Baillie.

Say what we will, you may be sure that ambition is an error; its wear and tear of heart are never recompensed —it steals away the freshness of life,— it deadens its vivid and social enjoyments,—it shuts our souls to our own youth,—and we are old ere we remember that we have made a fever and a labor of our raciest years.—Bulwer-Lytton.

There is no greater unreasonableness in the world than in the designs of ambition; for it makes the present certainly miserable, unsatisfactory, troublesome, and discontented, for the uncertain acquisition of an honor which nothing can secure; and, besides a thousand possibilities of miscarrying, it relies upon no greater certainty than our life; and when we are dead all the world sees who was the fool. —Jeremy Taylor.

Farewell, a long farewell, to all my greatness!
This is the state of man. To-day he puts
   forth
The tender leaves of hope; to-morrow blossoms,
And bears his blushing honors thick upon
   him;
The third day comes a frost, a killing frost.
      —Shakespeare.

It is a true observation of ancient writers, that as men are apt to be cast down by adversity, so they are easily satiated with prosperity, and that joy and grief produce the same effects. For whenever men are not obliged by necessity to fight they fight from ambition, which is so powerful a passion in the human breast that however high we reach we are never satisfied.—Machiavelli.

The cheat ambition, eager to espouse
Dominion, courts it with a lying show,
And shines in borrow'd pomp to serve a
   turn;
But the match made, the farce is at an end;
And all the hireling equipage of virtues,
Faith, honor, justice, gratitude and friend-
   ship,
Discharg'd at once.   —Jeffreys.

The wondrous architecture of the world,
And measure every wandering planet's
   course,
Still climbing after knowledge infinite,
And always moving as the restless spheres,
Will us to wear ourselves, and never rest
Until we reach the ripest fruit of all,
That perfect bliss and sole felicity,
The sweet fruition of a heavenly crown.
      —Marlowe.

The shadow, wheresoever it passes, leaves no track behind it; and of the greatest personages of the world, when they are once dead, then there remains no more than if they had never lived. How many preceding emperors of the Assyrian monarchy were lords of the world as well as Alexander! and now we remain not only ignorant of their monuments, but know not so much as their names. And of the same great Alexander, what have we at this day except the vain noise of his fame?— Jeremy Taylor.

On the summit see,
The seals of office glitter in his eyes;
He climbs, he pants, he grasps them! At
   his heels,
Close at his heels, a demagogue ascends,
And with a dexterous jerk soon twists him
   down,
And wins them, but to lose them in his turn.
      —Cowper.

Ambition is, of all other, the most contrary humor to solitude; and glory and repose are so inconsistent that they cannot possibly inhabit one and the same place; and for so much as I understand, those have only their arms and legs disengaged from the crowd, their mind and intention remain engaged behind more than ever.—Montaigne.

There is a kind of grandeur and respect which the meanest and most insignificant part of mankind endeavor to procure in the little circle of their friends and acquaintance. The poorest mechanic, nay, the man who lives upon common alms, gets him his set of admirers, and delights in that superiority which he enjoys over those who are in some respects beneath him. This ambition, which is natural to the soul of man, might, methinks, receive a very happy turn; and, if it were rightly directed, contribute as much to a person's advantage, as it generally does to his uneasiness and disquiet.—Addison.

This raging, vehement desire,
Of sovereignty no satisfaction finds;
But in the breasts of men doth ever roll
The restless stone of Sisyph, to torment them,
And as his heart, who stole the heav'nly fire,
The vulture gnaws, so doth that monster rent them;
Had they the world, the world would not content them.   —Earl of Sterling.

America

Child of the earth's old age.—Miss Langdon.

The home of the homeless all over the earth.—Street.

America, — half-brother of the world!—Bailey.

America is rising with a giant's strength. Its bones are yet but cartilages.—Fisher Ames.

I was born an American; I live an American; I shall die an American.—Daniel Webster.

America is a fortunate country. She grows by the follies of our European nations.—Napoleon.

Sail on, O Ship of State!
Sail on, O Union, strong and great.
        —Longfellow.

The enterprise of America precedes that of Europe, as the industry of England precedes that of the rest of Europe.—Beaconsfield.

America has begun her career at the culminating point of life, as Adam did at the age of thirty.—Mme. Swetchine.

Earth's biggest country's gut her soul
An' risen up earth's greatest nation.
        —Lowell.

Down to the Plymouth Rock, that had been to their feet as a doorstep
Into a world unknown—the corner-stone of a nation!   —Longfellow.

America has furnished to the world the character of Washington! And if our American institutions had done nothing else, that alone would have entitled them to the respect of mankind.—Daniel Webster.

Columbia, Columbia, to glory arise,
The queen of the world and the child of the skies!
Thy genius commands thee; with rapture behold,
While ages on ages thy splendors unfold.
        —Timothy Dwight.

England, our mother's mother! Come and see
A greater England here! O come and be
    At home with us, your children, for there runs
    The same blood in our veins as in your sons;
The same deep-seated love of liberty
Beats in our hearts. We speak the same good tongue;
Familiar with all songs your bards have sung,
Those large men, Milton, Shakespeare, both are ours.   —Stoddard.

Cease to brag to me of America, and its model institutions and constitutions. America, too, will have to strain its energies, crack its sinews, and all but break its heart, as the rest of us have had to do, in thousand-fold wrestle with the Pythons and muddemons, before it can become a habitation for the gods.—Carlyle.

Young man, there is America—which at this day serves for little more than to amuse you with stories of savage men and uncouth manners; yet shall, before you taste of death, show itself equal to the whole of that commerce which now attracts the envy of the world.—Burke.

Lo! body and soul!—this land!
Mighty Manhattan, with spires, and
The sparkling and hurrying tides, and the ships;
The varied and ample land—the South
And the North in the light—Ohio's shores, and flashing Missouri,
And ever the far-spreading prairies, covered with grass and corn.
—Walt Whitman.

Our country, whether bounded by the St. John's and the Sabine, or however otherwise bounded or described, and be the measurement more or less, —still our country, to be cherished in all our hearts, to be defended by all our hands.—Robert C. Winthrop.

Amiability

Amiability shines by its own light. —Horace.

Amiability is the redeeming quality of fools.—Miss Braddon.

How easy it is to be amiable in the midst of happiness and success!—Madame Swetchine.

We ought to regard amiability as the quality of woman, dignity that of man.—Cicero.

Amiability is very often a weakness, but the most unobjectionable one as a rule.—Lady Morgan.

Amiable people, while they are more liable to imposition in casual contact with the world, yet radiate so much of mental sunshine that they are reflected in all appreciative hearts.—Madame Deluzy.

That constant desire of pleasing, which is the peculiar quality of some, may be called the happiest of all desires in this, that it scarcely ever fails of attaining its ends, when not disgraced by affectation.—Fielding.

The amiable is a duty most certainly, but must not be exercised at the expense of any of the virtues. He who seeks to do the amiable always, can only be successful at the frequent expense of his manhood.—Simms.

Amnesty

Amnesty, that noble word, the genuine dictate of wisdom.—Æschines.

Amusement

No man is a hypocrite in his pleasures.—Dr. Johnson.

Encourage innocent amusement.—Addison.

The real character of a man is found out by his amusements.—Sir Joshua Reynolds.

Pastime passing excellent, if it be husbanded with modesty. — Shakespeare.

Amusement, to an observing mind, is study.—Beaconsfield.

A clear fire, a clean hearth, and the rigor of the game.—Lamb.

I am a great friend to public amusements; for they keep people from vice.—Samuel Johnson.

There is no such sport as sport by sport o'erthrown.—Shakespeare.

Any pleasure which takes and keeps the heart from God is sinful, and unless forsaken, will be fatal to the soul. —Richard Fuller.

Recreation is not the highest kind of enjoyment; but in its time and place it is quite as proper as prayer.—S. Irenæus Prime.

Cards were at first for benefits designed,
Sent to amuse, not to enslave the mind.
—Garrick.

People should be guarded against temptation to unlawful pleasures by furnishing them means of innocent ones.—Channing.

The mind ought sometimes to be amused, that it may the better return to thought, and to itself.—Phædrus.

Amusement allures and deceives us, and leads us down imperceptibly in thoughtlessness to the grave.—Pascal.

You can't live on amusement. It is the froth on water,—an inch deep, and then the mud!—George Macdonald.

When I play with my cat, who knows whether I do not make her more sport than she makes me?—Montaigne.

With spots quadrangular of diamond form,
Ensanguined hearts, clubs typical of strife,
And spades, the emblems of untimely
    graves.   —Cowper.

They are to religion like breezes of air to the flame,—gentle ones will fan it, but strong ones will put it out.—Rev. Dr. Thomas.

By sports like these are all their cares beguil'd,
The sports of children satisfy the child.
                    —Goldsmith.

So good things may be abused, and that which was first invented to refresh men's weary spirits.—Burton.

If those who are the enemies of innocent amusements had the direction of the world, they would take away the spring, and youth, the former from the year, the latter from human life. —Balzac.

The Eastern monarch who proclaimed a reward to him who should discover a new pleasure, would have deserved well of mankind had he stipulated that it should be blameless.—Whately.

Locke, whom there is no reason to suspect of being a favorer of idleness or libertinism, has advanced that whoever hopes to employ any part of his time with efficacy and vigor must allow some of it to pass in trifles.—Dr. Johnson.

We have all our playthings. Happy are they who are contented with those they can obtain; those hours are spent in the wisest manner that can easiest shade the ills of life, and are the least productive of ill consequences.—Lady Montagu.

Hail, blest Confusion! here are met
    All tongues, and times, and faces;
The Lancers flirt with Juliet,
    The Brahmin talks of races.
                    —Praed.

It is exceedingly deleterious to withdraw the sanction of religion from amusement. If we feel that it is all injurious we should strip the earth of its flowers and blot out its pleasant sunshine.—Chapin.

Let the world have their May-games, wakes, whetsunales, their dancings and concerts; their puppet-shows, hobby horses, tabors, bagpipes, balls, barley-breaks, and whatever sports and recreations please them best, provided they be followed with discretion.—Burton.

To find recreation in amusements is not happiness; for this joy springs from alien and extrinsic sources, and is therefore dependent upon and subject to interruption by a thousand accidents, which may minister inevitable affliction.—Pascal.

The habit of dissipating every serious thought by a succession of agreeable sensations is as fatal to happiness as to virtue; for when amusement is uniformly substituted for objects of moral and mental interest, we lose all that elevates our enjoyments above the scale of childish pleasures.—Anna Maria Porter.

Whatever amuses, serves to kill time, to lull the faculties, and to banish reflection. Whatever entertains, usually awakens the understanding or gratifies the fancy. Whatever diverts, is lively in its nature, and sometimes tumultuous in its effects.—Crabbe.

Analogy

The instincts of the ant are very unimportant, considered as the ant's; but the moment a ray of relation is seen to extend from it to man, and the little drudge is seen to be a monitor, a little body with a mighty heart, then all its habits, even that said to be recently observed, that it never sleeps, become sublime.—Emerson.

Anarchy

In a state of anarchy power is the measure of right.—Lucan.

Anarchy is the sure consequence of tyranny; for no power that is not limited by laws can ever be protected by them.—Milton.

The choking, sweltering, deadly, and killing rule of no rule; the consecration of cupidity and braying of folly, and dim stupidity and baseness, in most of the affairs of men. Slopshirts attainable three-halfpence cheaper by the ruin of living bodies and immortal souls.—Carlyle.

Bad as any government may be, it is seldom worse than anarchy.—Æsop.

Anatomy

It is shameful for man to rest in ignorance of the structure of his own body, especially when the knowledge of it mainly conduces to his welfare, and directs his application of his own powers.—Melancthon.

Ancestry

By blood a king, in heart a clown.
—Tennyson.

Breed is stronger than pasture.—George Eliot.

Some men by ancestry are only the shadow of a mighty name.—Lucan.

He who boasts of his lineage boasts of that which does not properly belong to him.—Seneca.

Whoever serves his country well has no need of ancestors.—Voltaire.

I am no herald to inquire of men's pedigrees; it sufficeth me if I know their virtues.—Sir P. Sidney.

Pride, in boasting of family antiquity, makes duration stand for merit.—Zimmermann.

People will not look forward to posterity, who never look backward to their ancestors.—Burke.

He who boasts of his descent, praises the deeds of another.—Seneca.

What is birth to a man if it shall be a stain to his dead ancestors to have left such an offspring?—Sir P. Sidney.

It is, indeed, a blessing, when the virtues of noble races are hereditary; and do derive themselves from the imitation of virtuous ancestors.—Nabb.

Philosophy does not regard pedigree; she did not receive Plato as a noble, but she made him so.—Seneca.

It is of no consequence of what parents any man is born, so that he be a man of merit.—Horace.

The man who has nothing to boast of but his illustrious ancestry is like a potato,—the only good belonging to him is underground.—Sir Thomas Overbury.

Great families of yesterday we show,
And lords whose parents were the Lord
knows who.   —Daniel De Foe.

From yon blue heaven above us bent, the grand old gardener and his wife smile at the claims of long descent.—Tennyson.

Our ancestors are very good kind of folks; but they are the last people I should choose to have a visiting acquaintance with.—Sheridan.

What can they see in the longest kingly line in Europe, save that it runs back to a successful soldier?—Walter Scott.

When real nobleness accompanies that imaginary one of birth, the imaginary seems to mix with real, and becomes real too.—Lord Greville.

It is better to be the builder of our own name than to be indebted by descent for the proudest gifts known to the books of heraldry.—Hosea Ballou.

He that boasts of his ancestors, the founders and raisers of a family, doth confess that he hath less virtue.—Jeremy Taylor.

___

The pride of ancestry is a superstructure of the most imposing height, but resting on the most flimsy foundation.—Colton.

___

They that on glorious ancestors enlarge,
Produce their debt, instead of their discharge. —Young.

___

Pedigrees seldom improve by age; the grandson is too often a weak infringement on the grandsire's patent.—H. W. Shaw.

___

If it is fortunate to be of noble ancestry, it is not less so to be such as that people do not care to be informed whether you are noble or ignoble.—Bruyère.

___

It is a shame for a man to desire honor because of his noble progenitors, and not to deserve it by his own virtue.—St. Chrysostom.

___

Nobility of birth is like a cipher; it has no power in itself, like wealth or talent; but it tells with all the power of a cipher when added to either of the other two.—J. F. Boyes.

___

We are very fond of some families because they can be traced beyond the Conquest, whereas indeed the farther back, the worse, as being the nearer allied to a race of robbers and thieves.—De Foe.

___

The happiest lot for a man as far as birth is concerned, is that it should be such as to give him but little occasion to think much about it.—Whately.

___

I am one who finds within me a nobility that spurns the idle pratings of the great, and their mean boasts of what their fathers were, while they themselves are fools effeminate.—Percival.

___

Birth and ancestry, and that which we have not ourselves achieved, we can scarcely call our own.—Ovid.

Some decent, regulated pre-eminence, some preference (not exclusive appropriation) given to birth, is neither unnatural nor unjust nor impolitic.—Burke.

___

Those who depend on the merits of their ancestors may be said to search in the roots of the tree for those fruits which the branches ought to produce.—Barrow.

___

He that to ancient wreaths can bring no more
From his own worth, dies bankrupt on the score. —Cleveland.

___

I have no urns, no dusty monuments;
No broken images of ancestors,
Wanting an ear, or nose; no forged tales
Of long descents, to boast false honors from.—Ben Jonson.

___

It is a revered thing to see an ancient castle not in decay; how much more to behold an ancient family which have stood against the waves and weathers of time!—Bacon.

___

High birth is a thing which I never knew any one to disparage except those who had it not; and I never knew any one to make a boast of it who had anything else to be proud of.—Bishop Warburton.

___

The origin of all mankind was the same; it is only a clear and good conscience that makes a man noble, for that is derived from heaven itself.—Seneca.

___

I make little account of genealogical trees. Mere family never made a man great. Thought and deed, not pedigree, are the passports to enduring fate.—General Skobeleff.

___

It has long seemed to me that it would be more honorable to our ancestors to praise them in words less, but in deeds to imitate them more.—Horace Mann.

___

Title and ancestry render a good man more illustrious, but an ill one more contemptible. Vice is infamous, though in a prince, and virtue honorable, though in a peasant.—Addison.

Pride of origin, whether high or low, springs from the same principle in human nature; one is but the positive, the other the negative, pole of a single weakness.—Lowell.

People who take no pride in the noble achievements of remote ancestors will never achieve anything worthy to be remembered with pride by remote descendants.—Macaulay.

The nobility of the Spencers has been illustrated and enriched by the trophies of Marlborough; but I exhort them to consider the "Faerie Queene," as the most priceless jewel of their coronet.—Gibbon.

It is with antiquity as with ancestry, nations are proud of the one, and individuals of the other; but if they are nothing in themselves, that which is their pride ought to be their humiliation.—Colton.

Of all vanities of fopperies, the vanity of high birth is the greatest. True nobility is derived from virtue, not from birth. Titles, indeed, may be purchased, but virtue is the only coin that makes the bargain valid.—Burton.

The generality of princes, if they were stripped of their purple and cast naked on the world, would immediately sink to the lowest rank of society, without a hope of emerging from their obscurity.—Gibbon.

The glory of ancestors sheds a light around posterity; it allows neither their good nor bad qualities to remain in obscurity.—Sallust.

Let him speak of his own deeds, and not of those of his forefathers. High birth is mere accident, and not virtue; for if reason had controlled birth, and given empire only to the worthy, perhaps Arbaces would have been Xerxes, and Xerxes Arbaces.—Metastasio.

Those who have nothing else to recommend them to the respect of others but only their blood, cry it up at a great rate, and have their mouths perpetually full of it. They swell and

vapor, and you are sure to hear of their families and relations every third word.—Charron.

Being well satisfied that, for a man who thinks himself to be somebody, there is nothing more disgraceful than to hold himself up as honored, not on his own account, but for the sake of his forefathers. Yet hereditary honors are a noble and splendid treasure to descendants.—Plato.

He that boasts of his ancestors confesses that he has no virtue of his own. No person ever lived for our honor; nor ought that to be reputed ours, which was long before we had a being; for what advantage can it be to a blind man to know that his parents had good eyes? Does he see one whit the better?—Charron.

Though you be sprung in direct line from Hercules, if you show a low-born meanness, that long succession of ancestors whom you disgrace are so many witnesses against you; and this grand display of their tarnished glory but serves to make your ignominy more evident.—Boileau.

In the founders of great families, titles or attributes of honor are generally correspondent with the virtues of the person to whom they are applied; but in their descendants they are too often the marks rather of grandeur than of merit. The stamp and denomination still continue, but the intrinsic value is frequently lost.—Addison.

The character of the reputed ancestors of some men has made it possible for their descendants to be vicious in the extreme, without being degenerate: and there are some hereditary strokes of character by which a family may be as clearly distinguished as by the blackest features of the human face.—Junius.

It is only shallow-minded pretenders who either make distinguished origin a matter of personal merit, or obscure origin a matter of personal reproach. Taunt and scoffing at the humble condition of early life affect nobody in

America but those who are foolish enough to indulge in them, and they are generally sufficiently punished by the published rebuke. A man who is not ashamed of himself need not be ashamed of his early condition.—Daniel Webster.

———

It was the saying of a great man, that if we could trace our descents, we should find all slaves to come from princes, and all princes from slaves; and fortune has turned all things topsy-turvy in a long series of revolutions; beside, for a man to spend his life in pursuit of a title, that serves only when he dies to furnish out an epitaph, is below a wise man's business.—Seneca.

———

Take the title of nobility which thou hast received by birth, but endeavor to add to it another, that both may form a true nobility. There is between the nobility of thy father and thine own the same difference which exists between the nourishment of the evening and of the morrow. The food of yesterday will not serve three for to-day, and will not give thee strength for the next.—Jamakchari.

———

There may be, and there often is, indeed, a regard for ancestry which nourishes only a weak pride; as there is also a care for posterity, which only disguises an habitual avarice, or hides the workings of a low and groveling vanity. But there is also a moral and philosophical respect for our ancestors, which elevates the character and improves the heart.—Daniel Webster.

———

If there be no nobility of descent, all the more indispensable is it that there should be nobility of ascent,—a character in them that bear rule so fine and high and pure that as men come within the circle of its influence they involuntarily pay homage to that which is the one pre-eminent distinction,—the royalty of virtue.—Bishop Henry C. Potter.

———

The pride of ancestry is a superstructure of the most imposing height, but resting on the most flimsy foundation. It is ridiculous enough to ob-

serve the hauteur with which the old nobility look down on the new. The reason of this puzzled me a little, until I began to reflect that most titles are respectable only because they are old; if new, they would be despised, because all those who now admire the grandeur of the stream would see nothing but the impurity of the source.—Colton.

———

No man is nobler born than another, unless he is born with better abilities and a more amiable disposition. They who make such a parade with their family pictures and pedigrees, are, properly speaking, rather to be called noted or notorious than noble persons. I thought it right to say this much, in order to repel the insolence of men who depend entirely upon chance and accidental circumstances for distinction, and not at all on public services and personal merit.—Seneca.

———

The power of perpetuating our property in our families is one of the most valuable and interesting circumstances belonging to it, and that which tends the most to the perpetuation of society itself. It makes our weakness subservient to our virtue; it grafts benevolence even upon avarice. The possession of family wealth and of the distinction which attends hereditary possessions (as most concerned in it), are the natural securities for this transmission.—Burke.

———

We sometimes see a change of expression in our companion, and say, his father or his mother comes to the windows of his eyes, and sometimes a remote relative. In different hours, a man represents each of several of his ancestors, as if there were seven or eight of us rolled up in each man's skin,—seven or eight ancestors at least, —and they constitute the variety of notes for that new piece of music which his life is.—Emerson.

Ancients

We derive all that is pardonable in us from ancient fountains.—Dryden.

———

The sages of old live again in us, and

in opinions there is a metempsychosis. —Glanvill.

The moderns cannot reach their beauties, but can avoid their imperfections.—Addison.

Those whom we call the ancients were in truth novices in all things, and properly constituted the infancy of mankind.—Prescott.

In taste and imagination, in the graces of style, in the arts of persuasion, in the magnificence of public works, the ancients were at least our equals.—Macaulay.

They left a great deal for the industry and sagacity of after ages.—Locke.

Anemone

Anemone, so well
Named of the wind, to which thou art all
free.   —George MacDonald.

From the soft wing of vernal breezes shed,
Anemones, auriculas, enriched
With shining meal o'er all their velvet
leaves.   —Thomson.

Anemones and seas of gold,
And new-blown lilies of the river,
And those sweet flow'rets that unfold
Their buds on Camadera's quiver.
    —Moore.

Thy subtle charm is strangely given,
My fancy will not let thee be—
Then poise not thus 'twixt earth and
heaven,
O white anemone!   —Elaine Goodale.

Within the woods,
Whose young and half transparent leaves
scarce cast
A shade, gray circles of anemones
Danced on their stalks.   —Bryant.

Angels

Angels and ministers of grace defend us!—Shakespeare.

Fools rush in where angels fear to tread.—Pope.

Like angel visits, few and far between.—Campbell.

We are never like angels till our passion dies.—Thomas Decker.

And flights of angels sing thee to thy rest!—Shakespeare.

Angels are bright still, though the brightest fell.—Shakespeare.

Millions of spiritual creatures walk the earth unseen, both when we sleep and when we wake.—Milton.

Angels boast ethereal vigor, and are formed from seeds of heavenly birth. —Virgil.

White wing'd angels meet the child
On the vestibule of life.
    —Mrs. E. Oakes Smith.

Angels contented with their face in heaven.
Seek not the praise of men.   —Milton.

A guardian angel o'er his life presiding,
Doubling his pleasures, and his cares dividing.   —Samuel Rogers.

So dear to heaven is saintly chastity,
That when a soul is found sincerely so
A thousand liveried angels lackey her.
    —Milton.

If you woo the company of the angels in your waking hours, they will be sure to come to you in your sleep. —G. D. Prentice.

We cannot let our angels go; we do not see that they only go out that archangels may come in.—Emerson.

The helmed Cherubim,
And sworded Seraphim,
Are seen in glittering ranks with wings dis-
play'd.   —Milton.

In this dim world of clouding cares,
We rarely know, till 'wildered eyes
See white wings lessening up the skies,
The angels with us unawares.
    —Gerald Massey.

How sweetly did they float upon the wings
Of silence through the empty-vaulted night,
At every fall smoothing the raven down
Of darkness till it smiled!   —Milton.

The angels may have wider spheres of action, may have nobler forms of duty; but right with them and with us is one and the same thing.—Chapin.

The guardian angel of life sometimes flies so high that man cannot see

it; but he always is looking down upon
us, and will soon hover nearer to us.
—Richter.

O, though oft oppressed and lonely,
  All my fears are laid aside,
If I but remember only
  Such as these have lived and died!
            —Longfellow.

Sweet souls around us watch us still,
  Press nearer to our side;
Into our thoughts, into our prayers,
  With gentle helpings glide.
        —Harriet Beecher Stowe.

For God will deign
To visit oft the dwellings of just men
Delighted, and with frequent intercourse
Thither will send his winged messengers
On errands of supernal grace. —Milton.

But all God's angels come to us disguised:
Sorrow and sickness, poverty and death,
One after other lift their frowning masks,
And we behold the Seraph's face beneath,
All radiant with the glory and the calm
Of having looked upon the front of God.
            —Lowell.

Around our pillows golden ladders rise,
  And up and down the skies,
With winged sandals shod,
The angels come, and go, the messengers of
  God!
Nor, though they fade from us, do they de-
  part—
It is the childly heart:
We walk as heretofore,
Adown their shining ranks, but see them
  nevermore.   —R. H. Stoddard.

Compare a Solomon, an Aristotle,
or an Archimedes, to a child that newly begins to speak, and they do not
more transcend such a one than the
angelical understanding exceeds theirs,
even in its most sublime improvements and acquisitions.—South.

Man hath two attendant angels,
  Ever waiting by his side,
With him wheresoe'er he wanders,
  Wheresoe'er his feet abide;
One to warn him when he darkleth,
  And rebuke him if he stray;
One to leave him to his nature,
  And so let him go his way.
            —Prince.

The accusing spirit, which flew up
to heaven's chancery with the oath,
blushed as he gave it in; and the recording angel, as he wrote it down,
dropped a tear upon the word and
blotted it out forever.—Sterne.

There are two angels that attend unseen
Each one of us, and in great books record
Our good and evil deeds. He who writes
  down
The good ones, after every action closes
His volume, and ascends with it to God.
The other keeps his dreadful day-book open
Till sunset, that we may repent; which
  doing,
The record of the action fades away,
And leaves a line of white across the page.
Now if my act be good, as I believe it,
It cannot be recalled. It is already
Sealed up in heaven, as a good deed ac-
  complished.
The rest is yours.   —Longfellow.

Anger

Let not the sun go down upon your
wrath.—Bible.

Temperate anger well becomes the
wise.—Philemon.

Anger is practical awkwardness.—
Colton.

Anger is a short madness.—Horace.

A temperate anger has virtue in it.—
Haliburton.

Men in rage strike those that wish
them best.—Shakespeare.

Abused patience turns to fury.—
Quarles.

Anger manages everything badly.—
Stadius.

Never anger made good guard for
itself.—Shakespeare.

Anger is self-immolation.—Phillips
Brooks.

Keep cool, and you command everybody.—St. Just.

Their rage supplies them with
weapons.—Virgil.

Like fragile ice anger passes away
in time.—Ovid.

He that will be angry for anything
will be angry for nothing.—Sallust.

Nursing her wrath to keep it warm.
—Burns.

When anger rushes, unrestrained, to action.—Savage.

He that would be angry and sin not must not be angry with anything but sin.—Secker.

Men often make up in wrath what they want in reason.—W. R. Alger.

People hardly ever do anything in anger, of which they do not repent.—Richardson.

To be in anger is impiety, but who is man that is not angry?—Shakespeare.

Anger is like a ruin, which, in falling upon its victim, breaks itself to pieces.—Seneca.

Whatsoever is worthy of their love is worth their anger.—Sir J. Denham.

There is no affectation in passion, for that putteth a man out of his precepts.—Bacon.

Anger is a transient hatred; or at least very like it.—South.

You may forgive, and so will I; but I will not forget, though I control my anger.—Colton.

Anger begins with folly, and ends with repentance.—Pythagoras.

When angry, count ten before you speak; if very angry, a hundred.—Jefferson.

Anger is like a full hot horse; who, being allowed his way, self-mettle tires him.—Shakespeare.

Anger is like rain which breaks itself whereon it falls.—Seneca.

And to be wroth with one we love
Doth work like madness in the brain.
—Coleridge.

An angry woman is vindictive beyond measure, and hesitates at nothing in her bitterness.—J. Petit-Senn.

Anger causes us often to condemn in one what we approve of in another.—Pasquier Quesnel.

Anger's my meat; I sup upon myself
And so shall starve with feeding.
—Shakespeare.

When a man is wrong and won't admit it, he always gets angry.—Haliburton.

He is a fool who cannot be angry; but he is a wise man who will not.—Seneca.

He best keeps from anger who remembers that God is always looking upon him.—Plato.

A countenance more in sorrow than in anger.—Shakespeare.

Heaven hath no rage like love to hatred turned, nor hell a fury like a woman scorned.—Congreve.

To be angry, is to revenge the fault of others upon ourselves.—Pope.

An angry man opens his mouth and shuts up his eyes.—Cato.

To abandon yourself to rage is often to bring upon yourself the fault of another.—Agapet.

To rule one's anger is well; to prevent it is better.—Edwards.

When anger rises, think of the consequences.—Confucius.

Violence in the voice is often only the death-rattle of reason in the throat.—J. F. Boyes.

Anger is one of the sinews of the soul.—Fuller.

The angriest person in a controversy is the one most liable to be in the wrong.—Tillotson.

Anger is not only the prevailing sin of argument, but its greatest stumbling-block.—Gladstone.

Anger has some claim to indulgence, and railing is usually a relief to the mind.—Junius.

An angry man is again angry with himself when he returns to reason.—Publius Syrus.

When one is in a good sound rage, it is astonishing how calm one can be.—Bulwer-Lytton.

It is he who is in the wrong who first gets angry.—William Penn.

A fit of anger is as fatal to dignity as a dose of arsenic is to life.—J. G. Holland.

A man deep-wounded may feel too much pain to feel much anger.—George Eliot.

Anger is blood, poured and perplexed into froth; but malice is the wisdom of our wrath.—Sir W. Davenant.

What most increases anger is the feeling that one is in the wrong.—Richter.

Anger turns the mind out of doors and bolts the entrance.—Plutarch.

Weak men are easily put out of humor. Oil freezes quicker than water.—Auerbach.

A woman moved is like a fountain troubled, muddy, ill-seeming, thick, bereft of beauty.—Shakespeare.

Convulsive anger storms at large; or pale
And silent, settles into full revenge.
—Thomson.

He submits himself to be seen through a microscope, who suffers himself to be caught in a fit of passion.—Lavater.

Our passions are like convulsion fits, which make us stronger for the time, but leave us weaker forever after.—Dean Swift.

The proud man hath no God; the envious man hath no neighbor; the angry man hath not himself.—Bishop Hall.

Scarce can I speak, my choler is so great. Oh! I could hew up rocks, and fight with flint.—Shakespeare.

He that contemns a shrew to the degree of not descending to words with her does worse than beat her.—L'Estrange.

Check and restrain anger. Never make any determination until you find it has entirely subsided.—Lord Collingwood.

If anger is not restrained, it is frequently more hurtful to us, than the injury that provokes it.—Seneca.

The elephant is never won by anger; nor must that man who would reclaim a lion take him by the teeth.—Dryden.

Have you not love enough to bear with me, when that rash humor which my mother gave me makes me forgetful.—Shakespeare.

Lamentation is the only musician that always, like a screech-owl, alights and sits on the roof of any angry man.—Plutarch.

He that is slow to anger is better than the mighty; and he that ruleth his spirit, than he that taketh a city.—Bible.

Anger is a noble infirmity, the generous failing of the just, the one degree that riseth above zeal, asserting the prerogative of virtue.—Tupper.

Anger is uneasiness or discomposure of the mind upon the receipt of any injury, with a present purpose of revenge.—Locke.

Give not reins to your inflamed passions; take time and a little delay; impetuosity manages all things badly.—Statius.

Anger is the most impotent passion that accompanies the mind of man; it effects nothing it goes about; and hurts the man who is possessed by it more than any other against whom it is directed.—Clarendon.

The most phlegmatic dispositions often contain the most inflammable spirits, as fire is struck from the hardest flints.—Hazlitt.

Anger ventilated often hurries towards forgiveness; anger concealed often hardens into revenge.—Bulwer-Lytton.

Must I give way and room to your rash choler? Shall I be frighted when a madman stares?—Shakespeare.

In the same degree in which a man's mind is nearer to freedom from all passion, in the same degree also is it nearer to strength.—Marcus Antoninus.

Bad temper is its own scourge. Few things are bitterer than to feel bitter. A man's venom poisons himself more than his victim.—Charles Buxton.

My rage is not malicious; like a spark
Of fire by steel inforced out of a flint
It is no sooner kindled, but extinct.
—Goffe.

Anger wishes all mankind had only one neck; love, that it had only one heart; grief, two tear-garlands; pride, two bent knees.—Richter.

If anger proceeds from a great cause, it turns to fury; if from a small cause, it is peevishness; and so is always either terrible or ridiculous. —Jeremy Taylor.

There is not in nature
A thing that makes a man so deform'd, so
  beastly,
As doth intemperate anger.   —Webster.

O that my tongue were in the thunder's
  mouth!
Then with a passion would I shake the
  world.   —Shakespeare.

Those passionate persons who carry their heart in their mouth are rather to be pitied than feared; their threatenings serving no other purpose than

to forearm him that is threatened.—Fuller.

I was angry with my friend:
I told my wrath, my wrath did end.
I was angry with my foe;
I told it not, my wrath did grow.
—Wm. Blake.

Anger requires that the offender should not only be made to grieve in his turn, but to grieve for that particular wrong which has been done by him.—Whately.

You are yoked with a lamb,
That carries anger as the flint bears fire;
Who, much enforced, shows a hasty spark,
And straight is cold again.—Shakespeare.

An angry man who suppresses his passions thinks worse than he speaks; and an angry man that will chide speaks worse than he thinks.—Bacon.

Anger blows out the lamp of the mind. In the examination of a great and important question, every one should be serene, slow-pulsed, and calm.—R. G. Ingersoll.

When anger rushes unrestrained to action, like a hot steed, it stumbles on its way. The man of thought strikes deepest and strikes safely.—Savage.

To be angry about trifles is mean and childish; to rage and be furious is brutish; and to maintain perpetual wrath is akin to the practice and temper of devils.—Dr. Watts.

Are you angry? Look at the child who has erred, he suspects no trouble, he dreams of no harm; you will borrow something of that innocence, you will feel appeased.—Chateaubriand.

There is no way but to meditate and ruminate well upon the effects of anger,—how it troubles man's life; and the best time to do this is to look back upon anger when the fit is thoroughly over.—Bacon.

The "last word" is the most dangerous of infernal machines; and the husband and wife should no more fight to get it than they would struggle for the possession of a lighted bomb-shell.—Douglas Jerrold.

The intoxication of anger, like that of the grape, shows us to others, but hides us from ourselves, and we injure our own cause, in the opinion of the world, when we too passionately and eagerly defend it.—Colton.

Angry and choleric men are as ungrateful and unsociable as thunder and lightning, being in themselves all storm and tempest; but quiet and easy natures are like fair weather, welcome to all.—Clarendon

---

As a conquered rebellion strengthens a government, or as health is more perfectly established by recovery from some diseases; so anger, when removed, often gives new life to affection.—Fielding.

Anger is like the waves of a troubled sea; when it is corrected with a soft reply, as with a little strand, it retires, and leaves nothing behind but froth and shells,—no permanent mischief.—Jeremy Taylor.

Anger is the most impotent passion that accompanies the mind of man. It effects nothing it goes about; and hurts the man who is possessed by it more than any other against whom it is directed.—Clarendon.

If a man meets with injustice, it is not required that he shall not be roused to meet it; but if he is angry after he has had time to think upon it, that is sinful. The flame is not wrong, but the coals are.—Beecher.

The round of a passionate man's life is in contracting debts in his passion, which his virtue obliges him to pay. He spends his time in outrage and acknowledgment, injury and reparation.—Johnson.

Never forget what a man has said to you when he was angry. If he has charged you with anything, you had better look it up. Anger is a bow that will shoot sometimes where another feeling will not.—Beecher.

Had I a careful and pleasant companion that should show me my angry face in a glass, I should not at all take it ill; to behold man's self so unnaturally disguised and dishonored will conduce not a little to the impeachment of anger.—Plutarch.

Anger and the thirst of revenge are a kind of fever; fighting and lawsuits, bleeding,—at least, an evacuation. The latter occasions a dissipation of money; the former, of those fiery spirits which cause a preternatural fermentation.—Shenstone.

For pale and trembling anger rushes in
With faltering speech, and eyes that wildly
    stare,
Fierce as the tiger, madder than the seas,
Desperate and armed with more than hu-
    man strength.   —Armstrong.

I never work better than when I am inspired by anger. When I am angry I can write, pray, and preach well; for then my whole temperament is quickened, my understanding sharpened, and all mundane vexations and temptations depart.—Luther.

Anger is implanted in us as sort of sting, to make us gnash with our teeth against the devil, to make us vehement against him, not to set us in array against each other.—Savage.

But curb thou the high spirit in thy breast,
For gentle ways are best.
                        —Homer.

Anger is an affected madness, compounded of pride and folly, and an intention to do commonly more mischief than it can bring to pass; and, without doubt, of all passions which actually disturb the mind of man, it is most in our power to extinguish, at least, to suppress and correct, our anger.—Clarendon.

Full many mischiefs follow cruel wrath;
Abhorred bloodshed and tumultuous strife
Unmanly murder and unthrifty scath,
Bitter despite, with rancor's rusty knife,
And fretting grief the enemy of life;
All these and many evils more, haunt ire.
                        —Spenser.

Be ye angry, and sin not; therefore all anger is not sinful; I suppose because some degree of it, and upon some occasions, is inevitable. It becomes sinful, or contradicts, however, the rule of Scripture, when it is conceived upon slight and inadequate provocation, and when it continues long.—Paley.

———

Alas! they had been friends in youth;
But whispering tongues can poison truth,
And constancy lives in realms above;
And life is thorny, and youth is vain;
And to be wroth with one we love
Doth work like madness in the brain.
           —Coleridge.

———

There is no passion that so much transports men from their right judgments as anger. No one would demur upon punishing a judge with death who should condemn a criminal upon the account of his own choler; why then should fathers and pedants be any more allowed to whip and chastise children in their anger? It is then no longer correction but revenge. Chastisement is instead of physic to children; and should we suffer a physician who should be animated against and enraged at his patient?—Montaigne.

———

When I myself had twice or thrice made a resolute resistance unto anger, the like befell me that did the Thebans; who, having once foiled the Lacedæmonians (who before that time had held themselves invincible), never after lost so much as one battle which they fought against them.—Plutarch.

Angling

Angling is an innocent cruelty.—George Parker.

———

Idle time not idly spent.—Sir Henry Wotton.

———

Angling is somewhat like poetry; men are to be born so.—Izaak Walton.

———

Everything appertaining to the angler's art is cowardly, cruel, treacherous, and cat-like.—Chatfield.

———

The pleasantest angling is to see the fish cut with her golden oars the silver stream, and greedily devour the treacherous bait.—Shakespeare.

Doubt not but angling will prove to be so pleasant, that it will prove to be, like virtue, a reward to itself.—Izaak Walton.

———

I have known a very good fisher angle diligently four or six hours for a river carp, and not have a bite.—Izaak Walton.

———

We really cannot see what equanimity there is in jerking a lacerated carp out of the water by the jaws, merely because it has not the power of making a noise; for we presume that the most philosophic of anglers would hardly delight in catching shrieking fish.—Leigh Hunt.

———

But should you lure
From his dark haunt, beneath the tangled roots
Of pendent trees, the monarch of the brook,
Behooves you then to ply your finest art.
           —Thomson.

———

The first men that our Saviour dear
Did choose to wait upon Him here,
Blest fishers were; and fish the last
Food was, that He on earth did taste:
I therefore strive to follow those,
Whom He to follow Him hath chose.
           —Izaak Walton.

———

O! the gallant fisher's life,
   It is the best of any:
'Tis full of pleasure, void of strife
   And 'tis beloved by many.
      Other joys
      Are but toys;
      Only this,
      Lawful is;
      For our skill
      Breeds no ill,
But content and pleasure.
           —Izaak Walton.

———

Though no participator in the joys of more vehement sport, I have a pleasure that I cannot reconcile to my abstract notions of the tenderness due to dumb creatures, in the tranquil cruelty of angling. I can only palliate the wanton destructiveness of my amusement by trying to assure myself that my pleasure does not spring from the success of the treachery I practise toward a poor little fish, but rather from that innocent revelry in the luxuriance of summer life which only anglers enjoy to the utmost.—Bulwer-Lytton.

In genial spring, beneath the quiv'ring
    shade,
Where cooling vapors breathe along the
    mead,
The patient fisher takes his silent stand,
Intent, his angle trembling in his hand;
With looks unmoved, he hopes the scaly
    breed,
And eyes the dancing cork and bending
    reed.   —Pope.

We may say of angling as Dr. Boteler said of strawberries, "Doubtless God could have made a better berry, but doubtless God never did;" and so, if I might be judge, God never did make a more calm, quiet, innocent recreation than angling.—Izaak Walton.

Animal

Animals are such agreeable friends; they ask no questions, pass no criticisms.—George Eliot.

If 't were not for my cat and dog, I think I could not live.—Ebenezer Elliott.

They rejoice each with their kind, lion with lioness, so fitly them in pairs thou hast combined.—Milton.

    Let cavillers deny
That brutes have reason; sure 'tis something
    more,
'Tis heaven directs, and stratagems inspires
Beyond the short extent of human thought.
    —Somerville.

There is in every animal's eye a dim image and gleam of humanity, a flash of strange light through which their life looks out and up to our great mystery of command over them, and claims the fellowship of the creature if not of the soul.—Ruskin.

Annihilation

Annihilation, as regards matter, is simply impossible.—Hosea Ballou.

Annihilation is an absurdity in terms.—Palissy.

Nothing whatever is annihilated; matter, like an eternal, still rolls on without any diminution.—Roucher.

Anticipation

Anticipation and Hope are born twins.—Rousseau.

The anticipation of evil courts evil.—Mme. Deluzy.

Nothing is so good as it seems beforehand.—George Eliot.

Troubles forereckoned are doubly suffered.—Bovee.

It is worse to apprehend than to suffer.—Bruyère.

Experience finds few of the scenes that lively hope designs.—Crabbe.

Oft expectation fails, and most oft there where most it promises.—Shakespeare.

We expect everything, and are prepared for nothing.—Madame Swetchine.

Thou tremblest before anticipated ills, and still bemoanest what thou never losest.—Goethe.

He who foresees calamities suffers them twice over.—Porteus.

All things that are, are with more spirit chased than enjoyed.—Shakespeare.

It is a great obstacle to happiness to expect too much.—Fontenelle.

Anticipate the difficult by managing the easy.—Lao-Tze.

The craving for a delicate fruit is pleasanter than the fruit itself.—Herder.

Suffering itself does less afflict the senses than the apprehension of suffering.—Quintilian.

What need a man forestall his date of grief, and run to meet what he would most avoid?—Milton.

I know that we often tremble at an empty terror; yet the false fancy brings a real misery.—Schiller.

Nothing is so great an adversary to those who make it their business to please as expectation.—Cicero.

All earthly delights are sweeter in expectation than enjoyment; but all spiritual pleasures more in fruition than expectation.—Feltham.

We can but ill endure, among so many sad realities, to rob anticipation of its pleasant visions.—Henry Giles.

It is expectation makes a blessing dear; heaven were not heaven if we knew what it were.—John Suckling.

There is nothing so wretched or foolish as to anticipate misfortunes. What madness is it in expecting evil before it arrives?—Seneca.

I would not anticipate the relish of any happiness, nor feel the weight of any misery, before it actually arrives.—Spectator.

I am giddy; expectation whirls me 'round.
The imaginary relish is so sweet
That it enchants my sense.
                    —Shakespeare.

We part more easily with what we possess, than with our expectations of what we wish for; because expectation always goes beyond enjoyment.—Henry Home.

Whatever advantage we snatch beyond a certain portion allotted us by nature, is like money spent before it is due, which, at the time of regular payment, will be missed and regretted.—Johnson.

To despond is to be ungrateful beforehand. Be not looking for evil. Often thou drainest the gall of fear while evil is passing by thy dwelling.—Tupper.

With every one, the expectation of a misfortune constitutes a dreadful punishment. Suffering then assumes the proportions of the unknown, which is the soul's infinite.—Balzac.

The events we most desire do not happen; or, if they do, it is neither in the time nor in the circumstances when they would have given us extreme pleasure.—Bruyère.

The problem is, whether a man constantly and strongly believing that such a thing shall be, it don't help anything to the effecting of the thing.—Bacon.

There are many things that are thorns to our hopes until we have attained them, and envenomed arrows to our hearts when we have.—Mirabeau.

There would be few enterprises of great labor or hazard undertaken, if we had not the power of magnifying the advantages which we persuade ourselves to expect from them.—Johnson.

Drawing near her death, she sent most pious thoughts as harbingers to heaven, and her soul saw a glimpse of happiness through the chinks of her sickness-broken body.—Thomas Fuller.

Things temporal are sweeter in the expectation, things eternal are sweeter in the fruition; the first shames thy hope, the second crowns it; it is a vain journey, whose end affords less pleasure than the way.—Quarles.

A man's desires always disappoint him; for though he meets with something that gives him satisfaction, yet it never thoroughly answers his expectation.—Rochefoucauld.

All fear is in itself painful, and when it conduces not to safety, is painful without use. Every consideration, therefore, by which groundless terrors may be removed adds something to human happiness.—Dr. Johnson.

The hours we pass with happy prospects in view are more pleasing than those crowned with fruition. In the first instance, we cook the dish to our own appetite; in the latter, Nature cooks it for us.—Goldsmith.

Such is the uncertainty of human affairs, that security and despair are equal follies; and as it is presumption and arrogance to anticipate triumphs, it is weakness and cowardice to prognosticate miscarriages.—Dr. Johnson.

It has been well said that no man ever sank under the burden of the day. It is when to-morrow's burden is added to the burden of to-day that the weight is more than a man can bear.—George Macdonald.

Men spend their lives in anticipations, in determining to be vastly happy at some period or other, when they have time. But the present time has one advantage over every other, it is our own.—Colton.

The pilot who is always dreading a rock or a tempest must not complain if he remain a poor fisherman. We must at times trust something to fortune, for fortune has often some share in what happens.—Metastasio.

In all worldly things that a man pursues with the greatest eagerness and intention of mind imaginable, he finds not half the pleasure in the actual possession of them, as he proposed to himself in the expectation.—South.

By anticipation we suffer misery and enjoy happiness before they are in being. We can set the sun and stars forward, or lose sight of them by wandering into those retired parts of eternity when the heavens and earth shall be no more.—Addison.

In proportion as our cares are employed upon the future, they are abstracted from the present, from the only time which we can call our own, and of which, if we neglect the apparent duties to make provision against visionary attacks, we shall certainly counteract our own purpose.—Dr. Johnson.

We are apt to rely upon future prospects, and become really expensive while we are only rich in possibility. We live up to our expectations, not to our possessions, and make a figure proportionable to what we may be, not what we are.—Addison.

Whichever way we look the prospect is disagreeable. Behind, we have left pleasures we shall never enjoy, and therefore regret; and before, we see pleasures which we languish to possess, and are consequently uneasy till we possess them.—Goldsmith.

Antiquity

Rich with the spoils of time.—Gray.

The rubbish of the past.—Mme. Louise Colet.

Antiquity is the aristocracy of history.—Dumas, Père.

The great men of antiquity were poor.—Lacordaire.

Antiquity! I like its ruins better than its reconstructions.—Joubert.

The sacred rust of twice ten hundred years.—Pope.

It is one proof of a good education, and of true refinement of feeling, to respect antiquity.—Mrs. Sigourney.

Time consecrates; and what is gray with age becomes religion.—Schiller.

Those we call the ancients were really new in everything.—Pascal.

Age shakes Athena's tower, but spares gray Marathon.—Byron.

Antiquity is a species of aristocracy with which it is not easy to be on visiting terms.—Madame Swetchine.

Nor rough, nor barren, are the winding ways
Of hoar Antiquity, but strewn with flowers.
—Thomas Warton.

The pyramids, doting with age, have forgotten the names of their founders. Fuller.

Cities, unlike human creatures, may grow to be so old that at last they will become new.—William Winter.

Those old ages are like the landscape that shows best in purple distance, all verdant and smooth, and bathed in mellow light.—Chapin.

How cunningly Nature hides every wrinkle of her inconceivable antiquity under roses and violets and morning dew!—Emerson.

We have a mistaken notion of antiquity, calling that so which in truth is the world's nonage.—Glanvill.

Some persons can never relish the full moon, out of respect for that venerable institution, the old one.—Douglas Jerrold.

It is with antiquity as with ancestry; nations are proud of the one, and individuals of the other.—Colton.

It is looked upon as insolence for a man to adhere to his own opinion against the current stream of antiquity.—Locke.

Time's gradual touch has mouldered into beauty many a tower, which when it frowned with all its battlements was only terrible.—Mason.

All those things that are now held to be of the greatest antiquity were at one time new; what we to-day hold up by example will rank hereafter as precedent.—Tacitus.

We have a maxim in the House of Commons, and written on the walls of our houses, that old ways are the safest and surest ways.—Sir E. Coke.

If the seal of time were to be the signet of truth, there is no absurdity, oppression, or falsehood that might not be revived as gospel; while the gospel itself would want the more ancient warrant of paganism.—Chatfield.

A thorough-paced antiquary not only remembers what all other people have thought proper to forget, but he also forgets what all other people think is proper to remember.—Colton.

When ancient opinions and rules of life are taken away, the loss cannot possibly be estimated. From that moment we have no compass to govern us; nor can we know distinctly to what port to steer.—Burke.

What subsists to-day by violence continues to-morrow by acquiescence, and is perpetuated by tradition; till at last the hoary abuse shakes the gray hairs of antiquity at us, and gives itself out as the wisdom of ages.—Edward Everett.

The volumes of antiquity, like medals, may very well serve to amuse the curious; but the works of the moderns, like the current coin of a kingdom, are much better for immediate use.—Goldsmith.

I do by no means advise you to throw away your time in ransacking, like a dull antiquarian, the minute and unimportant parts of remote and fabulous times. Let blockheads read what blockheads wrote.—Chesterfield.

History fades into fable; fact becomes clouded with doubt and controversy; the inscription moulders from the tablet; the statue falls from the pedestal. Columns, arches, pyramids, —what are they but heaps of sand; and their epitaphs but characters written in the dust?—Washington Irving.

Consider, for example, and you will find that almost all the transactions in the time of Vespasian differed little from those of the present day. You there find marrying and giving in marriage, educating children, sickness, death, war, joyous holidays, traffic, agriculture, flatterers, insolent pride, suspicions, laying of plots, longing for the death of others, newsmongers, lovers, misers, men canvassing for the consulship and for the kingdom; yet all these passed away, and are nowhere.—Marcus Antoninus.

Those were good old times, it may be thought, when baron and peasant feasted together. But the one could not read, and made his mark with a sword-pommel, and the other was held as dear as a favorite dog. Pure and simple times were those of our grandfathers, it may be. Possibly not so pure as we may think, however, and with a simplicity ingrained with some bigotry and a good deal of conceit.—Chapin.

_____

Antiquity, what is it else (God only excepted) but man's authority born some ages before us? Now for the truth of things time makes no alteration; things are still the same they are, let the time be past, present, or to come.

_____

Those things which we reverence for antiquity what were they at their first birth? Were they false?—time cannot make them true. Were they true?—time cannot make them more true. The circumstances therefore of time in respect of truth and error is merely impertinent.—John Hales.

_____

Antiquity! thou wondrous charm, what art thou? that, being nothing, art everything! When thou wert, thou wert not antiquity,—then thou wert nothing, but hadst a remoter antiquity, as thou calledst it to look back to with blind veneration; thou thyself being to thyself flat, jejune, modern! What mystery lurks in this retroversion? or what half Januses are we, that cannot look forward with the same idolatry with which we forever revert! The mighty future is as nothing, being everything! The past is everything, being nothing!—Lamb.

Anxiety

Over-confidence is as evil as undue anxiety.—Haliburton.

_____

Anxiety never yet successfully bridged over any chasm.—Ruffini.

_____

Nobody should ever look anxious except those who have no anxiety.—Beaconsfield.

_____

Generally we obtain very surely and very speedily what we are not too anxious to obtain.—Rousseau.

_____

Among those evils which befall us, there are many which have been more painful to us in the prospect than by their actual pressure.—Addison.

_____

Better to be despised for too anxious apprehensions than ruined by too confident a security.—Burke.

_____

Nothing in life is more remarkable than the unnecessary anxiety which we endure and generally occasion ourselves.—Beaconsfield.

_____

O foolish anxiety of wretched man, how inconclusive are the arguments which make thee beat thy wings below!—Dante.

_____

Anxiety is the poison of human life. It is the parent of many sins, and of more miseries. In a world where everything is doubtful, where you may be disappointed, and be blessed in disappointment, what means this restless stir and commotion of mind? Can your solicitude alter the cause or unravel the intricacy of human events?—Blair.

_____

Almost all men are over-anxious. No sooner do they enter the world than they lose that taste for natural and simple pleasures so remarkable in early life. Every hour do they ask themselves what progress they have made in the pursuit of wealth or honor; and on they go as their fathers went before them, till, weary and sick at heart, they look back with a sigh of regret to the golden time of their childhood.—Rogers.

_____

Anxiety has no place in the life of one of God's children. Christ's serenity was one of the most unmistakable signs of His filial trust. He was tired and hungry and thirsty and in pain; but we cannot imagine Him anxious or fretful. His mind was kept in perfect peace because it was stayed on God. The life lived by the faith of the Son of God will find His word kept: "My peace give I unto you."—Maltbie Babcock.

_____

It is not work that kills men; it is worry. Work is healthy; you can hardly put more upon a man than he can bear. Worry is rust upon the blade. It is not the revolution that destroys the machinery, but the friction. Fear secretes acids; but love and trust are sweet juices.—Beecher.

Apathy

A sort of living oblivion.—Horace Greeley.

In this sullen apathy neither true wisdom nor true happiness can be found.—Hume.

According to the Stoics, apathy meant the extinction of the passions by the ascendency of reason.—William Fleming.

There are some men formed with feelings so blunt that they can hardly be said to be awake during the whole course of their lives.—Burke.

Aphorism

Collect as pearls the words of the wise and virtuous.—Abd-el-Kader.

An epigram often flashes light into regions where reason shines but dimly.—Whipple.

Books are the beehives of thought; laconics the honey taken from them.—James Ellis.

Exclusively of the abstract sciences, the largest and worthiest portion of our knowledge consists of aphorisms; and the greatest and best of men is but an aphorism.—Coleridge.

I fancy mankind may come in time to write all aphoristically, except in narration; grow weary of preparation and connection and illustration, and all those arts by which a big book is made.—Dr. Johnson.

If these little sparks of holy fire which I have thus heaped up together do not give life to your prepared and already enkindled spirit, yet they will sometimes help to entertain a thought, to actuate a passion, to employ and hallow a fancy.—Jeremy Taylor.

Apology

No sensible person ever made an apology.—Emerson.

A very desperate habit; one that is rarely cured. Apology is only egotism wrong side out. Nine times out of ten, the first thing a man's companion knows of his short-comings is from his apology.—Holmes.

Apology is only egotism wrong side out.—O. W. Holmes.

There are occasions on which all apology is rudeness.—Dr. Johnson.

Apologies only account for the evil which they cannot alter.—Disraeli.

Apostacy

The kiss of the apostate was the most bitter earthly ingredient in the agonies which Christ endured.—E. L. Magoon.

Apostate, still thou err'st, nor end wilt find
Offering, from the paths of truth remote.
        —Milton.

Apothegm

Proverbs are potted wisdom.—Charles Buxton.

Apothegms form a short cut to much knowledge.—Hood.

All generalizations are dangerous, even this one.—Dumas, Fils.

The Sibyl, speaking with inspired mouth, sends her voice to remotest ages.—Heraclitus.

Quotations are best brought in to confirm some opinion controverted.—Swift.

Proverbs are, for the most part, rules of morals, and as such are often effective.—Rev. Dr. Sharp.

Aphorisms are portable wisdom, the quintessential extracts of thought and feeling.—W. R. Alger.

Apothegms are the most infallible mirror to represent a man truly what he is.—Plutarch.

The genius, wit, and spirit of a nation are discovered by their proverbs.—Bacon.

Short, isolated sentences were the mode in which ancient wisdom delighted to convey its precepts for the regulation of human conduct.—Bishop Warburton.

Apothegms are, in history, the same as the pearls in the sand, or the gold in the mine.—Erasmus.

What gems of painting or statuary are in the world of art, or what flowers are in the world of Nature, are gems of thought to the cultivated and thinking.—O. W. Holmes.

It is astonishing the influence foolish apothegms have upon the mass of mankind, though they are not unfrequently fallacies.—Sydney Smith.

Aphorisms, representing a knowledge broken, do invite men to inquire further; whereas methods carrying the show of a total do secure men, as if they were at furthest.—Bacon.

Out of monuments, names, words, proverbs, traditions, private records and evidences, fragments of stories, passages of books, and the like, we do save and recover somewhat from the deluge of time.—Bacon.

The little and short sayings of nice and excellent men are of great value, like the dust of gold, or the least sparks of diamonds.—Tillotson.

A man of maxims only is like a Cyclops with one eye, and that eye placed in the back of his head.—Coleridge.

He that lays down precepts for the governing of our lives, and moderating our passions, obliges humanity not only in the present, but in all future generations.—Seneca.

Thoughts take up no room. When they are right, they afford a portable pleasure, which one may travel with, without any trouble or encumbrance.—Jeremy Collier.

I am of opinion that there are no proverbial sayings which are not true, because they are all sentences drawn from experience itself, who is the mother of all sciences.—Cervantes.

We content ourselves to present to thinking minds the original seeds from whence spring vast fields of new thought, that may be further cultivated, beautified, and enlarged.—Chevalier Ramsay.

Few of the many wise apothegms which have been uttered, from the time of the seven sages of Greece to that of poor Richard, have prevented a single foolish action.—Macaulay.

The excellence of aphorisms consists not so much in the expression of some rare or abstruse sentiment, as in the comprehension of some useful truth in few words.—Johnson.

Under the veil of these curious sentences are hid those germs of morals which the masters of philosophy have afterwards developed into so many volumes.—Plutarch.

Ethical maxims are bandied about as a sort of current coin of discourse, and, being never melted down for use, those that are of base metal are never detected.—Bishop Whately.

A maxim is the exact and noble expression of an important and indisputable truth. Sound maxims are the germs of good; strongly imprinted in the memory, they nourish the will.—Joubert.

Abstracts, abridgments, summaries, etc., have the same use with burning-glasses,—to collect the diffused rays of wit and learning in authors, and make them point with warmth and quickness upon the reader's imagination.—Swift.

An epigram often flashes light into regions where reason shines but dimly. Holmes disposed of a bigot at once, when he compared his mind to the pupil of the eye,—the more light you let into it the more it contracts.—Whipple.

He may justly be numbered among the benefactors of mankind who contracts the great rules of life into short sentences, that may be easily impressed on the memory, and taught by frequent recollection to recur habitually to the mind.—Johnson.

A few words worthy to be remembered suffice to give an idea of a great mind. There are single thoughts that contain the essence of a whole volume, single sentences that have the beauties of a large work, a simplicity so finished and so perfect that it equals in merit and in excellence a large and glorious composition.—Joubert.

The wise men of old have sent most of their morality down to the stream of time in the light skiff of apothegm or epigram; and the proverbs of nations, which embody the common sense of nations, have the brisk concussion of the most sparkling wit.—Whipple.

Apparel

Let thy attyre bee comely, but not costly.—Lyly.

Costly thy habit as thy purse can buy,
But not express'd in fancy; rich, not gaudy;
For the apparel oft proclaims the man.
    —Shakespeare.

        She's adorned
Amply, that in her husband's eye looks
  lovely—
The truest mirror that an honest wife
Can see her beauty in! —John Tobin.

Dress drains our cellar dry,
And keeps our larder lean; puts out our
  fires.
And introduces hunger, frost, and woe,
Where peace and hospitality might reign.
    —Cowper.

Through tatter'd clothes small vices do appear;
Robes and furr'd gowns hide all. Plate sin
  with gold,
And the strong lance of justice hurtless
  breaks;
Arm it in rags, a pigmy's straw doth
  pierce it.   —Shakespeare.

      Her polish'd limbs,
Veil'd in a simple robe, their best attire;
Beyond the pomp of dress; for Loveliness
Needs not the foreign aid of ornament,
But is, when unadorn'd, adorn'd the most.
    —Thomson.

He that is proud of the rustling of his silks, like a madman, laughs at the rattling of his fetters. For indeed, Clothes ought to be our remembrancers of our lost innocency.—Fuller.

So for thy spirit did devise
Its maker seemly garniture,
Of its own essence parcel pure—
From grave simplicities a dress,
And reticent demureness,
And love encinctured with reserve;
Which the woven vesture would subserve.
For outward robes in their ostents
Should show the soul's habiliments.
Therefore I say—thou'rt fairer even so,
But better Fair I use to know.
    —Francis Thompson.

Apparitions

A dagger of the mind, a false creation,
Proceeding from the heat-oppressed brain?
    —Shakespeare.

So many ghosts, and forms of fright,
Have started from their graves to-night,
They have driven sleep from mine eyes
  away;
I will go down to the chapel and pray.
    —Longfellow.

Who gather round, and wonder at the tale
Of horrid apparition, tall and ghastly,
That walks at dead of night, or takes his
  stand
O'er some new-open'd grave; and (strange
  to tell!)
Evanishes at crowing of the cock.
    —Blair.

Now it is the time of night,
That the graves, all gaping wide,
Every one lets forth its sprite,
In the church-way paths to glide.
    —Shakespeare.

My people too were scared with eerie
  sounds,
A footstep, a low throbbing in the walls,
A noise of falling weights that never fell,
Weird whispers, bells that rang without a
  hand,
Door-handles turn'd when none was at the
  door,
And bolted doors that open'd of themselves;
And one betwixt the dark and light had
  seen
Her, bending by the cradle of her babe.
    —Tennyson.

Appearance

We take less pains to be happy than to appear so.—Rochefoucauld.

There is in us more of the appearance of sense and virtue than of the reality.—Marguerite de Valois.

A man may smile, and smile, and be a villain.—Shakespeare.

A miser grows rich by seeming poor; an extravagant man grows poor by seeming rich.—Shenstone.

There is no vice so simple, but assumes some mark of virtue on its outward parts.—Shakespeare.

Polished brass will pass upon more people than rough gold.—Chesterfield.

A man of the world must seem to be that he wishes to be.—Bruyère.

Men are like Geneva watches with crystal faces, which expose the whole movement.—Emerson.

Tangible language, which often tells more falsehoods than truths.—Abraham Lincoln.

Thy plain and open nature sees mankind
But in appearance, not what they are.
—Froude.

Even when the bird walks one feels that it has wings.—Lemierre.

Behavior is a mirror in which every one shows his image.—Goethe.

To succeed in the world, we must be foolish in appearance, but really wise.—Montesquieu.

How little do they see what is, who frame their hasty judgments upon that which seems!—Southey.

She looks as if butter wouldn't melt in her mouth.—Swift.

That gloomy outside, like a rusty chest, contains the shining treasure of a soul resolved and brave.—Dryden.

He has, I know not what
Of greatness in his looks, and of high fate
That almost awes me. —Dryden.

O place! O form, how often dost thou with thy case, thy habit, wrench awe from fools, and tie the wiser souls to thy false seeming!—Shakespeare.

There are no greater wretches in the world than many of those whom people in general take to be happy.—Seneca.

Appearances deceive
And this one maxim is a standing rule:
Men are not what they seem.—Havard.

An emperor in his nightcap will not meet with half the respect of an emperor with a crown.—Goldsmith.

Some men, like modern shops, hang everything in their show windows; when one goes inside, nothing is to be found.—Auerbach.

Men in general judge more from appearances than from reality. All men have eyes, but few have the gift of penetration.—Macchiavelli.

Weeds grow sometimes very much like flowers, and you can't tell the difference between true and false merely by the shape.—Paxton Hood.

He had a head which statuaries loved to copy, and a foot the deformity of which the beggars in the streets mimicked.—Macaulay.

We understood
Her by her sight; her pure and eloquent blood
Spoke in her cheeks, and so distinctly wrought.
That one might almost say her body thought. —Donne.

Within the oyster's shell uncouth
The purest pearl may hide,
Trust me you'll find a heart of truth
Within that rough outside.
—Mrs. Osgood.

'Tis not the fairest form that holds
The mildest, purest soul within;
'Tis not the richest plant that holds
The sweetest fragrance in. —Dawes.

A sweet attractive kinde of grace,
A full assurance given by lookes,
Continuall comfort in a face
The lineaments of gospell bookes.
—Matthew Royden.

By a kind of fashionable discipline, the eye is taught to brighten, the lip to smile, and the whole countenance to emanate with the semblance of friendly welcome, while the bosom is un-warmed by a single spark of genuine kindness and good-will.—Washington Irving.

In all professions every one af-fects a particular look and exterior, in order to appear what he wishes to be thought; so that it may be said the world's made up of appearances.—La Rochefoucauld.

Why should the sacred character of virtue Shine on a villain's countenance? Ye powers!
Why fix'd you not a brand on treason's front
That we might know t' avoid perfidious mortals. —Dennis.

In the condition of men, it fre-quently happens that grief and anxiety lie hid under the golden robes of pros-perity; and the gloom of calamity is cheered by secret radiations of hope and comfort; as in the works of na-ture, the bog is sometimes covered with flowers, and the mine concealed in the barren crags.—Johnson.

Surely you will not calculate any essential difference from mere appear-ances; for the light laughter that bub-bles on the lip often mantles over brackish depths of sadness, and the serious look may be the sober veil that covers a divine peace. You know that the bosom can ache beneath dia-mond brooches; and how many blithe hearts dance under coarse wool!—Chapin.

It is not every man that can afford to wear a shabby coat; and worldly wisdom dictates to her disciples the propriety of dressing somewhat beyond their means, but of living somewhat within them,—for every one sees how we dress, but none see how we live, except we choose to let them. But the truly great are, by universal suffrage, exempted from these trammels, and may live or dress as they please.—Colton.

In civilized society external advan-tages make us more respected. A man with a good coat upon his back meets with a better reception than he who

has a bad one. You may analyze this and say, What is there in it? But that will avail you nothing, for it is a part of a general system.—Johnson.

Appetite

Hunger is never delicate.—Dr. John-son.

Good cheer is no hindrance to a good life.—Aristippus.

Who can cloy the hungry edge of appetite?—Shakespeare.

A dinner lubricates business.—Lord Stowell.

Fat paunches have lean pates.—Shakespeare.

Reason should direct and appetite obey.—Cicero.

Turtle makes all men equal.—Bea-consfield.

Appetite comes with eating, says An-geston.—Rabelais.

If you are surprised at the number of our maladies, count our cooks.—Seneca.

It is difficult to speak to the belly because it has no ears.—Plutarch.

Hunger makes everything sweet ex-cept itself, for want is the teacher of habits.—Antiphanes.

Choose rather to punish your appe-tites than to be punished by them.—Tyrius Maximus.

Animals feed, man eats; the man of intellect alone knows how to eat.—Brillat-Savarin.

Who rises from a feast with that keen appetite that he sits down?—Shakespeare.

And gazed around them to the left and right
With the prophetic eye of appetite.
—Byron.

All philosophy in two words,—sus-tain and abstain.—Epictetus.

The table is the only place where we do not get weary during the first hour.—Brillat-Savarin.

Here is neither want of appetite nor mouths,
Pray heaven we be not scant of meat or mirth. —Scott.

Govern well thy appetite, lest Sin
Surprise thee, and her black attendant Death. —Milton.

Now good digestion wait on appetite,
And health on both! —Shakespeare.

Some men are born to feast, and not to fight; whose sluggish minds, even in fair honor's field, still on their dinner turn.—Joanna Baillie.

Doth not the appetite alter? A man loves the meat in his youth that he cannot endure in his age.—Shakespeare.

The destiny of nations depends upon the manner in which they feed themselves.—Brillat-Savarin.

The chief pleasure in eating does not consist in costly seasoning or exquisite flavor, but in yourself. Seek you for sauce in sweating.—Horace.

The stomach is a slave that must accept everything that is given to it, but which avenges wrongs as slyly as does the slave.—Emile Souvestre.

There are men whose stomachs are the clamorous creditors that sooner or later throw them into bankruptcy.—J. L. Basford.

The pleasures of eating deal with us like Egyptian thieves, who strangle those whom they embrace.—Seneca.

Oh cookery, cookery! that kills more than weapons, guns, wars, or poisons, and would destroy all, but that physic helps to make away some.—Anthony Brewer.

The ancients had a significant and truthful saying, that hunger was the best sauce for supper.—Rowland Hill.

For the sake of health, medicines are taken by weight and measure; so ought food to be, or by some similar rule.—Skelton.

A relish bestowed upon the poorer classes, that they may like what they eat; while it is seldom enjoyed by the rich, because they may eat what they like.—Chatfield.

Hunger is a cloud out of which falls a rain of eloquence and knowledge; when the belly is empty, the body becomes spirit; when it is full, the spirit becomes body.—Saadi.

These appetites are very humiliating weaknesses. That our grace depends so largely upon animal condition is not quite flattering to those who are hyperspiritual.—Beecher.

No man's body is as strong as his appetites, but Heaven has corrected the boundlessness of his voluptuous desires by stinting his strength and contracting his capacities.—Tillotson.

Our appetites, of one or another kind, are excellent spurs to our reason, which might otherwise but feebly set about the great ends of preserving and continuing the species.—Lamb.

His thirst he slakes at some pure neighboring brook,
Nor seeks for sauce where Appetite stands cook. —Churchill.

Seest thou how pale the sated guest rises from supper, where the appetite is puzzled with varieties? The body, too, burdened with yesterday's excess, weighs down the soul, and fixes to the earth this particle of the divine essence.—Horace.

The youth who follows his appetites too soon seizes the cup, before it has received its best ingredients, and by anticipating his pleasures, robs the remaining parts of life of their share, so that his eagerness only produces a manhood of imbecility and an age of pain.—Goldsmith.

There are so few invalids who are invariably and conscientiously untemptable by those deadly domestic enemies, sweetmeats, pastry, and gravies, that the usual civilities at a meal are very like being politely assisted to the grave.—Willis.

Applause

I would applaud thee to the very echo, that should applaud again.—Shakespeare.

A slowness to applaud betrays a cold temper or an envious spirit.—Hannah More.

The applause of a single human being is of great consequence.—Johnson.

A universal applause is seldom less than two thirds of a scandal.—L'Estrange.

O popular applause! what heart of man is proof against thy sweet, seducing charms?—Cowper.

Applause is the spur of noble minds, the end and aim of weak ones.—C. C. Colton.

You may fail to shine, in the opinion of others, both in your conversation and actions, from being superior as well as inferior to them.—Greville.

The praise we give to new comers into the world arises from the envy we bear to those who are established.—La Rochefoucauld.

Praise from the common people is generally false, and rather follows vain persons than virtuous ones.—Bacon.

When the million applaud you, seriously ask yourself what harm you have done; when they censure you, what good!—Colton.

The silence that accepts merit as the most natural thing in the world, is the highest applause.—Emerson.

Neither human applause nor human censure is to be taken as the test of truth; but either should set us upon testing ourselves.—Bishop Whately.

Flattery of the verbal kind is gross. In short, applause is of too coarse a nature to be swallowed in the gross, though the extract or tincture be ever so agreeable.—Shenstone.

They threw their caps
As they would hang them on the horns o' the moon,
Shouting their emulation. —Shakespeare.

Applause waits on success: the fickle multitude, like the light straw that floats along the street, glide with the current still, and follow fortune.—Franklin.

Such a noise arose as the shrouds make at sea in a stiff tempest, as loud and to as many tunes,—hats, cloaks, doublets, I think, flew up; and had their faces been loose, this day they had been lost.—Shakespeare.

Apple

The apple blossoms' shower of earl,
Though blent with rosier hue,
As beautiful as woman's blush,
As evanescent, too. —L. E. Lawdon.

What plant we in this apple tree?
Sweets for a hundred flowery springs
To load the May-wind's restless wings,
When, from the orchard-row, he pours
Its fragance though our open doors;
A world of blossoms for the bee,
Flowers for the sick girl's silent room,
For the glad infant sprigs of bloom,
We plant with the apple tree.
        —Bryant.

And what is more melancholy than the old apple-trees that linger about the spot where once stood a homestead, but where there is now only a ruined chimney rising out of a grassy and weed-grown cellar? They offer their fruit to every wayfarer—apples that are bitter-sweet with the moral of time's vicissitude.—Nath. Hawthorne.

Appreciation

By appreciation we make excellence in others our own property.—Voltaire.

The applause of a single human being is of great consequence.—Dr. Johnson.

Were she perfect, one would admire her more, but love her less.—Grattan.

Give tribute, but not oblation, to human wisdom.—Sir. P. Sidney.

It is only by loving a thing that you can make it yours.—George Macdonald.

Men should allow others' excellences, to preserve a modest opinion of their own.—Barrow.

To appreciate the noble is a gain which can never be torn from us.—Goethe.

To love her (Lady Elizabeth Hastings) was a liberal education.—Steele.

Men prize the thing ungained more than it is.—Shakespeare.

No man ever thought too highly of his nature or too meanly of himself.—Young.

It often happens that those of whom we speak least on earth are best known in heaven.—Caussin.

It is common, to esteem most what is most unknown.—Tacitus.

Neither the praise nor the blame is our own.—Cowley.

To praise great actions with sincerity may be said to be taking part in them.—Rochefoucauld.

It is a matter of the simplest demonstration, that no man can be really appreciated but by his equal or superior.—Ruskin.

He is a fool who is not for love and beauty. I speak unto the young, for I am of them and always shall be.—Bailey.

We are very much what others think of us. The reception our observations meet with gives us courage to proceed or damps our efforts.—Hazlitt.

You may fail to shine, in the opinion of others, both in your conversation and actions, from being superior, as well as inferior to them.—Greville.

It is with certain good qualities as with the senses; those who are entirely deprived of them can neither appreciate nor comprehend them.—Rochefoucauld.

Our companions please us less from the charms we find in their conversation than from those they find in ours.—Greville.

You think much too well of me as a man. No author can be as moral as his works, as no preacher is as pious as his sermons.—Richter.

Next to invention is the power of interpreting invention; next to beauty, the power of appreciating beauty.—Margaret Fuller Ossoli.

The silence that accepts merit as the most natural thing in the world is the highest applause.—Emerson.

There is no surer mark of the absence of the highest moral and intellectual qualities than a cold reception of excellence.—S. Bailey.

Contemporaries appreciate the man rather than the merit; posterity will regard the merit rather than the man.—Buxton.

We never know a greater character until something congenial to it has grown up within ourselves.—Channing.

He is incapable of a truly good action who knows not the pleasure in contemplating the good actions of others.—Lavater.

I do not know at first what it is that charms me. The men and things of to-day are wont to be fairer and truer in to-morrow's memory.—Thoreau.

Those who, from the desire of our perfection, have the keenest eye for our faults generally compensate for it by taking a higher view of our merits than we deserve.—J. F. Boyes.

In no time whatever can small critics entirely eradicate out of living men's hearts a certain altogether peculiar reverence for Great Men—genuine admiration, loyalty, adoration.—Carlyle.

Men are seldom underrated; the mercury in a man finds its true level in the eyes of the world just as certainly as it does in the glass of a thermometer.—H. W. Shaw.

Were not the eye made to receive the rays of the sun, it could not behold the sun; if the peculiar power of God lay not in us, how could the godlike charm us?—Goethe.

In an audience of rough people a generous sentiment always brings down the house. In the tumult of war both sides applaud an heroic deed.—T. W. Higginson.

Whatever the benefits of fortune are, they yet require a palate fit to relish and taste them; it is fruition, and not possession, that renders us happy.—Montaigne.

We are accustomed to see men deride what they do not understand; and snarl at the good and beautiful because it lies beyond their sympathies.—Goethe.

We must never undervalue any person. The workman loves not that his work should be despised in his presence. Now God is present everywhere, and every person is His work.—De Sales.

Praise is a debt we owe unto the virtues of others, and due unto our own from all whom malice hath not made mutes or envy struck dumb.—Sir Thomas Browne.

No good writer was ever long neglected; no great man overlooked by men equally great. Impatience is a proof of inferior strength, and a destroyer of what little there may be.—Landor.

I pity the man who can travel from Dan to Beersheba, and cry, " 'T is all barren!" And so it is, and so is all the world to him who will not cultivate the fruits it offers.—Sterne.

The more enlarged is our own mind, the greater number we discover of men of originality. Your commonplace people see no difference between one man and another.—Pascal.

In this world there is one godlike thing, the essence of all that ever was or ever will be of godlike in this world,—the veneration done to human worth by the hearts of men.—Carlyle.

To guard the mind against the temptation of thinking that there are no good people, say to them: "Be such as you would like to see others, and you will find those who resemble you."—Bossuet.

People do not always understand the motives of sublime conduct, and when they are astonished they are very apt to think they ought to be alarmed. The truth is none are fit judges of greatness but those who are capable of it.—Jane Porter.

It is very singular how the fact of a man's death often seems to give people a truer idea of his character, whether for good or evil, than they have ever possessed while he was living and acting among them.—Hawthorne.

Every man stamps his value on himself. The price we challenge for ourselves is given us. There does not live on earth the man, be his station what it may, that I despise myself compared with him. Man is made great or little by his own will.—Schiller.

Sometimes a common scene in nature—one of the common relations of life—will open itself to us with a brightness and pregnancy of meaning unknown before. Sometimes a thought of this kind forms an era in life. It changes the whole future course. It is a new creation.—Channing.

The charming landscape which I saw this morning is indubitably made up of some twenty or thirty farms. Miller owns this field, Locke that, and Manning the woodland beyond. But none of them owns the landscape. There is a property in the horizon which no man has but he whose eye can integrate all the parts, that is, the poet. This is the best part of these men's farms, yet to this their warranty-deeds give no title.—Emerson.

To feel, to feel exquisitely, is the lot of very many; it is the charm that lends a superstitious joy to fear. But to appreciate belongs to the few; to one or two alone, here and there, the blended passion and understanding that constitute in its essence worship. —Elizabeth Sheppard.

Nature and books belong to the eyes that see them. It depends on the mood of the man, whether he shall see the sunset or the fine poem. There are always sunsets, and there is always genius; but only a few hours so serene that we can relish nature or criticism. The more or less depends on structure or temperament. Temperament is the iron wire on which the beads are strung. Of what use is fortune or talent to a cold and defective nature?—Emerson.

We commend a horse for his strength, and sureness of foot, and not for his rich caparisons; a greyhound for his share of heels, not for his fine collar; a hawk for her wing, not for her jesses and bells. Why, in like manner, do we not value a man for what is properly his own? He has a great train, a beautiful palace, so much credit, so many thousand pounds a year, and all these are about him, but not in him.—Montaigne.

April

Oh, the lovely fickleness of an April day!
          —W. H. Gibson.

Old April wanes, and her last dewy morn
    Her death-bed steeps in tears; to hail the May
New blooming blossoms 'neath the sun are born,
And all poor April's charms are swept away.
          —Clare.

The children with the streamlets sing,
    When April stops at last her weeping;
And every happy growing thing
    Laughs like a babe just roused from sleeping,
          —Lucy Larcom.

There is no glory in star or blossom
    Till looked upon by a loving eye;
There is no fragrance in April breezes
    Till breathed with joy as they wander by.
          —Bryant.

Again the blackbirds sing; the streams
Wake, laughing, from their winter dreams,
And tremble in the April showers
The tassels of the maple flowers.
          —Whittier.

              When April winds
Grew soft, the maple burst into a flush
Of scarlet flowers. The tulip tree, high up,
Opened in airs of June her multitude
Of golden chalices to humming birds
And silken-wing'd insects of the sky.
          —Bryant.

Sweet April! many a thought
    Is wedded unto thee, as hearts are wed;
Nor shall they fail, till, to its autumn brought,
Life's golden fruit is shed.
          —Longfellow.

Every tear is answered by a blossom,
    Every sigh with songs and laughter blent,
Apple-blooms upon the breezes toss them,
    April knows her own, and is content.
          —Susan Coolidge.

Arbor Day (see Trees)

Arbor Day has fostered love of country.—B. G. Northrop.

It has been wisely suggested that each State should choose its own tree, which in every case should be one that will thrive best in its soil.—N. Y. Evangelist.

In all thickly peopled countries the forests no longer supply the necessities for wood by natural production.—Christian Work.

The opportunity should not be lost, which is afforded by the occasion, for illustrating and enforcing the thought that the universe, its creation, its arrangement, and all of its developing processes, are not due to human planning or oversight, but to the infinite wisdom and power of God.—A. S. Draper.

Arbor Day has brought about a revolution in American taste. From tree destroying we have come back to tree planting.—Johnhaird Wilson.

The tree of the field is man's life. "Then shall all the trees of the wood rejoice before the Lord." "The trees of the Lord are full of sap, the cedars of Lebanon which he hath planted; where the birds make their nests; as for the stork, the fir trees are her house."—Bible.

Woodman, spare that tree!
Touch not a single bough!
In youth it sheltered me,
And I'll protect it now.
'Twas my forefather's hand
That placed it near his cot,
There, woodman, let it stand;
Thy ax shall harm it not.
—George P. Morris.

What a noble gift to man are the Forests! What a debt of gratitude and admiration we owe to their beauty and their utility! How pleasantly the shadows of the wood fall upon our heads when we turn from the glitter and turmoil of the world of man!—Cooper.

The school children of New York State planted more than 200,000 trees within ten years from the time Arbor Day was recognized. Few similar efforts in years have been more thoroughly commendable than the effort to get our people practically to show their appreciation of the beauty and usefulness of trees.—A. S. Draper.

What earnest worker, with hand and brain for the benefit of his fellowmen, could desire a more pleasing recognition of his usefulness than the monument of a tree, ever growing, ever blooming, and ever bearing wholesome fruit?—Irving.

The great object to be attained through the observance of Arbor Day is the cultivation of a love for nature among children, with the confident expectation that thereby the needless destruction of the forests will be stayed, and the improvement of grounds about school buildings and residences will be promoted—A. S. Draper.

We know that our forests are in danger of being decimated by the ruthless strokes of the woodchopper's ax, and we know that to prevent that crisis, children, in the West especially, have been encouraged on this holiday to plant some tree or shrub to provide for future use and beauty.—Christian at Work.

Tree Planting on Arbor Day for economic purposes in the great West has given to the prairie States many thousand acres of new forests, and inspired the people with a sense of their great value, not only for economic purposes, but for climatic and meteorological purposes as well.—Warren Highley.

There is something nobly simple and pure in a taste for the cultivation of forest trees. It argues, I think, a sweet and generous nature to have this strong relish for the beauties of vegetation, and this friendship for the hardy and glorious sons of the forest. He who plants a tree looks forward to future ages, and plants for posterity. Nothing could be less selfish than this.—Irving.

The primary purpose of the Legislature in establishing "Arbor Day," was to develop and stimulate in the children of the Commonwealth a love and reverence for Nature as revealed in trees and shrubs and flowers. In the language of the statute, "to encourage the planting, protection and preservation of trees and shrubs" was believed to be the most effectual way in which to lead our children to love Nature and reverence Nature's God, and to see the uses to which these natural objects may be put in making our school grounds more healthful and attractive.—A. S. Draper.

So remarkable have been the results of Arbor Day in Nebraska, that its originator is gratefully recognized as the great benefactor of his State. Proofs of public appreciation of his grand work are found throughout the State. It glories in the old misnomer of the geographies, "The Great American Desert," since it has become so habitable and hospitable by cultivation and tree planting. Where, twenty years ago, the books said trees would not grow, the settler who does not plant them is the exception.—B. G. Northrop.

The Bible is full of trees; from the time when Adam and Eve sat under their shadow in Eden, on to that splendid vision of the New Jerusalem, where the tree of life bears twelve manner of fruits and its leaves are for the healing of the nations. Absalom's oak, and Elijah's juniper, and Jonah's gourd, and the sycamore which hoisted little Zaccheus into notice, are all familiar to every Sunday school scholar. Our Lord hung one of His most solemn parables on the boughs of a barren fig tree, and drew one of His most apt illustrations of the growth of His kingdom from the mustard which becomes tall enough for the birds to nestle in its branches.—Dr. Cuyler.

An eminent educator says: "Any teacher who has no taste for trees, shrubs, or flowers is unfit to be placed in charge of children." Arbor Day has enforced the same idea, especially in those States in which the pupils have cast their ballots on Arbor Day in favor of a State tree and State flower. Habits of observation have thus been formed which have led youth in their walks, at work or play, to recognize and admire our noble trees, and to realize that they are the grandest products of nature and form the finest drapery that adorns the earth in all lands.—B. G. Northrop.

In the olden times trees were planted about the home to commemorate events in the family. Grandfather's and grandmother's maple trees still stand in front of the old homestead gate. They were planted on their wedding day, many years ago. Large, grand trees they are now, and they have been the homes of generations of birds who have been reared amid their branches and taught how to use their wings, and each summer time they seem to increase in number. A new tree was planted when each little child came to gladden the home. They were called birthday trees. Here and there on the homestead grounds stand the memorial trees, planted when some of the loved ones went away from the home on earth to the Father's home above.—New York Evangelist.

Arbor Day has taken its place, and will no doubt hold its own among the holidays of the American people. It has done a wonderful work among children, not only in its influence as a practical factor in the beautifying of the yards and streets about the school buildings; but best of all has been the impetus given by it to the study of nature. The very fact that once every year the youth of our country may prepare for a day devoted to trees, has aroused them to observe and ask questions, and the coming generation will know more about them than did their fathers and mothers.—Churchman.

Let the people lay aside for a season the habitual activity of the day and devote sufficient time thereof to plant a forest, fruit or ornamental tree along the public highways and streams, in private and public parks, about the public schoolhouses and on the college grounds, in gardens and on the farms, thus promoting the pleasure, profit, and prosperity of the people of the State, providing protection against floods and storms, securing health and comfort, increasing that which is beautiful and pleasing to the eye, comforting to physical life, and elevating the mind and heart, and by associations and meetings excite public interest and give encouragement to this most commendable work.—Governor of Pennsylvania, Arbor Day Proclamation.

It appears that the woodland of the United States now covers 450,000,000 acres, or about twenty-six per cent of the whole area. Of this not less than 25,000,000 acres are cut over annually, a rate of destruction that will bring our forests to an end in eighteen years if there is no replanting. It is also stated that while the wood growing annually in the forests of the United States amounts to 12,000,000,000 cubic feet, the amount cut annually is 24,000,000,000 feet, and this does not include the amount destroyed by fire

The country's supply of timber, therefore, is being depleted at least twice as fast as it is being reproduced, and it is easy to see that unless this process is soon checked, it will not be many years before the country is suffering from a decrease in rainfall, and the consequent drying up of the streams.—Forestry Congress.

There's something in a noble tree—
What shall I say? a soul?
For 'tis not form, or aught we see
In leaf, or branch or bole.
Some presence, tho' not understood,
Dwells there always, and seems
To be acquainted with our mood,
And mingles in our dreams.
I would not say that trees at all
Were of our blood and race,
Yet, lingering where their shadows fall,
I sometimes think I trace
A kinship, whose far-reaching root
Grew when the world began,
And made them best of all things mute
To be the friends of man.

Children may not be able to understand the importance of trees in their aggregation as forests; however, they will, if allowed to assemble in a grove or park, be inspired with the idea that trees are one of the grandest products of God when they hear that without them the earth could never have produced the necessaries of life, and that with their destruction we could not keep up the sustained growth of the plants that feed man and animals. There is no more suitable subject for practical oral lessons, now common in most of our schools, than the nature of plants, and especially that of trees and the value of tree-planting.—Nicholas Jarchow.

It is encouraging to know that in so many places there is a growing tendency to purchase so-called waste lands and to hold them for the enjoyment of the people. We call to mind another region in Connecticut where the villagers are united in their interest to preserve all the rural charms of the neighborhood. Miles of highway have been purchased with no other purpose than to allow nature to frolic in her own free way by the roadside. Forests have been bought that they might be held for public enjoyment, and the feeling of the community is strong for the preservation of all wild spots which will help to satisfy the desire for beauty and repose.

Forest areas exercise a positive climatic influence upon the surrounding country. They modify the extremes of heat and cold, and render the temperature more equable throughout the year.

The deforesting of large areas of hilly and mountainous country affects to a very large extent the quantity of water that comes from springs and flows in rivers. The more apparent is this when the deforesting occurs on the head waters of important streams. Then the water power is destroyed or greatly impaired, navigation impeded, commerce interfered with, and droughts and floods are more frequent and more severe.

The interests of agriculture and horticulture are greatly subserved by the proper distribution of forest areas through their climatic and hydrographic influence.

A country, embracing within its borders the head waters of all the streams and rivers that interlace it, when stripped of its forest covering becomes a barren waste, incapable of supporting man or beast.—Warren Highley.

Arbor Day in the public schools is doing something toward the replenishing of treeless regions, restoring forest trees to their former habitation, and also toward the extermination of savagery toward all tree growth from the boys of this generation. Heredity from the slayers of trees in their fight with the primeval woods, will require heroic treatment. A boy with a hatchet is still a desolater, with an axe he is a scourge second only to the forest burner; when he grows to manhood his greed is proof against all sentiment or suggestion of remoter consequences. For centuries now the matchless forests of this country have been faced with the cry of "Kill! Kill!" There has been no mercy and no recourse. Slaughter has waged unhindered and unrebuked. Timber forests, with unlimited supply under care and culture, have been ruined. The waste has been more than the product. For bark, for charcoal and firewood, for fence posts and railroad ties, for lumber and shingles, for spars and ship timbers, for wooden - ware, matches, and even toothpicks, the woods have been flayed alive. We have wasted our inheritance until the resulting shame is beginning to show. Forest laws that are sharp and usable as axes are demanded. The ownership of woodland must not carry the right to abuse it. Lands that are important water preserves should be protected the same as public reservoirs. Private ownership which has proved detrimental to public interests should be suppressed by public purchases. All possible restraints must be put on the marauders and incendiaries of the woods. For toleration of this criminal treatment of trees has reached its limit. The sentiment of our people is ready to sustain the hand of justice in the defense of these true friends of man.—Christian Work.

Arbutus

Pure and perfect, sweet arbutus
Twines her rosy-tinted wreath.
　　　　—Elaine Goodale.

Now the tender, sweet arbutus,
Trails her blossom-clustered vines,
And the many-fingered cinquefoil
In the shadow hollow twines.
　　　　—Dora Read Goodale.

Darlings of the forest!
Blossoming alone
When Earth's grief is sorest
For her jewels gone—
Ere the last snow-drift melts your tender
buds have blown.　　—Rose T. Cooke.

Archæology

Archæology is not only the handmaid of history, it is also the conservator of art.—Lord Lytton.

Architecture

Architecture is the work of nations.—Ruskin.

The architect must not only understand drawing, but music.—Vitruvius,

Architecture is frozen music!—Madame de Staël.

A Gothic church is a petrified religion.—Coleridge.

Histories in blazonry and poems in stone.—Ouida.

The poetry of bricks and mortar.—Horace Greeley.

The architect built his great heart into those sculptured stones.—Longfellow.

Spires whose "silent finger points to heaven."—Wordsworth.

Greek architecture is the flowering of geometry.—Emerson.

A fabric huge
Rose, like an exhalation.　—Milton.

Earth proudly wears the Parthenon
As the best gem upon her zone.
　　　　—Emerson.

No workman steel, no pond'rous axes rung:
Like some tall palm the noiseless fabric
　　sprung.　　—Bishop Heber.

No person who is not a great sculptor or painter can be an architect. If he is not a painter or sculptor, he can only be a builder.—Ruskin.

Houses are built to live in, more than to look on; therefore let use be preferred before uniformity except where both may be had.—Bacon.

Thus when we view some well-proportion'd dome,
* 　* 　* 　* 　* 　*
No single parts unequally surprise,
All comes united to th' admiring eyes.
　　　　—Pope.

If cities were built by the sound of music, then some edifices would appear to be constructed by grave, solemn tones,—others to have danced forth to light fantastic airs.—Hawthorne.

We must note carefully what distinction there is between a healthy and a diseased love of change; for as it was in healthy love of change that the

Gothic architecture rose, it was partly in consequence of diseased love of change that it was destroyed.—Ruskin.

An instinctive taste teaches men to build their churches in flat countries with spire-steeples, which, as they cannot be referred to any other object, point as with silent finger to the sky and stars.—Coleridge.

Architecture is the art which so disposes and adorns the edifices raised by man, for whatsoever uses, that the sight of them may contribute to his mental health, power, and pleasure.—Ruskin.

It was stated * * * that the value of architecture depended on two distinct characters:—the one, the impression it receives from human power; the other, the image it bears of the natural creation.—Ruskin.

Better the rudest work that tells a story or records a fact, than the richest without meaning. There should not be a single ornament put upon great civic buildings, without some intellectual intention.—Ruskin.

I would have, then, our ordinary dwelling-houses built to last, and built to be lovely; as rich and full of pleasantness as may be within and without: * * * with such differences as might suit and express each man's character and occupation, and partly his history.—Ruskin.

The hasty multitude
Admiring enter'd, and the work some praise,
And some the architect: his hand was known
In heaven by many a tower'd structure high,
Where scepter'd angels held their residence,
And sat as princes.   —Milton.

In designing a house and gardens, it is happy when there is an opportunity of maintaining a subordination of parts; the house so luckily placed as to exhibit a view of the whole design. I have sometimes thought that there was room for it to resemble an epic or dramatic poem.—Shenstone.

The Gothic cathedral is a blossoming in stone, subdued by the insatiable demand of harmony in man. The mountain of granite blooms into an eternal flower, with the lightness and delicate finish as well as the aerial proportions and perspective of vegetable beauty.—Emerson.

Architecture exhibits the greatest extent of the difference from nature which may exist in works of art. It involves all the powers of design, and is sculpture and painting inclusively. It shows the greatness of man, and should at the same time teach him humility.—Coleridge.

The hand that rounded Peter's dome
And groined the aisles of Christian Rome,
Wrought in a sad sincerity:
Himself from God he could not free;
He builded better than he knew;
The conscious stone to beauty grew.
         —Emerson.

Möller, in his Essay on Architecture, taught that the building which was fitted accurately to answer its end would turn out to be beautiful, though beauty had not been intended. I find the like unity in human structures rather virulent and pervasive.—Emerson.

Grandeur * * * consists in form, and not in size: and to the eye of the philosopher, the curve drawn on a paper two inches long, is just as magnificent, just as symbolic of divine mysteries and melodies, as when embodied in the span of some cathedral roof.—Charles Kingsley.

Architecture is the printing-press of all ages, and gives a history of the state of the society in which it was erected, from the cromlech of the Druids to those toy-shops of royal bad taste,—Carlton House and the Brighton Pavilion. The Tower and Westminster Abbey are glorious pages in the history of time, and tell the story of an iron despotism, and the cowardice of unlimited power.—Lady Morgan.

Therefore when we build, let us think that we build (public edifices) forever. Let it not be for present delight, nor for present use alone, let it be such work as our descendants will thank us for, and let us think, as we lay stone on stone, that a time is to come when those stones will be held sacred because our hands have touched them, and that men will say as they look upon the labor and wrought substance of them, "See! this our fathers did for us."—Ruskin.

Argument

Let argument bear no unmusical sound.—Ben Jonson.

Neither irony nor sarcasm is argument.—Rufus Choate.

Argument is not always truth.—Kossuth.

Strong and bitter words indicate a weak cause.—Victor Hugo.

Silence is less injurious than a weak reply.—Colton.

I always get the better when I argue alone.—Goldsmith.

Argument should be politic as well as logical.—Lamartine.

In excessive altercation truth is lost.—Publius Syrus.

Keep cool; anger is not argument.—Daniel Webster.

Many can argue; not many converse.—Alcott.

Arguments out of a pretty mouth are unanswerable.—Addison.

In argument similes are like songs in love; they much describe; they nothing prove.—Prior.

Affect not little shifts and subterfuges to avoid the force of an argument.—Dr. Watts.

We are pleased with one who instantly assents to our opinions, but we love a proselyte.—Arthur Helps.

His conduct still right with his argument wrong.—Goldsmith.

Wise men argue causes, and fools decide them.—Anacharsis.

No argument can be drawn from the abuse of a thing against its use.—Latin.

Be calm in arguing; for fierceness makes error a fault, and truth discourtesy.—Herbert.

A man convinced against his will
Is of the same opinion still.
          —Butler.

Similes prove nothing, but yet greatly lighten and relieve the tedium of argument.—South.

Arguments, like children, should be like the subject that begets them.—Thomas Decker.

I have found you an argument; but I am not obliged to find you an understanding.—Samuel Johnson.

A knock-down argument; 'tis but a word and a blow.—Dryden.

He that is not open to conviction is not qualified for discussion.—Bishop Whately.

He who establishes his argument by noise and command shows that reason is weak.—Montaigne.

They that are more frequent to dispute be not always the best able to determine.—Hooker.

The devil can quote Scripture for his purpose.—Shakespeare.

One single positive weighs more,
You know, than negatives a score.
          —Prior.

In argument with men a woman ever
Goes by the worse, whatever be her cause.
          —Milton.

Never argue. In society nothing must be; give only results. If any person differs from you, bow, and turn the conversation.—Beaconsfield.

Insolence is not logic; epithets are the arguments of malice.—R. G. Ingersoll.

Who shall decide when doctors disagree, And sound casuists doubt like you and me? —Pope.

Nothing is more certain than that much of the force, as well as grace, of arguments or instructions depends on their conciseness.—Pope.

Gratuitous violence in argument betrays a conscious weakness of the cause, and is usually a signal of despair.—Junius.

In arguing, too, the parson owned his skill, For even tho' vanquish'd he could argue still. —Goldsmith.

The first race of mankind used to dispute, as our ordinary people do now-a-days, in a kind of wild logic, uncultivated by rule of art.—Addison.

Academical disputation gives vigor and briskness to the mind thus exercised, and relieves the languor of private study and meditation.—Dr. Watts.

There is no arguing with Johnson; for if his pistol misses fire, he knocks you down with the butt end of it.—Goldsmith.

Argument, as usually managed, is the worst sort of conversation; as it is generally in books the worst sort of reading.—Swift.

She hath prosperous art When she will play with reason and discourse, And well she can persuade. —Shakespeare.

As the scale of the balance must give way to the weight that presses it down, so the mind must of necessity yield to demonstration.—Cicero.

The skilful disputant well knows that he never has his enemy at more advantage than when, by allowing the premises, he shows him arguing wrong from his own principles.—Warburton.

There is no good in arguing with the inevitable. The only argument available with an east wind is to put on your overcoat.—Lowell.

Like doctors thus, when much dispute has past, We find our tenets just the same at last. —Pope.

No deeply rooted tendency was ever extirpated by adverse judgment. Not having originally been founded on argument, it cannot be destroyed by logic.—G. H. Lewes.

The soundest argument will produce no more conviction in an empty head than the most superficial declamation, as a feather and a guinea fall with equal velocity in a vacuum.—Colton.

Passionate expression and vehement assertion are no arguments, unless it be of the weakness of the cause that is defended by them, or of the man that defends it.—Chillingworth.

Examples I could cite you more; But be contented with these four; For when one's proofs are aptly chosen Four are as valid as four dozen. —Prior.

Reproachful speech from either side The want of argument supplied; They rail, reviled; as often ends The contests of disputing friends. —Gay.

An academical education, sir, bids me tell you, that it is necessary to establish the truth of your first proposition before you presume to draw inferences from it.—Junius.

Weak arguments are often thrust before my path; but although they are most unsubstantial, it is not easy to destroy them. There is not a more difficult feat known than to cut through a cushion with a sword.—Whately.

It is an excellent rule to be observed in all disputes, that men should give soft words and hard arguments; that they should not so much strive to vex as to convince each other.—Wilkins.

In a debate, rather pull to pieces the argument of thy antagonists than offer him any of thy own; for thus thou wilt fight him in his own country.—Fielding.

With temper calm and mild,
And words of soften'd tone,
He overthrows his neighbor's cause,
And justifies his own.
　　　—Vicksburg Whig.

There are some people as obtuse in recognizing an argument as they are in appreciating wit. You couldn't drive it into their heads with a hammer.—Douglas Jerrold.

If thou continuest to take delight in idle argumentation, thou mayest be qualified to combat with the sophists, but never know how to love with men. —Socrates.

It is in disputes as in armies; where the weaker side set up false lights, and make a great noise to make the enemy believe them more numerous and strong than they really are.—Swift.

Testimony is like an arrow shot from a long bow, the force of it depends on the strength of the hand that draws it. Argument is like an arrow from a cross-bow, which has equal force though drawn by a child.— Boyle.

Soon their crude notions with each other
　fought;
The adverse sect denied what this had
　taught;
And he at length the amplest triumph
　gain'd,
Who contradicted what the last maintain'd.
　　　—Prior.

Whenever you argue with another wiser than yourself, in order that others may admire your wisdom, they will discover your ignorance. When one imagines a discourse better than yourself, although you may be fully informed, yet do not start objections. —Saadi.

The first the Retort Courteous; the second the Quip Modest; the third the Reply Churlish; the fourth the Re-

proof Valiant; the fifth the Counter-check Quarrelsome; the sixth the Lie with Circumstance; the seventh the Lie Direct.—Shakespeare.

He'd undertake to prove, by force
Of argument, a man's no horse.
He'd prove a buzzard is no fowl,
And that a lord may be an owl,
A calf an alderman, a goose a justice,
And rooks, committeemen or trustees.
　　　—Butler.

I never love those salamanders that are never well but when they are in the fire of contentions. I will rather suffer a thousand wrongs than offer one. I have always found that to strive with a superior is injurious; with an equal, doubtful; with an inferior, sordid and base; with any, full of unquietness.—Bishop Hall.

When we would show any one that he is mistaken, our best course is to observe on what side he considers the subject,—for his view of it is generally right on this side,—and admit to him that he is right so far. He will be satisfied with this acknowledgment, that he was not wrong in his judgment, but only inadvertent in not looking at the whole case.—Pascal.

Treating your adversary with respect is giving him an advantage to which he is not entitled. The greatest part of men cannot judge of reasoning, and are impressed by character; so that, if you allow your adversary a respectable character, they will think that, though you differ from him, you may be in the wrong. Treating your adversary with respect is striking soft in a battle.—Dr. Johnson.

Be calm in argument; for fierceness makes
Error a fault, and truth discourtesy.
Why should I feel another man's mistakes
More than his sicknesses or poverty?
In love I should: but anger is not love,
Nor wisdom neither; therefore gently move.
Calmness is great advantage; he that lets
Another chafe may warm him at his fire,
Mark all his wand'rings and enjoy his frets,
As cunning fencers suffer heat to tire.
　　　—Herbert.

Where we desire to be informed 'tis good to contest with men above ourselves, but to confirm and establish our opinions, 'tis best to argue with judgments below our own, that the frequent spoils and victories over their reasons may settle in ourselves an esteem and confirmed opinion of our own.—Sir Thos. Browne.

Some men at the approach of a dispute neigh like horses. Unless there be an argument, they think nothing is doing. Some talkers excel in the precision with which they formulate their thoughts, so that you get from them somewhat to remember; others lay criticism asleep by a charm. Especially women use words that are not words,—as steps in a dance are not steps,—but reproduce the genius of that they speak of; as the sound of some bells makes us think of the bell merely, whilst the church chimes in the distance bring the church and its serious memories before us.—Emerson.

Aristocracy

An aristocracy is the true support of a monarchy.—Napoleon I.

By blood a king, in heart a clown.—Tennyson.

And lords whose parents were the Lord knows who!—De Foe.

You may depend upon it that there are as good hearts to serve men in palaces as in cottages.—Robert Owen.

I do not understand how an aristocracy can exist, unless it be distinguished by some quality which no other class of the community possesses.—Beaconsfield.

Turbulent, discontented men of quality, in proportion as they are puffed up with personal pride and arrogance, generally despise their own order.—Burke.

Where some think, and others do not, there is developed aristocracy. Where all have come to think we have democracy,—the government of the people by themselves.—Beecher.

Aristocracy has three successive ages,—the age of superiorities, the age of privileges, and the age of vanities;

having passed out of the first, it degenerates in the second, and dies away in the third.—Chateaubriand.

Amongst the masses—even in revolutions—aristocracy must ever exist; destroy it in nobility, and it becomes centred in the rich and powerful Houses of the Commons. Pull them down, and it still survives in the master and foreman of the workshop.—Guizot.

Army

For the army is a school in which the niggardly become generous, and the generous prodigal; and if there are some soldiers misers, they are a kind of monsters, but very rarely seen.—Cervantes.

The army is a good book to open to study human life. One learns there to put his hand to everything, to the lowest and highest things. The most delicate and rich are forced to see living nearly everywhere poverty, and to live with it, and to measure his morsel of bread and draught of water.—Alfred de Vigny.

Arrogance

Arrogance is the obstruction of wisdom.—Bion.

When men are most sure and arrogant, they are commonly the most mistaken, and have then given views to passion, without that proper deliberation and suspense which can alone secure them from the grossest absurdities.—Hume.

When Diogenes came to Olympia and perceived some Rhodian youths dressed with great splendor and magnificence, he said with a smile of contempt, "This is all arrogance." Afterwards some Lacedemonians came in his way, as mean and as sordid in their attire as the dress of the others was rich. "This," said he, "is also arrogance." —Ælian.

A man that loves to be peevish and paramount, and to play the sovereign at every turn, does but blast the blessings of life, and swagger away his own enjoyments; and not to enlarge upon the folly, not to mention the injustice of such a behavior, it is always the sign of a little, unbenevolent temper. It is disease and discredit all over, and there is no more greatness in it, than in the swelling of a dropsy.—Jeremy Collier.

What is so hateful to a poor man as the purse-proud arrogance of a rich one? Let fortune shift the scene, and make the poor man rich, he runs at once into the vice that he declaimed against so feelingly; these are strange contradictions in the human character. --Cumberland.

Art

The perfection of art is to conceal art.—Quintilian.

Art needs no spur beyond itself.—Victor Hugo.

Art does not imitate, but interpret. —Mazzini.

He that sips of many arts drinks of none.—Fuller.

The great artist is the slave of his ideal.—Bovee.

Art, however innocent, looks like deceiving.—Aaron Hill.

The inglorious arts of peace.—Andrew Marvell.

An artist should have more than two eyes.—Lamartine.

What is art? Nature concentrated. —Balzac.

Art is power.—Longfellow.

Unless art deceives, it is not art.— W. L. Reiner.

Every artist was first an amateur.—Emerson.

A picture is a poem without words. —Horace.

Art is the gift of God, and must be used unto His glory—Longfellow.

Art is not imitation, but illusion.—Charles Reade.

The highest art is artlessness.—F. A. Durivage.

The true artist can only labor con amore.—Victor Hugo.

Art may err, but nature cannot miss. —Dryden.

Art still followed where Rome's eagles flew.—Pope.

It was Homer who gave laws to the artist.—Francis Wayland.

The artist belongs to his work, not the work to the artist.—Novalis.

The first essential to success in the art you practice is respect for the art itself.—Bulwer-Lytton.

Seraphs share with thee knowledge; but art, O man, is thine alone!—Schiller.

Painters and poets have equal license in regard to everything.—Horace.

I think sculpture and painting have an effect to teach us manners, and abolish hurry.—Emerson.

Many persons feel art, some understand it; but few both feel and understand it.—Hillard.

The counterfeit and counterpart
Of Nature reproduced in art.
—Longfellow.

Art must anchor in nature, or it is the sport of every breath of folly.—Hazlitt.

The conscious utterance of thought, by speech or action, to any end, is art.—Emerson.

Beauty is at once the ultimate principle and the highest aim of art.—Goethe.

It is the end of art to inoculate men with the love of nature.—Beecher.

Greater completion marks the progress of art, absolute completion usually its decline.—Ruskin.

For Art is Nature made by Man
To Man the interpreter of God.
—Owen Meredith.

Art is indeed not the bread but the wine of life.—Jean Paul Richter.

Dead he is not, but departed—for the artist never dies.—Longfellow.

An amateur may not be an artist, though an artist should be an amateur.—Disraeli.

The true work of art is but a shadow of the divine perfection.—Michael Angelo.

The highest problem of any art is to cause by appearance the illusion of a higher reality.—Goethe.

In art, to express the infinite one should suggest infinitely more than is expressed.—Goethe.

In the fine arts, as in many other things, we know well only what we have not learned.—Chamfort.

No man can thoroughly master more than one art or science.—Hazlitt.

This is an art which does mend nature,—change it rather; but the art itself is nature.—Shakespeare.

The learned understand the reason of the art, the unlearned feel the pleasure.—Quintilian.

The mission of art is to represent nature not to imitate her. — W. M. Hunt.

It is only the educated who can produce or appreciate high art.—Marguerite de Valois.

There are certain epochs in art when simplicity is audacious originality.—Achilles Poincelot.

All things are artificial; for nature is the art of God.—Sir Thos. Browne.

In the study of the fine arts, they mutually assist each other.—Beaconsfield.

The object of art is to crystallize emotion into thought, and then to fix it in form.—François Delsarte.

Art is more godlike than science. Science discovers; art creates.—John Opie.

True art is but the anti-type of nature,—the embodiment of discovered beauty in utility.—James A. Garfield.

Art is a jealous thing; it requires the whole and entire man.—Michael Angelo.

There is a great affinity between designing and art.—Addison.

It is not the defects but the beauties which should form our criterion of judgment in all matters of art.—Chapin.

The ordinary true, or purely real, cannot be the object of the arts. Illusion on a ground of truth,—that is the secret of the fine arts.—Joubert.

A true artist should put a generous deceit on the spectators, and effect the noblest designs by easy methods.—Burke.

Art is based on a strong sentiment of religion,—on a profound and mighty earnestness; hence it is so prone to co-operate with religion.—Goethe.

Of every noble work the silent part is best; of all expression, that which cannot be expressed.—W. W. Story.

Art is the child of Nature; yes, her darling child, in whom we trace the features of the mother's face.—Longfellow.

Art, as far as it has ability, follows nature, as a pupil imitates his master; thus your art must be, as it were, God's grandchild.—Dante.

Art needs solitude or misery or passion. Lukewarm zephyrs wilt it. It is a rock-flower flourishing by stormy blasts and in stony soil.—Alex. Dumas.

In the art of design, color is to form what verse is to prose,—a more harmonious and luminous vehicle of the thought.—Mrs. Jameson.

The natural progress of the works of men is from rudeness to convenience, from convenience to elegance, and from elegance to nicety.—Dr. Johnson.

Art is the right hand of Nature. The latter has only given us being, the former has made us men.—Schiller.

Persons famous in the arts partake of the immortality of princes, and are upon a footing with them.—Francis I.

A work of art is said to be perfect in proportion as it does not remind the spectator of the process by which it was created.—Tuckerman.

It is only with the best judges that the highest works of art would lose none of their honor by being seen in their rudiments.—J. F. Boyes.

We speak of profane arts; but there are none properly such; every art is holy in itself; it is the son of Eternal Light.—Tegner.

That which exists in nature is a something purely individual and particular. Art, on the contrary, is essentially destined to manifest the general.—Schlegel.

Many young painters would never have taken their pencils in hand if they could have felt, known, and understood, early enough, what really produced a master like Raphael.—Goethe.

Ah! would that we could at once paint with the eyes! In the long way, from the eye, through the arm to the pencil, how much is lost!—Lessing.

From Egypt arts their progress made to Greece, wrapped in the fable of the golden fleece.—Sir J. Denham.

In old times men used their powers of painting to show the objects of faith; in later times they used the objects of faith that they might show their powers of painting.—Ruskin.

The enemy of art is the enemy of nature; art is nothing but the highest sagacity and exertions of human nature; and what nature will he honor who honors not the human?—Lavater.

Immortal art! where'er the rounded sky
Bends o'er the cradle where thy children lie,
Their home is earth, their herald every tongue.   —Holmes.

Artists may produce excellent designs, but they will avail little, unless the taste of the public is sufficiently cultivated to appreciate them.—George C. Mason.

The mother of useful arts is necessity; that of the fine arts is luxury. For father the former has intellect; the latter genius, which itself is a kind of luxury.—Schopenhauer.

All the arts, which have a tendency to raise man in the scale of being, have a certain common band of union, and are connected, if I may be allowed to say so, by blood-relationship with one another.—Cicero.

The highest art is always the most religious; and the greatest artist is always a devout man. A scoffing Raphael or Michael Angelo is not conceivable.—Blackie.

Around the mighty master came
The marvels which his pencil wrought,
Those miracles of power whose fame
Is wide as human thought.
      —Whittier.

Artists will sometimes speak of Rome with disparagement or indifference while it is before them; but no artist ever lived in Rome and then left it, without sighing to return.—Hillard.

Rules may teach us not to raise the arms above the head; but if passion carries them, it will be well done; passion knows more than art.—Baron.

The painter is, as to the execution of his work, a mechanic; but as to his conception, his spirit, and design, he is hardly below even the poet in liberal art.—Steele.

In art the Greeks were the children of the Egyptians. The day may yet come when we shall do justice to the high powers of that mysterious and imaginative people.—Beaconsfield.

One of the first principles of decorative art is that in all manufactures ornament must hold ·a place subordinate to that of utility; and when, by its exuberance, ornament interferes with utility, it is misplaced and vulgar. —G. C. Mason.

In art there is a point of perfection, as of goodness or maturity in nature; he who is able to perceive it, and who loves it, has perfect taste; he who does not feel it, or loves on this side or that, has an imperfect taste.—Bruyère.

The object of science is knowledge; the objects of art are works. In art, truth is the means to an end; in science, it is the only end. Hence the practical arts are not to be classed among the sciences.—Whewell.

The temple of art is built of words. Painting and sculpture and music are but the blazon of its windows, borrowing all their significance from the light, and suggestive only of the temple's use.—J. G. Holland.

The artist is the child in the popular fable, every one of whose tears was a pearl. Ah! the world, that cruel step-mother, beats the poor child the harder to make him shed more pearls. —Heinrich Heine.

Art itself, in all its methods, is the child of religion. The highest and best works in architecture, sculpture and painting, poetry and music, have been born out of the religion of Nature.—James Freeman Clarke.

The misfortune in the state is, that nobody can enjoy life in peace, but that everybody must govern; and in art, that nobody will enjoy what has been produced, but that every one wants to reproduce on his own account.—Goethe.

Art is a severe business; most serious when employed in grand and sacred objects. The artist stands higher than art, higher than the object. He uses art for his purposes, and deals with the object after his own fashion.—Goethe.

Winckelmann wished to live with a work of art as a friend. The saying is true of pen and pencil. Fresh lustre shoots from Lycidas in a twentieth perusal. The portraits of Clarendon are mellowed by every year of reflection.—Willmott.

When the painter wishes to represent an event, he cannot place before us too great a number of personages; but he cannot employ too few when he wishes to portray an emotion.—Joubert.

In sculpture did ever anybody call the Apollo a fancy piece? Or say of the Laocoön how it might be made different? A masterpiece of art has in the mind a fixed place in the chain of being, as much as a plant or a crystal. —Emerson.

All men are in some degree impressed by the face of the world; some men even to delight. This love of beauty is taste. Others have the same love in such excess that, not content with admiring, they seek to embody it in new forms. The creation of beauty is art.—Emerson.

Moral beauty is the basis of all true beauty. This foundation is somewhat covered and veiled in nature. Art brings it out, and gives it more transparent forms. It is here that art, when it knows well its power and resources, engages in a struggle with nature in which it may have the advantage.—Victor Cousin.

The study of art is a taste at once engrossing and unselfish, which may be indulged without effort, and yet has the power of exciting the deepest emotions,—a taste able to exercise and to gratify both the nobler and softer parts of our nature.—Guizot.

The one thing that marks the true artist is a clear perception and a firm, bold hand, in distinction from that imperfect mental vision and uncertain touch which give us the feeble pictures and the lumpy statues of the mere artisans on canvas or in stone.—O. W. Holmes.

Art employs method for the symmetrical formation of beauty, as science employs it for the logical exposition of truth; but the mechanical process is, in the last, ever kept visibly distinct, while in the first it escapes from sight amid the shows of color and the curves of grace.—Bulwer-Lytton.

Art does not imitate nature, but it founds itself on the study of nature,—takes from nature the selections which best accord with its own intention, and then bestows on them that which nature does not possess, viz. the mind and the soul of man.—Bulwer-Lytton.

The only kind of sublimity which a painter or sculptor should aim at is to express by certain proportions and positions of limbs and features that strength and dignity of mind, and vigor and activity of body, which enables men to conceive and execute great actions.—Burke.

The power of painter or poet to describe rightly what he calls an ideal thing depends upon its being to him not an ideal, but a real thing. No man ever did or ever will work well but either from actual sight or sight of faith.—Ruskin.

Art is the effort of man to express the ideas which nature suggests to him of a power above nature, whether that power be within the recesses of his own being, or in the Great First Cause of which nature, like himself, is but the effect.—Bulwer-Lytton.

There are two kinds of artists in this world; those that work because the spirit is in them, and they cannot be silent if they would, and those that speak from a conscientious desire to make apparent to others the beauty that has awakened their own admiration.—Anna Katharine Green.

Whatever may be the means, or whatever the more immediate end of any kind of art, all of it that is good agrees in this, that it is the expression of one soul talking to another, and is precious according to the greatness of the soul that utters it.—Ruskin.

It is a great mortification to the vanity of man that his utmost art and industry can never equal the meanest of Nature's productions, either for beauty or value. Art is only the underworkman, and is employed to give a few strokes of embellishment to those pieces which come from the hand of the master.—Hume.

The summit charms us, the steps to it do not; with the heights before our eyes, we like to linger in the plain. It is only a part of art that can be taught; but the artist needs the whole. He who is only half instructed speaks much and is always wrong; who knows it wholly is content with acting and speaks seldom or late.—Goethe.

I once asked a distinguished artist what place he gave to labor in art. "Labor," he in effect said, "is the beginning, the middle, and the end of art." Turning then to another—"And you," I inquired, "what do you consider as the great force in art?" "Love," he replied. In their two answers I found but one truth.—Bovee.

Art is a jealous mistress, and, if a man have a genius for painting, poetry, music, architecture, or philosophy, he makes a bad husband, and an ill provider, and should be wise in season, and not fetter himself with duties which will imbitter his days, and spoil him for his proper work.—Emerson.

Remember always, in painting as in eloquence, the greater your strength, the quieter will be your manner, and the fewer your words; and in painting, as in all the arts and acts of life.

the secret of high success will be found, not in a fretful and various excellence, but in a quiet singleness of justly chosen aim.—Ruskin.

The flitting sunbeam has been grasped and made to do man's bidding in place of the painter's pencil. And although Franklin tamed the lightning, yet not until yesterday has its instantaneous flash been made the vehicle of language; thus in the transmission of thought annihilating space and time.—Professor Robinson.

Art neither belongs to religion, nor to ethics; but, like these, it brings us nearer to the Infinite, one of the forms of which it manifests to us. God is the source of all beauty, as of all truth, of all religion, of all morality. The most exalted object, therefore, of art is to reveal in its own manner the sentiment of the Infinite.—Victor Cousin.

Those critics who, in modern times, have the most thoughtfully analyzed the laws of æsthetic beauty concur in maintaining that the real truthfulness of all works of imagination—sculpture, painting, written fiction—is so purely in the imagination, that the artist never seeks to represent the positive turth, but the idealized image of a truth.—Bulwer-Lytton.

Excellence in art is to be attained only by active effort, and not by passive impressions; by the manly overcoming of difficulties, by patient struggle against adverse circumstance, by the thrifty use of moderate opportunities. The great artists were not rocked and dandled into eminence, but they attained to it by that course of labor and discipline which no man need go to Rome or Paris or London to enter upon.—Hillard.

What a conception of art must those theorists have who exclude portraits from the proper province of the fine arts! It is exactly as if we denied that to be poetry in which the poet celebrates the woman he really loves. Portraiture is the basis and the touchstone of historic painting.—Schlegel.

Art is the microscope of the mind, which sharpens the wit as the other does the sight; and converts every object into a little universe in itself. Art may be said to draw aside the veil from nature. To those who are perfectly unskilled in the practice, unimbued with the principles of art, most objects present only a confused mass. —Hazlitt.

Art, not less eloquently than literature, teaches her children to venerate the single eye. Remember Matsys. His representations of miser-life are breathing. A forfeited bond twinkles in the hard smile. But follow him to an altar-piece. His Apostle has caught a stray tint from his usurer. Features of exquisite beauty are seen and loved; but the old nature of avarice frets under the glow of devotion. Pathos staggers on the edge of farce.—Willmott.

The perfection of an art consists in the employment of a comprehensive system of laws, commensurate to every purpose within its scope, but concealed from the eye of the spectator; and in the production of effects that seem to flow forth spontaneously, as though uncontrolled by their influence, and which are equally excellent, whether regarded individually, or in reference to the proposed result.—John Mason Good.

Every common dauber writes rascal and villain under his pictures, because the pictures themselves have neither character nor resemblance. But the works of a master require no index. His features and coloring are taken from nature. The impression they make is immediate and uniform; nor is it possible to mistake his characters. —Junius.

It is not so much in buying pictures as in being pictures, that you can encourage a noble school. The best patronage of art is not that which seeks for the pleasures of sentiment in a vague ideality, nor for beauty of form in a marble image, but that which educates your children into living heroes, and binds down the flights and the fondnesses of the heart into practical duty and faithful devotion.—Ruskin.

Now nature is not at variance with art, nor art with nature; they being both the servants of his providence. Art is the perfection of nature. Were the world now as it was the sixth day, there were yet a chaos. Nature hath made one world, and art another. In brief, all things are artificial; for nature is the art of God.—Sir Thomas Browne.

There is no more potent antidote to low sensuality than the adoration of the beautiful. All the higher arts of design are essentially chaste without respect to the object. They purify the thoughts as tragedy purifies the passions. Their accidental effects are not worth consideration,—there are souls to whom even a vestal is not holy.—Schlegel.

The study of art possesses this great and peculiar charm, that it is absolutely unconnected with the struggles and contests of ordinary life. By private interests, by political questions, men are deeply divided, and set at variance; but beyond and above all such party strifes, they are attracted and united by a taste for the beautiful in art.—Guizot.

Since I have known God in a saving manner, painting, poetry, and music have had charms unknown to me before. I have received what I suppose is a taste for them, or religion has refined my mind and made it susceptible of impressions from the sublime and beautiful. O, how religion secures the heightened enjoyment of those pleasures which keep so many from God, by their becoming a source of pride!—Henry Martyn.

The refining influence is the study of art, which is the science of beauty; and I find that every man values every scrap of knowledge in art, every observation of his own in it, every hint he has caught from another. For the laws of beauty are the beauty of beauty, and give the mind the same or a higher joy than the sight of it

gives the senses. The study of art is of high value to the growth of the intellect.—Emerson.

The names of great painters are like passing-bells: in the name of Velasquez you hear sounded the fall of Spain; in the name of Titian, that of Venice; in the name of Leonardo, that of Milan; in the name of Raphael, that of Rome. And there is profound justice in this, for in proportion to the nobleness of the power is the guilt of its use for purposes vain or vile; and hitherto the greater the art, the more surely has it been used, and used solely, for the decoration of pride or the provoking of sensuality.—Ruskin.

Artifice

To know to dissemble is the knowledge of kings.—Richelieu.

Artifice is allowed to deceive a rival; we may employ everything against our enemies.—Richelieu.

The ordinary employment of artifice is the mark of a petty mind; and it almost always happens that he who uses it to cover himself in one place uncovers himself in another.—Rochefoucauld.

Shallow artifice begets suspicion,
And like a cobweb veil, but thinly shades
The face of thy design, alone disguising
What should have ne'er been seen, imperfect mischief.   —Congreve.

Nature is mighty. Art is mighty. Artifice is weak. For nature is the work of a mightier power than man. Art is the work of man under the guidance and inspiration of a mightier power. Artifice is the work of mere man, in the imbecility of his mimic understanding.—Hare.

It is sometimes necessary to play the fool to avoid being deceived by cunning men.—La Rochefoucauld.

Ascension Day

Jesus went away not only to prepare a place for us, so that it will be ready for us as one by one we go home, but to prepare us for the place, to fit us for heavenly enjoyments and heavenly service.—Peloubet.

And it came to pass while He blessed them, He was parted from them, and carried up into heaven.—Bible.

So then after the Lord had spoken unto them, He was received up into heaven, and sat on the right hand of God.—Bible.

He is taken up, that He may fulfill His design in dying, and give the work of our salvation its last completing act.—John Flavel.

His ascension is not His separation from His people, but the ascension of His throne and the beginning of His reign as the head of the Church which "is His body, the fulness of Him that filleth all in all."—Rev. Com.

Christ "ascended," not to depart from earth, but to take the throne of His Kingdom on earth. "He sat down at the right hand of God." God's reign does not consist in sitting upon a distant throne! It consists in omnipresent power and authority. To sit at His right hand means to share His Authority and Omnipresence.—Talmadge Root.

Here was a magnificent triumph over the law of gravitation. Here was the royal ascent by which our Solomon went up to the house of the Lord. The everlasting gates lifted up their heads and the King of Glory entered in. It was all of a piece—His life, His death, His resurrection, His ascension, all were triumphs.—Rev. C. P. Eldridge.

The ascension of Elijah may be compared to the flight of a bird, which none can follow; the ascension of Christ is, as it were, a bridge between earth and heaven, laid down for all who are drawn to Him by His earthly existence.—Baumgarten.

When we see the only-begotten Son, clothed in a body like our own, exalted above all the heavens, in that sight we have before us the all-glorious and controlling center of all the spheres, the key which interprets the testimony of prophecy, the gathered first fruits of a new and redeemed world.—W. Pulsford.

Hail the day that sees Him rise,
Ravished from our wistful eyes!
Christ, awhile to mortals given,
Re-ascends His native heaven.
There the glorious triumph waits,
Lift your heads, eternal gates!
Wide unfold the radiant scene,
Take the King of glory in!
—Wesley.

See, the Conqueror mounts in triumph,
See the King in royal state,
Riding on the clouds His chariot
To His heavenly palace-gate;
Hark, the choirs of angel voices
Joyful halleluiahs sing,
And the portals high are lifted,
To receive their heavenly King.
—Wordsworth.

He is gone; a cloud of light
Has received Him from our sight;
High in heaven, where eye of men
Follows not, nor angels' ken;
Through the veils of time and space,
Passed in to the holiest place;
All the toil, the sorrow done,
All the battle fought and won.
—Dean Stanley.

With the ascent of the Saviour into heaven, from which this anniversary day receives its name, He has entered upon the real and undisputed possession of His royal reign, in which from this time on He rules over all things that are in heaven and on earth.—H. Kern.

His Ascension marked a stage in His revelation, but it only brought Him nearer to us. To have lingered among the early disciples would have limited His mission and sequestered Him from the later Church. As the Resurrection opened the grave, the Ascension opened heaven.—Evangelist.

Our first impressions are to consider the Ascension of our Lord as the very greatest event connected with His appearance on earth. To our own mind, undoubtedly, nothing could be so solemn, so exalting, as the changing this life for another: the putting off mortality and putting on immortality; and all this we connect with the thought of the removal from earth to heaven. —Thos. Arnold.

The Ascension was the appropriate bloom and culmination of the Resurrection. Had Christ, after the Resurrection, died a natural death, or had He simply disappeared from view into unknown obscurity, the Resurrection, as a proof of His divine power, and pledge of His undimmed and undiminished existence would have gone for nothing. And the Ascension of our Lord has some most precious lessons for us.—Homiletic Review.

In public, in the daylight, on holy Olivet, the Lord finished with glory the career which He began in obscurity. He finished His earthly career, but not His human life. His ascension perpetuated His incarnation. He did not evacuate His human body, but carried it with Him to the right hand of God—with its nail prints and its thorn scars. Touched with a feeling of our infirmities, our great Highpriest has passed into the heavens. There He ever liveth to make intercession for us. With His pierced hands He is able to save to the uttermost them that come unto God by Him.—R. S. Barrett.

To ascend on high must have meant for Christ a large increase of His quickening influence, more power to act beneficially on human minds and hearts, to purify and energize, to inspire and elevate, as hitherto He had not been able. That was His supreme ambition, the height for which He sighed; and was it not even thus that He went up gloriously at last from the cross and the grave, mounting from thence to be a greater saving and subliming force than He had ever been before, to beget repentance and remission of sins beyond what He had ever done?—S. A. Tipple.

By the Ascension all the parts of life are brought together in the oneness of their common destination. By the Ascension Christ in His Humanity is brought close to every one of us, and the words "in Christ," the very

charter of our faith, gain a present power. By the Ascension we are encouraged to work beneath the surface of things to that which makes all things capable of consecration. Then it is that the last element in our confession as to Christ's work speaks to our hearts. He is not only present with us as Ascended: He is active for us. We believe that He sitteth on the right hand of God the Father Almighty.—Bishop Westcott.

The ascension of Christ added distance to definiteness in worship. Definiteness we must have, as ever craving for a theophany, every instinct of idolatry proves. "Lord, show us the Father and it sufficeth us" is prompted by this feeling. The Incarnation is God's response to this human need. But imagine Jesus living on indefinitely after the resurrection, even under the earthly conditions which obtained during those forty days!

Worship demands the far distances of God; it protests against the little, the near, the material. It must love but it must look up. It cannot live without the note of spirituality and universality, if not mystery. The ascension, the passing of Christ within the veil, answers this need. So does a full-robed Christianity add to definiteness of knowledge the outreach of imagination and home.—Maltbie Babcock.

We celebrate this day the Ascension of our great Judge into heaven, where He sits upon His throne and has all the world before Him; every human soul, with its desires and aims, its thoughts, words, and works, whether they be good or bad. Every man who is running now his mortal race is from first to last before the eye of Him who as on this day ascended with human nature into heaven. Shall we grieve that the Visible Presence is withdrawn, and that there is no longer on earth the mighty and mysterious Personage who put away sin by the sacrifice of Himself and discomfited through dying the enemies of God and man? Not so! There is no reason for sorrow that He quits the earth on the wings of the wind. We could not detain Him below, we would have Him as our Mediator within the veil. This and this only, can secure to us those spiritual assistances through which we ourselves may climb the firmament.— H. Melvill.

Christ is already in that place of peace, which is all in all. He is on the right hand of God. He is hidden in the brightness of the radiance which issues from the everlasting throne. He is in the very abyss of peace, where there is no voice of tumult or distress, but a deep stillness—stillness, that greatest and most awful of all goods which we can fancy; that most perfect of joys, the utter profound, ineffable tranquillity of the Divine Essence. He has entered into His rest. That is our home; here we are on a pilgrimage, and Christ calls us to His many mansions which He has prepared.—J. H. Newman.

Aspiration

I have immortal longings in me.— Shakespeare.

The mere aspiration is partial realization.—Anna Cora Mowatt.

The movement of the species is upward.—Bancroft.

By steps we may ascend to God.— Milton.

O that I had wings like a dove!— Bible.

It is but a base, ignoble mind that mounts no higher than a bird can soar.—Shakespeare.

The heavens are as deep as our aspirations are high.—Thoreau.

No man can ever rise above that at which he aims.—Rev. A. A. Hodge.

A man—be the heavens ever praised!—is sufficient for himself.— Carlyle.

There is not a single heart but has its moments of longing.—Beecher.

Too low they build who build beneath the stars.—Young.

We cannot of ourselves estimate the degree of our success in what we strive for.—Bulwer-Lytton.

Oh for a muse of fire that would ascend the highest heaven of invention!—Shakespeare.

Aspirations after the holy,—the only aspiration in which the human soul can be assured that it will never meet with disappointment.—Maria M'Intosh.

Man ought always to have something which he prefers to life; otherwise life itself will appear to him tiresome and void.—Seume.

There is no sorrow I have thought more about than that,—to love what is great, and try to reach it, and yet to fail.—George Eliot.

O God, Thou art my God; early will I seek Thee; my soul thirsteth for Thee; my flesh longeth for Thee in a dry and thirsty land, where no water is.—Psalms.

It is not to taste sweet things, but to do noble and true things, and vindicate himself under God's heaven as a God-made man, that the poorest son of Adam dimly longs.—Carlyle.

The heart is a small thing, but desireth great matters. It is not sufficient for a kite's dinner, yet the whole world is not sufficient for it.—Quarles.

We learn to treasure what is above this earth; we long for revelation, which nowhere burns more purely and more beautifully than in the New Testament.—Goethe.

Father! forgive the heart that clings
Thus trembling to the things of time,
And bid my soul, on angel's wings
Ascend into a purer clime.
—Jane Roscoe.

It seems to me we can never give up longing and wishing while we are thoroughly alive. There are certain things we feel to be beautiful and good, and we must hunger after them. —George Eliot.

What we truly and earnestly aspire to be, that in some sense we are. The mere aspiration, by changing the frame of the mind, for the moment realizes itself.—Mrs. Jameson.

The negro king desired to be portrayed as white. But do not laugh at the poor African; for every man is but another negro king, and would like to appear in a color different from that with which Fate has bedaubed him.— Heinrich Heine.

There must be something beyond man in this world. Even on attaining to his highest possibilities, he is like a bird beating against his cage. There is something beyond, O deathless soul, like a sea-shell, moaning for the bosom of the ocean to which you belong!—Chapin.

Did you ever hear of a man who had striven all his life faithfully and singly towards an object, and in no measure obtained it? If a man constantly aspires, is he not elevated? Did ever a man try heroism, magnanimity, truth, sincerity, and find that there was no advantage in them,— that it was a vain endeavor?— Thoreau.

Aspiration, worthy ambition, desires for higher good for good ends,—all these indicate a soul that recognizes the beckoning hand of the good Father, who would call us homeward toward Himself.—J. G. Holland.

Assassination

Assassination is not argument.— Castelar.

There are moral as well as physical assassinations.—Voltaire.

Assassination makes only martyrs, not converts.—Lamartine.

If the assassination could trammel up the consequence, and catch, with his surcease, success; that but this blow might be the be-all and the end-all here,—but here, upon this bank and shoal of time, we'd jump the life to come.—Shakespeare.

Murder, like talent, seems occasionally to run in families.—G. H. Lewes.

Assassination has never changed the history of the world.—Beaconsfield.

Assertion

It is an impudent kind of sorcery, to attempt to blind us with the smoke, without convincing us that the fire has existed.—Junius.

Assertion, unsupported by fact, is nugatory; surmise and general abuse, in however elegant language, ought not to pass for proofs.—Junius.

Associates

A companion of fools shall be destroyed.—Proverbs xiii. 20.

He that walketh with wise men shall be wise.—Solomon.

Frequent the company of your betters.—Thackeray.

Friends are good,—good, if well chosen.—De Foe.

My friends! There are no friends. —Aristotle.

We encourage one another in mediocrity.—Lamb.

For my own part, I shall be glad to learn of noble men.—Shakespeare.

Company, villainous company, hath been the spoil of me.—Shakespeare.

It is a true proverb that if you live with a lame man you will learn to halt.—Plutarch.

It is best to be with those in time that we hope to be with in eternity.— Fuller.

Keep good company, and you shall be of the number.—George Herbert.

A man—be the heavens ever praised! —is sufficient for himself.—Carlyle.

He that walketh with wise men shall be wise.—Solomon.

We are far more liable to catch the vices than the virtues of our associates.—Diderot.

The company in which you will improve most will be least expensive to you.—Washington.

There are like to be short graces where the devil plays host.—Lamb.

Choose the company of your superiors whenever you can have it.—Lord Chesterfield.

Be not deceived; evil communications corrupt good manners.—Bible.

No man can be provident of his time, who is not prudent in the choice of his company.—Jeremy Taylor.

You may depend upon it that he is a good man whose intimate friends are all good.—Lavater.

We make others' judgment our own by frequenting their society.—Thomas Fuller.

If you always live with those who are lame, you will yourself learn to limp.—From the Latin.

If men wish to be held in esteem, they must associate with those only who are estimable.—Bruyère.

I set it down as a maxim, that it is good for a man to live where he can meet his betters, intellectual and social.—Thackeray.

Costly followers are not to be liked; lest while a man maketh his train longer, he makes his wings shorter.—Bacon.

It is meet that noble minds keep ever with their likes; for who so firm, that cannot be seduced?—Shakespeare.

A man should live with his superiors as he does with his fire,—not too near, lest he burn; nor too far off, lest he freeze.—Diogenes.

Those who are unacquainted with the world take pleasure in the intimacy of great men; those who are wiser dread the consequences.—Horace.

It is good discretion not to make too much of any man at the first; because one cannot hold out that proportion.—Bacon.

No man can possibly improve in any company for which he has not respect enough to be under some degree of restraint.—Chesterfield.

What is companionship where nothing that improves the intellect is communicated, and where the larger heart contracts itself to the model and dimension of the smaller?—Landor.

No company is far preferable to bad, because we are more apt to catch the vices of others than their virtues, as disease is far more contagious than health.—Colton.

Nothing is more deeply punished than the neglect of the affinities by which alone society should be formed, and the insane levity of choosing associates by others' eyes.—Emerson.

Constant companionship is not enjoyable, any more than constant eating. We sit too long at the table of friendship, when we outsit our appetites for each other's thoughts.—Bovee.

We gain nothing by being with such as ourselves. We encourage one another in mediocrity. I am always longing to be with men more excellent than myself.—Lamb.

He who comes from the kitchen, smells of its smoke; and he who adheres to a sect, has something of its cant; the college air pursues the student; and dry inhumanity him who herds with literary pedants.—Lavater.

It is expedient to have an acquaintance with those who have looked into the world; who know men, understand business, and can give you good intelligence and good advice when they are wanted.—Bishop Horne.

Associate with men of judgment, for judgment is found in conversation, and we make another man's judgment ours by frequenting his company.—Thomas Fuller.

It is certain that either wise bearing or ignorant carriage is caught, as men take disease, one of another; therefore let men take heed of their company.—Shakespeare.

A frequent intercourse and intimate connection between two persons make them so like, that not only their dispositions are moulded like each other, but their very face and tone of voice contract a certain analogy.—Lavater.

When we live habitually with the wicked, we become necessarily either their victim or their disciple; when we associate, on the contrary, with virtuous men, we form ourselves in imitation of their virtues, or, at least, lose every day something of our faults.—Agapet.

In all societies, it is advisable to associate if possible with the highest; not that the highest are always the best, but because, if disgusted there, we can at any time descend; but if we begin with the lowest, to ascend is impossible.—Colton.

A companion that feasts the company with wit and mirth, and leaves out the sin which is usually mixed with them, he is the man; and let me tell you, good company and good discourse are the very sinews of virtue.—Izaak Walton.

He that can enjoy the intimacy of the great, and on no occasion disgust them by familiarity, or disgrace himself by servility, proves that he is as perfect a gentleman by nature as his companions are by rank.—Colton.

It is hard to mesmerize ourselves, to whip our own top; but through sympathy we are capable of energy and endurance. Concert fires people to a certain fury of performance they can rarely reach alone.—Emerson.

Bad company is like a nail driven into a post, which, after the first and second blow, may be drawn out with little difficulty; but being once driven up to the head, the pincers cannot take hold to draw it out, but which can only be done by the destruction of the wood.—St. Augustine.

Be very circumspect in the choice of thy company. In the society of thine equals thou shalt enjoy more pleasure; in the society of thy superiors thou shalt find more profit. To be the best in the company is the way to grow worse; the best means to grow better is to be the worst there.—Quarles.

It is adverse to talent to be consorted and trained up with inferior minds and inferior companions, however high they may rank. The foal of the racer neither finds out his speed nor calls out his powers if pastured out with the common herd, that are destined for the collar and the yoke.—Colton.

Might I give counsel to any young hearer, I would say to him, try to frequent the company of your betters. In books and life is the most wholesome society; learn to admire rightly; the great pleasure of life is that. Note what the great men admire,—they admired great things; narrow spirits admire basely, and worship meanly.—Thackeray.

As there are some flowers which you should smell but slightly to extract all that is pleasant in them, and which, if you do otherwise, emit what is unpleasant and noxious, so there are some men with whom a slight acquaintance is quite sufficient to draw out all that is agreeable; a more intimate one would be unsatisfactory and unsafe.—Landor.

Association

There is no man who has not some interesting associations with particular scenes, or airs, or books, and who does not feel their beauty or sublimity enhanced to him by such connections.— Sir A. Alison.

There's not a wind but whispers of thy name;
And not a flow'r that grows beneath the moon,
But in its hues and fragrance tells a tale
Of thee, my love.   —Barry Cornwall.

Association is the delight of the heart, not less than of poetry. Alison observes that an autumn sunset, with its crimson clouds, glimmering trunks of trees, and wavering tints upon the grass, seems scarcely capable of embellishment. But if in this calm and beautiful glow the chime of a distant bell steal over the fields, the bosom heaves with the sensation that Dante so tenderly describes.—Willmott.

He whose heart is not excited upon the spot which a martyr has sanctified by his sufferings, or at the grave of one who has largely benefited mankind, must be more inferior to the multitude in his moral, than he can possibly be raised above them in his intellectual nature.—Southey.

How we delight to build our recollections upon some basis of reality,— a place, a country, a local habitation! how the events of life, as we look back upon them, have grown into the well-remembered background of the places where they fell upon us! Here is some sunny garden or summer lane, beautified and canonized forever with the flood of a great joy; and here are dim and silent places,—rooms always shadowed and dark to us, whatever they may be to others,—where distress or death came once, and since then dwells forevermore.—Washington Irving.

Whatever withdraws us from the power of our senses: whatever makes the past, the distant, or the future, predominate over the present, advances us in the dignity of thinking beings. Far from me, and far from my friends be such frigid philosophy as may conduct us indifferent and unmoved over any ground which has been dignified by wisdom, bravery, or virtue. That man is little to be envied whose patriotism would not gain force upon the plain of Marathon, or whose piety would not grow warmer among the ruins of Ionia.—Johnson

Assurance

Immoderate assurance is perfect licentiousness.—Shenstone.

Assurance never failed to get admission into the houses of the great. — Moore.

Assurance of hope is more than life, It is health, strength, power, vigor, activity, energy, manliness, beauty.— J. C. Ryle.

Assurance and intrepidity, under the white banner of seeming modesty, clear the way to merit that would otherwise be discouraged by difficulties. —Chesterfield.

True assurance makes a man more humble and self-denied, but presumptuous confidence puffs up with spiritual pride and self-conceit; the one excites to the practice of every commanded duty, but the other encourages sloth and indolence.—Fisher's Catechism.

There are believers who by God's grace, have climbed the mountains of full assurance and near communion, their place is with the eagle in his eyrie, high aloft; they are like the strong mountaineer, who has trodden the virgin snow, who has breathed the fresh, free air of the Alpine regions, and therefore his sinews are braced, and his limbs are vigorous; these are they who do great exploits, being mighty men, men of renown.—C. H. Spurgeon.

Let us rise into blest assurance that everywhere and forever we are enfolded, penetrated, guarded, guided, kept by the power of the Father and Friend, who can never forsake us;

and that all spirits who have begun to seek, know, love, and serve the All-Perfect One on earth shall be reunited in a celestial home, and be welcomed in a celestial home, and be welcomed together into the freedom of the universe, and the perpetual light of His presence.—W. E. Channing.

Astrology

Astrologers that future fates foreshow.—Pope.

———

Our jovial star reigned at his birth.
—Shakespeare.

———

Strange an astrologer should die without one wonder in the sky.—Swift.

———

No date prefixed directs me in the starry rubric set.—Milton.

———

Astrological prayers seem to me to be built on as good reason as the predictions.—Stillingfleet.

———

I will look on the stars and look on thee, and read the page of thy destiny.—L. E. Landon.

———

The astrologer who spells the stars, mistakes his globes, and in her bright eye interprets heaven's physiognomies.—John Cleaveland.

———

Do not Christians and Heathens, Jews and Gentiles, poets and philosophers, unite in allowing the starry influences?—Sir Walter Scott.

———

There's some ill planet reigns; I must be patient till the heavens look with an aspect favorable.—Shakespeare.

———

Figure-flingers and star-gazers pretend to foretell the fortunes of kingdoms, and have no foresight in what concerns themselves.—L'Estrange.

———

A wise man shall overrule his stars, and have a greater influence upon his own content than all the constellations and planets of the firmament.—Jeremy Taylor.

———

We speak of persons as jovial, as being born under the planet Jupiter or

Jove, which was the joyfullest star and the happiest augury of all. A gloomy person was said to be saturnine, as being born under the planet Saturn, who was considered to make those who owned his influence, and were born when he was in the ascendant, grave and stern as himself.—Trench.

Astronomy

An undevout astronomer is mad.—Young.

———

Astronomy is the science of the harmony of infinite expanse.—Lord John Russell.

———

And teach me how
To name the bigger light, and how the less,
That burn by day and night.
—Shakespeare.

Ye realms, yet unreveal'd to human sight,
Ye gods who rule the regions of the night,
Ye gliding ghosts permit me to relate
The mystic wonders of your silent state.
—Dryden.

———

The narrow sectarian cannot read astronomy with impunity. The creeds of his church shrivel like dried leaves at the door of the observatory.—Emerson.

———

The contemplation of celestial things will make a man both speak and think more sublimely and magnificently when he descends to human affairs.—Cicero.

———

These earthly god-fathers of heaven's lights
That give a name to every fixed star
Have no more profit of their shining nights
Than those that walk, and wot not what
they are. —Shakespeare.

The sun rejoicing round the earth, announced
Daily the wisdom, power and love of God.
The moon awoke, and from her maiden face,
Shedding her cloudy locks, looked meekly forth,
And with her virgin stars walked in the heavens—
Walked nightly there, conversing as she walked,
Of purity, and holiness, and God.
—Robert Pollok.

———

Astronomy is one of the sublimest fields of human investigation. The

mind that grasps its facts and principles receives something of the enlargement and grandeur belonging to
the science itself. It is a quickener
of devotion.—Horace Mann.

And God made two great lights, great for
their use
To man, the greater to have rule by day,
The less by night, altern.   —Milton.

I love to rove amidst the starry height,
To leave the little scenes of earth behind,
And let Imagination wing her flight
On eagle pinions swifter than the wind.
I love the planets in their course to trace;
To mark the comets speeding to the sun,
Then launch into immeasurable space,
Where, lost to human sight, remote they
run.
I love to view the moon, when high she
rides
Amidst the heav'ns, in borrowed lustre
bright;
To fathom how she rules the subject tides,
And how she borrows from the sun her
light.
O! these are wonders of th' Almighty
hand,
Whose wisdom first the circling orbits
planned.   —T. Rodd.

It does at first appear that an astronomer rapt in abstraction, while
he gazes on a star, must feel more
exquisite delight than a farmer who is
conducting his team.—Isaac Disraeli.

Atheism

The fool hath said in his heart,
There is no God.—Psalm xiv. 1.

By night an atheist half believes a
God.—Young.

No atheist, as such, can be a true
friend.—Bentley.

Atheism is rather in the life than in
the heart of man.—Francis Bacon.

No one is so much alone in the
world as a denier of God.—Richter.

Though a man declares himself an
atheist, it in no way alters his obligations.—Henry Ward Beecher.

Ingersoll's atheism can never become
an institution; it can never be more
than a destitution.—Robert Collyer.

Thank Heaven, the female heart
is untenantable by atheism.—Horace
Mann.

The thing formed says that nothing
formed it; and that which is made is,
while that which made it is not! The
folly is infinite.—Jeremy Taylor.

An atheist-laugh's a poor exchange
For Deity offended!   —Burns.

A little philosophy inclineth man's
mind to atheism, but depth in philosophy bringeth men's minds about to
religion.—Francis Bacon.

It is a fine observation of Plato, in
his Laws, that atheism is a disease of
the soul before it becomes an error
of the understanding.—Wm. Fleming.

God never wrought miracles to convince atheism, because His ordinary
works convince it.—Bacon.

The statements of atheists ought to
be perfectly clear of doubt. Now it is
not perfectly clear that the soul is
material.—Pascal.

Atheism is the result of ignorance
and pride, of strong sense and feeble
reasons, of good eating and ill living.—
Jeremy Collier.

An atheist is one of the most daring
beings in creation,—a contemner of
God, who explodes His laws by denying His existence.—John Foster.

Men are atheistical because they are
first vicious, and question the truth
of Christianity because they hate the
practice.—South.

As atheism is in all respects hateful, so in this, that it depriveth human
nature of the means to exalt itself
above human frailty.—Bacon.

There are few men so obstinate in
their atheism whom a pressing danger
will not reduce to an acknowledgment
of the divine power.—Plato.

They that deny a God destroy man's
nobility, for certainly man is of kin
to the beasts by his body; and if he

be not of kin to God by his spirit, he is a base and ignoble creature.—Francis Bacon.

Nothing enlarges the gulf of atheism more than the wide passage that lies between the faith and lives of men pretending to teach Christianity.—Stillingfleet.

Eyes which the preacher could not school,
By wayside graves are raised;
And lips say, "God be pitiful,"
That ne'er said "God be praised."
—Mrs. Browning.

When men live as if there were no God, it becomes expedient for them that there should be none; and then they endeavor to persuade themselves so.—Tillotson.

Atheism is a system which can communicate neither warmth nor illumination, except from those fagots which your mistaken zeal has lighted up for its destruction.—Colton.

The three great apostles of practical atheism, that make converts without persecuting, and retain them without preaching, are wealth, health, and power.—Colton.

The great atheists are, indeed, the hypocrites, which are ever handling holy things, but without feeling; so as they must need be cauterized in the end.—Bacon.

There is no being eloquent for atheism. In that exhausted receiver the mind cannot use its wings,—the clearest proof that it is out of its element. — Hare.

The owlet atheism, sailing on obscene wings across the noon, drops his blue-fringed lids, and shuts them close, and, hooting at the glorious sun in heaven, cries out, "Where is it?"—Coleridge.

That the universe was formed by a fortuitous concourse of atoms, I will no more believe than that the accidental jumbling of the alphabet would fall into a most ingenious treatise of philosophy.—Dean Swift.

I should like to see a man sober in his habits, moderate, chaste, just in his dealings, assert that there is no God; he would speak at least without interested motives; but such a man is not to be found.—Bruyère.

The footprint of the savage traced in the sand is sufficient to attest the presence of man to the atheist who will not recognize God, whose hand is impressed upon the entire universe.—Hugh Miller.

Whoever considers the study of anatomy, I believe, will never be an atheist; the frame of man's body, and coherence of his parts, being so strange and paradoxical, that I hold it to be the greatest miracle of nature.—Lord Herbert.

These are they
That strove to pull Jehovah from His throne,
And in the place of heaven's Eternal King
Set up the phantom, Chance. —Glynn.

Religion assures us that our afflictions shall have an end; she comforts us, she dries our tears, she promises us another life. On the contrary, in the abominable worship of atheism, human woes are the incense, death is the priest, a coffin the altar, and annihilation the Deity.—Chateaubriand.

Supposing all the great points of atheism were formed into a kind of creed, I would fain ask whether it would not require an infinite greater measure of faith than any set of articles which they so violently oppose. —Addison.

Settle it, therefore, in your minds, as a maxim never to be effaced or forgotten, that atheism is an inhuman, bloody, ferocious system, equally hostile to every useful restraint, and to every virtuous affection: that leaving nothing above us to excite awe, nor round us to awaken tenderness, it wages war with heaven and earth: its first object is to dethrone God, its next to destroy man.—Robert Hall.

One would fancy that the zealots in atheism would be exempt from the single fault which seems to grow out of the imprudent fervor of religion. But so it is, that irreligion is propagated with as much fierceness and contention, wrath and indignation, as if the safety of mankind depended upon it.—Addison.

The truly great consider, first, how they may gain the approbation of God, and, secondly, that of their own conscience. Having done this, they would then willingly conciliate the good opinion of their fellow-men. But the truly little reverse the thing. The primary object with them is to secure the applause of their fellow-men; and having effected this, the approbation of God and their own conscience may follow on as they can.—Colton.

Atheism can benefit no class of people; neither the unfortunate, whom it bereaves of hope, nor the prosperous, whose joys it renders insipid, nor the soldier, of whom it makes a coward, nor the woman whose beauty and sensibility it mars, nor the mother, who has a son to lose, nor the rulers of men, who have no surer pledge of the fidelity of their subjects than religion. —Chateaubriand.

Kircher, the astronomer, having an acquaintance who denied the existence of a Supreme Being, took the following method to convince him of his error. Expecting him on a visit, he placed a handsome celestial globe in a part of the room where it could not escape the notice of his friend, who, on observing it, inquired whence it came, and who was the maker. "It was not made by any person," said the astronomer. "That is impossible," replied the skeptic; "you surely jest." Kircher than took occasion to reason with his friend upon his own atheistical principles, explaining to him that he had adopted this plan with a design to show him the fallacy of his skepticism. "You will not," said he, "admit that this small body originated in mere chance, and yet you contend that those heavenly bodies, to which it bears only a faint and diminutive resemblance, came into existence without author or design."

He pursued this chain of reasoning till his friend was totally confounded, and cordially acknowledged the absurdity of his notions.

Athens

Athens, the eye of Greece, mother of arts
And eloquence.   —Milton.

Ancient of days! august Athena! where,
Where are thy men of might? thy grand in soul?
Gone—glimmering though the dream of things that were;
First in the race that led to glory's goal,
They won, and pass'd away—Is this the whole?   —Byron.

Attention

I never knew any man cured of inattention.—Swift.

In the power of fixing the attention lies the most precious of the intellectual habits.—Robert Hall.

Attention is the stuff that memory is made of, and memory is accumulated genius.—Lowell.

It is a way of calling a man a fool when no attention is given to what he says.—L'Estrange.

Lend thy serious hearing to what I shall unfold.   —Shakespeare.

It is difficult to instruct children because of their natural inattention; the true mode, of course, is to first make our modes interesting to them.— Locke.

Attention makes the genius; all learning, fancy, and science depend upon it. Newton traced back his discoveries to its unwearied employment. It builds bridges, opens new worlds, and heals diseases; without it taste is useless, and the beauties of literature are unobserved.—Willmott.

Attractiveness

The poetic element lying hidden in most women is the source of their magnetic attraction.—Victor Hugo.

The first duty of a woman is to be pretty.—Mme. de Girardin.

A poor beauty finds more lovers than husbands.—Geo. Herbert.

That hook of wiving, fairness which strikes the eye.—Shakespeare.

Her very frowns are fairer far than smiles of other maidens are.—Coleridge.

Nothing under heaven so strongly doth allure the sense of man, and all his mind possess, as beauty's love-bait.—Spenser.

Those who are formed to win general admiration are seldom calculated to bestow individual happiness.—Lady Blessington.

No woman can be handsome by the force of features alone, any more than she can be witty only by the help of speech.—Thomas Hughes.

I hold it to be the moral duty of women to make themselves beautiful in all lawful ways.—E. Lynn Linton.

The more sensible a woman is, supposing her not to be masculine, the more attractive she is in her proportionate power to entertain.—Leigh Hunt.

Women and flowers are made to be loved for their beauty and sweetness, rather than themselves to love.—Ninon de Lenclos.

On the attraction between man and woman society is based; but its refined is greater than its gross force, and its weight is like the gravitation of the globe.—Bartol.

A woman's natural quality is to attract, and having attracted to enchain; and how influential she may be for good or evil, the history of every age makes clear.—Mrs. H. R. Haweis.

There are other things besides beauty with which to captivate the hearts of men. The Italians have a saying: "Fair is not fair, but that which pleaseth."—Ninon de Lenclos.

To make the cunning artless, tame the rude, subdue the haughty, shake the undaunted soul; yea, put a bridle in the lion's mouth, and lead him forth as a domestic cur,—these are the triumphs of all-powerful beauty.—Joanna Baillie.

Rarity gives a charm: thus early fruits are most esteemed; thus winter roses obtain a higher price; thus coyness sets off an extravagant mistress: a door ever open attracts no young suitor.—Martial.

A pretty, silly, self-conceited woman will very often be far more courted, and seemingly far more liked and admired, than a woman of infinitely higher charms. All the while the men do not like her a tenth part as well.—Charles Buxton.

She carried about her an indefinable air of having been used to love, or admiration probably, of men as well as women, which the most exquisitely modest women will sometimes wear, and which is unmistakable as it is alluring to the eye.—Elizabeth Stuart Phelps.

Our poor eyes were so enriched as to behold, and our low hearts so exalted as to love, a maid who is such, that as the greatest thing the world can show is her beauty, so the least thing that may be praised in her is her beauty.—Sir P. Sidney.

August

In the parching August wind,
Cornfields bow the head,
Sheltered in round valley depths,
On low hills outspread.
—Christina G. Rossetti.

Dead is the air, and still! the leaves of the locust and walnut
Lazily hang from the boughs, inlaying their intricate outlines
Rather on space than the sky—on a tideless expansion of slumber.
—Bayard Taylor.

Authority

Even reproof from authority ought to be grave, and not taunting.—Bacon.

There is no fettering of authority.—Shakespeare.

Self-possession is the backbone of authority.—Haliburton.

A dog is obeyed in office.—Shakespeare.

Nothing is more gratifying to the mind of man than power of dominion.—Addison.

Though authority be a stubborn bear, yet he is oft led by the nose with gold.—Shakespeare.

The love of power and the love of liberty are in eternal antagonism.—J. Stuart Mill.

Every legitimate authority should respect its extent and its limits.—Joubert.

Authority, though it err like others, hath yet a kind of medicine in itself, that skins the vice of the top.—Shakespeare.

A man in authority is but as a candle in the wind, sooner wasted or blown out than under a bushel.—Beaumont and Fletcher.

The reason why the simpler sort are moved by authority is the consciousness of their own ignorance.—Hooker.

God, who prepares His work through ages, accomplishes it, when the hour is come, with the feeblest instruments.—Merle D'Aubigné.

Authority bears of a credent bulk
That no particular scandal once can touch;
But it confounds the breather.
                                    —Shakespeare.

All authority must be out of a man's self, turned * * * either upon an art, or upon a man.—Bacon.

Authority is by nothing so much strengthened and confirmed as by custom; for no man easily distrusts the things which he and all men have been always bred up to.—Sir W. Temple.

There is nothing sooner overthrows a weak head than opinion of authority, like too strong a liquor for a frail glass.—Sir P. Sidney.

Authority forgets a dying king,
Laid widow'd of the power in his eye
That bow'd the will.   —Tennyson.

Three means to fortify belief are experience, reason, and authority. Of these the more potent is authority; for belief upon reason or experience will stagger.—Bacon.

Mankind are apt to be strongly prejudiced in favor of whatever is countenanced by antiquity, enforced by authority, and recommended by custom.—Robert Hall.

                            Shall remain!
Hear you this Triton of the minnows?
    mark you
His absolute "shall"?   —Shakespeare.

An argument from authority is but a weak kind of proof,—it being but a topical probation, and an inartificial argument depending on naked asseveration.—Sir T. Browne.

                    Man, proud man!
Dress'd in a little brief authority:
Most ignorant of what he's most assur'd,
His glassy essence—like an angry ape
Plays such fantastic tricks before high heaven,
As make the angels weep.   —Shakespeare.

Meek young men grow up in libraries, believing it their duty to accept the views which Cicero, which Locke, which Bacon have given; forgetful that Cicero, Locke, and Bacon were only young men in libraries when they wrote these books.—Emerson.

Not from gray hairs authority doth flow,
Nor from bald heads, nor from a wrinkled brow;
But our past life, when virtuously spent,
Must to our age those happy fruits present.
                                    —Denham.

Authority is properly the servant of justice, and political powers are arbitrary and illegitimate if not based upon qualification for that service. This is the doctrine of the ethical derivation of authority or public

power, as opposed to that of an un-conditioned and inherent sovereignty.
—D. A. Wasson.

Thou hast seen a farmer's dog bark at a
  beggar,
And the creature run from the cur: There,
There, thou might'st behold the great image
  of authority;
A dog's obeyed in office.   —Shakespeare.

.   Authority intoxicates,
And makes mere sots of magistrates;
The fumes of it invade the brain,
And make men giddy, proud and vain;
By this the fool commands the wise;
The noble with the base complies;
The sot assumes the role of wit,
And cowards make the base submit.
                          —Butler.

Most of our fellow-subjects are
guided either by the prejudice of education or by a deference to the judgment of those who perhaps in their
own hearts disapprove the opinions
which they industriously spread among
the multitude.—Addison.

Authorship
And choose an author as you choose
a friend.—Wentworth Dillon.

Nature's chief masterpiece is writing well.—Sheffield, Duke of Buckingham.

Look, then, into thine heart and
write!—Longfellow.

All authors to their own defects are
blind.—Dryden.

None but an author knows an author's cares.—Cowper.

All writing comes by the grace of
God, and all doing and having.—Emerson.

Of all those arts in which the wise excel,
Nature's chief masterpiece is writing well.
                    —John Sheffield.

The only happy author in this world
is he who is below the care of reputation.—Washington Irving.

I believe that a man may write himself out of reputation when nobody
else can do it.—Thomas Paine.

Twenty to one offend more in writing too much than too little.—Roger
Ascham.

He who proposes to be an author
should first be a student.—Dryden.

Authors, like coins, grow dear as
they grow old.—Pope.

Young authors give their brains
much exercise and little food.—Joubert.

Satire lies respecting literary men
during their life, and eulogy does so
after their death.—Voltaire.

No man but a blockhead ever wrote
except for money.—Sam'l Johnson.

The chief glory of every people
arises from its authors.—Sam'l Johnson.

One hates an author that is all author; fellows in foolscap uniform
turned up with ink.—Byron.

Strength is not energy; some authors have more muscles than talent.—
Joubert.

Let your literary compositions be
kept from the public eye for nine years
at least.—Horace.

None but an author knows an author's
  cares,
Or fancy's fondness for the child she bears.
                          —Cowper.

Who does not more admire Cicero
as an author than as a consul of
Rome?—Addison.

The familiar writer is apt to be his
own satirist. Out of his own mouth
is he judged.—Whipple.

A man may write at any time if he
set himself doggedly to it.—Sam'l
Johnson.

Sound judgment is the ground of
writing well.—Roscommon.

In every author let us distinguish
the man from his works.—Voltaire.

There are authors in whose hand the pen becomes a magic wand: but they are few.—Lady Montagu.

The ink of the scholar is more sacred than the blood of the martyr.—Mohammed.

Devise, wit; write, pen; for I am for whole volumes in folio.—Shakespeare.

Authors are partial to their wit, 'tis true, But are not critics to their judgment, too? —Pope.

Authors now find, as once Achilles found, the whole is mortal if a part's unsound.—Young.

No author ever drew a character, consistent to human nature, but what he was forced to ascribe to it many inconsistencies.—Bulwer-Lytton.

We write from aspiration and antagonism, as well as from experience. We paint those qualities which we do not possess.—Emerson.

The two most engaging powers of an author are to make new things familiar, and familiar things new.—Thackeray.

Those authors who appear sometimes to forget they are writers, and remember they are men, will be our favorites.—Disraeli.

It is commonly the personal character of a writer which gives him his public significance.—Goethe.

They who, by speech or writing, present to the ear or eye of modesty any of the indecencies, are pests of society. —Beattie.

A man of moderate Understanding, thinks he writes divinely: A man of good Understanding, thinks he writes reasonably.—De La Bruyère.

Authors must not, like Chinese soldiers, expect to win victories by turning somersets in the air.—Longfellow.

*Never write on a subject without having first read yourself full on it;

and never read on a subject till you have thought yourself hungry on it.— Richter.

Nothing is so beneficial to a young author as the advice of a man whose judgment stands constitutionally at the freezing-point.—Douglas Jerrold.

Every author, in some degree, portrays himself in his works even be it against his will.—Goethe.

Successful writers learn at last what they should learn at first,—to be intelligently simple.—H. W. Shaw.

To write much, and to write rapidly, are empty boasts. The world desires to know what you have done, and not how you did it.—George Henry Lewes.

In every work regard the writer's end, Since none can compass more than they intend. —Pope.

A woman who writes, commits two sins: she increases the number of books, and decreases the number of women.—Alphonse Karr.

The writer, like a priest, must be exempted from secular labor. His work needs a frolic health; he must be at the top of his condition.—Emerson.

Perhaps the greatest lesson which the lives of literary men teach us is told in a single word: Wait!—Longfellow.

Peaceable times are the best to live in, though not so proper to furnish materials for a writer.—Addison.

If you once understand an author's character, the comprehension of his writings becomes easy.—Longfellow.

To expect an author to talk as he writes is ridiculous; or even if he did you would find fault with him as a pedant.—Hazlitt.

A man of letters is often a man with two natures,—one a book nature, the other a human nature. These often clash sadly.—Whipple.

Boileau's numbers are excellent, his expressions noble, his thoughts just, his language pure, and his sense close. —Dryden.

There is no author so poor who cannot be of some service, if only for a witness of his time.—Claude Fauchet.

The pen is the tongue of the hand; a silent utterer of words for the eye. —Henry Ward Beecher.

Sallust is indisputably one of the best historians among the Romans, both for the purity of his language and the elegance of his style.—Burke.

Of all unfortunate men one of the unhappiest is a middling author endowed with too lively a sensibility for criticism.—Disraeli.

Let authors write for glory or reward,
Truth is well paid, when she is sung and
  heard.   —R. Corbet.

For no man can write anything who does not think that what he writes is, for the time, the history of the world. —Emerson.

He who writes prose builds his temple to Fame in rubble; he who writes verses builds it in granite.—Bulwer-Lytton.

The success of many works is found in the relation between the mediocrity of the authors' ideas and that of the ideas of the public.—Chamfort.

There seems to be a strange affectation in authors of appearing to have done everything by chance.—Johnson.

Subtract from many modern poets all that may be found in Shakespeare, and trash will remain.—Colton.

No fathers or mothers think their own children ugly; and this self-deceit is yet stronger with respect to the offspring of the mind.—Cervantes.

Modern writers are the moons of literature; they shine with reflected light,—with light borrowed from the ancients.—Dr. Johnson.

From the moment one sets up for an author, one must be treated as ceremoniously, that is as unfaithfully, "as a king's favorite or a king."—Pope.

One writer excels at a plan or a title-page; another works away at the body of the book; and a third is a dab hand at an index.—Goldsmith.

Friend, howsoever thou camest by this book, I will assure thee thou wert least in my thoughts when I writ it.— Bunyan.

To write well is to think well, to feel well, and to render well; it is to possess at once intellect, soul, and taste.—Buffon.

Never write anything that does not give you great pleasure; emotion is easily propagated from the writer to the reader.—Joubert.

I have got my spindle and my distaff ready—my pen and mind—never doubting for an instant that God will send me flax.—J. G. Holland.

There is infinite pathos in unsuccessful authorship. The book that perishes unread is the deaf mute of literature.—Holmes.

The memory of other authors is kept alive by their works, but the memory of Johnson keeps many of his works alive.—Macaulay.

It is quite as much of a trade to make a book as to make a clock. It requires more than mere genius to be an author.—Bruyère.

The authors who affect contempt for a name in the world put their names to the books which they invite the world to read.—Cicero.

So idle are dull readers, and so industrious are dull authors, that puffed nonsense bids fair to blow unpuffed sense wholly out of the field.—Colton.

The author who speaks about his own books is almost as bad as a mother who talks about her own children.—Benj. Disraeli.

That writer does the most, who gives his reader the most knowledge, and takes from him the least time.—C. C. Colton.

Bacon is throughout, and especially in his essays, one of the most suggestive authors who ever wrote.—Whately.

People may be taken in once, who imagine that an author is greater in private life than other men.—Johnson.

Clear writers, like clear fountains, do not seem so deep as they are; the turbid looks most profound.—Landor.

A writer who attempts to live on the manufacture of his imagination is continually coquetting with starvation. —Whipple.

There are three difficulties in authorship—to write anything worth the publishing, to find honest men to publish it, and to get sensible men to read it.—Colton.

He that commeth in print because he woulde be knowen, is like the foole that commeth into the Market because he woulde be seen.—Lyly.

Whoever has set his whole heart upon book-making had better be sought in his works, for it is only the lees of his cup of life which he offers, in person, to the warm lips of his fellows.—Tuckerman.

And so I penned
It down, until at last it came to be
For length and breadth the bigness which
   you see.   —Bunyan.

The little mind who loves itself, will wr'te and think with the vulgar; but the great mind will be bravely eccentric, and scorn the beaten road, from universal benevolence.—Go'dsmith.

Peace be with the soul of that charitable and courteous author, who, for the common benefit of his fellow-authors, introduced the ingenious way of miscellaneous writing!—Shaftesbury.

This is the highest miracle of genius, that things which are not should be as though they were, that the imaginations of one mind should become the personal recollections of another.—Macaulay.

It is in vain a daring author thinks of attaining to the heights of Parnassus if he does not feel the secret influence of heaven and if his natal star has not formed him to be a poet.—Boileau.

Authorship is, according to the spirit in which it is pursued, an infamy, a pastime, a day-labor, a handicraft, an art, a science, a virtue.—Schlegel.

Every fool describes in these bright days his wondrous journey to some foreign court, and spawns his quarto, and demands your praise.—Byron.

There are both dull correctness and piquant carelessness; it is needless to say which will command the most readers and have the most influence.—Colton.

It was among the ruins of the capitol that I first conceived the idea of a work which has amused and exercised nearly twenty years of my life. —Gibbon.

I have observed that vulgar readers almost always lose their veneration for the writings of the genius with whom they have had personal intercourse.—Sir Egerton Brydges.

Our writings are so many dishes, our readers guests, our books like beauty; that which one admires another rejects; so are we approved as men's fancies are inclined.—Burton.

The most original modern authors are not so because they advance what is new, but simply because they know how to put what they have to say as if it had never been said before.— Goethe.

———

Herder and Schiller both in their youth intended to study as surgeons; but Destiny said, "No, there are deeper wounds than those of the body, —heal the deeper!" and they wrote.— Richter.

———

Would a writer know how to behave himself with relation to posterity? Let him consider in old books what he finds that he is glad to know, and what omissions he most laments.—Swift.

———

Whatever be the motives which induce men to write,—whether avarice or fame,—the country becomes more wise and happy in which they most serve for instructors.—Goldsmith.

———

Our favorites are few: since only what rises from the heart reaches it, being caught and carried on the tongues of men wheresoever love and letters journey.—Alcott.

———

The book that he has made renders its author this service in return, that so long as the book survives, its author remains immortal and cannot die. —Richard de Bury.

———

And, after all, it is style alone by which posterity will judge of a great work, for an author can have nothing truly his own but his style.—Isaac Disraeli.

———

The men, who labor and digest things most,
Will be much apter to despond than boast;
For if your author be profoundly good,
'Twill cost you dear before he's understood.
　　　　　—Wentworth Dillon.

Oh! rather give me commentators plain,
Who with no deep researches vex the brain;
Who from the dark and doubtful love to run,
And hold their glimmering tapers to the sun.　　　　　—Crabbe.

———

It is a doubt whether mankind are most indebted to those who, like Bacon and Butler, dig the gold from the mine of literature, or to those who, like

Paley, purify it, stamp it, fix its real value, and give it currency and utility. —Colton.

———

The great and good do not die even in this world. Embalmed in books, their spirits walk abroad. The book is a living voice. It is an intellect to which one still listens.—Sam'l Smiles.

———

True ease in writing comes from art, not chance,
As those move easiest who have learn'd to dance.　　　　　—Pope.

———

The book that a person is beginning to create or design contains within itself half a life, and God only knows what an expanse of futurity also.— Richter.

———

'Tis hard to say if greater want of skill
Appear in writing or in judging ill;
But, of the two less dang'rous is th' offence
To tire our patience than mislead our sense.
　　　　　—Pope.

———

His [Burke's] imperial fancy has laid all nature under tribute, and has collected riches from every scene of the creation and every walk of art.— Robert Hall.

———

Each change of many-colored life he drew,
Exhausted worlds and then imagined new;
Existence saw him spurn her bounded reign,
And panting Time toil'd after him in vain.
　　　　　—Samuel Johnson.

———

Authors are the vanguard in the march of mind, the intellectual backwoodsmen, reclaiming from the idle wilderness new territories for the thought and activity of their happier brethren.—Carlyle.

———

Dr. Johnson has said that the chief glory of a country arises from its authors. But then that is only as they are oracles of wisdom; unless they teach virtue, they are more worthy of a halter than of the laurel. —Jane Porter.

———

It is a fine simile in one of Mr. Congreve's prologues which compares a writer to a battering gamester that stakes all his winnings upon one cast, so that if he loses the last throw he is sure to be undone.—Addison.

This is the magnanimity of authorship, when a writer having a topic presented to him, fruitful of beauties for common minds, waives his privilege, and trusts to the judicious few for understanding the reason of his abstinence.—Lamb.

If authors cannot be prevailed upon to keep close to truth and instruction, by unvaried terms, and plain, unsophisticated argument, yet it concerns readers not to be imposed on.—Locke.

That author, however, who has thought more than he has read, read more than he has written, and written more than he has published, if he does not command success, has at least deserved it.—Colton.

But words are things, and a small drop of ink,
Falling, like dew, upon a thought produces
That which makes thousands, perhaps millions think.   —Byron.

Whatever an author puts between the two covers of his book is public property; whatever of himself he does not put there is his private property, as much as if he had never written a word.—Gail Hamilton.

It may be glorious to write
Thoughts that shall glad the two or three
High souls, like those far stars that come in sight
Once in a century.   —Lowell.

Whatever hath been written shall remain,
Nor be erased nor written o'er again:
The unwritten only still belong to thee:
Take heed, and ponder well what that shall be.   —Longfellow.

There are two things which I am confident I can do very well; one is an introduction to any literary work, stating what it is to contain, and how it should be executed in the most perfect manner.—Sam'l Johnson.

Nothing goes by luck in composition; it allows of no trick. The best you can write will be the best you are.

Every sentence is the result of a long probation. The author's character is read from title-page to end.—Thoreau.

Genius now and then produces a lucky trifle. We still read the Dove of Anacreon, and Sparrow of Catullus; and a writer naturally pleases himself with a performance which owes nothing to the subject.—Dr. Johnson.

For works of the mind really great there is no old age, no decrepitude. It is inconceivable that a time should come when Homer, Dante, Shakespeare, should not ring in the ears of civilized man.—Gladstone.

Spero Speroni explains admirably how an author who writes very clearly for himself is often obscure to his readers. "It is," he says, "because the author proceeds from the thought to the expression, and the reader from the expression to the thought."—Chamfort.

O thou who art able to write a book which once in the two centuries or oftener there is a man gifted to do, envy not him whom they name citybuilder, and inexpressibly pity him whom they name conqueror or cityburner.—Carlyle.

There is a natural disposition with us to judge an author's personal character by the character of his works. We find it difficult to understand the common antithesis of a good writer and a bad man.—Whipple.

Those authors into whose hands nature has placed a magic wand, with which they no sooner touch us than we forget the unhappiness in life, than the darkness leaves our soul, and we are reconciled to existence, should be placed among the benefactors of the human race.—Diderot.

Consult the acutest poets and speakers, and they will confess that their quickest and most admired conceptions were such as darted into their minds like sudden flashes of lightning, they know not how nor whence.—South.

There is infinite pathos in unsuccessful authorship. The book that perishes unread is the deaf-mute of literature. The great asylum of Oblivion is full of such, making inaudible signs to each other in leaky garrets and unattainable dusty upper shelves.—O. W. Holmes.

Indeed, unless a man can link his written thoughts with the everlasting wants of men, so that they shall draw from them as from wells, there is no more immortality to the thoughts and feelings of the soul than to the muscles and the bones.—Henry Ward Beecher.

He that writes
Or makes a feast, more certainly invites
His judges than his friends; there's not a guest
But will find something wanting or ill-drest.
—Sir R. Howard.

An author! 'Tis a venerable name!
How few deserve it, and what numbers claim!
Unblest with sense above their peers refin'd,
Who shall stand up, dictators to mankind?
Nay, who dare shine, if not in virtue's cause?
That sole proprietor of just applause.
—Young.

There is nothing more dreadful to an author than neglect; compared with which, reproach, hatred, and opposition are names of happiness; yet this worst, this meanest fate, every one who dares to write has reason to fear.—Johnson.

That an author's work is the mirror of his mind is a position that has led to very false conclusions. If Satan himself were to write a book it would be in praise of virtue, because the good would purchase it for use, and the bad for ostentation.—Colton.

For all the practical purposes of life, truth might as well be in a prison as in the folio of a schoolman; and those who release her from her cobwebbed shelf and teach her to live with men have the merit of liberating, if not of discovering, her.—Colton.

Authors may be divided into falling stars, planets, and fixed stars: the first have a momentary effect; the second have a much longer duration; but the third are unchangeable, possess their own light, and work for all time.—Schopenhauer.

For popular purposes, at least, the aim of literary artists should be similar to that of Rubens in his landscapes, of which, without neglecting the minor traits or finishing, he was chiefly solicitous to present the leading effect, or what we may call the inspiration.—W. B. Clulow.

Dear authors! suit your topics to your strength,
And ponder well your subject, and its length;
Nor lift your load, before you're quite aware
What weight your shoulders will, or will not, bear.
—Byron.

The faults of a brilliant writer are never dangerous on the long run; a thousand people read his work who would read no other; inquiry is directed to each of his doctrines; it is soon discovered what is sound and what is false; the sound become maxims, and the false beacons.—Bulwer-Lytton.

The motives and purposes of authors are not always so pure and high, as, in the enthusiasm of youth, we sometimes imagine. To many the trumpet of fame is nothing but a tin horn to call them home, like laborers from the field, at dinner-time, and they think themselves lucky to get the dinner.—Longfellow.

The triumphs of the warrior are bounded by the narrow theatre of his own age; but those of a Scott or a Shakespeare will be renewed with greater and greater lustre in ages yet unborn, when the victorious chieftain shall be forgotten, or shall live only in the song of the minstrel and the page of the chronicler.—Prescott.

I believe that there is much less difference between the author and his works than is currently supposed; it is usually in the physical appearance of the writer,—his manners, his mien, his exterior,—that he falls short of the ideal a reasonable man forms of him—rarely in his mind.—Bulwer-Lytton.

The wickedness of a loose or profane author, in his writings, is more atrocious than that of the giddy libertine or drunken ravisher; not only because it extends its effects wider (as a pestilence that taints the air is more destructive than poison infused in a draught), but because it is committed with cool deliberation.—Johnson.

It is commonly the personal character of a writer which gives him his public significance. It is not imparted by his genius. Napoleon said of Corneille, "Were he living I would make him a king;" but he did not read him. He read Racine, yet he said nothing of the kind of Racine.—Goethe.

How many great ones may remember'd be,
Which in their days most famously did
   flourish,
Of whom no word we hear, nor sign
   now see,
But as things wip'd out with a sponge do
   perish,
Because the living cared not to cherish
No gentle wits, through pride or covetize,
Which might their names forever memorize!
                              —Spenser.

Certain I am that every author who has written a book with earnest forethought and fondly cherished designs will bear testimony to the fact that much which he meant to convey has never been guessed at in any review of his work; and many a delicate beauty of thought, on which he principally valued himself, remains, like the statue of Isis, an image of truth from which no hand lifts the veil.—Bulwer-Lytton.

Every author, indeed, who really influences the mind, who plants in it -thoughts and sentiments which take root and grow, communicates his character. Error and immorality—two words for one thing, for error is the immorality of the intellect, and immorality the error of the heart—these escape from him if they are in him,

and pass into the recipient mind through subtle avenues invisible to consciousness.—Whipple.

Nature I believe in. True art aims to represent men and women, not as my little self would have them, but as they appear. My heroes and heroines I want not extreme types, all good or all bad; but human, mortal—partly good, partly bad. Realism I need. Pure mental abstractions have no significance for me.—Ouida.

The wonderful fortune of some writers deludes and leads to misery a great number of young people. It cannot be too often repeated that it is dangerous to enter upon a career of letters without some other means of living. An illustrious author has said in these times, "Literature must not be leant on as upon a crutch; it is little more than a stick."—J. Petit-Senn.

As for my labors, if they can but wear one impertinence out of human life, destroy a single vice, or give a morning's cheerfulness to an honest mind—in short, if the world can be but one virtue the better, or in any degree less vicious, or receive from them the smallest addition to their innocent diversions—I shall not think my pains, or indeed my life, to have been spent in vain.—Steele.

Living authors, therefore, are usually bad companions. If they have not gained character, they seek to do so by methods often ridiculous, always disgusting; and if they have established a character, they are silent for fear of losing by their tongue what they have acquired by their pen—for many authors converse much more foolishly than Goldsmith, who have never written half so well.—Colton.

Professed authors who overestimate their vocation are too full of themselves to be agreeable companions. The demands of their egotism are inveterate. They seem to be incapable of that abandon which is the requisite condition of social pleasure; and bent upon winning a tribute of admiration, or some hint which they can turn to the account of pen-craft, there is seldom in their company any of the delightful unconsciousness which harmonizes a circle.—Tuckerman.

We may observe in humorous authors that the faults they chiefly ridicule have often a likeness in themselves. Cervantes had much of the knight-errant in him; Sir George Etherege was unconsciously the Fopling Flutter of his own satire; Goldsmith was the same hero to chambermaids, and coward to ladies that he has immortalized in his charming comedy; and the antiquarian frivolities of Jonathan Oldbuck had their resemblance in Jonathan Oldbuck's creator. —Bulwer-Lytton.

Autumn

Autumn is the harvest of greedy death.—Juvenal.

The year's last, loveliest smile.— Bryant.

The Indian summer—the dead summer's soul!—Mary Clemmer.

Autumn, in his leafless bowers, is waiting for the winter's snow.—Whittier.

Behold congenial Autumn comes,
The Sabbath of the year! —Logan.

When bounteous autumn rears her head, he joys to pull the ripened pear. —Dryden.

Wild is the music of autumnal winds amongst the faded woods.—Wordsworth.

The misty earth below is wan and drear,
The baying winds chase all the leaves away,
As cruel hounds pursue the trembling deer;
It is a solemn time, the sunset of the year.
—R. H. Stoddard.

All-cheering plenty, with her flowing horn,
Led yellow Autumn, wreath'd with nodding
corn. —Burns.

When summer gathers up her robes of glory, and like a dream of beauty glides away.—Sarah Helen Whitman.

The spring, the summer, the chill autumn, angry winter, change their wonted liveries.—Shakespeare.

The teeming autumn, big with rich increase, bearing the wanton burden of the prime.—Shakespeare.

Autumn wins you best by this, its mute
Appeal to sympathy for its decay.
—Robert Browning.

The tints of autumn—a mighty flower garden, blossoming under the spell of the enchanter, Frost.—Whittier.

The year growing ancient,
Nor yet on summer's death, nor on the
birth
Of trembling winter. —Shakespeare.

As fall the light autumnal leaves, one still the other following, till the bough strews all its honors.—Dante.

Crown'd with the sickle and the wheaten
sheaf,
While Autumn, nodding o'er the yellow
plain,
Comes jovial on. —Thomson.

The lands are lit with all the autumn blaze of golden-rod, and everywhere the purple asters nod and bend and wave and flit.—Helen Hunt.

To her bier comes the year, not with weeping and distress, as mortals do; but to guide her way to it, all the trees have torches lit.—Lucy Larcom.

How strange and awful is the synthesis of life and death in the gusty winds and falling leaves of an autumnal day!—Coleridge.

Thrice happy time,
Best portion of the various year, in which
Nature rejoiceth, smiling on her works
Lovely, to full perfection wrought.
—Phillips.

It was Autumn, and incessant
Piped the quails from shocks and sheaves,
And, like living coals, the apples
Burned among the withering leaves.
—Longfellow.

However constant the visitations of sickness and bereavement, the fall of the year is most thickly strewn with the fall of human life.—James Martineau.

Boughs are daily rifled
By the gusty thieves,
And the book of Nature
Getteth short of leaves.
—Hood.

The melancholy days are come, the saddest of the year,
Of wailing winds, and naked woods, and meadows brown and sear. —Bryant.

Every season hath its pleasures;
Spring may boast her flowery prime,
Yet the vineyard's ruby treasures
Brighten Autumn's sob'rer time.
—Moore.

The year's in the wane;
There is nothing adorning;
The night has no eve,
And the day has no morning;
Cold winter gives warning!
—Hood.

The pale descending year, yet pleasing still, a gentler mood inspires; for now the leaf incessant rustles from the mournful grove, oft startling such as, studious, walk below, and slowly circles through the waving air.—Thomson.

Divinest Autumn! who may paint thee best,
Forever changeful o'er the changeful globe?
Who guess thy certain crown, thy favorite crest,
The fashion of thy many-colored robe?
—R. H. Stoddard.

Autumn's earliest frost had given
To the woods below
Hues of beauty, such as heaven
Lendeth to its bow;
And the soft breeze from the west
Scarcely broke their dreamy rest.
—Whittier.

But see the fading, many color'd woods,
Shade deep'ning over shade, the country round
Imbrown; crowded umbrage, dusk and dun,
Of every hue, from wan declining green
To sooty dark. —Thomson.

Who is there who, at this season, does not feel his mind impressed with a sentiment of melancholy? or who is able to resist that current of thought, which, from such appearances of decay, so naturally leads him to the solemn imagination of that inevitable fate which is to bring on alike the decay of life, of empire, and of nature itself?—Sir A. Alison.

Season of mists and mellow fruitfulness!
Close bosom-friend of the maturing sun;
Conspiring with him how to load and bless
With fruit the vines that round the thatch-eaves run;
To bend with apples the moss'd cottage trees,
And fill all fruit with ripeness to the core.
—Keats.

O Autumn, laden with fruit, and stained
With the blood of the grape, pass not, but sit
Beneath my shady roof; there thou mayst rest
And tune thy jolly voice to my fresh pipe,
And all the daughters of the year shall dance!
Sing now the lusty song of fruits and flowers. —William Blake.

The summer's throbbing chant is done
And mute the choral antiphon;
The birds have left the shivering pines
To flit among the trellised vines,
Or fan the air with scented plumes
Amid the love-sick orange blooms,
And thou art here alone—alone—
Sing, little bird! the rest have flown.
—O. W. Holmes.

Then came the autumne, all in yellow clad,
As though he joy'd in his plenteous store,
Laden with fruits that made him laugh, full glad
That he had banished hunger, which tofore
Had by the belly oft him pinched sore;
Upon his head a wreath that was enrol'd
With ears of corne of every sort, he bore,
And in his hand a sickle did he holde,
To reape the ripened fruit the which the earth had yold. —Spenser.

What visionary tints the year puts on,
When falling leaves falter through motionless air
Or numbly cling and shiver to be gone!
How shimmer the low flats and pastures bare,
As with her nectar Hebe Autumn fills
The bowl between me and those distant hills,
And smiles and shakes abroad her misty, tremulous hair! —Lowell.

A moral character is attached to autumnal scenes; the leaves falling like our years, the flowers fading like our hours, the clouds fleeting like our illusions, the light diminishing like our intelligence, the sun growing colder like our affections, the rivers becoming frozen like our lives—all bear secret relations to our destinies.—Chateaubriand.

Yellow, mellow, ripened days,
  Sheltered in a golden coating;
O'er the dreamy listless haze,
  White and dainty cloudlets floating;
Winking at the blushing trees,
  And the sombre, furrowed fallow;
Smiling at the airy ease
  Of the southward flying swallow.
Sweet and smiling are thy ways,
Beauteous, golden Autumn days.
        —Will Carleton.

However constant the visitations of sickness and bereavement, the fall of the year is most thickly strewn with the fall of human life. Everywhere the spirit of some sad power seems to direct the time; it hides from us the blue heavens, it makes the green wave turbid; it walks through the fields, and lays the damp ungathered harvest low; it cries out in the night wind and the shrill hail; it steals the summer bloom from the infant cheek; it makes old age shiver to the heart; it goes to the churchyard, and chooses many a grave.—James Martineau.

Avarice

The love of money is the root of all evil.—I Timothy vi. 10.

Avarice is the vice of declining years.—George Bancroft.

There is thy gold; worse poison to men's souls.—Shakespeare.

Avarice is always poor.—Dr. Johnson.

If you wish to remove avarice you must remove its mother, luxury.—Cicero.

Avarice, where it has full dominion, excludes every other passion.—Gladstone.

Avarice is insatiable, and is always pushing on for more.—L'Estrange.

A captive fettered at the oar of gain.—Falconer.

To be thankful for what we grasp exceeding our proportion, is to add hypocrisy to injustice.—Lamb.

Poverty is in want of much, but avarice of everything.—Publius Syrus.

Avarice increases with the increasing pile of gold.—Juvenal.

Wealth in the gross is death, but life diffus'd,
As poison heals, in just proportion us'd.
        —Pope.

Avarice is the miser's dream, as fame is the poet's.—Hazlitt.

Those who covet much suffer from the want.—Horace.

It is surely very narrow policy that supposes money to be the chief good.—Johnson.

Avarice is more opposite to economy than liberality.—Rochefoucauld.

How quickly nature falls into revolt when gold becomes her object!—Shakespeare.

Some o'erenamor'd of their bags run mad,
Groan under gold, yet weep for want of
  bread.   —Young.

Avarice is to the intellect what sensuality is to the morals.—Mrs. Jameson.

The avaricious man is kind to no person, but he is most unkind to himself.—John Kyrle.

You despise a man for avarice; but you do not hate him.—Dr. Johnson.

It is natural to covet just what we have not.—Achilles Poincelot.

Poverty wants some, luxury many, and avarice all things.—Cowley.

In plain truth, it is not want, but rather abundance, that creates avarice.—Montaigne.

Avarice is only prudence and economy pushed to excess.—Chatfield.

When money is unreasonably coveted, it is a disease of the mind which is called avarice.—Cicero.

So for a good old-gentlemanly vice,
I think I must take up with avarice.
—Byron.

Avarice is always poor, but poor by her own fault.—Johnson.

The love of pelf increases with the pelf.—Juvenal.

To me avarice seems not so much a vice as a deplorable piece of madness.—Sir Thomas Browne.

There is no vice which mankind carries to such wild extremes as that of avarice.—Swift.

What must be the wealth that avarice, aided by power, cannot exhaust!—James Otis.

This avarice sticks deeper; grows with more pernicious root than summer-seeding lust.—Shakespeare.

It is but shaping the bribe to the taste, and every one has his price.—Richardson.

Why Mammon sits before a million hearths
Where God is bolted out from every house.
—Bailey.

And in his lap a masse of coyne he told
And turned upside down, to feede his eye
And covetous desire with his huge treasury.
—Spenser.

When all the sins are old in us,
And go upon crutches, covetousness
Does but lie in her cradle. —Decker.

O cursed lust of gold; when for thy sake
The fool throws up his interest in both worlds,
First starved in this, then damn'd in that to come. —Blair.

Some men make fortunes, but not to enjoy them; for, blinded by avarice, they live to make fortunes.—Juvenal.

If, of all vices, avarice is the most generally detested, it is the effect of an avidity common to all men.—Helvetius.

'Tis strange the miser should his cares employ
To gain those riches he can ne'er enjoy.
—Pope.

Expel avarice, the mother of all wickedness, who, always thirsty for more, opens wide her jaws for gold.—Claudianus.

A poor spirit is poorer than a poor purse. A very few pounds a year would ease a man of the scandal of avarice.—Swift.

Some men are called sagacious, merely on account of their avarice; whereas a child can clench its fist the moment it is born.—Shenstone.

Avarice starves its possessor to fatten those who come after, and who are eagerly awaiting the demise of the accumulator.—Greville.

Avarice is the most opposite of all characters to that of God Almighty, whose alone it is to give and not receive.—Shenstone.

The lust of avarice has so totally seized upon mankind that their wealth seems rather to possess them than they possess their wealth.—Pliny.

Many have been ruined by their fortunes; many have escaped ruin by the want of fortune. To obtain it, the great have become little, and the little great.—Zimmermann.

There are two considerations which always imbitter the heart of an avaricious man—the one is a perpetual thirst after more riches, the other the prospect of leaving what he has already acquired.—Fielding.

Because men believe not in Providence, therefore they do so greedily scrape and hoard. They do not believe in any reward for charity, therefore they will part with nothing.—Barrow.

Avarice in old age is foolish; for what can be more absurd than to increase our provisions for the road, the nearer we approach to our journey's end?—Cicero.

He sat amid his bags, and, with a look
Which hell might be ashamed of, drove the poor
Away unalmsed; and midst abundance died—
Sorest of evils!—died of utter want.
—Pollok.

All the good things of this world are no further good to us than as they are of use; and whatever we may heap up to give to others, we enjoy only as much as we can use, and no more.—De Foe.

We are at best but stewards of what we falsely call our own; yet avarice is so insatiable that it is not in the power of liberality to content it.—Seneca.

It is by bribing, not so often by being bribed, that wicked politicians bring ruin on mankind. Avarice is a rival to the pursuits of many.—Burke.

It is one of the worst effects of prosperity to make a man a vortex instead of a fountain; so that, instead of throwing out, he learns only to draw in.—Beecher.

Parsimony is enough to make the master of the golden mines as poor as he that has nothing; for a man may be brought to a morsel of bread by parsimony as well as profusion.—Henry Home.

He who is always in a hurry to be wealthy and immersed in the study of augmenting his fortune has lost the arms of reason and deserted the post of virtue.—Horace.

Study rather to fill your mind than your coffers; knowing that gold and silver were originally mingled with dirt, until avarice or ambition parted them.—Seneca.

The avaricious man is like the barren, sandy ground of the desert, which sucks in all the rain and dews with greediness, but yields no fruitful herbs or plants for the benefit of others.—Zeno.

There grows
In my most ill-compos'd affection such
A stanchless avarice, that, were I king,
I should cut off the nobles for their lands,
—Shakespeare.

The objects of avarice and ambition differ only in their greatness. A miser is as furious about a halfpenny as the man of ambition about the conquest of a kingdom.—Adam Smith.

Extreme avarice is nearly always mistaken; there is no passion which is oftener further away from its mark, nor upon which the present has so much power to the prejudice of the future.—La Rochefoucauld.

The character of covetousness is what a man generally acquires more through some niggardliness or ill grace in little and inconsiderable things, than in expenses of any consequence.—Pope.

The avarice of the miser may be termed the grand sepulchre of all his other passions, as they successively decay. But unlike other tombs, it is enlarged by repletion and strengthened by age.—Colton.

In all the world there is no vice
Less prone t' excess than avarice;
It neither cares for food nor clothing;
Nature's content with little—that with nothing.
—Butler.

Avarice has ruined more men than prodigality, and the blindest thoughtlessness of expenditure has not destroyed so many fortunes as the calculating but insatiable lust of accumulation.—Colton.

It may be remarked for the comfort of honest poverty that avarice reigns most in those who have but few good qualities to recommend them. This is a weed that will grow in a barren soil.—Hughes.

Avarice often produces opposite effects; there is an infinite number of people who sacrifice all their property to doubtful and distant expectations; others despise great future advantages to obtain present interests of a trifling nature.—Rochefoucauld.

Avarice begets more vices than Priam did children, and like Priam survives them all. It starves its keeper to surfeit those who wish him dead, and makes him submit to more mortifications to lose heaven than the martyr undergoes to gain it.—Colton.

Avarice is generally the last passion of those lives of which the first part has been squandered in pleasure, and the second devoted to ambition. He that sinks under the fatigue of getting wealth lulls his age with the milder business of saving it.—Dr. Johnson.

Objects close to the eye shut out much larger objects on the horizon; and splendors born only of the earth eclipse the stars. So a man sometimes covers up the entire disc of eternity with a dollar, and quenches transcendent glories with a little shining dust. —Chapin.

Avarice is a uniform and tractable vice; other intellectual distempers are different in different constitutions of mind. That which soothes the pride of one will offend the pride of another, but to the favor of the covetous bring money, and nothing is denied.—Johnson.

It would not be more unreasonable to transplant a favorite flower out of black earth into gold dust than it is for a person to let money-getting harden his heart into contempt, or into impatience, of the little attentions, the merriments and the caresses of domestic life.—Mountford.

The lust of gold succeeds the lust of conquest;
The lust of gold, unfeeling and remorseless!
The last corruption of degenerate man.
    —Dr. Johnson.

It is not the nature of avarice to be satisfied with anything but money. Every passion that acts upon mankind has a peculiar mode of operation.

Many of them are temporary and fluctuating; they admit of cessation and variety. But avarice is a fixed, uniform passion.—Thomas Paine.

It is a bitter thought to an avaricious spirit that by and by all these accumulations must be left behind. We can only carry away from this world the flavor of our good or evil deeds.—Beecher.

Riches, like insects, when conceal'd they lie,
Wait but for wings, and in their season fly.
Who sees pale Mammon pine amidst his store,
Sees but a backward steward for the poor;
This year a reservoir, to keep and spare;
The next a fountain, spouting thro' his heir
In lavish streams to quench a country's thirst,
And men and dogs shall drink him till they burst.   —Pope.

The love of gold that meanest rage,
And latest folly of man's sinking age,
Which, rarely venturing in the van of life,
While nobler passions wage their heated strife,
Comes skulking last with selfishness and fear
And dies collecting lumber in the rear!
    —Moore.

When a miser contents himself with giving nothing, and saving what he has got, and is in other respects guilty of no injustice, he is, perhaps, of all bad men the least injurious to society; the evil he does is properly nothing more than the omission of the good he might do. If, of all the vices, avarice is the most generally detested, it is the effect of an avidity common to all men; it is because men hate those from whom they can expect nothing. The greedy misers rail at sordid misers.—Helvetius.

Had covetous men, as the fable goes of Briareus, each of them one hundred hands, they would all of them be employed in grasping and gathering, and hardly one of them in giving or laying out, but all in receiving, and none in restoring; a thing in itself so monstrous that nothing in nature besides is like it, except it be death and the grave—the only things I know which are always carrying off the spoils of the world and never making restitution. For otherwise all the parts of the universe, as they borrow of one another, so they still pay what they borrow, and that by so just and well-balanced an equality that their payments always keep pace with their receipts.—Dryden.

It is impossible to conceive any contrast more entire and absolute than that which exists between a heart glowing with love to God, and a heart in which the love of money has cashiered all sense of God—His love, His presence, His glory; and which is no sooner relieved from the mockery of a tedious round of religious formalism than it reverts to the sanctuaries where its wealth is invested, with an intenseness of homage surpassing that of the most devout Israelite who ever, from a foreign land, turned his longing eyes toward Jerusalem. — Richard Fuller.

Aversion

I do not love thee, Doctor Fell,
The reason why, I cannot tell;
But this alone I know full well
I do not love thee, Doctor Fell.
—Tom Brown.

As well the noble savage of the field
Might tamely couple with the fearful ewe;
Tigers might engender with the timid deer;
Wild, muddy boars defile the cleanly ermine,
Or vultures sort with doves; as I with thee.
—Lee.

Awe

A heavenly awe overshadowed and encompassed, as it still ought, and must, all earthly business whatsoever. —Carlyle.

I cannot tell what you and other men
Think of this life; but for my single self,
I had as lief not be as live to be
In awe of such a thing as I myself.
—Shakespeare.

Awkwardness

Awkwardness is a more real disadvantage than it is generally thought to be; it often occasions ridicule, it always lessens dignity.—Chesterfield.

Not all the pumice of the polish'd town
Can smooth the roughness of the barnyard
   clown;
Rich, honor'd, titled, he betrays his race
By this one mark—he's awkward in his face.
—Holmes.

Awkward, embarrassed, stiff, without the
   skill
Of moving gracefully or standing still,
One leg, as if suspicious of his brother,
Desirous seems to run away from t'other.
—Churchill.

What's a fine person, or a beauteous face,
Unless deportment gives them decent grace?
Blessed with all other requisites to please,
Some want the striking elegance of ease;
The curious eye their awkward movement
   tires:
They seem like puppets led about by wires.
—Churchill.

B

Babbler

They always talk who never think.—Prior.

Who think too little, and who talk too much.—Dryden.

It is a shame for the tongue to cast itself upon the uncertain pardon of other's ears.—Bishop Hall.

Fie! what a spendthrift he is of his tongue!—Shakespeare.

Those who have few things to attend to are great babblers; for the less men think, the more they talk.—Montesquieu.

Tut! tut! my lord! we will not stand to prate;
Talkers are no good doers, be assured;
We go to use our hands, and not our tongues. —Shakespeare.

Babe — Babyhood

Fragile beginnings of a mighty end.—Mrs. Norton.

Incipient beings.—Carlyle.

A babe is a mother's anchor.—Beecher.

A link between angels and men.—Tupper.

Heaven lies about us in our infancy!—Wordsworth.

Of all the joys that brighten suffering earth, what joy is welcomed like a new-born child?—Mrs. Norton.

As living jewels dropped unstained from heaven.—Pollock.

A tight little bundle of wailing and flannel,
Perplex'd with the newly found fardel of life. —Fred. Locker.

A sweet new blossom of humanity, fresh fallen from God's own home to flower on earth.—Gerald Massey.

Bent o'er her babe, her eye dissolved in dew;
The big drops, mingling with the milk he drew. —John Langhorne.

The little babe up in his arms he bent, who with sweet pleasure and bold blandishment 'gan smile.—Spenser.

Sweet babe, in thy face
Soft desires I can trace,
Secret joys and secret smiles,
Little pretty infant wiles.
—William Blake.

Hush, my dear, lie still and slumber,
Holy angels guard thy bed!
Heavenly blessings without number
Gently falling on thy head.
—Watts.

But what am I?
An infant crying in the night:
An infant crying for the light:
And with no language but a cry.
—Tennyson.

A babe in a house is a well-spring of pleasure, a messenger of peace and love, a resting-place for innocence on earth, a link between angels and men.—Tupper.

The coarsest father gains a new impulse to labor from the moment of his baby's birth; he scarcely sees it when awake, and yet it is with him all the time. Every stroke he strikes is for his child. New social aims, new moral motives, come vaguely up to him.— T. W. Higginson.

Sweet sleep, with soft down
Weave thy brows an infant crown!
Sweet sleep, angel mild,
Hover o'er my happy child.
—William Blake.

It is curious to see how a self-willed, haughty girl, who sets her father and mother and all at defiance, and can't be managed by anybody, at once finds her master in a baby. Her sister's child will strike the rock and set all her affections flowing.—Charles Buxton.

Good Christian people, here lies for you an inestimable loan;—take all heed thereof, in all carefulness employ it;—with high recompense, or else with heavy penalty will it one day be required back.—Carlyle.

When you fold your hands, Baby Louise!
Your hands like a fairy's, so tiny and fair,
With a pretty, innocent, saintlike air,
Are you trying to think of some angel-taught prayer
You learned above, Baby Louise?
—Margaret Eytinge.

Beat upon mine, little heart! beat, beat!
Beat upon mine! you are mine, my sweet!
All mine from your pretty blue eyes to your feet,
My sweet!   —Tennyson.

Suck, baby! suck! mother's love grows by giving:
Drain the sweet founts that only thrive by wasting!
Black manhood comes when riotous guilty living
Hands thee the cup that shall be death in tasting.   —Charles Lamb.

Welcome to the parents the puny struggler, strong in his weakness, his little arms more irresistible than the soldier's, his lips touched with persuasion which Chatham and Pericles in manhood had not. His unaffected lamentations when he lifts up his voice on high, or, more beautiful, the sobbing child—the face all liquid grief, as he tries to swallow his vexation—

soften all hearts to pity and to mirthful and clamorous compassion.—Emerson.

Her beads while she numbered,
The baby still slumbered,
And smiled in her face, as she bended her knee;
Oh! bless'd be that warning,
My child, thy sleep adorning,
For I know that the angels are whispering with thee.   —Samuel Lover.

O child! O new-born denizen
Of life's great city! on thy head
The glory of the morn is shed,
Like a celestial benison!
Here at the portal thou dost stand,
And with thy little hand
Thou openest the mysterious gate
Into the future's undiscovered land.
—Longfellow.

How lovely he appears! his little cheeks
In their pure incarnation, vying with
The rose leaves strewn beneath them.
And his lips, too,
How beautifully parted! No; you shall not
Kiss him; at least not now; he will wake soon—
His hour of midday rest is nearly over.
—Byron.

What is the little one thinking about?
Very wonderful things, no doubt;
Unwritten history!
Unfathomed mystery!
Yet he laughs and cries, and eats and drinks,
And chuckles and crows, and nods and winks,
As if his head were as full of kinks
And curious riddles as any sphinx!
—J. G. Holland.

Look! how he laughs and stretches out his arms,
And opens wide his blue eyes upon thine,
To hail his father; while his little form
Flutters as winged with joy. Talk not of pain!
The childless cherubs well might envy thee
The pleasures of a parent.   —Byron.

He smiles and sleeps!—sleep on
And smile, thou little, young inheritor
Of a world scarce less young: sleep on and smile!
Thine are the hours and days when both are cheering
And innocent!   —Byron.

It is well for us that we are born babies in intellect. Could we understand half what mothers say and do to their infants, we should be filled with a conceit of our own importance, which would render us insupportable through life. Happy the boy whose mother is tired of talking nonsense to him before he is old enough to know the sense of it.—Hare.

Babe (Death of)

And thou hast stolen a jewel, Death!
Shall light thy dark up like a star.
A beacon kindling from afar
Our light of love and fainting faith.
        —Gerald Massey.

A little soul scarce fledged for earth
Takes wing with heaven again for goal,
Even while we hailed as fresh from birth
A little soul.   —Swinburne.

You scarce could think so small a thing
  Could leave a loss so large;
Her little light such shadow fling
  From dawn to sunset's marge.
In other springs our life may be
  In bannered bloom unfurled,
But never, never match our wee
  White Rose of all the world.
        —Gerald Massey.

When the baby died,
    On every side
Rose strangers' voices, hard and harsh and
  loud.
The baby was not wrapped in any shroud.
The mother made no sound. Her head
  was bowed
That men's eyes might not see
    Her misery.   —Helen Hunt.

He seemed a cherub who had lost his way
And wandered hither, so his stay
With us was short, and 'twas most meet
That he should be no delver in earth's clod,
Nor need to pause and cleanse his feet
To stand before his God:
O blest word—Evermore!   —Lowell.

When the baby died we said,
With a sudden secret dread;
"Death be merciful and pass;
Leave the other!"—but alas!
While we watched he waited there,
One foot on the golden stair,
One hand beckoning at the gate,
Till the home was desolate.
        —Nora Perry.

Those who have lost an infant are never, as it were, without an infant child. Their other children grow up to manhood and womanhood, and suffer all the changes of mortality; but this one alone is rendered an immortal child; for death has arrested it with his kindly harshness, and blessed it into an eternal image of youth and innocence.—Leigh Hunt.

Bachelor

When I said I would die a bachelor, I did not think I should live till I were married.—Shakespeare.

I have no wife or children, good or bad, to provide for; a mere spectator of other men's fortunes and adventures, and how they play their parts; which, methinks, are diversely presented unto me, as from a common theatre or scene.—Burton.

A man unattached and without wife, if he have any genius at all, may raise himself above his original position, may mingle with the world of fashion, and hold himself on a level with the highest; this is less easy for him who is engaged; it seems as if marriage put the whole world in their proper rank.—Bruyère.

Backsliding

I never yet have heard of a good man having fallen when he was trying to do Christ's will and trusting on Christ's help. Every fall without one exception came from venturing upon sinful ground or from venturing upon self-support.—T. L. Cuyler.

When we read or hear how some professed Christian has turned defaulter, or lapsed into drunkenness, or slipped from the communion table into open disgrace, it simply means that a human arm has broken. The man has forsaken the everlasting arms.—T. L. Cuyler.

The Master will not keep His hand under our arms when we go on forbidden ground. Presumptuous Peter needed a sharp lesson, and he got it. That bitter cry at the foot of the stairs bespoke an awful fall. How many such are rising daily into God's listening ears.—T. L. Cuyler.

Ballads

I knew a very wise man that believed that * * * if a man were permitted to make all the ballads, he need not care who should make the laws of a nation.—Andrew Fletcher.

Vocal portraits of the national mind.—Lamb.

Ballads are the gypsy children of song, born under green hedgerows, in the leafy lanes and by-paths of literature, in the genial summer-time.—Longfellow.

A well-composed song strikes the mind and softens the feelings, and produces a greater effect than a moral work, which convinces our reason, but does not warm our feelings, nor effect the slightest alteration in our habits.—Napoleon.

I love a ballad but even too well; if it be doleful matter, merrily set down, or a very pleasant thing indeed, and sung lamentably.—Shakespeare.

Ballot

A weapon that comes down as still
As snow-flakes fall upon the sod;
But executes a freeman's will,
As lightning does the will of God;
And from its force, nor doors nor locks
Can shield you—'tis the ballot-box.
—J. Pierpont.

Baptism

Only what coronation is in an earthly way, baptism is in a heavenly way; God's authoritative declaration in material form of a spiritual reality.—F. W. Robertson.

What is baptism but a declaration of our misery by sin, our need of Christ, and a badge of our belonging to Him.—W. D. Paden.

Bargain

A dear bargain is always disagreeable, particularly as it is a reflection upon the buyer's judgment.—Pliny.

The modern craze for bargains has often inflicted great hardships upon a certain class of humble toilers.—Douglas.

What is the disposition which makes men rejoice in good bargains? There are few people who will not be benefited by pondering over the morals of shopping.—Beecher.

I'll give thrice so much land,
To any well deserving friend;
But in the way of bargain, mark me,
I'll cavil on the ninth part of a hair.
—Shakespeare.

Baseness

Some kinds of baseness are nobly undergone.—Shakespeare.

Every base occupation makes one sharp in its practice, and dull in every other.—Sir P. Sidney.

There is a law of neutralization of forces, which hinders bodies from sinking beyond a certain depth in the sea; but in the ocean of baseness, the deeper we get, the easier the sinking.—Lowell.

Bashfulness

The scarlet hue of modesty.—Laténa.

Awkwardness in full dress.—Ninon de Lenclos.

A shy face is better than a forward heart.—Cervantes.

Twin sister of awkwardness.—Mrs. Barbauld.

Bashfulness is an ornament to youth, but a reproach to old age.—Aristotle.

Diffidence and awkwardness are antidotes to love.—Hazlitt.

Mere bashfulness without merit is awkwardness.—Addison.

Conceit not so high a notion of any as to be bashful and impotent in their presence.—Fuller.

Modesty is the graceful, calm virtue of maturity; bashfulness the charm of vivacious youth.—Mary Wollstonecraft.

Bashfulness may sometimes exclude pleasure, but seldom opens any avenue to sorrow or remorse.—Dr. Johnson.

Bashfulness is not becoming to maidenhood, though modesty always is. —Marguerite de Valois.

The most curious offspring of shame is shyness.—Sydney Smith.

So sweet the blush of bashfulness
Even pity scarce can wish it less.
—Byron.

A tardiness in Nature, which often leaves the history unspoke, that it intends to do.—Shakespeare.

Bashfulness is more frequently connected with good sense than we find assurance; and impudence, on the other hand, is often the mere effect of downright stupidity.—Shenstone.

She felt his flame; but deep within her breast, in bashful coyness or in maiden pride, the soft return concealed.—Thomson.

We must prune it with care, so as only to remove the redundant branches, and not injure the stem, which has its root in the generous sensitiveness to shame.—Plutarch.

As those that pull down private houses adjoining to the temples of the gods, prop up such parts as are contiguous to them; so, in undermining bashfulness, due regard is to be had to adjacent modesty, good-nature and humanity.—Plutarch.

Bashfulness is a great hindrance to a man, both in uttering his sentiments and in understanding what is proposed to him; 't is therefore good to press forward with discretion, both in discourse and company of the better sort. —Bacon.

There are two distinct sorts of what we call bashfulness; this, the awkwardness of a booby, which a few steps into the world will convert into the pertness of a coxcomb; that, a consciousness, which the most delicate feelings produce, and the most extensive knowledge cannot always remove. —Mackenzie.

Nor do we accept as genuine the person not characterized by this blushing bashfulness, this youthfulness of heart, this sensibility to the sentiment of suavity and self-respect. Modesty is bred of self-reverence. Fine manners are the mantle of fair minds. None are truly great without this ornament.—Alcott.

Women who are the least bashful are not unfrequently the most modest; and we are never more deceived than when we would infer any laxity of principle from that freedom of demeanor which often arises from a total ignorance of vice.—Colton.

Battle — Battlefield

The next dreadful thing to a battle lost is a battle won.—Wellington.

Troops of heroes undistinguished die.—Addison.

As well the soldier dieth who standeth still, as he that gives the bravest onset.—Sir P. Sidney.

When Greeks join'd Greeks, then was the
    tug of war;
The labor'd battle sweat, and conquest bled.
—Lee.

Hand to hand and foot to foot,
Nothing there save death, was mute;
Stroke and thrust, and flash, and cry
For quarter or for victory,
Mingle there with the volleying thunder.
—Byron.

It was a goodly sight to see the embattled pomp, as with the step of stateliness the barbed steeds came on, to see the pennons rolling their long waves before the gale, and banners, broad and bright, tossing their blazonry.— Southey.

That awful pause, dividing life from death
Struck for an instant on the hearts of men,
Thousands of whom were drawing their
    last breath!
A moment all will be life again.
* * * * one moment more,
The death-cry drowning in the battle's roar.
—Byron.

The cannons have their bowels full of wrath; and ready mounted are they to spit forth their iron indignation against your walls.—Shakespeare.

The fame of a battlefield grows with its years; Napoleon storming the Bridge of Lodi, and Wellington surveying the towers of Salamanca, affect us with fainter emotions than Brutus reading in his tent at Philippi, or Richard bearing down with the English chivalry upon the white armies of Saladin.—Willmott.

This day hath made
Much work for tears in many a English mother,
Whose sons lie scatter'd on the bleeding ground;
Many a widow's husband grovelling lies,
Coldly embracing the discolor'd earth.
—Shakespeare.

Then after length of time, the labouring swains,
Who turn the turfs of those unhappy plains,
Shall rusty piles from the plough'd furrows take,
And over empty helmets pass the rake;
Amazed at antique titles on the stones,
And mighty relics of gigantic bones.
—Dryden.

Then more fierce
The conflict grew; the din of arms—the yell
Of savage rage—the shriek of agony—
The groan of death, commingled in one sound
Of undistinguish'd horrors; while the sun,
Retiring slow beneath the plain's far verge,
Shed o'er the quiet hills his fading light.
—Southey.

Hark! the death-denouncing trumpet sounds
The fatal charge, and shouts proclaim the onset;
Destruction rushes dreadful to the field,
And bathes itself in blood; havoc let loose
Now undistinguish'd rages all around,
While ruin, seated on her dreary throne,
Sees the plain strewed with subjects truly hers,
Breathless and cold.   —Havard.

Therewith they gan, both furious and fell,
To thunder blowes, and fiercely to assaile
Each other, bent his enemy to quell,
That with their force they perst both plate and maile,
And made wide furrows in their fleshes fraile,
That it would pitv any living eie,
Large floods of blood adowne their sides did raile,
But floods of blood could not them satisfie:
Both hongred after death; both chose to win or die.   —Spenser.

From camp to camp, through the foul womb of night,
The hum of either army stilly sounds,
That the fixed sentinels almost receive
The secret whispers of each other's watch;
Fire answers fire; and through their paly flames,
Each battle sees the other's umbered face:
Steed threatens steed in high and boastful neighs,
Piercing the night's dull ear; and from the tents,
The armourers accomplishing the knights,
With busy hammers closing rivets up,
Give dreadful note of preparation.
—Shakespeare.

Here you might see
Barons and peasants on th' embattled field,
Slain or half dead, in one huge ghastly heap
Promiscuously amass'd. With dismal groans,
And ejaculation, in the pangs of death,
Some call for aid, neglected; some o'erturn'd
In the fierce shock lie gasping, and expire,
Trampled by fiery coursers: Horror thus,
And wild uproar, and desolation reign'd
Unrespited.   —Philips.

Beard

Beard was never the true standard of brains.—Fuller.

Beards, in olden times, were the emblems of wisdom and piety.—Macaulay.

He that hath a beard is more than a youth; And he that hath none is less than a man.
—Shakespeare.

How many cowards wear yet upon their chins the beards of Hercules and frowning Mars!—Shakespeare.

. There is great truth in Alphonse Karr's remark that modern men are ugly because they do not wear their beards.—G. A. Sala.

Beau

A beau is everything of a woman but the sex, and nothing of a man beside it.—Fielding.

Beauty

The fringe of the garment of the Lord.—Bailey.

The beautiful attracts the beautiful.
—Leigh Hunt.

All the beauty of the world, 'tis but skin deep.—Ralph Venning.

Rare is the union of beauty and virtue.—Juvenal.

How goodness heightens beauty!—Hannah More.

Beauty draws us with a single hair.—Pope.

Beauty is a short-lived tyranny.—Socrates.

Trust not too much to an enchanting face.—Virgil.

All orators are dumb, when beauty pleadeth.—Shakespeare.

Beautiful coquettes· are quacks of love.—Rochefoucauld.

Beauty can inspire miracles.—Beaconsfield.

Beauty is a possession not our own.—Bion.

The beauty seen is partly in him who sees it.—Bovee.

Beauty is a frail good.—Ovid.

Beauty,—the fading rainbow's pride.—Halleck.

Whatever is beautiful is also profitable.—Willmott.

Beauty provoketh thieves sooner than gold.—Shakespeare.

Beauty is the purgation of superfluities.—Michael Angelo.

Beauty lives with kindness.—Shakespeare.

A flower that dies when first it begins to bud.—Shakespeare.

Beauty doth varnish age.—Shakespeare.

The body charms because the soul is seen.—Young.

Beauty's choicest mirror is an admiring eye.—J. L. Basford.

A heaven of charms divine Nausicaa lay.—Homer.

Beauty is Nature's brag.—Milton.

Too fair to worship, too divine to love.—Henry Hart Milman.

The beautiful is never plentiful.—Emerson.

Expression is the mystery of beauty.—Bulwer-Lytton.

Mortal beauty stings while it delights.—Bovee.

The beautiful is always severe.—Ségur.

Beauty is power; a smile is its sword.—Charles Reade.

A lovely girl is above all rank.—Charles Buxton.

Beauty is always queen.—Joseph II.

Beauty vanishes; virtue is lasting.—Goethe.

Beauty is a delightful prejudice.—Theocritus.

Accuracy is essential to beauty.—Emerson.

Beauty is an accidental and transient good.—Richardson.

Beauty is its own excuse for being.—Emerson.

Beauty and wisdom are rarely conjoined.—Petronius Arbiter.

Nature was here so lavish of her store,
That she bestow'd until she had no more.
—Brown.

Without the smile from partial beauty won,
O, what were man! a world without a sun!
—Campbell.

Beauty is truth, truth beauty—that is all
Ye know on earth, and all ye need to know.
—Keats.

The mate for beauty should be a man and not a money chest.—Bulwer.

A handsome woman is a jewel; a good woman is a treasure.—Saadi.

I pray Thee, O God, that I may be beautiful within.—Socrates.

Exquisite beauty resides rather in the female form than face, where it is also more lasting.—Lamartine.

'Tis the eternal law,
That first in beauty should be first in might.
—Keats.

It is beauty that begins to please, and tenderness that completes the charm.—Fontenelle.

The essence of the beautiful is unity in variety.—Mendelssohn.

Beauty is the index of a larger fact than wisdom.—O. W. Holmes.

Her overpowering presence made you feel
It would not be idolatry to kneel.
—Byron.

That is the best part of beauty which a picture cannot express.—Bacon.

The criterion of true beauty is that it increases on examination; if false, that it lessens.—Greville.

In days of yore nothing was holy but the beautiful.—Schiller.

Beauty is worse than wine; it intoxicates both the holder and the beholder.—Zimmermann.

Beauty itself is but the sensible image of the Infinite.—Bancroft.

Oesser taught me that the ideal of beauty is simplicity and tranquillity.—Goethe.

Is beauty vain because it will fade? Then are earth's green robe and heaven's light vain.—Pierpont.

What's true beauty but fair virtue's face,—virtue made visible in outward grace?—Young.

Beauty is like an almanac; if it lasts a year, it is well.—Rev. T. Adam.

There is a self-evident axiom, that she who is born a beauty is half married.—Ouida.

It is seldom that beautiful persons are otherwise of great virtue.—Bacon.

Eyes raised toward heaven are always beautiful, whatever they be.—Joseph Joubert.

The good is always beautiful, the beautiful is good!—Whittier.

Beauty, without virtue, is like a flower without perfume.—From the French.

In the forming of female friendships beauty seldom recommends one woman to another.—Fielding.

Beauty can afford to laugh at distinctions; it is itself the greatest distinction.—Bovee.

Even virtue is more fair when it appears in a beautiful person.—Virgil.

There is no beauty on earth which exceeds the natural loveliness of woman.—J. Petit-Senn.

Beauty can give an edge to the bluntest sword.—Sir P. Sidney.

There is nothing that makes its way more directly to the soul than beauty.—Addison.

The most natural beauty in the world is honesty and moral truth.—Shaftesbury.

Beauty is no local deity, like the Greek and Roman gods, but omnipresent.—Bartol.

There is no more potent antidote to low sensuality than the adoration of beauty.—Schlegel.

Beauty comes, we scarce know how, as an emanation from sources deeper than itself.—Shairp.

Might but the sense of moral evil be as strong in me as is my delight in external beauty!—Dr. Arnold.

For beauty is the bait which with delight doth man allure, for to enlarge his kind.—Spenser.

O, how much more doth beauty beauteous seem, by that sweet ornament which truth doth give!—Shakespeare.

To give pain is the tyranny,—to make happy the true empire of beauty. —Steele.

A lovely being, scarcely formed or moulded, A rose with all its sweetest leaves yet folded. —Byron.

In life, as in art, the beautiful moves in curves.—Bulwer-Lytton.

Few have borne unconsciously the spell of loveliness.—Whittier.

Beauty, without kindness, dies unenjoyed and undelighting.—Johnson.

Beauty soon grows familiar to the lover, Fades in his eye, and palls upon the sense. —Addison.

There's nothing that allays an angry mind So soon as a sweet beauty. —Beaumont and Fletcher.

And all the carnal beauty of my wife Is but skin-deep.   —Sir Thomas Overbury.

Heat cannot be separated from fire, or beauty from the eternal.—Dante.

Thou who hast
The fatal gift of beauty.
—Byron.

If eyes were made for seeing,
Then beauty is its own excuse for being.
—Emerson.

Liking is not always the child of beauty; but whatsoever is liked, to the liker is beautiful.—Sir P. Sidney.

Beauty is an exquisite flower, and its perfume is virtue.—Ruffini.

A daughter of the gods, divinely tall, And most divinely fair.
—Tennyson.

We call comeliness a mischance in the first respect, which belongs principally to the face.—Montaigne.

The soul, by an instinct stronger than reason, ever associates beauty with truth.—Tuckerman.

A queen devoid of beauty is not queen; She needs the royalty of beauty's mien.
—Victor Hugo.

The beautiful rests on the foundations of the necessary.—Emerson.

In beauty, faults conspicuous grow; The smallest speck is seen on snow.
—Gay.

'Tis beauty truly blent, whose red and white Nature's own sweet and cunning hand laid on.   —Shakespeare.

Beauty is a witch, against whose charms faith melteth into blood.— Shakespeare.

Beauty is such a fleeting blossom, how can wisdom rely upon its momentary delight?—Seneca.

Beauty's tears are lovelier than her smiles.—Campbell.

Whatever beauty may be, it has for its basis order, and for its essence unity.—Father André.

'Tis not a lip, or eye, we beauty call, But the joint force and full result of all.
—Pope.

Beauty is God's handwriting,—a wayside sacrament.—Milton.

Beauty is the first present Nature gives to women, and the first it takes away.—Méré.

We give our best affections to the beautiful, only our second best to the useful.—Bovee.

Half light, half shade, she stood a sight to make an old man young.— Tennyson.

All beauty does not inspire love. Some please the sight without captivating the affections.—Cervantes.

Unity and simplicity are the two true sources of beauty. Supreme beauty resides in God.—Winckelmann.

Even beauty may present a prism wearying to the eye.—Prince de Ligne.

Such another peerless queen only could her mirror show.—Emerson.

Beauty and health are the chief sources of happiness.—Beaconsfield.

Beauty is a beam from heaven that dazzles blind our reason.—Campbell.

Beauty is but a flower which wrinkles will devour.—Thomas Nash.

What delights us in visible beauty is the invisible.—Marie Ebner-Eschenbach.

True features make the beauty of a face, and true proportions the beauty of architecture.—Shaftesbury.

An appearance of delicacy, and even of fragility, is almost essential to beauty.—Burke.

Is beauty beautiful, or is it only our eyes that make it so?—Thackeray.

Her beauty hangs upon the cheek of night, as a rich jewel in an Ethiop's ear.—Shakespeare.

Beauty is at once the ultimate and the highest aim of art.—Goethe.

It is impossible that beauty should ever distinctly appreciate itself.—Goethe.

If there is a fruit that can be eaten raw, it is beauty.—Alphonse Karr.

Rarely do we meet in one combined, a beauteous body and a virtuous mind.—Juvenal.

Beauty itself doth itself persuade the eyes of men without an orator.—Shakespeare.

In the recognition of beauty, the eye takes the most delight in color.—Addison.

Lord Bacon makes beauty to consist of grace and motion.—Lady Montagu.

Venus, thy eternal sway all the race of men obey.—Euripides.

Beautiful works do not intoxicate, but they enchant.—Joubert.

Beauties, whether male or female, are generally the most untractable people of all others.—Steele.

Beauty intoxicates the eye, as wine does the body; both are morally fatal if indulged.—J. G. Saxe.

Good nature will always supply the absence of beauty; but beauty cannot supply the absence of good nature.—Addison.

'T is a powerful sex; they were too strong for the first, the strongest, and the wisest man that was.—Howell.

Beauty or unbecomingness is of more force to draw or deter invitation than any discourses which can be made to them.—Locke.

You may keep your beauty and your health, unless you destroy them yourself, or discourage them to stay with you, by using them ill.—Sir W. Temple.

Beauty is nothing else but a just accord and mutual harmony of the members, animated by a healthful constitution.—Dryden.

You may not, cannot, appropriate beauty. It is the wealth of the eye, and a cat may gaze upon a king.—Theodore Parker.

The beautiful is a manifestation of secret laws of Nature, which, but for this appearance, had been forever concealed from us.—Goethe.

The very first discovery of beauty strikes the mind with an inward joy, and spreads a cheerfulness and delight through all its faculties.—Addison.

Beauty and sadness always go together. Nature thought Beauty too rich to go forth upon the earth without a meet alloy.—George MacDonald

What is really beautiful needs no adorning. We do not grind down the pearl upon a polishing stone.—Sataka.

Man has still more desire for beauty than knowledge of it; hence the caprices of the world.—X. Doudan.

As amber attracts a straw, so does beauty admiration, which only lasts while the warmth continues.—Robert Burton.

Though color be the lowest of all the constituent parts of beauty, yet it is vulgarly the most striking.—Joseph Spence.

Beauty deceives women in making them establish on an ephemeral power the pretensions of a whole life.—Bignicourt.

Though we travel the world over to find the beautiful, we must carry it with us, or we find it not.—Emerson.

It is the saddest of all things that even one human soul should dimly perceive the beauty that is ever around us, a perpetual benediction.—Mrs. L. M. Child.

Expression is of more consequence than shape; it will light up features otherwise heavy.—Sir C. Bell.

Female beauties are as fickle in their faces as in their minds; though casualties should spare them, age brings in a necessity of decay.—Boyle.

Every trait of beauty may be traced to some virtue, as to innocence, candor, generosity, modesty, and heroism. —St. Pierre.

Do not idolatrize; beauty's a flower,
Which springs and withers almost in an
   hour.   —Wm. Smith.

If thou marry beauty, thou bindest thyself all thy life for that which, perchance, will neither last nor please thee one year.—Raleigh.

If virtue accompany it, it is the heart's paradise; if vice associate it, it is the soul's purgatory.—Quarles.

We do love beauty at first sight; and we do cease to love it, if it is not accompanied by amiable qualities.— Lydia Maria Child.

Such harmony in motion, speech and air,
That without fairness, she was more than
   fair.   —Crabbe.

                          Loveliness
Needs not the foreign aid of ornament,
But is when unadorn'd adorn'd the most.
                          —Thomson.

Beauty is an outward gift which is seldom despised except by those to whom it has been refused.—Gibbon.

Beauty is Nature's coin, must not be hoarded,
But must be current, and the good thereof
Consists in mutual and partaken bliss.
                          —Milton.

The beauty that addresses itself to the eyes is only the spell of the moment; the eye of the body is not always that of the soul.—Georges Sand.

Remember that the most beautiful things in the world are the most useless; peacocks and lilies, for instance. —Ruskin.

                The beautiful seems right
By force of beauty, and the feeble wrong
Because of weakness.
                          —E. B. Browning.

There's nothing ill can dwell in such a
   temple:
If the ill spirit have so fair a house,
Good things will strive to dwell with't.
                          —Shakespeare.

The first distinction among men, and the first consideration that gave one precedence over another, was doubtless the advantage of beauty.—Montaigne.

Naught under heaven so strongly doth allure the sense of man, and all his mind possess, as beauty's love-bait. —Spenser.

Love that has nothing but beauty to keep it in good health is short-lived, and apt to have ague fits.—Erasmus.

A beautiful woman is the hell of the soul, the purgatory of the purse, and the paradise of the eyes.—Fontenelle.

The dower of great beauty has always been misfortune, since happiness and beauty do not agree together.—Calderon.

Where the mouth is sweet and the eyes intelligent, there is always the look of beauty, with a right heart.—Leigh Hunt.

No woman can be handsome by the force of features alone, any more than she can be witty only by the help of speech.—Hughes.

The sense of beauty is intuitive, and beauty itself is all that inspires pleasure without, and aloof from, and even contrarily to interest.—Coleridge.

A beautiful form is better than a beautiful face; it gives a higher pleasure than statues or pictures; it is the finest of the fine arts.—Emerson.

The perception of the beautiful is gradual, and not a lightning revelation; it requires not only time, but some study.—Ruffini.

The very beautiful rarely love at all. Those precious images are placed above the reach of the passions.—Landor.

Beauty is a great gift of heaven; not for the purpose of female vanity, but a great gift for one who loves, and wishes to be beloved.—Miss Edgeworth.

Methinks a being that is beautiful becometh more so as it looks on beauty, the eternal beauty of undying things.—Byron.

Affect not to despise beauty, no one is freed from its dominion; but regard is not a pearl of price, it is fleeting as the bow in the clouds.—Tupper.

Where rivulets dance their wayward round, and beauty born of murmuring sound shall pass into her face.—Wordsworth.

The common foible of women who have been handsome is to forget that they are no longer so.—Rochefoucauld.

Beauty attracts us men, but if, like an armed magnet it is pointed with gold or silver beside, it attracts with tenfold power.—Richter.

What place is so rugged and so homely that there is no beauty, if you only have a sensibility to beauty?—Beecher.

Thus was beauty sent from heaven, the lovely ministress of truth and good in this dark world.—Akenside.

Beauty, like truth and justice, lives within us; like virtue, and like moral law, it is a companion of the soul.—Bancroft.

That is true beauty which has not only a substance, but a spirit; a beauty that we must intimately know, justly to appreciate.—Colton.

O human beauty, what a dream art thou, that we should cast our life and hopes away on thee!—Barry Cornwall.

Every good picture is the best of sermons and lectures. The sense informs the soul. Whatever you have, have beauty.—Sydney Smith.

Beautiful as sweet! and young as beautiful! and soft as young! and gay as soft! and innocent as gay!—Young.

Beauty hath no lustre save when it gleameth through the crystal web that purity's fine fingers weave for it.—Maturin.

By cultivating the beautiful, we scatter the seeds of heavenly flowers; by doing good, we foster those already belonging to humanity.—Howard.

Lovely sweetness is the noblest power of woman, and is far fitter to prevail by parley than by battle.—Sir P. Sidney.

That which is striking and beautiful is not always good, but that which is good is always beautiful.—Ninon de Lenclos.

To cultivate the sense of the beautiful is but one, and the most effectual, of the ways of cultivating an appreciation of the Divine goodness.—Bovee.

Not more the rose, the queen of flowers,
Outblushes all the bloom of bower,
Than she unrivall'd grace discloses;
The sweetest rose, where all are roses.
—Moore.

Exalt your passion by directing and settling it upon an object the due contemplation of whose loveliness may cure perfectly all hurts received from mortal beauty.—Boyle.

A beautiful face fires our imagination, and we see higher virtue and intelligence in it than we can detect in its owner's head or heart when we descend to calm inspection.—Charles Reade.

There is more or less of pathos in all true beauty. The delight it awakens has an indefinable, and, as it were, luxurious sadness, which is perhaps one element of its might.—Tuckerman.

The greatest truths are wronged if not linked with beauty; and they win their way most surely and deeply into the soul when arrayed in this their natural and fit attire.—Channing.

Yet even this hath this inconvenience in it—that it makes its possessor neglect the furnishing of the mind with nobleness. Nay, it oftentimes is a cause that the mind is ill.—Feltham.

The sense of beauty enters into the highest philosophy, as in Plato. The highest poet must be a philosopher, accomplished like Dante, or intuitive like Shakespeare.—Gladstone.

O, if so much beauty doth reveal
Itself in every vein of life and nature,
How beautiful must be the Source itself,
The Ever Bright One. —Tegner.

Mark her majestic fabric; she's a temple
Sacred by birth, and built by hands divine;
Her soul's the Deity that lodges there;
Nor is the pile unworthy of the God.
—Dryden.

It is only through the morning gate of the beautiful that you can penetrate into the realm of knowledge. That

which we feel here as beauty we shall one day know as truth.—Schiller.

A look of intelligence in men is what regularity of features is in women; it is a style of beauty to which the most vain may aspire.—La Bruyère.

There's beauty all around our paths, if but
our watchful eyes
Can trace it 'midst familiar things, and
through their lowly guise.
—Mrs. Hemans.

There should be, methinks, as little merit in loving a woman for her beauty as in loving a man for his prosperity; both being equally subject to change.—Pope.

Beauty in a modest woman is like fire at a distance, or like a sharp sword; neither doth the one burn, nor the other wound those that come not too near them.—Cervantes.

Every year of my life I grow more convinced that it is wisest and best to fix our attention on the beautiful and good and dwell as little as possible on the dark and the base.—Cecil.

In the true mythology, Love is an immortal child, and Beauty leads him as a guide; nor can we express a deeper sense than when we say, Beauty is the pilot of the young soul.—Emerson.

True beauty dwells in deep retreats,
Whose veil is unremoved
Till heart with heart in concord beats,
And the lover is beloved.
—Wordsworth.

The divine right of beauty is the only divine right a man can acknowledge, and a pretty woman the only tyrant he is not authorized to resist.—Junius.

The useful encourages itself; for the multitude produce it, and no one can dispense with it: the beautiful must be encouraged; for few can set it forth, and many need it.—Goethe.

He who cannot see the beautiful side is a bad painter, a bad friend, a bad lover; he cannot lift his mind and his heart so high as goodness.—Joubert.

Beauty is the mark God sets on virtue. Every natural action is graceful. Every heroic act is also decent, and causes the place and the bystanders to shine.—Emerson.

Something of the severe hath always been appertaining to order and to grace; and the beauty that is not too liberal is sought the most ardently, and loved the longest.—Landor.

Who doth not feel, until his failing sight
Faints into dimness with its own delight,
His changing cheek, his sinking heart confess,
The might—the majesty of Loveliness?
—Byron.

Beauty! thou pretty plaything! dear deceit,
That steals so softly o'er the stripling's heart
And gives it a new pulse unknown before!
—Blair.

He will always see the most beauty whose affections are warmest and most exercised, whose imagination is the most powerful, and who has most accustomed himself to attend to the objects by which he is surrounded.—Lord Jeffrey.

The essence of all beauty, I call love,
The attribute, the evidence, and end,
The consummation to the inward sense
Of beauty apprehended from without,
I still call love. —E. B. Browning.

An agreeable figure and winning manner, which inspire affection without love, are always new. Beauty loses its relish, the graces never, after the longest acquaintance, they are no less agreeable than at first.—Henry Home.

Beauty is as summer fruits, which are easy to corrupt and cannot last; and for the most part it makes a dissolute youth, and an age a little out of countenance; but if it light well, it makes virtues shine and vice blush.—Bacon.

The contemplation of beauty in nature, in art, in literature, in human character, diffuses through our being a soothing and subtle joy, by which the heart's anxious and aching cares are softly smiled away.—Whipple.

Beauty is the true prerogative of women, and so peculiarly their own, that our sex, though naturally requiring another sort of feature, is never in its lustre but when puerile and beardless, confused and mixed with theirs.—Montaigne.

Contrast increases the splendor of beauty, but it disturbs its influence; it adds to its attractiveness, but diminishes its power.—Ruskin.

Beauty is a fairy; sometimes she hides herself in a flower-cup, or under a leaf, or creeps into the old ivy, and plays hide-and-seek with the sunbeams, or haunts some ruined spot, or laughs out of a bright young face.—G. A. Sala.

To make the cunning artless, tame the rude, subdue the haughty, shake the undaunted soul; yea, put a bridle in the lion's mouth, and lead him forth as a domestic cur, these are the triumphs of all-powerful beauty.—Joanna Baillie.

How much wit, good-nature, indulgences, how many good offices and civilities, are required among friends to accomplish in some years what a lovely face or a fine hand does in a minute!—Bruyère.

An Indian philosopher, being asked what were, according to his opinion, the two most beautiful things in the universe, answered: The starry heavens above our heads, and the feeling of duty in our hearts.—Bossuet.

Happily there exists more than one kind of beauty. There is the beauty of infancy, the beauty of youth, the beauty of maturity, and, believe me, ladies and gentlemen, the beauty of age.—G. A. Sala.

No better cosmetics than a severe temperance and purity, modesty and humility, a gracious temper and calmness of spirit; no true beauty without the signature of these graces in the very countenance.—John Ray.

We may say of agreeableness, as distinct from beauty, that it consists in a symmetry of which we know not the rules, and a secret conformity of the features to each other, as also to the air and complexion of the person.—Rochefoucauld.

The most natural beauty in the world is honesty and moral truth. For all beauty is truth. True features make the beauty of a face, and true proportions the beauty of architecture; as true measures that of harmony and music.—Shaftesbury.

In all things that live there are certain irregularities and deficiencies which are not only signs of life, but sources of beauty. No human face is exactly the same in its lines on each side, no leaf perfect in its lobes, no branch in its symmetry.—Ruskin.

How intoxicating is the triumph of beauty, and how right it is to name it queen of the universe! How many courtiers, how many slaves, have submitted to it! But, alas! why must it be that what flatters our senses almost always deceives our souls?—Madame de Surin.

There is no more potent antidote to low sensuality than the adoration of beauty. All the higher arts of design are essentially chaste, without respect of the object. They purify the thoughts, as tragedy, according to Aristotle, purifies the passions.—Schlegel.

Sometimes there are living beings in nature as beautiful as in romance. Reality surpasses imagination; and we see breathing, brightening, and moving before our eyes sights dearer to our hearts than any we ever beheld in the land of sleep.—Jane Austen.

Beauty is a dangerous property, tending to corrupt the mind of the wife, though it soon loses its influence over the husband. A figure agreeable and engaging, which inspires affection, without the ebriety of love, is a much safer choice.—Henry Home.

Beauty has been the delight and torment of the world ever since it began. The philosophers have felt its influence so sensibly that almost every one of them has left some saying or other which intimates that he knew too well the power of it.—Steele.

Beauty too often sacrifices to fashion. The spirit of fashion is not the beautiful, but the wilful; not the graceful, but the fantastic; not the superior in the abstract, but the superior in the worst of all concretes,—the vulgar.—Leigh Hunt.

One of the old philosophers calls beauty a silent fraud, because it imposes upon us without the help of language. But I think Carneades spoke as much like a philosopher as any of them, though more like a lover, when he called it "royalty without force."—Steele.

In ourselves, rather than in material nature, lie the true source and life of the beautiful. The human soul is the sun which diffuses light on every side, investing creation with its lovely hues, and calling forth the poetic element that lies hidden in every existing thing.—Mazzini.

For converse among men, beautiful persons have less need of the mind's commending qualities. Beauty in itself is such a silent orator, that it is ever pleading for respect and liking, and by the eyes of others is ever sending to their hearts for love.—Feltham.

The flower which blossoms to-day and is withered to-morrow,—is it at all more actual than the colors of the rainbow? Or rather are those less actual? Beauty is the most fleeting thing upon earth, yet immortal as the spirit from which it blooms.—De Wette.

Her cheek had the pale pearly pink
Of sea shells, the world's sweetest tint, as though
She lived, one-half might deem, on roses sopp'd
In pearly dew.　　　　　—Bailey.

Truth is the foundation and the reason of the perfection of beauty, for of whatever stature a thing may be, it cannot be beautiful and perfect, unless it be truly what it should be, and possess truly all that it should have. —La Rochefoucauld.

Beauty, like ice, our footing does betray;
Who can tread sure on the smooth, slippery way?
Pleased with the surface, we glide swiftly on,
And see the dangers that we cannot shun.
—Dryden.

Give me a look, give me a face,
That makes simplicity a grace;
Robes loosely flowing, hair as free!
Such sweet neglect more taketh me,
Than all the adulteries of art;
That strike mine eyes, but not my heart.
—Ben Jonson.

Beauty, sweet love, is like the morning dew,
Whose short refresh upon tender green,
Cheers for a time, but till the sun doth show,
And straight is gone, as it had never been.
—Daniel.

Beauty is only truly irresistible when it shows us something less transitory than itself; when it makes us dream of that which charms life beyond the fugitive moment which seduces us. It is necessary for the soul to feel it when the senses have perceived it. The soul never wearies; the more it admires, the more it is exalted.—Mme. de Krudener.

Like other beautiful things in this world, its end (that of a shaft) is to be beautiful; and, in proportion to its beauty, it receives permission to be otherwise useless. We do not blame emeralds and rubies because we cannot make them into heads of hammers. —Ruskin.

She walks in beauty, like the night
Of cloudless climes and starry skies;
And all that's best of dark and bright
Meet in her aspect and her eyes;
Thus mellow'd to that tender light
Which Heaven to gaudy day denies.
—Byron.

It was a very proper answer to him who asked why any man should be delighted with beauty, that it was a question that none but a blind man could ask; since any beautiful object doth so much attract the sight of all men, that it is in no man's power not to be pleased with it.—Clarendon.

---

* * * for beauty stands
In the admiration only of weak minds
Led captive. Cease to admire, and all her plumes
Fall flat and shrink into a trivial toy,
At every sudden slighting quite abash'd.
—Milton.

'Twas not the fading charms of face
That riveted Love's golden chain;
It was the high celestial grace
Of goodness that doth never wane—
Whose are the sweets that never pall,
Delicious, pure, and crowning all.
—Abraham Coles.

A thing of beauty is a joy forever;
Its loveliness increases; it will never
Pass into nothingness; but still will keep
A bower quiet for us, and a sleep
Full of sweet dreams, and health, and quiet breathing.
—Keats.

Her glossy hair was cluster'd o'er a brow
Bright with intelligence, and fair and smooth;
Her eyebrow's shape was like the aërial bow,
Her cheek all purple with the beam of youth,
Mounting, at times, to a transparent glow,
As if her veins ran lightning. —Byron.

Exquisite beauty resides with God. Unity and simplicity, joined together in different organs, are the principal sources of beauty. It resides in the good, the honest, and in the useful to the highest physical and intellectual degree.— Winkelman.

There is scarcely a single joy or sorrow within the experience of our fellow-creatures which we have not tasted; yet the belief in the good and beautiful has never forsaken us. It has been medicine to us in sickness, richness in poverty, and the best part of all that ever delighted us in health and success.—Leigh Hunt.

What is beauty? Not the show
Of shapely limbs and features. No.
These are but flowers
That have their dated hours
To breathe their momentary sweets, then go.
'Tis the stainless soul within
That outshines the fairest skin.
—Sir A. Hunt.

I am of opinion that there is nothing so beautiful but that there is something still more beautiful, of which this is the mere image and expression,—a something which can neither be perceived by the eyes, the ears, nor any of the senses; we comprehend it merely in the imagination.—Cicero.

O, it is the saddest of all things that even one human soul should dimly perceive the beauty that is ever around us, "a perpetual benediction!" Nature, that great missionary of the Most High, preaches to us forever in all tones of love, and writes truth in all colors, on manuscripts illuminated with stars and flowers.—Mrs. L. M. Child.

Take the whole sex together, and you find that those who have the strongest possession of men's hearts are not eminent for their beauty. You see it often happen that those who engage men to the greatest violence are such as those who are strangers to them would take to be remarkably defective for that end.—John Hughes.

Nothing is arbitrary, nothing is insulated in beauty. It depends forever on the necessary and the useful. The plumage of the bird, the mimic plumage of the insect, has a reason for its rich colors in the constitution of the animal. Fitness is so inseparable an accompaniment of beauty, that it has been taken for it.—Emerson.

The human heart yearns for the beautiful in all ranks of life. The beautiful things that God makes are His gift to all alike. I know there are many of the poor who have fine feeling and a keen sense of the beautiful, which rusts out and dies because they are too hard pressed to procure it any gratification.—Mrs. Stowe.

Who has not experienced how, on near acquaintance, plainness becomes beautified, and beauty loses its charm, exactly according to the quality of the heart and mind? And from this cause am I of opinion that the want of outward beauty never disquiets a noble nature or will be regarded as a misfortune. It never can prevent people from being amiable and beloved in the highest degree.—Fredrika Bremer.

Those critics who, in modern times, have the most thoughtfully analyzed the laws of æsthetic beauty, concur in maintaining that the real truthfulness of all works of imagination—sculpture, painting, written fiction—is so purely in the imagination, that the artist never seeks to represent the positive truth, but the idealized image of a truth.—Bulwer-Lytton.

Oh, talk as we may of beauty as a thing to be chiselled from marble or wrought out on canvas, speculate as we may upon its colors and outlines, what is it but an intellectual abstraction, after all? The heart feels a beauty of another kind; looking through the outward environment, it discovers a deeper and more real loveliness.—Whittier.

Gaze not on beauty too much, lest it blast thee; nor too long, lest it blind thee; nor too near, lest it burn thee. If thou like it, it deceives thee; if thou love it, it disturbs thee; if thou hunt after it, it destroys thee. If virtue accompany it, it is the heart's paradise; if vice associate it, it is the soul's purgatory. It is the wise man's bonfire, and the fool's furnace.—Quarles.

No man receives the true culture of a man in whom the sensibility to the beautiful is not cherished; and I know of no condition in life from which it should be excluded. Of all luxuries this is cheapest and the most at hand; and it seems to me to be the most important to those conditions where coarse labor tends to give a grossness to the mind.—Channing.

When I approach
Her loveliness, so absolute she seems,
And in herself complete, so well to know
Her own, that what she wills to do or say,
Seems wisest, virtuousest, discretest, best;
All higher knowledge in her presence falls
Degraded. Wisdom in discourse with her
Loses, discount'nanc'd, and like folly shows.
—Milton.

Beauty of form affects the mind, but then it must be understood that it is not the mere shell that we admire; we are attracted by the idea that this shell is only a beautiful case adjusted to the shape and value of a still more beautiful pearl within. The perfection of outward loveliness is the soul shining through its crystalline covering.—Jane Porter.

Beauty has so many charms, one knows not how to speak against it; and when it happens that a graceful figure is the habitation of a virtuous soul, when the beauty of the face speaks out the modesty and humility of the mind, and the justness of the proportion raises our thoughts up to the heart and wisdom of the great Creator, something may be allowed it, —and something to the embellishments which set it off; and yet, when the whole apology is read, it will be found at last that beauty, like truth, never is so glorious as when it goes the plainest.—Sterne.

Beauty is an all-pervading presence. It unfolds to the numberless flowers of the spring; it waves in the branches of the trees and the green blades of grass; it haunts the depths of the earth and the sea, and gleams out in the hues of the shell and the precious stone. And not only these minute objects, but the ocean, the mountains, the clouds, the heavens, the stars, the rising and setting sun, all overflow with beauty.—Channing.

Around her shone
The nameless charms unmark'd by her alone.
The light of love, the purity of grace,
The mind, the music breathing from her face,
The heart whose softness harmonized the whole,
And, oh! that eye was in itself a soul.
—Byron.

Not faster in the summer's ray,
The spring's frail beauty fades away,
Than anguish and decay consume,
The smiling virgin's rosy bloom.
Some beauty's snatch'd each day, each hour;
For beauty is a fleeting flower;
Then how can wisdom e'er confide
In beauty's momentary pride?
—Elphinstone.

There is a certain period of the soul-culture when it begins to interfere with some of the characters of typical beauty belonging to the bodily frame, the stirring of the intellect wearing down the flesh, and the moral enthusiasm burning its way out to heaven,

through the emaciation of the earthen vessel; and there is, in this indication of subduing the mortal by the immortal part, an ideal glory of perhaps a purer and higher range than that of the more perfect material form. We conceive, I think, more nobly of the weak presence of Paul than of the fair and ruddy countenance of David. —Ruskin.

What's female beauty but an air divine,
Through which the mind's all gentle graces shine?
They, like the sun, irradiate all between;
The body charms because the soul is seen.
Hence men are often captives of a face—
They know not why—of no peculiar grace;
Some forms, though bright, no mortal man can bear;
Some none resist, though not exceeding fair.
—Young.

Beauty is but a vain and doubtful good,
A shining glass, that fadeth suddenly;
A flower that dies, when first it 'gins to bud;
A brittle glass, that's broken presently;
A doubtful good, a gloss, a glass, a flower,
Lost, faded, broken, dead within an hour.
And as good lost is seld or never found,
As fading gloss no rubbing will refresh,
As flowers dead lie wither'd on the ground,
As broken glass no cement can redress,
So beauty blemish'd once, for ever's lost,
In spite of physic, painting, pain and cost.
—Shakespeare.

Ye tradeful merchants! that with weary toil,
Do seek most precious things to make you gaine,
And both the Indies of their treasures spoil;
What needeth you to seek so far in vain?
For lo! my love doth in herself contain
All this world's riches that may far be found;
If saphyrs, lo! her eyes be saphyrs plain;
If rubies, lo! her lips be rubies sound;
If pearls, her teeth be pearls, both pure and round;
If ivory, her forehead's ivory I ween;
If gold, her locks are finest gold on ground;
If silver, her fair hands are silver sheen;
But that which fairest is, but few behold,
Her mind, adorn'd with virtues manifold.
—Spenser.

Socrates called beauty a short-lived tyranny; Plato, a privilege of nature; Theophrastus, a silent cheat; Theocritus, a delightful prejudice; Carneades, a solitary kingdom; Domitian said, that nothing was more grateful; Aristotle affirmed that beauty was better than all the letters of recommendation in the world; Homer, that 'twas a glorious gift of nature, and Ovid, alluding to him, calls it a favor bestowed by the gods.—From the Italian.

Beauty depends more upon the movement of the face, than upon the form of the features when at rest. Thus a countenance habitually under the influence of amiable feelings, acquires a beauty of the highest order, from the frequency with which such feelings are the originating causes of the movement or expressions which stamp their character upon it.—Mrs. S. C. Hall.

Bed

The bed has become a place of luxury to me! I would not exchange it for all the thrones in the world.—Napoleon I.

O bed! O bed! delicious bed!
That heaven upon earth to the weary head.
　　　　　—Hood.

　　　　Sweet pillows, sweetest bed;
A chamber deaf to noise, and blind to light;
A rosy garland, and a weary head.
　　　　　—Sir Philip Sidney.

In bed we laugh, in bed we cry;
And born in bed, in bed we die;
The near approach a bed may show
Of human bliss to human woe.
　　　　　—Isaac De Benserade.

　　　　　　Oh! thou gentle scene
Of sweet repose; where by th' oblivious draught
Of each sad toilsome day to peace restor'd.
Unhappy mortals lose their woes awhile.
　　　　　—Thomson.

There should be hours for necessities, not for delights; times to repair our nature with comforting repose, and not for us to waste these times.—Shakespeare.

Night is the time for rest;
How sweet when labours close,
To gather round an aching breast
The curtain of repose;
Stretch the tir'd limbs, and lay the head
Down on our own delightful bed.
　　　　　—James Montgomery.

It is a delicious moment, certainly, that of being well nestled in bed, and feeling that you shall drop gently to sleep. The good is to come, not past;

the limbs have just been tired enough to render the remaining in one posture delightful; the labor of the day is gone.—Leigh Hunt.

Bed is a bundle of paradoxes; we go to it with reluctance, yet we quit it with regret; and we make up our minds every night to leave it early, but we make up our bodies every morning to keep it late.—Colton.

Bees

Many-colored, sunshine-loving, spring-betokening bee! yellow bee, so mad for love of early-blooming flowers!—Professor Wilson.

How doth the little busy bee
Improve each shining hour,
And gather honey all the day,
From every opening flower.
　　　　　—Watts.

Even bees, the little alms-men of spring bowers,
Know there is richest juice in poison-flowers.
　　　　　—Keats.

Look on the bee upon the wing 'mong flowers;
How brave, how bright his life! then mark him hiv'd,
Cramp'd, cringing in his self-built, social cell,
Thus it is in the world-hive; most where men
Lie deep in cities as in drifts.　—Bailey.

The pedigree of honey
　Does not concern the bee;
　A clover, any time, to him
　Is aristocracy.
　　　　　—Emily Dickinson.

His labor is a chant,
　His idleness a tune,
Oh, for a bee's experience
　Of clovers and of noon!
　　　　　—Emily Dickinson.

　　　　Listen! O, listen!
Here ever hum the golden bees
Underneath full-blossomed trees,
At once with glowing fruit and flowers crowned.—Lowell.

The bee is enclosed, and shines preserved, in a tear of the sisters of Phaëton, so that it seems enshrined in its own nectar. It has obtained a worthy reward for its great toils; we may suppose that the bee itself would have desired such a death.—Martial.

"O bees, sweet bees!" I said; "that nearest
  field
Is shining white with fragrant immortelles.
Fly swiftly there and drain those honey
  wells."
             —Helen Hunt.

The wild bee reels from bough to bough
  With his furry coat and his gauzy wing,
Now in a lily cup, and now
  Setting a jacinth bell a-swing,
    In his wandering.
             —Oscar Wilde.

Bees work for man, and yet they never
  bruise
  Their Master's flower, but leave it having
    done,
As fair as ever and as fit to use;
  So both the flower doth stay and honey
  run.   —Herbert.

The careful insect 'midst his works I view,
Now from the flowers exhaust the fragrant
  dew,
With golden treasures load his little thighs,
And steer his distant journey through the
  skies.   —Gay.

The little bee returns with evening's gloom,
  To join her comrades in the braided hive,
Where, housed beside their mighty honey-
  comb,
  They dream their polity shall long survive.
    —Charles (Tennyson) Turner.

The honey-bee that wanders all day long
The field, the woodland, and the garden o'er,
To gather in his fragrant winter store,
Humming in calm content his winter song,
Seeks not alone the rose's glowing breast,
The lily's dainty cup, the violet's lips,
But from all rank and noxious weeds he sips
The single drop of sweetness closely pressed
Within the poison chalice.
    —Anne C. Lynch Botta.

      So work the honey-bees;
Creatures, that by a rule in nature teach
The art of order to a peopled kingdom.
They have a king and officers of sorts;
Where some, like magistrates, correct at
  home;
Others, like merchants, venture trade abroad;
Others, like soldiers, armed in their stings,
Make boot upon the summer's velvet buds;
Which pillage they, with merry march, bring
  home,
To the tent royal of their emperor;
Who, busied in his majesty, surveys
The singing masons building roofs of gold;
The civil citizens kneading up the honey;
The poor mechanic porters crowding in
Their heavy burdens at his narrow gate;
The sad-ey'd justice, with his surly hum,
Delivering o'er to executors pale
The lazy yawning drone.   —Shakespeare.

Beggar

He who begs timidly courts a refusal.—Seneca.

Aspiring beggary is wretchedness itself.—Goldsmith.

Sturdy beggars can bear stout de-
nials.—Colton.

The real beggar is indeed the true
and only king.—Lessing.

Better a living beggar than a buried
emperor.—La Fontaine.

To get thine ends, lay bashfulnesse aside;
Who feares to aske, doth teach to be deny'd.
             —Herrick.

A beggar that is dumb, you know,
May challenge double pity.
             —Sir Walter Raleigh.

The adage must be verified—
That beggars mounted, run their horse to
death.   —Shakespeare.

Though our donations are made to
please ourselves, we insist upon those
who receive our alms being pleased
with them.—Zimmermann.

Well, whiles I am a beggar I will rail
And say, there is no sin but to be rich;
And being rich, my virtue then shall be
To say, there is no vice but beggary.
             —King John.

A beggar through the world am I,
From place to place I wander by.
Fill up my pilgrim's scrip for me,
For Christ's sweet sake and charity.
             —Lowell.

He makes a beggar first that first relieves
  him;
Not us'rers make more beggars where they
  live
Than charitable men that use to give.
             —Heywood.

His house was known to all the vagrant
  train,
He chid their wanderings but reliev'd their
  pain;
The long remembered beggar was his guest,
Whose beard descending swept his aged
  breast.   —Goldsmith.

He is never out of the fashion, or
limpeth awkwardly behind it. He is
not required to put on court mourning.

He weareth all colors, fearing none.
His costume hath undergone less
change than the Quaker's. He is the
only man in the universe who is not
obliged to study appearances.—Lamb.

Beggar!—the only free men of our common-
wealth,
Free above scot-free, that observe no laws,
Obey no governor, use no religion,
But what they draw from their own ancient
custom,
Or constitute themselves, yet are no rebels.
—Broome.

Art thou a man, and shams't thou not to
beg,
To practice such a servile kind of life?
Why, were thy education ne'er so mean,
Having thy limbs, a thousand fairer courses
Offer themselves to thy election.
Either the wars might still supply thy wants,
Or service of some virtuous gentleman,
Or honest labour; nay, what can I name
But would become thee better than to beg?
But men of thy condition feed on sloth,
As doth the beetle on the dung she breeds
in;
Not caring how the metal of your minds
Is eaten with the rust of idleness.
Now, after me, what e'er he be, that should
Believe a person of thy quality,
While thou insist in this loose desp'rate
course,
I would esteem the sin not thine, but his.
—Ben Jonson.

In every civilized society there is
found a race of men who retain the
instincts of the aboriginal cannibal
and live upon their fellow-men as a
natural food.—Bulwer-Lytton.

Beginnings

What's well begun, is half done.—
Horace.

The principal part of everything is
the beginning.—Law Maxim.

Whatever begins, also ends.—Seneca.

The distance is nothing; it is only
the first step that costs.—Mme. du
Deffand.

The beginnings of all things are
small.—Cicero.

Still thou knowest that in the ardor
of pursuit men lose sight of the goal
from which they start.—Schiller.

Begin whatever you have to do: the
beginning of a work stands for the
whole.—Ausonius.

Thou beginnest better than thou
endest. The last is inferior to the
first.—Ovid.

Everything that has a beginning
comes to an end.—Quintilian.

Resist beginnings: it is too late to
employ medicine when the evil has
grown strong by inveterate habit.—
Ovid.

Begin; to begin is half the work.
Let half still remain; again begin this,
and thou wilt have finished.—Ausonius.

Behavior

Behavior is the theory of manners
practically applied.—Mme. Necker.

Behavior is a mirror, in which everyone shows his image.—Goethe.

Levity of behavior is the bane of all
that is good and virtuous.—Seneca.

Venus herself, if she were bold,
would not be Venus.—Apuleius.

Women should be doubly careful of
their conduct, since appearances often
injure them as much as real faults.—
Abbé Girard.

Wise men read very sharply all of
your private history in your look and
gait and behavior.—Emerson.

Oddities and singularities of behavior may attend genius; when they do,
they are its misfortunes and its blemishes. The man of true genius will be
ashamed of them; at least he will
never affect to distinguish himself by
whimsical peculiarities.—S. W. Temple.

Any man shall speak the better
when he knows what others have said,
and sometimes the consciousness of his
inward knowledge gives a confidence to
his outward behavior, which of all
other is the best thing to grace a man
in his carriage.—Feltham.

Never put off till to-morrow what you can do to-day.

Never trouble another for what you can do yourself.

Never spend your money before you have it.

Never buy what you do not want because it is cheap.

Pride costs us more than hunger, thirst, and cold.

We seldom repent having eaten too little.

Nothing is troublesome that we do willingly.

How much pain the evils have cost us that have never happened!

Take things always by the smooth handle.

When angry, count ten before you speak; if very angry, a hundred.—Jefferson.

Belief

What ardently we wish we soon believe.—Young.

He who knows most believes the least.—Buckle.

What ardently we wish, we soon believe.—Young.

Now God be praised, that to believing souls,
Gives light in darkness, comfort in despair!
                              —Shakespeare.

He that will believe only what he can fully comprehend, must have a very long head, or a very short creed.—C. C. Colton.

Nothing is so firmly believed as what we least know.—Montaigne.

The region of the senses is the unbelieving part of the human soul.—George MacDonald.

You believe that easily which you hope for earnestly.—Terence.

The practical effect of a belief is the real test of its soundness.—Froude.

Men believe that willingly which they wish to be true.—Cæsar.

Being alone when one's belief is firm, is not to be alone.—Auerbach.

Belief consists in accepting the affirmations of the soul; unbelief, in denying them.—Emerson.

When in God thou believest, near God thou wilt certainly be.—C. G. Leland.

All I have seen teaches me to trust the Creator for all I have not seen.—Emerson.

We are slow to believe that which if believed would hurt our feelings.—Ovid.

You do not believe, you only believe that you believe.—Coleridge.

The want of belief is a defect which ought to be concealed where it cannot be overcome.—Swift.

The more sincere we are in our belief, as a rule, the less demonstrative we are.—Beecher.

Belief is not a matter of choice, but of conviction.—R. G. Ingersoll.

Happy the man who sees a God employed in all the good and ills that checker life.—Cowper.

Till their own dreams at length deceive 'em,
And oft repeating, they believe 'em.
                              —Prior.

Begin by regarding every thing from a moral point of view, and you will end by believing in God.—Dr. Arnold.

And to add greater honours to his age
Than man could give him, he died fearing
  God.   —Shakespeare.

'Tis with our judgments as our watches; none
Are just alike, yet each believes his own.
                              —Pope.

O thou, whose days are yet all spring,
  Faith, blighted once, is past retrieving;
Experience is a dumb, dead thing;
  The victory's in believing.   —Lowell.

Intellectually the difficulties of unbelief are as great as those of unbelief, while morally the argument is wholly on the side of belief.—Dr. T. Arnold.

Men ascribe a great value in the sight of God to their barren belief. Why are we so anxious that our neighbor should have our faith and not our practice?—Richter.

For fools are stubborn in their way,
As coins are harden'd by th' allay;
And obstinacy's ne'er so stiff
As when 'tis in a wrong belief.
—Butler.

If you wish to be assured of the truth of Christianity, try it. Believe, and if thy belief be right, that insight which gradually transmutes faith into knowledge will be the reward of thy belief.—S. T. Coleridge.

It is a singular fact that most men of action incline to the theory of fatalism, while the greater part of men of thought believe in providence.—Balzac.

To believe is to be happy; to doubt is to be wretched. To believe is to be strong. Doubt cramps energy. Belief is power. Only so far as a man believes strongly, mightily, can he act cheerfully, or do any thing that is worth the doing.—F. W. Robertson.

There are three means of believing, —by inspiration, by reason, and by custom. Christianity, which is the only rational institution, does yet admit none for its sons who do not believe by inspiration.—Pascal.

They that deny a God destroy man's nobility; for certainly man is of kin to the beasts by his body; and, if he be not of kin to God by his spirit, he is a base and ignoble creature.—Bacon.

The great desire of this age is for a doctrine which may serve to condense our knowledge, guide our researches, and shape our lives, so that conduct may really be the consequence of belief.—G. H. Lewes.

The man who goes through life with an uncertain doctrine not knowing what he believes, what a poor, powerless creature he is! He goes around through the world as a man goes down through the street with a poor, wounded arm, forever dodging people he meets on the street for fear they may touch him.—Phillips Brooks.

A man may be a heretic in the truth; and if he believe things only because his pastor says so, or the assembly so determines, without knowing other reason, though his belief be true, yet the very truth he holds becomes his heresy.—Milton.

They believed—faith, I'm puzzled—I think
I may call
Their belief a believing in nothing at all,
Or something of that sort; I know they all
went
For a general union of total dissent.
—Lowell.

When, in your last hour (think of this), all faculty in the broken spirit shall fade away, and sink into inanity, —imagination, thought, effort, enjoyment,—then will the flower of belief, which blossoms even in the night, remain to refresh you with its fragrance in the last darkness.—Richter.

I am not afraid of those tender and scrupulous consciences, who are ever cautious of professing and believing too much; if they are sincerely in the wrong, I forgive their errors, and respect their integrity. The men I am afraid of are the men who believe everything, subscribe to everything, and vote for everything.—Bishop Shipley.

If that impression does not remain on this intrepid and powerful people, into whose veins all nations pour their mingling blood it will be our immense calamity. Public action, without it, will lose the dignity of consecration. Eloquence, without it, will miss what is loftiest, will give place to a careless and pulseless disquisition, or fall to the flatness of political slang. Life, without it, will lose its sacred and mystic charm. Society, without it, will fail of inspirations, and be drowned in an animalism whose rising tides will keep pace with its wealth.—R. S. Storrs.

Bells

For bells are the voice of the church;
They have tones that touch and search
The hearts of young and old.
—Longfellow.

The music nighest bordering upon heaven.—Lamb.

Ring out the old, ring in the new,
Ring, happy bells, across the snow.
—Tennyson.

Ring out the darkness of the land,
Ring in the Christ that is to be.
—Tennyson.

That all-softening, overpowering knell,
The tocsin of the soul—the dinner bell.
—Byron.

When o'er the street the morning peal is flung
From yon tall belfry with the brazen tongue,
Its wide vibrations, wafted by the gale,
To each far listener tell a different tale.
—Holmes.

And the Sabbath bell,
That over wood and wild and mountain dell
Wanders so far, chasing all thoughts unholy
With sounds most musical, most melancholy.
—Samuel Rogers.

Those evening bells! those evening bells!
How many a tale their music tells,
Of youth, and home, and that sweet time,
When last I heard their soothing chime!
—Tom Moore.

There is in souls a sympathy with sounds;
How soft the music of those village bells,
Falling at intervals upon the ear
In cadence sweet, now dying all away.
—Cowper.

Bell, thou soundest merrily,
When the bridal party
To the church doth hie!
Bell, thou soundest solemnly,
When, on Sabbath morning,
Fields deserted lie!
—Longfellow.

The bells themselves are the best of preachers,
Their brazen lips are learned teachers,
From their pulpits of stone, in the upper air,
Sounding aloft, without crack or flaw,
Shriller than trumpets under the Law,
Now a sermon and now a prayer.
—Longfellow.

The cheerful Sabbath bells, wherever heard,
Strike pleasant on the sense, most like the voice
Of one, who from the far-off hills proclaims
Tidings of good to Zion. —Charles Lamb.

And this be the vocation fit,
For which the founder fashioned it;
High, high above earth's life, earth's labor
E'en to the heaven's blue vault to soar.
To hover as the thunder's neighbor,
The very firmament explore.
To be a voice as from above
Like yonder stars so bright and clear,
That praise their Maker as they move,
And usher in the circling year.
Tun'd be its metal mouth alone
To things eternal and sublime.
And as the swift wing'd hours speed on
May it record the flight of time!—Schiller.

Hear the mellow wedding bells,
Golden bells!
What a world of happiness their harmony foretells
Through the balmy air of night .
How they ring out their delight!
From the molten golden notes,
And all in tune
What a liquid ditty floats
To the turtle-dove that listens while she gloats
On the moon! —Poe.

Benevolence

Rare benevolence, the minister of God.—Carlyle.

Giving is true having.—Spurgeon.

Learn the luxury of doing good.—Goldsmith.

Great minds, like heaven, are pleased in doing good.—Rowe.

Our opportunities to do good are our talents.—Dr. Mather.

A noble deed is a step towards heaven.—J. G. Holland.

Honor the Lord with thy substance.

Benevolent people are always cheerful.—Father Taylor.

Try to be of some use to others.—Bishop Hall.

Be charitable before wealth makes thee covetous.—Sir Thomas Browne.

A benefit is estimated according to the mind of the giver.—Seneca.

You will find people ready enough to do the Samaritan without the oil and twopence.—Sydney Smith.

Whatever we give to the wretched, we lend to fortune.—Seneca.

Carve your name on hearts, and not on marble.—Spurgeon.

When my friends are one-eyed, I look at their profile.—Joubert.

Genuine benevolence is not stationary, but peripatetic. It goeth about doing good.—Nevins.

How quickly a truly benevolent act is repaid by the consciousness of having done it!—Hosea Ballou.

Every charitable act is a stepping stone toward heaven.—Beecher.

The lower a man descends in his love, the higher he lifts his life.—W. R. Alger.

And chiefly for the weaker by the wall,
You bore that lamp of sane benevolence.
—Meredith.

Good, the more communicated, more abundant grows.—Milton.

Benevolence and feeling ennoble the most trifling actions.—Thackeray.

The more we give to others, the more are we increased.—Lao-Tze.

Our hands we open of our own free will, and the good flies, which we can never recall.—Goethe.

Liberality consists less in giving profusely than in giving judiciously.—Bruyère.

We should do good whenever we can and do kindness at all times, for at all times we can.—Joubert.

We should be careful that our benevolence does not exceed our means. —Cicero.

Doing good is the only certainly happy action of a man's life.—Sir P. Sidney.

The office of liberality consisteth in giving with judgment.—Cicero.

The secret pleasure of a generous act, is the great mind's great bribe.—Dryden.

As often as we do good, we offer sacrifice to God.—Aristotle.

A poor man served by thee shall make thee rich.—Mrs. Browning.

He who waits to do a great deal of good at once, will never do anything.—Samuel Johnson.

Men resemble the gods in nothing so much as in doing good to their fellow creatures.—Cicero.

While selfishness joins hands with no one of the virtues, benevolence is allied to them all.—Goldsmith.

The entire world shall be populous with that action which saves one soul from despair.—Omar Khayam.

Good deeds in this life are coals raked up in embers, to make a fire next day.—Sir T. Overbury.

Being myself no stranger to suffering, I have learned to relieve the sufferings of others.—Virgil.

It is in contemplating man at a distance that we become benevolent.—Bulwer-Lytton.

Better to expose ourselves to ingratitude than fail in assisting the unfortunate.—Du Cœur.

He believed that he was born, not for himself, but for the whole world.—Lucan.

The Romans assisted their allies and friends, and acquired friendships by giving rather than receiving kindness. —Sallust.

If you realize an incentive to do a good thing, an act of benevolence, do it at once; do not put it off until to-morrow.—Henry Horne.

For his bounty, there was no winter in 't; an autumn 't was that grew the more by reaping.—Shakespeare.

A benefit consists not in what is done or given, but in the intention of the giver or doer.—Seneca.

Be generous, and pleasant-tempered, and forgiving; even as God scatters favors over thee, do thou scatter over the people.—Saadi.

There is no use of money equal to that of beneficence; here the enjoyment grows upon reflection.—Mackenzie.

Doubtless that is the best charity which, Nilus-like, hath the several streams thereof seen, but the fountain concealed.—Rev. T. Gouge.

Nothing is so wholesome, nothing does so much for people's looks, as a little interchange of the small coin of benevolence.—Ruffini.

————amid life's quests
That seems but worthy one—to do men
  good.   —Bailey.

The greatest pleasure I know is to do a good action by stealth, and to have it found out by accident.—Lamb.

The best portion of a good man's life,—his little, nameless, unremembered acts of kindness and of love.—Wordsworth.

That is fine benevolence, finely executed, which, like the Nile, comes from hidden sources.—Colton.

Every virtue carries with it its own reward, but none in so distinguished and pre-eminent a degree as benevolence.

There is no beautifier of complexion or form or behavior, like the wish to scatter joy and not pain around us.—Emerson.

Proportion thy charity to the strength of thy estate, lest God proportion thy estate to the weakness of thy charity.—Quarles.

True benevolence is to love all men. Recompense injury with justice, and kindness with kindness.—Confucius.

Every fresh act of benevolence is the herald of deeper satisfaction; every charitable act a stepping-stone towards heaven.—Beecher.

By doing good with his money, a man, as it were, stamps the image of God upon it, and makes it pass current for the merchandise of heaven.—Rutledge.

So quickly sometimes has the wheel turned round, that many a man has lived to enjoy the benefit of that charity which his own piety projected.—Laurence Sterne.

Time is short, your obligations are infinite. Are your houses regulated, your children instructed, the afflicted relieved, the poor visited, the work of piety accomplished?—Massillon.

It is another's fault if he be ungrateful, but is mine if I do not give. To find one thankful man I will oblige a great many that are not so.—Seneca.

When thou seest thine enemy in trouble, curl not thy whiskers in contempt; for in every bone there is marrow, and within every jacket there is a man.—Saadi.

The disposition to give a cup of cold water to a disciple is a far nobler property than the finest intellect. Satan has a fine intellect, but not the image of God.—Howells.

The lessons of prudence have charms,
  And slighted, may lead to distress;
But the man whom benevolence warms
  Is an angel who lives but to bless.
              —Bloomfield.

The only way to be loved is to be and to appear lovely; to possess and display kindness, benevolence, tenderness; to be free from selfishness and to be alive to the welfare of others.—Jay.

God will excuse our prayers for ourselves whenever we are prevented from them by being occupied in such good works as to entitle us to the prayers of others.—Colton.

We know who is benevolent by quite other means than the amount of subscription to soup societies. It is only low merits that can be enumerated.—Emerson.

The paternal and filial duties discipline the heart, and prepare it for the love of all mankind. The intensity of private attachment encourages, not prevents, universal benevolence.—Coleridge.

The benevolent affections owe much of their vigor to the frequency with which they are exercised, and to the pleasure by which they are attended.—Dr. Parr.

The conqueror is regarded with awe, the wise man commands our esteem, but it is the benevolent man who wins our affection.—From the French.

And 'tis not sure so full a benefit
Freely as freely to require.
A bounteous act hath glory following it,
They cause the glory that the act desire.
—Lady Carew.

A beneficent person is like a fountain watering the earth, and spreading fertility; it is, therefore, more delightful and more honorable to give than to receive.—Epicurus.

Beneficence is a duty. He who frequently practices it, and sees his benevolent intentions realized, at length comes really to love him to whom he has done good.—Kane.

He that does good to another does good also to himself, not only in the consequence, but in the very act; for the consciousness of well-doing is in itself ample reward.—Seneca.

There is scarcely a man who is not conscious of the benefits which his own mind has received from the performance of single acts of benevolence. How strange that so few of us try a course of the same medicine!—J. F. Boyes.

There cannot be a more glorious object in creation than a human being replete with benevolence, meditating in what manner he might render himself most acceptable to his Creator by doing most good to His creatures.—Fielding.

The poor must be wisely visited and liberally cared for, so that mendicity shall not be tempted into mendacity, nor want exasperated into crime.—Robert C. Winthrop.

The charities of life are scattered everywhere, enameling the vales of human beings as the flowers paint the meadows. They are not the fruit of study, nor the privilege of refinement, but a natural instinct.—Bancroft.

The great Howard was so fully engaged in works of active benevolence, that, unlike Baxter, whose knees were calcined by prayer, he left himself but little time to pray. Thousands were praying for him.—Colton.

Open your hands, ye whose hands are full! The world is waiting for you! The whole machinery of the Divine beneficence is clogged by your hard hearts and rigid fingers. Give and spend, and be sure that God will send; for only in giving and spending do you fulfill the object of His sending.—J. G. Holland.

Never did any soul do good but it came readier to do the same again, with more enjoyment. Never was love or gratitude or bounty. practiced but with increasing joy, which made the practicer still more in love with the fair act.—Shaftesbury.

No sincere desire of doing good need make an enemy of a single human being; that philanthropy has surely a flaw in it which cannot sympathize with the oppressor equally as with the oppressed.—Lowell.

Poverty is the load of some, and wealth is the load of others, perhaps the greater load of the two. It may weigh them to perdition. Bear the load of thy neighbor's poverty, and let him bear with thee the load of thy wealth. Thou lightenest thy load by lightening his.—St. Augustine.

The opportunity of making happy is more scarce than we imagine; the punishment of missing it is, never to meet with it again; and the use we make of it leaves us an eternal sentiment of satisfaction or repentance.—Rousseau.

Never try to save out of God's cause; such money will canker the rest. Giving to God is no loss; it is putting your substance in the best bank. Giving is true having, as the old gravestone said of the dead man "What I spent I had, what I saved I lost, what I gave I have."—C. H. Spurgeon.

There is no bounty to be showed to such
As have real goodness: Bounty is
A spice of virtue; and what virtuous act
Can take effect on them that have no power
Of equal habitude to apprehend it?
—Ben Jonson.

As there are none so weak that we may venture to injure them with impunity, so there are none so low that they may not at some time be able to repay an obligation. Therefore, what benevolence would dictate, prudence would confirm.—Colton.

There is nothing that requires so strict an economy as our benevolence. We should husband our means as the agriculturist his manure, which, if he spread over too large a superficies, produces no crop,—if over too small a surface, exuberates in rankness and in weeds.—Colton.

Never lose a chance of saying a kind word. As Collingwood never saw a vacant place in his estate but he took an acorn out of his pocket and popped it in, so deal with your compliments through life. An acorn costs nothing; but it may sprout into a prodigious bit of timber.—Thackeray.

Animated by Christian motives and directed to Christian ends, it shall in no wise go unrewarded: here, by the testimony of an approving conscience; hereafter, by the benediction of our blessed Redeemer, and a brighter inheritance in His Father's house.—Bishop Mant.

The generous pride of virtue,
Disdains to weigh too nicely the returns
Her bounty meets with—like the liberal gods,
From her own gracious nature she bestows,
Nor stops to ask reward.   —Thomson.

Men are not only prone to forget benefits; they even hate those who have obliged them, and cease to hate those who have injured them. The necessity of revenging an injury, or of recompensing a benefit seems a slavery to which they are unwilling to submit.—La Rochefoucauld.

The true source of cheerfulness is benevolence. The pursuits of mankind are commonly frigid and contemptible, and the mistake comes, at last, to be detected. But virtue is a charm that never fades. The soul that perpetually overflows with kindness and sympathy will always be cheerful.—Parke Godwin.

Rich people who are covetous are like the cypress-tree,—they may appear well, but are fruitless; so rich persons have the means to be generous, yet some are not so, but they should consider they are only trustees for what they possess, and should show their wealth to be more in doing good than merely in having it.—Bishop Hall.

There do remain dispersed in the soil of human nature divers seeds of goodness, of benignity, of ingenuity, which, being cherished, excited, and quickened by good culture, do, by common experience, thrust out flowers very lovely, and yield fruits very pleasant of virtue and goodness.—Barrow.

I have heard of a monk who in his cell had a glorious vision of Jesus revealed to him. Just then a bell rang, which called him away to distribute loaves of bread among the poor beggars at the gate. He was sorely tried as to whether he should lose a scene so inspiring. He went to his act of mercy; and when he came back the vision remained more glorious than ever.—T. L. Cuyler.

Every man who becomes heartily and understandingly a channel of the Divine beneficence is enriched through every league of his life. Perennial satisfaction springs around and within him with perennial verdure. Flowers of gratitude and gladness bloom all along his pathway, and the melodious gurgle of the blessings he bears is echoed back by the melodious waves of the recipient stream.—J. G. Holland.

He is good that does good to others. If he suffers for the good he does, he is better still; and if he suffers from them to whom he did good, he is arrived to that height of goodness that nothing but an increase of his sufferings can add to it; if it proves his death, his virtue is at its summit—it is heroism complete.—Bruyère.

Thy love shall chant itself its own beatitudes, after its own life working. A child-kiss, set on thy sighing lips, shall make thee glad; a poor man, served, by thee, shall make thee rich; a rich man, helped by thee, shall make thee strong; thou shalt be served thyself by every sense of service which thou renderest.—E. B. Browning.

My God, grant that my bounty may be a clear and transparent river, flowing from pure charity, and uncontaminated by self-love, ambition, or interest. Thanks are due not to me, but Thee, from whom all I possess is derived. And what are the paltry gifts for which my neighbor forgets to thank me, compared with the immense blessings for which I have so often forgotten to be grateful to Thee!—Gotthold.

You are so to put forth the power that God has given you; you are so to give, and sacrifice to give, as to earn the eulogium pronounced on the woman, "She hath done what she could." Do it now. It is not a safe thing to leave a generous feeling to the cooling influences of a cold world. If you intend to do a mean thing, wait till to-morrow; if you are to do a noble thing, do it now,—now!—Rev. Dr. Guthrie.

Think not the good,
The gentle deeds of mercy thou hast done,
Shall die forgotten all; the poor, the pris-'ner,
The fatherless, the friendless, and the widow,
Who daily own the bounty of thy hand,
Shall cry to heav'n and pull a blessing on thee.   —Rowe.

A life of passionate gratification is not to be compared with a life of active benevolence. God has so constituted our nature that a man cannot be happy unless he is, or thinks he is, a means of good. Judging from our own experi-

ence, we cannot conceive of a picture of more unutterable wretchedness than is furnished by one who knows that he is wholly useless in the world.—Rev. Erskine Mason.

The difference of the degrees in which the individuals of a great community enjoy the good things of life has been a theme of declaration and discontent in all ages; and it is doubtless our paramount duty, in every state of society, to alleviate the pressure of the purely evil part of this distribution, as much as possible, and, by all the means we can devise, secure the lower links in the chain of society from dragging in dishonor and wretchedness.—Herschel.

Beneficence is a duty. He who frequently practices it, and sees his benevolent intentions realized, at length comes really to love him to whom he has done good. When, therefore, it is said, "Thou shalt love thy neighbor as thyself," it is not meant, thou shalt love him first and do him good in consequence of that love, but thou shalt do good to thy neighbor; and this thy beneficence will engender in thee that love to mankind which is the fulness and consummation of the inclination to do good.—Kant.

Benevolence is not in word and in tongue, but in deed and in truth. It is a business with men as they are, and with human life as drawn by the rough hand of experience. It is a duty which you must perform at the call of principle; though there be no voice of eloquence to give splendor to your exertions, and no music of poetry to lead your willing footsteps through the bowers of enchantment. It is not the impulse of high and ecstatic emotion. It is an exertion of principle. You must go to the poor man's cottage, though no verdure flourish around it, and no rivulet be nigh to delight you by the gentleness of its murmurs. If you look for the romantic simplicity of fiction you will be disappointed; but it is your duty to persevere in spite of every discouragement. Benevolence is not merely a feeling but a principle; not a dream of rapture for the fancy to indulge in, but a business for the hand to execute.—Chalmers.

Bereavement

A genuine faith lifts us above the bitterness of grief; a sense of Christ's living presence takes away all unbearable loneliness even when we are most alone. In our darkest hours, to know that our lost friend is still living, still loving us, still ours, in the highest and best sense, must be unspeakably consoling.—A. H. K.

Believe me, it is no time for words when the wounds are fresh and bleeding; no time for homilies when the lightning's shaft has smitten, and the man lies stunned and stricken. Then let the comforter be silent; let him sustain by his presence, not by his preaching; by his sympathetic silence, not by his speech.—George C. Lorimer.

Bible

All Scripture is given by inspiration of God.—Bible.

It speaks no less than God in every line.—Dryden.

A noble book! all men's book!—Carlyle.

This book of stars lights to eternal bliss.—George Herbert.

The Bible is common-sense inspired.—R. Howells.

Bibles laid open, millions of surprises.—George Herbert.

What can be nobler than the idea it gives us of the Supreme Being?—Addison.

The Bible stands alone in human literature in its elevated conception of manhood, in character and conduct.—Henry Ward Beecher.

Good, the more communicated, more abundant grows.—Milton.

Out from the heart of Nature rolled the burdens of the Bible old.—Emerson.

Within that awful volume lies
The mystery of mysteries. —Scott.

Like the needle to the north pole, the Bible points to heaven.—R. B. Nichol.

Other books we may read and criticise. To the Scriptures we must bow the entire soul, with all its faculties.—E. N. Kirk.

The Bible is to religion what the Iliad is to poetry.—Joubert.

The help, the guide, the balm of souls perplexed.—Arbuthnot.

The history of every man should be a Bible.—Novalis.

Even the style of the Scriptures is more than human.—Steele.

Nobody ever outgrows Scripture; the book widens and deepens with our years.—Spurgeon.

O may my understanding ever read
This glorious volume, which thy wisdom made. —Dr. Young.

If thou desire to profit, read with humility, simplicity, and faithfulness; nor even desire the repute of learning.—Thomas à Kempis.

The books of men have their day and grow obsolete. God's word is like Himself, "the same yesterday, to-day, and forever."—R. Payne Smith.

The Bible is the most thought-suggesting book in the world. No other deals with such grand themes.—Herrick Johnson.

If the Bible is God's word, and we believe it, let us handle it with reverence.—John B. Gough.

A stream where alike the elephant may swim and the lamb may wade.—Gregory the Great.

The word of God tends to make large-minded, noble-minded men.—Henry Ward Beecher.

When you read the sacred Scriptures, or any other book, never think how you read, but what you read.—John Kemble.

The Bible is a window in this prison-world, through which we may look into eternity.—Timothy Dwight.

With the history of Moses no book in the world, in point of antiquity, can contend.—Tillotson.

Every leaf is a spacious plain; every line a flowing brook; every period a lofty mountain.—Hervey.

The best evidence of the Bible's being the word of God is to be found between its covers. It proves itself. —Charles Hodge.

The Scriptures were written, not to make us astronomers, but to make us saints.—Matthew Henry.

The Bible abounds in plain truth, expressed in plain language; in this it surpasses all other books.—Whelpley.

Merely reading the Bible is no use at all without we study it thoroughly, and hunt it through, as it were, for some great truth.—D. L. Moody.

One gem from that ocean is worth all the pebbles from earthly streams. —Robert McCheyne.

Intense study of the Bible will keep any man from being vulgar in point of style.—Coleridge.

A loving trust in the Author of the Bible is the best preparation for a wise study of the Bible.—H. Clay Trumbull.

If God is a reality, and the soul is a reality, and you are an immortal being, what are you doing with your Bible shut?—Herrick Johnson.

And in that charter reads with sparkling eyes,
Her title to a treasure in the skies.
—Cowper.

When you are reading a book in a dark room, and come to a difficult part, you take it to a window to get more light. So take your Bibles to Christ. —Robert McCheyne.

The reason why we find so many dark places in the Bible is, for the most part, because there are so many dark places in our hearts.—A. Tholuck.

The Scripture is to be its own interpreter, or rather the Spirit speaking in it; nothing can cut the diamond but the diamond; nothing can interpret Scripture but Scripture.—Richard Watson.

The grand old Book of God still stands; and this old earth, the more its leaves are turned over and pondered, the more it will sustain and illustrate the Sacred word.—James D. Dana.

The English Bible—a book which, if every thing else in our language should perish, would alone suffice to show the whole extent of its beauty and power. —T. B. Macaulay.

If there be any thing in my style of thought to be commended, the credit is due to my kind parents in instilling into my mind an early love of the Scriptures.—Daniel Webster.

The Old and New Testaments contain but one scheme of religion. Neither part of this scheme can be understood without the other.—Richard Cecil.

Let your daughter have first of all the book of Psalms for holiness of heart, and be instructed in the Proverbs of Solomon for her godly life. —St. Jerome.

What other book besides the Bible could be heard in public assemblies from year to year, with an attention that never tires, and an interest that never cloys?—Robert Hall.

There was plainly wanting a divine revelation to recover mankind out of their universal corruption and degeneracy.—Dr. Samuel Clarke.

Here there is milk for babes, whilst there is manna for Angels; truth level with the mind of a peasant, truth soaring beyond the reach of a Seraph. —Rev. Hugh Stowell.

The Bible alone of all the books in the world, instead of uttering the opinions of the successive ages that produced it, has been the antagonist of these opinions.—Stuart Robinson.

The Bible is God's chart for you to steer by, to keep you from the bottom of the sea, and to show you where the harbor is, and how to reach it without running on rocks or bars.—H. W. Beecher.

In the Bible the ignorant may learn all requisite knowledge, and the most knowing may learn to discern their ignorance.—Boyle.

The most learned, acute, and diligent student cannot, in the longest life, obtain an entire knowledge of this one volume.—Sir Walter Scott.

The Scriptures teach us the best way of living, the noblest way of suffering, and the most comfortable way of dying.—Flavel.

There never was found, in any age of the world, either religion or law that did so highly exalt the public good as the Bible.—Bacon.

I call the Book of Job, apart from all theories about it, one of the grandest things ever written with pen.—Carlyle.

It is not simply a theological treatise, a code of laws, a religious homily, but the Bible—the book—while the only book for the soul, the best book for the mind.—Herrick Johnson.

A Bible and a newspaper in every house, a good school in every district —all studied and appreciated as they merit—are the principal support of virtue, morality and civil liberty.—Franklin.

It has God for its author, salvation for its end, and truth, without any mixture of error, for its matter: it is all pure, . all sincere, nothing too much, nothing wanting.—Locke.

There are no songs comparable to the songs of Zion, no orations equal to those of the prophets, and no politics like those which the Scriptures teach.—Milton.

Learn the Bible through the Bible, the Old through the New Testament;

either can only be understood by the needs of thy own heart.—John von Müller.

Do you know a book that you are willing to put under your head for a pillow when you lie dying? Very well; that is the book you want to study while you are living. There is but one such book in the world.—Joseph Cook.

I never saw a useful Christian who was not a student of the Bible. If a man neglects his Bible, he may pray and ask God to use him in His work; but God cannot make much use of him, for there is not much for the Holy Ghost to work upon.—D. L. Moody.

Give the Bible the place in your families to which it is justly entitled, and then, through the unsearchable riches of Christ, many a household among you may hereafter realize that most blessed consummation, and appear a whole family in heaven.—H. A. Boardman.

The word of God is solid; it will stand a thousand readings; and the man who has gone over it the most frequently and the most carefully is the surest of finding new wonders there.—James Hamilton.

All that has been done to weaken the foundation of an implicit faith in the Bible, as a whole, has been at the expense of the sense of religious obligation, and at the cost of human happiness.—J. G. Holland.

God in tender indulgence to our different dispositions, has strewed the Bible with flowers, dignified it with wonders, and enriched it with delight. —James Hervey.

It is not hard for any man who hath a Bible in his hand to borrow good words and holy sayings in abundance; but to make them his own is a work of grace only from above.—Milton.

Does not the passage of Moses and the Israelites into the Holy Land yield incomparably more poetic variety than the voyages of Ulysses or Æneas?—Cowley.

Then for the style, majestic and divine,
It speaks no less than God in every line;
Commanding words; whose force is still the same
As the first fiat that produced our frame.
—Dryden.

Whence but from Heaven, could men unskill'd in arts,
In several ages born, in several parts,
Weave such agreeing truths? or how, or why
Should all conspire to cheat us with a lie?
—Dryden.

The increasing influence of the Bible is marvelously great, penetrating everywhere. It carries with it a tremendous power of freedom and justice guided by a combined force of wisdom and goodness.—Mori.

A glory gilds the sacred page,
Majestic like the sun,
It gives a light to every age;
It gives, but borrows none.
—Cowper.

All human discoveries seem to be made only for the purpose of confirming more strongly the truths come from on high, and contained in the sacred writings.—Herschel.

There is no passion that is not finely expressed in those parts of the inspired writings which are proper for divine songs and anthems.—Addison.

As the telescope is not a substitute for, but an aid to, our sight, so revelation is not designed to supersede the use of reason, but to supply its deficiencies.—Whately.

I am heartily glad to witness your veneration for a book which to say nothing of its holiness or authority, contains more specimens of genius and taste than any other volume in existence.—W. S. Landor.

In Job and the Psalms we shall find more sublime ideas, more elevated language, than in any of the heathen versifiers of Greece or Rome.—Dr. Watts.

We glory most in the fact, that Scripture so commends itself to the conscience, and experience so bears out the Bible, that the gospel can go the round of the world, and carry with it, in all its travel, its own mighty credentials.—Henry Melvill.

Wherever public worship has been established and regularly maintained, idolatry has vanished from the face of the earth. There is not now a temple to a heathen god where the word of God is read.—Bishop Simpson.

It is impossible to look into the Bible with the most ordinary attention without feeling that we have got into a moral atmosphere quite different from that which we breathe in the world, and in the world's literature.—Thomas Erskine.

High above all earthly lower happiness the blessedness of the eight Beatitudes towers into the heaven itself. They are white with the snows of eternity; they give a space, a meaning, a dignity to all the rest of the earth over which they brood.—Dean Stanley.

Wherever God's word is circulated, it stirs the hearts of the people, it prepares for public morals. Circulate that word, and you find the tone of morals immediately changed. It is God speaking to man.—Bishop Simpson.

The Bible, as a revelation from God, was not designed to give us all the information we might desire, nor to solve all the questions about which the human soul is perplexed, but to impart enough to be a safe guide to the haven of eternal rest.—Albert Barnes.

A man may read the figure on the dial, but he cannot tell how the day goes unless the sun shines on the dial; we may read the Bible over, but we cannot learn to purpose till the Spirit of God shine into our hearts.—Rev. T. Watson.

As the profoundest philosophy of ancient Rome and Greece lighted her taper at Israel's altar, so the sweetest strains of the pagan muse were swept from harps attuned on Zion's hill.—Bishop Thomson.

The Bible begins gloriously with Paradise, the symbol of youth, and ends with the everlasting kingdom, with the holy city. The history of every man should be a Bible.—Novalis.

Scholars may quote Plato in studies, but the hearts of millions shall quote the Bible at their daily toil, and draw strength from its inspiration, as the meadows draw it from the brook.—Conway.

O Word of God incarnate ...
It is the golden casket
Where gems of truth are stored;
It is the heaven-drawn picture
Of Thee, the Living Word.
—William W. How.

So far as I ever observed God's dealings with my soul, the flights of preachers sometimes entertained me, but it was Scripture expressions which did penetrate my heart, and in a way peculiar to themselves.—J. Brown of Haddington.

The Bible is the most betrashed book in the world. Coming to it through commentaries is much like looking at a landscape through garret windows, over which generations of unmolested spiders have spun their webs.—Beecher.

I will answer for it, the longer you read the Bible, the more you will like it: it will grow sweeter and sweeter; and the more you get into the spirit of it, the more you will get into the spirit of Christ.—Romaine.

The Bible is a precious storehouse, and the Magna Charta of a Christian. There he reads of his Heavenly Father's love, and of his dying Saviour's legacies. There he sees a map of his travels through the wilderness, and a landscape, too, of Canaan.—Berridge.

Christianity claims that the supernatural is as reasonable as the natural, that man himself is supernatural as truly as he is natural, and that the

Bible is so clearly the word of God by proofs that are unanswerable, that it is unreasonable to disbelieve its divine truths.—A. E. Kittredge.

I have carefully and regularly perused the Holy Scriptures, and am of opinion that the volume contains more sublimity, purer morality, more important history, and finer strains of eloquence, than can be collected from all other books, in whatever language they may have been written.—Sir William Jones.

In the poorest cottage are books,—is one book, wherein for several thousands of years the spirit of man has found light and nourishment and an interpreting response to whatever is deepest in him.—Carlyle.

There are two books laid before us to study, to prevent our falling into error; first, the volume of the Scriptures, which reveal the will of God; then the volume of the Creatures, which express His power.—Bacon.

There is not a book on earth so favorable to all the kind and to all the sublime affections, or so unfriendly to hatred and persecution, to tyranny, injustice, and every sort of malevolence, as the Gospel.—Beattie.

They who are not induced to believe and live as they ought by those discoveries which God hath made in Scriptures would stand out against any evidence whatever, even that of a messenger sent express from the other world.—Atterbury.

Men cannot be well educated without the Bible. It ought, therefore, to hold the chief place in every situation of learning throughout Christendom; and I do not know of a higher service that could be rendered to this republic than the bringing about this desirable result.—Dr. Nott.

It is belief in the Bible, the fruits of deep meditation, which has served me as the guide of my moral and literary life. I have found capital safely invested and richly productive of interest, although I have sometimes made but a bad use of it.—Goethe.

The translators of the Bible were masters of an English style much fitter for that work than any we see in our present writings; the which is owing to the simplicity that runs through the whole.—Swift.

The life-boat may have a tasteful bend and beautiful decoration, but these are not the qualities for which I prize it; it was my salvation from the howling sea! So the interest which a regenerate soul takes in the Bible is founded on a personal application to the heart of the saving truth which it contains.—J. W. Alexander.

For more than a thousand years the Bible, collectively taken, has gone hand in hand with civilization, science, law; in short, with the moral and intellectual cultivation of the species, always supporting and often leading the way.—Coleridge.

The Bible is a book of faith, and a book of doctrine, and a book of morals, and a book of religion, of special revelation from God: but it is also a book which teaches man his own individual responsibility, his own dignity, and his equality with his fellow man.—Daniel Webster.

In morality there are books enough written both by ancient and modern philosophers, but the morality of the Gospel doth so exceed them all that to give a man a full knowledge of true morality I shall send him to no other book than the New Testament.—Locke.

The pure and noble, the graceful and dignified, simplicity of language is nowhere in such perfection as in the Scriptures and Homer. The whole book of Job, with regard both to sublimity of thought and morality, exceeds, beyond all comparison, the most noble parts of Homer.—Pope.

If you are ever tempted to speak lightly or think lightly of it, just sit down and imagine what this world would be without it. No Bible! A wound and no cure, a storm and no covert, a condemnation and no shrift, a lost eternity and no ransom! Alas for us if this were all; alas for us if the

ladder of science were the only stair to lead us up to God!—R. R. Meredith.

The Bible is not only the revealer of the unknown God to man, but His grand interpreter as the God of nature. In revealing God it has given us the key that unlocks the profoundest mysteries of creation, the clew by which to thread the labyrinth of the universe, the glass through which to look from nature up to nature's God.—L. J. Halsey.

The Psalms are an everlasting manual to the soul; the book of its immortal wishes, its troubles, its aspirations, and its hopes; sung in every tongue, and in every age; destined to endure while the universe of God has light, harmony, or grandeur, while man has religion or sensibility, while language has sublimity or sweetness.—Henry Giles.

As the moon, though darkened with spots, gives us a much greater light than the stars that seem all-luminous, so do the Scriptures afford more light than the brightest human authors. In them the ignorant may learn all requisite knowledge, and the most knowing may learn to discern their ignorance.—Boyle.

I use the Scriptures, not as an arsenal to be resorted to only for arms and weapons, but as a matchless temple, where I delight to contemplate the beauty, the symmetry, and the magnificence of the structure, and to increase my awe and excite my devotion to the Deity there preached and adored.—Boyle.

My own experience is that the Bible is dull when I am dull. When I am really alive, and set in upon the text with a tidal pressure of living affinities, it opens, it multiplies discoveries, and reveals depths even faster than I can note them. The worldly spirit shuts the Bible; the Spirit of God makes it a fire, flaming out all meanings and glorious truths.—Horace Bushnell.

All flesh is grass, and all the goodliness thereof is as the flower of the field; the grass withereth, the flower fadeth; because the spirit of the Lord bloweth upon it; surely the people is grass. The grass withereth, the flower fadeth, but the word of our God shall stand forever.—Isaiah xl. 6.

Within that awful volume lies
The mystery of mysteries!
Happiest they of human race,
To whom God has granted grace
To read, to fear, to hope, to pray,
To lift the latch and force the way;
And better had they ne'er been born,
Who read to doubt, or read to scorn.
—Scott.

All systems of morality are fine. The Gospel alone has exhibited a complete assemblage of the principles of morality divested of all absurdity. It is not composed, like your creed, of a few commonplace sentences put in bad verse. Do you wish to see that which is really sublime? Repeat the Lord's Prayer.—Napoleon I.

At the time when that odious style which deforms the writings of Hall and of Lord Bacon was almost universal, had appeared that stupendous work, the English Bible,—a book which, if everything else in our language should perish, would alone suffice to show the whole extent of its beauty and power.—Macaulay.

If an uninterested spectator, after a careful perusal of the New Testament, were asked what he conceived to be its distinguishing characteristic, he would reply, without hesitation, "That wonderful spirit of philanthropy by which it is distinguished." It is a perpetual commentary on that sublime aphorism, "God is love."—Robert Hall.

The main condition is that the spiritual ear should be open to overhear and patiently take in, and the will ready to obey that testimony which, I believe, God bears in every human heart, however dull, to those great truths which the Bible reveals. This, and not logic, is the way to grow in religious knowledge, to know that the truths of religion are not shadows, but deep realities.—J. C. Shairp.

How admirable and beautiful is the simplicity of the Evangelists! They never speak injuriously of the enemies of Jesus Christ, of His judges, nor of His executioners. They report the facts without a single reflection. They comment neither on their Master's mildness when He was smitten, nor on His constancy in the hour of His ignominious death, which they thus describe: "And they crucified Jesus." —Racine.

What is the Bible in your house? It is not the Old Testament, it is not the New Testament, it is not the Gospel according to Matthew, or Mark, or Luke, or John; it is the Gospel according to William; it is the Gospel according to Mary; it is the Gospel according to Henry and James; it is the Gospel according to your name. You write your own Bible.—Beecher.

The Saviour who flitted before the patriarchs through the fog of the old dispensation, and who spake in time past to the fathers by the prophets, articulate but unseen, is the same Saviour who, on the open heights of the Gospel, and in the abundant daylight of this New Testament, speaks to us. Still all along it is the same Jesus, and that Bible is from beginning to end, all of it, the word of Christ.—James Hamilton.

The Bible is a treasure. It contains enough to make us rich for time and eternity. It contains the secret of happy living. It contains the key of heaven. It contains the title-deeds of an inheritance incorruptible, and that fadeth not away. It contains the pearl of great price. Nay, in so far as it reveals them as the portion of us sinful worms, it contains the Saviour and the living God Himself.—James Hamilton.

The Bible is a warm letter of affection from a parent to a child; and yet there are many who see chiefly the severer passages. As there may be fifty or sixty nights of gentle dews in one summer, that will not cause as much remark as one hailstorm of half an hour, so there are those who are more struck by those passages of the Bible that announce the indignation of God than by those that announce His affection.—T. DeWitt Talmage.

The parable of the prodigal son, the most beautiful fiction that ever was invented; our Saviour's speech to His disciples, with which He closed His earthly ministrations, full of the sublimest dignity and tenderest affection, surpass everything that I ever read; and like the spirit by which they were dictated, fly directly to the heart.— Cowper.

This Bible, then, has a mission, grander than any mere creation of God; for in this volume are infinite wisdom, and infinite love. Between its covers are the mind and heart of God; and they are for man's good, for his salvation, his guidance, his spiritual nourishment. If now I neglect my Bible, I do my soul a wrong; for the fact of this Divine message is evidence that I need it.—A. E. Kittredge.

The Bible is the treasure of the poor, the solace of the sick, and the support of the dying; and while other books may amuse and instruct in a leisure hour, it is the peculiar triumph of that book to create light in the midst of darkness, to alleviate the sorrow which admits of no other alleviation, to direct a beam of hope to the heart which no other topic of consolation can reach; while guilt, despair, and death vanish at the touch of its holy inspiration.— Robert Hall.

I cannot look around me without being struck with the analogy observable in the works of God. I find the Bible written in the style of His other books of Creation and Providence. The pen seems in the same hand. I see it, indeed, write at times mysteriously in each of these books; thus I know that mystery in the works of God is only another name for my ignorance. The moment, therefore, that I become humble, all becomes right.—Richard Cecil.

There are many persons of combative tendencies, who read for ammunition, and dig out of the Bible iron for balls. They read, and they find nitre and charcoal and sulphur for powder. They read, and they find cannon. They read, and they make portholes and embrasures. And if a man does not believe as they do, they look upon him as an enemy, and let fly the Bible at him to demolish him. So men turn the word of God into a vast arsenal, filled with all manner of weapons, offensive and defensive.—H. W. Beecher.

Many will say, "I can find God without the help of the Bible, or church, or minister." Very well. Do so if you can. The Ferry Company would feel no jealousy of a man who should prefer to swim to New York. Let him do so if he is able, and we will talk about it on the other shore; but probably trying to swim would be the thing that would bring him quickest to the boat. So God would have no jealousy of a man's going to heaven without the aid of the Bible, or church, or minister; but let him try to do so, and it will be the surest way to bring him back to them for assistance.—Beecher.

The Book, this Holy Book, on every line,
Mark'd with the seal of high divinity,
On every leaf bedew'd with drops of love
Divine, and with the eternal heraldry
And signature of God Almighty stamp'd
From first to last; this ray of sacred light,
This lamp, from off the everlasting throne,
Mercy took down, and in the night of time
Stood, casting on the dark her gracious bow;
And evermore beseeching men with tears
And earnest sighs, to read, believe and live.
—Pollok.

Eighteen centuries have passed since the Bible was finished. They have been centuries of great changes. In their course the world has been wrought over into newness at almost every point. But to-day the text of the Scriptures, after copyings almost innumerable and after having been tossed about through ages of ignorance and tumult, is found by exhaustive criticism to be unaltered in every important particular—there being not a single doctrine, nor duty, nor fact of any grade, that is brought into question by variations of readings—a fact that stands alone in the history of such ancient literature.—E. F. Burr.

We may persuade men that are infidels to receive the Scriptures as the word of God by rational arguments drawn from their antiquity; the heavenliness of the matter; the majesty of the style; the harmony of all the parts though written in different ages; the exact accomplishment of prophecies;

the sublimity of the mysteries and matters contained in the word; the efficacy and power of it, in the conviction and conversion of multitudes; the scope of the whole,—to guide men to attain their chief end,—the glory of God in their own salvation; and the many miracles wrought for the confirmation of the truth of the doctrines contained in them.—Fisher's Catechism.

A single book has saved me; but that book is not of human origin. Long had I despised it, long had I deemed it a class-book for the credulous and ignorant, until, having investigated the Gospel of Christ, with an ardent desire to ascertain its truth or falsity, its pages proffered to my inquiries the simplest knowledge of man and nature, and the simplest and at the same time the most exalted system of moral ethics. Faith, hope and charity were enkindled in my bosom; and every advancing step strengthened me in the conviction that the morals of this book are as infinitely superior to human morals as its oracles are superior to human opinions—M. L. Bautin.

Parents, I urge you to make the Bible the sweetest, the dearest book to your children; not by compelling them to read so many chapters each day, which will have the effect of making them hate the Bible, but by reading its pages with them, and by your tender parental love, so showing them the beauty of its wondrous incidents, from the story of Adam and Eve to the story of Bethlehem and Calvary, that no book in the home will be so dear to your children as the Bible; and thus you will be strengthening their minds with the sublimest truths, storing their hearts with the purest love, and sinking deep in their souls solid principles of righteousness, whose divine stones no waves of temptation can ever move. —A. E. Kittredge.

The Bible has been my guide in perplexity, and my comfort in trouble. It has roused me when declining, and animated me in languor. Other writings may be good, but they want certainty and force. The Bible carries its own credentials along with it, and proves spirit and life to the soul, In other writings I hear the words of a stranger or a servant. In the Bible I hear the language of my Father and my friend. Other books contain only the picture of bread. The Bible presents me with real manna, and feeds me with the bread of life.

You will want a book which contains not man's thoughts, but God's—not a book that may amuse you, but a book that can save you—not even a book that can instruct you, but a book on which you can venture an eternity—not only a book which can give relief to your spirit, but redemption to your soul—a book which contains salvation, and conveys it to you, one which shall at once be the Saviour's book and the sinner's.—John Selden.

Bigotry

Bigotry is chronic dogmatism.— Horace Greeley.

All looks yellow to the jaundiced eye. —Pope.

Bigotry dwarfs the soul by shutting out the truth.—Chapin.

Bigotry murders religion to frighten folks with her ghost.—Colton.

Every sect clamors for toleration when it is down.—Macaulay.

A man who stole the livery of the court of heaven to serve the devil in.— Pollok.

There is no tariff so injurious as that with which sectarian bigotry guards its commodities.—Chapin.

To follow foolish precedents, and wink
With both our eyes is easier than to think.
—Cowper.

The superstition in which we were brought up never loses its power over us, even after we understand it.— Lessing.

A proud bigot, who is vain enough to think that he can deceive even God by affected zeal, and throwing the veil of holiness over vices, damns all mankind by the word of his power,—Boileau.

A man must be excessively stupid, as well as uncharitable, who believes there is no virtue but on his own side. —Addison.

The bigot is like the pupil of the eye, the more light you put upon it, the more it will contract.—O. W. Holmes.

Show me the man who would go to heaven alone if he could, and in that man I will show you one who will never be admitted into heaven.—Feltham.

Unwillingness to acknowledge whatever is good in religion foreign to our own has always been a very common trait of human nature; but it seems to me neither generous nor just.—Mrs. L. M. Child.

Mr. T. sees religion, not as a sphere, but as a line; and it is the identical line in which he is moving. He is like an African buffalo,—sees right forward, but nothing on the right hand or on the left.—John Foster.

Persecuting bigots may be compared to those burning lenses which Lenhenhoeck and others composed from ice; by their chilling apathy they freeze the suppliant; by their fiery zeal they burn the sufferer.—Colton.

Soon their crude notions with each other fought,
The adverse sect, deny'd what this had taught,
And he at length the amplest triumph gain'd,
Who contradicted what the last maintain'd.
—Prior.

She has no head, and cannot think; no heart, and cannot feel. When she moves, it is in wrath; when she pauses, it is amid ruin; her prayers are curses—her God is a demon—her communion is death—her vengeance is eternity—her decalogue written in the blood of her victims; and if she stops for a moment in her infernal flight, it is upon a kindred rock, to whet her vulture fang for a more sanguinary desolation.—Daniel O'Connell.

The doctrine which, from the very first origin of religious dissensions, has been held by bigots of all sects, when condensed into a few words and stripped of rhetorical disguise, is simply this: I am in the right, and you are in the wrong. When you are the stronger, you ought to tolerate me, for it is your duty to tolerate truth; but when I am the stronger, I shall persecute you, for it is my duty to persecute error.—Macaulay.

Biography

There is properly no history, only biography.—Emerson.

Biography is the best form of history.—H. W. Shaw.

Some one calls biography the home aspect of history.—Beecher.

A true delineation of the smallest man is capable of interesting the greatest man.—Carlyle.

One anecdote of a man is worth a volume of biography.—Channing.

A life that is worth writing at all is worth writing minutely.—Longfellow.

To be ignorant of the lives of the most celebrated men of antiquity is to continue in a state of childhood all our days.—Plutarch.

The great lesson of biography is to show what man can be and do at his best. A noble life put fairly on record acts like an inspiration to others.—Samuel Smiles.

The cabinets of the sick and the closets of the dead have been ransacked to publish private letters and divulge to all mankind the most secret sentiments of friendship.—Pope.

Our Grub-street biographers watch for the death of a great man like so many undertakers on purpose to make a penny of him.—Addison.

Occasionally a single anecdote opens a character; biography has its comparative anatomy, and a saying or a sentiment enables the skilful hand to construct the skeleton.—Willmott.

The lives of great men cannot be writ with any tolerable degre of elegance or exactness within a short time after their decease.—Addison.

My advice is to consult the lives of other men as we would a looking-glass, and from thence fetch examples for our own imitation.—Terence.

Rich as we are in biography, a well-written life is almost as rare as a well-spent one; and there are certainly many more men whose history deserves to be recorded than persons willing and able to record it.—Carlyle.

Of all the species of literary composition, perhaps biography is the most delightful. The attention concentrated on one individual gives a unity to the materials of which it is composed, which is wanting in general history.—Robert Hall.

I should dread to disfigure the beautiful ideal of the memories of illustrious persons with incongruous features, and to sully the imaginative purity of classical works with gross and trivial recollections.—Wordsworth.

History can be formed from permanent monuments and records; but lives can only be written from personal knowledge, which is growing every day less, and in a short time is lost forever.—Dr. Johnson.

Biographies of great, but especially of good men are most instructive and useful as helps, guides, and incentives to others. Some of the best are almost equivalent to gospels,—teaching high living, high thinking, and energetic action, for their own and the world's good.—Samuel Smiles.

Biography, especially the biography of the great and good, who have risen by their own exertions from poverty and obscurity to eminence and usefulness, is an inspiring and ennobling study. Its direct tendency is to reproduce the excellence it records.—Horace Mann.

The parallel circumstances and kindred images to which we readily conform our minds are, above all other writings, to be found in the lives of particular persons, and therefore no species of writing seems more worthy of cultivation than biography.—Dr. Johnson.

As in the case of painters, who have undertaken to give us a beautiful and graceful figure, which may have some slight blemishes, we do not wish them to pass over such blemishes altogether, nor yet to mark them too prominently. The one would spoil the beauty, and the other destroy the likeness of the picture.—Plutarch.

The business of the biographer is often to pass slightly over those performances and incidents which produce vulgar greatness, to lead the thoughts into domestic privacies, and display the minute details of daily life, where exterior appendages are cast aside, and men excel each other only by prudence and virtue.—Dr. Johnson.

Of all studies, the most delightful and the most useful is biography. The seeds of great events lie near the surface; historians delve too deep for them. No history was ever true. Lives I have read which, if they were not, had the appearance, the interest, and the utility of truth.—Landor.

Much that is published as a novel is only anonymous biography. Many a man who is a bore in conversation may have qualities which give indescribable charms to narrative; and the egotist, if he only have the art to conceal his identity, can then hold the reader by the powerful grasp of sympathy.—R. S. Mackenzie.

As it often happens that the best men are but little known, and consequently cannot extend the usefulness of their examples a great way, the biographer is of great utility, as, by communicating such valuable patterns to the world, he may perhaps do a more extensive service to mankind than the person whose life originally afforded the pattern.—Fielding.

Birds

A bird of the air shall carry the voice, and that which hath wings shall tell the matter.—Ecclesiastes.

The little birds have God for their caterer.—Cervantes.

Was never secret history but birds tell it in the bowers.—Emerson.

I was always a lover of soft-winged things.—Victor Hugo.

Hear how the birds, on ev'ry blooming spray,
With joyous musick wake the dawning day!
—Pope.

And hark, how blithe the throstle sings! He, too, is no mean preacher.—Wordsworth.

Teach me, O lark! with thee to greatly rise, to exalt my soul and lift it to the skies. —Burke.

Fowls, by winter forced, forsake the floods, and wing their hasty flight to happier lands.—Dryden.

With sonorous notes
Of every tone, mix'd in confusion sweet,
Our forest rings. —Carlos Wilcox.

A light broke in upon my soul—
It was the carol of a bird;
It ceased—and then it came again
The sweetest song ear ever heard.
—Byron.

The birds, great Nature's happy commoners, that haunt in woods, in meads, and flowery gardens, rifle the sweets and taste the choicest fruits.—Rowe.

See the enfranchised bird, who wildly springs,
With a keen sparkle in his glowing eye
And a strong effort in his quivering wings,
Up to the blue vault of the happy sky.
—Mrs. Norton.

Do you ne'er think what wondrous beings these?
Do you ne'er think who made them, and who taught
The dialect they speak, where melodies
Alone are the interpreters of thought?
Whose household words are songs in many keys,
Sweeter than instrument of man e'er caught!
—Longfellow.

The nightingale, if he should sing by day, when every goose is cackling, would be thought no better a musician than the wren. How many things by season seasoned are to their right praise and true perfection!—Shakespeare.

Birds, the free tenants of earth, air, and ocean,
Their forms all symmetry, their motions grace,
In plumage delicate and beautiful,
Thick without burthen, close as fish's scales,
Or loose as full blown poppies on the gale;
With wings that seem as they'd a soul within them,
They bear their owners with such sweet enchantment. —James Montgomery.

Birth — Birthplace

Birth is a shadow. Courage, self-sustained, outlords succession's phlegm, and needs no ancestors.—Aaron Hill.

We forget the origin of a parvenu if he remembers it; we remember it if he forgets it.—J. Petit-Senn.

A noble birth and fortune, though they make not a bad man good, yet they are a real advantage to a worthy one, and place his virtues in a fairer light.—Lillo.

Called to the throne by the voice of the people, my maxim has always been, A career open to talent without distinction of birth. It is this system of equality for which the European oligarchy detests me.—Napoleon.

While man is growing, life is in decrease;
And cradles rock us nearer to the tomb.
Our birth is nothing but our death begun.
—Young.

No distinction is 'tween man and man,
But as his virtues add to him a glory
Or vices cloud him. —Habbington.

What is birth to a man if it shall be a stain to his dead ancestors to have left such an offspring?—Sir P. Sidney.

When real nobleness accompanies that imaginary one of birth, the imaginary seems to mix with real, and becomes real, too.—Greville.

High birth is a gift of fortune which should never challenge esteem towards those who receive it, since it costs them neither study nor labor.—Bruyère.

Custom forms us all; our thoughts, our morals, our most fixed belief, are consequences of our place of birth.—Aaron Hill.

———

Verily, I swear, it is better to be lowly born, and range with humble livers in content, than to be perked up in a glistering grief, and wear a golden sorrow.—Shakespeare.

———

I've learned to judge of men by their own deeds;
I do not make the accident of birth
The standard of their merit. —Mrs. Hale.

———

Whatever strengthens our local attachments is favorable both to individual and national character, our home, our birthplace, our native land. Think for a while what the virtues are which arise out of the feelings connected with these words, and if you have any intellectual eyes, you will then perceive the connection between topography and patriotism.—Southey.

———

Our birth is but a sleep and a forgetting;
The soul that rises with us, our life's Star,
Hath had elsewhere its setting,
And cometh from afar;
Not in entire forgetfulness,
And not in utter nakedness,
But trailing clouds of glory, do we come
From God, who is our home.
Heaven lies about us in our infancy.
*   *   *   *   *   *
At length the man perceives it die away,
And fade into the light of common day.
—Wordsworth.

———

Those who wish to forget painful thoughts do well to absent themselves for a while from the ties and objects that recall them; but we can be said only to fulfill our destiny in the place that gave us birth.—Hazlitt.

Birthday

Heaven give you many, many merry days!—Shakespeare.

———

And send him many years of sunshine days!—Shakespeare.

———

And more such days as these to us befall!—Shakespeare.

———

This day shall change all griefs and quarrels into love.—Shakespeare.

Oh! be thou blest with all that Heaven can send,
Long health, long youth, long pleasure—
    and a friend.
    —Pope.

———

Pleas'd to look forward, pleas'd to look behind,
And count each birthday with a grateful mind.
    —Pope.

———

    The day
For whose returns, and many, all these pray;
And so do I.   —B. Jonson.

———

The birth of a child is the imprisonment of a soul.—Simms.

———

Is that a birthday? 'tis, alas! too clear;
'Tis but the funeral of the former year.
    —Pope.

———

Yet all I've learnt from hours rife
  With painful brooding here,
Is, that amid this mortal strife,
  The lapse of every year
But takes away a hope from life,
  And adds to death a fear.
    —Hoffman.

———

My birthday!—what a different sound
  That word had in my youthful ears;
And how each time the day comes round,
  Less and less white its mark appears.
    —Moore.

———

Believing hear, what you deserve to hear,
Your birthday as my own to me is dear.
Blest and distinguish'd days! which we
    should prize
The first, the kindest bounty of the skies.
But yours gives most; for mine did only
    lend
Me to the world; yours gave to me a friend.
    —Martial.

———

As this auspicious day began the race
Of ev'ry virtue join'd with ev'ry grace;
May you, who own them, welcome its return,
Till excellence, like yours, again is born.
The years we wish, will half your charms
    impair;
The years we wish the better half will spare;
The victims of your eyes will bleed no more,
But all the beauties of your mind adore.
    —Jeffrey.

Blackbird

The birds have ceased their songs,
All save the blackbird, that from yon tall
    ash,
'Mid Pinkie's greenery, from his mellow
    throat,
In adoration of the setting sun,
Chants forth his evening hymn. —Moir.

O Blackbird! sing me something well:
While all the neighbors shoot thee round,
I keep smooth plats of fruitful ground,
Where thou may'st warble, eat and dwell.
—Tennyson.

Golden Bill! Golden Bill!
Lo, the peep of day;
All the air is cool and still,
From the elm-tree on the hill,
Chant away:
*   *   *   *   *   *
Let thy loud and welcome lay
Pour alway
Few notes but strong.
—Montgomery.

How sweet the harmonies of the afternoon!
The Blackbird sings along the sunny breeze
His ancient song of leaves, and summer boon;
Rich breath of hayfields streams thro' whispering trees;
And birds of morning trim their bustling wings,
And listen fondly—while the Blackbird sings. —Frederick Tennyson.

Blacksmith

And he sang: "Hurra for my handiwork!"
And the red sparks lit the air;
Not alone for the blade was the bright steel made;
And he fashioned the first ploughshare.
—Chas. Mackay.

Under a spreading chestnut tree
The village smithy stands;
The smith a mighty man is he,
With large and sinewy hands;
And the muscles of his brawny arms
Are strong as iron bands.
—Longfellow.

And the smith his iron measures hammered to the anvil's chime;
Thanking God, whose boundless wisdom makes the flowers of poesy bloom
In the forge's dust and cinders, in the tissues of the loom. —Longfellow.

Blame

Man only blames himself in order that he may be praised.—La Rochefoucauld.

A man takes contradiction and advice much more easily than people think, only he will not bear it when violently given, even though it be well founded. Hearts are flowers, they remain open to the soft-falling dew, but shut up in the violent downpour of rain.—Richter.

Blandishment

The maiden's blush lights the volcano in the lover's heart.—De Finod.

Charms strike the sight, but merit wins the soul.—Pope.

One only needs to see a smile in a white crape bonnet in order to enter the palace of dreams.—Victor Hugo.

For beauty is the bait which, with delight, doth man allure for to enlarge his kind.—Spenser.

Expression alone can invest beauty with supreme and lasting command over the eye.—Fuseli.

Admiration and love are like being intoxicated with champagne; judgment and friendship are like being enlivened. —Dr. Johnson.

Her eyes, her lips, her cheeks, her shape, her features, seem to be drawn by Love's own hand; by Love himself in love.—Dryden.

Her face had a wonderful fascination in it. It was such a calm, quiet face, with the light of the rising soul shining so peacefully through it.—Longfellow.

The most fascinating women are those that can most enrich the everyday moments of existence. In a particular and attaching sense, they are those that can partake our pleasures and our pains in the liveliest and most devoted manner. Beauty is little without this; with it she is triumphant.—Leigh Hunt.

In the age of chivalry it was the beauty of woman alone that wrestled successfully against barbarism. She softened the rude manners of the warriors, and inspired the valorous knight with courage, generosity and honor, thus civilizing by the influence of her charms those whose hearts could not be touched by any other human power.—Alexander Walker.

Blessedness

True blessedness consisteth in a good life and a happy death.—Solon.

He alone is blessed who never was born.—Prior.

The harvest song of inward peace.—Mrs. Barbauld.

'T is not for mortals always to be blest.—Armstrong.

Blest is he whose heart is the home of the great dead and their great thoughts.—Bailey.

Blessedness is a whole eternity older than damnation.—Richter.

And let me tell you that every misery I miss is a new blessing.—Izaak Walton.

Blessedness consists in the accomplishment of our desires, and in our having only regular desires.—St. Augustine.

There is in man a higher than love of happiness; he can do without happiness, and instead thereof find blessedness.—Carlyle.

The beloved of the Almighty are the rich who have the humility of the poor, and the poor who have the magnanimity of the rich.—Saadi.

Blessings

Ill blows the wind that profits nobody.—Shakespeare.

Fall silently like dew on roses.—Dryden.

The blessing of the Lord, it maketh rich, and He addeth no sorrow with it.—Proverbs x. 22.

I dimly guess, from blessings known, of greater out of sight.—Whittier.

Blessings star forth forever; but a curse is like a cloud, it passes.—Bailey.

The benediction of these covering heavens fall on their heads like dew.—Shakespeare.

Words are as they are taken, and things are as they are used. There are even cursed blessings.—Bishop Hall.

A man's best things are nearest him, lie close about his feet.—R. M. Milnes.

Our blessings are the least heeded, because the most common events of life.—Hosea Ballou.

We mistake the gratuitous blessings of heaven for the fruits of our own industry.—L'Estrange.

How blessings brighten as they take their flight!—Young.

For blessings ever wait on virtuous deeds,
And though a late, a sure reward succeeds.
—Congreve.

Blessings on him who invented sleep.—Cervantes.

Reflect upon your present blessings, of which every man has many; not on your past misfortunes, of which all men have some.—Dickens.

To heal divisions, to relieve the oppress'd,
In virtue rich; in blessing others, bless'd.
—Homer.

Men live best upon a little; Nature has given to all the privilege of being happy, if they but knew how to use their gifts.—Claudianus.

Amid my list of blessings infinite,
Stands this the foremost, "That my heart has bled."
—Young.

Prosperity is the blessing of the Old Testament;
Adversity is the blessing of the New.
—Bacon.

Of many imagined blessings it may be doubted whether he that wants or possesses them had more reason to be satisfied with his lot.—Dr. Johnson.

Even the best things ill used become evils; and, contrarily, the worst things used well prove good.—Bishop Hall.

The blessings of fortune are the lowest; the next are the bodily advantages of strength and health; but the superlative blessings, in fine, are those of the mind.—L'Estrange.

The good things of life are not to be had singly, but come to us with a mixture; like a school-boy's holiday, with a task affixed to the tail of it.—Charles Lamb.

Not to understand a treasure's worth,
Till time has stolen away the slightest good,
Is cause of half the poverty we feel,
And makes the world the wilderness it is.
—Cowper.

It is too generally true that all that is required to make men unmindful what they owe to God for any blessing is that they should receive that blessing often enough and regularly enough.
—Bishop Whately.

Blessings we enjoy daily; and for most of them, because they be so common, most men forget to pay their praises; but let not us, because it is a sacrifice so pleasing to Him that made the sun and us, and still protects us, and gives us flowers and showers and meat and content.—Izaak Walton.

Blessings be with them, and eternal praise
Who gave us nobler loves, and nobler cares,
The poets, who on earth have made us heirs
Of truth and pure delight, by heavenly lays.
—Wordsworth.

Nothing raises the price of a blessing like its removal; whereas it was its continuance which should have taught us its value. There are three requisitions to the proper enjoyment of earthly blessings,—a thankful reflection on the goodness of the Giver, a deep sense of our unworthiness, a recollection of the uncertainty of long possessing them. The first would make us grateful; the second, humble; and the third, moderate.—Hannah More.

Heaven may have happiness as utterly unknown to us as the gift of perfect vision would be to a man born blind. If we consider the inlets of pleasure from five senses only, we may be sure that the same Being who created us could have given us five hundred, if He had pleased.—Colton.

Blindness

O loss of sight, of thee I most complain!
Blind among enemies, O worse than chains,
Dungeon, or beggary, or decrepit age!
—Milton.

None so blind as those that will not see.—Mathew Henry.

He that is strucken blind cannot forget
The precious treasure of his eyesight lost.
—Shakespeare.

But love is blind, and lovers cannot see
The pretty follies that themselves commit.
—Shakespeare.

O dark, dark, dark, amid the blaze of noon,
Irrecoverably dark! total eclipse,
Without all hope of day. —Milton.

He whom nature thus bereaves,
Is ever fancy's favourite child;
For thee enchanted dreams she weaves
Of changeful beauty, bright and wild.
—Mrs. Osgood.

Oh, say! what is that thing called light,
Which I must ne'er enjoy?
What are the blessings of the sight?
Oh, tell your poor blind boy!
—Colley Cibber.

Ye have a world of light,
When love in the loved rejoices;
But the blind man's home is the house of night,
And its beings are empty voices.
—Bulwer.

These eyes tho' clear
To outward view of blemish or of spot,
Bereft of light, their seeing have forgot,
Nor to their idle orbs doth sight appear
Of sun, or moon, or star, throughout the year,
Or man, or woman. Yet I argue not
Against Heaven's hand or will, nor have a jot
Of heart or hope; but still bear up and steer
Right onward. —Milton.

O happiness of blindness! now no beauty
Inflames my lust; no other's goods my envy,
Or misery my pity; no man's wealth
Draws my respect; nor poverty my scorn,
Yet still I see enough! man to himself
Is a large prospect, raised above the level
Of his low creeping thoughts; if then I have
A world within myself, that world shall be
My empire; there I'll reign, commanding freely,
And willingly obey'd, secure from fear
Of foreign forces, or domestic treasons.
—Denham.

The blindness of men is the most dangerous effect of their pride; it seems to nourish and augment it; it deprives them of knowledge of remedies which can solace their miseries and can cure their faults.—La Rochefoucauld.

This fellow must have a rare understanding;
For nature recompenseth the defects
Of one part with redundance in another;
Blind men have excellent memories, and the tongue
Thus indisposed, there's treasure in the intellect.   —Shirley.

Bliss

The bliss that can be told is but half-bliss.—Bulwer-Lytton.

And for our country 'tis a bliss to die.—Homer.

Every one speaks of it,—who has known it?—Mme. Necker.

Pure felicity is reserved for the heavenly life; it grows not in an earthly soil.—Chapin.

Who falls from all he knows of bliss, cares little into what abyss.—Byron.

The way to bliss lies not on beds of down,
And he that had no cross deserves no crown.
                              —Quarles.

Some place the bliss in action, some in ease,
Those call it pleasure, and contentment these.   —Pope.

Though duller thoughts succeed, the bliss e'en of a moment still is bliss.—Joanna Baillie.

Vain, very vain, my weary search to find
That bliss which only centres in the mind.
                              —Goldsmith.

Domestic happiness, thou only bliss
Of Paradise, that has survived the fall!
                              —Cowper.

We may anticipate bliss, but who ever drank of that enchanted cup unalloyed?—Colton.

Condition, circumstance, is not the thing;
Bliss is the same in subject or in king.
                              —Pope.

Health is the vital principle of bliss,
And exercise of health.   —Thomson.

The happiest woman sees not gladness alone reflected from her mirror;
its surface will inevitably be sometimes dimmed with sighs.—Mme. Louise Colet.

Alas! by some degree of woe
  We every bliss must gain;
The heart can ne'er a transport know,
  That never feels a pain.
                              —Lord Lyttleton.

Bliss in possession will not last;
Remember'd joys are never past;
At once the fountain, stream, and sea,
They were,—they are,—they yet shall be.
                              —Montgomery.

Blockhead

Heaven and earth fight in vain against a dunce!—Schiller.

A blockhead cannot come in, nor go away, nor sit, nor rise, nor stand, like a man of sense.—Bruyère.

There never was any party, faction, sect, or cabal whatsoever, in which the most ignorant were not the most violent; for a bee is not a busier animal than a blockhead.—Pope.

Blood

Blood is a juice of rarest quality.—Goethe.

There is no caste in blood.—Edwin Arnold.

Blood follows blood.—De Foe.

Some kind of pace may be got out of the veriest jade by the near prospect of oats; but the thoroughbred has the spur in his blood.—Lowell.

Noble blood! bah! What blood is more noble or so pure as that of the lion? And yet he is only a brute. It is merit, education and virtue, not blood, that lift men above the level of the brutes.—Michael le Faucheur.

Bluebell

Oh! roses and lilies are fair to see;
But the wild bluebell is the flower for me.
                              —Louisa A. Meredith.

Hang-head Bluebell,
Bending like Moses' sister over Moses,
Full of a secret that thou dar'st not tell!
                              —George MacDonald.

Bluebird

Whither away, Bluebird,
Whither away?
The blast is chill, yet in the upper sky,
Thou still canst find the color of thy wing,
The hue of May.
Warbler, why speed thy southern flight? ah,
why,
Thou too, whose song first told us of the
Spring?
Whither away?
—E. C. Stedman.

Bluntness

I have neither wit, nor words, nor worth,
Nor actions, nor utterance, nor the power
of speech,
To stir men's blood: I only speak right on.
—Shakespeare.

This is some fellow,
Who having been prais'd for bluntness, doth
affect
A saucy roughness, and constrains the garb,
Quite from his nature: he can't flatter, he!
An honest mind and plain,—he must speak
truth!
And they will take it so; if not he's plain.
These kind of knaves I know, which in this
plainness
Harbor more craft, and far corrupter ends,
Than twenty silly, ducking observants,
That stretch their duty nicely.
—Shakespeare.

Blushes

The heart's meteors tilting in the
face.—Shakespeare.

Blushes are the rainbow of modesty.
—Mme. Necker.

The sunset glow of self-possession.—
Chamfort.

Young roses kindled into thought.—
Moore.

Blushing is the livery of virtue.—
Bacon.

Blushes are the echo of sensibility.—
Mme. de Salm.

The glow of the angel in woman.—
Mrs. Balfour.

Innocence is not accustomed to blush.
—Molière.

The lily and the rose in her fair face
striving for precedence.—N. P. Willis.

Blushes cannot be counterfeited.—
Marguerite de Valois.

The man that blushes is not quite a
brute.—Young.

Do good by stealth, and blush to find
it fame.—Pope.

Such war of white and red within
her cheeks.—Shakespeare.

The bloom of young desire and purple light of love.—Gay.

A blush is the sign which Nature
hangs out to show where chastity and
honor dwell.—Gotthold.

Men blush less for their crimes than
for their weaknesses and vanity.—La
Bruyère.

The lilies faintly to the roses yield,
As on thy lovely cheek, they struggling vie.
—Hoffman.

The rose was budded in her cheek,
just opening to the view.—Mallet.

The inconvenience or the beauty of
the blush, which is the greater?—
Madame Necker.

One blushes oftener from the wounds
of self-love than from modesty.—Mme.
Guibert.

The blush is beautiful, but it is some
times inconvenient.—Goldoni.

Like the last beam of evening thrown
on a white cloud, just seen and gone.—
Walter Scott.

They teach us to dance; O that they
could teach us to blush, did it cost a
guinea a glow!—Madame Deluzy.

Playful blushes, that seemed nought
But luminous escapes of thought.
—Moore.

The ambiguous livery worn alike by
modesty and shame.—Mrs. Balfour.

A blush is no language; only a dubious flag-signal which may mean either
of two contradictories.—George Eliot

On her cheek blushes the richness of an autumn sky with ever-shifting beauty.—Longfellow.

Like the faint streaks of light broke loose from darkness, and dawning into blushes.—Dryden.

The rising blushes, which her cheek o'erspread,
Are opening roses in the lily's bed.
—Gay.

The eloquent blood spoke in her cheeks, and so distinctly wrought, you might have almost said her body thought.—Donne.

The blush is nature's alarm at the approach of sin, and her testimony to the dignity of virtue.—Fuller.

Troubled blood through his pale face was seen to come and go, with tidings from his heart, as it a running messenger had been.—Spenser.

Bid the cheek be ready with a blush, modest as Morning when she coldly eyes the youthful Phœbus.—Shakespeare.

A faint blush melting through the light of thy transparent cheek like a rose-leaf bathed in dew.—Whittier.

From every blush that kindles in thy cheeks,
Ten thousand little loves and graces spring
To revel in the roses. —Nicholas Rowe.

Once he saw a youth blushing, and addressed him, "Courage, my boy; that is the complexion of virtue."—Diogenes Lærtius.

Such a blush
In the midst of brown was born,
Like red poppies grown with corn.
—Hood.

Her cheeks blushing, and withal, when she was spoken to, a little smiling, were like roses when their leaves are with a little breath stirred.—Sir P. Sidney.

Had he not long read the heart's hushed secret in the soft, dark eye, lighted at his approach, and on the cheek, coloring all crimson at his lightest look?—L. E. Landon.

The bold defiance of a woman is the certain sign of her shame,—when she has once ceased to blush, it is because she has too much to blush for.—Talleyrand.

An Arab, by his earnest gaze,
Has clothed a lovely maid with blushes;
A smile within his eyelids plays
And into words his longing gushes.
—Wm. R. Alger.

One day, a daughter of Aristotle, Pythias by name, was asked what color pleased her most. She replied, "The color with which modesty suffuses the face of simple, inoffensive men."—Joubert.

Give me the eloquent cheek,
When blushes burn and die
Like thine its changes speak,
The spirit's purity. —Mrs. Osgood.

Forgot the blush that virgin fears impart
To modest cheeks, and borrowed one from art.
—Cowper.

I pity bashful men, who feel the pain
Of fancied scorn and undeserved disdain,
And bear the marks upon a blushing face
Of needless shame, and self-impos'd disgrace.
—Cowper.

The blushing cheek speaks modest mind,
The lips befitting words most kind,
The eye does tempt to love's desire,
And seems to say 'tis "Cupid's fire."
—Harrington.

———the blush is formed—and flies—
Nor owns reflection's calm control;
It comes, it deepens—fades and dies,
A gush of feeling from the soul.
—Mrs. Dinnies.

By noting of the lady I have mark'd
A thousand blushing apparitions
To start into her face, a thousand innocent shames,
In angel whiteness bear away those blushes.
—Shakespeare.

Who has not seen that feeling born of flame
Crimson the cheek at mention of a name?
The rapturous touch of some divine surprise
Flash deep suffusion of celestial dyes:
When hands clasped hands, and lips to lips were pressed,
And the heart's secret was at once confessed?
—Abraham Coles.

Girls blush, sometimes, because they are
   alive,
Half wishing they were dead to save the
   shame.
The sudden blush devours them, neck and
   brow;
They have drawn too near the fire of life,
   like gnats,
And flare up bodily, wings and all.
   —E. B. Browning.

Though looks and words, by the
strong mastery of his practiced will,
are overruled, the mounting blood betrays an impulse in its secret spring
too deep for his control.—Southey.

Blustering

A killing tongue and a quiet sword.
—Shakespeare.

Splitting the air with noise.—Shakespeare.

The devil may be bullied, but not the
Deity.—W. R. Alger.

Loudness is impotence.—Lavater.

Ever the characteristic manners of
cowardice.—Edward Everett.

Bold at the council board, but cautious in the field.—Dryden.

The empty vessel makes the greatest
sound.—Shakespeare.

They that have voice of lions and act
of hares,—are they not monsters?—
Shakespeare.

Without big words, how could many
people say small things?—J. Petit-
Senn.

A brave man is sometimes a des-
perado; a bully is always a coward.—
Haliburton.

Wine and the sun will make vinegar
without any shouting to help them.—
George Eliot.

True courage scorns to vent her
prowess in a storm of words; and to
the valiant action speaks alone.—Smollett.

There are braying men in the world,
as well as braying asses; for what is

loud and senseless talking any other
than a way of braying?—L'Estrange.

The insignificant, the empty, is usually the loud; and after the manner of
a drum, is louder even because of its
emptiness.—Carlyle.

It is with narrow-souled people as
with narrow-necked bottles; the less
they have in them, the more noise they
make in pouring it out.—Pope.

That, of course, they are many in
number, or that, after all, they are,
other than the little, shriveled, meagre,
hopping, though loud and troublesome,
insects of the hour.—Burke.

What art thou? Have not I
An arm as big as thine? A heart as big?
Thy words, I grant, are bigger, for I wear
   not
My dagger in my mouth. —Shakespeare.

For highest looks have not the highest mind,
   Nor haughty words most full of highest
      thought;
But are like bladders blown up with the
   wind,
That being prick'd evanish into nought.
   —Spenser.

Because half a dozen grasshoppers
under a fern make the field ring with
their importunate chink, whilst thousands of great cattle, reposing beneath
the shadow of the British oak, chew
the cud and are silent, pray do not
imagine that those who make the noise
are the only inhabitants of the field.—
Burke.

Those that are the loudest in their
threats are the weakest in the execution of them. In springing a mine,
that which has done the most extensive
mischief makes the smallest report;
and again, if we consider the effect of
lightning, it is probable that he that is
killed by it hears no noise; but the
thunderclap which follows, and which
most alarms the ignorant, is the surest
proof of their safety.—Colton.

Boasting

Where boasting ends, there dignity
begins.—Young.

The less people speak of their greatness the more we think of it.—Bacon.

No more delay, vain boaster, but begin.—Dryden.

Where there is much pretension, much has been borrowed; nature never pretends.—Lavater.

It will come to pass that every braggart shall be found an ass.—Shakespeare.

The honor is overpaid when he that did the act is commentator.—Shirley.

Commonly they use their feet for defense, whose tongue is their weapon.—Sir P. Sidney.

Fools carry their daggers in their open mouths.—H. W. Shaw.

A gentleman that loves to hear himself talk will speak more in a minute than he will stand to in a month.—Shakespeare.

With all his tumid boasts, he's like the sword-fish, who only wears his weapon in his mouth.—Madden.

Self-laudation abounds among the unpolished; but nothing can stamp a man more sharply as ill-bred.—Charles Buxton.

The man that once did sell the
  lion's skin
While the beast lived, was killed
  with hunting him.—Shakespeare.

We wound our modesty, and make foul the clearness of our deservings, when of ourselves we publish them.—Shakespeare.

Conceit, more rich in matter than in words,
Brags of his substance, not of ornament:
They are but beggars that can count their
  worth.   —Shakespeare.

Men of real merit, and whose noble and glorious deeds we are ready to acknowledge, are yet not to be endured when they vaunt their own actions.—Æschines.

Boasting and bravado may exist in the breast even of the coward, if he is successful through a mere lucky hit; but a just contempt of an enemy can alone arise in those who feel that they are superior to their opponent by the prudence of their measures.—Thucydides.

There is this benefit in brag, that the speaker is unconsciously expressing his own ideal. Humor him by all means, draw it all out, and hold him to it.—Emerson.

Lord Bacon told Sir Edward Coke when he boasted, "The less you speak of your greatness, the more I shall think of it." Mirrors are the accompaniments of dandies, not heroes. The men of history were not perpetually looking in the glass to make sure of their own size. Absorbed in their work they did it, and did it so well that the wondering world saw them to be great, and labeled them accordingly.—Rev. S. Coley.

I know them, yea,
And what they weigh, even to the utmost
  scruple;
Scambling, out-facing, fashion-mong'ring
  boys,
That lie, and cog, and flout, deprave, and
  slander,
Go antickly, and show outward hideousness,
And speak off half a dozen dangerous words,
How they might hurt their enemies, if they
  durst;
And this is all.   —Shakespeare.

One man affirms that he has rode post a hundred miles in six hours: probably it is a lie; but supposing it to be true, what then? Why, he is a very good post-boy; that is all. Another asserts, and probably not without oaths, that he has drunk six or eight bottles of wine at a sitting; out of charity I will believe him a liar; for, if I do not, I must think him a beast.—Chesterfield.

Bobolink

Modest and shy as a nun is she;
  One weak chirp is her only note;
Braggarts and prince of braggarts is he,
  Pouring boasts from his little throat.
            —Bryant.

Robert of Lincoln's Quaker wife,
  Pretty and quiet, with plain brown wings,
Passing at home a patient life,
  Broods in the grass while her husband
  sings.   —Bryant.

When Nature had made all her birds,
  With no more cares to think on,
She gave a rippling laugh and out
  There flew a bobolink. —C. P. Cranch.

Bobolink! that in the meadow,
  Or beneath the orchard's shadow,
Keepest up a constant rattle
Joyous as my children's prattle,
Welcome to the north again.
  —Thos. Hill.

Out of the fragrant heart of bloom,
  The bobolinks are singing;
Out of the fragrant heart of bloom
The apple-tree whispers to the room,
"Why art thou but a nest of gloom
While the bobolinks are singing?"
  —W. D. Howells.

Body

What! know ye not that your body
is the temple of the Holy Ghost which
is in you, which ye have of God; and
ye are not your own?—Cor. vi, 19.

For of the soul the body form doth take,
For soul is form, and doth the body make.
  —Spenser.

Our body is a well-set clock, which
keeps good time; but if it be too much
or indiscreetly tampered with, the
alarum runs out before the hour.—
Bishop Hall.

Every physician knows, though metaphysicians know little about it, that
the laws which govern the animal machine are as certain and invariable as
those which guide the planetary system, and are as little within the control
of the human being who is subject
to them.—Priestley.

These limbs,—whence had we them;
this stormy force; this life-blood, with
its burning passion? They are dust
and shadow—a shadow system gathered round our me; wherein through
some moments or years, the divine
essence is to be revealed in the flesh.
—Carlyle.

God made the human body, and it is
by far the most exquisite and wonderful organization which has come to us
from the Divine hand. It is a study
for one's whole life. If an undevout
astronomer is mad, an undevout phys-
iologist is still madder.—Beecher.

Boldness

Fortune befriends the bold.—Dryden.

Fools rush in where angels fear to
tread.—Pope.

We make way for the man who
boldly pushes past us.—Bovee.

Carried away by the irresistible influence which is always exercised over
men's minds by a bold resolution in
critical circumstances.—Guizot.

It deserves to be considered that
boldness is ever blind, for it sees not
dangers and inconveniences. Whence
it is bad in council though good in
execution. The right use of bold persons, therefore, is that they never command in chief, but serve as seconds,
under the direction of others. For in
council it is good to see dangers, and
in execution not to see them unless
they are very great.—Bacon.

Bondage

A bond is necessary to complete our
being, only we must be careful that
the bond does not become bondage.—
Mrs. Jameson.

Bondage is hoarse, and may not
speak aloud.—Shakespeare.

Books

Books are embalmed minds.—Bovee.

A book is the only immortality.—
Rufus Choate.

A true book is an inspiration.—
Alexander H. Everett.

The medicine of the mind.—Dio-
dorus.

Books wind into the heart.—Hazlitt.

Law dies; books never.—Bulwer-
Lytton.

The virtue of books is to be read-
able.—Emerson.

Good books are true friends.—Bacon.

Medicine for the soul.—Inscription
over the door of the library at Thebes.

The monument of vanished mindes.
—Sir Wm. Davenant.

Books are not seldom talismans and spells.—Cowper.

Go, litel boke! go litel myn tregedie!
—Chaucer.

Books which are no books.—Charles Lamb.

A book may be as great a thing as a battle.—Disraeli.

Not many but good books.—Bayard Taylor.

Books, the children of the brain.—Swift.

My library was dukedom large enough.—Shakespeare.

Begin by reading thyself rather than books.—Rumi.

Deep versed in books and shallow in himself.—Milton.

Books are a languid pleasure.—Montaigne.

Beware you be not swallowed up in books.—John Wesley.

A multitude of books distracts the mind.—Seneca.

Books are sepulchres of thought.—Longfellow.

The worth of a book is a matter of expressed juices.—Bovee.

There is no book so poor that it would not be a prodigy if wholly made by a single man.—Johnson.

Learning hath gained most by those books by which printers have lost.—Fuller.

The last thing that we discover in writing a book is to know what to put at the beginning.—Pascal.

Every man is a volume if you know how to read him.—Channing.

There is nothing so imperishable as a book.—James Hain Friswell.

A good book is the best of friends, —the same to-day and forever.—Tupper.

Books are the legacies that a great genius leaves to mankind.—Addison.

We prize books, and they prize them most who are themselves wise.—Emerson.

There is no past so long as books shall live.—Bulwer-Lytton.

Next to acquiring good friends, the best acquisition is that of good books.
—Colton.

Great books, like large skulls, have often the least brains.—W. B. Clulow.

Those faithful mirrors, which reflect to our mind the minds of sages and heroes.—Gibbon.

We are as liable to be corrupted by books as by companions.—Fielding.

Books,—lighthouses erected in the great sea of time.—Whipple.

There was a time when the world acted upon books. Now books act upon the world.—Joubert.

It is always easy to shut a book, but not quite so easy to get rid of a lettered coxcomb.—Colton.

A small number of choice books are sufficient.—Voltaire.

Without grace no book can live, and with it the poorest may have its life prolonged.—Horace Walpole.

Books are true friends that will never flatter nor dissemble: be you but true to yourself, . . . and you shall need no other comfort.—Bacon.

Reading maketh a full man, conference a ready man, and writing an exact man.—Bacon.

He hath never fed of the dainties that are bred in a book.—Shakespeare.

No book can be so good, as to be profitable when negligently read.—Seneca.

Tis pleasant, sure, to see one's name in print;
A book's a book, although there's nothing in 't.   —Byron.

A taste for books, which is still the pleasure and glory of my life.—Gibbon.

The burning soul, the burden'd mind,
In books alone companions find.
                        ——Mrs. Hale.

It is a sure evidence of a good book if it pleases us more and more as we grow older.—Lichtenberg.

Every great book is an action, and every great action is a book.—Martin Luther.

Books are the best things, well used; abused, among the worst.—Emerson.

Come, and take choice of all my library,
And so beguile thy sorrow.
                        —Shakespeare.

              'Tis in books the chief
Of all perfections to be plain and brief.
                        —Butler.

Books cannot always please, however good,
Minds are not ever craving for their food.
                        —Crabbe.

When a new book comes out, I read an old one.—Rogers.

How science dwindles, and how volumes swell!—Young.

A first book has some of the sweetness of a first love.—Willmott.

The true University of these days is a collection of books.—Carlyle.

A book should be luminous, but not voluminous.—Bovee.

Books must follow sciences, and not sciences books.—Bacon.

Wise books for half the truths they hold are honored tombs.—George Eliot.

Books are the ever-burning lamps of accumulated wisdom.—G. W. Curtis.

These hoards of wealth you can unlock at will.—Wordsworth.

Some books are to be tasted, others to be swallowed, and some few to be chewed and digested.—Bacon.

Let every man, if possible, gather some good books under his roof.—Channing.

Books think for me. I can read anything which I call a book.—Lamb.

It is not with the living that we should live, but with the dead.—Chamfort.

Let us digest them; otherwise they enter our memory, but not our minds.—Seneca.

A blessing on the printer's art!—
Books are the mentors of the heart.
                        —Mrs. Hale.

Books that you may carry to the fire, and hold readily in your hand, are the most useful after all.—Johnsoniana.

In proportion as society refines, new books must ever become more necessary.—Goldsmith.

"Books," says my lord Bacon, "should have no patrons but truth and reason."—Colton.

Some said, John, print it, others said, Not so;
Some said, it might do good, others said, No.   —Bunyan

The pleasant books, that silently among our household treasures take familiar places.—Longfellow.

Old wood to burn, old wine to drink, old friends to trust, old books to read.—Alonzo of Arragon.

Books bear him up awhile, and make him try to swim with bladders of philosophy.—Rochester.

Come, my best friends, my books! and lead me on.—Cowley.

All the known world, excepting only savage nations, is governed by books. —Voltaire.

The great objection to new books is that they prevent our reading old ones.—Joubert.

I entrench myself in my books, equally against sorrow and the weather.—Leigh Hunt.

That is a good book which is opened with expectation and closed with profit.—Alcott.

Some books are only cursorily to be tasted of.—Fuller.

Books that are books are all that you want, and there are but half a dozen in any thousand.—Thoreau.

The writings of the wise are the only riches our posterity cannot squander.—Landor.

It is nearly an axiom that people will not be better than the books they read.—Dr. Potter.

All books grow homilies by time; they are Temples, at once, and Landmarks.
                    —Bulwer-Lytton.

In the highest civilization the book is still the highest delight.—Emerson.

"There is no book so bad," said the bachelor, "but something good may be found in it."—Cervantes.

Thou art a plant sprung up to wither never.
But, like a laurel, to grow green forever.
                    —Herrick.

A man will turn over half a library to make one book.—Samuel Johnson.

Books are the immortal sons deifying their sires.—Plato.

The love of books is a love which requires neither justification, apology, nor defence.—Langford.

Every book is, in an intimate sense, a circular-letter to the friends of him who writes it.—R. L. Stevenson.

For books are as meats and viands are; some of good, some of evil substance.—Milton.

Leaving us heirs to amplest heritages
Of all the best thoughts of the greatest sages,
And giving tongues unto the silent dead!
                    —Longfellow.

No matter what his rank or position may be, the lover of books is the richest and the happiest of the children of men.—Langford.

We call some books immortal! Do they live?
If so, believe me, Time hath made them pure.
In Books, the veriest wicked rest in peace.
                    —Bulwer-Lytton.

As you grow ready for it, somewhere or other you will find what is needful for you in a book.—George MacDonald.

A good book is fruitful of other books; it perpetuates its fame from age to age, and makes eras in the lives of its readers.—Alcott.

Books, like proverbs, receive their chief value from the stamp and esteem of ages through which they have passed.—Sir W. Temple.

The quantity of books in a library is often a cloud of witnesses of the ignorance of the owner.—Oxenstiern.

Worthy books are not companions, they are solitudes; we lose ourselves in them, and all our cares.—Bailey.

If a book come from the heart, it will contrive to reach other hearts; all art and authorcraft are of small amount to that.—Carlyle.

A book may be compared to the life of your neighbor. If it be good, it cannot last too long; if bad, you cannot get rid of it too early.—H. Brooke.

He who loves not books before he comes to thirty years of age will hardly love them enough afterwards to understand them.—Clarendon.

That wonderful book, while it obtains admiration from the most fastidious critics, is loved by those who are too simple to admire it.—Macaulay.

Some books are drenched sands, on which a great soul's wealth lies all in heaps, like a wrecked argosy.—Alexander Smith.

That book in many's eyes doth share the glory,
That in gold clasps locks in the golden story. —Shakespeare.

Employ your time in improving yourselves by other men's documents: so shall you come easily by what others have labored hard for.—Socrates.

Old books, as you well know, are books of the world's youth, and new books are the fruits of its age.—O. W. Holmes.

The images of men's wits and knowledge remain in books, exempted from the worry of time and capable of perpetual renovation.—Bacon.

All that mankind has done, thought, gained, or been,—it is lying as in magic preservation in the pages of books.—Carlyle.

Strong as man and tender as woman, they welcome you in every mood, and never turn from you in distress. —J. A. Langford.

Pray thee, take care, that tak'st my book in hand,
To read it well; that is to understand. —Ben Jonson.

The foolishest book is a kind of leaky boat on a sea of wisdom; some of the wisdom will get in anyhow.— O. W. Holmes.

In every man's memory, with the hours when life culminated are usually associated certain books which met his views.—Emerson.

If time is precious, no book that will not improve by repeated readings deserves to be read at all.—Carlyle.

The greatest pleasure in life is that of reading while we are young. I have had as much of this pleasure perhaps as any one.—Hazlitt.

Books should to one of these four ends conduce,
For wisdom, piety, delight, or use.
—Sir John Denham.

How many books there are whose reputation is made that would not obtain it were it now to make!— Joubert.

Many books owe their success to the good memories of their authors and the bad memories of their readers.— Colton.

Books are the negative pictures of thought, and the more sensitive the mind that receives their images, the more nicely the finest lines are reproduced.—Holmes.

He that studies books alone, will know how things ought to be; and he that studies men will know how things are.—Colton.

We should have a glorious conflagration if all who cannot put fire into their works would only consent to put their works into the fire.—Colton.

In the best books great men talk to us, give us their most precious thoughts, and pour their souls into ours.—Channing.

Books are men of higher stature, and the only men that speak aloud for future times to hear.—Mrs. Browning.

A good book is the precious lifeblood of a master spirit, embalmed and treasured up on purpose to a life beyond life.—Milton.

God be thanked for books. They are the voices of the distant and the dead, and make us heirs of the spiritual life of past ages.—Channing.

Here, in the country, my books are my sole occupation; books my sure solace, and refuge from frivolous cares. Books the calmers, as well as the instruction of the mind.—Mrs. Inchbald.

As good almost kill a man as kill a good book; who kills a man kills a reasonable creature, God's image; but he who destroys a good book kills reason itself.—Milton.

It is with books as with men: a very small number play a great part; the rest are confounded with the multitude.—Voltaire.

It is thought and digestion which makes books serviceable, and gives health and vigor to the mind.—Thomas Fuller.

If a book really wants the patronage of a great name, it is a bad book; and if it be a good book, it wants it not.—Colton.

Men often discover their affinity to each other by the mutual love they have for a book.—Samuel Smiles.

A book! oh, rare one! be not, as in this fangled world, a garment nobler than it covers.—Shakespeare.

He who loveth a book will never want a faithful friend, a wholesome counsellor, a cheerful companion, or an effectual comforter.—Barrow.

Books, we know,
Are a substantial world, both pure and good;
Round these, with tendrils strong as flesh and blood,
Our pastime and our happiness will grow.
—Wordsworth.

The scholar only knows how dear these silent yet eloquent companions of pure thoughts and innocent hours become in the season of adversity.—Washington Irving.

In books lies the soul of the whole Past Time; the articulate audible voice of the Past, when the body and material substance of it has altogether vanished like a dream.—Carlyle.

Books are the legacies that genius leaves to mankind, to be delivered down from generation to generation, as presents to the posterity of those that are yet unborn.—Addison.

It is books that teach us to refine our pleasures when young, and which, having so taught us, enable us to recall them with satisfaction when old.—Leigh Hunt.

Books are necessary to correct the vices of the polite; but those vices are ever changing, and the antidote should be changed accordingly—should still be new.—Goldsmith.

Many books require no thought from those who read them, and for a simple reason,—they made no such demand upon those who wrote them.—Colton.

It is chiefly through books that we enjoy intercourse with superior minds; and these invaluable communications are within the reach of all.—Mme. de Genlis.

If the crowns of all the kingdoms of Europe were laid down at my feet in exchange for my books and my love of reading, I would spurn them all.—Fénelon.

When a book raises your spirit, and inspires you with noble and courageous feelings, seek for no other rule to judge the work by; it is good, and made by a good workman.—Bruyère.

Our favorites are few; since only what rises from the heart reaches it, being caught and carried on the tongues of men wheresoever love and letters journey.—Alcott.

There is a kind of physiognomy in the titles of books no less than in the faces of men, by which a skilful observer will as well know what to expect from the one as the other.—Butler.

Books are the true levellers. They give to all who faithfully use them the society, the spiritual presence, of the best and greatest of our race.—Channing.

The profit of books is according to the sensibility of the reader. The profoundest thought or passion sleeps as in a mine, until an equal mind and heart finds and publishes it.—Emerson.

When self-interest inclines a man to print, he should consider that the purchaser expects a pennyworth for his penny, and has reason to asperse his honesty if he finds himself deceived.—Shenstone.

Do not believe that a book is good, if in reading it thou dost not become more contented with thy existence, if it does not rouse up in thee most generous feelings.—Lavater.

To buy books only because they were published by an eminent printer, is much as if a man should buy clothes that did not fit him, only because made by some famous tailor.—Pope.

The past but lives in words; a thousand ages were blank if books had not evoked their ghosts, and kept the pale, unbodied shades to warn us from fleshless lips.—Bulwer-Lytton.

If the secret history of books could be written, and the author's private thoughts and meanings noted down alongside of his story, how many insipid volumes would become interesting, and dull tales excite the reader.—Thackeray.

Books, to judicious compilers, are useful,—to particular arts and professions absolutely necessary,—to men of real science they are tools; but more are tools to them.—Johnson.

Many a man lives a burden upon the earth; but a good book is the precious life-blood of a master spirit, embalmed and treasured up on purpose for a life beyond life.—Milton.

Homeliness is almost as great a merit in a book as in a house, if the reader would abide there. It is next to beauty, and a very high art.—Thoreau.

Plays and romances sell as well as books of devotion, but with this difference,—more people read the former than buy them, and more buy the latter than read them.—T. Hughes.

Men love better books which please them than those which instruct. Since

their ennui troubles them more than their ignorance, they prefer being amused to being informed.—L'Abbé Dubois.

Most books fail, not so much from a want of ability in their authors, as from an absence in their productions of a thorough development of their ability.—Bovee.

Books are faithful repositories, which may be awhile neglected or forgotten, but when they are opened again, will again impart their instruction.—Jonson.

Without books God is silent, justice dormant, natural science at a stand, philosophy lame, letters dumb, and all things involved in Cimmerian darkness.—Bartholin.

Those who are conversant with books well know how often they mislead us when we have not a living monitor at hand to assist us in comparing practice with theory.—Junius.

I like books. I was born and bred among them, and have the easy feeling when I get in their presence, that a stable-boy has among horses.—O. W. Holmes.

Gentlemen use books as gentlewomen handle their flowers, who in the morning stick them in their heads, and at night strawe them at their heeles.—Lyly.

Oh, but books are such safe company! They keep your secrets well; they never boast that they made your eyes glisten, or your cheek flush, or your heart throb.—Mrs. S. P. Parton.

Properly speaking, we learn from those books only that we cannot judge. The author of a book that I am competent to criticise would have to learn from me.—Goethe.

Silent companions of the lonely hour,
Friends, who can alter or forsake,
Who for inconstant roving have no power,
And all neglect, perforce, must calmly
    take.   —Mrs. Norton.

I have somewhere seen it observed that we should make the same use of a book that the bee does of a flower: she steals sweets from it, but does not injure it.—Colton.

Nothing ought to be more weighed than the nature of books recommended by public authority. So recommended, they soon form the character of the age.—Burke.

No man writes a book without meaning something, though he may not have the faculty of writing consequentially and expressing his meaning.—Addison.

Of all the things which man can do or make here below, by far the most momentous, wonderful, and worthy are the things we call books.—Carlyle.

Be as careful of the books you read as of the company you keep, for your habits and character will be as much influenced by the former as the latter.—Paxton Hood.

I love to lose myself in other men's minds. When I am not walking, I am reading; I cannot sit and think. Books think for me.
—Charles Lamb.

The pleasant books, that silently among Our household treasures take familiar places, And are to us as if a living tongue Spake from the printed leaves or pictured faces!
—Longfellow.

In the poorest cottage are Books: is one Book, wherein for several thousands of years the spirit of man has found light, and nourishment, and an interpreting response to whatever is Deepest in him.—Carlyle.

After the pleasure of possessing books there is hardly anything more pleasant than that of speaking of them, and of communicating to the public the innocent richness of thought which we have acquired by the culture of letters.—Nodier.

It is with books as with women, where a certain plainness of manner and of dress is more engaging than that glare of paint and airs and apparel which may dazzle the eye, but reaches not the affections.—Hume.

A book is a friend whose face is constantly changing. If you read it when you are recovering from an illness, and return to it years after, it is changed surely, with the change in yourself.—Andrew Lang.

Books are the true metempsychosis, —they are the symbol and presage of immortality. The dead men are scattered, and none shall find them. Behold they are here! they do but sleep. —Beecher.

He that will have no books but those that are scarce evinces about as correct a taste in literature as he would do in friendship who would have no friends but those whom all the rest of the world have sent to Coventry.—Colton.

There are persons who flatter themselves that the size of their works will make them immortal. They pile up reluctant quarto upon solid folio, as if their labors, because they are gigantic, could contend with truth and heaven! —Junius.

I armed her against the censures of the world; showed her that books were sweet unreproaching companions to the miserable, and that if they could not bring us to enjoy life, they would at least teach us to endure it.—Goldsmith.

To divert at any time a troublesome fancy, run to thy books; they presently fix thee to them, and drive the other out of thy thoughts. They always receive thee with the same kindness.—Fuller.

Mankind are creatures of books, as well as of other circumstances; and such they eternally remain,—proofs, that the race is a noble and believing race, and capable of whatever books can stimulate.—Leigh Hunt.

Some new books it is necessary to read,—part for the information they contain, and others in order to acquaint one's self with the state of literature in the age in which one lives; but I would rather read too few than too many.—Lord Dudley.

Nothing can supply the place of books. They are cheering or soothing companions in solitude, illness, affliction. The wealth of both continents would not compensate for the good they impart.—Channing.

The Wise
(Minstrel or Sage), out of their books are clay;
But in their books, as from their graves they rise,
Angels—that, side by side, upon our way,
Walk with and warn us!
—Bulwer-Lytton.

Many readers judge of the power of a book by the shock it gives their feelings,—as some savage tribes determine the power of their muskets by their recoil; that being considered best which fairly prostrates the purchaser. —Longfellow.

There is this value in books, that they enable us to converse with the dead. There is something in this beyond the mere intrinsic worth of what they have left us.—Brydges.

In looking round me seeking for miserable resources against the heaviness of time, I open a book, and I say to myself, as the cat to the fox: I have only one good turn, but I need no other.—Madame Necker.

A man ought to inquire and find out what he really and truly has an appetite for; what suits his constitution; and that, doctors tell him, is the very thing he ought to have in general. And so with books.—Carlyle.

Learning is more profound
When in few solid authors 't may be found;
A few good books, digested well, do feed
The mind; much cloys, and doth ill humors breed.   —Robert Heath.

In science, read, by preference, the newest works; in literature, the oldest. The classic literature is always modern. New books revive and redecorate old ideas; old books suggest and invigorate new ideas.—Bulwer-Lytton.

What a joy is there in a good book, writ by some great master of thought, who breaks into beauty as in summer the meadow into grass and dandelions

and violets, with geraniums and manifold sweetness.—Theodore Parker.

We ought to regard books as we do sweetmeats, not wholly to aim at the pleasantest, but chiefly to respect the wholesomest; not forbidding either, but approving the latter most.—Plutarch.

No man should consider so highly of himself as to think he can receive but little light from books, nor so meanly as to believe he can discover nothing but what is to be learned from them.—Dr. Johnson.

My favorite books have a personality and complexion as distinctly drawn as if the author's portrait were framed into the paragraphs and smiled upon me as I read his illustrated pages.—Alcott.

Books, dear books.
Have been, and are my comforts; morn and night,
Adversity, prosperity, at home,
Abroad, health, sickness—good or ill report,
The same firm friends; the same refreshment rich,
And source of consolation. —Dr. Dodd.

By cultivating an interest in a few good books which contain the result of the toil or the quintessence of the genius of some of the most gifted thinkers of the world, we need not live on the marsh and in the mists. The slopes and ridges invite us.—T. Starr King.

Some future strain, in which the muse shall tell
How science dwindles, and how volumes swell.
How commentators each dark passage shun,
And hold their farthing candle to the sun.
—Young.

Of many large volumes the index is the best portion and the usefullest. A glance through the casement gives whatever knowledge of the interior is needful. An epitome is only a book shortened; and as a general rule, the worth increases as the size lessens.—Willmott.

One must be rich in thought and character to owe nothing to books, though preparation is necessary to profitable reading; and the less reading is better than more;—book-struck men are of all readers least wise, however knowing or learned.—Alcott.

The books which help you most are those which make you think the most. The hardest way of learning is by easy reading: but a great book that comes from a great thinker—it is a ship of thought, deep freighted with truth and with beauty.—Theodore Parker.

We ought to reverence books, to look at them as useful and mighty things. If they are good and true, whether they are about religion or politics, farming, trade, or medicine, they are the message of Christ, the maker of all things, the teacher of all truth.—Rev. C. Kingsley.

Books are not absolutely dead things, but do contain a progeny of life in them to be as active as that soul was whose progeny they are; nay, they do preserve as in a vial the purest efficacy and extraction of that living intellect that bred them.—Milton.

Good books are to the young mind what the warming sun and the refreshing rain of spring are to the seeds which have lain dormant in the frosts of winter. They are more, for they may save from that which is worse than death, as well as bless with that which is better than life.—Horace Mann.

There are many virtues in books, but the essential value is the adding of knowledge to our stock by the record of new facts, and, better, by the record of intuitions which distribute facts, and are the formulas which supersede all histories.—Emerson.

In a well-written book we are presented with the maturest reflections, or the happiest flights of a mind of uncommon excellence. It is impossible that we can be much accustomed to such companions without attaining some resemblance to them.—William Godwin.

You, O Books, are the golden vessels of the temple, the arms of the clerical

militia with which the missiles of the most wicked are destroyed; fruitful olives, vines of Engaddi, fig-trees knowing no sterility; burning lamps to be ever held in the hand.—Richard Aungervyle.

Books, like friends, should be few, and well chosen. Thou mayst as well expect to grow strong by always eating as wiser by always reading. Too much overcharges nature, and turns more into disease than nourishment. 'Tis thought and digestion which makes books serviceable, and gives health and vigor to the mind.—Fuller.

There is no such thing as a worthless book, though there are some far worse than worthless; no book that is not worth preserving, if its existence may be tolerated: as there may be some men whom it may be proper to hang, but none who should be suffered to starve.—Coleridge.

Books are a part of man's prerogative
In formal ink, they thought and voices hold,
That we to them our solitude may give,
And make time present travel that of old,
Our life fame pieceth longer at the end,
And books it farther backward doth extend.   —Sir Thomas Overbury.

They are for company the best friends, in Doubts Counsellors, in Damps Comforters, Time's Prospective, the Home Traveller's Ship or Horse, the busie Man's best Recreation, the Opiate of idle Weariness, the Mindes best Ordinary, Nature's Garden and Seed-plot of Immortality.—Bulstrode Whitelocke.

When I would know thee * * * my
      thought looks
Upon thy well-made choice of friends and
      books;
Then do I love thee, and behold thy ends
In making thy friends books, and thy books
      friends.   —Ben Jonson.

If I were to pray for a taste which would stand by me under every variety of circumstances, and be a source of happiness and cheerfulness to me through life, and a shield against its ills, however things might go amiss, and the world frown upon me, it would be a taste for reading.—Herschel.

Many books belong to sunshine, and should be read out of doors. Clover, violets, and hedge roses breathe from their leaves; they are most lovable in cool lanes, along field paths, or upon stiles overhung by hawthorn, while the blackbird pipes, and the nightingale bathes its brown feathers in the twilight copse.—Willmott.

Books are the best of things, well used; abused, among the worst. What is the right use? What is the one end, which all means go to effect? They are for nothing but to inspire. I had better never see a book than to be warped by its attraction clean out of my own orbit, and made a satellite instead of a system.—Emerson.

In comparing men and books, one must always remember this important distinction,—that one can put the books down at any time. As Macaulay says, "Plato is never sullen, Cervantes is never petulant, Demosthenes never comes unseasonably, Dante never stays too long,"—Willis.

The silent power of books is a great power in the world; and there is a joy in reading them which those alone can know who read them with desire and enthusiasm. Silent, passive, and noiseless though they be, they may yet set in action countless multitudes, and change the order of nations.—Henry Giles.

Books, as Dryden has aptly termed them, are spectacles to read nature. Æschylus and Aristotle, Shakespeare and Bacon, are priests who preach and expound the mysteries of man and the universe. They teach us to understand and feel what we see, to decipher and syllable the hieroglyphics of the senses. —Hare.

To divert myself from a troublesome fancy, it is but to run to my books; they presently fix me to them, and drive the other out of my thoughts, and do not mutiny to see that I have only recourse to them for want of other more real, natural, and lively conveniences; they always receive me with the same kindness.—Montaigne.

A book becomes a mirror, with the author's face shining over it. Talent only gives an imperfect image,—the broken glimmer of a countenance. But the features of genius remain unruffled. Time guards the shadow. Beauty, the spiritual Venus,—whose children are the Tassos, the Spensers, the Bacons,—breathes the magic of her love, and fixes the face forever.—Willmott.

In you are sent
The types of Truths whose life is The to Come;
In you soars up the Adam from the fall;
In you the Future as the Past is given—
Ev'n in our death ye bid us hail our birth—
Unfold these pages, and behold the Heaven,
Without one grave-stone left upon the Earth.   —Bulwer-Lytton.

Books are delightful when prosperity happily smiles; when adversity threatens, they are inseparable comforters. They give strength to human compacts, nor are grave opinions brought forward without books. Arts and sciences, the benefits of which no mind can calculate, depend upon books. —Richard Aungervyle.

A wise man will select his books, for he would not wish to class them all under the sacred name of friends. Some can be accepted only as acquaintances. The best books of all kinds are taken to the heart, and cherished as his most precious possessions. Others to be chatted with for a time, to spend a few pleasant hours with, and laid aside, but not forgotten.— Langford.

Books are a guide in youth, and an entertainment for age. They support us under solitude, and keep us from becoming a burden to ourselves. They help us to forget the crossness of men and things, compose our cares and our passions, and lay our disappointments asleep. When we are weary of the living, we may repair to the dead, who have nothing of peevishness, pride or design in their conversation.—Jeremy Collier.

As friends and companions, as teachers and consolers, as recreators and amusers, books are always with us, and always ready to respond to our wants. We can take them with us in our wanderings, or gather them around us at our firesides. In the lonely wilderness, and the crowded city, their spirit will be with us, giving a meaning to the seemingly confused movements of humanity, and peopling the desert with their own bright creations. —Langford.

Knowledge of books is like that sort of lantern which hides him who carries it, and serves only to pass through secret and gloomy paths of his own; but in the possession of a man of business it is as a torch in the hand of one who is willing and able to show those who are bewildered the way which leads to their prosperity and welfare.—Steele.

The diffusion of these silent teachers —books—through the whole community is to work greater effects than artillery, machinery, and legislation. Its peaceful agency is to supersede stormy revolutions. The culture which it is to spread, whilst an unspeakable good to the individual, is also to become the stability of nations.—Channing.

What is a great love of books? It is something like a personal introduction to the great and good men of all past time. Books, it is true, are silent as you see them on their shelves; but, silent as they are, when I enter a library I feel as if almost the dead were present, and I know if I put questions to these books they will answer me.— John Bright.

Books, of which the principles are diseased or deformed, must be kept on the shelf of the scholar, as the man of science preserves monsters in glasses. They belong to the study of the mind's morbid anatomy, and ought to be accurately labelled. Voltaire will still be a wit, notwithstanding he is a scoffer; and we may admire the brilliant spots and eyes of the viper, if we acknowledge its venom and call it a reptile.—Willmott.

I have ever gained the most profit, and the most pleasure also, from the books which have made me think the most: and, when the difficulties have once been overcome, these are the books which have struck the deepest root, not only in my memory and understanding, but likewise in my affections.—J. C. and A. W. Hare.

Books are faithful repositories, which may be awhile neglected or forgotten, but when they are opened again, will again impart their instruction. Memory, once interrupted, is not to be recalled; written learning is a fixed luminary, which, after the cloud that had hidden it has passed away, is again bright in its proper station. Tradition is but a meteor, which, if it once falls, cannot be rekindled.—Johnson.

Books, says Lord Bacon, can never teach us the use of books; the student must learn by commerce with mankind to reduce his speculations to practice. No man should think so highly of himself as to think he can receive but little light from books; no one so meanly, as to believe he can discover nothing but what is to be learned from them.—Johnson.

Let us consider how great a commodity of doctrine exists in books; how easily, how secretly, how safely they expose the nakedness of human ignorance without putting it to shame. These are the masters who instruct us without rods and ferules, without hard words and anger, without clothes or money. If you approach them, they are not asleep; if investigating you interrogate them, they conceal nothing; if you mistake them, they never grumble; if you are ignorant, they cannot laugh at you.—Richard de Bury.

Golden volumes! richest treasures,
Objects of delicious pleasures!
You my eyes rejoicing please,
You my hands in rapture seize!
Brilliant wits and musing sages,
Lights who beam'd through many ages!
Left to your conscious leaves their story,
And dared to trust you with their glory;
And now their hope of fame achiev'd,
Dear volumes! you have not deceived!
            —Isaac Disraeli.

Great books are not in everybody's reach; and though it is better to know them thoroughly, than to know them only here and there; yet it is a good work to give a little to those who have neither the time nor means to get more. Let every book-worm, when, in any fragrant scarce old tome, he discovers a sentence, a story, and illustration that does his heart good, hasten to give it.—Coleridge.

And as for me, though than I konne but
    lyte,
On bokes for to rede I me delyte,
And to hem yeve I feyth and ful credence,
And in myn herte have hem in reverence
So hertely, that ther is game noon,
That fro my bokes maketh me to goon,
But yt be seldome on the holy day.
Save, certeynly, when that the monthe of
    May
Is comen, and that I here the foules synge,
And that the floures gynnen for to sprynge,
Farwel my boke, and my devocion.
          —Chaucer.

      We get no good
By being ungenerous, even to a book,
And calculating profits—so much help
By so much reading. It is rather when
We gloriously forget ourselves, and plunge
Soul-forward, headlong, into a book's pro-
    found,
Impassioned for its beauty, and salt of
    truth—
'Tis then we get the right good from a
    book.   —E. B. Browning.

Books have always a secret influence on the understanding; we cannot at pleasure obliterate ideas: he that reads books of science, though without any desire fixed of improvement, will grow more knowing; he that entertains himself with moral or religious treatises, will imperceptibly advance in goodness; the ideas which are often offered to the mind, will at last find a lucky moment when it is disposed to receive them.—Samuel Johnson.

        ———The place that does
Contain my books, the best companions, is
To me a glorious court, where hourly I
Converse with the old sages and philoso-
    phers;
And sometimes for variety, I confer
With kings and emperors, and weigh their
    counsels;
Calling their victories, if unjustly got,
Unto a strict account; and in my fancy,
Deface their ill-plac'd statutes.
          —Fletcher.

It is saying less than the truth to affirm that an excellent book (and the remark holds almost equally good of a

Raphael as of a Milton) is like a well-chosen and well-tended fruit tree. Its fruits are not of one season only. With the due and natural intervals, we may recur to it year after year, and it will supply the same nourishment and the same gratification, if only we ourselves return to it with the same healthful appetite.—Coleridge.

Bores

The smaller the calibre of mind, the greater the bore of a perpetually open mouth.—O. W. Holmes.

Society is now one polished horde,
Formed of two mighty tribes, the Bores and
    Bored.   —Byron.

The secret of making one's self tiresome is not to know when to stop.—Voltaire.

Got the ill name of augurs because they were bores.—Lowell.

He says a thousand pleasant things—
But never says "Adieu."—J. G. Saxe.

A tedious person is one a man would leap a steeple from.—Ben Jonson.

The biggest bore of all is he who is overflowing with congratulations.—Hood.

Those wanting wit, affect gravity and go by the name of solid men.—Dryden.

Bores are not to be got rid of except by rough means. They are to be scraped off like scales from a fish.—Bovee.

The bore is the same eating dates under the cedars of Lebanon as over a plate of baked beans in Beacon Street.—O. W. Holmes.

We are almost always wearied in the company of persons with whom we are not permitted to be weary.—Rochefoucauld.

The bore is usually considered a harmless creature, or of that class of irrational bipeds who hurt only themselves.—Maria Edgeworth.

There are some kinds of men who cannot pass their time alone; they are the flails of occupied people.—M. de Bonald.

There are few wild beasts more to be dreaded than a communicative man having nothing to communicate.—Bovee.

It is one of the vexatious mortifications of a studious man to have his thoughts disordered by a tedious visit.—L'Estrange.

The symptoms of compassion and benevolence in some people are like those minute-guns which warn you that you are in deadly peril.—Mme. Swetchine.

He will steal himself into a man's favor and for a week escape a great deal of discoveries; but when you find him out, you have him ever after—Shakespeare.

Never hold any one by the button or the hand in order to be heard out; for if people are unwilling to hear you, you had better hold your tongue.—Chesterfield.

> O, he's as tedious
> As is a tired horse, a railing wife;
> Worse than a smoky house; I had rather live
> With cheese and garlic in a windmill, far,
> Than feed on cates, and have him talk to me,
> In any summer-house in Christendom.
> —Shakespeare.

It is to be hoped that, with all the modern improvements, a mode will be discovered of getting rid of bores; for it is too bad that a poor wretch can be punished for stealing your pocket-handkerchief or gloves, and that no punishment can be inflicted on those who steal your time, and with it your temper and patience, as well as the bright thoughts that might have entered into your mind (like the Irishman who lost the fortune before he had got it), but were frightened away by the bore.—Byron.

Borrowing

No remedy against this consumption of the purse; borrowing only lingers and lingers it out, but the disease is incurable.—Shakespeare.

The borrower runs in his own debt.—Emerson.

Debt is a bottomless sea—Carlyle.

Borrowing from Peter to pay Paul.—Cicero.

Neither a borrower nor a lender be:
For loan oft loses both itself and friend,
And borrowing dulls the edge of husbandry.
—Shakespeare.

Who borrow much, then fairly make it known, and damn it with improvements not their own.—Young.

To forget, or pretend to do so, to return a borrowed article, is the meanest sort of petty theft.—Dr. Johnson.

The reason why borrowed books are so seldom returned to their owners is that it is much easier to retain the books than what is in them.—Montaigne.

If you lend a person any money, it becomes lost for any purpose as one's own. When you ask for it back again, you may find a friend made an enemy by your kindness. If you begin to press still further, either you must part with that which you have intrusted, or else you must lose that friend.—Plautus.

Few have borrowed more freely than Gray and Milton; but with a princely prodigality, they have repaid the obscure thoughts of others, with far brighter of their own—like the ocean, which drinks up the muddy water of the rivers from the flood, but replenishes them with the clearest from the shower.—Colton.

Charles Lamb, tired of lending his books, threatened to chain Wordsworth's poems to his shelves, adding: "For of those who borrow, some read slow; some mean to read, but don't read; and some neither read nor mean to read, but borrow, to leave you an opinion of their sagacity. I must do my money-borrowing friends the justice to say that there is nothing of this caprice or wantonness of alienation in them. When they borrow my money, they never fail to make use of it."—Talfourd.

You should only attempt to borrow from those who have but few of this world's goods, as their chests are not of iron, and they are, besides, anxious to appear wealthier than they really are.—Heinrich Heine.

Boston

Boston State-house is the hub of the solar system. You couldn't pry that out of a Boston man if you had the tire of all creation straightened out for a crow-bar.—O. W. Holmes.

The sea returning day by day
  Restores the world-wide mart.
So let each dweller on the Bay
  Fold Boston in his heart
Till these echoes be choked with snows
Or over the town blue ocean flows.
            —Emerson.

Bounty

From bounty issues power.—Akenside.

Our bounty, like a drop of water, disappears, when diffus'd too widely. Goldsmith.

The superfluous blossoms on a fruit tree are meant to symbolize the large way God loves to do pleasant things.—Beecher.

O blessed bounty, giving all content!
The only fautress of all noble arts
That lend'st success to every good intent.
A grace that rests in the most godlike
  hearts,
By heav'n to none but happy souls infus'd
Pity it is, that e'er thou wast abus'd.
            —Drayton.

Boyhood

Ah! happy years! once more who would
  not be a boy!   —Byron.

Ye tiny elves, that guiltless sport,
Like linnets in the bush,
Ye little know the ill ye court,
When manhood is your wish!
The losses, the crosses,
That active men engage;
The fears all, the tears all,
Of dim declining age.   —Burns.

Brains

The human brain is the highest bloom of the whole organic metamorphosis of the earth.—Schelling.

When God endowed human beings with brains, He did not intend to guarantee them.—Montesquieu.

Stern men, with empires in their brains.—Lowell.

Oh, rare the headpiece, if but brains were there!—Phædrus.

Not Hercules could have knocked out his brains, for he had none.—Shakespeare.

With curious art the brain, too finely
  wrought,
Preys on herself, and is destroyed by
  thought.   —Churchill.

An excellent scholar: One that hath a head fill'd with calves' brains without any sage in them.—Webster.

When a strong brain is weighed with a true heart, it seems to me like balancing a bubble against a wedge of gold.—O. W. Holmes.

There are brains so large that they unconsciously swamp all individualities which come in contact or too near, and brains so small that they cannot take in the conception of any other individuality as a whole, only in part or parts.—Mrs. Jameson.

The brain is the palest of all the internal organs, and the heart the reddest. Whatever comes from the brain carries the hue of the place it came from, and whatever comes from the heart carries the heat and color of its birthplace.—Holmes.

Individuals possessing moderate-sized brains easily find their proper sphere, and enjoy in it scope for all their energy. In ordinary circumstances they distinguish themselves, but they sink when difficulties accumulate around them. Persons with large brains, on the other hand, do not readily attain their appropriate place; common occurrences do not rouse or call them forth.—George Combe.

Bravery

God helps the brave.—Schiller.

Fortune favors the brave.—Terence.

A brave soul is a thing which all things serve.—Alex. Smith.

None but the brave deserves the fair.—Dryden.

A brave man may fall but cannot yield.

True bravery is quiet, undemonstrative.—Sir P. Sidney.

The brave man may yield to a braver man.

The brave find a home in every land.—Ovid.

Brave men are brave from the very first.—Corneille.

The brave are parsimonious of threats.—Kossuth.

'Tis late before the brave despair.—Thomson.

Bravery is often too sharp a spur.—Kossuth.

Brave deeds are most estimable when hidden.—Pascal.

General Taylor never surrenders.—Thos. L. Crittenden.

The bravest men are subject most to chance.—Dryden.

That's a valiant flea that dares eat his breakfast on the lip of a lion.—Shakespeare.

A brave man is clear in his discourse, and keeps close to truth.—Aristotle.

A true knight is fuller of gay bravery in the midst than in the beginning of danger.—Sir P. Sidney.

We come to know best what men are, in their worse jeopardies.—Daniel.

Brave men do not boast nor bluster. Deeds, not words, speak for such.—Rivarol.

Women commiserate the brave, and men the beautiful.—Landor.

Who bravely dares must sometimes risk a fall.—Smollett.

He's truly valiant that can wisely suffer the worst that man can breathe.—Shakespeare.

The best hearts, Trim, are ever the bravest, replied my uncle Toby.—Sterne.

The brave
Love mercy, and delight to save.
—Gay.

Come one, come all! this rock shall fly
From its firm base as soon as I.
—Scott.

What will not woman, gentle woman, dare when strong affection stirs her spirit up?—Southey.

The truly brave are soft of heart and eyes, and feel for what their duty bids them do.—Byron.

It is besides necessary that whoever is brave should be a man of great soul.—Cicero.

'Tis more brave
To live, than to die.
—Lord Lytton.

What's brave, what's noble,
Let's do it after the high Roman fashion,
And make death proud to take us.
—Shakespeare.

In adversity it is easy to despise life; he is truly brave who can endure a wretched life.—Martial.

Nature often enshrines gallant and noble hearts in weak bosoms—oftenest, God bless her!—in female breasts.—Dickens.

True bravery is shown by performing, without witnesses, what one might be capable of doing before all the world.—Rochefoucauld.

Life may be given in many ways, and loyalty to truth be sealed as bravely in the closet as the field.—Lowell.

Who combats bravely is not therefore brave: He dreads a death-bed like the meanest slave. —Pope.

Dare to do something worthy of transportation and a prison, if you mean to be anybody.—Juvenal.

He is not worthy of the honeycomb That shuns the hive because the bees have stings. —Shakespeare.

Without a sign his sword the brave man draws, And asks no omen but his country's cause. —Homer.

The brave and bold persist even against fortune; the timid and cowardly rush to despair through fear alone.—Tacitus.

Physical bravery is an animal instinct; moral bravery is a much higher and truer courage.—Wendell Phillips.

No man can be brave who thinks pain the greatest evil; nor temperate, who considers pleasure the highest good.—Cicero.

Bravery is a cheap and vulgar quality, of which the brightest instances are frequently found in the lowest savage.—Chatfield.

Fight valiantly to-day; and yet I do thee wrong to mind thee of it, for thou art framed of the firm truth of valor. —Shakespeare.

People glorify all sorts of bravery except the bravery they might show on behalf of their nearest neighbors. George Eliot.

There is no love-broker in the world can more prevail in man's commendation with woman than report of valor. —Shakespeare.

The brave man, indeed, calls himself lord of the land, through his iron, through his blood.—Arndt.

What valor were it, when a cur doth grin, for one to thrust his hand between his teeth, when he might spurn him with his foot away?—Shakespeare.

I know not how, but martial men are given to love. I think it is but as they are given to wine; for perils commonly ask to be paid in pleasures. Bacon.

Song of the brave, how thrills thy tone As when the organ's music rolls; No gold rewards, but song alone, The deeds of great and noble souls. —Bürger.

That courage which arises from the sense of our duty, and from the fear of offending Him that made us, acts always in a uniform manner, and according to the dictates of right reason.—Addison.

There's a brave fellow! There's a man of pluck! A man who's not afraid to say his say, Though a whole town's against him. —Longfellow.

At the bottom of a good deal of the bravery that appears in the world there lurks a miserable cowardice. Men will face powder and steel because they cannot face public opinion. —Chapin.

The brave man is not he who feels no fear, for that were stupid and irrational; but he whose noble soul its fear subdues, and bravely dares the danger which it shrinks from.—Joanna Baillie.

The heroic example of other days is in great part the source of the courage of each generation; and men walk up composedly to the most perilous enterprises, beckoned onward by the shades of the brave that were.—Arthur Helps.

The bravery founded upon the hope of recompense, upon the fear of punishment, upon the experience of success, upon rage, upon ignorance of dangers, is common bravery, and does not merit the name. True bravery proposes a just end, measures the dangers, and, if it is necessary, the affront, with coldness.—Francis la Noue.

The brave man seeks not popular applause,
Nor, overpower'd with arms, deserts his
cause,
Unsham'd, though foil'd, he does the best
he can,
Force is of brutes, but honor is of man.
—Dryden.

Cato the elder, when somebody was praising a man for his foolhardy bravery, said "that there was an essential difference between a really brave man and one who had merely a contempt for life."—Plutarch.

O friends, be men; so act that none may
feel
Ashamed to meet the eyes of other men.
Think each one of his children and his wife,
His home, his parents, living yet or dead.
For them, the absent ones, I supplicate,
And bid you rally here, and scorn to fly.
—Homer.

Intrepidity is an extraordinary strength of soul, which raises it above the troubles, disorders and emotions which the sight of great perils can arouse in it; by this strength heroes maintain a calm aspect and preserve their reason and liberty in the most surprising and terrible accidents.—La Rochefoucauld.

The truly brave,
When they behold the brave oppressed with
odds,
Are touched with a desire to shield and
save—
A mixture of wild beasts and demi-gods
Are they—now furious as the sweeping
wave,
Now moved with pity; even as sometimes
nods
The rugged tree unto the summer wind,
Compassion breathes along the savage mind.
—Byron.

Courage is incompatible with the fear of death; but every villain fears death; therefore, no villain can be brave. He may, indeed, possess the courage of the rat, and fight with desperation when driven into a corner, * * * * * yet the glare of a courage thus elicited by danger, where fear conquers fear, is not to be compared to that calm sunshine which constantly cheers and illuminates the breast of him, who builds his confidence on virtuous principles.—Colton.

Brevity

Brevity is the soul of wit.—Shakespeare.

Concentration alone conquers.—Charles Buxton.

A downright fact may be briefly told.—Ruskin.

I will be brief.—Shakespeare.

A verse may find him whom a sermon flies.—George Herbert.

Brevity is a great praise of eloquence.—Cicero.

The one prudence in life is concentration.—Emerson.

Whatever precepts you give, be short.—Horace.

Aiming at brevity, I become obscure. —Horace.

The fewer words, the better prayer. —Luther.

A parsimony of words prodigal of sense.—Disraeli.

Brevity is the child of silence, and is a credit to its parentage.—H. W. Shaw.

Brevity never fatigues; therefore, brevity is always a welcome guest.—Théophile Gautier.

We must be brief when traitors brave the field.—Shakespeare.

Rather to excite your judgment briefly than to inform it tediously.—Bacon.

Great captains do never use long orations when it comes to the point of execution.—Sir P. Sidney.

Cervantes speaks of potted wisdom as "short sentences drawn from a long experience."—Charles Buxton.

It is safe to make a choice of your thoughts, scarcely ever safe to express them all.—Barrow.

Brevity is very good, when we are, or are not, understood.—Butler.

You may get a large amount of truth into a brief space.—Beecher.

The wisdom of nations lies in their proverbs, which are brief and pithy.—William Penn.

My tongue within my lips I rein,
For who talks much must talk in vain.
—Gay.

The more you say, the less people remember. The fewer the words, the greater the profit.—Fénelon.

The more an idea is developed, the more concise becomes its expression; the more a tree is pruned, the better is the fruit.—Alfred Bougeart.

Generally, downright fact may be told in a plain way; and we want downright facts, at the present, more than anything else.—Ruskin.

If you would be pungent, be brief; for it is with words as with sunbeams—the more they are condensed the deeper they burn.—Southey.

General observations drawn from particulars are the jewels of knowledge, comprehending great store in a little room.—Locke.

A little plot of ground thick sown is better than a great field which, for the most part of it, lies fallow.—Bishop Norris.

Brevity is the best recommendation of a speech, not only in the case of a senator, but in that, too, of an orator.—Cicero.

I saw one excellency was within my reach—it was brevity; and I determined to obtain it.—Jay.

Since brevity is the soul of wit, and tediousness the limbs and outward flourishes—I will be brief.—Shakespeare.

Brevity and conciseness are the parents of conviction. The leaden bullet is more fatal than when multiplied into shot.—Hosea Ballou.

Brevity in writing is what charity is to all other virtues—righteousness is nothing without the one, nor authorship without the other.—Sydney Smith.

I would fain coin wisdom—mould it, I mean, into maxims, proverbs, sentences, that can easily be retained and transmitted.—Joubert.

When a man has no design but to speak plain truth, he may say a great deal in a very narrow compass.—Steele.

It is not a great Xerxes army of words, but a compact Greek ten thousand that march safely down to posterity.—Lowell.

Brevity is the body and soul of wit. It is wit itself, for it alone isolates sufficiently for contrasts; because redundancy or diffuseness produces no distinctions.—Jean Paul Richter.

And there's one rare strange virtue in their speeches,
The secret of their mastery—they are short.
—Halleck.

A sentence well couched takes both the sense and understanding. I love not those cart-rope speeches that are longer than the memory of man can fathom.—Feltham.

Was there ever anything written by mere man that was wished longer by its readers, excepting Don Quixote, Robinson Crusoe and the Pilgrim's Progress?—Dr. Johnson.

With vivid words your just conceptions grace,
Much truth compressing in a narrow space;
Then many shall peruse. but few complain,
And envy frown, and critics snarl in vain.
—Pindar.

The seven wise men of Greece, so famous for their wisdom all the world over, acquired all that fame, each of them, by a single sentence consisting of two or three words.—South.

The Grecian's maxim would indeed be a sweeping clause in literature; it would reduce many a giant to a pygmy, many a speech to a sentence, and many a folio to a primer.—Colton.

It is the work of fancy to enlarge, but of judgment to shorten and contract; and therefore this must be as far above the other as judgment is a greater and nobler faculty than fancy or imagination.—South.

Talk to the point, and stop when you have reached it. The faculty some possess of making one idea cover a quire of paper is not good for much. Be comprehensive in all you say or write. To fill a volume upon nothing is a credit to nobody; though Lord Chesterfield wrote a very clever poem upon nothing.—John Neal.

It is excellent discipline for an author to feel that he must say all he has to say in the fewest possible words, or his reader is sure to skip them; and in the plainest possible words, or his reader will certainly misunderstand them. Generally, also, a downright fact may be told in a plain way; and we want downright facts at present more than anything else.—Ruskin.

Bribery

All men have their price.—Ascribed to Walpole.

Judges and senates have been bought for gold.—Pope.

The universe would not be rich enough to buy the vote of an honest man.—St. Gregory.

Who thinketh to buy villainy with gold, Shall ever find such faith so bought—so sold. —Shakespeare.

Our supple tribes repress their patriot throat And ask no questions but the price of vote. —Samuel Johnson.

It is a great mistake to suppose that bribery and corruption, although they may be very convenient for gratifying the ambition or the vanity of individuals, have any great effect upon the fortunes or the power of parties. And it is a great mistake to suppose that bribery and corruption are means by which power can either be obtained or retained.—Beaconsfield.

'Tis pleasant purchasing our fellow-creatures;
And all are to be sold, if you consider
Their passions, and are dext'rous; some by features
Are bought up, others by a warlike leader;
Some by a place—as tend their years or natures;
The most by ready cash—but all have prices,
From crowns to kicks, according to their vices. —Byron.

Petitions, not sweetened with gold, are but unsavory and oft refused; or, if received, are pocketed, not read.—Massinger.

Silver, though white,
Yet it draws black lines; it shall not rule my palm
There to mark forth its base corruption. —Middleton and Rowley.

Bride

New dressed and blooming as a bridal maid.—Walter Harte.

O, happy youth! for whom thy fate reserved so fair a bride.—Dryden.

Evasive of the bridal day, she gives fond hopes to all, and all with hope deceives.—Pope.

A thin aerial veil is drawn o'er beauty's face, seeming to hide, more sweetly shows the blushing bride.—Crashaw.

The man who builds and wants wherewith to pay, provides a home from which to run away.—Young.

The bride, lovely herself, and lovely by her side a bevy of bright nymphs, with sober grace came glittering like a star, and took her place.—Dryden.

In ancient Bœotia brides were carried home in vehicles whose wheels were burned at the door, in token that they would never again be needed.—T. W. Higginson.

He laid him down and slept, and from his side a woman in her magic beauty rose; dazzled and charmed, he called that woman "bride," and his first sleep became his last repose.— Besser.

Up, up, fair bride ! and call thy stars from out their several boxes; take thy rubies, pearls, and diamonds forth, and make thyself a constellation of them all.—Donne.

Brooks

Sweet are the little brooks that run
O'er pebbles glancing in the sun,
Singing in soothing tones.
—Hood.

I chatter, chatter, as I flow
To join the brimming river,
For men may come and men may go,
But I go on forever.   —Tennyson.

Brook! whose society the poet seeks,
Intent his wasted spirits to renew;
And whom the curious painter doth pursue
Through rocky passes, among flowery creeks,
And tracks thee dancing down thy water-
breaks.   —Wordsworth.

Thou hastenest down between the hills to
meet me at the road,
The secret scarcely lisping of thy beautiful
abode
Among the pines and mosses of yonder
shadowy height,
Where thou dost sparkle into song, and fill
the woods with light.
—Lucy Larcom.

Brotherhood

Infinite is the help man can yield to man.—Carlyle.

Nature has inclined us to love men. —Cicero.

Man, man, is thy brother, and thy father is God.—Lamartine.

We must love men, ere to us they will seem worthy of our love.— Shakespeare.

To live is not to live for one's self alone; let us help one another.— Menander.

Kings and their subjects, masters and slaves find a common level in two places—at the foot of the cross and in the grave.—C. C. Colton.

However wretched a fellow-mortal may be, he is still a member of our common species.—Seneca.

The universe is but one great city, full of beloved ones, divine and human, by nature endeared to each other.— Epictetus.

If we love one another, nothing, in truth, can harm us, whatever mischances may happen.—Longfellow.

Give bread to a stranger, in the name of the universal brotherhood which binds together all men under the common father of nature.—Quintilian.

Be kindly affectioned one to another with brotherly love; in honor preferring one another.—Bible.

The era of Christianity—peace, brotherhood, the Golden Rule as applied to governmental matters—is yet to come, and when it comes, then, and then only, will the future of nations be sure.—Kossuth.

We are members of one great body. Nature planted in us a mutual love, and fitted us for a social life. We must consider that we were born for the good of the whole.—Seneca.

Enough of good there is in the lowest estate to sweeten life; enough of evil in the highest to check presumption; enough there is of both in all estates, to bind us in compassionate brotherhood, to teach us impressively that we are of one dying and one immortal family.—Henry Giles.

The race of mankind would perish, did they cease to aid each other. From the time that the mother binds the child's head till the moment that some kind assistant wipes the death-damp from the brow of the dying, we cannot exist without mutual help. All, therefore, that need aid have a right to ask it from their fellow-mortals; no one who holds the power of granting can refuse it without guilt.—Walter Scott.

My friends, let us try to follow the Saviour's steps; let us remember all day long what it is to be men; that it is to have every one whom we meet for our brother in the sight of God; that it is this, never to meet anyone, however bad he may be, for whom we cannot say: "Christ died for that man, and Christ cares for him still. He is precious in God's eyes, and he shall be precious in mine also."—Charles Kingsley.

God has taught in the Scriptures the lesson of a universal brotherhood, and man must not gainsay the teaching. Shivering in the ice-bound or scorching in the tropical regions; in the lap of luxury or in the wild hardihood of the primeval forest; belting the globe in a tired search for rest, or quieting through life in the heart of ancestral woods; gathering all the decencies around him like a garment, or battling in fierce raid of crime against a world which has disowned him, there is an inner humanness which binds me to that man by a primitive and indissoluble bond. He is my brother, and I cannot dissever the relationship. He is my brother, and I cannot release myself from the obligation to do him good.—Wm. M. Punshon.

Jesus throws down the dividing prejudices of nationality, and teaches universal love without distinction of race, merit or rank. A man's neighbor, henceforth, was every one who needed help, even an enemy. All men, from the slave to the highest, were sons of one Father in heaven, and should feel and act toward each other, as brethren. No human standard of virtue would suffice; no imitations of the loftiest examples among men. Moral perfection had been recognized alike by heathen and Jews, as found only in likeness to the Divine, and that Jesus proclaims as, henceforth, the one ideal for all humanity. With a sublime enthusiasm and brotherly love for the race, He rises above his age, and announces a common Father of all mankind, and one grand spiritual ideal in resemblance to Him.—J. C. Geikie.

Brute

A singular fact, that, when man is a brute, he is the most sensual and loathsome of all brutes.—Hawthorne.

Notwithstanding that natural love in brutes is much more violent and intense than in rational creatures, Providence has taken care that it should be no longer troublesome to the parent than it is useful to the young; for so soon as the wants of the latter cease, the mother withdraws her fondness, and leaves them to provide for themselves.—Addison.

Building

Too low they build who build beneath the stars.—Dr. Young.

Old houses mended cost little less than new before they're ended.—Cibber.

All below is strength, and all above is grace.—Dryden.

The building fitted accurately to answer its end will turn out to be admirable.—Müller.

Ah, to build, to build! that is the noblest art of all the arts.—Longfellow.

The man who builds, and wants wherewith to pay,
Provides a home from which to run away.
—Dr. Young.

The Gothic cathedral is a blossoming in stone, subdued by the insatiable demand of harmony in man.—Emerson.

Which of you, intending to build a tower, sitteth not down first and counteth the cost, whether he have sufficient to finish it?—Bible.

Never build after you are five and forty; have five years' income in hand before you lay a brick; and always calculate the expense at double the estimate.—Kett.

Like one who draws the model of a house beyond his power to build it, who, half through, gives o'er, and leaves his part-created cost a naked subject to the weeping clouds.—Shakespeare.

In designing a house and gardens, it is happy when there is an opportunity of maintaining a subordination of parts; the house so luckily placed as to exhibit a view of the whole design.— Shenstone.

———

When we mean to build,
We first survey the plot, then draw the model;
And when we see the figure of the house,
Then must we rate the cost of the erection;
Which if we find outweighs ability,
What do we then, but draw anew the model
In fewer offices; or, at least, desist
To build at all? —Shakespeare.

———

Houses are built to live in more than to look on; therefore let use be preferred before uniformity, except where both may be had.—Bacon.

Burlesque

Satire is the right hand of burlesque.—Voltaire.

———

Cervantes smiled Spain's chivalry away.—Byron.

———

A burlesque word is often a powerful sermon.—Boileau.

———

It is a sin to be a mocker.—Shakespeare.

———

The guerilla weapon of political warfare.—Horace Greeley.

———

The keenest of political weapons.—Bryant.

———

Often most telling and often most unfair; stimulated by want of a juster argument.—W. R. Alger.

———

What caricature is in painting, burlesque is in writing; and in the same manner the comic writer and painter correlate to each other; as in the former, the painter seems to have the advantage, so it is in the latter infinitely on the side of the writer. For the monstrous is much easier to paint than describe, and the ridiculous to describe than paint.— Fielding.

Burns

And Burns—though brief the race he ran,
Though rough and dark the paths he trod,
Lived—died—in form and soul a man,
The image of his God.
—Fitz-Greene Halleck.

Business

Neither above nor below his business.—Tacitus.

———

Shoemaker, stick to your last.— Pliny.

———

Avoid as much as possible multiplicity of business.—Bishop Wilson.

———

Few people do business well who do nothing else.—Chesterfield.

———

I attend to the business of other people, having lost my own.—Horace.

———

To business that we love, we rise betimes and go to it with delight.— Shakespeare.

———

A man who cannot mind his own business is not fit to be trusted with the king's.—Saville.

———

Every man has business and desire, such as it is.—Shakespeare.

———

The master looks sharpest to his own business.—Phædrus.

———

Do you fear to trust the word of a man whose honesty you have seen in business?—Terence.

———

Hasty and adventurous schemes are at first view flattering, in execution difficult and in the issue disastrous.— Livy.

———

That which is everybody's business is nobody's business.—Izaak Walton.

———

Let every one engage in the business with which he is best acquainted. —Propertius.

———

The most important part of every business is to know what ought to be done.—Columella.

———

All inconsiderate enterprises are impetuous at first, but soon languish.— Tacitus.

———

It very seldom happens to a man that his business is his pleasure.—Dr. Johnson.

———

Business despatched is business well

done; but business hurried is business ill done.—Bulwer-Lytton.

Physicians attend to the business of physicians and workmen handle the tools of workmen.—Horace.

The old proverb about having too many irons in the fire is an abominable old lie. Have all in, shovel, tongs, and poker.—Adam Clarke.

Have you so much leisure from your own business that you can take care of other people's that does not at all belong to you?—Terence.

Not because of any extraordinary talents did he succeed, but because he had a capacity on a level for business and not above it.—Tacitus.

Success in business is seldom owing to uncommon talents or original power which is untractable and self-willed, but to the greatest degree of commonplace capacity.—Hazlitt.

Men of great parts are often unfortunate in the management of public business, because they are apt to go out of the common road by the quickness of their imagination.—Swift.

Formerly when great fortunes were only made in war, war was a business; but now, when great fortunes are only made by business, business is war.—Bovee.

Never shrink from doing anything which your business calls you to do. The man who is above his business may one day find his business above him.—Drew.

Call on a business man at business times only, and on business, transact your business and go about your business, in order to give him time to finish his business.—Duke of Wellington.

The great secret both of health and successful industry is the absolute yielding up of one's consciousness to the business and diversion of the hour —never permitting the one to infringe in the least degree upon the other.— Sismondi.

Business is the salt of life, which not only gives a grateful smack to it, but dries up those crudities that would offend, preserves from putrefaction and drives off all those blowing flies that would corrupt it.—Feltham.

To men addicted to delights, business is an interruption; to such as are cold to delights, business is an entertainment. For which reason it was said to one who commended a dull man for his application: "No thanks to him; if he had no business, he would have nothing to do."—Steele.

He that attends to his interior self,
That has a heart, and keeps it; has a mind
That hungers, and supplies it; and who
    seeks
A social, not a dissipated life,
Has business.   —Cowper.

It is very sad for a man to make himself servant to a thing, his manhood all taken out of him by the hydraulic pressure of excessive business. I should not like to be merely a great doctor, a great lawyer, a great minister, a great politician—I should like to be also something of a man.— Theodore Parker.

Business in a certain sort of men is a mark of understanding, and they are honored for it. Their souls seek repose in agitation, as children do by being rocked in a cradle. They may pronounce themselves as serviceable to their friends as troublesome to themselves. No one distributes his money to others, but every one therein distributes his time and his life. There is nothing of which we are so prodigal as of those two things, of which to be thrifty would be both commendable and useful.—Montaigne.

Rare almost as great poets, rarer, perhaps, than veritable saints and martyrs, are consummate men of business. A man, to be excellent in this way, requires a great knowledge of character, with that exquisite tact which feels unerringly the right moment when to act. A discreet rapidity must pervade all the movements of his thought and action. He must be singularly free from vanity, and is generally found to be an enthusiast who has the art to conceal his enthusiasm.—Helps.

Business is religion, and religion is business. The man who does not make a business of his religion has a religious life of no force, and the man who does not make a religion of his business has a business life of no character. The world is God's workshop; the raw materials are His; the ideals and patterns are His; our hands are "the members of Christ," our reward His recognition. Blacksmith or banker, draughtsman or doctor, painter or preacher, servant or statesman, must work as unto the Lord, not merely making a living, but devoting a life. This makes life sacramental, turning its water into wine. This is twice blessed, blessing both the worker and the work.—Maltbie Babcock.

Busybodies

They learn to be idle, wandering about from house to house; and not only idle, but tattlers also, and busybodies, speaking things which they ought not.—Bible.

A person who is too nice an observer of the business of the crowd, like one who is too curious in observing the labor of the bees, will often be stung for his curiosity.—Pope.

He is a treacherous supplanter and underminer of the peace of all families and societies. This being a maxim of an unfailing truth, that nobody ever pries into another man's concerns but with a design to do, or to be able to do him a mischief.—South.

His tongue, like the tail of Samson's foxes, carries firebrands, and is enough to set the whole field of the world on a flame. Himself begins table-talk of his neighbor at another's board, to whom he bears the first news, and adjures him to conceal the reporter; whose choleric answer he returns to his first host, enlarged with a second edition; so as it used to be done in the fight of unwilling mastiffs, he claps each on the side apart, and provokes them to an eager conflict.—Bishop Hall.

Butcher

The butcher in his killing clothes.—Walt Whitman.

Whoe'er has gone thro' London street,
Has seen a butcher gazing at his meat,
    And how he keeps
    Gloating upon a sheep's
Or bullock's personals, as if his own;
    How he admires his halves
    And quarters—and his calves,
As if in truth upon his own legs grown.
            —Hood.

Buttercup

The buttercups, bright-eyed and bold,
Held up their chalices of gold
To catch the sunshine and the dew.
            —Julia C. R. Dorr.

The buttercups across the field
Made sunshine rifts of splendor.
            —D. M. Mulock.

All will be gay when noontide wakes anew
The buttercups, the little children's dower.
            —Robert Browning.

When buttercups are blossoming,
The poets sang, 'tis best to wed:
So all for love we paired in spring—
Blanche and I—ere youth had sped.
            —E. C. Stedman.

And O the buttercups! that field
    O' the cloth of gold, where pennons swam—
Where France set up his lilied shield,
    His oriflamb,
And Henry's lion-standard rolled:
    What was it to their matchless sheen,
    Their million million drops of gold
    Among the green!   —Jean Ingelow.

Butterfly

I'd be a butterfly, born in a bower,
Where roses and lilies and violets meet.
            —Thomas Haynes Bayly.

The gold-barr'd butterflies to and fro
    And over the waterside wander'd and wove
As heedless and idle as clouds that rove
And rift by the peaks of perpetual snow.
            —Joaquin Miller.

With the rose the butterfly's deep in love,
    A thousand times hovering round;
But round himself, all tender like gold,
    The sun's sweet ray is hovering found.
            —Heine.

Much converse do I find in thee,
Historian of my infancy!
Float near me; do not yet depart!
Dead times revive in thee:
Thou bring'st, gay creature as thou art!
A solemn image to my heart.
            —Wordsworth.

C

Calamities

Calamity was ordained for man.—Sir W. Davenant.

Calamity is man's true touchstone.—Beaumont and Fletcher.

Calamity is the test of integrity.—Richardson.

Bear calamities with meekness.—Euripides.

Of some calamity we can have no relief but from God alone; and what would men do, in such a case, if it were not for God?—Tillotson.

How wisely fate ordain'd for human kind
Calamity! which is the perfect glass,
Wherein we truly see and know ourselves.
                                    —Davenant.

When any calamity has been suffered the first thing to be remembered is, how much has been escaped.—Johnson.

Know, he that foretells his own calamity, and makes events before they come, twice over doth endure the pains of evil destiny.—Sir W. Davenant.

It is from the level of calamities, not that of every-day life, that we learn impressive and useful lessons.—Thackeray.

Do not insult calamity:
It is a barb'rous grossness to lay on
The weight of scorn, where heavy misery
Too much already weighs men's fortunes
    down.   —Daniel.

'Tis only from the belief of the goodness and wisdom of a Supreme Being that our calamities can be borne in that manner which becomes a man.—Mackenzie.

Differences, we know, are never so effectually laid asleep as by some common calamity; an enemy unites all to whom he threatens danger.—Dr. Johnson.

A vulgar man, in any ill that happens to him, blames others; a novice in philosophy blames himself; and a philosopher blames neither the one nor the other.—Epictetus.

If you tell your troubles to God, you put them into the grave; they will never rise again when you have committed them to Him. If you roll your burden anywhere else, it will roll back again like the stone of Sisyphus.—Spurgeon.

Times of general calamity and confusion have ever been productive of the greatest minds. The purest ore is produced from the hottest furnace, and the brightest thunderbolt is elicited from the darkest storm.—Colton.

The willow which bends to the tempest, often escapes better than the oak which resists it; and so in great calamities, it sometimes happens that light and frivolous spirits recover their elasticity and presence of mind sooner than those of a loftier character.—Sir Walter Scott.

Calm

The holy calm that leads to heavenly musing.—Rogers.

The tempest is o'er-blown, the skies are
clear,
And the sea charm'd into a calm so still
That not a wrinkle ruffles her smooth face.
—Dryden.

See me, how calm I am.
Ay, people are generally calm at the misfortunes of others. —Goldsmith.

How calm—how beautiful comes on
The stilly hour, when storms have gone,
When warring winds have died away
And clouds, beneath the dancing ray
Melt off and leave the land and sea,
Sleeping in bright tranquillity. —Moore.

'Tis noon—a calm, unbroken sleep
Is on the blue waves of the deep;
A soft haze, like a fairy dream,
Is floating over wood and stream;
And many a broad magnolia flower,
Within its shadowy woodland bower,
Is gleaming like a lovely star.
—George D. Prentice.

Gradual sinks the breeze,
Into a perfect calm; that not a breath
I heard to quiver thro' the closing woods,
Or rustling turn the many twinkling leaves,
Of aspen tall. The uncurling floods dif-
fus'd
In glassy breadth, seen through delusive
lapse
Forgetful of their course. 'Tis silence all,
And pleasing expectation. —Thomson.

Calumny

Cutting honest throats by whispers.
—Walter Scott.

Something of calumny always sticks.
—C. Boileau.

Calumny is only the noise of madmen.—Diogenes.

Virtue itself escapes not calumnious
strokes.—Shakespeare.

There are calumnies against which
even innocence loses courage.—Napoleon.

To persevere in one's duty and to
be silent is the best answer to calumny.—Washington.

Back-wounding calumny the whitest
virtue strikes.—Shakespeare.

Do you never look at yourself when
you abuse another person?—Plautus.

Calumny will sear virtue itself;
these shrugs, these hums and ha's.—
Shakespeare.

Those who ought to be secure from
calumny are generally those who avoid
it least.—Stanislaus.

Be thou as chaste as ice, as pure
as snow, thou shalt not escape calumny.—Shakespeare.

One triumphs over calumny only by
disdaining it.—Mme. de Maintenon.

There are persons always standing
ready to believe a scandal.—Ovid.

Nothing is so swift as calumny;
nothing is more easily uttered; nothing more readily received; nothing
more widely dispersed.—Cicero.

I never think it necessary to repeat
calumnies; they are sparks, which, if
you do not blow them, will go out of
themselves.—Boerhaave.

Neglected, calumny soon expires;
show that you are hurt, and you give
it the appearance of truth.—Tacitus.

False praise can please, and calumny af-
fright
None but the vicious, and the hypocrite.
—Horace.

If the calumniator bespatters and
belies me, I will endeavor to convince
him by my life and manners, but not
by being like him.—South.

Calumny is a vice of curious constitution; trying to kill it keeps it
alive; leave it to itself and it will die
a natural death.—Thomas Paine.

His calumny is not only the greatest
benefit a rogue can confer on us, but
the only service he will perform for
nothing.—Lavater.

A single seed of fact will produce in
a season or two a harvest of calumnies; but sensible men will pay no
attention to them.—Froude.

The upright, if he suffer calumny
to move him, fears the tongue of man
more than the eye of God.—Colton.

He that lends an easy and credulous ear to calumny is either a man of very ill morals or has no more sense and understanding than a child.—Menander.

___

I am beholden to calumny, that she hath so endeavored and taken pains to belie me. It shall make me set a surer guard on myself, and keep a better watch upon my actions.—Ben Jonson.

___

A nickname a man may chance to wear out; but a system of calumny, pursued by a faction, may descend even to posterity. This principle has taken full effect on this state favorite. —Isaac Disraeli.

___

Calumny is like the wasp which worries you, and which it is not best to try to get rid of unless you are sure of slaying it; for otherwise it returns to the charge more furious than ever.—Chamfort.

___

The men who convey and those who listen to calumnies should, if I could have my way, all hang, the tale-bearers by their tongues, the listeners by their ears.—Plautus.

___

Calumny crosses oceans, scales mountains and traverses deserts, with greater ease than the Scythian Abaris, and like him, rides upon a poisoned arrow.—Colton.

___

No might nor greatness in mortality
Can censure 'scape; back-wounding calumny
The whitest virtue strikes : what king so strong
Can tie the gall up in the slanderous tongue?
—Shakespeare.

___

The calumniator is like the dragon that pursued a woman, but, not being able to overtake her, opened his mouth and threw a flood after her to drown her.—Edward Blunt.

___

I never listen to calumnies, because if they are untrue I run the risk of being deceived, and if they be true, of hating persons not worth thinking about.—Montesquieu.

___

The pure in heart are slow to credit calumnies, because they hardly comprehend what motives can be inducements to the alleged crimes.—Jane Porter.

___

Close thine ear against him that shall open his mouth secretly against another; if thou receive not his words, they fly back and wound the reporter : if thou receive them, they flee forward and wound the receiver.—Quarles.

___

Calumniators are those who have neither good hearts nor good understandings. We ought not to think ill of any one till we have palpable proof; and even then we should not expose them to others.—Colton.

___

Like the tiger, that seldom desists from pursuing man after having once preyed upon human flesh, the reader who has once gratified his appetite with calumny makes ever after the most agreeable feast upon murdered reputations!—Goldsmith.

___

The celebrated Boerhaave, who had many enemies, used to say that he never thought it necessary to repeat their calumnies. "They are sparks," said he, "which, if you do not blow them, will go out of themselves."— Disraeli.

___

It is like the Greek fire used in ancient warfare, which burnt unquenched beneath the water; or like the weeds which, when you have extirpated them in one place, are sprouting forth vigorously in another spot, at the distance of many hundred yards; or, to use the metaphor of St. James, it is like the wheel which catches fire as it goes, and burns with fiercer conflagration as its own speed increases.— F. W. Robertson.

___

Calumny is a monstrous vice: for, where parties indulge in it, there are always two that are actively engaged in doing wrong, and one who is subject to injury. The calumniator inflicts wrong by slandering the absent : he who gives credit to the calumny before he has investigated the truth is equally implicated. The person traduced is doubly injured—first by him who propagates, and secondly by him who credits the calumny.—Herodotus.

Canary

Bird of the amber beak,
Bird of the golden wing!
Thy dower is thy carolling;
Thou hast not far to seek
Thy bread, nor needest wine
To make thy utterance divine;
Thou art canopied and clothed
And unto Song betrothed.
          —E. C. Stedman.

Sing away, ay, sing away,
    Merry little bird,
Always gayest of the gay,
Though a woodland roundelay
    You ne'er sung nor heard;
Though your life from youth to age
Passes in a narrow cage.
          —D. M. Mulock.

Thou should'st be carolling thy Maker's
    praise,
Poor bird! now fetter'd, and here set to
    draw,
With graceless toil of beak and added claw,
The meager food that scarce thy want
    allays!
And this—to gratify the gloating gaze
Of fools, who value nature not a straw,
But know to prize the infraction of her law
And hard perversion of her creatures'
    ways!
Thee the wild woods await, in leaves attired,
Where notes of liquid utterance should en-
    gage
Thy bill, that now with pain scant forage
    earns.   —Julian Fane.

Candor

Candor is the brightest gem of criticism.—Disraeli.

Plain dealing is easiest and best.—
Jane Porter.

In simple and pure soul I come to
you.—Shakespeare.

I can promise to be candid, but I
cannot promise to be impartial.—
Goethe.

He speaks home; you may relish him
more in the soldier than in the scholar.
—Shakespeare.

Candor may be considered as a compound of justice and the love of truth.
—J. Abercrombie.

Candor is the seal of a noble mind,
the ornament and pride of man, the
sweetest charm of woman, the scorn
of rascals and the rarest virtue of
sociability.—Bentzel-Sternaů.

'Tis great—'tis manly to disdain disguise,
It shows our spirit, or it proves our
    strength.   —Young.

          Make my breast
Transparent as pure crystal, that the world,
Jealous of me, may see the foulest thought
My heart does hold.   —Buckingham.

There is but one way I know of
conversing safely with all men; that
is, not by concealing what we say or
do, but by saying or doing nothing that
deserves to be concealed.—Pope.

He who, when called upon to speak
a disagreeable truth, tells it boldly
and has done, is both bolder and
milder than he who nibbles in a low
voice and never ceases nibbling.—Lavater.

Give me the avowed, the erect, the manly
    foe;
Bold I can meet—perhaps may turn his
    blow;
But of all plagues, good heaven, thy wrath
    can send,
Save, save, oh! save me from the candid
    friend.   —George Canning.

The brave do never shun the light;
Just are their thoughts, and open are their
    tempers;
Truly without disguise they love and hate;
Still are they found in the fair face of day,
And heav'n and men are judges of their
    actions.   —Rowe.

A man should never be ashamed to
own he has been in the wrong, which
is but saying, in other words, that he
is wiser to-day than he was yesterday.—Pope.

          You talk to me in parables.
You may have known that I'm no wordy
    man,
Fine speeches are the instruments of
    knaves
Or fools that use them, when they want
    good sense;
But honesty
Needs no disguise nor ornament: be plain.
          —Otway.

Some frauds succeed from the apparent candor, the open confidence, and
the full blaze of ingenuousness that is
thrown around them. The slightest

mystery would excite suspicion and ruin all. Such stratagems may be compared to the stars; they are discoverable by darkness and hidden only by light.—Colton.

If anything in my conversation has merited your regard, I think it must be the openness and freedom with which I commonly express my sentiments. You are too wise a man not to know that such freedom is not without its use.—Burke.

Cant

Cant is the twin sister of hypocrisy. —Beecher.

Cant is the parrot talk of a profession.—Coleridge.

Cant is not the vehicle, but the substitute of thought.—Robert Hall.

The affectation of some late authors to introduce and multiply cant words is the most ruinous corruption in any language.—Swift.

Cant is the voluntary overcharging or prolongation of a real sentiment; hypocrisy is the setting up a pretension to a feeling you never had and have no wish for.—Hazlitt.

'Tis too much prov'd—that, with devotion's visage
And pious action, we do sugar o'er
The devil himself.   —Shakespeare.

To wear long faces, just as if our Maker
The God of goodness, was an undertaker,
Well pleas'd to wrap the soul's unlucky mien
In sorrow's dismal crape or bombazine.
                         —Dr. Wolcot.

Is not cant the materia prima of the devil, from which all falsehoods, imbecilities, abominations, body themselves, from which no true thing can come? For cant is itself properly a doubledistilled lie, the second power of a lie.—Carlyle.

Those people are often the least worldly on whom they who make the loudest boast of their unworldliness seek basely to affix that opprobrious epithet. For they walk the world with a heart pure as it is cheerful; they are, by that unpretending purity, saved from infection; as there are as many fair and healthy faces to be seen in the smoke and stir of cities as in the rural wilds, so also are there as many fair and healthy spirits.—Professor Wilson.

There is such a thing as a peculiar word or phrase cleaving as it were to the memory of the writer or speaker, and presenting itself to his utterance at every turn. When we observe this, we call it a cant word or a cant phrase. —Paley.

The superabundance of phrases appropriated by some pious authors to the subject of religion, and never applied to any other purpose, has not only the effect of disgusting persons of taste, but of obscuring religion itself.—Robert Hall.

Caprice

Men are nearly as capricious as women.—Chamfort.

Caprice in woman is the antidote to beauty.—Bruyère.

Woman is a miracle of divine contradictions.—Michelet.

A woman's fitness comes by fits.— Shakespeare.

It is not always like to like in love. Titania loved the weaver Bottom, with the ass's head.—Anthony Trollope.

There is a vein of inconsistency in every woman's heart, within whose portals love hath entered.—Mme. Deluzy.

How wayward is this foolish love, that, like a testy babe, will scratch the nurse and presently, all humble, kiss the rod.—Shakespeare.

There is a proverb in the South that a woman laughs when she can, and weeps when she pleases.—J. Petit-Senn.

Love has a way of cheating itself consciously, like a child who plays at solitary hide-and-seek; it is pleased with assurances that it all the while disbelieves.—George Eliot.

There are women so hard to please that it would seem as if nothing less than an angel would suit them; and hence it comes that they often encounter devils.—Marguerite de Valois.

Sing of the nature of women, and then the song shall be surely full of variety,—old crotchets and most sweet closes. It shall be humorous, grave, fantastical, amorous, melancholy, sprightly,—one in all, all in one.—Marston.

"One might almost fear," writes a thoughtful woman, "seeing how the women of to-day are lightly stirred up to run after some new fashion or faith, that heaven is not so near to them as it was to their mothers and grandmothers."—Samuel Smiles.

Cards

A snug and friendly game at cards. —Cowper.

Patience and shuffle the cards.—Cervantes.

I must complain the cards are ill-shuffled till I have a good hand.—Swift.

Have I not here the best cards for the game,
To win this easy match? —Shakespeare.

Call them again, my lord, and accept their suit.—Shakespeare.

Whist, then, delightful whist, my theme shall be.—A. Thompson.

Care

I am sure care's an enemy to life. —Shakespeare.

As rust eats iron, so care eats the heart.—A. Ricard.

To carry care to bed is to sleep with a pack on your back.—Haliburton.

Care, admitted as guest, quickly turns to be master.—Bovee.

Cast all your care on God; that anchor holds.—Tennyson.

Many of our cares are but a morbid way of looking at our privileges.—Sir Walter Scott.

Second-hand cares, like second-hand clothes, come easily off and on.—Dickens.

Care that is once enter'd into the breast Will have the whole possession ere it rest.
—Johnson.

Care to our coffin adds a nail, no doubt; And every grin so merry draws one out.
—Dr. Wolcot.

Care keeps his watch in every old man's eye, And where care lodges, sleep will never lie.
—Shakespeare.

Some must watch while some must sleep, so runs the world away.—Shakespeare.

Providence has given us hope and sleep as a compensation for the many cares of life.—Voltaire.

Care seeks out wrinkled brows and hollow eyes, and builds himself caves to abide in them.—Beaumont and Fletcher.

Care is no cure, but rather corrosive for things that are not to be remedied.—Shakespeare.

Care may acquire wealth, which, when acquired, care must guard and worry about.—Quesnel.

But can the noble mind for ever brood, The willing victim of a weary mood, On heartless cares that squander life away, And cloud young Genius bright'ning into day?
—Campbell.

O, polished perturbation! golden care that keepest the ports of slumber open wide to many a watchful night!—Shakespeare.

Black care sits behind all sorts of horses, and gives a trink-gilt to postilions all over the map.—Thackeray.

All cares appear twice as large as they really are, owing to their emptiness and darkness; and so is it with the grave.—Richter.

Cares are often more difficult to thrown off than sorrows; the latter die with time, the former grow upon it.—Richter.

He who climbs above the cares of this world and turns his face to his God, has found the sunny side of life.—Spurgeon.

God gives us power to bear all the sorrows of His making; but He does not give us power to bear the sorrows of our own making, which the anticipation of sorrow most assuredly is.—Alexander Maclaren.

Our cares are the mothers, not only of our charities and virtues, but of our best joys and most cheering and enduring pleasures.—Simms.

Eat not thy heart; which forbids to afflict our souls, and waste them with vexatious cares.—Plutarch.

Why art thou troubled and anxious about many things? One thing is needful—to love Him and to sit attentively at His feet.—Fénelon.

He that taketh his own cares upon himself loads himself in vain with an uneasy burden. I will cast all my cares on God; He hath bidden me; they cannot burden Him.—Bishop Hall.

I could lie down like a tired child,
And weep away the life of care
Which I have borne, and yet must bear.
—Shelley.

Begone, old Care, and I prithee begone
    from me;
For i' faith, old Care, thee and I shall
    never agree.   —Playford.

Although my cares do hang upon my soul
Like mines of lead, the greatness of my
    spirit
Shall shake the sullen weight off.
—Clapthorne.

I met a brother who, describing a friend of his, said he was like a man who had dropped a bottle and broken it, and put all the pieces in his bosom,

where they were cutting him perpetually.—H. W. Beecher.

But human bodies are sic fools,
For a' their colleges and schools,
That when nae real ills perplex them,
They make enow themselves to vex them.
—Burns.

And the night shall be filled with music,
    And the cares that infest the day
Shall fold their tents like the Arabs,
    And as silently steal away.
—Longfellow.

All creatures else a time of love possess,
Man only clogs with care his happiness,
And while he should enjoy his part of bliss,
With thoughts of what may be, destroys
    what is.   —Dryden.

Quick is the succession of human events; the cares of to-day are seldom the cares of to-morrow; and when we lie down at night, we may safely say to most of our troubles, "Ye have done your worst, and we shall meet no more."—Cowper.

Still though the headlong cavalier,
O'er rough and smooth, in wild career,
    Seems racing with the wind;
His sad companion, ghastly pale,
And darksome as a widow's veil,
    Care keeps her seat behind. —Horace.

Men do not avail themselves of the riches of God's grace. They love to nurse their cares, and seem as uneasy without some fret as an old friar would be without his hair girdle. They are commanded to cast their cares upon the Lord, but even when they attempt it, they do not fail to catch them up again, and think it meritorious to walk burdened.—Beecher.

Carelessness

Carelessness does more harm than a want of knowledge.—Franklin.

If you will fling yourself under the wheels, Juggernaut will go over you; depend upon it.—Thackeray.

Childish, imbecile carelessness is enough to render any man poor, without the aid of a single positive vice.—Francis Wayland.

Carelessness is inexcusable, and merits the inevitable sequence.—Froude.

Caricature

Nothing conveys a more inaccurate idea of a whole truth than a part of a truth so prominently brought forth as to throw the other parts into shadow. This is the art of caricature; and by the happy use of that art you might caricature the Apollo Belvidere.—Bulwer-Lytton.

A farce is that in poetry which grotesque (caricature) is in painting. The persons and actions of a farce are all unnatural, and the manners false, that is, inconsistent with the characters of mankind; and grotesque painting is the just resemblance of this.—Dryden.

The great moral satirist, Hogarth, was once drawing in a room where many of his friends were assembled, and among them my mother. She was then a very young woman. As she stood by Hogarth, she expressed a wish to learn to draw caricature. "Alas, young lady," said Hogarth, "it is not a faculty to be envied! Take my advice, and never draw caricature; by the long practice of it, I have lost the enjoyment of beauty. I never see a face but distorted; I never have the satisfaction to behold the human face divine." We may suppose that such language from Hogarth would come with great effect; his manner was very earnest, and the confession is well deserving of remembrance.—Bishop Sandford.

Carpentry

The carpenter dresses his plank—the tongue of his fore-plane whistles its wild ascending lisp.—Walt Whitman.

The house-builder at work in cities or anywhere,
The preparatory jointing, squaring, sawing, mortising,
The hoist-up of beams, the push of them in their places, laying them regular,
Setting the studs by their tenons in the mortises, according as they were prepared,
The blows of the mallets and hammers.
    —Walt Whitman.

Are the tools without, which the carpenter puts forth his hands to, or are they and all the carpentry within himself; and would he not smile at the notion that chest or house is more than he?—Cyrus A. Bartol.

Castles in the Air

A sigh can shatter a castle in the air. —W. R. Alger.

No tribute is laid on castles in the air.—Churchill.

Leave glory to great folks. Ah, castles in the air cost a vast deal to keep up!—Bulwer-Lytton.

Leaving the wits the spacious air,
With license to build castles there.
    —Swift.

Charming Alnaschar visions! it is the happy privilege of youth to construct you.—Thackeray.

Thus we build on the ice, thus we write on the waves of the sea; the waves roaring pass away, the ice melts, and away goes our palace, like our thoughts.—Herder.

If you have built castles in the air, your work need not be lost; that is where they should be. Now put the foundations under them.—Thoreau.

Ever building, building to the clouds, still building higher, and never reflecting that the poor narrow basis cannot sustain the giddy tottering column.—Schiller.

Happy season of virtuous youth, when shame is still an impassable barrier, and the sacred air-cities of hope have not shrunk into the mean clay hamlets of reality; and man, by his nature, is yet infinite and free.—Carlyle.

In all assemblies, though you wedge them ever so close, we may observe this peculiar property, that over their heads there is room enough; but how to reach it is the difficult point. To this end the philosopher's way in all ages has been by erecting certain edifices in the air.—Swift.

Cat

Mrs. Crupp had indignantly assured him that there wasn't room to swing a cat there; but as Mr. Dick justly observed to me, sitting down on the foot of the bed, nursing his leg, "You know, Trotwood, I don't want to swing a cat. I never do swing a cat. Therefore what does that signify to me!"—Dickens.

If 'twere not for my cat and dog,
I think I could not live.
—Ebenezer Elliott.

Confound the cats! All cats—alway—
Cats of all colors, black, white, gray;
By night a nuisance and by day—
    Confound the cats!
      —Dobbin.

It has been the providence of nature to give this creature nine lives instead of one.—Pilpay.

Cause

A rotten cause abides no handling.—Shakespeare.

God hides Himself behind causes.—Charles Rollin.

God befriend us, as our cause is just.—Shakespeare.

A noble cause doth ease much a grievous case.—Sir Philip Sidney.

To all facts there are laws,
The effect has its cause, and I mount to
    the cause.   —Lord Lytton.

I would seek unto God and unto God would I commit my cause.—Bible.

The first springs of great events, like those of great rivers, are often mean and little.—Swift.

In war events of importance are the result of trivial causes.—Cæsar.

The cause is hidden, but the result is known.—Ovid.

Happy the man who has been able to learn the causes of things.—Virgil.

We know the effects of many things, but the cause of few; experience, therefore, is a surer guide than imagination, and inquiry than conjecture.—Colton.

Every effect doth, after a sort, contain, or at least resemble, the cause from which it proceedeth.—Hooker.

Small are the seeds fate does unheeded sow
Of slight beginnings to important ends.
—Davenant.

It becomes extremely hard to disentangle our idea of the cause from the effect by which we know it.—Burke.

The great chain of causes, which, linking one to another, even to the throne of God Himself, can never be unraveled by any industry of ours.—Burke.

Those physical difficulties which you cannot account for, be very slow to arraign; for he that would be wiser than Nature would be wiser than God.—Jeremy Bentham.

The general idea of cause is that without which another thing, called the effect, cannot be. The final cause is that for the sake of which anything is done.—Lord Morpeth.

To legislate each duty, were to count
Drops of a stream that issue from one fount.
God gives, since all effects are in their cause,
For narrow prescripts universal laws.
    —Abraham Coles.

Small causes are sufficient to make a man uneasy, when great ones are not in the way; for want of a block, he will stumble at a straw.—Swift.

Caution

Hasten slowly.—Augustus Cæsar.

Pitchers have ears.—Shakespeare.

Little boats should keep near shore.—Franklin.

The cautious seldom err.—Confucius.

Caution is the lower story of prudence.—Carlyle.

All is to be feared where all is to be lost.—Byron.

Caution, though very often wasted, is a good risk to take.—H. W. Shaw.

Among mortals second thoughts are wisest.—Euripides.

A hare is not caught with a drum.—La Fontaine.

Be cautious and bold.—Rothschild.

Be slow of tongue and quick of eye.—Cervantes.

Caution is the eldest child of wisdom.—Victor Hugo.

It is a good thing to learn caution by the misfortunes of others.—Publius Syrius.

Man's caution often into danger turns, and his guard falling crushes him to death.—Young.

When clouds are seen, wise men put on their cloaks.—Shakespeare.

Who 'scapes the snare
Once, has a certain caution to beware.
—Chapman.

Open your mouth and purse cautiously, and your stock of wealth and reputation shall, at least in repute, be great.—Zimmermann.

The way out of our narrowness may not be so easy as the way in. The weasel that creeps into the corn-bin has to starve himself before he can leave by the same passage.—Bartol.

I knew a wise man who had it for a by-word when he saw men hasten to a conclusion: "Stay a little, that we may make an end the sooner."—Bacon.

Trust none,
For oaths are straws, men's faiths are wafer cakes,
And hold-fast is the only dog.
—Shakespeare.

The wound of peace is surety,
Surety secure; but modest doubt is called
The beacon of the wise, the 'tent that searches
To the bottom of the worst.
—Shakespeare.

When you have need of a needle, you move your fingers delicately, with a wise caution. Use the same precaution with the inevitable dullness of life; give attention; keep yourself from imprudent precipitation; and do not take it by the point.—Rance.

But now so wise and wary was the knight
By trial of his former harms and cares,
That he descry'd and shunned still his slight;
The fish, that once was caught, new bait will hardly bite.   —Spenser.

The bird alighteth not on the spread net when it beholds another bird in the snare. Take warning by the misfortunes of others, that others may not take example from you.—Saadi.

Celibacy

No man can either live piously or die righteous without a wife.—Richter.

Marriage has in it less of beauty, but more of safety, than the single life.—Jeremy Taylor.

"As to marriage or celibacy, let a man take which course he will," says Socrates, "he will be sure to repent."—Colton.

God has set the type of marriage through creation. Each creature seeks its perfection in another.—Luther.

Alas! many an enamored pair have courted in poetry, and after marriage lived in prose.—John Foster.

Thales was reputed to be one of the wise men who made answer to the question when a man should marry: "A young man not yet, an old man not at all."—Bacon.

It happens, as with cages: the birds without despair to get in, and those within despair of getting out.—Montaigne.

Even supposing there were some spiritual advantage in celibacy, it ought to be completely voluntary.—Whately.

Might I have had my own will, I would not have married Wisdom herself, if she would have had me.—Montaigne.

Though bachelors be the strongest stakes, married men are the best binders in the hedge of the commonwealth.—Thomas Fuller.

They that have grown old in a single state are generally found to be morose, fretful, and captious,—tenacious of their own practices and maxims.—Dr. Johnson.

Unmarried men are best friends, best masters, best servants, but not always best subjects; for they are light to run away, and almost all fugitives are of that condition.—Bacon.

Celerity

Celerity is the lazy man's enemy.—R. Lowe.

Celerity wins the race.—Sir John Astley.

Celerity is never more admired
Than by the negligent.
—Shakespeare.

There is no secrecy comparable to celerity; like the motion of a bullet in the air, it flies so swift that it outruns the eye.—Bacon.

The Italians say it is not necessary to be a stag; but we ought not to be a tortoise.—Beaconsfield.

Cemeteries

The Christian cemetery is a memorial and a record. It is not a mere field in which the dead are stowed away unknown; it is a touching and beautiful history, written in family burial plots, in mounded graves, in sculptured and inscribed monuments. It tells the story of the past,—not of its institutions, or its wars, or its ideas, but of its individual lives,—of its men and women and children, and of its household. It is silent, but eloquent; it is common, but it is unique. We find no such history elsewhere; there are no records in all the wide world in which we can discover so much that is suggestive, so much that is pathetic and impressive.—Joseph Anderson.

Censure

Censure is the tax a man pays to the public for being eminent.—Swift.

The villain's censure is extorted praise.—Pope.

The death of censure is the death of genius.—Simms.

There is no defense against reproach except obscurity.—Addison.

Censure pardons the ravens, but rebukes the doves.—Juvenal.

The censure of those that are opposed to us is the nicest commendation that can be given us.—St. Evremond.

Censure is often useful, praise often deceitful.—Churchill.

We must not stint our necessary actions in the fear to cope malicious censurers.—Shakespeare.

Censure is like the lightning which strikes the highest mountains.—Balthasar Gracian.

The readiest and surest way to get rid of censure is to correct ourselves.—Demosthenes.

He that accuses all mankind of corruption ought to remember that he is sure to convict only one.—Burke.

We do not like our friends the worse because they sometimes give us an opportunity to rail at them heartily. Their faults reconcile us to their virtues.—Hazlitt.

Few persons have sufficient wisdom to prefer censure which is useful to them to praise which deceives them.—La Rochefoucauld.

Others proclaim the infirmities of a great man with satisfaction and complacence, if they discover none of the like in themselves.—Addison.

These men (chronic fault-finders) should consider that it is their envy which deforms everything, and that the ugliness is not in the object, but in the eye.—Steele.

Invective may be a sharp weapon, but overuse blunts its edge. Even when the denunciation is just and true it is an error of art to indulge it too long.—Tyndall.

When the tongue is the weapon, a man may strike where he cannot reach; and a word shall do execution both further and deeper than the mightiest blow.—South.

To arrive at perfection, a man should have very sincere friends, or inveterate enemies; because he would be made sensible of his good or ill conduct either by the censures of the one or the admonitions of the others.—Diogenes.

Some men's censures are like the blasts of rams' horns before the walls of Jericho; all a man's fame they lay level at one stroke, when all they go upon is only conceit, without any certain basis.—J. Beaumont.

Horace appears in good humor while he censures, and therefore his censure has the more weight as supposed to proceed from judgment, not from passion.—Young.

It is undoubtedly true, though it may seem paradoxical,—but, in general, those who are habitually employed in finding and displaying faults are unqualified for the work of reformation.—Burke.

O that the too censorious world would learn
This wholesome rule, and with each other bear;
But man, as if a foe to his own species,
Takes pleasure to report his neighbors' faults.
Judging with rigor every small offense,
And prides himself in scandal. Few there are
Who injured take the part of the transgressor
And plead his pardon ere he deigns to ask it.   —Haywood.

It is harder to avoid censure than to gain applause; for this may be done by one great or wise action in an age. But to escape censure a man must pass his whole life without saying or doing one ill or foolish thing.—Hume.

There are but three ways for a man to revenge himself of the censure of the world,—to despise it, to return the like, or to endeavor to live so as to avoid it; the first of these is usually pretended, the last is almost impossible, the universal practice is for the second.—Swift.

Plutarch tells us of an idle and effeminate Etrurian who found fault with the manner in which Themistocles had conducted a recent campaign. "What," said the hero in reply, "have you, too, something to say about war, who are like the fish that has a sword, but no heart?" He is always the severest censor on the merits of others who has the least worth of his own.—E. L. Magoon.

He that abuses his own profession will not patiently bear with any one else who does so. And this is one of our most subtle operations of self-love. For when we abuse our own profession, we tacitly except ourselves; but when another abuses it, we are far from being certain that this is the case.—Colton.

It is a folly for an eminent man to think of escaping censure, and a weakness to be affected with it. All the illustrious persons of antiquity, and indeed of every age in the world, have passed through this fiery persecution. There is no defense against reproach but obscurity; it is a kind of concomitant to greatness, as satires and invectives were an essential part of a Roman triumph.—Addison.

Ceremony

Ceremonies are the outworks of manners.—Chesterfield.

Truth and ceremony are two things.—Marcus Antoninus.

What art thou, thou idol ceremony?
What kind of god art thou, that suffer'st more
Of mortal griefs than do thy worshippers?
   —Shakespeare.

There are ceremonious bows that repel one like a cudgel.—Bovee.

When love begins to sicken and decay it useth an enforced ceremony.—Shakespeare.

Ceremony is all backbone.—Haliburton.

> To feed were best at home;
> From thence the sauce to meat is ceremony;
> Meeting were bare without it.
> —Shakespeare.

Candlesticks and incense not being portable into the maintop, the sailor perceives these decorations to be, on the whole, inessential to a maintop mass. Sails must be set and cables bent, be it never so strict a saint's day; and it is found that no harm comes of it. Absolution on a lee-shore must be had of the breakers, it appears, if at all; and they give plenary and brief without listening to confession.—Ruskin.

> Ceremony was but devis'd at first
> To set a gloss on faint deeds, hollow welcomes,
> Recanting goodness, sorry ere 'tis shown.
> —Shakespeare.

Forms and regularity of proceeding, if they are not justice, partake much of the nature of justice, which, in its highest sense, is the spirit of distributive order.—Hare.

If we use no ceremony towards others, we shall be treated without any. People are soon tired of paying trifling attentions to those who receive them with coldness, and return them with neglect.—Hazlitt.

As ceremony is the invention of wise men to keep fools at a distance, so good breeding is an expedient to make fools and wise men equal.—Steele.

> What infinite heart's ease
> Must kings neglect, that private men enjoy?
> And what have kings that privates have not too,
> Save ceremony, save general ceremony?
> —Shakespeare.

> O ceremony, show me but thy worth!
> What is thy soul of adoration?
> Art thou aught else but place, degree, and form,
> Creating awe and fear in other men?
> —Shakespeare.

Ceremony keeps up things; 'tis like a penny glass to a rich spirit, or some

excellent water; without it the water were spilt, and the spirit lost.—Selden.

Chance

Chance governs all.—Milton.

Chance is a nickname for Providence.—Chamfort.

Time and chance happeneth to them all.—Bible.

The generality of men have, like plants, latent properties, which chance brings to light.—Rochefoucauld.

Chance generally favors the prudent. —Joubert.

Chance is a second master.—Pliny the Elder.

Such is the chance of war.—Homer.

How slight a chance may raise or sink a soul!—Bailey.

Chance is a word void of sense; nothing can exist without a cause.— Voltaire.

Chance is blind and is the sole author of creation.—Saintine.

Chance corrects us of many faults that reason would not know how to correct.—Rochefoucauld.

Discouragement seizes us only when we can no longer count on chance.— George Sand.

The opposites of apparent chance are constancy and sensible interposition.—Paley.

Chance often gives us that which we should not have presumed to ask.—Lamartine.

Chance never helps those who do not help themselves.—Sophocles.

I have set my life upon a cast, and I will stand the hazard of the die.— Shakespeare.

Chance is a kind of god, for it preserves many things which we do not observe.—Menander.

Chance happens to all, but to turn chance to account is the gift of few.—Bulwer-Lytton.

The mines of knowledge are oft laid bare through the forked hazel wand of chance.—Tupper.

Chance is but the pseudonyme of God for those particular cases which He does not choose to subscribe openly with His own sign-manual,—Coleridge.

Nature goes on her way, and all that to us seems an exception is really according to order.—Goethe.

To talk of luck and chance only shows how little we really know of the laws which govern cause and effect.—Hosea Ballou.

Many shining actions owe their success to chance, though the general or statesman runs away with the applause.—Lord Kames.

Chance is but a mere name, and really nothing in itself; a conception of our minds, and only a compendious way of speaking.—Bentley.

I do not believe such a quality as chance exists. Every incident that happens must be a link in a chain.—Beaconsfield.

How often events, by chance and unexpectedly, come to pass, which you had not dared even to hope for!—Terence.

Chance is always powerful; let your hook always be cast. In a pool where you least expect it there will be a fish.—Ovid.

There is no such thing as chance; and what seems to us merest accident springs from the deepest source of destiny.—Schiller.

Although men flatter themselves with their great actions, they are not so often the result of a great design as of chance.—La Rochefoucauld.

There is no doubt such a thing as chance, but I see no reason why Provi-

dence should not make use of it.—Simms.

But as the unthought-on accident is guilty
To what we wildly do, so we profess
Ourselves to be the slaves of chance, and flies
Of every wind that blows.
—Shakespeare.

All nature is but art unknown to thee,
All chance, direction, which thou canst not see.—Pope.

There must be chance in the midst of design; by which we mean that events which are not designed necessarily arise from the pursuit of events which are designed.—Paley.

As the ancients wisely say
Have a care o' th' main chance,
And look before you ere you leap;
For as you sow y'are like to reap.
—Butler.

To admit that there is any such thing as chance, in the common acceptation of the term, would be to attempt to establish a power independent of God.—Colton.

What can be more foolish than to think that all this rare fabric of heaven and earth could come by chance, when all the skill of art is not able to make an oyster!—Jeremy Taylor.

Be not too presumptuously sure in any business; for things of this world depend upon such a train of unseen chances that if it were in man's hands to set the tables, yet is he not certain to win the game.—George Herbert.

Chance never writ a legible book; chance never built a fair house; chance never drew a neat picture; it never did any of these things, nor ever will; nor can it be without absurdity supposed able to do them; which yet are works very gross and rude, very easy and feasible, as it were, in comparison to the production of a flower or a tree.—Barrow.

It is strictly and philosophically true in Nature and reason that there is no such thing as chance or accident; it being evident that these words do not signify anything really existing, anything that is truly an agent or the cause of any event; but they signify merely men's ignorance of the real and immediate cause.—Adam Clarke.

Can that which is not shape, shape the
    things that are?
Is chance omnipotent—resolve me why
The meanest shellfish, and the noblest
    brute,
Transmit their likeness to the years that
    come?   —Dilnot Sladden.

Chance is a term we apply to events to denote that they happen without any necessary or foreknown cause. When we say a thing happens by chance, we mean no more than that its cause is unknown to us, and not, as some vainly imagine, that chance itself can be the cause of anything.—C. Buck.

Chance will not do the work—Chance sends
    the breeze;
But if the pilot slumber at the helm,
The very wind that wafts us towards the
    port
May dash us on the shelves.—The steers-
    man's part is vigilance,
Blow it or rough or smooth.   —Scott.

There are chords in the human heart—strange varying strings—which are only struck by accident; which will remain mute and senseless to appeals the most passionate and earnest, and respond at last to the slightest casual touch. In the most insensible or childish minds there is some train of reflection which art can seldom lead or skill assist, but which will reveal itself, as great truths have done, by chance, and when the discoverer has the plainest and simplest end in view.—Dickens.

Surely no man can reflect, without wonder, upon the vicissitudes of human life arising from causes in the highest degree accidental and trifling. If you trace the necessary concatenation of human events a very little way back, you may perhaps discover that a person's very going in or out of a door has been the means of coloring with misery or happiness the remaining current of his life.—Lord Greville.

Change

I am not what I once was.—Horace.

All things human change.—Tennyson.

Nought may endure but mutability.—Shelley.

Revolutions are not made; they come.—Wendell Phillips.

Do not think that years leave us and find us the same!—Lord Lytton.

Change still doth reign, and keep the greater sway.—Spenser.

Change generally pleases the rich.—Horace.

And one by one in turn, some grand mis-
    take
Casts off its bright skin yearly like the
    snake.   —Byron.

What I possess I would gladly retain; change amuses the mind, yet scarcely profits.—Goethe.

In this world of change, nought which comes stays, and nought which goes is lost.—Mme. Swetchine.

    All things must change
To something new, to something strange.
        —Longfellow.

"Passing away" is written on the world, and all the world contains.—Mrs. Hemans.

As hope and fear alternate chase
Our course through life's uncertain race.
        —Scott.

Earth changes, but thy soul and God stand sure.—Robert Browning.

        To the mind,
Which is itself, no changes bring surprise
        —Byron.

Nothing maintains its bloom forever; age succeeds age.—Cicero.

Bodies are slow of growth, but are rapid in their dissolution.—Tacitus.

As the rolling stone gathers no moss, so the roving heart gathers no affections.—Mrs. Jameson.

The lazy ox wishes for horse-trappings, and the steed wishes to plough.
—Horace.

The stone that is rolling can gather no moss.
Who often removeth is suer of loss.
—Tusser.

He pulls down, he builds up, he changes squares into circles.—Horace.

The world is a scene of changes, and to be constant in nature were inconstancy.—Cowley.

I am not now
That which I have been. —Byron.

The great world spins forever down the ringing grooves of change.—Tennyson.

Manners with fortunes, humors turn with climes,
Tenets with books and principles with times. —Pope.

Changing hands without changing measures is as if a drunkard in a dropsy should change his doctors, and not his diet.—Saville.

There is nothing in the world that remains unchanged. All things are in perpetual flux, and every shadow is seen to move.—Ovid.

Weep not that the world changes—did it keep
A stable, changeless state, it were cause indeed to weep. —Bryant.

Believe, if thou wilt, that mountains change their places, but believe not that man changes his nature.—Mohammed.

Alack, this world
Is full of change, change, change—nothing but change! —D. M. Mulock.

This world is not for aye, nor 'tis not strange
That even our loves should with our fortunes change. —Shakespeare.

Can any one find out in what condition his body will be, I do not say a year hence, but this evening?—Cicero.

There is nothing better fitted to delight the reader than change of circumstances and varieties of fortune.—Cicero.

The world goes up and the world goes down,
And the sunshine follows the rain;
And yesterday's sneer and yesterday's frown
Can never come over again.
—Charles Kingsley.

He is less likely to be mistaken who looks forward to a change in the affairs of the world than he who regards them as firm and stable.—Guicciardini.

All that's bright must fade—
The brightest still the fleetest;
All that's sweet was made
But to be lost when sweetest.
—Moore.

'Tis well to be merry and wise,
'Tis well to be honest and true;
'Tis well to be off with the old love
Before you are on with the new.
—Maturin.

Weary the cloud falleth out of the sky,
Dreary the leaf lieth low.
All things must come to the earth by and by,
Out of which all things grow.
—Lord Lytton.

Thus times do shift; each thing his turne does hold;
New things succeed, as former things grow old. —Herrick.

Gather ye rosebuds while ye may,
Old Time is still a flying;
And that same flower that blooms to-day,
To-morrow shall be dying. —Herrick.

As the blessings of health and fortune have a beginning, so they must also find an end. Everything rises but to fall, and increases but to decay.—Sallust.

Ships, wealth, general confidence—
All were his;
He counted them at break of day,
And when the sun set! where were they?
—Byron.

Everything that is created is changed by the laws of man; the earth does not know itself in the revolution of years; even the races of man assume various forms in the course of ages.—Manilius.

So many great nobles, things, administrations,
So many high chieftains, so many brave nations,
So many proud princes, and powers so splendid,
In a moment, a twinkling, all utterly ended.
—Abraham Coles.

We do not know either unalloyed happiness or unmitigated misfortune. Everything in this world is a tangled yarn; we taste nothing in its purity; we do not remain two moments in the same state. Our affections as well as bodies, are in a perpetual flux.—Rousseau.

Time fleeth on,
Youth soon is gone,
Naught earthly may abide;
Life seemeth fast,
But may not last—
It runs as runs the tide.—Leland.

To-day is not yesterday; we ourselves change; how can our works and thoughts if they are always to be the fittest, continue always the same? Change, indeed, is painful; yet ever needful; and if memory have its force and worth, so also has hope.—Carlyle.

Joy comes and goes, hope ebbs and flows
Like the wave;
Change doth unknit the tranquil strength of men.
Love lends life a little grace,
A few sad smiles; and then,
Both are laid in one cold place,
In the grave.
—Matthew Arnold.

This is the state of man: To-day he puts forth
The tender leaves of hope; to-morrow blossoms,
And bears his blushing honors thick upon him;
The third day comes a frost, a killing frost,
And, when he thinks, good easy man, full surely
His greatness is a-ripening, nips his root
And then he falls, as I do.—Shakespeare.

The life of any one can by no means be changed after death; an evil life can in no wise be converted into a good life, or an infernal into an angelic life; because every spirit, from head to foot, is of the character of his love, and, therefore, of his life; and to convert this life into its opposite would be to destroy the spirit utterly.—Swedenborg.

Such are the vicissitudes of the world, through all its parts, that day and night, labor and rest, hurry and retirement, endear each other; such are the changes that keep the mind in action: we desire, we pursue, we obtain, we are satiated; we desire something else and begin a new pursuit.—Johnson.

All things that we ordained festival,
Turn from their office to black funeral;
Our instruments to melancholy bells,
Our wedding cheer to a sad burial feast,
Our solemn hymns to sullen dirges change,
Our bridal flowers serve for a buried corse,
And all things change them to the contrary. —Shakespeare.

Perfection is immutable. But for things imperfect, change is the way to perfect them. It gets the name of wilfulness when it will not admit of a lawful change to the better. Therefore constancy without knowledge cannot be always good. In things ill it is not virtue, but an absolute vice.—Feltham.

Character

Nothing endures but personal qualities.—Walt Whitman.

Character is a perfectly educated will.—Novalis.

The man that makes a character makes foes.—Young.

No talent, but yet a character.—Heine.

Character makes its own destiny.—Mrs. Campbell Praed.

The great hope of society is individual character.—Channing.

Character must be kept bright as well as clean.—Chesterfield.

Character is very much a matter of health.—Bovee.

Human improvement is from within outward.—Froude.

Our character is our will; for what we will we are.—Archbishop Manning.

Weakness of character is the only defect which cannot be amended.—Rochefoucauld.

No change of circumstances can repair a defect of character.—Emerson.

Happiness is not the end of life; character is.—Beecher.

You must look into people as well as at them.—Chesterfield.

We are sometimes as different from ourselves as we are from others.—Rochefoucauld.

As your enemies and your friends, so are you.—Lavater.

In this world a man must either be anvil or hammer.—Longfellow.

Character lives in a man, reputation outside of him.—J. G. Holland.

Character is what nature has engraven in us; can we then efface it?—Voltaire.

Character is the diamond that scratches every other stone.—Bartol.

Character is centrality, the impossibility of being overthrown.—Emerson.

A good name is better than precious ointment.—Eccles. vii. 1.

The most striking characters are sometimes the product of an infinity of little accidents.—Danton.

The fine tints and fluent curves which constitute beauty of character.—Bulwer-Lytton.

The most careful reasoning characters are very often the most easily abashed.—Mme. de Staël.

Every one is as God made him, and often a great deal worse.—Cervantes.

Talent is nurtured in solitude; char- acter is formed in the stormy billows of the world.—Goethe.

Men and brethren, a simple trust in God is the most essential ingredient in moral sublimity of character.—Richard Fuller.

Individuality is everywhere to be guarded and honored as the root of all good.—Jean Paul Richter.

Actions, looks, words, steps from the alphabet by which you may spell characters.—Lavater.

Our character is but the stamp on our souls of the free choice of good or evil we have made through life.—J. C. Geikie.

Character is moral order seen through the medium of an individual nature.—Emerson.

Characters never change. Opinions alter,—characters are only developed.—Disraeli.

Strong characters are brought out by change of situation, and gentle ones by permanence.—Richter.

All men are like in their lower natures; it is in their higher characters that they differ.—Bovee.

I'm called away by particular business. But I leave my character behind me.—Sheridan.

Every one is least known to himself, and it is very difficult for a man to know himself.—Cicero.

Many persons carry about their character in their hands, not a few under their feet.—Murillo.

You may depend upon it that he is a good man whose intimate friends are all good.—Lavater.

Only what we have wrought into our character during life can we take away with us.—Humboldt.

I have learned by experience that no man's character can be eventually injured but by his own acts.—Rowland Hill.

Character gives splendor to youth, and awe to wrinkled skin and grey hairs.—Emerson.

Fine natures are like fine poems; a glance at the first two lines suffices for a guess into the beauty that waits you if you read on.—Bulwer-Lytton.

Learn now of the treachery of the Greeks, and from one example the character of the nation may be known. —Virgil.

The true greatness of nations is in those qualities which constitute the greatness of the individual.—Charles Sumner.

Give me the character and I will forecast the event. Character, it has in substance been said, is "victory organized."—Bovee.

Love, hope, fear, faith,—these make humanity;
These are its sign, and note, and character.
—Robert Browning.

Every man has in himself a continent of undiscovered character. Happy is he who acts the Columbus to his own soul.—Sir J. Stevens.

Not in the clamor of the crowded street,
Not in the shouts and plaudits of the throng,
But in ourselves, are triumph and defeat.
—Longfellow.

Character is higher than intellect. * * * A great soul will be strong to live, as well as to think.—Emerson.

Every man has three characters—that which he exhibits, that which he has, and that which he thinks he has. —Alphonse Karr.

There is a kind of character in thy life,
That to the observer doth thy history
Fully unfold. —Shakespeare.

There are peculiar ways in men, which discover what they are, through the most subtle feints and closest disguises.—La Bruyère.

In all our reasonings concerning men

we must lay it down as a maxim that the greater part are moulded by circumstances.—Robert Hall.

We do not judge men by what they are in themselves, but by what they are relatively to us.—Mme. Swetchine.

As the present character of a man, so his past, so his future. Who recollects distinctly his past adventures knows his destiny to come.—Lavater.

To judge human character rightly, a man may sometimes have very small experience, provided he has a very large heart.—Bulwer-Lytton.

It is by presence of mind in untried emergencies that the native metal of a man is tested.—Lowell.

The most brilliant qualities become useless when they are not sustained by force of character.—Ségur.

Circumstances form the character; but, like petrifying matters, they harden while they form.—Landor.

He is truly great that is little in himself, and that maketh no account of any height of honors.—Thomas à Kempis.

He whose life seems fair, if all his errors and follies were articled against him, would seem vicious and miserable. —Jeremy Taylor.

A good character when established should not be rested in as an end, but only employed as a means of doing still further good.—Atterbury.

There never has been a great and beautiful character, which has not become so by filling well the ordinary and smaller offices appointed of God.— Horace Bushnell.

It is in men as in soils where sometimes there is a vein of gold which the owner knows not of.—Swift.

Character, like porcelain ware, must be printed before it is glazed. There can be no change after it is burned in. —Beecher.

Character is made up of small duties faithfully performed—of self-denials, of self-sacrifices, of kindly acts of love and duty.—Anon.

Character shows itself apart from genius as a special thing. The first point of measurement of any man is that of quality.—T. W. Higginson.

Let the character as it began be preserved to the last; and let it be consistent with itself.—Horace.

Everything that happens to us leaves some trace behind; everything contributes imperceptibly to make us what we are.—Goethe.

Certain trifling flaws sit as disgracefully on a character of elegance as a ragged button on a court dress.—Lavater.

This is that which we call character,—a reserved force which acts directly by presence, and without means.—Emerson.

Never does a man portray his own character more vividly than in his manner of portraying another.—Richter.

Individual character is in the right that is in strict consistence with itself. Self-contradiction is the only wrong.—Schiller.

We are not that we are, nor do we treat or esteem each other for such, but for that we are capable of being.—Thoreau.

When you have discovered a stain in yourself, you eagerly seek for and gladly find stains in others.—Auerbach.

The man who consecrates his hours
By vig'rous effort and an honest aim,
At once he draws the sting of life and
    death;
He walks with nature, and her paths are
    peace. —Young.

There is in every man a certain feeling that he has been what he is from all eternity, and by no means become such in time.—Schelling.

Those with whom we can apparently become well acquainted in a few moments are generally the most difficult to rightly know and to understand.—Hawthorne.

He that is good will infallibly become better, and he that is bad will as certainly become worse; for vice, virtue, and time are three things that never stand still.—Colton.

Conflict, which rouses up the best and highest powers in some characters, in others not only jars the whole being, but paralyzes the faculties.—Mrs. Jameson.

Many men build as cathedrals were built,—the part nearest the ground finished, but that part which soars toward heaven, the turrets and the spires, forever incomplete.—Beecher.

In common discourse we denominate persons and things according to the major part of their character; he is to be called a wise man who has but few follies.—Watts.

Character is not cut in marble; it is not something solid and unalterable. It is something living and changing, and may become diseased as our bodies do.—George Eliot.

Whatever capacities there may be for enjoyment or for suffering in this strange being of ours, and God only knows what they are, they will be drawn out wholly in accordance with character.—Mark Hopkins.

Some characters are like some bodies in chemistry; very good, perhaps, in themselves, yet fly off and refuse the least conjunction with each other.—Lord Greville.

Fame is what you have taken,
  Character's what you give;
When to this truth you waken,
  Then you begin to live.
    —Bayard Taylor.

It was observed of Elizabeth that she was weak herself, but chose wise counsellors; to which it was replied, that to choose wise counsellors was, in a prince, the highest wisdom.—Colton.

Character is the spiritual body of the person, and represents the individualization of vital experience, the conversion of unconscious things into self-conscious men.—Whipple.

Whoe'er amidst the sons
Of reason, valor, liberty and virtue,
Displays distinguished merit, is a noble
Of Nature's own creating.   —Thomson.

A man's character is like his shadow which sometimes follows, and sometimes precedes him, and which is occasionally longer, occasionally shorter than he is.—From the French.

The best rules to form a young man are to talk little, to hear much, to reflect alone upon what has passed in company, to distrust one's own opinions, and value others that deserve it. —Sir William Temple.

Those who quit their proper character to assume what does not belong to them are, for the greater part, ignorant both of the character they leave and of the character they assume.—Burke.

Man can have strength of character only as he is capable of controlling his faculties; of choosing a rational end; and, in its pursuit, of holding fast to his integrity against all the might of external nature.—Mark Hopkins.

In society every man is taken for what he gives himself out to be; but he must give himself out to be something. Better to be slightly disagreeable than altogether insignificant.—Goethe.

There are many persons of whom it may be said that they have no other possession in the world but their character, and yet they stand as firmly upon it as any crowned king.—Samuel Smiles.

Rugged strength and radiant beauty—
These were one in Nature's plan;
Humble toil and heavenward duty—
These will form the perfect man.
—Sarah J. Hale.

The effect of character is always to command consideration. We sport and toy and laugh with men or women who have none, but we never confide in them.—Simms.

A German writer observes: "The noblest characters only show themselves in their real light. All others act comedy with their fellow-men even unto the grave."—Lady Blessington.

I hope I shall always possess firmness and virtue enough to maintain what I consider the most enviable of all titles, the character of an "honest man."—George Washington.

In our relations with the people around us, we forgive them more readily for what they do, which they can help, than for what they are, which they cannot help.—Mrs. Jameson.

What is the true test of character, unless it be its progressive development in the bustle and turmoil, in the action and reaction of daily life?—Goethe.

These two things, contradictory as they may seem, must go together,—manly dependence and manly independence, manly reliance and manly self-reliance.—Wordsworth.

The most accomplished persons have usually some defect, some weakness in their characters, which diminishes the lustre of their brighter qualifications.—Junius.

It is amusing to detect character in the vocabulary of each person. The adjectives habitually used, like the inscriptions on a thermometer, indicate the temperament.—Tuckerman.

The keen spirit
Seizes the prompt occasion—makes the thought
Start into instant action, and at once
Plans and performs, resolves and executes.
—Hannah More.

It is in the relaxation of security; it is in the expansion of prosperity; it is in the hour of dilatation of the heart, and of its softening into festivity and pleasure, that the real character of men is discerned.—Burke.

As there is much beast and some devil in man, so is there some angel and some God in him. The beast and the devil may be conquered, but in this life never destroyed.—Coleridge.

Your disposition will be suitable to that which you most frequently think on; for the soul is, as it were, tinged with the color and complexion of its own thoughts.—Marcus Antoninus.

A man who shows no defect is a fool or a hypocrite, whom we should mistrust. There are defects so bound to fine qualities that they announce them,—defects which it is well not to correct.—Joubert.

Duke Chartres used to boast that no man could have less real value for character than himself, yet he would gladly give twenty thousand pounds for a good one, because he could immediately make double that sum by means of it.—Colton.

Where the vivacity of the intellect and the strength of the passions exceed the development of the moral faculties the character is likely to be embittered or corrupted by extremes, either of adversity or prosperity.—Mrs. Jameson.

A man is what he is, not what men say he is. His character no man can touch. His character is what he is before his God and his Judge; and only himself can damage that. His reputation is what men say he is. That can be damaged; but reputation is for time, character is for eternity.—John B. Gough.

The two most precious things this side the grave are our reputation and our life. But it is to be lamented that the most contemptible whisper may deprive us of the one, and the weakest weapon of the other.—Colton.

Should any man tell you that a mountain had changed its place, you are at liberty to doubt it if you think fit; but if any one tells you that a man has changed his character, do not believe it.—Mahomet.

Each man forms his duty according to his predominant characteristic; the stern require an avenging judge; the gentle, a forgiving father. Just so the pygmies declared that Jove himself was a pygmy.—Bulwer-Lytton.

Joy and grief decide character. What exalts prosperity? what imbitters grief? what leaves us indifferent? what interests us? As the interest of man, so his God,—as his God, so he.—Lavater.

As fire when thrown into water is cooled down and put out, so also a false accusation when brought against a man of the purest and holiest character boils over and is at once dissipated and vanishes.—Cicero.

A man's character is the reality of himself: his reputation, the opinion others have formed about him; character resides in him, reputation in other people; that is the substance, this is the shadow.—Beecher.

The noblest contribution which any man can make for the benefit of posterity is that of a good character. The richest bequest which any man can leave to the youth of his native land is that of a shining, spotless example.—Winthrop.

It is a common error, of which a wise man will beware, to measure the worth of our neighbor by his conduct towards ourselves. How many rich souls might we not rejoice in the knowledge of, were it not for our pride!—Richter.

To know a people's character, we must see it at its homes, and look chiefly to the humbler abodes where that portion of the people dwells which makes the broad basis of the national prosperity.—Kossuth.

There are beauties of character which, like the night-blooming cereus, are closed against the glare and turbulence of every-day life, and bloom only in shade and solitude, and beneath the quiet stars.—Tuckerman.

A man is known to his dog by the smell, to his tailor by the coat, to his friend by the smile; each of these know him, but how little or how much depends on the dignity of the intelligence. That which is truly and indeed characteristic of the man is known only to God.—Ruskin.

Although genius always commands

admiration, character most secures re-spect. The former is more the product of the brain, the latter of heart-power; and in the long run it is the heart that rules in life.—Samuel Smiles.

Grit is the grain of character. It may generally be described as heroism materialized,—spirit and will will thrust into heart, brain, and backbone, so as to form part of the physical substance of the man.—Whipple.

He that has light within his own clear
   breast,
May sit i' th' centre, and enjoy bright day:
But he that hides a dark soul, and foul
   thoughts,
Benighted walks under the mid-day sun;
Himself is his own dungeon. —Milton.

Character halts without aid of the imagination, which our classes in Shakespeare and Browning, music and drawing, recognize not only as amusement and by-play of the mind, but a co-ordinate power. Its work is unhappily styled fiction; for to idealize is to realize.—Bartol.

The highest of characters, in my estimation, is his who is as ready to pardon the moral errors of mankind as if he were every day guilty of some himself; and at the same time as cautious of committing a fault as if he never forgave one.—Pliny the Younger.

The only equitable manner in my opinion, of judging the character of a man is to examine if there are personal calculations in his conduct; if there are not, we may blame his manner of judging, but we are not the less bound to esteem him.—Madame de Staël.

He's truly valiant that can wisely suffer
The worst that man can breathe;
And make his wrongs his outsides,
To wear them like his raiment, carelessly;
And ne'er prefer his injuries to his heart,
To bring it into danger. —Shakespeare.

Never get a reputation for a small perfection if you are trying for fame in a loftier area. The world can only judge by generals, and it sees that those who pay considerable attention to minutiæ seldom have their minds

occupied with great things.—Bulwer-Lytton.

A good character is, in all cases, the fruit of personal exertion. It is not inherited from parents, it is not created by external advantages, it is no necessary appendage of birth, wealth, talents or station; but it is the result of one's own endeavors.—Hawes.

As nature made every man with a nose and eyes of his own, she gave him a character of his own, too; and yet we, O foolish race! must try our very best to ape some one or two of our neighbors, whose ideas fit us no more than their breeches!—Thackeray.

Remedy your deficiencies, and your merits will take care of themselves. Every man has in him good and evil. His good is his valiant army, his evil is his corrupt commissariat; reform the commissariat and the army will do its duty.—Bulwer-Lytton.

The amiable and the severe, Mr. Burke's sublime and beautiful, by different proportions, are mixed in every character. Accordingly, as either is predominant, men imprint the passions of love or fear. The best punch depends on a proper mixture of sugar and lemons.—Shenstone.

It is not what a man gets, but what a man is that he should think of. He should first think of his character and then of his condition. He that has character need have no fears about his condition. Character will draw after it condition. Circumstances obey principles.—Beecher.

Many men are mere warehouses full of merchandise—the head, the heart, are stuffed with goods. * * * There are apartments in their souls which were once tenanted by taste, and love, and joy, and worship, but they are all deserted now, and the rooms are filled with earthy and material things.—Henry Ward Beecher.

Character is the product of daily, hourly actions, and words and thoughts; daily forgivenesses, unselfishness, kindnesses, sympathies, charities, sacrifices for the good of others, struggles against temptation, submissiveness under trial. Oh, it is these, like the blending colors in a picture or the blending notes of music which constitute the man.—J. R. Macduff.

Brains and character rule the world. The most distinguished Frenchman of the last century said: "Men succeed less by their talents than their character." There were scores of men a hundred years ago who had more intellect than Washington. He outlives and overrides them all by the influence of his character.—Wendell Phillips.

The craft with which the world is made runs also into the mind and character of men. No man is quite sane; each has a vein of folly in his composition, a slight determination of blood to the head, to make sure of holding him hard to some one point which Nature has taken to heart.—Emerson.

It is an error common to many to take the character of mankind from the worst and basest amongst them; whereas, as an excellent writer has observed, nothing should be esteemed as characteristical of a species but what is to be found amongst the best and the most perfect individuals of that species.—Fielding.

We should not be too hasty in bestowing either our praise or censure on mankind, since we shall often find such a mixture of good and evil in the same character, that it may require a very accurate judgment and a very elaborate inquiry to determine on which side the balance turns.—Fielding.

We must have a weak spot or two in a character before we can love it much. People that do not laugh or cry, or take more of anything than is good for them, or use anything but dictionary words, are admirable subjects for biographies. But we don't always care most for those flat-pattern flowers that press best in the herbarium.—Holmes.

Modern engineers, after having erected a viaduct, insist upon subjecting it to a severe strain by a formal trial trip before allowing it to be opened for public traffic, and it would almost seem that God, in employing moral agents for the carrying out of His purposes, secures that they shall be tested by some dreadful ordeal before He fully commits to them the work which He wishes them to perform.—Wm. M. Taylor.

Ordinary people regard a man of a certain force and inflexibility of character as they do a lion. They look at him with a sort of wonder—perhaps they admire; but they will, on no account, house with him. The lap dog, who wags his tail and licks the hand and cringes at the nod of every stranger, is a much more acceptable companion to them.—Merkel.

Avoid connecting yourself with characters whose good and bad sides are unmixed and have not fermented together; they resemble vials of vinegar and oil; or palletts set with colors; they are either excellent at home and insufferable abroad, or intolerable within doors and excellent in public; they are unfit for friendship, merely because their stamina, their ingredients of character are too single, too much apart; let them be finely ground up with each other, and they are incomparable.—Lavater.

Every man has at times in his mind the ideal of what he should be, but is not. This ideal may be high and complete, or it may be quite low and insufficient; yet in all men that really seek to improve, it is better than the actual character. * * * Man never falls so low that he can see nothing higher than himself.—Theodore Parker.

Formed on the good old plan,
A true and brave and downright honest man!
He blew no trumpet in the market-place,
Nor in the church with hypocritic face
Supplied with cant the lack of Christian grace;
Loathing pretense, he did with cheerful will
What others talked of while their hands were still.   —Whittier.

Very great personages are not likely to form very just estimates either of others or of themselves; their knowledge of themselves is obscured by the flattery of others; their knowledge of others is equally clouded by circumstances peculiar to themselves. For in the presence of the great, the modest are sure to suffer from too much diffidence, and the confident from too much display.—Colton.

A great character, founded on the living rock of principle, is, in fact, not a solitary phenomenon, to be at once perceived, limited and described. It is a dispensation of Providence, designed to have not merely an immediate but a continuous, progressive and never-ending agency. It survives the man who possessed it; survives his age —perhaps his country, his language. —Ed. Everett.

Character is always known. Thefts never enrich; alms never impoverish; murder will speak out of stone walls. The least admixture of a lie— for example, the taint of vanity, any attempt to make a good impression, a favorable appearance—will instantly vitiate the effect. But speak the truth and all nature and all spirits help you with unexpected furtherance. —Emerson.

Instead of saying that man is the creature of circumstance, it would be nearer the mark to say that man is the architect of circumstance. It is character which builds an existence out of circumstance. Our strength is measured by our plastic power. From the same materials one man builds palaces, another hovels; one warehouses, another villas; bricks and mortar are mortar and bricks until the architect can make them something else.—Carlyle.

Decision of character is one of the most important of human qualities, philosophically considered. Speculation, knowledge, is not the chief end of man; it is action. * * * "Give us the man," shout the multitude, "who will step forward and take the responsibility." He is instantly the idol, the lord and the king among men. He, then, who would command among his fellows, must excel them more in energy of will than in power of intellect.—Burnap.

There are some characters who appear to superficial observers to be full of contradiction, change and inconsistency, and yet they that are in the secret of what such persons are driving at, know that they are the very reverse of what they appear to be, and that they have one single object in view, to which they as pertinaciously adhere through every circumstance of change, as the hound to the hare, through all her mazes and doublings. We know that a windmill is eternally at work to accomplish one end, although it shifts with every variation of the weather-cock, and assumes ten different positions in a day.—Colton.

Charity

For charity shall cover the multitude of sins.—Bible.

Charity is the scope of all God's commands.—Chrysostom.

He is truly great who hath a great charity.—Thomas à Kempis.

Charity, which renders good for bad, blessings for curses.—Shakespeare.

What we frankly give, forever is our own.—Granville.

They serve God well who serve His creatures.—Mrs. Norton.

As the purse is emptied the heart is filled.—Victor Hugo.

True charity, a plant divinely nurs'd.—Cowper.

And learn the luxury of doing good. —Goldsmith.

Gently to hear, kindly to judge.— Shakespeare.

That comes too late that comes for the asking.—Seneca.

Charity is a virtue of the heart and not of the hands.—Addison.

Gifts and alms are the expressions, not the essence, of this virtue.— Addison.

Charity is an eternal debt and without limit.—Pasquier Quesnel.

Be charitable and indulgent to every one but yourself.—Joubert.

But when thou doest alms, let not thy left hand know what thy right hand doeth.—Matthew vi. 3.

Did universal charity prevail, earth would be a heaven and hell a fable.—Colton.

Charity resembleth fire, which inflameth all things it toucheth.—Erasmus.

We are rich only through what we give, and poor only through what we refuse.—Madame Swetchine.

That charity which is the perfection and ornament of religion.—Addison.

The drying up a single tear has more
Of honest fame, than shedding seas of gore.
—Byron.

An effort made for the happiness of others lifts us above ourselves.—L. M. Child.

No communication or gift can exhaust genius or impoverish charity.—Lavater.

Faith and hope themselves shall die, while deathless charity remains.—Prior.

A friar who asks alms for God's sake begs for two.—Calderon.

You must have a genius for charity as well as for anything else.—Thoreau.

Alas for the rarity of Christian charity under the sun.—Hood.

The place of charity, like that of God, is everywhere.—Professor Vinet.

You find people ready enough to do the Samaritan, without the oil and twopence.—Sydney Smith.

A poor man serv'd by thee, shall make thee rich.—Mrs. Browning.

There can be no Christianity where there is no charity.—Colton.

To pity distress is but human; to relieve it is Godlike.—Horace Mann.

I will chide no breather in the world but myself; against whom I know most faults.—Shakespeare.

Wherever the tree of beneficence takes root, it sends forth branches beyond the sky!—Saadi.

A tear for pity and a hand
Open as day for melting charity.
—Shakespeare.

There is no dearth of charity in the world in giving, but there is comparatively little exercised in thinking and speaking.—Sir Philip Sidney.

For true charity
Though ne'er so secret finds its just reward.
—May.

Charity ever finds in the act reward, and needs no trumpet in the receiver.—Beaumont and Fletcher.

Large charity doth never soil, but only whitens soft white hands.—Lowell.

That charity which longs to publish itself, ceases to be charity.—Hutton.

The secret pleasure of a generous act is the great mind's great bribe.—Dryden.

The smallest act of charity shall stand us in great stead.—Atterbury.

True charity is liable to excesses and transports.—Massillon.

My poor are my best patients. God pays for them.—Boerhaave.

A hand as fruitful as the land that feeds us; His dew falls everywhere.—Shakespeare.

'Tis not enough to help the feeble up, But to support him after.—Shakespeare.

The highest exercise of charity is charity towards the uncharitable.—Buckminster.

The heart of a girl is like a convent—the holier the cloister, the more charitable the door.—Bulwer-Lytton.

Cast thy bread upon the waters; for thou shalt find it after many days. —Bible.

It is fruition, and not possession, that renders us happy.—Montaigne.

It was sufficient that his wants were known, True charity makes other's wants its own. —Robert Danborne.

And now abideth faith, hope, charity, these three; but the greatest of these is charity.—Bible.

No sound ought to be heard in the church but the healing voice of Christian charity.—Burke.

A woman who wants a charitable heart wants a pure mind.—Haliburton.

Nothing will make us so charitable and tender to the faults of others as by self-examination thoroughly to know our own.—Fénelon.

Good is no good, but if it be spend, God giveth good for none other end. —Spenser.

The charities that soothe and heal and bless, lie scattered at the feet of men like flowers.—Wordsworth.

There is no virtue can be sooner missed or later welcomed; it begins the rest, and sets them all in order.— Middleton.

Give to him that asketh thee; and from him that would borrow of thee turn not thou away.—Matthew.

He who receives a good turn should never forget it; he who does one should never remember it.—Charron.

Defer not charities till death. He who does so is rather liberal of another man's substance than his own. —Stretch.

With malice toward none, with charity for all, with firmness in the right—as God gives us to see the right

—let us strive on to finish the work we are in.—Abraham Lincoln.

How white are the fair robes of charity, as she walketh amid the lowly habitations of the poor!—Hosea Ballou.

Posthumous charities are the very essence of selfishness, when bequeathed by those who, when alive, would part with nothing.—Colton.

Earth has not a spectacle more glorious or more fair to show than this —love tolerating intolerance; charity covering, as with a vail, even the sin of the lack of charity.—F. W. Robertson.

Charity is that sweet-smelling savor of Jesus Christ, which vanishes and is extinguished from the moment that it is exposed.—Massillon.

Charity itself consists in acting justly and faithfully in whatever office, business and employment a person is engaged in.—Swedenborg.

Ah! what a divine religion might be found out if charity were really made the principle of it instead of faith!—Shelley.

It is wicked to withdraw from being useful to the needy, and cowardly to give way to the worthless.—Epictetus.

A rich man without charity is a rogue; and perhaps it would be nc difficult matter to piove that he is also a fool.--Fielding.

Our possessions are wholly in our performances. He owns nothing to whom the world owes nothing.— Simms.

It is with charity as with money —the more we stand in need of it, the less we have to give away.—Bovee.

Prayer carries us half way to God, fasting brings us **to** the door of His palace and alms-giving procures us admission.—Koran.

A man should fear when he enjoys only what good he does publicly Is it not the publicity, rather than the charity, that he loves?—Beecher.

In all works of liberality something more is to be considered besides the occasion of the givers; and that is the occasion of the receivers.—Thomas Sprat.

In giving alms, let us rather look at the needs of the poor than his claim to your charity.—J. Petit-Senn.

True charity is spontaneous and finds its own occasion; it is never the offspring of importunity, nor of emulation.—Hosea Ballou.

We should give as we would receive, cheerfully, quickly and without hesitation; for there is no grace in a benefit that sticks to the fingers.—Seneca.

Charity is a flower not naturally of earthly growth, and it needs manuring with a promise of profit.—Ouida.

That charity is bad which takes from independence its proper pride, from mendicity its salutary shame.—Southey.

It is good to be charitable; but to whom? That is the point. As to the ungrateful, there is not one who does not at last die miserable.—La Fontaine.

Great minds, like heaven, are pleased in doing good, though the ungrateful subjects of their favors are barren in return.—Rowe.

The spirit of the world encloses four kinds of spirits, diametrically opposed to charity—the spirit of resentment, spirit of aversion, spirit of jealousy and the spirit of indifference.—Bossuet.

Why should not our solemn duties and our hastening end render us so united that personal contention would be impossible, in a general sympathy, quickened by the breath of a forbearing and pitying charity?—Henry Giles.

Charity in various guises is an in-

truder the poor see often; but courtesy and delicacy are visitants with which they are seldom honored.—Ouida.

In charity to all mankind, bearing no malice or ill-will to any human being, and even compassionating those who hold in bondage their fellow-men, not knowing what they do.—John Quincy Adams.

He that rightly understands the reasonableness and excellency of charity will know that it can never be excusable to waste any of our money in pride and folly.—William Law.

If thou neglectest thy love to thy neighbor, in vain thou professest thy love to God; for by thy love to God, the love to thy neighbor is begotten, and by the love to thy neighbor thy love to God is nourished.—Francis Quarles.

Though we may sometimes unintentionally bestow our beneficence on the unworthy, it does not take from the merit of the act. For charity doth not adopt the vices of its objects.—Fielding.

Our true acquisitions lie only in our charities. We gain only as we give. There is no beggar so destitute as he who can afford nothing to his neighbor.—Simms.

I would have none of that rigid circumspect charity which is never done without scrutiny, and which always mistrusts the truth of the necessities laid open to it.—Massillon.

Charity is a principle of prevailing love to God and good will to men which effectually inclines one endued with it to glorify God and to do good to others.—Cruden.

Heaven be their resource who have no other but the charity of the world, the stock of which, I fear, is no way sufficient for the many great claims which are hourly made upon it.—Sterne.

Use every man after his desert, and

who shall 'scape whipping? Use them after your own honor and dignity; the less they deserve, the more merit is in your bounty.—Shakespeare.

Even the wisdom of God hath not suggested more pressing motives, more powerful incentives to charity, than these, that we shall be judged by it at the last dreadful day.—Atterbury.

What we employ in charitable uses during our lives is given away from ourselves; what we bequeath at our death is given from others only, as our nearest relations.—Atterbury.

Beneficence is a duty. He who frequently practices it, and sees his benevolent intentions realized, at length comes really to love him to whom he has done good.—Kant.

Be not frightened at the hard words "imposition," "imposture;" give, and ask no questions. Cast thy bread upon the waters. Some have, unawares, entertained angels.—Lamb.

Then gently scan your brother man,
Still gentler, sister woman;
Though they may gang a gennin' wrang,
To step aside is human. —Burns.

A beggar through the world am I—
From place to place I wander by,
Fill up my pilgrim's scrip for me,
For Christ's sweet sake and charity.
—Lowell.

It maketh God man, and man God; things temporal, eternal; mortal, immortal; it maketh an enemy a friend, a servant a son, vile things glorious, cold hearts fiery, and hard things liquid.—St. Bonaventura.

In faith and hope the world will disagree,
But all mankind's concern is charity;
All must be false that thwart this one great end,
And all of God that bless mankind or mend.
—Pope.

As every lord giveth a certain livery to his servants, charity is the very livery of Christ. Our Saviour, Who is the Lord above all lords, would have His servants known by their badge, which is love.—Latimer.

Charity is that rational and constant affection which makes us sacrifice ourselves to the human race, as if we were united with it, so as to form one individual, partaking equally in its adversity and prosperity.—Confucius.

When I die, I should be ashamed to leave enough to build me a monument if there were a wanting friend above ground. I would enjoy the pleasure of what I give by giving it alive and seeing another enjoy it.—Pope.

I have no respect for that self-boasting charity which neglects all objects of commiseration near and around it, but goes to the end of the earth in search of misery, for the purpose of talking about it.—George Mason.

The charities of life are scattered everywhere, enamelling the vales of human beings as the flowers paint the meadows. They are not the fruit of study, nor the privilege of refinement, but a natural instinct.—Bancroft.

He who has never denied himself for the sake of giving has but glanced at the joys of charity. We owe our superfluity, and to be happy in the performance of our duty we must exceed it.—Mme. Swetchine.

I thank heaven I have often had it in my power to give help and relief, and this is still my greatest pleasure. If I could choose my sphere of action now, it would be that of the most simple and direct efforts of this kind.—Niebuhr.

The last, best fruit which comes to late perfection, even in the kindliest soul, is tenderness toward the hard, forbearance toward the unforbearing, warmth of heart toward the cold, philanthropy toward the misanthropic.—Richter.

In giving of thy alms, inquire not so much into the person, as his necessity. God looks not so much upon the merits of him that requires, as into the manner of him that relieves; if the man deserve not, thou hast given it to humanity.—Quarles.

I have much more confidence in the charity which begins in the home and diverges into a large humanity, than in the world-wide philanthropy which begins at the outside of our horizon to converge into egotism.—Mrs. Jameson.

When thy brother has lost all that he ever had, and lies languishing, and even gasping under the utmost extremities of poverty and distress, dost thou think to lick him whole again only with thy tongue?—South.

Poplicola's doors were opened on the outside, to save the people even the common civility of asking entrance; where misfortune was a powerful recommendation, and where want itself was a powerful mediator.—Dryden.

Shall we repine at a little misplaced charity—we who could no way foresee the effect—when an all-knowing, all-wise Being showers down every day His benefits on the unthankful and undeserving?—Atterbury.

The desire of power in excess caused the angels to fall; the desire of knowledge in excess caused man to fall; but in charity there is no excess, neither can angel or man come in danger by it.—Bacon.

To complain that life has no joys while there is a single creature whom we can relieve by our bounty, assist by our counsels or enliven by our presence, is to lament the loss of that which we possess, and is just as irrational as to die of thirst with the cup in our hands.—Fitzosborne.

Flatter not thyself in thy faith to God, if thou wantest charity for thy neighbor; and think not thou hast charity for thy neighbor, if thou wantest faith to God; where they are not both together, they are both wanting; they are both dead, if once divided.—Quarles.

And when Christ came to implant in human bosoms pure, disinterested Christian charity, He brought it as an exotic from heaven, and God had to coin a name for it, for there was no word in all the polyglots of earth that would properly describe it. The thing itself was a thing unknown until the angels heralded it and Jesus brought it.

Goodness answers to the theological virtue charity, and admits no excess but error. The desire of power in excess caused the angels to fall; the desire of knowledge in excess caused man to fall; but in charity there is no excess; neither can angel nor man come in danger by it.—Bacon.

The best thing to give to your enemy is forgiveness; to an opponent, tolerance; to a friend, your heart; to your child, a good example; to a father, deference; to your mother, conduct that will make her proud of you; to yourself, respect; to all men, charity.—Mrs. Balfour.

Proportion thy charity to the strength of thy estate, lest God proportion thy estate to the weakness of thy charity: let the lips of the poor be the trumpet of thy gift, lest in seeking applause, thou lose thy reward. Nothing is more pleasing to God than an open hand and a close mouth.—Quarles.

In silence, * * *
Steals on soft-handed Charity,
Tempering her gifts, that seem so free,
By time and place,
Till not a woe the bleak world see,
But finds her grace.   —Keble.

There is a debt of mercy and pity of charity and compassion, of relief and succor due to human nature, and payable from one man to another; and such as deny to pay it the distressed in the time of their abundance may justly expect it will be denied themselves in a time of want. "With what measure you mete it shall be measured to you again."—Burkitt.

Charity suffereth long, and is kind; charity envieth not; charity vaunteth not itself, is not puffed up, doth not behave itself unseemly, seeketh not her own, is not easily provoked, thinketh no evil; rejoiceth not in iniquity, but rejoiceth in the truth; beareth all things, believeth all things, hopeth all things, endureth all things.—Bible.

'Mongst all your virtues
I see not charity written, which some call
The first born of religion; and I wonder,
I cannot see it in yours. Believe it, sir,
There is no virtue can be sooner miss'd
Or later welcom'd; it begins the rest,
And sets them all in order.—Middleton.

I have learned from Jesus Christ Himself what charity is, and how we ought to practise it; for He says: "By this shall all men know that ye are My disciples, if ye love one another." Never can I, therefore, please myself in the hope that I may obtain the name of a servant of Christ if I possess not a true and unfeigned charity within me.—St. Basil.

Whoever would entitle himself after death through the merits of his Redeemer, to the noblest of rewards, let him serve God throughout life in this most excellent of all duties, doing good to our brethren. Whoever is sensible of his offences, let him take this way especially of evidencing his repentance.—Archbishop Secker.

True charity, a plant divinely nursed,
Fed by the love from which it rose at first,
Thrives against hope, and in the rudest scene,
Storms but enliven its unfading green;
Exub'rant is the shadow it supplies,
Its fruit on earth, its growth above the skies.   —Cowper.

Let shining Charity adorn your zeal,
The noblest impulse generous minds can feel.   —Aaron Hill.

Would'st thou from sorrow find a sweet relief,
Or is thy heart oppress'd with woe untold?
Balm would'st thou gather for corroding grief?—
Pour blessings round thee, like a shower of gold.   —Carlos Wilcox.

It is an old saying, that charity begins at home; but this is no reason it should not go abroad. A man should live with the world as a citizen of the world; he may have a preference for the particular quarter or square, or even alley, in which he lives, but he should have a generous feeling for the welfare of the whole.—Cumberland.

The soul of the truly benevolent man does not seem to reside much in his own body. Its life, to a great extent, is a mere reflex of the lives of others. It migrates into their bodies, and identifying its existence with their existence, finds its own happiness in increasing and prolonging their pleasures, in extinguishing or solacing their pains.—Horace Mann.

If there be a pleasure on earth which angels cannot enjoy, and which they might almost envy man the possession of, it is the power of relieving distress—if there be a pain which devils might pity man for enduring, it is the death-bed reflection that we have possessed the power of doing good, but that we have abused and perverted it to purposes of ill.—Colton.

Active beneficence is a virtue of easier practice than forbearance after having conferred, or than thankfulness after having received a benefit. I know not, indeed, whether it be a greater and more difficult exercise of magnanimity, for the one party to act as if he had forgotten, or for the other as if he constantly remembered the obligation.—Canning.

Shut not thy purse-strings always against painted distress. Act a charity sometimes. When a poor creature (outwardly and visibly such) comes before thee, do not stay to inquire whether the "seven small children," in whose name he implores thy assistance, have a veritable existence. Rake not into the bowels of unwelcome truth to save a halfpenny. It is good to believe him.—Lamb.

In all other human gifts and passions, though they advance nature, yet they are subject to excess; but charity alone admits no excess. For so we see, by aspiring to be like God in power the angels transgressed and fell; by aspiring to be like God in knowledge man transgressed and fell; but by aspiring to be like God in goodness or love, neither man nor angel ever did or shall transgress. For unto that imitation we are called.—Bacon.

Think not you are charitable if the love of Jesus and His brethren be not purely the motive of your gifts. Alas! you might not give your superfluities, but "bestow all your goods to feed the poor;" you might even "give your body to be burned" for them, and yet be utterly destitute of charity, if self-seeking, self-pleasing or self-ends guide you; and guide you they must, until the love of God be by the Holy Ghost shed abroad in your heart.—Haweis.

O chime of sweet Saint Charity,
  Peal soon that Easter morn
When Christ for all shall risen be,
  And in all hearts new-born!
That Pentecost when utterance clear
  To all men shall be given,
When all shall say My Brother here,
  And hear My Son in heaven!
                          —Lowell.

The shepherds led the pilgrims to Mount Charity, where they showed them a man that had a bundle of cloth lying before him, out of which he cut coats and garments for the poor that stood about him; yet his bundle or roll of cloth was never the less. Then said they: "What should this be?" "This is," said the shepherds, "to show you that he who has a heart to give of his labor to the poor shall never want wherewithal. 'He that watereth shall be watered himself.' And the cake that the widow gave to the prophet did not cause that she had the less in her barrel."—Bunyan.

That charity alone endures • which flows from a sense of duty and a hope in God. This is the charity that treads in secret those paths of misery from which all but the lowest of human wretches have fled; this is that charity which no labor can weary, no ingratitude detach, no horror disgust; that toils, that pardons, that suffers; that is seen by no man, and honored by no man, but, like the great laws of Nature, does the work of God in silence, and looks to a future and better world for its reward.—Sydney Smith.

Almost all the virtues that can be named are enwrapt in one virtue of charity and love:—"for it suffereth long," and so it is longanimity; it "is kind," and so it is courtesy;

it "vaunteth not itself," and so it is modesty; it "is not puffed up," and so it is humility; it "is not easily provoked," and so it is lenity; it "thinketh no evil," and so it is simplicity; it "rejoiceth in the truth," and so it is verity; it "beareth all things," and so it is fortitude; it "believeth all things," and so it is faith; it "hopeth all things," and so it is confidence; it "endureth all things," and . so it is patience; it "never faileth," and so it is perseverance.—Chillingworth.

Charm

Expression alone can invest beauty with conquering charms.—Fuseli.

Unhappy sex, whose beauty is your snare.—Dryden.

They dazzle our eyes as they fly to our hearts.—Burns.

She whom smiles and tears make equally lovely may command all hearts. —Lavater.

A beautiful woman is the paradise of the eyes.—Fontenelle.

The most beautiful object in the world, it will be allowed, is a beautiful woman.—Macaulay.

Charming women can true converts make; we love the precept for the teacher's sake.—Franklin.

When she passed it seemed like the ceasing of exquisite music.—Longfellow.

A lovely countenance is the fairest of all sights, and the sweetest harmony is the sound of the voice of her whom we love.—Bruyère.

A beautiful hand is an excellent thing in woman; it is a charm that never palls: and better than all, it is a means of fascinating that never disappears.—Beaconsfield.

There is neither spirit nor persistency enough in the whole range of masculine humanity, with but a few rare exceptions, to withstand the artillery of a magnificent woman's charms.—Dr. J. V. C. Smith.

Dean Swift proposed to tax beauty, and to leave every lady to rate her own charms; he said the tax would be cheerfully paid and very productive.—Frederic Saunders.

Charms which, like flowers, lie on the surface and always glitter, easily produce vanity; hence women, wits, players, soldiers, are vain, owing to their presence, figure and dress. On the contrary, other excellences, which lie down like gold and are discovered with difficulty, leave their possessors modest and proud.—Richter.

Chastity

Modesty and chastity are twins.—Mrs. Jameson.

She that has that is clad in complete steel.—Milton.

Of chastity, the ornaments are chaste.—Shakespeare.

The woman that deliberates is lost.—Addison.

As chaste as is the bud ere it be blown.—Shakespeare.

To the pure all things are pure.—Shelley.

Whiter than new snow on a raven's back.—Shakespeare.

Chastity is the seal of grace.—Lady Huntington.

Chastity, like piety, is a uniform grace.—Richardson.

As chaste as unsunn'd snow.—Shakespeare.

Chastity is the ermine of woman's soul.—Queen Elizabeth.

Let women paint their eyes with tints of chastity.—Tertullian.

Chastity, once lost, cannot be recalled; it goes only once.—Ovid.

As pure as a pearl,
And as perfect; a noble and innocent girl.
—Lord Lytton.

A woman's character is as delicate as her eye; it can bear no flaw.—G. A. Sala.

For violets plucked, the sweetest showers will ne'er make grow again.—Byron.

A man defines his standing at the court of chastity by his views of women.—Alcott.

Not the mountain ice, congealed to crystals, is so frosty chaste as thy victorious soul, which conquers man, and man's proud tyrant, passion.—Dryden.

Vanity bids all her sons be brave, and all her daughters chaste and courteous.—Sterne.

The most chaste woman may be the most voluptuous, if she truly loves.—Mirabeau.

The supreme sway of chastity over the senses makes her queenly.—Joubert.

There needs not strength to be added to inviolate chastity; the excellency of the mind makes the body impregnable.—Sir P. Sidney.

That chastity of look which seems to hang a veil of purest light over all her beauties, and by forbidding most inflames desire.—Young.

The soul whose bosom lust did never touch
Is God's fair bride; and maidens' souls are
such.   —Decker.

The soul that is the abode of chastity acquires an energy which enables her to surmount with ease the obstacles that lie along the path of duty.— Joubert.

A beautiful and chaste woman is

the perfect workmanship of God, and the true glory of angels, the rare miracle of earth, and the sole wonder of the world.—Hermes.

So dear to heaven is saintly chastity,
That, when a soul is found sincerely so,
A thousand liveried angels lackey her,
Driving far off each thing of sin and guilt.
—Milton.

Consider what importance to society the chastity of women is. Upon that all the property in the world depends. We hang a thief for stealing a sheep; but the unchastity of a woman transfers sheep and farm and all from the right owner.—Dr. Johnson.

A pure mind in a chaste body is the mother of wisdom and deliberation, sober counsels and ingenuous actions, open deportment and sweet carriage, sincere principles and unprejudicate understanding, love of God and self-denial, peace and confidence, holy prayers and spiritual comfort, and a pleasure of spirit infinitely greater than the sottish pleasure of unchastity.—Jeremy Taylor.

In Goethe's drama, Iphigenia defends her chastity, ascribing her firmness to the gods. "No god hath said this: thine own heart hath spoken," answered Thoas, the king. "They only speak to us through our heart," she replies. "Have not I the right to hear them too?" he rejoins. "Thy storm of passion drowns the gentle whisper," adds the maiden, and closes all debate.—Bartol.

Nothing makes a woman more esteemed by the opposite sex than chastity; whether it be that we always prize those most who are hardest to come at, or that nothing besides chastity, with its collateral attendants, truth, fidelity, and constancy, gives the man a property in the person he loves, and consequently endears her to him above all things.—Addison.

Cheerfulness

He who sings frightens away his ills.—Cervantes.

Let cheerfulness on happy fortune wait.—Dryden.

Be thou of good cheer.—Bible.

Nature designed us to be of good cheer.—Douglas Jerrold.

A good laugh is sunshine in a house.—Thackeray.

Cheerfulness is an offshoot of goodness and of wisdom.—Bovee.

The inborn geniality of some people amounts to genius.—Whipple.

A light heart lives long.—Shakespeare.

A merry heart goes all the day,
A sad tires in a mile.—Shakespeare.

A man he seems of cheerful yesterdays and confident to-morrows.—Wordsworth.

Cheerfulness is health; the opposite, melancholy, is disease.—Haliburton.

Cheerfulness is the friend and helper of all good graces, and the absence of it is certainly a vice.—Aughey.

The way to cheerfulness is to keep our bodies in exercise and our minds at ease.—Steele.

Cheerful at morn he wakes from short repose,
Breathes the keen air, and carols as he goes.   —Goldsmith.

A merry heart doeth good like a medicine; but a broken spirit drieth the bones.—Bible.

Cheerful looks make every dish a feast, and it is that which crowns a welcome.—Massinger.

The most manifest sign of wisdom is continued cheerfulness.—Montaigne.

What can the Creator see with greater pleasure than a happy creature?—Lessing.

The creed of the true saint is to make the best of life, and make the most of it.—Chapin.

An ounce of cheerfulness is worth a

pound of sadness to serve God with.—Fuller.

The burden becomes light which is cheerfully borne.—Ovid.

If there is a virtue in the world at which we should always aim, it is cheerfulness.—Bulwer-Lytton.

The soul that perpetually overflows with kindness and sympathy will always be cheerful.—Parke Godwin.

Cheerfulness is full of significance; it suggests good health, a clear conscience, and a soul at peace with all human nature.—Charles Kingsley.

Such a man, truly wise, creams off Nature, leaving the sour and the dregs for philosophy and reason to lap up.—Swift.

The cheerful live longest in life, and after it, in our regards. Cheerfulness is the offshot of goodness.—Bovee.

The habit of looking on the best side of every event is worth more than a thousand pounds a year.—Johnson.

I like the laughter that opens the lips and the heart,—that shows at the same time pearls and the soul.—Victor Hugo.

Wondrous is the strength of cheerfulness, altogether past calculation its powers of endurance.—Carlyle.

Cheerfulness is like money well expended in charity; the more we dispense of it, the greater our possession.—Victor Hugo.

Not by constraint or severity shall you have access to true wisdom, but by abandonment and childlike mirthfulness.—Thoreau.

Cheerfulness ought to be the *viaticum vitæ* of their life to the old; age without cheerfulness is a Lapland winter without a sun.—Colton.

Inner sunshine warms not only the heart of the owner, but all who come in contact with it.—J. T. Fields.

Cheerfulness is also an excellent wearing quality. It has been called the bright weather of the heart.—Samuel Smiles.

I have found the saying of the ancients true, that better is a bright comrade on a weary road than a horse-litter.—Charles Reade.

God is glorified, not by our groans, but our thanksgivings; and all good thought and good action claim a natural alliance with good cheer.—Whipple.

Let us be of good cheer, remembering that the misfortunes hardest to bear are those which never happen.—Lowell.

Youth will never live to age unless they keep themselves in breath with exercise, and in heart with joyfulness.—Sir P. Sidney.

If the soul be happily disposed, every thing becomes capable of affording entertainment, and distress will almost want a name.—Goldsmith.

To be free-minded and cheerfully disposed at hours of meat and sleep and of exercise is one of the best precepts of long lasting.—Bacon.

You find yourself refreshed by the presence of cheerful people. Why not make earnest effort to confer that pleasure on others?—L. M. Child.

Between levity and cheerfulness there is a wide distinction; and the mind which is most open to levity is frequently a stranger to cheerfulness.—Blair.

Sweetness of spirit and sunshine is famous for dispelling fears and difficulties; patience is a mighty help to the burden-bearer.—James Hamilton.

If good people would but make their goodness agreeable, and smile instead of frowning in their virtue, how many would they win to the good cause!—Archbishop Usher.

I have always preferred cheerfulness to mirth. The latter I consider as an art, the former as a habit of mind. Mirth is short and transient, cheerfulness fixed and permanent.—Addison.

The lightsome countenance of a friend giveth such an inward decking to the house where it lodgeth, as proudest palaces have cause to envy the gilding.—Sir P. Sidney.

The mind that is cheerful in its present state, will be averse to all solicitude as to the future, and will meet the bitter occurrences of life with a placid smile.—Horace.

To be happy, the passions must be cheerful and gay, not gloomy and melancholy. A propensity to hope and joy is real riches; one to fear and sorrow, real poverty.—Hume.

A cheerful, easy, open countenance will make fools think you a good-natured man, and make designing men think you an undesigning one.—Chesterfield.

As in our lives so also in our studies, it is most becoming and most wise, so to temper gravity with cheerfulness, that the former may not imbue our minds with melancholy, nor the latter degenerate into licentiousness.—Pliny.

Cheerfulness is just as natural to the heart of a man in strong health as color to his cheek; and wherever there is habitual gloom, there must be either bad air, unwholesome food, improperly severe labor, or erring habits of life.—Ruskin.

True joy is a serene and sober motion: and they are miserably out that take laughing for rejoicing; the seat of it is within, and there is no cheerfulness like the resolutions of a brave mind.—Seneca.

There is no Christian duty that is not to be seasoned and set off with cheerishness, which in a thousand outward and intermitting crosses may yet be done well, as in this vale of tears.—Milton.

Cheerfulness is, in the first place, the best promoter of health. Repining

and secret murmurs of heart give imperceptible strokes to those delicate fibres of which the vital parts are composed.—Addison.

Mirth is like a flash of lightning that breaks through a gloom of clouds and glitters for a moment. Cheerfulness keeps up a daylight in the mind, filling it with a steady and perpetual serenity.—Johnson.

You find yourself refreshed by the presence of cheerful people. Why not make earnest effort to confer that pleasure on others? You will find half the battle is gained if you never allow yourself to say anything gloomy.—Mrs. L. M. Child.

Be thou like the bird perched upon some frail thing, although he feels the branch bending beneath him, yet loudly sings, knowing full well that he has wings.—Mme. de Gasparin.

O God, animate us to cheerfulness! May we have a joyful sense of our blessings, learn to look on the bright circumstances of our lot, and maintain a perpetual contentedness.—Channing.

Cheerfulness charms us with a spell that reaches into eternity; and we would not exchange it for all the soulless beauty that ever graced the fairest form on earth.—Anna Cleaves.

Had she been light, like you,
Of such a merry, nimble, stirring spirit,
She might ha' been a grandam ere she died;
And so may you; for a light heart lives long.   —Shakespeare.

I have observed that in comedies the best actor plays the droll, while some scrub rogue is made the fine gentleman or hero. Thus it is in the farce of life. Wise men spend their time in mirth; it is only fools who are serious.—Bolingbroke.

A cheerful temper spreads like the dawn, and all vapors disperse before it. Even the tear dries on the cheek, and the sigh sinks away half-breathed when the eye of benignity beams upon the unhappy.—Jane Porter.

Cheerfulness bears the same friendly regard to the mind as to the body; it banishes all anxious care and discontent, soothes and composes the passions and keeps them in a perpetual calm.—Addison.

Cheerfulness is always to be kept up if a man is out of pain; but mirth, to a prudent man, should always be accidental. It should naturally arise out of the occasion, and the occasion seldom be laid for it.—Steele.

A cheerful temper, joined with innocence, will make beauty attractive, knowledge delightful and wit goodnatured. It will lighten sickness, poverty and affliction, convert ignorance into an amiable simplicity, and render deformity itself agreeable.—Addison.

I live in a constant endeavor to fence against the infirmities of illhealth, and other evils of life, by mirth; being firmly persuaded that every time a man smiles, but much more when he laughs, it adds something to his fragment of life.—Sterne.

Cheerfulness sharpens the edge and removes the rust from the mind. A joyous heart supplies oil to our inward machinery, and makes the whole of our powers work with ease and efficiency; hence it is of the utmost importance that we maintain a contented, cheerful, genial disposition.—Aughey.

Let me play the fool; with mirth and laughter let old wrinkles come; and let my liver rather heat with wine than my heart cool with mortifying groans. Why should a man whose blood is warm within sit like his grandsire cut in alabaster, sleep when he wakes, and creep into the jaundice by being peevish?—Shakespeare.

Levity may be the forced production of folly or vice; cheerfulness is the natural offspring of wisdom and virtue only. The one is an occasional agitation; the other a permanent habit. The one degrades the character; the other is perfectly consistent with the dignity of reason and the steady and manly spirit of religion.—Blair.

Nothing will supply the want of sunshine to peaches, and, to make knowledge valuable, you must have the cheerfulness of wisdom. Whenever you are sincerely pleased you are nourished. The joy of the spirit indicates its strength. All healthy things are sweet-tempered. Genius works in sport, and goodness smiles to the last.—Emerson.

Every human soul has a germ of some flowers within; and they would open if they could only find sunshine and free air to expand in. I always told you that not having enough of sunshine was what ailed the world. Make people happy, and there will not be half the quarrelling or a tenth part of the wickedness there is.—Mrs. L. M. Child.

I have told you of the Spaniard who always put on his spectacles when about to eat cherries, that they might look bigger and more tempting. In like manner I make the most of my enjoyments; and though I do not cast my eyes away from my troubles, I pack them in as little compass as I can for myself, and never let them annoy others.—Southey.

When Goethe says that in every human condition foes lie in wait for us, "invincible only by cheerfulness and equanimity," he does not mean that we can at all times be really cheerful, or at a moment's notice; but that the endeavor to look at the better side of things will produce the habit, and that this habit is the surest safeguard against the danger of sudden evils.—Leigh Hunt.

Cheerfulness is a friend to grace, it puts the heart in tune to praise God. Uncheerful Christians, like the spies, bring an evil report on the good land; others suspect there is something unpleasant in religion, that they who profess it hang their harps upon the willows and walk so dejectedly. Be serious, yet cheerful. Rejoice in the Lord always.—Rev. T. Watson.

There seem to be some persons, the favorites of fortune and darlings of nature, who are born cheerful. "A star danced" at their birth. It is no superficial visibility, but a bountiful and beneficent soul that sparkles in their eyes and smiles on their lips. Their inborn geniality amounts to genius,—the rare and difficult genius which creates sweet and wholesome character, and radiates cheer.—Whipple.

The industrious bee does not stop to complain that there are so many poisonous flowers and thorny branches in his road, but buzzes on, selecting the honey where he can find it, and passing quietly by the places where it is not. There is enough in this world to complain about and find fault with, if men have the disposition. We often travel on a hard and uneven road; but with a cheerful spirit, and a heart to praise God for His mercies, we may walk therein with comfort, and come to the end of our journey in peace.—Dewey.

Give us, O give us, the man who sings at his work! Be his occupation what it may, he is equal to any of those who follow the same pursuit in silent sullenness. He will do more in the same time,—he will do it better, —he will persevere longer. One is scarcely sensible of fatigue whilst he marches to music. The very stars are said to make harmony as they revolve in their spheres. Wondrous is the strength of cheerfulness, altogether past calculation its powers of endurance. Efforts, to be permanently useful, must be uniformly joyous,—a spirit all sunshine,—graceful from very gladness,—beautiful because bright.—Carlyle.

I cannot tell how much I esteem and admire your good and happy temperament. What folly not to take advantage of circumstances, and enjoy gratefully the consolations which God sends us after the afflictive dispensations which He sometimes sees proper to make us feel! It seems to me to be a proof of great wisdom to submit with resignation to the storm, and enjoy the calm when it pleases Him to give it us again.—Madame de Sévigné.

A cheerful spirit is one of the most valuable gifts ever bestowed upon humanity by a kind Creator. It is the sweetest and most fragrant flower of the Spirit, that constantly sends out its beauty and fragrance, and blesses everything within its reach. It will sustain the soul in the darkest and most dreary places of this world. It will hold in check the demons of despair, and stifle the power of discouragement and hopelessness. It is the brightest star that ever cast its radiance over the darkened soul, and one that seldom sets in the gloom of morbid fancies and forboding imaginations.—Aughey.

Child (Death of)

Think of your child, then, not as dead, but as living; not as a flower that has withered, but as one that is transplanted, and touched by a divine hand, is blooming in richer colors and sweeter shades than those of earth.—Hooker.

Better that the light cloud should fade away into heaven with the morning breath, than travail through the weary day to gather in darkness, and in storm.—Bulwer.

Ye have lost a child—nay, she is not lost to you, who is found to Christ; she is not sent away, but only sent before; like unto a star, which going out of our sight, doth not die and vanish, but shineth in another hemisphere.—Rutherford.

When our children die, we drop them into the unknown, shuddering with fear. We know that they go out from us, and we stand, and pity, and wonder. If we receive news that a hundred thousand dollars had been left them by some one dying, we should be thrown into an ecstasy of rejoicing; but when they have gone home to God, we stand, and mourn, and pine, and wonder at the mystery of Providence.—H. W. Beecher.

The dying boy said: "Father, don't you weep for me; when I get to heaven I will go straight to Jesus and tell Him that ever since I can remember you have tried to lead me to Him." I would rather have my children say that of me after I am gone; or if they die before me, I would rather they should take that message to the Master than to have a monument over me reaching to the skies.—D. L. Moody.

How can a mother's heart feel cold or weary
Knowing her dearer self safe, sheltered, warm?
How can she feel her road too dark or dreary,
Who knows her treasure sheltered from the storm?
How can she sin? Our hearts may be unheeding,
Our God forgot, our holy saints defied;
But can a mother hear her dead child pleading,
And thrust those little angel hands aside?
—A. A. Proctor.

It will be hard for you not to ask why this must be. God knows why, and that may be as good to us as though we knew a thousand reasons. I pray God to hold you quiet and patient and uncomplaining, and help you bear the weight of this seemingly unintelligible sorrow. I hope you will remember that this is the only world in which a Christian can suffer, and suffer patiently and meekly. We cannot suffer by and by. God helps us to glorify Him now, when we can.—Maltbie Babcock.

My heart goes out to you—twice over—for the sorrow that has come to you, and for the thought that I could perhaps be a help to you. That shows that you see already one reason why sorrow comes—you turn to me, because I have tasted the same cup. Some day someone will come to you, and you will "comfort with the comfort wherewith you yourself have been comforted." Perfect sympathy cannot spring from the imagination. Only they who have suffered can really sympathize. I am sure you are saying, like the little child in the dark, "Speak, Lord, for Thy servant heareth." The worst of all losses is a lost sorrow, for then all is lost. Your little child is safe, and I believe your sorrow is safe, too, for you are your Father's child, and you want to please Him. I would not ask "why" if I were you. "How" is a better word—how can I glorify Thee, how well can I show those who know

me how the Father can help His child. God's will is not to be borne, but ever to be done. Now you are to do His will under new, hard, distressing and depressing circumstances. If we were pagans, we might hide ourselves and our despair, but we are Christians who say "Our Father" and hear our Saviour's words, "Because I live ye shall live also."—Maltbie Babcock.

Childhood

The child is father of the man.—Wordsworth.

Heaven lies about us in our infancy. —Wordsworth.

A child is an angel dependent on man.—Count de Maistre.

Children are the to-morrow of society.—Whately.

Childhood is the sleep of reason.—Rousseau.

Childhood, whose very happiness is love.— L. E. L. Erinna.

In bringing up a child, think of its old age.—Joubert.

As each one wishes his children to be so they are.—Terence.

The childhood shows the man
As morning shows the day.—Milton.

Better to be driven out from among men than to be disliked of children.—R. H. Dana.

Let nothing foul to either eye or ear reach those doors within which dwells a boy.—Juvenal.

The dutifulness of children is the foundation of all virtues.—Cicero.

Who can foretell for what high cause
This darling of the gods was born?
—Andrew Marvell.

Childhood has no forebodings; but then, it is soothed by no memories of outlived sorrow.—George Eliot.

Children have more need of models than of critics.—Joubert.

Every child walks into existence through the golden gate of love.—Beecher.

The training of children is a profession where we must know to lose time in order to gain it.—Rousseau.

Parents deserve reproof when they refuse to benefit their children by severe discipline.—Petronius Arbiter.

But still I dream that somewhere there must be
The spirit of a child that waits for me.
　　　　　　　—Bayard Taylor.

It is better to keep children to their duty by a sense of honor and by kindness than by fear.—Terence.

To a mother, a child is everything; but to a child, a parent is only a link in the chain of her existence.—Lord Beaconsfield.

Children have neither past nor future; and that which seldom happens to us, they rejoice in the present.—La Bruyère.

Man to the last is but a froward child;
So eager for the future, come what may,
And to the present so insensible.—Rogers.

Thine are the hours and days when both are cheering
And innocent. 　　　　　—Byron.

Happy child! the cradle is still to thee a vast space; but when thou art a man the boundless world will be too small for thee.—Schiller.

Children are the keys of Paradise;
They alone are good and wise,
　Because their thoughts, their very lives,
　are prayer. 　　—R. H. Stoddard.

We should treat children as God does us, who makes us happiest when He leaves us under the influence of innocent delusions.—Goethe.

I love these little people; and it is not a slight thing when they, who are so fresh from God, love us.—Dickens.

Children sweeten labors, but they make misfortunes more bitter; they increase the cares of life, but they mitigate the remembrance of death.—Bacon.

A simple child,
That lightly draws its breath,
And feels its life in every limb,
What should it know of death?
　　　　　　—Wordsworth.

Oh, for boyhood's time of June,
Crowding years in one brief moon,
When all things I heard or saw,
Me, their master, waited for.
　　　　　　　—Whittier.

Alas! regardless of their doom,
　The little victims play;
No sense have they of ills to come,
　Nor care beyond to-day. 　—Gray.

Oh, would I were a boy again,
When life seemed formed of sunny years,
And all the heart then knew of pain
　Was wept away in transient tears!
　　　　　　—Mark Lemon.

The tear down childhood's cheek that flows
Is like the dewdrop on the rose,
When next the summer breeze comes by
And waves the bush, the flower is dry.
　　　　　　　—Scott.

"Beware," said Lavater, "of him who hates the laugh of a child." "I love God and little children," was the simple yet sublime sentiment of Richter.—Mrs. Sigourney.

While here at home, in shining day,
We round the sunny garden play,
Each little Indian sleepy-head
Is being kissed and put to bed.
　　　　—Robert Louis Stevenson.

In winter I get up at night
And dress by yellow candle-light.
In summer, quite the other way,
I have to go to bed by day.
　　　　—Robert Louis Stevenson.

If there is anything that will endure
The eye of God, because it still is pure,
It is the spirit of a little child,
Fresh from His hand, and therefore undefiled. 　　—R. H. Stoddard.

I do not like punishments. You will never torture a child into duty; but a sensible child will dread the frown of a judicious mother more than all the rods, dark rooms, and scolding schoolmistresses in the universe.—H. K. White.

That season of childhood, when the soul, on the rainbow bridge of fancy, glides along, dry-shod, over the walls and ditches of this lower earth.—Richter.

No man can tell but he that loves his children how many delicious assents make a man's heart dance in the pretty conversation of those dear pledges.—Jeremy Taylor.

Ah! what would the world be to us
If the children were no more?
We should dread the desert behind us
Worse than the dark before.
    —Longfellow.

A man shall see, where there is a house full of children, one or two of the eldest restricted, and the youngest ruined by indulgence; but in the midst, some that are, as it were, forgotten, who many times, nevertheless, prove the best.—Bacon.

But still when the mists of doubt prevail,
And we lie becalmed by the shores of age,
We hear from the misty troubled shore
The voice of the children gone before,
Drawing the soul to its anchorage.
    —Bret Harte.

Ay, these young things lie safe in our hearts just so long
As their wings are in growing; and when these are strong
They break it, and farewell! the bird flies!
    —Lord Lytton.

Oh, when I was a tiny boy
My days and nights were full of joy.
My mates were blithe and kind!
No wonder that I sometimes sigh
And dash the teardrop from my eye
To cast a look behind!   —Hood.

Pointing to such, well might Cornelia say,
When the rich casket shone in bright array,
"These are my Jewels!" Well of such as he,
When Jesus spake, well might the language be,
"Suffer these little ones to come to me!"
    —Samuel Rogers.

A creature undefiled by the taint of the world, unvexed by its injustice,

unwearied by its hollow pleasures; a being fresh from the source of light, with something of its universal lustre in it. If childhood be this, how holy the duty to see that in its onward growth it shall be no other!—Douglas Jerrold.

Do ye hear the children weeping, O my brothers,
Ere the sorrow comes with years?
They are leaning their young heads against their mothers,
And that cannot stop their tears.
    —E. B. Browning.

Perhaps there lives some dreamy boy, untaught
In schools, some graduate of the field or street,
Who shall become a master of the art,
An admiral sailing the high seas of thought
Fearless and first, and steering with his fleet
For lands not yet laid down in any chart.
    —Longfellow.

If a boy is not trained to endure and to bear trouble, he will grow up a girl; and a boy that is a girl has all a girl's weakness without any of her regal qualities. A woman made out of a woman is God's noblest work; a woman made out of a man is His meanest.—Beecher.

An infallible way to make your child miserable is to satisfy all his demands. Passion swells by gratification; and the impossibility of satisfying every one of his demands will oblige you to stop short at last, after he has become a little headstrong.—Henry Home.

When the lessons and tasks are all ended,
And the school for the day is dismissed,
The little ones gather around me,
To bid me good night and be kissed;
Oh, the little white arms that encircle
My neck in their tender embrace;
Oh, the smiles that are halos of heaven,
Shedding sunshine of love on my face.
    —Charles M. Dickinson.

When a child can be brought to tears, not from fear of punishment, but from repentance for his offence, he needs no chastisement. When the tears begin to flow from grief at one's own conduct, be sure there is an angel nestling in the bosom.—Horace Mann.

A child's eyes, those clear wells of undefiled thought—what on earth can be more beautiful? Full of hope, love and curiosity, they meet your own. In prayer, how earnest; in joy, how sparkling; in sympathy, how tender! The man who never tried the companionship of a little child has carelessly passed by one of the great pleasures of life, as one passes a rare flower without plucking it or knowing its value.—Mrs. Norton.

Children, ay, forsooth
They bring their own love with them when they come,
But if they come not there is peace and rest;
The pretty lambs! and yet she cries for more;
Why, the world's full of them, and so is heaven—
They are not rare.   —Jean Ingelow.

A truthful page is childhood's lovely face,
Whereon sweet Innocence has record made—
An outward semblance of the young heart's grace,
Where truth, and love, and trust are all portrayed.   —Shillaber.

Behold, my lords,
Although the print be little, the whole matter
And copy of the father, eye, nose, lip,
The trick of 's frown, his forehead, nay, the valley,
The pretty dimples of his chin and cheek; his smiles;
The very mould and frame of hand, nail, finger.   —Shakespeare.

You hear that boy laughing? You thing he's all fun;
But the angels laugh, too, at the good he has done.
The children laugh loud as they troop to his call,
And the poor man that knows him laughs loudest of all!   —O. W. Holmes.

Dare we let children grow up with no vital contact with the Saviour, never intentionally and consciously put into His arms? Not to bring them to Him, not to teach them to walk toward Him, as soon as they can walk toward anyone, is wronging a child beyond words. The terrible indictment uttered by the Lord, "Them that were entering in ye hindered," and the millstone warning for offending little ones, are close akin to the deserts of those who ruin a man's whole day of life by wronging his morning hours. Not to help a child to know the saving power of Christ is to hold back a man from salvation.—Maltbie Babcock.

They are idols of hearts and of households;
They are angels of God in disguise;
His sunlight still sleeps in their tresses;
His glory still gleams in their eyes.
Oh, those truants from home and from heaven,
They have made me more manly and mild,
And I know now how Jesus could liken
The kingdom of God to a child.
   —Dickens.

The least and most imperceptible impressions received in our infancy have consequences very important, and of a long duration. It is with these first impressions, as with a river whose waters we can easily turn, by different canals, in quite opposite courses, so that from the insensible direction the stream receives at its source, it takes different directions, and at last arrives at places far distant from each other; and with the same facility we may, I think, turn the minds of children to what direction we please.—Locke.

Children

Fragile beginnings of a mighty end. —Mrs. Norton.

Children like olive plants round about thy table.—Psalm cxxviii. 3.

A rose with all its sweetest leaves yet folded.—Byron.

Living jewels, dropped unstained from heaven.—Pollok.

Children are what the mothers are. —Landor.

Childhood is the sleep of reason.— Rousseau.

A child is an angel dependent on man.—Count de Maistre.

Childhood has no forebodings; but then it is soothed by no memories of outlived sorrow.—George Eliot.

Children are the to-morrow of society.—Whately.

The child is father of the man.—Wordsworth.

Heaven lies about us in our infancy.—Wordsworth.

Unblown flowers, new-appearing sweets.—Shakespeare.

Dispel not the happy delusions of children.—Goethe.

Children blessings seem, but torments are.—Otway.

Just as the twig is bent the tree is inclined.—Pope.

Your little child is your only true democrat.—Mrs. Stowe.

The sports of children satisfy the child.—Goldsmith.

In bringing up a child, think of its old age.—Joubert.

Children have more need of models than of critics.—Joseph Joubert.

Childhood shows the man, as morning shows the day.—Milton.

The smallest children are nearest to God, as the smallest planets are nearest the sun.—Richter.

Children are like grown people; the experience of others is never of any use to them.—Daudet.

Call not that man wretched, who whatever ills he suffers, has a child to love.—Southey.

Children are God's apostles, day by day sent forth to preach of love and hope and peace.—Lowell.

The clew of our destiny, wander where we will, lies at the cradle foot.—Richter.

Never educate a child to be a gentleman or lady alone, but to be a man, a woman.—Herbert Spencer.

Children will grow up substantially what they are by nature—and only that.—Mrs. H. B. Stowe.

Never despair of a child. The one you weep the most for at the mercy-seat may fill your heart with the sweetest joys.—T. L. Cuyler.

Nothing has a better effect upon children than praise.—Sir P. Sidney.

Many children, many cares; no children, no felicity.—Bovee.

The scenes of childhood are the memories of future years.—J. O. Choules.

What gift has Providence bestowed on man, that is so dear to him as his children?—Cicero.

Do not try to produce an ideal child; it would find no fitness in this world.—Herbert Spencer.

The children of to-day will be the architects of our country's destiny in 1900.—James A. Garfield.

Childhood is like a mirror, which reflects in after life the images first presented to it.—Samuel Smiles.

Train up a child in the way he should go, and when he is old he will not depart from it.—Proverbs xxii. 6.

How sharper than a serpent's tooth it is
To have a thankless child.—Shakespeare.

The bearing and training of a child is woman's wisdom.—Tennyson.

His little children, climbing for a kiss, welcome their father's late return at night.—Dryden.

Behold the child, by nature's kindly law
Pleased with a rattle, tickled with a straw.
—Pope.

A mother's love, in a degree, sanctifies the most worthless offspring.—Hosea Ballou.

The glorified spirit of the infant is as a star to guide the mother to its own blissful clime.—Mrs. Sigourney

Where children are, there is the golden age.—Novalis.

Childhood, who like an April morn appears, Sunshine and rain, hopes clouded o'er with fears.—Churchill.

A torn jacket is soon mended; but hard words bruise the heart of a child. —Longfellow.

We speak of educating our children. Do we know that our children also educate us?—Mrs. Sigourney.

Truly there is nothing in the world so blessed or so sweet as the heritage of children.—Mrs. Oliphant.

A woman's natural protector is less an aged father or tall brother than a very young child.—Mme. de Girardin.

The death of a child occasions a passion of grief and frantic tears, such as your end, brother reader, will never inspire.—Thackeray.

I would not have children much beaten for their faults, because I would not have them think bodily pain the greatest punishment.—Locke.

In the man whose childhood has known caresses, there is always a fibre of memory that can be touched to gentle issues.—George Eliot.

There is another accidental advantage in marriage, which has also fallen to my share; I mean the having a multitude of children.—Steele.

It seems impossible they should ever grow to be men, and drag the heavy artillery along the dusty road of life. —Longfellow.

Who is not attracted by bright and pleasant children, to prattle, to creep, and to play with them?—Epictetus.

I love these little people; and it is not a slight thing when they, who are so fresh from God, love us.—Dickens.

As soft wax is apt to take the stamp of the seal, so are the minds of young children to receive the instruction imprinted on them.—Plutarch.

A man looketh on his little one as a being of better hope; in himself ambition is dead, but it hath a resurrection in his son.—Tupper.

The whining schoolboy, with his satchel and shining morning face, creeping like snail unwillingly to school.—Shakespeare.

Jesus was the first great teacher of men who showed a genuine sympathy for childhood. When He said "Of such is the kingdom of heaven," it was a revelation.—Eggleston.

God has given you your child, that the sight of him, from time to time, might remind you of His goodness, and induce you to praise Him with filial reverence.—Christian Scriver.

Blessed be the hand that prepares a pleasure for a child, for there is no saying when and where it may bloom forth.—Douglas Jerrold.

Children have neither past nor future; and, what scarcely ever happens to us, they enjoy the present.—Bruyère.

Let us be men with men, and always children before God; for in His eyes we are but children. Old age itself, in presence of eternity, is but the first moment of a morning.—Joseph Joubert.

In praising or loving a child, we love and praise not that which is, but that which we hope for.—Goethe.

I have often thought what a melancholy world this would be without children, and what an inhuman world without the aged.—Coleridge.

The training of children is a profession where we must know to lose time in order to gain it.—Rousseau.

Precious Saviour! come in spirit, and lay Thy strong, gentle grasp of love on our dear boys and girls, and keep these our lambs from the fangs of the wolf.—T. L. Cuyler.

Children are the keys of Paradise.
 * * * They alone are good and wise, Because their thoughts, their very lives are prayer.   —Stoddard.

We should treat children as God does us, who makes us happiest when He leaves us under the influence of innocent delusions.—Goethe.

Happy child! the cradle is still to thee a vast space; become a man, and the boundless world will be too small to thee.—Schiller.

What in us the women leave uncultivated, children cultivate when we retain them near us.—Goethe.

It is better to keep children to their duty, by a sense of honor, and by kindness, than by fear and punishment. —Tertullian.

Let your children be as so many flowers, borrowed from God. If the flowers die or wither, thank God for a summer loan of them.—Rutherford.

Children generally hate to be idle; all the care then is that their busy humor should be constantly employed in something of use to them.—Locke.

I seem, for my own part, to see the benevolence of the Deity more clearly in the pleasures of very young children than in anything else in the world.— Paley.

Then gathering 'round his bed, they climb to share
His kisses, and with gentle violence there, Break in upon a dream not half so fair.
            —Rogers.

The sacred books of the ancient Persians say, "If you would be holy, instruct your children, because all the good acts they perform will be imputed to you."—Montesquieu.

A house is never perfectly furnished for enjoyment unless there is a child in it rising three years old, and a kitten rising three weeks.—Southey.

Children must be rendered reasonable, but not reasoners. The first thing to teach them is that it is reasonable for them to obey, and unreasonable for them to dispute.—Joubert.

A child's existence is a bright, soft element of joy, out of which, as in Prospero's Island, wonder after wonder bodies itself forth, to teach by charming.—Rodney.

Ah! what would the world be to us, If the children were no more? We should dread the desert behind us Worse than the dark before.
            —Longfellow.

As in the Master's spirit you take into your arms the little ones, His own everlasting arms will encircle them and you. He will pity both their and your simplicity; and as in unseen presence He comes again, His blessing will breathe upon you.—James' Hamilton.

"A fig-tree looking on a fig-tree becometh fruitful," says the Arabian proverb. And so it is with children; their first great instructor is example. —Samuel Smiles.

In trying to teach children a great deal in a short time, they are treated not as though the race they were to run was for life, but simply a three-mile heat.—Horace Mann.

"Beware," said Lavater, "of him who hates the laugh of a child." "I love God and little children," was the simple yet sublime sentiment of Richter.—Mrs. Sigourney.

Children are very nice observers, and they will often perceive your slightest defects. In general, those who govern children forgive nothing in them, but everything in themselves.— Fénelon.

Is the world all grown up? Is childhood dead? Or is there not in the bosom of the wisest and the best some of the child's heart left, to respond to its earliest enchantments?—Lamb.

We should amuse our evening hours of life in cultivating the tender plants, and bringing them to perfection, before they are transplanted to a happier clime.—Washington.

Children sweeten labors, but they make misfortunes more bitter; they increase the cares of life, but they mitigate the remembrance of death.—Bacon.

While childhood, and while dreams, producing childhood, shall be left, imagination shall not have spread her holy wings totally to fly the earth.—Lamb.

One of the greatest pleasures of childhood is found in the mysteries which it hides from the skepticism of the elders, and works up into small mythologies of its own.—O. W. Holmes.

The first duty toward children is to make them happy. If you have not made them happy, you have wronged them; no other good they may get can make up for that.—Charles Buxton.

Call not that man wretched, who whatever else he suffers as to pain inflicted, or pleasure denied, has a child for whom he hopes and on whom he doats.—Coleridge.

Who feels injustice, who shrinks before a slight, who has a sense of wrong so acute, and so glowing a gratitude for kindness, as a generous boy?—Thackeray.

That season of childhood, when the soul, on the rainbow bridge of fancy, glides along, dry-shod, over the walls and ditches of this lower earth.—Richter.

Oft too the mind well pleased surveys,
Its progress from its childish days;
See how the current upwards ran,
And reads the child o'er in the man.
—Lloyd.

To season them, and win them early to the love of virtue and true labor, are any flattering seducement or vain principle seize them wandering, some easy and delightful book of education should be read to them.—Milton.

Beware of fatiguing them by ill-judged exactness. If virtue offer itself to a child under a melancholy and constrained aspect, if liberty and license present themselves under an agreeable form, all is lost, your labor is in vain.—Fénelon.

If I were to choose among all gifts and qualities that which, on the whole, makes life pleasantest, I should select the love of children. No circumstance can render this world wholly a solitude to one who has this possession.—T. W. Higginson.

I hardly know so melancholy a reflection as that parents are necessarily the sole directors of the management of children, whether they have or have not judgment, penetration or taste to perform the task.—Lord Greville.

The child's grief throbs against the round of its little heart as heavily as the man's sorrow; and the one finds as much delight in his kite or drum as the other in striking the springs of enterprise or soaring on the wings of fame.—Chapin.

A man shall see, where there is a house full of children, one or two of the eldest restricted, and the youngest ruined by indulgence; but in the midst, some that are, as it were, forgotten, who many times, nevertheless, prove the best.—Bacon.

A large portion of Christ's miracles of love were wrought at the urgent request of parents for their suffering children. Is that ear gone deaf today? Will He not do for our children's souls what He did for the bodies of the ruler's daughter, and the dead youth at Nain?—T. L. Cuyler.

Of all the sights which can soften and humanize the heart of men, there is none that ought so surely to reach it as that of innocent children, enjoying the happiness which is their proper and natural portion.—Southey.

I never hear parents exclaim impatiently, "Children, you must not make so much noise," that I do not think how soon the time may come when, beside the vacant seat, those parents would give all the world, could they hear once more the ringing laughter which once so disturbed them.—A. E. Kittredge.

Delightful task! to rear the tender thought,
To teach the young idea how to shoot,
To pour the fresh instruction o'er the mind,
To breathe the enlivening spirit and to fix
The generous purpose in the glowing
   breast! —Thomson.

What art can paint or gild any object in after life with the glow which nature gives to the first baubles of childhood? · St. Peter's cannot have the magical power over us that the red and gold covers of our first picture-book possessed.—Emerson.

The children of the poor are so apt to look as if the rich would have been over-blest with such! Alas for the angel capabilities, interrupted so soon with care, and with after life so sadly unfulfilled?—Willis.

Children are the hands by which we take hold of heaven. By these tendrils we clasp it and climb thitherward. And why do we think that we are separated from them? We never half knew them, nor in this world could.—Beecher.

I do not like punishments. You will never torture a child into duty; but a sensible child will dread the frown of a judicious mother more than all the rods, dark rooms, and scolding schoolmistresses in the universe.—H. K. White.

Good Christian people, here lies for you an inestimable loan: take all heed thereof, in all carefulness employ it: with high recompense, or else with heavy penalty, will it one day be required back.—Carlyle.

The plays of natural lively children are the infancy of art. Children live in a world of imagination and feeling.

They invest the most insignificant object with any form they please, and see in it whatever they wish to see.—Oehlenschläger.

We are but children, the things that we do
Are as sports of a babe to the Infinite view,
That sees all our weakness, and pities it, too.
And oh! when aweary, may we be so blest
As to sink, like an innocent child, to our rest,
And feel ourselves clasped to the Infinite breast. —F. Burge Smith.

A mother once asked a clergyman when she should begin the education of her child, which she told him was then four years old. "Madam," was the reply, "you have lost three years already. From the very first smile that gleams over an infant's cheek, your opportunity begins."—Whately.

Our children that die young are like those spring bulbs which have their flowers prepared beforehand, and leave nothing to do but to break ground, and blossom, and pass away. Thank God for spring flowers among men, as well as among the grasses of the field.—Beecher.

Happy season of childhood! Kind Nature, that art to all a bountiful mother; that visitest the poor man's hut with auroral radiance; and for thy nursling hast provided a soft swathing of love and infinite hope wherein he waxes and slumbers, danced round by sweetest dreams!—Carlyle.

If a boy is not trained to endure and to bear trouble, he will grow up a girl; and a boy that is a girl has all a girl's weakness without any of her regal qualities. A woman made out of a woman is God's noblest work: a woman made out of a man is His meanest.—Beecher.

When a child can be brought to tears, not from fear of punishment, but from repentance for his offence, he needs no chastisement. When the tears begin to flow from grief at one's own conduct, be sure there is an angel nestling in the bosom.—Horace Mann.

An infallible way to make your child miserable is to satisfy all his demands. Passion swells by gratification; and the impossibility of satisfying every one of his demands will oblige you to stop short at last, after he has become a little headstrong.—Henry Home.

And yet we check and chide
The airy angels as they float about us,
With rules of so-called wisdom, till they grow
The same tame slaves to custom and the world. —Mrs. Osgood.

Look how he laughs and stretches out his arms,
And opens wide his blue eyes upon thine,
To hail his father: while his little form
Flutters as wing'd with joy. Talk not of pain!
The childless cherubs well might envy thee
The pleasures of a parent. —Byron.

Train them to virtue; habituate them to industry, activity, and spirit. Make them consider every vice as shameful and unmanly. Fire them with ambition to be useful. Make them disdain to be destitute of any useful knowledge. Fix their ambition upon great and solid objects, and their contempt upon little, frivolous, and useless ones.—John Adams.

Thine was the shout! the song! the burst of joy!
Which sweet from childhood's rosy lip resoundeth;
Thine was the eager spirit nought could cloy,
And the glad heart from which all grief reboundeth. —Mrs. Norton.

I can endure a melancholy man, but not a melancholy child; the former, in whatever slough he may sink, can raise his eyes either to the kingdom of reason or of hope; but the little child is entirely absorbed and weighed down by one black poison-drop of the present.—Mrs. Norton.

As hardly anything can accidentally touch the soft clay without stamping its mark on it, so hardly any reading can interest a child, without contributing in some degree, though the book itself be afterwards totally forgotten, to form the character.—Whately.

It always grieves me to contemplate the initiation of children into the ways of life when they are scarcely more than infants. It checks their confidence and simplicity, two of the best qualities that heaven gives them, and demands that they share our sorrows before they are capable of entering into our enjoyments.—Dickens.

I know that a sweet child is the sweetest thing in nature, not even excepting the delicate creatures which bear them; but the prettier the kind of a thing is, the more desirable it is that it should be pretty of its kind. One daisy differs not much from another in glory; but a violet should look and smell the daintiest.—Lamb.

A creature undefiled by the taint of the world, unvexed by its injustice, unwearied by its hollow pleasures; a being fresh from the source of light, with something of its universal lustre in it. If childhood be this, how holy the duty to see that in its onward growth it shall be no other!—Douglas Jerrold.

To aid thy mind's development—to watch
Thy dawn of little joys—to sit and see
Almost thy very growth—to view thee catch
Knowledge of objects—wonders yet to thee!
To hold thee lightly on a gentle knee,
And print on thy soft cheek a parent's kiss.

A child's eyes, those clear wells of undefiled thought—what on earth can be more beautiful? Full of hope, love and curiosity, they meet your own. In prayer, how earnest; in joy, how sparkling; in sympathy, how tender! The man who never tried the companionship of a little child has carelessly passed by one of the great pleasures of life, as one passes a rare flower without plucking it or knowing its value.—Mrs. Norton.

Be very vigilant over thy child in the April of his understanding, lest the frost of May nip his blossoms. While he is a tender twig, straighten him; whilst he is a new vessel, season him; such as thou makest him, such commonly shalt thou find him. Let his first lesson be obedience, and his second shall be what thou wilt.—Quarles.

Their future may, perchance, appear dark to others; but to their fearless gaze it looms up brilliant and beautiful as the walls of a fairy palace. There is no tear which a mother's gentle hand cannot wipe away, no wound that a mother's kiss cannot heal, no anguish which the sweet murmuring of her soft, low voice cannot soothe.—Esaias Tegner.

They are idols of hearts and of households;
They are angels of God in disguise;
His sunlight still sleeps in their tresses;
His glory still gleams in their eyes.
Oh, those truants from home and from heaven,
They have made me more manly and mild,
And I know now how Jesus could liken
The kingdom of God to a child.
        —Dickens.

Be ever gentle with the children God has given you; watch over them constantly; reprove them earnestly, but not in anger. In the forcible language of Scripture, "Be not bitter against them." "Yes, they are good boys," I once heard a kind father say. "I talk to them very much, but do not like to beat my children—the world will beat them." It was a beautiful thought, though not elegantly expressed.—Elihu Burritt.

Above all things endeavor to breed them up in the love of virtue, and that holy plain way of it which we have lived in, that the world in no part of it get into my family. I had rather they were homely than finely bred as to outward behavior; yet I love sweetness mixed with gravity, and cheerfulness tempered with sobriety.—William Penn.

Bring your little children to the Saviour. Place them in His arms. Devote them to His service. Born in His camp, let them wear from the first His colors. Taking advantage of timely opportunities, and with all tenderness of spirit, seek to endear them to the Friend of Sinners, the Good Shepherd of the lambs, the loving Guardian of the little children. And not only teach them, but govern them. And in order to govern them, govern yourselves.—James Hamilton.

God sends children for another purpose than merely to keep up the race—to enlarge our hearts, to make us unselfish, and full of kindly sympathies and affections; to give our souls higher aims, and to call out all our faculties to extended enterprise and exertion; to bring round our fireside bright faces and happy smiles, and loving, tender hearts. My soul blesses the Great Father every day, that He has gladdened the earth with little children.—Mary Howitt.

A child is man in a small letter, yet the best copy of Adam before he tasted of Eve or the apple; and he is happy whose small practice in the world can only write his character. His soul is yet a white paper unscribbled with observations of the world, wherewith at length it becomes a blurred note-book. He is purely happy because he knows no evil, nor hath made means by sin to be acquainted with misery.—Bishop Earle.

If there is anything that will endure
The eye of God because it still is pure,
It is the spirit of a little child,
Fresh from His hand, and therefore undefiled.
Nearer the gate of Paradise than we,
Our children breathe its airs, its angels see;
And when they pray God hears their simple prayer,
Yea, even sheathes His sword, in judgment bare.   —Stoddard.

Children, like dogs, have so sharp and fine a scent that they detect and hunt out everything—the bad before all the rest. They also know well enough how this or that friend stands with their parents; and as they practice no dissimulation whatever, they serve as excellent barometers by which to observe the degree of favor or disfavor at which we stand with their parents.—Goethe.

Bring together all the children of the universe, you will see nothing in them but innocence, gentleness, and fear; were they born wicked, spiteful, and cruel, some signs of it would come from them; as little snakes strive to bite, and little tigers to tear. But nature having been as sparing of offensive weapons to man as to pigeons and rabbits, it cannot have given them an instinct to mischief and destruction.—Voltaire.

I know he's coming by this sign,
  That baby's almost wild;
See how he laughs and crows and starts—
  Heaven bless the merry child!
He's father's self in face and limb,
And father's heart is strong in him.
Shout, baby, shout! and clap thy hands,
For father on the threshold stands.
          —Mary Howitt.

The least and most imperceptible impressions received in our infancy, have consequences very important, and of a long duration. It is with these first impressions, as with a river whose waters we can easily turn, by different canals, in quite opposite courses, so that from the insensible direction the stream receives at its source, it takes different directions, and at last arrives at places far distant from each other; and with the same facility we may, I think, turn the minds of children to what direction we please.—Locke.

Children's Day (Sunday School)

And they brought young children to Him, that He should touch them; and His disciples rebuked those that brought them. But when Jesus saw it, He was much displeased, and said unto them, Suffer the little children to come unto Me, and forbid them not; for of such is the kingdom of God. Verily I say unto you, whosoever shall not receive the kingdom of God as a little child, he shall not enter therein. And He took them up in His arms, put His hands upon them, and blessed them.—Bible.

Children are the lambs of the flock. Christ said to the church, "Feed my lambs." The lambs belong to the sheep and the sheep to the shepherd.—Rev. J. J. Barnhardt.

Dr. Holmes was asked when the training of a child should begin. "A hundred years before it is born," he replied. This is a strong way of putting the truth that the training of children should begin with the training of their grandparents.—S. E. Wishard, D. D.

Anything we do to hinder a child from coming to Jesus greatly displeases our dear Lord. He cries to us, "Stand off. Let them alone. Let them come to Me, and forbid them not."—Spurgeon.

The children should have a part in public services. By enlisting their activities we shall incite them to attendance, for children love to go where they can use their powers.—J. F. Cowan.

Little works, little thoughts, little loves, little prayers for little Christians, and larger and larger as the years grow.—Rev. Chas. H. Parkhurst.

And let me say only this one word more: that the little things that a little Christian does are not overlooked any more than the larger things that an older Christian does.—Rev. Chas. H. Parkhurst.

Shepherd of tender youth,
Guiding in love and truth,
  Through devious ways;
Christ, our triumphant King,
We come Thy name to sing,
And here our children bring,
  To shout Thy praise.
          —St. Ambrose.

Among the old Romans there prevailed the touching custom of holding the face of every new born babe toward the heavens, signifying by their presenting its forehead to the stars that it was to look above the world into celestial glories. That was only a vain superstition; but Christ has taught us how to realize the old Pagan yearning.—Dr. L. A. Banks.

I will say broadly that I have more confidence in the spiritual life of the children that I have received into this church than I have in the spiritual condition of the adults thus received. I will even go further than that, and say that I have usually found a clearer knowledge of the gospel and a warmer love of Christ in the child-converts than in the man-converts. I will even astonish you still more by saying that I have sometimes met with a deeper spiritual experience in children of ten and twelve than I have in certain persons of fifty and sixty.—Spurgeon.

Do not others expect from children more perfect conduct than they themselves exhibit? If a gracious child should lose his temper or act wrongly in some trifling thing through forgetfulness, straightway he is condemned as a little hypocrite by those who are a long way from being perfect themselves. Jesus says, "Take heed that ye despise not one of these little ones."—Spurgeon.

When children ask you questions about gray hairs, and wrinkles in the face, and sighs that have no words, and smiles too bright to be carved upon the radiant face by the hands of hypocrisy—when they ask you about kneeling at the altar, speaking into the vacant air, and uttering words to an unseen and in an invisible Presence—when they interrogate you about your great psalms, and hymns, and anthembursts of thankfulness, what is your reply to these? Do not be ashamed of the history. Keep steadily along the line of fact. Say what happened to you, and magnify God in the hearing of the inquirer.—Rev. Joseph Parker.

Ought there to be room in the bonds of church-fellowship for the great mass of average boys and girls who, by judicious training and careful Christian nurture, may be induced very early to give their hearts to God? Aye, we believe with all our heart there ought to be such a place. We believe that before many years there will be such a place in every true church, and it will be just as much expected that many young children will form part of the membership of every church as that there will be gray-haired men and women there.—Rev. F. E. Clark, D. D.

Children should be educated in and into the church. Whatever our theory may be of the spiritual relation of the child to the church, this is certain and true: That children should be consecrated to God from their birth. Of such is the kingdom of heaven. We

should assume this as the normal state of the case and treat the child accordingly. He should be trained in the nurture and admonition of the Lord. His first intelligent lesson should be of God and worship. The happiest hours of child-life should be in learning of the way to God through Jesus Christ.—Rev. S. Irenæus Prime, D. D.

But these dear boys and girls— there is something to be made out of them. If now they yield themselves to Christ they may have a long, happy, and holy day before them in which they may serve God with all their hearts. Who knows what glory God may have of them? Heathen lands may call them blessed. Whole nations may be enlightened by them. O brethren and sisters, let us estimate children at their true valuation, and we shall not keep them back, but we shall be eager to lead them to Jesus at once.—Spurgeon.

"Suffer that little children come to Me,
Forbid them not." Emboldened by His words,
The mothers onward press; but, finding vain
The attempt to reach the Lord, they trust their babes
To strangers' hands; the innocents, alarmed
Amid the throng of faces all unknown,
Shrink, trembling, till their wandering eyes discern
The countenance of Jesus, beaming love
And pity; eager then they stretch their arms,
And, cowering, lay their heads upon His breast.   —James Grahame.

Few special days in the average Sunday school are looked forward to with such eager expectancy on the part of the scholars as Children's Day. Even fathers and mothers, big brothers and sisters, who perhaps seldom enter church doors, go then if at no other time. With many schools it is practically the end of a year's work and an anniversary corresponding to Commencement Day in our public schools. But in every school it may be a day of unusual opportunity for presenting the joy of the Christ-life and the friendship of the All-Loving One to many who perhaps are not reached at other times during the year.—**New Century Teachers' Monthly.**

Some kind hearts have lived in every generation, but it is only within a few years that the older Christians have come into such perfect love and sympathy with children's needs as to set apart a Sunday for their especial benefit. Those who planned the grand day seem to enjoy it as much as the little ones, for the churches are full of grown-up people, many of them with silvery hair and wrinkled faces; but many of the wrinkles seem to be smoothed out by the happy, fresh looks that come over them when the children's voices are heard taking a prominent part in the worship. We older ones can testify that Children's Day has benefited us in many ways, and is the Sunday of the whole year which we enjoy the best.—Susan Teall Perry.

For you, a boy or girl, to be a Christian will be for you to be as nearly as you can like what Jesus was when He was at your age. That is one reason why it is worth so much to us to have a Jesus that began in the cradle and gradually grew up. If we had a Jesus that was already a man when He came, and hadn't stopped to be a baby and a boy, we should hardly have known what to say to the children about these things; we might have had to say that only grown-up men and women could be Christians. But now we have Jesus all the way along, from eighteen inches up, so that we can say to any one, "You can be a Christian by being as nearly as you can like what Jesus was at your age."—Rev. Chas. H. Parkhurst.

Go, then, ye happy children,
And love Him more and more!
He holds a cup of blessing,
And in it He will pour
All joy and pleasure for you;
And from this day of flowers
Ye all may work for Jesus
And bless this world of ours.
Oh, may the King of children
Be crowned of all His own;
On this sweet day of beauty
Be every heart His throne!
—Rev. Dwight Willis.

As we look and listen we hear with our hearts the cry of myriads of children pleading for the bread of life. What response shall we make to this

lifted signal? The offering of Children's Day will measure our love, our gratitude, our appreciation of the divine movement of Providence and of the grand and awful time in which we are living. Let every one, then, give as God has prospered him, and additional Sabbath school missionaries will go forth to many a wilderness, and the solitary place will be glad for them and blossom as the rose.—James A. Worden, D. D.

Most of you will have a very happy Children's Day, we trust; but there will be many of Christ's little ones who will have to be at home on beds of sickness and pain, and cannot go to the Lord's house and worship Him among the beautiful flowers and loving friends who will make everything so attractive. Remember such ones. Carry them flowers and some sweet, helpful words, to make the day less burdensome to them. There may be others obliged to stay away, who have not suitable clothes to wear, because of their poverty. Seek out such and overcome any hindrances in their way that you can, so that as many as possible of Christ's little ones may gather together in His courts on that especial day.—Susan Teall Perry.

Well may the Church keep Children's Day,
And thus draw near the Son,
Who gained His richest human realm,
When children's hearts were won.
Well may the Church keep Children's Day,
And thus draw near the skies,
For in the children's sunny hearts,
The light of heaven lies.
Well may the Church keep Children's Day,
She keeps her greatness then,
E'en now the Christ uplifts a child,
Above all sinful men.
Oh, happy day! Oh, heavenly hour!
When thus the Church shall stand,
Like Christ with smile and touch of grace,
Amid the children's band. Amen.
—George Edward Martin.

And so sweetly adapted is the child-mind to the Gospel and the Gospel to the child-mind that they cheerfully coalesce, and the babe's milk is not more palatable and nutritious than is the bread of life to the new-born soul. No one can say how soon a child may intelligently apprehend the divine truth. Many saints of God have no memory of the period in their early lives when Christ was not dear to their hearts. When they were born from above they do not remember any more than they can recollect the moment when they first breathed the breath of life. It is not so with all; perhaps not so with the most. But the true theory of the Gospel is that children should be brought up on it, as their daily food; be nurtured by it; renewed by the Holy Spirit, and made heirs of salvation.—Rev. S. Irenæus Prime, D. D.

———

Were we more anxious about the children we would do more work of a Christian kind. The old man seems to be beyond our reach, but the little child seems to be made for Christ. It would seem—do not let us shrink from the term—natural for every little child to put out his arms to cling to the Child of Bethlehem. Save the children and you will purify society; expend your solicitude upon the young, opening, tender life, and you shall see the result of your concern after many days. Services should be constituted for children; the old people have had the sanctuary too long; their ears are sated with eloquence; their minds are stored with names that never turn into inspirations; churches might be built for children, and preachers trained to speak to them alone. We have reversed all things and thus have gone astray. * * * * A poet says he was nearer heaven in his childhood than he ever was in after days, and he sweetly prayed that he might return through his yesterdays and through his childhood back to God. That is chronologically impossible—locally and physically not to be done, and yet that is the very miracle which is to be performed in the soul—in the spirit; we must be "born again."—Rev. Joseph Parker.

———

So with the children. It is even more important that religious exercises should not be made irksome and burdensome to them. Too much of a good thing is bad for them. I would not require them to be all the livelong day in a treadmill of religious work. They will be disgusted and hate the service, which should be always attractive to them and a delight. It is a serious question with ministers how to make the pulpit useful and pleasant to the young. Preachers with the gift of talking to children—a gift not so rare as is often thought—sometimes give a brief discourse to the children before the regular sermon. The objection to that practice is that children take it as their portion and dismiss the sermon that follows from their attention altogether. Now the art of talking to children does not consist in baby-talk or little stories or poor jokes. A man need not be a mountebank in order to interest the young in what he is saying. Children are not fools. If a man is simple in his words and earnest in his manner, children will hear with attention and get instruction from a sermon that is designed for the whole people.—Rev. S. Irenæus Prime, D. D.

Chivalry

The age of chivalry has gone, and one of calculators and economists has succeeded.—Burke.

———

Collision is as necessary to produce virtue in men as it is to elicit fire in inanimate matter; and chivalry is the essence of virtue.—Lord John Russell.

Choice

Choose you this day whom ye shall serve.—Bible.

———

Preferment goes by letter and affection.—Shakespeare.

———

There's a small choice in rotten apples.—Shakespeare.

———

Follow thou thy choice.—William Cullen Bryant.

———

The measure of choosing well is whether a man likes what he has chosen.—Lamb.

———

So much to win, so much to lose,
No marvel that I fear to choose.
—Miss Landon.

———

Be ignorance thy choice where knowledge leads to woe.—Beattie.

God offers to every mind its choice between truth and repose.—Emerson.

When to elect there is but one,
'Tis Hobson's choice; take that or none.
—Thomas Ward.

Life often presents us with a choice of evils, rather than of goods.—C. C. Colton.

Still to ourselves in every place consigned
Our own felicity we make or find.
—Goldsmith.

The strongest principle of growth lies in human choice.—George Eliot.

Rather than be less
Car'd not to be at all.   —Milton.

When better cherries are not to be had,
We needs must take the seeming best of bad.
—Daniel.

A wise man likes that best, that is itself;
Not that which only seems, though it look fairer.
—Middleton.

Choose always the way that seems the best, however rough it may be. Custom will render it easy and agreeable.—Pythagoras.

Give house-room to the best; 'tis never known
Verture and pleasure both to dwell in one.
—Herrick.

But for us there are moments, O, how solemn, when destiny trembles in the balance, and the preponderance of either scale is by our own choice.— Mark Hopkins.

I will not choose what many men desire,
Because I will not jump with common spirits,
And rank me with the barbarous multitudes.
—Shakespeare.

"Thy royal will be done—'tis just,"
Replied the wretch, and kissed the dust;
"Since, my last moments to assuage,
Your majesty's humane decree
Has deigned to leave the choice to me,
I'll die, so please you, of old age."
—Horace Smith.

You must make your choice whether to hold on to some thing which can-not save you, or let go, and fall into the hands of the Lord.—Ichabod Spencer.

God has so framed us as to make freedom of choice and action the very basis of all moral improvement, and all our faculties, mental and moral, resent and revolt against the idea of coercion.—Wm. Matthews.

Christ

Behold the Lamb of God, which taketh away the sin of the world!— Bible.

Surely He hath borne our griefs and carried our sorrows.—Bible.

All power is given unto me in heaven and in earth.—Bible.

In His love and in His pity he redeemed them.—Bible.

Jesus Christ is, in the noblest and most perfect sense, the realized ideal of humanity.—Herder.

Jesus Christ was more than man.— Napoleon I.

In Him dwelleth the fullness of the Godhead bodily.—Coloss. ii. 9.

How free from everything like art were the reasonings and language of Christ.—David Thomas.

The absence of sentimentalism in Christ's relations with men is what makes His tenderness so exquisitely touching.—Phillips Brooks.

At His birth a star, unseen before in heaven, proclaims Him come.— Milton.

Rejecting the miracles of Christ, we still have the miracle of Christ Himself.—Bovee.

Christ came not to talk about a beautiful light, but to be that light— not to speculate about virtue, but to be virtue.—H. G. Taylor.

Christ wrought out His perfect obedience as a man, through temptation, and by suffering.—Alexander Maclaren.

From first to last, Jesus is the same; always the same—majestic and simple, infinitely severe and infinitely gentle. —Napoleon Bonaparte.

Certainly, no revolution that has ever taken place in society can be compared to that which has been produced by the words of Jesus Christ. —Mark Hopkins.

If you (to General Bertrand) do not perceive that Jesus Christ is God, very well; then I did wrong to make you a general.—Napoleon I.

In darkness there is no choice. It is light that enables us to see the differences between things; and it is Christ that gives us light.—J. C. and A. W. Hare.

Christ was either the grandest, guiltiest of impostors, by a marvelous and most subtle refinement of wickedness, or He was God manifest in the flesh.—Herrick Johnson.

I have read in Plato and Cicero sayings that are very wise and very beautiful; but I never read in either of them, "Come unto me, all ye that labor and are heavy laden."—St. Augustine.

God be thanked for that good and perfect gift, the gift unspeakable: His life, His love, His very self in Jesus Christ.—Maltbie Babcock.

If the life and death of Socrates were those of a sage, the life and death of Jesus were those of a God.— Rousseau.

His name shall be called Wonderful, Counsellor, the Mighty God, the Everlasting Father, the Prince of Peace.— Isaiah ix. 6.

Whoever would fully and feelingly understand the words of Christ, must endeavor to conform his life wholly to the life of Christ.—Thomas à Kempis.

Unlike all other founders of a religious faith, Christ had no selfishness, no desire of dominance.—William Howitt.

The miracles of Christ were studiously performed in the most unostentatious way. He seemed anxious to veil His majesty under the love with which they were wrought.—W. E. Channing.

The name of Christ—the one great word well worth all languages in earth or heaven.—Bailey.

He that condescended so far, and stooped so low, to invite and bring us to heaven, will not refuse us a gracious reception there.—Robert Boyle.

If Christ is the wisdom of God and the power of God in the experience of those who trust and love Him, there needs no further argument of His divinity.—H. W. Beecher.

Are we proud and passionate, malicious and revengeful? Is this to be like-minded with Christ, who was meek and lowly?—Tillotson.

The best of men that ever wore earth about Him was a sufferer, a soft, meek, patient, humble, tranquil spirit; the first true gentleman that ever breathed.—Decker.

In His death He is a sacrifice, satisfying for our sins; in the resurrection, a conqueror; in the ascension, a king; in the intercession, a high priest.—Luther.

The Saviour of mankind Himself, in whose blameless life malice could find no act to impeach, has been called in question for words spoken.—Macaulay.

God never gave man a thing to do concerning which it were irreverent to ponder how the Son of God would have done it.—George MacDonald.

Those who have minutely studied the character of the Saviour will find it difficult to determine whether there is most to admire or to imitate in it—there is so much of both.

He came, bringing with Him the knowledge that God is a Being of infinite goodness; that the service required of mankind is not a service of form or ceremony, but a service of obedience.—J. A. Froude.

Hail to the King of Bethlehem,
Who weareth in His diadem
The yellow crocus for the gem
Of His authority.　—Longfellow.

The sacrifice of Christ has rendered it just for Him to forgive sin; and whenever we are led to repent of and to forsake it, even the righteousness of God is declared in the pardon of it. —Robert Hall.

That image, or rather that Person, so human, yet so entirely divine, has a power to fill the imagination, to arrest the affections, to deepen and purify the conscience, which nothing else in the world has.—J. C. Shairp.

Poor shepherdless sheep! It was his delight, as the Good Shepherd, to lead them to rich pastures; and as they sat and stood around Him they forgot their bodily wants in the beauty and power of His words.—J. Cunningham Geikie.

The tears of Christ are the pity of God. The gentleness of Jesus is the long-suffering of God. The tenderness of Jesus is the love of God. "He that hath seen Me hath seen the Father."—Alexander Maclaren.

Whatever Jesus is, the glorious Godhead is; and to have fellowship with the Son is to have fellowship with the Father. To know the love of Christ is to be filled with all the fullness of God.—James Hamilton.

The incarnation of God is a necessity of human nature. If we really and truly have a Father, we must be able to clasp His feet in our penitence, and to lean on His breast in our weary sorrowfulness.—Charles F. Deems.

Remember that vision on the Mount of Transfiguration; and let it be ours, even in the glare of earthly joys and brightnesses, to lift up our eyes, like those wondering three, and see no man any more, save Jesus only.—Alexander Maclaren.

As to Jesus of Nazareth, my opinion of whom you particularly desire, I think the system of morals and His religion, as He left them to us, is the best the world ever saw, or is likely to see.—Benjamin Franklin.

As human voice and instrument blend in one harmony, as human soul and body blend in each act of feeling, thought, or speech, so, as far as we can know, divinity and humanity act together in the thought and heart and act of the one Christ.—A. A. Hodge

---

The Christian world has a Leader, the contemplation of whose life and sufferings must administer comfort in affliction, while the sense of His power and omnipotence must give them humiliation in prosperity.—Steele.

The sages and heroes of history are receding from us, and history contracts the record of their deeds into a narrower and narrower page. But time has no power over the name and deeds and words of Jesus Christ.—Channing.

But chiefly Thou,
Whom soft-eyed Pity once led down from heaven
To bleed for man, to teach him how to live,
And, oh! still harder lesson! how to die.
　　　　　—Bishop Porteus.

In those holy fields,
Over whose acres walk'd those blessed feet
Which, fourteen hundred years ago, were nail'd
For our advantage on the bitter cross.
　　　　　—Shakespeare.

He, the Holiest among the mighty, and the Mightiest among the holy, has lifted with His pierced hands empires off their hinges, has turned the stream of centuries out of its channel, and still governs the ages.—Richter.

Alexander, Cæsar, Charlemagne and I myself have founded empires; but upon what do these creations of our genius depend? Upon force. Jesus alone founded His empire upon love; and to this very day millions would die for Him.—Napoleon I.

The nature of Christ's existence is mysterious, I admit; but this mystery meets the wants of man. Reject it, and the world is an inexplicable riddle; believe it, and the history of our race is satisfactorily explained.—Napoleon.

All the glory and beauty of Christ are manifested within, and there He delights to dwell; His visits there are frequent, His condescension amazing, His conversation sweet, His comforts refreshing; and the peace that He brings passeth all understanding.— Thomas à Kempis.

Lovely was the death Of Him whose life was Love! Holy with power He on the thought-benighted Skeptic beamed Manifest Godhead. —Coleridge.

Men who neglect Christ, and try to win heaven through moralities, are like sailors at sea in a storm, who pull, some at the bowsprit and some at the mainmast, but never touch the helm. —Beecher.

It was necessary for the Son to disappear as an outward authority, in order that He might reappear as an inward principle of life. Our salvation is no longer God manifested in a Christ without us, but as a "Christ within us, the hope of glory."—F. W. Robertson.

Every unfulfilled aspiration of humanity in the past; all partial representation of perfect character; all sacrifices, nay, even those of idolatry, point to the fulfillment of what we want, the answer to every longing— the type of perfect humanity, the Lord Jesus Christ.—F. W. Robertson.

Unlike all other founders of a religious faith, Christ had no selfishness, no desire of dominance; and His system, unlike all other systems of worship, was bloodless, boundlessly beneficent, and—most marvelous of all— went to break all bonds of body and soul, and to cast down every temporal and every spiritual tyranny.—William Howitt.

No other fame can be compared with that of Jesus. He has a place in the human heart that no one who ever lived has in any measure rivaled. No name is pronounced with a tone of such love and veneration. All other laurels wither before His. His are ever kept fresh with tears of gratitude. —W. E. Channing.

Christ's whole life on earth was the assertion and example of true manliness—the setting forth in living act and word what man is meant to be, and how he should carry himself in this world of God—one long campaign in which the "temptation" stands out as the first great battle and victory.— Thomas Hughes.

Christ's miracles were vivid manifestations to the senses that He is the Saviour of the body—and now as then the issues of life and death are in His hands—that our daily existence is a perpetual miracle. The extraordinary was simply a manifestation of God's power in the ordinary.—F. W. Robertson.

You never get to the end of Christ's words. There is something in them always behind. They pass into proverbs—they pass into laws—they pass into doctrines—they pass into consolations; but they never pass away, and, after all the use that is made of them, they are still not exhausted.—Dean Stanley.

Christ is the Good Physician. There is no disease He cannot heal; no sin He cannot remove; no trouble He cannot help. He is the Balm of Gilead, the Great Physician who has never yet failed to heal all the spiritual maladies of every soul that has come unto Him in faith and prayer.—Aughey.

I find the life of Christ made up of two parts; a part I can sympathize with as a man, and a part on which I gaze; a beam sent down from heaven which I can see and love, and another beam shot into the infinite, that I cannot comprehend.—Barr.

Star unto star speaks light, and world to world
Repeats the passage of the universe
To God; the name of Christ—the one great word
Well worth all languages in earth or heaven.   —Bailey.

Who did leave His Father's throne,
To assume thy flesh and bone?
Had He life, or had He none?
If He had not liv'd for thee,
Thou hadst died most wretchedly
And two deaths had been thy fee.
—Herbert.

The most destructive criticism has not been able to dethrone Christ as the incarnation of perfect holiness. The waves of a tossing and restless sea of unbelief break at His feet, and He stands still the supreme model, the inspiration of great souls, the rest of the weary, the fragrance of all Christendom, the one divine flower in the garden of God.—Herrick Johnson.

Our Lord's miracles were all essential parts of His one consistent life. They were wrought as evidences not only of His power, but of His mercy. They were throughout moral in their character, and spiritual in the ends contemplated by them. They were in fact embodiments of His whole character, exemplars of His whole teaching, emblems of His whole mission.—James McCosh.

Christ pitied because He loved, because He saw through all the wretchedness, and darkness, and bondage of evil; that there was in every human soul a possibility of repentance, of restoration; a germ of good, which, however stifled and overlaid, yet was capable of recovery, of health, of freedom, of perfection.—Dean Stanley.

It is the grandeur of Christ's character which constitutes the chief power of His ministry, not His miracles or teachings apart from His character. The greatest triumph of the Gospel is Christ Himself—a human body become the organ of the Divine nature, and revealing, under the conditions of an earthly life, the glory of God.—Horace Bushnell.

The "wise men" were journeying to the manger—we to the throne. They to see a babe—we to look upon the King in His beauty. They to kneel and worship—we to sit with Him on His throne. That trembling star shone for them through the darkness of the night, lighting their way—Jesus is always with us, our star of hope; and the pathway is never dark where He leads; for He giveth "songs in the night."—A. E. Kittredge.

Great occasions rally great principles, and brace the mind to a lofty bearing, a bearing that is even above itself. But trials that make no occasion at all, leave it to show the goodness and beauty it has in its own disposition. And here precisely is the superhuman glory of Christ as a character, that He is just as perfect, exhibits just as great a spirit in little trials as in great ones.—Horace Bushnell.

On the head of Christ are many crowns. He wears the crown of victory; He wears the crown of sovereignty; He wears the crown of creation; He wears the crown of providence; He wears the crown of grace; He wears the crown of glory—for every one of His glorified people owes his honor, happiness and blessedness to Him.—Aughey.

Newton supposed that all matter attracted other matter inversely according to the square of the distance; and the hypothesis was found to account for the whole movements of the heavenly bodies; which all became verifications of what Newton supposed to be the law of the solar system. Adopt the hypothesis that Jesus was what He is represented, and the whole of the books and the history becomes a verification.—James McCosh.

When has the world seen a phenomenon like this?—a lonely uninstructed youth, coming from amid the moral darkness of Galilee, even more distinct from His age, and from everything around Him, than a Plato would be rising up in some wild tribe in Oregon, assuming thus a position at the head of the world and maintaining it, for eighteen centuries, by the pure self-evidence of His life and doctrine.—Horace Bushnell.

Christ's divinity accounts for His exaltation to the right hand of God, justifies the worship of angels and the confidence of mankind. It makes clear His right to the throne of the universe, and enables the mind to understand why He is exalted in providence, in grace, and in judgment. It is the unifying truth that harmonizes all other teachings of Christianity, and renders the entire system symmetrical and complete.—George C. Lorimer.

From the moment of His self-dedication, when He threw His cares away, and went forth not knowing where to lay His head, the whole energy which others spend on interests of their own was poured into His human and Divine affections, and filled His life with an enthusiasm resistless and unique. However quiet His words, it is impossible not to feel the tender depths from which they come.—James Martineau.

He walked into Judæa eighteen hundred years ago; His sphere melody, flowing in wild native tones, took captive the ravished souls of men, and, being of a truth sphere melody, still flows and sounds, though now with thousandfold accompaniments and rich symphonies, through all our hearts, and modulates and divinely leads them.—Carlyle.

Across the chasm of eighteen hundred years Jesus Christ makes a demand which is beyond all others difficult to satisfy. He asks that for which a philosopher may often seek in vain at the hands of his friends, or a father of his children, or a bride of her spouse, or a man of his brother. He asks for the human heart; he will have it entirely to himself; he demands it unconditionally, and forthwith his demand is granted. Wonderful!—Napoleon I.

It was before Deity embodied in a human form, walking among men, partaking of their infirmities, leaning on their bosoms, weeping over their graves, slumbering in the manger, bleeding on the cross, that the prejudices of the synagogue, and the doubts of the academy, and the pride of the portico, and the fasces of the lictor, and the swords of thirty legions were humbled in the dust.—Macaulay.

Philosophical argument, especially that drawn from the vastness of the universe, in comparison with the insignificance of this globe, has sometimes shaken my reason for the faith that is in me; but my heart has always assured and reassured me that the gospel of Jesus Christ must be a divine reality. The Sermon on the Mount cannot merely be a human production. This belief enters into the very depth of my conscience.—Daniel Webster.

This it is that gives a majesty so pure and touching to the historic figure of Christ; self-abandonment to God, uttermost surrender, without reserve or stipulation, to the guidance of the Holy Spirit from the Soul of souls; pause in no darkness, hesitation in no perplexity, recoil in no extremity of anguish, but a gentle unfaltering hold of the invisible Hand, of the Only Holy and All Good—these are the features that have made Jesus of Nazareth the dearest and most sacred image to the heart of so many ages.—James Martineau.

Think of the majesty of that moment in this dying world's history, when Jesus Christ declared that to the Christian death was only a sleep. Outside of that small dwelling in Capernaum, a great race of men rushed and toiled as they harassed continents and seas; mighty events marshaled themselves into annals and pageants. What was inside? In one inconspicuous chamber of a now forgotten house, man's Redeemer, unobserved, martyred man's final enemy, There Immanuel subdued death forever.—C. S. Robinson.

What is our hope but the indwelling Spirit of Christ, to bring every thought into captivity to the obedience of Christ, to inspire every word and deed by His love? Then will "broken lights" blend in steady shining, the fractional be summed up in the integral, and life, unified and beautified by the central Christ, radiate God's glory, and shine with divine effulgence.—Maltbie Babcock.

Christ was placed midmost in the world's history; and in that central position He towers like some vast mountain to heaven—the farther slope stretching backward toward the creation, the hither slope toward the consummation of all things. The ages before look to Him with prophetic gaze; the ages since behold Him by historic faith; by both He is seen in common as the brightness of the Father's glory, and the unspeakable gift of God to the race.

In Christ we see the strength of achievement, and the strength of endurance. He moved with a calm majesty, like the sun. The bloody sweat, and the crown of thorns, and the cross, were full in His eyes; but He was obedient unto death. In His perfect self-sacrifice we see the perfection of strength; in the love that prompted it we see the perfection of beauty. This combination of self-sacrifice and love must be commenced in every Christian; and when it shall be in its spirit complete in him, then will he also be perfect in strength and beauty.—Mark Hopkins.

We believe that to Christ belongs creative power—that "without Him was not anything made which was made." We believe that from Him

came all life at first. In Him life was as in its deep source. He is the fountain of life. We believe that as no being comes into existence without His creative power, so none continues to exist without His sustaining energy. We believe that the history of the world is but the history of His influence, and that the centre of the whole universe is the cross of Cavalry.—Alexander Maclaren.

Other sages have spoken to me of God. But from whom could I have learned the essence of divine perfection as from Him, who was in a peculiar sense the Son, representative, and image of God—who was especially an incarnation of the unbounded love of the Father? And from what other teacher could I have learned to approach the Supreme Being with that filial spirit, which forms the happiness of my fellowship with Him? From other seers I might have heard of heaven; but when I behold in Jesus the spirit of heaven, dwelling actually on earth, what a new comprehension have I of that better world!—W. E. Channing.

Jesus Christ was born in a stable; He was obliged to fly into Egypt; thirty years of His life were spent in a workshop; He suffered hunger, thirst, and weariness; He was poor, despised, and miserable; He taught the doctrines of heaven, and no one would listen. The great and the wise persecuted and took Him, subjected Him to frightful torments, treated Him as a slave, and put Him to death between two malefactors, having preferred to give liberty to a robber, rather than to suffer Him to escape. Such was the life which our Lord chose; while we are horrified at any kind of humiliation, and cannot bear the slightest appearance of contempt.—Fénelon.

If we carried with us more distinctly than we do that one simple thought that in all human joys, in all the apparently self-forgetting tenderness, of that Lord, who had a heart for every sorrow, and an ear for every complaint, and a hand open as day and full of melting charity for every need—that

Christ   275   **Christ**

in every moment of that life in the boyhood, in the dawning manhood, in the maturity of His growing power—there was always present one black shadow, toward which He ever went straight with the consent of His will and the clearest eye, we should understand something more of how the life as well as the death was a sacrifice for us sinful men.—Alexander Maclaren.

"And whatsover ye do in word or deed—all in the name of the Lord Jesus." "Do" does not belong there. There is more than doing in life. Thinking, speaking, hoping, planning, dreaming—all are to be in the name of the Lord Jesus. His love and life are to color and shape our ambitions and accomplishments. In Him, as a plant in soil, in rain and sunshine, we are to live, growing up by Him and into Him. In His name we are to work, to pray, to suffer, to rejoice, and at last to go home. It is only another way of saying, "For me to live is Christ." —Maltbie Babcock.

Christ's method is divine. His words have the charm of antiquity with the freshness of yesterday; the simplicity of a child with the wisdom of a God; the softness of kisses from the lip of love, and the force of the lightning rending the tower. His parables are like groups of matchless statuary; His prayers like an organ peal floating round the world and down the ages, echoed by the mountain peaks and plains into rich and varied melody, in which all devout hearts find their noblest feelings at once expressed, sustained, refined. His truths are self-evidencing. They fall into the soul as seed into the ground, to rest and germinate. He speaks, and all nature and life become vocal with theology.—Edward Thomson.

All the virtues which appeared in Christ shone brightest in the close of His life, under the trials He then met. Eminent virtue always shows brightest in the fire. Pure gold shows its purity chiefly in the furnace. It was chiefly under those trials which Christ endured in the close of His life that

His love to God, His honor of God's majesty, His regard to the honor of His law, His spirit of obedience, His humility, contempt of the world, His patience, meekness, and spirit of forgiveness towards men, appeared. Indeed, everything that Christ did to work out redemption for us appears mainly in the close of His life. Here mainly is His satisfaction for sin, and here chiefly is His merit of eternal life for sinners, and here chiefly appears the brightness of His example which He has set us for imitation.—Jonathan Edwards.

He stands alone in unapproachable grandeur. Nineteen centuries roll away, and His character so lives that He inspires millions of men with impassioned love. Other men may seem to be children of their surroundings; He became what He was despite His surroundings, and is the only one who can say in truth and holiness, "Do as I have done." He, the ideal, the perfect one of our race, appears in an age when such an ideal could not have been developed in act—could not have been conceived in thought. In the theory of development the perfection of humanity is the final result of man's history ages hence. Christ therefore is the great miracle which more than any other establishes the fact of miracles. Christ Himself is proof of His own miracles.—Reynolds.

Jesus! How does the very word overflow with sweetness, and light, and love, and life; filling the air with odors, like precious ointment poured forth; irradiating the mind with a glory of truths on which no fear can live, soothing the wounds of the heart with a balm that turns the sharpest anguish into delicious peace, shedding through the soul a cordial of immortal strength. Jesus! the answer to all our doubts, the spring of all our courage, the earnest of all our hopes, the charm omnipotent against all our foes, the remedy for all weakness, the supply of all our wants, the fullness of all our desires. Jesus! at the mention of whose name every knee shall bow and every tongue confess. Jesus! our power: Jesus! our righteousness,

our sanctification, our redemption—
Jesus! our elder brother, our blessed
Lord and Redeemer. Thy name is the
most transporting theme of the church,
as they sing going up from the valley
of tears, to their home on the mount
of God; Thy name shall ever be the
richest chord in the harmony of
heaven, while the angels and the redeemed unite their exulting, adoring
songs around the throne of God.—
George W. Bethune.

How easily and contentedly we
speak of Jesus Christ as our example.
Do we realize what it means? If we
did, it would revolutionize our life.
Do we begin to know our Bible as He
did? Do we begin to pray as He did?
How thoughtful He was for others,
how patient toward dullness, how
quiet under insult! Think of what it
meant for Him to take a basin and
towel like a slave and wash the disciples' feet! Do we stoop to serve?
Can anyone say of us, as was said of
Him, that we go about "doing good"?
Think of His words, servants of His,
"I have given you an example, that ye
should do as I have done to you."
"Christlike" is a word often on our
lips. Do not speak it too lightly. It
is the heart of God's predestination.
It is our high calling.

There has appeared in this, our day,
a man of great virtue, named Jesus
Christ, who is yet living amongst us,
and with the Gentiles is accepted as a
prophet of truth, but His own disciples
call Him the Son of God. He raiseth
the dead, and cureth all manner of
diseases; a man of stature somewhat
tall and comely, with a very reverend
countenance; such as the beholder may
both love and fear; his hair is of the
color of a filbert, full ripe, and plain
down to His ears, but from His ears
downwards somewhat curled, and
more orient of color, waving about His
shoulders. In the midst of His head
goeth a seam or partition of hair, after
the manner of the Nazarites; His forehead very smooth and plain; His face,
nose and mouth so framed as nothing
can be reprehended; His beard somewhat thick, agreeable to the hair of
His head for color, not of any great

length, but forked in the middle; of
an innocent and mature look; His eyes
gray, clear and quick. In reproving,
He is terrible; in admonishing, courteous and fair spoken, pleasant in
speech, amidst gravity. It cannot be
remembered that any have seen Him
laugh, but many have seen Him weep.
In proportion of body, well shaped
and straight; His hands and arms
most beauteous to behold; in speaking, very temperate, modest and wise;
a man of singular virtue, surpassing
the children of men.—Publius Len-
tulus.

Christ is a rare jewel, but men
know not His value; a sun which ever
shines, but men perceive not His
brightness, nor walk in His light. He
is a garden full of sweets, a hive full
of honey, a sun without a spot, a star
ever bright, a fountain ever full, a
brook which ever flows, a rose which
ever blooms, a foundation which never
yields, a guide who never errs, a friend
who never forsakes. No mind can
fully grasp His glory; His beauty, His
worth, His importance, no tongue can
fully declare. He is the source of all
good, the fountain of every excellency,
the mirror of perfection, the light of
heaven, the wonder of the earth, time's
masterpiece, and eternity's glory; the
sun of bliss, the way of life, and life's
fair way. "He is altogether lovely,"
says the saint; a morning without
clouds, a day without night, a rose
without a thorn; His lips drop like
the honeycomb, His eyes beam tenderness, His heart gushes love. The
Christian is fed by His hands, carried
in His heart, supported by His arm,
nursed in His bosom, guided by His
eye, instructed by His lips, warmed by
His love; His wounds are his life, His
smile the light of his path, the health
of his soul, his rest and heaven below.
—Balfern.

Christ (Death of)

If Socrates died like a sage, Jesus
died like a God.—Rousseau.

The death of the Son of God is a
single and most perfect sacrifice and
satisfaction for sins; of infinite value
and price, abundantly sufficient to ex-

piate the sins of the whole world.—Synod of Dort.

He was Himself forsaken that none of His children might ever need to utter His cry of loneliness.—J. H. Vincent.

Herein is love, not that we loved God, but that He loved us, and sent His son to be the propitiation for our sins.—Bible.

The sufferings and death of Jesus Christ are a substitution for the endless punishment of all who truly believe on Him.—Adams.

When Jesus knew that it was not possible for the cup to pass from Him, with love to God He held it fast, and with love to man He drank it all.—Alexander Dickson.

In this awfully stupendous manner, at which Reason stands aghast, and Faith herself is half confounded, was the grace of God to man at length manifested.—Richard Hurd.

In the beauty of the lilies Christ was born
   across the sea,
With a glory in His bosom that transfigures
   you and me:
As He died to make men holy, let us die to
   make men free. —Julia Ward Howe.

The whole history of Israel, its ritual and its government, is explicable only as it is typical of the spiritual Israel, of the sacrifice on Cavalry, of the precious blood which alone can wash away sin.—A. E. Kittredge.

My friends, there is one spot on earth where the fear of death, of sin, and of judgment need never trouble us, the only safe spot on earth where the sinner can stand—Calvary.—D. L. Moody.

I have always considered the atonement to be characteristic of the Gospel as a system of religion. Strip it of that doctrine, and you reduce it to a scheme of morality, excellent indeed, and such as the world never before saw; but to man in the present state

of his faculties, absolutely impracticable.—Thomas, Earl of Kinnoul.

Christ's sacrifice stands in glorious proportions with the work to be done. Nothing else or less would suffice. It is a work supernatural, transacted in the plane of nature; and what but such a work could restore the broken order of the soul under evil?—Horace Bushnell.

"Having loved His own which were in the world, He loved them to the end." Often had they been faithless; and now, while addressing them, He knows that they will all in a few hours forsake Him. Yet He trusts them; He commits His cause to their keeping. And we must love as He loved.—Richard Fuller.

O, let us understand that the power of Christianity lies not in a hazy indefiniteness, not in shadowy forms, not so much even in definite truths and doctrines, but in the truth and the doctrine. There is but one Christ crucified. All the gathered might of the infinite God is in that word.—Herrick Johnson.

Other men have said, "If I could only live, I would establish and perpetuate an empire." This Christ of Galilee says, "My death shall do it." Other martyrs have died in simple fidelity to truth. This martyr dies that He may make His truth mighty over all hearts. He was a man; but was He only a man?—Herrick Johnson.

In agony unknown He bleeds away His life; in terrible throes He exhausts His soul. "Eloi! Eloi! lama sabachthani?" And then see! they pierce His side, and forthwith runneth out blood and water! This is the shedding of blood, the terrible pouring out of blood, without which, for you and the whole human race, there is no remission.—C. H. Spurgeon.

It was in His parting sorrow—that Jesus asked His disciples to remember Him; and never was entreaty of affection answered so; for ever since has

His name been breathed in morning and evening prayers that none can count, and has brought down some gift of sanctity and peace on the anguish of bereavement, and the remorse of sin.—James Martineau.

God's beloved Son, leaving the echoes of His cries upon the mountains and the traces of His weary feet upon the streets, shedding His tears over the tombs and His blood upon Golgotha, associating His life with our homes, and His corpse with our sepulchres, shows us how we, too, may be sons in the humblest vale of life, and sure of sympathy in heaven amid the deepest wrongs and sorrows of earth.—Edward Thomson.

As we look upon that agony and those tearful prayers, let us not only look with thankfulness; but let that kneeling Saviour teach us that in prayer alone can we be forearmed against our lesser sorrows; that strength to bear flows into the heart that is opened in supplication; and that a sorrow which we are made able to endure is more truly conquered than a sorrow which we avoid.—Alexander Maclaren.

It was not until Jesus had cried, "It is finished," and from His riven side the soldier's spear had fetched the blood and water; it was not till then that the fountain sealed of Incarnate Love became the fountain opened of Redeeming merit, and that the Siloah began to flow, which ever since has flowed adown the oracles of God.—James Hamilton.

But now, the sounds of infancy, always nearest the heart, and sure to come to the lips in our deepest emotion, returned in His anguish; and in words which He had learned at His mother's knee, His heart uttered its last wail—"Eloi! Eloi! lama sabachthani?" "My God! My God! why hast Thou forsaken me?"—J. Cunningham Geikie.

Grant, O Lord, that as we are baptized into the death of Thy blessed Son our Saviour Jesus Christ, so by continual mortifying our corrupt affections, we may be buried with Him; and that through the grave, and gate of death, we may pass to our joyful resurrection; for His merits, who died, and was buried, and rose again for us, Thy Son Jesus Christ our Lord. Amen.—Book of Common Prayer.

The study of everything that stands connected with the death of Christ, whether it be in the types of the ceremonial law, the predictions of the prophets, the narratives of the gospels, the doctrines of the epistles, or the sublime vision of the Apocalypse, this is the food of the soul, the manna from heaven, the bread of life. This is "meat indeed" and "drink indeed."—John Angel James.

A moment more, and all was over. The cloud had passed as suddenly as it rose. Far and wide, over the vanquished throngs of His enemies, with a loud voice, as if uttering His shout of eternal victory before entering into His glory, He cried, "It is finished!" Then, more gently, came the words, "Father, into Thy hands I commend my spirit." A moment more, and there arose a great cry, as of mortal agony; the head fell. He was dead.—J. Cunningham Geikie.

All other great men are valued for their lives; He, above all, for His death, around which mercy and truth, righteousness and peace, God and man are reconciled; for the cross is the magnet which sends the electric current through the telegraph between earth and heaven, and makes both Testaments thrill, through the ages of the past and future, with living, harmonious, and saving truth.—Edward Thomson.

The world cannot bury Christ. The earth is not deep enough for His tomb, the clouds are not wide enough for His winding-sheet; He ascends into the heavens, but the heavens cannot contain Him. He still lives—in the church which burns unconsumed with His love; in the truth that reflects His image; in the hearts which burn

as He talks with them by the way.—
Edward Thomson.

By Thine hour of dire despair;
By Thine agony of prayer;
By the cross, the nail, the thorn,
Piercing spear, and torturing scorn;
By the gloom that veiled the skies
O'er the dreadful sacrifice;
Listen to our humble cry,
Hear our solemn Litany.
—Sir Robert Grant.

He was alone; alone, enduring the curse for us; alone, "bearing our sins in His own body on the tree," and exhausting the fierceness of eternal justice; alone, without succor from man; alone, without one strengthening whisper from angel; above all, alone, without one ray from His Father's countenance. And that expiring cry, "My God! My God! why hast Thou forsaken me?" was the bitter, dreary, dismal, piercing wail of a soul utterly deserted—wrapped, shrouded in essential unmitigated desolation.—Richard Fuller.

I entreat you to devote one solemn hour of thought to a crucified Saviour —a Saviour expiring in the bitterest agony. Think of the cross, the nails, the open wounds, the anguish of His soul. Think how the Son of God became a man of sorrows and acquainted with grief, that you might live forever. Think as you lie down upon your bed to rest, how your Saviour was lifted up from the earth to die. Think amid your plans and anticipations of future gaiety what the redemption of your soul has cost, and how the dying Saviour would wish you to act. His wounds plead that you will live for better things.—Albert Barnes.

He planted His cross in the midst of the mad and roaring current of selfishness, aggravated to malignity, and uttered from it the mighty cry of expiring love. And the waters heard Him, and from that moment they began to be refluent about His cross. From that moment, a current deeper and broader and mightier began to set heavenward; and it will continue to be deeper and broader and mightier till its glad waters shall encompass the

earth, and toss themselves as the ocean. And not alone did earth hear the cry. It pierced the regions of immensity. Heaven heard it, and hell heard it, and the remotest star shall hear it, testifying to the love of God in His unspeakable gift, and to the supremacy of that blessedness of giving which could be reached only through death—the death of the cross.—Mark Hopkins.

When the Father would give men the light of the knowledge of His glory, how does He proceed? To what does He turn men's gaze? Not to His mighty works; not to creative or providential wonders; not to geological or astronomical facts; not to the data on which Paley and Bell and other admirable writers build up their argument from design; not to the still greater wonder of mind, but to "the face of Jesus Christ," that face that was more marred than any man's; that endured the ruffian blows; down which the blood drops trickled; that looked down on a mocking crowd from an ignominious cross.—John Hall.

Christ (Resurrection of)

Having made an expiation for sins, He is set down on God's right hand forever. There is no more that even Immanuel can do. This is Love's extremest effort, God's last and greatest gift, God's own sacrifice. Can there be any escape for those who neglect so great salvation?—James Hamilton.

In His discourses, His miracles, His parables, His sufferings, His resurrection, He gradually raises the pedestal of His humanity before the world, but under a cover, until the shaft reaches from the grave to the heavens, when He lifts the curtain, and displays the figure of a man on a throne, for the worship of the universe; and clothing His church with His own power, He authorizes it to baptize and to preach remission of sins in His own name.—Edward Thomson.

Step by step, He had raised their conceptions of Him nearer the unspeakable grandeur of His true nature and work. At first the Teacher, He had, after a time, by gradual disclosures, revealed Himself as the Son of God veiled in the form of man; and, now, since His crucifixion and resurrection, He had taught them to see in Him the Messiah, exalted to immortal and Divine majesty, as the conqueror of death and the Lord of all. —James Hamilton.

But who is this that cometh from the tomb, with dyed garments from the bed of death? He that is glorious in His appearance, walking in the greatness of strength? It is thy Prince, O Zion! Christian, it is your Lord! He hath trodden the wine-press alone; He hath stained His raiment with blood; but now as the first-born from the womb of nature, He meets the morning of His resurrection. He arises, a conqueror from the grave; He returns with blessings from the world of spirits; He brings salvation to the sons of men. Never did the returning sun usher in a day so glorious! It was the jubilee of the universe!

Christ (Saviour)

The blood of Jesus Christ His Son cleanseth us from all sin.

Unless you live in Christ, you are dead to God.—Rowland Hill.

No man cometh unto the Father, but by me.—Bible.

In danger Christ lashes us to Himself, as the Alpine guides do when there is perilous ice to get over.— Alexander Maclaren.

Christ wants to lead men by their love, their personal love to Him, and the confidence of His personal love to them.—Horace Bushnell.

The Lord Jesus Christ would have the whole world to know that though He pardons sin, He will not protect it. —Joseph Alleine.

Jesus did all the saving-work. He brought the cross to our level. Get saved by looking to Him, and then live to God.—W. P. Mackay.

Jesus is the true manifestation of God, and He is manifested to be the regenerating power of a divine life.— Horace Bushnell.

Jesus Christ hath brought life and immortality to light through the Gospel.

And I, if I be lifted up from the earth, will draw all men unto Me.— Bible.

A man may go to heaven without health, without riches, without honors, without learning, without friends; but he can never go there without Christ. —John Dyer.

He who thinks he hath no need of Christ, hath too high thoughts of himself. He who thinks Christ cannot help him, hath too low thoughts of Christ.—J. M. Mason.

Never be afraid to bring the transcendent mysteries of our faith, Christ's life and death and resurrection, to the help of the humblest and commonest of human wants.—Phillips Brooks.

You may be a dreadful failure. Christ is a divine success. "Who shall lay anything to the charge of God's elect? It is God that justifieth."— Edward Thomson.

No glory of the Eternal One is higher than this, "Mighty to save;" no name of God is more adorable than that of "Saviour;" no place among the servants of God can be so glorious as that of an instrument of salvation.— William Arthur.

Sun of my soul, Thou Saviour dear,
It is not night if Thou be near;
Oh, may no earth-born cloud arise,
To hide Thee from Thy servant's eyes.
—John Keble.

Christ's voice sounds now for each of us in loving invitation; and dead in sin and hardness of heart though we be, we can listen and live. Christ Himself, my brother, sows the seed now. Do you take care that it falls not on, but in, your souls.—Alexander Maclaren.

———

On Thee alone my hope relies,
Beneath Thy cross I fall;
My Lord! my Life! my Sacrifice!
My Saviour! and my All!
—Anne Steele.

———

Because many who are called by the Gospel do not repent nor believe in Christ, but perish in unbelief, this does not arise from defect or insufficiency of the sacrifice offered by Christ, but from their own fault.—Synod of Dort.

———

Christ is known only by them that receive Him into their love, their faith, their deep want; known only as He is enshrined within, felt as a divine force, breathed in the inspirations of the secret life.—Horace Bushnell.

———

Beloved, you that have faith in the fountain, frequent it. Beware of two errors which are very natural and very disastrous; beware of thinking any sin too great for it; beware of thinking any sin too small.—James Hamilton.

———

Our sins are debts that none can pay but Christ. It is not our tears, but His blood; it is not our sighs, but His sufferings, that can testify for our sins. Christ must pay all, or we are prisoners forever.—Thomas Brooks.

———

It was the custom of the Roman emperors, at their triumphal entrance, to cast new coins among the multitudes; so doth Christ, in His triumphal ascension into heaven, throw the greatest gifts for the good of men that were ever given.—T. Goodwin.

———

There is truth in Jesus which is terrible, as well as truth that is soothing; terrible, for He shall be Judge as well as Saviour; and ye cannot face Him, ye cannot stand before Him, unless ye now give ear to His invitation.—Henry Melvill.

———

Christ sends His Spirit, not only to help, but to lead us on, so that we build better than we know. We come freely into His methods; we are made to carry out His plan. This is the guarantee of an eternal success.—M. B. Riddle.

———

Christ puts Himself at the head of the mystic march of the generations; and, like the mysterious angel that Joshua saw in the plain by Jericho, makes the lofty claim, "Nay, but as the captain of the Lord's host am I come up."—Alexander Maclaren.

———

Jesus does not drive His followers on before, as a herd of unwilling disciples, but goes before Himself, leading them into paths that He has trod, and dangers He has met, and sacrifices He has borne Himself, calling them after Him and to be only followers.—Horace Bushnell.

———

Christ is the great burden bearer—the Lamb of God who beareth the sin of the world; but in order to enjoy the benefit of His interposition, I must distinctly and for myself take advantage of it. Conscious of my lost estate, I must seek a personal share in the common salvation.—James Hamilton.

———

Be sure that Christ is not behind you, but before, calling and drawing you on. This is the liberty, the beautiful liberty of Christ. Claim your glorious privilege in the name of a disciple; be no more a servant, when Christ will own you as a friend.—Horace Bushnell.

———

As this brook not only washes off impurities, but overwhelms them, so that they can no longer be found, even so Thy Divine mercy, and the stream of my Saviour's blood, not only purge away, but extinguish my sins, sweeping them into the depths of the sea, where through all eternity they shall be remembered no more.—Christian Scriver.

———

Go to the family where darkness and suspicion and jealousy and disorder reign, and if they will but receive Christ, mark how light and confidence and order and peace spring up. Go to the regions of superstition and idolatry, and see what transformations are effected by Jesus.—Edward Thomson.

From behind the shadow of the still small voice—more awful than tempest or earthquake—more sure and persistent than day and night—is always sounding full of hope and strength to the weariest of us all, "Be of good cheer, I have overcome the world."—Thomas Hughes.

And what is the joy of Christ? The joy and delight which springs forever in His great heart, from feeling that He is forever doing good; from loving all, and living for all; from knowing that if not all, yet millions on millions are grateful to Him, and will be forever.—Charles Kingsley.

When a man begins to apprehend the first approach of grace, pardon, and mercy by Jesus Christ to his soul; when he is convinced of his utter unworthiness and desert of hell, and can never expect anything from a just and holy God but damnation, how do the first dawnings of mercy melt and humble him!—John Flavel.

Grieve not the Christ of God, who redeems us; and remember that we grieve Him most when we will not let Him pour His love upon us, but turn a sullen, unresponsive unbelief towards His pleading grace, as some glacier shuts out the sunshine from the mountain-side with its thick-ribbed ice.—Alexander Maclaren.

As a child walking over a slippery and dangerous path cries out, "Father, I am falling!" and has but a moment to catch his father's hand, so every believer sees hours when only the hand of Jesus comes between him and the abysses of destruction.—T. L. Cuyler.

Compassionate Saviour! We welcome Thee to our world. We welcome Thee to our hearts. We bless Thee for the Divine goodness Thou hast brought from heaven; for the souls Thou hast warmed with love to man, and lifted up in love to God; for the efforts of divine philanthropy

which Thou hast inspired; and for that hope of a pure celestial life, through which Thy disciples triumph over death.—W. E. Channing.

Reader, if Christ is yours, and you are Christ's, is there anything on which you may more confidently repose than that Jesus is making continual intercession for you, ever displaying the merits of His cross and precious blood, not only for the church at large, but for thee, even for sinful thee?—G. W. Mylne.

Brethren, is not this the Saviour that you need? one who can save you from the utmost depths of depravity, in the utmost corner of the earth, on the utmost inch of time? One who can save you amidst the utmost urgency of fierce temptations, and who in the uttermost extreme of exhausted nature, when heart and flesh do faint and fail, completes the work, and seals the salvation for evermore?—James Hamilton.

You have only to cast your life-long guilt, your ungodliness, your evil thoughts and wicked words, your sinful soul itself, into this crime-canceling, sin-annihilating, soul-cleansing Fountain, in order to obliterate from God's creation your foul transgressions, and yet leave the Divine perfection fair as ever. The sin which a Saviour's blood dissolves is the only sin which, after being once committed, is totally extinguished.—James Hamilton.

"My burden is light," said the blessed Redeemer, a light burden indeed, which carries him that bears it. I have looked through all nature for a resemblance of this, and seem to find a shadow of it in the wings of a bird, which are indeed borne by the creature, and yet support her flight towards heaven.—St. Bernard.

What do we know about the world unseen? What reasonings, what curiosity, what misgivings there have been concerning that impenetrable mystery! Out of this mystery and vagueness and vastness comes the human form of the

Divine Redeemer. He assures us that there is an unmixed and endless life, and that all we have to do to secure it is to trust ourselves to Him who came to declare it and to confer it.—William Adams.

It is not the thinker who is the true king of men, as we sometimes hear it proudly said. We need one who will not only show, but be the Truth; who will not only point, but open and be the Way; who will not only communicate thought, but give, because He is the Life. Not the rabbi's pulpit, nor the teacher's desk, still less the gilded chairs of earthly monarchs, least of all the tents of conquerors, are the throne of the true king. He rules from the cross.—Alexander Maclaren.

Happy those who are able in truth to say, "My Lord and my God!" Here is the true bond of union. Here is the noblest inspiration of life. Strength for work. Comfort in trouble. Hope in death. Here is what gives eternity itself its chief interest and joy. There we shall behold the King in His beauty. And when we shall see Him as He is, and shall be like Him, with what ecstasy of love and gratitude and joy shall we cry, "My Lord and my God!"—William Forsythe.

I feel my disease, and I feel that my want of alarm and lively affecting conviction forms its most obstinate ingredient; I try to stir up the emotion, and feel myself harassed and distressed at the impotency of my own meditations. But why linger without the threshold in the face of a warm and urgent invitation? "Come unto me." Do not think it is your office to heal one part of the disease, and Christ's to heal the remainder.—Thomas Chalmers.

The hoary centuries are full of Him; the echoes of His sweet voice are heard to-day; His love has perfumed the past eighteen hundred years, and He lives to-day, as the Head of His church; He lives to-day, the object of the warmest adoration, the most passionate love, for whom millions would die this very hour. Empires have fallen, thrones have crumbled; but Jesus lives, His empire extending every day, His throne gaining new trophies of His grace.—A. E. Kittredge.

The enthronement of Christ over the minds of men is steadily going forward. His kingdom embraces the princes in the realm of mind. It embraces the nations of highest civilization. They are all beneath the cross. It is maintained by simple authority. Other mental monarchs rule by logic; Christ's word is law—it is satisfying to His subjects. His truth in the hands of His disciples, like the bread He broke upon the mountains, is an ample supply for the millions that gather at His table.—Edward Thomson.

Yes, we have throned Him in our minds and hearts—the cynosure of our wandering thoughts—the monarch of our warmest affections, hopes, desires. This we have done. And the more we meditate upon His astonishing love, His amazing sacrifice, the more we feel that if we had a thousand minds, hearts, souls, we would crown Him Lord of all. Living we will live in Him, for Him, to Him. Dying, we will clasp Him in our arms, and, with Simeon, welcome death as the consummation of bliss.—Richard Fuller.

Thus the word reveals the divine essence; His incarnation makes that life, that love, that light, which is eternally resident in God obvious to souls that steadily contemplate Himself. These terms life, love, light—so abstract, so simple, so suggestive—meet in God; but they meet also in Jesus Christ. They do not only make Him the centre of a philosophy; they belong to the mystic language of faith more truly than to the abstract terminology of speculative thought. They draw hearts to Jesus; they invest Him with a higher than any intellectual beauty.—H. P. Liddon.

My only comfort is that I with body and soul, both in life and death, am not my own, but belong to my faithful

Saviour Jesus Christ, who with His precious blood hath fully satisfied for all my sins, and delivered me from all the power of the devil; and so preserves me, that without the will of my heavenly Father, not a hair can fall from my head; yea, that all things must be subservient to my salvation. And, therefore, by His holy spirit, He also assures me of eternal life, and makes me sincerely willing and ready, henceforth to live unto Him.—Heidelberg Catechism.

We believe that the salvation of sinners is wholly of grace; through the mediatorial offices of the Son of God; who, by the appointment of the Father, freely took upon Him our nature, yet without sin; honored the divine law by His personal obedience, and by His death made a full atonement for sins; that having risen from the dead He is now enthroned in heaven; and uniting in His wonderful person the tenderest sympathies with divine perfections, He is every way qualified to be a suitable, a compassionate, and an all-sufficient Saviour.—Baptist Church Manual.

Christ is the head of all things. Everything lies open before His eye, everything is sustained by His power, and everything is disposed of by His wisdom. Not a sparrow can fall to the ground without His notice and permission. Oh, to see Jesus in all things! Oh, to see everything at the disposal of Jesus! Oh, to see that all things are directed, controlled, and overruled by Christ alone! May this calm my mind, compose my spirit, and produce holy resignation in my soul! If Jesus arranges all, sends all, directs all, overrules all, then all things must work together for good to them that love God.—James Smith.

If you are really anxious to learn the way to God, He has not left Himself without a witness, nor you without a teacher. Go to the recorded Christ, and look at that history; listen to those words which survive in the gospels. And go to the living Christ, to Him who has said, "I am the light of the world, he that followeth me shall not walk in darkness, but shall have the light of life." And dim as may be your outset—more of night than morning in your twilight, as you follow on you shall know the Lord, and with the light that radiates from Himself, your path will shine brighter and brighter unto the perfect day.—James Hamilton.

Christian

A Christian is the highest style of man.—Young.

A Christian is God Almighty's gentleman.—J. C. Hare.

The disciples were called Christians first at Antioch.—The Acts.

Whatever makes men good Christians, makes them good citizens.—Daniel Webster.

The purified righteous man has become a coin of the Lord, and has the impress of his King stamped upon him.—Clement of Alexandria.

Being in Christ, it is safe to forget the past; it is possible to be sure of the future; it is possible to be diligent in the present.—Alexander Maclaren.

Christians have burnt each other, quite persuaded
That all the apostles would have done as they did.   —Byron.

A greater absurdity cannot be thought of than a morose, hard-hearted, covetous, proud, malicious Christian.—Jonathan Edwards.

Christians are called saints, for their holiness; believers, for their faith; brethren, for their love; disciples, for their knowledge.—Fuller.

A child of God should be a visible beatitude, for joy and happiness, and a living doxology, for gratitude and adoration.—C. H. Spurgeon.

There is nothing that will make you a Christian indeed, but a taste of the sweetness of Christ.—Rutherford.

The Christian life is not hearing nor knowing, but doing.—Rev. S. L. Dickey.

I never knew any man in my life who could not bear another's misfortunes perfectly like a Christian.—Pope.

It was a deep true thought which the old painters had, when they drew John as likest to his Lord. Love makes us like.—Alexander Maclaren.

Servant of God, well done, well hast thou fought
The better fight.   —Milton.

A virtuous and a Christian-like conclusion, To pray for them that have done scathe to us.   —Shakespeare.

The greatness of God is the true rebuke to the littleness of men. The greatness of Christ is the true rebuke to the littleness of Christians.—Dean Stanley.

A Christian is a man in Christ. "If any man be in Christ." A Christian is a man for Christ. "Glorify God in your body and spirit which are God's." —Richard Fuller.

A Christian in this world is but gold in the ore; at death the pure gold is melted out and separated and the dross cast away and consumed.—Flavel.

If all were perfect Christians, individuals would do their duty; the people would be obedient to the laws, the magistrates incorrupt, and there would be neither vanity nor luxury in such a state.—Rousseau.

Christian work is something more than furnishing food and raiment and shelter. It is also teaching men of God, of Christ, of heaven, of sin, of love, of justice, of brotherhood.

Christ, in that place He hath put you, hath intrusted you with a dear pledge, which is His own glory, and hath armed you with His sword to keep the pledge, and make a good account of it to God.—Rutherford.

The last, best fruit that comes to perfection, even in the kindliest soul, is tenderness toward the hard; forbearance toward the unforbearing; warmth of heart toward the cold; and philanthropy toward the misanthropic.—Jean Paul Richter.

Like the cellar-growing vine is the Christian who lives in the darkness and bondage of fear. But let him go forth, with the liberty of God, into the light of love, and he will be like the plant in the field, healthy, robust, and joyful.—H. W. Beecher.

The weakest believer is a member of Christ as well as the strongest; and the weakest member of the body mystically shall not perish. Christ will cut off rotten members, but not weak members.—Watson.

Ordinary human motives will appeal in vain to the ears which have heard the tones of the heavenly music; and all the pomp of life will show poor and tawdry to the sight that has gazed on the vision of the great white throne and the crystal sea.—Alexander Maclaren.

It is more to the honor of a Christian soldier, by faith to overcome the world, than by a monastical vow to retreat from it; and more for the honor of Christ, to serve Him in a city than to serve Him in a cell.—Matthew Henry.

Persons of mean understandings, not so inquisitive, nor so well instructed, are made good Christians, and by reverence and obedience, implicitly believe, and abide by their belief.— Montaigne.

The sum of the whole matter is this: He who is one in will and heart with God is a Christian. He who loves God is one in will and heart with Him. He who trusts Christ loves God. That is Christianity in its ultimate purpose and result. That is Christianity in its means and working forces. That is Christianity in its starting point and foundation.—Alexander Maclaren.

He that will deserve the name of a Christian must be such a man as excelleth through the knowledge of Christ and His doctrine; in modesty and righteousness of mind, in constancy of life, in virtuous fortitude, and in maintaining sincere piety toward the one and the only God, who is all in all.—Eusebius.

Many there are who, while they bear the name of Christians, are totally unacquainted with the power of their divine religion. But for their crimes the Gospel is in no wise answerable. Christianity is with them a geographical, not a descriptive, appellation.—Faber.

Yes—rather plunge me back in pagan night,
And take my chance with Socrates for bliss,
Than be the Christian of a faith like this,
Which builds on heavenly cant its earthly
    sway,
And in a convert mourns to lose a prey.
    —Moore.

Health is a great blessing—competence obtained by honorable industry is a great blessing—and a great blessing it is to have kind, faithful, and loving friends and relatives; but, that the greatest of all blessings, as it is the most ennobling of all privileges, is to be indeed a Christian.—Coleridge.

The Christian life is not an engagement by contract between the Master and His servant. It is the union of two hearts—that of the Saviour and the saved—by the endearing ties of the most intimate love.

The great comprehensive truths written in letters of living light on every page of our history are these: Human happiness has no perfect security but freedom; freedom none but virtue; virtue none but knowledge; and neither freedom nor virtue has any vigor of immortal hope, except in the principles of Christian faith, and in the sanctions of the Christian religion.—Aughey.

Now see what a Christian is, drawn by the hand of Christ. He is a man on whose clear and open brow God has set the stamp of truth; one whose very eye beams bright with honor; in whose very look and bearing you may see freedom, manliness, veracity; a brave man—a noble man—frank, generous, true, with, it may be, many faults; whose freedom may take the form of impetuosity or rashness, but the form of meanness never.—F. W. Robertson.

A Christian is a believer in Jesus. He believes that if he only throws his own lost and sinful soul on the Redeemer, there is in His sacrifice sufficient merit to cancel all his guilt, and in His heart sufficient love to undertake the keeping of his soul for all eternity. He believes that Jesus is a Saviour. He believes that His heart is set on His people's holiness, and that it is only by making them new creatures, pure-minded, kind-hearted, unselfish, devout, that He can fit them for a home and a life like His own, that He can fit them for the occupations and enjoyments of heaven. And believing all this he prays and labors after holiness.—James Hamilton.

He that can apprehend and consider vice with all her baits and seeming pleasures, and yet abstain, and yet distinguish, and yet prefer that which is truly better, he is the true way-faring Christian. I cannot praise a fugitive and cloistered virtue unexercised and unbreathed that never sallies out and sees her adversary, but slinks out of the race, where that immortal garland is to be run for, not without dust and heat.—Milton.

These—lowliness, meekness, long-suffering, loving forbearance—quiet, unpretending, unshowy virtues, are amongst the best means for promoting true unity in the church of God. Who is the most useful Christian? Not as a rule he who has the most transcendent genius, brilliant talents, and commanding eloquence, but he who has the most of this quiet, loving, forbearing spirit. The world may do without its Niagara, whose thundering roar and majestic rush excite the highest amazement of mankind, but it cannot spare the thousand rivulets that glide unseen and unheard every moment through the earth, imparting life, and verdure, and beauty wherever they go. And so the church may do without its men of splendid abilities, but it cannot do without its men of tender, loving, forbearing souls.—David Thomas.

Putting the soul into trifles. Let us remember that greatness of action depends on two other kinds of greatness; on our appreciation of the greatness of the occasion when it can be done. It has been well said, by an eminent French writer, that the true calling of a Christian is not to do extraordinary things, but to do ordinary things in an extraordinary way. The most trival tasks can be accomplished in a noble, gentle, regal spirit, which overrides and puts aside all petty, paltry feelings, and which elevates all little things.—Dean Stanley.

Christianity

There is no social life outside of Christendom.—Wm. H. Seward.

Christianity is a battle, not a dream. —Wendell Phillips.

Christendom, as an effect, must be accounted for. It is too large for a mortal cause.—Bishop Huntington.

Christianity ruined emperors, but saved peoples.—Alfred de Musset.

Christianity is completed Judaism, or it is nothing.—Beaconsfield.

Christianity commands us to pass by injuries; policy to let them pass by us. —Franklin.

The Christian faith is a grand cathedral with divinely pictured windows.—Hawthorne.

The pure and benign light of revelation has had a meliorating influence on mankind.—Washington.

I desire no other evidence of the truth to Christianity than the Lord's Prayer.—Madame de Staël.

Christianity is intensely practical. She has no trait more striking than her common sense.—Charles Buxton.

God must have loved the plain people; He made so many of them.— Abraham Lincoln.

Every Christian is born great because he is born for heaven.—Massillon.

Give us more and more of real Christianity, and we shall need less of its evidences.

Christianity is not so much the advent of a better doctrine as of a perfect character.—Horace Bushnell.

Without the way, there is no going; without the truth, there is no knowing; without the life, there is no living.— Thomas à Kempis.

Our Christianity is a name, a shadow, unless we resemble Him who, being the incarnate God, was incarnate goodness.—Aughey.

Though the living man can wear a mask and carry on deceit, the dying Christian cannot counterfeit.—Cumberland.

The other world is as to this like the east to the west. We cannot approach the one without turning away from the other.—Abd-el-Kader.

He who is truly a good man is more than half way to being a Christian, by whatever name he is called.—South.

There was never law, or sect, or opinion, did so much magnify goodness as the Christian religion doth.—Bacon.

In becoming Christians, though we love some persons more than we did, let us love none less.—Gambold.

I would give nothing for the Christianity of a man whose very dog and cat were not the better for his religion. —Rowland Hill.

Christianity was the temple that was to be eternal; and on it, as unconscious builders, men were laboring in all the ages from the creation.—Bishop Foss.

Christianity, which is always true to the heart, knows no abstract virtues, but virtues resulting from our wants, and useful to all.—Chateaubriand.

The church limits her sacramental services to the faithful. Christ gave Himself upon the cross, a ransom for all.—Pascal.

The whole of Christianity is comprised in three things—to believe, to love, and to obey Jesus. These are things, however, which we must be learning all our life.—Christian Scriver.

The peculiar doctrine of Christianity is that of a universal sacrifice and perpetual propitiation.—Dr. Johnson.

Christianity is the companion of liberty in all its conflicts, the cradle of its infancy and the divine source of its claims.—De Tocqueville.

Ours is a religion jealous in its demands, but how infinitely prodigal in its gifts! It troubles you for an hour, it repays you by immortality.—Bulwer-Lytton.

If Christianity were only a development, then Christ was not needed. If Christianity were only a scheme of morals, then the divine incarnation was a thing superfluous.—Herrick Johnson.

The real difficulty with thousands in the present day is not that Christianity has been found wanting, but that it has never been seriously tried.—H. P. Liddon.

Other sciences may strengthen certain faculties of the soul; some the intellect, some the imagination, some the memory; but Christianity strengthens the soul itself.

When Christianity is received, it stimulates the faculties, and calls forth new ideas, new motives and new sentiments. It has been the mother of all modern education.—James McCosh.

There is no inevitable connection between Christianity and cynicism. Truth is not a salad, is it, that you must always dress it with vinegar?—Wm. M. Punshon.

I always have had, and always shall have, a profound regard for Christianity, the religion of my fathers, and for its rights, its usages and observances.—Henry Clay.

The introduction of Christianity, which, under whatever form, always confers such inestimable benefits on mankind, soon made a sensible change in these rude and fierce manners.—Burke.

The whole history of Christianity proves that she has indeed little to fear from persecution as a foe, but much to fear from persecution as an ally.—Macaulay.

Christianity may produce agitation, anger, tumult as at Ephesus; but the diffusion of the pure gospel of Christ, and the establishment of the institutions of honesty and virtue, at whatever cost, is a blessing to mankind.—Albert Barnes.

It is a refiner as well as a purifier of the heart; it imparts correctness of perception, delicacy of sentiment, and all those nicer shades of thought and feeling which constitute elegance of mind.—Mrs. John Sanford.

If ever Christianity appears in its power, it is when it erects its trophies upon the tomb; when it takes up its votaries where the world leaves them; and fills the breast with immortal hope in dying moments.—Robert Hall.

Christianity is within a man, even as he is gifted with reason; it is associated with your mother's chair, and with the first remembered tones of her blessed voice.—Coleridge.

Christianity is, above all other religions ever known, a religion of sacrifice. It is a religion founded on the greatest of all sacrifices, the sacrifice of the Incarnation, culminating in the sacrifice on Calvary.—Dean Stanley.

Our religion is not Christianity so much as Christ. Our gospel is the knowledge, not of a system, but the saving knowledge of a personal Saviour.—Aughey.

Christianity, Christ, heaven, hell, the judgment, sin, holiness, God,— these, and whether they be true or false, and our personal relations to them, whether they be right or wrong, are things to know about, not to be doubting or guessing about.—Herrick Johnson.

The distinction between Christianity and all other systems of religion consists largely in this, that in these other men are found seeking after God, while Christianity is God seeking after man. —Thomas Arnold.

A Christianity which will not help those who are struggling from the bottom to the top of society needs another Christ to die for it.—Beecher.

Christianity has no ceremonial. It has forms, for forms are essential to order; but it disdains the folly of attempting to reinforce the religion of the heart by the antics of the mind.— Rev. Dr. Croly.

Personal Christianity is not a creed, however orthodox; not a ritualism, however Scriptural; not a profession, however outwardly consistent; not a service, however seemingly useful; but is Christ in man.

He that loves Christianity better than truth will soon love his own sect or party better than Christianity, and will end by loving himself better than all.—Coleridge.

Christ was *vitæ magister*, not *scholæ;* and he is the best Christian whose heart beats with the purest pulse towards heaven; not he whose head spinneth out the finest cobwebs.— Cudworth.

Christianity alone inspires and guides progress; for the progress of man is movement toward God, and movement toward God will ensure a gradual unfolding of all that exalts and adorns man.—Mark Hopkins.

Christianity teaches us to moderate our passions; to temper our affections toward all things below; to be thankful for the possession, and patient under loss, whenever He who gave shall see fit to take away.—Sir Wm. Temple.

Christianity is more than history; it is also a system of truths. Every event which its history records, either is a truth, or suggests a truth, or expresses a truth which man needs to assent to or to put into practice.— Noah Porter.

It awes by the majesty of its truths. it agitates by the force of its compunctions, it penetrates the heart by the tenderness of its appeals, and it casts over the abyss of thought, the shadow of its eternal grandeur.— Henry Giles.

Where science speaks of improvement, Christianity speaks of renovation; where science speaks of development, Christianity speaks of sanctification; where science speaks of progress, Christianity speaks of perfection.—Aughey.

Christian graces are like perfumes; the more they are pressed, the sweeter they smell; like stars that shine brightest in the dark; like trees, the more they are shaken, the deeper root they take, and the more fruit they bear.— Rev. John Mason.

Great books are written for Christianity much oftener than great deeds are done for it. City libraries tell us of the reign of Jesus Christ, but city streets tell us of the reign of Satan.— Horace Mann.

Alas! how has the social spirit of Christianity been perverted by fools at one time, and by knaves and bigots at another; by the self-tormentors of the cell, and the all-tormentors of the conclave!—Colton.

Christianity does not consist in a proud priesthood, a costly church, an imposing ritual, a fashionable throng, a pealing organ, loud responses to the creed, and reiterated expressions of reverence for the name of Christ; but in the spirit of filial trust in God, and ardent, impartial, overflowing love to man.—T. J. Mumford.

Look back to the cross, and the disciples gazing on it in terror from afar, and then look around on the nations that are influenced by the faith that there centres—and note the change! Then take these elements, established in history, and calculate the orbit Christianity is to fill.—R. S. Storrs.

We are blessed with a faith, which calls into action the whole intellectual man; which prescribes a reasonable service; which challenges the investigation of its evidences; and which, in the doctrine of immortality, invests the mind of man with a portion of the dignity of Divine intelligence.—Edward Everett.

A man can no more be a Christian without facing evil and conquering it than he can be a soldier without going to battle, facing the cannon's mouth, and encountering the enemy in the field.—Chapin.

A few persons of an odious and despised country could not have filled the world with believers, had they not shown undoubted credentials from the divine person who sent them on such a message.—Addison.

Christianity taught the capacity, the element, to love the All-perfect without a stingy bargain for personal happiness. It taught that to love Him was happiness,—to love Him in others' virtues.—Emerson.

It happened very providentially, to the honor of the Christian religion, that it did not take its rise in the dark illiterate ages of the world, but at a time when arts and sciences were at their height.—Addison.

Christianity is no mere scheme of doctrine or of ethical practice, but is instead a kind of miracle, a power out of nature and above, descending into it; a historically supernatural move-

ment on the world, that is visibly entered into it, and organized to be an institution in the person of Jesus Christ.—Horace Bushnell.

Christian faith is a grand cathedral, with divinely pictured windows. Standing without you see no glory, nor can possibly imagine any. Nothing is visible but the merest outline of dusky shapes. Standing within all is clear and defined; every ray of light reveals an army of unspeakable splendors.—John Ruskin.

The greatest, strongest, mightiest plea for the church of God in the world is the existence of the Spirit of God in its midst, and the works of the Spirit of God are the true evidences of Christianity. They say miracles are withdrawn, but the Holy Spirit is the standing miracle of the church of God to-day.—C. H. Spurgeon.

The strong argument for the truth of Christianity is the true Christian; the man filled with the Spirit of Christ. The best proof of Christ's resurrection is a living church, which itself is walking in a new life, and drawing life from Him who hath overcome death.—Christlieb.

Christianity, contrasted with the Jewish system of emblems, is truth in the sense of reality, as substance is opposed to shadows, and, contrasted with heathen mythology, is truth as opposed to falsehood.—Whately.

Christianity is the only true and perfect religion, and in proportion as mankind adopt its principles and obey its precepts, they will be wise and happy. And a better knowledge of this religion is to be acquired by reading the Bible than in any other way.—Benjamin Rush.

Public charities and benevolent associations for the gratuitous relief of every species of distress, are peculiar to Christianity; no other system of civil or religious policy has originated them; they form its highest praise and characteristic feature.—Colton.

Had it been published by a voice from heaven, that twelve poor men, taken out of boats and creeks, without any help of learning, should conquer the world to the cross, it might have been thought an illusion against all reason of men; yet we know it was undertaken and accomplished by them.—Stephen Charnock.

Christianity is indeed peculiarly fitted to the more improved stages of society, to the more delicate sensibilities of refined minds, and especially to that dissatisfaction with the present state which always grows with the growth of our moral powers and affections.—Channing.

Christianity has found its triumphs and shown its fruits in every nation and tribe upon the globe; and its results have been in every case the same. Virtue, social order, prosperity, blessedness, the elevation and improvement, in all respects, of the human life, are the uniform and exclusive inheritance of those who receive the Gospel.—J. H. Seelye.

If Christianity has really come from heaven, it must renew the whole life of man; it must govern the life of nations no less than that of individuals; it must control a Christian when acting in his public and political capacity as completely as when he is engaged in the duties which belong to him as a member of a family circle.—H. P. Liddon.

Read a work on the "Evidences of Christianity," and it may become highly probable that Christianity, are true. This is an opinion. Feel God. Do His will, till the Absolute Imperative within you speaks as with a living voice, "Thou shalt, and thou shalt not;" and then you do not think, you know that there is a God.—F. W. Robertson.

Here is Christianity. Whence came it? What is it? It is a force in the world, a prodigious force. It has revolutionized society. It has lifted man out of himself. It has changed the face of the world. There it lies, imbedded in more than eighteen centuries of human history; and history

of no mean sort, the best record of the race.—Herrick Johnson.

Christianity has carried civilization along with it, whithersoever it has gone; and, as if to show that the latter does not depend on physical causes, some of the countries the most civilized in the days of Augustus are now in a state of hopeless barbarism.—Hare.

We have now in our possession three instruments of civilization, unknown to antiquity. These are the art of printing; free representative government; and, lastly, a pure and spiritual religion, the deep fountain of generous enthusiasm, the mighty spring of bold and lofty designs, the great sanctuary of moral power.—Edward Everett.

When I see how fragmentary the structure of religious knowledge was left by nature, when I see how inadequate all the labors of man had proved for its completion,—and when I look at the glorious and completed dome reared by Christianity, I cannot but feel that other than human hands have been employed in its structure.—Mark Hopkins.

Now, the whole world hears
Or shall hear,—surely shall hear, at the last,
Though men delay, and doubt, and faint, and fail,—
That promise faithful:—"Fear not, little flock!
It is your Father's will and joy, to give
To you, the Kingdom"!
     —Matthew Arnold.

The relations of Christians to each other are like the several flowers in a garden that have upon each the dew of heaven, which, being shaken by the wind, they let fall the dew at each other's roots, whereby they are jointly nourished, and become nourishers of one another.—Bunyan.

The introduction of the Christian religion into the world has produced an incalculable change in history. There had previously been only a history of nations—there is now a history of mankind: and the idea of an education of human nature as a whole,—an education the work of Jesus Christ

Himself—is become like a compass for the historian, the key of history, and the hope of nations.—D'Aubigné.

I have been young, but now am old. I have spent a whole lifetime in battling against infidelity with the weapons of apologetic science; but I have become ever more and more convinced that the way to the heart does not lie through the head; and that the only way to conversion of the head lies through a converted heart which already tastes the living fruits of the Gospel.—A. Tholuck.

Christianity depends finally on consciousness and experience. From other departments of the mind she may retire at times or seem to, but never from this. Sitting here, if allowed to, on the throne of the soul, she occasionally walks into the other rooms and sets them in order; and accustomed to her presence, sooner or later the soul finds every department flooded with her light.—E. O. Haven.

Christianity is perfect, men are imperfect. Now a perfect consequence cannot spring from an imperfect principle. Christianity, therefore, is not the work of man. If Christianity is not the work of man, it can have come from none but God. If it came from God, men cannot have acquired a knowledge of it except by revelation. Therefore, Christianity is a revealed religion.—Chateaubriand.

The real security of Christianity is to be found in its benevolent morality, in its exquisite adaptation to the human heart, in the facility with which its scheme accommodates itself to the capacity of every human intellect, in the consolation which it bears to every house of mourning, in the light with which it brightens the great mystery of the grave.—Macaulay.

It is the truth divine, speaking to our whole being: occupying, calling into action, and satisfying man's every faculty, supplying the minutest wants of his being, and speaking in one and the same moment to his reason, his conscience and his heart. It is the light of reason, the life of the heart, and the strength of the will.—Pierre.

All who have been great and good without Christianity would have been much greater and better with it. If there be, amongst the sons of men, a single exception to this maxim, the divine Socrates may be allowed to put in the strongest claim. It was his high ambition to deserve, by deeds, not by creeds, an unrevealed heaven, and by works, not by faith, to enter an unpromised land.—Colton.

Nature never gives to a living thing capacities not particularly meant for its benefit and use. If Nature gives to us capacities to believe that we have a Creator whom we never saw, of whom we have no direct proof, who is kind and good and tender beyond all that we know of kindness and goodness and tenderness on earth, it is because the endowment of capacities to conceive a Being must be for our benefit and use; it would not be for our benefit and use if it were a lie.—Bulwer-Lytton.

All the graces of Christianity always go together. They so go together that where there is one, there are all, and where one is wanting, all are wanting. Where there is faith, there are love, and hope, and humility; and where there is love, there is also trust; and where there is a holy trust in God, there is love to God; and where there is a gracious hope, there also is a holy fear of God.—Jonathan Edwards.

Now you say, alas! Christianity is hard; I grant it; but gainful and happy. I contemn the difficulty when I respect the advantage. The greatest labors that have answerable requitals are less than the least that have no regard. Believe me, when I look to the reward, I would not have the work easier. It is a good Master whom we serve, who not only pays, but gives; not after the proportion of our earnings, but of His own mercy.—Bishop Hall.

No religion ever appeared in the world whose natural tendency was so much directed to promote the peace and happiness of mankind. It makes right reason a law in every possible definition of the word. And therefore, even supposing it to have been purely a human invention, it had been the most amiable and the most useful invention that was ever imposed on mankind for their good.—Lord Bolingbroke.

As to the Christian religion, besides the strong evidence which we have for it, there is a balance in its favor from the number of great men who have been convinced of its truth after a serious consideration of the question. Grotius was an acute man, a lawyer, a man accustomed to examine evidence, and he was convinced. Grotius was not a recluse, but a man of the world, who certainly had no bias on the side of religion. Sir Isaac Newton set out an infidel, and came to be a very firm believer.—Johnson.

Ordinarily rivers run small at the beginning, grow broader and broader as they proceed, and become widest and deepest at the point where they enter the sea. It is such rivers that the Christian's life is like. But the life of the mere worldly man is like those rivers in Southern Africa, which, proceeding from mountain freshets, are broad and deep at the beginning, and grow narrower and more shallow as they advance. They waste themselves by soaking into the sands, and at last they die out entirely. The farther they run the less there is of them.—Beecher.

Christianity excludes malignity, subdues selfishness, regulates the passions, subordinates the appetites, quickens the intellect, exalts the affections. It promotes industry, honesty, truth, purity, kindness. It humbles the proud, exalts the lowly, upholds law, favors liberty, is essential to it, and would unite men in one great brotherhood. It is the breath of life to social and civil well-being here, and spreads the azure of that heaven into whose unfathomed depths the eye of faith loves to look.—Mark Hopkins.

We say, then, that Christianity is adapted to the intellect, because its spirit coincides with that of true philosophy; because it removes the incu-

bus of sensuality and low vice; because of the place it gives to truth; because it demands free inquiry; because its mighty truths and systems are brought before the mind in the same way as the truths and systems of nature; because it solves higher problems than nature can; and because it is so communicated as to be adapted to every mind.—Mark Hopkins.

In what consists the entire of Christianity but in this,—that feeling an utter incapacity to work out our own salvation, we submit our whole selves, our hearts, and our understandings, to the Divine disposal; and that, relying upon God's gracious assistance, ensured to our honest endeavors to obtain it, through the mediation of Jesus Christ, we look up to Him, and to Him alone, for safety? Nay, what is the very notion of religion, but this humble reliance upon God?—Archbishop Magee.

Christians are continually tempted to do what all controversy solicits them to do; namely, to argue; as if their business was to establish, in the light of the understanding, certain conclusions to which every rational person must assent. But this is to put the main point, the attractive action of God Himself out of the question. If the end of God be what we hold it to be, to bring human souls to Himself, then the means He actually employs must be living and spiritual. They are likely to be infinitely various and subtle; but they will deal principally with the conscience and the affections.—J. Llewelyn Davies.

The patriarchal, the Jewish, and the Christian dispensations, are evidently but the unfolding of one general plan. In the first we see the folded bud; in the second the expanded leaf; in the third the blossom and the fruit. And now, how sublime the idea of a religion thus commencing in the earliest dawn of time; holding on its way through all the revolutions of kingdoms and the vicissitudes of the race; receiving new forms, but always identical in spirit; and, finally, expanding and embracing in one great brotherhood the whole family of man! Who can doubt that such a religion was from God?—Mark Hopkins.

No, there is nothing on the face of the earth that can, for a moment, bear a comparison with Christianity as a religion for man. Upon this the hope of the race hangs. From the very first, it took its position, as the pillar of fire, to lead the race onward. The intelligence and power of the race are with those who have embraced it; and now, if this, instead of proving indeed a pillar of fire from God, should be found but a delusive meteor, then nothing will be left to the race but to go back to a darkness that may be felt, and to a worse than Egyptian bondage.—Mark Hopkins.

We live in the midst of blessings, till we are utterly insensible to their greatness, and of the source from which they flow. We speak of our civilization, our arts, our freedom, our laws, and forget entirely how large a share of all is due to Christianity. Blot Christianity out of the page of man's history, and what would his laws have been?—what his civilization? Christianity is mixed up with our very being and our daily life; there is not a familiar object round us which does not wear its mark, not a being or a thing which does not wear a different aspect, because the light of Christian hope is on it; not a law which does not owe its truth and gentleness to Christianity, not a custom, which cannot be traced, in all its holy and healthful parts, to the Gospel.—Rose.

Christianity bears all the marks of a divine original; it came down from heaven, and its gracious purpose is to carry us up thither. Its author is God; it was foretold from the beginning, by prophecies, which grew clearer and brighter as they approached the period of their accomplishment. It was confirmed by miracles, which continued until the religion they illustrated was established. It was ratified by the blood of its author; its doctrines are pure, sublime, consistent; its precepts just and holy; its worship is spiritual; its service reasonable and rendered practicable by the offers of divine aid to human weakness. It is sanctioned by the promise of eternal happiness to the faithful, and the threat of everlasting misery to the disobedient.—Hannah More.

Since its introduction, human nature has made great progress, and society experienced great changes; and in this advanced condition of the world, Christianity, instead of losing its application and importance, is found to be more and more congenial and adapted to man's nature and wants. Men have outgrown the other institutions of that period when Christianity appeared, its philosophy, its modes of warfare, its policy, its public and private economy; but Christianity has never shrunk as intellect has opened, but has always kept in advance of men's faculties, and unfolded nobler views in proportion as they have ascended. The highest powers and affections which our nature has developed, find more than adequate objects in this religion. Christianity is indeed peculiarly fitted to the more improved stages of society, to the more delicate sensibilities of refined minds, and especially to that dissatisfaction with the present state, which always grows with the growth of our moral powers and affections.—Channing.

Outside of Christianity there have been grand spectacles of activity and force, brilliant phenomena of genius and virtue, generous attempts at reform, learned mythological systems, and beautiful mythological poems, but no real profound or fruitful regeneration of humanity and society. Jesus Christ from His cross accomplishes what erewhile in Asia and Europe, princes and philosophers, the powerful of the earth, and sages, attempted without success. He changes the moral and the social state of the world. He pours into the souls of men new enlightenment and new powers. For all classes, for all human conditions, He prepares destinies before His advent unknown. He liberates them at the same time that He lays down rules for their guidance: He quickens them and stills them. He places the Divine law and human liberty face to face, and yet still in harmony. He offers an effectual remedy for the evil which weighs upon humanity; to sin He opens the path of salvation, to unhappiness, the door of hope.—Guizot.

Since the revelation of Christianity, all moral thought has been sanctified by religion. Religion has given it a purity, a solemnity, a sublimity, which even among the noblest of the heathen, we shall look for in vain. The knowledge which shone only by fits and dimly on the eyes of Socrates and Plato, "that rolled in vain to find the light," has descended over many lands into "the huts where poor men lie"— and thoughts are familiar there, beneath the low and smoky roofs, higher far than ever flowed from the lips of Grecian sage meditating among the magnificence of his pillared temples. The whole condition and character of the human being in Christian countries has been raised up to a loftier elevation; and he may be looked at in the face without a sense of degradation, even when he wears the aspect of poverty and distress. Since that religion was given us, and not before, has been felt the meaning of that sublime expression, "The Brotherhood of Man."—John Wilson.

While Christianity is speaking in languages more numerous, by tongues more eloquent, in nations more populous than ever before; marshaling better troops, with richer harmony; shrinking from no foe, rising triumphant from every conflict; shaking down the towers of old philosophies that exalt themselves against God; making the steam-press rush under the demand for her Scriptures, and the steam-horse groan under the weight of her charities; emancipating the enslaved, civilizing the lawless, refining literature, inspiring poetry; sending forth art and science no longer clad in soft raiment to linger in king's palaces, but as hardy prophets of God to make earth bud and blossom as the rose; giving God-like breadth and freedom and energy to the civilization that bears its name, elevating savage islands into civilized states, leading forth Christian martyrs from the mountains of Madagascar, turning the clubs of cannibals into the railings of the altars before which Fiji savages call upon Jesus; repeating the Pentecost, "by

many an ancient river and many a palmy plain;" thundering at the seats of ancient paganism; sailing all waters, cabling all oceans, scaling all mountains in the march of its might, and ever enlarging the diameter of those circles of light which it has kindled on earth, and which will soon meet in a universal illumination,—you call it a failure! A little more such failure, and we shall have, over all the globe, the new heavens and new earth wherein dwelleth righteousness.—Edward Thomson.

Christianity is not a voice in the wilderness, but a life in the world. It is not an idea in the air, but feet on the ground, going God's way. It is not an exotic to be kept under glass, but a hardy plant to bear twelve manner of fruits in all kinds of weather. Fidelity to duty is its root and branch. Nothing we can say to the Lord, no calling Him by great or dear names, can take the place of the plain doing of His will. We may cry out about the beauty of eating bread with Him in His kingdom, but it is wasted breath and a rootless hope, unless we plow and plant in His kingdom here and now. To remember Him at His table and to forget Him at ours, is to have invested in bad securities. There is no substitute for plain, every-day goodness.—Maltbie Babcock.

Christmas

For unto you is born this day in the city of David a Saviour, which is Christ the Lord.—Luke ii. 11.

I will honor Christmas in my heart, and try to keep it all the year.— Charles Dickens.

A good conscience is a continual Christmas.—Franklin.

'Tis the season for kindling the fire of hospitality in the hall, the genial fire of charity in the heart.—W. Irving.

It is good to be children sometimes, and never better than at Christmas when its mighty Founder was a child Himself.—Dickens.

This day shall change all griefs and quarrels into love.—Shakespeare.

The belfries of all Christendom now roll along the unbroken song of peace on earth, good will to men!—Longfellow.

———

At Christmas play, and make good cheer, For Christmas comes but once a year.
—Tusser.

———

The mistletoe hung in the castle hall, The holly branch shone on the old oak wall.
—Thos. Haynes Bayly.

———

The church-bells of innumerable sects are all chime-bells to-day, ringing in sweet accordance throughout many lands, and awaking a great joy in the heart of our common humanity.—E. H. Chapin.

———

Heap on more wood! the wind is chill; But let it whistle as it will, We'll keep our Christmas merry still.
—Scott.

———

The time draws near the birth of Christ: The moon is hid; the night is still; The Christmas bells from hill to hill Answer each other in the mist.
—Tennyson.

———

Hail to the King of Bethlehem, Who weareth in His diadem The yellow crocus for the gem Of His authority!
—Longfellow.

———

For little children everywhere A joyous season still we make; We bring our precious gifts to them, Even for the dear child Jesus' sake.
—Phebe Cary.

———

Be merry all, be merry all, With holly dress the festive hall; Prepare the song, the feast, the ball, To welcome merry Christmas.
—W. R. Spencer.

———

It is the Christmas time: And up and down 'twixt heaven and earth, In glorious grief and solemn mirth, The shining angels climb.
—D. M. Mulock.

———

At Christmas-tide the open hand Scatters its bounty o'er sea and land, And none are left to grieve alone, For Love is heaven and claims its own.
—Margaret E. Sangster.

———

The kindness of Christmas is the kindness of Christ. To know that God so loved us as to give us His Son for our dearest Brother, has brought human affection to its highest tide on the day of that Brother's birth. If God so loved us, how can we help loving one another?—Maltbie Babcock.

———

Hark! the herald angels sing, Glory to the new-born King: Peace on earth, and mercy mild, God and sinners reconciled.
—Charles Wesley.

———

No trumpet-blast profaned The hour in which the Prince of Peace was born; No bloody streamlet stained Earth's silver rivers on that sacred morn.
—Bryant.

———

I heard the bells on Christmas Day Their old, familiar carols play, And wild and sweet The words repeat Of peace on earth, good-will to men!
—Longfellow.

———

Glory to God in the highest, and on earth peace, good will toward men.

———

Heathenism had proved unequal to the wants of men; and it was when the most thoughtful among the Pagans were turned away from its hollow mockeries and misleading altars that the anthem of the angels broke clear and loud above the slopes of Bethlehem: "Glory to God in the highest! Peace on earth and good will toward men!"—Wm. M. Taylor, D. D.

———

To-day the whole Christian world prostrates itself in adoration around the crib of Bethlehem and rehearses in accents of love a history which precedes all time and will endure throughout eternity. As if by an instinct of our higher, spiritual nature, there well up from the depths of our hearts, emotions which challenge the power of human expression. We seem to be lifted out of the sphere of natural endeavor to put on a new life and to stretch forward in desire to a blessedness which, though not palpable, is eminently real.—Cardinal Gibbons.

———

To realize this purpose—to change humanity, to triumph over evil, and to honor the Father by a union never to be broken of the Father and the many sons who should be brought unto glory —this was the thought which filled the mind of Jesus Christ. This is the meaning of Christmas; and as we love God with soul and mind and strength, and prove our divine sonship by good will and kindness toward all our fellow-men, we shall realize the divine idea of our Master and unite in His blessed work.—Observer.

In the past, Christ was, in the genealogies, stepping Bethlehemward. Every time a new descendant in the covenant-line was born, the voice of prophecy shouted: "Christ is coming!" As ancestor was added to ancestor, the voice waxed louder and louder. Thus the shout was repeated and repeated until at last the angels and the magi and the shepherds and the watchers in the Temple answered back that shout with the gladder and louder shout, "Christ has come!" That is the Christmas shout which to-day Church of God throws to Church of God all through Christendom.—David Gregg, D. D.

We therefore welcome our Christmas in December. The "worship of Christ" could not have a better setting than amid the domestic festivities, social forces, and generous and man helping deeds of our merry Christmas-tide. In no more fitting way can we say farewell to the closing year, and All hail! to the new. "Christ is born." We therefore must put off the old man —his moroseness and selfishness, his sadness and despair, his peevishness and fretfulness, his feebleness and decay—and put on the new man, which, after Christ, is created in true joy, large faith, energetic service, lowly duty, devout obedience, and death-daring self-sacrifice.—John Clifford.

God framed the history of the world in view of the coming of Jesus Christ. In the very beginning He chose a family whose line of descent should run directly from Eden to Bethlehem. This family God took into covenant with Himself, and the promise of the covenant was that of its seed Christ should be born in the fulness of time. This covenant-line runs through the whole of the Old Testament as the

golden thread runs through the beautiful fabric. Everything centres in this covenant-line. It unifies the Old Testament. It is the cord upon which the pearls of history are strung. Keep this in mind, and it will explain a thousand mysteries and perplexities in reading the ld Testament.—David Gregg, D. D.

It is the most human and kindly of seasons, as fully penetrated and irradiated with the feeling of human brotherhood, which is the essential spirit of Christianity, as the month of June with sunshine and the balmy breath of roses.—Geo. W. Curtis.

O little town of Bethlehem!
How still we see thee lie;
Above thy deep and dreamless sleep,
The silent stars go by.
Yet, in thy dark street shineth
The everlasting Light;
The hopes and fears of all the years,
Are met in thee, to-night.
—Phillips Brooks.

Blessed be God for His unspeakable gift. We need Him. Souls desire Him as the hart panteth after the water brooks. He came to the world in the fullness of time. He comes at this advent season to us. To-day may be for some soul the fullness of time. Let us open the gates and admit Him, that this Christ may be our Christ forever; that living with Him and dying with Him, we may also be glorified together with Him.—David J. Burrell, D. D.

But now the Prince of Peace has come—He of whom it was said that "in His days there shall be abundance of peace." Now "mercy and truth are met together; righteousness and peace have kissed each other." Now "old things are passed away; behold, all things are become new;" and "all things are of God, who hath reconciled us to himself by Jesus Christ, and hath given to us the ministry of reconciliation; to wit, that God was in Christ, reconciling the world unto Himself."

The herald angels are singing still, and we hear their "Peace on earth, good will to men," once more, as we have often done. What can we do but answer back in glad strains: "Unto us a child is born, unto us a son is given: and the government shall be upon his shoulder; and His name shall be called Wonderful, Counselor, The mighty God, The everlasting Father, The Prince of Peace"? It is His presence that fills our homes with mirth and song. If he will come again, turning life's water into wine, touching our sick that they may be healed, cleansing, pardoning, blessing us all—as He will if we make room for Him—then, indeed, we must be glad.—Christian at Work.

The universal joy of Christmas is certainly wonderful. We ring the bells when princes are born, or toll a mournful dirge when great men pass away. Nations have their red-letter days, their carnivals and festivals, but once in the year and only once, the whole world stands still to celebrate the advent of a life. Only Jesus of Nazareth claims this world-wide, undying remembrance. You cannot cut Christmas out of the Calendar, nor out of the heart of the world.—Anon.

The earth has grown old with its burden of care,
But at Christmas it always is young;
The heart of the jewel burns lustrous and fair,
And its soul, full of music, breaks forth on the air
When the song of the angels is sung.

It is coming, Old Earth, it is coming to-night!
On the snowflakes which cover thy sod
The feet of the Christ-child fall gentle and white,
And the voice of the Christ-child tells out with delight
That mankind are the children of God.
—Phillips Brooks.

If we were to fancy a wholly Christianized world, it would be a world inspired by the spirit of Christmas—a bright, friendly, beneficent, generous, sympathetic, mutually helpful world. A man who is habitually mean, selfish, narrow, is a man without Christmas in his soul. Let us cling to Christmas all the more as a day of the spirit which in every age some souls have believed to be the possible spirit of human society. The earnest faith

and untiring endeavor which see in Christmas a forecast are more truly Christian, surely, than the pleasant cynicism of Atheists, etc., which smiles upon it as the festival of a futile hope. Meanwhile we may reflect that from good natured hopelessness to a Christmas world may not be farther than from star dust to a solar system. —George William Curtis.

We see Jesus in the manger. We adore Him; we worship Him; we glorify Him. We stand oppressed before such love—a love stronger than death—a love so strong that it did die that we might live. We thank Thee for the sweetness of human love, but how could we ever have dared to think that such love was in the heart of God for us! We look on nature and see Thy beauty and Thy majesty, but we are afraid, for we have sinned. And then we learn that Thou has sent Thy Son, to be bone of our bone, flesh of our flesh; and before such inconceivable love we can only worship and adore. We are so weary of our failures and our slow growth toward Thee. Cleanse us deeply from sin, strengthen our moral purposes.—Maltbie Babcock.

The lovely legends of the day; the stories and the songs and the half-fairy lore that gather around it; the ancient traditions of dusky woods and mystic rites; the magnificence or simplicity of Christian observance, from the pope in his triple tiara, borne upon his portative throne in gorgeous state to celebrate pontifical high mass at the great altar of St. Peter's, to George Herbert humbly kneeling in his rustic church at Bemerton, or to the bare service in some missionary chapel upon the American frontier; the lighting of Christmas trees and hanging up of Christmas stockings, the profuse giving, the happy family meetings, the dinner, the game, the dance—they are all the natural signs and symbols, the flower and fruit, of Christmas. For Christmas is the day of days which declares the universal human consciousness that peace on earth comes only from good will to men.—Geo. W. Curtis.

The whole air at the first Christmastide was tremulous with joy. It was a time for holy song, for inspired pæan, for seraphic song. Let joy come still to our homes and hearts. Christ gives brightness and beauty, gladness and glory, to the whole circle of life and duty. Come, Lord Jesus, there shall be room for Thee in our homes. Once there was none in the inn, but only in the stable; now our best is Thine. Only honor us with Thy beneficent presence. Let us away with strife at this season; now is the time to speak kindly words. Let us not carry into the new year the enmities of the old; let not the harsh notes of contention come into the heavenly song of peace. Christ came to give peace, and from Heaven's throne to-day He bends to give peace to all who trust Him. He was the only person ever born into the world who had His choice as to how He should come. He might have come man, as did the first Adam; He came a babe. He inserted Himself into our race at its lowest and weakest point. If He were to lift the race He must get under it. He glorified the cradle; He beautified boyhood; He sanctified motherhood.—Robert S. MacArthur, D. D.

For us, however, in these northern climes, and with our traditions and associations, Christmas could not well be better placed than where it is. Nature is in slumber, as if in death—fit picture of the sleep of man till roused to righteousness by the voice of the new-born Babe of Bethlehem. Life is at its lowest, and death reigns, or seems to reign, everywhere. Saving the thick-berried holly, the mistletoe, dear to Druid priests, the laurel, and the yew, the trees are bared, and the warblers of the sky avoid their desolate branches. We are driven inward. The fireside is the centre of a thousand charms. Home is clothed in its most beautiful garments. We are forced to the conclusion that we need other help than Mother Earth can give us. Our hearts open instinctively to heaven and its message, and with willing feet we haste to do the will of Him "Who, though He was rich, yet for our sakes became poor."

Christians, stand at Bethlehem and open every door and window of your being Christward. Look backward. Look forward. Magnify Bethlehem. Recount to your souls the things for which it stands. It stands for the "fulness of time." It stands for the fulfilment of glorious predictions. It stands for the realization of those burning hopes which made the heroic men of the past. It stands for the coming of the Son of God Himself into our nature. It stands for the glorious past and for the more glorious future. As the dawn carries in it the full day, it carries in it the salvation of man, and the triumph of the right over the wrong, and the coming millennial glory of the kingdom of Jesus Christ.

When we comprehend the backward and forward reach of Bethlehem, we do not wonder that all that is grand crowds around the Cradle-Manger. It is worthy of all. Let the Star shine. Let the Magi give gifts. Let the Shepherds worship. Let the angel-faces flash out from the great dome overhead. Let the church-bells chime. Let the sacred harps and organs respond to the masterhand that sweeps their strings and flies over their keys, and let them turn the common air into praise. Let Christmas carols roll over this wide earth, and echo among the stars. Let the great universe of God jubilate. Let everything in Heaven and earth shout, "Hosanna to the Son of David; blessed is He that cometh in the name of the Lord; Hosanna in the Highest." While all this takes place, see to it, O my soul, that thou carriest thyself to Bethlehem, to receive, and to love, and to trust, and to worship. Be thou certainly there; and while there recognize Christ, honor Christ, reincarnate Christ, and call Christ God.—David Gregg, D. D.

We ring the bells and we raise the strain.
We hang up garlands everywhere
And bid the tapers twinkle fair,
And feast and frolic—and then we go
     Back to the same old lives again.
            —Susan Coolidge.

Never deny the babies their Christmas! It is the shining seal set upon a year of happiness. Let them believe in Santa Claus, or St. Nicholas, or Kriss Kringle, or whatever name the jolly Dutch saint bears in your religion.—Marion Harland.

Let Christmas be a bright and happy day; but let its brightness come from the radiance of the star of Bethlehem, and its happiness be found in Christ, the sinner's loving Saviour.—H. G. Den.

Some say, that ever 'gainst that season comes,
Wherein our Saviour's birth is celebrated,
The bird of dawning singeth all night long,
And then, they say no spirit can walk abroad,
So hallow'd and so gracious is the time.
—Shakespeare.

Blow, bugles of battle, the marches of peace;
East, west, north, and south let the long quarrel cease;
Sing the song of great joy that the angels began,
Sing of glory to God and of good-will to man!
—Whittier.

England was merry England, when
Old Christmas brought his sports again.
'Twas Christmas broach'd the mightiest ale;
'Twas Christmas told the merriest tale;
A Christmas gambol oft could cheer
The poor man's heart through half the year.
—Scott.

What babe new born is this that in a manger cries?
Near on her lowly bed his happy mother lies.
Oh, see the air is shaken with white and heavenly wings—
This is the Lord of all the earth, this is the King of Kings. —R. W. Gilder.

God rest ye, little children; let nothing you affright,
For Jesus Christ, your Saviour, was born this happy night;
Along the hills of Galilee the white flocks sleeping lay,
When Christ, the Child of Nazareth, was born on Christmas Day.
—D. M. Mulock.

'Twas the night before Christmas, when all through the house
Not a creature was stirring,—not even a mouse;
The stockings were hung by the chimney with care,
In hopes that St. Nicholas soon would be there. —Clement C. Moore.

I have always thought of Christmas time, when it has come round apart from the veneration due to its sacred name and origin, if anything belonging to it can be apart from that—as a good time; a kind, forgiving, charitable, pleasant time.—Charles Dickens.

This is the month, and this the happy morn,
Wherein the Son of Heaven's eternal King,
Of wedded maid and virgin mother born,
Our great redemption from above did bring,
For so the holy sages once did sing,
That He our deadly forfeit should release,
And with His Father work us a perpetual peace. —Milton.

How bless'd, how envied, were our life,
Could we but scape the poulterer's knife!
But man, curs'd man, on Turkeys preys,
And Christmas shortens all our days:
Sometimes with oysters we combine,
Sometimes assist the savory chine;
From the low peasant to the lord,
The Turkey smokes on every board.
—Gay.

God rest you, merry gentlemen,
Let nothing you dismay,
For Jesus Christ our Saviour
Was born upon this day,
To save us all from Satan's power
When we were gone astray.
O tidings of comfort and joy,
For Jesus Christ our Saviour was
Born on Christmas Day.
—Old English Carol.

O most illustrious of the days of time!
Day full of joy and benison to earth
When Thou wast born, sweet Babe of Bethlehem!
With dazzling pomp descending angels sung
Good will and peace to men, to God due praise,
Who on the errand of salvation sent
Thee, Son Beloved! of plural Unity
Essential part, made flesh that mad'st all worlds. —Abraham Coles.

Ring out, ye crystal spheres!
Once bless our human ears,
If ye have power to touch our senses so;
And let your silver chime
Move in melodious time,
And let the bass of Heaven's deep organ blow;
And with your ninefold harmony
Make up full consort to the angelic symphony. —Milton.

The death of Christ is a great mystery; His birth is even a greater. That He should live a human life at all, is stranger than that, so living, He should die a human death. I can scarce get past His cradle in my wondering, to wonder at His cross. The infant Jesus is, in some views, a greater marvel than Jesus with the purple robe and the crown of thorns.—Crichton.

___

The chief charm of Christmas is its simplicity. It is a festival that appeals to everyone, because every one can understand it. * * * A genuine fellowship pervades our common life—a fellowship whose source is our common share in the gift of the world's greatest Life which was given to the whole world.—Arthur Reed Kimball.

Chrysanthemum

Chrysanthemums from gilded argosy
Unload their gaudy scentless merchandise.
—Oscar Wilde.

___

Fair gift of Friendship! and her ever bright
And faultless image! welcome now thou art,
In thy pure lovel'ness—thy robes of white,
Speaking a moral to the feeling heart;
Unscattered by heats—by wintry blasts unmoved—
Thy strength thus tested—and thy charms improved. —Anna Peyre Dinnies.

Church

Spires whose "silent finger points to heaven."—Wordsworth.

___

The way to preserve the peace of the church is to preserve the purity of it.—Matthew Henry.

___

Built God a church and laughed His word to scorn.—Cowper.

___

The mission of the Church is to seek and to save them that are lost.—Aughey.

___

Some to church repair, not for the doctrine, but the music there.—Pope.

___

Who builds a church to God, and not to fame,
Will never mark the marble with his name.
—Pope.

___

Everywhere, through all generations and ages of the Christian world, no church ever perceived the Word of God to be against it.—Hooker.

An itch of disputing will prove the scab of churches.—Sir Henry Wotton.

___

What is a church? Our honest sexton tells,
'Tis a tall building, with a tower and bells.
—Crabbe.

___

A little thing will keep them from the house of God who have no desire to go to it.—Aughey.

Fond fools
Promise themselves a name from building churches.   —Randolph.

___

Surely the church is a place where one day's truce ought to be allowed to the dissensions and animosities of mankind.—Burke.

I never yet have known the Spirit of God to work where the Lord's people were divided.—D. L. Moody.

Division has done more to hide Christ from the view of men than all the infidelity that has ever been spoken.—George MacDonald.

A lazy, indolent church tends toward unbelief; an earnest, busy church, in hand-to-hand conflict with sin and misery, grows stronger in faith.—John Hall.

The union of Church and State is not to make the Church political, but the State religious.—Lord Eldon.

The Church limits her sacramental services to the faithful. Christ gave Himself upon the cross a ransom for all.—Pascal.

___

The church is made up of individuals. It can do nothing except as its members work, and work together.—Aughey.

___

To support those of your rights authorized by Heaven, destroy everything rather than yield; that is the spirit of the Church.—Boileau.

The church may go through her dark ages, but Christ is with her in the midnight; she may pass through her fiery furnace, but Christ is in the midst of the flame with her.—C. H. Spurgeon.

I believe that the root of almost every schism and heresy from which the Christian church has ever suffered, has been the effort of men to earn, rather than to receive, their salvation. —John Ruskin.

The Church has a good stomach; she has swallowed down whole countries, and has never known a surfeit; the Church alone can digest such ill-gotten wealth.—Goethe.

What makes a church a den of thieves? A dean and chapter, and white sleeves. —Butler.

Wherever God erects a house of prayer, The Devil always builds a chapel there: And 'twill be found upon examination, The latter has the largest congregation. —De Foe.

The perfect world, by Adam trod, Was the first temple—built by God— His fiat laid the corner stone, And heaved its pillars, one by one. —Willis.

"What is a church?" Let truth and reason speak; They would reply—"The faithful pure and meek, From Christian folds, the one selected race, Of all professions, and in every place." —Crabbe.

When once thy foot enters the church, beware— God is more there than thou: for thou art there Only by His permission. Then beware, And make thyself all reverence and fear. —Herbert.

It is better to have a plain, substantial building, with no extravagance about it, but without a debt, than to have the most splendid specimen of Gothic architecture that is overlaid by a mortgage.—Wm. M. Taylor.

We have houses of God built in defiance of the laws of God. On the walls of one of these monstrosities I saw this most appropriate motto: "This is the house of God; how dreadful is this place!"—Prof. Sheppard.

Doubts about the fundamentals of the Gospel exist in certain churches, I am told, to a large extent. My dear friends, where there is a warm-hearted church, you do not hear of them. I never saw a fly light on a red-hot plate.—C. H. Spurgeon.

Persecution has not crushed it, power has not beaten it back, time has not abated its force, and, what is most wonderful of all, the abuses and treasons of its friends have not shaken its stability.—Horace Bushnell.

One family—we dwell in Him, One church above, beneath, Though now divided by the stream, The narrow stream of death. —Charles Wesley.

Steele has observed that there is this difference between the Church of Rome and the Church of England,— the one professes to be infallible, the other to be never in the wrong.—Colton.

Why should we crave a hallow'd spot? An altar is in each man's cot, A church in every grove that spreads Its living roof above our heads. —Wordsworth.

An instinctive taste teaches men to build their churches in flat countries with spire steeples, which, as they cannot be referred to any other object, point as with silent finger to the sky and stars.—Coleridge.

Jesus organized the church, which is His vineyard. He commands all to go into the vineyard and work. All who are united to Christ by faith, and are thus members of His mystical body, should be members of His visible church.—Aughey.

And this is the mission of the church—not civilization, but salvation—not better laws, purer legislation, social elevation, human equality, and liberty, but first, the "kingdom of God and His righteousness;" regenerated hearts, and all other things will follow.—A. E. Kittredge.

They who would grow in grace, must love the habitation of God's house. It is those that are planted in the courts of the Lord who shall flourish, and not those that are occasionally there.—John Angel James.

There ought to be such an atmosphere in every Christian church that a man going there and sitting two hours should take the contagion of heaven, and carry home a fire to kindle the altar whence he came.—Beecher.

There is nothing more pitiable than a soulless, sapless, shriveled church, seeking to thrive in a worldly atmosphere, rooted in barren professions, bearing no fruit, and maintaining only the semblance of existence; such a church cannot long survive.—George C. Lorimer.

Do you recall the laughter of the Philistines at the helpless Sampson—You can hear the echo of that laughter to-day, as the church, shorn of her strength by her own sin, is an object of ridicule to the world, who cry in derision, "Where is your boasted triumph and your Millennial glory?"—A. E. Kittredge.

How long must the church live before it will learn that strength is won by action, and success by work, and that all this immeasurable feeding without action and work is a positive damage to it—that it is the procurer of spiritual obesity, gout, and debility.—J. G. Holland.

Antedating our history, possessing and illumining the hearts of the founders of liberty in our free land, and constantly exerting the soul-equalizing and soul-elevating principles of the gospel of Christ as they fall from Sabbath to Sabbath on the masses of the people, the Christian church stands before all men as the pillar and ground of civil liberty in the world.—W. H. Perrine.

To be of no church is dangerous. Religion, of which the rewards are distant, and which is animated only by Faith and Hope, will glide by degrees out of the mind, unless it be invigorated and reimpressed by external ordinances, by stated calls to worship, and the salutary influence of example.—Johnson.

Under the term Church, I understand a body or collection of human persons, professing faith in Christ, gathered together in several places of the world, for worship of the same God, and united into the same corporation.—Bishop Pearson.

As in Noah's ark there were the clean and the unclean, raven and dove, leopard and kid, the cruel lion with the gentle lamb; so in the Church of Christ on earth you will find the same diversities and differences of human character.—Rev. Dr. Guthrie.

And she (the Roman Catholic Church) may still exist in undiminished vigor, when some traveller from New Zealand shall, in the midst of a vast solitude, take his stand on a broken arch of London Bridge to sketch the ruins of St. Paul's.—Macaulay.

In the true, original, catholic, evangelical religion of Jesus Christ, and in this alone, all the divided religions of Christendom find their union, their repose, their support. Find out His mind, His character, His will; and in His greatness we shall rise above our littleness; in His strength we shall lose our weakness; in His peace we shall forget our discord.—Dean Stanley.

The church is a sort of hospital for men's souls, and as full of quackery as the hospital for their bodies. Those who are taken into it live like pensioners in their Retreat or Sailors' Snug Harbor, where you may see a row of religious cripples sitting outside in sunny weather.—Thoreau.

In the Church of Christ one little worker can mar the whole by failing to fulfill his office. There is a place for each. Find your place if you are not already in it, and obey the Saviour's command, "Go work in my vineyard"—the command of a king which you disobey at the peril of losing the reward of the faithful.—Aughey.

So, from generation to generation, the spiritual church is rising upwards toward its perfection; and, though one after another the workmen pass away, the fabric remains, and the great Master-builder carries on the undertaking. Be it ours to build in our portion in a solid and substantial manner, so that they who come after us may be at once thankful for our thoroughness, and inspired by our example.—Wm. M. Taylor.

What is the average type of a counterfeit church? A hammock, attached on one side to the cross, and, on the other, held and swung to and fro by the forefinger of Mammon; its freight of nominal Christians elegantly moaning meanwhile over the evils of the times, and not at ease unless fanned by eloquence and music, and sprinkled by social adulations into perfumed, unheroic slumber.—Joseph Cook.

Let the church come to God in the strength of a perfect weakness, in the power of a felt helplessness and a child-like confidence, and then, either she has no strength, and has no right to be, or she has a strength that is infinite. Then and thus, will she stretch out the rod over the seas of difficulty that lie before her, and the waters shall divide, and she shall pass through, and sing the song of deliverance.—Mark Hopkins.

I know that with consecration on the part of believers, separation from the world, disentanglement from enslaving sins, and a mighty baptism of the Holy Spirit, the church would become a conquering power in the world, not by its constructed theology, not by its Sabbath services, not by its arguments to convince the intellect, but by its simple story of Jesus' love, by the Cross, the Cross—God's hammer, God's fire.—A. E. Kittredge.

Men say their pinnacles point to heaven. Why, so does every tree that buds, and every bird that rises as it sings. Men say their aisles are good for worship. Why, so is every mountain glen and rough sea-shore. But this they have of distinct and indisputable glory,—that their mighty walls were never raised, and never shall be, but by men who love and aid each other in their weakness.—Ruskin.

The clearest window that ever was fashioned, if it is barred by spiders' webs, and hung over with carcasses of insects, so that the sunlight has forgotten to find its way through, of what use can it be? Now, the Church is God's window; and if it is so obscured by errors that its light is darkness, how great is that darkness!—Beecher.

When I go to the house of God I do not want amusement; I want the doctrine which is according to godliness. I want to hear the remedy against the harassing of my guilt and the disorder of my affections. I want to be led from weariness and disappointment to that goodness which filleth the hungry soul. I want to have light upon the mystery of Providence; to be taught how the judgments of the Lord are right; how I shall be prepared for duty and for trial; how I may fear God all the days of my life, and close them in peace.—John M. Mason.

The church itself has got to go outside of its own borders and carry the Gospel to every creature, or it is no church of Christ; and any mutual improvement club which thinks that by reading its Shakespeare, or by acting its pretty tableaux, or by having this or that little reading from Spenser and from Chaucer, it is going to lift itself up into any higher order of culture or life, is wholly mistaken, unless as an essential part of its duty, it goes out into the world, finds those that are falling down, and lifts them up to the majesty of freemen, who are sons of God.—Edward E. Hale.

Then might ye see
Cowls, hoods, and habits with their wearers
  tost
And flutter'd into rags; then reliques,
  beads,
Indulgences, dispenses, pardons, bulls,
The sport of winds; all these upwhirl'd
  aloft
Fly to the rearward of the world far off
Into a limbo large and broad, since called
The paradise of fools.   —Milton.

The church is not a select circle of the immaculate, but a home where the outcast may come in. It is not a palace with gate attendants and challenging sentinels along the entrance-ways holding off at arm's-length the stranger, but rather a hospital where the broken-hearted may be healed, and where all the weary and troubled may find rest and take counsel together.—Aughey.

Any church which forsakes the regular and uniform for the periodical and spasmodic service of God, is doomed to decay; any church which relies for its spiritual strength and growth entirely upon seasons of "revival," will very soon have no genuine revivals to rely on. Our holy God will not conform His blessings to man's moods and moral caprice. If a church is declining, it may require a "revival" to restore it; but what need was there of its declining?—T. L. Cuyler.

In dim cathedrals, dark with vaulted gloom,
What holy awe invests the sacred tomb!
There pride will bow, and anxious care expand,
And creeping avarice come with open hand;
The gay can weep, the impious can adore,
From morn's first glimmerings on the chancel floor
Till dying sunset shed his crimson stains
Through the faint halos of the iris'd panes.
      —O. W. Holmes.

Look on this edifice of marble made—
How fair it swells, too beautiful to fade.
See what fine people in its portals crowd,
Smiling and greeting, talking, laughings loud!
What is it? Surely not a gay exchange,
Where wit and beauty social joys arrange;
Not a grand shop, where late Parisian styles
Attract rich buyers from a thousand miles?
But step within; no need of further search.
Behold, admire a fashionable church!
Look how its oriel window glints and gleams,
What tinted light magnificently streams
On the proud pulpit, carved with quaint device,
Where velvet cushions, exquisitely nice,
Press'd by the polish'd preacher's dainty hands,
Hold a large volume clasp'd by golden bands.   —Park Benjamin.

The one injurious and fatal fact of our present church work is the barrier between the churches and the poorest classes. The first thing for us to do is to demolish this barrier. The impression is abroad among the poor that they are not wanted in the churches. This impression is either

correct or incorrect. If it is correct, then there is no missionary work, for us who are pastors, half so urgent as the conversion of our congregations to Christianity. If it is incorrect, we are still guilty before God in that we have allowed such an impression to go abroad; and we are bound to address ourselves, at once and with all diligence, to the business of convincing the poor people that they are wanted, and will be made welcome in the churches. —W. Gladden.

Congregations must justify their existence. If they only bring people together to be "very much pleased," why, the lecture bureaus will contract for all that. "Did you worship? Were you edified? Did the Lord speak to you? Did you speak to Him? Do you mean more seriously to be pure, honest, upright, generous, manly, holy, from what you did and heard to-day?" These are the questions which the best part of mankind feel to be proper, and to which we must have affirmative replies.—John Hall.

Churchyard

There lay the warrior and the son of song,
   And there—in silence till the judgment day—
The orator, whose all-persuading tongue
   Had mov'd the nations with resistless sway.   —Mrs. Norton.

Strange things, the neighbours say, have happen'd there:
Wild shrieks have issued from the hollow tombs,
Dead men have come again, and walk'd about;
And the great bell has toll'd unrung, untouch'd.
Such tales their cheer at wake or gossiping,
When it draws near to 'witching time of night.   —Blair.

Yet there are graves, whose rudely shapen sod
Bears the fresh footprints where the sexton trod;
Graves where the verdure has not dar'd to shoot,
Where the chance wildflower has not fix'd its root,
Whose slumbering tenants, dead without a name,
The eternal record shall at length proclaim
Pure as the holiest in the long array
Of hooded, mitred, or tiara'd clay!
      —O. W. Holmes.

The solitary, silent, solemn scene,
Where Cæsars, heroes, peasants, hermits lie,
Blended in dust together; where the slave
Rests from his labors; where th' insulting
  proud
Resigns his power, the miser drops his
  hoard,
Where human folly sleeps.   —Dyer.

Circles

The eye is the first circle; the horizon which it forms is the second; and throughout nature this primary figure is repeated without end. It is the highest emblem in the cipher of the world.—Emerson.

I watch'd the little circles die;
They past into the level flood.
                —Tennyson.

As the small pebble stirs the peaceful lake;
The centre mov'd, a circle straight succeeds,
Another still, and still another spreads.
                —Pope.

Glory is like a circle in the water,
Which never ceaseth to enlarge itself,
Till, by broad spreading, it disperse to
  nought.   —Shakespeare.

Circles in water as they wider flow
The less conspicuous in their progress grow,
And when at last they trench upon the
  shore,
Distinction ceases and they're view'd no
  more.   —Crabbe.

Circles and right lines limit and close all bodies, and the mortal rightlined circle must conclude and shut up all.—Sir Thomas Browne.

Circumspection

Persons who want experience should be extremely cautious how they depart from those principles which have been received generally, because founded on solid reasons, and how they deviate from those customs which have obtained long, because in their effect they have proved good: thus circumspect should all persons be, who cannot yet have acquired much practical knowledge of the world: lest, instead of becoming what they anxiously wish to become, more beneficial to mankind than those who have preceded them, they should actually though inadvertently be instrumental towards occasioning some of the worst evils that can . befall human society.—Bishop Huntingford.

Circumstances

Circumstances alter cases.—Haliburton.

Circumstances! I make circumstances.—Napoleon I.

Cause and effect are the chancellors of God.—Emerson.

Circumstances over which I have no control.—Wellington (Duke of).

The happy combination of fortuitous circumstances.—Scott.

It is circumstances (difficulties) which show what men are.—Epictetus.

We are surrounded, ambushed, by the robber troops of circumstances.—Hafiz.

How truly are we the dupes of show and circumstances!—Washington Irving.

The education of circumstances is superior to that of tuition.—Wordsworth.

The same wind that carries one vessel into port may blow another off shore.—Bovee.

Man is not the creature of circumstances,
Circumstances are the creatures of men.
                —Benj. Disraeli.

It is our relation to circumstances that determines their influence upon us.—Bovee.

Superiority to circumstances is one of the most prominent characteristics of great men.—Horace Mann.

Who does the best his circumstance allows, does well, acts nobly; angels could no more.—Young.

A prudent man should neglect no circumstances.—Sophocles.

Sure, occasion is the father of most that is good in us.--Thackeray.

Thus neither the praise nor the blame is our own.—Cowper.

And grasps the skirts of happy chance,
And breasts the blows of circumstance.
—Tennyson.

Circumstances are the rulers of the weak; they are but the instruments of the wise.—Samuel Lover.

Men are the sport of circumstance, when
The circumstances seem the sport of men.
—Byron.

To give and to lose is nothing; but to lose and to give still is the part of a great mind.—Seneca.

For these attacks do not contribute to make us frail but rather show us to be what we are.—Thomas à Kempis.

I am the very slave of circumstance
And impulse—borne away with every breath.
—Byron.

What saves the virtue of many a woman is that protecting god, the impossible.—Balzac.

Circumstance, that unspiritual god and miscreator, makes and helps along our coming evils.—Byron.

He is happy whose circumstances suit his temper; but he is more excellent who can suit his temper to any circumstances.—Hume.

A man is not little when he finds it difficult to cope with circumstances, but when circumstances overmaster him.—Goethe.

When Fate wills that something should come to pass, she sends forth a million of little circumstances to clear and prepare the way.—Thackeray.

To what fortuitous occurrence do we not owe every pleasure and convenience of our lives.—Goldsmith.

Man is not the creature of circumstances, circumstances are the creatures of man. We are free agents, and man is more powerful than matter.—Beaconsfield.

Change a virtue in its circumstances and it becomes a vice; change a vice in its circumstances, and it becomes a virtue. Regard the same quality from two sides; on one it is a fault, on the other a merit. The essential of a man is found concealed far below these moral badges.—Taine.

Thus we see, too, in the world that some persons assimilate only what is ugly and evil from the same moral circumstances which supply good and beautiful results—the fragrance of celestial flowers—to the daily life of others.—Nath. Hawthorne.

When the Gauls laid waste Rome, they found the senators clothed in their robes, and seated in stern tranquillity in their curule chairs; in this manner they suffered death without resistance or supplication. Such conduct was in them applauded as noble and magnanimous; in the hapless Indians it was reviled as both obstinate and sullen. How truly are we the dupes of show and circumstances! How different is virtue, clothed in purple and enthroned in state, from virtue, naked and destitute, and perishing obscurely in a wilderness.—Washington Irving.

Instead of saying that man is the creature of circumstances, it would be nearer the mark to say that man is the architect of circumstance. It is character which builds an existence out of circumstance. Our strength is measured by our plastic power. From the same material one man builds palaces, another hovels; one warehouses, another villas.—G. H. Lewes.

Cities — Citizen

In the busy haunts of men.—Mrs. Hemans.

Even cities have their graves!—Longfellow.

Far from gay cities, and the ways of men.—Homer.

The people are the city.—Coriolanus.

If you would know and not be known, live in a city.—Colton.

I always seem to suffer some loss of faith on entering cities.—Emerson.

Before man made us citizens, great Nature made us men.—Lowell.

Towered cities please us then,
And the busy hum of men.
　　　　　　—Milton.

Like Melrose Abbey, large cities should especially be viewed by moonlight.—Willis.

Cities force growth, and make men talkative and entertaining, but they make them artificial.—Emerson.

Cities give us collision. 'Tis said London and New York take the nonsense out of a man.—Emerson.

Great towns are but a large sort of prison to the soul, like cages to birds, or pounds to beasts.—Charron.

I have found by experience that they who have spent all their lives in cities contract not only an effeminacy of habit, but of thinking.—Goldsmith.

The number of objects we see from living in a large city amuses the mind like a perpetual raree-show, without supplying it with any ideas.—Hazlitt.

I live not in myself, but I become
Portion of that around me; and to me
High mountains are a feeling, but the hum
Of human cities torture.　　—Byron.

Take heed what you say, sir.
An hundred honest men! why, if there were
So many i' th' city, 'twere enough to forfeit
Their charter.　　　　—Shirley.

Men, by associating in large masses, as in camps and in cities, improve their talents, but impair their virtues, and strengthen their minds, but weaken their morals.—Colton.

If you suppress the exorbitant love of pleasure and money, idle curiosity, iniquitous pursuits and wanton mirth, what a stillness would there be in the greatest cities.—Bruyère.

The city an epitome of the social world. All the belts of civilization intersect along its avenues. It contains the products of every moral zone. It is cosmopolitan, not only in a national, but a spiritual sense.—Chapin.

The union of men in large masses is indispensable to the development and rapid growth of the higher faculties of men. Cities have always been the fireplaces of civilization whence light and heat radiated out into the dark cold world.—Theodore Parker.

Dante might choose his home in all the wide beautiful world; but to be out of the streets of Florence was exile to him. Socrates never cared to go beyond the bounds of Athens. The great universal heart welcomes the city as a natural growth of the eternal forces.—F. B. Sanborn.

A great city whose image dwells on the memory of man is the type of some great idea. Rome represents conquest; faith hovers over Jerusalem; and Athens embodies the pre-eminent quality of the antique world-art.—Beaconsfield.

There is such a difference between the pursuits of men in great cities that one part of the inhabitants lives to little other purpose than to wonder at the rest. Some have hopes and fears, wishes and aversions, which never enter into the thoughts of others, and inquiry is laboriously exerted to gain that which those who possess it are ready to throw away.—Johnson.

The conditions of city life may be made healthy, so far as the physical constitution is concerned; but there is connected with the business of the city so much competition, so much rivalry, so much necessity for industry, that I think it is a perpetual, chronic, wholesale violation of natural law. There are ten men that can succeed in the country, where there is one that can succeed in the city.—Beecher.

I bless God for cities. Cities have been as lamps of life along the pathway of humanity and religion. Within them science has given birth to her noblest discoveries. Behind their walls freedom has fought her noblest battles. They have stood on the surface of the earth like great breakwaters, rolling back or turning aside the swelling tide of oppression. Cities, indeed, have been the cradles of human liberty. They have been the active centres of almost all church and state reformation.—Rev. Dr. Guthrie.

The most delicate beauty in the mind of women is, and ever must be, an independence of artificial stimulants for content. It is not so with men. The links that bind men to capitals belong to the golden chain of civilization,—the chain which fastens all our destinies to the throne of Jove. And hence the larger proportion of men in whom genius is pre-eminent have preferred to live in cities, though some of them have bequeathed to us the loveliest pictures of the rural scenes in which they declined to dwell. —Bulwer-Lytton.

Our large trading cities bear to me very nearly the aspect of monastic establishments in which the roar of the mill-wheel and the crane takes the place of other devotional music, and in which the worship of Mammon and Moloch is conducted with a tender reverence and an exact propriety; the merchant rising to his Mammon matins with the self-denial of an anchorite, and expiating the frivolities into which he may be beguiled in the course of the day by late attendance at Mammon vespers.—Ruskin.

Civility

Civility is but a desire to receive civility, and to be esteemed polite.—La Rochefoucauld.

Whilst thou livest keep a good tongue in thy head.—Shakespeare.

A good word is an easy obligation, but not to speak ill, requires only our silence, which costs us nothing.—Tillotson.

The insolent civility of a proud man is, if possible, more shocking than his rudeness could be; because he shows you, by his manner, that he thinks it mere condescension in him; and that his goodness alone bestows upon you what you have no pretense to claim.— Chesterfield.

Civilization

Extremes produce reaction. Beware that our boasted civilization does not lapse into barbarism.—Rivarol.

The ultimate tendency of civilization is towards barbarism.—Hare.

Barbarism recommences by the excess of civilization.—Lamartine.

A sufficient measure of civilization is the influence of good women.—Emerson.

Increased means and increased leisure are the two civilizers of men.— Beaconsfield.

Nations, like individuals, live and die; but civilization cannot die.—Mazzini.

Mankind's struggle upwards, in which millions are trampled to death, that thousands may mount on their bodies.—Mrs. Balfour.

The truest test of civilization is not the census, nor the size of cities, nor the crops; no, but the kind of man the country turns out.—Emerson.

Ever since there has been so great a demand for type, there has been much less lead to spare for cannonballs.—Bulwer-Lytton.

The most civilized people are as near to barbarism as the most polished steel is to rust. Nations, like metals, have only a superficial brilliancy.—Rivarol.

Civilization, or that which is so called, has operated two ways to make one part of society more affluent and the other part more wretched than would have been the lot of either in a natural state.—Thomas Paine.

No attribute so well befits the exalted seat supreme, and power's disposing hand, as clemency. Each crime must from its quality be judged; and pity there should interpose, where malice is not the aggressor.—Sir William Jones.

There is often no material difference between the enjoyment of the highest ranks and those of the rudest stages of society. If the life of many a young English nobleman, and an Iroquois in the forest, or an Arab in the desert are compared, it will be found that their real sources of happiness are nearly the same.—Sir A. Alison.

Such is the diligence with which, in countries completely civilized, one part of mankind labor for another, that wants are supplied faster than they can be formed, and the idle and luxurious find life stagnate for want of some desire to keep it in motion. This species of distress furnishes a new set of occupations; and multitudes are busied from day to day in finding the rich and the fortunate something to do.—Johnson.

A semi-civilized state of society, equally removed from the extremes of barbarity and of refinement, seems to be that particular meridian under which all the reciprocities and gratuities of hospitality do most readily flourish and abound. For it so happens that the ease, the luxury, and the abundance of the highest state of civilization, are as productive of selfishness, as the difficulties, the privations, and the sterilities of the lowest.—Colton.

We are but too apt to consider things in the state in which we find them, without sufficiently adverting to the causes by which they have been produced, and possibly may be upheld. Nothing is more certain than that our manners, our civilization, and all the good things which are connected with civilization, have, in this European world of ours, depended for ages upon two principles, and were indeed the result of both combined. I mean the spirit of a gentleman and the spirit of religion. The nobility and the clergy, the one by profession, the other by patronage, kept learning in existence even in the midst of arms and confusion. Learning paid back what it received to nobility and priesthood, and paid it back with usury by enlarging their ideas and furnishing their minds.—Burke.

Cleanliness

If dirt was trumps, what hands you would hold!—Charles Lamb.

Let thy mind's sweetness have its operation upon thy body, clothes, and habitation.—George Herbert.

Cleanliness may be defined to be the emblem of purity of mind.—Addison.

Certainly this is a duty, not a sin. 'Cleanliness is indeed next to godliness."—John Wesley.

Even from the body's purity, the mind Receives a secret, sympathetic aid.
　　　　　　　　　—Thomson.

For cleanness of body was ever esteemed to proceed from a due reverence to God, to society, and to ourselves.—Bacon.

So great is the effect of cleanliness upon man, that it extends even to his moral character. Virtue never dwelt long with filth; nor do I believe there ever was a person scrupulously attentive to cleanliness, who was a consummate villain.—Rumford.

Beauty commonly produces love, but cleanliness preserves it. Age itself is not unamiable while it is preserved clean and unsullied; like a piece of metal constantly kept smooth and bright, we look on it with more pleasure than on a new vessel cankered with rust.—Addison.

Clematis

Where the woodland streamlets flow,
　Gushing down a rocky bed,
Where the tasselled alders grow,
　Lightly meeting overhead,
When the fullest August days
　Give the richness that they know,
　　Then the wild clematis comes,
　　With her wealth of tangled blooms.
Reaching up and drooping low,
But when Autumn days are here,
　And the woods of Autumn burn,
Then her leaves are black and sere,
　Quick with early frosts to turn!
As the golden Summer dies,
　So her silky green has fled,
　　And the smoky clusters rise
　　As from fires of sacrifice,—
Sacred incense to the dead!
　　　　　　　—Dora Read Goodale.

Clemency

In general, indulgence for those we know is rarer than pity for those we know not.—Rivarol.

To be good to the vile is to throw water into the sea.—Cervantes.

Clemency alone makes us equal to the gods.—Claudianus.

Tender-handed stroke a nettle, and it stings you for your pains.—Aaron Hill.

Forgiveness, that noblest of all self-denial, is a virtue which he alone who can practise in himself can willingly believe in another.—Colton.

Clemency, which we make a virtue of, proceeds sometimes from vanity, sometimes from indolence, often from fear, and almost always from a mixture of all three.—Rochefoucauld.

No attribute
So well befits th' exalted seat supreme,
And power's disposing hand as clemency.
Each crime must from its quality be judged;
And pity there should interpose, where malice
Is not th' aggressor.—Sir William Jones.

The little I have seen of the world teaches me to look upon the errors of others in sorrow, not in anger. When I take the history of one poor heart that has sinned and suffered, and represent to myself the struggles and temptations it has passed through, the brief pulsations of joy, the feverish inquietude of hope and fear, the pressure of want, the desertion of friends, I would fain leave the erring soul of my fellow-man with Him from whose hand it came.—Longfellow.

Clergyman

The true clergyman is a reflex of his Master.—André Dacier.

The defects of a preacher are soon spied.—Luther.

He—the country parson—is not witty or learned or eloquent, but holy.—George Herbert.

The clergyman who lives in the city may have piety, but he must have taste.—Emerson.

The pulpit is a clergyman's parade; the parish is his field of active service.—Southey.

If you would lift me you must be on a higher ground.—Emerson.

There is nothing noble in a clergyman but burning zeal for the salvation of souls.—William Law.

Recollect for your encouragement the reward that awaits the faithful minister.—Robert Hall.

Embryos and idiots, eremites and friars,
White, black, and grey, with all their trumpery.   —Milton.

Around his form his loose long robe was thrown,
And wrapt a breast bestowed on heaven alone.   —Byron.

There goes the parson, oh illustrious spark!
And there, scarce less illustrious, goes the clerk.   —Cowper.

I never saw, heard, nor read, that the clergy were beloved in any nation where Christianity was the religion of the country.—Swift.

As there are certain mountebanks and quacks in physic, so there are much the same also in divinity.—South.

Nothing is more detestable than a professed declaimer who retails his discourses as a quack does his medicines.—Massillon.

I do not envy a clergyman's life as an easy life, nor do I envy the clergyman who makes it an easy life.—Dr. Johnson.

The Christian messenger cannot think too highly of his Prince, or too humbly of himself.—Colton.

From such apostles, oh ye mitred heads,
Preserve the church; and lay not careless hands
On skulls that cannot teach, and will not learn.   —Cowper.

There are passages of the Bible that are soiled forever by the touches of the hands of ministers who delight in the cheap jokes they have left behind them.—Phillips Brooks.

The ascendency of the sacerdotal order was long the ascendency which naturally and properly belonged to intellectual superiority.—Macaulay.

Suppose, however, that something like moderation were visible in this political sermon, yet politics and the pulpit are terms that have little agreement.—Burke.

Ev'n children followed with endearing wile
And pluck'd his gown to share the good
man's smile.   —Goldsmith.

Love and meekness, lord,
Become a churchman better than ambition:
Win straying souls with modesty again,
Cast none away.   —Shakespeare.

Make not the church to us an instrument
Of bondage, to yourselves of liberty:
Obedience there confirms your government,
Our sovereigns, God's subalterns, you be.
            —Lord Brooks.

The proud he tamed, the penitent he cheered,
Nor to rebuke the rich offender feared;
His preaching much, but more his practice
    wrought,
A living sermon of the truths he taught.
            —Dryden.

At church with meek and unaffected grace,
His looks adorn'd the venerable place;
Truth from his lips prevail'd with double
    sway,
And fools, who came to scoff, remain'd to
    pray.   —Goldsmith.

He that negotiates between God and man,
As God's ambassador, the grand concerns
Of judgment and of mercy, should beware
Of lightness in his speech.   —Cowper.

I venerate the man, whose heart is warm,
Whose hands are pure, whose doctrine and
    whose life
Coincident, exhibit lucid proof
That he is honest in the sacred cause.
            —Cowper.

He was a shepherd and no mercenary,
And though he holy was and virtuous,
He was to sinful men full piteous;
His words were strong, but not with anger
    fraught;
A love benignant he discreetly taught.
To draw mankind to heaven by gentleness
And good example was his business.
            —Chaucer.

Others of graver mien, behold, adorn'd
With holy ensigns, how sublime they
    move,
And bending oft their sanctimonious eyes,
Take homage of the simple-minded throng;
Ambassadors of heaven!   —Akenside.

The life of a conscientious clergyman is not easy. I have always consid-ered a clergyman as the father of a larger family than he is able to maintain. I would rather have chancery suits upon my hands than the cure of souls.—Dr. Johnson.

Do not, as some ungracious pastors do,
Show me the steep and thorny way to
    heaven;
Whilst, like a puff'd and reckless libertine,
Himself the primrose path of dalliance
    treads,
And recks not his own road.
            —Shakespeare.

In man or woman, but far most in man,
And most of all in man that ministers,
And serves the altar, in my soul I loathe
All affectation. 'Tis my perfect scorn:
Object of my implacable disgust.
            —Cowper.

It never was a prosperous world
Since priests have interfer'd with temporal
    matters;
The custom of their ancestors they slight,
And change their shirts of hair for robes of
    gold;
Thus luxury and interest rule the church,
Whilst piety and conscience dwell in caves.
            —Bancroft.

Their sheep have crusts, and they the
    bread;
The chips and they the cheer:
They have the fleece, and eke the flesh,
(O seely sheep the while!)
The corn is theirs—let others thresh,
Their hands they may not file.
            —Spenser.

His talk was now of tythes and dues;
He smok'd his pipe, and read the news;
Knew how to preach old sermons next,
Vamp'd in the preface and the text;
At christenings well could act his part,
And had the service all by heart;
Wish'd women might have children fast,
And thought whose sow had farrow'd last;
Against dissenters would repine,
And stood up firm for right divine;
Found his head fill'd with many a system,
But classic authors—he ne'er miss'd 'em.
            —Swift.

Your Lordship and your Grace, what schooi
    can teach
A rhetoric equal to those parts of speech?
What need of Homer's verse, or Tully's
    prose,
Sweet interjections! if he learn but those?
Let rev'rend churls his ignorance rebuke.
Who starve upon a dog's ear'd Pentateuch,
The Parson knows enough who knows a
    Duke.   —Cowper.

Behold the picture! Is it like? Like
whom?·
The things that mount the rostrum with a
skip
And then skip down again. Pronounce a
text,
Cry hem; and reading what they never
wrote,
Just fifteen minutes huddle up their work,
And with a well-bred whisper close the
scene.   —Cowper.

If we must pray,
Rear in the streets bright altars to the
gods,
Let virgin's hands adorn the sacrifice;
And not a grey-beard forging priest come
here,
To pry into the bowels of their victim,
And with their dotage mad the gaping
world.   —Lee.

Near yonder copse, where once the garden
smil'd,
And still where many a garden flower grows
wild,
There, where a few torn shrubs the place
disclose,
The village preacher's modest mansion rose.
A man he was to all the country dear,
And passing rich with forty pounds a year;
Remote from towns he ran his godly race,
Nor e'er had chang'd nor wish'd to change
his place;
Unskilful he to fawn, or seek for power,
By doctrines fashion'd to the varying hour;
Far other aims his heart had learn'd to
prize.
More bent to raise the wretched than to
rise.   —Goldsmith.

Cleverness

We can be more clever than one,
but not more clever than all.—La
Rochefoucauld.

To know how to hide one's ability
is great skill.—La Rochefoucauld.

Climate

The institutions of a country depend in great measure on the nature
of its soil and situation. Many of
the wants of man are awakened or
supplied by these circumstances. To
these wants, manners, laws, and religion must shape and accommodate
themselves. The division of land, and
the rights attached to it, alter with
the soil: the laws relating to its produce, with its fertility. The manners
of its inhabitants are in various ways
modified by its position. The religion
of a miner is not the same as the faith

of a shepherd, nor is the character of
the ploughman so war-like as that of
the hunter. The observant legislator
follows the direction of all these various circumstances. The knowledge of
the natural advantages or defects of a
country thus form an essential part of
political science and history.—Justus
Moser.

Clouds

Those playful fancies of the mighty
sky.—Smith.

The clouds,—the only birds that
never sleep.—Victor Hugo.

Those clouds are angels' robes.—That fiery
west
Is paved with smiling faces.
    —Charles Kingsley.

They are fair resting-places
For the dear weary dead on their way up to
heaven.   —Joaquin Miller.

Clouds on clouds, in volumes driven,
Curtain round the vault of heaven.
    —Thomas Love Peacock.

When clouds appear like rocks and towers,
The earth's refreshed by frequent showers.
    —Old Weather Rhyme.

If woolly fleeces spread the heavenly way,
No rain, be sure, disturbs the summer's
day.   —Old Weather Rhyme.

The hooded clouds, like friars,
Tell their beads in drops of rain.
    —Longfellow.

Yonder cloud
That rises upward always higher,
A looming bastion fringed with fire.
    —Tennyson.

That look'd
As though an angel, in his upward flight,
Had left his mantle floating in mid-air.
    —Joanna Baillie.

The clouds consign their treasure to the
fields,
And, softly shaking on the dimpled pool
Prelusive drops, let all their moisture flow,
In large effusion o'er a freshen'd world.
    —Thomson.

When scattered clouds are resting
on the bosoms of hills, it seems as if
one might climb into the heavenly region, earth being so intermixed with

sky, and gradually transformed into it.
—Hawthorne.

We often praise the evening clouds,
   And tints so gay and bold,
But seldom think upon our God,
   Who tinged these clouds with gold.
                              —Scott.

Bathed in the tenderest purple of distance,
Tinted and shadowed by pencils of air,
Thy battlements hang o'er the slopes and
   the forests,
Seats of the Gods in the limitless ether,
Looming sublimely aloft and afar.
                        —Bayard Taylor.

            Now a cloud,
Massive and black, strides up; the angry
   gleam
Of the red lightning cleaves the frowning
   folds.   —Street.

         Wafted up,
The stealing cloud with soft grey blinds
   the sky
And in its vapory mantle onward steps
The summer shower.   —Street.

Ye clouds, that are the ornament of heaven,
Who give to it its gayest shadowings
And its most awful glories; ye who roll
In the dark tempest, or at dewy evening
Bow low in tenderest beauty;—ye are to us
A volume full of wisdom.   —Percival.

A cloud lay cradled near the setting sun;
A gleam of crimson tinged its braided
   snow;
         *   *   *   *   *
Tranquil its spirit seemed and floated slow;
Even in its very motion there was rest;
While every breath of eve that chance to
   blow
Wafted the traveller to the beauteous west.
                        —John Wilson.

Cloud-walls of the morning's gray
Faced with amber column,
Crowned with crimson cupola
From a sunset solemn.
May-mists, for the casements, fetch,
Pale and glimmering,
With a sunbeam hid in each,
And a smell of spring.
                        —Mrs. Browning.

O, it is pleasant, with a heart at ease,
Just after sunset, or by moonlight skies,
To make the shifting clouds be what you
   please,
Or let the easily persuaded eyes
Own each quaint likeness issuing from the
   mould
Of a friend's fancy.   —Coleridge.

Sometimes we see a cloud that's dragonish;
A vapour, sometimes, like a bear or lion,
A tower'd citadel, a pendant rock,
A forked mountain, or blue promontory,
With trees upon't, that nod unto the world,
And mock our eyes with air.
                        —Shakespeare.

I bring fresh showers for the thirsting
   flowers,
   From the seas and the streams;
I bear light shade for the leaves when laid
   In their noonday dreams.
From my wings are shaken the dews that
   waken
   The sweet buds every one,
When rocked to rest on their mother's
   breast,
   As she dances about the sun.
I wield the flail of the lashing hail,
   And whiten the green plains under,
And then again I dissolve it in rain,
   And laugh as I pass in thunder.
                        —Shelley.

         I loved the Clouds.
Fire-fringed at dawn, or red with twilight
   bloom,
Or stretched above, like isles of leaden
   gloom
In heaven's vast deep, or drawn in belts of
   gray,
Or dark blue walls along the base of day;
Or snow-drifts luminous at highest noon,
Ragged and black in tempests, veined with
   lightning,
And when the moon was brightening.
Impearled and purpled by the changeful
   moon.   —R. H. Stoddard.

Color

Color is, in brief terms, the type of
love. Hence it is especially connected
with the blossoming of the earth; and
again, with its fruits; also, with the
spring and fall of the leaf, and with
the morning and evening of the day, in
order to show the waiting of love
about the birth and death of man.—
Ruskin.

The little may contrast with the
great, in painting, but cannot be said
to be contrary to it. Oppositions of
colors contrast; but there are also
colors contrary to each other, that is,
which produce an ill effect because
they shock the eye when brought very
near it.—Voltaire.

The fact is, that of all God's gifts
to the sight of man, color is the holiest,
the most divine, the most solemn. We

speak rashly of gay color and sad color, for color cannot at once be good and gay. All good color is in some degree pensive, the loveliest is melancholy, and the purest and most thoughtful minds are those which love color the most.—Thomas Starr King.

Comet

Comets importing change of times and states,
Brandish your crystal tresses in the sky
And with them scourge the bad revolting stars.　　　—Shakespeare.

Lo! from the dread immensity of space
Returning, with accelerated course,
The rushing comet to the sun descends:
And as he sinks below the shading earth,
With awful train projected o'er the heavens,
The guilty nations tremble.—Thomson.

Stranger of Heaven, I bid thee hail!
Shred from the pall of glory riven
That flashest in celestial gale—
Broad pennon of the King of Heaven
Whate'er portends thy front of fire
And streaming locks so lovely pale;
Or peace to man, or judgments dire
Stranger of Heaven, I bid thee hail.　　　—Hogg.

Hast thou ne'er seen the comet's flaming light?
Th' illustrious stranger passing, terror sheds
On gazing nations, from his fiery train
Of length enormous, takes his ample round
Through depths of ether; coasts unnumber'd worlds,
Of more than solar glory; doubles wide
Heaven's mighty cape; and then re-visits earth,
From the long travel of a thousand years.　　　—Young.

Lone traveller through the fields of air,
What may thy presence here portend?
Art come to greet the planets fair,
As friend greets friend?
Whate'er thy purpose, thou dost teach
Some lessons to the humble soul;
Though far and dim thy pathway reach,
Yet still thy goal
Tends to the fountain of that light
From whence thy golden beams are won;
So should we turn, from earth's dark night,
To God our sun.　　　—Mrs. Hale.

Comfort

Of all created comforts, God is the lender; you are the borrower, not the owner.—Rutherford.

Comfort and indolence are cronies.—Hood.

For in a dearth of comforts, we art taught
To be contented with the least.
　　　—Sir W. Davenant.

Comfort—'tis for ease and quiet;
It sleeps upon the down of sweet content,
In the sound bed of industry and health.
　　　—Havard.

Comfort, like the golden sun,
Dispels the sullen shade with her sweet influence,
And cheers the melancholy house of care.
　　　—Rowe.

The comforts we enjoy here below are not like the anchor in the bottom of the sea that holds fast in a storm, but like the flag upon the top of the mast that turns with every wind.—Rev. Christopher Love.

The chief secret of comfort lies in not suffering trifles to vex us, and in prudently cultivating an undergrowth of small pleasures, since very few great ones are let on long leases.—Aughey.

It is a little thing to speak a phrase of common comfort, which by daily use has almost lost its sense; yet on the ear of him who thought to die unmourned it will fall like choicest music.—Talfourd.

Giving comfort under affliction requires that penetration into the human mind. joined to that experience which knows how to soothe, how to reason, and how to ridicule; taking the utmost care never to apply those arts improperly.—Fielding.

Sweet as refreshing dews or summer showers,
To the long parching thirst of drooping flowers;
Grateful as fanning gales to fainting swains
And soft as trickling balm to bleeding pains.
Such are thy words.　　　—Gay.

I want a sofa, as I want a friend, upon which I can repose familiarly. If you can't have intimate terms and freedom with one and the other, they are of no good.—Thackeray.

In the exhaustless catalogue of Heaven's mercies to mankind, the power we have of finding some germs of comfort in the hardest trials must ever occupy the foremost place; not only because it supports and upholds us when we most require to be sustained, but because in this source of consolation there is something, we have reason to believe, of the Divine Spirit; something of that goodness which detects, amidst our own evil doings, a redeeming quality; something, which even in our fallen nature, we possess in common with the angels; which had its being in the old time when they trod the earth, and linger on it yet in pity.—Dickens.

Command — Commander

A brave captain is as a root, out of which (as branches) the courage of his soldiers doth spring.—Sir Philip Sidney.

It is better to have a lion at the head of an army of sheep, than a sheep at the head of an army of lions.—De Foe.

He stopp'd the fliers:
And, by his rare example, made the coward
Turn terror into sport; as waves before
A vessel under sail, so men obey'd,
And fell below his stem. —Shakespeare.

Truly, a command of gall cannot be obeyed like one of sugar. A man must require just and reasonable things, if he would see the scales of obedience properly trimmed. From orders which are improper, springs resistance, which is not easily overcome.—Basil.

Commendation

Commend a fool for his wit, or a knave for his honesty, and they will receive you into their bosom.—Fielding.

Commerce

Commerce has made all winds her mistress.—Sterling.

God is making commerce His missionary.—Joseph Cook.

The first inventions of commerce are, like those of all other arts, cunning and short-sighted.—Curran.

More pernicious nonsense was never devised by man than treaties of commerce.—Beaconsfield.

Commerce defies every wind, outrides every tempest, and invades every zone.—Bancroft.

Commerce is the equalizer of the wealth of nations.—Gladstone.

It may almost be held that the hope of commercial gain has done nearly as much for the cause of truth as even the love of truth.—Bovee.

The care of our national commerce redounds more to the riches and prosperity of the public than any other act of government.—Addison.

Commerce links all mankind in one common brotherhood of mutual dependence and interests.—James A. Garfield.

As soon as the commercial spirit acquires vigor, and begins to gain an ascendant in any society, we discern a new genius in its policy, its alliances, its wars, and its negotiations.—Dr. W. Robertson.

Commerce can never be at a stop while one man wants what another can supply; and credit will never be denied, while it is likely to be repaid with profit.—Dr. Johnson.

Whatever has a tendency to promote the civil intercourse of nations by an exchange of benefits is a subject as worthy of philosophy as of politics.—Thomas Paine.

Chiefly the sea-shore has been the point of departure to knowledge, as to commerce. The most advanced nations are always those who navigate the most.—Emerson.

A well regulated commerce is not, like law, physic, or divinity, to be overstocked with hands; but, on the contrary, flourishes by multitudes, and gives employment to all its professors.—Addison.

Next to the pastoral came the agricultural life. When you add to that the manufacturing phase of development, society begins to fill out, and needs but wings to fly, and commerce is its wings.—Beecher.

Commerce is no other than the traffic of two individuals, multiplied on a scale of number; and, by the same rule that Nature intended the intercourse of two, she intended that of all!—Thomas Paine.

There are no more useful members in a commonwealth than merchants. They knit mankind together in a mutual intercourse of good offices, distribute the gifts of Nature, find work for the poor, and wealth to the rich, and magnificence to the great.—Addison.

A statesman may do much for commerce, most by leaving it alone. A river never flows so smoothly, as when it follows its own course, without either aid or check. Let it make its own bed, it will do so better than you can.

Commerce, however we may please ourselves with the contrary opinion, is one of the daughters of fortune, inconstant and deceitful as her mother. She chooses her residence where she is least expected, and shifts her abode when her continuance is, in appearance, most firmly settled.—Johnson.

As Egypt does not on the clouds rely
But to the Nile owes more than to the sky;
So what our earth and what our heaven denies
Our ever constant friend, the sea supplies.
The taste of hot Arabia's spice we know,
Free from the scorching sun that makes it grow;
Without the worm in Persia's silks we shine;
And without planting, drink of every vine,
To dig for wealth we weary not our limbs.
Gold, though the heaviest metal hither swims,
Ours is the harvest where the Indians mow.
We plough the deep, and reap what others sow.   —Waller.

Commerce tends to wear off those prejudices which maintain distinction and animosity between nations. It softens and polishes the manners of

men. It unites them by one of the strongest of all ties—the desire of supplying their mutual wants. It disposes them to peace, by establishing in every State an order of citizens bound by their interest to be the guardians of public tranquillity. As soon as the commercial spirit acquires vigor, and begins to gain an ascendant in any society, we begin to discern a new genius in its policy, its alliances, its wars, and its negotiations.—Robertson.

Nature seems to have taken a particular care to disseminate her blessings among the different regions of the world, with an eye to their mutual intercourse and traffic among mankind, that the nations of the several parts of the globe might have a kind of dependence upon one another and be united together by their common interest.—Addison.

Common Sense

Common sense is very uncommon.—Horace Greeley.

Common sense is in spite of, not because of age.—Lord Thurlow.

Common sense is nature's gift, but reason is an art.—Beattie.

Common sense, alas in spite of our educational institutions, is a rare commodity.—Bovee.

If common sense has not the brilliancy of the sun, it has the fixity of the stars.—Fernan Caballero.

Good sense, disciplined by experience and inspired by goodness, issues in practical wisdom.—Samuel Smiles.

Common sense is in spite of, not the result of, education—Victor Hugo.

Common sense is instinct, and enough of it is genius.—H. W. Shaw.

Common sense is the favorite daughter of Reason.—H. W. Shaw.

Common sense is only a modification of talent. Genius is an exaltation of it: the difference is, therefore, in the degree, not nature.—Bulwer-Lytton.

The aim of all intellectual training for the mass of the people should be to cultivate common sense.—J. Stuart Mill.

———

Common sense is the average sensibility and intelligence of men undisturbed by individual peculiarities.—W. R. Alger.

———

Common sense has given to words their ordinary signification, and common sense is the genius of mankind.—Guizot.

———

Common sense in one view is the most uncommon sense. While it is extremely rare in possession, the recognition of it is universal. All men feel it, though few men have it.—H. N. Hudson.

———

Fine sense and exalted sense are not half as useful as common sense. There are forty men of wit for one man of sense. And he that will carry nothing about him but gold will be every day at a loss for readier change. —Pope.

———

Sydney Smith playfully says that common sense was invented by Socrates, that philosopher having been one of its most conspicuous exemplars in conducting the contest of practical sagacity against stupid prejudice and illusory beliefs.—Whipple.

———

Common sense is science exactly so far as it fulfils the ideal of common sense; that is, sees facts as they are, or at any rate without the distortion of prejudice, and reasons from them in accordance with the dictates of sound judgment.—Huxley.

———

To act with common sense, according to the moment, is the best wisdom I know; and the best philosophy, to do one's duties, take the world as it comes, submit respectfully to one's lot, bless the goodness that has given us so much happiness with it, whatever it is, and despise affectation.—Horace Walpole.

———

In most old communities there is a common sense even in sensuality. Vice itself gets gradually digested into a

system, is amenable to certain laws of conventional propriety and honor, has for its object simply the gratification of its appetites, and frowns with quite a conservative air on all new inventions, all untried experiments in iniquity.—Whipple.

———

Common sense punishes all departures from her, by forcing those who rebel into a desperate war with all facts and experience, and into a still more terrible civil war with each other and with themselves.—Colton.

Commonwealth

We will renew the times of peace and justice,
Condensing in a fair free commonwealth;
Not rash equality, but equal rights,
Proportion'd like the columns of the temple
Giving and taking strength reciprocal,
And making firm the whole with grace and beauty;
So that no part could be removed without
Infringement of the general symmetry.
—Byron.

Communion

All Christian power springs from communion with God, and from the indwelling of divine grace.—Aughey.

———

If we show the Lord's death at Communion, we must show the Lord's life in the world. If it is a Eucharist on Sunday, it must prove on Monday that it was also a Sacrament.—Maltbie Babcock.

———

This do in remembrance of me.—I Cor. xi. 24.

———

We should come to the Lord's table with the confident expectation of meeting Christ there, of receiving there a blessing.—Rev. Chas. A. Savage.

———

The Lord's Supper is the central act of Christian worship. It is a prophecy, pledge, and prelude to that "supper table of the Lamb," when we shall sit down with Abraham and Isaac and Jacob in the kingdom of our Father. —Rev. Gerard B. F. Hallock.

———

I agree with you that the communion with the invisible saints must be more of a dream than a reality. But we have a right to dream dreams, if they are not contradicted by the evident laws of God's word, or God's world.—Maltbie Babcock.

We should look to the Sacrament for a special revelation of Christ and His truth. The purpose of the communion service is to afford us an opportunity to take into our spiritual natures something from the outside.—Rev. Chas. A. Savage.

A consciousness of guilt does not disqualify one. We come to the Lord's table because we know that we are sinners trusting only in the death and work of Jesus Christ. No matter how great one's consciousness of guilt, if he is penitent and is seeking strength to live a Christian life, the Lord's table is the very place for him.—Smith Baker, D. D.

The Lord's Supper comes to us like a ring plucked off from Christ's finger, or a bracelet from His arm; or rather like His picture from His breast, delivered to us with such words as these, "As oft as you look on this, remember me."—John Flavel.

Especially in acts of sacramental communion with his Lord does the Christian gather up and consecrate the powers of his life-long communion with heaven. Then it is that he has most vivid impressions of the nearness of God to his soul, a most comfortable assurance of strength for his need.—Mackarness.

The Lord's Supper has been greatly instrumental in keeping His cause alive. It is the voice of all believers preaching the Lord's death till He come. He who believes that the Lord did come and die for us, and will come again and take us to Himself, will not hesitate to regard this last request of our Lord and Saviour.—Chas. F. Deems, D. D.

We want to look at the Lord's Supper as an ordinance of thanksgiving, that we may have greater desire and pleasure and profit in its celebration. God unfolds to us the different attributes of this beautiful ordinance, that we may be attracted to it. He means every attribute to be a per-

suasive argument enforcing obedience to the command: "This do in remembrance of me."—David Gregg, D. D.

"We do not presume to come to this Thy table, O merciful Lord, trusting in our own righteousness, but in Thy manifold and great mercies. We are not worthy so much as to gather up the crumbs under Thy table. But thou art the same Lord, Whose property is always to have mercy," etc.—Book of Common Prayer.

It is a love feast, emphasizing Christ's love for us, and ours to Him and to one another. Sin parts men, but in Christ we have brotherhood. We are to love the world, but in a different way our Christian brothers. "This is My commandment, That ye love one another."

It is a pledge of glory, a foretaste of the marriage supper of the Lamb. The glory is in heaven, and we must wait for it, but we are heirs of it.—Howard Crosby, D. D.

Let us remember that the Lord's Supper is an ordinance given to the friends of Jesus Christ who have entered upon the saved life, and intended to help them realize their privileges. The Lord's Supper takes the most terrible facts of history and experience, and groups them with the grandest of realities in such a way that our souls break forth into hallelujahs.—David Gregg, D. D.

Bread of the world, in mercy broken,
Wine of the soul, in mercy shed,
By whom the words of life were spoken,
And in whose death our sins are dead:

Look on the heart by sorrow broken,
Look on the tears by sinners shed;
And be Thy feast to us the token
That by Thy grace our souls are fed.
—Reginald Heber.

The proper attitude to assume with relation to the Lord's Supper is a golden mean between idolatry and indifference.—Rev. Chas. A. Savage.

Historians are unanimous in their testimony that from the beginning this sacrament was viewed as a great mystery, to which was attached profound doctrinal significance and the highest spiritual efficacy. With the visible elements, it was believed, were mystically the body and blood of the Lord. Those who in faith partook of this Supper enjoyed essential communion with Christ.—Prof. E. J. Wolf, D. D.

Indifference to the Sacrament casts contempt on an ordinance instituted by our Saviour Himself, and one that is full of holy meaning. An idolatrous reverence for it not only violates the Second Commandment, but dishonors Christ.—Rev. Chas. A. Savage.

The Lord's Supper may be made more profitable for us if we emphasize it as a bond of brotherhood. A communion with Christ, it is also a communion with each other, and not only among the few gathered within the walls of a single sanctuary; it is the fellowship of the ages. In the name of our common Christ, "encompassed by so great a cloud of witnesses," we sit with them in heavenly places whenever we come to the Communion Table of our Lord.—Rev. Chas. A. Savage.

Bread of Heaven, on Thee I feed,
For Thy flesh is meat indeed;
Ever may my soul be fed
With this true and living bread;
Day by day with strength supplied,
Through the life of Him who died.

Vine of Heaven, Thy blood supplies
This blest cup of sacrifice;
'Tis Thy wounds my healing give;
To Thy cross I look and live.
Thou my Life, O let me be
Rooted, grafted, built on Thee.
—Josiah Conder.

Coming by faith, and thus truly partaking of the bread and the wine, we receive anew the assurance that we are pardoned sinners. We receive increased grace to confirm our Christian habits and to quicken them in their exercise. We receive the earnest of eternal bliss and joy. Most precious foretastes of the heavenly happiness are here bestowed upon a lively faith. A bunch of grapes from the heavenly Eshcol is pressed by the Lord into the sacramental cup. We have food to eat that the world knows not of.—Rev. M. Patterson, D. D.

It is certainly not desirable that improper persons should take the sacrament of the Lord's Supper; but there are many who injure their spiritual characters and diminish their spiritual enjoyment by failing to obey the request of our dying Lord. About to die, He tenderly asked every man who believed that He was dying for the world to do this in remembrance of Him. It is a most simple request; the observance of it in a similar spirit would increase the joy and power of all who wish well the cause of Christianity.

This will appear as we notice what the Lord's Supper signifies. (a) It is a memorial of Christ's life and death. (b) It is a symbol of Christ's work. (c) It represents the union of all God's people; at the table of the Lord all human souls are on a level. (d) Again, it represents the soul's constant dependence upon Christ for strength. Christ is the daily bread of life to the soul. (e) It represents the mystic union of Christ and His people; He lives in them and they in Him. (f) The Lord's Supper is a special communion with Christ, when in a particular manner He reveals Himself to the believing heart.—Smith Baker, D. D.

Thus may we abide in union,
With each other and the Lord,
And possess in sweet communion
Joys which earth cannot afford.
—Rev. John Newton.

Let us come, then, hungering and thirsting for the body and blood of the Lord. He will be present to satisfy the spiritual desires of which He is Himself the author. It would be no feast without Himself. Mere common bread, mere common wine, mere meeting with one another, would this sacrament be unless Jesus Himself were here. "He must break the bread, if it is to nourish my soul. He must pour out the wine, if it is to refresh and gladden me." And we doubt not that He will do this. We come in obedience to His command, and we rely upon His promise. We will seek to commune under their influence, and then we will go away from the table joyfully and exultingly declaring: "As the apple-tree among the trees of the wood, so is my Beloved among the sons. I sat down under his shadow with great delight, and his fruit was sweet to my taste."

God, in giving us what we pray for because we pray, and in refusing to give what we fail to ask for, deals with us as a loving father. He cultivates that living sympathy and communion between our hearts and His own which is necessary to our happiness and growth in grace.—C. E. Babb, D. D.

He walks in the presence of God that converses with Him in frequent prayer and communion; that runs to Him with all his necessities, that asks counsel of Him in all his doubtings, that opens all his wants to Him; weeps before Him for all his sins; and that asks remedy and support for all his weakness, that fears Him as a Judge, reverences Him as a Lord, and obeys Him as a Father.

If a friend is the one who summons us to our best, then is not Jesus Christ our best friend, and should we not think of the Communion as one of His chief appeals to us to be our best? The Lord's Supper looks not back to our past with a critical eye, but to our future, with a hopeful one. The Master appeals from what we have been to what we may be. He bids us come, not because He sees we are better than we have been, but because He wants us to be. To stay away because our hearts are cold is to refuse to go to the fire till we are warm.—Maltbie Babcock.

Ye do well to remember that habitual affectionate communion with God, asking Him for all good which is needed, praising Him for all that is received, and trusting Him for future supplies, prevents anxious cares, inspires peace, calmness and composure, and furnishes a delight surpassing all finite comprehension.—Aughey.

Communism

Communism means barbarism.—Lowell.

The law cannot equalize men in spite of Nature—Vauvenargues.

Communism is plunder legalized.—Mary Trimmer.

There may be community of material possessions, but there can never be community of love or esteem.—Dr. Johnson.

Communism possesses a language which every people can understand. Its elements are hunger, envy, death. —Heinrich Heine.

You cannot place mediocrity on a par with culture and intelligence; consequently communism is impossible.—Perley Poore.

One who has yearnings for equal division of unequal earnings. Idler or bungler, he is willing to fork out his penny and pocket your shilling.—Ebenezer Elliott.

Cæsar was Rome's escape from communism. I expect no Cæsar; I find on our map no Rubicon. But then I expect to see communistic madness rebuked and ended.—Prof. Hitchcock.

Levellers wish to level down as far as themselves, but they cannot bear levelling up to themselves. They would all have some people under them; why not then have some people above them?—Dr. Johnson.

Company — Companions

Wicked companions invite us to hell. —Fielding.

A pleasant companion is as good as a coach.—Swift.

He that toucheth pitch shall be defiled therewith.—Bible.

Company, villanous company, hath been the spoil of me.—Shakespeare.

There are like to be short graces where the devil plays host.—Lamb.

The freer you feel yourself in the presence of another, the more free is he.—Lavater.

No man can be provident of his time who is not prudent in the choice of his company.—Jeremy Taylor.

No possession is gratifying without a companion.—Seneca.

A companion is but another self; wherefore it is an argument that a man is wicked if he keep company with the wicked.—St. Clement.

No man in effect doth accompany with others but he learneth, ere he is aware, some gesture, voice, or fashion.—Bacon.

No man can possibly improve in any company for which he has not respect enough to be under some degree of restraint.—Chesterfield.

Our companions please us less from the charms we find in their conversation than from those they find in ours.—Fulke Greville.

We have been born to associate with our fellow-men, and to join in community with the human race.—Cicero.

It is certain that either wise bearing or ignorant carriage is caught as men take diseases one of another; therefore, let men take heed of their company.—Shakespeare.

No company is far preferable to bad, because we are more apt to catch the vices of others than virtues, as disease is far more contagious than health.—Colton.

Let them have ever so learned lectures of breeding, that which will most influence their carriage will be the company they converse with, and the fashion of those about them.—Locke.

Without good company all dainties
Lose their true relish, and like painted grapes,
Are only seen, not tasted. —Massinger.

Be cautious with whom you associate, and never give your company or your confidence to persons of whose good principles you are not certain.—Bishop Coleridge.

Men or women that are greedy of acquaintance, or hasty in it, are oftentimes snared in ill company before they are aware, and entangled so, that they cannot easily get loose from it after, when they would.—Sir Matthew Hale.

Nature has left every man a capacity of being agreeable, though not of shining in company; and there are a hundred men sufficiently qualified for both, who, by a very few faults, that they might correct in half an hour, are not so much as tolerable.—Swift.

Take rather than give the tone to the company you are in. If you have parts you will show them more or less upon every subject; and if you have not, you had better talk sillily upon a subject of other people's than of your own choosing.—Chesterfield.

The most agreeable of all companions is a simple, frank man, without any high pretensions to an oppressive greatness; one who loves life, and understands the use of it; obliging alike at all hours; above all, of a golden temper and steadfast as an anchor. For such an one we gladly exchange the greatest genius, the most brilliant wit, the profoundest thinker.—Lessing.

Bad company is like a nail driven into a post, which, after the first or second blow, may be drawn out with little difficulty; but being once driven up to the head, the pincers cannot take hold to draw it out, but which can only be done by the destruction of the wood.—Augustine.

We should ever have it fixed in our memories that, by the character of those whom we choose for our friends, our own is likely to be formed, and will certainly be judged by the world. We ought, therefore, to be slow and cautious in contracting intimacy; but when a virtuous friendship is once established, we must ever consider it a sacred engagement.—Blair.

Comparisons

Comparisons are odious.—Burton.

Comparisons do ofttime great grievance.—John Lydgate.

The superiority of some men is merely local. They are great, because their associates are little.—Johnson.

Like master, like man.—Chevalier
Bayard.

In virtues nothing earthly could surpass her,
Save thine "incomparable oil," Macassar!
        —Byron.

There's some are fou o' love divine,
There's some are fou o' brandy.
        —Burns.

Compare her face with some that I shall
  show,
And it will make thee think thy swan a
  crow.   —Shakespeare.

Thus I knew that pups are like dogs,
and kids like goats; so I used to compare great things with small.—Virgil.

What, is the jay more precious than the
  lark,
Because his feathers are more beautiful?
Or is the adder better than the eel,
Because his painted skin contents the eye?
        —Shakespeare.

When two persons do the self-same
thing, it oftentimes falls out that in
the one it is criminal, in the other it
is not so; not that the thing itself is
different, but he who does it.—Terence.

Is it possible your pragmatical worship should not know that the comparisons made between wit and wit,
courage and courage, beauty and
beauty, birth and birth, are always
odious and ill taken?—Cervantes.

When the moon shone, we did not
see the candle, so doth the greater
glory dim the less; a substitute shines
brightly as a king, until a king be
by; and then his state empties itself,
as doth an inland brook into the main
of waters.—Shakespeare.

It's wiser being good than bad;
  It's safer being meek than fierce:
It's fitter being sane than mad.
  My own hope is, a sun will pierce
The thickest cloud earth ever stretched;
That, after Last, returns the First,
Though a wide compass round be fetched;
  That what began best, can't end worst,
  Nor what God blessed once, prove ac-
    curst.   —Robert Browning.

The botanist looks upon the astronomer as a being unworthy of his regard; and he that is growing great
and happy by electrifying a bottle
wonders how the world can be engaged by trifling prattle about war and
peace.—Johnson.

Yet why repine? I have seen mansions on the verge of Wales that convert my farm-house into a Hampton
Court, and where they speak of a
glazed window as a great piece of
magnificence. All things figure by
comparison.—Shenstone.

Compassion

Compassion, the fairest associate of
the heart.—Paine.

Man may dismiss compassion from his heart,
But God will never.   —Cowper.

There never was any heart truly
great and generous that was not also
tender and compassionate.—South.

It is the crown of justice, and the
glory, where it may kill with right,
to save with pity.—Beaumont and
Fletcher.

Compassion to an offender who has
grossly violated the laws is, in effect,
a cruelty to the peaceable subject who
has observed them.—Junius.

O, heavens! can you hear a good man
  groan,
And not relent, or not compassion him?
        —Shakespeare.

Poor naked wretches, wheresoe'er you are,
That bide the pelting of this pitiless storm,
How shall your houseless heads and unfed
  sides,
Your loop'd and window'd raggedness, de-
  fend you
From seasons such as these? Oh, I have
  ta'en
Too little care of this! Take physic, pomp;
Expose thyself to feel what wretches feel;
That thou may'st shake the superflux to
  them,
And show the heavens more just.
        —Shakespeare.

Want of compassion (however inaccurate observers have reported to the
contrary) is not to be numbered among
the general faults of mankind. The
black ingredient which fouls our disposition is envy. Hence our eyes, it
is to be feared, are seldom turned up

to those who are manifestly greater, better, wiser, or happier than ourselves, without some degree of malignity, while we commonly look downward on the mean and miserable with sufficient benevolence and pity.—Fielding.

Compassion is an emotion of which we ought never to be ashamed. Graceful, particularly in youth, is the tear of sympathy, and the heart that melts at the tale of woe. We should not permit ease and indulgence to contract our affections, and wrap us up in a selfish enjoyment; but we should accustom ourselves to think of the distresses of human life, of the solitary cottage, the dying parent, and the weeping orphan. Nor ought we ever to sport with pain and distress in any of our amusements, or treat even the meanest insect with wanton cruelty.—Blair.

Complacency

Complaisance renders a superior amiable, an equal agreeable, and an inferior acceptable.—Addison.

Complacency is a coin by the aid of which all the world can, for want of essential means, pay his club-bill in society. It is necessary, finally, that it may lose nothing of its merits, to associate judgment and prudence with it.—Voltaire.

Complaisance, though in itself it be scarce reckoned in the number of moral virtues, is that which gives a lustre to every talent a man can be possessed of. It was Plato's advice to an unpolished writer that he should sacrifice to the graces. In the same manner I would advise every man of learning, who would not appear in the world a mere scholar or philosopher, to make himself master of the social virtue which I have here mentioned.—Addison.

Complaining

Complaint is more contemptible than pitiful.—Bovee.

We lose the right of complaining sometimes by forbearing it; but we often treble the force.—Sterne.

Complaint is the largest tribute heaven receives.—Swift.

The usual fortune of complaint is to excite contempt more than pity.—Johnson.

We are too prone to find fault; let us look for some of the perfections.—Schiller.

Constant complaint is the poorest sort of pay for all the comforts we enjoy.—Franklin.

Every one must see daily instances of people who complain from a mere habit of complaining.—Graves.

I have always despised the whining yelp of complaint, and the cowardly feeble resolve.—Burns.

I will not be as those who spend the day in complaining of headache, and the night in drinking the wine that gives the headache.—Goethe.

Our condition never satisfies us; the present is always the worst. Though Jupiter should grant his request to each, we should continue to importune him.—La Fontaine.

To tell thy mis'ries will no comfort breed;
Men help thee most, that think thou hast no need;
But if the world once thy misfortunes know,
Thou soon shalt lose a friend and find a foe.   —Randolph.

All our murmurings are so many arrows shot at God Himself, and they will return upon our own hearts; they reach not Him, but they will hit us; they hurt not Him, but they will wound us; therefore it is better to be mute than to murmur; it is dangerous to provoke a consuming fire.—Aughey.

Compensation

No evil is without its compensation.—Seneca.

One golden day redeems a weary year.—Celia Thaxter.

'Tis always morning somewhere in the world.—Richard Hengest Horne.

It is some compensation for great evils that they enforce great lessons.—Bovee.

Whoever makes great presents expects great presents in return.—Martial.

When the first is plucked, a second will not be wanting.—Virgil.

Since we are exposed to inevitable sorrows, wisdom is the art of finding compensation.—Lévis.

The equity of Providence has balanced peculiar sufferings with peculiar enjoyments.—Dr. Johnson.

If the poor man cannot always get meat, the rich man cannot always digest it.—Henry Giles.

'Tis toil's reward, that sweetens industry,
As love inspires with strength the enrap-
tur'd thrush.   —Ebenezer Elliott.

What we gave, we have:
What we spent, we had:
What we left, we lost.
—Epitaph of Edward, Earl of Devon.

If poverty makes man groan, he yawns in opulence. When fortune exempts us from labor, nature overwhelms us with time.—Rivarol.

The fiercest agonies have shortest reign;
And after dreams of horror, comes again
The welcome morning with its rays of
peace.   —William Cullen Bryant.

The rose does not bloom without thorns. True; but would that the thorns did not outlive the rose!—Richter.

We read on the forehead of those who are surrounded by a foolish luxury that Fortune sells what she is thought to give.—La Fontaine.

There is a day of sunny rest
For every dark and troubled night;
And grief may hide an evening guest,
But joy shall come with early light.
—William C. Bryant.

When fate has allowed to any man more than one great gift, accident or necessity seems usually to contrive that one shall encumber and impede the other.—Swinburne.

The poor eat always more relishable food than the rich; hunger makes the dishes sweet, and this occurs almost never with rich people.—Mahabharata.

Curses always recoil on the head of him who imprecates them. If you put a chain around the neck of a slave, the other end fastens itself around your own.—Emerson.

Nothing is pure and entire of a piece. All advantages are attended with disadvantages. A universal compensation prevails in all conditions of being and existence.—Hume.

Whatever difference may appear in the fortunes of mankind, there is, nevertheless, a certain compensation of good and evil which makes them equal.—Rochefoucauld.

O weary hearts! O slumbering eyes!
O drooping souls, whose destinies
Are fraught with fear and pain,
Ye shall be loved again.
   —Longfellow.

If the gatherer gathers too much, Nature takes out of the man what she puts into his chest; swells the estate, but kills the owner. Nature hates monopolies and exceptions.—Emerson.

And light is mingled with the gloom,
  And joy with grief;
Divinest compensations come,
Through thorns of judgment mercies bloom
In sweet relief.   —Whittier.

We devote the activity of our youth to revelry and the decrepitude of our old age to repentance: and we finish the farce by bequeathing our dead bodies to the chancel, which when living, we interdicted from the church—Colton.

There is a third silent party to all our bargains. The nature and soul of things takes on itself the guaranty of the fulfilment of every contract, so that honest service cannot come to loss.—Emerson.

If I have lost anything it was incidental; and the less money, the less trouble; the less favor, the less envy, —nay, even in those cases which put us out of our wits, it is not the loss itself, but the estimate of the loss that troubles us.—Seneca.

Universally, the better gold the worse man. The political economist defies us to show any gold mine country that is traversed by good roads, or a shore where pearls are found on which good schools are erected.— Emerson.

Under the storm and the cloud to-day,
And to-day the hard peril and pain—
To-morrow the stone shall be rolled away,
For the sunshine shall follow the rain.
Merciful Father, I will not complain,
I know that the sunshine shall follow the rain.   —Joaquin Miller.

Where there is much general deformity nature has often, perhaps generally, accorded some one bodily grace even in over-measure. So, no doubt, with the intellect and disposition, only it is frequently less apparent, and we give ourselves but little trouble to discover it.—J. F. Boyes.

As some tall cliff that lifts its awful form,
Swells from the vale, and midway leaves the storm,
Though round its breast the rolling clouds are spread,
Eternal sunshine settles on its head.
    —Goldsmith.

Earth gets its price for what Earth gives us,
The beggar is taxed for a corner to die in;
The priest has his fee who comes and shrives us,
We bargain for the graves we lie in;
At the devil's booth are all things sold,
Each ounce of dross costs its ounce of gold;
For a cap and bells our lives we pay,
Bubbles we buy with a whole soul's tasking,
'Tis heaven alone that is given away,
'Tis only God may be had for the asking,
No price is set on the lavish summer;
June may be had by the poorest comer.
    —Lowell.

As there is no worldly gain without some loss, so there is no worldly loss without some gain. If thou hast lost thy wealth, thou hast lost some trouble with it; if thou art degraded from thy honor, thou art likewise freed from the stroke of envy; if sickness hath

blurred thy beauty, it hath delivered thee from pride. Set the allowance against the loss, and thou shalt find no loss great; he loses little or nothing that reserves himself.—Quarles.

Compliments

Compliments are only lies in court clothes.

—Current among men
Like coin, the tinsel clink of compliment.
    —Tennyson.

A compliment is usually accompanied with a bow, as if to beg pardon for paying it—J. C. and A. W. Hare

Deference is the most complicate, the most indirect, and the most elegant of all compliments.—Shenstone.

He who sports compliments, unless he takes good aim, may miss his mark, and be wounded by the recoil of his own weapon.—Haliburton.

When two people compliment each other with the choice of anything, each of them generally gets that which he likes least.—Pope.

A woman * * * always feels herself complimented by love, though it may be from a man incapable of winning her heart, or perhaps even her esteem.—Abel Stevens.

Banish all compliments but single truth,
From every tongue, and every shepherd's heart,
Let them use still persuading, but no art.
    —Beaumont and Fletcher.

Though all compliments are lies, yet because they are known to be such, nobody depends on them, so there is no hurt in them; you return them in the same manner you receive them; yet it is best to make as few as one can.— Lady Gethin.

Treachery oft lurks
In compliments. You have sent so many posts
Of undertakings, they outride performance;
And make me think your fair pretences aim
At some intended ill, which my prevention
Must strive to avert.   —Nabb.

Compliments and flattery oftenest excite my contempt by the pretension they imply; for who is he that assumes to flatter me? To compliment often implies an assumption of superiority in the complimenter. It is, in fact, a subtle detraction.—Thoreau.

Compliments of congratulation are always kindly taken, and cost nothing but pen, ink and paper. I consider them as draughts upon good breeding, where the exchange is always greatly in favor of the drawer.—Chesterfield.

Compromise

Compromise makes a good umbrella, but a poor roof; it is a temporary expedient, often wise in party politics, almost sure to be unwise in statesmanship.—Lowell.

Compulsion

Force is the agent which ignorance uses for making his followers do the actions to which they are disinclined by nature; and (like an attempt to make water ascend above its level) the moment the agent ceases to act, the same instant does the operation cease.—Combe.

Concealment

If rich, it is easy enough to conceal your wealth; but if poor, it is not quite so easy to conceal your poverty. We shall find that it is less difficult to hide a thousand guineas than one hole in our coat.—Colton.

To conceal anything from those to whom I am attached, is not in my nature. I can never close my lips where I have opened my heart.—Dickens.

Conceit

Be not wise in your own conceits.—Bible.

Be not righteous overmuch.—Bible.

Conceit in weakest bodies strongest works.—Shakespeare.

I am not in the roll of common men.—Shakespeare.

Wind puffs up empty bladders; opinion, fools.—Socrates.

The art of making much show with little substance.—Macaulay.

Self-made men are most always apt to be a little too proud of the job.—H. W. Shaw.

The world knows only two, that's Rome and I.—Ben Jonson.

Every man, however little, makes a figure in his own eyes.—Henry Home.

Conceit may puff a man up, but never prop him up.—Ruskin.

Faith, that's as well said as if I had said it myself.—Swift.

Nature has sometimes made a fool, but a coxcomb is always of a man's own making.—Addison.

The certain way to be cheated is to fancy one's self more cunning than others.—Charron.

He who gives himself airs of importance exhibits the credentials of impotence.—Lavater.

The weakest spot in every man is where he thinks himself to be the wisest.—Emmons.

No man was ever so much deceived by another as by himself.—Lord Greville.

The more any one speaks of himself, the less he likes to hear another talked of.—Lavater.

A man who is proud of small things shows that small things are great to him.—Madame de Girardin.

The miller imagines that the corn grows only to make his mill turn.—Goethe.

One whom the music of his own vain tongue doth ravish like enchanting harmony.—Shakespeare.

We think our fathers fools, so wise we grow;
Our wiser sons, no doubt, will thing us so.
—Pope.

Strong conceit, like a new principle, carries all easily with it, when yet above common-sense.—Locke.

I say that conceit is just as natural a thing to human minds as a centre to a circle.—Holmes.

Seest thou a man wise in his own conceit? There is more hope of a fool than of him.—Bible.

Man believes himself always greater than he is, and is esteemed less than he is worth.—Goethe.

A strong conceit is . rich; so most men deem:
If not to be, 'tis comfort yet to seem.
—Marston.

The best of lessons, for a good many people, would be to listen at a keyhole. It is a pity for such that the practice is dishonorable.—Madame Swetchine.

Self-love is better than any gilding to make that seem gorgeous wherein ourselves be parties.—Sir P. Sidney.

The cuckoo drinks the celestial juice of the mango-tree, and is not proud; the frog drinks swamp-water, and quacks with conceit.—Varuki.

Conceit and confidence are both of them cheats; the first always imposes on itself, the second frequently deceives others too.—Zimmermann.

How wise are we in thought! how weak in practice! our very virtue, like our will, is—nothing.—Shirley.

Conceited people are never without a certain degree of harmless satisfaction wherewith to flavor the waters of life.—Madame Deluzy.

It is the admirer of himself, and not the admirer of virtue, that thinks himself superior to others.—Plutarch.

Men are found to be vainer on account of those qualities which they fondly believe they have than of those which they really have.—Voiture.

A man—poet, prophet, or whatever he may be—readily persuades himself of his right to all the worship that is voluntarily tendered.—Hawthorne.

We go and fancy that everybody is thinking of us. But he is not; he is like us—he is thinking of himself.—Charles Reade.

A man who is always well satisfied with himself is seldom so with others, and others as little pleased with him.—La Rochefoucauld.

One's self-satisfaction is an untaxed kind of property, which it is very unpleasant to find depreciated.—George Eliot.

Those who differ most from the opinions of their fellow-men are the most confident of the truth of their own.—Mackintosh.

Conceit is to nature what paint is to beauty; it is not only needless, but impairs what it would improve.—Pope.

Everything without tells the individual that he is nothing; everything within persuades him that he is everything.—X. Doudan.

I've never any pity for conceited people, because I think they carry their comfort about with them.—George Eliot.

There is scarcely any man, how much soever he may despise the character of a flatterer, but will condescend in the meanest manner to flatter himself.—Fielding.

Conceited men often seem a harmless kind of men, who, by an overweening self-respect, relieve others from the duty of respecting them at all.—Beecher.

None are so seldom found alone, and are so soon tired of their own company, as those coxcombs who are on the best terms with themselves.—Colton.

Conceit is the most contemptible and one of the most odious qualities in the world. It is vanity driven from all other shifts, and forced to appeal to itself for admiration.—Hazlitt.

Every man deems that he has precisely the trials and temptations which are the hardest of all for him to bear; but they are so, because they are the very ones he needs.—Richter.

No wonder we are all more or less pleased with mediocrity, since it leaves us at rest, and gives the same comfortable feeling as when one associates with his equals.—Goethe.

It is a fact which escapes no one, that, generally speaking, whoso is acquainted with his worth has but a little stock to cultivate acquaintance with.—Carlyle.

Conceit, more rich in matter than in words, Brags of his substance, not of ornament: They are but beggars that can count their worth. —Shakespeare.

An eagerness and zeal for dispute on every subject, and with every one, shows great self-sufficiency, that never-failing sign of great self-ignorance.— Lord Chatham.

Drawn by conceit from reason's plan How vain is that poor creature man; How pleas'd in ev'ry paltry elf To prate about that thing himself. —Churchill.

We judge of others for the most part by their good opinion of themselves; yet nothing gives such offense or creates so many enemies, as that extreme self-complacency or supercili-ousness of manner, which appears to set the opinion of every one else at defiance.—Hazlitt.

Be very slow to believe that you are wiser than all others; it is a fatal but common error. Where one has been saved by a true estimation of another's weakness, thousands have been destroyed by a false appreciation of their own strength.—Colton.

This self-conceit is a most dangerous shelf Where many have made shipwreck unawares; He who doth trust too much unto himself Can never fail to fall in many snares. —Earl of Stirling.

All affectation and display proceed from the supposition of possessing something better than the rest of the world possesses. Nobody is vain in possessing two legs and two arms; because that is the precise quantity of either sort of limb which everybody possesses.—Sydney Smith.

Whoe'er imagines prudence all his own, Or deems that he hath powers to speak and judge Such as none other hath, when they are known, They are found shallow. —Sophocles.

They say it was Liston's firm belief, that he was a great and neglected tragic actor; they say that every one of us believes in his heart, or would like to have others believe, that he is something which he is not.—Thackeray.

A school of art or of anything else is to be looked on as a single individual, who keeps talking to himself for a hundred years, and feels an extreme satisfaction with his own circle of favorite ideas, be they ever so silly.— Goethe.

Men educate each other in reason by contact or collision, and keep each other sane by the very conflict of their separate hobbies. Society as a whole is the deadly enemy of the particular crotchet of each, and solitude is almost the only condition in which the acorn of conceit can grow to the oak of perfect self-delusion.—Whipple.

Nature descends down to infinite smallness. Great men have their parasites; and, if you take a large buzzing blue-bottle fly, and look at it in a microscope, you may see twenty or thirty little ugly insects crawling about it, which, doubtless, think their fly to be the bluest, grandest, merriest, most important animal in the universe, and are convinced the world would be at an end if it ceased to buzz.—Sydney Smith.

Conceit is just as natural a thing to human minds as a centre is to a circle. But little-minded people's thoughts move in such small circles that five minutes' conversation gives you an arc long enough to determine their whole curve. An arc in the movement of a large intellect does not differ sensibly from a straight line.—Holmes.

But the conceit of one's self and the conceit of one's hobby are hardly more prolific of eccentricity than the conceit of one's money. Avarice, the most hateful and wolfish of all the hard, cool, callous dispositions of selfishness, has its own peculiar caprices and crotchets. The ingenuities of its meanness defy all the calculations of reason, and reach the miraculous in subtlety. —Whipple.

Success seems to be that which forms the distinction between confidence and conceit. Nelson, when young, was piqued at not being noticed in a certain paragraph of the newspapers, which detailed an action wherein he had assisted. "But never mind," said he, "I will one day have a gazette of my own."—Colton.

Talk about conceit as much as you like, it is to human character what salt is to the ocean; it keeps it sweet and renders it endurable. Say rather it is like the natural unguent of the seafowl's plumage, which enables him to shed the rain that falls on him and the wave in which he dips. When one has had all his conceit taken out of him, when he has lost all his illusions, his feathers will soon soak through, and he will fly no more.—Holmes.

Conciliation

Agree with thine adversary quickly while thou art in the way with him.—Bible.

It is the part of a prudent man to conciliate the minds of others, and to turn them to his own advantage.—Cicero.

Conduct

A man, like a watch, is to be valued for his manner of going.—William Penn.

The integrity of men is to be measured by their conduct, not by their professions.—Junius.

And let men so conduct themselves in life As to be always strangers to defeat.
—Cicero.

The conduct of men depends upon the temperament, not upon a bunch of musty maxims.—Beaconsfield.

No books are so legible as the lives of men; no character so plain as their moral conduct.—Aughey.

Take heed lest passion sway
Thy judgment to do aught which else free-will
Would not admit.   —Milton.

Those virtues which cost us dear prove that we love God; those which are easy to us prove that He loves us. —J. Petit-Senn.

To do evil is more within the reach of every man, in public as in private life, than to do good.—Dr. Parr.

All the while thou livest ill, thou hast the trouble, distraction, inconveniences of life, but not the sweets and true use of it.—Fuller.

That conduct sometimes seems ridiculous, in the eyes of the world, the secret reasons for which, may, in reality, be wise and solid.—Rochefoucauld.

I would, God knows, in a poor woodman's hut
Have spent my peaceful days, and shared my crust
With her who would have cheer'd me, rather far
Than on this throne; but being what I am,
I'll be it nobly.   —Joanna Baillie.

Have more than thou showest,
Speak less than thou knowest,
Lend less than thou owest,
Learn more than thou trowest,
Set less than thou throwest.
                —Shakespeare.

Obey thy parents, keep thy word justly; swear not; commit not with man's sworn spouse; set not thy sweet heart on proud array. * * * Keep thy foot out of brothels, thy pen from lenders' books.—Shakespeare.

It is not enough that you can form, nay, and follow, the most excellent rules for conducting yourself in the world. You must also know when to deviate from them, and where lies the exception.—Greville.

I will govern my life, and my thoughts, as if the whole world were to see the one, and to read the other;

for what does it signify to make anything a secret to my neighbor, when to God (who is the searcher of our hearts) all our privacies are open?—Seneca.

Only add
Deeds to thy knowledge answerable, add faith,
Add virtue, patience, temperance, add love,
By name to come call'd charity, the soul
Of all the rest; then wilt thou not be loath
To leave this Paradise, but shalt possess
A Paradise within thee, happier far.
—Milton.

As in walking it is your great care not to run your foot upon a nail, or to tread awry, and strain your leg; so let it be in all the affairs of human life, not to hurt your mind or offend your judgment. And this rule, if observed carefully in all your deportment, will be a mighty security to you in your undertakings.—Epictetus.

Confession

Confess yourself to heaven;
Repent what's past; avoid what is to come.
—Shakespeare.

Why does no man confess his vices? Because he is yet in them; it is for a waking man to tell his dream.—Seneca.

A man should never be ashamed to own he has been in the wrong, which is but saying, in other words, that he is wiser to-day than he was yesterday.—Pope.

If thou wouldst be justified, acknowledge thy injustice; he that confesses his sin begins his journey toward salvation; he that is sorry for it mends his pace; he that forsakes it is at his journey's end.—Quarles.

Come, now again thy woes impart,
Tell all thy sorrows, all thy sin;
We cannot heal the throbbing heart,
Till we discern the wounds within.
—Crabbe.

Unless we realize our sins enough to call them by name, it is hardly worth while to say anything about them at all. When we pray for forgiveness, let us say, "my temper," or "untruthfulness," or "pride," "my selfishness, my cowardice, indolence, jealousy, revenge, impurity." To recognize our sins, we must look them in the face and call them by their right names, however hard. Honesty in confession calls for definiteness in confession.—Maltbie Babcock.

Confidence

Society is built upon trust.—South.

Self-trust is the essence of heroism.—Emerson.

Security is mortal's chiefest enemy.—Shakespeare.

Be not confident and affirmative.—Jeremy Taylor.

For they can conquer who believe they can.—Dryden.

Trust not him that hath once broken faith.—Shakespeare.

Confidence is nowhere safe.—Virgil.

Confidence is a plant of slow growth in an aged bosom.—William Pitt.

He knows little who will tell his wife all he knows.—Thomas Fuller.

He who has lost confidence can lose nothing more.—Boiste.

Thou know'st how fearless is my trust in thee.—Miss L. E. Landon.

He is safe who admits no one to his confidence.—Rochefoucauld.

Confidence imparts a wonderful inspiration to its possessor.—Milton.

Be as just and gracious unto me,
As I am confident and kind to thee.
—Shakespeare.

He that wold not when he might,
He shall not when he wold-a.
—Percy.

Your wisdom is consum'd in confidence.
Do not go forth to-day. —Shakespeare.

Fields are won by those who believe in the winning.—T. W. Higginson.

Wise men have but few confidants, and cunning ones none.—H. W. Shaw.

He who believes in nobody knows that he himself is not to be trusted.—Auerbach.

Confidence in another man's virtue is no slight evidence of a man's own.—Montaigne.

Confidence in conversation has a greater share than wit.—Rochefoucauld.

It is almost always to save telling a great deal that women tell a little to their husbands.—Rochebrune.

Surely modesty never hurt any cause; and the confidence of man seems to me to be much like the wrath of man.—Tillotson.

Trust him little who praises all, him less who censures all, and him least who is indifferent about all.—Lavater.

A noble heart, like the sun, showeth its greatest confidence in its lowest estate.—Sir P. Sidney.

Trust him with little who, without proofs, trusts you with everything, or, when he has proved you, with nothing. —Lavater.

Confidence is that feeling by which the mind embarks in great and honorable courses with a sure hope and trust in itself.—Cicero.

Confidence, as opposed to modesty and distinguished from decent assurance, proceeds from self-opinion, and is occasioned by ignorance and flattery. —Jeremy Collier.

He who does not respect confidence, will never find happiness in his path. The belief in virtue vanishes from his heart, the source of nobler actions becomes extinct in him.—Auffenberg.

Whatever distrust we may have of the sincerity of those who converse with us, we always believe they will tell us more truth than they do to others.—La Rochefoucauld.

The hearing ear is always found close to the speaking tongue; and no genius can long or often utter anything which is not invited and gladly entertained by men around him.—Emerson.

We may have the confidence of another without possessing his heart. If his heart be ours, there is no need of revelation or of confidence,—all is open to us.—Du Cœur.

To reveal imprudently the spot where we are most sensitive and vulnerable is to invite a blow. The demigod Achilles admitted no one to his confidence.—Madame Swetchine.

There is something captivating in spirit and intrepidity, to which we often yield as to a resistless power; nor can he reasonably expect the confidence of others who too apparently distrusts himself.—Hazlitt.

It is unjust and absurd of persons advancing in years, to expect of the young that confidence should come all and only on their side; the human heart, at whatever age, opens only to the heart that opens in return.—Miss Edgeworth.

I see before me the statue of a celebrated minister, who said that confidence was a plant of slow growth. But I believe, however gradual may be the growth of confidence, that of credit requires still more time to arrive at maturity.—Benj. Disraeli.

Where there is any good disposition, confidence begets faithfulness; but distrust, if it do not produce treachery, never fails to destroy every inclination to evince fidelity. Most people disdain to clear themselves from the accusations of mere suspicion.—Jane Porter.

Most frequently we make confidants from vanity, a love of talking, a wish to win the confidence of others, and to make an exchange of secrets.—La Rochefoucauld.

Never put much confidence in such as put no confidence in others. A man prone to suspect evil is mostly looking in his neighbor for what he sees in himself. As to the pure all things are pure, even so to the impure all things are impure.—Hare.

Confidence always pleases those who receive it. It is a tribute we pay to their merit, a deposit we commit to their trust, a pledge that gives them a claim upon us, a kind of dependence to which we voluntarily submit.—La Rochefoucauld.

All confidence which is not absolute and entire is dangerous; there are few occasions but where a man ought either to say all or conceal all; for how little soever you have revealed of your secret to a friend, you have already said too much if you think it not safe to make him privy to all particulars.—J. Beaumont.

Confidence is conqueror of men; victorious
  both over them and in them;
The iron will of one stout heart shall make
  a thousand quail:
A feeble dwarf, dauntlessly resolved, will
  turn the tide of battle,
And rally to a nobler strife the giants that
  had fled.   —Tupper.

There is a kind of greatness which does not depend upon fortune; it is a certain manner that distinguishes us, and which seems to destine us for great things; it is the value we insensibly set upon ourselves; it is by this quality that we gain the deference of other men, and it is this which commonly raises us more above them, than birth, rank, or even merit itself.—La Rochefoucauld.

Let not the quietness of any man's temper, much less the confidence he has in thy honesty and goodness, tempt thee to contrive any mischief against him; for the more securely he relies on thy virtue, and the less mistrust he has of any harm from thee, the greater wickedness will it be to entertain even the thought of doing him an injury.—Bishop Patrick.

People have generally three epochs in their confidence in man. In the first they believe him to be everything that is good, and they are lavish with their friendship and confidence. In the next, they have had experience, which has smitten down their confi-dence, and they then have to be careful not to mistrust every one, and to put the worst construction upon everything. Later in life, they learn that the greater number of men have much more good in them than bad, and that even when there is cause to blame, there is more reason to pity than condemn; and then a spirit of confidence again awakens within them.—Fredrikå Bremer.

When young, we trust ourselves too much, and we trust others too little when old. Rashness is the error of youth, timid caution of age. Manhood is the isthmus between the two extremes; the ripe and fertile season of action, when alone we can hope to find the head to contrive, united with the hand to execute.—Colton.

Confirmation

Believe and be confirmed.—Milton.

Confirmation is a most solemn and important ordinance.—Bishop Oxenden.

Whether confirmation be a sacrament or not, it is no use to dispute; and if it be disputed, it cannot follow that it is not of very great use and holiness.—Jeremy Taylor.

Conjecture

Our conjectures are like our hopes. —Jane Taylor.

Conjecture as to things useful is good; but conjecture as to what it would be useless to know, such as whether men went upon all-four, is very idle.—Dr. Johnson.

Conquest

I came, I saw, I conquered.—Julius Cæsar.

Self-conquest is the greatest of victories.—Plato.

How grand is victory, but how dear! —Boufflers.

He conquers twice who conquers himself in victory.—Syrus.

We triumph without glory when we conquer without danger.—Corneille.

You will hardly conquer, but conquer you must.—Ovid.

Yield to him who opposes you; by yielding you conquer.—Ovid.

He who surpasses or subdues mankind must look down on the hate of those below.—Byron.

Anticipation leads the way to victory, and is the spur to conquest.—Chamfort.

Then fly betimes, for only they
Conquer love that run away.
—Thomas Carew.

A victory is twice itself when the achiever brings home full numbers.—Shakespeare.

The more acquisitions the government makes abroad, the more taxes the people have to pay at home.—Thomas Paine.

Know that the slender shrub which is seen to bend, conquers when it yields to the storm.—Metastasio.

It is the right of war for conquerors to treat those whom they have conquered according to their pleasure.—Cæsar.

Brave conquerors! for so you are
That war against your own affections,
And the huge army of the world's desires.
—Shakespeare.

Great things thro' the greatest hazards are achiev'd,
And then they shine.
—Beaumont and Fletcher.

I claim by right
Of conquest; for when kings make war,
No law betwixt two sov'reigns can decide,
But that of arms, where fortune is the judge,
Soldiers the lawyers, and the bar the field.
—Dryden.

Hannibal knew better how to conquer than how to profit by the conquest; and Napoleon was more skilful in taking positions than in maintaining them. As to reverses, no general can presume to say that he may not be defeated; but he can, and ought to say, that he will not be surprised.—Colton.

Conscience

A still, small voice.—I Kings xix. 12

Conscience is a thousand swords.—Shakespeare.

The only infallible judge.—Hosea Ballou.

Conscience is the voice of God in the soul.—Aughey.

The soft whispers of the God in man.—Young.

Conscience is justice's best minister.—Lady Montagu.

Conscience is its own counsellor.—South.

Man's conscience is the oracle of God!—Byron.

There is no college for the conscience.—Theodore Parker.

God's vicegerent in the soul.—Buchan.

The pulse of reason.—Coleridge.

Reason deceives us often; conscience never.—Rousseau.

No infallible oracle out of the breast.—Rev. Dr. Hedge.

The conscience is more wise than science.—Lavater.

Let his tormentor conscience find him out.—Milton.

The great theatre for virtue is conscience.—Cicero.

How awful is that hour when conscience stings.—Percival.

Conscience is the sentinel of virtue.—Johnson.

A wounded conscience is able to unparadise paradise itself.—Fuller.

Conscience is God's deputy in the soul.—Rev. T. Adams.

Conscience is the chamber of justice.—Origen.

What exile from himself can flee?—Byron.

The sense of right.—Dr. Watson.

A good conscience is a continual Christmas.—Franklin.

The thundering voice that wrings, in one dark, damning moment, crimes of years!—Percival.

No evil is intolerable but a guilty conscience.—Channing.

Conscience is its own readiest accuser.—Chapin.

The still small voice is wanted.—Cowper.

The torture of a bad conscience is the hell of a living soul.—Calvin.

A sound conscience is a brazen wall of defense.—From the Latin.

Trust that man in nothing who has not a conscience in everything.—Sterne.

Good conscience is sometimes sold for money, but never bought with it.—Aughey.

Despotic conscience rules our hopes and fears.—Ovid.

A good conscience is the best looking-glass of heaven.—Cudworth.

The most exacting jailer is our own conscience.—J. Petit-Senn.

The only incorruptible thing about us.—Fielding.

Conscience is a sacred sanctuary where God alone may enter as judge.—Lamennais.

By the verdict of his own breast no guilty man is ever acquitted.—Juvenal.

The tribunal of conscience exists independent of edicts and decrees.—Burke.

One self-approving hour whole years outweighs.—Pope.

No outward change need trouble him who is inwardly serene.—Hosea Ballou.

Conscience has no more to do with gallantry than it has with politics.—Sheridan.

The conscience of the dying belies their life.—Vauvenargues.

Many a lash in the dark doth conscience give the wicked.—Boston.

Rules of society are nothing, one's conscience is the umpire.—Madame Dudevant.

A man of integrity will never listen to any reason against conscience.—Home.

The sweetest cordial we receive at last,
Is conscience of our virtuous actions past.
—Goffe.

Suspicion always haunts the guilty mind;
The thief doth fear each bush an officer.
—Shakespeare.

The mind conscious of innocence despises false reports; but we are always ready to believe a scandal.—Ovid.

The Unknown is an ocean. What is conscience? The compass of the Unknown.—Joseph Cook.

Heed the still, small voice that so seldom leads us wrong, and never into folly.—Mme. du Deffand.

I feel within me a peace above all earthly dignities, a still and quiet conscience.—Shakespeare.

Conscience is but a word that cowards use,
Devised at first to keep the strong in awe.
—Shakespeare.

Labor to keep alive in your breast that little spark of celestial fire, called Conscience.—George Washington.

Most men are afraid of a bad name, but few fear their consciences.—Pliny.

Nor ear can hear nor tongue can tell
The tortures of that inward hell!
—Byron.

Conscience serves us especially to judge of the actions of others.—J. Petit-Senn.

Conscience is harder than our enemies,
Knows more, accuses with more nicety.
—George Eliot.

Ah, what a sign it is of evil life,
Where death's approach is seen so terrible!
—Shakespeare.

The conscience is the inviolable asylum of the liberty of man.—Napoleon.

No man ever offended his own conscience but first or last it was revenged upon him for it.—South.

I seek no better warrant than my own conscience.—Sir P. Sidney.

Conscience is the reason employed about questions of right and wrong.—Whewell.

What we call conscience, in many instances, is only a wholesome fear of the constable.—Bovee.

Conscience warns us as a friend before it punishes us as a judge.—Stanislaus.

The great chastisement of a knave is not to be known, but to know himself.—J. Petit-Senn.

Let us be thankful for health and competence, and, above all, for a quiet conscience.—Izaak Walton.

Leave her to heaven and to those thorns that in her bosom lodge, to prick and sting her.—Shakespeare.

Conscience is the living law, and honor is to this law what piety is to religion.—Boufflers.

There is no evil which we cannot face or fly from but the consciousness of duty disregarded.—Daniel Webster.

Conscience and wealth are not always neighbors.—Massinger.

Be fearful only of thyself, and stand in awe of none more than thine own conscience.—Burton.

In matters of conscience first thoughts are best; in matters of prudence last thoughts are best.—Rev. Robert Hall.

We never do evil so effectually as when we are led to do it by a false principle of conscience.—Pascal.

If you should escape the censure of others, hope not to escape your own.—Henry Home.

There is in man a conscienc which outlives the sensations, reso utions, and emotions of the hour, and rises above them all.—Edward Thomson.

Conscience is that peculiar faculty of the soul which may be called the religious instinct.—Samuel Smiles.

The voice of conscience is so delicate that it is easy to stifle it; but it is also so clear that it is impossible to mistake it.—Madame de Staël.

The virtuous mind that ever walks attended
By a strong siding champion, Conscience.
—Harrison.

See from behind her secret stand
The sly informer minutes ev'ry fault
And her dread diary with horror fills.
—Young.

A good conscience is the palace of Christ; the temple of the Holy Ghost; the paradise of delight; the standing Sabbath of the saints.—Augustine.

There is one court whose "findings" are incontrovertible, and whose sessions are held in the chambers of our own breast.—Hosea Ballou.

Conscience is merely our own judgment of the moral rectitude or turpitude of our own actions.—Locke.

What other dungeon is so dark as one's own heart? What jailer so inexorable as one's self?—Hawthorne.

Our secret thoughts are rarely heard except in secret. No man knows what conscience is until he understands what solitude can teach him concerning it.—Joseph Cook.

Foul whisp'rings are abroad; and unnat'ral deeds
Do breed unnat'ral troubles: infected minds
To their deaf pillows will discharge their secrets.   —Shakespeare.

Every one of us, whatever his speculative opinions, knows better than he practices, and recognizes a better law than he obeys.—James A. Froude.

He that hath a scrupulous conscience is like a horse that is not well weighed; he starts at every bird that flies out of the hedge.—Selden.

I believe that we cannot live better than in seeking to become better, nor more agreeably than having a clear conscience.—Socrates.

A guilty conscience is like a whirlpool, drawing in all to itself which would otherwise pass by.—Fuller.

O conscience, into what abyss of fears and horrors hast thou driven me, out of which I find no way, from deep to deeper plunged.—Milton.

O the wound of conscience is no scar, and time cools it not with his wing, but merely keeps it open with his scythe.—Richter.

Conscience is the mirror of our souls, which represents the errors of our lives in their full shape.—Bancroft.

There is no class of men so difficult to be managed in a state, as those whose intentions are honest, but whose consciences are bewitched.—Napoleon.

We should have all our communications with men, as in the presence of God; and with God, as in the presence of men.—Colton.

Conscience, that boon companion who sets a man free under the strong breastplate of innocence, that bids him on and fear not.—Dante.

I am more afraid of my own heart than of the pope and all his cardinals. I have within me the great pope, self.—Luther.

Our faults afflict us more than our good deeds console. Pain is ever uppermost in the conscience as in the heart.—Madame Swetchine.

Conscience, that vicegerent of God in the human heart, whose "still small voice" the loudest revelry cannot drown.—W. H. Harrison.

A man never outlives his conscience, and that, for this cause only, he cannot outlive himself.—South.

There is no future pang can deal that justice on the self-condemned he deals on his own soul.—Byron.

That conscience approves of and attests such a course of action, is itself alone an obligation—Butler.

The true grandeur of humanity is in moral elevation, sustained, enlightened, and decorated by the intellect of man.—Charles Sumner.

Be this thy brazen bulwark, to keep a clear conscience, and never turn pale with guilt.—Horace.

Light as a gossamer is the circumstance, which can bring enjoyment to a conscience, which is not its own accuser.—W. Carleton.

Liberty of conscience (when people have consciences) is rightly considered the most indispensable of liberties.—Chambers.

Thrice is he arm'd, that hath his quarrel just;
And he but naked, though lock'd up in steel,
Whose conscience with injustice is corrupted.   —Shakespeare.

Who has a heart so pure but some uncleanly apprehensions keep leets and law-days, and in session sit with meditations awful?—Shakespeare.

Happy is the man who renounces everything which may bring a stain or burden upon his conscience.—Thomas à Kempis.

A quiet conscience makes one so serene!
Christians have burnt each other, quite persuaded
That all the apostles would have done as
  they did.   —Byron.

Why should not conscience have vacation,
As well as other courts o' th' nation?
Have equal power to adjourn,
Appoint appearance, and return?
              —Butler.

A man's first care should be to avoid the reproaches of his own heart; his next, to escape the censures of the world.—Addison.

Conscience is a blushing, shame-faced spirit that mutinies in a man's bosom; it fills one full of obstacles.—Shakespeare.

Conscience never commands nor forbids anything authentically, but there is some law of God which commands and forbids it first.—South.

A man can bear a world's contempt when he has that within which says he's worthy. When he contemns himself, there burns the hell.—Alexander Smith.

It is often easier to justify one's self to others than to respond to the secret doubts that arise in one's own bosom.—Mrs. Oliphant.

If we regulate our conduct according to our own convictions, we may safely disregard the praise or censure of others.—Pascal.

Conscience is a coward; and those faults it has not strength enough to prevent it seldom has justice enough to accuse.—Goldsmith.

The authority of conscience stands founded upon its vicegerency and deputation under God.—South.

The most miserable pettifogging in the world is that of a man in the court of his own conscience.—Beecher.

Merit and good works is the end of man's motion, and conscience of the same is the accomplishment of man's rest.—Bacon.

I must leave you to the satisfaction of your own conscience, which, though a silent panegyric, is yet the best.—Dryden.

As the blush is the signal of innocence, so is serenity of manner the token of a quiet conscience.—Mme. Necker.

Undoubtedly we render our consciences callous by evil indulgences; but we cannot entirely subdue that still, small voice.—Beecher.

Thus conscience does make cowards of us
  all;
And thus the native hue of resolution
Is sicklied o'er with the pale cast of
  thought.   —Shakespeare.

As the mind of each man is conscious of good or evil, so does he conceive within his breast hope or fear, according to his actions.—Ovid.

Man, wretched man, whene'er he stoops to
  sin,
Feels, with the act, a strong remorse within.
              —Juvenal.

The Past lives o'er again
In its effects, and to the guilty spirit
The ever-frowning Present is its image.
              —Coleridge.

It is as bad to clip conscience as to clip coin; it is as bad to give a counterfeit statement as a counterfeit bill.—Chapin.

Be more careful of your conscience than of your estate. The latter can be bought and sold; the former never.—Hosea Ballou.

Trust me no tortures which the poets feign
Can match the fierce unutterable pain
He feels, who night and day devoid of rest
Carries his own accuser in his breast.
              —Gifford.

Better be with the dead, whom we, to gain our place, have sent to peace, than on the torture of the mind to lie in restless ecstasy.—Shakespeare.

Yet still there whispers the small voice within,
Heard thro' gain's silence, and o'er glory's din;
Whatever creed be taught or land be trod,
Man's conscience is the oracle of God!
—Byron.

Here, here it lies; a lump of lead by day;
And in my short distracted nightly slumbers,
The hag that rides my dreams.
—Dryden.

Though thy slumber may be deep.
Yet thy spirit will not sleep;
There are shades that will not vanish,
There are thoughts thou canst not banish.
—Byron.

A man who sells his conscience for his interest, will sell it for his pleasure. A man who will betray his country, will betray his friend.—Miss Edgeworth.

Even in the fiercest uproar of our stormy passions, conscience, though in her softest whispers, gives to the supremacy of rectitude the voice of an undying testimony.—Chalmers.

Let a prince be guarded with soldiers, attended by councillors, and shut up in forts; yet if his thoughts disturb him, he is miserable.—Plutarch.

If thou wouldst be informed what God has written concerning thee in Heaven look into thine own bosom, and see what graces He hath there wrought in thee.—Fuller.

But, at sixteen, the conscience rarely gnaws
So much, as when we call our old debts in
At sixty years, and draw the accounts of evil,
And find a deuced balance with the devil.
—Byron.

The color of the king doth come and go,
Between his purpose and his conscience,
Like heralds 'twixt two dreadful battles set:
His passion is so ripe, it needs must break.
—Shakespeare.

He that hath a blind conscience which sees nothing, a dead conscience which feels nothing, and a dumb conscience which says nothing, is in as miserable a condition as a man can be on this side of hell.—Patrick Henry.

In the commission of evil, fear no man so much as thyself; another is but one witness against thee, thou art a thousand; another thou mayest avoid, thyself thou canst not. Wickedness is its own punishment.—Quarles.

A man, so to speak, who is not able to bow to his own conscience every morning is hardly in a condition to respectfully salute the world at any other time of the day.—Douglas Jerrold.

What Conscience dictates to be done,
Or warns me not to do;
This teach me more than Hell to shun,
That more than Heav'n pursue.
—Pope.

Oh! think what anxious moments pass between
The birth of plots, and their last fatal periods,
Oh! 'tis a dreadful interval of time,
Filled up with horror all, and big with death!
—Addison.

Some persons follow the dictates of their conscience only in the same sense in which a coachman may be said to follow the horses he is driving.—Whately.

The world will never be in any manner of order or tranquillity until men are firmly convinced that conscience, honor and credit are all in one interest; and that without the concurrence of the former the latter are but impositions upon ourselves and others.—Steele.

It is a man's own dishonesty, his crimes, his wickedness, and boldness, that takes away from him soundness of mind; these are the furies, these the flames and firebrands, of the wicked.—Cicero.

Remorse of conscience is like an old wound; a man is in no condition to fight under such circumstances. The pain abates his vigor and takes up too much of his attention.—Jeremy Collier.

Preserve your conscience always soft and sensitive. If but one sin force its way into that tender part of the soul and dwell there, the road is paved for a thousand iniquities.—Watts.

Man is naturally more desirous of a quiet and approving, than of a vigilant and tender conscience,—more desirous of security than of safety.—Whately.

Our conscience is a fire within us, and our sins as the fuel; instead of warming, it will scorch us, unless the fuel be removed, or the heat of it allayed by penitential tears.—Dr. Mason.

Conscience and covetousness are never to be reconciled; like fire and water they always destroy each other, according to the predominancy of the element.—Jeremy Collier.

A good conscience is never lawless in the worst regulated state, and will provide those laws for itself which the neglect of legislators had forgotten to supply.—Fielding.

A man's own conscience is his sole tribunal, and he should care no more for that phantom "opinion" than he should fear meeting a ghost if he crossed the churchyard at dark.—Bulwer-Lytton.

Conscience is a great ledger book in which all our offences are written and registered, and which time reveals to the sense and feeling of the offender.—Burton.

A tender conscience is an inestimable blessing; that is, a conscience not only quick to discern what is evil, but instantly to shun it, as the eyelid closes itself against the mote.—Rev. N. Adams.

Oh the difference of divers men in the tenderness of their consciences! Some are scarcely touched with a wound, while others are wounded with a touch therein.—Thomas Fuller.

Let not your peace rest in the utterances of men, for whether they put a good or bad construction on your conduct does not make you other than you are.—Thomas à Kempis.

I have somewhere read that conscience not only sits as witness and

judge within our bosoms, but also forms the prison of punishment.—Hosea Ballou.

Now conscience wakes despair
That slumber'd, wakes the bitter memory,
Of what he was, what is, what must be
Worse; if worst deeds, worse sufferings
must ensue.   —Milton.

A good conscience is to the soul what health is to the body; it preserves a constant ease and serenity within us, and more than countervails all the calamities and afflictions that can possibly befall us.—Addison.

The breast of a good man is a little heaven commencing on earth; where the Deity sits enthroned with unrivaled influence, every subjugated passion, "like the wind and storm, fulfilling his word."—Colton.

Oh! Conscience! Conscience! Man's most
faithful friend,
Him canst thou comfort, ease, relieve, defend:
But if he will thy friendly checks forego,
Thou art, oh! woe for me, his deadliest foe!
                          —Crabbe.

Conscience is a clock which, in one man, strikes aloud and gives warning; in another, the hand points silently to the figure, but strikes not. Meantime, hours pass away, and death hastens, and after death comes judgment.—Jeremy Taylor.

He that has light within his own clear
breast,
May sit i' the centre, and enjoy bright day;
But he that hides a dark soul, and foul
thoughts,
Benighted walks under the mid-day sun;
Himself is his own dungeon.
                          —Milton.

To say that we have a clear conscience is to utter a solecism; had we never sinned we should have had no conscience. Were defeat unknown, neither would victory be celebrated by songs of triumph.—Carlyle.

He that loses his conscience has nothing left that is worth keeping. Therefore be sure you look to that, and in the next place look to your health; and if you have it, praise God and value it next to a good conscience. —Izaak Walton.

A good conscience is a port which is landlocked on every side, where no winds can possibly invade. There a man may not only see his own image, but that of his Maker, clearly reflected from the undisturbed waters.— Dryden.

Be what it may, let the first whisper of the internal monitor be listened to as an oracle, as the still small voice which Elijah heard when he wrapped his face in his mantle, recognizing it to be the voice of God.—Robert Hall.

Conscience is, at once, the sweetest and most troublesome of guests. It is the voice which demanded Abel of his brother, or that celestial harmony which vibrated in the ears of the martyrs, and soothed their sufferings.— Madame Swetchine.

God, in His wrath, has not left this world to the mercy of the subtlest dialectician; and all arguments are happily transitory in their effect when they contradict the primal intuitions of conscience and the inborn sentiments of the heart.—Whipple.

We are born to lose and to perish, to hope and to fear, to vex ourselves and others; and there is no antidote against a common calamity but virtue; for the foundation of true joy is in the conscience.—Seneca.

Oh! I have past a miserable night!
So full of fearful dreams, of ugly sights,
That as I am a Christian faithful man,
I would not spend another such a night,
Though 't were to buy a world of happy
  days!   —Shakespeare.

No outward tryanny can reach the mind. If conscience plays the tyrant, it would be greatly for the benefit of the world that she were more arbitrary, and far less placable than some men find her.—Junius.

The moral conscience is a truly primitive faculty; it is a particular manner of feeling which corresponds to the goodness of moral actions, as taste is a manner of feeling which cor-

responds to beauty. Love men, immolate error.—St. Augustine.

The impulse which directs to right conduct, and deters from crime, is not only older than the ages of nations and cities, but coeval with that Divine Being who sees and rules both heaven and earth.—Cicero.

Who born so poor,
Of intellect so mean, as not to know
What seem'd the best; and knowing not to
  do?
As not to know what God and conscience
  bade,
And what they bade not able to obey?
                          —Pollok.

Not all the glory, all the praise,
That decks the hero's prosperous days,
The shout of men, the laurel crown,
The pealing anthems of renown,
May conscience' dreadful sentence drown.
                          —Mrs. Holford.

Alas, that we should be so unwilling to listen to the still and holy yearnings of the heart! A god whispers quite softly in our breast, softly yet audibly; telling us what we ought to seek and what to shun.—Goethe.

When Conscience wakens who can with her
  strive?
Terrors and troubles from a sick soul drive?
Naught so unpitying as the ire of sin,
The inappeas'ble Nemesis within.
                          —Abraham Coles.

Be fearful only of thyself; and stand in awe of none more than thine own conscience. There is a Cato in every man; a severe censor of his manners. And he that reverences this judge will seldom do anything he need repent of.—Fuller.

Be mine that silent calm repast,
A conscience cheerful to the last:
That tree which bears immortal fruit,
Without a canker at the root;
That friend which never fails the just,
When other friends desert their trust.
                          —Dr. Cotton.

Every man, however good he may be, has a yet better man dwelling in him, which is properly himself, but to whom nevertheless he is often unfaithful. It is to this interior and less mutable being that we should attach ourselves,

not to the changeable, every-day man.
—Wilhelm von Humboldt.

Conscience is that faculty which perceives right and wrong in actions, approves or disapproves them, anticipates their consequences under the
moral administration of God, and is
thus either the cause of peace or of
disquietude of mind.—Rev. S. Conn,
D. D.

'Tis ever thus
With noble minds, if chance they slide to
  folly;
Remorse stings deeper, and relentless con-
science
Pours more gall into the bitter cup
Of their severe repentance.   —Mason.

Shall be more sweet than all the joys
  Amongst us mortal men.
Then shalt thou find but one refuge
  Which comfort can retain;
A guiltless conscience pure and clear
  From touch of sinful stain.
              —Brandon.

To be satisfied with the acquittal of
the world, though accompanied with
the secret condemnation of conscience,
this is the mark of a little mind; but
it requires a soul of no common stamp
to be satisfied with its own acquittal,
and to despise the condemnation of the
world.—Colton.

What a fool is he who locks his door
to keep out spirits, who has in his
own bosom a spirit he dares not meet
alone; whose voice, smothered far
down, and piled over with mountains
of earthliness, is yet like the forewarning trumpet of doom!—Mrs.
Stowe.

He fears not dying—'tis a deeper fear,—
The thunder-peal cries to his conscience—
  "Hear"!
The rushing winds from memory lift the
  veil,
And in each flash his sins, like spectres pale,
Freed, from their dark abode, his guilty
  breast,
Shriek in his startled ear—"Death is not
  rest"!   —Mrs. Hale.

It is quite certain that, if from
childhood men were to begin to follow
the first intimations of conscience,
honestly to obey them and carry them
out into act, the power of conscience

would be so strengthened and improved within them, that it would soon
become, what it evidently is intended
to be, "a connecting principle between
the creature and the Creator."—J. C.
Shairp.

Give me another horse,—bind up my
  wounds,
Have mercy, Jesu!—soft;—I did but
  dream.—
O coward conscience, how dost thou afflict me!—
The lights burn blue.—It is now dead midnight.
Cold fearful drops stand on my fearful
  flesh.
What do I fear? myself?
            —Shakespeare.

What a strange thing an old dead
sin laid away in a secret drawer of
the soul is? Must it some time or
other be moistened with tears, until it
comes to life again, and begins to stir
in our consciousness, as the dry wheat-
animalcule, looking like a grain of
dust, becomes alive if it is wet with a
drop of water?—Holmes.

A palsy may as well shake an oak,
or a fever dry up a fountain, as either
of them shake, dry up, or impair the
delight of conscience. For it lies
within, it centres in the heart, it
grows into the very substance of the
soul, so that it accompanies a man to
his grave; he never outlives it.—South.

Conscience is too great a power in
the nature of man to be altogether
subdued; it may be for a time repressed and kept dormant; but conjectures there are in human life which
awaken it, and when once reawakened,
it flashes on the sinner's mind with all
the horrors of an invisible ruler and
a future judgment.—Blair.

A good conscience fears no witnesses, but a guilty conscience is solicitous even in solitude. If we do
nothing but what is honest, let all the
world know it; but if otherwise, what
does it signify to have nobody else
know it so long as I know it myself?
Miserable is he who slights that witness!—Seneca.

Conscience signifies that knowledge
which a man hath of his own thoughts

and actions; and because, if a man judgeth fairly of his actions by comparing them with the law of God, his mind will approve or condemn him; this knowledge or conscience may be both an accuser and a judge.—Swift.

Conscience is a judge in every man's breast, which none can cheat or corrupt, and perhaps the only incorrupt thing about him; yet, inflexible and honest as this judge is (however polluted the bench on which he sits), no man can, in my opinion, enjoy any applause which is not there adjudged to be his due.—Fielding.

A man's first care should be to avoid the reproaches of his own heart; his next, to escape the censures of the world. If the last interferes with the former, it ought to be entirely neglected; but otherwise there cannot be a greater satisfaction to an honest mind, than to see those approbations which it gives itself seconded by the applause of the public.—Addison.

A Witness.
Consider all thy actions and take heed
On stolen bread, tho' it is sweet to feed.
Sin, like a bee, unto thy hive may bring
A little honey but expect the sting.
Thou may'st conceal thy sin by cunning art,
But conscience sits a witness in thy heart,
Which will disturb thy peace, thy rest undo,
For that is witness, judge, and prison too.
—Watkins.

Were men so enlightened and studious of their own good as to act by the dictates of their reason and reflection, and not the opinion of others, conscience would be the steady ruler of human life, and the words truth, law, reason, equity, and religion could be but synonymous terms for that only guide which makes us pass our days in our own favor and approbation.—Steele.

It is a blushing, shame-faced spirit, that mutinies in a man's bosom; it fills one full of obstacles; it made me once restore a purse of gold that by chance I found; it beggars any man that keeps it; it is turned out of all towns and cities for a dangerous thing; and every man that means to live well

endeavors to trust to himself, and live without it.—Shakespeare.

Conscience is justice's best minister; it threatens, promises, rewards, and punishes and keeps all under control; the busy must attend to its remonstrances, the most powerful submit to its reproof, and the angry endure its upbraidings. While conscience is our friend all is peace; but if once offended farewell the tranquil mind.—Mrs. Montagu.

In the wildest anarchy of man's insurgent appetites and sins there is still a reclaiming voice,—a voice which, even when in practice disregarded, it is impossible not to own; and to which, at the very moment that we refuse our obedience, we find that we cannot refuse the homage of what ourselves do feel and acknowledge to be the best, the highest principles of our nature.—Chalmers.

The good or evil we confer on others very often, I believe, recoils on ourselves; for as men of a benign disposition enjoy their own acts of beneficence equally with those to whom they are done, so there are scarce any natures so entirely diabolical as to be capable of doing injuries without paying themselves some pangs for the ruin which they bring on their fellow-creatures.—Fielding.

The most reckless sinner against his own conscience has always in the background the consolation that he will go on in this course only this time, or only so long, but that at such a time he will amend. We may be assured that we do not stand clear with our own consciences so long as we determine or project, or even hold it possible, at some future time to alter our course of action.—Fichte.

As the stag which the huntsman has hit flies through bush and brake, over stock and stone, thereby exhausting his strength but not expelling the deadly bullet from his body; so does experience show that they who have troubled consciences run from place to place, but carry with them wherever they go their dangerous wounds.—Gotthold.

Conscience is the voice of the soul, the passions are the voice of the body. Is it astonishing that often these two languages contradict each other, and then to which must we listen? Too often reason deceives us; we have only too much acquired the right of refusing to listen to it; but conscience never deceives us; it is the true guide of man; it is to man what instinct is to the body, which follows it, obeys nature, and never is afraid of going astray.—Rousseau.

An old historian says about the Roman armies that marched through a country, burning and destroying every living thing, "They make a solitude, and they call it peace." And so men do with their consciences. They stifle them, sear them, forcibly silence them, somehow or other; and then, when there is a dead stillness in the heart, broken by no voice of either approbation or blame, but doleful, like the unnatural quiet of a deserted city, then they say, "It is peace;" and the man's uncontrolled passions and unbridled desires dwell solitary in the fortress of his own spirit! You may almost attain to that.—Alexander Maclaren.

Although there is nothing so bad for conscience as trifling, there is nothing so good for conscience as trifles. Its certain discipline and development are related to the smallest things. Conscience, like gravitation, takes hold of atoms. Nothing is morally indifferent. Conscience must reign in manners as well as morals, in amusements as well as work. He only who is "faithful in that which is least" is dependable in all the world.—Maltbie Babcock.

Consecration

See that you receive Christ with all your heart. As there is nothing in Christ that may be refused, so there is nothing in you from which He must be excluded.—John Flavel.

If you want to live in this world, doing the duty of life, knowing the blessings of it, doing your work heartily, and yet not absorbed by it, remember that the one power whereby you can so act is, that all shall be con-

secrated to Christ, and done for His sake.—Alexander Maclaren.

Teach us, Master, how to give
  All we have and are to Thee;
Grant us, Saviour, while we live,
  Wholly, only Thine to be.
        —F. R. Havergal.

God consecrates us with His Spirit; whom He adopts, He anoints; whom He makes sons, He makes saints; He doth not only give them a new name, but a new nature. God turns the wolf into a lamb; He makes the heart humble and gracious; He works such a change as if another soul did dwell in the same body.—T. Watson.

Seek to make life henceforth a consecrated thing; that so, when the sunset is nearing, with its murky vapors and lowering skies, the very clouds of sorrow may be fringed with golden light. Thus will the song in the house of your pilgrimage be always the truest harmony. It will be composed of no jarring, discordant notes; but with all its varied tones will form one sustained, life-long melody; dropped for a moment in death, only to be resumed with the angels, and blended with the everlasting cadences of your Father's house.—J. R. Macduff.

Consequences

As thou sowest, so shalt thou reap.—Cicero.

As the dimensions of the tree are not always regulated by the size of the seed, so the consequences of things are not always proportionate to the apparent magnitude of those events that have produced them.—Colton.

Conservatism

A conservative is a man who will not look at the new moon, out of respect for that "ancient institution," the old one.—Douglas Jerrold.

The conservative may clamor against reform, but he might as well clamor against the centrifugal force. He sighs for the "good old times,"—he might as well wish the oak back into the acorn.—Chapin.

A conservative young man has wound up his life before it was unreeled. We expect old men to be conservative; but when a nation's young men are so, its funeral bell is already rung.—Beecher.

We are reformers in spring and summer; in autumn and winter we stand by the old; reformers in the morning, conservers at night. Reform is affirmative, conservatism negative; conservatism goes for comfort, reform for truth.—Emerson.

Conservatism is a very good thing; but how many conservatives announce principles which might have shocked Dick Turpin, or nonsensicalities flat enough to have raised contempt in Jerry Sneak!—Whipple.

Consideration

That should be maturely considered which can be decided but once.

Consideration, like an angel came
And whipp'd the offending Adam out of him,
Leaving his body as a paradise,
To envelope and contain celestial spirits.
— Shakespeare.

Better it is toward the right conduct of life, to consider what will be the end of a thing, than what is the beginning of it: for what promises fair at first may prove ill, and what seems at first a disadvantage, may prove very advantageous.—Wells.

Consistency

The foible of weak minds.—Emerson.

Without consistency there is no moral strength.—Owen.

Consistency is the bugbear that frightens little minds.—Emerson.

With consistency a great soul has simply nothing to do. He may as well concern himself with his shadow on the wall.—Emerson.

To be rational is so glorious a thing that two-legged creatures generally content themselves with the title.—Locke.

A foolish consistency is the hobgoblin of little minds, adored by little

statesmen and philosophers and divines.—Emerson.

As flowers always wear their own colors and give forth their own fragrance every day alike, so should Christians maintain their character at all times and under all circumstances.—Beecher.

We feel something like respect for consistency even in error. We lament the virtue that is debauched into a vice; but the vice that affects a virtue becomes the more detestable.—Thomas Paine.

Tush! tush! my lassie, such thoughts resigne,
Comparisons are cruele:
Fine pictures suit in frames as fine,
Consistencie's a jewell.
—Jolly Robyn-Roughhead.

Gineral C. is a dreffle smart man:
    He's been on all sides that give places or pelf;
But consistency still wuz a part of his plan;
He's been true to one party, and that is, himself;—
    So John P.
    Robinson, he
Sez he shall vote for Gineral C.
—Lowell.

Consolation

God has commanded time to console the unhappy.—Joubert.

For grief is crowned with consolation.—Shakespeare.

And empty heads console with empty sound.—Pope.

In a healthy state of the organism all wounds have a tendency to heal.—Madame Swetchine.

For every bad there might be a worse; and when one breaks his leg, let him be thankful it was not his neck.—Bishop Hall.

Consolation heals without contact; somewhat like the blessed air which we need but to breathe.—Madame Swetchine.

Apt words have power to suage the tumors of a troubled mind.—Milton.

If a man makes me keep my distance, the comfort is he keeps his own at the same time.—Swift.

Prosperity is not without many fears and distastes, and Adversity is not without comforts and hopes.—Bacon.

Consolation indiscreetly pressed upon us, when we are suffering undue affliction, only serves to increase our pain, and to render our grief more poignant.—Rousseau.

One should never be very forward in offering spiritual consolations to those in distress. These, to be of any service, must be self-evolved in the first instance.—Coleridge.

All are not taken! there are left behind
Living Beloveds, tender looks to bring,
And make the daylight still a happy thing,
And tender voices, to make soft the wind.
    —E. B. Browning.

Whoever can turn his weeping eyes to heaven has lost nothing; for there above is everything he can wish for here below. He only is a loser who persists in looking down on the narrow plains of the present time.—Richter.

Before an affliction is digested, consolation ever comes too soon; and after it is digested, it comes too late; but there is a mark between these two, as fine almost as a hair, for a comforter to take aim at.—Sterne.

Queen Elizabeth, in her hard, wise way, writing to a mother who had lost her son, tells her that she will be comforted in time; and why should she not do for herself what the mere lapse of time will do for her?—Bentley.

Sprinkled along the waste of years
Full many a soft green isle appears:
Pause where we may upon the desert road,
Some shelter is in sight, some sacred safe abode.
    —Keble.

As the bosom of earth blooms again and again, having buried out of sight the dead leaves of autumn, and loosed the frosty bands of winter; so does the heart, in spite of all that melancholy poets write, feel many renewed springs and summers. It is a beautiful and a blessed world we live in, and whilst that life lasts, to lose the enjoyment of it is a sin.—A. W. Chambers.

Nothing does so establish the mind amidst the rollings and turbulence of present things, as a look above them and a look beyond them,—above them, to the steady and good hand by which they are ruled; and beyond them, to the sweet and beautiful end to which, by that hand, they will be brought.—Jeremy Taylor.

Conspiracy

Conspiracies no sooner should be formed
Than executed.   —Addison.

For all things are less dreadful than they
  seem.   —Wordsworth.

    Conspiracies
Like thunder-clouds, should in a moment
  form
And strike, like lightning, ere the sound is
  heard.   —Dowe.

Oh think what anxious moments pass between
The birth of plots, and their last fatal periods;
Oh! 'tis a dreadful interval of time,
Fill'd up with horror, and big with death.
    —Addison.

Between the acting of a dreadful thing,
And the first motion, all the interim is
Like a phantasma, or a hideous dream;
The genius and the mortal instruments
Are then in council; and the state of man,
Like to a little kingdom, suffers then
The nature of an insurrection.
    —Shakespeare.

    O conspiracy!
Shams't thou to show thy dangerous brow
  by night,
When evils are most free? O, then by day,
Where wilt thou find a cavern dark enough
To mask thy monstrous visage? Seek none,
  conspiracy,
Hide it in smiles and affability:
For if thou put thy native semblance on,
Not Erebus itself were dim enough
To hide thee from prevention.
    —Shakespeare.

Constancy

Constancy is a saint without a worshiper.—Boufflers.

Constancy is the complement of all the other human virtues.—Mazzini.

Constancy is the chimera of love.—Vauvenargues.

Were man but constant, he were perfect.—Shakespeare.

The lasting and crowning privilege of friendship is constancy.—South.

'Tis often constancy to change the mind.—Hoole.

Without constancy, there is neither love, friendship, nor virtue in the world.—Addison.

True constancy no time no power can move;
He that hath known to change, ne'er knew to love.
—Gay.

The constancy of the wise is only the art of keeping disquietude to one's self.—Rochefoucauld.

I am constant as the northern star, of whose true-fixed and resting quality there is no fellow in the firmament.—Shakespeare.

A good man it is not mine to see; could I see a man possessed of constancy, that would satisfy me.—Confucius.

The mountain rill
Seeks with no surer flow the far bright sea,
Than my unchang'd affections flow to thee.
—Park Benjamin.

Now from head to foot
I am marble-constant: now the fleeting moon
No planet is of mine.   —Shakespeare.

Sooner shall this blue ocean melt to air,
Sooner shall earth resolve itself to sea,
Than I resign thine image, Oh my fair!
Or think of anything, excepting thee.
—Byron.

The love that is kept in the beauty of trust,
Cannot pass like the foam from the seas,
Or a mark that the finger hath trac'd in the dust,
Where 't is swept by the breath of the breeze.   —Mrs. Welby.

There are two kinds of constancy in love, one arising from incessantly finding in the loved one fresh objects to love, the other from regarding it as a point of honor to be constant.—La Rochefoucauld.

Out upon it! I have lov'd
Three whole days together;
And am like to love three more,
If it prove fair weather.
—Sir John Suckling.

Changeless march the stars above,
Changeless morn succeeds to even;
And the everlasting hills
Changeless watch the changeless heaven.
—Charles Kingsley.

————I have won
Thy heart, my gentle girl! but it hath been
When that soft eye was on me; and the love
I told beneath the evening influence,
Shall be as constant as its gentle star.
—Willis.

Oh, the heart, that has truly loved, never forgets,
But as truly loves on to the close,
As the sun-flower turns on her god, when he sets,
The same look which she turn'd when he rose.   —Moore.

There is nothing but death
Our affections can sever,
And till life's latest breath
Love shall bind us for ever.
—Percival.

Then come the wild weather, come sleet or come snow,
We will stand by each other, however it blow.
Oppression, and sickness, and sorrow, and pain
Shall be to our true love as links to the chain.   —Longfellow.

Tell him I love him yet,
As in that joyous time;
Tell him I ne'er forget,
Though memory now be crime.
—Praed.

Though youth be past, and beauty fled,
The constant heart its pledge redeems,
Like box, that guards the flowerless bed
And brighter from the contrast seems.
—Mrs. Hale.

Whatever is genuine in social relations endures, despite of time, error, absence, and destiny; and that which has no inherent vitality had better die at once. A great poet has truly declared that constancy is no virtue, but a fact.—Tuckerman.

First shall the heaven's bright lamp forget
  to shine,
The stars shall from the azur'd sky decline:
First shall the orient with the west shake
  hand,
The centre of the world shall cease to
  stand:
First wolves shall league with lambs, the
  dolphins fly,
The lawyer and physician fees deny;
The Thames with Tagus shall exchange her
  bed,
My mistress' locks with mine shall first
  turn red;
First heav'n shall lie below, and hell above,
Ere I inconstant to my Delia prove.
          —Howell.

Constitution

A constitution is not a thing in name only, but in fact. It has not an ideal but a real existence, and wherever it cannot be produced in a visible form, there is none. A constitution is a thing antecedent to a government, and a government is only the creature of a constitution. The constitution of a country is not the act of its government, but of a people constituting a government. It is the body of elements to which you refer, and quote article by article, and contains the principles on which the government shall be established—the form in which it shall be organized—the powers it shall have—the mode of elections—the duration of Congress—and, in fine, everything that relates to the complete organization of a civil government, and the principles on which it shall act, and by which it shall be bound. A constitution is to a government, therefore, what the laws made by that government are to a court of judicature. The court of judicature does not make laws, neither can it alter them; it only acts in conformity to the laws made; and the government is in like manner governed by the constitution.—Paine.

Contemplation

The act of contemplation then creates the thing contemplated.—Isaac Disraeli.

In order to improve the mind, we ought less to learn than to contemplate.—Descartes.

There is no lasting pleasure but contemplation; all others grow flat and insipid upon frequent use; and when a man hath run through a set of vanities, in the declension of his age, he knows not what to do with himself, if he cannot think; he saunters about from one dull business to another, to wear out time; and hath no reason to value Life but because he is afraid of death.—Burnet.

When holy and devout religious men
Are at their beads, 'tis hard to draw them
  thence;
So sweet is zealous contemplation.
          —Shakespeare.

A contemplative life has more the appearance of a life of piety than any other; but it is the divine plan to bring faith into activity and exercise.—Cecil.

Contempt

Contempt leaves a deeper scar than anger.

Contempt is frequently regulated by fashion.—Zimmermann.

Those only are despicable who fear to be despised.—La Rochefoucauld.

An Englishman fears contempt more than death.—Goldsmith.

O, what a deal of scorn looks beautiful in the contempt and anger of his lip!—Shakespeare.

None but the contemptible are apprehensive of contempt.—Rochefoucauld.

Who can refute a sneer?—Paley.

Contempt is the only way to triumph over calumny.—Madame de Maintenon.

I find my familiarity with thee has bred contempt.—Cervantes.

Contemptuous people are sure to be contemptible.—Chamfort.

Nothing, says Longinus, can be great, the contempt of which is great.—Addison.

You may not despise any man, nor spurn anything.—Rabbi Ben Azai.

Nothing so contemptible as habitual contempt.—E. L. Magoon.

———

Contempt putteth an edge upon anger more than the hurt itself.—Bacon.

———

Contempt is a kind of gangrene which, if it seizes one part of a character, corrupts all the rest by degrees.—Johnson.

———

No man can fall into contempt but those who deserve it.—Johnson.

———

There is no room in the universe for the least contempt or pride; but only for a gentle and a reverent heart.—James Martineau.

———

The spirit of contempt is the true spirit of Antichrist; for no other is more directly opposed to Christ.—Henry Giles.

———

Christ saw much in this world to weep over, and much to pray over; but He saw nothing in it to look upon with contempt.—E. H. Chapin.

———

I have unlearned contempt; it is a sin that is engendered earliest in the soul, and doth beset it like a poison worm feeding on all its beauty.—Willis.

———

It is often more necessary to conceal contempt than resentment; the former is never forgiven, but the latter is sometimes forgotten.—Chesterfield.

———

Speak with contempt of no man. Every one hath a tender sense of reputation. And every man hath a sting, which he may, if provoked too far, dart out at one time or other.—Burton.

———

He hears
On all sides, from innumerable tongues
A dismal universal hiss, the sound
Of public scorn.   —Milton.

———

He who feels contempt for any living thing hath faculties that he hath never used, and thought with him is in its infancy.—Wordsworth.

———

If there be no great love in the beginning, yet heaven may decrease it upon better acquaintance, when we are married and have more occasion to know one another; I hope, upon familiarity will grow more contempt.—Shakespeare.

———

What valor were it, when a cur doth grin, for one to thrust his hand between his teeth, when he might spurn him with his foot away?—Shakespeare.

———

Contempt is not a thing to be despised. It may be borne with a calm and equal mind, but no man, by lifting his head high, can pretend that he does not perceive the scorns that are poured down on him from above.—Burke.

———

There is no action in the behavior of one man toward another of which human nature is more impatient than of contempt, it being the undervaluing of a man upon a belief of his utter uselessness and inability.—South.

———

Ah, there is nothing more beautiful than the difference between the thought about sinful creatures which is natural to a holy being, and the thought about sinful creatures which is natural to a self-righteous being. The one is all contempt; the other, all pity.—Alexander Maclaren.

———

Wrongs are often forgiven, but contempt never is. Our pride remembers it forever. It implies a discovery of weaknesses, which we are much more careful to conceal than crimes. Many a man will confess his crimes to a common friend, but I never knew a man who would tell his silly weaknesses to his most intimate one.—Chesterfield.

———

Men are much more unwilling to have their weaknesses and their imperfections known than their crimes; and if you hint to a man that you think him silly, ignorant, or even ill-bred or awkward, he will hate you more and longer than if you tell him plainly that you think him a rogue.—Chesterfield.

———

Contempt of others is the truest symptom of a base and bad heart,—while it suggests itself to the mean and the vile, and tickles their little fancy on every occasion, it never enters the great and good mind but on the strongest motives; nor is it then a welcome guest,—affording only an uneasy sensation, and bringing always with it a mixture of concern and compassion.— Fielding.

Contempt naturally implies a man's esteeming of himself greater than the person whom he contemns; he therefore that slights, that contemns an affront is properly superior to it; and he conquers an injury who conquers his resentments of it. Socrates, being kicked by an ass, did not think it a revenge proper for Socrates to kick the ass again.—South.

Content — Contentment

The harvest song of inward peace. —Whittier.

Our content is our best having.— Shakespeare.

Contentment opes the source of every joy.—Beattie.

Contentment, parent of delight.— Green.

The noblest mind the best contentment has.—Spenser.

The fewer desires, the more peace.— Thomas Wilson.

Contentment is natural wealth; luxury, artificial poverty.—Socrates.

He is well paid that is well satisfied.—Shakespeare.

Contentment is better than divinations or visions.—Landor.

Contentment, as it is a short road and pleasant, has great delight and little trouble.—Epictetus.

A contented heart is an even sea in the midst of all storms.

Contentment gives a crown where fortune hath denied it.—Ford.

I have learned in whatsoever state I am therewith to be content.—Bible.

Fortify yourself with contentment, for this is an impregnable fortress.— Epictetus.

We only see in a lifetime a dozen faces marked with the peace of a contented spirit.—Henry Ward Beecher.

Mutual content is like a river, which must have its banks on either side.— Le Sage.

Contentment with to-day's lot makes candidacy for a better lot to-morrow. —Charles H. Parkhurst.

The great quality of Dulness is to be unalterably contented with itself. —Thackeray.

O Contentment, make me rich! for without thee there is no wealth.— Saadi.

Show me a thoroughly contented person, and I will show you a useless one.—H. W. Shaw.

Naught is had, all is spent, where our desire is got without content.— Shakespeare.

Without content, we shall find it almost as difficult to please others as ourselves.—Greville.

May I always have a heart superior, with economy suitable, to my fortune. —Shenstone.

Content is to the mind like moss to a tree; it bindeth it up so as to stop its growth.—Halifax.

That is true plenty, not to have, but not to want riches.—St. Chrysostom.

It is right to be contented with what we have, but never with what we are. —Sir James Mackintosh.

He is richest who is content with the least; for content is the wealth of nature.—Socrates.

The rarest feeling that ever lights a human face is the contentment of a loving soul.—Henry Ward Beecher.

A man who finds no satisfaction in himself seeks for it in vain elsewhere. —Rochefoucauld.

He that commends me to mine own content Commends me to the thing I cannot get.
—Shakespeare.

Unless we find repose within ourselves, it is vain to seek it elsewhere. —Hosea Ballou.

Contentment is, after all, simply refined indolence.—Haliburton.

Contentment consisteth not in adding more fuel, but in taking away some fire.—Fuller.

A mind content both crown and kingdom is.—Robert Greene.

It is not for man to rest in absolute contentment.—Southey.

To be content with little is difficult; to be content with much, impossible.— Marie Ebner-Eschenbach.

When the best things are not possible, the best may be made of those that are.—Hooker.

Let him who has enough ask for nothing more.—Horace.

If you are content, you have enough to live comfortably.—Plautus.

Be happy ye, whose fortunes are already completed.—Virgil.

Learn this of me, where'er thy lot doth fall, Short lot, or not, to be content with all.
—Herrick.

Content dwells with him, for his mind is fed,
And temperance has driven out unrest.
—Willis.

Each good mind doubles his own free content,
When in another's use they give it vent.
—Sir Giles Goosecap.

Contentment travels rarely with fortune, but follows virtue even in misfortune.—Marie Leszczinski.

Enjoy your own life without comparing it with that of another.—Condorcet.

To be content with what we possess is the greatest and most secure of riches.—Cicero.

Contentment, rosy, dimpled maid,
Thou brightest daughter of the sky.
—Lady Manners.

All things on earth thus change, some up, some down;
Content's a kingdom, and I wear that crown.
—Heywood.

Lord of himself, though not of lands;
And having nothing, yet hath all.
—Sir Henry Wotton.

A Man he seems of cheerful yesterdays And confident to-morrows. —Wordsworth.

If we are at peace with God and our own conscience, what enemy among men need we fear?—Hosea Ballou.

There are two sorts of content; one is connected with exertion, the other with habits of indolence. The first is a virtue; the other, a vice.—Mrs. Maria Edgeworth.

To secure a contented spirit, measure your desires by your fortune, and not your fortune by your desires.— Jeremy Taylor.

True contentment depends not upon what we have; a tub was large enough for Diogenes, but a world was too little for Alexander.—C. C. Colton.

I have often said that all the unhappiness of men comes from not knowing how to remain quiet in a chamber.—Pascal.

What is the highest secret of victory and peace? To will what God wills, and strike a league with destiny.— W. R. Alger.

I earn that I eat, get that I wear; owe no man hate, envy no man's happiness; glad of other men's good, content with my harm.—Shakespeare.

Poor and content is rich, and rich enough; but riches, fineless, is as poor as winter to him that ever fears he shall be poor.—Shakespeare.

Contentment is not happiness. An oyster may be contented. Happiness is compounded of richer elements.—Bovee.

Take the good with the evil, for ye all are the pensioners of God, and none may choose or refuse the cup His wisdom mixeth.—Tupper.

That happy state of mind, so rarely possessed, in which we can say, "I have enough," is the highest attainment of philosophy.—Zimmermann.

He is happy whose circumstances suit his temper; but he is more excellent who can suit his temper to any circumstances.—Hume.

For mine own part, I could be well content
To entertain the lag-end of my life
With quiet hours.   Shakespeare.

Few things are needed to make a wise man happy; nothing can make a fool content; that is why most men are miserable.—La Rochefoucauld.

Content thyself to be obscurely good;
When vice prevails, and impious men bear sway,
The post of honor is a private station.
—Addison.

Let's live with that small pittance which we have;
Who covets more is evermore a slave.
—Herrick.

Contentment is a pearl of great price and whoever procures it at the expense of ten thousand desires makes a wise and a happy purchase.—Balguy.

I am quite my own master, agreeably lodged, perfectly easy in my circumstances. I am contented with my situation, and happy because I think myself so.—Le Sage.

My God, give me neither poverty nor riches; but whatsoever it may be Thy will to give, give me with it a heart

which knows humbly to acquiesce in what is Thy will.—Christian Scriver.

If two angels were sent down from heaven,—one to conduct an empire, and the other to sweep a street,—they would feel no inclination to change employments.—John Newton.

Learn to be pleased with everything, with wealth so far as it makes us beneficial to others; with poverty, for not having much to care for; and with obscurity, for being unenvied.—Plutarch.

The highest point outward things can bring unto, is the contentment of the mind; with which no estate can be poor, without which all estates will be miserable.—Sir P. Sidney.

There is some help for all the defects of fortune; for, if a man cannot attain to the length of his wishes, he may have his remedy by cutting of them shorter.—Cowley.

None is poor but the mean in mind, the timorous, the weak, and unbelieving; none is wealthy but the affluent in soul, who is satisfied and floweth over.—Tupper.

Happy the heart to whom God has given enough strength and courage to suffer for Him, to find happiness in simplicity and the happiness of others.—Lavater.

One who is contented with what he has done will never become famous for what he will do. He has lain down to die. The grass is already growing over him.—Bovee.

"What you demand is here, or at Ulubræ." You traverse the world in search of happiness, which is within the reach of every man; a contented mind confers it on all.—Horace.

We can console ourselves for not having great talents as we console ourselves for not having great places. We can be above both in our hearts.—Vauvenargues.

Alas! if the principles of contentment are not within us, the height of station and worldly grandeur will as soon add a cubit to a man's stature as to his happiness.—Sterne.

My crown is in my heart, not on my head;
Not deck'd with diamonds, and Indian stones,
Nor to be seen: my crown is call'd content;
A crown it is that seldom kings enjoy.
—Shakespeare.

What happiness the rural maid attends,
In cheerful labor while each day she spends!
She gratefully receives what Heav'n has sent,
And, rich in poverty, enjoys content.
—Gay.

I do not think that the road to contentment lies in despising what we have not got. Let us acknowledge all good, all delight that the world holds, and be content without it.—George MacDonald.

It is not by change of circumstances, but by fitting our spirits to the circumstances in which God has placed us, that we can be reconciled to life and duty.—F. W. Robertson.

An elegant Sufficiency, Content,
Retirement, rural Quiet, Friendship, Books,
Ease and alternate Labor, useful Life,
Progressive Virtue, and approving Heaven!
—Thomson.

Dear little head, that lies in calm content
Within the gracious hollow that God made
In every human shoulder, where He meant
Some tired head for comfort should be laid.   Celia Thaxter.

I swear, 't is better to be lowly born,
And range with humble livers in content,
Than to be perk'd up in a glistering grief,
And wear a golden sorrow.
—Shakespeare.

He, fairly looking into life's account,
Saw frowns and favours were of like amount;
And viewing all—his perils, prospects, purse,
He said, "content;—'t is well it is no worse."   —Crabbe.

Contentment furnishes constant joy. Much covetousness, constant grief. To the contented, even poverty is joy. To the discontented, even wealth is a vexation.—Ming Sum Paou Keën.

We shall be made truly wise if we be made content; content, too, not only with what we can understand, but content with what we do not understand,—the habit of mind which theologians call, and rightly, faith in God.—Charles Kingsley.

Yes! in the poor man's garden grow
Far more than herbs and flowers,
Kind thoughts, contentment, peace of mind,
And joy for weary hours.
—Mary Howitt.

This is the charm, by sages often told,
Converting all it touches into gold:
Content can soothe, where'er by fortune placed,
Can rear a garden in the desert waste.
—Henry Kirke White.

I would do what I pleased; and, doing what I pleased, I should have my will; and, having my will, I should be contented; and, content, there is no more to be desired; and when there is no more to desire, there is an end of it.—Cervantes.

Content is the best opulence, because it is the pleasantest, and the surest. The richest man is he who does not want that which is wanting to him; the poorest is the miser, who wants that which he has.—Paul Chatfield, M. D.

The chief secret of comfort lies in not suffering trifles to vex us, and in prudently cultivating our undergrowth of small pleasures, since very few great ones, alas! are let on long leases. —Sharp.

Every one is well or ill at ease, according as he finds himself! not he whom the world believes, but he who believes himself to be so, is content; and in him alone belief gives itself being and reality.—Montaigne.

It conduces much to our content if we pass by those things which happen to our trouble, and consider that which is pleasing and prosperous; that by the representation of the better the worse may be blotted out.—Jeremy Taylor.

If we will take the good we find, asking no questions, we shall have heaping measures. The great gifts are not got by analysis. Everything good is on the highway. The middle region of our being is the temperate zone.—Emerson.

Contentment produces, in some measure, all those effects which the alchemist usually ascribes to what he calls the philosopher's stone; and if it does not bring riches, it does the same thing by banishing the desire for them.—Addison.

A contented mind is the greatest blessing a man can enjoy in this world; and if in the present life his happiness arises from the subduing of his desires, it will arise in the next from the gratification of them.—Addison.

Seeming contentment is real discontent, combined with indolence or self-indulgence, which, while taking no legitimate means of raising itself, delights in bringing others down to its own level.—Mill.

With the civilized man contentment is a myth. From the cradle to the grave he is forever longing and striving after something better, an indefinable something, some new object yet unattained.—Wm. Matthews.

Happy the life, that in a peaceful stream,
Obscure. unnoticed through the vale has flow'd;
The heart that ne'er was charm'd by fortune's gleam
Is ever sweet contentment's blest abode.
        —Percival.

He that troubles not himself with anxious thoughts for more than is necessary, lives little less than the life of angels, whilst by a mind content with little, he imitates their want of nothing.—Cave.

O calm, hush'd, rich content,
Is there a being, blessedness, without thee?
How soft thou down'st the couch where thou dost rest,
Nectar to life thou sweet ambrosian feast.
        —Marston.

That man lives happy and in command of himself, who from day to day can say I have lived. Whether clouds

obscure, or the sun illumines the following day, that which is past is beyond recall.—Horace.

Since every man who lives is born to die,
And none can boast sincere felicity,
With equal mind what happens let us bear,
Nor grieve too much for things beyond our care.
Like pilgrims, to th' appointed place we tend;
The world's an inn, and death the journey's end.   —Dryden.

The point of aim for our vigilance to hold in view is to dwell upon the brightest parts in every prospect, to call off the thoughts when running upon disagreeable objects, and strive to be pleased with the present circumstances surrounding us.—Rev. J. Tucker.

A sense of contentment makes us kindly and benevolent to others; we are not chafed and galled by cares which are tyrannical because original. We are fulfilling our proper destiny, and those around us feel the sunshine of our own hearts.—Bulwer-Lytton.

With more of thanks and less of thought,
  I strive to make my matters meet;
To seek what ancient sages sought,
  Physic and food in sour and sweet,
To take what passes in good part,
And keep the hiccups from the heart.
        —John Byrom.

We'll therefore relish with content,
Whate'er kind Providence has sent,
  Nor aim beyond our pow'r;
For, if our stock be very small,
'Tis prudent to enjoy it all,
  Nor lose the present hour.
        —Nathaniel Cotton.

A voice of greeting from the wind was sent,
The mists enfolded me with soft white arms,
The birds did sing to lap me in content,
The rivers wove their charms,
And every little daisy in the grass
Did look up in my face, and smile to see me pass.   —R. H. Stoddard.

What tho' we quit all glittering pomp and greatness,
The busy noisy flattery of courts,
We should enjoy content, in that alone
Is greatness, power, wealth, honour, all summ'd up.   —Powell.

We cannot be young twice; we cannot turn upon our steps, and go back to gather the garlands we gathered ten years ago. And, therefore, with a gaze over on the cross upon the distant hills, and a remembrance always of the shadow land that lies beyond, let us endeavor to be contented with small things, and to make ourselves happy in the pleasantness of simple pleasures.—Holme Lee.

I press to bear no haughty sway;
  I wish no more than may suffice:
I do no more than well I may,
  Look what I lack, my mind supplies;
Lo, thus I triumph like a king,
  My mind's content with anything.
          —Byrd.

There is a jewel which no Indian mine can
  buy,
No chemic art can counterfeit;
It makes men rich in greatest poverty,
Makes water wine, turns wooden cups to
  gold,
The homely whistle to sweet music's strain;
Seldom it comes, to few from heaven sent,
That much in little—all in naught—content.
          —Wilbye.

Think'st thou the man whose mansions hold
The wordling's pomp and miser's gold,
  Obtains a richer prize
Than he who, in his cot at rest,
Finds heavenly peace a willing guest,
And bears the promise in his breast
  Of treasure in the skies?
          —Mrs. Sigourney.

I say to thee be thou satisfied. It is recorded of the hares that with a general consent they went to drown themselves out of a feeling of their misery; but when they saw a company of frogs more fearful than they were, they began to take courage and comfort again. Confer thine estate with others.—Burton.

Sweet are the thoughts that savour of content;
The quiet mind is richer than a crown;
Sweet are the nights in careless slumber
  spent;
The poor estate scorns fortune's angry
  frown;
Such sweet content, such minds, such sleep,
  such bliss,
Beggars enjoy, when princes oft do miss.
          —Robert Greene.

For no chance is evil to him who is content, and to a man nothing is miserable unless it is unreasonable. No man can make another man to be his slave unless he hath first enslaved himself to life and death. No pleasure or pain, to hope or fear; command these passions, and you are freer than the Parthian kings.—Jeremy Taylor.

Happy the man, of mortals happiest he,
Whose quiet mind from vain desires is free;
Whom neither hopes deceive, nor fears torment.
But lives at peace, within himself content;
In thought, or act, accountable to none
But to himself, and to the gods alone.
          —Geo. Granville.

If men knew what felicity dwells in the cottage of a godly man, how sound he sleeps, how quiet his rest, how composed his mind, how free from care, how easy his position, how moist his mouth, how joyful his heart, they would never admire the noises, the diseases, the throngs of passions, and the violence of unnatural appetites that fill the house of the luxurious and the heart of the ambitious.—Jeremy Taylor.

Lo now, from idle wishes clear,
  I make the good I may not find;
Adown the stream I gently steer,
  And shift my sail with every wind.
And half by nature, half by reason,
  Can still with pliant heart prepare,
The mind, attuned to every season,
  The merry heart that laughs at care.
          —H. M. Milman.

In Paris a queer little man you may see,
  A little man all in gray;
Rosy and round as an apple is he,
Content with the present whate'er it may be,
While from care and from cash he is equally
  free,
  And merry both night and day!
"Ma foi! I laugh at the world," says he,
"I laugh at the world, and the world laughs
  at me!"
What a gay little man in gray.
          —Beranger.

Contentment is not satisfaction. It is the grateful, faithful, fruitful use of what we have, little or much. It is to take the cup of Providence, and call upon the name of the Lord. What the cup contains is its contents. To get all there is in the cup is the act and art of contentment. Not to drink because one has but half a cup, or because one does not like its flavor, or because some one else has silver to one's own glass, is to lose the contents; and that is the penalty, if not the meaning of discontent. No one is discontented who employs and enjoys to the utmost what he has. It is high philosophy to say, we can have just what we like, if we like what we have; but this much at least can be done, and this is contentment,—to have the most and best in life, by making the most and best of what we have.—Maltbie Babcock.

To be contented,—what, indeed, is it? Is it not to be satisfied,—to hope for nothing, to aspire to nothing, to strive for nothing,—in short to rest in inglorious ease, doing nothing for your country, for your own or others' material, intellectual, or moral improvement, satisfied with the condition in which you or they are placed? Such a state of feeling may do very well where nature has fixed an inseparable and ascertained barrier,—a "thus far shalt thou go and no farther,"—to our wishes, or where we are troubled by ills past remedy. In such cases it is the highest philosophy not to fret or grumble, when, by all our worrying and self-teasing, we cannot help ourselves a jot or tittle, but only aggravate and intensify an affliction that is incurable. To soothe the mind down into patience is then the only resource left us, and happy is he who has schooled himself thus to meet all reverses and disappointments. But in the ordinary circumstances of life this boasted virtue of contentment, so far from being laudable, would be an evil of the first magnitude. It would be, in fact, nothing less than a trigging of the wheels of all enterprise,—a cry of "Stand still!" to the progress of the whole social world.—Wm. Matthews.

Contention

In excessive altercation, truth is lost.—Syrus.

Religious contention is the devil's harvest.—La Fontaine.

Great contests generally excite great animosities.—Livy.

He that wrestles with us strengthens our nerves, and sharpens our skill. Our antagonist is our helper.—Burke.

Contention is a hydra's head; the more they strive the more they may: and as Praxiteles did by his glass, when he saw a scurvy face in it, brake it in pieces: but for that one he saw many more as bad in a moment.—Burton.

When two discourse, if the one's anger rise,
The man who lets the contest fall is wise.
—Plutarch.

Contentions fierce,
Ardent, and dire, spring from no petty cause. —Scott.

Great contest follows, and much learned dust
Involves the combatants; each claiming truth,
And truth disclaiming both. —Cowper.

A quarrel is quickly settled when deserted by one party: there is no battle unless there be two.—Seneca.

Birds in their little nests agree:
And 'tis a shameful sight,
When children of one family
Fall out, and chide, and fight.
—Isaac Watts.

Contention, like a horse
Full of high feeding, madly hath broke loose, -
And bears down all before him.
—Shakespeare.

Even as a broken mirror, which the glass
In every fragment multiplies, and makes
A thousand images of one that was
The same, and still the more, the more it breaks. —Byron.

Some say, compared to Bononcini,
That Mynheer Handel's but a ninny;
Others aver,—that he to Handel
Is scarcely fit to hold a candle:
Strange all this difference should be,
'Twixt tweedle-dum and tweedle-dee?
—John Byrom.

Thus when a barber and collier fight,
The barber beats the luckless collier—white;
The dusty collier heaves his ponderous sack,
And, big with vengeance, beats the barber—black.
In comes the brick-dust man, with grime o'erspread,
And beats the collier and the barber—red;
Black, red, and white, in various clouds are toss'd,
And in the dust they raise the combatants are lost. —Christopher Smart.

Contradiction

We must not contradict, but instruct him that contradicts us; for a madman is not cured by another running mad also.—Antisthenes.

Contrast

Shadow owes its birth to light.—Gay.

Nature hath meal and bran, contempt and grace.—Shakespeare.

The rose and the thorn, sorrow and gladness, are linked together.—Saadi.

Where there is much light the shadow is deep.—Goethe.

Do not speak of your happiness to a man less fortunate than yourself.—Plutarch.

A learned man is a tank; a wise man is a spring.—W. R. Alger.

The coldest bodies warm with opposition, the hardest sparkle in collision.—Junius.

Look here, upon this picture, and on this,
The counterfeit presentment of two
brothers. —Shakespeare.

The superiority of some men is merely local. They are great because their associates are little.—Johnson.

Some people with great merit are very disgusting; others with great faults are very pleasing.—Rochefoucauld.

Strange as it may seem, the most ludicrous lines I ever wrote have been written in the saddest mood.—Cowper.

The presence of the wretched is a burden to the happy; and alas! the happy still more so to the wretched.—Goethe.

Those that are good manners at the court are as ridiculous in the country as the behavior of the country is most mockable at the court.—Shakespeare.

Is the jay more precious than the lark because his feathers are more beautiful? Or is the adder better than the eel because his painted skin contents the eye?—Shakespeare.

The good often sigh more over little faults than the wicked over great. Hence an old proverb, that the stain appears greater according to the brilliancy of what it touches.—Palmieri.

Cruel men are the greatest lovers of mercy, avaricious men of generosity, and proud men of humility; that is to say, in others, not in themselves.—Colton.

Men and statues that are admired in an elevated situation have a very different effect upon us when we approach them; the first appear less than we imagined them, the last bigger.—Lord Greville.

By Heaven! upon the same man, as upon a vine-planted mount, there grow more kinds of wine than one; on the south side something little worse than nectar, on the north side something little better than vinegar.—Richter.

If there be light, then there is darkness; if cold, then heat; if height, depth also; if solid, then fluid; hardness and softness, roughness and smoothness, calm and tempest, prosperity and adversity, life and death.—Pythagoras.

As the rose-tree is composed of the sweetest flowers and the sharpest thorns,—as the heavens are sometimes overcast, alternately tempestuous and serene; so is the life of man intermingled with hopes and fears, with joy and sorrows, with pleasure and with pains.—Burton.

All things are double, one against another. Good is set against evil, and life against death; so is the godly against the sinner, and the sinner against the godly. Look upon all the works of the Most High, and there are two and two, one against another.—Bible.

Joy and grief are never far apart. In the same street the shutters of one house are closed, while the curtains of the next are brushed by shadows of the dance. A wedding-party returns from church, and a funeral winds to its door. The smiles and the sadness of life are the tragi-comedy of Shakespeare. Gladness and sighs brighten and dim the mirror he beholds.—Willmott.

Controversy

Where violence reigns, reason is weak.—Chamfort.

Fierceness makes error a fault and truth discourtesy.—George Herbert.

He who is not open to conviction is not qualified for discussion.—Whately.

Wise men argue causes, and fools decide them.—Anacharsis.

All disputation makes the mind deaf; and when people are deaf, I am dumb.—Joubert.

To think everything disputable is a proof of a weak mind and captious temper.—Beattie.

Controversy, though always an evil in itself, is sometimes a necessary evil. —Whately.

No great advance has ever been made in science, politics, or religion, without controversy.—Lyman Beecher.

When men differ in any matter of belief, let them meet each other manfully.—F. Wayland.

Doubtless there are times when controversy becomes a necessary evil. But let us remember that it is an evil.— Dean Stanley.

Disputation carries away the mind from that calm and sedate temper which is so necessary to contemplate truth.—Dr. Watts.

The precipitancy of disputation, and the stir and noise of passions that usually attend it, must needs be prejudicial to verity.—Glanvill.

There is no dispute managed without passion, and yet there is scarce a dispute worth a passion.—Sherlock.

It is very unfair in any writer to employ ignorance and malice together, because it gives his answerer double work.—Swift.

If a cause be good, the most violent attack of its enemies will not injure it so much as an injudicious defence of it by its friends.—Colton.

It is humbling to mankind to contemplate men capable of grasping eternal truths, fencing and debating in trivialities, like gladiators fighting with flies.—M. Nisard.

Suspense of judgment and exercise of charity were safer and seemlier for Christian men than the hot-pursuit of these controversies.—Hooker.

However some may affect to dislike controversy, it can never be of ultimate disadvantage to the interests of truth or the happiness of mankind.— Robert Hall.

It is almost always the unhappiness of a victorious disputant to destroy his own authority by claiming too many consequences, or diffusing his proposition to an indefensible extent.—Dr. Johnson.

He could raise scruples dark and nice,
And after solve 'em in a trice;
As if divinity had catch'd
The itch on purpose to be scratch'd.
—Butler.

Men of many words sometimes argue for the sake of talking; men of ready tongues frequently dispute for the sake of victory; men in public life often debate for the sake of opposing the ruling party, or from any other motive than the love of truth.—Crabbe.

When civil dudgeon first grew high,
And men fell out, they knew not why;
When hard words, jealousies, and fears
Set folk together by the ears,
And made them fight, like mad or drunk,
For dame Religion, as for punk.
—Butler.

What Tully said of war may be applied to disputing: "It should be always so managed as to remember that the only true end of it is peace." But generally true disputants are like true sportsmen,—their whole delight is in the pursuit; and the disputant no more cares for the truth than the sportsman for the hare.—Pope.

There is no learned man but will confess he hath much profited by reading controversies,—his senses awakened, his judgment sharpened, and the truth which he holds firmly established. If then it be profitable for him to read, why should it not at least be tolerable and free for his adversary to write? In logic they teach that contraries laid together, more evidently appear; it follows then, that all controversy being permitted, falsehood will appear more false, and truth the more true; which must needs conduce much to the general confirmation of an implicit truth. —Milton.

We are more inclined to hate one another for points on which we differ, than to love one another for points on which we agree. The reason perhaps is this: when we find others that agree with us, we seldom trouble ourselves to confirm that agreement; but when we chance on those who differ from us, we are zealous both to convince and to convert them. Our pride is hurt by the failure, and disappointed pride engenders hatred.—Colton.

Conversation

The soul of conversation is sympathy.—Hazlitt.

Unconstraint is the grace of conversation.—Dr. Johnson.

Silence is one great art of conversation.—Hazlitt.

The less men think, the more they talk.—Montesquieu.

Many can argue, not many converse.—A. Bronson Alcott.

Conversation is a game of circles.— Emerson.

All men, well interrogated, answer well.—Plato.

Debate is masculine; conversation is feminine.—A. Bronson Alcott.

With thee conversing I forget the way.—Gay.

With thee conversing I forget all time.—Milton.

Repose is as necessary in conversation as in a picture.—Hazlitt.

Be silent always, when you doubt your sense,
And speak, tho' sure, with seeming diffidence.   —Pope.

The best of life is conversation.— Emerson.

Discourse, the sweeter banquet of the mind.—Homer.

The secret of tiring is to say everything that can be said on the subject. —Voltaire.

Conceit causes more conversation than wit.—La Rochefoucauld.

Conversation is an abandonment to ideas, a surrender to persons.—A. Bronson Alcott.

Conversation is the vent of character as well as of thought.—Emerson.

Reasonable men are the best dictionaries of conversation.—Goethe.

Conversation is the laboratory and workshop of the student.—Emerson.

Conversation is an art in which a man has all mankind for competitors. —Emerson.

Conversation enriches the understanding, but solitude is the school of genius.—Gibbon.

His conversation does not show the minute hand; but he strikes the hour very correctly.—Sam'l Johnson.

Speak little and well, if you wish to be considered as possessing merit.— From the French.

Good discourse sinks differences and seeks agreements.—A. Bronson Alcott.

It is good to rub and polish our brain against that of others.—Montaigne.

Egotists cannot converse, they talk to themselves only.—A. Bronson Alcott.

In conversation avoid the extremes of forwardness and reserve.—Cato.

Form'd by thy converse, happily .o steer From grave to gay, from lively to severe. —Pope.

Conversation, which, when it is best, is a series of intoxications.—Emerson.

Questioning is not the mode of conversation among gentlemen.—Sam'l Johnson.

A great thing is a great book, but greater than all is the talk of a great man.—Earl of Beaconsfield.

While we converse with her, we mark No want of day, nor think it dark. —Waller.

The first ingredient in conversation is truth, the next good sense, the third good humor, and the fourth wit.—Sir W. Temple.

In the sallies of badinage a polite fool shines; but in gravity he is as awkward as an elephant disporting. —Zimmermann.

The perfection of conversational intercourse is when the breeding of high life is animated by the fervor of genius. —Leigh Hunt.

There is no arena is which vanity displays itself under such a variety of forms as in conversation.—Pascal.

One of the first observations to make in conversation is the state, or the character, and the education of the person to whom we speak.— Madame Necker.

It is by speech that many of our best gains are made. A large part of the good we receive comes to us in conversation.—Washington Gladden.

Our companions please us less from the charms we find in their conversation than from those they find in ours. —Lord Greville.

Amongst such as out of cunning hear all and talk little, be sure to talk less; or if you must talk, say little. —La Bruyère.

There are three things in speech that ought to be considered before some things are spoken—the manner, the place and the time.—Southey.

Topics of conversation among the multitude are generally persons, sometimes things, scarcely ever principles. —W. B. Clulow.

Not only to say the right thing in the right place, but, far more difficult still, to leave unsaid the wrong thing at the tempting moment.—G. A. Sala.

The perfection of conversation is not to play a regular sonata, but, like the Æolian harp, to await the inspiration of the passing breeze.—Burke.

A single conversation across the table with a wise man is better than ten years' study of books.—Longfellow.

The art of conversation is to be prompt without being stubborn, to refute without argument, and to clothe great matters in a motley garb.— Beaconsfield.

As it is the characteristic of great wits to say much in few words, so it is of small wits to talk much and say nothing.—Rochefoucauld.

Method is not less requisite in ordinary conversation than in writing, provided a man would talk to make himself understood.—Addison.

Debate is angular, conversation circular and radiant of the underlying unity.—A. Bronson Alcott.

The extreme pleasure we take in talking of ourselves should make us fear that we give very little to those who listen to us.—La Rochefoucauld.

Conversation stock being a joint and common property, every one should take a share in it; and yet there may be societies in which silence will be our best contribution.—Paul Chatfield, M. D.

The fool only is troublesome. A man of sense perceives when he is agreeable or tiresome; he disappears the very minute before he would have been thought to have stayed too long. —La Bruyère.

The great charm of conversation consists less in the display of one's own wit and intelligence than in the power to draw forth the resources of others.—Bruyère.

You must originate, and you must sympathize; you must possess, at the same time, the habit of communicating and the habit of listening. The union is rather rare, but irresistible.— Beaconsfield.

No one will ever shine in conversation who thinks of saying fine things; to please, one must say many things indifferent, and many very bad.— Francis Lockier.

He who sedulously attends, pointedly asks, calmly speaks, coolly answers, and ceases when he has no more to say, is in possession of some of the best requisites of man.—Lavater.

Never hold any one by the button or the hand in order to be heard out; for if people are unwilling to hear you, you had better hold your tongue than them.—Chesterfield.

Conversation is interesting in proportion to the originality of the central ideas which serve as pivots, and the fitness of the little facts and observations which are contributed by the talkers.—Hamerton.

A dearth of words a woman need not fear;
But 'tis a task indeed to learn to hear:
In that the skill of conversation lies;
That shows or makes you both polite and
    wise.   —Young.

Conversation never sits easier upon us than when we now and then discharge ourselves in a symphony of laughter, which may not improperly be called the chorus of conversation.— Steele.

In conversation, humor is more than wit, easiness more than knowledge; few desire to learn, or think they need it; all desire to be pleased, or, at least, to be easy.—Sir W. Temple.

Those who speak always and those who never speak are equally unfit for friendship. A good proportion of the talent of listening and speaking is the base of social virtues.—Lavater.

The fullest instruction, and the fullest enjoyment are never derived from books, till we have ventilated the ideas thus obtained, in free and easy chat with others—Wm. Matthews.

They would talk of nothing but high life and high-lived company, with other fashionable topics, such as pictures, taste, Shakespeare, and the musical glasses.—Goldsmith.

Conversation should be pleasant without scurrility, witty without affectation, free without indecency, learned without conceitedness, novel without falsehood.—Shakespeare.

To speak well supposes a habit of attention which shows itself in the thought; by language we learn to think, and above all to develop thought.—Bonstetten.

Men of great conversational powers almost universally practice a sort of lively sophistry and exaggeration which deceives for the moment both themselves and their auditors.—Macaulay.

But conversation, choose what theme we
    may,
And chiefly when religion leads the way,
Should flow, like waters after summer
    show'rs,
Not as if raised by mere mechanic powers.
          —Cowper.

In private conversation between intimate friends, the wisest men very often talk like the weakest; for indeed the talking with a friend is nothing else but thinking aloud.—Addison.

There is nothing by which a man exasperates most people more than by displaying a superior ability or brilliancy in conversation. They seem pleased at the time, but their envy makes them curse him at their hearts.—Johnson.

I never, with important air,
In conversation overbear.
* * * * * * *
My tongue within my lips I rein;
For who talks much must talk in vain.
—Gay.

If it were not for respect for human opinions, I would not open my window to see the Bay of Naples for the first time, whilst I would go five hundred leagues to talk with a man of genius whom I had not seen.—Mme. de Staël.

One of the best rules in conversation is, never say a thing which any of the company can reasonably wish we had rather left unsaid. Let the sage reflections of these philosophic minds be cherished.—Swift.

If conversation be an art, like painting, sculpture, and literature, it owes its most powerful charm to nature; and the least shade of formality or artifice destroys the effect of the best collection of words.—Tuckerman.

The secret of pleasing in conversation is not to explain too much everything; to say them half and leave a little for divination is a mark of the good opinion we have of others, and nothing flatters their self-love more.—Rochefoucauld.

One thing which makes us find so few people who appear reasonable and agreeable in conversation is, that there is scarcely any one who does not think more of what he is about to say than of answering precisely what is said to him.—La Rochefoucauld.

Silence is one great art of conversation. He is not a fool who knows when to hold his tongue; and a person may gain credit for sense, eloquence, wit, who merely says nothing to lessen the opinion which others have of these qualities in themselves.—Hazlitt.

Jeffrey, in conversation, was like a skilful swordsman flourishing his weapon in the air; while Mackintosh, with a thin sharp rapier, in the middle of his evolutions, ran him through the body.—Sir A. Alison.

Among the arts of conversation no one pleases more than mutual deference or civility, which leads us to resign our own inclinations to those of our companions, and to curb and conceal that presumption and arrogance so natural to the human mind.—Hume.

The great secret of succeeding in conversation is to admire little, to hear much; always to distrust our own reason, and sometimes that of our friends; never to pretend to wit, but to make that of others appear as much as possibly we can; to hearken to what is said, and to answer to the purpose.—Benjamin Franklin.

It is given to few persons to keep this secret well. Those who lay down rules too often break them, and the safest we are able to give is to listen much, to speak little, and to say nothing that will ever give ground for regret.—La Rochefoucauld.

When we are in the company of sensible men, we ought to be doubly cautious of talking too much, lest we lose two good things, their good opinion and our own improvement; for what we have to say we know, but what they have to say we know not.—Colton.

Some men are very entertaining for a first interview, but after that they are exhausted, and run out; on a second meeting we shall find them flat and monotonous; like hand-organs, we have heard all their tunes.—Colton.

Abstruse and mystic thoughts you must express with painful care, but seeming easiness.—Wentworth Dillon.

It is a secret known but to few, yet of no small use in the conduct of life, that when you fall into a man's conversation, the first thing you should consider is, whether he has a greater inclination to hear you, or that you should hear him.—Steele.

There is nothing so delightful as the hearing, or the speaking of truth. For this reason, there is no conversation so agreeable as that of the man of integrity, who hears without any intention to betray, and speaks without any intention to deceive.—Plato.

These high wild hills and rough uneven ways,
Draw out our miles and make them wearisome;
And yet your fair discourse hath been as sugar,
Making the hard way sweet and delectable.
—Shakespeare

Conversation opens our views, and gives our faculties a more vigorous play; it puts us upon turning our notions on every side, and holds them up to a light that discovers those latent flaws which would probably have lain concealed in the gloom of unagitated abstraction.—Melmoth.

The tone of good conversation is brilliant and natural; it is neither tedious nor frivolous; it is instructive without pedantry, gay without tumultuousness, polished without affection, gallant without insipidity, waggish without equivocation.—Rousseau.

He is so full of pleasant anecdote;
So rich, so gay, so poignant in his wit,
Time vanishes before him as he speaks,
And ruddy morning through the lattice peeps
Ere night seems well begun.
—Joanna Baillie.

Wise, cultivated, genial conversation is the last flower of civilization, and the best result which life has to offer us,—a cup for gods, which has no repentance. Conversation is our account of ourselves. All we have, all we can, all we know, is brought into play, and as the reproduction in finer form, of all our havings.—Emerson.

Discretion of speech is more than eloquence; and to speak agreeably to him with whom we deal, is more than to speak in good words or in good order. A good continued speech,

without a good speech of interlocution, shows slowness; and a good reply, or second speech, without a good settled speech, showeth shallowness and weakness.—Bacon.

One would think that the larger the company is in which we are engaged, the greater variety of thoughts and subjects would be started into discourse; but, instead of this we find that conversation is never so much straightened and confined, as in numerous assemblies.—Addison.

With good and gentle-humored hearts
I choose to chat where'er I come
Whate'er the subject be that starts.
But if I get among the glum
I hold my tongue to tell the truth
And keep my breath to cool my broth.
—John Byrom.

There is a sort of knowledge beyond the power of learning to bestow, and this is to be had in conversation; so necessary is this to the understanding the characters of men, that none are more ignorant of them than those learned pedants whose lives have been entirely consumed in colleges and among books; for however exquisitely human nature may have been described by writers the true practical system can be learned only in the world.—Fielding.

In my whole life I have only known ten or twelve persons with whom it was pleasant to speak,—i. e., who keep to the subject, do not repeat themselves, and do not talk of themselves; men who do not listen to their own voice, who are cultivated enough not to lose themselves in commonplaces, and, lastly, who possess tact and good taste enough not to elevate their own persons above their subjects.—Metternich.

There is speaking well, speaking easily, speaking justly and speaking seasonably: It is offending against the last, to speak of entertainments before the indigent; of sound limbs and health before the infirm; of houses and lands before one who has not so much as a dwelling; in a word, to speak of your prosperity before the miserable; this conversation is cruel, and the comparison which naturally arises in them betwixt their condition and yours is excruciating.—La Bruyère.

————

One could take down a book from a shelf ten times more wise and witty than almost any man's conversation. Bacon is wiser, Swift more humorous, than any person one is likely to meet with; but they cannot chime in with the exact frame of thought in which we happen to take them down from our shelves. Therein lies the luxury of conversation: and when a living speaker does not yield us that luxury, he becomes only a book on two legs.—Campbell.

————

Solitary reading will enable a man to stuff himself with information; but, without conversation, his mind will become like a pond without an outlet —a mass of unhealthy stagnature. It is not enough to harvest knowledge by study; the wind of talk must winnow it, and blow away the chaff; then will the clear, bright grains of wisdom be garnered, for our own use or that of others.—Wm. Matthews.

————

The progress of a private conversation betwixt two persons of different sexes is often decisive of their fate, and gives it a turn very distinct perhaps from what they themselves anticipated. Gallantry becomes mingled with conversation, and affection and passion come gradually to mix with gallantry. Nobles, as well as shepherd swains, will, in such a trying moment, say more than they intended; and queens, like village maidens, will listen longer than they should.—Walter Scott.

————

Conversation is the music of the mind, an intellectual orchestra, where all the instruments should bear a part, but where none should play together. Each of the performers should have a just appreciation of his own powers, otherwise an unskilful novice who might usurp the first fiddle, would infallibly get into a scrape. To prevent these mistakes, a good master of the band will be very particular in the assortment of the performers; if too dissimilar, there will be no harmony, if too few, there will be no variety;

and if too numerous, there will be no order, for the presumption of one prater, might silence the eloquence of a Burke, or the wit of a Sheridan, as a single kettle-drum would drown the finest solo of a Gionowich or a Jordini.—Colton.

————

He that questioneth much shall learn much, and content much; but especially if he apply his questions to the skill of the persons whom he asketh; for he shall give them occasion to please themselves in speaking, and himself shall continually gather knowledge; but let his questions not be troublesome, for that is fit for a poser; and let him be sure to leave other men their turn to speak; nay, if there be any that would reign and take up all the time, let them find means to take them off, and bring others on,—as musicians used to do with those that dance too long galliards. If you dissemble sometimes your knowledge of that you are thought to know, you shall be thought, another time, to know that you know not.—Bacon.

Conversion

Lord, what wilt Thou have me to do?—Bible.

————

It is slow work to be born again.—Beecher.

————

As to the value of conversion God alone can judge.—Goethe.

————

A man to be converted has to give up his will, his ways, and his thoughts.—D. L. Moody.

————

The time when I was converted was when religion became no longer a duty, but a pleasure.—Prof. Lincoln.

————

It is pleasant to see a notorious profligate seized with a concern for religion, and converting his spleen into zeal.—Addison.

————

These, by obtruding the beginning of a change for the entire work of new life, will fall under the former guilt.—Henry Hammond.

————

My observation continues to confirm me more and more in the opinion that to experience religion is to experience the truth of the great doctrines of divine grace.—Ichabod Spencer.

Palaces and pyramids are reared by laying one brick, or block, at a time; and the kingdom of Christ is enlarged by individual conversions.—Aughey.

You cannot find, I believe, a case in the Bible where a man is converted without God's calling in some human agency—using some human instrument.—D. L. Moody.

Every man or woman who turns to Christ must bear in mind that they are breaking with their old master, and enlisting under a new leader. Conversion is a revolutionary process.—T. L. Cuyler.

Conversion by the Holy Spirit is a spiritual illumination of the soul. God's grace lights up the dark heart. And when a man has once been kindled at the cross of Christ, he is bound to shine.—T. L. Cuyler.

Conversion is the act of joining our hands to the pierced hand of the crucified Saviour. The new life begins with the taking of Christ's hand, and His taking hold, in infinite love, of our weak hands.—T. L. Cuyler.

The evidence of our acceptance in the Beloved arises in proportion to our love, to our repentance, to our humility, to our faith, to our self-denial, to our delight in duty. Other evidence than this the Bible knows not—God has not given.—Gardiner Spring.

In what way, or by what manner of working, God changes a soul from evil to good, how He impregnates the barren rock—the priceless gems and gold —is to the human mind an impenetrable mystery, in all cases alike. —Coleridge.

The most zealous converters are always the most rancorous when they fail of producing conversion.—Colton.

Conversion is not, as some suppose, a violent opening of the heart by grace, in which will, reason and judgment are all ignored or crushed. The reason is not blinded, but enlightened;

and the whole man is made to act with a glorious liberty which it never knew till it fell under the restraints of grace. —C. H. Spurgeon.

This is always the way in which the reality of Christian conversion evidences itself. It makes the selfish man charitable; the churlish, liberal; and implants in the soul, which hitherto has cared only for the things belonging to himself, a disposition to seek also the things of others.—William Adams.

Conversion goes on more prosperously in Tanjore and other provinces, where there are no Europeans, than in Tranquebar, where they are numerous; for we find that European example in the large towns is the bane of Christian instruction.—Rev. Dr. Buchanan.

As to the value of conversions, God alone can judge. God alone can know how wide are the steps which the soul has to take before it can approach to a community with Him, to the dwelling of the perfect, or to the intercourse and friendship of higher natures.—Goethe.

"Follow me!" The publican "rose up." This implies immediate action. It was now or never with him. So you must act with prompt obedience. He did the first thing Jesus bade him do. Are you willing to do as much? If not, you are deciding against Christ, and that means death. —T. L. Cuyler.

In every sound convert the judgment is brought to approve of the laws and ways of Christ, and subscribe to them as most righteous and reasonable; the desire of the heart is to know the whole mind of Christ; the free and resolved choice of the heart is determined for the ways of Christ, before all the pleasures of sin, and prosperities of the world; it is the daily care of his life to walk with God. —Joseph Alleine.

I have known men who thought the object of conversion was to cleanse them as a garment is cleansed, and that when they are converted they were to be hung up in the Lord's wardrobe, the door of which was to be shut, so that no dust could get at them. A coat that is not used the moths eat; and a Christian who is hung up so that he shall not be tempted, the moths eat him; and they have poor food at that.—Beecher.

Should you suffer your weary soul this day to sink into the arms of that Saviour who rejoices to pardon and is mighty to save, the first entrance of such a word, and the first response of such a faith, would be the date of your better life and the commencement of your union to Christ. The graft has taken. At first the juncture may be very slight—a single thread or fiber—and it is not till you try to part them that you find that they are knit together; that their life is one, and that the force which plucks away the graft must also wound the vine. And your faith may yet be no more than a single filament. It may be only one point of attachment by which you are joined to the Lord Jesus. It may be only one solitary sentence, one isolated invitation or promise, of which you have undoubting hold. But hold it fast. If it be the word of Jesus, cling to it.—Aughey.

Conviction

I will listen to any one's convictions, but pray keep your doubts to yourself. —Goethe.

Conviction is oftener the child of Temperament than of Reason.—Mme. de Lambert.

Conviction is the conscience of the mind.—Chamfort.

What man in his right mind would conspire his own hurt? Men are beside themselves when they transgress against their convictions.—William Penn.

No human power can force the intrenchments of the human mind: compulsion never persuades; it only makes hypocrites.—Fénelon.

To remember that once we were near the salvation of Christ, so near that our right hand might have touched and taken it, and after all that hand was withheld; this is a memory which will enhance remorse forever.— William Adams.

True conviction of sin—how difficult it is, when its appearances and modes of life are so fair, when it twines itself so cunningly about, or creeps so insidiously into, our amiable qualities, and sets off its internal disorders by so many outward charms and attractions. —Horace Bushnell.

It is no certain evidence, that because the conscience feels the weight of sin, the heart is humbled on account of it; that because the conscience approves of the rectitude of the Divine justice, the heart bows to the Divine sovereignty. The most powerful conviction of sin, therefore, is not conclusive evidence of Christian character.—Gardiner Spring.

Coquette

All women seem by nature to be coquettes.—Rochefoucauld.

Coquetry is the champagne of love. —Hood.

Coquetry is the art of successful deception.—Mme. Louise Colet.

Coquetry is love without conscience. —Mathieu Moté.

The most effective coquetry is innocence.—Lamartine.

What careth she for hearts when once possessed?—Byron.

By her we first were taught the wheedling art.—Gay.

New vows to plight, and plighted vows to break.—Dryden.

Though it is pleasant weaving nets, it is wiser to make cages.—Moore.

It is a species of coquetry to make a parade of never practising it.—La Rochefoucauld.

God created the coquette as soon as He had made the fool.—Victor Hugo.

Women know not the whole of their coquetry.—La Rochefoucauld.

Coquetry is the desire to inspire love without experiencing it yourself.—Mme. de Brade.

Provocation is one of the arts of coquetry for which virtue often pays the penalty.—Lingrée.

There is but one antidote for coquetry,—true love.—Mme. Deluzy.

All's one to her; above her fan she'd make sweet eyes to Caliban.—Aldrich.

The maid whom now you court in vain
Will quickly run in quest of man.
—Horace.

Mincing she was, as is a wanton colt,
Sweet as a flower and upright as a bolt.
—Chaucer.

The greatest miracle of love is the cure of coquetry.—La Rochefoucauld.

She lik'd his soothing lutes, his presents more,
And granted kisses, but would grant no more. —Gay.

Bright as the sun her eyes the gazers strike,
And, like the sun, they shine on all alike.
—Pope.

A modern writer likens coquettes to those hunters who do not eat the game which they have successfully pursued. —Miss Braddon.

A flirt is like a dipper attached to a hydrant; every one is at liberty to drink from it, but no one desires to carry it away.—N. P. Willis.

The ladies—Heaven bless them!—are, as a general rule, coquettes from babyhood upwards.—Thackeray.

Women find it far more difficult to overcome their inclination to coquetry than to overcome their love.—Rochefoucauld.

It is, as it were, born in maidens that they should wish to please everything that has eyes.—Solomon Gessner.

An accomplished coquette excites the passions of others in proportion as she feels none herself.—Hazlitt.

Faints into airs and languishes with pride;
On the rich quilt sinks with becoming woe,
Wrapt in a gown for sickness and for show.
—Pope.

Heartlessness and fascination, in about equal quantities, constitute the receipt for forming the character of a coquette.—Mme. Deluzy.

From loveless youth to unrespected age
No passion gratified, except her rage;
So much the fury still outran the wit,
The pleasure miss'd her, and the scandal hit.
—Pope.

For a woman to be at once a coquette and a bigot is more than the humblest of husbands can bear; she should mercifully choose between the two.—Bruyère.

The life of a coquette is one constant lie; and the only rule by which you can form any correct judgment of them is that they are never what they seem.—Fielding.

The coquette has companions, indeed, but no lovers,—for love is respectful and timorous; and where among her followers will she find a husband?—Dr. Johnson.

How happy could I be with either,
Were t'other dear charmer away!
But while ye thus tease me together,
To neither a word will I say. —Gay.

Like a lovely tree
She grew to womanhood, and between whiles
Rejected several suitors, just to learn
How to accept a better in his turn.
—Byron.

"With every pleasing, every prudent part,
Say, What can Chloe want?"—she wants a heart.
She speaks, behaves, and acts just as she ought;
But never, never reach'd one generous thought. —Pope.

Coquetry is the essential characteristic, and the prevalent humor of women; but they do not all practise it, because the coquetry of some is re-

strained by fear or by reason.—La
Rochefoucauld.

The vain coquette each suit disdains,
And glories in her lover's pains;
With age she fades—each lover flies,
Contemn'd, forlorn, she pines and dies.
—Gay.

Would you teach her to love?
For a time seem to rove;
At first she may frown in a pet;
But leave her awhile,
She shortly will smile,
And then you may win your coquette.
—Byron.

Now Laura moves along the joyous crowd,
Smiles in her eyes, and simpers in her lips;
To some she whispers, others speaks aloud;
To some she curtsies, and to some she dips.
—Byron.

Ye belles, and ye flirts, and ye pert little
things,
Who trip in this frolicsome round,
Pray tell me from whence this impertinence
springs,
The sexes at once to confound?
—Whitehead.

See how the world its veterans reward!
A youth of frolics, an old age of cards;
Fair to no purpose, artful to no end,
Young without lovers, old without a friend;
A fop their passion but their prize a sot,
Alive ridiculous, and dead forgot!
—Pope.

Coquetry whets the appetite; flirtation depraves it. Coquetry is the
thorn that guards the rose—easily
trimmed off when once plucked. Flirtation is like the slime on water-
plants, making them hard to handle,
and when caught, only to be cherished
in slimy waters.—Ik Marvel.

She who only finds her self-esteem
In others' admiration, begs an alms;
Depends on others for her daily food,
And is the very servant of her slaves;
Tho' oftentimes, in a fantastic hour,
O'er men she may a childish pow'r exert,
Which not ennobles but degrades her state.
—Joanna Baillie.

Coquettes are but too rare. It is a
career that requires great abilities,
infinite pains, a gay and airy spirit.
'T is the coquette who provides all
the amusements,—suggests the riding-
party, plans the picnic, gives and
guesses charades, acts them. She is

the stirring element amid the heavy
congeries of social atoms,—the soul of
the house, the salt of the banquet.—
Beaconsfield.

Such is your cold coquette, who can't say
"No,"
And won't say "Yes," and keeps you on and
off-ing
On a lee-shore, till it begins to blow,
Then sees your heart wreck'd, with an in-
ward scoffing.
—Byron.

Then in a kiss she breath'd her various arts,
Of trifling prettily with wounded hearts;
A mind for love, but still a changing mind,
The lisp affected, and the glance design'd;
The sweet confusing blush, the secret wink,
The gentle swimming walk, the courteous
sink;
The stare for strangeness fit, for scorn the
frown
For decent yielding, looks declining down;
The practis'd languish, where well-feign'd
desire
Would own its melting in a mutual fire;
Gay smiles to comfort; April showers to
move;
And all the nature, all the art of love.
—Parnell.

A coquette is one that is never to be
persuaded out of the passion she has
to please, nor out of a good opinion
of her own beauty: time and years she
regards as things that only wrinkle
and decay other women, forgetting
that age is written in the face, and
that the same dress which became her
when she was young now only makes
her look older.—Bruyère.

Corner Stone Laying

To whom coming, as unto a living
stone, disallowed indeed of men, but
chosen of God, and precious.—I Pet.
ii. 4.

Christ is the foundation of all our
hopes for time and for eternity. Oh,
build on this divine foundation! All
other foundations are sinking sand.—
Robert S. MacArthur, D. D.

These fair stones remind us that ere
long it will be our privilege to worship God in a place of greater beauty
and dignity than has thus far been
our lot.—S. C. Edsall.

May the influence of this great
church be found for Christ in every
part of this world!—Cortland Myers.

May the whole structure be one of the treasures opened by wise men for the incarnate Christ. May every passer-by hear echoing from its walls the angelic song, "Behold, I bring you good tidings of great joy."—Cortland Myers.

May this temple have for its corner-stone Christ in theology, Christ in worship, Christ in work, Christ in character—four-sided, square, and perfect. May there not be one square foot of standing-room for the preacher who takes one verse from the Bible or one star from the brow of the Christ. May form and superstition and idolatry be banished from its worship, and lines never be drawn between the worshipers. Over every one of its nine entrances let the chisel cut that large gospel word, "Whosoever."—Cortland Myers.

Corporations

They cannot commit treason, nor be outlawed, nor excommunicate, for they have no souls.—Sir Edward Coke.

You never expected justice from a company, did you? They have neither a soul to lose, nor a body to kick.—Lord Thurlow.

Corruption

Loathsome canker lives in sweetest bud.—Shakespeare.

The more corrupt the state, the more laws.—Tacitus.

——I have seen corruption boil and bubble 'Till it o'errun the stew. —Shakespeare.

Be certain that he who has betrayed thee once will betray thee again.—Lavater.

A corrupt judge does not carefully search for the truth.—Horace.

E'en grave divines submit to glittering gold, The best of consciences are bought and sold. —Dr. Wolcot.

O that estates, degrees, and offices were not derived corruptly! and that clear honor were purchased by the merit of the wearer!—Shakespeare.

I have been young and am now old, and have not yet known an untruthful man to come to a good end.—Auerbach.

Our supple tribes repress their patriot throats, And ask no questions but the price of votes. —Dr. Johnson.

He that accuses all mankind of corruption ought to remember that he is sure to convict only one.—Burke.

Whoso seeks an audit here Propitious, pays his tribute, game or fish, Wild fowl or venison, and his errand speeds. —Cowper.

And conscience, truth and honesty are made To rise and fall, like other wares of trade. —Moore.

He who tempts, though in vain, at last asperses The tempted with dishonor foul, supposed Not incorruptible of faith, not proof Against temptation. —Milton.

Corruption is a tree, whose branches are Of an unmeasurable length: they spread Ev'rywhere; and the dew that drops from thence Hath infected some chairs and stools of authority. —Beaumont and Fletcher.

When rogues like these (a sparrow cries) To honours and employments rise, I court no favor, ask no place, For such preferment is disgrace. —Gay.

Here let those reign, whom pensions can incite, To vote a patriot black, a courtier white, Explain their country's dear-bought rights away, And plead for pirates in the face of day. —Dr. Johnson.

There is something in corruption which, like a jaundiced eye, transfers the color of itself to the object it looks upon, and sees everything stained and impure.—Thomas Paine.

This mournful truth is everywhere confess'd, Slow rises worth by poverty depress'd: But here more slow, where all are slaves to gold, Where looks are merchandise, and smiles are sold. —Dr. Johnson.

Men by associating in large masses, as in camps, and in cities, improve their talents, but impair their virtues, and strengthen their minds, but weaken their morals; thus a retrocession in the one is too often the price they pay for a refinement in the other.—Colton.

At length corruption, like a general flood,
(So long by watchful ministers withstood,)
Shall deluge all; and avarice creeping on,
Spread like a low-born mist, and blot the sun.   —Pope.

Like a young eagle who has lent his plume,
To fledge the shaft by which he meets his
  doom,
See their own feathers pluck'd, to wing the
  dart,
Which rank corruption destines for their
  heart!   —Moore.

Hence, wretched nation! all thy woes arise,
Avow'd corruption, licens'd perjuries,
Eternal taxes, treaties for a day,
Servants that rule, and senates that obey.
     —Lord Lyttleton.

The impious man, who sells his country's
  freedom
Makes all the guilt of tyranny his own.
His are her slaughters, her oppressions his;
Just heav'n! reserve your choicest plagues
  for him,
And blast the venal wretch.

     —Martyn.

But though bare merit might in Rome appear
The strongest plea for favour, 'tis not here;
We form our judgment in another way;
And they will best succeed, who best can
  pay;
Those, who would gain the votes of British
  tribes,
Must add to force of merit, force of bribes.
     —Churchill.

'Tis pleasant purchasing our fellow-creatures,
And all are to be sold if you consider
Their passions, and are dext'rous; some by
  features
Are bought up, others by a warlike leader;
Some by a place, as tend their years or
  natures;
The most by ready cash—but all have prices,
From crowns to kicks, according to their
  vices.   —Byron.

Examine well his milk-white hand, the palm is hardly clean,—but here and there an ugly smutch appears. Foh! It was a bribe that left it. He has touched corruption.—Cowper.

For, firm within, and while at heart untouch'd,
Ne'er yet by force was freedom overcome.
But soon as independence stoops the head,
To vice-enslaved, and vice-created wants,
Then to some foul corrupting-hand, whose
  waste
Their craving lusts with fatal bounty feeds,
They fall a willing, undefended prize;
From man to man th' infectious softness
  runs,
Till the whole state unnerved in slavery
  sinks.   —Thomson.

If, ye powers divine!
Ye mark the movements of this nether world
And bring them to account, crush, crush,
  those vipers,
Who, singled out by a community
To guard their rights, shall, for a grasp of
  air,
Or paltry office, sell 'em to the foe.
     —Miller.

Counsel

In the multitude of counsellors there is safety.—Proverbs xi. 14.

Good counsels observed are chains of grace.—Thomas Fuller.

Let no man value at little price a virtuous woman's counsel.—George Chapman.

The best receipt—best to work and best to take—is the admonition of a friend.—Bacon.

When all is done, the help of good counsel is that which setteth business straight.—Bacon.

They say that the best counsel is that of woman.—Calderon.

Bosom up my counsel,
You'll find it wholesome.—Shakespeare.

Hasty counsels are generally followed by repentance.—Laberius.

And if the blind lead the blind, both shall fall into the ditch.—Bible.

Harsh counsels have little or no effect; they are like hammers which are always repulsed by the anvil.—Helvetius.

I will adhere to the counsels of good men, although misfortune and death should be the consequence.—Cicero.

I can easier teach twenty what were good to be done, than be one of the twenty to follow mine own teaching.— Shakespeare.

Counsel and conversation is a good second education, that improves all the virtues and corrects all the vices.— Clarendon.

Let no man presume to give advice to others that has not first given counsel to himself.—Seneca.

Good counsels observed are chains to grace, which neglected, prove halters to strange undutiful children.— Fuller.

And cast
O'er erring deeds and thoughts a heav'nly hue
Of words, like sunbeams, dazzling as they pass'd.   —Byron.

The secret counsels of princes are a troublesome burden to such as have only to execute them.—Montaigne.

Though I may not be able to inform men more than they know, yet I may give them the occasion to consider.— Sir W. Temple.

Ah, gentle dames! it gars me greet,
To think how monie counsels sweet,
How monie lengthened sage advices,
The husband frae the wife despises.
    —Burns.

A man takes contradiction and advice much more easily than people think, only he will not bear it when violently given, even though it be well founded.—Richter.

I pray thee, cease thy counsel,
Which falls into mine ears as profitless
As water in a sieve.   —Shakespeare.

Consult your friend on all things, especially on those which respect yourself. His counsel may then be useful, where your own self-love might impair your judgment.—Seneca.

Countenance

The countenance may be rightly defined as the title page which heralds the contents of the human volume, but like other title pages, it sometimes puzzles, often misleads, and often says nothing to the purpose.—Wm. Matthews.

The cheek
Is apter than the tongue to tell an errand.
    —Shakespeare.

A countenance more
In sorrow than in anger.—Shakespeare.

Yea this man's brow, like to a tragic leaf,
Foretells the nature of a tragic volume.
    —Shakespeare.

A sweet attractive kind of grace,
   A full assurance given by looks,
Continual comfort in a face,
   The lineaments of Gospel books—
I trow that countenance cannot lye
Whose thoughts are legible in the eye.
    —Spenser.

Physically, they exhibited no indication of their past lives and characters. The greatest scamp had a Raphael face, with a profusion of blonde hair; Oakhurst, a gambler, had the melancholy character and intellectual abstraction of a Hamlet; the coolest and most courageous man was scarcely over five feet in height, with a soft voice, and an embarrassed manner.— Bret Harte.

Country — Country Life

Sunny spots of greenery.—Coleridge.

Far from the gay cities, and the ways of men.—Homer.

Men are taught virtue and a love of independence by living in the country.—Menander.

If country life be healthful to the body, it is no less so to the mind.— Ruffini.

Nor rural sights alone, out rural sounds
Exhilarate the spirit, and restore
The tone of languid Nature. —Cowper.

Sir, when you have seen one green field, you have seen all green fields. Let us walk down Cheapside.—Johnson.

I consider it the best part of an education to have been born and brought up in the country.—Alcott.

One gets sensitive about losing mornings after getting a little used to them with living in the country. Each one of these endlessly varied daybreaks is an opera but once performed.—Willis.

———

This pure air
Braces the listless nerves, and warms the blood:
I feel in freedom here. —Joanna Baillie.

———

Scenes must be beautiful which daily view'd
Please daily, and whose novelty survives
Long knowledge and the scrutiny of years.
—Cowper.

———

Secure and free they pass their harmless hours,
Gay as the birds that revel in the grove,
And sing the morning up. —Tate.

———

Ye sacred Nine! that all my soul possess . . .
Bear me, O bear me to sequestered scenes,
The bow'ry mazes, and surrounding greens. —Pope.

———

The city reveals the moral ends of being, and sets the awful problem of life. The country soothes us, refreshes us, lifts us up with religious suggestion.—Chapin.

———

To one who has been long in city pent,
'Tis very sweet to look into the fair
And open face of heaven,—to breathe a prayer
Full in the smile of the blue firmament.
—Keats.

———

And as I read
I hear the crowing cock, I hear the note
Of lark and linnet, and from every page
Rise odors of ploughed field or flowery mead. —Longfellow.

———

Thus is nature's vesture wrought
Too instruct our wandering thought;
Thus she dresses green and gay
To disperse our cares away. —Dyer.

———

From the white-thorn the May-flower shed
Its dewy fragrance round our head;
Not Ariel lived more merrily
Under the blossom'd bough than we.
—Scott.

———

There is virtue in country houses, in gardens and orchards, in fields, streams, and groves, in rustic recreations and plain manners, that neither cities nor universities enjoy.—Alcott.

Nature I'll court in her sequester'd haunts,
By mountain, meadow, streamlet, grove, or cell;
Where the pois'd lark his evening ditty chants,
And health, and peace, and contemplation dwell. —Smollett.

———

Mine be a cot beside the hill;
A beehive's hum shall soothe my ear;
A willowy brook, that turns a mill,
With many a fall, shall linger near.
—Sam'l Rogers.

———

Within the sun-lit forest,
Our roof the bright blue sky,
Where fountains flow, and wild flowers blow,
We lift our hearts on high.
—Ebenezer Elliott.

———

Give me, indulgent gods! with mind serene,
And guiltless heart, to range the sylvan scene;
No splendid poverty, no smiling care,
No well-bred hate, or servile grandeur there.
—Young.

———

The fields did laugh, the flowers did freshly spring,
The trees did bud and early blossoms bore,
And all the quire of birds did sweetly sing,
And told that gardin's pleasures in their caroling. —Spenser.

———

A wilderness of sweets; for nature here
Wanton'd as in her prime, and play'd at will
Her virgin fancies, pouring forth more sweets;
Wild above rule or art, enormous bliss.
—Milton.

———

O happy if ye knew your happy state,
Ye rangers of the fields! whom nature's boon
Cheers with her smiles, and ev'ry element
Conspires to bless. —Somerville.

———

Oh knew he but his happiness, of men
The happiest he! who far from public rage,
Deep in the vale, with a choice few retir'd
Drinks the pure pleasures of the rural life.
—Thomson.

———

There health, so wild and gay, with bosom bare
And rosy cheek, keen eye, and flowing hair,
Trips with a smile the breezy scene along
And pours the spirit of content in song.
—Dr. Wolcot.

———

In those vernal seasons of the year, when the air is calm and pleasant, it were an injury and sullenness against nature not to go out and see her riches, and partake in her rejoicing with heaven and earth.—Milton.

God made the country, and man made the town;
What wonder then, that health and virtue, gifts,
That can alone make sweet the bitter draught
That life holds out to all, should most abound,
And least be threatened in the fields and groves?   —Cowper.

And see the country, far diffused around,
One boundless blush, one white impurpled shower
Of mingled blossoms! where the raptured eye
Hurries from joy to joy.   —Thomson.

As a light,
And pliant harebell swinging in the breeze
On some grey rock—its birth-place—so had I
Wanton'd, fast-rooted in the ancient tower
Of my beloved country, wishing not
A happier fortune, than to wither there.
    —Wordsworth.

Here too dwells simple truth; plain innocence;
Unsullied beauty; sound unbroken youth,
Patient of labour, with a little pleas'd;
Health ever blooming; unambitious toil,
Calm contemplation; and poetic ease.
    —Thomson.

This is a beautiful life now, privacy,
The sweetness and the benefit of essence;
I see there is no man but may make his paradise,
And it is nothing but his love and dotage
Upon the world's foul joys that keeps him out on't.   —Beaumont and Fletcher.

They love the country, and none else, who seek
For their own sake its silence and its shade.
Delights which who would leave, that has a heart
Susceptible of pity, or a mind
Cultured and capable of sober thought.
    —Cowper.

Ask any school-boy up to the age of fifteen where he would spend his holidays. Not one in five hundred will say, "In the streets of London," if you give him the option of green fields and running waters. It is, then, a fair presumption that there must be something of the child still in the character of the men or the women whom

---

the country charms in maturer as in dawning life.—Bulwer-Lytton.

Under a tuft of shade that on the green
Stood whisp'ring soft, by a fresh fountain side
They sat them down; and after no more toil
Of their sweet gard'ning labour than suffic'd
To recommend cool zephyr, and made ease
More easy, wholesome thirst and appetite
More grateful, to their supper fruits they fell.   —Milton.

How various his employments, whom the world
Calls idle, and who justly in return
Esteems that busy world an idler too!
Friends, books, a garden, and perhaps his pen,
Delightful industry enjoyed at home,
And Nature in her cultivated trim,
Dressed to his taste, inviting him abroad.
    —Cowper.

Now the summer's in prime
Wi' the flowers richly blooming,
And the wild mountain thyme
A' the moorlands perfuming.
To own dear native scenes
Let us journey together,
Where glad innocence reigns
'Mang the braes o' Balquhither.
    —Robert Tannahill.

O, when I am safe in my sylvan home,
I mock at the pride of Greece and Rome;
And when I am stretch'd beneath the pines
When the evening star so holy shines,
I laugh at the lore and pride of man,
At the Sophist's schools, and the learned clan;
For what are they all in their high conceit,
When man in the bush with God may meet?
    —R. W. Emerson.

I'm weary of my lonely hut
And of its blasted tree,
The very lake is like my lot,
So silent constantly—
I've liv'd amid the forest gloom
Until I almost fear—
When will the thrilling voices come
My spirit thirsts to hear?   —Willis.

There is a something in the pleasures of the country that reaches much beyond the gratification of the eye—a something that invigorates the mind, that erects its hopes, that allays its perturbations, that mellows its affections; and it will generally be found that our happiest schemes, and wisest resolutions, are formed under the mild influence of a country scene, and the

soft obscurities of rural retirement.—
Roberts.

Ever charming, ever new,
When will the landscape tire the view?
The fountains fall, the rivers flow
The woody valleys, warm and low,
The windy summit, wild and high,
Roughly rushing on the sky!
The pleasant seat, the ruin'd tower,
The naked rock, the shady bower,
The town and village, dome and farm,
Each gave each a double charm,
As pearls upon an Ethiop's arm. —Dyer.

Abused mortals! did you know
Where joy, heart's-ease, and comforts grow;
You'd scorn proud towers,
And seek them in these bowers,
Where winds sometimes our woods perhaps
   may shake,
But blustering care could never tempest
   make,
Nor murmurs e'er come nigh us,
Saving of fountains that glide by us.
    —Sir W. Raleigh.

Your love in a cottage is hungry,
Your vine is a nest for flies—
Your milkmaid shocks the graces,
And simplicity talks of pies!
You lie down to your shady slumber,
And wake with a bug in your ear;
And your damsel that walks in the morning
Is shod like a mountaineer.
    —N. P. Willis.

None can describe the sweets of country life,
But those blest men that do enjoy and taste
   them.
Plain husbandmen, tho' far below our pitch,
Of fortune plac'd, enjoy a wealth above us;
To whom the earth with true and bounteous
   justice,
Free from war's cares, returns an easy food,
They breathe the fresh and uncorrupted air,
And by clear brooks enjoy untroubled sleeps.
Their state is fearless and secure, enrich'd
With several blessings, such as greatest
   kings
Might in true justice envy, and themselves
Would count too happy, if they truly knew
   them.   —May.

Seldom shall we see in cities, courts,
and rich families, where men live plen-
tifully and eat and drink freely, that
perfect health, that athletic soundness
and vigor of constitution which is commonly seen in the country, in poor
houses and cottages, where nature is
their cook, and necessity their caterer,
and where they have no other doctor
but the sun and fresh air, and that

such a one as never sends them to
the apothecary.—South.

Country (Love of)

He who loves not his country can
love nothing.—Johnson.

There's no glory like his who saves
his country.—Tennyson.

They love their land because it is their own,
And scorn to give aught other reason why.
    —Halleck.

The accent of our native country
dwells in the heart and mind, as well
as on the tongue.—La Rochefoucauld.

Oh, Christ! it is a goodly sight to see
What Heaven hath done for this delicious
   land!   —Byron.

Land of my sires! what mortal hand
Can e'er untie the filial band
That knits me to thy rugged strand!—Scott.

I fancy the proper means of increasing the love we bear our native country is to reside some time in a foreign
one.—Shenstone.

The infant, on first opening his eyes,
ought to see his country, and to the
hour of his death never to lose sight
of it.—Rousseau.

Thou, O my country hast thy foolish ways!
Too apt to purr at every stranger's praise,
But if the stranger touch thy modes or laws,
Off goes the velvet and out come the claws.
    —Holmes.

Breathes there the man with soul so dead,
Who never to himself hath said,
This is my own, my native land!
Whose heart hath ne'er within him burn'd,
As home his footsteps he hath turn'd,
From wandering on a foreign strand!
    —Scott.

O beautiful and grand,
My own, my native land!
   Of thee I boast:
Great empire of the west,
The dearest and the best,
Made up of all the rest,
   I love thee most.
    —Abraham Coles.

There ought to be a system of manners in every nation which a well-
informed mind would be disposed to
relish. To make us love our country,

our country ought to be lovely.—Burke.

***

Our hearts, our hopes, are all with thee,
Our hearts, our hopes, our prayers, our tears,
Our faith triumphant o'er our fears,
Are all with thee,—are all with thee!
—Longfellow.

***

Had I a dozen sons, each in my love alike, I had rather have eleven die nobly for their country, than one voluptuously surfeit out of action.—Shakespeare.

***

Stand
Firm for your country, and become a man Honour'd and lov'd: It were a noble life, To be found dead, embracing her.
—Johnson.

***

Our country! in her intercourse with foreign nations, may she always be in the right; but our country, right or wrong.—Stephen Decatur.

Courage

God holds with the strong.—Mazzini.

***

The best hearts are ever the bravest.
—Sterne.

***

Courage is adversity's lamp.—Vauvenargues.

***

To bear is to conquer our fate.—Campbell.

***

Courage leads to heaven; fear, to death.—Seneca.

***

Much danger makes great hearts most resolute.—Marston.

***

A courage to endure and to obey.
—Tennyson.

***

Courage never to submit or yield.
—Milton.

***

Courage mounteth with occasion.—Shakespeare,

***

A man of courage is also full of faith.—Cicero.

***

A stout heart may be ruined in fortune but not in spirit.—Victor Hugo.

***

Courage is fire, and bullying is smoke.—Beaconsfield.

***

The first mark of valor is defence.
—Sir P. Sidney.

***

Whatever enlarges hope will exalt courage.—Johnson.

***

Treason seldom dwells with courage.
—Sir Walter Scott.

***

A spirit superior to every weapon.—Ovid.

***

Hold the Fort! I am coming.—Gen. W. T. Sherman.

***

Courage in danger is half the battle.
—Plautus.

***

Fortune and Love befriend the bold.
—Ovid.

***

Courage of the soldier awakes the courage of woman.—Emerson.

***

Courage is temperamental, scientific, ideal.—Emerson.

***

Half a man's wisdom goes with his courage.—Emerson.

***

It is courage that vanquishes in war, and not good weapons.—Cervantes.

***

Courage makes a man more than himself; for he is then himself plus his valor.—W. R. Alger.

***

True courage scorns to vent her prowess in a storm of words.—Smollett.

***

True valor, friends, on virtue founded strong,
Meets all events alike.
—Mallet.

***

I dare do all that may become a man:
Who dares do more is none.
—Shakespeare.

***

Come one, come all! this rock shall fly
From its firm base as soon as I.
—Scott.

***

Courage consists not in blindly overlooking danger, put in seeing it and conquering it.—Richter.

Few persons have courage enough to appear as good as they really are.—J. C. and A. W. Hare.

God is the brave man's hope and not the coward's excuse.—Plutarch.

There is no courage but in innocence; no constancy but in an honest cause.—Southern.

Courage is, on all hands, considered as an essential of high character.—Froude.

It is in great dangers that we see great courage.—Regnard.

Fortune can take away riches, but not courage.—Seneca.

True courage is like a kite; a contrary wind raises it higher.—J. Petit-Senn.

Courage without discipline is nearer beastliness than manhood.—Sir P. Sidney.

But screw your courage to the sticking place,
And we'll not fail.   —Shakespeare.

Most men have more courage than even they themselves think they have.—Greville.

The mind I sway by, and the heart I bear,
Shall never sagg with doubt, nor shake with fear.   —Shakespeare.

Whate'er betides, by destiny 't is done,
And better bear like men, than vainly seek to shun.   —Dryden.

I rather tell thee what is to be fear'd,
Than what I fear; for always I am Cæsar.
        —Shakespeare.

The man who has never been in danger cannot answer for his courage.—La Rochefoucauld.

Why, courage, then! what cannot be avoided
'Twere childish weakness to lament or fear.
        —Shakespeare.

Courage conquers all things: it even gives strength to the body.—Ovid.

Hail, Cæsar, those who are about to die salute thee.—Suetonius.

Cowards may fear to die; but courage stout,
Rather than live in snuff, will be put out.
        —Sir Walter **Raleigh.**

He has not learned the lesson of life who does not every day surmount a fear.—Emerson.

The charm of the best courages is that they are inventions, inspirations, flashes of genius.—Emerson.

Courage is generosity of the highest order, for the brave are prodigal of the most precious things.—Colton.

If we survive danger, it steels our courage more than anything else.—Niebuhr.

The soul, secure in her existence, smiles
At the drawn dagger, and defies its point.
        —Addison.

Small in number, but their valor tried in war, and glowing.—Virgil.

Courage is a virtue of no doubtful seeming; there can be no contradiction, no diversity of opinion, about it.—Richter.

Courage, when it is not heroic self-sacrifice, is sometimes a modification and sometimes a result of faith.—J. C. and A. W. Hare.

To bear other people's afflictions, every one has courage enough and to spare.—Benjamin Franklin.

Courage, like cowardice, is undoubtedly contagious, but some persons are not liable to catch it.—George D. Prentice.

When moral courage feels that it is in the right, there is no personal daring of which it is incapable.—Leigh Hunt.

Without courage there cannot be truth, and without truth there can be no other virtue.—Sir Walter Scott.

Who hath not courage to revenge will never find generosity to forgive.—Henry Home.

Be courageous. Be independent. Only remember where the true courage and independence come from.—Phillips Brooks.

Go on and increase in valor, O boy! this is the path to immortality.—Virgil.

Stand fast * * * And all temptation to transgress repel.
—Milton.

Whenever you do what is holy, be of good cheer, knowing that God Himself takes part with rightful courage.—Menander.

Conscience in the soul is the root of all true courage. If a man would be brave, let him learn to obey his conscience.—James F. Clarke.

A real spirit Should neither court neglect, nor dread to bear it. —Byron.

He who loses wealth loses much; he who loses a friend loses more; but he that loses his courage loses all.—Cervantes.

Brave spirits are a balsam to themselves, There is a nobleness of mind that heals Wounds beyond salves. —Cartwright.

True fortitude is seen in great exploits That justice warrants, and that wisdom guides; All else is tow'ring phrenzy and distraction.
—Addison.

It does not matter a feather whether a man be supported by patron or client, if he himself wants courage.—Plautus.

My heart is firm: There's nought within the compass of humanity But I would dare and do. —Sir A. Hunt.

Before putting yourself in peril, it is necessary to foresee and fear it; but when one is there, nothing remains but to despise it.—Fénelon.

It is not our criminal actions that require courage to confess, but those which are ridiculous and foolish.—Rousseau.

Not only does the bull attack its foe with its crooked horns, but the injured sheep will fight its assailant.—Propertius.

He hath borne himself beyond the promise of his age, doing, in the figure of a lamb, the feats of a lion.—Shakespeare.

True valor Lies in the mind, the never-yielding purpose, Nor owns the blind award of giddy fortune.
—Thomson.

The wounded gladiator forswears all fighting, but soon forgetting his former wound resumes his arms.—Ovid.

There is no impossibility to him who stands prepared to conquer every hazard; the fearful are the failing.—Mrs. S. J. Hale.

The conscience of every man recognizes courage as the foundation of manliness, and manliness as the perfection of human character.—Thomas Hughes.

Courage is a quality so necessary for maintaining virtue, that it is always respected even when it is associated with vice.—Dr. Johnson.

Troops would never be deficient in courage, if they could only know how deficient in it their enemies were.—Wellington.

Fear to do base, unworthy things is valor; if they be done to us, to suffer them is valor too.—Ben Jonson.

The smallest worm will turn being trodden on, And doves will peck in safeguard of their brood. —Shakespeare.

Courage consists not in hazarding without fear, but being resolutely minded in a just cause.—Plutarch.

Consult the honor of religion more, and your personal safety less. Is it for the honor of religion (think you) that Christians should be as timorous as hares to start at every sound?—John Flavel.

Remember, now, when you meet your antagonist, do everything in a mild, agreeable manner. Let your courage be as keen, but, at the same time, as polished as your sword.—Sheridan.

———

A valiant man
Ought not to undergo or tempt a danger,
But worthily, and by selected ways;
He undertakes by reason, not by chance.
—Ben Jonson.

To struggle when hope is banished!
To live when life's salt is gone!
To dwell in a dream's that vanished!
To endure, and go calmly on!

I wonder is it because men are cowards in heart that they admire bravery so much, and place military valor so far beyond every other quality for reward and worship.—Thackeray.

———

The most sublime courage I have ever witnessed has been among that class too poor to know they possessed it, and too humble for the world to discover it.—H. W. Shaw.

The brave man seeks not popular applause,
Nor, overpower'd with arms, deserts his cause;
Unsham'd, though foil'd, he does the best he can,
Force is of brutes, but honor is of man.
—Dryden.

———

The moral courage that will face obloquy in a good cause is a much rarer gift than the bodily valor that will confront death in a bad one.—Chatfield.

———

I argue not
Against heaven's hand or will, nor bate a jot
Of heart or hope; but still bear up and steer
Right onward.   —Milton.

———

This is the way to cultivate courage: First, by standing firm on some conscientious principle, some law of duty. Next, by being faithful to truth and right on small occasions and common events. Third, by trusting in God for help and power.—James F. Clarke.

———

Tender handed stroke a nettle,
And it stings you for your pains;
Grasp it like a man of mettle,
And it soft as silk remains.
—Aaron Hill.

To do an evil actior is base; to do a good action without incurring danger is common enough; but it is the part of a good man to do great and noble deeds, though he risks every thing.—Plutarch.

———

Let us, then, be up and doing,
With a heart for any fate;
Still achieving, still pursuing,
Learn to labor and to wait.
—Longfellow.

———

The brave man is not he who feels no fear,
For that were stupid and irrational;
But he, whose noble soul its fear subdues,
And bravely dares the danger nature shrinks from.   —Joanna Baillie.

To hope for safety in flight, when you have turned away from the enemy the arms by which the body is defended, is indeed madness. In battle those who are most afraid are always in most danger; but courage is equivalent to rampart.—Sallust.

———

The truest courage is always mixed with circumspection; this being the quality which distinguishes the courage of the wise from the hardiness of the rash and foolish.—Jones of Nayland.

———

Ah, never shall the land forget
How gush'd the life-blood of the brave,
Gush'd warm with hope and courage yet,
Upon the soil they fought to save!
—Bryant.

The human race are sons of sorrow born;
And each must have his portion. Vulgar minds
Refuse or cranch beneath their load: the brave
Bears theirs without repining.
—Mallet and Thomson.

A brave man thinks no one his superior who does him an injury; for he has it then in his power to make himself superior to the other by forgiving it.—Pope.

Courage is poorly housed that dwells in numbers; the lion never counts the herd that are about him, nor weighs how many flocks he has to scatter.—Aaron Hill.

He holds no parley with unmanly fears,
Where duty bids he confident steers,
Faces a thousand dangers at her call,
And, trusting to his God, surmounts them
   all.   ı   —Cowper.

True courage but from opposition grows;
And what are fifty, what a thousand slaves,
Match'd to the sinew of a single arm
That strikes for liberty?   —Brooke.

Courage is like the diamond,—very brilliant; not changed by fire, capable of high polish, but except for the purpose of cutting hard bodies, useless.—Colton.

The intent and not the deed
Is in our power; and, therefore, who dares
  greatly
Does greatly.   —Brown.

Women and men of retiring timidity are cowardly only in dangers which affect themselves, but the first to rescue when others are endangered.—Richter.

The wise and active conquer difficulties
By daring to attempt them: sloth and folly
Shiver and shrink at sight of toil and
  hazard,
And make the impossibility they fear.
      —Rowe.

Oh fear not in a world like this,
And thou shalt know ere long,
Know how sublime a thing it is
To suffer and be strong.
      —Longfellow.

All desp'rate hazards courage do create,
As he plays frankly, who has least estate;
Presence of mind, and courage in distress,
Are more than armies, to procure success.
      —Dryden.

Courage, considered in itself or without reference to its causes, is no virtue, and deserves no esteem. It is found in the best and the worst, and is to be judged according to the quali-ties from which it springs and with which it is conjoined.—Channing.

Courage is generosity of the highest order, for the brave are prodigal of the most precious things. Our blood is nearer and .dearer to us than our money, and our life than our estate.—Colton.

Courage and modesty are the most unequivocal of virtues, for they are of a kind that hypocrisy cannot imitate; they too have this quality in common, that they are expressed by the same color.—Goethe.

Courage ought to be guided by skill, and skill armed by courage. Neither should hardiness darken wit, nor wit cool hardiness. Be valiant as men despising death, but confident as unwonted to be overcome.—Sir P. Sidney.

Courage is incompatible with the fear of the death; but every villain fears death: therefore no villain can be brave. He may, indeed, possess the courage of a rat, and fight with desperation, when driven into a corner.—Colton.

A thousand hearts are great within my
  bosom:
Advance our standards, set upon our foes;
Our ancient word of courage, fair St.
  George,
Inspire us with the spleen of fiery dragons!
Upon them! Victory sits upon our helms.
      —Shakespeare.

What though the field be lost!
All is not lost; the ungovernable will,
And study of revenge, immortal hate,
And courage never to submit or yield;
And what is else not to be overcome.
      —Milton.

No thought of flight,
None of retreat, no unbecoming deed
That argued fear; each on himself relied,
As only in his arm the moment lay
Of victory.   —Milton.

I like to read about Moses best, in th' Old Testament. He carried a hard business well through, and died when other folks were going to reap the fruits; a man must have courage to look after his life so, and think what'll come of it after he's dead and gone.—George Eliot.

Courage multiplies the chances of success by sometimes making opportunities, and always availing itself of them; and in this sense Fortune may be said to favor fools by those who, however prudent in their opinion, are deficient in valor and enterprise.—Coleridge.

Courage is always greatest when blended with meekness; intellectual ability is most admirable when it sparkles in the setting of a modest self-distrust; and never does the human soul appear so strong as when it foregoes revenge and dares to forgive an injury.—Chapin.

True courage is the result of reasoning. A brave mind is always impregnable. Resolution lies more in the head than in the veins, and a just sense of honor and of infamy, of duty and of religion, will carry us farther than all the force of mechanism.—Jeremy Collier.

Let us not despair too soon, my friend. Men's words are ever bolder than their deeds, and many a one who now appears resolute to meet every extremity with eager zeal, will on a sudden find in their breast a heart which he wot not of.—Schiller.

Not to the ensanguin'd field of death alone
Is valor limited: she sits serene
In the deliberate council, sagely scans
The source of action: weighs, prevents, provides,
And scorns to· count her glories, from the feats
Of brutal force alone.   —Smollett.

A valiant man
Ought not to undergo, or tempt a danger,
But worthily, and by selected ways,
He undertakes with reason, not by chance.
His valor is the salt t' his other virtues,
They're all unseason'd without it.
        —Ben Jonson.

What we want is men with a little courage to stand up for Christ. When Christianity wakes up, and every child that belongs to the Lord is willing to speak for Him, is willing to work for Him, and, if need be, willing to die for Him, then Christianity will advance, and we shall see the work of the Lord prosper.—D. L. Moody.

There is a contemptibly quiet path for all those who are afraid of the blows and clamor of opposing forces. There is no honorable fighting for a man who is not ready to forget that he has a head to be battered and a name to be bespattered. Truth wants no champion who is not as ready to be struck as to strike for her.—J. G. Holland.

Yet it may be more lofty courage dwells
In one weak heart which braves an adverse fate,
Than his whose ardent soul indignant swells,
Warm'd by the fight, or cheer'd through high debate.   —Mrs. Norton.

True courage has so little to do with anger, that there lies always the strongest suspicion against it where this passion is highest. The true courage is the cool and calm. The bravest of men have the least of brutal bullying insolence, and in the very time of danger are found the most serene, pleasant, and free.—Shaftesbury.

Physical courage, which despises all danger, will make a man brave in one way; and moral courage, which despises all opinion, will make a man brave in another. The former would seem most necessary for the camp, the latter for council; but to constitute a great man, both are necessary.—Colton.

Courage, so far as it is a sign of race, is peculiarly the mark of a gentleman or a lady; but it becomes vulgar if rude or insensitive, while timidity is not vulgar, if it be a characteristic of race or fineness of make. A fawn is not vulgar in being timid, nor a crocodile "gentle" because courageous.—Ruskin.

True courage is cool and calm. The bravest of men have the least of a brutal bullying insolence, and in the very time of danger are found the most serene and free. Rage, we know, can make a coward forget himself and fight. But what is done in fury or anger can never be placed to the account of courage.—Shaftesbury.

When by and by the din of war 'gan pierce
His ready sense; then straight his doubled spirit
Re-quicken'd what in flesh was fatigate,
And to the battle came he; where he did
Run reeking o'er the lives of men, as if
'Twere a perpetual spoil; and till we call'd
Both field and city ours he never stood
To ease his breath with panting.
—Shakespeare.

An intrepid courage is at best but a holiday kind of virtue, to be seldom exercised, and never but in cases of necessity; affability, mildness, tenderness, and a word which I would fain bring back to its original signification of virtue, I mean good-nature, are of daily use; they are the bread of mankind and staff of life.—Dryden.

True courage is not the brutal force
Of vulgar heroes, but the firm resolve
Of virtue and of reason. He who thinks
Without their aid to shine in deeds of arms
Builds on a sandy basis his renown;
A dream, a vapor, or an ague-fit,
May make a coward of him.—Whitehead.

Courage enlarges, cowardice diminishes resources. In desperate straits the fears of the timid aggravate the dangers that imperil the brave. For cowards the road of desertion should be left open. They will carry over to the enemy nothing but their fears. The poltroon, like the scabbard, is an encumbrance when once the sword is drawn.—Bovee.

What! shall one monk, scarcely known beyond his cell,
Front Rome's far-reaching bolts, and scorn her frown?
Brave Luther answered "Yes"; that thunder's swell
Rocked Europe, and discharmed the triple crown. —Lowell.

Courage that grows from constitution very often forsakes a man when he has occasion for it, and, when it is only a kind of instinct in the soul, breaks out on all occasions without

judgment or discretion. That courage which proceeds from the sense of our duty, and from the fear of offending Him that made us, acts always in a uniform manner, and according to the dictates of right reason.—Addison.

Like a mountain lone and bleak,
With its sky-encompass'd peak,
    Thunder riven,
Lifting its forehead bare,
Through the cold and blighting air,
    Up to heaven,
Is the soul that feels its woe,
And is nerv'd to bear the blow.
—Mrs. Hale.

"Be bold!" first gate; "Be bold, be bold, and evermore be bold," second gate; "Be not too bold!" third gate.—Inscription on the Gates of Busyrane.

Write on your doors the saying wise and old,
"Be bold! be bold!" and everywhere—"Be bold;
Be not too bold!" Yet better the excess
Than the defect; better the more than less;
Better like Hector in the field to die,
Than like a perfumed Paris turn and fly.
—Longfellow.

O friends, be men, and let your hearts be strong,
And let no warrior in the heat of fight
Do what may bring him shame in others' eyes;
For more of those who shrink from shame are safe
Than fall in battle, while with those who flee
Is neither glory nor reprieve from death.
—Homer.

None of the prophets old,
So lofty or so bold!
No form of danger shakes his dauntless breast;
In loneliness sublime
He dares confront the time,
And speak the truth, and give the world no rest:
No kingly threat can cowardize his breath,
He with majestic step goes forth to meet his death. —Abraham Coles.

Religion gives a man courage. * * * I men the higher moral courage which can look danger in the face unawed and undismayed; the courage that can encounter loss of ease, of wealth, of friends, of your own good name; the courage that can face a world full of howling and of scorn—

ay, of loathing and of hate; can see all this with a smile, and, suffering it all, can still toil on, conscious of the result, yet fearless still.—Theodore Parker.

In the whole range of earthly experience, no quality is more attractive and ennobling than moral courage. Like that mountain of rock which towers aloft in the Irish Sea, the man possessed of this principle is unmoved by the swelling surges which fret and fume at his feet. And yet, unlike that same Ailsa Craig, he is sensitive beyond measure to every adverse influence—battling against it, and triumphing over it by a power which proceeds from God's throne, and pervades his entire being.—J. McC. Holmes.

Courage, the highest gift, that scorns to bend
To mean devices for a sordid end.
Courage—an independent spark from heaven's bright throne,
By which the soul stands raised, triumphant, high, alone.
Great in itself, not praises of the crowd,
Above all vice, it stoops not to be proud.
Courage, the mighty attribute of powers above,
By which those great in war are great in love.
The spring of all brave acts is seated here,
As falsehoods draw their sordid birth from fear. —Farquhar.

Courage, by keeping the senses quiet and the understanding clear, puts us in a condition to receive true intelligence, to make computations upon danger, and pronounce rightly upon that which threatens us. Innocence of life, consciousness of worth, and great expectations, are the best foundations of courage. These ingredients make a richer cordial than youth can prepare; they warm the heart at eighty, and seldom fail in operation.—Elmes.

Let him not imagine who aims at greatness that all is lost by a single adverse cast of fortune; for if fortune has at one time the better of courage, courage may afterwards recover the advantage. He who is prepossessed with the assurance of overcoming at least overcomes the fear of failure; whereas he who is apprehensive of losing loses, in reality, all hopes of subduing. Boldness and power are such inseparable companions that they appear to be born together; and when once divided, they both decay and die at the same time.—Archbishop Venn.

Court — Courtiers

A court is an assemblage of noble and distinguished beggars.—Talleyrand.

The court does not render a man contented, but it prevents his being so elsewhere.—Bruyère.

The caterpillars of the commonwealth,
Which I have sworn to weed and pluck away. —Shakespeare.

Courts can give nothing to the wise and good,
But scorn of pomp, and love of solitude. —Young.

Poor wretches that depend
On greatness' favor, dream as I have done;
Wake, and find nothing. —Shakespeare.

Not a courtier, although they wear their faces to the bent of the king's looks, hath a heart that is not glad at the thing they scowl at.—Shakespeare.

They smile and bow, and hug, and shake the hand,
E'en while they whisper to the next assistant
Some curs'd plot to blast its owner's head. —Beller.

A lazy, proud, unprofitable crew,
The vermin gender'd from the rank corruption
Of a luxurious state. —Cumberland.

Fly from the court's pernicious neighborhood;
Where innocence is sham'd, and blushing modesty
Is made the scorner's jest; where hate, deceit,
And deadly ruin wear the mask of beauty,
And draw deluded fools with shows of pleasure. —Rowe.

The chief requisites for a courtier are a flexible conscience and an inflexible politeness.—Lady Blessington.

I am no courtier, no fawning dog of state,
To lick and kiss the hand that buffets me;
Nor can I smile upon my guest and praise
His stomach, when I know he feeds on
poison,
And death disguised sits grinning at my
table.   —Sewell.

Live loath'd and long,
Most smiling, smooth, detested parasites,
Courteous destroyers, affable wolves, meek
bears,
You fools of fortune, trencher friends,
time's flies,
Cap and knee slaves, vapors, and minute
jacks.   —Shakespeare.

Men that would blush at being thought
sincere,
And feign, for glory, the few faults they
want;
That love a lie, where truth would pay as
well;
As if to them, vice shone her own reward.
                                          —Young.

How many men
Have spent their blood in their dear coun-
try's service,
Yet now pine under want; while selfish
slaves,
That even would cut their throats whom
now they fawn on,
Like deadly locusts, eat the honey up,
Which those industrious bees so hardly
toil'd for.   —Otway.

Those that go up hill, use to bow,
Their bodies forward, and stoop low
To poise themselves, and sometimes creep,
When th' way is difficult and steep:
So those at court, that do address,
By low ignoble offices,
Can stoop at anything that's base,
To wriggle into trust and grace,
Are like to rise to greatness sooner,
Than those that go by worth and honor.
                                         —Butler.

See there he comes, th' exalted idol comes!
The circle's form'd, and all his fawning
slaves
Devoutly bow to earth; from every mouth
The nauseous flattery flows, which he re-
turns
With promises which die as soon as born.
Vile intercourse, where virtue has no place!
Frown but the monarch, all his glories
fade;
He mingles with the throng, outcast, un-
done,
The pageant of a day; without one friend
To soothe his tortur'd mind; all, all are
fled,
For though they bask'd in his meridian ray,
The insects vanish as his beams decline.
                                       —Somerville.

Courtesy
I am the very pink of courtesy.—
Shakespeare.

Approved valor is made precious by
natural courtesy.—Sir P. Sidney.

A churlish courtesy rarely comes
but either for gain or falsehood.—Sir
P. Sidney.

There is no outward sign of courtesy that does not rest on a deep
moral foundation.—Goethe.

O dissembling courtesy! how fine
this tyrant can tickle where she
wounds!—Shakespeare.

The small courtesies sweeten life;
the greater ennoble it.—Bovee.

What fairer cloak than courtesy for
fraud?—Earl of Stirling.

Nothing costs less nor is cheaper
than compliments of civility.—Cervantes.

Civility is a desire to receive civility, and to be accounted well-bred.—
Rochefoucauld.

When my friends are blind of one
eye, I look at them in profile.—Joubert.

Whilst thou livest, keep a good
tongue in thy head.—Shakespeare.

Courtesy is a duty public servants
owe to the humblest member of the
public.—Lord Lytton.

We must be as courteous to a man
as we are to a picture, which we are
willing to give the advantage of a
good light.—Emerson.

There is a courtesy of the heart; it
is allied to love. From it springs the
purest courtesy in the outward behavior.—Goethe.

If ever I should affect injustice, it
would be in this, that I might do
courtesies and receive none.—Feltham.

Life is not so short but that there is always time enough for courtesy.—Emerson.

A moral, sensible, and well-bred man
Will not affront me, and no other can.
—Cowper.

A good word is an easy obligation; but not to speak ill requires only our silence, which costs us nothing.—Tillotson.

Courtesy which oft is sooner found in lowly sheds, with smoky rafters, than in tapestry halls and courts of princes, where it first was named.—Milton.

When we are saluted with a salutation, salute the person with a better salutation, or at least return the same, for God taketh an account of all things.—Koran.

The whole of heraldry and of chivalry is in courtesy. A man of fine manners shall pronounce your name with all the ornament that titles of nobility could ever add.—Emerson.

By a union of courtesy and talent an adversary may be made to grace his own defeat, as the sandal-tree perfumes the hatchet that cuts it down.—Chatfield.

This Florentine's a very saint, so meek
And full of courtesy, that he would lend
The devil his cloak, and stand i' th' rain
himself. —Davenant.

As the sword of the best-tempered metal is the most flexible; so the truly generous are most pliant and courteous in their behavior to their inferiors.—Fuller.

Ill seemes (sayd he) if he so valiant be,
That he should be so sterne to stranger wight;
For seldom yet did living creature see
That courtesie and manhood ever disagree.
—Spenser.

Hail! ye small sweet courtesies of life, for smooth do ye make the road of it, like grace and beauty, which beget inclinations to love at first sight; it is ye who open the door and let the stranger in.—Sterne.

Shepherd, I take thy word,
And trust thy honest offer'd courtesy,
Which oft is sooner found in lowly sheds
With smoky rafters, than in tap'stry halls,
And courts of princes. —Milton.

When Zachariah Fox, the great merchant of Liverpool, was asked by what means he contrived to realize so large a fortune as he possessed, his reply was: "Friend, by one article alone, and in which thou mayest deal too, if thou pleasest,—it is civility."—Bentley.

How sweet and gracious, even in common speech,
Is that fine sense which men call Courtesy!
Wholesome as air and genial as the light,
Welcome in every clime as breath of flowers—
It transmutes aliens into trusting friends,
And gives its owner passport round the globe. —James T. Fields.

Courtesy, like grace and beauty, that which begets liking and inclination to love one another at the first sight, and in the very beginning of our acquaintance and familiarity; and, consequently, that which first opens the door for us to better ourselves by the example of others, if there be anything in the society worth notice.—Montaigne. •

Courtesy is a science of the highest importance. It is, like grace and beauty in the body, which charm at first sight, and lead on to further intimacy and friendship, opening a door that we may derive instruction from the example of others, and at the same time enabling us to benefit them by our example, if there be anything in our character worthy of imitation.—Montaigne.

Great talents, such as honor, virtue, learning, and parts, are above the generality of the world, who neither possess them themselves, nor judge of them rightly in others; but all people are judges of the lesser talents, such as civility, affability, and an obliging, agreeable address and manner, because they feel the good effects of them, as making society easy and pleasing.—Chesterfield.

Nothing is a courtesy unless it be meant us, and that friendly and lovingly. We owe no thanks to rivers that they carry our boats, or winds that they be favoring and fill our sails, or meats that they be nourishing; for these are what they are necessarily. Horses carry us, trees shade us; but they know it not.—Ben Jonson.

Courtship

The pleasantest part of a man's life.—Addison.

She most attracts who longest can refuse.—Aaron Hill.

See how the skilful lover spreads his toils.—Stillingfleet.

She half consents• who silently denies.—Ovid.

Men dream in courtship, but in wedlock wake!—Pope.

A feast is more fatal to love than a fast.—Colton.

Ah, fool! faint heart fair lady ne'er could win.—Spenser.

What a woman says to her lover should be written on air or swift water.—Catullus.

The acceptance of favors from the other sex is a woman's first step towards self-committal.—Mme. de Puisieux.

So, with decorum all things carried,
Miss frown'd, and blush'd, and then was
   married.   —Goldsmith.

O, that I were a glove upon that hand,
That I might touch that cheek!
          —Shakespeare.

She is a woman, therefore may be woo'd;
She is a woman, therefore may be won.
          —Shakespeare.

That man that has a tongue, I say, is no man if with his tongue he cannot win a woman.—Shakespeare.

A woman that wishes to retain her suitor must keep him in the trenches.—Colton.

Men are April when they woo, December when they wed.—Shakespeare.

I knelt, and with the fervor of a lip unused to the cool breath of reason, told my love.—Willis.

With women worth the being won,
The softest lover ever best succeeds.
          —Hill.

It is your virtue, being men, to try;
And it is ours, by virtue to deny.
          —Drayton.

Who listens once will listen twice; her heart be sure is not of ice, and one refusal no rebuff.—Byron.

A fellow who lives in a windmill has not a more whimsical dwelling than the heart of a man that is lodged in a woman.—Congreve.

Every man in the time of courtship and in the first entrance of marriage, puts on a behavior like my correspondent's holiday suit.—Addison.

Courtship consists in a number of quiet attentions, not so pointed as to alarm, nor so vague as not to be understood.—Sterne.

If you cannot inspire a woman with love of you, fill her above the brim with love of herself; all that runs over will be yours.—Colton.

A man is in no danger so long as he talks his love; but to write it is to impale himself on his own pothooks.—Douglas Jerrold.

I profess not to know how women's hearts are wooed and won. To me they have always been matters of riddle and admiration.—Washington Irving.

God has put into the heart of man love and the boldness to sue, and into the heart of woman fear and the courage to refuse.—Marguerite de Valois.

When a woman is deliberating with herself whom she shall choose of many near each other in other pretensions, certainly he of the best understanding is to be preferred.—Steele.

Now from the world,
Sacred to sweet retirement, lovers steal,
And pour their souls in transport.
—Thomson.

Into these ears of mine,
These credulous ears, he pour'd the sweetest words
That art or love could frame.—Beaumont.

Rejected lovers need never despair! There are four-and-twenty hours in a day, and not a moment in the twenty-four in which a woman may not change her mind.—De Finod.

The Greek epigram intimates that the force of love is not shown by the courting of beauty, but where the like desire is inflamed for one who is ill-favored.—Emerson.

If fathers are sometimes sulky at the appearance of the destined son-in-law, is it not a fact that mothers become sentimental and, as it were, love their own loves over again——Thackeray.

Tom hinted at his dislike at some trifle his mistress had said; she asked him how he would talk to her after marriage if he talked at this rate before.—Addison.

She that with poetry is won,
Is but a desk to write upon;
And what men say of her they mean
No more than on the thing they lean.
—Butler.

He that would win his dame must do
As love does when he draws his bow;
With one hand thrust the lady from,
And with the other pull her home.
—Butler.

Wooing thee, I found thee of more value
Than stamps in gold or sums in sealed bags;
And 'tis the very riches of thyself
That now I aim at.   —Shakespeare.

How would that excellent mystery, wedded life, irradiate the world with its blessed influences, were the generous impulses and sentiments of courtship but perpetuated in all their exuberant fullness during the sequel of marriage!—Frederic Saunders.

Women are angels, wooing:
Things won are done; joy's soul lies in the doing:
That she beloved knows naught, that knows not this—
Men prize the thing ungained more than it is.   —Shakespeare.

Do proper homage to thine idol's eyes,
But not too humbly, or she will despise
Thee and thy suit though told in moving tropes;
Disguise even tenderness, if thou art wise.
—Byron.

Like a lovely tree
She grew to womanhood, and between whiles
Rejected several suitors, just to learn
How to accept a better in his turn.
—Byron.

Like conquering tyrants you our breasts invade,
Where you are pleas'd to ravage for awhile;
But soon you find new conquests out and leave .
The ravag'd province ruinate and bare.
—Otway.

There is, sir, a critical minute in
Ev'ry man's wooing, when his mistress may
Be won, which if he carelessly neglect
To prosecute, he may wait long enough
Before he gain the like opportunity.
—Marmion.

The pleasantest part of a man's life is generally that which passes in courtship, provided his passion be sincere, and the party beloved kind with discretion. Love, desire, hope, all the pleasing emotions of the soul, rise in the pursuit.—Addison.

He that can keep handsomely within rules, and support the carriage of a companion to his mistress, is much more likely to prevail than he who lets her see the whole relish of his life depends upon her. If possible, therefore, divert your mistress rather than sigh for her.—Steele.

Let a woman once give you a task, and you are hers, heart and soul; all your care and trouble lend new charms to her for whose sake they are taken,

To rescue, to revenge, to instruct, or protect a woman is all the same as to love her.—Richter.

If she do frown, 'tis not in hate of you,
But rather to beget more love in you:
If she do chide, 'tis not to have you gone;
For why, the fools are mad if left alone.
Take no repulse, whatever she doth say;
For—get you gone—she doth not mean—
   away.   —Shakespeare.

Every man ought to be in love a few times in his life, and to have a smart attack of the fever. You are better for it when it is over: the better for your misfortune, if you endure it with a manly heart; how much the better for success, if you win it and a good wife into the bargain!—Thackeray.

Courtship is a fine bowling-green turf, all galloping round and sweethearting, a sunshine holiday in summer time; but when once through matrimony's turnpike, the weather becomes wintry, and some husbands are seized with a cold, aguish fit, to which the faculty give the name of indifference.—G. A. Stevens.

His folded flock secure, the shepherd home
Hies merry-hearted; and by turns relieves
The ruddy milk-maid of her brimming pail;
The beauty whom perhaps his witless heart,
Unknowing what the joy-mix'd anguish
   means,
Sincerely loves, by that best language shown
Of cordial glances, and obliging deeds.
    —Thomson.

And otherwhyles with amorous delights
And pleasing toyes he would her entertaine,
Now singing sweetly to surprise her
   sprights,
Now making layes of love and lover's paine,
Bransles, ballads, virelayes, and verses
   vaine!
Oft purposes, oft riddles, he devys'd;
And thousands like which flowed in his
   braine,
With which he fed her fancy, and entys'd
To take to his new love, and leave her old
   despys'd.   —Spenser.

Maggie and Stephen were in that stage of courtship which makes the most exquisite moment of youth, the freshest blossom-time of passion,—when each is sure of the other's love, but no formal declaration has been made, and all is mutual divination, exalting the most trivial words, the lightest gestures, into thrills delicate and delicious as wafted jasmine scent. —George Eliot.

Say that she rail; why then I'll tell her
   plain,
She sings as sweetly as a nightingale;
Say that she frown; I'll say she looks as
   clear
As morning roses, newly wash'd with dew;
Say she be mute and will not speak a word,
Then I'll commend her volubility
And say she uttereth piercing eloquence.
    —Shakespeare.

O days remember'd well! remember'd all!
The bitter sweet, the honey and the gall;
Those garden rambles in the silent night,
Those trees so shady, and that moon so
   bright,
That thickset alley by the arbor clos'd,
That woodbine seat where we at last re
   pos'd;
And then the hopes that came and then
   were gone,
Quick as the clouds beneath the moon past
   on.   —Crabbe.

A town, before it can be plundered and deserted, must first be taken p;and in this particular Venus has borrowed a law from her consort Mars. A woman that wishes to retain her suitor must keep him in the trenches; for this is a siege which the besieger never raises for want of supplies, since a feast is more fatal to love than a fast, and a surfeit than a starvation. Inanition may cause it to die a slow death, but repletion always destroys it by a sudden one.—Colton.

Covetousness

Covetousness, which is idolatry.—
—Bible.

The soul of man is infinite in what it covets.—Ben Jonson.

The covetous man.—Horace.

We never desire earnestly what we desire in reason.—La Rochefoucauld.

To the covetous man life is a nightmare, and God lets him wrestle with it as best he may.—Henry Ward Beecher.

Covetousness is ever attended with solicitude and anxiety.—Benjamin Franklin.

He deservedly loses his own property, who covets that of another.—Phædrus.

Those who give not till they die show that they would not then if they could keep it any longer.—Bishop Hall.

Covetousness swells the principal to no purpose, and lessens the use to all purposes.—Jeremy Taylor.

The covetous man heaps up riches, not to enjoy them, but to have them.—Tillotson.

The covetous person lives as if the world were made altogether for him, and not he for the world.—South.

The covetous man explores the whole world in pursuit of a subsistence, and fate is close at his heels.—Saadi.

Some men are so covetous, as if they were to live forever; and others so profuse, as if they were to die the next moment.—Aristotle.

The things which belong to others please us more, and that which is ours, is more pleasing to others.—Syrus.

Take heed and beware of covetousness; for a man's life consisteth not in the abundance of the things which he possesseth.—Bible.

Covetous men need money least, yet they most affect it; but prodigals, who need it most have the least regard for it.—Alexander Wilson.

Why are we so blind? That which we improve, we have, that which we hoard is not for ourselves.—Madame Deluzy.

Covetousness, by a greediness of getting more, deprives itself of the true end of getting; it loses the enjoyment of what it has got.—Sprat.

When all sins are old in us, and go upon crutches, covetousness does but then lie in her cradle.—Decker.

When workmen strive to do better than well, they do confound their skill in covetousness.—Shakespeare.

Covetousness is a sort of mental gluttony, not confined to money, but craving honor, and feeding on selfishness.—Chamfort.

Covetousness, like a candle ill made, smothers the splendor of a happy fortune in its own grease.—F. Osborn.

Poor in abundance, famished at a feast, man's grief is but his grandeur in disguise, and discontent is immortality.—Young.

Those that much covet are with gain so fond,
That what they have not, that which they possess,
They scatter and unloose it from their bond,
And so, by hoping more, they have but less.
—Shakespeare.

The only sovereign remedy is to give Christ the pre-eminence in our hearts; for then we shall undervalue all temporal things in comparison of Him.—Fisher's Catechism.

The covetous man is like a camel with a great hunch on his back; heaven's gate must be made higher and broader, or he will hardly get in.—Thomas Adams.

The only instance of a despairing sinner left upon record in the New Testament is that of a treacherous and greedy Judas.

Covetousness, like jealousy, when it has once taken root, never leaves a man but with his life.—Thomas Hughes.

If money be not thy servant, it will be thy master. The covetous man cannot so properly be said to possess wealth, as that it may be said to possess him.—Bacon.

The covetous man pines in plenty, like Tantalus up to the chin in water, and yet thirsty.—Rev. T. Adams.

Where necessity ends, desire and curiosity begin; and no sooner are we supplied with everything nature can demand than we sit down to contrive artificial appetites.—Johnson.

Of covetousness we may truly say that it makes both the Alpha and Omega in the devil's alphabet, and that it is the first vice in corrupt nature which moves, and the last which dies.—South.

To think well of every other man's condition, and to dislike our own, is one of the misfortunes of human nature. "Pleased with each other's lot, our own we hate."—Burton.

He that visits the sick, in hopes of a legacy, let him be never so friendly in all other cases, I look upon him in this, to be no better than a raven, that watches a weak sheep only to peck out its eyes.—Seneca.

Although the beauties, riches, honors, sciences, virtues, and perfections of all men living were in the present possession of one, yet somewhat above and beyond all this would still be sought and earnestly thirsted for.—Hooker.

Covetousness teaches men to be cruel and crafty, industrious and evil, full of care and malice; and after all this, it is for no good to itself, for it dares not spend those heaps of treasure which it has snatched.—Jeremy Taylor.

Covetous men are fools, miserable wretches, buzzards, madmen, who live by themselves, in perpetual slavery, fear, suspicion, sorrow, discontent, with more of gall than honey in their enjoyments; who are rather possessed by their money than possessors of it. —Burton.

A circle cannot fill a triangle, so neither can the whole world, if it were to be compassed, the heart of man; a man may as easily fill a chest with grace as the heart with gold. The air fills not the body, neither doth money the covetous mind of man.—Spenser.

Suppose a more complete assemblage of sublunary enjoyments, and a more perfect system of earthly felicity than ever the sun beheld, the mind of man would instantly devour it, and, as if it was still empty and unsatisfied, would require something more.—Leighton.

I am not covetous for gold,
Nor care I who doth feed upon my cost;
It yearns me not if men my garments wear;
Such outward things dwell not in my desires:
But if it be a sin to covet honor
I am the most offending soul alive.
—Shakespeare.

The covetous man heaps up riches, not to enjoy them, but to have them; and starves himself in the midst of plenty, and most unnaturally cheats and robs himself of that which is his own; and makes a hard shift, to be as poor and miserable with a great estate, as any man can be without it. —Tillotson.

It was with good reason that God commanded through Moses that the vineyard and harvest were not to be gleaned to the last grape or grain; but something to be left for the poor. For covetousness is never to be satisfied; the more it has, the more it wants. Such insatiable ones injure themselves, and transform God's blessings into evil.—Luther.

There is not a vice which more effectually contracts and deadens the feelings, which more completely makes a man's affections center in himself, and excludes all others from partaking in them, than the desire of accumulating possessions. When the desire has once gotten hold on the heart, it shuts out all other considerations, but such as may promote its views. In its zeal for the attainment of its end, it is not delicate in the choice of means. As it closes the heart, so also it clouds the understanding. It cannot discern between right and wrong; it takes evil for good, and good for evil; it calls darkness light, and light darkness. Beware, then, of the beginning of covetousness, for you know not where it will end.—Bishop Mant.

Cow

A cow is a very good animal in the field; but we turn her out of a garden.—Samuel Johnson.

Coward — Cowardice

Cowards die many times before their death.—Shakespeare.

All men would be cowards if they durst.—Earl of Rochester.

Cowards have no luck.—Elizabeth Kulman.

Cruel people are ever cowards in emergency.—Swift.

To wish for death is a coward's part.—Ovid.

Cowardice, the dread of what will happen.—Epictetus.

A plague of all cowards, I say.—Shakespeare.

A coward's fear can make a coward valiant.—Owen Feltham.

It is the misfortune of worthy people that they are cowards.—Voltaire.

What masks are these uniforms to hide cowards!—Duke of Wellington.

The craven's fear is but selfishness, like his merriment.—Whittier.

A cowardly cur barks more fiercely than it bites.—Quintus Curtius Rufus.

A coward; a most devout coward; religious in it.—Shakespeare.

It is only in little matters that men are cowards.—W. H. Herbert.

The native hue of resolution is sicklied o'er with the pale cast of thought.—Shakespeare.

Commonly they use their feet for defence, whose tongue is their weapon. Sir P. Sidney.

To see what is right and not to do it is want of courage.—Confucius.

Fear is the virtue of slaves; but the heart that loveth is willing.—Longfellow.

Mankind are dastardly when they meet with opposition.—Franklin.

The coward never on himself relies, But to an equal for assistance flies.
—Crabbe.

Cowards falter, but danger is often overcome by those who nobly dare.—Queen Elizabeth.

Strange that cowards cannot see that their greatest safety lies in dauntless courage.—Lavater.

Plenty and peace breed cowards; hardness ever of hardiness is mother.—Shakespeare.

Cowards fear to die; but courage stout, Rather than live in snuff, will be put out.
—Sir Walter Raleigh.

A coward is the kindest animal; 'Tis the most forgiving creature in a fight.
—Dryden.

That same man that rennith awaie, Maie again fight, an other daie.
—Erasmus.

I would give all my fame for a pot of ale and safety.—Shakespeare.

When all the blandishments of life are gone, The coward sneaks to death, the brave live on.
—Dr. Sewell.

Cowards are cruel, but the brave Love mercy, and delight to save.
—Gay.

Fear is my vassal, when I frown he flies; A hundred times in life a coward dies.
—Marston.

But look for ruin when a coward wins; For fear and cruelty are ever twins.
—Aleyn.

When desperate ills demand a speedy cure, distrust is cowardice, and prudence folly.—Dr. Johnson.

Men lie, who lack courage to tell truth—the cowards!—Joaquin Miller.

My valor is certainly going!—it is sneaking off!—I feel it oozing out, as it were, at the palms of my hands.— Sheridan.

Go—let thy less than woman's hand
Assume the distaff—not the brand.
—Byron.

He who fears to venture as far as his heart urges and his reason permits, is a coward; he who ventures further than he intended to go, is a slave.— Heine.

The man that lays his hand on woman,
Save in the way of kindness, is a wretch
Whom 'twere gross flattery to name a
coward. —Tobin.

All mankind is one of these two cowards—either to wish to die when he should live, or live when he should die.—Sir Robert Howard.

It is the coward who fawns upon those above him. It is the coward that is insolent whenever he dares be so.—Junius.

It is vain for the coward to fly; death follows close behind; it is by defying it that the brave escape.—Voltaire.

For cowards the road of desertion should be left open. They will carry over to the enemy nothing but their fears.—Bovee.

Dangers are light, if they seem light; and more dangers have deceived men than forced them.—Bacon.

Some are brave men one day and cowards another, as great captains have often told me, from their own experience and observation.—**Sir W. Temple.**

Dost thou now fall over to my foes?
Thou wear a lion's hide! doff it for shame,
And hang a calf's skin on those recreant
limbs. —Shakespeare.

To be afraid is the miserable condition of a coward. To do wrong, or omit to do right from fear, is to superadd delinquency to cowardice.—David Dudley Field.

Cowardice encroaches fast upon such as spend their lives in company of persons higher than themselves.— Dr. Johnson.

Cowardice is not synonymous with prudence. It often happens that the better part of discretion is valor.— Hazlitt.

The coward wretch whose hand and heart
Can bear to torture aught below,
Is ever first to quail and start
From slightest pain or equal foe.
—Eliza Cook.

He who fights and runs away
May live to fight another day.
But he who is in battle slain,
Can never rise to fight again.
—Goldsmith.

If cowardice were not so completely a coward as to be unable to look steadily upon the effects of courage, he would find that there is no refuge so sure as dauntless valor.—Jane Porter.

Lie not, neither to thyself, nor man, nor God. Let mouth and heart be one; beat and speak together, and make both felt in action. It is for cowards to lie.—George Herbert.

It is a law of nature that faint-hearted men should be the fruit of luxurious countries, for we never find that the same soil produces delicacies and heroes.—Herodotus.

To die, and thus avoid poverty or love, or anything painful, is not the part of a brave man, but rather of a coward; for it is cowardice to avoid trouble, and the suicide does not undergo death because it is honorable, but in order to avoid evil.—Aristotle.

What is in reality cowardice and faithlessness, we call charity, and consider it the part of benevolence sometimes to forgive men's evil practice for the sake of their accurate faith, and sometimes to forgive their confessed heresy for the sake of their admirable practice.—Ruskin.

The fact is, that to do anything in this world worth doing, we must not stand back shivering and thinking of the cold and danger, but jump in and scramble through as well as we can.—Sydney Smith.

The courage that grows from constitution very often forsakes a man when he has occasion for it; and when it is only a kind of instinct in the soul, it breaks out on all occasions, without judgment or discretion.—Addison.

How many cowards, whose hearts are all as false
As stairs of sand, wear yet upon their chins
The beards of Hercules and frowning Mars,
Who, inward search'd, have livers white as milk.   —Shakespeare.

When the passengers gallop by as if fear made them speedy, the cur follows them with an open mouth; let them walk by in confident neglect, and the dog will not stir at all; it is a weakness that every creature takes advantage of.—J. Beaumont.

Cowards die many times before their deaths:
The valiant never taste of death but once.
Of all the wonders that I yet have heard,
It seems to me most strange that men should fear;
Seeing that death, a necessary end,
Will come when it will come.
                    —Shakespeare.

He
That kills himself to avoid misery, fears it,
And, at the best, shows but a bastard valor.
This life's a fort committed to my trust,
Which I must not yield up, till it be forced;
Nor will I. He's not valiant that dares die,
But he that boldly bears calamity.
                    —Massinger.

Thou slave, thou wretch, thou coward!
Thou little valiant, great in villainy!
Thou ever strong upon the stronger side!
Thou Fortune's champion, that dost never fight
But when her humorous ladyship is by
To teach thee safety.   —Shakespeare.

The reign of terror to which France submitted has been more justly termed "the reign of cowardice." One knows not which most to execrate,—the nation that could submit to suffer such atrocities, or that low and blood-thirsty demagogue that could inflict them. France, in succumbing to such a wretch as Robespierre, exhibited, not her patience, but her pusillanimity.—Colton.

A great deal of talent is lost in the world for want of a little courage. Every day sends to their graves a number of obscure men who have only remained in obscurity because their timidity has prevented them from making a first effort.—Sydney Smith.

Coxcomb

Once a coxcomb, always a coxcomb. —Dr. Johnson.

A coxcomb is the blockhead's man of merit.—La Bruyère.

A coxcomb is ugly all over with the affectation of the fine gentleman.—Johnson.

A coxcomb is four-fifths affectation and one-fifth vanity.—Haliburton.

A man of sense and gravity is less apt to succeed with a fine woman than the gay, the giddy, the flattering coxcomb.—Henry Horne.

                    This is he
That kiss'd away his hand in courtesy;
This is the ape of form, monsieur the nice,
That when he plays at tables, chides the dice
In honorable terms; nay, he can sing
A mean most meanly; and in ushering,
Mend him who can; the ladies call him, sweet;
The stairs, as he treads on them, kiss his feet.   —Shakespeare.

He was perfum'd like a milliner:
And 'twixt his finger and his thumb he held
A pouncet-box, which ever and anon
He gave his nose: and still he smil'd and talk'd;
And as the soldiers bore dead bodies by,
He call'd them untaught knaves, unmannerly,
To bring a slovenly unhandsome corpse
Betwixt the wind and his nobility.
                    —Shakespeare.

A vulgar man is captious and jealous; eager and impetuous about trifles. He suspects himself to be slighted, and thinks everything that is said meant at him.—Chesterfield.

All the world says of a coxcomb that he is a coxcomb; but no one dares to say so to his face, and he dies without knowing it.—Bruyère.

None are so seldom found alone, and are so soon tired of their own company, as those coxcombs who are on the best terms with themselves.—Colton.

A coxcomb begins by determining that his own profession is the first; and he finishes by deciding that he is the first of his profession.—Colton.

Craft

When the fox hath once got in his nose,
He'll soon find means to make the body
    follow. —Shakespeare.

For he
That sows in craft does reap in jealousy.
    —Middleton.

That for ways that are dark
And for tricks that are vain,
The heathen Chinee is peculiar.
    —Bret Harte.

This is the fruit of craft:
Like him that shoots up high, looks for the shaft,
And finds it in his forehead.—Middleton.

Creation

Creation is great, and cannot be understood.—Carlyle.

All are but parts of one stupendous whole,
Whose body Nature is, and God the soul.
    —Pope.

Silently as a dream the fabric rose;
No sound of hammer or of saw was there.
    —Cowper.

As Thou has created me out of mingled air and glitter, I thank Thee for it.—Rückert.

God only opened His hand to give flight to a thought that He had held imprisoned from eternity.—Timothy Titcomb.

God may rationally be supposed to have framed so great and admirable an automaton as the world for special ends and purposes.—Robert Boyle.

A spontaneous production is against matter of fact; a thing without example, not only in man, but the vilest of weeds.—Bentley.

The chain that's fixed to the throne of Jove,
On which the fabric of our world depends,
One link dissolved, the whole creation ends.
    —Edmund Waller.

One God, one law, one element,
And one far-off divine event,
To which the whole creation moves.
    —Tennyson.

Though to recount almighty works
What words of tongue or seraph can suffice,
Or heart of man suffice to comprehend?
    —Milton.

Open, ye heavens, your living doors; let in
The great Creator from His work return'd
Magnificent, His six days' work, a world!
    —Milton.

Had I been present at the creation, I would have given some useful hints for the better ordering of the universe.—Alphonso the Wise.

Nature, they say, doth dote,
And cannot make a man
Save on some worn-out plan,
Repeating us by rote. —Lowell.

The wisdom and goodness of the Maker plainly appears in the parts of this stupendous fabric, and the several degrees and ranks of creatures in it.—Locke.

A wonder it must be, that there should be any man found so stupid as to persuade himself that this most beautiful world could be produced by the fortuitous concourse of atoms.—John Ray.

God is a worker: He has thickly strewn
Infinity with grandeur: God is love:
He shall wipe away creation's tears,
And all the worlds shall summer in His
    smile. —Smith.

No man saw the building of the New Jerusalem, the workmen crowded together, the unfinished walls and unpaved streets; no man heard the clink of trowel and pickaxe; it descended out of heaven from God.—Seeley.

It became Him who created it to set it in order; and if he did so, it is unphilosophical to seek for any other origin of the world, or to pretend that it might arise out of a chaos by the mere laws of Nature.—Newton.

Through knowledge we behold the world's creation,
How in his cradle first he fostered was;
And judge of Nature's cunning operation,
How things she formed of a formless mass.
—Spenser.

What cause
Moved the Creator in His holy rest
Through all eternity so late to build
In chaos, and, the work begun, how soon
Absolved. —Milton.

Whoever considers the study of anatomy I believe will never be an atheist; the frame of man's body and coherence of his parts being so strange and paradoxical that I hold it to be the greatest miracle of Nature.—Herbert of Cherbury.

In the vast, and the minute, we see
The unambiguous footsteps of the God,
Who gives its lustre to an insect's wing
And wheels His throne upon the rolling worlds. —Cowper.

From harmony, from heavenly harmony,
This universal frame began:
From harmony, to harmony,
Through all the compass of the notes it ran,
The diapason closing full in man.
—Dryden.

Then tower'd the palace, then in awful state
The temple rear'd its everlasting gate.
No workman steel, no ponderous axes rung,
Like some tall palm the noiseless fabric sprung. —Bishop Heber.

Let no presuming impious railer tax
Creative wisdom as if aught was form'd
In vain, or not for admirable ends.
Shall little haughty ignorance pronounce
His works unwise of which the smallest part
Exceeds the narrow vision of his mind?
—Thomson.

The heavens declare the glory of God, and the firmament showeth His handiwork. Day unto day uttereth speech, and night unto night showeth knowledge. There is no speech nor language where their voice is not heard—Bible.

For wonderful indeed are all His works,
Pleasant to know, and worthiest to be all
Had in remembrance always with delight;
But what created mind can comprehend
Their number, or the wisdom infinite
That brought them forth, but hid their causes deep? —Milton.

The spacious firmament on high,
With all the blue ethereal sky,
And spangled heavens, a shining frame
Their great Original proclaim.
*   *   *   *   *   *
Forever singing as they shine
The hand that made us is divine.
—Addison.

How often might a man, after he had jumbled a set of letters in a bag, fling them out upon the ground before they would fall into an exact poem,—yea, or so much as make a good discourse in prose? And may not a little book be as easily made by chance as this great volume of the world?—Tillotson.

From nature's constant or eccentric laws,
The thoughtful soul this general inference draws,
That an effect must pre-suppose a cause;
And, while she does her upward flight sustain,
Touching each link of the continued chain,
At length she is oblig'd and forc'd to see
A first, a source, a life, a Deity;
Which has forever been, and must forever be. —Prior.

The ever varying brilliancy and grandeur of the landscape, and the magnificence of the sky, sun, moon and stars, enter more extensively into the enjoyment of mankind than we, perhaps ever think, or can possibly apprehend, without frequent and extensive investigation. This beauty and splendour of the objects around us, it is ever to be remembered, is not necessary to their existence, nor to what we commonly intend by their usefulness. It is therefore to be regarded as a source of pleasure, gratuitously superinduced upon the general nature of the objects themselves, and in this light, a testimony of the divine goodness, peculiarly affecting.—Dwight.

We cannot look around us, without being struck by the surprising variety and multiplicity of the sources of beauty of creation, produced by form, or by colour, or by both united. It is scarcely too much to say, that every object in nature, animate or inanimate, is in some manner beautiful, so largely has the Creator provided for our pleasures, through the sense of sight. It is rare to see anything, which is in itself distasteful, or disagreeable to the eye, or repulsive.—Macculloch.

Credit — Creditor

Public credit is suspicion asleep.—Thomas Paine.

What is bought is cheaper than a gift.—Cervantes.

If confidence is a plant of slow growth, credit is one which matures much more slowly—Beaconsfield.

Lose not thine own for want of asking for it; 'twill get thee no thanks.—Fuller.

Blest paper-credit! last and best supply!
That lends corruption lighter wings to fly.
—Pope.

Every man's credit and consequence are proportioned to the sums which he holds in his chest.—Juvenal.

The creditor whose appearance gladdens the heart of a debtor may hold his head in sunbeams and his foot on storms.—Lavater.

Creditors have better memories than debtors; and creditors are a superstitious sect, great observers of set days and times.—Franklin.

Private credit is wealth; public honor is security. The feather that adorns the royal bird supports its flight; strip him of his plumage, and you pin him to the earth.—Junius.

He smote the rock of the national resources, and abundant streams of revenue gushed forth. He touched the dead corpse of Public Credit, and it sprung upon its feet.—Daniel Webster.

We have now learned that rashness and imprudence will not be deterred from taking credit; let us try whether fraud and avarice may be more easily restrained from giving it.—Dr. Johnson.

Credit is a matter so subtle in its essence, that, as it may be obtained almost without reason, so, without reason, may it be made to melt away.—Anthony Trollope.

The most trifling actions that affect a man's credit are to be regarded. The sound of your hammer at five in the morning or nine at night, heard by a creditor, makes him easy six months longer; but if he sees you at a billiard table, or hears your voice at a tavern, when you should be at work, he sends for his money the next day.—Franklin.

There is nothing in this world so fiendish as the conduct of a mean man when he has the power to revenge himself upon a noble one in adversity. It takes a man to make a devil; and the fittest man for such a purpose is a snarling, waspish, red-hot, fiery creditor.—Beecher.

Credulity

Your noblest natures are most credulous.—Chapman.

Quick believers need broad shoulders—George Herbert.

Credulity thinks others short-sighted.—Abbé Guerguil.

The only disadvantage of an honest heart is credulity.—Sir P. Sidney.

You believe that easily which you hope for earnestly.—Terence.

It is as wise to moderate our belief as our desires.—Landor.

We believe easily what we fear or what we desire.—La Fontaine.

When credulity comes from the heart it does no harm to the intellect. —Joubert.

Credulity is perhaps a weakness almost inseparable from eminently truthful characters.—Tuckerman.

I wish I was as sure of anything as Macaulay is of everything.—William Windham.

I cannot spare the luxury of believing that all things beautiful are what they seem.—Halleck.

Generous souls
Are still most subject to credulity.
—Davenant.

We believe at once in evil; we only believe in good upon reflection. Is not this sad?—Madame Deluzy.

Ignorant people are to be caught by the ears as one catches a pot by the handle.—From the French.

Men are most apt to believe what they least understand; and through the lust of human wit obscure things are more easily credited.—Pliny.

Women are sometimes drawn in to believe against probability by the unwillingness they have to doubt their own merit.—Richardson.

O credulity, thou hast as many ears as fame has tongues, open to every sound of truth as of falsehood.—Havard.

Let us believe neither half of the good people tell us of ourselves, nor half the evil they say of others.—J. Petit-Senn.

The incredulous are the most credulous. They believe the miracles of Vespasian that they may not believe those of Moses.—Pascal.

The more gross the fraud, the more glibly will it go down, and the more greedily will it be swallowed, since folly will always find faith wherever impostors will find impudence.—Bovee.

To be deceived by our enemies and betrayed by our friends is not to be borne; yet are we often content to be served so by ourselves. — Rochefoucauld.

The greatest and saddest defect is not credulity, but an habitual forgetfulness that our science is ignorance. —Thoreau.

The general goodness which is nourished in noble hearts makes every one think that strength of virtue to be in another whereof they find assured foundation in themselves.—Sir P. Sidney.

Superstition is certainly not the characteristic of this age. Yet some men are bigoted in politics who are infidels in religion. Ridiculous credulity!—Junius.

It is a curious paradox that precisely in proportion to our own intellectual weakness will be our credulity as to those mysterious powers assumed by others.—Colton.

Credulity is the common failing of inexperienced virtue, and he who is spontaneously suspicious may be justly charged with radical corruption.—Johnson.

What believer sees a disturbing omission or infelicity? The text, whether of prophet or of poet, expands for whatever we can put into it; and even his bad grammar is sublime.—George Eliot.

A man must have a good deal of vanity who believes, and a good deal of boldness who affirms, that all the doctrines he holds are true, and all he rejects are false.—Franklin.

In all places, and in all times, those religionists who have believed too much have been more inclined to violence and persecution than those who have believed too little.—Colton.

What the light of your mind, which is the direct inspiration of the Almighty, pronounces incredible, that, in God's name, leave uncredited. At your peril do not try believing that!—Carlyle.

We all know that a lie needs no other grounds than the invention of the liar; and to take for granted as truth all that is alleged against the fame of others is a species of credulity that men would blush at on any other subject.—Jane Porter.

O credulity,
Security's blind nurse, the dream of fools,
The drunkard's ape, that feeling for his way
Ev'n when he thinks, in his deluded sense
To snatch at safety, falls without defence.
—Mason.

Blessed credulity, thou great great god of error,
Thou art the strong foundation of huge wrongs,
To thee give I my vows and sacrifice;
By thee, great deity, he doth believe
Falsehoods, that falsehood's self could not invent;
And from that misbelief doth draw a course
T' o'erwhelm e'en virtue, truth and sanctity.
Let him go on, blest stars, 'tis meet he fall,
Whose blindfold judgment hath no guide at all.
—Machen.

It is a curious paradox that precisely in proportion to our own intellectual weakness will be our credulity, to those mysterious powers assumed by others; and in those regions of darkness and ignorance where man cannot effect even those things that are within the power of man, there we shall ever find that a blind belief in feats that are far beyond those powers has taken the deepest root in the minds of the deceived, and produced the richest harvest to the knavery of the deceiver.—Colton.

Fear, if it be not immoderate, puts a guard about us that does watch and defend us; but credulity keeps us naked, and lays us open to all the sly assaults of ill-intending men: it was a virtue when man was in his innocence; but since his fall, it abuses those that own it.—Feltham.

Creed

Life is one, religion one, creeds are many and diverse.—A. Bronson Alcott.

He that will believe only what he can fully comprehend must have a very long head or a very short creed. —Colton.

Call your opinions your creed, and you will change it every week. Make your creed simply and broadly out of the revelation of God, and you may keep it to the end.—Phillips Brooks.

Shall I ask the brave soldier who fights by my side
In the cause of mankind, if our creeds agree?
Shall I give up the friend I have valued and tried,
If he kneel not before the same altar with me?
—Moore.

In politics, as in religion, it so happens that we have less charity for those who believe the half of our creed than for those who deny the whole of it, since if Servetus had been a Mahomedan he would not have been burnt by Calvin.—Colton.

And so the Word had breath, and wrought
With human hands the creed of creeds
In loveliness of perfect deeds
More strong than all poetic thought.
—Tennyson.

Crime

One crime is everything; two nothing. —Madame Deluzy.

Responsibility prevents crimes.— Burke.

Crimes generally punish themselves. —Oliver Goldsmith.

For all guilt is avenged on earth.— Goethe.

Fear follows crime, and is its punishment.—Voltaire.

Every crime destroys more Edens than our own.—Hawthorne.

Those who are themselves incapable of great crimes are ever backward to suspect others.—Rochefoucauld.

Purposelessness is the fruitful mother of crime.—Charles H. Parkhurst.

No crime has been without a precedent.—Seneca.

Well does Heaven have care that no man secures happiness by crime.—Alfieri.

Most people fancy themselves innocent of those crimes of which they cannot be convicted.—Seneca.

How oft the sight of means to do ill deeds
Makes ill deeds done.   —Shakespeare.

He who does not prevent a crime when he can, encourages it.—Seneca.

One crime is concealed by the commission of another.—Seneca.

Society prepares the crime; the criminal commits it.—Buckle.

Crime succeeds by sudden despatch; honest counsels gain vigor by delay.—Tacitus.

For he that but conceives a crime in thought,
Contracts the danger of an actual fault.
                    —Creech.

If poverty is the mother of crimes, want of sense is the father.—La Bruyère.

He who overlooks one crime invites the commission of another.—Syrus.

Whoever commits a crime strengthens his enemy.—Daniel O'Connell.

Crimes sometimes shock us too much; vices almost always too little.—Hare.

Those magistrates who can prevent crime, and do not, in effect encourage it.—Cato.

Most crimes are sanctioned in some form or other when they take grand names.—Ouida.

A man who has no excuse for crime is indeed defenseless!—Bulwer-Lytton.

Every crime will bring remorse to the man who committed it.—Juvenal.

For whoever meditates a crime is guilty of the deed.—Juvenal.

To be at peace in crime! ah, who can thus flatter himself?—Voltaire.

You are not to do evil that good may come of it.—Law Maxim.

Many commit the same crimes with a very different result. One bears a cross for his crime; another a crown.—Juvenal.

Crimes lead one into another; they who are capable of being forgers are capable of being incendiaries.—Burke.

No matter how you seem to fatten on a crime, that can never be good for the bee which is bad for the hive.—Emerson.

There are crimes which become innocent and even glorious through their splendor, number and excess.—Rochefoucauld.

Between the acting of a dreadful thing
And the first motion, all the interim is
Like a phantasma, or a hideous dream.
                    —Shakespeare.

But many a crime deemed innocent on earth
Is registered in heaven; and these no doubt
Have each their record, with a curse annex'd.
                    —Cowper.

Foul deeds will rise,
Though all the earth o'erwhelm them, to men's eyes.   —Shakespeare.

The perfection of a thing consists in its essence; there are perfect criminals, as there are men of perfect probity.—La Roche.

Man's crimes are his worst enemies, following,
Like shadows, till they drive his steps into
The pit he dug.   —Creon.

Where have you ever found that man who stopped short after the perpetration of a single crime?—Juvenal.

For the credit of virtue we must admit that the greatest misfortunes of men are those into which they fall through their crimes.—La Rochefoucauld.

———

It is supposable that, in the eyes of angels, a struggle down a dark lane and a battle of Leipsic differ in nothing but excess of wickedness.—Willmott.

———

We want a state of things in which crime will not pay, a state of things which allows every man the largest liberty compatible with the liberty of every other man.—Emerson.

'Tis no sin love's fruits to steal;
But the sweet thefts to reveal;
To be taken, to be seen,
These have crimes accounted been.
     —Ben Jonson.

———

     Every crime
Has, in the moment of its perpetration,
Its own avenging angel—dark misgiving,
An ominous sinking at the inmost heart.
     —Coleridge.

———

The contagion of crime is like that of the plague. Criminals collected together corrupt each other; they are worse than ever when at the termination of their punishment they re-enter society.—Napoleon.

———

There is no den in the wide world to hide a rogue. Commit a crime, and the earth is made of glass. Commit a crime, and it seems as if a coat of snow fell on the ground, such as reveals in the woods the track of every partridge and fox, and squirrel and mole.—Emerson.

———

We are easily shocked by crimes which appear at once in their full magnitude; but the gradual growth of our wickedness, endeared by interest and palliated by all the artifices of self-deceit, gives us time to form distinctions in our favor.—Dr. Johnson.

———

Small crimes always precede great crimes. Whoever has been able to transgress the limits set by law may afterwards violate the most sacred rights; crime, like virtue, has its degrees, and never have we seen timid innocence pass suddenly to extreme licentiousness.—Racine.

———

Of all the adult male criminals in London, not two in a hundred have entered upon a course of crime who have lived an honest life up to the age of twenty; almost all who enter upon a course of crime do so between the ages of eight and sixteen.—Earl of Shaftesbury.

———

If little faults, proceeding on distemper,
Shall not be wink'd at, how shall we stretch
  our eye
When capital crimes, chew'd, swallow'd, and
  digested,
Appear before us?   —Shakespeare.

———

Oh how will crime engender crime! throw
  guilt
Upon the soul, and like a stone cast on
The troubled waters of a lake,
'Twill form in circles round succeeding
  round,
Each wider than the first.
     —Colman the Younger.

Crisis

Things at the worst will cease, or else climb upward to what they were before.—Shakespeare.

———

In great straits, and when hope is small, the boldest counsels are the safest.—Livy.

———

There is always a moment in the pyramid of our lives when the apex is reached.—Ninon de Lenclos.

———

There is a moment of difficulty and danger at which flattery and falsehood can no longer deceive, and simplicity itself can no longer be misled.—Junius.

———

The nearer any disease approaches to a crisis, the nearer it is to a cure. Danger and deliverance make their advances together; and it is only in the last push that one or the other takes the lead.—Thomas Paine.

Critic — Criticism

Criticism is our weak point.—Goethe.

———

Criticism is not construction, it is observation.—George William Curtis.

Criticism is easy, and art is difficult. —P. N. Destouches.

For I am nothing if not critical.— Shakespeare.

I criticise by creation, not by finding fault.—Michael Angelo.

Cavil you may, but never criticise. —Pope.

Sir, there is no end of negative criticism.—Johnson.

He wreathed the rod of criticism with roses.—Disraeli.

Ten censure wrong for one who writes amiss.—Pope.

It is much easier to be critical than to be correct.—Beaconsfield.

Hold their farthing candle to the sun.—Young.

A wise scepticism is the first attribute of a good critic.—Lowell.

Good by reason of its exceeding badness.—Macaulay.

You know who the critics are? The men who have failed in literature and art.—Disraeli.

Spite of all the criticising elves, those who make us feel must feel themselves.—Churchill.

Whoever thinks a faultless piece to see, Thinks what ne'er was, nor is, nor e'er shall be.   —Pope.

In truth it may be laid down as an almost universal rule that good poets are bad critics.—Macaulay.

The most noble criticism is that in which the critic is not the antagonist so much as the rival of the author.— Isaac Disraeli.

The eyes of critics, whether in commending or carping, are both on one side, like a turbot's.—Landor.

It is a maxim with me that no man was ever written out of reputation but by himself.—Bentley.

But you with pleasure own your errors past, And make each day a critic on the last. —Pope.

Of all the cants in this canting world, deliver me from the cant of criticism.—Sterne.

Let those teach others who themselves excel; and censure freely, who have written well.—Pope.

It is easy to criticise an author, but it is difficult to appreciate him.—Vauvenargues.

Criticism often takes from the tree caterpillars and blossoms together.— Richter.

Those readiest to criticise are often least able to appreciate.—Joubert.

The strength of criticism lies only in the weakness of the thing criticised.— Longfellow.

Those who do not read criticism will rarely merit to be criticised.—Isaac Disraeli.

It is the heart that makes the critic, not the nose.—Max Müller.

The man who becomes a critic by trade ceases, in reality, to be one at all.—Tuckerman.

I had rather be hissed for a good verse than applauded for a bad one.— Victor Hugo.

The press, the pulpit, and the stage, Conspire to censure and expose our age. —Wentworth Dillon.

Blame where you must, be candid where you can, And be each critic the good-natured man. —Goldsmith

Sympathy is the first condition of criticism; reason and justice presuppose, at their origin, emotion.—Amiel

A critic must accept what is best in a poet, and thus become his best encourager.—Stedman.

A critic should be a pair of snuffers. He is oftener an extinguisher, and not seldom a thief.—J. C. and A. W. Hare.

An over-readiness to criticise or to depreciate a minister of Christ is proof of a lack of devotion to Christ.—H. Clay Trumbull.

The pleasure of criticism takes from us that of being deeply moved by very beautiful things.—Bruyère.

The generous Critic fann'd the Poet's fire,
And taught the world with reason to admire. —Pope.

To what base ends, and by what abject ways,
Are mortals urg'd through sacred lust of praise!
Ah, ne'er so dire a thirst of glory boast,
Nor in the critic let the man be lost.
 —Pope.

Criticism is a study by which men grow important and formidable at very small expense.—Dr. Johnson.

Comparative criticism teaches us that moral and æsthetic defects are more nearly related than is commonly supposed.—Lowell.

The purity of the critical ermine, like that of the judicial, is often soiled by contact with politics.—Whipple.

The rule in carving holds good as to criticism : never cut with a knife what you can cut with a spoon.—Charles Buxton.

He whose first emotion, on the view of an excellent production, is to undervalue it, will never have one of his own to show.—Aiken.

Who shall dispute what the reviewers say?
Their word's sufficient; and to ask a reason,
In such a state as theirs, is downright
treason. —Churchill.

A poet that fails in writing becomes often a morose critic. The weak and insipid white wine makes at length excellent vinegar.—Shenstone.

The severest critics are always those who have either never attempted, or who have failed in original composition.—Hazlitt.

How many people would like to get up in a social prayer-meeting to say a few words for Christ, but there is such a cold spirit of criticism in the church that they dare not do it.

Get your enemies to read your works in order to mend them, for your friend is so much your second self that he will judge too like you.—Pope.

There is scarcely a good critic of books born in our age, and yet every fool thinks himself justified in criticising persons.—Bulwer-Lytton.

If a faultless poem could be produced, I am satisfied it would tire the critics themselves, and annoy the whole reading world with the spleen.—Walter Scott.

It behooves the minor critic who hunts for blemishes to be a little distrustful of his own sagacity.—Junius.

Criticism, as it was first introduced by Aristotle, was meant as a standard of judging well.—Johnson.

Criticism even should not be without its charms. When quite devoid of all amenities, it is no longer literary.—Joubert.

Critics are sentinels in the grand army of letters, stationed at the corners of newspapers and reviews, to challenge every new author.—Longfellow.

Not all on books their criticism waste; the genius of a dish some justly taste, and eat their way to fame.—Young.

Though by whim, envy, or resentment led,
They damn those authors whom they never
read. —Churchill.

The floods of nonsense printed in the form of critical opinions seem to me a chief curse of the times, a chief obstacle to true culture.—George Eliot.

Reviewers are forever telling authors they can't understand them. The author might often reply: Is that my fault?—J. C. and A. W. Hare.

It may be observed of good writing, as of good blood, that it is much easier to say what it is composed of than to compose it.—Colton.

Criticism is as often a trade as a science; it requiring more health than wit, more labor than capacity, more practice than genius.—Bruyère.

It is ridiculous for any man to criticise on the works of another who has not distinguished himself by his own performances.—Addison.

What a blessed thing it is that nature, when she invented, manufactured and patented her authors, contrived to make critics out of the chips that were left!—Holmes.

Why will you be always sallying out to break lances with other people's wind-mills, when your own is not capable of grinding corn for the horse you ride?—J. G. Holland.

Criticism is above all a gift, an intuition, a matter of tact and *flair;* it cannot be taught or demonstrated—it is an art.—Amiel.

When I read rules of criticism I inquire immediately after the works of the author who has written them, and by that means discover what it is he likes in a composition.—Addison.

All truth is valuable, and satirical criticism may be considered as useful when it rectifies error and improves judgment. He that refines the public taste is a public benefactor.—Johnson.

Grant me patience, just Heaven! Of all the cants which are canted in this canting world—though the cant of hypocrites may be the worst—the cant of criticism is the most tormenting.—Laurence Sterne.

Properly speaking, we learn from those books only that we cannot judge.

The author of a book that I am competent to criticise would have to learn from me.—Goethe.

Of his shallow species there is not a more unfortunate, empty and conceited animal than that which is generally known by the name of a critic.—Addison.

A servile race
Who, in mere want of fault, all merit place;
Who blind obedience pay to ancient schools,
Bigots to Greece, and slaves to musty rules.
—Churchill.

In the world's affairs there is no design so great or good but it will take twenty wise men to help it forward a few inches; and a single fool can stop it.—Ruskin.

We rarely meet with persons that have true judgment; which, to many, renders literature a very tiresome knowledge. Good judges are as rare as good authors.—St. Evremond.

Is it in destroying and pulling down that skill is displayed? The shallowest understanding, the rudest hand, is more than equal to that task.—Burke.

Critics must excuse me if I compare them to certain animals called asses, who, by gnawing vines, originally taught the great advantage of pruning them.—Shenstone.

Neither praise nor blame is the object of true criticism. Justly to discriminate, firmly to establish, wisely to prescribe and honestly to award—these are the true aims and duties of criticism.—Simms.

Damn with faint praise, assent with civil leer,
And, without sneering, teach the rest to sneer;
Willing to wound, and yet afraid to strike,
Just hint a fault, and hesitate dislike.
—Pope.

To be a mere verbal critic is what no man of genius would be if he could; but to be a critic of true taste and feeling is what no man without genius could be if he would.—Colton.

He who would reproach an author for obscurity should look into his own mind to see whether it is quite clear there. In the dusk the plainest writing is illegible.—Goethe.

The opinion of the great body of the reading public is very materially influenced even by the unsupported assertions of those who assume a right to criticise.—Macaulay.

If men of wit and genius would resolve never to complain in their works of critics and detractors, the next age would not know that they ever had any.—Swift.

Thou shalt not write, in short, but what I
   choose.
This is true criticism, and you may kiss,
Exactly as you please, or not, the rod.
      —Byron.

Criticism is not religion, and by no process can it be substituted for it. It is not the critic's eye, but the child's heart that most truly discerns the countenance that looks out from the pages of the gospel.—J. C. Shairp.

It is quite cruel that a poet cannot wander through his regions of enchantment without having a critic forever, like the Old Man of the Sea, upon his back.—Moore.

Those fierce inquisitors of wit, the critics, spare no flesh that ever writ; but just as tooth-drawers find among the rout their own teeth work in pulling others out.—Samuel Butler.

Critics on verse, as squibs on triumphs
   wait,
Proclaim their glory, and augment the state;
Hot, envious, noisy, proud, the scribbling
   fry
Burn, hiss, and bounce, waste paper, ink,
   and die.   —Young.

He was in Logic a great critic,
Profoundly skilled in Analytic;
He could distinguish, and divide
A hair 'twixt south and southwest side.
      —Butler.

The critic's first labor is the task of distinguishing between men, as history and their works display them, and the

ideals which one and another have conspired to urge upon his acceptance. —Stedman.

Critics to plays for the same end resort
That surgeons wait on trials in a court;
For innocence condemn'd they've no re-
   spect,
Provided they've a body to dissect.
      —Congreve.

It is advantageous to an author that his book should be attacked as well as praised. Fame is a shuttlecock. If it be struck only at one end of the room it will soon fall to the ground. To keep it up it must be struck at both ends.—Johnson.

The great contention of criticism is to find the faults of the moderns and the beauties of the ancients. While an author is yet living we estimate his powers by his worst performance, and when he is dead we rate them by his best.—Johnson.

Men of great talents, whether poets or historians, seldom escape the attacks of those who, without ever favoring the world with any production of their own, take delight in criticising the works of others.—Cervantes.

A critic is never too severe when he only detects the faults of an author. But he is worse than too severe when, in consequence of this detection, he presumes to place himself on a level with genius.—Landor.

A true critic ought rather to dwell upon excellences than imperfections, to discern the concealed beauties of a writer, and communicate to the world such things as are worth their observation.—Addison.

I never knew a critic who made it his business to lash the faults of other writers that was not guilty of greater himself—as the hangman is generally a worse malefactor than the criminal that suffers by his hand.—Addison.

Men have commonly more pleasure in the criticism which hurts than in that which is innocuous, and are more tolerant of the severity which breaks hearts and ruins fortunes than of that which falls impotently on the grave.—Ruskin.

———

Censure and criticism never hurt anybody. If false, they can't hurt you unless you are wanting in manly character; and if true, they show a man his weak points, and forewarn him against failure and trouble.—Gladstone.

———

Modern criticism discloses that which it would fain conceal, but conceals that which it professes to disclose; it is therefore read by the discerning, not to discover the merits of an author, but the motives of his critic.—Colton.

———

There is a certain race of men that either imagine it their duty, or make it their amusement, to hinder the reception of every work of learning or genius, who stand as sentinels in the avenues of fame, and value themselves upon giving ignorance and envy the first notice of a prey.—Johnson.

———

Of all mortals a critic is the silliest; for, inuring himself to examine all things whether they are of consequence or not, never looks upon anything but with a design of passing sentence upon it; by which means he is never a companion, but always a censor.—Steele.

———

The exercise of criticism always destroys for a time our sensibility to beauty by leading us to regard the work in relation to certain laws of construction. The eye turns from the charms of nature to fix itself upon the servile dexterity of art.—Alison.

———

Doubtless criticism was originally benignant, pointing out the beauties of a work rather than its defects. The passions of men have made it malignant, as the bad heart of Procrustes turned the bed, the symbol of repose, into an instrument of torture.—Longfellow.

———

There is a certain meddlesome spirit which, in the garb of learned research, goes prying about the traces of history, casting down its monuments, and marring and mutilating its fairest trophies. Care should be taken to vindicate great names from such pernicious erudition.—Washington Irving.

———

As soon

Seek roses in December—ice in June,
Hope, constancy in wind, or corn in chaff;
Believe a woman or an epitaph,
Or any other thing that's false, before
You trust in critics.   —Byron.

———

The critic is a literary educator, a professor of literature with a class which embraces the entire reading community. He is to instruct, if he can; he is to judge fairly and to "give his own to each;" but his main business is to stimulate the minds of people, to conduct a live conversation with the public concerning the books they are reading.—E. S. Nadal.

———

Reviewers are usually people who would have been poets, historians, biographers, etc., if they could; they have tried their talents at one or the other, and have failed; therefore they turn critics.—Coleridge.

———

The most exquisite words and finest strokes of an author are those which very often appear the most doubtful and exceptionable to a man who wants a relish for polite learning; and they are those which a sour undistinguishing critic generally attacks with the greatest violence.—Addison.

———

Critics are a kind of freebooters in the republic of letters—who, like deer, goats and divers other graminivorous animals, gain subsistence by gorging upon buds and leaves of the young shrubs of the forest, thereby robbing them of their verdure, and retarding their progress to maturity.—Washington Irving.

———

A true critic, in the perusal of a book, is like a dog at a feast, whose thoughts and stomach are wholly set upon what the guests fling away, and consequently is apt to snarl most when there are the fewest bones.—Swift.

Professional critics are incapable of distinguishing and appreciating either diamonds in the rough state or gold in bars. They are traders, and in literature know only the coins that are current. Their criticism has scales and weights, but neither crucible nor touchstone.—Joubert.

There are some books and characters so pleasant, or rather which contain so much that is pleasant, that criticism is perplexed or silent. The hounds are perpetually at fault among the sweet-scented herbs and flowers that grow at the base of Etna.—J. F. Boyes.

Nature fits all her children with something to do,
He who would write and can't write, can surely review;
Can set up a small booth as critic and sell us his
Petty conceit and his pettier jealousies.
         —Lowell.

It is not enough for a reader to be unprejudiced. He should remember that a book is to be studied, as a picture is hung. Not only must a bad light be avoided, but a good one obtained. This taste supplies. It puts a history, a tale, or a poem in a just point of view, and there examines the execution.—Willmott.

The critic, as he is currently termed, who is discerning in nothing but faults, may care little to be told that this is the mark of unamiable dispositions or of bad passions; but he might not feel equally easy were he convinced that he thus gives the most absolute proofs of ignorance and want of taste.—Macculloch.

Critics are a kind of wild flies, that breed
In wild fig trees, and when they're grown up feed
Upon the raw fruit of the nobler kind,
And by their nibbling on the outer rind,
Open the pores, and make way for the sun
To ripen it sooner than he would have done.   —Butler.

Criticism is like champagne, nothing more execrable if bad, nothing more excellent if good; if meagre, muddy,

vapid and sour, both are fit only to engender colic and wind; but if rich, generous and sparkling, they communicate a genial glow to the spirits, improve the taste, and expand the heart.—Colton.

Some critics are like chimney-sweepers; they put out the fire below, and frighten the swallows from their nests above; they scrape a long time in the chimney, cover themselves with soot, and bring nothing away but a bag of cinders, and then sing from the top of the house as if they had built it. —Longfellow.

It is necessary a writing critic should understand how to write. And though every writer is not bound to show himself in the capacity of critic, every writing critic is bound to show himself capable of being a writer; for if he be apparently impotent in this latter kind, he is to be denied all title or character in the other.—Shaftesbury.

The fangs of a bear, and the tusks of a wild boar, do not bite worse and make deeper gashes than a goose-quill sometimes; no, not even the badger himself, who is said to be so tenacious of his bite that he will not give over his hold till he feels his teeth meet and the bones crack.—Howell.

'Tis not the wholesome sharp morality,
Or modest anger of a satiric spirit,
That hurts or wounds the body of a state,
But the sinister application
Of the malicious, ignorant, and base
Interpreter; who will distort and strain
The general scope and purpose of an author
To his particular and private spleen.
        —Ben Jonson.

Malherbe, on hearing a prose work of great merit much extolled, dryly asked if it would reduce the price of bread. Neither was his appreciation of poetry much higher, when he observed that a good poet was of no more use to the church or the state than a good player at ninepins.—Colton.

Criticism must never be sharpened into anatomy. The delicate veins of fancy may be traced, and the rich blood that gives bloom and health to the complexion of thought be resolved into its elements. Stop there. The life of the imagination, as of the body, disappears when we pursue it.—Willmott.

___

We should be wary what persecution we raise against the living labors of public men, how we spill that seasoned life of man, preserved and stored up in books, since we see a kind of homicide may be thus committed, sometimes a martyrdom; and if it extend to the whole impression, a kind of massacre, whereof the execution ends not in the slaying of an elemental life, but strikes at the ethereal and fifth essence, the breath of reason itself; slays an immortality rather than a life.—Milton.

___

How good it would be if we could learn to be rigorous in judgment of ourselves, and gentle in our judgment of our neighbors! In remedying defects, kindness works best with others, sternness with ourselves. It is easy to make allowances for our faults, but dangerous; hard to make allowances for others' faults, but wise. "If thy hand offend thee, cut it off," is a word for our sins; for the sins of others, "Father, forgive them."—Maltie Babcock.

___

A man must serve his time to ev'ry trade,
Save censure; critics all are ready made:
Take hackney'd jokes from Miller, got by rote,
With just enough of learning to misquote;
A mind well skill'd to find or forge a fault,
A turn for punning—call it Attic salt—
Fear not to lie—'twill seem a lucky hit;
Shrink not from blasphemy—'twill pass for wit;
Care not for feeling, pass your proper jest—
And stand a critic, hated, yet caress'd.
　　　　　　　　　　　　　　—Byron.

___

One interesting feature of criticism is seen in the ease with which it discovers what Addison called the specific quality of an author. In Livy, it will be the manner of telling the story; in Sallust, personal identification with the character; in Tacitus, the analysis of the deed into its motive. If the same test be applied to painters, it will find the prominent faculty of Correggio to be manifested in harmony of effect; of Poussin, in the sentiment of his landscapes; and of Raffaelle, in the general comprehension of his subject.—Willmott.

___

The malignant deity Criticism dwelt on the top of a snowy mountain in Nova Zembla; Momus found her extended in her den upon the spoils of numberless volumes half devoured. At her right sat Ignorance, her father and husband, blind with age; at her left Pride, her mother, dressing her up in the scraps of paper herself had torn. There was Opinion, her sister, light of foot, hoodwinked and headstrong, yet giddy and perpetually turning. About her played her children, Noise and Impudence, Dullness and Vanity, Positiveness, Pedantry and Ill Manners.—Swift.

___

A critic was of old a glorious name,
Whose sanction handed merit up to fame;
Beauties as well as faults he brought to view,
His judgment great, and great his candor too.
No servile rules drew sickly taste aside;
Secure he walked, for nature was his guide.
But now, O strange reverse! our critics bawl
In praise of candor with a heart of gall,
Conscious of guilt, and fearful of the light;
They lurk enshrouded in the veil of night;
Safe from destruction, seize th' unwary prey,
And stab like bravoes, all who come that way.   —Churchill.

___

In the whole range of literature nothing is more entertaining, and, I might add, more instructive, than sound, legitimate criticism, the disinterested convictions of a man of sensibility, who enters rather into the spirit, than the letter of his author, who can follow him to the height of his compass, and while he sympathizes with every brilliant power and genuine passion of the poet, is not so far carried out of himself as to indulge his admiration at the expense of his judgment, but who can afford us the double pleasure of being first pleased with his author, and secondly with himself, for having given us such just and incontrovertible reason for our approbation.—Colton.

Crocus

Hail to the King of Bethlehem,
Who weareth in His diadem
The yellow crocus for the gem
Of His authority! —Longfellow.

Welcome, wild harbinger of spring!
To this small nook of earth;
Feeling and fancy fondly cling
Round thoughts which owe their birth
To thee, and to the humble spot
Where chance has fixed thy lowly lot.
—Bernard Barton.

Cross

Welcome, welcome, cross of Christ, if Christ be with it.—Rutherford.

How soon would faith freeze without a cross!—Rutherford.

Weak Christians are afraid of the shadow of the cross.—Thomas Brooks.

There is an immeasurable distance between submission to the cross and acceptance of it.—Charlotte Elizabeth Tonna.

Losses and crosses are heavy to bear; but when our hearts are right with God, it is wonderful how easy the yoke becomes.—C. H. Spurgeon.

If Jesus bore the cross, and died on it for me, ought I not to be willing to take it up for Him?—D. L. Moody.

The cross is not only imposed upon the saints as their burden, but bequeathed unto them as their legacy. It is given unto them as an honor and privilege.—Richard Alleine.

He who tears down the cross, what is there left to lift him to heaven? The church claiming to be a Christian church is false to the title, if she make the cross of Christ of none effect.—Herrick Johnson.

O, cross of my bleeding Lord, may I meditate on thee more, may I feel thee more, may I resolve to know nothing but thee.—Richard Fuller.

All you have really to do is to keep your back as straight as you can; and not think about what is upon it. The real and essential meaning of "virtue" is that straightness of back.—John Ruskin.

Dear Lord, forgive my sinful, foolish fears
And give me daily, strengthening grace,
I pray,
And one thing more I ask with humble tears,
Take not my cross away.
—Susan O. Curtis.

We must bear our crosses; self is the greatest of them all. If we die in part every day of our lives, we shall have but little to do on the last. O how utterly will these little daily deaths destroy the power of the final dying!—Fénelon.

And now my cross is all supported—
Part on my Lord, and part on me;
But as He is so much the stronger,
He seems to bear it—I go free.
—Anna Warner.

In the cross of Christ I glory,
Towering o'er the wrecks of time;
All the light of sacred story
Gathers round its head sublime.
—John Bowring.

When our will runs parallel with the will of God, no cross is formed; but when our will runs counter to God's will, a cross is formed which is heavy to be borne.—Aughey.

There is no man that goeth to heaven but he must go by the cross. The cross is the standing way-mark which all they that go to glory must pass by.—Aughey.

The cross is the center of the world's history; the incarnation of Christ and the crucifixion of our Lord are the pivot round which all the events of the ages revolve. The testimony of Christ was the spirit of prophecy, and the growing power of Jesus is the spirit of history.—Alexander Maclaren.

And how high is Christ's cross? As high as the highest heaven, and the throne of God, and the bosom of the Father—that bosom out of which forever proceed all created things. Ay, as high as the highest heaven! for—if you will receive it—when Christ hung upon the cross, heaven came down on earth, and earth ascended into heaven. —Charles Kingsley.

Nothing like one honest look, one honest thought of Christ upon His cross. That tells us how much He has been through, how much He endured, how much He conquered, how much God loved us, who spared not His only begotten Son, but freely gave Him for us. Dare we doubt such a God? Dare we murmur against such a God?— Charles Kingsley.

A cross borne in simplicity, without the interference of self-love to augment it, is only half a cross. Suffering in this simplicity of love, we are not only happy in spite of the cross, but because of it; for love is pleased in suffering for the Well Beloved, and the cross which forms us into His image is a consoling bond of love.—Fénelon.

To deny one's self, to take up the cross, denotes something immeasurably grander than self-imposed penance or rigid conformity to a divine statute. It is the surrender of self to an ennobling work, an absolute subordination of personal advantages and of personal pleasures for the sake of truth and the welfare of others, and a willing acceptance of every disability which their interests may entail.—George C. Lorimer.

There under the cross is the sinner's sanctuary—there, my friend, is the place for you and me. The first smiling look we shall get from God will be when looking unto Jesus; and the first time that we shall experience the alacrity of a lightened conscience, the relief and elasticity of the great life-burden lifted off, will be when we have laid our sins on the Lamb of God.— James Hamilton.

Christianity without the cross is nothing. The cross was the fitting close of a life of rejection, scorn and defeat. But in no true sense have

these things ceased or changed. Jesus is still He whom man despiseth, and the rejected of men. The world has never admired Jesus, for moral courage is yet needed in every one of its high places by him who would "confess" Christ. The "offense" of the cross, therefore, has led men in all ages to endeavor to be rid of it, and to deny that it is the power of God in the world.—William H. Thomson.

God makes crosses of great variety; He makes some of iron and lead, that look as if they must crush; some of straw, that seem so light, and yet are no less difficult to carry; some He makes of precious stones and gold, that dazzle the eye and excite the envy of spectators, but in reality are as well able to crucify as those which are so much dreaded.—Aughey.

Thou, Everlasting Strength, hast set Thyself forth to bear our burdens. May we bear Thy cross, and bearing that, find there is nothing else to bear; and touching that cross, find that instead of taking away our strength, it adds thereto. Give us faith for darkness, for trouble, for sorrow, for bereavement, for disappointment; give us a faith that will abide though the earth itself should pass away—a faith for living, a faith for dying.—H. W. Beecher.

To do Thy holy will;
  To bear Thy cross;
To trust Thy mercy still,
  In pain or loss;
Poor gifts are these to bring,
  Dear Lord, to Thee,
Who hast done everything
  For me!
      —George Cooper.

Nothing but the cross of Christ can so startle the spiritual nature from its torpor, as to make it an effectual counterpoise to the debasing and sensual tendencies of the race. Favored by temperament and education, individuals may measurably escape; but if the race is to triumph in the conflict between the flesh and the spirit, between the lower propensities and the higher nature, they must, as Constantine is said to have done, see the cross, and on it the motto, "*In hoc signo vinces.*" By this sign we conquer.—Mark Hopkins.

At the foot of the cross, in all humility and in all adoration, we have learned at once the depth and the height of human nature; we have learned to think all wisdom but foolishness for the knowledge of Christ; all purity but sin, unwashed by His atonement; all hope in earth, of all hopes the most miserable, but in the faith of His most blessed resurrection; content to bear the struggles of life, at His command; and submitting to the grave, with a consciousness that it can sting no more.—George Croly.

Crow

To shoot at crows is powder flung away.—Gay.

Even the blackest of them all, the crow,
Renders good service as your man-at-arms,
Crushing the beetle in his coat of mail,
And crying havoc on the slug and snail.
                          —Longfellow.

If the old shower-foretelling crow
  Croak not her boding note in vain,
To-morrow's eastern storm shall strow
The woods with leaves, with weeds the
  main.   —Francis Horace.

Crown

Uneasy lies the head that wears a crown.—Shakespeare.

Within the hollow crown
That rounds the mortal temples of a king,
Keeps death his court; and there the antick
  sits,
Scoffing his state, and grinning at his pomp.
                          —Shakespeare.

A crown
Golden in show, is but a wreath of thorns;
Brings dangers, troubles, cares, and sleepless nights
To him who wears the regal diadem,
When on his shoulders each man's burden
  lies;
For therein stands the office of a king,
His honor, virtue, merit, and chief praise,
That for the public all this weight he bears.
                          —Milton.

Cruelty

Detested sport, that owes its pleasures to another's pain.—Cowper.

Cruelty and fear shake hands together.—Balzac.

All just laws condemn cruelty.—Calderon.

All cruelty springs from weakness.—Seneca.

I must be cruel, only to be kind.—Shakespeare.

A good thing can't be cruel.—Dickens.

Much more may a judge overweigh himself in cruelty than in clemency.—Sir P. Sidney.

An infallible characteristic of meanness is cruelty.—Dr. Johnson.

It is cruelty to be humane to rebels, and humanity is cruelty.—Attributed to Charles IX.

Cruelty is the highest pleasure to the cruel man; it is his love.—Landor.

The cruelty of the effeminate is more dreadful than that of the hardy.—Lavater.

———those whose cruelty makes many
  mourn
Do by the fires, which they first kindle,
  burn.   —Earl of Stirling.

A stony adversary, an inhuman wretch,
Uncapable of pity, void and empty
From any dram of mercy. —Shakespeare.

The man who prates about the cruelty of angling will be found invariably to beat his wife.—Christopher North.

Let me be cruel, not unnatural; I will speak daggers to her; but use none; my tongue and soul in this be hypocrites.—Shakespeare.

Cruelty, like every other vice, requires no motive outside of itself; it only requires opportunity. — George Eliot.

Cruelty, if we consider it as a crime, is the greatest of all; if we consider it

as a madness, we are equally justifiable in applying to it the readiest
and the surest means of oppression.—
Landor.

O Saxon cruelty! how it cheers my
heart to think that you dare not attempt such a thing again! — Daniel
O'Connell.

We ought never to sport with pain
and distress in any of our amusements,
or treat even the meanest insect with
wanton cruelty.—Blair.

Cruelty in all countries is the companion of anger; but there is only one,
and never was another on the globe,
where she coquets both with anger and
mirth.—Landor.

I would not enter on my list of
friends (though graced with polished
manners and fine sense, yet wanting
sensibility) the man who needlessly
sets foot upon a worm.—Cowper.

Cruelty is no more the cure of
crimes than it is the cure of sufferings.
Compassion, in the first instance, is
good for both; I have known it to
bring compunction when nothing else
would.—Landor.

That cruelty which children are permitted to show to birds and other animals will most probably exert itself on
their fellow creatures when at years of
maturity.—Richardson.

Men so noble,

However faulty, yet should find respect
For what they have been; 'tis a cruelty
To load a falling man.   —Shakespeare.

Nothing is so pregnant as cruelty;
so multifarious, so rapid, so ever teeming a mother is unknown to the animal
kingdom; each of her experiments provokes another and refines upon the
last; though always progressive, yet
always remote from the end.—Lavater.

When the cruel fall into the hands
of the cruel, we read their fate with
horror, not with pity. Sylla commanded the bones of Marius to be
broken, his eyes to be pulled out, his
hands to be cut off, and his body to be
torn in pieces with pinchers; and
Catiline was the executioner. "A piece
of cruelty," says Seneca, "only fit for
Marius to suffer, Catiline to execute,
and Sylla to command."—Colton.

Cuckoo

Sweet bird! thy bower is ever green,
  Thy sky is ever clear;
Thou hast no sorrow in thy song,
  No winter in thy year!
          —John Logan.

The merry cuckow, messenger of spring,
His trumpet shrill hath thrice already
  sounded.   —Spenser.

Oh, could I fly, I'd fly with thee!
  We'd make, with joyful wing,
Our annual visit o'er the globe,
  Companions of the spring.
          —John Logan.

O blithe newcomer! I have heard,
I hear thee and rejoice;
O cuckoo! shall I call thee Bird,
Or but a wandering Voice?
          —Wordsworth.

List—'twas the cuckoo—O with what de-
  light
Heard I that voice! and catch it now,
  though faint,
Far off and faint, and melting into air,
Yet not to be mistaken. Hark again!
Those louder cries give notice that the bird,
Although invisible as Echo's self,
Is wheeling hitherward. —Wordsworth.

Culinary — Cooks

Cookery is become an art, a noble
science; cooks are gentlemen.—Burton.

Heaven sends us good meat, but the
devil sends us cooks.—David Garrick.

Cultivation — Culture

Meditation is culture.—Earl of Beaconsfield.

Men of culture are the true apostles
of equality.—Matthew Arnold.

Reading makes a full man, conference a ready man, and writing an exact man.—Bacon.

Partial culture runs to the ornate;
extreme culture to simplicity.—Bovee

Cultivation to the mind is as necessary as food is to the body.—Cicero.

Many-sidedness of culture makes our vision clearer and keener in particulars.—Lowell.

Great culture is often betokened by great simplicity.—Mme. Deluzy.

Culture is like wealth; it makes us more ourselves, it enables us to express ourselves.—Hamerton.

The foundation of culture, as of character, is at last the moral sentiment.—Emerson.

Unless above himself he can erect himself, how poor a thing is man!—Daniel.

Greece appears to be the fountain of knowledge; Rome of elegance.—Dr. Johnson.

Culture is then properly described not as having its origin in curiosity, but as having its origin in the love of perfection; it is a study of perfection.—Matthew Arnold.

A man's nature runs either to herbs or weeds; therefore let him seasonably water the one and destroy the other.—Lady Gethin.

Man is born barbarous—he is ransomed from the condition of beasts only by being cultivated.—Lamartine.

It matters little whether a man be mathematically or philologically or artistically cultivated, so he be but cultivated.—Goethe.

That is true cultivation which gives us sympathy with every form of human life, and enables us to work most successfully for its advancement.—Henry Ward Beecher.

As the soil, however rich it may be, cannot be productive without culture, so the mind, without cultivation, can never produce good fruit.—Seneca.

I am very sure that any man of common understanding may, by culture, care, attention and labor, make himself whatever he pleases, except a great poet.—Chesterfield.

The highest purpose of intellectual cultivation is to give a man a perfect knowledge and mastery of his own inner self; to render our consciousness its own light and its own mirror.—Novalis.

A well-cultivated mind is, so to speak, made up of all the minds of preceding ages; it is only one single mind which has been educated during all this time.—Fontenelle.

Though men of delicate taste be rare, they are easily to be distinguished in society by the soundness of their understanding, and the superiority of their faculties above the rest of mankind.—Hume.

It is very rare to find ground which produces nothing; if it is not covered with flowers, with fruit trees and grains, it produces briers and pines. It is the same with man; if he is not virtuous, he becomes vicious.—Bruyère.

Culture, far from giving us freedom, only develops, as it advances, new necessities; the fetters of the physical close more tightly around us, so that the fear of loss quenches even the ardent impulse toward improvement, and the maxims of passive obedience are held to be the highest wisdom of life.—Schiller.

The great law of culture is, Let each become all that he was created capable of being; expand, if possible, to his full growth; resisting all impediments, casting off all foreign, especially all noxious adhesions, and show himself at length in his own shape and stature be these what they may.—Carlyle.

The only worthy end of all learning, of all science, of all life, in fact, is that human beings should love one another better. Culture merely for culture's sake can never be anything but a sap-less root, capable of producing at best a shriveled branch.—John Walter Cross.

High culture always isolates, always drives men out of their class, and makes it more difficult for them to share naturally and easily the common class-life around them. They seek the few companions who can understand them, and when these are not to be had within a traversable distance, they sit and work alone.—Hamerton.

Not that the moderns are born with more wit than their predecessors, but, finding the world better furnished at their coming into it, they have more leisure for new thoughts, more light to direct them, and more hints to work upon.—Jeremy Collier.

The prosperity of a country depends, not on the abundance of its revenues, nor on the strength of its fortifica-tions, nor on the beauty of its public buildings; but it consists in the num-ber of its cultivated citizens, in its men of education, enlightenment and character.—Luther.

Whatever expands the affections, or enlarges the sphere of our sympathies —whatever makes us feel our relation to the universe, and all that it inherits, in time and in eternity, to the great and beneficent Cause of all, must un-questionably refine our nature, and ele-vate us in the scale of being.—Chan-ning.

There is no reason why the brown hand of labor should not hold Thom-son as well as the sickle. Ornamental reading shelters and even strengthens the growth of what is merely useful. A cornfield never returns a poorer crop because a few wild-flowers bloom in the hedge. The refinement of the poor is the triumph of Christian civiliza-tion.—Willmott.

Where no interest is taken in sci-ence, literature and liberal pursuits, mere facts and insignificant criticisms

necessarily become the themes of dis-course; and minds, strangers alike to activity and meditation, become so limited as to render all intercourse with them at once tasteless and op-pressive.—Mme. de Staël.

What sort of tree is there which will not, if neglected, grow crooked and unfruitful; what but will, if rightly ordered, prove productive and bring its fruit to maturity? What strength of body is there which will not lose its vigor and fall to decay by laziness, nice usage, and debauchery?—Plutarch.

The earth flourishes, or is overrun with noxious weeds and brambles, as we apply or withhold the cultivating hand. So fares it with the intellectual system of man. If you are a parent, then, consider that the good or ill dis-positions and principles you please to cultivate in the mind of your infant may hereafter preserve a nation in prosperity, or hang its fate on the point of the sword.—Horace Mann.

There are few delights in any life so high and rare as the subtle and strong delight of sovereign art and poetry; there are none more pure and more sublime. To have read the greatest works of any great poet, to have beheld or heard the greatest works of any great painter or musician, is a posses-sion added to the best things of life.— Swinburne.

Culture looks beyond machinery, cul-ture hates hatred; culture has one great passion—the passion for sweet-ness and light. It has one even yet greater, the passion for making them all prevail. It is not satisfied till we all come to a perfect man; it knows that the sweetness and light of the few must be imperfect until the raw and unkindly masses of humanity are touched with sweetness and light.— Matthew Arnold.

It does not try to reach down to the level of inferior classes; it does not try to win them for this or that sect of its own, with ready-made judgments and watchwords of its own. It seeks to do away with classes, to make the best that has been taught and known in the world current everywhere, to make all men live in an atmosphere of sweetness and light, where they may use ideas, as it uses them itself, freely—nourished, and not bound by them.—Matthew Arnold.

The wealthy and the noble, when they expend large sums in decorating their houses with the rare and costly efforts of genius, with busts from the chisel of a Canova and with cartoons from the pencil of a Raphael, are to be commended, if they do not stand still here, but go on to bestow some pains and cost, that the master himself be not inferior to the mansion, and that the owner be not the only thing that is little, amidst everything else that is great.—Colton.

Culture implies all which gives the mind possession of its own powers, as languages to the critic, telescope to the astronomer. Culture alters the political status of an individual. It raises a rival royalty in a monarchy. 'Tis king against king. It is ever the romance of history in all dynasties—the co-presence of the revolutionary force in intellect. It creates a personal independence which the monarch cannot look down, and to which he must often succumb.—Emerson.

To the highest culture, evenness of development, resulting in roundness and symmetry, is essential. The ideal man possesses, in addition to all his other qualities, that quality which is figured in the bloom of the flowering plant, in the fragrance of blossoms, in the blush and flavor of fruit—a quality which cannot be counterfeited any more than you can counterfeit a flower's perfume, which cannot be hidden any more than you can hide the fragrance of an orchard in May. It is the precious flavor of the ripened man. As the full fragrance of the apple, as the velvety cheek of the peach, comes only when the fruit has reached its highest development, so this quality comes only as the result of that wise self-enlargement, that deliberate cath-olicity, that cultivated charity of opinion, which characterizes the man of culture.—Joseph Anderson.

Cunning

Cunning is the dwarf of wisdom.—W. R. Alger.

_____

Stratagem is the right hand of cunning.—G. W. Curtis.

_____

Cunning has only private selfish aims.—Addison.

_____

Cleverness and cunning are incompatible.—Byron.

_____

In a great business there is nothing so fatal as cunning management.—Junius.

_____

Cunning and treachery are the offspring of incapacity.—La Rochefoucauld.

_____

All my own experience of life teaches me the contempt of cunning, not the fear.—Mrs. Jameson.

_____

A cunning man overreaches no one half as much as himself.—Beecher.

_____

Cunning pays no regard to virtue, and is but the low mimic of reason.—Bolingbroke.

_____

Cunning is the art of concealing our own defects, and discovering other people's weaknesses.—Hazlitt.

_____

Knowledge without justice ought to be called cunning rather than wisdom.—Plato.

_____

When the fox hath once got in his nose, he'll soon find means to make the body follow.—Shakespeare.

_____

The bounds of a man's knowledge are easily concealed, if he has but prudence.—Goldsmith.

_____

The fox is very cunning, but he is more cunning who catches the fox.—Calderon.

_____

Cunning cheats itself wholly, and other people partially.—Cervantes.

The very cunning conceal their cunning; the indifferently shrewd boast of it.—Bovee.

Cunning is none of the best nor worst qualities. It floats between virtue and vice.—Bruyère.

Cunning is the intensest rendering of vulgarity, absolute and utter.—Ruskin.

The most sure method of subjecting yourself to be deceived is to consider yourself more cunning than others.—La Rochefoucauld.

Nobody was ever so cunning as to conceal their being so; and everybody is shy and distrustful of crafty men.—Locke.

We should do by our cunning as we do by our courage—always have it ready to defend ourselves, never to offend others.—Greville.

Hurry and cunning are the two apprentices of despatch and skill; but neither of them ever learn their master's trade.—Colton.

Surely the continual habit of dissimulation is but a weak and sluggish cunning, and not greatly politic.—Bacon.

Cunning differs from widom as twilight from open day.—Dr. Johnson.

Whoever appears to have much cunning has in reality very little; being deficient in the essential article, which is, to hide cunning.—Henry Home.

This is the fruit of craft; like him that shoots up high, looks for the shaft, and finds it in his forehead.—Middleton.

Cunning leads to knavery; it is but a step from one to the other, and that very slippery; lying only makes the difference; add that to cunning, and it is knavery.—La Bruyère.

It is a remarkable circumstance in reference to cunning persons that they are often deficient not only in comprehensive, far-sighted wisdom, but even in prudent, cautious circumspection.—Whately.

Those who are overreached by our cunning are far from appearing to us as ridiculous as we appear to ourselves when the cunning of others has overreached us.—Rochefoucauld.

The animals to whom nature has given the faculty we call cunning know always when to use it, and use it wisely; but when man descends to cunning he blunders and betrays.—Thomas Paine.

Cunning is only the mimic of discretion, and may pass upon weak men, in the same manner as vivacity is often mistaken for wit, and gravity for wisdom.—Addison.

The greatest of all cunning is to seem blind to the snares which we know to be laid for us. Men are never so easily deceived as while they are endeavoring to deceive others.—Rochefoucauld.

The common practice of cunning is the sign of a small genius; it almost always happens that those who use it to cover themselves in one place lay themselves open in another.—Rochefoucauld.

Cunning is none of the best nor worst qualities; it floats between virtue and vice; there is scarce any exigence where it may not, and perhaps ought not to be supplied by prudence.—Bruyère.

Taking things not as they ought to be, but as they are, I fear it must be allowed that Macchiavelli will always have more disciples than Jesus.—Colton.

It has been a sort of maxim that the greatest art is to conceal art; but I know not how, among some people we meet with, their greatest cunning is to appear cunning.—Steele.

We take cunning for a sinister or crooked wisdom; and certainly there is a great difference between a cunning man and a wise man, not only in point of honesty, but in point of ability.—Bacon.

All my own experience of life teaches me the contempt of cunning, not the fear. The phrase "profound cunning" has always seemed to me a contradiction in terms. I never knew a cunning mind which was not either shallow or on some point diseased.—Mrs. Jameson.

Cunning has only private selfish aims, and sticks at nothing which may make them succeed. Discretion has large and extended views, and, like a well-formed eye, commands a whole horizon; cunning is a kind of short-sightedness, that discovers the minutest objects which are near at hand, but is not able to discern things at a distance.—Addison.

The whole power of cunning is privative; to say nothing, and to do nothing, is the utmost of its reach. Yet men, thus narrow by nature and mean by art, are sometimes able to rise by the miscarriages of bravery and the openness of integrity, and, watching failures and snatching opportunities, obtain advantages which belong to higher characters.—Johnson.

Cupid

That blind, rascally boy that abuses every one's eyes, because his own are out.—Shakespeare.

Cupid is a knavish lad,
Thus to make poor females mad.
—Shakespeare.

Love, well thou knowest, no partnership allows; Cupid averse rejects divided vows.—Prior.

Love is a child that talks in broken language, yet then he speaks most plain.—Dryden.

The wounds invisible that Love's keen arrows make.—Shakespeare.

Thou art figured blind, and yet we borrow our best sight from thee.—Massinger.

Love looks not with the eyes, but with the mind,
And therefore is wing'd Cupid painted blind.   —Shakespeare.

There is music in the beauty, and the silent note which Cupid strikes, far sweeter than the sound of an instrument.—Sir Thomas Browne.

There is an English song beginning, "Love knocks at the door." He knocks less often than he finds it open.—Mme. Swetchine.

Love is ever busy with his shuttle, is ever weaving into life's dull warp bright, gorgeous flowers, and scenes Arcadian.—Longfellow.

According to the Asiatics, Cupid's bow is strung with bees which are apt to sting, sometimes fatally, those who meddle with it.—Miss Edgeworth.

This senior-junior, giant-dwarf, Dan Cupid:
Regent of love rhymes, lord of folded arms,
The anointed sovereign of sighs and groans,
Liege of all loiterers and malcontents.
—Shakespeare.

Before the birth of Love, many fearful things took place through the empire of necessity; but when this god was born, all things rose to men.—Socrates.

Cupid is a casuist,
A mystic and a cabalist—
Can your lurking thought surprise,
And interpret your device. * * *
Heralds high before him run;
He has ushers many a one;
He spreads his welcome where he goes,
And touches all things with his rose.
All things wait for and divine him—
How shall I dare to malign him?
—Emerson.

We say love is blind, and the figure of Cupid is drawn with a bandage around his eyes. Blind—yes, because he does not see what he does not like; but the sharpest-sighted hunter in the universe is Love for finding what he seeks, and only that.—Emerson.

In the true mythology, Love is an immortal child, and Beauty leads him as guide; nor can we express a deeper sense than when we say Beauty is the pilot of the young soul.—Emerson.

Love can take what shape he pleases; and when once begun his fiery inroad in the soul, how vain the after knowledge which his presence gives! We weep or rave; but still he lives, and lives master and lord, amidst pride and tears and pain.—Barry Cornwall.

Curiosity

A penny for your thought.—Swift.

The over curious are not over wise.—Massinger.

Curiosity is the thirst of the soul.—Dr. Johnson.

I loathe that low vice, curiosity.—Byron.

Curiosity is lying in wait for every secret.—Emerson.

Curiosity is one of the forms of feminine bravery.—Victor Hugo.

Curiosity is thought on its entering edge.—Charles H. Parkhurst.

Curiosity is a little more than another name for hope.—J. C. and A. W. Hare.

He who would pry behind the scenes oft sees a counterfeit.—Dryden.

The curiosity of knowing things has been given to man for a scourge.—Bible.

Curiosity is as much the parent of attention as attention is of memory.—Whately.

The enquiring spirit will not be controll'd,
We would make certain all, and all behold.
—Sprague.

Men are more inclined to ask curious questions than to obtain necessary instruction.—Pasquier Quesnel.

Ask me no questions, and I'll tell you no fibs.—Goldsmith.

Talk to him of Jacob's ladder, and he would ask the number of steps.—Douglas Jerrold.

Curiosity has lost more young girls than love.—Mme. de Puisieux.

The first and simplest emotion which we discover in the human mind is curiosity.—Burke.

The first vice of the first woman was curiosity, and it runs through the whole sex.—Richardson.

Curiosity in children Nature has provided to remove the ignorance they were born with.—Locke.

Curiosity is one of the permanent and certain characteristics of a vigorous intellect.—Johnson.

People of a lively imagination are generally curious, and always so when a little in love.—Longfellow.

Avoid him who from mere curiosity asks three questions running about a thing that cannot interest him.—Lavater.

Curiosity is a kernel of the forbidden fruit, which still sticketh in the throat of a natural man, sometimes to the danger of his choking.—Fuller.

O this itch of the ear, that breaks out at the tongue! Were not curiosity so over-busy, detraction would soon be starved to death.—Douglas Jerrold.

Inquisitive people are the funnels of conversation; they do not take in anything for their own use, but merely to pass it to another.—Steele.

No heart is empty of the humor of curiosity, the beggar being as attentive in his station to an improvement of knowledge as the prince.—Osborn.

The world is the book of women. What knowledge they may possess is acquired by watchful observation rather than by reading.—Rousseau.

The knowledge that women lack stimulates their imagination; the knowledge that men possess blunts theirs.—Mme. de Sartory.

Talkativeness has another plague attached to it, even curiosity; for praters wish to hear much that they may have much to say.—Plutarch.

Curiosity is, in great and generous minds, the first passion and the last, and perhaps always predominates in proportion to the strength of the contemplative faculties.—Dr. Johnson.

Man is distinguished not only by his reason, but also by this singular passion, from all other animals.—Thomas Hobbes.

Curiosity, or the love of knowledge, has a very limited influence, and requires youth, leisure, education, genius and example to make it govern any person.—Hume.

Who forces himself on others is to himself a load. Impetuous curiosity is empty and inconstant. Prying intrusion may be suspected of whatever is little.—Lavater.

Of all the faculties of the human mind, curiosity is that which is the most fruitful or the most barren in effective results, according as it is well or badly directed.—Palmieri.

He that questioneth much shall learn much, and content much; but especially if he apply his questions to the skill of the persons whom he asketh.—Bacon.

As those things which engage us merely by their novelty cannot attach us for any length of time, curiosity is the most superficial of all the affections.—Burke.

A person who is too nice an observer of the business of the crowd, like one who is too curious in observing the labor of the bees, will often be stung for his curiosity.—Pope.

There are different kinds of curiosity —one of interest, which causes us to learn that which would be useful to us, and the other of pride which springs from a desire to know that of which others are ignorant.—Rochefoucauld.

There is philosophy in the remark that every man has in his own life follies enough, in the performance of his duty deficiencies enough, in his own mind trouble enough, without being curious after the affairs of others.—Dibdin.

Curiosity is the most superficial of all the affections; it changes its object perpetually; it has an appetite which is very sharp, but very easily satisfied, and it has always an appearance of giddiness, restlessness and anxiety.—Burke.

Curiosity is a languid principle, where access is easy and gratification is immediate; remoteness and difficulty are powerful incentives to its vigorous and lasting operation.—Munro.

Curiosity is the direct incontinency of the spirit. Knock therefore at the door before you enter upon your neighbor's privacy; and remember that there is no difference between entering into his house and looking into it.—Jeremy Taylor.

Inquire not too much into your bosom companion's griefs, nor compel him to tell all the tale of his life. Much and all will be told to those that do not ask; and you shall have the secrets into which you do not pry.—Bartol.

The curiosity of an honorable mind willingly rests there, where the love of truth does not urge it farther onward, and the love of its neighbor bids it stop; in other words, it willingly stops at the point where the interests of truth do not beckon it onward, and charity cries, Halt!—Coleridge.

Curiosity is but vanity. Oftenest one wishes to know but to talk of it. Otherwise one would not go to sea if he were never to say anything about it, and for the sole pleasure of seeing, without hope of ever communicating what he has seen.—Pascal.

Curse

A curse is like a cloud—it passes.—Bailey.

Curses are like young chickens,
And still come home to roost!
—Lytton.

We let our blessings get mouldy, and then call them curses.—Beecher.

Oh! I will curse thee till thy frighted soul
Runs mad with horror. —Lee.

Down to the dust! and as thou rott'st away,
Even worms shall perish on thy poisonous clay. —Byron.

All the infections that the sun sucks up
From bogs, fens, flats, on Prosper fall, and make him
By inch-meal a disease! —Shakespeare.

Whip me, ye devils,
Blow me about in winds, roast me in sulphur,
Wash me in steep-down gulfs of liquid fire.
—Shakespeare.

May the grass wither from thy feet; the woods
Deny thee shelter! earth a home! the dust
A grave! the sun his light! and heaven her God! —Byron.

Plagues and palsy,
Disease and pestilence consume the robber,
Infect his blood, and wither ev'ry pow'r.
—Brown.

But no, I will not curse them: thro' the world
A curse will follow them, like the black plague,
Tracking their footsteps ever—day and night,
Morning and eve, summer and winter—ever. —Proctor.

Dinna curse him, sir; I have heard a good man say that a curse was like a stone flung up to the heavens, and maist like to return on his head that sent it.—Walter Scott.

You nimble lightnings, dart your blinding flames
Into her scornful eyes!—Infect her beauty,
You fen-suck'd fogs, drawn by the powerful sun,
To fall and blister her pride!
—Shakespeare.

Villains, vipers, damn'd without redemption;
Dogs, easily won to fawn on any man;
Snakes in my heart-blood warm'd, that sting my heart;
Three Judases, each one thrice worse than Judas. —Shakespeare.

May never glorious sun reflex his beams
Upon the country where you make abode!
But darkness and the gloomy shade of death
Environ you till mischief and despair
Drive you to break your necks, or hang yourselves. —Shakespeare.

Poison be their drink!
Gall, worse than gall, the daintiest meat that they taste!—
Their softest touch as smart as lizards' stings!
Their music frightful as the serpent's hiss!
And boding screech-owls make the concert full! —Shakespeare.

All the contagion of the south light on you,
You shames of Rome! you herd of—boils and plagues
Plaster you o'er; that you may be abhorr'd
Further than seen, and one infect another
Against the wind a mile! —Shakespeare.

Custom

Custom is the law of fools.—Vanburgh.

Custom does often reason overrule.
—Rochester.

Custom doth make dotards of us all.
—Carlyle.

Custom is the best interpreter of laws.—Law Maxim.

Custom is held to be as a law.—Law Maxim.

Experience is the mother of custom.
—Henry Ward Beecher.

Ancient custom is always held or regarded as law.—Law Maxim.

Custom reconciles to everything.—Burke.

How use doth breed a habit in a man!—Shakespeare.

As the world leads we follow.—Seneca.

A deep meaning often lies in old customs.—Schiller.

Custom, though never so ancient, without truth, is but an old error.—Cyprian.

Custom calls me to 't—
What custom wills, in all things should we
do 't?   —Shakespeare.

There is nothing more nearly permanent in human life than a well-established custom.—Joseph Anderson.

Be not so bigoted to any custom as to worship at the expense of truth.—Zimmermann.

Great things astonish us, and small dishearten us. Custom makes both familiar.—De La Bruyère.

To follow foolish precedents, and wink
With both our eyes, is easier than to think.
          —Cowper.

Habit with him was all the test of truth,
"It must be right: I've done it from my
youth."   —Crabbe.

There is no tyrant like custom, and no freedom where its edicts are not resisted.—Bovee.

The ancients tell us what is best; but we must learn of the moderns what is fittest.—Franklin.

Custom may lead a man into many errors; but it justifies none.—Fielding.

Custom is the tyranny of the lower human faculties over the higher.—Mme. Necker.

The way of the world is to make laws, but follow customs.—Montaigne.

Strange customs do not thrive in foreign soil.—Schiller.

It is a custom,
More honor'd in the breach than the ob·
servance.   —Shakespeare.

The breach of custom
Is breach of all.
          —Shakespeare.

Custom, which diminishes the intense, increases the moderate, pleasures.—Ramsay.

The custom of the manor and the place must be observed.—Law Maxim.

Custom, 'tis true, a venerable tyrant
O'er servile man extends her blind do·
minion.   —Thomson.

There are not unfrequently substantial reasons underneath for customs that appear to us absurd.—Charlotte Bronte.

The tyrant custom, most grave senators,
Hath made the flinty and steel couch of
war
My thrice-driven bed of down.
          —Shakespeare.

New customs,
Though they be never so ridiculous,
Nay, let 'em be unmanly, yet are followed.
          —Shakespeare.

The laws of conscience, which we pretend to be derived from nature, proceed from custom.—Montaigne.

The influence of custom is incalculable; dress a boy as a man and he will at once change his own conception of himself.—Bayle St. John.

Choose always the way that seems the best, however rough it may be. Custom will render it easy and agreeable.—Pythagoras.

The custom and fashion of to-day will be the awkwardness and outrage of to-morrow. So arbitrary are these transient laws.—Dumas.

The customs and fashions of men change like leaves on the bough, some of which go and others come.—Dante.

Can there be any greater dotage in the world than for one to guide and direct his courses by the sound of a bell, and not by his own judgment.— Rabelais.

Man yields to custom as he bows to fate.
In all things ruled—mind, body and estate;
In pain or sickness, we for cure apply
To them we know not, and we know not why. —Crabbe.

Custom forms us all.
Our thoughts, our morals, our most fix'd belief
Are consequences of our place of birth.
—Hill.

The slaves of custom and established mode,
With pack-horse constancy, we keep the road
Crooked or straight, through quags or thorny dells,
True to the jingling of our leader's bells.
—Cowper.

Men commonly think according to their inclinations, speak according to their learning and imbibed opinions; but generally act according to custom. —Bacon.

Custom is the great leveller. It corrects the inequality of fortune by lessening equally the pleasures of the prince and the pains of the peasant.— Henry Home.

Their origin is commonly unknown; for the practice often continues when the cause has ceased, and concerning superstitious ceremonies it is in vain to conjecture; for what reason did not dictate, reason cannot explain.—Dr. Johnson.

Such dupes are men to custom, and so prone
To rev'rence what is ancient, and can plead
A course of long observance for its use,
That even servitude, the worst of ills,
Because deliver'd down from sire to son,
Is kept and guarded as a sacred thing!
—Cowper.

Be not too rash in the breaking of an inconvenient custom; as it was gotten, so leave it by degrees. Danger attends upon too sudden alterations; he that pulls down a bad building by the great may be ruined by the fall,

but he that takes it down brick by brick may live to build a better.— Quarles.

Custom is the law of one description of fools, and fashion of another; but the two parties often clash—for precedent is the legislator of the first, and novelty of the last. Custom, therefore, looks to things that are past, and fashion to things that are present.— Colton.

When all moves equally (says Pascal), nothing seems to move, as in a vessel under sail; and when all run by common consent into vice, none appear to do so. He that stops first, views as from a fixed point the horrible extravagance that transports the rest.—Colton.

Parents fear the destruction of natural affection in their children. What is this natural principle so liable to decay? Habit is a second nature, which destroys the first. Why is not custom nature? I suspect that this nature itself is but a first custom, as custom is a second nature.—Pascal.

Custom is a violent and treacherous school mistress. She, by little and little, slyly and unperceived, slips in the foot of her authority; but having by this gentle and humble beginning, with the benefit of time, fixed and established it, she then unmasks a furious and tyrannic countenance, against which we have no more the courage or the power so much as to lift up our eyes.—Montaigne.

Cynic — Cynicism

There is so much trouble in coming into the world, and so much more, as well as meanness, in going out of it, that it is hardly worth while to be here at all.—Lord Bolingbroke.

Don't hang a dismal picture on the wall, and do not daub with sables and glooms in your conversation. Don't be a cynic and disconsolate preacher. Don't bewail and bemoan. Omit the negative propositions. Nerve us with incessant affirmatives. Don't waste yourself in rejection, nor bark against the bad, but chant the beauty of the good. When that is spoken which has a right to be spoken, the chatter and the criticism will stop. Set down nothing that will not help somebody.—Emerson.

———

I do not know the man I should avoid
So soon as that spare Cassius. He reads
   much;
He is a great observer, and he looks
Quite through the deeds of men: he loves
   no plays,
As thou dost, Antony; he hears no music;
Seldom he smiles; and smiles in such a
   sort
As if he mocked himself and scorned his
   spirit
That could be moved to smile at anything.
                        —Shakespeare.

———

Indifference to all the actions and passions of mankind was not supposed to be such a distinguished quality at that time, I think. I have known it very fashionable indeed. I have seen it displayed with such success that I have encountered some fine ladies and gentlemen who might as well have been born caterpillars.—Dickens.

———

The cynic is one who never sees a good quality in a man, and never fails to see a bad one. He is the human owl, vigilant in darkness and blind to light, mousing for vermin, and never seeing noble game. The cynic puts all human actions into two classes—openly bad and secretly bad. All virtue and generosity and disinterestedness are merely the appearance of good; but selfish at the bottom. He holds that no man does a good thing except for profit. The effect of his conversation upon your feelings is to chill and sear them; to send you away sour and morose. His criticisms and hints fall indiscriminately upon every lovely thing, like frost upon flowers.—Beecher.

———

Nil admirari is the motto which men of the world always affect. They think it vulgar to wonder, or be enthusiastic. They have so much corruption and so much charlatanism that they think the credit of all high qualities must be delusive.—Sir Egerton Brydges.

Cypress

Dark tree! still sad when others' grief is
   fled,
The only constant mourner o'er the dead.
                        —Byron.

D

Daffodil

Daffodils
That come before the swallow dares,
and take
The winds of March with beauty;
violets, dim,
But sweeter than the lids of Juno's eyes,
Or Cytherea's breath.   —Shakespeare.

Dainties

Such dainties to them, their health it might
hurt;
It's like sending them ruffles, when wanting a shirt.   —Goldsmith.

Daisy

The poet's darling.—Wordsworth.

Thou unassuming commonplace
Of nature.   —Wordsworth.

That well by reason men it call may
The daisie, or els the eye of the day,
The emprise, and floure of floures all.
·   —Chaucer.

Small service is true service while it lasts:
Of humblest friends, bright creature! scorn
not one:
The daisy, by the shadow that it casts,
Protects the lingering dewdrop from the
sun.   —Wordsworth.

Myriads of daisies have shown forth in
flower
Near the lark's nest, and in their natural
hour
Have passed away; less happy than the one
That, by the unwilling ploughshare, died to
prove
The tender charm of poetry and love.
—Wordsworth.

Wee, modest, crimson-tipped flow'r,
Thou's met me in an evil hour;
For I maun crush amang the stoure
Thy slender stem:
To spare thee now is past my pow'r,
Thou bonnie gem.—Burns.

Of all the floures in the mede,
Than love I most these floures white and
rede,
Soch that men callen daisies in our toun.
—Chaucer.

Dancing

No man in his senses will dance.—
Cicero.

Those elegant delights of jig and
vaulting.—Elijah Fenton.

All are not merry that dance lightly.
—George Herbert.

Come, knit hands, and beat the ground
In a light fantastic round.   —Milton.

To brisk notes in cadence beating
Glance their many-twinkling feet. —Gray.

While his off-heel, insidiously aside,
Provokes the caper which he seems to chide.
—Sheridan.

Come and trip it as ye go,
On the light fantastic toe.
—Milton.

Others import yet nobler arts from France,
Teach kings to fiddle, and make senates
dance.   —Pope.

They who love dancing too much
seem to have more brains in their feet
than their head, and think to play the
fool with reason.—Terence.

Dance, laugh, and be merry; but be
also innocent.—Théodore Barrière.

Social dissipation, as witnessed in
the ball-room, is the abettor of pride,
the instigator of jealousy, it is the
sacrificial altar of health, it is the
defiler of the soul, it is the avenue of
lust and it is the curse of every town
in America.—Talmage.

The dancing pair, that simply sought
renown,
By holding out, to tire each other
down. —Goldsmith.

But O, she dances such a way!
No sun upon an Easter-day,
Is half so fine a sight.
—Sir John Suckling.

And the dancing has begun now,
And the dancers whirl round gaily
In the waltz's giddy mazes,
And the ground beneath them
trembles. —Heine.

Fashionable dances as now carried
on are revolting to every feeling of
delicacy and propriety and are fraught
with the greatest danger to millions.
—Horace Bushnell.

Charity balls are a curse. The
name is a subtle argument in favor of
their existence, but if ever anything
belied its name, it is a charity ball.—
Geo. F. Hall.

Well was it said by a man of sagacity that dancing was a sort of privileged and reputable folly, and that the
best way to be convinced of this was
to close the ears and judge of it by
the eyes alone.—Gotthold.

On with the dance! let joy be uncon-
fined!
No sleep till morn, when youth and
pleasure meet,
To chase the glowing hours with flying feet. —Byron.

The gymnasium of running, walking on stilts, climbing, etc., steels and
makes hardy single powers and muscles, but dancing, like a corporeal
poesy, embellishes, exercises, and
equalizes all the muscles at once.—
Richter.

The rout is Folly's circle, which she
draws
With magic wand. So potent is the
spell,
That none decoy'd into that fatal ring,
Unless by heaven's peculiar grace,
escape.
There we grow early gray, but never
wise. —Cowper.

The ball-room is one way and a
very broad way, too, to ruin. May
God help every lover of the race to
sound a note of alarm both to those
already astray and to those who thus
far have not set foot in the slippery
path.—Hall.

Alike all ages: dames of ancient days
Have led their children through the
mirthful maze;
And the gay grandsire, skill'd in gestic
lore,
Has frisked beneath the burden of
threescore. —Goldsmith.

Merrily, merrily whirled the wheels of
the dizzying dances
Under the orchard-trees and down the
path to the meadows;
Old folk and young together, and children mingled among them.
—Longfellow.

Where wildness and disorder are
visible in the dance, there Satan,
death and all kinds of mischief are
likewise upon the floor. For this reason I could wish that the dance of
death were painted on the walls of all
ball-rooms, in order to warn the dancers, not by the levity of their deportment, to provoke the God of righteousness to visit them with a sudden
judgment.—Gotthold.

No amusement seems more to have
a foundation in our nature. The animation of youth overflows spontaneously in harmonious movements.
The true idea of dancing entitles it to
favor. Its end is to realize perfect
grace in motion; and who does not
know that a sense of the graceful is
one of the higher faculties of our nature?—Channing.

I saw her at a country ball;
There when the sound of flute and
fiddle
Gave signal sweet in that old hall,
Of hands across and down the
middle.
Hers was the subtlest spell by far
Of all that sets young hearts ro-
mancing;
She was our queen, our rose, our star;
And when she danced—oh, heaven,
her dancing! —Praed.

A thousand hearts beat happily; and
when
Music arose with its voluptuous
swell,
Soft eyes look'd love to eyes which
spake again,
And all went merry as a marriage
bell. —Byron.

And beautiful maidens moved down in
the dance,
With the magic of motion and sunshine of glance;
And white arms wreathed lightly, and
tresses fell free
As the plumage of birds in some tropical tree. —Whittier.

He who esteems the Virginia reel
A bait to draw saints from their spiritual weal,
And regards the quadrille as a far
greater knavery
Than crushing His African children
with slavery,
Since all who take part in a waltz or
cotillon
Are mounted for hell on the devil's
own pillion,
Who, as every true orthodox Christian
well knows,
Approaches the heart through the door
of the toes. —Lowell.

The uniform testimony of all religious specialists is that as the love of
dancing increases, the love of the Lord
and his work decreases. The spirit
of the dance is not the spirit of the
Master. If the one be harbored the
other will not remain. Where the experiment is tried of retaining both, a
horrible muddle is the result, a corruption that disgraces the holy vocation wherewith we are called. The
dance is a deadly poison to the higher
life and he who professing Christianity takes it into his spiritual system
wounds our Lord afresh, and by the
act classes himself with the traitors
of old who killed the world's only hope
by nailing Christ to the cross.—Sam
Jones.

I love these rural dances—from my
heart I love them. This world, at
best, is full of care and sorrow; the
life of a poor man is so stained with
the sweat of his brow, there is so
much toil and struggling and anguish

and disappointment here below, that I
gaze with delight on a scene where all
those are laid aside and forgotten, and
the heart of the toil-worn peasant
seems to throw off its load.—Longfellow.

I love to go and mingle with the young
In the gay festal room—when every
heart
Is beating faster than the merry tune,
And their blue eyes are restless, and
their lips
Parted with eager joy, and their round
cheeks
Flush'd with the beautiful motion of
the dance. —Willis.

And then he danced—all foreigners
excel
The serious Angles in the eloquence
Of pantomine—he danced, I say, right
well
With emphasis, and also with good
sense—
A thing in footing indispensable:
He danced without theatrical pretence,
Not like a ballet-master in the van
Of his drill'd nymphs, but like a gen-
tleman. —Byron.

What may we expect of people who
work all day and dance all night?
After a while they will be thrown on
society nervous, exhausted imbeciles.—
Talmage.

I wish that I could marshall all the
young to an appreciation of the fact
that you have an earnest work in life
and your amusements and recreations
are only to help you along in that
work.—Talmage.

Chaste were his steps, each kept
within due bound,
And elegance was sprinkled o'er his
figure;
Like swift Camilla, he scarce skimm'd
the ground,
And rather held in than put forth his
vigor.
And then he had an ear for music's
sound,
Which might defy a crotchet critic's
rigor.
Such classic pas—sans flaws—set off
our hero,
He glanced like a personified Bolero.
—Byron.

Once on a time, the wight Stupidity
For his throne trembled,
When he discovered in the brains of men
Something like thoughts assembled,
And so he searched for a plausible plan—
One of validity—
And racked his brains, if rack his brains he
   can,
None having, or a very few!
At last he hit upon a way
For putting to rout,
And driving out
From our dull clay
These same intruders new—
This Sense, these Thoughts, these Specula-
   tive ills—
What could he do? He introduced qua-
   drilles.   —Ruskin.

Such pains, such pleasures now alike are
   o'er,
And beaus and etiquette shall soon exist
   no more
   At their speed behold advancing
   Modern men and women dancing;
Step and dress alike express
Above, below, from heel to toe,
Male and female awkwardness.
Without a hoop, without a ruffle,
One eternal jig and shuffle,
Where's the air and where's the gait?
Where's the feather in the hat?
Where the frizzed toupee? and where
Oh! where's the powder for the hair?
      —Catherine Fanshawe.

Dandy

Dandyism is a species of genius.—
Hazlitt.

Dandyism is refined vulgarity.—G.
F. Goss.

Clothes form the intellect of the
dandy.—H. W. Shaw.

All finery is a sign of littleness.—
Lavater.

Dandies, when first-rate, are generally very agreeable men.—Bulwer-
Lytton.

Oh! save me, ye powers, from these pinks
   of the nation,
These tea-table heroes! these lords of creation.   —Salmagundi.

A dandy is a clothes-wearing man—
a man whose trade, office, and existence consist in the wearing of clothes.
Every faculty of his soul, spirit, person and purse is heroically consecrated

to this one object—the wearing of
clothes wisely and well; so that, as
others dress to live, he lives to dress.
—Carlyle.

A fool may have his coat embroidered with gold, but it is a fool's coat
still.—Rivarol.

Danger

Danger comes the sooner when it is
despised.—Syrus.

That danger which is despised arrives the soonest.—Laberius.

For danger levels man and brute
And all are fellows in their need.
      —Dryden.

The absent danger greater still appears
Less fears he, who is near the thing he
   fears.   —Daniel.

Man is never watchful enough
against dangers that threaten him
every hour.—Horace.

In extreme danger, fear turns a deaf
ear to every feeling of pity.—Cæsar.

Danger for danger's sake is senseless.—Leigh Hunt.

Our dangers and delights are near allies,
From the same stem the rose and prickle
   rise.   —Aleyn.

Speak, speak, let terror strike slaves mute,
Much danger makes great hearts most resolute.   —Marston.

Nothing is strong that may not be
endangered even by the weak.—Quintus Curtius Rufus.

If we must fall, we should boldly
meet the danger.—Tacitus.

He is safe from danger who is on
his guard even when safe.—Syrus.

He knows that the man is overcome
ingloriously who is overcome without
danger.—Seneca.

Thou dwarf dressed up in giant's
clothes, that showest far off still
greater than thou art.—Suckling.

There is no person who is not dangerous for some one.—Mme. de Sévigné.

Keep together here, lest, running thither,
We unawares run into danger's mouth.
—Milton.

Constant exposure to dangers will breed contempt for them.—Seneca.

Let every eye negotiate for itself, and trust no agent.—Shakespeare.

Danger levels man and brute, and all are fellows in their need.—Byron.

It is the danger which is least expected that soonest comes to us.—Voltaire.

Out of this nettle, danger, we pluck this flower, safety.—Shakespeare.

We have scotch'd the snake, not kill'd it,
She'll close, and be herself! whilst our poor malice
Remains in danger of her former tooth.
—Shakespeare.

A timid person is frightened before a danger, a coward during the time, and a courageous person afterwards.—Richter.

Fools and sensible men are equally innocuous. It is in the half fool and the half wise that the danger lies.—Goethe.

Danger knows full well,
That Cæsar is more dangerous than he:
We are two lions litter'd in one day,
And I the elder and more terrible.
—Shakespeare.

What is danger
More than the weakness of our apprehensions?
A poor cold part o' th' blood; who takes it hold of?
Cowards and wicked livers: valiant minds
Were made the masters of it.
—Beaumont and Fletcher.

A man's opinion of danger varies at different times, in consequence of an irregular tide of animal spirits; and he is actuated by considerations which he dares not avow.—Smollett.

It is better to meet danger than to wait for it. He that is on a lee shore, and foresees a hurricane, stands out to sea and encounters a storm to avoid a shipwreck.—Colton.

Let the fear of a danger be a spur to prevent it; he that fears otherwise gives advantage to the danger; it is less folly not to endeavor the prevention of the evil thou fearest than to fear the evil which thy endeavor cannot prevent.—Quarles.

Thou little know'st
What he can brave, who, born and nurst
In danger's paths, has dared her worst!
Upon whose ear the signal-word
Of strife and death is hourly breaking;
Who sleeps with head upon the sword
His fever'd hand must grasp in waking.
—Moore.

Dangers are no more light if they once seem light, and more dangers have deceived men than forced them; nay, it were better to meet some dangers half-way, though they come nothing near, than to keep too long a watch upon their approaches; for if a man watch too long it is odds he will fall fast asleep.—Bacon.

He led on; but thoughts
Seem'd gathering round which troubled him. The veins
Grew visible upon his swarthy brow,
And his proud lip was press'd as if with pain.
He trod less firmly; and his restless eye
Glanc'd forward frequently, as if some ill
He dared not meet were there.—Willis.

We should never so entirely avoid danger as to appear irresolute and cowardly; but, at the same time, we should avoid unnecessarily exposing ourselves to danger, than which nothing can be more foolish.—Cicero.

Daring

Fortune helps the bold.—Virgil.

I dare do all that may become a man;
Who dares do more, is none.
—Shakespeare.

And what he greatly thought, he nobly dared.—Homer.

By daring, great fears are concealed.
—Lucan.

Be bolde, be bolde, and everywhere be bolde.—Spenser.

Dare to act! Even Venus aids the bold.—Tibullus.

A decent boldness ever meets with friends.—Homer.

And what they dare to dream of, dare to do.—Lowell.

In great straits and when hope is small, the boldest counsels are the safest.—Livy.

And dar'st thou then
To beard the lion in his den,
The Douglas in his hall? —Scott.

He either fears his fate too much,
Or his deserts are small,
That dares not put it to the touch
To gain or lose it all.
—Marquis of Montrose.

He that climbs the tall tree has won right to the fruit,
He that leaps the wide gulf should prevail in his suit. —Scott.

No one reaches a high position without daring.—Syrus.

Darkness

Darkness which may be felt.—Bible.

Darkness visible.—Milton.

Weep, for the light is dead.—Schiller.

At one stride comes the dark.—Coleridge.

Darkness, thou first great parent of us all,
Thou art our great original!
—Yalden.

Lo! darkness bends down like a mother of grief
On the limitless plain, and the fall of her hair
It has mantled a world.
—Joaquin Miller.

There is no darkness but ignorance. —Shakespeare.

The repose of darkness is deeper on the water than on the land.—Victor Hugo.

Melt, and dispel, ye spectre doubts that roll
Cimmerian darkness o'er the parting soul.
—Campbell.

There is such a thing as the pressure of darkness.—Victor Hugo.

Daughter

Good daughters make good mothers. —Abigail G. Whittlesey.

Still harping on my daughter.—Shakespeare.

A daughter is an embarrassing and ticklish possession.—Menander.

Marry your daughters betimes, lest they marry themselves.—Burleigh.

With a little hoard of maxims preaching down a daughter's heart.—Tennyson.

If thy daughter marry well, thou hast found a son; if not, thou hast lost a daughter.—Quarles.

Happy is it to place a daughter; yet it pains a father's heart when he delivers to another's house a child, the object of his tender care.—Euripides.

To a father waxing old, nothing is dearer than a daughter; sons have spirits of a higher pitch, but less inclined to endearing fondness.—Euripides.

If a daughter you have, she's the plague of your life,
No peace shall you know though you've buried your wife!
At twenty she mocks at the duty you taught her—
Oh, what a plague is an obstinate daughter!
—Sheridan.

Trust to me, judicious mother: do not make of your daughter an honest man, as if to give the lie to Nature; make her an honest woman, and be assured that she will be of more worth both to herself and to us.—Rousseau.

See, indeed, that your daughter is thoroughly grounded and experienced in household duties; but take care, through religion and poetry, to keep her heart open to heaven.—Richter.

Who can describe the transports of a heart truly parental on beholding a daughter shoot up like some fair and modest flower, and acquire, day after day, fresh beauty and growing sweetness, so as to fill every eye with pleasure and every heart with admiration? —Fordyce.

When a mother, as fond mothers will, vows that she knows every thought in her daughter's heart, I think she pretends to know a great deal too much.—Thackeray.

Dawn

There is no solemnity so deep, to a right-thinking creature, as that of dawn.—Ruskin.

The morning steals upon the night,
Melting the darkness. —Shakespeare.

Yon grey lines
That fret the clouds are messengers of day.
—Shakespeare.

The dawn is overcast, the morning lowers,
And heavily in clouds brings on the day.
—Addison.

The quiet night, now dappling, 'gan to wane,
Dividing darkness from the dawning main.
—Byron.

Night's candles are burnt out, and jocund day
Stands tiptoe on the misty mountain-tops.
—Shakespeare.

The gray-eyed morn smiles on the frowning night,
Checkering the eastern clouds with streaks of light. —Shakespeare.

The day begins to break, and night is fled,
Whose pitchy mantle over-veil'd the earth.
—Shakespeare.

Look, the morn, in russet mantle clad,
Walks o'er the dew of yon high eastern hill. —Shakespeare.

The sun had not risen, but the vault of heaven was rich with the winning softness that "brings and shuts the day," while the whole air was filled with the carols of birds, the hymns of the feathered tribe.—James Fenimore Cooper.

Look, the gentle day,
Before the wheels of Phœbus, round about
Dapples the drowsy east with spots of gray.
—Shakespeare.

The eastern gate, all fiery red,
Opening on Neptune, with fair blessed beams,
Turns into yellow gold his salt-green streams. —Shakespeare.

Faster and more fast,
O'er night's brim, day boils at last;
Boils, pure gold, o'er the cloud-cup's brim.
—Robert Browning.

See the dapple coursers of the morn
Beat up the light with their bright silver hoofs,
And chase it through the sky.
—Marston.

Night's swift dragons cut the clouds full fast,
And yonder shines Aurora's harbinger;
At whose approach, ghosts, wand'ring here and there,
Troop home to churchyards.
—Shakespeare.

'Tis beautiful, when first the dewy light
Breaks on the earth! while yet the scented air
Is breathing the cool freshness of the night
And the bright clouds a tint of crimson wear. —Elizabeth M. Chandler.

At last the golden oriental gate
Of greatest heaven 'gan to open fair;
And Phœbus, fresh as bridegroom to his mate,
Came dancing forth shaking his dewy hair,
And hurl'd his glist'ing beams through gloomy air. —Spenser.

Color, in the outward world, answers to feeling in man; shape, to thought; motion, to will. The dawn of day is the nearest outward likeness of an act of creation; and it is, therefore, also the closest type in nature for that in us which most approaches to creation—the realization of an idea by an act of the will.—John Sterling.

Day

Sufficient unto the day is the evil thereof.—Bible.

Each day is the scholar of yesterday.—Publius Syrus.

A day for God to stoop, and man to soar.—Tennyson.

One of the heavenly days that cannot die.—Wordsworth.

No day is without its innocent hope.—Ruskin.

Thinking of the days that are no more.—Tennyson.

He who has lived a day has lived an age.—Bruyère.

One glance of Thine creates a day.—Watts.

The spirit walks of every day deceased.—Young.

What is a day to an immortal soul!
A breath, no more. —T. B. Aldrich.

One day, with life and heart,
Is more than time enough to find a world.
—James Russell Lowell.

The long days are no happier than the short ones.—Bailey.

Frail empire of a day!
That with the setting sun extinct is lost.
—Somerville.

Not all Apollo's Pythian treasures hold can bribe the poor possession of a day.—Homer.

Days, that need borrow
No part of their good morrow
From a fore-spent night of sorrow.
—Richard Crashaw.

The sun is in the heaven; and the proud day, attended with the pleasures of the world, is all too wanton.—Shakespeare.

Boast not thyself of to-morrow; for thou knowest not what a day may bring forth.—Bible.

One day spent well, and agreeably to your precepts, is preferable to an eternity of error.—Yonge.

O beautiful, awful summer day, what hast thou given, what taken away?—Longfellow.

Philip. Madam, a day may sink or save a realm.
Mary. A day may save a heart from breaking too. —Tennyson.

What hath this day deserv'd? what hath it done,
That it in golden letters should be set
Among the high tides in the calendar?
—Shakespeare.

Day is a snow-white Dove of heaven
That from the East glad message brings:
Night is a stealthy, evil Raven,
Wrapt to the eyes in his black wings.
—T. B. Aldrich.

Day is the Child of Time,
And Day must cease to be:
But Night is without a sire,
And cannot expire,
One with Eternity.
—R. H. Stoddard.

Sweet day, so cool, so calm, so bright,
The bridal of the earth and sky,
The dew shall weep thy fall to-night;
For thou must die. —Herbert.

How troublesome is day!
It calls us from our sleep away;
It bids us from our pleasant dreams awake,
And sends us forth to keep or break
Our promises to pay.
How troublesome is day!
—Thomas Love Peacock.

O summer day beside the joyous sea!
O summer day so wonderful and white,
So full of gladness and so full of pain!
Forever and forever shalt thou be
To some the gravestone of a dead delight,
To some the landmark of a new domain.
—Longfellow.

Blest power of sunshine! genial day!
What balm, what life is in thy ray;
To feel thee is such real bliss,
That had the world no joy but this,
To sit in sunshine calm and sweet—
It were a world too exquisite,
For man to leave it for the gloom,
The deep cold shadow of the tomb.
—Moore.

Enjoy the blessings of this day if God sends them; and the evils bear patiently and sweetly. For this day only is ours; we are dead to yesterday, and we are not born to to-morrow.—Jeremy Taylor.

The days are made on a loom whereof the warp and woof are past and future time. They are majestically dressed, as if every god brought a thread to the skyey web.—Emerson.

Dead

Let the dead bury their dead.—Bible.

De mortuis nil nisi bonum.—Of the dead be nothing said but what is good.—Riley.

Death puts an end to rivalship and competition. The dead can boast no advantage over us, nor can we triumph over them.—Hazlitt.

He who hath bent him o'er the dead,
Ere the first day of death is fled—
The first dark day of nothingness,
The last of danger and distress,
(Before Decay's effacing fingers,
Have swept the lines where beauty lingers)—
And mark'd the mild angelic air,
The rapture of repose that's there.
             —Byron.

We hold reunions, not for the dead, for there is nothing in all the earth that you and I can do for the dead. They are past our help and past our praise. We can add to them no glory, we can give to them no immortality. They do not need us, but forever and forever more we need them.—Garfield.

Death

Death is the crown of life.—Young.

Not dead, but gone before.—Samuel Rogers.

Death is the gate of life.—Bailey.

Death is another life.—Bailey.

Death comes but once.—Beaumont and Fletcher.

Every moment of life is a step towards death.—Corneille.

Death is a mighty, universal truth.—Dickens.

God's finger touched him, and he slept.—Tennyson.

Passing through Nature to eternity.—Shakespeare.

Death is the quiet haven of us all.—Wordsworth.

God giveth quietness at last.—Whittier.

In the midst of life we are in death.—Burial Service.

Death levels all things.—Claudianus.

O death! thou gentle end of human sorrows.—Rowe.

The blind cave of eternal night.—Shakespeare.

Where all life dies death lives.—Milton.

There are remedies for all things but death.—Carlyle.

Death is Life's high meed.—Keats.

Death hath a thousand doors to let out life.—Massinger.

A man can die but once.—Shakespeare.

I want to meet my God awake.—Carlyle.

Death will have his day.—Shakespeare.

Tell me, my soul! can this be death?—Pope.

Death robs the rich and relieves the poor.—J. L. Basford.

I must sleep now.—Dying words of Byron.

Thou hast all seasons for thine own, O death!—Mrs. Hemans.

Cruel as death and hungry as the grave.—Thomson.

Death, thou art infinite; it is life is little.—Bailey.

What can they suffer that do not fear to die?—Plutarch.

This is the last of earth! I am content.—John Quincy Adams.

The breathing miracle into silence passed!—Gerald Massey.

Dear beauteous death, the jewel of the just.—Henry Vaughan.

Death is the greatest evil, because it cuts off hope.—Hazlitt.

Death ready stands to interpose his dart.—Milton.

Death loves a shining mark, a signal blow.—Young.

The young may die, but the old must!—Longfellow.

Heaven gives its favorites early death.—Byron.

Is it then so sad a thing to die?—Virgil.

Tired he sleeps, and life's poor play is o'er.—Pope.

Death lays his icy hand on kings.—Shirley.

The sense of death is most in apprehension.—Shakespeare.

Death is a release from and an end of all pains.—Seneca.

'Tis long since death had the majority.—Blair.

If some men died and others did not, death would indeed be a most mortifying evil.—Bruyère.

Death, as the psalmist saith, is certain to all; all shall die.—Shakespeare.

Just death, kind umpire of men's miseries.—Shakespeare.

Death is the last limit of all things.—Horace.

Good men but see death, the wicked taste it.—Ben Jonson.

Death is not an end. It is a new impulse.—Henry Ward Beecher.

Man makes a death, which nature never made.—Young.

It is infamy to die, and not be missed.—Carlos Wilcox.

The most happy ought to wish for death.—Seneca.

Though death be poor, it ends a mortal woe.—Shakespeare.

The relations of all living end in separation.—Mahabharata.

He that dies pays all debts.—Shakespeare.

The sleeping partner of life—a change of existence.—Paul Chatfield.

Men fear death as children fear to go in the dark.—Bacon.

To have to die is a distinction of which no man is proud.—Alexander Smith.

He that dies this year is quit for the next.—Shakespeare.

There are few die well that die in a battle.—Shakespeare.

Death's but a path that must be trod,
If man would ever pass to God.
         —Parnell.

Kings and mightiest potentates must die,
For that's the end of human misery.
         —Shakespeare.

Ah! surely nothing dies but something mourns.—Byron.

That which is so universal as death must be a benefit.—Schiller.

Is death the last sleep? No, it is the last final awakening.—Walter Scott.

Death gives us sleep, eternal youth, and immortality.—Richter.

I heard that God had called your mother home to heaven. It will seem more than ever like home to you now.—Babcock.

It is not I who die, when I die, but my sin and misery.—Gotthold.

I have often thought of death, and I find it the least of all evils.—Jeremy Taylor.

All my possessions for a moment of time.—Last words of Queen Elizabeth.

I regret not death. I am going to meet my friends in another world.—Ariosto.

No king nor nation one moment can retard the appointed hour.—Dryden.

The farthest from the fear are often nearest to the stroke of fate.—Young.

What is death, after all? We leave only mortals behind us.—Ninon de Lenclos.

The eyes of our souls only then begin to see when our bodily eyes are closing.—William Law.

That golden key that opes the palace of eternity.—Milton.

Death is the waiting-room where we robe ourselves for immortality.—Spurgeon.

One may live as a conquerer, a king, or a magistrate; but he must die as a man.—Daniel Webster.

Death, so called, is a thing that makes men weep,
And yet a third of life is pass'd in sleep.
—Byron.

How much of love lies buried in dusty graves!—F. A. Durivage.

The heart is the first part that quickens, and the last that dies.—John Ray.

Gone before
To that unknown and silent shore.
—Charles Lamb.

We are dying from our very birth, and our end hangs on our beginning.—Manilius.

Dead! God, how much there is in that little word!—Byron.

Faith builds a bridge across the gulf of death.—Young.

Death is a black camel, which kneels at the gates of all.—Abd-el-Kader.

Soon as man, expert from time, has found the key of life, it opes the gates of death.—Young.

He that cuts off twenty years of life
Cuts off so many years of fearing death.
—Horace.

The air is full of farewells to the dying,
And mournings for the dead.
—Longfellow.

Jesus does not want us to say, "dead," for, He said, "all live unto Him," though they seem dead to us.—Babcock.

Life is the jailer, death the angel sent to draw the unwilling bolts and set us free.—Lowell.

How wonderful is Death, Death and his brother Sleep!   —Shelley.

Pale death enters with impartial step the cottages of the poor and the palaces of the rich.—Horace.

Men drop so fast, ere life's mid stage we tread,
Few know so many friends alive, as dead.
—Young.

It were well to die if there be gods, and sad to live if there be none.—Marcus Antoninus.

How wonderful is Death, Death and his brother Sleep!—Shelley.

To' how many is the death of the beloved the parent of faith!—Bulwer-Lytton.

———

Death lies on her like an untimely frost Upon the sweetest flower of all the field.
—Shakespeare.

———

Men may live fools, but fools they cannot die.—Young.

———

Death is the ultimate boundary of human matters.—Horace.

———

We turn to dust, and all our mightiest works die too.—Cowper.

———

The ancients dreaded death: the Christian can only fear dying.—J. C. and A. W. Hare.

———

Yes, death—the hourly possibility of it—death is the sublimity of life.—Mountford.

———

The finest day of life is that on which one quits it.—Frederick the Great.

———

Death rides on every passing breeze, He lurks in every flower.
—Bishop Heber.

———

The first dark day of nothingness. The last of danger and distress.
—Byron.

———

There is no fireside, howsoe'er defended, but has one vacant chair!—Longfellow.

———

To fear death is the way to live long; to be afraid of death is to be long a dying.—Quarles.

———

There is nothing certain in man's life but this, that he must lose it.—Owen Meredith.

———

Knowledge by suffering endureth, And life is perfected by Death.
—Mrs. Browning.

———

Death in itself is nothing; but we fear To be we know not what, we know not where. —Dryden.

———

Death hath no advantage but where it comes a stranger.—Jeremy Taylor,

Death comes to us, under many conditions, with all the welcome serenity of sleep.—Hosea Ballou.

———

There is no death. The thing that we call death Is but another, sadder name for life.
—Stoddard.

———

No better armor against the darts of death than to be busied in God's service.—Thomas Fuller.

———

Can honor's voice provoke the silent dust, or flattery soothe the dull, cold ear of death?—Gray.

———

The hour conceal'd and so remote the fear, Death still draws nearer, never seeming near. —Pope.

———

We understand death for the first time when he puts his hand upon one whom we love.—Mme. de Staël.

———

The good die first; and they whose hearts are dry as summer dust burn to the socket.—Wordsworth.

———

For in that sleep of death what dreams may come. —Shakespeare.

———

When a few years are come, then I shall go the way whence I shall not return.—Bible.

———

He gave his honours to the world again, His blessed part to heaven, and slept in peace. —Shakespeare.

———

Before decay's effacing fingers have swept the lines where beauty lingers.—Byron.

———

The tall, the wise, the reverend head, Must lie as low as ours.
—Isaac Watts.

———

We thought her dying while she slept, and sleeping when she died.—Hood.

———

You who come my grave to view, A moment stop and think, That I am in eternity, And you are on the brink.—Epitaph.

———

You should not fear, nor yet should you wish for your last day.—Martial

But, oh! fell Death's untimely frost,
That nipt my flower sae early.
—Burns.

To our graves we walk
In the thick footprints of departed men.
—Alex. Smith.

It is only to those who have never
lived that death ever can seem beautiful.—Ouida.

My sole defense against the natural
horror which death inspires is to love
beyond it.—Mme. Swetchine.

Nor virtue, wit, or beauty, could
preserve from death's hand this their
heavenly mould.—Carew.

Death has made
His darkness beautiful with thee.
—Tennyson.

Of no distemper, of no blast he died
But fell like autumn fruit that mellow'd
long. —Dryden.

Death borders upon our birth; and
our cradle stands in our grave.—
Bishop Hall.

Good-bye, proud world; I'm going home:
Thou art not my friend, and I'm not thine.
—Emerson.

The shadow cloak'd from head to foot,
Who keeps the keys of all the creeds.
—Tennyson.

That last day does not bring extinction to us, but change of place.—
Cicero.

Death is a friend of ours; and he
that is not ready to entertain him is
not at home.—Bacon.

The uncertainty of death is, in effect,
the great support of the whole system
of life.—Johnson.

It is silliness to live when to live is
a torment; and then we have a prescription to die when death is our
physician.—Shakespeare.

It is the cause, and not the death,
that makes the martyr.—Napoleon I.

I looked, and behold a pale horse;
and his name that sat on him was
Death.—Bible.

Death but supplies the oil for the
inextinguishable lamp of life.—Coleridge.

Death is the ugly fact which Nature has to hide, and she hides it well.
—Alexander Smith.

There are countless roads on all
sides to the grave.—Cicero.

Early, bright, transient, chaste as morning
dew,
She sparkled, was exhal'd, and went to
heaven. —Young.

Death never happens but once, yet
we feel it every moment of our lives.—
La Bruyère.

If one was to think constantly of
death the business of life would stand
still.—Johnson.

Death comes equally to us all, and
makes us all equal when it comes.—
Donne.

Before mine eyes in opposition sits
Grim Death, my son and foe.
—Milton.

Death is appalling to those of the
most iron nerves, when it comes quietly
and in the stillness and solitude of
night.—James Fenimore Cooper.

Death * * * openeth the gate
to good fame, and extinguisheth envy.
—Bacon.

Those only can thoroughly feel the
meaning of death who know what is
perfect love.—George Eliot.

Death is the universal salt of states;
Blood is the base of all things—law and
war. —Bailey.

Death is easier to bear without
thinking of it, than the thought of
death without peril.—Pascal.

He only half dies who leaves an image of himself in his sons.—Goldoni.

The angel of Death has been abroad throughout the land; you may almost hear the beating of his wings.—John Bright.

Neither the sun nor death can be looked at steadily.—La Rochefoucauld.

There is a remedy for everything but death, who, in spite of our teeth, will take us in his clutches.—Cervantes.

Men have died from time to time, and worms have eaten them, but not for love.—Shakespeare.

This day which thou fearest so much, and which thou callest thy last, is the birthday of an eternity.—Seneca.

Is it courage in a dying man to go, in weakness and in agony, to affront an almighty and eternal God?—Pascal.

Going out into life—that is dying. Christ is the door out of life.—Henry Ward Beecher.

In the capacious urn of death, every name is shaken.—Horace.

He who fears death has already lost the life he covets.—Cato.

The time will come to every human being when it must be known how well he can bear to die.—Johnson.

Death is the dropping of the flower that the fruit may swell.—Beecher.

Death is dreadful to the man whose all is extinguished with his life; but not to him whose glory never can die. —Cicero.

Though in midst of life we be
Snares of death surround us.
—Martin Luther.

Life is the triumph of our mouldering clay; death, of the spirit infinite! divine!—Young.

To a father, when his child dies, the future dies; to a child, when his parents die, the past dies.—Auerbach.

Not where death hath power may love be blest.—Mrs. Hemans.

The gods conceal from men the happiness of death, that they may endure life.—Lucan.

That evil can never be great which is the last.—Cornelius Nepos.

A death-like sleep,
A gentle wafting to immortal life.
—Milton.

Here is my journey's end, here is my birth,
And very sea-mark of my utmost sail.
—Shakespeare.

There is no finite life except unto death; no death except unto higher life.—Bunsen.

A short death is the sovereign good hap of human life.—Pliny.

Death is an equal doom to good and bad, the common inn of rest.—Spenser.

Death? Translated into the heavenly tongue, that word means life!—Beecher.

It is uncertain at what place death awaits thee. Wait thou for it at every place.—Seneca.

The tongues of dying men enforce attention, like deep harmony.—Shakespeare.

Death and love are the two wings which bear man from earth to heaven. —Michael Angelo.

Death is as the foreshadowing of life. We die that we may die no more. —Hooker.

The last enemy that shall be destroyed is death.—Bible.

If Socrates died like a sage, Jesus died like a God.—Rousseau.

Believe that each day is the last to shine upon thee.—Horace.

The whole life of a philosopher is the meditation of his death.—Cicero.

If I must die, I will encounter darkness as a bride, and hug it in mine arms.—Shakespeare.

Death possesses a good deal of real estate, namely, the graveyard in every town.—Hawthorne.

Let no man fear to die, we love to sleep all,
And death is but the sounder sleep.
—Beaumont.

When beggars die, there are no comets seen;
The heavens themselves blaze forth the death of princes. —Shakespeare.

He that hath a will to die by himself,
Fears it not from another.
—Shakespeare.

The sands are number'd, that make up my life;
Here must I stay, and here my life must end. —Shakespeare.

That death is best which comes appropriately at a ripe age.—Propertius.

Death only this mysterious truth unfolds,
The mighty soul how small a body holds.
—Dryden.

Look forward a little further to the period when all the noise and tumult and business of this world shall have closed forever.—J. G. Pike.

When I lived, I provided for everything but death; now I must die, and am unprepared.—Cæsar Borgia.

The world recedes; it disappears!
Heaven opens on my eyes! —Pope.

And when obedient nature knows his will,
A fly, a grapestone, or a hair can kill.
—Prior.

An honorable death is better than a dishonorable life.—Tacitus.

Death has left on her,
Only the beautiful. —Hood.

He who does not fear death cares naught for threats.—Corneille.

What! is there no bribing death?—Dying words of Cardinal Beaufort.

The long sleep of death closes our scars, and the short sleep of life our wounds.—Jean Paul Richter.

The divinity who rules within us forbids us to leave this world without his command.—Cicero.

No evil is honorable: but death is honorable; therefore death is not evil.—Zeno.

There is no death! What seems so is transition.—Longfellow.

This I ask, is it not madness to kill thyself in order to escape death!—Martial.

On this side and on that, men see their friends
Drop off like leaves in autumn. —Blair.

Who knows that 'tis not life which we call death, and death our life on earth?—Euripides.

Nothing in his life
Became him like the leaving it.
—Shakespeare.

Thou fool, what is sleep but the image of death? Fate will give an eternal rest.—Ovid.

Men must endure their going hence,
Even as their coming hither.
—Shakespeare.

Death alone discloses how insignificant are the puny bodies of men.—Juvenal.

All our days travel toward death, and the last one reaches it.—Montaigne.

Who now travels that dark path to the bourne from which they say no one returns.—Catullus.

Teach him how to live,
And, oh! still harder lesson! how to die.
—Bishop Porteus.

To die at the command of another is to die twice.—Syrus.

Wherever I look there is nothing but the image of death.—Ovid.

Death is not grievous to me, for I shall lay aside my pains by death.—Ovid.

___

Sleep the sleep that knows not breaking, Morn of toil, nor night of waking.
—Scott.

___

Sometimes death is a punishment; often a gift; it has been a favor to many.—Seneca.

___

Beauty is fading, nor is fortune stable; sooner or later death comes to all.—Propertius.

___

When death gives us a long lease of life, it takes as hostages all those whom we have loved.—Mme. Necker.

___

The character wherewith we sink into the grave at death is the very character wherewith we shall reappear at the resurrection.—Thomas Chalmers.

___

Death is a silent, peaceful genius, who rocks our second childhood to sleep in the cradle of the coffin.—Chatfield.

___

Death, remembered, should be like a mirror, who tells us life is but a breath; to trust it, error.—Shakespeare.

___

Death shuns the naked throat and proffered breast; he flies when called to be a welcome guest.—Sir Charles Sedley.

___

Death is a stage in human progress, to be passed as we would pass from childhood to youth, or from youth to manhood, and with the same consciousness of an everlasting nature.—Sears.

___

And when no longer we can see Thee, may we reach out our hands, and find Thee leading us through death to immortality and glory.—H. W. Beecher.

___

The knell, the shroud, the mattock, and the grave, the deep, damp vault, the darkness and the worm.—Young.

Whatever crazy sorrow saith, no life that breathes with human breath has ever truly longed for death.—Tennyson.

___

Like other tyrants, death delights to smite what, smitten, most proclaims the pride of power and arbitrary nod.—Young.

___

Nothing can we call our own but death, and that small model of the barren earth which serves as paste and cover to our bones.—Shakespeare.

___

Death, of all estimated evils, is the only one whose presence never incommoded anybody, and which only causes concern during its absence.—Arcesilaus.

___

Setting is preliminary to brighter rising; decay is a process of advancement; death is the condition of higher and more fruitful life.—Chapin.

___

We sometimes congratulate ourselves at the moment of waking from a troubled dream—it may be so the moment after death.—Hawthorne.

___

Death is the only monastery; the tomb is the only cell, and the grave that adjoins the convent is the bitterest mock of its futility.—Bulwer-Lytton.

___

To the Christian, these shades are the golden haze which heaven's light makes, when it meets the earth, and mingles with its shadows.—H. W. Beecher.

___

Remember to think of your departed mother always as living, just away in another room of our Father's house.—Babcock.

___

Whatever stress some may lay upon it, a death-bed repentance is but a weak and slender plank to trust our all on.—Sterne.

___

Death is like thunder in two particulars; we are alarmed at the sound of it; and it is formidable only from that which preceded it.—C. C. Colton.

He that always waits upon God is ready whenever He calls. Neglect not to set your accounts even; he is a happy man who so lives as that death at all times may find him at leisure to die.—Owen Feltham.

Dead is she? No; rather let us call ourselves dead, who tire so soon in the service of the Master whom she has gone to serve forever.—W. S. Smart.

Death, which hateth and destroyeth a man, is believed; God, which hath made him and loves him, is always deferred.—Sir Walter Raleigh.

It seems to be remarkable that death increases our veneration for the good, and extenuates our hatred for the bad.—Johnson.

Death is not an end, but a transition crisis. All the forms of decay are but masks of regeneration—the secret alembics of vitality.—Chapin.

To close the eyes, and give a seemly comfort to the apparel of the dead, is poverty's holiest touch of nature.—Dickens.

The reconciling grave swallows distinction first, that made us foes, that all alike lie down in peace together.—Shakespeare.

It seems as though, at the approach of a certain dark hour, the light of heaven infills those who are leaving the light of earth.—Victor Hugo.

The darkness of death is like the evening twilight; it makes all objects appear more lovely to the dying.—Richter.

Birth into this life was the death of the embryo life that preceded, and the death of this will be birth into some new mode of being.—Rev. Dr. Hedge.

Earth has one angel less, and heaven one more since yesterday. Already, kneeling at the throne, she has received her welcome, and is resting on the bosom of her Saviour.—Hawthorne.

To neglect at any time preparation for death is to sleep on our post at a siege; to omit it in old age is to sleep at an attack.—Johnson.

In the destroyer's steps there spring up bright creations that defy his power and his dark path becomes a way of light to heaven.—Dickens.

We bury love; forgetfulness grows over it like grass; that is a thing to weep for, not the dead.—Alexander Smith.

'Tis the cessation of our breath.
Silent and motionless we lie;
And no one knoweth more than this.
—Longfellow.

If life be a pleasure, yet, since death also is sent by the hand of the same Master, neither should that displease us.—Michael Angelo.

Of all the evils of the world which are reproached with an evil character, death is the most innocent of its accusation.—Jeremy Taylor.

Approach thy grave like one that wraps the drapery of his couch about him, and lies down to pleasant dreams.—Bryant.

Death came with friendly care, the opening bud to heaven conveyed, and bade it blossom there.—Coleridge.

The premeditation of death is the premeditation of liberty; he who has learnt to die has forgot to serve.—Montaigne.

I look upon death to be as necessary to our constitution as sleep. We shall rise refreshed in the morning.—Franklin.

Death is not the monarch of the dead, but of the dying. The moment he obtains a conquest, he loses a subject.—Thomas Paine.

Let us live like those who expect to die, and then we shall find that we feared death only because we were unacquainted with it.—William Wake.

'Tis the only discipline we are born for; all studies else are but as circular lines, and death the center where they all must meet.—Massinger.

The night comes on that knows not morn,
When I shall cease to be all alone,
To live forgotten, and love forlorn.
—Tennyson.

Death is not rare, alas! nor burials few,
And soon the grassy coverlet of God
Spreads equal green above their ashes pale.
—Bayard Taylor.

Death is delightful. Death is dawn—
The waking from a weary night
Of fevers unto truth and light.
—Joaquin Miller.

All that tread
The globe are but a handful to the tribes
That slumber in its bosom. —Bryant.

Then Sleep and Death, two twins of winged race,
Of matchless swiftness, but of silent pace.
—Homer.

Like a led victim, to my death I'll go,
And, dying, bless the hand that gave the blow. —Dryden.

Men in general do not live as if they looked to die; and therefore do not die as if they looked to live.—Manton.

By medicine life may be prolong'd, yet death
Will seize the doctor too. —Shakespeare.

Death is a commingling of eternity with time; in the death of a good man, eternity is seen looking through time.—Goethe.

Death is the liberator of him whom freedom cannot release, the physician of him whom medicine cannot cure, and the comforter of him whom time cannot console.—Colton.

It is as natural to die as to be born; and to a little infant, perhaps, the one is as painful as the other.—Bacon.

It is by no means a fact that death is the worst of all evils; when it comes it is an alleviation to mortals who are worn out with sufferings.—Metastasio.

Death is the only physician, the shadow of his valley the only journeying that will cure us of age and the gathering fatigue of years.—George Eliot.

The happiest of pillows is not that which love first presses! it is that which death has frowned on and passed over.—Landor.

A few feet under the ground reigns so profound a silence, and yet so much tumult on the surface!—Victor Hugo.

Oh, God! it is a fearful thing
To see the human soul take wing
In any shape, in any mood!
—Byron.

Death rides in triumph,—fell destruction
Lashes his fiery horse, and round about him
His many thousand ways to let out souls.
—Beaumont and Fletcher.

To die, I own, is a dread passage—terrible to nature, chiefly to those who have, like me, been happy.—Thomson.

How short is human life; the very breath,
Which frames my words, accelerates my death. —Hannah More.

Death itself is less painful when it comes upon us unawares than the bare contemplation of it, even when danger is far distant.—Pascal.

Suns may set and rise; we, when our short day is closed, must sleep on during one never-ending night.—Catullus.

To die is landing on some silent shore,
Where billows never break nor tempests roar;
Ere well we feel the friendly stroke 'tis o'er. —Sir Samuel Garth.

O mighty Cæsar! dost thou lie so low? Are all thy conquests, glories, triumphs, spoils, shrunk to this little measure?—Shakespeare.

If thou expect death as a friend, prepare to entertain it; if thou expect death as an enemy, prepare to overcome it; death has no advantage, but when it comes a stranger.—Quarles,

Man should ever look to his last day, and no one should be called happy before his funeral.—Ovid.

Lay her i' the earth;
And from her fair and unpolluted flesh
May violets spring!   —Shakespeare.

A man after death is not a natural but a spiritual man; nevertheless he still appears in all respects like himself.—Swedenborg.

Death upon his face
Is rather shine than shade,
A tender shine by looks beloved made.
—Mrs. Browning.

I fled, and cried out Death!
Hell trembled at the hideous name, and sigh'd
From all her caves, and back resounded Death.   —Milton.

Death to the Christian is the funeral of all his sorrows and evils, and the resurrection of all his joys.—Aughey.

He whom the gods love dies young, while he is in health, has his senses and his judgment sound.—Plautus.

When at last the angels come to convey your departing spirit to Abraham's bosom, depend upon it, however dazzling in their newness they may be to you, you will find that your history is no novelty, and you yourself no stranger to them.—James Hamilton.

So we fall asleep in Jesus. We have played long enough at the games of life, and at last we feel the approach of death. We are tired out, and we lay our heads back on the bosom of Christ, and quietly fall asleep.—H. W. Beecher.

Reflect on death as in Jesus Christ, not as without Jesus Christ. Without Jesus Christ it is dreadful, it is alarming, it is the terror of nature. In Jesus Christ it is fair and lovely, it is good and holy, it is the joy of saints. —Pascal.

The most heaven-like spots I have ever visited have been certain rooms in which Christ's disciples were await-ing the summons of death. So far from being a "house of mourning," I have often found such a house to be a vestibule of glory.—T. L. Cuyler.

How well he fell asleep!
Like some proud river, widening toward the sea;
Calmly and grandly, silently and deep,
Life joined eternity.—S. T. Coleridge.

When darkness gathers over all,
And the last tottering pillars fall,
Take the poor dust Thy mercy warms,
And mould it into heavenly forms.
—O. W. Holmes.

Death cannot come
To him untimely who is fit to die;
The less of this cold world, the more of heaven;
The briefer life, the earlier immortality.
—Millman.

Drawing near her death, she sent most pious thoughts as harbingers to heaven; and her soul saw a glimpse of happiness through the chinks of her sickness-broken body.—Thomas Fuller.

It is impossible that anything so natural, so necessary, and so universal as death should ever have been designed by Providence as an evil to mankind.—Swift.

Certainly the contemplation of death, as the wages of sin, and passage to another world, is holy and religious; but the fear of it, as a tribute due unto Nature, is weak.—Bacon.

He that would die well must always look for death, every day knocking at the gates of the grave; and then the grave shall never prevail against him to do him mischief.—Jeremy Taylor.

Death is so genuine a fact that it excludes falsehoods, or betrays its emptiness; it is a touchstone that proves the gold, and dishonors the baser metal.—Hawthorne.

Seek such union to the Son of God as, leaving no present death within, shall make the second death impossible, and shall leave in all your future only that shadow of death which men call dissolution, and which the gospel calls sleeping in Jesus.—James Hamilton.

All was ended now, the hope and the fear and the sorrow, all the aching of heart, the restless, unsatisfied longing, all the dull, deep pain, and constant anguish of patience.—Longfellow.

When the dust of death has choked a great man's voice, the common words he said turn oracles, the common thoughts he yoked like horses draw like griffins.—Mrs. Browning.

The weariest and most loathed worldly life that age, ache, penury, and imprisonment can lay on nature is a paradise to what we fear of death.— Shakespeare.

Soon for me the light of day
Shall forever pass away;
Then from sin and sorrow free,
Take me, Lord, to dwell with Thee.
                —Doane.

Love masters agony; the soul that seemed
Forsaken feels her present God again
   And in her Father's arms
   Contented dies away.
              —John Keble.

Many persons sigh for death when it seems far off, but the inclination vanishes when the boat upsets, or the locomotive runs off the track, or the measles set it.—T. W. Higginson.

We die every day; every moment deprives us of a portion of life and advances us a step toward the grave; our whole life is only a long and painful sickness.—Massillon.

The fear of approaching death, which in youth we imagine must cause inquietude to the aged, is very seldom the source of much uneasiness.—Hazlitt.

O Death, what are thou? nurse of dreamless slumbers freshening the fevered flesh to a wakefulness eternal. —Tupper.

Everything dies, and on this spring morning, if I lay my ear to the ground, I seem to hear from every point of the

compass the heavy step of men who carry a corpse to its burial.—Madame de Gasparin.

Death makes a beautiful appeal to charity. When we look upon the dead form, so composed and still, the kindness and the love that are in us all come forth.—Chapin.

There is nothing of evil in life for him who rightly comprehends that death is no evil; to know how to die delivers us from all subjection and constraint.—Montaigne.

Death is as near to the young as to the old; here is all the difference: death stands behind the young man's back, before the old man's face.—Rev. T. Adams.

Cullen whispered in his last moments: "I wish I had the power of writing or speaking, for then I would describe to you how pleasant a thing it is to die."—Dr. Derby.

Death to a good man is but passing through a dark entry, out of one little dusky room of his Father's house into another that is fair and large, lightsome and glorious, and divinely entertaining.—Adam Clarke.

All life is surrounded by a great circumference of death; but to the believer in Jesus, beyond this surrounding death is a boundless sphere of life. He has only to die once to be done with death forever.—James Hamilton.

How beautiful it is for a man to die on the walls of Zion! to be called like a watch-worn and weary sentinel, to put his armor off, and rest in heaven. —N. P. Willis.

Death opens the gate of fame, and shuts the gate of envy after it; it unlooses the chain of the captive, and puts the bondsman's task into another man's hand.—Sterne.

When a man dies they who survive him ask what property he has left behind. The angel who bends over the dying man asks what good deeds he has sent before him.—Koran.

Life's race well run,
Life's work well done,
Life's crown well won,
Now comes rest.
—President Garfield's Epitaph.

The churchyard is the market-place where all things are rated at their true value, and those who are approaching it talk of the world and its vanities with a wisdom unknown before.—Baxter.

There are such things as a man shall remember with joy upon his death-bed; such as shall cheer and warm his heart even in that last and bitter agony.—South.

If human love hath power to penetrate the veil—and hath it not?—then there are yet living here a few who have the blessedness of knowing that an angel loves them.—Hawthorne.

We look at death through the cheap-glazed windows of the flesh, and believe him the monster which the flawed and cracked glass represents him.—Lowell.

I have heard that death takes us away from ill things, not from good. I have heard that when we pronounce the name of man we pronounce the belief of immortality.—Emerson.

To die,—to sleep,—
No more;—and by a sleep to say we end
The heart-ache, and the thousand natural shocks
That flesh is heir to. —Shakespeare.

And there at Venice gave
His body to that pleasant country's earth,
And his pure soul unto his captain Christ,
Under whose colours he had fought so long.
—Shakespeare.

How oft, when men are at the point of death,
Have they been merry! which their keepers call
A lightning before death. —Shakespeare.

Nature intends that, at fixed periods, men should succeed each other by the instrumentality of death. We shall never outwit Nature; we shall die as usual.—Fontenelle.

The world recedes; it disappears!
Heav'n opens on my eyes! my ears
With sounds seraphic ring:
Lend, lend your wings! I mount! I fly!
—Pope.

The prince, who kept the world in awe,
The judge, whose dictate fix'd the law,
The rich, the poor, the great, the small,
Are levell'd; death confounds 'em all.
—Gay.

The world will turn when we are earth
As though we had not come nor gone;
There was no lack before our birth,
When we are gone there will be none.
—Omar Khayyam.

Strange—is it not?—that of the myriads who
Before us passed the door of Darkness through,
Not one returns to tell us of the road
Which to discover we must travel too.
—Omar Khayyam.

For thee, O now a silent soul, my brother,
Take at my hands this garland and farewell.
Thin is the leaf, and chill the wintry smell,
And chill the solemn earth, a fatal mother.
—Swinburne.

Death! to the happy thou art terrible;
But how the wretched love to think of thee,
O thou true comforter! the friend of all
Who have no friend beside!
—Southey.

There is no Death! What seems so is transition;
This life of mortal breath
Is but a suburb of the life elysian,
Whose portal we call death.
—Longfellow.

Death is the port where all may refuge find,
The end of labor, entry into rest;
Death hath the bounds of misery confin'd
Whose sanctuary shrouds affliction best.
—Earl of Stirling.

O death! the poor man's dearest friend,
The kindest and the best!
Welcome the hour, my aged limbs
Are laid with thee at rest! —Burns.

What is certain in death is somewhat softened by what is uncertain; it is an indefiniteness in the time.

which holds a certain relation to the infinite, and what is called eternity.—La Bruyère.

And thou art terrible—the tear,
The groan, the knell, the pall, the bier;
And all we know, or dream, or fear
Of agony, are thine.   —Halleck.

When we see our enemies and friends gliding away before us, let us not forget that we are subject to the general law of mortality, and shall soon be where our doom will be fixed forever.—Dr. Johnson.

As man, perhaps, the moment of his breath,
Receives the lurking principle of death;
The young disease, that must subdue at length,
Grows with his growth, and strengthens with his strength.   —Pope.

His last day places man in the same state as he was before he was born; nor after death has the body or soul any more feeling than they had before birth.—Pliny the Elder.

She thought our good-night kiss was given,
And like a lily her life did close;
Angels uncurtain'd that repose,
And the next waking dawn'd in heaven.
—Gerald Massey.

Then with no fiery throbbing pain,
No cold gradations of decay,
Death broke at once the vital chain,
And freed his soul the nearest way.
—Samuel Johnson.

The soul too soft its ills to bear,
Has left our mortal hemisphere,
And sought in better world the meed
To blameless life by heaven decreed.
—Scott.

But whether on the scaffold high,
Or in the battle's van,
The fittest place where man can die
Is where he dies for man.
—Michael J. Barry.

Dust, to its narrow house beneath!
Soul, to its place on high!
They that have seen thy look in death,
No more may fear to die.
—Mrs. Hemans.

As the films of clay are removed from our eyes, Death loses the false aspect of the spectre, and we fall at last into its arms as a wearied child upon the bosom of its mother.—Bulwer.

But since, howe'er protracted, death will come,
Why fondly study, with ingenious pains,
To put it off?—To breathe a little longer
Is to defer our fate, but not to shun it.
—Hannah More.

First our pleasures die—and then
Our hopes, and then our fears—and when
These are dead, the debt is due,
Dust claims dust—and we die too.
—Shelley.

There is a Reaper whose name is Death,
And with his sickle keen,
He reaps the bearded grain at a breath,
And the flowers that grow between.
—Longfellow.

What day, what hour, but knocks at human hearts,
To wake the soul to sense of future scenes?
Deaths stand like Mercurys, in every way,
And kindly point us to our journey's end.
—Dr. Young.

Death is the king of this world: 'tis his park
Where he breeds life to feed him. Cries of pain
Are music for his banquet.
—George Eliot.

And, as she looked around, she saw how Death, the consoler,
Laying his hand upon many a heart, had healed it forever.   —Longfellow.

Death comes to all. His cold and sapless hand
Waves o'er the world, and beckons us away.
Who shall resist the summons?
—Thomas Love Peacock.

How shocking must thy summons be, O death!
To him that is at ease in his possessions;
Who, counting on long years of pleasure here,
Is quite unfurnish'd for that world to come!
—Blair.

Two hands upon the breast,
And labor's done;
Two pale feet cross'd in rest,
The race is won. —D. M. Mulock.

The truth of it is, there is nothing in history which is so improving to the reader as those accounts which we meet with of the death of eminent persons and of their behavior in that dreadful season.—Addison.

But the grave is not deep; it is the shining tread of an angel that seeks us. When the unknown hand throws the fatal dart at the end of man, then boweth he his head and the dart only lifts the crown of thorns from his wounds.—Richter.

Brethren, we are all sailing home; and by and by, when we are not thinking of it, some shadowy thing (men call it death), at midnight, will pass by, and will call us by name, and will say, "I have a message for you from home; God wants you; heaven waits for you."—H. W. Beecher.

Death is the wish of some, the relief of many, and the end of all. It sets the slave at liberty, carries the banished man home, and places all mortals on the same level, insomuch that life itself were a punishment without it.—Seneca.

He that always waits upon God is ready whensoever He calls. Neglect not to set your accounts even; he is a happy man who so lives as that death at all times may find him at leisure to die.—Feltham.

When you take the wires of the cage apart, you do not hurt the bird, but help it. You let it out of its prison. How do you know that death does not help me when it takes the wires of my cage down?—that it does not release me, and put me into some better place, and better condition of life?—Bishop Randolph S. Foster.

Death is a mighty mediator. There all the flames of rage are extinguished, hatred is appeased, and angelic pity, like a weeping sister, bends with gentle and close embrace over the funeral urn.—Schiller.

"Come and see how a Christian can die," said the dying sage to his pupil: how would it do to say, "Come and see how an infidel can die?"—How would it have done for Voltaire to say

this, who, in his panic at the prospect of eternity, offered his physician half his fortune for six weeks more of life?—James Hamilton.

Against specious appearances we must set clear convictions, bright and ready for use. When death appears as an evil, we ought immediately to remember that evils are things to be avoided, but death is inevitable.—Epictetus.

O, if the deeds of human creatures could be traced to their source, how beautiful would even death appear; for how much charity, mercy, and purified affection would be seen to have their growth in dusty graves!—Dickens.

What is our death but a night's sleep? For as through sleep all weariness and faintness pass away and cease, and the powers of the spirit come back again, so that in the morning we arise fresh and strong and joyous; so at the Last Day we shall rise again as if we had only slept a night, and shall be fresh and strong.—Martin Luther.

If life has not made you by God's grace, through faith, holy—think you, will death without faith do it? The cold waters of that narrow stream are no purifying bath in which you may wash and be clean. No! no! as you go down into them, you will come up from them.—Alexander Maclaren.

Let death and exile, and all other things which appear terrible, be daily before your eyes, but death chiefly; and you will never entertain any abject thought, nor too eagerly covet anything.—Epictetus.

Feasts and business and pleasure and enjoyments seem great things to us, whilst we think of nothing else; but as soon as we add death to them they all sink into an equal littleness.—William Law.

At the last, when we die, we have the dear angels for our escort on the way. They who can grasp the whole world in their hands can surely also guard our souls, that they make that last journey safely.—Luther.

There is a sweet anguish springing up in our bosoms when a child's face brightens under the shadow of the waiting angel. There is an autumnal fitness when age gives up the ghost; and when the saint dies there is a tearful victory.—Chapin.

If I were a writer of books, I would compile a register, with the comment of the various deaths of men; and it could not but be useful, for who should teach men to die would at the same time teach them to live.—Montaigne.

Death alone of the gods loves not gifts, nor do you need to offer incense or libations; he cares not for altar nor hymn; the goddess of Persuasion alone of the gods has no power over him.—Horace.

Can we wonder that men perish and are forgotten, when their noblest and most enduring works decay? Death comes even to monumental structures, and oblivion rests on the most illustrious names.—Marcus Antoninus.

The bed of death brings every human being to his pure individuality; to the intense contemplation of that deepest and most solemn of all relations, the relation between the creature and his Creator.—Daniel Webster.

We so converse every night with the image of death that every morning we find an argument of the resurrection. Sleep and death have but one mother, and they have one name in common.—Jeremy Taylor.

Nature has lent us life, as we do a sum of money; only no certain day is fixed for payment. What reason then to complain if she demands it at pleasure, since it was on this condition that we received it?—Cicero.

I scarcely know how it is, but the deaths of children seem to me always less premature than those of older persons. Not that they are in fact so, but it is because they themselves have little or no relation to time or maturity.—Barry Cornwall.

To mourn deeply for the death of another loosens from myself the petty desire for, and the animal adherence to life. We have gained the end of the philosopher, and view without shrinking the coffin and the pall.—Bulwer-Lytton.

Who knows we have not lived before
 In forms that felt delight and pain?
If death is not the open door
 Through which we pass to life again?
 —David Banks Sickels.

Few people know death, we only endure it, usually from determination, and even from stupidity and custom; and most men only die because they know not how to prevent dying.—La Rochefoucauld.

The boast of heraldry, the pomp of power,
And all that beauty, all that wealth e'er
 gave,
Await alike the inevitable hour,
The paths of glory lead but to the grave.
 —Gray.

Thy day without a cloud hath pass'd,
 And thou wert lovely to the last;
 Extinguish'd not decay'd!
As stars that shoot along the sky
Shine brightest as they fall from high.
 —Byron.

 Can that man be dead
Whose spiritual influence is upon his kind?
He lives in glory; and his speaking dust
Has more of life than half its breathing
 moulds. —Miss Landon.

Let us not doubt that God has a father's pity towards us, and that in the removal of that which is dearest to us He is still loving and kind. Death separates, but it also unites. It reunites whom it separates.—Abraham Coles.

Philosophy has often attempted to repress insolence by asserting that all conditions are leveled by death; a position which, however it may deject the happy, will seldom afford much comfort to the wretched.—Dr. Johnson.

What is death but a ceasing to be what we were before? We are kindled, and put out, we die daily; nature that begot us expels us, and a better and safer place is provided for us.—Seneca.

Where the brass knocker, wrapt in flannel band,
Forbids the thunder of the footman's hand,
Th' upholder, rueful harbinger of death,
Waits with impatience for the dying breath.
—Gay.

One destin'd period men in common have,
The great, the base, the coward, and the brave,
All food alike for worms, companions in the grave.
—Lord Lansdowne.

Then fell upon the house a sudden gloom,
A shadow on those features fair and thin;
And softly, from that hushed and darkened room,
Two angels issued, where but one went in.
—Longfellow.

The hand that unnerved Belshazzar derived its most horrifying influence from the want of a body, and death itself is not formidable in what we do know of it, but in what we do not. —Colton.

Eyes, look your last!
Arms, take your last embrace! and lips O you
The doors of breath, seal with a righteous kiss
A dateless bargain to engrossing death.
—Shakespeare.

Death wounds to cure: we fall; we rise; we reign!
Spring from our fetters; fasten in the skies;
Where blooming Eden withers in our sight:
Death gives us more than was in Eden lost.
This king of terrors is the prince of peace.
—Young.

Every man at time of Death,
Would fain set forth some saying that may live
After his death and better humankind;
For death gives life's last word a power to live,
And, like the stone-cut epitaph, remain
After the vanished voice, and speak to men.
—Tennyson.

I am not in the least surprised that your impression of death becomes more lively, in proportion as age and infirmity bring it nearer. God makes use of this rough trial to undeceive us in re-spect to our courage, to make us feel our weakness, and to keep us in all humility in His hands.—Fénelon.

The moment in which the spirit meets death is perhaps like the moment in which it is embraced in sleep. I suppose it never happened to any one to be conscious of the immediate transition from the waking to the sleeping state.—Mrs. Jameson.

The world is full of resurrections. Every night that folds us up in darkness is a death; and those of you that have been out early, and have seen the first of the dawn, will know it—the day rises out of the night like a being that has burst its tomb and escaped into life.—George MacDonald.

When the veil of death has been drawn between us and the objects of our regard, how quick-sighted do we become to their merits, and how bitterly do we remember words, or even looks, of unkindness which may have escaped in our intercourse with them.—Bishop Heber.

No man but knows that he must die; he knows that in whatever quarter of the world he abides—whatever be his circumstances—however strong his present hold of life—however unlike the prey of death he looks—that it is his doom beyond reverse to die.—Stebbing.

Cowards die many times before their deaths;
The valiant never taste of death but once.
Of all the wonders that I yet have heard,
It seems to me most strange that men should fear;
Seeing that death, a necessary end,
Will come, when it will come.
—Shakespeare.

The world recedes; it disappears;
Heav'n opens on my eyes; my ears
With sounds seraphic ring:
Lend, lend your wings! I mount! I fly!
O Grave! where is thy victory?
O Death! where is thy sting? —Pope.

All that nature has prescribed must be good; and as death is natural to us, it is absurdity to fear it. Fear loses its purpose when we are sure it cannot preserve us, and we should draw resolution to meet it from the impossibility to escape it.—Steele.

O Earth, so full of dreary noises!
O men, with wailing in your voices!
O delved gold, the wailer's heap!
O strife, O curse, that o'er it fall!
God makes a silence through you all,
And "giveth His beloved, sleep."
—Mrs. Browning.

Yet 'twill only be a sleep:
When, with songs and dewy light,
Morning blossoms out of Night,
She will open her blue eyes
'Neath the palms of Paradise,
While we foolish ones shall weep.
—Edward Rowland Sill.

Sure 'tis a serious thing to die! My soul!
What a strange moment must it be, when, near
Thy journey's end, thou hast the gulf in view!
That awful gulf, no mortal e'er repass'd
To tell what's doing on the other side.
—Blair.

Death never takes one alone, but two!
Whenever he enters in at a door,
Under roof of gold or roof of thatch,
He always leaves it upon the latch,
And comes again ere the year is o'er,
Never one of a household only.
—Longfellow.

It is hard
To feel the hand of death arrest one's steps,
Throw a chill blight o'er all one's budding hopes,
And hurl one's soul untimely to the shades
Lost in the gaping gulf of blank oblivion.
—Kirk White.

A true philosopher
Makes death his common practice, while he lives,
And every day by contemplation strives
To separate the soul, far as he can,
From off the body. —May.

All at rest now—all dust!—wave flows on wave,
But the sea dries not! What to us the grave?
It brings no real homily; we sigh,
Pause for a while, and murmur, "All must die!"
Then rush to pleasure, action, sin, once more,
Swell the loud tide, and fret unto the shore! —The New Timon.

And now, with busy, but noiseless process, the Comforter is giving the last finish to the sanctifying work, and making the heir of glory meet for home, till, at a given signal, the portal opens, and even the numb body feels the burst of blessedness as the rigid features smile and say, "I see Jesus," then leave the vision pictured on the pale but placid brow.—James Hamilton.

Death is the tyrant of the imagination. His reign is in solitude and darkness, in tombs and prisons, over weak hearts and seething brains. He lives, without shape or sound, a phantasm, inaccessible to sight or touch— a ghastly and terrible apprehension.— Barry Cornwall.

The birds of the air die to sustain thee; the beasts of the field die to nourish thee; the fishes of the sea die to feed thee. Our stomachs are their common sepulchre. Good God! with how many deaths are our poor lives patched up! how full of death is the life of momentary man!—Quarles.

There is before the eyes of men, on the brink of dissolution, a glassy film, which death appears to impart, that they may have a brief prospect of eternity when some behold the angels of light, while others have the demons of darkness before them.—Cockton.

Oh that we may all be living in such a state of preparedness, that, when summoned to depart, we may ascend the summit whence faith looks forth on all that Jesus hath suffered and done, and exclaiming, "We have waited for Thy salvation, O Lord," lie down with Moses on Pisgah, to awake with Moses in paradise.—Henry Melvill.

Death brings us again to our friends. They are waiting for us, and we shall not be long. They have gone before us, and are like the angels in heaven. They stand upon the borders of the grave to welcome us with the countenance of affection which they wore on earth,—yet more lovely, more radiant, more spiritual.—Longfellow.

"Paid the debt of nature." No; it is not paying a debt; it is rather like bringing a note to the bank to obtain solid gold for it. In this case you bring this cumbrous body which is nothing worth, and which you could not wish to retain long; you lay it down, and receive for it from the eternal treasures—liberty, victory, knowledge, rapture.—Foster.

For the fear of death is indeed the pretence of wisdom, and not real wisdom, being a pretended knowledge of the unknown; and no one knows whether death, which men in their fear apprehend to be the greatest evil, may not be the greatest good. Is there not here conceit of knowledge, which is a disgraceful sort of ignorance?—Plato.

The death-bed of the just is yet undrawn
By mortal hand—it merits a divine.
Angels should paint it—angels ever there—
There on a post of honour and of joy.
A death-bed's a detector of the heart;—
Here tired dissimulation drops her mask:
Virtue alone has majesty in death.
                              —Young.

I live,
But live to die: and living, see no thing
To make death hateful, save an innate clinging,
A loathsome and yet all invincible
Instinct of life, which I abhor, as I
Despise myself, yet cannot overcome—
And so I live.   —Byron.

All buildings are but monuments of death,
All clothes but winding-sheets for our last knell,
All dainty fattings for the worms beneath,
All curious music but our passing bell:
Thus death is nobly waited on, for why?
All that we have is but death's livery.
                              —Shirley.

For I know that Death is a guest divine,
Who shall drink my blood as I drink this wine;
And he cares for nothing! a king is he—
Come on, old fellow, and drink with me!
With you I will drink to the solemn past,
Though the cup that I drain should be my last.   —-William Winter.

Death is but a word to us. One's own experience alone can teach us the real meaning of the word. The sight of the dying does little. What one sees of them is merely what precedes death: dull unconsciousness is all we see. Whether this be so,—how and when the spirit wakes to life again,—this is what all wish to know, and what never can be known until it is experienced.—Wilhelm von Humboldt.

Divinely fair as thine, O never more
Would strong hearts break o'er biers. There sleeps to-night
A sacred sweetness on thy silent lips,
A solemn light upon thy ample brow,
That I can never, never hope to find
Upon a living face.   —Smith.

'Tis not the stoic's lesson got by rote,
The pomp of words, and pedant dissertation,
That can support thee in that hour of terror.
Books have taught cowards to talk nobly of it;
But when the trial comes, they start and stand aghast.   —Rowe.

None who e'er knew her can believe her dead;
Though, should she die, they deem it well might be
Her spirit took its everlasting flight
In summer's glory, by the sunset sea,
That onward through the Golden Gate is fled.
Ah, where that bright soul is cannot be night.   —R. W. Gilder.

So his life has flow'd
From its mysterious urn a sacred stream,
In whose calm depth the beautiful and pure
Alone are mirror'd, which though shapes of ill
May hover round its surface glides in light,
And takes no shadow from them.
                              —Talfourd.

It is very singular, how the fact of a man's death often seems to give people a truer idea of his character, whether for good or evil, than they have ever possessed while he was living and acting among them. Death is so genuine a fact that it excludes falsehood or betray its emptiness; it is a touch-stone that proves the gold, and dishonors the baser metal.—Hawthorne.

O eloquent, just and mightie Death! whom none could advise, thou hast perswaded; what none hath dared, thou hast done; and whom all the world hath flattered, thou only hast cast out of the world and despised: thou hast drawne together all the farre stretchéd greatnesse, all the pride, crueltie and ambition of men, and covered it all over with these two narrow words, *Hic jacet!*—Sir Walter Raleigh.

It unfortunately happens that no man believes that he is likely to die soon. So every one is much disposed to defer the consideration of what ought to be done on the supposition of such an emergency; and while nothing is so uncertain as human life, so nothing is so certain as our assurance that we shall survive most of our neighbors. —Aughey.

I have seen those who have arrived at a fearless contemplation of the future, from faith in the doctrine which our religion teaches. Such men were not only calm and supported, but cheerful in the hour of death; and I never quitted such a sick chamber without a hope that my last end might be like theirs.—Sir Henry Halford.

Then 'tis our best, since thus ordain'd to die,
To make a virtue of necessity.
Take what he gives, since to rebel is vain,
The bad grows better which we well sustain,
And could we choose the time and choose aright,
'Tis best to die, our honor at the height.
—Dryden.

Living is death; dying is life. We are not what we appear to be. On this side of the grave we are exiles, on that citizens; on this side orphans, on that children; on this side captives, on that freemen;. on this side disguised, unknown, on that disclosed and proclaimed as the sons of God.—Beecher.

Dying visions of angels and Christ and God and heaven are confined to credibly good men. Why do not bad men have such visions? They die of all sorts of diseases; they have nervous temperaments; they even have creeds and hopes about the future which they cling to with very great tenacity; why do not they rejoice in some such glorious illusions when they go out of the world?—E. F. Burr.

Death, whether it regards ourselves or others, appears less terrible in war than at home. The cries of women and children, friends in anguish, a dark room, dim tapers, priests and physicians, are what affect us the most on the death-bed. Behold us already more than half dead and buried. —Henry Home.

Who is it that called time the avenger, yet failed to see that death was the consoler. What mortal afflictions are there to which death does not bring full remedy? What hurts of hope and body does it not repair? "This is a sharp medicine," said Raleigh, speaking of the axe, "but it cures all disorders."—Simms.

He that dies in an earnest pursuit is like one that is wounded in hot blood; who, for the time, scarce feels the hurt; and therefore a mind fixed and bent upon somewhat that is good doth avert the dolors of death; but above all, believe it, the sweetest canticle is, "Lord, now lettest Thou Thy servant depart in peace."—Bacon.

The day of our decease will be that of our coming of age; and with our last breath we shall become free of the universe. And in some region of infinity, and from among its splendors, this earth will be looked back on like a lowly home, and this life of ours be remembered like a short apprenticeship to duty.—Mountford.

Could we but know one in a hundred of the close approachings of the skeleton, we should lead a life of perpetual shudder. Often and often do his bony fingers almost clutch our throat, or his foot is put out to give us a cross buttock. But a saving arm pulls him back ere we have seen so much as his shadow.—Prof. Wilson.

Friend to the wretch whom every friend forsakes, I woo thee, Death! Life and its joys I leave to those that prize them. Hear me, O gracious God! At Thy good time let Death approach; I reck not, let him but come in genuine form, not with Thy vengeance armed, too much for man to bear.—Bishop Porteus.

When death strikes down the innocent and young, for every fragile form from which he lets the panting spirit free, a hundred virtues rise, in shapes of mercy, charity, and love, to walk the world and bless it. Of every tear that sorrowing mortals shed on such green graves, some good is born, some gentler nature comes.—Dickens.

And when, in the evening of life, the golden clouds rest sweetly and invitingly upon the golden mountains, and the light of heaven streams down through the gathering mists of death, I wish you a peaceful and abundant entrance into that world of blessedness, where the great riddle of life will be unfolded to you in the quick consciousness of a soul redeemed and purified.—J. G. Holland.

Let dissolution come when it will, it can do the Christian no harm, for it will be but a passage out of a prison into a palace: out of a sea of troubles into a haven of rest; out of a crowd of enemies to an innumerable company of true, loving, and faithful friends; out of shame, reproach, and contempt, into exceeding great and eternal glory. —Bunyan.

Death did not first strike Adam, the first sinful man, nor Cain, the first hypocrite, but Abel, the innocent and righteous. The first soul that met with death, overcame death; the first soul that parted from earth went to heaven. Death argues not displeasure, because he whom God loved best dies first, and the murderer is punished with living.—Bishop Hall.

Death reigns in all the portions of our time. The autumn with its fruits provides disorders for us, and the winter's cold turns them into sharp diseases, and the spring brings flowers to strew our hearse, and the summer gives green turf and brambles to bind upon our graves. Calentures and surfeit, cold and agues, are the four quarters of the year, and all minister

to death; and you can go no whither but you tread upon ' a dead man's bones.—Bishop Taylor.

There are flowers which only yield their fragrance to the night; there are faces whose beauty only fully opens out in death. No more wrinkles; no drawn, distorted lineaments; an expression of extreme humility, blended with gladness of hope; a serene brightness, and an ideal straightening of the outline, as if the Divine finger, source of supreme beauty, had been laid there.—Madame de Gasparin.

The more we sink into the infirmities of age, the nearer we are to immortal youth. All people are young in the other world. That state is an eternal spring, ever fresh and flourishing. Now, to pass from midnight into noon on the sudden, to be decrepit one minute and all spirit and activity the next, must be a desirable change. To call this dying is an abuse of language. —Jeremy Collier.

The realm of death seems an enemy's country to most men, on whose shores they are loathly driven by stress of weather; to the wise man it is the desired port where he moors his bark gladly, as in some quiet haven of the Fortunate Isles; it is the golden west into which his sun sinks, and, sinking, casts back a glory upon the leaden cloud-tack which had darkly besieged his day.—Lowell.

Ephemera die all at sunset, and no insect of this class has ever sported in the beams of the morning sun. Happier are ye, little human ephemera! Ye played only in the ascending beams, and in the early dawn, and in the eastern light; ye drank only of the prelibations of life; hovered for a little space over the world of freshness and of blossoms; and fell asleep in innocence before yet the morning dew was exhaled;—Richter.

Among the poor, the approach of dissolution is usually regarded with a quiet and natural composure, which it is consolatory to contemplate, and which is as far removed from the dead palsy of unbelief as it is from the delirious raptures of fanaticism. Theirs is a true, unhesitating faith, and they are willing to lay down the burden of a weary life, in the sure and certain hope of a blessed immortality.—Southey.

Men fear death, as children fear the dark; and as that natural fear in children is increased by frightful tales, so is the other. Groans, convulsions, weeping friends, and the like show death terrible; yet there is no passion so weak but conquers the fear of it, and therefore death is not such a terrible enemy. Revenge triumphs over death, love slights it, honor aspires to it, dread of shame prefers it, grief flies to it, and fear anticipates it.—Bacon.

Death comes equally to us all, and makes us all equal when it comes. The ashes of an oak in a chimney are no epitaph of that, to tell me how high or how large that was; it tells me not what flocks it sheltered while it stood, nor what men it hurt when it fell. The dust of great persons' graves is speechless, too; it says nothing, it distinguishes nothing.—Donne.

All death in nature is birth, and at the moment of death appears visibly the rising of life. There is no dying principle in nature, for nature throughout is unmixed life, which, concealed behind the old, begins again and develops itself. Death as well as birth is simply in itself, in order to present itself ever more brightly and more like to itself.—Fichte.

Sometimes, I think, the angel Death
　Comes down from realms above,
And grants to souls unfit for flight
　More time to learn God's love.

Sometimes, I think, the pitying tears,
　Like rain on parching sod,
Bring forth new life from wasted years,
　And bring a soul to God. —J. C. H.

We hold death, poverty, and grief for our principal enemies; but this death, which some repute the most dreadful of all dreadful things, who does not know that others call it the only secure harbor from the storms and tempests of life, the sovereign good of nature, the sole support of liberty, and the common and sudden remedy of all evils?—Montaigne.

If I had thought thou couldst have died
　I might not weep for thee;
But I forgot, when by thy side,
　That thou couldst mortal be;
It never through my mind had passed,
　That time would e'er be o'er
When I on thee should look my last,
　And thou shouldst smile no more!
　　　　　　　—Chas. Wolfe.

The golden ripple on the wall came back again, and nothing else stirred in the room. The old, old fashion! The fashion that came in with our first garments, and will last unchanged until our race has run its course, and the wide firmament is rolled up like a scroll. The old, old fashion—Death! Oh, thank God, all who see it, for that older fashion yet—of Immortality!—Dickens.

One may live as a conqueror, a king or a magistrate; but he must die as a man. The bed of death brings every human being to his pure individuality; to the intense contemplation of that deepest and most solemn of all relations, the relation between the creature and his Creator. Here it is that fame and renown cannot assist us; that all external things must fail to aid us; that even friends, affection and human love and devotedness cannot succor us.—Webster.

So live, that, when thy summons comes to join
The innumerable caravan, that moves
To that mysterious realm, where each shall take
His chamber in the silent halls of death,
Thou go not, like the quarry-slave at night,
Scourged to his dungeon; but sustain'd and sooth'd
By an unfaltering trust, approach thy grave,
Like one that draws the drapery of his couch
About him, and lies down to pleasant dreams. 　　　　　—Bryant.

When a friend is carried to his grave, we at once find excuses for every weakness, and palliation of every fault. We recollect a thousand endearments, which before glided off our minds without impression, a thousand favors unrepaid, a thousand duties unperformed; and wish, vainly wish, for his return, not so much that we may receive as that we may bestow happiness, and recompense that kindness which before we never understood.—Dr. Johnson.

It is an exquisite and beautiful thing in our nature, that, when the heart is touched and softened by some tranquil happiness or affectionate feeling, the memory of the dead comes over it most powerfully and irresistibly. It would seem almost as though our better thoughts and sympathies were charms, in virtue of which the soul is enabled to hold some vague and mysterious intercourse with the spirits of those whom we loved in life. Alas! how often and how long may these patient angels hover around us, watching for the spell which is so soon forgotten!—Dickens.

When I remember all
  The friends so link'd together,
I've seen around me fall,
  Like leaves in wintry weather;
I feel like one who treads alone
  Some banquet hall deserted,
Whose lights are fled, whose garlands dead,
  And all but he departed.
        —Tom Moore.

Ye living soldiers of the mighty war,
  Once more from roaring cannon and the
    drums
And bugles blown at morn, the summons
  comes:
Forget the halting limb, each wound and
  scar:
Once more your Captain calls to you;
  Come to his last review!
        —R. W. Gilder.

Out—out are the lights—out all!
  And, over each quivering form,
The curtain, a funeral pall,
  Comes down with the rush of a storm,
And the angels, all pallid and wan,
  Uprising, unveiling, affirm
That the play is the tragedy, "Man,"
  And its hero the Conqueror Worm.
        —Poe.

Our respect for the dead, when they are just dead, is something wonderful,

and the way we show it more wonderful still. We show it with black feathers and black horses; we show it with black dresses and black heraldries; we show it with costly obelisks and sculptures of sorrow, which spoil half of our beautiful cathedrals. We show it with frightful gratings and vaults, and lids of dismal stone, in the midst of the quiet grass; and last, and not least, we show it by permitting ourselves to tell any number of falsehoods we think amiable or credible in the epitaph.—Ruskin.

Ay, but to die, and go we know not where;
To lie in cold obstruction, and to rot:
This sensible warm motion to become
A kneaded clod; and the delighted spirit
To bathe in fiery floods, or to reside
In thrilling regions of thick-ribbed ice;
To be imprison'd in the viewless winds,
And blown with restless violence round
  about
The pendant world.   —Shakespeare.

O Death, what art thou? a Lawgiver that
  never altereth,
Fixing the consummating seal, whereby the
  deeds of life become established;
O Death, what art thou? a stern and silent
  usher,
Leading to the judgment for Eternity, after
  the trial scene of Time;
O Death, what art thou? an husbandman
  that reapeth always,
Out of season, as in season, with the sickle
  in his hand.   —Tupper.

He who died at Azan sends
This to comfort all his friends:
Faithful friends! It lies I know
Pale and white and cold as snow;
And ye say, "Abdallah's dead"!
Weeping at the feet and head,
I can see your falling tears,
I can hear your sighs and prayers;
Yet I smile and whisper this:
I am not the thing you kiss.
Cease your tears and let it lie;
It was mine—it is not I.
        —Edwin Arnold.

To what base uses may we return! Why may not imagination trace the noble dust of Alexander, till it find it stopping a bunghole? As thus: Alexander died, Alexander was buried, Alexander returneth to dust; the dust is earth: of earth we make loam. And why of that loam, whereto he was con-

verted, might they not stop a beer
barrel?—Shakespeare.

But know that thou must render up the
    dead,
And with high interest too! they are not
    thine
But only in thy keeping for a season,
Till the great promis'd day of restitution;
When loud diffusive sound of brazen
    trump
Of strong-lung'd cherub shall alarm thy
    captives,
And rouse the long, long sleepers into life,
Daylight and liberty.   —Blair.

The dead are like the stars, by day
  Withdrawn from mortal eye,
But not extinct, they hold their way
  In glory through the sky:
Spirits from bondage thus set free,
Vanish amidst immensity,
Where human thought, like human sight,
Fails to pursue their trackless flight.
    —James Montgomery.

We do not die wholly at our deaths:
we have mouldered away gradually
long before. Faculty after faculty,
interest after interest, attachment
after attachment disappear; we are
torn from ourselves while living, year
after year sees us no longer the same,
and death only consigns the last fragment of what we were to the grave.—
Hazlitt.

Death should come
Gently to one of gentle mould, like thee,
As light winds, wandering through groves
    of bloom,
Detach the delicate blossoms from the tree,
Close thy sweet eyes calmly, and without
    pain,
And we will trust in God to see thee yet
    again.   —Bryant.

Why should man's high aspiring mind
Burn in him with so proud a breath;
When all his haughty views can find
In this world, yield to death;
The fair, the brave, the vain, the wise,
The rich, the poor, the great, the small,
Are each but worms' anatomies,
To strew his quiet hall.   —Marvel.

For the death of the righteous is
like the descending of ripe and wholesome fruits from a pleasant and florid
tree. Our senses entire, our limbs
unbroken, without horrid tortures;
after provision made for our children,
with a blessing entailed upon posterity,
in the presence of our friends, our
dearest relatives closing our eyes and
binding our feet, leaving a good name
behind us.—Jeremy Taylor.

What is death? Oh! what is death?
'Tis slumber to the weary—
  'Tis rest to the forlorn—
'Tis shelter to the dreary—
  'Tis peace amid the storm—
'Tis the entrance to our home—
  'Tis the passage to that God
Who bids His children come,
  When their weary course is trod.
Such is death! yes, such is death.
    —Anon.

Yet tell me, frighted senses! what is death?
Blood only stopp'd, and interrupted breath;
The utmost limit of a narrow span,
And end of motion, which with life began,
And smoke that rises from the kindling
    fires
Is seen this moment and the next expires;
As empty clouds by rising winds are toss'd
Their fleeting forms scarce sooner found
    than lost.   —Prior.

All that tread
The globe are but a handful to the tribes
That slumber in its bosom. Take the wings
Of morning, and the Barcan desert pierce,
Or lose thyself in the continuous woods
Where rolls the Oregon, and hears no sound
Save his own dashings,—yet the dead are
    there;
And millions in those solitudes, since first
The flight of years began, have laid them
    down
In their last sleep: the dead reign there
    alone.   —Bryant.

It is not strange that that early
love of the heart should come back, as
it so often does when the dim eye is
brightening with its last light. It is
not strange that the freshest fountains
the heart has ever known in its wastes
should bubble up anew when the life-
blood is growing stagnant. It is not
strange that a bright memory should
come to a dying old man, as the sunshine breaks across the hills at the
close of a stormy day; nor that in the
light of that ray, the very clouds that
made the day dark should grow gloriously beautiful.—Hawthorne.

Do we not all, in this very hour, recall a death-bed scene in which some
loved one has passed away? And, as
we bring to mind the solemn reflec-

tions of that hour, are we not ready to hear and to heed the voice with which a dying wife once addressed him who stood sobbing by her side: "My dear husband, live for one thing, and only one thing; just one thing,—the glory of God, the glory of God!"—E. P. Tenney.

Beloved in the Lord, if you only will lay hold of the Saviour's strength, and cast yourself entirely on His kind arms, with His dying grace He will do wonders for you in the dying hour. A great trembling may come upon you when you think of going down to tread the verge of Jordan; "for ye have not passed this way heretofore." But Jesus has; and you shall see His footprints on the shore. He will be your guide unto death, and through death.—Alexander Dickson.

I do not know why a man should be either regretful or afraid, as he watches the hungry sea eating away this "bank and shoal of time" upon which he stands, even though the tide has all but reached his feet—if he knows that God's strong hand will be stretched forth to him at the moment when the sand dissolves from under him, and will draw him out of many waters, and place him high above the floods on the stable land where there is "no more sea."—Alexander Maclaren.

What is death
To him who meets it with an upright heart?
A quiet haven, where his shatter'd bark
Harbours secure, till the rough storm is past,
Perhaps a passage overhung with clouds,
But at its entrance, a few leagues beyond
Opening to kinder skies and milder suns,
And seas pacific as the soul that seeks them.
—Hurdis.

Every day His servants are dying modestly and peacefully—not a word of victory on their lips; but Christ's deep triumph in their hearts—watching the slow progress of their own decay, and yet so far emancipated from personal anxiety that they are still able to think and plan for others, not knowing that they are doing any great thing. They die, and the world hears nothing of them; and yet theirs was the completest victory. They came to the battle field, the field to which they had been looking forward all their lives, and the enemy was not to be found. There was no foe to fight with.—F. W. Robertson.

What a power has Death to awe and hush the voices of this earth! How mute we stand when that presence confronts us, and we look upon the silence he has wrought in a human life! We can only gaze, and bow our heads, and creep with our broken stammering utterances under the shelter of some great word which God has spoken, and in which we see through the history of human sorrow the outstretching and overshadowing of the eternal arms.—W. W. Battershall.

My friend, there will come one day to you a Messenger, whom you cannot treat with contempt. He will say, "Come with me;" and all your pleas of business cares and earthly loves will be of no avail. When his cold hand touches yours, the key of the counting-room will drop forever, and he will lead you away from all your investments, your speculations, your bank-notes and real estate, and with him you will pass into eternity, up to the bar of God. You will not be too busy to die.—A. E. Kittredge.

Death can never interrupt a faithful Christian life. When we feel the touch upon our shoulder and hear the word whispered in our ear, we may be at our work or on a journey, walking the street or asleep in our beds, praying at church or fishing in the country. What difference does it make? We are trying to please our God in what is our business just then. Sacred places and times have no superior advantage for the dying. Sacredness is in the motive of the heart that would do everything as unto the Lord, dying along with the rest. As heaven is still the glad doing of God's will, where is there any interruption?—Maltbie Babcock.

However dreary we may have felt life to be here, yet when that hour comes—the winding up of all things, the last grand rush of darkness on our spirits, the hour of that awful sudden wrench from all we have ever known or loved, the long farewell to sun, moon, stars, and light—brother man, I ask you this day, and I ask myself humbly and fearfully, "What will then be finished? When it is finished, what will it be? Will it be the butterfly existence of pleasure, the mere life of science, a life of uninterrupted sin and self-gratification, or will it be 'Father, I have finished the work which Thou gavest me to do?' "—F. W. Robertson.

We shall be in the midst of some great work, when the tools shall drop from our relaxing fingers, and we shall work no more; we shall be planning some mighty project—house, business, society, book—when in one shattering moment all our thoughts shall perish. Life shall seem strong in us when we shall find that it is done. Oh, how happy they to whom all that remains is immortality; happy you who have that confidence in the Saviour, that, although nature start at the sudden midnight cry, "The Bridegroom cometh!" faith shall answer, the moment that we remember who He is, "Even so, come, Lord Jesus!" —James Hamilton.

When we come to die, we shall be alone. From all our worldly possessions we shall be about to part. Worldly friends—the friends drawn to us by our position, our wealth, or our social qualities,—will leave us as we enter the dark valley. From those bound to us by stronger ties—our kindred, our loved ones, children, brothers, sisters, and from those not less dear to us who have been made our friends because they and we are the friends of the same Saviour,— from them also we must part. Yet not all will leave us. There is One who "sticketh closer than a brother"—One who having loved His own which are in the world loves them to the end.— Albert Barnes.

"God giveth His beloved sleep;" and in that peaceful sleep, realities, not dreams, come round their quiet rest, and fill their conscious spirits and

their happy hearts with blessedness and fellowship. In His own time He will make the eternal morning dawn, and the hand that kept them in their slumbers shall touch them into waking, and shall clothe them when they arise according to the body of His own glory; and they, looking into His face, and flashing back its love, its light, its beauty, shall each break forth into singing as the rising light of that unsetting day touches their transfigured and immortal heads, in the triumphant thanksgiving, "I am satisfied, for I awake in Thy likeness."—Alexander Maclaren.

Death is a great preacher of deathlessness. The protest of the soul against death, its reversion, its revulsion, is a high instinct of life. Dissatisfaction in his world who satisfieth the desire of every living thing has a grip on the future. As far as this goes, he has the least assurance of immortality who can be best satisfied with eating and drinking and "things"; he has the surest hope of ongoings and far distances who does not live by bread alone, whose eye is looking over the shoulder of things, whose ear hears mighty waters rolling evermore, who has "hopes naught can satisfy below." The limits of which death makes us aware, make us aware of life's limitlessness. The wing whose stretch touches the bars of its cage knows it was meant for an ampler ether and diviner air."—Maltbie Babcock.

No man who is fit to live need fear to die. Poor, timorous, faithless souls that we are! How we shall smile at our vain alarms when the worst has happened! To us here, death is the most terrible thing we know. But when we have tasted its reality, it will mean to us birth, deliverance, a new creation of ourselves. It will be what health is to the sick man. It will be what home is to the exile. It will be what the loved one given back is to the bereaved. As we draw near to it, a solemn gladness should fill our hearts. It is God's great morning lighting up the sky. Our fears are the terror of children in the night. The night with its terrors, its darkness, its feverish dreams, is passing away; and when we awake, it will be into the sunlight of God.—George S. Merriam.

Debt

Debt is the worst poverty.—M. G. Lichtwer.

He that dies pays all debts.—Shakespeare.

A church debt is the devil's salary. —Beecher.

Who goes a-borrowing goeth a-sorrowing.—Tusser.

A small debt makes a debtor; a heavy one makes an enemy.—Publius Syrus.

If I owe Smith ten dollars, and God forgives me, that doesn't pay Smith.— R. G. Ingersoll.

Rather go to bed supperless than rise in debt.—Benjamin Franklin.

Many delight more in giving of presents than in paying their debts.— Sir P. Sidney.

Debt is like any other trap, easy enough to get into, but hard enough to get out of.—H. W. Shaw.

I hold every man a debtor to his profession.—Bacon.

Wilt thou seal up the avenues of ill? Pay every debt as if God wrote the bill! —Emerson.

Lose not thy own for want of asking for it; it will get thee no thanks.— Fuller.

Debt is the secret foe of thrift, as vice and idleness are its open enemies. —Aughey.

The ghost of many a veteran bill Shall hover around his slumbers. —Holmes.

Industry pays debts, while despair increaseth them.—Benjamin Franklin.

A national debt, if it is not excessive, will be to us a national blessing. —Alex. Hamilton.

The man who never has money enough to pay his debts has too much of something else.—J. L. Basford.

Creditors have better memories than debtors; and creditors are a superstitious sect, great observers of set days and times.—Franklin.

Debt is the fatal disease of republics, the first thing and the mightiest to undermine government and corrupt the people.—Wendell Phillips.

Paying of debts is, next to the grace of God, the best means in the world to deliver you from a thousand temptations to sin and vanity.—Delany.

Run not into debt, either for wares sold or money borrowed; be content to want things that are not of absolute necessity, rather than to run up the score.—Sir M. Hale.

Man hazards the condition and loses the virtues of freeman, in proportion as he accustoms his thoughts to view without anguish or shame his lapse into the bondage of debtor.—Lytton.

Debt is to man what the serpent is to the bird; its eye fascinates, its breath poisons, its coil crushes sinew and bone, its jaw is the pitiless grave. —Bulwer-Lytton.

Small debts are like small shot,— they are rattling on every side, and can scarcely be escaped without a wound; great debts are like cannon, of loud noise but little danger.—Johnson.

A public debt is a kind of anchor in the storm; but if the anchor be too heavy for the vessel, she will be sunk by that very weight which was intended for her preservation.—Colton.

Never be argued out of your soul, never be argued out of your honor, and never be argued into believing that soul and honor do not run a terrible risk if you limp into life with the load of a debt on your shoulders.—Bulwer-Lytton.

To one that is not callous, a state of debt and embarrassment is a state of positive misery; the sufferer is as one haunted by an evil spirit, and his heart can know neither rest nor peace till it is cast out.—Bridges.

At the time we were funding our national debt, we heard much about "a public debt being a public blessing," that the stock representing it was a creation of active capital for the ailment of commerce, manufactures and agriculture.—Thomas Jefferson.

Debt, grinding debt, whose iron face the widow, the orphan, and the sons of genius fear and hate; debt, which consumes so much time, which so cripples and disheartens a great spirit with cares that seem so base, is a preceptor whose lessons cannot be foregone, and is needed most by those who suffer from it most.—Emerson.

Debt haunts the mind; a conversation about justice troubles it; the sight of a creditor fills it with confusion; even the sanctuary is not a place of refuge. The borrower is servant to the lender. Independence, so essential to the virtues and pleasures of a man, can only be maintained by setting bounds to our desires, and owing no man anything. A habit of boundless expense undermines and destroys the virtues even in the mind where they seem to dwell. It becomes difficult and at last impossible to pay punctually. When a man of sensibility thinks of the low rate at which his word must henceforth pass, he is little in his own eyes; but difficulties prompt him to study deceiving as an art, and at last he lies to his creditors without a blush. How desolate and how woeful does his mind appear, now that the fence of truth is broken down! Friendship is next dissolved. He felt it once; he now insinuates himself by means of professions and sentiments which were once sincere. He seizes the moment of unsuspecting affection to ensnare the friends of his youth, borrowing money which he never will pay, and binding them *for debts which they must hereafter answer. At this rate he sells the virtuous pleasures of loving and being beloved. He swallows up the provisions of aged parents, and the portion of sisters and brethren. The loss of truth is followed by the loss of humanity. His calls are still importunate. He proceeds to fraud and walks on precipices. Ingenuity, which in a better cause might have illustrated his name, is exerted to evade the law, to deceive the world, to cover poverty with the appearance of wealth, to sow unobserved the seeds of fraud.—Chartery.

A man who owes a little can clear it off in a very little time, and, if he is a prudent man, will; whereas a man, who by long negligence, owes a great deal, despairs of ever being able to pay, and therefore never looks into his accounts at all.—Chesterfield.

Decay

Mutability is written upon all things.—Rivarol.

I sorrow that all fair things must decay.—Halleck.

A gilded halo hovering round decay. —Byron.

Ruins in some countries indicate prosperity, in others decay.—R. Anderson.

In the sweetest bud
The eating canker dwells.
—Shakespeare.

An age that melts with unperceiv'd decay,
And glides in modest innocence away.
—Samuel Johnson.

Nature strips her garment gay,
And wears the vesture of decay.
—Logan.

A worm is in the bud of youth,
And at the root of age. —Cowper.

Man passes away; his name perishes from record and recollection; his history is as a tale that is told, and his

very monument becomes a ruin.—
Washington Irving.

My way of life
Is fall'n into the sear and yellow leaf.
—Shakespeare.

Before decay's effacing fingers
Have swept the lines where beauty lingers.
—Byron.

Can we wonder that men perish and
are forgotten when their noblest and
most enduring works decay?—Ausonius.

Devouring Time and envious Age,
all things yield to you; and with lingering death you destroy, step by step,
with venomed tooth whatever you attack.—Ovid.

All that's bright must fade,—
The brightest still the fleetest;
All that's sweet was made
But to be lost when sweetest.
—Moore.

He that loves a rosy cheek,
Or a coral lip admires,
Or from star-like eyes doth seek
Fuel to maintain his fires;—
As old Time makes these decay,
So his flames must waste away.
—Thomas Carew.

There seems to be a constant decay
of all our ideas; even of those which
are struck deepest, and in minds the
most retentive, so that if they be not
sometimes renewed by repeated exercises of the senses, or reflection on
those kinds of objects which at first
occasioned them, the print wears out,
and at last there remains nothing to
be seen.—Locke.

It is sad
To see the light of beauty wane away,
Know eyes are dimming, bosoms shrivelling,
feet
Losing their springs, and limbs their lily
roundness;
But it is worse to feel the heart-spring
gone,
To lose hope, care not for the coming
thing,
And feel all things go to decay within us.
—Bailey.

History fades into fable; fact becomes clouded with doubt and controversy; the inscription moulders from
the tablet: the statue falls from the
pedestal. Columns, arches, pyramids,
what are they but heaps of sand; and
their epitaphs, but characters written
in the dust?—Irving.

Deceit — Deception

Life is the art of being well-deceived.
—Hazlitt.

We are our own aptest deceiver.—
Goethe.

We are never deceived; we deceive
ourselves.—Goethe.

It is a double pleasure to deceive the
deceiver.—La Fontaine.

The best of women are hypocrites.—
Thackeray.

Yet still we hug the dear deceit.—
Nathaniel Cotton.

Wiles and deceit are female qualities.—Æschylus.

A pious fraud.—Ovid.

Trust not in him that seems a saint.
—Fuller.

Trust not to outward show.—Juvenal.

Gold all is not that doth golden
seem.—Spenser.

We are easily fooled by that which
we love.—Molière.

Our distrust of another justifies his
deceit.—La Rochefoucauld.

Think not I am what I appear.—
Byron.

If the world will be gulled, let it be
gulled.—Burton.

It is a pity that we so often succeed
in our endeavors to deceive each other.
—Empress Irene.

Oh, that deceit should dwell in such
a gorgeous palace!—Shakespeare.

The cunning man uses deceit, but the more cunning man shuns deception.—Adam Ferguson.

Of darkness visible so much be lent, as half to show, half veil, the deep intent.—Pope.

But every thyng which schyneth as the gold, Nis nat gold, as that I have herd it told.
—Chaucer.

Deadly poisons are often concealed under sweet honey.—Ovid.

With such deceits he gained their easy hearts, too prone to credit his perfidious arts.—Dryden.

There is nothing more contemptible than a bald man who pretends to have hair.—Martial.

Perhaps it was right to dissemble your love, But why did you kick me down stairs?
—J. P. Kemble.

O, what a tangled web we weave, When first we practise to deceive.
—Scott.

No man was ever so much deceived by another as by himself.—Lord Greville.

Of all the evil spirits abroad at this hour in the world, insincerity is the most dangerous.—Froude.

Who makes the fairest show means most deceit.—Pericles.

There is a demand in these days for men who can make wrong conduct appear right.—Terence.

Cheats easily believe others as bad as themselves; there is no deceiving them, nor do they long deceive.—La Bruyère.

We must distinguish between speaking to deceive and being silent to be reserved.—Voltaire.

Ah, that deceit should steal such gentle shapes, and with a virtuous visor hide deep vice!—Shakespeare.

You should not live one way in private, another in public.—Syrus.

We never deceive for a good purpose; knavery adds malice to falsehood.—Bruyère.

The surest way of making a dupe is to let your victim suppose you are his.—Bulwer-Lytton.

We deceive and flatter no one by such delicate artifices as we do our own selves.—Schopenhauer.

The first and worst of all frauds is to cheat one's self. All sin is easy after that.—Bailey.

Nothing is more easy than to deceive one's self, as our affections are subtle persuaders.—Demosthenes.

In olden times an enemy was sometimes poisoned by a bouquet,—deceit sugar-coated.—Latimer.

People would not long remain in social life if they were not the dupes of each other.—Rochefoucauld.

Men, like musical instruments, seem made to be played upon.—Bovee.

False face must hide what the false heart doth know.—Shakespeare.

He carries a stone in one hand, and offers bread with the other.—Plautus.

No one has deceived the whole world, nor has the whole world ever deceived any one.—Pliny the Younger.

It is the act of a bad man to deceive by falsehood.—Cicero.

Even the world, that despises simplicity, does not profess to approve of duplicity.—Trench.

Look to her, Moor; if thou hast eyes to see: She has deceiv'd her father, and may thee.
—Shakespeare.

You tread on smoldering fires covered by deceitful ashes.—Horace.

To know how to dissemble is the knowledge of kings.—Richelieu.

Pretexts are not wanting when one wishes to use them.—Goldoni.

Stamps God's own name upon a lie just made,
To turn a penny in the way of trade.
—Cowper.

Dissimulation creeps gradually into the minds of men.—Cicero.

Things are not always what they seem; first appearances deceive many.—Phædrus.

The smooth speeches of the wicked are full of treachery.—Phædrus.

It is not being deceived, but undeceived, that renders us miserable.—Mme. Sophie Arnould.

Hypocrisy is the homage which vice renders to virtue.—La Rochefoucauld.

Don't tell me of deception; a lie is a lie, whether it be a lie to the eye or a lie to the ear.—Dr. Johnson.

If mankind were only just what they pretend to be, the problem of the millennium would be immediately solved.—H. W. Shaw.

When I was stamp'd, some coiner with his tools
Made me a counterfeit.   —Shakespeare.

Hateful to me as are the gates of hell is he who, hiding one thing in his heart, utters another.—Bryant.

A cunning woman is her own mistress because she confides in no one. She who deceives others anticipates deceit, and guards herself.—Ninon de Lenclos.

There is no quality so contrary to any nature which one cannot affect, and put on upon occasion, in order to serve an interest.—Swift.

Artifice is allowable in deceiving a rival; we may employ everything against our enemies.—Richelieu.

There is less misery in being cheated than in that kind of wisdom which perceives, or thinks it perceives, that all mankind are cheats.—Chapin.

All deception in the course of life is, indeed, nothing else but a lie reduced to practice and falsehood passing from words into things.—South.

There is no killing the suspicion that deceit has once begotten.—George Eliot.

Though thy face is glossed with specious art, thou retainest the cunning fox beneath thy vapid breast.—Persius.

Skilled in every trick, a worthy heir of his paternal craft, he would make black look white, and white look black.—Ovid.

Men are so simple, and yield so much to necessity, that he who will deceive will always find him who will lend himself to be deceived.—Machiavelli.

Deceit is the false road to happiness; and all the joys we travel through to vice, like fairy banquets, vanish when we touch them.—Aaron Hill.

We are so accustomed to masquerade ourselves before others that we end by deceiving ourselves.—Rochefoucauld.

It many times falls out that we deem ourselves much deceived in others because we first deceived ourselves.—Sir P. Sidney.

Mankind in the gross is a gaping monster, that loves to be deceived, and has seldom been disappointed.—Mackenzie.

'Tis not my talent to conceal my thoughts,
Or carry smiles and sunshine in my face,
When discontent sits heavy at my heart.
—Addison.

Cheaters must get some credit before they can cozen, and all falsehood, if not founded in some truth, would not be fixed in any belief.—Fuller.

Dissimulation was his masterpiece; in which he so much excelled that men were not ashamed of being deceived but twice by him.—Clarendon.

I hate all explanations; they who make them deceive either themselves or the other party,—generally both.—Goethe.

The silly when deceived exclaim loudly; the fool complains; the honest man walks away and is silent.—La Noue.

There are falsehoods which represent truth so well that it would be judging ill not to be deceived by them.—Rochefoucauld.

It is as easy to deceive one's self without perceiving it as it is difficult to deceive others without their finding it out.—Rochefoucauld.

He seem'd
For dignity compos'd and high exploit:
But all was false and hollow. —Milton.

We have few faults that are not more excusable in themselves than are the means which we use to conceal them.—Rochefoucauld.

Men are such dupes by choice, that he who would impose upon others never need be at a loss to find ready victims.—Balzac.

With one hand he put
A penny in the urn of poverty,
And with the other took a shilling out.
    —Pollok.

Shut, shut the door, good John! fatigu'd I said;
Tie up the knocker, say I'm sick, I'm dead.
    —Pope.

You think him to be your dupe; if he feigns to be so, who is the greater dupe, he or you?—La Bruyère.

It is in disputes as in armies; where the weaker side sets up false lights, and makes a great noise, to make the enemy believe them more numerous and strong than they really are.—Swift.

Trust him not with your secrets, who, when left alone in your room, turns over your papers.—Lavater.

Smooth runs the water, where the brook is deep;
And in his simple show he harbors treason.
The fox barks not, when he would steal the lamb.   —Shakespeare.

All false practices and affections of knowledge are more odious to God, and deserve to be so to men, than any want or defect of knowledge can be.—Sprat.

If a misplaced admiration shows imbecility, an affected criticism shows vice of character. Expose thyself rather to appear a beast than false.—Diderot.

There can be no greater labor than to be always dissembling; there being so many ways by which a smothered truth is apt to blaze and break out.—South.

Many an honest man practices upon himself an amount of deceit sufficient, if practised upon another, and in a little different way, to send him to the state prison.—Bovee.

The true motives of our actions, like the real pipes of an organ, are usually concealed; but the gilded and hollow pretext is pompously placed in the front for show.—Colton.

Sigh no more, ladies, sigh no more,
Men were deceivers ever;
One foot in sea, and one on shore;
To one thing constant never.
    —Shakespeare.

It is dishonorable to say one thing and think another; how much more dishonorable to write one thing and think another.—Seneca.

No man for any considerable period can wear one face to himself and another to the multitude without finally getting bewildered as to which may be true.—Hawthorne.

An evil soul producing holy witness
Is like a villain with a smiling cheek;
A goodly apple rotten at the heart;
O, what a goodly outside falsehood hath!
—Shakespeare.

It is a pity we so often succeed in our attempts to deceive each other, for our double-dealing generally comes down upon ourselves. To speak a lie or to act a lie is alike contemptible in the sight of God and man.—Everton.

The deceptions which the two sexes play off upon each other bring as many ill-sorted couples into the bonds of Hymen as ever could be done by the arbitrary pairing of a legal matchmaker.—Byron.

He was justly accounted a skilful poisoner who destroyed his victims by bouquets of lovely and fragrant flowers. The art has not been lost; nay, is practised every day,—by the world.—Latimer.

As that gallant can best affect a pretended passion for one woman who has no true love for another, so he that has no real esteem for any of the virtues can best assume the appearance of them all.—Colton.

A false mind is false in everything, just as a cross eye always looks askant. But one may err once, nay, a hundred times, without being double-minded. There can never be mental duplicity where there is sincerity.—Joubert.

The life of a woman is a long dissimulation. Candor, beauty, freshness, virginity, modesty,—woman has each of these but once. When lost, she must simulate them the rest of her life.—Rétif de la Bretonne.

The life even of a just man is a round of petty frauds; that of a knave a series of greater. We degrade life by our follies and vices, and then complain that the unhappiness which is

only their accompaniment is inherent in the constitution of things.—Bovee.

Deceit and falsehood, whatever conveniences they may for a time promise or produce, are, in the sum of life, obstacles to happiness. Those who profit by the cheat distrust the deceiver; and the act by which kindness was sought puts an end to confidence.—Johnson.

Of all the agonies in life, that which is most poignant and harrowing—that which for the time annihilates reason, and leaves our whole organization one lacerated, mangled heart—is the conviction that we have been deceived where we placed all the trust of love.—Bulwer-Lytton.

He who attempts to make others believe in means which he himself despises is a puffer; he who makes use of more means than he knows to be necessary is a quack; and he who ascribes to those means a greater efficacy than his own experience warrants is an impostor.—Lavater.

I follow a more easy, and, in my opinion, a wiser course, namely—to inveigh against the levity of the female sex, their fickleness, their double-dealing, their rotten promises, their broken faith, and, finally, their want of judgment in bestowing their affections.—Cervantes.

For he who has acquired the habit of lying or deceiving his father, will do the same with less remorse to others. I believe that it is better to bind your children to you by a feeling of respect, and by gentleness, than by fear.—Terence.

Think'st thou there are no serpents in the world
But those who slide along the grassy sod,
And sting the luckless foot that presses them?
There are who in the path of social life
Do bask their spotted skins in Fortune's sun,
And sting the soul.
—Joanna Baillie.

Some frauds succeed from the apparent candor, the open confidence, and the full blaze of ingenuousness that is thrown around them. The slightest mystery would excite suspicion, and ruin all. Such stratagems may be compared to the stars, they are discoverable by darkness and hidden only by light.—Colton.

The world is still deceiv'd with ornament,
In law, what plea so tainted and corrupt,
But, being season'd with a gracious voice,
Obscures the show of evil? In religion,
What damned error, but some sober brow
Will bless it and approve it with a text,
Hiding the grossness with fair ornament?
                              —Shakespeare.

What man so wise, what earthly wit so ware,
As to descry the crafty cunning train,
By which deceit doth mask in visor fair,
And cast her colours dyed deep in grain,
To seem like truth, whose shape she well can feign,
And fitting gestures to her purpose frame,
The guiltless man with guile to entertain?
                              —Spenser.

Of Adam's first wife, Lilith, it is told
(The witch he loved before the gift of Eve)
That ere the snakes, her sweet tongue could deceive
And her enchanted hair was the first gold—
And still she sits, young while the earth is old
And, subtly of herself contemplative,
Draws men to watch the bright net she can weave,
Till heart and body and life are in its hold.
                —Dante Gabriel Rossetti.

Man is nothing but insincerity, falsehood, and hypocrisy, both in regard to himself and in regard to others. He does not wish that he should be told the truth, he shuns saying it to others; and all these moods, so inconsistent with justice and reason, have their roots in his heart.—Pascal.

December

In cold December fragrant chaplets blow,
And heavy harvests nod beneath the snow.
                              —Pope.

In a drear-nighted December,
Too happy, happy brook,
Thy bubblings ne'er remember
Apollo's summer look;
But with a sweet forgetting,
They stay their crystal fretting,
Never, never petting
About the frozen time. —Keats.

December drops no weak, relenting tear,
By our fond Summer sympathies en-
snared,
Nor from the perfect circle of the year
Can even Winter's crystal gems be
spared.   —C. P. Cranch.

In December ring
Every day the chimes;
Loud the gleemen sing
In the streets their merry rhymes.
Let us by the fire
Ever higher
Sing them till the night expire!
                              —Longfellow.

Shout now! The months with loud acclaim,
Take up the cry and send it forth;
May breathing sweet her Spring perfumes,
November thundering from the North.
With hands upraised, as with one voice,
They join their notes in grand accord;
Hail to December! say they all,
It gave to Earth our Christ the Lord!
                              —J. K. Hoyt.

Decency

The laws of decency enforce themselves.—Mme. Louise Colet.

Decency renders all things tolerable.
—De Gerando.

Delicacy is the parent of decency.—
Mme. Deluzy.

Decency is not defined by statute, but the laws of instinct are stronger.—
Duclos.

Too great a display of delicacy can and does sometimes infringe upon decency.—Balzac.

Caprice in women often infringes upon the rules of decency.—Bruyère.

A woman without a degree of decency and delicacy is unsexed.—C. M. Yonge.

No law reaches it, but all right-minded people observe it.—Chamfort.

Decency is the least of all laws, yet the law which is most strictly observed.—Rochefoucauld.

If once a woman breaks through the barriers of decency, her case is desperate; and if she goes greater lengths than the men, and leaves the pale of propriety farther behind her, it is because she is aware that all return is prohibited, and by none so strongly as by her own sex.—Colton.

Virtue and decency are so nearly related that it is difficult to separate them from each other but in our imagination.—Tully.

As beauty of body, with an agreeable carriage, pleases the eye, and that pleasure consists in that we observe all the parts with a certain elegance are proportioned to each other; so does decency of behavior which appears in our lives obtain the approbation of all with whom we converse, from the order, consistency, and moderation of our words and actions.—Steele.

Decision

I'll not budge an inch.—Shakespeare.

Here I stand; I can do no otherwise. God help me. Amen.—Martin Luther.

I am here; I shall remain here.—Marshal MacMahon.

All may do what has by man been done.—Young.

For what I will, I will, and there an end.—Shakespeare.

Joking decides great things,
Stronger and better oft than earnest can.
—Milton.

He only is a well-made man who has a good determination.—Emerson.

And her yes, once said to you,
Shall be Yes for evermore.
—E. B. Browning.

The souls of men of feeble purpose are the graveyards of good intentions.

Heaven never helps the man who will not act.—Shakespeare.

I take one decisive and immediate step, and resign my all to the suffi-

ciency of my Saviour.—Thomas Chalmers.

I hate to see things done by halves. If it be right, do it boldly; if it be wrong, leave it undone.—Gilpin.

When desperate ills demand a speedy cure, distrust is cowardice and prudence folly.—Johnson.

There is no mistake; there has been no mistake; and there shall be no mistake.—Duke of Wellington.

Advise well before you begin; and when you have decided, act promptly. —Sallust.

Take time to deliberate; but when the time for action arrives, stop thinking and go in.—Andrew Jackson.

The power of uncontrollable decision is of the most delicate and dangerous nature.—James A. Bayard.

Choose a firm cloud before it fall, and in it
Catch, ere she change, the Cynthia of this
minute. —Pope.

Men must decide on what they will not do, and then they are able to act with vigor in what they ought to do.— Mencius.

Sighs, groans, and tears proclaim his inward pains,
But the firm purpose of his heart remains.
—Dryden.

The woman who is resolved to be respected can make herself to be so even amidst an army of soldiers.—Cervantes.

Once to every man and nation come the moment to decide,
In the strife of Truth with Falsehood, for the good or evil side. —Lowell.

The keen spirit
Seizes the prompt occasion—makes the thought
Start into instant action, and at once
Plans and performs, resolves and executes!
—Hannah More.

Firmness, both in sufferance and exertion, is a character which I would wish to possess. I have always despised the whining yelp of complaint and the cowardly, feeble resolve.—Robert Burns.

Decision is a vastly important thing with a convicted sinner. He must choose, or he must be lost. If he will not do it, he may expect the Divine Spirit to depart from him, and leave him to his own way.—Ichabod Spencer.

A man who has not learned to say "no"—who is not resolved that he will take God's way in spite of every dog that can bark at him, in spite of every silvery voice that can woo him aside—will be a weak and wretched man till he dies.—Alexander Maclaren.

I reverence the individual who understands distinctly what he wishes; who unweariedly advances, who knows the means conducive to his object, and can seize and use them.—Goethe.

There is nothing more to be esteemed than a manly firmness and decision of character. I like a person who knows his own mind and sticks to it; who sees at once what is to be done in given circumstances and does it.—Hazlitt.

Decide not rashly. The decision made
Can never be recalled. The Gods implore not,
Plead not, solicit not; they only offer
Choice and occasion, which once being passed
Return no more. Dost thou accept the gift? —Longfellow.

In such a world as this, with such hearts as ours, weakness is wickedness in the long run. Whoever lets himself be shaped and guided by anything lower than an inflexible will, fixed in obedience to God, will in the end be shaped into a deformity, and guided to wreck and ruin.—Alexander Maclaren.

For a few brief days the orchards are white with blossoms. They soon turn to fruit, or else float away, useless and wasted, upon the idle breeze.

So will it be with present feelings. They must be deepened into decision, or be entirely dissipated by delay.—T. L. Cuyler.

There is a tide in the affairs of men,
Which, taken at the flood, leads on to fortune;
Omitted, all the voyage of their life
Is bound in shallows and in miseries;
And we must take the current when it serves,
Or lose our ventures. —Shakespeare.

To be energetic and firm where principle demands it, and tolerant in all else, is not easy. It is not easy to abhor wickedness, and oppose it with every energy, and at the same time to have the meekness and gentleness of Christ, becoming all things to all men for the truth's sake. The energy of patience, the most godlike of all, is not easy.—Mark Hopkins.

Whatever we think out, whatever we take in hand to do, should be perfectly and finally finished, that the world, if it must alter, will only have to spoil it; we have then nothing to do but unite the severed, to recollect and restore the dismembered.—Goethe.

Then to side with Truth is noble when we
share her wretched crust,
Ere her cause bring fame and profit, and
'tis prosperous to be just;
Then it is the brave man chooses, while the
coward stands aside,
Doubting in his abject spirit, till his Lord
is crucified. —James Russell Lowell.

Once to every man and nation comes the
moment to decide,
In the strife of Truth with Falsehood, for
the good or evil side;
Some great cause, God's new Messiah offering each the bloom or blight,
Parts the goats upon the left hand, and the
sheep upon the right;
And the choice goes by forever 'twixt that
darkness and that light.
—James Russell Lowell

Men first make up their minds (and the smaller the mind the sooner made up), and then seek for the reasons; and if they chance to stumble upon a good reason, of course they do not reject it. But though they are right, they are only right by chance.—Whately.

Decoration Day

"It is the purpose of the commander-in-chief to inaugurate this observance with the hope that it will be kept up from year to year while a survivor of the war remains to honor the memory of the departed."—Gen. Logan.

The army of Grant and the army of Lee are together. They are one now in faith, in hope, in fraternity, in purpose, and in an invincible patriotism. And, therefore, the country is in no danger. In justice strong, in peace secure, and in devotion to the flag all one.—William McKinley.

We honor our heroic and patriotic dead by being true men, as true men by faithfully fighting the battles of our day as they fought the battles of their day.—David Gregg, D. D.

Let no vandalism of avarice or neglect, no ravages of time, testify to the present or to the coming generations, that we have forgotten, as a people, the cost of a free and undivided republic.—Gen. John A. Logan.

Other lands have had heroes, but ours were more—they were saviors, and by their sacrifices have saved the greatest land under the shining sun.—Rev. H. W. Bolton.

There is a shrine in the temple of ages, where lie forever embalmed the memories of such as have deserved well of their country and their race.—Col. John Mason Brown.

Soldiers of the Republic, the battles of the present are identical with the battles of the past. The form of warfare only is changed. The moral conflicts waged in our nation are as truly battles as were the conflicts of Gettysburg and Lookout Mountain.—David Gregg, D. D.

So long as its sons are willing to die for their motherland, so long will it endure to shelter and bless them and their children. At the hour when a people shall be unwilling to abide this test, they will find that they have no longer a country worth saving.—Capt. F. J. Babson.

It is good for us to be here. He who reverently and gratefully makes a pilgrimage to the spot where lies the patriot soldier, who gave his life for his country and for freedom, and for the expression of those emotions places a violet upon the soldier's grave, has received a re-consecration to the work which belongs to the citizen and the patriot.

It is but natural that flowers should give expression to our love for the departed; theirs is an oratory that speaks in perfumed silence. Joy and sorrow have their appropriate expression in these mute yet eloquent letters of "the blooming alphabet of creation."—A. T. Slade, Esq.

The immortal Lincoln bowed in prayer, and plead Heaven's almighty aid, vowing the proclamation of freedom through all the land to all the inhabitants thereof; and though the assassin's deadly arm cut short his high career, his soul went up to God with four million broken manacles in its hand.—American Wesleyan.

It is instructive to read the arguments of the statesmen of forty years ago; but the war settled the issue, and no State nor combination of States can extricate itself from the loving grasp of all the States. "United we stand." "Divided" we cannot be. *E Pluribus Unum.*—Christian Advocate.

The Union army demonstrated the stability of representative government. In the estimation of Europe the American Republic was an experiment. Would it go to pieces by the earthquake shock of civil war? Jealous kings said "Yes," but when the red lips of Grant's cannon thundered "No!" thrones trembled.—Rev. C. E. Allison.

Memorial Day is one of the most significant and beautiful occasions of the year. It shows the sentiment of the people toward those who gave their lives for a good cause, and it teaches a lesson in patriotism which is without a parallel.—Rev. C. E. Allison.

No more shall the war-cry sever,
  Or the widening rivers be red;
Our anger is banished forever
  When are laureled the graves of our dead!
  Under the .sod and the dew,
    Waiting the judgment-day—
  Love and tears for the Blue,
  Tears and love for the Gray.
      —F. M. Finch.

The passions of the titanic struggle will finally enter upon the sleep of oblivion, and only its splendid accomplishments for the cause of human freedom and a united nation, stronger and richer in patriotism because of the great strife, will be remembered.—General James Longstreet.

This precious slumbering dust, when animate, leaving the peaceful pursuits of life, sundering the ties of friendship and love, and assuming the habiliments of the soldier, incurred exposure, hardship, fatigue, danger, death, inspired by no such love of glory, but rather by the consciousness which animated the hero of Trafalgar, "Our country expects every man to do his duty."—Capt. W. H. Sweet.

For no such wretched end did our heroes die. In their last will and testament, sealed with their blood, they have bequeathed to us, as their dying legacy, a union stronger, nobler, freer than ever. "The blood of the martyrs is the seed of the church." By the gift of these men, and such as these, we have henceforth a more homogeneous country and a grander and higher civilization.—E. B. Fairfield.

Let us cherish their memories and treasure up their deeds! Let us gather their ashes into the urn of immortality, and write every name on the national roll of honor! Our country's soil gives them all sepulture. They sleep beneath the Stripes and Stars, revered by a race freed from bondage, and the liberty-loving masses of the whole world.—J. E. Patterson.

Alas, many who went forth to the deadly fray returned not, save encoffined for the tomb, or smitten with a mortal wound or deadly disease, which claimed their lives at length. Over the memory of these, we drop the tear of affection, and strew above their sleeping dust the fragrant emblems of a nation's undying gratitude, and chant again their funeral requiem.—American Wesleyan.

Here sleeps heroic dust! It is meet that a redeemed nation should come, to pay it homage at such tombs, wreathing the memory of its patriot dead in the emblems of grateful affection. These grass-grown mounds, these flower-decked graves, awake the memories of the past, and the history of our nation's perils and its triumphs comes crowding on us here.—American Wesleyan.

Through all history, from the beginning, a noble army of martyrs have fought fiercely and fallen bravely for that unseen mistress, their country. So, through all history, to the end, as long as men believe in God, that army must still march and fall, recruited only from the flower of mankind, cheered only by their own hope of humanity, strong or ly in the confidence of their cause.—George William Curtis.

When the war began thousands of young men, the flower of American youth, were looking out of college halls upon a future bright with professional honors. They flung books aside and seized rifles. They became "History's Graduates." Hundreds of thousands of young Americans were anticipating a future replete with the profits and emoluments which reward business genius and integrity. Straightway they abandoned cherished life plans in order to defend free institutions.—Rev. Chas. E. Allison.

And every village graveyard will have its green mounds, that shall need no storied monument to clothe them with a peculiar consecration—graves that hold the dust of heroes—graves that all men approach with reverent steps—graves out of whose solemn silence shall whisper inspiring voices, telling the young from generation to generation how great is their country's worth and cost, and how noble and beautiful it was to die for it.—Putnam.

As we honor their patriotism, emulate their example, glorify their heroism, and teach our children the sacredness of the great cause in which they offered up their young lives, let us scatter over their graves the brightest beauties of life—the glad tokens of a blessed immortality. And may the service, now inaugurated, be perpetuated through each recurring year, so long as the republic shall stand.—Captain G. C. Mitchell.

It is very pleasant to have the opportunity to grasp the friendly hand of those who thought so diametrically opposite, thirty years ago. It proves time not only heals, but also cools the blood, gives more mature judgment, enabling each to overlook the past, and while we do not claim to forget those dark hours in our life, nor withdraw an iota, nor impugn the motives or sincerity of an opponent, we can each forgive, and while we let the dead past bury its dead, rejoice in the sunshine of the present, that brings comfort and happiness to all parts of our native land, as we remember above and over all else, we are American citizens.—Rev. Clark Wright.

We are assembled to-day to call the roll of the honored dead anew, and to lay a fresh tribute of love and gratitude upon their graves. The occasion is complete in itself. It needs no help of speech to make it memorable. These eloquent flags waving at so many headstones, with no stripe erased, and no star obscured; these bayonets gleaming in the sunshine; these echoing cannon, this tap of drums; these beautiful flowers borne by loving hands, contributed by loving hearts; these sacred memories baptizing us all; speak to us to-day more eloquently than man can speak, in a language which we can all understand.—Rev. J. B. Moore.

'Tis quite enough for grief and shame,
 That such a strife e'er smote the land;
And quite enough for praise and fame,
 That Union, Law, and Freedom stand.
Forgive the strife, wash out the shame
 In Lethe's unrevealing river;
But build a monument to 'fame,
 And glorify these dead forever.
                    —J. W. Gordon.

Strew the fair garlands where slumber the
    dead,
Ring out the strains like the swell of the
    sea;
Heart-felt the tribute we lay on each bed:
Sound o'er the brave the refrain of the
    free,
Sound the refrain of the loyal and free,
Visit each sleeper and hallow each bed:
Waves the starred banner from sea-coast to
    sea;
Grateful the living and honored the dead.
                    —S. F. Smith.

The light that shines from a patriot's grave is a pure and holy light, and while we are guided by it we shall never go into the paths of treason and rebellion. Let that light illuminate our pathway, and the noble example of the dead strengthen our love of country and devotion to duty. When patriotism in the hearts of the people is dead all is lost. It is the life-blood and soul of the national existence, the animating fire which makes a people great, and their history grand and beautiful.

They pass before us like a long procession coming from their camping grounds amid the cemeteries, the battlefields, the graveyards of the south. To us they are no longer dead, they live—we can almost hear their well-known voices as with flashing eye, active limb, courageous lion hearts, once more they are with us, side by side, the blue, the gray, the private, the officer; on they pass, those who died at Roanoke, at Camden, at South Mountain, at Antietam, at Fredericksburg, and the battlefields of the south. Hayes and McComas, Kimbal, Sturges, Gadsden, Hamilton, Barnett, Wright, Reno, Jackson and Burnside, Grant and Lee.—Rev. Clark Wright.

With no jealousies to indulge and no envy to gratify, we seek to draw a lesson from the past that shall be to our future a beacon and a guide. To the sleeping martyrs, whose graves billow every battlefield, it matters little what we may now say or do. Our tender offerings of affection will be lost upon their mounds, and the sweet aroma of our scented flowers be uselessly exhaled to air, save as we revive our faith in the doctrines which they defended, and our zeal in the cause for which they died.—Col. John P. Jackson.

These saved the Union—union which had perished
But for the courage which their deeds revealed;
No stripes were taken from the flag they cherished,
No star was blotted from its azure field.

The old survivors of that fight victorious,
Some still remain, yet leave us one by one;
They die, but never die their actions glorious—
They die, but lives the work so nobly done.   —Thomas Dunn English.

You who went forth with a mother's benediction; you who bade farewell to the children who received your last embrace at the place of embarkation; you who faced the enemy so boldly in the charge; you who died amid the carnage of battle alone, alone, while the very stars of God seemed to look in pity upon you. O yes, you, you, my countrymen, whether from Georgia or New York, to-night, these—the remnant of more than 2,000 men—these your comrades gathered here, salute you as we bring to mind your faithfulness as soldiers, and rejoice with you that our country has passed from the hurricane to the calm; from out of all that crash, of which we were part, to liberty, union, brotherly love, and peace.—Rev. Clark Wright.

In the book of nature, where every emotional, mental, and spiritual quality of humanity may find its correspondence and illustrations, flowers represent good affections, thoughts, and intentions toward others. As the flower precedes the fruit, and gives notice of its coming, so good thoughts, affections, and intentions precede and give promise of deeds in love to others. These cherished dead are now beyond the reach of our good deeds; to bring fruits to them would be vain, but to indulge good thoughts and affections toward them should enlarge our souls and wake in our breasts a more vigorous determination to sacrifice ourselves for the good of others.—Rev. Homer Everett.

The asperities and alienations engendered by the great struggle between freedom and slavery have largely passed away, and those who participated as soldiers on both sides, who are still living, fraternize with each other as brothers and fellow-citizens of one common country, on whose glorious banner is inscribed forever *E pluribus unum*. It is meet that those who sacrificed and died in the struggle, or who sacrificed and have since died, should be remembered and honored for the invaluable service they have rendered their country and humanity. Let the graves of the dead soldiers be decorated with flowers and wreaths of laurel, and the memory of their noble deeds revived anew in oratory and song.—Selected.

How sleep the brave who sink to rest,
With all their country's wishes blessed;
When Spring, with dewy fingers cold,
Returns to deck their hallow'd mold,
She there shall dress a sweeter sod,
Than Fancy's feet have ever trod.

By fairy hands their knell is rung,
By forms unseen their dirge is sung;
There Honor comes, a pilgrim gray,
To bless the turf that wraps their clay;
And Freedom shall awhile repair,
To dwell a weeping hermit there.
                                              —Collins.

Then as oft as the 30th of May returns with time's annual round let a grateful nation remember its dead, and with a floral offering decorate the tombs of its fallen heroes, while the dropping tear moistens the cold sod that covers their sleeping dust. To them we owe the liberty we enjoy; to them we owe the preservation of our institutions; and shall we not hold them in grateful remembrance? And though we may often differ in opinion, let us here be united. In God's name let us respect and love the dead who have died for us. Let this beautiful custom be perpetuated until the day shall become hallowed in the history of freedom. It carries with it the idea of our loss and the dear cost of liberty. It brings fresh to mind the deeds of our country's martyrs, it keeps alive and warm the greatest principles for which our sires poured out their blood, on which our republic is based.—Gen. John A. Logan.

Cover the thousands who sleep far away—
Sleep where their friends can not find them to-day;
They who in mountain, and hillside and dell
Rest where they wearied, and lie where they fell.
Softly the grass-blade creeps round their repose;
Sweetly above them the wild flow'ret blows;
Zephyrs of freedom fly gently o'erhead,
Whispering names for the patriot dead.
Cover the faces that motionless lie,
Shut from the blue of the glorious sky;
Faces once lighted with smiles of the gay—
Faces now marred with the frown of decay.
Eyes that beamed friendship and love to your own;
Lips that sweet thoughts of affection made known;
Brows you have soothed in the day of distress;
Cheeks you have flushed by the tender caress.
Faces that brightened at War's stirring cry;
Faces that streamed when they bade you good-by.
Faces that glowed in the battle's red flame,
Paling for naught, till the Death Angel came.
Cover them over—yes, cover them over—
Parent, and husband, and brother, and lover:
Kiss in your hearts these dead heroes of ours,
And cover them over with beautiful flowers!
—Will Carleton.

For love of country they accepted death, and thus resolved all doubts, and made immortal their patriotism and their virtue. For the noblest man that lives there still remains a conflict. He must still withstand the assaults of time and fortune, must still be assailed with temptations, before which lofty natures have fallen; but with these the conflict ended, the victory was won, when death stamped on them the great seal of heroic character, and closed a record which years can never blot.—Rev. C. E. Allison.

When the life of the nation was attempted, when the cause of liberty and human rights called for their aid, they rushed forth to rally under the banner they loved, with grand singleness of purpose and heroic devotion—leaving all behind them, to meet toil and danger, hunger, sickness, wounds, and death, for nothing but the sublime satisfaction of doing their duty to their country and to mankind.—Gen. Carl Schurz.

The best men we had in each of these two regiments are not visibly present with us now; the best and truest of our number lie buried on the battlefields of the south; some were clad in gray, some in blue; no towering monument marks their resting place, nor massive monolith stands sentinel. Buried where they fell, baptizing the soil with their blood, forever consecrating the ground, making it holy, while their life and death tell the world the story of how an American will fight, and if necessary die for what he believes to be the right.—Rev. Clark Wright.

From age to age the honorable fame of this patriotic army will endure. It will not decrease, but rather increase with the flow of years. When the passions of the times are stilled in the grave and the men of this generation have passed away from the earth, the gathering plaudits of coming generations will greet the memory of the men who in a great crisis saved the national life.—Rev. Franklin Moore, D. D.

But the patriot dead are not only those who wore the blue and marched under the flag; not alone their graves do we honor. There were patriots who at home upheld the soldier's heart and inspired him to duty. There were the women, who gave their loved ones, who breathed up prayers for their safety and return, whose needles stitched for them, whose hands wrought for them, whose letters cheered them, whose love forever embodied itself in something that should comfort and relieve them. The memory of those patriot women we too would honor, and did we know where their bodies sleep, their graves we would decorate.

The martyrs of all ages are illustrious, not so much by virtue of their personal position and merits as from the fact that the great cause for which they suffered and sacrificed themselves has reflected upon them its own imperishable luster and glory. And if any cause can confer honor upon its defenders and martyrs, surely the cause for which these men suffered is such a one.—Rev. William McKinley.

As a flash of lightning in a midnight tempest reveals the abysmal horrors of the sea, so did the flash of the first gun disclose the awful abyss into which rebellion was ready to plunge us. In a moment the fire was lighted in twenty million hearts. In a moment we were the most warlike nation on the earth. In a moment we were not merely a people with an army— we were a people in arms. The nation was in column—not all at the front, but all in the array. I love to believe that no heroic sacrifice is ever lost; that the characters of men are molded and inspired by what their fathers have done; that treasured up in American souls are all the unconscious influences of the great deeds of the Anglo-Saxon race, from Agincourt to Bunker Hill. It was such an influence that led a young Greek, two thousand years ago, when musing on the battle of Marathon, to exclaim, "The trophies of Miltiades will not let me sleep!" Could these men be silent in 1861; these, whose ancestors had felt the inspiration of battle on every field where civilization had fought in the last thousand years? Read their answer in this green turf. Each for himself gathered up the cherished purposes of life—its aims and ambitions, its dearest affections—and flung all, with life itself, into the scale of battle.—James A. Garfield.

A shot fired at the old flag aroused the anger of a great people. Who can describe those historic years? The heavens were suddenly black. Fierce eagles of war flew across the lurid clouds. The awful storm rolled thunders along the sky. Reverberating, they shook the Atlantic coast and the banks of the Mississippi. They crashed over Antietam, Vicksburg, and Gettysburg. Forked lightnings played among the clouds around Lookout Mountain. Fire ran along upon the ground in Tennessee, and in Virginia, swamps and rivers were turned to blood. It was the nation's midnight. The death angel was abroad with unsheathed sword. There was a great cry in the land, for there was not a house among half a million where there was not one dead. Four years the storm raged. The iron hail rattled incessantly, prostrating armed men, and crushing woman's tender heart. It was a deluge of blood. Then muttering thunders ceased; the clouds broke away, and out of the blue sky a dove came, and lo! in her mouth was an olive leaf. More than a quarter of a century has passed. Peace still abides. "Over the cannon's mouth the spider weaves his web." But while mighty people are busied with great enterprises, they do not forget—cannot forget—the brave men who purchased peace by their valor and blood.—Rev. Chas. E. Allison.

Great God! We thank Thee for this home,
  This bounteous birthland of the free,
Where wanderers from afar may come,
  And breathe the air of liberty;
Still may her flowers untrampled spring,
  Her harvests wave, her cities rise,
And yet, till time shall fold her wing,
  Remain earth's loveliest paradise.

Give me the death of those
  Who for their country die;
And oh, be mine like their repose,
  As cold and low they lie.
Their loveliest mother earth
  Enshrines the fallen brave;
In her sweet lap who gave them birth,
  They find a tranquil grave.
          —Col. T. A. Green.

We hear much of the language of flowers. With them we crown the head of childhood, and deck the brow of beauty. They bring to the sick chamber the cheering remembrance of the grand expanse of strength and loveliness that is spread abroad without. They grace the festival. They soothe the grief of the funeral. They tell the deepest secrets of love, and pass into the cells of memory, never to be forgotten. But where have flowers ever been applied by man to a nobler, fitter purpose than by us to-day? Have we not done well to give the sweetest products of our native land to the memory of those who died to defend it? May not these flowers best spend the brief hour of their unassuming lives in doing honor to heroes, and wither and meet death on the graves of the truest hearts that ever bled?— Rev. W. H. Dana.

Their heroic deeds take rank in that grandeur whose full appreciation requires the lapse of thoughtful years. Their greatness, heartily as it is recognized now, will grow more in splendor as the fruits of their victory shall fall in successive years to enrich the nation's history. It has happened to them as to all prominent actors in either religious or political contests, that the excellency of their deeds could not be fully discovered until the smoke and dust of battle had been swept away. In such time the aspirations of slandering enemies and the jealousy of lukewarm associates, and the timidity of friends in faintly claiming deserved praise, all conspire in withholding that generous award of honor which after generations take delight in bestowing. Thus the generations to come will continue the repetition of the tributes to these patriots which we have this day observed, rehearsing with ever-increasing praise the moral grandeur of their deeds.—Rev. Mr. Baumme.

But one way is open to the people of this country who would estimate the value of the services rendered by the union soldiers, living or dead. It is to try to imagine what the result would have been had the union been divided. There would have been two nations instead of one; twice as many foreign diplomats within the territory as now; twice as many possibilites of foreign complications; and much more

than twice as much difficulty in settling them, while the influence of each fragment would be much less than half the amount exercised by the whole. Those who had a common ancestry which had been represented in the same halls of legislation, had cheered the same flag and fought together— not against each other—for freedom— would have been strangers and foreigners, aliens from the commonwealth of which Washington was the father. Mutual jealousies would make standing armies necessary, and war clouds would ever have lowered upon the political horizon. It was the valor of our soldiers that stood between the people of the United States and these evils.—New York Christian Advocate.

When we look at our vast country with all its resources of wealth and power, at our system of free government with all the appliances for further advancement in greatness and intelligence, reaching as it does from ocean to ocean, with its fields, and mines, and streams, its hills and valleys, smiling in the sunlight of freedom, inviting the poor and oppressed of all lands to come and occupy them, to plow and reap, to build and grow, and be happy—when we look at all this and think what we would have been had the rebellion proved a success, we feel that our comrades did not die in vain, and we feel that this is but a small token, indeed, of the love that we ought to show their memories. What tender emotions are awakened to-day in our minds as we bend over the silent, yet eloquent, mounds where the American soldier sleeps his last sleep.—Rev. J. F. Meredith.

Dedication

To be a living member of the church of Christ, and to enjoy its privileges is the highest honor God can confer on a man.—A. F. Behrends.

Strength is power in action. Beauty is the assemblage of all graces. The strength and the beauty, being connected with God's sanctuary, must be divine strength and divine beauty. In what, then, consist this strength and beauty which so emphasize and make distinctive His sanctuary?—Rev. W. B. Stevens.

Solomon closed the prayer with which he dedicated the temple with these words: "Now, my God, let, I beseech Thee, Thine eyes be open, and let Thine ears be attent unto the prayer that is made in this place. Now therefore arise, O Lord God, into Thy resting-place, Thou, and the ark of Thy strength: let Thy priests, O Lord God, be clothed with salvation, and let Thy saints rejoice in goodness."—Rev. W. B. Stevens.

_____

Behold this temple to Thy praise,
  Make it Thy very own;
Here knit our waiting souls in one,
  And bind us to Thy throne.

Come, Lord, and with Thy presence fill
  This consecrated place;
Come, gather here through all the years
  The trophies of Thy grace.

_____

Great benefits are conferred by the churches upon communities in the educational advantages they afford, the moral life they impart the basal fluence they exert, and the power of their associations upon individual lives in the formation of character.—Bishop E. G. Andrews.

_____

The consecration is a solemn transaction between God and the parish, as well as between the bishop and the parish—the parish, through its vestry and by a legal instrument, making the building over to God through the hands of the bishop; and God graciously accepting the gift and ratifying the transaction by the bishop's sentence of consecration, which declares it "separated henceforth from all unhallowed, ordinary, and common uses, and dedicated to the sole service of Almighty God." Henceforth this edifice is no more yours, but God's. Given to Him by your corporate and legal act, His name has been recorded here, His presence will be vouchsafed here, and each one of you, as you enter into these courts, can say with joyous hearts, "Strength and beauty are in His sanctuary."—Rev. W. B. Stevens.

In the sanctuary the strength of God's promises comes out with intense force. In the sanctuary do we find the strength of divine praise, when the swelling voices of the whole congregation ascend as the voice of many waters; and the strength of fervent prayer, when "all the people" with one mouth breathe the same prayers, which rise as a cloud of incense from the whole congregation. Thus I might go on and show that there is no conceivable strength that the soul needs which is not found in the sanctuary of the Lord.—Rev. W. B. Stevens.

_____

Such in spirit is our prayer to-day. Make this house, O Lord God, Thy resting-place. Let the Christian priesthood which ministers here, like the Levitical priesthood of the temple, be clothed with salvation, ever showing forth the sacrificial death of Christ, as well as His perfect life in all its divine glory and beauty; and let Thy saints, Thy devout people, who worship here, ever rejoice in God's goodness, and shout aloud His praises in the beauty of holiness. Thus shall the services of this house prepare us for the higher services of the house not made with hands, eternal in the heavens; and may this edifice prove to many successive generations of worshipers, as they pass in long procession through these courts, none other but the house of God and the very gate of heaven.—Rev. W. B. Stevens.

_____

Especially is there "beauty" in the sanctuary when Christ, the "One altogether lovely," shines out of Zion, itself "the perfection of beauty." When He reveals Himself there, in all the fullness of His grace and in all the freeness of His salvation, then indeed do we "sit down under his shadow with great delight," and our hearts, transported with His loveliness, exclaim, "He brought me to the banqueting-house, and His banner over me was love." Let us now sum up in a few sentences the principal ideas of strength and beauty which are found in the sanctuary: Strength, in the strong doctrines, which uphold, like columns, the overarching dome of divine truth. Beauty, in the worship of holiness, which is celebrated therein. Strength, in the Bible, God's majestic voice speaking to us from the lectern, the font, and the table.—Rev. W. B. Stevens.

It cannot be too strongly emphasized, in this day of secularism on the one hand and the love of a sensuous ceremonial on the other, that the true strength of the church does not lie in its historic continuity with the apostles' days; does not lie in its great creeds; does not lie in its hallowed liturgy; does not lie in its learned ministry; does not lie in its churches and cathedrals—it may have all these, and yet, like the apostolic church of Sardis, have a name to live, and yet be dead. Its apostolic ministry may be apostolic in lineage and not in spirit; its grand creeds may be but great petrifactions of orthodox faith; its venerable liturgy may be but the embroidered cerements of a corpse; its beautiful churches and basilicas may be but mausoleums of a lifeless worship. What the church must have, and by which only it can live, is the constant, realized, positive indwelling of the Holy Ghost. All our worship, all our teaching, must be subordinated to this divine Spirit.—Rev. W. B. Stevens.

Deeds

Deeds alone suffice.—Whittier.

Deeds, not words.—Beaumont and Fletcher.

'Tis deeds must win the prize.—Shakespeare.

Deeds survive the doers.—Horace Mann.

The gods see the deeds of the righteous.—Ovid.

Give me the ready hand rather than the ready tongue.—Garibaldi.

Men do not value a good deed unless it brings a reward.—Ovid.

"He wishes well" is worthless, unless the deed go with it.—Plautus.

Great things are not accomplished by idle dreams, but by years of patient study.—Aughey.

Contemplation is necessary to generate an object, but action must propagate it.—Feltham.

Heaven ne'er helps the man who will not help himself.—Sophocles.

A stirring dwarf we do allowance give before a sleeping giant.—Shakespeare.

The deeds of men never escape the gods.—Ovid.

Noble deeds that are concealed are most esteemed.—Pascal.

Foul deeds will rise,
Though all the earth o'erwhelm them, to men's eyes.
—Shakespeare.

Blessings ever wait on virtuous deeds,
And, though a late, a sure reward succeeds.
—Congreve.

Who doth right deeds
Is twice born, and who doeth ill deeds vile.
—Edwin Arnold.

How far that little candle throws his beams!
So shines a good deed in a naughty world.
—Shakespeare.

The flighty purpose never is o'ertook,
Unless the deed go with it.
—Shakespeare.

Things of to-day?
Deeds which are harvest for Eternity!
—Ebenezer Elliott.

Our deeds determine us as much as we determine our deeds.—George Eliot.

Go put your creed into your deed,
Nor speak with double tongue.
—Emerson.

For as one star another far exceeds,
So souls in heaven are placed by their deeds.
—Robert Greene.

Your deeds are known,
In words that kindle glory from the stone.
—Schiller.

Our deeds are like children born to us; they live and act apart from our own will. Children may be strangled, but deeds never.—George Eliot.

Little deeds of kindness, little words of love,
Make our earth an Eden like the heaven above. —Julia A. Carney.

A mighty deed is like the Heaven's thunder, That wakes the nation's slumberers from their rest. —Raupach.

'Tis not what man Does which exalts him, but what man Would do.
—Robert Browning.

However resplendent an action may be, it should not be accounted great unless it is the result of a great design.—La Rochefoucauld.

I on the other side
Us'd no ambition to commend my deeds;
The deeds themselves, though mute, spoke loud the doer. —Milton.

We are our own fates. Our own deeds
Are our doomsmen. Man's life was made
Not for men's creeds,
But men's actions. —Lord Lytton.

A word that has been said may be unsaid; it is but air. But when a deed is done, it cannot be undone, nor can our thoughts reach out to all the mischiefs that may follow.—Longfellow.

One improper word or act will neutralize the effect of many good ones; and one base deed, after years of noble service, will cover them all with shame.—Aughey.

So our lives
In acts exemplarie, not only winne
Ourselves good Names, but doth to others give
Matter for virtuous Deedes, by which wee live. —George Chapman.

Every one may know that to will and not to do, when there is opportunity, is in reality not to will; and that to love what is good and not to do it, when it is possible, is in reality not to love it. Will, which stops short of action, and love, which does not do the good that is loved, is a mere thought separate from will and love, which vanishes and comes to nothing. —Swedenborg.

Defeat

Defeat serves to enlighten us.—Lavater.

It is defeat which educates us.—Emerson.

Defeat is a school in which truth always grows strong.—Beecher.

Defeat should never be a source of discouragement, but rather a fresh stimulus.—South.

Ah! what seeds for a paradise I bore in my heart, of which birds of prey have robbed me.—Richter.

What is defeat? Nothing but education, nothing but the first step to something better.—Wendell Phillips.

Thirsting for the golden fountain of the fable, from how many streams have we turned away, weary and in disgust?—Bulwer-Lytton.

Such a numerous host
Fled not in silence through the frighted deep,
With ruin upon ruin, rout on rout,
Confusion worse confounded. —Milton.

There is something solid and doughty in the man that can rise from defeat, the stuff of which victories are made in due time, when we are able to choose our position better, and the sun is at our back.—Lowell.

No man is defeated without some resentment which will be continued with obstinacy while he believes himself in the right, and asserted with bitternes, if even to his own conscience he is detected in the wrong.—Johnson.

We mortals, men and women, devour many a disappointment between breakfast and dinner-time; keep back the tears and look a little pale about the lips, and in answer to inquiries say, "Oh, nothing!" Pride helps us; and pride is not a bad thing when it only urges us to hide our own hurts—not to hurt others.—George Eliot.

Defects

If we had no defects ourselves, we should not take so much pleasure in noting those of others.—La Rochefoucauld.

In the intercourse of life we please, often, more by our defects than by our good qualities.—La Rochefoucauld.

Defence

In cases of defence, 'tis best to weigh
The enemy more mighty than he seems;·
So the proportions of defence are fill'd;
Which of a weak and niggardly projection
Doth, like a miser, spoil his coat with
 scanting a little cloth.—Shakespeare.

Deference

Deference often shrinks and withers as much upon the approach of intimacy as the sensitive plant does upon the touch of one's finger.—Shenstone.

Deference is the most complicate, the most indirect, and the most elegant of all compliments.—Shenstone.

Defiance

Then, Bolingbroke, as low as to thy heart,
Through the false passage of thy throat,
 thou liest.   —Shakespeare.

Come one, come all—this rock shall fly
From its firm base as soon as I.
     —Scott.

Why, I will fight with him upon this theme
Until my eyelids will no longer wag.
     —Shakespeare.

If thou deny'st it, twenty times thou liest;
And I will turn thy falsehood to thy heart,
Where it was forged, with my rapier's point.
     —Shakespeare.

I do defy him, and I spit at him;
Call him—a slanderous coward, and a villain:
Which to maintain, I would allow him odds;
And meet him, were I ty'd to run a-foot,
Even to the frozen ridges of the Alps.
     —Shakespeare.

If thou but frown on me, or stir thy foot,
Or teach thy hasty spleen to do me shame,
I'll strike thee dead. Put up thy sword
 betime,
Or I'll so maul you and your toasting-iron,
That you shall think the devil has come
 from hell.   —Shakespeare.

Who sets me else? by heaven I'll throw at
 all;
I have a thousand spirits in one breast,
To answer twenty thousand such as you.
     —Shakespeare.

I had rather chop this hand off at a blow,
And with the other fling it at thy face,
Than bear so low a sail, to strike to thee.
     —Shakespeare.

Though all around is dark and cheerless,
 And on high my star looks pale,
My heart is steadfast still and fearless,
 Still my lips disdain to wail.
My spirit still stands up undaunted,
 Still I on myself rely;
No craven thought my brain e'er haunted,
 Fate and Fortune I defy!
    —Frazer's Magazine.

Deformity

Do you suppose we owe nothing to Pope's deformity? He said to himself, "If my person be crooked, my verses shall be straight."—Hazlitt.

In nature there's no blemish but the mind;
None can be call'd deform'd but the un-
 kind:
Virtue is beauty; but the beauteous evil
Are empty trunks, o'er-flourish'd by the
 devil.
     —Shakespeare.

 Deformity of the heart I call
 The worst deformity of all;
 For what is form, or what is face,
 But the soul's index, or its case?
     —Colton.

Deformity is either natural, voluntary or adventitious, being either caused by God's unseen Providence (by men nicknamed chance), or by men's cruelty.—Fuller.

Deform'd, unfinish'd, sent before my time
Into this breathing world, scarce half made
 up,
And that so lamely and unfashionably,
That dogs bark at me, as I halt by them.
But I,—that am not shap'd for sportive
 tricks,
Nor made to court an amorous looking-
 glass;
I that am rudely stamp'd, and want love's
 majesty,
To strut before a wanton ambling nymph.
     —Shakespeare.

From whence comes it that a cripple in body does not irritate us, and that a crippled mind enrages us? It is because a cripple sees that we go right, and a distorted mind says that it is we who go astray. But for that we

should have more pity and less rage.
—Pascal.

Deformity is daring;
It is its essence to o'ertake mankind
By heart and soul, and make itself the
    equal—
Ay, the superior of the rest. There is
A spur in its halt movements, to become
All that the others cannot, in such things
As still are free for both, to compensate
For stepdame Nature's avarice at first.
                                    —Byron.

Nature herself started back when thou wert
    born,
And cried, "the work's not mine."
The midwife stood aghast; and when she
    saw
Thy mountain back and thy distorted legs,
Thy face itself,
Half-minted with the royal stamp of man,
And half o'ercome with beast, she doubted
    long
Whose right in thee were more;
And know not if to burn thee in the flames
Were not the holier work.   —Lee.

Why, love forswore me in my mother's
    womb:
And, for. I should not deal in her soft laws,
She did corrupt frail nature with some bribe
To shrink mine arm up like a wither'd
    shrub,
To make an envious mountain on my back,
Where sits deformity to make my body;
To shape my legs of an unequal size;
To disproportion me in every part,
Like to a chaos, or an unlick'd bear-whelp,
That carries no impression like the dam.
And am I then a man to be belov'd?
                              —Shakespeare.

Am I to blame, if nature threw my body
In so perverse a mould! yet when she cast
Her envious hand upon my supple joints,
Unable to resist, and rumpled them
On heaps in their dark lodging; to revenge
Her bungled work, she stamped my mind
    . more fair,
And as from chaos, huddled and deform'd,
The gods struck fire, and lighted up the
    lamps
That beautify the sky; so she inform'd
This ill-shap'd body with a daring soul,
And, making less than man, she made me
    more.   —Lee.

Many a man has risen to eminence
under the powerful reaction of his
mind in fierce counter-agency to the
scorn of the unworthy, daily evoked by
his personal defects, who with a handsome person would have sunk into the
luxury of a careless life under the

tranquillizing smiles of continual admiration.—De Quincey.

Degeneracy

O, that a mighty man of such descent,
Of such possessions, and so high esteem,
Should be infused with so foul a spirit!
                              —Shakespeare.

What a falling off was there.
                              —Shakespeare.

In an age remarkable for good reasoning and bad conduct, for sound
rules and corrupt manners, when virtue fills our heads, but vice our hearts;
when those who would fain persuade
us that they are quite sure of heaven,
appear in no greater hurry to go there
than other folks, but put on the livery
of the best master only to serve the
worst;—in an age when modesty herself is more ashamed of detection than
delinquency; when independence of
principle consists in having no principle on which to depend; and free
thinking, not in thinking freely, but
in being free from thinking; in an age
when patriots will hold anything except
their tongues; keep anything except
their word; and lose nothing patiently
except their character;—to improve
such an age must be difficult; to instruct it dangerous; and he stands no
chance of amending it who cannot at
the same time amuse it.—Colton.

Delay

Delay is as hateful as it is dangerous.—Holcroft.

Dull not device by coldness and delay.—Shakespeare.

Every delay that postpones our joys
is long.—Ovid.

Lingering labors come to naught.—
Robert Southwell.

All delays are dangerous in war.—
Dryden.

Away with delay; the chance of
great fortune is short-lived.—Silius
Italicus.

He that riseth late must tread all
day, and shall scarce overtake his business at night.—Benjamin Franklin.

Defer no time, delays have dangerous ends.—Shakespeare.

The opportunity is often lost by deliberating.—Syrus.

What reason could not avoid has often been cured by delay.—Seneca.

Your gift is princely, but it comes too late,
And falls like sunbeams on a blasted blossom.   —Suckling.

Every delay is too long to one who is in a hurry.—Seneca.

Away with delay—it always injures those who are prepared.—Lucan.

When a man's life is at stake no delay is too long.—Juvenal.

One man by delay restored the state, for he preferred the public safety to idle report.—Ennius.

Late, late, so late! but we can enter still.
Too late, too late! ye cannot enter now.
                              —Tennyson.

Ah! nothing is too late
Till the tired heart shall cease to palpitate.
                              —Longfellow.

He that gives time to resolve gives leisure to deny, and warning to prepare.—Quarles.

Some one speaks admirably of "the well-ripened fruit of sage delay."—Balzac.

The procrastinator is not only indolent and weak, but commonly false, too; most of the weak are false.—Lavater.

He who prorogues the honesty of to-day till to-morrow will probably prorogue his to-morrows to eternity.—Lavater.

Be wise to-day; 't is madness to defer;
Next day the fatal precedent will plead
Thus on, till wisdom is push'd out of life.
                              —Young.

When the death of a human being may be the consequence, no delay that is afforded is long.—Law Maxim.

Meet the disorder in the outset, the medicine may be too late, when the disease has gained ground through delay.—Ovid.

O my good lord, that comfort comes too
    late;
'T is like a pardon after execution:
That gentle physic, given in time, had cur'd
    me,
But now I'm past all comfort here but
    prayers.   —Shakespeare.

Procrastination is the thief of time; year after year it steals, till all are fled, and to the mercies of a moment leaves the vast concerns of an eternal scene.—Young.

Our greatest actions, or of good or evil,
The hero's and the murderer's spring at
    once
From their conception: O! how many
    deeds
Of deathless virtue and immortal crime
The world had wanted, had the actor said,
I will do this to-morrow.
                         —Lord John Russell.

Shun delays, they breed remorse;
Take thy time, while time is lent thee;
Creeping snails have weakest force;
Fly their fault, lest thou repent thee;
Good is best when soonest wrought,
Ling'ring labours come to naught.
Hoist up sail while gale doth last,
Tide and wind stay no man's pleasure;
Seek not time, when time is past,
Sober speed is wisdom's leisure,
After-wits are dearly bought,
Let thy fore-wit guide thy thought.
                         —Robert Southwell.

Time drinketh up the essence of every great and noble action, which ought to be performed, and is delayed in the execution.—Vishnu Sarma.

Delicacy

Delicacy is the genuine tint of virtue.—Marguerite de Valois.

Delicacy in woman is strength.—Lichtenberg.

Delicacy is an attribute of heaven.—James Ellis.

Delicacy is to affectation what grace is to beauty.—Mme. de Maintenon.

Delicacy is to the affections what grace is to the beauty.—Degerando.

If you destroy delicacy and a sense of shame in a young girl, you deprave her very fast.—Mrs. Stowe.

Delicacy is the coquetry of truth; fastidiousness is the prudery of falsehood.—H. W. Shaw.

Delicacy is to the mind what fragrance is to the fruit.—Achilles Poincelot.

The dependant who cultivates delicacy in himself very little consults his own tranquillity.—Dr. Johnson.

An appearance of delicacy is inseparable from sweetness and gentleness of character.—Mrs. Sigourney.

The hand of little employment hath the daintier sense.—Shakespeare.

An appearance of delicacy, and even of fragility, is almost essential to beauty.—Burke.

Love lessens woman's delicacy, and increases man's.—Richter.

In delicate souls love never presents itself but under the veil of esteem.—Mme. Roland.

It is against womanhood to be forward in their own wishes.—Sir P. Sidney.

True delicacy, that most beautiful heart-leaf of humanity, exhibits itself most significantly in little things.—Mary Howitt.

The finest qualities of our nature, like the bloom on fruits, can be preserved only by the most delicate handling.—Thoreau.

To a woman of delicate feeling the most persuasive declaration of love consists in the embarrassment of the lover.—Laténa.

A fine lady is a squirrel-headed thing, with small airs and small notions; about as applicable to the business of life as a pair of tweezers to the clearing of a forest.—George Eliot.

Women could take part in the processions, the songs, the dances, of old religion; no one fancied their delicacy was impaired by appearing in public for such a cause.—Margaret Fuller Ossoli.

Weak men often from the very principle of their weakness derive a certain susceptibility, delicacy and taste which render them, in those particulars, much superior to men of stronger and more consistent minds, who laugh at them.—Greville.

The commonest man, who has his ounce of sense and feeling, is conscious of the difference between a lovely, delicate woman and a coarse one. Even a dog feels a difference in her presence.—George Eliot.

Friendship, love, and piety ought to be handled with a sort of mysterious secrecy; they ought to be spoken of only in the rare moments of perfect confidence, to be mutually understood in silence. Many things are too delicate to be thought; many more, to be spoken.—Novalis.

There is a certain delicacy which in yielding conquers; and with a pitiful look makes one find cause to crave help one's self.—Sir P. Sidney.

Delight

A sip is the most that mortals are permitted from any goblet of delight.—A. Bronson Alcott.

I am convinced that we have a degree of delight, and that no small one, in the real misfortunes and pains of others.—Burke.

These violent delights have violent ends
And in their triumph die, like fire and
        powder,
Which as they kiss consume.
                        —Shakespeare.

A voice of greeting from the wind was
        sent;
    The mists enfolded me with soft white
        arms;
The birds did sing to lap me in content,
    The rivers wove their charms,—
And every little daisy in the grass
Did look up in my face, and smile to see me
        pass!   —R. H. Stoddard.

The last excessive feelings of delight are always grave.—Leigh Hunt.

Delusion

The worst deluded are the self-deluded.—Bovee.

Delusions, like dreams, are dispelled by our awaking to the stern realities of life.—A. R. C. Dallas.

Delusion produces not one mischief the less because it is universal.—Burke.

When our vices quit us, we flatter ourselves with the belief that it is we who quit them.—Rochefoucauld.

Were we perfectly acquainted with the object, we should never passionately desire it.—Rochefoucauld.

No man is happy without a delusion of some kind. Delusions are as necessary to our happiness as realities.—Bovee.

You think a man to be your dupe; if he pretends to be so, who is the greatest dupe—he or you?—Bruyère.

We are always living under some delusion, and instead of taking things as they are, and making the best of them, we follow an ignis fatuus, and lose, in its pursuit, the joy we might attain.—James Ellis.

Demagogue

We strive as hard to hide our hearts from ourselves as from others, and always with more success; for in deciding upon our own case we are both judge, jury, and executioner, and where sophistry cannot overcome the first, or flattery the second, self-love is always ready to defeat the sentence by bribing the third.—Colton,

I do despise these demagogues that fret
The angry multitude; they are but as
The froth upon the mountain wave—the bird
That shrieks upon the sullen tempest's
   wing,　　　—Sir A. Hunt.

Democracy

Democracy means not "I am as good as you are," but "You are as good as I am."—Theodore Parker,

Your little child is the only true democrat.—Mrs. Stowe.

Democracy is a mischievous dream.—O. A. Brownson.

The love of democracy is that of equality.—Montesquieu.

In Europe democracy is a falsehood.—Metternich.

Democracies are prone to war, and war consumes them.—William H. Seward.

Democracy is the government of the people, by the people, for the people.—Lincoln.

In every village there will arise a miscreant to establish the most grinding tyranny by calling himself the people.—Sir Robert Peel.

Christ was the first true democrat that ever breathed, as the old dramatist Dekkar said he was the first true gentleman.—Lowell.

Democracy will itself accomplish the salutary universal change from delusive to real, and make a new blessed world of us by and by.—Carlyle.

If there were a people consisting of gods, they would be governed democratically. So perfect a government is not suitable to men.—Rousseau.

Democracy is always the work of kings. Ashes, which in themselves are sterile, fertilize the land they are cast upon.—Landor.

The idea of bringing all men on an equality with each other has always been a pleasant dream; the law cannot equalize men in spite of nature.—Vauvenargues.

I cannot help concurring with the opinion that an absolute democracy, no more than absolute monarchy, is to be reckoned among the legitimate forms of government.—Burke.

He was a democrat in the best sense, earnestly desiring the elevation of the people to a higher plane of intellectual and moral life, as well as their political emancipation.—Hamerton.

Democracy is the healthful life-blood which circulates through the veins and arteries, which supports the system, but which ought never to appear externally, and as the mere blood itself.—Coleridge.

To govern according to the sense, and agreeably to the interests of the people is a great and glorious object of government. This object cannot be obtained but through the medium of popular election, and popular election is a mighty evil.—Burke.

Lycurgus being asked why he, who in other respects appeared to be so zealous for the equal rights of men, did not make his government democratical rather than oligarchical, "Go you," replied the legislator, "and try a democracy in your own house."—Plutarch.

It is the most beautiful truth in morals that we have no such thing as a distinct or divided interest from our race. In their welfare is ours, and by choosing the broadest paths to effect their happiness we choose the surest and the shortest to our own.—Bulwer-Lytton.

A father of the church said that property was theft, many centuries before Proudhon was born. Bourdaloue reaffirmed it. Montesquieu was the inventor of national workshops and of the theory that the state owed every man a living. Nay, was not the church herself the first organized democracy?—Lowell.

There is still another inconveniency in conquests made by democracies; their government is ever odious to the conquered states. It is apparently monarchical, but in reality it is more oppressive than monarchy, as the experience of all ages and countries evinces.—Montesquieu.

That is the best government which desires to make the people happy, and knows how to make them happy.

Neither the inclination nor the knowledge will suffice alone; and it is difficult to find them together. Pure democracy, and pure democracy alone, satisfies the former condition of this great problem.—Macaulay.

"It is a great blessing," says Pascal, "to be born a man of quality, since it brings one man as far forward at eighteen or twenty as another man would be at fifty, which is a clear gain of thirty years." These thirty years are commonly wanting to the ambitious characters of democracies. The principle of equality, which allows every man to arrive at everything, prevents all men from rapid advancement.—De Tocqueville.

A love of the republic in a democracy is a love of the democracy, as the latter is that of equality. A love of the democracy is likewise that of frugality. Since every individual ought here to enjoy the same happiness, and the same advantages, they should consequently taste the same pleasures and form the same hopes, which cannot be expected but from a general frugality.—Montesquieu.

Denial

The more a man denies himself the more he shall receive from heaven.—Horace.

They that do much themselves deny,
Receive more blessings from the sky.
—Creech.

To have what we want is riches, but to be able to do without it is power.

There are many seasons in a man's life—and the more exalted and responsible his position, the more frequently do these seasons recur—when the voice of duty and the dictates of feeling are opposed to each other; and it is only the weak and the wicked who yield that obedience to the selfish impulses of the heart which is due to reason and honor.—Aughey.

Denominationalism

Old religious factions are volcanoes burned out; on the lava and ashes and squalid scoriæ of old eruptions grow the peaceful olive, the cheering vine and the sustaining corn.—Edmund Burke.

O for less of an abstract, controversial Christianity, and more of a living, loving, personal Christ.—Richard Fuller.

It is not the actual differences of Christian men that do the mischief, but the mismanagement of those differences.—Philip Henry.

I do not want the walls of separation between different orders of Christians to be destroyed, but only lowered, that we may shake hands a little easier over them.—Rowland Hill.

Sects differ; but, with few exceptions they agree not only that a life of unselfish love will insure heaven, but that repentance and faith are the way by which one enters into this path of life.—The Independent.

God grant that we may contend with other churches as the vine with the olive, which of us shall bear the best fruit; but not as the brier with the thistle, which of us shall be most unprofitable.—Lord Bacon.

It is neither possible nor desirable to make all men think alike. Variety is the very basis of harmony; and, in the sphere of ecclesiastical experience, oneness of feeling is vastly preferable to unanimity of belief. The voice of God, however, as uttered in the events and experiences of the past hundred years, enjoins upon the private membership of the church the culture of that "unity of the Spirit" which is begotten of the Holy Ghost, and which derives from its Divine Author the life in which it resides, the elements of which it is composed, and the impulses under which it acts.—J. McC. Holmes.

Were we all one body, we should lose the tremendous stimulation that comes from the present arrangement, and I fear that our uniformity would become the uniformity of death and the tomb.—George C. Lorimer.

If God allows us to remain Methodist, Baptist, or Episcopalian, it may be on account of the unconverted, that they may be without excuse; that every type of man may be confronted with a corresponding type of doctrine and of method. Surely there are means adapted to your state, and ministries fitted to your peculiar temperament.—George C. Lorimer.

Dentistry (Toothache)

One said a tooth-drawer was a kind of unconscionable trade, because his trade was nothing else but to take away those things whereby every man gets his living.—Hazlitt.

For there was never yet philosopher
That could endure the toothache patiently.
　　　　　　　　　—Shakespeare.

Those cherries fairly do enclose
　Of orient pearl a double row,
Which, when her lovely laughter shows,
　They look like rosebuds fill'd with snow.
　　　　　　　　　—Howe.

My curse upon thy venom'd stang,
That shoots my tortured gums alang;
And through my lugs gies monie a twang,
　Wi' gnawing vengeance,
Tearing my nerves wi' bitter pang,
　Like racking engines!　　　—Burns.

Dependence

There is no one subsists by himself alone.—Feltham.

God has made no one absolute.—Feltham.

Man is the circled oak; woman the ivy.—Aaron Hill.

Depend on no man, on no friend, but him who can depend on himself.—Lavater.

Heaven's eternal wisdom has decreed that man of man should ever stand in need.—Theocritus.

The greatest man living may stand in need of the meanest, as much as the meanest does of him.—Fuller.

Thou shalt know by experience how salt the savor is of others' bread, and how sad a path it is to climb and descend another's stairs.—Dante.

No degree of knowledge attainable by man is able to set him above the want of hourly assistance.—Johnson.

Dependence is a perpetual call upon humanity, and a greater incitement to tenderness and pity than any other motive whatever.—Addison.

People may live as much retired from the world as they please; but sooner or later, before they are aware, they will find themselves debtor or creditor to somebody.—Goethe.

He who imagines he can do without the world deceives himself much; but he who fancies the world cannot do without him is still more mistaken.—Rochefoucauld.

There is none made so great but he may both need the help and service, and stand in fear of the power and unkindness, even of the meanest of mortals.—Seneca.

In an arch each single stone which, if severed from the rest, would be perhaps defenceless is sufficiently secured by the solidity and entireness of the whole fabric, of which it is a part.—Boyle.

The beautiful must ever rest in the arms of the sublime. The gentle needs the strong to sustain it, as much as the rock-flowers need rocks to grow on, or the ivy the rugged wall which it embraces.—Mrs. Stowe.

Dependence goes somewhat against the grain of a generous mind; and it is no wonder that it should do so, considering the unreasonable advantage which is often taken of the inequality of fortune.—Jeremy Collier.

We are never without a pilot. When we know not how to steer, and dare not hoist a sail, we can drift. The current knows the way, though we do not. The ship of heaven guides itself, and will not accept a wooden rudder.—Emerson.

That acknowledgment of weakness which we make in imploring to be relieved from hunger and from temptation is surely wisely put in our daily prayer. Think of it, you who are rich, and take heed how you turn a beggar away.—Thackeray.

When we consider how weak we are in ourselves, yea, the very strongest of us, and how assaulted, we may justly wonder that we can continue one day in the state of grace; but when we look on the strength by which we are guarded, the power of God, then we see the reason of our stability to the end; for omnipotency supports us, and the everlasting arms are under us.—Leighton.

How beautifully is it ordered, that as many thousands work for one, so must every individual bring his labor to make the whole! The highest is not to despise the lowest, nor the lowest to envy the highest; each must live in all and by all. Who will not work neither shall he eat. So God has ordered that men, being in need of each other, should learn to love each other, and bear each other's burdens. —G. A. Sala.

I hate dependence on another's will,
Which changes with the breath of ev'ry whisper,
Just as the sky and weather with the winds:
Nay, with the winds, as they blow east or west,
To make his temper pleasant or unpleasant:
So are our wholesome or unwholesome days. —Crown.

Life is a system of relations rather than a positive and independent existence; and he who would be happy himself and make others happy must carefully preserve these relations. He cannot stand apart in surly and haughty egotism; let him learn that he is as much dependent on others as others are on him.—G. A. Sala.

Deportment

What's a fine person, or a beauteous face,
Unless deportment gives them decent grace?
Blest with all other requisites to please,
Some want the striking elegance of ease;
The curious eye their awkward movement tires;
They seem like puppets led about by wires.
  —Churchill.

Depravity

God's love seemed lost upon him.—Bailey.

There is not a beast of the field but may trust his nature and follow it; certain that it will lead him to the best of which he is capable. But as for us, our only invincible enemy is our nature.—William Arthur.

Human nature is said by many to be good; if so, where have social evils come from? For human nature is the only moral nature in that corrupting thing called "society." Every example set before the child of to-day is the fruit of human nature. It has been planted on every possible field—among the snows that never melt; in temperate regions, and under the line; in crowded cities, in lonely forests; in ancient seats of civilization, in new colonies; and in all these fields it has, without once failing, brought forth a crop of sins and troubles.—William Arthur.

Those that hold the doctrine of native depravity do not believe that there is a mass of corrupt matter lodged in the heart, which sends off noxious exhalations, like a dead body. But they maintain that the soul has entirely lost the image of God in which it was originally created; that there is nothing pure or good remaining in it; that in consequence of the withdrawment of those special Divine influences which were given to our first parents, the proper balance of the power is destroyed, they have lost their conformity to the law of God; and the holy dispositions, which were at first implanted in the soul, have given place to sinful dispositions, which are the source of all actual transgression.—H. A. Boardman.

If we take away this foundation, that man is by nature foolish and sinful, fallen short of the glorious image of God, the Christian system falls at once; nor will it deserve as honorable an appellation as that of a cunningly devised fable.—John Wesley.

We believe that man was created in holiness, under the law of his Maker; but by voluntary transgression fell from that holy and happy state; in consequence of which all mankind are now sinners, not by constraint, but choice; being by nature utterly void of that holiness required by the law of God, positively inclined to evil; and therefore under just condemnation to eternal ruin, without defense or excuse.—Baptist Church Manual.

Deserts

Use every man after his desert, and who should escape whipping? Use them after your own honor and dignity; the less they deserve, the more merit is in your bounty.—Shakespeare.

Design

When any great design thou dost intend,
Think on the means, the manner, and the end.   —Denham.

Honest designs
Justly resemble our devotions,
Which we must pay and wait for the reward.
    —Sir Robert Howard.

He that intends well, yet deprives himself
Of means to put his good thoughts into deed,
Deceives his purpose of the due reward.
    —Beaumont and Fletcher.

When men's intents are wicked, their guilt haunts them,
But when they are just they're arm'd, and nothing daunts them.   —Middleton.

Desire

Can one desire too much of a good thing?—Shakespeare.

Life is a race; desire the goal.—Ramsay.

Perish the lore that deadens young desire!—Beattie.

Desires are the pulse of the soul.—Manton.

Heart's-ease is a flower which blooms from the grave of desire.—W. R. Alger.

Sordid desires are the children of indulgence.—J. L. Basford.

Happy the man who early learns the wide chasm that lies between his wishes and his powers!—Goethe.

We never desire ardently what we desire rationally.—Rochefoucauld.

We trifle when we assign limits to our desires, since nature has set none.—Bovee.

Each man has his own desires; all do not possess the same inclinations.—Persius.

We are always striving for things forbidden, and coveting those denied us.—Ovid.

It is easier to suppress the first desire than to satisfy all that follow it.—Franklin.

The desires of man increase with his acquisitions.—Dr. Johnson.

It is much easier to suppress the first desire than to satisfy those that follow.—Rochefoucauld.

It is not wishing and desiring to be saved will bring men to heaven; hell's mouth is full of good wishes.—Thomas Shepard.

Desire is the uneasiness a man finds in himself upon the absence of anything whose present enjoyment carries the idea of delight with it.—Lavater.

In moderating, not in satisfying desires, lies peace.—Heber.

What we seek, we shall find; what we flee from, flees from us.—Emerson.

What we wish for in youth comes in heaps to us in old age.—Goethe.

But O! for the touch of a vanish'd hand,
And the sound of a voice that is still!
—Tennyson.

We grow like flowers, and bear desire,
The odor of the human flowers.
R. H. Stoddard.

It is better to desire than to enjoy, to love than to be loved.—Hazlitt.

Keep you in the rear of your affection, out of the shot and danger of desire.—Shakespeare.

Troubles advance upon us rapidly; our desires travel in the opposite direction.—Alfred Mercier.

The shadows of our own desires stand between us and our better angels, and thus their brightness is eclipsed.—Dickens.

Some desire is necessary to keep life in motion, and he whose real wants are supplied must admit those of fancy.—Johnson.

As a general thing we obtain very surely and very speedily what we are not too anxious to obtain.—Rousseau.

There is no inborn longing that shall not be fulfilled. I think that is as certain as the forgiveness of sins.—George MacDonald.

Ah! *Vanitas vanitatum!* Which of us is happy in this world? Which of us has his desire, or, having it, is satisfied?—Thackeray.

When our desires are fulfilled, we never fail to realize the wealth of imagination and the paucity of reality.—Ninon de Lenclos.

O that I might have my request; and that God would grant me the thing that I long for.—Bible.

However rich or elevated, a nameless something is always wanting to our imperfect fortune.—Horace.

I have
Immortal longings in me.
—Shakespeare.

Before we passionately desire anything which another enjoys, we should examine into the happiness of its possessor.—Rochefoucauld.

The reason that many men want their desires is because their desires want reason. He may do what he will that will do but what he may.—Warwick.

He who desires naught will always be free.—Lefebvre-Laboulaye.

Unlawful desires are punished after the effect of enjoying; but impossible desires are punished in the desire itself. —Sir P. Sidney.

Where necessity ends, curiosity begins; and no sooner are we supplied with everything that Nature can demand than we sit down to contrive artificial appetites.—Dr. Johnson.

Our desires always increase with our possessions. The knowledge that something remains yet unenjoyed impairs our enjoyment of the good before us.—Dr. Johnson.

The desire of the moth for the star—
Of the night for the morrow—
The devotion to something afar
From the sphere of our sorrow.
—Shelley.

O fierce desire, the spring of sighs and tears,
Reliev'd with want, impoverish'd with store,
Nurst with vain hopes, and fed with doubtful fears,
Whose force withstood, increaseth more and more! —Brandon.

Every desire is a viper in the bosom, who while he was chill was harmless; but when warmth gave him strength, exerted it in poison.—Johnson.

As long as the heart preserves desire, the mind preserves illusions.—Chateaubriand.

Ere yet we yearn for what is out of our reach, we are still in the cradle. When wearied out with our yearnings, desire again falls asleep; we are on the death-bed.—Bulwer-Lytton.

Our nature is inseparable from desires, and the very word "desire" (the craving for something not possessed) implies that our present felicity is not complete.—Hobbes.

There is nothing capricious in nature. In nature the implanting of a desire indicates that the gratification of that desire is in the constitution of the creature that feels it.—Emerson.

By annihilating the desires, you annihilate the mind. Every man without passions has within him no principle of action, nor motive to act.—Helvetius.

The passions and desires, like the two twists of a rope, mutually mix one with the other, and twine inextricably round the heart; producing good if moderately indulged; but certain destruction if suffered to become inordinate.—Burton.

He who can wait for what he desires takes the course not to be exceedingly grieved if he fails of it; he, on the contrary, who labors after a thing too impatiently thinks the success when it comes is not a recompense equal to all the pains he has been at about it. —Bruyère.

How large are our desires! and yet how few
Events are answerable! So the dew,
Which early on the top of mountains stood,
Meaning, at least, to imitate a flood;
When once the sun appears, appears no more,
And leaves that parch'd which was too moist before. —Gomersall.

Thou blind man's mark; thou fool's self-chosen snare,
Fond fancy's scum, and dregs of scatter'd thoughts;
Band of all evils; cradle of causeless care;
Thou web of ill, whose end is never wrought;
Desire! Desire! I have too dearly bought
With price of mangled mind thy worthless ware,
Too long, too long, asleep thou hast me brought,
Who shouldst my mind to higher things prepare. —Sir P. Sidney.

Every desire bears its death in its very gratification. Curiosity languishes under repeated stimulants, and novelties cease to excite and surprise, until at length we cannot wonder even at a miracle.—Washington Irving.

Desolation

There is no creature loves me;
And if I die no soul shall pity me.
—Shakespeare.

No soul is desolate as long as there is a human being for whom it can feel trust and reverence.—George Eliot.

On rolls the stream with a perpetual sigh;
The rocks moan wildly as it passes by;
Hyssop and wormwood border all the strand,
And not a flower adorns the dreary land.
—Bryant.

I alone am left on earth!
To whom nor relative nor blood remains,
No! not a kindred drop that runs in human
veins. —Campbell.

Gone—flitted away,
Taken the stars from the night and the sun
from the day!
Gone, and a cloud in my heart.
—Tennyson.

No one is so accursed by fate,
No one so utterly desolate,
But some heart, though unknown,
Responds unto his own.
—Longfellow.

What is the worst of woes that wait on age?
What stamps the wrinkle deeper on the
brow?
To view each loved one blotted from life's
page,
And be alone on earth, as I am now.
—Byron.

Desolate! Life is so dreary and desolate.
Women and men in the crowd meet and
mingle,
Yet with itself every soul standeth single,
Deep out of sympathy moaning its moan;
Holding and having its brief exultation;
Making its lonesome and low lamentation;
Fighting its terrible conflicts alone.
—Alice Cary.

The fountain of my heart dried up within
me,—
With nought that loved me, and with nought
to love,
I stood upon the desert earth alone.
And in that deep and utter agony,
Though then, then even most unfit to die
I fell upon my knees and prayed for death.
—Maturin.

Unhappy he! who from the first of joys,
Society, cut off, is left alone
Amid this world of death. Day after day,
Sad on the jutting eminence he sits,
And views the main that ever toils below;
Still fondly forming in the farthest verge,
Where the round ether mixes with the wave,
Ships, dim-discovered, dropping from the
clouds;
At evening, to the setting sun he turns
A mournful eye, and down his dying heart
Sinks helpless. —Thomson.

Despair

God has prohibited despair.—Mme.
Swetchine.

Despair defies even despotism.—
Byron.

Despair is free.—Bulwer-Lytton.

Despair is infidelity and death.—
Whittier.

Despair makes victims sometimes
victors.—Bulwer-Lytton.

Despair swallows up cowardice.—
Hazlitt.

There is a very life in our despair.
—Byron.

For me—I hold no commerce with
despair!—Dawes.

Despair is the greatest of our errors.
—Vauvenargues.

That last dignity of the wretched.—
Henry Giles.

And doubt, a greater mischief than
despair.—Sir J. Denham.

Despair is a dauntless hero.—Holcroft.

Despair is the conclusion of fools.—
Beaconsfield.

It is late before the brave despair.
—Thomson.

Rage is for little wrongs; despair is
dumb.—Hannah More.

All hope abandon, ye who enter here.
—Dante.

The mild despairing of a heart resigned.—Coleridge.

Dreadful is their doom, whom doubt has
driven
To censure fate, and pious hope forego.
—Beattie.

He is the truly courageous man who
never desponds.—Confucius.

He that despairs measures Providence by his own little contracted model.—South.

Lean abstinence, pale grief, and haggard care,
The dire attendants of forlorn despair.
　　　　　　　　　—Pattison.

Religion converts despair, which destroys, into resignation, which submits. —Lady Blessington.

My loss is such as cannot be repair'd,
And to the wretched, life can be no mercy.
　　　　　　　　　—Dryden.

Despair is the damp of hell; rejoicing is the serenity of heaven.—Donne.

When pain can't bless, heaven quits us in despair.—Young.

Despair is a great incentive to honorable death.—Quintus Curtius Rufus.

Even every ray of hope destroyed and not a wish to gild the gloom.—Burns.

A speculative despair is unpardonable where it is our duty to act.—Burke.

Some noble spirits mistake despair for content.—Willis.

Sick in the world's regard, wretched and low.—Shakespeare.

Beware of desperate steps. The darkest day, live till to-morrow, will have passed away.—Cowper.

No change, no pause, no hope! Yet I endure.—Shelley.

Despair gives the shocking ease to the mind that a mortification gives to the body.—Lord Greville.

Despair doth strike as deep a furrow in the brain as mischief or remorse.—Barry Cornwall.

Hope, withering, fled—and Mercy sighed farewell.　　　　　—Byron.

The fear that kills, and hope that is unwilling to be fed.—Wordsworth.

There are circumstances in which despair does not imply inactivity.—Burke.

O Lucius, I am sick of this bad world!
The day-light and the sun grow painful to me.　　　　　　—Addison.

Wouldst thou unlock the door to cold despair and knowing pensiveness? —George Herbert.

There's no dew left on the daisies and clover; there's no rain left in heaven.—Jean Ingelow.

It is impossible for that man to despair who remembers that his Helper is omnipotent.—Jeremy Taylor.

Mr. Fearing had, I think, a slough of despond in his mind, a slough that he carried everywhere with him, or else he could never have been as he was.—John Bunyan.

The fact that God has prohibited despair gives misfortune the right to hope all things, and leaves hope free to dare all things.—Madame Swetchine.

All hope is lost of my reception into grace; what worse? For where no hope is left, is left no fear.—Milton.

Farewell hope, and with hope farewell fear;
Farewell remorse; all good to me is lost;
Evil, be thou my good!　　　—Milton.

Talk not of comfort —'tis for lighter ills,
　*　　*　　*　　*　　*　　*
I will indulge my sorrow, and give way
To all the pangs and fury of despair.
　　　　　　　　　—Addison.

I am one whom the vile blows and buffets of the world have so incensed that I am reckless what I do to spite the world.—Shakespeare.

O God! O God! How weary, stale, flat, and unprofitable seem to me all the uses of this world!—Shakespeare.

Where Christ brings His cross He brings His presence; and where He is none are desolate, and there is no room for despair.—Mrs. Browning.

To doubt is worse than to have lost;
and to despair is but to antedate those
miseries that must fall on us.—Massinger.

Despair defies even despotism; there
is that in my heart would make its
way through hosts with leveled spears.
—Byron.

Consider how the desperate fight;
Despair strikes wild,—but often fatal too—
And in the mad encounter wins success.
—Havard.

To tell men that they cannot help
themselves is to fling them into recklessness and despair.—Froude.

Hark! to the hurried question of Despair:
"Where is my child?"—an Echo answers—
     "Where?"   .   —Byron.

My day is closed! the gloom of night
is come! a hopeless darkness settles
over my fate.—Joanna Baillie.

There are some vile and contemptible men who, allowing themselves to
be conquered by misfortune, seek a
refuge in death.—Agathon.

To him whose spirit is bowed down
by the weight of piercing sorrow, the
day and night are both of the same
color.—Dschami.

---

     *   *   *   then black despair,
The shadow of a starless night, was thrown
Over the world in which I moved alone.
—Shelley.

Though plunged in ills and exercised in
     care,
Yet never let the noble mind despair.
—Phillips.

There is no despair so absolute as
that which comes with the first moments of our first great sorrow, when
we have not yet known what it is to
have suffered and be healed, to have
despaired and have recovered hope.—
George Eliot.

He that despairs degrades the Deity,
and seems to intimate that He is insufficient, or not just to His word;
and in vain hath read the scriptures,
the world, and man.—Feltham.

Despair, thou hast the noblest issues
of all ill, which frailty brings us to;
for to be worse we fear not, and who
cannot lose is ever a frank gamester.
—Sir Robert Howard.

To despond is to be ungrateful beforehand. Be not looking for evil.
Often thou drainest the gall of fear
while evil is passing thy dwelling.—
Tupper.

Considering the unforeseen events of
this world, we should be taught that
no human condition should inspire
men with absolute despair.—Fielding.

No man's credit can fall so low but
that, if he bear his shame as he should
do, and profit by it as he ought to do,
it is in his own power to redeem his
reputation.—Lord Nottingham.

I would not despair unless I knew
the irrevocable decree was passed; saw
my misfortune recorded in the book of
fate, and signed and sealed by necessity.—Jeremy Collier.

          Now cold despair
To livid paleness turns the glowing red;
His blood, scarce liquid, creeps within his
     veins,
Like water which the freezing wind constrains.   —Dryden.

The passage of Providence lies
through many crooked ways; a despairing heart is the true prophet of
approaching evil; his actions may
weave the webs of fortune, but not
break them.—Quarles.

Despair is like forward children,
who, when you take away one of their
playthings, throw the rest into the
fire for madness. It grows angry with
itself, turns its own executioner, and
revenges its misfortunes on its own
head.—Charron.

Alas for him who never sees
The stars shine through his cypress-trees!
Who, hopeless, lays his dead away,
Nor looks to see the breaking day
Across the mournful marbles play!
—Whittier.

Despair makes a despicable figure,
and descends from a mean original.

'Tis the offspring of fear, of laziness and impatience; it argues a defect of spirit and resolution, and oftentimes of honesty, too. I would not despair unless I saw misfortune recorded in the book of fate, and signed and sealed by necessity.—Collier.

The world goes whispering to its own,
"This anguish pierces to the bone;"
And tender friends go sighing round,
"What love can ever cure this wound?"
My days go on, my days go on.
    —E. B. Browning.

Oh, break, my heart! poor bankrupt, break at once!
To prison, eyes, ne'er look on liberty!
Vile earth, to earth resign; end motion here;
And thou and Romeo press one heavy bier!
    —Shakespeare.

A broken heart is a distemper which kills many more than is generally imagined, and would have a fair title to a place in the bills of mortality, did it not differ in one instance from all other diseases, namely, that no physicians can cure it.—Fielding.

Of all faults the greatest is the excess of impious terror, dishonoring divine grace. He who despairs wants love, wants faith; for faith, hope, and love are three torches which blend their light together, nor does the one shine without the other.—Metastasio.

I am one . . . whom the foul blows . . .
Have so incensed, that I am reckless what I do to spite the world.
    And I another,
So weary with disaster, tugg'd with fortune,
That I would set my life on any chance
To mend it, or be rid of it.—Shakespeare.

Despair of ever being saved, "except thou be born again," or of seeing God "without holiness," or of having part in Christ except thou "love Him above father, mother, or thy own life." This kind of despair is one of the first steps to heaven.—Baxter.

Disordered nerves are the origin of much religious despair, when the individual does not suspect it; and then the body and mind have a reciprocal influence upon each other, and it is difficult to tell which influences the other most. The physician is often blamed, when the fault lies with the minister. Depression never benefits body or soul. We are saved by hope. —Ichabod Spencer.

Lachrymal counsellors, with one foot in the cave of despair, and the other invading the peace of their friends, are the paralyzers of action, the pests of society, and the subtlest homicides in the world; they poison with a tear; and convey a dagger to the heart while they press you to their bosoms.—Jane Porter.

   Look on me in my sleep,
Or watch my watchings—come and sit by me!
My solitude is solitude no more,
But peopled with the furies;—I have gnash'd
My teeth in darkness till returning morn,
Then cursed myself till sunset;—I have pray'd
For madness as a blessing—'tis denied me.
    —Byron.

   Let her rave,
And prophesy ten thousand thousand horrors;
I could join with her now, and bid 'em come;
They fit the present fury of my soul.
The stings of love and rage are fix'd within,
And drive me on to madness. Earthquakes, whirlwinds,
A general wreck of nature now would please me.   —Rowe.

As a general rule, those who are dissatisfied with themselves will seek to go out of themselves into an ideal world. Persons in strong health and spirits, who take plenty of air and exercise, who are "in favor with their stars," and have a thorough relish of the good things of this life, seldom devote themselves in despair to religion or the muses. Sedentary, nervous, hypochondriacal people, on the contrary, are forced, for want of an appetite for the real and substantial, to look out for a more airy food and speculative comforts.—Hazlitt.

Despatch

Despatch is the soul of business.— Chesterfield.

Business is bought at a dear hand where there is small despatch.—Bacon.

The swiftest despatch seems slow to desire.—Publius Syrus.

Reason and right give the quickest despatch.—Feltham.

Crimes succeed by sudden despatch; honest counsels gain vigor by delay.—Tacitus.

Generally it is good to commit the beginning of all great actions to Argus with his hundred eyes, and the end to Briareus with his hundred hands—first to watch, and then to speed.—Bacon.

To choose time is to save time; and an unseasonable motion is but beating the air. There be three parts of business—the preparation, the debate or examination, and the perfection; whereof, if you look for despatch, let the middle only be the work of many, and the first and last the work of few.—Bacon.

Despatch is taking time by the ears; hurry is taking it by the end of the tail.—H. W. Shaw.

Despondency

Sorrow comes soon enough without despondency. It does a man no good to carry around a lightning-rod to attract trouble.—Aughey.

Open your heart to sympathy, but close it against despondency. The flower which opens to receive the dew shuts against the rain.—Aughey.

All day the darkness and the cold
Upon my heart have lain,
Like shadows on the winter sky,
Like frost upon the pane. —Whittier.

The recollection of one upward hour
Hath more in it to tranquilize and cheer
The darkness of despondency, than years
Of gayety and pleasure.   —Percival.

No thought within her bosom stirs,
  But wakes some feeling dark and dread;
God keep thee from a doom like hers,
  Of living when the hopes are dead.
               —Phœbe Carey.

Some persons depress their own minds, despond at the first difficulty;

and conclude that making any progress in knowledge, farther than serves their ordinary business, is above their capacities.—Locke.

My heart is very tired—my strength is low—
My hands are full of blossoms pluck'd before
Held dead within them till myself shall die.
               —Mrs. Browning.

To believe a business impossible is the way to make it so. How many feasible projects have miscarried through despondency, and been strangled in their birth by a cowardly imagination.—Jeremy Collier.

Despondency is not a state of humility; on the contrary, it is the vexation and despair of a cowardly pride—nothing is worse; whether we stumble or whether we fall, we must only think of rising again and going on in our course.—Fénelon.

Life is a warfare; and he who easily desponds deserts a double duty—he betrays the noblest property of man, which is dauntless resolution; and he rejects the providence of that All-Gracious Being who guides and rules the universe.—Jane Porter.

Despotism

Honor is unknown in despotic states.—Montesquieu.

A despot has always some good moments.—Voltaire.

Fear must rule in a despotism.—Kossuth.

Despotism and freedom of the press cannot exist together.—Gambetta.

Arbitrary power is but the first natural step from anarchy, or the savage life.—Swift.

Despotism is often the effort of nature to cure herself from a worse disease.—Robert Lord Lytton.

Despotism can no more exist in a nation until the liberty of the press be destroyed than the night can happen before the sun is set.—Colton.

Despotism sits nowhere so secure as under the effigy and ensigns of ʟreedom.—Landor.

———

Despotism is the only form ʊʄ government which may, with safety to itself, neglect the education of its infant poor.—Bishop Horsley.

———

In times of anarchy one may seem a despot in order to be a saviour.—Mirabeau.

———

It is odd to consider the connection between despotism and barbarity, and how the making one person more than man makes the rest less.—Addison.

———

When men have become heartily wearied of licentious anarchy, their eagerness has been proportionately great to embrace the opposite extreme of rigorous despotism.—Whately.

———

When the savages of Louisiana wish to have fruit, they cut the tree at the bottom and gather the fruit. That is exactly a despotic government.—Montesquieu.

———

As virtue is necessary in a republic, and honor in a monarchy, fear is what is required in a despotism. As for virtue, it is not at all necessary, and honor would be dangerous there.—Montesquieu.

———

Travelers describe a tree in the island of Java whose pestiferous exhalations blight every tiny blade of grass within the compass of its shade. So it is with despotism.—Ruffini.

———

Many of the greatest tyrants on the records of history have begun their reigns in the fairest manner. But the truth is, this unnatural power corrupts both the heart and the understanding.—Burke.

———

I will believe in the right of one man to govern a nation despotically when I find a man born into the world with boots and spurs, and a nation born with saddles on their backs.—Algernon Sidney.

———

There is something among men more capable of shaking despotic power than lightning, whirlwind, or earthquake; that is, the threatened indignation of the whole civilized world.—Daniel Webster.

———

Despots govern by terror. They know that he who fears God fears nothing else; and therefore they eradicate from the mind, through their Voltaire, their Helvetius, and the rest of that infamous gang, that only sort of fear which generates true courage.—Burke.

———

Then shall they seek to avail themselves of names,
Places and titles, and with these to join
Secular pow'r though feigning still to act
By spiritual, to themselves appropriating
The spirit of God, promis'd alike and given
To all believers; and from that pretence
Spiritual laws by carnal pow'r shall force
On every conscience; laws which none shall find
Left them enroll'd, or what the spirit within
Shall on the heart engrave.   —Milton.

———

It is difficult for power to avoid despotism. The possessors of rude health; the individualities cut out by a few strokes, solid for the very reason that they are all of a piece; the complete characters whose fibers have never been strained by a doubt; the minds that no questions disturb and no aspirations put out of breath—these, the strong, are also the tyrants.—Mme. de Gasparin.

Destiny

Alas! we are the sport of destiny.—Thackeray.

———

Destiny is always dark.—George Herbert.

———

Destiny is our will, and our will is nature.—Disraeli.

———

How circumscribed is woman's destiny!—Goethe.

———

We are but as the instrument of heaven.—Owen Meredith.

———

Marriage is ever made by destiny.—Chapman.

———

Men must work, and women must weep.—Charles Kingsley.

Hanging and wiving goes by destiny.
—Shakespeare.

Every man meets his Waterloo at last.—Wendell Phillips.

If we cannot shape our destiny there is no such thing as witchcraft.—Beaconsfield.

What a glorious thing human life is, * * * and how glorious man's destiny!—Longfellow.

For some must watch, while some must sleep;
So runs the world away. —Shakespeare.

All, soon or late, are doom'd that path to tread. —Homer.

That which God writes on thy forehead thou wilt come to.—Koran.

When I shun Scylla, your father, I fall into Charybdis, your mother.
—Shakespeare.

Vast, colossal destiny, which raises man to fame, though it may also grind him to powder!—Schiller.

What unknown power governs men! On what feeble causes do their destinies hinge!—Voltaire.

Resist as much as thou wilt; heaven's ways are heaven's ways.—Lessing.

Woman is born for love, and it is impossible to turn her from seeking it. —Margaret Fuller Ossoli.

Destiny bears us to our lot, and destiny is perhaps our own will.—Disraeli.

What fates impose, that men must needs abide.—Shakespeare.

Our deeds determine us, as much as we determine our deeds.—George Eliot.

We are all sure of two things, at least; we shall suffer. and we shall all die.—Goldsmith.

No man of woman born, coward or brave, can shun his destiny.—Bryant.

'Tis man himself makes his own god and his own hell.—Bailey.

Everything is done by immutable laws, and our destiny is already recorded.—Voltaire.

Each thing, both in small and in great, fulfilleth the task which destiny hath set down.—Hippocrates.

Maids must be wives and mothers to fulfill the entire and holiest end of woman's being.—Frances Anne Kemble.

If the course of human affairs be considered, it will be seen that many things arise against which heaven does not allow us to guard.—Machiavelli.

There are but two future verbs which man may appropriate confidently and without pride: "I shall suffer," and "I shall die."—Madame Swetchine.

Our minds are as different as our faces; we are all traveling to one destination—happiness; but few are going by the same road.—Colton.

That which is not allotted the hand cannot reach, and what is allotted will find you wherever you may be.—Saadi.

Stern is the onlook of necessity. Not without a shudder may the hand of man grasp the mysterious urn of destiny.—Schiller.

Life treads on life, and heart on heart;
We press too close in church and mart
To keep a dream or grave apart.
—E. B. Browning.

Man supposes that he directs his life and governs his actions, when his existence is irretrievably under the control of destiny.—Goethe.

No living man can send me to the shades
Before my time; no man of woman born,
Coward or brave, can shun his destiny.
—Homer.

That each thing, both in small and in great, fulfilleth the task which destiny hath set down.—Hippocrates.

Death and life have their determined appointments; riches and honor depend upon heaven.—Confucius.

Would the face of nature be so serene and beautiful if man's destiny were not equally so.—Thoreau.

Can man or woman choose duties? No more than they can choose their birthplace, or their father and mother. —George Eliot.

The heart of silver falls ever into the hands of brass. The sensitive herb is eaten as grass by the swine.— Ouida.

That old miracle—Love-at-first-sight— Needs no explanations. The heart reads aright
Its destiny sometimes.   —Owen Meredith.

They who talk much of destiny, their birth-star, etc., are in a lower dangerous plane, and invite the evil they fear. —Emerson.

Art and power will go on as they have done—will make day out of night, time out of space, and space out of time.—Emerson.

He whom the gods love dies young, while he is in health, has his senses and his judgment sound.—Plautus.

To be a Prodigal's favourite,—then, worse truth,
A Miser's Pensioner,—behold our lot!
—Wordsworth.

Unseen hands delay
The coming of what oft seems close in ken,
And, contrary, the moment, when we say
" 'Twill never come!" comes on us even then.   —Lord Lytton.

Alas! how easily things go wrong!
A sigh too deep, or a kiss too long,
And then comes a mist and a weeping rain,
And life is never the same again.
—George MacDonald.

Oh blindness to the future! kindly given,
That each may fill the circle mark'd by heav'n;
Who sees with equal eye, as God of all,
A hero perish, or a sparrow fall. —Pope.

And all the bustle of departure— sometimes sad, sometimes intoxicating

—just as fear or hope may be inspired by the new chances of coming destiny. —Madame De Staël.

Alas! what stay is there in human state,
Or who can shun inevitable fate?
The doom was written, the decree was past,
Ere the foundations of the world were cast.
—Dryden.

We met, hand to hand,
We clasped hands close and fast,
As close as oak and ivy stand;
But it is past:
Come day, come night, day comes at last.
—Christina G. Rossetti.

All has its date below; the fatal hour
Was register'd in Heav'n ere time began.
We turn to dust, and all our mightiest works
Die too.   —Cowper.

For I am a weed,
Flung from the rock, on Ocean's foam, to sail,
Where'er the surge may sweep, the tempest's breath prevail.   —Byron.

The scapegoat which we make responsible for all our crimes and follies; a necessity which we set down for invincible, when we have no wish to strive against it.—Mrs. Balfour.

The seed ye sow, another reaps;
The wealth ye find, another keeps;
The robes ye weave, another wears;
The arms ye forge, another bears.
—Shelley.

I know that nothing comes to pass but what God appoints; our fate is decreed, and things do not happen by chance, but every man's portion of joy and sorrow is predetermined.— Seneca.

Seek not to know what must not be reveal'd;
Joys only flow where Fate is most conceal'd;
Too busie man wou'd find his Sorrows more,
If future Fortunes he shou'd know before;
For by that knowledge of his Destiny
He would not live at all, but always die.
—Dryden.

Men are what their mothers made them. You may as well ask a loom which weaves huckabuck why it does not make cashmere as to expect poetry from this engineer or a chemical discovery from that jobber.—Emerson.

Philosophers never stood in need of Homer or the Pharisees, to be convinced that everything is done by immutable laws, that everything is settled, that everything is a necessary effect of some previous cause.—Voltaire.

"It is destiny"—phrase of the weak human heart; dark apology for every error. The strong and the virtuous admit no destiny. On earth, guides conscience; in heaven, watches God. And destiny is but the phantom we invoke to silence the one, to dethrone the other.—Bulwer-Lytton.

And this is woman's fate: all her affections are called into life by winning flatteries, and then thrown back upon themselves to perish; and her heart, her trusting heart, filled with weak tenderness, is left to bleed or break!—L. E. Landon.

There are certain events which to each man's life are as comets to the earth, seemingly strange and erratic portents; distinct from the ordinary lights which guide our course and mark our seasons, yet true to their own laws, potent in their own influences.—Bulwer-Lytton.

Ships that pass in the night, and speak each other in passing,
Only a signal shown and a distant voice in the darkness:
So on the ocean of life we pass and speak one another,
Only a look and a voice, then darkness again and a silence.   —Longfellow.

The irrevocable Hand
That opes the year's fair gate, doth ope and shut
The portals of our earthly destinies;
We walk through blindfold, and the noiseless doors
Close after us forever.   —D. M. Mulock.

Like warp and woof all destinies
Are woven fast,
Linked in sympathy like the keys
Of an organ vast.
Pluck one thread, and the web ye mar;
Break but one
Of a thousand keys, and the paining jar
Through all will run.   —Whittier.

Take life too seriously, and what is it worth? If the morning wake us to no new joys, if the evening bring us

not the hope of new pleasures, is it worth while to dress and undress? Does the sun shine on me to-day that I may reflect on yesterday? That I may endeavor to foresee and to control what can neither be foreseen nor controlled—the destiny of to-morrow?—Goethe.

Farewell! a long farewell, to all my greatness!
This is the state of man: to-day he puts forth
The tender leaves of hope; to-morrow blossoms,
And bears his blushing honours thick upon him:
The third day comes a frost, a killing frost,
And, when he thinks, good easy man, full surely
His greatness is a-ripening, nips his root,
And then he falls, as I do.
                          —Shakespeare.

The wheels of nature are not made to roll backward; everything presses on toward Eternity; from the birth of Time an impetuous current has set in, which bears all the sons of men toward that interminable ocean. Meanwhile heaven is attracting to itself whatever is congenial to its nature, is enriching itself by the spoils of earth, and collecting within its capacious bosom, whatever is pure, permanent and divine.—Robert Hall.

Determination

Muse not that I thus suddenly proceed;
For what I will, I will, and there's an end.
                          —Shakespeare.

Although
The air of paradise did fan the house,
And angels offic'd all; I will be gone.
                          —Shakespeare.

I'll speak to it, though hell itself should gape,
And bid me hold my peace. —Shakespeare.

Detraction

Black detraction will find faults where they are not.—Massinger.

The low desire, the base design
That makes another's virtues less.
                          —Longfellow.

Detraction's a bold monster, and fears not
To wound the fame of princes, if it find
But any blemish in their lives to work on.
                          —Massinger.

A third interprets motions, looks, and eyes;
At every word a reputation dies.—Pope.

Mankind praise against their will,
And mix as much detraction as they can.
—Dr. Young.

'Tis not the wholesome sharp morality,
Or modest anger of a satiric spirit,
That hurts or wounds the body of a state,
But the sinister application
Of the malicious, ignorant, and base
Interpreter, who will distort and strain
The general scope and purpose of an author
To his particular and private spleen.
—Ben Jonson.

Devil

The devil has his elect.—Carlyle.

Accursed be he who plays with the
devil.—Schiller.

Every newspaper editor owes tribute to the devil.—La Fontaine.

He must have a long spoon that eats
with the devil.—Marlowe.

He must needs go that the devil
drives.—Shakespeare.

The devil can cite scripture for his
purpose.—Shakespeare.

The devil hath power to assume a
pleasing shape.—Shakespeare.

The prince of darkness is a gentleman.—Sir John Suckling.

Where God hath a temple, the devil
will have a chapel.—Burton.

The devil is an ass, I do acknowledge it.—Ben Jonson.

The devil was sick, the devil a saint would
be;
The devil was well, the devil a saint was he.
—Rabelais.

For, where God built a church
there the devil would also build a
chapel. They imitated the Jews also
in this, namely, that as the Most
Holiest was dark, and had no light,
even so and after the same manner did
they make their shrines dark where
the devil made answer. Thus is the
devil ever God's ape.—Martin Luther.

What, man! defy the devil? Consider, he's an enemy to mankind.—
Shakespeare.

Satan; so call him now, his former name
Is heard no more in heaven.   —Milton.

The Devil, my friends, is a woman just now.
'Tis a woman that reigns in Hell.
—Lord Lytton.

Go, poor devil, get thee gone; why
should I hurt thee? This world surely is wide enough to hold both thee
and me.—Sterne.

The devil is not, indeed, perfectly
humorous, but that is only because he
is the extreme of all humor.—Coleridge.

No man means evil but the devil,
and we shall know him by his horns.—
Shakespeare.

From his brimstone bed, at break of day,
A-walking the Devil is gone,
To look at his little snug farm of the world,
And see how his stock went on.
—Southey.

With grave
Aspect he rose, and in his rising seem'd
A pillar of state; deep on his front engraven
Deliberation sat and public care;
And princely counsel in his face yet shone,
Majestic though in ruin.   —Milton.

If the devil take a less hateful shape
to us than to our fathers, he is as busy
with us as with them.—Lowell.

Black it stood as night,
Fierce as ten furies, terrible as hell,
And shook a dreadful dart; what seem'd his
head
The likeness of a kingly crown had on.
Satan was now at hand.   —Milton.

I call'd the devil, and he came,
And with wonder his form did I closely
scan;
He is not ugly, and is not lame,
But really a handsome and charming man.
A man in the prime of life is the devil,
Obliging, a man of the world, and civil;
A diplomatist too, well skill'd in debate,
He talks quite glibly of church and state.
—Heine.

Satan is to be punished eternally in
the end, but for a while he triumphs.
—B. R. Haydon.

The meanest thing in the world is—the devil.—Henry Ward Beecher.

Let me say "amen" betimes, lest the devil cross my prayer.—Shakespeare.

It is Lucifer,
The son of mystery;
And since God suffers him to be,
He, too, is God's minister,
And labors for some good
By us not understood. —Longfellow.

The devil shall have his bargain; for he was never yet a breaker of proverbs —he will give the devil his due.—Shakespeare.

Devotion

Devotion, like fire, goeth upward. —Zoroaster.

Complete self-devotion is woman's part.—Macaulay.

A woman whom we truly love is a religion.—Mme. de Girardin.

All is holy where devotion kneels.—Holmes.

Devotion's self shall steal a thought from heaven.—Pope.

That fabric rises high as heaven whose basis on devotion stands.—Prior.

Many waters cannot quench love, neither can the floods drown it.—Bible.

Like Dian's kiss, unasked, unsought, love gives itself, but is not bought.—Longfellow.

Thy love to me was wonderful, passing the love of woman.—Bible.

One grain of incense with devotion offer'd 'S beyond all perfumes of Sabæan spices.
—Massinger.

Love without reverence and enthusiasm is only friendship.—George Sand.

Oh, only those whose souls have felt this one idolatry can tell how precious is the slightest thing affection gives and hallows.—L. E. Landon.

Real inward devotion knows no prayer but that arising from the depths of its own feelings.—Humboldt.

To feel, to love, to suffer, to devote herself, will always be the text of the life of woman.—Balzac.

Those who make use of devotion as a means and end generally are hypocrites.—Goethe.

The life of a devotee is a crusade of which the heart is the Holy Land.—Alfred de Musset.

The woman who has too easily and ardently yielded her devotion will find that its vitality, like a bright fire, soon consumes itself.—Rivarol.

Man may content himself with the applause of the world and the homage paid to his intellect, but woman's heart has holier idols.—George Eliot.

The perfect disinterestedness and self-devotion of which men seem incapable, but which is sometimes found in women.—Macaulay.

Devotion, when it does not lie under the check of reason, is apt to degenerate into enthusiasm.—Addison.

Seeming devotion does but gild a knave,
That's neither faithful, honest, just, nor brave;
But where religion does with virtue join,
It makes a hero like an angel shine.
—Waller.

As down in the sunless retreats of the ocean
Sweet flowers are springing no mortal can see,
So deep in my soul the still prayer of devotion
Unheard by the world, rises silent to Thee.
—Moore.

The secret heart is fair devotion's temple; there the saint, even on that living altar, lights the flame of purest sacrifice, which burns unseen, not unaccepted.—Hannah More.

Devotion is like the candle which Michael Angelo used to take in his pasteboard cap, so as not to throw his shadow upon the work in which he was engaged.—Phillips Brooks.

Love is not love which alters when it alteration finds; love alters not with his brief hours and weeks, but bears it out even to the edge of doom.—Shakespeare.

All who wait upon the Lord shall rise higher and higher upon the mighty pinions of strong devotion, and with the unblinking eye of faith, into the regions of heavenly-mindedness, and shall approach nearer and nearer to God, the Sun of our spiritual day.—John Angel James.

The best part of a woman's love is worship; but it is hard to her to be sent away with her precious spikenard rejected, and her long tresses, too, that were let fall, ready to soothe the wearied feet.—George Eliot.

Private devotions and secret offices of religion are like the refreshing of a garden with the distilling and petty drops of a water-pot; but addressed from the temple are like rain from heaven.—Jeremy Taylor.

I find no quality so easy for a man to counterfeit as devotion, though his life and manner are not conformable to it; the essence of it is abstruse and occult, but the appearances easy and showy.—Montaigne.

The days of chivalry are not gone, notwithstanding Burke's grand dirge over them; they live still in that far-off worship paid by many a youth and man to the woman of whom he never dreams that he shall touch so much as her little finger, or the hem of her robe.—George Eliot.

There are other books in a man's library besides Ovid, and after dawdling ever so long at a woman's knee, one day he gets up and is free. We have all been there; we have all had the fever—the strongest and the smallest, from Samson, Hercules, Rinaldo, downward: but it burns out, and you get well.—Thackeray.

Devout

To worship rightly is to love each other, each smile a hymn, each kindly deed a prayer.—Whittier.

Some persons are so devotional they have not one bit of true religion in them.—B. R. Haydon.

There is a divine depth in silence. We meet God alone.—F. W. Robertson.

"Draw nigh to God, and He will draw nigh to you." Keep near to the fountain-head and "with joy shall ye draw water out of the wells of salvation."—Gardiner Spring.

The inward sighs of humble penitence rise to the ear of heaven, when pealèd hymns are scattered with the sounds of common air.—Joanna Baillie.

This is the spirit of prayer—sincere, humble, believing, submissive. Other prayer than this the Bible does not require—God will not accept.—Gardiner Spring.

Other hope had she none, nor wish in life,
but to follow
Meekly, with reverent steps, the sacred feet of her Saviour. —Longfellow.

The Christian life is a long and continual tendency of our hearts towards that eternal goodness which we desire upon earth.—Fénelon.

It is not he who knows most, nor he who hears most, nor yet he who talks most, but he who exercises grace most, who has most communion with God.—Thomas Brooks.

The hand is rais'd, the pledge is given,
One monarch to obey, one creed to own,
That monarch, God; that creed, His word alone. —Sprague.

The Christian is not always praying; but within his bosom is a heaven-kindled love—fires of desire, fervent longings—which make him always ready to pray, and often engage him in prayer.—Thomas Guthrie.

Our activity should consist in placing ourselves in a state of susceptibility to Divine impressions, and pliability to all the operations of the Eternal Word.—Madame Guyon.

The inward sighs of humble penitence
Rise to the ear of Heaven, when peal'd
  hymns .
Are scatter'd with the sounds of common
  air.   —Joanna Baillie.

Like earth, awake, and warm, and bright
  With joy the spirit moves and burns;
So up to thee! O Fount of Light!
  Our light returns.   —John Sterling.

He who receives a sacrament does
not perform a good work; he receives
a benefit. In the mass we give Christ
nothing; we only receive from Him.—
Luther.

Thou, when thou prayest, enter into
thy closet, and when thou hast shut
the door pray to thy Father, which
is in secret; and thy Father, which
seeth in secret, shall reward thee openly.—Bible.

That holy, humble, meek, modest,
retiring Form, sometimes called the
Spirit of Prayer, has been dragged
from the closet, and so rudely handled
by some of her professed friends that
she has not only lost all her wonted
loveliness, but is now stalking the
street, in some places, stark mad.—
Nettleton.

Only in the sacredness of inward
silence does the soul truly meet the
secret, hiding God. The strength of
resolve, which afterward shapes life,
and mixes itself with action, is the
fruit of those sacred, solitary moments.
There is a divine depth in silence.
We meet God alone.—F. W. Robertson.

The Christian life is a long and
continual tendency of our hearts
toward that eternal goodness which
we desire on earth. All our happiness
consists in thirsting for it. Now this
thirst is prayer. Ever desire to approach your Creator, and you will
never cease to pray. Do not think it
necessary to pronounce many words.—
Fénelon.

There are two principal points of
attention necessary for the preservation of this constant spirit of prayer
which unites us with God; we must
continually seek to cherish it, and we

must avoid everything that tends to
make us lose it.—Fénelon.

Dew
Earth's liquid jewelry, wrought of
air.—Bailey.

Dew depends not on Parliament.—
James Otis.

None can give us dew but God.—
Bishop Reynolds.

The dew-bead gem, of earth and sky
begotten.—George Eliot.

Liquid pearl.—Shakespeare.

And every dew-drop paints a bow.—
Tennyson.

The dew waits for no voice to call
it to the sun.—Rev. Joseph Parker.

As fresh as morning dew distill'd
on flowers.—Shakespeare.

Every dew-drop and rain-drop had a
whole heaven within it.—Longfellow.

Gems which adorn the beauteous
tresses of the weeping morn.—Poole.

Dew-drops are the gems of morning
but the tears of mournful eve!—Coleridge.

Those tears of the sky for the loss of
the sun.—Chesterfield.

I must go seek some dew-drops here,
And hang a pearl in every cowslip's ear.
           —Shakespeare.

'Tis of the tears which stars weep,
sweet with joy.—Bailey.

Or stars of morning, dew-drops which the
  sun
Impearls on every leaf and every flower.
           —Milton.

The starlight dews all silently their
tears of love instill.—Byron.

Hushed as the falling dews, whose
noiseless showers impearl the folded
leaves of evening flowers.—Congreve.

That same dew, which sometime on
the buds was wont to swell, like round

and orient pearls, stood now within
the pretty flowerets' eyes, like tears
that did their own disgrace bewail.—
Shakespeare.

Within the rose I found a trembling tear,
Close curtained in a gloom of crimson night
By tender petals from the outer light.
—Boyesen.

The dew-drop in the breeze of morn,
Trembling and sparkling on the thorn,
Falls to the ground, escapes the eye,
Yet mounts on sunbeams to the sky.
—Montgomery.

Dew-drops, Nature's tears, which she
Sheds in her own breast for the fair which
die.
The sun insists on gladness; but at night,
When he is gone, poor Nature loves to weep.
—Bailey.

See how the orient dew
Shed from the bosom of the morn
Into the blowing roses
(Yet careless of its mansion new
For the clear region where 'twas born)
Round in itself incloses,
And in its little globe's extent
Frames, as it can, its native element.
—Andrew Marvell.

A globe of dew
Filling, in the morning new,
Some eyed flower, whose young leaves
waken
On an unimagined world;
Constellated suns unshaken,
Orbits measureless are furl'd
In that frail and fading sphere,
With ten millions gathered there
To tremble, gleam and disappear.
—Shelley.

There is dew in one flower and not
in another, because one opens its cup
and takes it in, while the other closes
itself and the drop runs off. So God
rains goodness and mercy as wide as
the dew, and if we lack them, it is because we do not open our hearts to receive them.—Aughey.

Diary

A man's diary is a record in youth
of his sentiments, in middle age of his
actions, in old age of his reflections.
—J. Q. Adams.

Diet

Things sweet to taste prove in digestion sour.—Shakespeare.

Simple diet is best.—Pliny.

Unquiet meals make ill digestion.—
Shakespeare.

Many dishes bring many diseases.—
Pliny.

One meal a day is enough for a
lion, and it ought to suffice for a man.
—Dr. George Fordyce.

Now, good digestion wait on appetite,
And health on both! —Shakespeare.

A fig for your bill of fare; show me
your bill of company.—Swift.

Free-livers on a small scale, who are
prodigal within the compass of a
guinea.—Washington Irving.

It was Dean Swift who ignored the
bill of fare, and asked for a bill of the
company.—N. P. Willis.

In general, mankind, since the improvement of cookery, eat about twice
as much as nature requires.—Franklin.

The chief pleasure (in eating) does
not consist in costly seasoning or exquisite flavor, but in yourself. Do
you seek for sauce by sweating.—
Horace.

A chine of honest bacon would please
my appetite more than all the marrow-
puddings, for I like them better plain,
having a very vulgar stomach.—
Dryden.

If thou wouldst preserve a sound
body, use fasting and walking; if a
healthful soul, fasting and praying;
walking exercises the body, praying
exercises the soul, fasting cleanses
both.—Quarles.

Food, improperly taken, not only
produces original diseases, but affords
those that are already engendered both
matter and sustenance; so that, let the
father of disease be what it may, In-

temperance is certainly its mother.—Burton.

Your worm is your only emperor for diet; we fat all creatures else to fat us, and we fat ourselves for maggots.—Shakespeare.

All courageous animals are carnivorous, and greater courage is to be expected in a people, such as the English, whose food is strong and hearty, than in the half starved commonalty of other countries.—Sir W. Temple.

Difficulties

Out of difficulties grow miracles.—Bruyère.

It is difficulties which give birth to miracles.—Rev. Dr. Sharpe.

How strangely easy difficult things are!—Charles Buxton.

Difficulties strengthen the mind, as well as labor does the body.—Seneca.

Many things difficult to design prove easy to performance.—Sam'l Johnson.

To bear adversity with an equal mind is both the sign and glory of a brave spirit.—Quarles.

It is the surmounting of difficulties that makes heroes.—Kossuth.

There is such a choice of difficulties, that I own myself at a loss how to determine.—James.

The illustration which solves one difficulty by raising another, settles nothing.—Horace.

There are few difficulties that hold out against real attacks; they fly, like the visible horizon, before those who advance.

Wisdom is not found with those who dwell at their ease; rather nature, when she adds brain, adds difficulty.—Emerson.

The greatest difficulties lie where we are not looking for them.—Goethe.

It is as hard to come, as for a camel to thread the postern of a needle's eye.—Shakespeare.

Difficulties, by bracing the mind to overcome them, assist cheerfulness, as exercise assists digestion.—Bovee.

Every noble acquisition is attended with its risks; he who fears to encounter the one must not expect to obtain the other.—Metastasio.

The three things most difficult are—to keep a secret, to forget an injury, and to make good use of leisure.—Chilo.

Difficulty excites the mind to the dignity which sustains and finally conquers misfortunes, and the ordeal refines while it chastens.—Aughey.

There is no merit where there is no trial; and, till experience stamps the mark of strength, cowards may pass for heroes, faith for falsehood.—Aaron Hill.

Fortune is the best school of courage when she is fraught with anger, in the same way as winds and tempests are the school of the sailorboy.—Metastasio.

Difficulties are God's errands; and when we are sent upon them we should esteem it a proof of God's confidence—as a compliment from God.—Beecher.

What is difficulty? Only a word indicating the degree of strength requisite for accomplishing particular objects; a mere notice of the necessity for exertion; a bugbear to children and fools; only a mere stimulus to men.—Samuel Warren.

The more powerful the obstacle, the more glory we have in overcoming it; and the difficulties with which we are met are the maids of honor which set off virtue.—Molière.

Accustom yourself to master and overcome things of difficulty; for if you observe, the left hand for want of practice is insignificant, and not adapted to general business; yet it holds the bridle better than the right, from constant use.—Pliny.

Our energy is in proportion to the resistance it meets. We can attempt nothing great but from a sense of the difficulties we have to encounter; we can persevere in nothing great but from a pride in overcoming them.—Hazlitt.

Difficulty is a severe instructor, set over us by the supreme ordinance of a paternal guardian and legislator, who knows us better than we know ourselves, as He loves us better too. He that wrestles with us strengthens our nerves and sharpens our skill. Our antagonist is our helper.—Burke.

The wise and active conquer difficulties
By daring to attempt them; sloth and folly
Shiver and shrink at sight of toil and hazard,
And make the impossibility they fear.
—Rowe.

Hath fortune dealt thee ill cards? let wisdom make thee a good gamester. In a fair gale, every fool may sail, but wise behavior in a storm commends the wisdom of a pilot; to bear adversity with an equal mind is both the sign and glory of a brave spirit.—Quarles.

Difficulties are things that show what men are. In case of any difficulty remember that God, like a gymnastic trainer, has pitted you against a rough antagonist. For what end? That you may be an Olympic conqueror, and this cannot be without toil.—Epictetus.

It is not every calamity that is a curse, and early adversity is often a blessing. Perhaps Madame de Maintenon would never have mounted a throne had not her cradle been rocked in a prison. Surmounted obstacles not only teach, but hearten us in our future struggles; for virtue must be learnt, though, unfortunately, some of the vices come as it were by inspiration.—Rev. Dr. Sharpe.

Diffidence

Diffidence is a sort of false modesty.—Thackeray.

Diffidence is not always innocence.—Mme. Necker.

Mere bashfulness without merit is awkward.—Thomas Hughes.

We are as often duped by diffidence as by confidence.—Chesterfield.

Persons extremely reserved are like old enamelled watches, which had painted covers, that hindered your seeing what o'clock it was.—Walpole.

A tardiness in nature,
Which often leaves the history unspoke,
That it intends to do. —Shakespeare.

Diffidence may check resolution and obstruct performance, but compensates its embarrassments by more important advantages; it conciliates the proud, and softens the severe; averts envy from excellence, and censure from miscarriage.—Johnson.

Dignity

Ease with dignity.—Cicero.

Dignity and love do not blend.—Mme. Necker.

All celebrated people lose on a close view.—Napoleon I.

There is even the dignity of vice.—Rivarol.

Dignity increases more easily than it begins.—Seneca.

Dignity and love were never yet boon companions.—Fielding.

Dignity consists not in possessing honors, but in deserving them.—Aristotle.

Dignity and love do not blend well, nor do they continue long together.—Ovid.

Dignity of manner always conveys a sense of reserved force.—Alcott.

Let none presume to wear an undeserved dignity.—Shakespeare.

As vivacity is the gift of woman, gravity is that of man.—Addison.

There is a healthful hardiness about real dignity that never dreads contact and communion with others, however humble.—Washington Irving.

Grace was in all her steps, heaven in her eye,
In every gesture dignity and love.
—Milton.

True dignity is never gained by place,
And never lost when honours are withdrawn. —Massinger.

A fit of anger is as fatal to dignity as a dose of arsenic to life.—J. G. Holland.

The nearer we approach great men, the clearer we see that they are men.—Bruyère.

Clay and clay differs in dignity, whose dust is both alike.—Shakespeare.

Dignity is often a veil between us and the real truth of things.—Whipple.

It is of very little use in trying to be dignified, if dignity is no part of your character.—Bovee.

She is calm because she is the mistress of her subject,—the secret of self-possession.—Beaconsfield.

The dignity of truth is lost with much protesting.—Ben Jonson.

True dignity is his whose tranquil mind virtue has raised above the things below.—Beattie.

In order that she may be able to give her hand with dignity, she must be able to stand alone.—Margaret Fuller Ossoli.

Remember this,—that there is a proper dignity and proportion to be observed in the performance of every act of life.—Marcus Aurelius.

She hath a natural, wise sincerity, a simple truthfulness; and these have lent her a dignity as moveless as the centre.—Lowell.

Men possessing minds which are morose, solemn, and inflexible enjoy generally a greater share of dignity than of happiness.—Bacon.

It is at once the thinnest and most effective of all the coverings under which duncedom sneaks and skulks.—Whipple.

We have exchanged the Washingtonian dignity for the Jeffersonian simplicity, which was in truth only another name for the Jeffersonian vulgarity.—Bishop Henry C. Potter.

Dignity of position adds to dignity of character, as well as to dignity of carriage. Give us a proud position, and we are impelled to act up to it.—Bovee.

True dignity abides with him alone who, in the silent hour of inward thought, can still suspect and still revere himself in lowliness of heart.—Wordsworth.

The dignity of man into your hands is given;
Oh, keep it well, with you it sinks or lifts itself to heaven. —Schiller.

True dignity is his whose tranquil mind
Virtue has raised above the things below;
Who, every hope and fear to heaven resign'd
Shrinks not, though fortune aims her deadliest blow. —Beattie.

With grave
Aspect he rose, and in his rising seem'd
A pillar of state; deep on his front engraven
Deliberation sat, and public care;
And princely counsel in his face yet shone
Majestic, though in ruin. Sage he stood,
With Atlantean shoulders, fit to bear
The weight of mightiest monarchies; his look
Drew audience and attention still as night
Or summer's noontide air. —Milton.

Lord Chatham and Napoleon were as much actors as Garrick or Talma. Now, an imposing air should always be taken as evidence of imposition. Dignity is often a veil between us and the real truth of things.—Whipple.

Digression

Digressions incontestibly are the sunshine; they are the life, the soul of reading.—Sterne.

Diligence

Diligence is the mother of good fortune.—Cervantes.

Diligence, above all, is the mother of good luck.—Samuel Smiles.

Who makes quick use of the moment, is a genius of prudence.—Lavater.

That which ordinary men are fit for, I am qualified in; and the best of me is diligence.—Shakespeare.

What we hope ever to do with ease we may learn first to do with diligence.—Johnson.

It is want of diligence rather than want of means that causes most failures.—Alfred Mercier.

Prefer diligence before idleness, unless you esteem rust above brightness. —Plato.

The more the marble wastes, the more the statue grows.—Michael Angelo.

The expectations of life depend upon diligence; and the mechanic that would perfect his work, must first sharpen his tools.—Confucius.

Like clocks, one wheel another on must drive,
Affairs by diligent labors only thrive.
    —Chapman.

To be rich be diligent; move on
Like heav'ns great movers that enrich the earth;
Whose moment's sloth would show the world undone;
And make the spring straight bury all her birth.
Rich are the diligent who can command
Time—nature's stock.   —Davenant.

As he that lives longest lives but a little while, every man may be certain that he has no time to waste. The duties of life are commensurate to its duration; and every day brings its task, which, if neglected, is doubled on the morrow.—Dr. Johnson.

Diligence is the mother of good luck, and God gives all things to industry. Then plough deep while sluggards sleep, and you shall have corn to sell and to keep.—Benjamin Franklin.

Diligence which, as it avails in all things, is also of the utmost moment in pleading causes. Diligence is to be particularly cultivated by us; it is to be constantly exerted; it is capable of effecting almost everything.—Cicero.

Dimples

Then did she lift her hands unto his chin,
And praise the pretty dimpling of his skin.
    —Beaumont.

In each cheek appears a pretty dimple;
Love made those hollows; if himself were slain
He might be buried in a tomb so simple;
Foreknowing well, if there he came to lie,
Why, there Love lived, and there he could not die.   —Shakespeare.

Dinner — Dining

The tocsin of the soul—the dinner bell!—Byron.

He fell upon whate'er was offer'd, like
A priest, a shark, an alderman, or pike.
    —Byron.

When dinner has oppress'd one,
I think it is perhaps the gloomiest hour
Which turns up out of the sad twenty-four.
    —Byron.

Their various cares in one great point combine
The business of their lives, that is—to dine.
    —Young.

All human history attests
That happiness for man—the hungry sinner—
Since Eve ate apples, much depends on dinner!
    —Byron.

'Twas a public feast and public day—
Quite full, right dull, guests hot, and dishes cold,
Great plenty, much formality, small cheer,
And everybody out of their own sphere.
    —Byron.

A good dinner sharpens wit, while it softens the heart.—Doran.

Before dinner men meet with great inequality of understanding; and those who are conscious of their inferiority have the modesty not to talk; when they have drunk wine, every man feels himself happy, and loses that modesty, and grows impudent and vociferous; but he is not improved; he is only not sensible of his defects.—Johnson.

Dirt

Dirt is not dirt, but only something in the wrong place.—Lord Palmerston.

Dirt has been shrewdly termed "misplaced material."—Victor Hugo.

By those who look close to the ground dirt will be seen. I hope I see things from a greater distance.— Dr. Johnson.

I confess I could never see any good reason why dirt should always be a necessary concomitant of poverty.— W. G. Clark.

In Nature there is no dirt, everything is in the right condition; the swamp and the worm, as well as the grass and the bird,—all is there for itself. Only because we think that all things have a relation to us, do they appear justifiable or otherwise.—Auerbach.

"Ignorance," says Ajax, "is a painless evil"; so, I should think, is dirt, considering the merry faces that go along with it.—George Eliot.

Disappointment

Disappointment is the nurse of wisdom.—Sir Bayle Roche.

Disappointment is often the salt of life.—Theodore Parker.

O world, how many hopes thou dost engulf!—Alfred de Musset.

Bearing a life-long hunger in his heart.—Tennyson.

Thus ever fade my fairy dreams of bliss.—Byron.

How Disappointment tracks the steps of Hope!—L. E. Landon.

Disappointments are to the soul what a thunder-storm is to the air.— Schiller.

Oh! that a dream so sweet, so long enjoy'd, Should be so sadly, cruelly destroy'd!
—Moore.

As distant prospects please us, but when near
We find but desert rocks and fleeting air.
—Sir Sam'l Garth.

His early dreams of good outstripp'd the truth,
And troubled manhood follow'd baffled youth.
—Byron.

Life is as tedious as a twice-told tale, vexing the dull ear of a drowsy man.—Shakespeare.

Women suffer more from disappointment than men, because they have more of faith and are naturally more credulous.—Marguerite de Valois.

Of all the uses of adversity which are sweet, none are sweeter than those which grow out of disappointed love.—Henry Taylor.

Disappointment to a noble soul is what cold water is to burning metal; it strengthens, tempers, intensifies, but never destroys it.—Eliza Tabor.

Life often seems like a long shipwreck, of which the debris are friendship, glory, and love; the shores of existence are strewn with them.— Mme. de Staël.

Man must be disappointed with the lesser things of life before he can comprehend the full value of the greater.—Bulwer-Lytton.

Oft expectation fails, and most oft there where it most promises; and oft it hits where hope is coldest, and despair most sits.—Shakespeare.

We mount to heaven mostly on the ruins of our cherished schemes, finding our failures were successes.—Alcott.

Mean spirits under disappointment, like small beer in a thunder-storm, always turn sour.—Randolph.

When we meet with better fare than was expected, the disappointment is overlooked even by the scrupulous. When we meet with worse than was expected, philosophers alone know how to make it better.—Zimmermann.

Impell'd with steps unceasing to pursue
Some fleeting good, that mocks me with the view,
That, like the circle bounding earth and skies,
Allures from far, yet, as I follow, flies.
—Goldsmith.

A thousand years a poor man watched
Before the gate of Paradise:
But while one little nap he snatched,
It oped and shut. Ah! was he wise?
—Wm. R. Alger.

It never yet happened to any man since the beginning of the world, nor ever will, to have all things according to his desire, or to whom fortune was never opposite and adverse.—Burton.

In the light of eternity we shall see that what we desired would have been fatal to us, and that what we would have avoided was essential to our well-being.—Fénelon.

The best-laid schemes o' mice and men,
Gang aft a-gley,
And leave us nought but grief and pain,
For promised joy. —Burns.

O! ever thus from childhood's hour,
I've seen my fondest hopes decay;
I never loved a tree or flower,
But 'twas the first to fade away!
—Moore.

Out of the same substances one stomach will extract nutriment, another poison; and so the same disappointments in life will chasten and refine one man's spirit, and embitter another's.—Wm. Matthews.

It is generally known that he who expects much will be often disappointed; yet disappointment seldom cures us of expectation, or has any other effect than that of producing a moral sentence or peevish exclamation.—Johnson.

He that will do no good offices after a disappointment must stand still, and do just nothing at all. The plough goes on after a barren year; and while the ashes are yet warm, we raise a new house upon the ruins of a former.—Seneca.

It is sometimes of God's mercy that men in the eager pursuit of worldly aggrandizement are baffled; for they are very like a train going down an inclined plane,—putting on the brake is not pleasant, but it keeps the car on the track.—Beecher.

An old man once said, "When I was young I was poor; when old I became rich; but in each condition I found disappointment. When the faculties of enjoyment were, I had not the means; when the means came, the faculties were gone."—Madame de Gasparin.

It is folly to pretend that one ever wholly recovers from a disappointed passion. Such wounds always leave a scar. There are faces I can never look upon without emotion, there are names I can never hear spoken without almost starting.—Longfellow.

Full little knowest thou that hast not tried,
What hell it is in suing long to bide:
To loose good dayes, that might be better spent;
To waste long nights in pensive discontent;
To speed to-day, to be put back to-morrow;
To feed on hope, to pine with feare and sorrow. —Spenser.

Young ladies may have been crossed in love, and have had their sufferings, their frantic moments of grief and tears, their wakeful nights, and so forth: but it is only in very sentimental novels that people occupy themselves perpetually with that passion, and I believe what are called broken hearts are a very rare article indeed.—Thackeray.

The darling schemes and fondest hopes of man are frequently frustrated by time. While sagacity contrives, patience matures, and labor industriously executes, disappointment laughs at the curious fabric, formed by so many efforts, and gay with so many brilliant colors, and, while the artists imagin the work arrived at the moment of completion, brushes away the beautiful web, and leaves nothing behind.—Dwight.

Welcome, Disappointment! Thy hand is cold and hard, but it is the hand of a friend. Thy voice is stern and harsh, but it is the voice of a friend. Oh, there is something sublime in calm endurance, something sublime in the resolute, fixed purpose of suffering without complaining, which makes disappointment oftentimes better than success!—Longfellow.

Disaster

Disasters teach us humility.—St. Anselm.

Defeat may be victory in disguise. —Longfellow.

The cruelest foe is a masked benefactor. The wars which make history so dreary have served the cause of truth and virtue.—Emerson.

It is in periods of apparent disaster, during the sufferings of whole generations, that the greatest improvement in human character has been effected. —Sir A. Alison.

When the foot of the mountain is enveloped in mist, the mountain appears to us much loftier than it is; so also when the ground and basis of a disaster is not clear to us.—Auerbach.

Discernment

Lynx-eyed toward our equals, and moles to ourselves.—La Fontaine.

Good men can more easily see through bad men than the latter can the former.—Jean Paul Richter.

The rarest things in world, next to a spirit of discernment, are diamonds and pearls.—La Bruyère.

There seems to be no part of knowledge in fewer hands than that of discerning when to have done.—Swift.

Discernment is a power of the understanding in which few excel. Is not that owing to its connection with impartiality and truth? for are not prejudice and partiality blind?—Greville.

If you give me six lines written by the hand of the most honest of men, I will find something in them which will hang him.—Richelieu.

To succeed in the world, it is much more necessary to possess the penetration to discern who is a fool than to discover who is a clever man.—Talleyrand.

The idiot, the Indian, the child, and unschooled farmer's boy stand nearer to the light by which nature is to be read, than the dissector or the antiquary.—Emerson.

Simple creatures, whose thoughts are not taken up, like those of educated people, with the care of a great museum of dead phrases, are very quick to see the live facts which are going on about them.—Holmes.

Discipline

It is never wise to slip the bands of discipline.—Lew Wallace.

A stern discipline pervades all nature, which is a little cruel that it may be very kind.—Spenser.

No pain, no palm; no thorns, no throne; no gall, no glory; no cross, no crown.—William Penn.

No evil propensity of the human heart is so powerful that it may not be subdued by discipline.—Seneca.

Train up a child in the way he should go; and when he is old he will not depart from it.—Bible.

We have all to be laid upon an altar; we have all, as it were, to be subjected to the action of fire.—G. J. W. Melville.

The strength one can eke from little, who knows till he has been subjected to the trial?—Lew Wallace.

Has it never occurred to us, when surrounded by sorrows, that they may be sent to us only for our instruction, as we darken the cages of birds when we wish to teach them to sing.—Richter.

He that hath wife and children hath given hostages to fortune, for they are impediments to great enterprises, either of virtue or mischief. * * * Certainly wife and children are a kind of discipline of humanity.—Bacon.

A dull axe never loves grindstones, but a keen workman does; and he puts his tool on them in order that it may be sharp. And men do not like grinding; but they are dull for the purposes which God designs to work out with them, and therefore He is grinding them.—Beecher.

The heart must be divorced from its idols. Age does a great deal in curing the man of his frenzy; but if God has a special work for a man, he takes a shorter and sharper course with him. This grievous loss is only a further and more expensive education for the work of the ministry; it is but saying more closely, "Will you pay the price?"—Cecil.

Discipline, like the bridle in the hand of a good rider, should exercise its influence without appearing to do so; should be ever active, both as a support and as a restraint, yet seem to lie easily in hand. It must always be ready to check or to pull up, as occasion may require; and only when the horse is a runaway should the action of the curb be perceptible.

Discontent

What is more miserable than discontent?—Shakespeare.

Men would be angels; angels would be gods.—Pope.

Discontent is the want of self-reliance: it is infirmity of will.—Emerson.

We love in others what we lack ourselves, and would be everything but what we are.—R. H. Stoddard.

O thoughts of men accurst! Past and to come seems best; things present, worst.—Shakespeare.

The lazy ox wishes for horse-trappings, and the steed wishes to plough. —Horace.

'T is not my talent to conceal my thoughts, or carry smiles and sunshine in my face when discontent sits heavy at my heart.—Addison.

Discontent is the source of all trouble, but also of all progress in individuals and in nations.—Auerbach.

That which makes people dissatisfied with their condition is the chimerical idea they form of the happiness of others.—Thomson.

It happens as with cages; the birds without despair to get in, and those within despair of getting out.—Montaigne.

Man hath a weary pilgrimage,
 As through the world he wends;
On every stage, from youth to age,
 Still discontent attends. —Southey.

Such is the emptiness of human enjoyment that we are always impatient of the present. Attainment is followed by neglect, and possession by disgust.—Dr. Johnson.

How does it happen, Mæcenas, that no one is content with that lot in life which he has chosen, or which chance has thrown in his way, but praises those who follow a different course?—Horace.

There's discontent from sceptre to the swain
And from the peasant to the king again,
The whatsoever in thy will afflict thee,
Or in thy pleasure seem to contradict thee,
Give it a welcome as a wholesome friend
That would instruct thee to a better end.
Since no condition from defect is free,
Think not to find what here can never be.
   —Nicholes.

Discontents are sometimes the better part of our life. I know not well which is the most useful; joy I may choose for pleasure, but adversities are the best for profit; and sometimes those do so far help me, as I should, without them, want much of the joy I have.—Feltham.

It's hardly in a body's power
To keep at times, frae being sour,
To see how things are shar'd;
How best o' chiels are whyles in want,
While coofs on countless thousands rant,
And ken na how to wear't. —Burns.

Against our peace we arm our will;
Amidst our plenty something still,
For horses, houses, pictures planting,
To thee, to me, to him is wanting;
That cruel something unpossest
Corrodes and leavens all the rest,
That something if we could obtain,
Would soon create a future pain.
     —Prior.

The malcontent is neither well, full nor fasting; and though he abounds with complaints, yet nothing dislikes him but the present; for what he condemns while it was, once passed, he magnifies and strives to recall it out of the jaw of time. What he hath he seeth not, his eyes are so taken up with what he wants; and what he sees he careth not for, because he cares so much for that which is not.—Bishop Hall.

Men are merely on a lower or higher stage of an eminence, whose summit is God's throne, infinitely above all; and there is just as much reason for the wisest as for the simplest man being discontent with his position, as respects the real quantity of knowledge he possesses.—Ruskin.

Discord

A modicum of discord is the very spice of courtship.—Chamfort.

Discord oft in music makes the sweeter lay.—Spenser.

Untimely conduct is the discord of manners.—Mme. Louise Colet.

How sour sweet music is,
When time is broke, and no proportion kept!
     —Shakespeare.

Unity, agreement, is always silent or soft-voiced; it is only discord that loudly proclaims itself.—Carlyle.

Our life is full of discord; but by forbearance and virtue this same discord can be turned to harmony.—James Ellis.

From hence, let fierce contending nations know
What dire effects from civil discord flow.
     —Addison.

Discord, a sleepless hag, who never dies,
With snipe-like nose and ferret-glowing eyes
Lean sallow cheeks, long chin, with beard supplied,
Poor crackling joints, and wither'd parchment hide,
As if old drums, worn out with martial din,
Had clubb'd their yellow heads to form her skin. —Peter Pindar.

The peacemakers shall be called the sons of God, who came to make peace between God and man. What then shall the sowers of discord be called, but the children of the devil? And what must they look for but their father's portion?—St. Bernard.

Discoveries

A new principle is an inexhaustible source of new views.—Vauvenargues.

All great discoveries are made by men whose feelings run ahead of their thinkings.—Charles H. Parkhurst.

Obedience does not stop for mystery, but, going on, sees twilight brighten into day. How can wheat and corn become energy to think, and love, and work? Who can tell, but who can doubt? When we obey God's laws, it is as if an angel troubled the water, and instantly life and power emerge. Loyalty discovers. It is not merely the illumination, but the transfiguration of life; a brave departure, and then a discovery; "Westward-ho," and then a new world.

It is a mortifying truth, and ought to teach the wisest of us humility, that many of the most valuable discoveries have been the result of chance, rather than of contemplation, and of accident, rather than of design.—Colton.

Discovery Day

The spirit of Columbus hovers over us to-day.—Chauncey Depew.

The Old World owes scarcely less to Columbus than the New.—Rev. W. W. Wilson.

Every man has in himself a continent of undiscovered character. Happy is he who acts the Columbus to his own soul.—Theo. L. Cuyler, D. D.

And he went out not knowing whither he went.—Bible.

I will command your fleet and discover for you new realms.—Columbus.

Neither realism nor romance furnishes a more striking and picturesque figure than that of Christopher Columbus. The mystery about his origin heightens the charm of his story.—Chauncey Depew.

It was for Columbus, when the right hour struck, forced and propelled by this fresh life, to reveal the land where these new principles were to be brought, and where the awaited trial of the new civilization was to be made.—Chauncey Depew.

The tomb of the Saviour was a narrow and empty vault, precious only for its memories of the supreme tragedy of the centuries, but the new continent was to be the home and temple of the living God.—Chauncey Depew.

Columbus stood in his age as the pioneer of progress and achievement. The system of universal education is in our age the most prominent and salutary feature of the spirit of enlightenment, and it is peculiarly appropriate that the schools be made by the people the center of the day's demonstration, Let the national flag float over every school-house in the country, and the exercises be such as shall impress upon our youth the patriotic duties of American citizenship.—Benjamin Harrison.

England of late has been the elect nation, but now the star of empire is passing westward to this land. There is no question but that now and in the future this land is to be the elect nation under God for solving the problems of liberty, of the amelioration of mankind, and of the best Christian civilization.—Rev. M. M. Smith.

If we claim heritage in Bacon, Shakespeare and Milton, we also acknowledge that it was for liberties guaranteed Englishmen by sacred charters our fathers triumphantly fought. While wisely rejecting throne and caste and privilege and an Established Church in their new-born state, they adopted the substance of English liberty and the body of English law. —Chauncey Depew.

A great revolution has happened— a revolution made, not by chopping and changing of power in any of the existing states, but by the appearance of a new species, in a new part of the globe. It has made as great a change in all the relations and balances and gravitations of power as the appearance of a new planet would in the system of the solar world.—Burke.

Columbus was an Abraham, for he went out not knowing whither he went. Columbus was a Moses, for he endured as seeing Him who is invisible. Only the man of faith is the man of power. Only he who can see the invisible can do the impossible. God grant that to-day in that bark we may be wafted by God's blessing, and may land at last on the shores of Heaven, where we shall sing a sweeter Te Deum than that which awoke the echoes on the soil of virgin America, or those amid the splendors of the court at Barcelona.—Rev. R. S. Mac-Arthur.

He, too, went out not knowing whither he went, and he never fully knew; he died under an utter misapprehension of the nature of the country he had visited and of the character of the discoveries he had made. He, too, realized the necessity of great faith, and of divine guidance. God went before Abraham, and before even Columbus, altho he was a very imperfect man, as truly as when by the pillar of cloud by day, and the pillar of fire by night, He went before the children of Israel on their weary march.—Rev. R. S. MacArthur, D. D.

Till the English-speaking and God-fearing colonists came there were none who dwelt on this continent who had thoughts worth keeping alive in the world. If all the ideas our forerunners had were utterly dropped out of history men would not miss them. These people lived after a fashion, but what did they stand for? What principles, what causes were incarnate in them? People who only live must die the death. It is Heaven's law.—Bishop Haygood.

Columbus died in utter ignorance of the true nature of his discovery. He supposed he had found India, but never knew how strangely God had used him. So God piloted the fleet. The great discoverer, with all his heroic virtues, did not know whither he went. "He sailed for the back door of Asia, and landed at the front door of America, and knew it not." He never settled the continent. Thus far and no farther, said the Lord. His providence was over all.—Rev. L. J. Burrill, D. D.

From the discovery of the New World, the mercantile spirit has been rapidly gaining upon its old antagonist; and the establishment upon these shores of our Republic, whose union was the immediate result of commercial necessities, whose independence found its original impulse in commercial oppression, and of whose Constitution the regulation of commerce was the first leading idea, may be regarded as the epoch at which the martial spirit finally lost its supremacy, which, it is believed and trusted, it can never again acquire.—Robert C. Winthrop.

His perseverance never failed; when rejected at Genoa, rejected at Venice, rejected in Portugal, delayed in England and delayed in Spain, he still persevered, amid all the trials of his immortal voyage until on the morning of the 12th of October, 1492, he saw the sand glistening on the shores of the New World, and in a little while heard one of the men on the

Pinta call out, "Land! land!" and a new world was discovered.

Our country for the World! we sing,
But in no worldly way:
Our country to the Lord we bring
And fervent for her pray:
God make her true; God make her pure;
God make her wise and good;
And through her may the Christ make sure
Man's world-wide Brotherhood!
America! America!
'Gainst wrong thy might be hurled;
For thee we lift our loud Huzza!
Our Country for the World!
—Denis Wortman, D. D.

Ours is the last experiment among the nations. Other nations may possibly arise and mar their future or make it, but it is in no undue spirit of self-importance that we say to-day that no other nation can arise with so great an inheritance and so great opportunities as the God of Nations has given us. Great danger lurks in our country's rapid growth in material wealth. The rich are growing richer and the poor poorer, and all are selfish. I hope that the problem of our civilization may be solved without bloodshed.—Rev. Dr. Rainsford.

All hail, Columbus, discoverer, dreamer, hero, and apostle! We here, of every race and country, recognize the horizon which bounded his vision and the infinite scope of his genius. The voice of gratitude and praise for all the blessings which have been showered upon mankind by his adventure is limited to no language, but is uttered in every tongue. Neither marble nor brass can fitly form his statue. Continents are his monument, and unnumbered millions present and to come, who enjoy in their liberties and their happiness the fruits of his faith, will reverently guard and preserve, from century to century, his name and fame.—World's Best Orations.

The history of the connection of the Spaniards with the Indians of the New World shows that, far from being actuated by a desire for the spiritual welfare of the unfortunate red men, their sole purpose was to use them as instruments for gaining wealth, regardless of their health or even of their lives. History does not contain a blacker record than the dealings of the Spaniards with the Indians. Columbus himself set the example in Hayti, when he and his companions ruthlessly butchered the miserable savages simply to create terror. The pages of Las Casas are full of the records of deeds of which demons should be ashamed. —St. Louis Advocate.

Without a parallel in history the name of Christopher Columbus stands alone, and like some great oak towering above the forest trees, so does he stand far in advance of his age with a work which is the most important since the birth of the Saviour of mankind. And I believe that as surely as men have been chosen by God for any work, so surely was he the chosen vessel to reveal the marvels of a New World to the wondering vision of the Old.—Rev. E. S. Holloway.

Force was the factor in the government of the world when Christ was born, and force was the source and exercise of authority both by Church and State when Columbus sailed from Palos. The Wise Men traveled from the East toward the West under the guidance of the Star of Bethlehem. The spirit of the equality of all men before God and the law moved westward from Calvary with its revolutionary influence upon old institutions, to the Atlantic Ocean. Columbus carried it westward across the seas.—Chauncey M. Depew.

He wrote the sacred name of Christ on his banner and gave Him all honor. He landed on the shores of this New World dressed in the resplendent robes of an admiral, with a sword in one hand and the banner of Christ in the other. The company fell upon their knees and praised God for His wonderful goodness. This New World was consecrated to God from the very moment of its first discovery. This country is a Christian land; the highest authority has recently pronounced it to be a Christian land, and it ought to be recognized as a Christian land, and the holy Sabbath be observed. Woe to us as a people if we lower our flag, if we dishonor our history, if we forsake our God!—Rev. R. S. Mac-Arthur, D. D.

We, therefore, on this anniversary of America, present the Public School as the proudest and noblest expression of the principle of enlightenment which Columbus grasped by faith. We uplift the system of free and universal education as the master-force which, under God, has been informing each of our generations with the peculiar truths of Americanism. America, therefore, gathers her sons around the schoolhouse to-day as the institution closest to the people, most characteristic of the people, and fullest of hope for the people. To-day America's fifth century begins. The world's twentieth century will soon be here. To the thirteen millions now in the American schools the command of the coming years belongs. We, the youth of America, who to-day unite to march as one army under the sacred flag, understand our duty. We pledge ourselves that the flag shall not be stained, and that America shall mean equal opportunity and justice for every citizen, and brotherhood for the world.—Francis Bellamy.

What are we here for? I answer, as a Christian—as one who believes in God and his Christ, and therefore does not despair of man. We are here to build a Christian nation. Nothing less would vindicate the wisdom of the Creator in preparing such a country; nothing less vindicate the Providence that first settled these shores with English-speaking Christian men and women, by divine laws of life driving hence and away the people who would not use their gifts; nothing less than a Christian state makes life worth living for us or our children,—Bishop Haygood.

Columbus is always a good subject for meditation. His piety, his courage, his confidence in Providence and in himself, his ceaseless industry, his enterprise and indomitable self-control are strongly marked in every step of his romantic and extraordinary career. Had he been a man who could be turned from his high purpose by dis couragements his name would be unknown to-day. His life and work are a monument to faith and determination. He felt within him the power to do, and he had the courage to dare.—N. Y. Herald.

Many blessings and advantages were bequeathed to all nations by the discoveries of the great captain: First, in securing large space for the multiplying millions of the Old World; second, in affording opportunity for experiments in government, unburdened by the evil traditions and prejudices which have so often defeated efforts toward political equality; and, third, in liberating the world's thought and sympathies by showing how men of all creeds and conceits might dwell together in the same political household in perfect good will.—Dr. Rylance.

The advent of the United States as a Sixth Power in the world has made obsolete all the traditions and diplomacy that have known only the Five Great Powers of Europe. Six months have made the United States one of the greatest factors in the history of the future by making this Nation the disinterested champion of freedom in the world. The die is cast. There can be no retreat, no drawing back. It is demanded of our Government and people, that they shall take their place in the councils of the nations, and inaugurate and carry out, in the spirit of disinterestedness, a Christian policy and diplomacy, in accomplishing the extraordinary task providentially assigned to them.—Gregory.

We are to-day treading in the same steps that other historic republics have taken and regretted—luxury and extravagance attending upon wealth, general laxity in morality and religion, jealousies and discontents incident to poverty among the masses, bitter conflicts between political parties, abuse heaped upon public servants, favors shown to the most dangerous classes when they can be used to promote party interests. These were the reasons why the historic republics fell into degradation, disgrace, and death. The greatest danger threatening our republic to-day is promiscuous immigration, and from this giant evil flow many perils, chief among which is the wholesale placing of the sacred ballot in the hands of those who have as yet done nothing entitling them to American citizenship. More than one republic has been wrecked on this rock. —Rev. C. H. Parkhurst.

Among the thoughts suggested by this day the first is one of humiliation. As a people we are disposed to brag and boast and have an inordinate confidence in our powers. We are possessed with an idea that American ingenuity can accomplish anything. We regard our own things as far the best in the world, our own institutions as the most perfect. But if we come to view things with an unprejudiced eye and to pass judgment free from self-interest, we must say that, as a rule, our own things are not the best, the productions of our skilled labor are not always equal to those of older countries. The only things we have any shadow of reason to boast of are those things the production of which we have nothing to do with, namely, those things which are our natural resources and are the gift of God.—Rev. J. Nevitt Steele.

My native land, my native land,
  To her my thoughts will fondly turn;
For her the warmest hopes expand,
  For her the heart with fears will yearn.
Oh, may she keep her eye, like thee,
  Proud eagle of the rocky wild,
Fixed on the sun of Liberty,
  By rank, by faction, unbeguiled;
Remembering still the rugged road
Our venerable fathers trod,
When they through toil and danger pressed
To gain their glorious bequest,
And from each lip the caution fell
To those who followed, "Guard it well."
                              —Col. S.

Before Columbus and the one hundred and twenty men embarked on board the Santa Maria, the Pinta, and the Nina, on their eventful voyage, what did they do? Took the Sacrament of our Lord Jesus Christ. Coming in sight of land, what song goes up from all three decks? "Gloria in Excelsis." What did they first do stepping from shipboard to solid ground? All knelt in prayer, consecrating the

New World to God. What did the Huguenots do, landing in the Carolinas; and the Hollanders, landing in New York; and the Puritans, landing in New England? With bent knees, uplifted faces and heaven-beseeching prayer, they took possession of this Continent for God. How did they open the First American Congress? With prayer in the name of Christ. Beside that, see what God has done for us. Open the map of our North American Continent, and see how the land was shaped for immeasurable prosperities. Behold the navigable rivers, greater and more numerous than those of any other land, running down to the sea in all directions—prophecy of large manufactures and easy commerce. Look at the great ranges of mountains, timbered with wealth on the tops and sides, and metaled with wealth underneath; 180,000 square miles of coal; 180,000 square miles of iron. The land so contoured that extreme weather seldom lasts more than three days. For the most of the year the climate is bracing, and favorable for brawn and brain. All fruits, all minerals, all harvests. Scenery which displays an autumnal pageantry which no other land pretends to rival. No South American earthquakes. No Scotch mists. No English fogs. No Egyptian plagues. No Germanic divisions. The happiest people on the earth are the people of the United States. The poor man has more chance, the industrious man more opportunity. How good God was to our fathers! How good God is to us and our children!

Discretion

Great ability without discretion comes almost invariably to a tragic end.—Gambetta.

Even in a hero's heart
Discretion is the better part.
—Churchill.

Discretion and hard valor are the twins of honor. — Beaumont and Fletcher.

To make another person hold his tongue, be you first silent.—Seneca.

The better part of valor is discretion.—Shakespeare.

Discretion in speech is more than eloquence.—Bacon.

If thou art a master, be sometimes blind; if a servant, sometimes deaf.—Fuller.

Neither coquetry nor love is imbued with discretion.—Mme. Sophie Arnould.

Remember the divine saying, He that keepeth his mouth, keepeth his life.—Sir Walter Raleigh.

Let's teach ourselves that honourable stop,
Not to outsport discretion. —Shakespeare.

All persons are not discreet enough to know how to take things by the right handle.—Cervantes.

Partake of love as a temperate man partakes of wine; do not become intoxicated.—Alfred de Musset.

Let your own discretion be your tutor: suit the action to the word, the word to the action.—Shakespeare.

I have seen the day of wrong through the little hole of discretion.—Shakespeare.

A sound discretion is not so much indicated by never making a mistake as by never repeating it.—Bovee.

In a state where discretion begins, law, liberty, and safety end.—Junius.

Discretion is the salt, and fancy the sugar of life; the one preserves, the other sweetens it.—Bovee.

The better part of valour is discretion; in the which better part I have saved my life.—Shakespeare.

Discreet women have sometimes neither eyes nor ears.--Mme. Deluzy.

There are many more shining qualities in the mind of man, but there is none so useful as discretion.—Addison.

What is denominated discretion in man we call cunning in brutes.—La Fontaine.

Discretion is the perfection of reason, and a guide to win all the duties of life.—Addison.

Never join with your friend when he abuses his horse or his wife, unless the one is about to be sold, and the other to be buried.—Colton.

For 'tis not good that children should know any wickedness : old folks, you know, have discretion, as they say, and know the world.—Shakespeare.

Discretion is more necessary to women than eloquence, because they have less trouble to speak well than to speak little.—Father du Bosc.

There are three things that ought to be considered before some things are spoken,—the manner, the place, and the time.—Southey.

Had Windham possessed discretion in debate, or Sheridan in conduct, they might have ruled their age.—Swift.

Some delicate matters must be treated like pins, because if they are not seized by the right end, we get pricked. —J. Petit-Senn.

Without discretion, people may be overlaid with unreasonable affection, and choked with too much nourishment.—Jeremy Collier.

If a cause be good, the most violent attack of its enemies will not injure it so much as an injudicious defence of it by its friends.—Colton.

Open your purse and your mouth cautiously ; and your stock of wealth and reputation shall, at least in repute, be great.—Zimmermann.

Swift calls discretion low prudence ; it is high prudence, and one of the most important elements entering into either social or political life.—Chapin.

There is no talent so useful towards rising in the world, or which puts men more out of the reach of fortune, than discretion, a species of lower prudence.—Swift.

If we look into communities and divisions of men, we observe that the discreet man, not the witty, nor the learned, nor the brave, guides the conversation, and gives measure to society. —Addison.

Quoth he, That man is sure to lose,
That fouls his hands with dirty foes;
For where no honor's to be gain'd,
'Tis thrown away in being maintain'd.
                                        —Butler.

You are old;
Nature in you stands on the very verge
Of her confine: you should be ruled and led
By some discretion, that discerns your state
Better than you yourself. —Shakespeare.

I do not contend against the advantages of distrust. In the world we live in, it is but too necessary. Some of old called it the very sinews of discretion.—Burke.

The greatest parts, without discretion, as observed by an elegant writer, may be fatal to their owner ; as Polyphemus, deprived of his eyes, was only the more exposed on account of his enormous strength and stature.—Addison.

Jest not openly at those that are simple, but remember how much thou art bound to God, who hath made thee wiser. Defame not any woman publicly, though thou know her to be evil ; for those that are faulty cannot endure to be taxed, but will seek to be avenged of thee ; and those that are not guilty cannot endure unjust reproach.—Sir Walter Raleigh.

Always man needs woman for his friend. He needs her clearer vision, her subtler insight, her softer thought, her winged soul, her pure and tender heart. Always woman needs man to be her friend. She needs the vigor of his purpose, the ardor of his will, his calmer judgment, his braver force of action, his reverence and his devotion. —Mary Clemmer

There is no talent so useful towards rising in the world, or which puts men more out of the power of fortune, than that quality generally possessed by the dullest sort of men, and in common speech called "discretion,"—a species of lower prudence, by the assistance of which people of the meanest intellectuals pass through the world in great tranquillity, neither giving nor taking offence. For want of a reasonable infusion of this aldermanly discretion, everything fails.—Swift.

Discretion is the perfection of reason, and a guide to us in all the duties of life; cunning is a kind of instinct, that only looks out after our immediate interests and welfare. Discretion is only found in men of strong sense and good understanding; cunning is often to be met with in brutes themselves, and in persons who are but the fewest removes from them.—Bruyère.

Discrimination

I will buy with you, sell with you, talk with you, walk with you, and so following, but I will not eat with you, drink with you, nor pray with you.—Shakespeare.

You ought to choose both physician and friend, not the most agreeable, but the most useful.—Epictetus.

Discussion

The bitter clamor of two eager tongues.—Shakespeare.

Religious contention is the devil's harvest.—La Fontaine.

Free and fair discussion will ever be found the firmest friend to truth.—George Campbell.

Men are never so likely to settle a question rightly as when they discuss it freely.—Macaulay.

The fair way of conducting a dispute is to exhibit, one by one, the arguments of your opponent, and, with each argument, the precise and specific answer you are able to make to it.—Paley.

The skilful disputant well knows that he never has his enemy at more advantage than when, by allowing the premises, he shows him arguing wrong from his own principles.—Warburton.

Of a certain class of disputants it has been wittily observed that their conclusions are always right and their reasons for them invariably wrong.—J. C. Jeaffreson.

Whoever is afraid of submitting any question, civil or religious, to the test of free discussion, is more in love with his own opinion than with truth.—Bishop Watson.

The great enemy of knowledge is not error, but inertness. All that we want is discussion; and then we are sure to do well, no matter what our blunders may be. One error conflicts with another, each destroys its opponent, and truth is evolved.—Buckle.

Disease

Disease is the retribution of outraged Nature.—Hosea Ballou.

Disease is a hot-house plant.—Haller.

Desperate diseases need desperate cures.—Proverb.

Just disease to luxury succeeds.—Pope.

Sickness seizes the body from bad ventilation.—Ovid.

Against diseases here the strongest fence,
Is the defensive virtue, abstinence.
—Herrick.

That dire disease, whose ruthless power
Withers the beauty's transient flower.
—Goldsmith.

This sickness doth infect
The very life-blood of our enterprise.
—Shakespeare.

O, he's a limb, that has but a disease;
Mortal, to cut it off; to cure it, easy.
—Shakespeare.

He who cures a disease may be the skilfullest, but he that prevents it is the safest physician.—T. Fuller.

Diseases of the mind impair the bodily powers.—Ovid.

A wounded heart can with difficulty be cured.—Goethe.

It is not the disease but neglect of the remedy which generally destroys life.—From the Latin.

Diseases desperate grown
By desperate appliance are reliev'd,
Or not at all.   —Shakespeare.

Before the curing of a strong disease, even in the instant of repair and health, the fit is strongest.—Shakespeare.

Decay and disease are often beautiful, like the pearly tear of the shellfish and the hectic glow of consumption.—Thoreau.

A bodily disease which we look upon as whole and entire within itself, may, after all, be but a symptom of some ailment in the spiritual part.—Nath. Hawthorne.

Diseases crucify the soul of man, attenuate our bodies, dry them, wither them, shrivel them up like old apples, make them as so many anatomies.—Burton.

The surest road to health, say what they will,
Is never to suppose we shall be ill.
Most of those evils we poor mortals know
From doctors and imagination flow.
            —Churchill.

So when a raging fever burns,
We shift from side to side by turns;
And 'tis a poor relief we gain,
To change the place but keep the pain.
            —Watts.

As man, perhaps, the moment of his breath,
Receives the lurking principle of death,
The young disease, that must subdue at length,
Grows with his growth, and strengthens with his strength.   —Pope.

The canker which the trunk conceals is revealed by the leaves, the fruit, or the flower.—Metastasio.

Disenchantment

A blaze first pleases and then tires the sight.—Dr. Johnson.

Which of us that is thirty years old has not had his Pompeii? Deep under ashes lies Life, Youth, the careless sports, the pleasures and passions, the darling joy.—Thackeray.

Year by year, more and more of the world gets disenchanted. Even the icy privacy of the arctic and antarctic circles is invaded. We have played Jack Horner with our earth, till there is never a plum left in it.—Lowell.

Disgrace

No one can disgrace us but ourselves.—J. G. Holland.

Disgrace is the synonym of discovery.—Alfred de Musset.

Come, Death, and snatch me from disgrace.—Bulwer-Lytton.

Dishonor is like the Aaron's Beard in the hedgerows; it can only poison if it be plucked.—Ouida.

Reason bears disgrace, courage combats it, patience surmounts it.—Mme. de Sévigné.

Disgrace is immortal, and living even when one thinks it dead.—Plautus.

That only is a disgrace to a man which he has deserved to suffer.—Phædrus.

Could he with reason murmur at his case
Himself sole author of his own disgrace?
            —Cowper.

Whatever disgrace we may have deserved, it is almost always in our power to re-establish our character.—La Rochefoucauld.

The unbought grace of life, the cheap defence of nations, the nurse of manly sentiment and heroic enterprise, is gone!—Burke.

It is disgraceful when the passers-by exclaim, "O ancient house, alas, how unlike is thy present master to thy former one."—Cicero.

And wilt thou still be hammering treachery,
To tumble down thy husband and thyself
From top of honour to disgrace's feet?
     —Shakespeare.

Since you go where all have gone before, why do you torment your disgraceful life with such mean ambitions, O miser?—Phædrus.

Disguise

We become so accustomed to disguise ourselves to others, that at last we are disguised to ourselves.—La Rochefoucauld.

'Tis great, 'tis manly, to disdain disguise;
It shows our spirit, or it proves our strength.
     —Young.

Were we to take as much pains to be what we ought to be as we do to disguise what we really are, we might appear like ourselves without being at the trouble of any disguise at all.—Rochefoucauld.

Disguise, I see, thou art a wickedness,
Wherein the pregnant enemy does much.
How easy is it for the proper false
In women's waxen hearts to set their forms!
Alas, our frailty is the cause, not we:
For, such as we are made of, such are we.
     —Shakespeare.

Men would not live long in society, were they not the mutual dupes of each other.—Rochefoucauld.

Dishonesty

Ill-gotten wealth is never stable.—Euripides.

Who purposely cheats his friend, would cheat his God.—Lavater.

What is dishonestly got vanishes in profligacy.—Cicero.

The gains of the wicked bring short-lived pleasure, but afterwards long-continued grief.—Antiphanes.

Dishonor waits on perfidy. A man should blush to think a falsehood; it is the crime of cowards.—Johnson.

Dishonesty is a forsaking of permanent for temporary advantages.—Bovee.

Dishonesty is so grasping it would deceive God Himself, were it possible.—Bancroft.

Dishonest men conceal their faults from themselves as well as others; honest men know and confess them.—Rochefoucauld.

It is hard to say which of the two we ought most to lament,—the unhappy man who sinks under the sense of his dishonor, or him who survives it.—Junius.

That which is won ill, will never wear well, for there is a curse attends it, which will waste it; and the same corrupt dispositions which incline men to the sinful ways of getting, will incline them to the like sinful ways of spending.—Matthew Henry.

If you attempt to beat a man down and to get his goods for less than a fair price, you are attempting to commit burglary, as much as though you broke into his shop to take the things without paying for them. There is cheating on both sides of the counter, and generally less behind it than before it.—Beecher.

I have known a vast quantity of nonsense talked about bad men not looking you in the face. Don't trust that conventional idea. Dishonesty will stare honesty out of countenance any day in the week, if there is anything to be got by it.—Dickens.

Disinterestedness

How difficult it is to get men to believe that any other man can or does act from disinterestedness!—B. R. Haydon.

Men of the world hold that it is impossible to do a disinterested action, except from an interested motive; for the sake of admiration, if for no grosser, more tangible gain. Doubtless they are also convinced that, when the sun is showering light from the sky, he is only standing there to be stared at.

———

The slightest emotion of disinterested kindness that passes through the mind, improves and refreshes that mind, producing generous thought and noble feeling. We should cherish kind wishes, for a time may come when we may be enabled to put them in practice.—Miss Mitford.

Disobedience

Wherever there is authority, there is a natural inclination to disobedience.—Haliburton.

———

Of man's first disobedience, and the fruit
Of that forbidden tree, whose mortal taste
Brought death into the world, and all our
woe.   —Milton.

———

    She is peevish, sullen, froward,
Proud, disobedient, stubborn, lacking duty;
Neither regarding that she is my child,
Nor fearing me as if I were her father.
            —Shakespeare.

Disparagement

They praise, and they admire, they know not
    what,
And know not whom, but as one leads the
    other,
And what delight to be by such extoll'd,
To live upon their tongues, and be their
    talk,
Of whom to be dispraised were no small
    praise?   —Milton.

———

My mistress' eyes are nothing like the sun;
Coral is far more red than her lips' red:
If snow be white, why then her breasts are
    dun;
If hairs be wires, black wires grow on her
    head.
I have seen roses damask'd, red and white,
But no such roses see I in her cheeks;
And in some perfumes is there more delight
Than in the breath that from my mistress
    reeks.
I love to hear her speak; yet well I know
That music hath a far more pleasing sound:
I grant, I never saw a goddess go;
My mistress, when she walks, treads on the
    ground.   —Shakespeare.

Disparity

Crabbed age and youth cannot live together:
Youth is full of pleasance, age is full of
    care;
Youth like summer morn, age like winter
    weather;
Youth like summer brave, age like winter
    bare;
Youth is full of sport, age's breath is short;

Youth is nimble, age is lame:
Youth is hot and bold, age is weak and cold;
Youth is wild, and age is tame.
            —Shakespeare.

Display

Display is as false as it is costly.—Franklin.

———

They that govern most make least noise.—Selden.

———

Narrow waists and narrow minds go together.—Chamfort.

———

She who desires to see, desires also to be seen.—Cervantes.

———

Loud-dressing men and women have also loud characters.—Haliburton.

———

People newly emerged from obscurity generally launch out into indiscriminate display.—Jean Ingelow.

———

A fop of fashion is the mercer's friend, the tailor's fool, and his own foe.—Lavater.

———

Display is like shallow water, where you can see the muddy bottom.—Alphonse Karr.

———

The lowest people are generally the first to find fault with show or equipage; especially that of a person lately emerged from his obscurity. They never once consider that he is breaking the ice for themselves.—Shenstone.

———

If a young lady has that discretion and modesty without which all knowledge is little worth, she will never make an ostentatious parade of it, because she will rather be intent on acquiring more than on displaying what she has.—Hannah More.

———

I have often reflected within myself on this unaccountable humor in womankind of being smitten with everything that is showy and superficial, and on the numberless evils that befall the sex from this light fantastical disposition.—Addison.

———

The horses which make the most show are, in general, those which advance the least. It is the same with men; and we ought not to confound that perpetual agitation which exhausts itself in vain efforts, with the activity which goes right to the end.— Baron de Stassart.

Beauty gains little, and homeliness and deformity lose much, by gaudy attire. Lysander knew this when he refused the rich garments that the tyrant Dionysius proffered to his daughter, saying that they were fit only to make unhappy faces more remarkable.—Zimmermann.

Dispute

Could we forbear dispute, and practice love,
We should agree, as angels do above.
—Waller.

The pain of dispute exceeds by much its utility. All disputation makes the mind deaf; and when people are deaf I am dumb.—Joubert.

'Tis strange how some men's tempers suit,
Like bawd and brandy, with dispute,
That for their own opinions stand fast,
Only to have them claw'd and canvass'd.
—Butler.

The more discussion the better, if passion and personality be eschewed; and discussion, even if stormy, often winnows truth from error—a good never to be expected in an uninquiring age.—Channing.

Some say, compared to Bononcini,
That Mynheer Handel's but a ninny;
Others aver that he to Handel
Is scarcely fit to hold a candle.
Strange that all this diff'rence should be
'Twixt Tweedledum and Tweedledee.
—J. Byrom.

It is true there is nothing displays a genius, I mean a quickness of genius, more than a dispute; as two diamonds, encountering, contribute to each other's luster. But perhaps the odds is much against the man of taste in this particular.—Shenstone.

Dissatisfaction

Let not the stream of your life be a murmuring stream.—Aughey.

Opposition embitters the enthusiast, but never converts him.—Schiller.

The fastidious are unfortunate; nothing can satisfy them.—La Fontaine.

Dissension

Dissensions, like small streams at first begun,
Unseen they rise, but gather as they run.
—Garth.

Civil dissension is a viperous worm
That gnaws the bowels of the commonwealth.
—Shakespeare.

If they perceive dissension in our looks
And that within ourselves we disagree,
How will their grudging stomachs be provoked
To wilful disobedience and rebel!
—Shakespeare.

Alas! how light a cause may move
Dissension between hearts that love!
Hearts that the world in vain had tried,
And sorrow but more closely tied;
That stood the storm, when waves were rough,
Yet in a sunny hour fall off. —Moore.

Dissimulation

All men wear a disguised habit.— Terence.

We endeavor to conceal our vices under the disguise of the opposite virtues.—Fielding.

When my love swears that she is made of truth,
I do believe her, though I know she lies.
—Shakespeare.

He who knows not how to dissimulate knows not how to rule.—Metellus of Macedon.

Away and mock the time with fairest show;
False face must hide what false heart doth know.
—Shakespeare.

Thus 'tis with all—their chief and constant care
Is to seem everything but what they are.
—Goldsmith.

We are so much accustomed to disguise ourselves to others that at length we disguise ourselves to ourselves.— Rochefoucauld.

Dissimulation, even the most innocent in its nature, is ever productive of embarrassment; whether the design is evil or not artifice is always danger-

ous and almost inevitably disgraceful.
—La Bruyère.

Dissimulation is the only thing that
makes society possible; without its
amenities the world would be a bear-
garden.—Ouida.

Dissimulation is but a faint kind of
policy or wisdom; for it asketh a
strong wit and a strong heart to know
when to tell truth, and to do it; therefore, it is the weaker sort of politicians that are the greatest dissem-
blers.—Bacon.

Dissimulation in youth is the forerunner of perfidy in old age; its first
appearance is the fatal omen of growing depravity and future shame. It
degrades parts and learning, obscures
the luster of every accomplishment and
sinks us into contempt. The path of
falsehood is a perplexing maze. After
the first departure from sincerity, it is
not in our power to stop; one artifice unavoidably leads on to another,
till, as the intricacy of the labyrinth
increases, we are left entangled in our
snare.—Blair.

Dissolution

Like the baseless fabric of this vision,
The cloud-capped towers, the gorgeous pal-
    aces,
The solemn temples, the great globe itself,
Yea, all which it inherit, shall dissolve;
And, like this insubstantial pageant faded,
Leave not a rack behind. —Shakespeare.

Distance

Distance sometimes endears friendship and absence sweeteneth it.—
Howell.

'Tis distance lends enchantment to the view,
And robes the mountain in its azure hue.
    —Campbell.

Wishes, like painted landscapes, best de-
    light,
Whilst distance recommends them to the
    sight.
Plac'd afar off, they beautiful appear:
But show their coarse and nauseous colors
    near. —Dr. Yalden.

She pleased while distant, but when
near she charm'd.—Shenstone.

Distinction

Distinction, with a broad and powerful fan, puffing at all, winnows the
light away.—Shakespeare.

There's but the twinkling of a star
Between a man of peace and war;
A thief and justice, fool and knave,
A huffing off'cer and a slave;
A crafty lawyer and a pickpocket,
A great philosopher and a blockhead;
A formal preacher and a player,
A learn'd physician and man-slayer.
    —Butler.

All that causes one man to differ
from another is a very slight thing.
What is it that is the origin of beauty
or ugliness, health or weakness, ability
or stupidity? A slight difference in
the organs, a little more or a little less
bile. Yet this more or less is of infinite importance to men; and when
they think otherwise they are mistaken.—Vauvenargues.

All our distinctions are accidental;
beauty and deformity, though personal
qualities, are neither entitled to praise
nor censure; yet it so happens that
they color our opinion of those qualities to which mankind have attached
responsibility.—Zimmermann.

Distrust

What loneliness is more lonely than
distrust?—George Eliot.

In love the deceit generally outstrips
the distrust.—Rochefoucauld.

The best use one can make of his
mind is to distrust it.—Fénelon.

A usurper always distrusts the
whole world.—Alfieri.

Doubt the man who swears to his
devotion.—Mme. Louise Colet.

Women distrust men too much in
general, and too little in particular.—
Commerson.

It is difficult for a woman to try to
be anything good when she is not believed in.—George Eliot.

Jealousy lives upon distrust, becomes madness, or ceases entirely,

when we pass from doubt to certainty. —Rochefoucauld.

The saddest thing that can befall a soul is when it loses faith in God and woman.
—Alexander Smith.

This feeling of distrust is always the last which a great mind acquires; he is deceived for a long time.—Racine.

Excessive distrust is not less hurtful than its opposite. Most men become useless to him who is unwilling to risk being deceived.—Vauvenargues.

Zoroaster said, when in doubt abstain; but this does not always apply. At cards, when in doubt take the trick. —H. W. Shaw.

Self-reliance is demanded in woman; the supreme fall of falls is the first doubt of one's self.—Mme. de Gasparin.

As health lies in labor, and there is no royal road to it but through toil, so there is no republican road to safety but in constant distrust.—Wendell Phillips.

Three things a wise man will not trust,
The wind, the sunshine of an April day,
And woman's plighted faith. —Southey.

A certain amount of distrust is wholesome, but not so much of others as of ourselves; neither vanity nor conceit can exist in the same atmosphere with it.—Madame Necker.

The doubts of love are never to be wholly overcome; they grow with its various anxieties, timidities, and tenderness, and are the very fruits of the reverence in which the admired object is beheld.—Jane Porter.

Self-distrust is the cause of most of our failures. In the assurance of strength there is strength, and they are the weakest, however strong, who have no faith in themselves or their powers.—Bovee.

Nothing is more certain of destroying any good feeling that may be cherished towards us than to show distrust. To be suspected as an enemy is often enough to make a man become so; the whole matter is over, there is no farther use of guarding against it. On the contrary, confidence leads us naturally to act kindly, we are affected by the good opinion which others entertain of us, and we are not easily induced to lose it.— Madame de Sévigné.

Divinity

There's a Divinity that shapes our ends,
Rough-hew them how we will.
—Shakespeare.

Docility

A docile disposition will, with application, surmount every difficulty.— Manilius.

Doctor

An ignorant doctor is the aide-de-camp of death.—Abu Avicenna.

By medicine life may be prolonged, yet death
Will seize the doctor, too.—Shakespeare.

It is not much trouble to doctor sick folks, but to doctor healthy ones is troublesome.—H. W. Shaw.

Though fancy may be the patient's complaint, necessity is often the doctor's.—Zimmermann.

The doctor is not unfrequently death's pilot-fish.—G. D. Prentice.

Doctrine

Live to explain thy doctrine by thy life.—Prior.

The question is not whether a doctrine is beautiful, but whether it is true.—Guesses at Truth.

All sects seem to me to be right in what they assert, and wrong in what they deny.—Goethe.

Every one cleaves to the doctrine he has happened upon, as to a rock against which he has been thrown by tempest. —Cicero.

Doctrine is nothing but the skin of truth set up and stuffed.—Beecher.

How absurd to try to make two men think alike on matters of religion, when I cannot make two timepieces agree!—Charles V.

Go put your creed into your deed
Nor speak with double tongue.
—Emerson.

"Orthodoxy, my Lord," said Bishop Warburton, in a whisper—"orthodoxy is my doxy—heterodoxy is another man's doxy."—Joseph Priestly.

Doctrine is something that is taught. Applied to religion it is something that God teaches.—Joseph Shipps.

He knew how to weaken his divinity, on occasion, as well as an old housewife to weaken her tea, lest it should keep people awake.—O. W. Holmes.

The Athanasian creed is the most splendid ecclesiastical lyric ever poured forth by the genius of man.—Benj. Disraeli.

Logic has its use and metaphysics has its use, but neither of them is of much help in the making of a creed.—Talmage.

That doctrine which rectifies the conscience, purifies the heart and produces love to God and men is necessarily true.—Walker.

In religion as in politics it so happens that we have less charity for those who believe half our creed, than for those who deny the whole of it.—Colton.

I move for a creed for all our denominations made out of Scripture quotations, pure and simple. That would be impregnable against infidelity and Appolyonic assault. That would be beyond human criticism. Let us make it simpler and plainer for people to get into the Kingdom of God.—Talmage.

Religion, as embodied in the character and conduct of its disciples, cannot survive without doctrinal purity. In the absence of this element, religious feeling inevitably decays; while even religious necessity becomes a thing of naught.—J. McC. Holmes.

Doctrine is the framework of life; it is the skeleton of truth, to be clothed and rounded out by the living graces of a holy life. It is only the lean creature whose bones become offensive.—A. J. Gordon.

Go on your knees before God. Bring all your idols; bring self-will, and pride, and every evil lust before Him, and give them up. Devote yourself, heart and soul, to His will; and see if you do not "know of the doctrine."—H. W. Beecher.

The question is not whether a doctrine is beautiful, but whether it is true. When we want to go to a place, we don't ask whether the road leads through a pretty country, but whether it is the right road, the road pointed out by authority, the turnpike-road.—Hare.

Don't turn your back upon your doctrinal doubts and difficulties. Go up to them and examine them. Perhaps the ghastly object which looks to you in the twilight like a sheeted ghost may prove to be no more than a table-cloth hanging upon a hedge.—A. H. Boyd.

Shall I ask the brave soldier, who fights by my side
In the cause of mankind, if our creeds agree?
Shall I give up the friend I have valued and tried,
If he kneel not before the same altar with me?
From the heretic girl of my soul should I fly,
To seek somewhere else a more orthodox kiss?
No! perish the hearts, and the laws that try
Truth, valor, or love, by a standard like this!
—Moore.

As those wines which flow from the first treading of the grape are sweeter and better than those forced out by the press, which gives them the roughness of the husk and stone, so are those doctrines best and sweetest which flow from a gentle crush of the scriptures,

and are not wrung into controversies
and commonplaces.—Bacon.

And after hearing what our Church can say,
If still our reason runs another way,
That private reason, 'tis more just to curb,
Than by disputes the public peace disturb;
For points obscure are of small use to
learn,
But common quiet is mankind's concern.
—Dryden.

We are not called on to believe this
or that doctrine which may be proposed to us till we can do so from
honest conviction. But we are called
on to trust—to trust ourselves to God,
being sure that He will lead us right
—to keep close to Him—and to trust
the promises which He whispers
through our conscience; this we can
do, and we ought to do.—J. C. Shairp.

Dog

Every dog must have his day.—
Swift.

Let Hercules himself do what he may,
The cat will mew, and dog will have his day.
—Shakespeare.

I am his highness' dog at Kew;
Pray tell me, sir, whose dog are you?
—Pope.

Let dogs delight to bark and bite,
For God hath made them so;
Let bears and lions growl and fight,
For 'tis their nature to.   —Watts.

And in that town a dog was found,
As many dogs there be,
Both mongrel, puppy, whelp and hounu,
And curs of low degree.   —Goldsmith.

I have a dog of Blenheim birth,
With fine long ears and full of mirth;
And sometimes, running o'er the plain,
He tumbles on his nose:
But quickly jumping up again
Like lightning on he goes!   —Ruskin.

Ay, in the catalogue ye go for men;
As hounds, and greyhounds, mongrels,
spaniels, curs,
Shoughs, water-rugs, and demi-wolves, are
'clept
All by the name of dogs: the valued file
Distinguishes the swift, the slow, the
subtle,
The housekeeper, the hunter, every one
According to the gift which bounteous na-
ture
Hath in him closed.   —Shakespeare.

We are two travelers, Roger and I.
Roger's my dog—come here, you scamp!
Jump for the gentleman—mind your eye!
Over the table—look out for the lamp!
The rogue is growing a little old;
Five years we've tramped through wind and
weather,
And slept out-doors when nights were cold,
And ate and drank and starved together.
—John T. Trowbridge.

Dogmatism

Nothing can be more unphilosophical
than to be positive or dogmatical on
any subject.—Hume.

They utter all they think with violence.—Ben Jonson.

When men are the most sure and
arrogant, they commonly are the most
mistaken.—Hume.

Those who differ most from the
opinions of their fellow men are the
most confident of the truth of their
own.—Mackintosh.

He who is certain, or presumes to
say he knows, is, whether he be mistaken or in the right, a dogmatist.—
William Fleming.

Those who refuse the long drudgery
of thought, and think with the heart
rather than the head, are ever the most
fiercely dogmatic in tone.—Bayne.

It is a wrong use of my understanding to make it the rule and measure of
another man's—a use which it is
neither fit for nor capable of.—Locke.

A dogmatical spirit inclines a man
to be censorious of his neighbors.
Every one of his opinions appears to
him written, as it were, with sunbeams, and he grows angry that his
neighbors do not see it in the same
light. He is tempted to disdain his
correspondents as men of low and dark
understandings because they do not believe what he does.—Watts.

Nothing can be more unphilosophical
than to be positive or dogmatical on
any subject; and even if excessive
scepticism could be maintained it
would not be more destructive to all
just reasoning and inquiry. When

men are the most sure and arrogant, they are commonly the most mistaken, and have there given reins to passion, without that proper deliberation and suspense which can alone secure them from the grossest absurdities.—Hume.

Domesticity

Home joys are blessed of heaven.—Seneca.

Home is the sacred refuge of our life.—Dryden.

Home is the chief school of human virtue.—Channing.

A cottage will hold as much happiness as would stock a palace.—James Hamilton.

Home should be the center of joy, equatorial and tropical.—Beecher.

Silence and chaste reserve is woman's genuine praise, and to remain quiet within the house.—Euripides.

Apelles used to paint a good housewife on a snail, to import that she was home-keeping.—James Howell.

Domestic happiness, thou only bliss of paradise that hath survived the fall.—Cowper.

The sober comfort, all the peace which springs from the large aggregate of little things.—Hannah More.

Lord Lyttleton says true domestic bliss shuns too strong a light.—J. C. Hare.

A prince wants only the pleasure of private life to complete his happiness.—Bruyère.

Women do act their part when they do make their ordered houses know them.—Sheridan Knowles.

A woman is not a woman until she has been baptized in her love and devotion to home and children.—Mrs. F. C. Croly.

The nest may be constructed, so far as the sticks go, by the male bird; but only the hen can line it with moss and down!—Frances Power Cobbe.

The grandest of heroic deeds are those which are performed within four walls and in domestic privacy.—Richter.

Only so far as a man is happily married to himself is he fit for married life, and family life generally.—Novalis.

The parted bosom clings to wonted home, if aught that's kindred cheer the welcome hearth.—Byron.

Domestic happiness is the end of almost all our pursuits, and the common reward of all our pains.—Fielding.

The domestic man, who loves no music so well as his kitchen clock, and the airs which the logs sing to him as they burn on the hearth, has solaces which others never dream of.—Emerson.

The only fountain in the wilderness of life, where man drinks of water totally unmixed with bitterness, is that which gushes for him in the calm and shady recess of domestic life.—William Penn.

The best school of discipline is home. Family life is God's own method of training the young, and homes are very much as women make them.—Samuel Smiles.

She was little known beyond her home; but there she silently spread around her that soft, pure light, the preciousness of which is never fully understood till it is quenched.—Channing.

Oh, trebly blest the placid lot of those whose hearth foundations are in pure love laid, where husband's breast with tempered ardor glows, and wife, oft mother, is in heart a maid!—Euripides.

The man at the head of the house can mar the pleasure of the household, but he cannot make it; that must rest with the woman, and it is her great privilege.—Arthur Helps.

Housekeepers, homemakers, wives, and mothers are fundamental social relations, which rest upon woman's characteristics, physical, mental, and moral.—R. Herbert Newton.

A house kept to the end of prudence is laborious without joy; a house kept to the end of display is impossible to all but a few women, and their success is dearly bought.—Emerson.

No money is better spent than what is laid out for domestic satisfaction. A man is pleased that his wife is dressed as well as other people, and the wife is pleased that she is dressed. —Johnson.

Our notion of the perfect society embraces the family as its center and ornament. Nor is there a paradise planted until the children appear in the foreground, to animate and complete the picture.—Alcott.

Father, mother, child, are the human trinity, whose substance must not be divided nor its persons confounded. As well reconstruct your granite out of the grains it is disintegrated into as society out of the dissolution of wedded love.—Bartol.

If a woman is not fit to manage the internal matters of a house, she is fit for nothing, and should never be put in a house or over a house, any way. Good housekeeping lies at the root of all the real ease and satisfaction in existence.—Harriet Prescott Spofford.

Men talk in raptures of youth and beauty, wit and sprightliness; but after seven years of union not one of them is to be compared to good family management, which is seen at every meal, and felt every hour in the husband's purse.—Witherspoon.

Domestic happiness is the end of almost all our pursuits, and the common reward of all our pains. When men find themselves forever barred from this delightful fruition, they are lost to all industry, and grow careless of all their worldly affairs. Thus they become bad subjects, bad relations, bad friends, and bad men.—Fielding.

Dominion Day

We are nere a nation, composed of the most heterogeneous elements— Protestants and Catholics, English, French, German, Irish, Scotch, every one, let it be remembered, with his traditions, with his prejudices. In each of these conflicting antagonistic elements, however, there is a common spot of patriotism, and the only true policy is that which reaches that common patriotism and makes it vibrate in all toward common ends and common aspirations.—Wilfrid Laurier.

Ye sons of Canada, awake!
Stretch forth the mighty arm of toil;
Embattle, beautify the soil
Your fathers won by brave turmoil;
And, while your glory swells, behold
Your virgin empire still unfold
Her halcyon hope, her wealth untold.
    —A. M. Taylor.

Blest land of peace!—O may'st thou ever be
Even as now the land of liberty!
Treading serenely thy bright upward road,
Honored of nations, and approved of God!
On thy fair front emblazoned clear and bright—
Freedom, fraternity, and equal right!
    —Pamelia S. Vining.

One hundred years have passed away since the conquest of Quebec, but here we sit, the children of the victor and the vanquished, all avowing hearty attachment to the British crown, all earnestly deliberating how we shall best extend the blessings of British institutions; how a great people may be established on this continent, in close and hearty connection with Great Britain. Where, sir, in the page of history, shall we find a parallel to this? Will it not stand as an imperishable monument to the generosity of British rule? And it is not in Canada alone that this scene has been witnessed. Four other colonies are at this moment occupied as we are—declaring their hearty love for the parent state, and deliberating with us how they may best discharge the great duty entrusted to their hands, and give their aid in developing the teeming resources of these vast possessions.—Hon. George Brown.

We should strengthen the faith of our people in their own future, the faith of every Canadian in Canada, and of every province in its sister province. This faith wrongs no one; burdens no one; menaces no one; dishonors no one; and, as it was said of old, faith moves mountains, so I venture reverently to express my own belief that if the difficulties of our future as a dominion were as high as the peaks of the Alps or Andes, yet that the pure patriotic faith of a united people would be all sufficient to overcome and ultimately to triumph over all such difficulties.—Hon. D'Arcy McGee.

We wear no haughty tyrant's chain—
  We bend no servile knee,
When to the mistress of the main
  We pledge our fealty.
She binds us with the cords of love—
  All others we disown;
The rights we owe to God above
  We yield to Him alone.
May He our future course direct
  By His unerring hand;
Our laws and liberties protect,
  And bless our native land!
            —Helen M. Johns.

Here's to the land of the rock and the pine;
Here's to the land of the raft and the river!
Here's to the land where the sunbeams shine,
And the night that is bright with the north-light's quiver!
Here's to the land of the ax and the hoe!
Here's to the stalwarts that give them their glory—
With stroke upon stroke, and with blow upon blow,
The might of the forest has passed into story!   —William Wye Smith.

Other countries have seen their territories enlarged and their destinies determined by trouble and war, but no blood has stained the bonds which have knit together your free and order-loving populations, and yet in this brief period, so brief in the life of a nation, you have attained to a union whose characteristics from sea to sea are the same. A judicature above suspicion, a strong central government to direct all national interests, the toleration of all faiths with favor to none, a franchise recognizing the rights of labor by the exclusion only of the idler, a government ever susceptible to the change of public opinion and ever open, through a responsible ministry, to the scrutiny of the people—these are the features of your rising power.—Lord Lorne.

He must have a dull and sluggish soul who can look without emotion on the quiet graves of the early settlers of this country, who can tread upon their moldering bones without a thought of their privations and their toils, who can, from their tombs, look out upon the rural loveliness—the fruitfulness and peace by which he is surrounded, nor drop a tear to the memories of the dead, who won, by the stoutness of their hearts, and the sweat of their brows, the blessings their children have only to cherish and enjoy.

Why should not these three great branches of the family flourish, under different systems of government, it may be, but forming one grand whole, proud of a common origin and of their advanced civilization? The clover lifts its trefoil leaves to the evening dew, yet they draw their nourishment from a single stem. Thus distinct, and yet united, let us live and flourish. Why should we not? For nearly two thousand years we were one family. Our fathers fought side by side at Hastings, and heard the curfew toll. They fought in the same ranks for the sepulchre of our Saviour. In the earlier and later civil wars, we can wear our white and red roses without a blush, and glory in the principles those conflicts established. Our common ancestors won the great charter and the bill of rights—established free parliaments, the habeas corpus, and trial by jury. Our jurisprudence comes down from Coke and Mansfield to Marshall and Story, rich in knowledge and experience which no man can divide. From Chaucer to Shakespeare our literature is a common inheritance. Tennyson and Longfellow write in one language, which is enriched by the genius developed on either side of the Atlantic. In the great navigators from Cortereal to Hudson, and in all their "moving accidents by flood and field" we have a common interest.—Joseph Howe.

Awake, my country, the hour of dreams is
  done.
Doubt not, nor dread the greatness of thy
  fate,
Tho' faint souls fear the keen, confronting
  sun
And fain would bid the morn in splendor
  wait!
Tho' dreamers wrapped in starry visions
  cry:
"Lo, yon thy future, yon thy faith, thy
  fame!"
And stretch vain hands to stars. Thy fame
  is nigh,
Here in Canadian hearth, and home and
  name;
This name which yet shall grow till all the
  nations know
Us for a patriot people, heart and hand,
Loyal to our native hearth, our native land.
        —C. D. Roberts.

What can we say as to our future? What of our destiny? Our destiny under a kind Providence will be just what we will make it. It rests in our own hands. We may in the face of all our advantages mar it if we will. As it is with individual destiny, so is it with national destiny; we are largely the architects of our own fortunes. We have laid, as I have shown, deep and safe and broad foundations for a bright future. What country can show legislation more advanced or leading up to better results than ours? In what land do we find a people enjoying more fully than we do the rights of self-government, or where is there a people more fitted to be entrusted with that precious right? Our laws have been well administered. Our courts of justice have won the unlimited confidence of the people. Imbued with the healthy sentiment which has prevailed in the mother land for centuries, attached to her forms of government, cherishing her precedents and traditions, we have passed from childhood to youth. We are approaching manhood, and its strength and vigor must depend upon ourselves. What is needed, then? We must appease interprovincial jealousies; we must modify

mere local patriotism; we must cultivate an increased national feeling and show in every way we can that we have crossed the line of youth and pupilage.—Richard Harcourt.

Doubt

Doubt indulged soon becomes doubt realized.—F. R. Havergal.

When you doubt, abstain.—Zoroaster.

Human knowledge is the parent of doubt.—Lord Greville.

Doubt is the accomplice of tyranny.—Amiel.

When in doubt, lean to the side of mercy.—Cervantes.

Misgive that you may not mistake.—Whately.

Doubt is hell in the human soul.—Mme. de Gasparin.

To be once in doubt is once to be resolved.—Shakespeare.

Our distrust justifies the deceit of others.—Rochefoucauld.

Doubt is the vestibule of faith.—Colton.

Doubt is the shadow of truth.—Bailey.

I love sometimes to doubt, as well as know.—Dante.

Man was not made to question, but adore.—Young.

There lives more faith in honest doubt,
Believe me, than in half the creeds.
        —Tennyson.

Doubt comes in at the window when inquiry is denied at the door.—Prof. Jowett.

Doubting charms me not less than knowledge.—Dante.

Every body drags its shadow, and every mind its doubt.—Victor Hugo.

Never do anything, concerning the rectitude of which you have a doubt.
—Pliny, Junior.

I run the gauntlet of a file of doubts,
Each one of which down hurls me to the
ground.   —Bailey.

Who never doubted never half believed,
Where doubt there truth is—'tis her
shadow.   —Bailey.

To believe with certainty we must begin to doubt.—Stanislaus.

A bitter and perplexed "What shall I do?"
Is worse to man than worse necessity.
—Coleridge.

Many with trust, with doubt few, are undone.—Greville.

Modest doubt is call'd
The beacon of the wise.
—Shakespeare.

Uncertain ways unsafest are,
And doubt a greater mischief than despair.
—Sir John Denham.

Who knows most, doubts most; entertaining hope means recognizing fear.—-Browning.

Doubt springs from the mind; faith is the daughter of the soul.—J. Petit-Senn.

Galileo called doubt the father of invention; it is certainly the pioneer.
—Bovee.

No sadder proof can be given by a man of his own littleness than disbelief in great men.—Carlyle.

There is no weariness like that which rises from doubting. It is unfixed reason.—South.

Faith keeps many doubts in her pay. If I could not doubt, I should not believe.—Thoreau.

Doubt follows white-winged hope with trembling steps.—Balzac.

The doubts of an honest man contain more moral truth than the profession of faith of people under a worldly yoke.—X. Doudan.

We know accurately only when we know little; with knowledge doubt increases.—Goethe.

You prove but too clearly that seeking to know
Is too frequently learning to doubt.
—Madame Deshoulières.

Our doubts are traitors
And make us lose the good we oft might win,
By fearing to attempt.   —Shakespeare.

Weary the path that does not challenge reason. Doubt is an incentive to truth, and patient inquiry leadeth the way.—Hosea Ballou.

Servile doubt argues an impotence of mind, that says we fear because we dare not meet misfortunes.—Aaron Hill.

To doubt is worse than to have lost; and to despair is but to antedate those miseries that must fall on us.—Massinger.

But the gods are dead—
Ay, Zeus is dead, and all the gods but Doubt,
And Doubt is brother devil to Despair!
—John Boyle O'Reilly.

In contemplation, if a man begin with certainties, he shall end in doubts, but if he will be content to begin with doubts, he shall end in certainties.—Bacon.

Can that which is the greatest virtue in philosophy, doubt (called by Galileo the father of invention), be in religion what the priests term it, the greatest of sins?—Bovee.

The wound of peace is surety, surety secure; but modest doubt is called the beacon of the wise; the tent that searches to the bottom of the worst.—Shakespeare.

Doubt thou the stars are fire;
Doubt that the sun doth move;
Doubt truth to be a liar;
But never doubt I love.
—Shakespeare.

To doubt is a misfortune, but to seek when in doubt is an indispensable duty. So he who doubts and seeks not is at once unfortunate and unfair.—Pascal.

———

Fain would I but I dare not; I dare, and yet I may not;
I may, although I care not for pleasure when I play not.—Sir Walter Raleigh.

———

Remember Talleyrand's advice, "If you are in doubt whether to write a letter or not, don't!" The advice applies to many doubts in life besides that of letter-writing.—Bulwer-Lytton.

———

Known mischiefs have their cure; but doubts have none;
And better is despair than fruitless hope
Mix'd with a killing fear.   —May.

———

Beware of doubt—faith is the subtle chain
Which binds us to the infinite: the voice
Of a deep life within, that will remain
Until we crowd it thence.
—Mrs. E. Oakes Smith.

———

Give unqualified assent to no propositions but those the truth of which is so clear and distinct that they cannot be doubted. The enunciation of this first great commandment of science consecrated doubt.—Huxley.

———

People, when asked if they are Christians, give some of the strangest answers you ever heard. Some will say if you ask them: "Well—well—well, I—I hope I am." Suppose a man should ask me if I am an American. Would I say: "Well, I—well, I—I hope I am?"—D. L. Moody.

———

The clear, cold question chills to frozen doubt;
Tired of beliefs, we dread to live without;
O then, if reason waver at thy side,
Let humbler Memory be thy gentle guide,
Go to thy birth-place, and, if faith was there,
Repeat thy father's creed, thy mother's prayer.   —O. W. Holmes.

———

To get rid of your doubts, part with your sin. Put away your intemperance, your dishonesty, your unlawful ways of making money, your sensuality, your falsehood, acted or spoken, and see if a holy life be not the best disperser of unwelcome doubts, and

new obedience the most certain guide to fresh assurance.—James Hamilton.

———

There is no weariness like that which rises from doubting, from the perpetual jogging of unfixed reason. The torment of suspense is very great; and as soon as the wavering, perplexed mind begins to determine, be the determination which way soever, it will find itself at ease.—South.

———

Nothing is more perplexing than the power, but nothing is more durable than the dynasty of doubt; for he reigns in the hearts of all his people, but gives satisfaction to none of them, and yet he is the only despot who can never die while any of his subjects live.—Colton.

———

When we are in doubt and puzzle out the truth by our own exertions, we have gained a something that will stay by us, and which will serve us again. But, if to avoid the trouble of the search, we avail ourselves of the superior information of a friend, such knowledge will not remain with us; we have not bought, but borrowed it.—Colton.

———

Life's sunniest hours are not without
The shadow of some lingering doubt—
Amid its brightest joys will steal
Spectres of evil yet to feel—
Its warmest love is blent with fears,
Its confidence a trembling one—
Its smile—the harbinger of tears—
Its hope—the change of April's sun!
A weary lot—in mercy given,
To fit the chastened soul for heaven.
—Whittier.

———

Cold hearts are not anxious enough to doubt. Men who love will have their misgivings at times; that is not the evil. But the evil is, when men go on in that languid, doubting way, content to doubt, proud of their doubts, morbidly glad to talk about them, liking the romantic gloom of twilight, without the manliness to say, "I must and will know the truth." That did not John the Baptist. Brethren, John appealed to Christ.—F. W. Robertson.

———

You ask bitterly, like Pontius Pilate, "What is truth?" In such an hour

what remains? I reply, "Obedience."
Leave those thoughts for the present.
Act—be merciful and gentle—honest;
force yourself to abound in little services; try to do good to others; be true
in the duty that you know. That
must be right, whatever else is uncertain. And by all the laws of the
human heart, by the word of God, you
shall not be left to doubt. Do that
much of the will of God which is plain
to you, and "You shall know of the
doctrine, whether it be of God."—
F. W. Robertson.

———

Of the terrible doubt of appearances,
Of the uncertainty after all, that we may
  be deluded,
That maybe reliance and hope are but speculations after all,
That maybe indentity beyond the grave is a
  beautiful fable only,
Maybe the things I perceive, the animals,
  plants, men, hills, shining and flowing
  waters,
The skies of day and night, colors, densities,
  forms, maybe these are (as doubtless
  they are) only apparitions, and the real
  something has yet to be known.
          —Walt. Whitman.

———

Fear not to confront realities. The
Saviour lives; and the first joy that
you will give to Him is when, leaving
off your false excuses, you throw yourself with a full heart and empty hands
into His arms of mercy. The Saviour
lives; and were you now to die looking for salvation only from that
Friend of Sinners, verily this day
should you be with Him in a better
than Adam's paradise. The Saviour
lives; and in full sympathy with that
wondrous lover of men's souls, the
Holy Spirit is even now ready if be-
sought to begin His sanctifying process in your mind. The Saviour lives;
and even now He stretches out toward
you an arm which, if you only grasp
in thankful love, your faith shall
strengthen while you cling, and it will
be from no weakness in that arm, if
you are not ere long exalted to a point
of holy attainment which at this moment you view with despair, and by
and by to that region of unveiled realities where you will ask in wonder
at yourself, "Wherefore did I doubt?"
—James Hamilton.

Dove

And there my little doves did sit
  With feathers softly brown
And glittering eyes that showed their right
To general Nature's deep delight.
          —E. B. Browning.

———

The thrustelcok made eek hir lay,
The wode dove upon the spray
She sang ful loude and cleere.
          —Chaucer.

———

As when the dove returning bore the mark
Of earth restored to the long laboring ark;
The relics of mankind, secure of rest,
Oped every window to receive the guest,
And the fair bearer of the message bless'd.
          —Dryden.

———

Oh! when 'tis summer weather,
And the yellow bee, with fairy sound,
The waters clear is humming round,
And the cuckoo sings unseen,
And the leaves are waving green—
  Oh! then 'tis sweet,
  In some retreat,
To hear the murmuring dove,
With those whom on earth alone we love,
And to wind through the greenwood to-
  gether.   —Rev. Wm. Lisle Bowles.

Drama

The drama is the book of the people.
—Willmott.

———

The drama's laws the drama's patrons give,
For we that live to please, must please to
  live.   —Dr. Johnson.

———

A passion for the dramatic art is
inherent in the nature of man.—Edwin
Forrest.

———

All the world's a stage, and all the
men and women merely players.—
Shakespeare.

———

It is remarkable how virtuous and
generously disposed every one is at a
play.—Hazlitt.

———

The seat of wit, when one speaks as
a man of the town and the world, is
the playhouse.—Steele.

———

The real object of the drama is the
exhibition of the human character.—
Macaulay.

———

Men of wit, learning and virtue
might strike out every offensive or unbecoming passage from plays.—Swift.

The drama is the looking-glass in which we see the hideousness of vice and the beauties of virtue.—Frances Anne Kemble.

Dramatical or representative poesy is, as it were, a visible history; for it sets out the image of things as if they were present.—Bacon.

The propriety of thoughts and words, which are the hidden beauties of a play, are but confusedly judged in the vehemence of action.—Dryden.

I maintain, against the enemies of the stage, that patterns of piety, decently represented, may second the precepts.—Dryden.

There is so much of the glare and grief of life connected with the stage that it fills me with most solemn thoughts.—Henry Giles.

The business of the dramatist is to keep himself out of sight, and to let nothing appear but his characters. As soon as he attracts notice to his personal feelings, the illusion is broken. —Macaulay.

On the Greek stage a drama, or acted story, consisted in reality of three dramas, called together a trilogy, and performed consecutively in the course of one day.—Coleridge.

Every movement of the theater by a skilful poet is communicated, as it were, by magic, to the spectators; who weep, tremble, resent, rejoice, and are inflamed with all the variety of passions which actuate the several personages of the drama.—Hume.

The drama embraces and applies all the beauties and decorations of poetry. The sister arts attend and adorn it. Painting, architecture, and music are her handmaids. The costliest lights of a people's intellect burn at her show. All ages welcome her.—Willmott.

The tragedy of "Hamlet" is critically considered to be the masterpiece of dramatic poetry; and the tragedy of "Hamlet" is also, according to the testimony of every sort of manager, the play of all others which can invariably be depended on to fill a theater.—G. A. Sala.

The dramatist, like the poet, is born, not made. * * * There must be inspiration back of all true and permanent art, dramatic or otherwise, and art is universal: there is nothing national about it. Its field is humanity, and it takes in all the world; nor does anything else afford the refuge that is provided by it from all troubles and all the vicissitudes of life.—William Winter.

The drama is not a mere copy of nature, not a facsimile. It is the free running hand of genius, under the impression of its liveliest wit or most passionate impulses, a thousand times adorning or feeling all as it goes; and you must read it, as the healthy instinct of audiences almost always does, if the critics will let them alone, with a grain of allowance, and a tendency to go away with as much of it for use as is necessary, and the rest for the luxury of laughter, pity, or poetical admiration.—Leigh Hunt.

Dreams

The visions of a busy brain.— Joanna Baillie.

The fickle pensioners of Morpheus' train.—Milton.

Our waking dreams are fatal.— Young.

But if, as morning rises, dreams are true.—Dante.

A change came o'er the spirit of my dream.—Byron.

His fancy lost in pleasant dreams. —Addison.

Yet eat in dreams, the custard of the day.—Pope.

A dream itself is but a shadow.— Shakespeare.

For dhrames always go by conthraries, my dear.—Samuel Lover.

Ground not upon dreams, you know they are ever contrary.—Thos. Middleton.

Sleep brings dreams; and dreams are often most vivid and fantastical before we have yet been wholly lost in slumber.—Robert Montgomery Bird.

Dreams are excursions into the limbo of things, a semi-deliverance from the human prison.—Amiel.

Our dreams drench us in sense, and sense steeps us again in dreams.—A. Bronson Alcott.

But dreams full oft are found of real events
The form and shadows. —Joanna Baillie.

As a wild maiden, with love-drinking eyes, sees in sweet dreams a beaming youth of glory.—Alexander Smith.

Like the dreams,
Children of night, of indigestion bred.
—Churchill.

The dreamer is a madman quiescent, the madman is a dreamer in action.—F. H. Hedge.

Regard not dreams, since they are but the images of our hopes and fears.—Cato.

We are near waking when we dream that we dream.—Novalis.

Let not our babbling dreams affright our souls.—Shakespeare.

When monarch reason sleeps, this mimic wakes.—Dryden.

For his dreams, I wonder he's so simple to trust the mockery of unquiet slumbers.—Shakespeare.

If I may trust the flattering truth of sleep,
My dreams presage some joyful news at hand.   —Shakespeare.

When we die, we shall find we have not lost our dreams; we have only lost our sleep.—Richter.

In waking whispers and repeated dreams, to hint pure thoughts and warn the favored soul.—Thomson.

Dreams where thought, in fancy's maze, runs mad.—Young.

Dreams are like portraits; and we find they please because they are confessed resemblances.—Crabbe.

In sleep, when fancy is let loose to play,
Our dreams repeat the wishes of the day.
—Claudius.

Till their own dreams at length deceive 'em,
And, oft repeating, they believe 'em.
—Prior.

Beneath closed lids and folds of deepest shade we think we see.—N. L. Frothingham.

Friday night's dreams on Saturday told
Are sure to come true—be they never so old.   —Old Sayings.

There are a kind of men so loose of soul
That in their sleep will utter their affairs.
—Shakespeare.

I have had a most rare vision. I have had a dream—past the wit of man to say what dream it was.—Shakespeare.

The day seems long, but night is odious; no sleep, but dreams; no dreams but visions strange.—Sir P. Sidney.

Alas! that dreams are only dreams!
That fancy cannot give
A lasting beauty to those forms,
Which scarce a moment live!
—Rufus Dawes.

What studies please, what most delight,
And fill men's thoughts, they dream them
o'er at night.   —Creech.

Sorrow returned with the dawning of morn, and the voice in my dreaming ear melted away.—Campbell.

Every one turns his dreams into realities as far as he can; man is cold as ice to the truth, hot as fire to falsehood.—La Fontaine.

We are such stuff
As dreams are made on, and our little life
Is rounded with a sleep. —Shakespeare.

In this retirement of the mind from the senses, it retains a yet more incoherent manner of thinking, which we call dreaming.—Locke.

As dreams are the fancies of those that sleep, so fancies are but the dreams of those awake.—Sir T. P. Blount.

True, I talk of dreams,
Which are the children of an idle brain,
Begot of nothing but vain fantasy.
—Shakespeare.

A body may as well lay too little as too much stress upon a dream; but the less he heed them the better.—L'Estrange.

Nothing so much convinces me of the boundlessness of the human mind as its operations in dreaming.—W. B. Clulow.

For never yet one hour in his bed
Have I enjoyed the golden dew of sleep,
But have been waked by his timorous
dreams.   —Shakespeare.

Dreaming is an act of pure imagination, attesting in all men a creative power which, if it were available in waking, would make every man a Dante or a Shakespeare.—F. H. Hedge.

I'll dream no more—by manly mind
Not even in sleep is will resigned.
My midnight orisons said o'er,
I'll turn to rest, and dream no more.
—Scott.

Dreams are the children of an idle brain, begot of nothing but vain fantasy; which is as thin of substance as the air, and more inconstant than the wind.—Shakespeare.

Divinity hath oftentimes descended
Upon our slumbers, and the blessed troupes
Have, in the calm and quiet of the soule,
Conversed with us.   —Shirley.

That holy dream—that holy dream,
While all the world were chiding,
Hath cheered me as a lovely beam
A lonely spirit guiding.   —Poe.

I believe it to be true that dreams are the true interpreters of our inclinations; but there is art required to sort and understand them.—Montaigne.

What the tender and poetic youth dreams to-day, and conjures up with inarticulate speech, is to-morrow the vociferated result of public opinion, and the day after is the character of nations.—Emerson.

Dreams are rudiments
Of the great state to come. We dream
About to happen.   —Bailey.
what is

One of those passing rainbow dreams,
Half light, half shade, which fancy's beams
Paint on the fleeting mists that roll,
In trance or slumber, round the soul!
—Moore.

Some dreams we have are nothing else but dreams,
Unnatural and full of contradictions;
Yet others of our most romantic schemes
Are something more than fictions.
—Hood.

The dream
Dreamed by a happy man, when the dark east,
Unseen, is brightening to his bridal morn.
—Tennyson.

'Twas but a dream—let it pass—let it vanish like so many others!
What I thought was a flower is only a weed, and is worthless.
—Longfellow.

In blissful dream, in silent night,
There came to me, with magic might,
With magic might, my own sweet love,
Into my little room above.   —Heine.

Dream after dream ensues;
And still they dream that they shall still succeed;
And still are disappointed.   —Cowper.

The chambers in the house of dreams
Are fed with so divine an air,
That Time's hoar wings grow young therein,
And they who walk there are most fair.
—Francis Thomson.

Dreams, which, beneath the hov'ring shades of night,
Sport with the ever-restless minds of men,
Descend not from the gods. Each busy brain
Creates its own.—Thomas Love Peacock.

Dreams are the bright creatures of poem and legend, who sport on the earth in the night season, and melt away with the first beam of the sun, which lights grim care and stern reality on their daily pilgrimage through the world.—Dickens.

In this world of dreams, I have chosen my part.
To sleep for a season and hear no word
Of true love's truth or of light love's art,
Only the song of a secret bird.
—Swinburne.

If we can sleep without dreaming, it is well that painful dreams are avoided. If, while we sleep, we can have any pleasing dreams, it is as the French say, *tant gagné*, so much added to the pleasure of life.—Franklin.

Dreams in their development have breath,
And tears, and tortures, and the touch of joy,
They have a weight upon our waking thoughts,
They take a weight from off our waking toils,
They do divide our being. —Byron.

Oh! I have pass'd a miserable night,
So full of ugly sights, of ghastly dreams,
That, as I am a Christian faithful man,
I would not spend another such a night,
Though 'twere to buy a world of happy days. —Shakespeare.

And yet, as angels in some brighter dreams
Call to the soul when man doth sleep,
So some strange thoughts transcend our wonted dreams,
And into glory peep. —Vaughan.

When to soft Sleep we give ourselves away,
And in a dream as in a fairy bark
Drift on and on through the enchanted dark
To purple daybreak—little thought we pay
To that sweet bitter world we know by day.
—T. B. Aldrich.

We are somewhat more than ourselves in our sleep; and the slumber of the body seems to be but the waking of the soul. It is the ligation of sense, but the liberty of reason; and our waking conceptions do not match the fancies of our sleeps.—Sir Thomas Browne.

I believe that everyone, some time or other, dreams that he is reading papers, books, or letters; in which case the invention prompts so readily that the mind is imposed upon, and mistakes its own suggestions for the composition of another.—Addison.

As one who in some frightful dream would shun
His pressing foe, labors in vain to run
And his own slowness in his sleep bemoans.
In short thick sighs, weak cries, and tender groans. —Dryden.

I dreamt my lady came and found me dead,
(Strange dream! that gives a dead man leave to think),
And breath'd such life with kisses in my lips
That I reviv'd, and was an emperor.
—Shakespeare.

Sweet sleep be with us, one and all!
And if upon its stillness fall
The visions of a busy brain,
We'll have our pleasure o'er again,
To warm the heart, to charm the sight,
Gay dreams to all! good night, good night.
—Joanna Baillie.

What was your dream?
It seemed to me that a woman in white raiment, graceful and fair to look upon, came towards me and calling me by name said:
On the third day, Socrates, thou shalt reach the coast of fertile Phthia.
—Plato.

The fisher droppeth his net in the stream,
And a hundred streams are the same as one;
And the maiden dreameth her love-lit dream;
And what is it all, when all is done?
The net of the fisher the burden breaks
And always the dreaming the dreamer wakes. —Alice Cary.

And the dream that our mind had sketched in haste
Shall others continue, but never complete.
For none upon earth can achieve his scheme;
The best as the worst are futile here:
We wake at the self-same point of the dream—
All is here begun, and finished elsewhere. —Victor Hugo.

In dreams we are true poets; we create the persons of the drama; we give them appropriate figures, faces, costumes; they are perfect in their organs, attitudes, manners; moreover they speak after their own characters, not ours; and we listen with surprise to what they say.—Emerson.

Dreams ought to produce no conviction whatever on philosophical minds. If we consider how many dreams are dreamt every night, and how many events occur every day, we shall no longer wonder at those accidental coincidences which ignorance mistakes for verifications.—Colton.

Thy spirit within thee hath been so at war,
And thus hath so bestirr'd thee in thy sleep
That beads of sweat have stood upon thy brow
Like bubbles in a late-disturbed stream:
And in thy face strange motions have appear'd,
Such as we see when men restrain their breath
On some great sudden haste.
    —Shakespeare.

Those dreams, that on the silent night intrude,
And with false flitting shades our minds delude,
Jove never sends us downward from the skies;
Nor can they from infernal mansions rise;
But are all mere productions of the brain,
And fools consult interpreters in vain.
    —Swift.

Metaphysicians have been learning their lessons for the last four thousand years, and it is high time that they should now begin to teach us something. Can any of the tribe inform us why all the operations of the mind are carried on with undiminished strength and activity in dreams, except the judgment, which alone is suspended and dormant?—Colton.

Dress

The dress does not make the monk.—Rabelais.

Dress changes the manners.—Voltaire.

A saint in crape is twice a saint in lawn.—Pope.

Dress is an index of your contents.—Lavater.

She bears a duke's revenues on her back.—Shakespeare.

His dress was a volcano of silk with lava buttons.—Sydney Smith.

Ridiculous modes, invented by ignorance, and adopted by folly.—Smollett.

Dress does not give knowledge.—Yriarte.

Out of clothes out of countenance, out of countenance out of wit.—Ben Jonson.

Oft in dreams invention we bestow to change a flounce or add a furbelow.—Pope.

No man is esteemed for gay garments but by fools and women.—Sir Walter Raleigh.

Eat to please thyself, but dress to please others.—Franklin.

Who seems most hideous when adorned the most.—Ariosto.

The only medicine which does women more good than harm is dress.—Richter.

It is not every man who can afford to wear a shabby coat.—Colton.

In the matter of dress one should always keep below one's ability.—Montesquieu.

In clothes clean and fresh there is a kind of youth with which age should surround itself.—Joubert.

No real happiness is found
In trailing purple o'er the ground.
    —Parnell.

Gay mellow silks her mellow charms infold, and nought of Lyce but herself is old.—Young.

My dear, your everlasting blue velvet quite tires me.—Thackeray.

The fashion wears out more apparel than the man.—Shakespeare.

Next to dressing for a rout or ball, undressing is a woe.—Byron.

In cloths cheap handsomeness doth bear the bell.—George Herbert.

The wanton lawns, more soft and white than milk.—Beaumont and Fletcher.

Beauty, like truth, never is so glorious as when it goes plainest.—Sterne.

There can be no kernel in this light nut; the soul of this man is in his clothes.—Shakespeare.

There is not so variable a thing in nature as a lady's head-dress.—Addison.

Dress is the great business of all women, and the fixed idea of some.—Alphonse Karr.

An ugly woman in a rich habit set out with jewels nothing can become.—Dryden.

When a soldier is hit by a cannon-ball, rags are as becoming as purple.—Thoreau.

Here's such a plague every morning, with buckling shoes, gartering, combing and powdering.—Farquhar.

Be plain in dress, and sober in your diet;
In short, my deary, kiss me! and be quiet.
—Lady M. W. Montagu.

The plainer the dress, with greater luster does beauty appear.—Lord Halifax.

As soon as a woman begins to dress "loud," her manners and conversation partake of the same element.—Haliburton.

There are female dandies as well as clothes-wearing men; and the former are as objectionable as the latter.—Carlyle.

There are some women who require much dressing, as some meats must be highly seasoned to make them palatable.—Rochebrune.

Worldly wisdom dictates to her disciples the propriety of dressing somewhat beyond their means, but of living somewhat within them.—Colton.

If a woman were about to proceed to her execution, she would demand a little time to perfect her toilet.—Chamfort.

Too great carelessness, equally with excess in dress, multiplies the wrinkles of old age, and makes its decay still more conspicuous.—Bruyère.

Let Harlequin be taken with a fit of the colic, and his trappings will have to serve that mood too.—Thoreau.

And why take ye thought for raiment? Consider the lilies of the field, how they grow: they toil not, neither do they spin.—Bible.

We sacrifice to dress till household joys and comforts cease. Dress drains our cellar dry, and keeps our larder lean.—Cowper.

Costly thy habit as thy purse can buy, but not expressed in fancy; rich, not gaudy; for the apparel oft proclaims the man.—Shakespeare.

Oh, fair undress, best dress! It checks no vein, but every flowing limb in pleasure drowns, and heightens ease with grace.—Thomson.

Sturdy swains, in clean array, for rustic dance prepare, mixed with the buxom damsels hand in hand.—John Phillips.

A fine coat is but a livery when the person who wears it discovers no higher sense than that of a footman.—Addison.

As you treat your body, so your house, your domestics, your enemies, your friends. Dress is a table of your contents.—Lavater.

The peacock in all his pride does not display half the colors that appear in the garments of a British lady when she is dressed.—Addison.

Nothing can embellish a beautiful face more than a narrow band that indicates a small wound drawn crosswise over the brow.—Richter.

In the indications of female poverty there can be no disguise. No woman dresses below herself from caprice.—Lamb.

The vanity of loving fine clothes and new fashions, and valuing ourselves by them, is one of the most childish pieces of folly that can be.—Sir Matthew Hale.

A rich dress adds but little to the beauty of a person. It may possibly create a deference, but that is rather an enemy to love.—Shenstone.

I am convinced that if the virtuosi could once find out a world in the moon, with a passage to it, our women would wear nothing but what directly came from thence.—Swift.

A man's appearance falls within the censure of every one that sees him; his parts and learning very few are judges of.—Steele.

We believe that the dress that shows taste and sentiment is elevating to the home, and is one of the most feminine means of beautifying the world.—Miss Oakey.

We may hold it slavish to dress according to the judgment of fools and the caprice of coxcombs; but are we not ourselves both when we are singular in our attire?—Chatfield.

Those who think that in order to dress well it is necessary to dress extravagantly or grandly make a great mistake. Nothing so well becomes true feminine beauty as simplicity.—George D. Prentice.

Those who are incapable of shining out by dress would do well to consider that the contrast between them and their clothes turns out much to their disadvantage.—Shenstone.

He that is proud of the rustling of his silks, like a madman, laughs at the rattling of his fetters; for, indeed, clothes ought to be our remembrancers of our lost innocency.—Thomas Fuller.

That the women of the Old Testament were dressed with oriental richness there is no doubt, nor are they censured for so arraying themselves.—Charlotte M. Yonge.

Women always show more taste in adorning others than themselves; and the reason is that their persons are like their hearts—they read another's better than they can their own.—Richter.

A lady of genius will give a genteel air to her whole dress by a well-fancied suit of knots, as a judicious writer gives a spirit to a whole sentence by a single expression.—Gay.

Rich apparel has strange virtues; it makes him that hath it without means esteemed for an excellent wit; he that enjoys it with means puts the world in remembrance of his means.—Ben Jonson.

What, is the jay more precious than the lark,
Because his feathers are more beautiful?
Or is the adder better than the eel,
Because his painted skin contents the eye?
—Shakespeare.

Our purses shall be proud, our garments poor:
For 'tis the mind that makes the body rich;
And as the sun breaks through the darkest clouds,
So honor peereth in the meanest habit.
—Shakespeare.

Women overrate the influence of fine dress and the latest fashions upon gentlemen; and certain it is that the very expensiveness of such attire frightens the beholder from all ideas of matrimony.—Abba Goold Woolson.

Her polish'd limbs,
Veil'd in a simple robe, their best attire,
Beyond the pomp of dress; for loveliness
Needs not the foreign aid of ornament,
But is, when unadorn'd, adorn'd the most.
—Thomson.

It is well known that a loose and easy dress contributes much to give to both sexes those fine proportions of body that are observable in the Grecian statues, and which serve as models to our present artists.—Rousseau.

I have heard with admiring submission the experience of the lady who declared that the sense of being well dressed gives a feeling of inward tranquillity which religion is powerless to ·bestow.—Emerson.

Through tattered clothes small vices do appear; robes and furred gowns hide all. Plate sin with gold, and the strong lance of justice hurtless breaks; arm it in rags, a pygmy's straw doth pierce it.—Shakespeare.

Good dressing includes a suggestion of poetry. One nowhere more quickly detects sentiment than in dress. A well-dressed woman in a room should fill it with poetic sense, like the perfume of flowers.—Miss Oakey.

Let women paint their eyes with tints of chastity, insert into their ears the word of God, tie the yoke of Christ around their necks, and adorn their whole persons with the silk of sanctity and the damask of devotion.—Tertullian.

Be neither too early in the fashion, nor too long out of it, nor too precisely in it; what custom hath civilized is become decent, till then ridiculous; where the eye is the jury thy apparel is the evidence.—Quarles.

To this end, nothing is to be more carefully consulted than plainness. In a lady's attire this is the single excellence; for to be what some people call fine, is the same vice, in that case, as to be florid is in writing or speaking. —Addison.

Many shiver from want of defence against the cold; but there is vastly more suffering among the rich from absurd and criminal modes of dress, which fashion has sanctioned, than among the poor from deficiency of raiment.—Channing.

Love in modern times has been the tailor's best friend. Every suitor of the nineteenth century spends more than his spare cash on personal adornment. A faultless fit, a glistening hat, tight gloves, and tighter boots pro-

claim the imminent peril of his position.—G. A. Sala.

Next to clothes being fine, they should be well made, and worn easily; for a man is only the less genteel for a fine coat, if, in wearing it, he shows a regard for it, and is not as easy in it as if it was a plain one.—Chesterfield.

Virgil has very finely touched upon the female passion for dress and shows, in the character of Camilla; who, though she seems to have shaken off all the other weaknesses of her sex, is still described as a woman in this particular.—Addison.

Beauty gains little, and homeliness and deformity lose much, by gaudy attire. Lysander knew this was in part true, and refused the rich garments that the tyrant Dionysius proffered to his daughters, saying "that they were fit only to make unhappy faces more remarkable."—Zimmermann.

Dress has a moral effect upon the conduct of mankind. Let any gentleman find himself with dirty boots, old surtout, soiled neckcloth and a general negligence of dress, and he will in all probability find a corresponding disposition by negligence of address.—Sir Jonah Barrington.

In Athens the ladies were not gaudily but simply arrayed, and we doubt whether any ladies ever excited more admiration. So also the noble old Roman matrons, whose superb forms were gazed on delightedly by men worthy of them, were always very plainly dressed.—George D. Prentice.

Men of quality never appear more amiable than when their dress is plain. Their birth, rank, title and its appendages are at best invidious; and as they do not need the assistance of dress, so, by their disclaiming the advantage of it, they make their superiority sit more easy.—Shenstone.

Processions, cavalcades, and all that fund of gay frippery, furnished out by tailors, barbers, and tire-women, me·

chanically influence the mind into veneration; an emperor in his nightcap would not meet with half the respect of an emperor with a crown.—Goldsmith.

I have always a sacred veneration for any one I observe to be a little out of repair in his person, as supposing him either a poet or a philosopher; because the richest minerals are ever found under the most ragged and withered surfaces of the earth.—Swift.

A simple garb is the proper costume of the vulgar; it is cut for them, and exactly suits their measure; but it is an ornament for those who have filled up their lives with great deeds. I liken them to beauty in dishabille, but more bewitching on that account.—Bruyère.

The person whose clothes are extremely fine I am too apt to consider as not being possessed of any superiority of fortune, but resembling those Indians who are found to wear all the gold they have in the world in a bob at the nose.—Goldsmith.

A majority of women seem to consider themselves sent into the world for the sole purpose of displaying dry goods, and it is only when acting the part of an animated milliner's block that they feel they are performing their appropriate mission.—Abba Goold Woolson.

Beauty in dress, as in other things, is largely relative. To admit this is to admit that a dress which is beautiful upon one woman may be hideous worn by another. Each should understand her own style, accept it, and let the fashion of her dress be built upon it.—Miss Oakey.

Never teach false modesty. How exquisitely absurd to teach a girl that beauty is of no value, dress of no use! Beauty is of value; her whole prospects and happiness in life may often depend upon a new gown or a becoming bonnet; if she has five grains of common sense she will find this out. The great thing is to teach her their proper value.—Sydney Smith.

A French woman is a perfect architect in dress: she never, with Gothic ignorance, mixes the orders; she never tricks out a snobby Doric shape with Corinthian finery; or, to speak without metaphor, she conforms to general fashion only when it happens not to be repugnant to private beauty.—Goldsmith.

The gracious and self-sacrificing and womanly women of our revolution wore dresses cut lower than those of their great-granddaughters, as any portrait gallery will show. The dress is indefensible, but let us not be too ready to condemn the wearer for worse sins than thoughtlessness and vanity.—Mrs. L. G. Calhoun.

A gentleman's taste in dress is, upon principle, the avoidance of all things extravagant. It consists in the quiet simplicity of exquisite neatness; but, as the neatness must be a neatness in fashion, employ the best tailor; pay him ready money, and, on the whole, you will find him the cheapest.—Bulwer-Lytton.

No man ever stood lower in my estimation for having a patch in his clothes; yet I am sure there is greater anxiety to have fashionable, or at least clean and unpatched clothes, than to have a sound conscience. I sometimes try my acquaintances by some such test as this—who could wear a patch, or two extra seams only, over the knee.—Thoreau.

As long as there are cold and nakedness in the land around you, so long can there be no question at all but that splendor of dress is a crime. In due time, when we have nothing better to set people to work at, it may be right to let them make lace and cut jewels: but as long as there are any who have no blankets for their beds, and no rags for their bodies, so long it is blanket-making and tailoring we must set people to work at, not lace.—Ruskin.

It is the saying of an old divine, "Two things in my apparel I will chiefly aim at—commodiousness and decency; more than these is not commendable, yet I hate an effeminate spruceness as much as a fantastic disorder. A neglected comeliness is the best ornament." It is said of the celebrated Mr. Whitfield that he always was very clean and neat, and often said pleasantly "that a minister of the gospel ought to be without a spot."— J. Beaumont.

As the index tells us the contents of stories and directs to the particular chapter, even so does the outward habit and superficial order of garments (in man or woman) give us a taste of the spirit, and demonstratively point (as it were a manual note from the margin) all the internal quality of the soul ; and there cannot be a more evident, palpable, gross manifestation of poor, degenerate, dunghilly blood and breeding than a rude, unpolished, disordered, and slovenly outside.—Massinger.

I would rather have a young fellow too much than too little dressed ; the excess on that side will wear off, with a little age and reflection ; but if he is negligent at twenty, he will be a sloven at forty, and stink at fifty years old. Dress yourself fine where others are fine, and plain where others are plain ; but take care always that your clothes are well made and fit you, for otherwise they will give you a very awkward air.—Chesterfield.

Drink, Drunkenness

Habitual intoxication is the epitome of every crime.—Douglas Jerrold.

Drunkenness is nothing else than a voluntary madness.—Seneca.

Drink, pretty creature, drink !— Wordsworth.

Some folks are drunk, yet do not know it.—Prior.

Troops of furies march in the drunkard's triumph.—Zimmermann.

The drunkard and the glutton shall come to poverty.—Prov. 23 : 21.

Woe unto them that rise up early in the morning that they may follow strong drink.—Bible.

A drunkard is unprofitable for any kind of good service.—Plato.

Every inordinate cup is unbless'd, and the ingredient is a devil.—Shakespeare.

Thirst teaches all animals to drink, but drunkenness belongs only to man. —Fielding.

The axe of intemperance has lopped off his green boughs and left him a withered trunk.—Swift.

There is scarcely a crime before me that is not directly or indirectly caused by strong drink.—Judge Coleridge.

'Tis pity wine should be so deleterious, For tea and coffee leave us much more serious. —Byron.

Inspiring bold John Barleycorn, What dangers thou canst make us scorn. —Burns.

The sight of a drunkard is a better sermon against that vice than the best that was ever preached upon that subject.—Saville.

A vine bears three grapes—the first of pleasure, the second of drunkenness, and the third of repentance.— Anacharsis.

The drunkard forfeits man and doth divest All wordly right, save what he hath by beast. —Herbert.

The bliss of the drunkard is a visible picture of the expectation of the dying atheist, who hopes no more than to lie down in the grave with the "beasts that perish."—Jane Porter.

If a man is right, all the bombardment of the world for five, ten, twenty, forty years will only strengthen him in his position. So that all you have to do is to keep yourself right. Never mind the world. Let it say what it will. It can do you no damage. But as soon as it is whispered "he drinks," and it can be proved, he begins to go down. What clerk can get a position with such a reputation? What store wants him? What Church of God wants him for a member? What dying man wants him for an executor? "He drinks!"—Talmage.

Now to rivulets from the mountains
Point the rods of fortune-tellers;
Youth perpetual dwells in fountains,
Not in flasks, and casks, and cellars.
—Longfellow.

There shall be, in England, seven half-penny loaves sold for a penny; the three-hooped pot shall have ten hoops; and I will make it felony to drink small beer.—Shakespeare.

Woe to him that giveth his neighbor drink, that puttest thy bottle to him and makest him drunken.—Hab. 2 : 15.

When he is best, he is little worse than a man; and when he is worst he is little better than a beast.—Shakespeare.

The first draught a man drinks ought to be for thirst, the second for nourishment, the third for pleasure, the fourth for madness.

Man has evil as well as good qualities peculiar to himself. Drunkenness places him as much below the level of the brutes as reason elevates him above them.—Sir G. Sinclair.

People say, "Do not regard what he says now he is in liquor." Perhaps it is the only time he ought to be regarded: *Aperit prae cordia liber.*—Shenstone.

Those men who destroy a healthful constitution of body by intemperance and an irregular life do as manifestly kill themselves as those who hang or poison or drown themselves.—Shakespeare.

Almighty God! If it be thy will that man should suffer, whatever seemeth good in thy sight impose upon me. Let the bread of affliction be given to me to eat. Take from me the friends of my confidence. Let the cold hut of poverty be my dwelling-place and the wasting hand of disease inflict its painful torments. Let me sow in the whirlwind and reap in the storm. Let

those have me in derision who are younger than I. Let the passing away of my welfare be like the fleeting of a cloud and the shouts of my enemies like the rushing of waters. When I anticipate good, let evil annoy me. When I look for light, let darkness come upon me. Do all this, but save me, merciful God! Save me from the fate of a drunkard.—Talmage.

I drank: I liked it not: 'twas rage,
'twas noise,
An airy scene of transitory joys.
In vain I trusted that the flowing bowl
Would banish sorrow and enlarge the
soul. —Prior.

Some of the domestic evils of drunkenness are houses without windows, gardens without fences, fields without tillage, barns without roofs, children without clothing, principles, morals or manners.—Franklin.

Drunkenness is a flattering devil, a sweet poison, a pleasant sin, which whosoever hath hath not himself; which whosoever doth commit doth not commit sin, but he himself is wholly sin.—St. Augustine.

Call things by their right names. * * * Glass of brandy and water! That is the current, but not the appropriate, name; ask for a glass of liquid fire and distilled damnation.—Robert Hall.

O that men should put an enemy in their mouths to steal away their brains! that we should with joy, pleasance, revel, and applause, transform ourselves into beasts!—Shakespeare.

As long as you make drinking respectable, drinking customs will prevail, and the plowshare of death, drawn by terrible disasters, will go on turning up this whole continent, from end to end, with the long, deep, awful furrow of drunkards' graves.—Talmage.

I will ask him for my place again: he shall tell me I am a drunkard. Had I as many mouths as Hydra, such an answer would stop them all. To be now a sensible man, by and by a fool, and presently a beast. O strange! Every inordinate cup is unblessed, and the ingredient is a devil. —Shakespeare.

A monster such as never ranged African thicket or Hindustan jungle hath traced this land, and with bloody maw hath strewn the continent with the mangled carcasses of whole generations; and there are tens of thousands of fathers and mothers who could hold up the garment of their slain boy, truthfully exclaiming, "It is my son's coat; that evil beast, Intemperance, hath devoured him."— Talmage.

Oli.—What's a drunken man like, fool?

Clo.—Like a drowned man, a fool, and a madman; one draught above heat makes him a fool, the second mads him, and a third drowns him.— Shakespeare.

The thirsty Earth soaks up the Rain, And drinks, and gapes for Drink again;
The Plants suck in the Earth and are With constant Drinking fresh and fair.   —Cowley.

Thou sparkling bowl! thou sparkling bowl!
Through lips of bards thy brim may press,
And eyes of beauty o'er thee roll,
And song and dance they power confess—
I will not touch thee; for there clings A scorpion to thy side that stings.   —John Pierpont.

Oh! if you could only hear Intemperance with drunkards' bones drumming on the top of the wine cask the Dead March of immortal souls, you would go home and kneel down and pray God that rather than your children should ever become the victims of this evil habit, you might carry them out to Greenwood and put them down in the last slumber, waiting for the flowers of spring to come over the grave—sweet prophecies of the resurrection. God hath a balm for such a wound, but what flower of comfort ever grew on the blasted heath of a drunkard's sepulcher?—Talmage.

All excess is ill, but drunkenness is of the worst sort. It spoils health, dismounts the mind, and unmans men. It reveals secrets, is quarrelsome, lascivious, impudent, dangerous and bad. —William Penn.

Drunkenness is the vice of a good constitution or of a bad memory—of a constitution so treacherously good that it never bends till it breaks; or of a memory that recollects the pleasures of getting intoxicated, but forgets the pains of getting sober.—Colton.

If a man's innate self-respect will not save him from habitual, disgusting intoxication, all the female influences in the universe would not avail. Man's will, like woman's, is stronger than the affections, and once subjugated by vice, all eternal influences will be futile.—Miss Evans.

The rum fiend would like to go and hang up a skeleton in your beautiful house so that, when you opened the front door to go in, you would see it in the hall; and, when you sat at your table you would see it hanging from the wall; and, when you opened your bedroom you would find it stretched upon your pillow; and, waking at night, you would feel its cold hand passing over your face and pinching at your heart. There is no home so beautiful but it may be devastated by the awful curse.—Talmage.

It were better for a man to be subject to any vice than to drunkenness; for all other vanities and sins are recovered, but a drunkard will never shake off the delight of beastliness.— Sir Walter Raleigh.

Your friends avoid you, brutishly transform'd
They hardly know you, or if one remains
To wish you well, he wishes you in heaven.   —Armstrong.

Beware of drunkenness, lest all good men beware of thee; where drunkenness reigns, there reason is an exile, virtue a stranger, God an enemy; blasphemy is wit, oaths are rhetoric, and secrets are proclamations.—Quarles.

Intemperance is a dangerous companion. It throws many people off their guard, betrays them to a great many indecencies, to ruinous passions, to disadvantages in fortune; makes them discover secrets, drive foolish bargains, engage in play, and often to stagger from the tavern to the stews. —Jeremy Collier.

The longer it possesseth a man the more he will delight in it, and the elder he groweth the more he shall be subject to it; for it dulleth the spirits, and destroyeth the body as ivy doth the old tree, or as the worm that engendereth in the kernal of the nut.— Sir Walter Raleigh.

The habit of using ardent spirits by men in office has occasioned more injury to the public, and more trouble to me, than all other causes. Were I to commence my administration again, the first question I would ask respecting a candidate for office would be, Does he use ardent spirits?—Jefferson.

Man with raging drink inflam'd,
Is far more savage and untamed;
Supplies his loss of wit and sense
With barb'rousness and insolence;
Believes himself, the less he's able
The more heroic and formidable.
—Butler.

The costliest thing on earth is the drunkard's song. It costs ruin of body. It costs ruin of mind, It costs ruin of soul. Go right down among the residential streets of any city and you can find once beautiful and luxurious homesteads that were expended in this destructive music. The lights have gone out in the drawing-room the pianos have ceased the pulsation of their keys, the wardrobe has lost its last article of appropriate attire. The Belshazzarean feast has left nothing but the broken pieces of the crushed chalices. There it stands, the ghastliest thing on earth, the remnant of a drunkard's home. The costliest thing on earth is sin. The most expensive of all music is the Song of the Drunkards. It is the highest tariff, of nations—not a protective tariff, but a tariff of doom, a tariff of woe, a tariff of death.—Talmage.

Drunkenness is not only the cause of crime, but it is crime; and if any encourage drunkenness for the sake of the profit derived from the sale of drink, they are guilty of a form of moral assassination as criminal as any that has ever been practiced by the braves of any country or of any age.—Ruskin.

Drunkenness! Does it not jingle the burglar's key? Does it not whet the assassin's knife? Does it not cock the highwayman's pistol? Does it not wave the incendiary's torch? Does it not send the physician reeling into the sickroom; and the minister with his tongue thick into the pulpit? Did not an exquisite poet, from the very top of his fame, fall a gibbering sot, into the gutter, on his way to be married to one of the fairest daughters of New England, and at the very hour the bride was decking herself for the altar; and did he not die of delirium tremens, almost unattended, in a hospital? Tamerlane asked for one hundred and sixty thousand skulls with which to build a pyramid to his own honor. He got the skulls, and built the pyramid. But if the bones of all those who have fallen as a prey to dissipation could be piled up, it would make a vaster pyramid.—Talmage.

The young man who thinks he can drink "just a little" because others do, and not be in danger of a drunkard's grave, should look around him to fearful examples to be found on the streets of every large city and many small ones. Even if you succeed in keeping within the limits of "moderate drinking" your example to those who are unfortunately not so strong-willed should ever be borne in mind. Help the weaker brother. Think not of self alone. Remember the Golden Rule.—George D. R. Hubbard.

Let no company or respect ever draw you to excess in drink, for be you well assured, that if ever that possess you, you are instantly drunk to all the respects your friends will otherwise pay you, and shall by unequal staggering paces go to your grave with confusion of face, as well in them that love you as in yourself; and, therefore abhor all company that

might entice you that way.—Lord
Strafford.

It weaks the brain, it spoils the memory,
Hasting on age, and wilful poverty;
It drowns thy better parts, making thy
   name
To foes a laughter, to thy friends a shame.
'Tis virtue's poison and the bane of trust,
The match of wrath, the fuel unto lust.
Quite leave this vice, and turn not to 't
   again,
Upon presumption of a stronger brain;
For he who holds more wine than others
   can,
I rather count a hogshead than a man.
     —Randolph.

Of all vices take heed of drunkenness; other vices are but fruits of disordered affections—this disorders, nay,
banishes reason; other vices but impair the soul—this demolishes her two
chief faculties, the understanding and
the will; other vices make their own
way—this makes way for all vices;
he that is a drunkard is qualified for
all vice.—Quarles.

Drowning

O Lord, methought, what pain it was to
   drown,
What dreadful noise of water in mine ears!
What sights of ugly death within mine
   eyes!
Methought I saw a thousand fearful
   wracks;
A thousand men that fishes gnaw'd upon;
Wedges of gold, great anchors, heaps of
   pearl,
Inestimable stones, unvalued jewels,
All scattered in the bottom of the sea;
Some lay in dead men's skulls; and in those
   holes
Where eyes did once inhabit, there were
   crept,
As 'twere in scorn of eyes, reflecting gems.
     —Shakespeare.

Drudgery

The everyday cares and duties,
which men call drudgery, are the
weights and counterpoises of the clock
of time; giving its pendulum a true
vibration and its hands a regular motion; and when they cease to hang
upon its wheels, the pendulum no
longer swings, the hands no longer
move, the clock stands still.—Longfellow.

Duelling

Since bodily strength is but a servant to the mind, it were very barbarous and preposterous that force
should be made judge over reason.—
Sir P. Sidney.

If all seconds were as averse to
duels as their principals, very little
blood would be shed in that way.—
Colton.

It has a strange, quick jar upon the ear,
   That cocking of a pistol, when you know
A moment more will bring the sight to bear
Upon your person, twelve yards off or
     so.
     —Byron.

Some fiery fop, with new commission vain,
Who sleeps on brambles till he kills his
   man;
Some frolic drunkard, reeling from a feast,
Provokes a broil, and stabs you for a jest.
     —Dr. Johnson.

Ah me! what perils do environ
The man that meddles with cold iron!
What plaguy mischiefs and mishaps
Do dog him still with after-claps.
     —Butler.

Duelling, though barbarous in civilized, is a highly civilized institution
among barbarous people; and when
compared to assassination, is a prodigious victory gained over human
passions.—Sydney Smith.

Do not cherish that daring vice for
which the whole age suffers—these
private duels—which had their first
original from the French and for
which to this day we're justly censured, are banished from all civil government.—Beaumont and Fletcher.

Men engage in it compell'd by force,
And fear, not courage, is its proper source,
The fear of tyrant custom, and the fear
Lest fops should censure us, and fools
   should sneer.
     *   *   *   *   *
Am I to set my life upon a throw
Because a bear is rude and surly?—No—
A moral, sensible, and well-bred man
Will not affront me, and no other can.
     —Cowper.

With respect to duels, indeed, I have
my own ideas. Few things in this
surprising world strike me with more
surprise. Two little visual spectra of
men, hovering with insecure enough
cohesion in the midst of the unfathomable, and to dissolve therein, at any

rate, very soon, make pause at the distance of twelve paces asunder, whirl around, and simultaneously, by the cunningest mechanism, explode one another into dissolution; and, off-hand, become air, and non-extant—the little spitfires!—Carlyle.

Dullness

The worst of it is, dullness is catching.—Douglas Jerrold.

Glory and gain the industrious tribe pro-
voke;
And gentle dullness ever loves a joke.
—Pope.

There are some heads which have no windows, and the day can never strike from above; nothing enters from heavenward.—Joubert.

For of a truth stupidity is strong, most strong, as the poet Schiller sings, "Against stupidity the very gods fight invictorious."—Carlyle.

The head of dullness, unlike the tail of the torpedo, loses nothing of the benumbing and lethargizing influence, by reiterated discharges.—Colton.

What a comfort a dull but kindly person is, to be sure, at times! A ground-glass shade over a gas lamp does not bring more solace to our dazzled eyes than such a one to our minds.—Holmes.

A dull man is so near a dead man that he is hardly to be ranked in the list of the living; and as he is not to be buried whilst he is half alive, so he is as little to be employed whilst he is half dead.—Saville.

Duplicity

Where nature's end of language is declined,
And men talk only to conceal the mind.
—Young.

Damn with faint praise, assent with civil
leer,
And, without sneering, teach the rest to
sneer;
Willing to wound, and yet afraid to strike,
Just hint a fault, and hesitate dislike.
—Pope.

I, I, I myself, sometimes, leaving the fear of heaven on the left hand,

and hiding mine honor in my necessity, am fain to shuffle, to hedge, and to lurch.—Shakespeare.

O, what may man within him hide,
Though angel on the outward side.
—Shakespeare.

One dupe is as impossible as one twin.—John Sterling.

Duty

Stern daughter of the voice of God!
—Wordsworth.

Duties are ours; events are God's.
—Cecil.

Duty is the demand of the hour.—Goethe.

Simple duty hath no place for fear.
—Whittier.

Who escapes a duty avoids a gain.
—Theodore Parker.

Consult duty, not events.—Annesly.

Man cannot choose his duties.—George Eliot.

New occasions teach new duties.—James Russell Lowell.

Men must be either the slaves of duty, or the slaves of force.—Joseph Joubert.

The reward of one duty is the power to fulfill another.—George Eliot.

Do the duty which lies nearest to thee.—Goethe.

Fear is not a lasting teacher of duty.—Cicero.

God never imposes a duty without giving the time to do it.—Ruskin.

Every subject's duty is the king's; but every subject's soul is his own.—Shakespeare.

Life is of little value unless it be consecrated by duty.—Samuel Smiles.

Perish discretion when it interferes with duty.—Hannah More.

The sense of duty pursues us ever. —Joseph Cook.

Thanks to the gods; my boy has done his duty.—Addison.

England expects every man to do his duty.—Horatio Nelson.

Not liberty but duty is the condition of existence.—Mathilde Blind.

There is no moment without some duty.—Cicero.

We have an intuitive sense of our duty.—Swift.

The doing of things from duty is but a stage on the road to the kingdom of truth and love.—George MacDonald.

Hath the spirit of all beauty
Kissed you in the path of duty?
—Anna Katharine Green.

There are not good things enough in life to indemnify us for the neglect of a single duty.—Madame Swetchine.

None should expect to prosper who go out of the way of duty.—Aughey.

There is nothing in the universe I fear but that I shall not know all my duty, or shall fail to do it.—Mary Lyon.

Knowledge is the hill which few may hope to climb; duty is the path that all may tread.—Lewis Morris.

Cold duty's path is not so blithely trod
Which leads the mournful spirit to its God.
—William Herbert.

When I'm not thank'd at all, I'm thank'd enough:
I've done my duty, and I've done no more.
—Fielding.

Knowledge of our duties is the most useful part of philosophy.—Whately.

The most fruitful and elevating influence I have ever seemed to meet

has been my impression of obligation to God.—Daniel Webster.

The latest gospel in this world is, know thy work and do it.—Carlyle.

Duty only frowns when you flee from it; follow it, and it smiles upon you.—Elizabeth, Queen of Roumania.

Let us not run out of the path of duty, lest we run into the way of danger.—Rowland Hill.

He who can at all times sacrifice pleasure to duty approaches sublimity. —Lavater.

Never anything can be amiss, when simpleness and duty tender it.—Shakespeare.

As birds are made to fly and rivers to run, so the soul to follow duty.— Ramayana.

Every duty we omit obscures some truth we should have known.— Ruskin.

To what gulfs a single deviation from the track of human duties leads! —Byron.

Every mission constitutes a pledge of duty.—Mazzini.

Do well the duty that lies before you.—Pittachus.

In doing what we ought we deserve no praise, because it is our duty.—St. Augustine.

Zeal and duty are not slow;
But on occasion's forelock watchful wait.
—Milton.

Men love to hear of their power, but have an extreme disrelish to be told their duty.—Burke.

Whether your time calls you to live or die, do both like a prince.—Sir P. Sidney.

Every one regards his duty as a troublesome master from whom he would like to be free.—La Roche,

The true way to render ourselves happy is to love our duty and find in it our pleasure.—Mme. de Motteville.

Then on! then on! where duty leads,
My course be onward still.
—Bishop Heber.

You will always find those who think they know your duty better than you know it.—Emerson.

Duty grows everywhere—like children, like grass.—Emerson.

Nothing is properly one's duty but what is also one's interest.—Bishop Wilkins.

Not once or twice in our rough island story,
The path of duty was the way to glory.
—Tennyson.

Every duty, even the least duty, involves the whole principle of obedience.—Archbishop Manning.

Thy sum of duty let two words contain—. . . be humble and be just.—Prior.

It is thy duty oftentimes to do what thou wouldst not; thy duty, too, to leave undone that thou wouldst do.—Thomas à Kempis.

There is no evil which we cannot face or fly from but the consciousness of duty disregarded.—Daniel Webster.

The last pleasure in life is the sense of discharging our duty.—Hazlitt.

Such duty as the subject owes the prince,
Even such a woman oweth to her husband.
—Shakespeare.

In common things the law of sacrifice takes the form of positive duty.—Froude.

Our grand business is, not to see what lies dimly at a distance, but to do what lies clearly at hand.—Thomas Carlyle.

A nation, as an individual, has duties to fulfill appointed by God and His moral law.—Earl of Beaconsfield.

Duty—the command of heaven, the eldest voice of God.—Charles Kingsley.

Duty, especially out of the domain of love, is the veriest slavery in the world.—Timothy Titcomb.

They do well, or do their duty, who with alacrity do what they ought.—La Bruyère.

Our duty is to be useful, not according to our desires but according to our powers.—Amiel.

I am not aware that payment, or even favors, however gracious, bind any man's soul and conscience in questions of highest morality and highest importance.—Charles Kingsley.

When any duty is to be done, it is fortunate for you if you feel like doing it; but, if you do not feel like it, that is no reason for not doing it.—W. Gladden.

Brethren, life is passing; youth goes, strength decays. But duty performed, work done for God—this abides forever, this alone is imperishable.—Richard Fuller.

Man is saved by love and duty, and by the hope that springs from duty, or rather from the moral facts of consciousness, as a flower springs from the soil.—Amiel.

The pleasure a man of honor enjoys in the consciousness of having performed his duty is a reward he pays himself for all his pains.—La Bruyère.

I have learned that to do one's next duty is to take a step toward all that is worth possessing.—J. G. Holland.

Only when the voice of duty is silent, or when it has already spoken, may we allowably think of the consequences of a particular action.—Hare.

A deliberate rejection of duty prescribed by already recognized truth cannot but destroy, or at least impair most seriously the clearness of our mental vision.—H. P. Liddon.

Duty is what goes most against the grain, because in doing that we do only what we are strictly obliged to, and are seldom much praised for it.— La Bruyère.

Let men of all ranks, whether they are successful or unsuccessful, whether they triumph or not—let them do their duty, and rest satisfied. —Plato.

The constant duty of every man to his fellows is to ascertain his own powers and special gifts, and to strengthen them for the help of others. —John Ruskin.

The primal duties shine aloft like stars;
The charities that soothe, and heal, and
    bless,
Are scattered at the feet of man, like
    flowers.   —Wordsworth.

Stern duties need not speak sternly. He who stood firm before the thunder worshipped the "still small voice." —Sidney Dobell.

It is one of the worst of errors to suppose that there is any other path of safety except that of duty.— Aughey.

Whatever our place allotted to us by Providence, that for us is the post of honor and duty. God estimates us, not by the position we are in, but by the way in which we fill it.—T. Edwards.

Let no guilty man escape, if it can be avoided. No personal consideration should stand in the way of performing a public duty.—Ulysses S. Grant.

Duty does not consist in suffering everything, but in suffering everything for duty. Sometimes, indeed, it is our duty not to suffer.—Professor Vinet.

Do your duty, and don't swerve from it. Do that which your con-science tells you to be right, and leave the consequences to God.—B. R. Haydon.

Duty is one and invariable: it requires no impossibilities, nor can it ever be disregarded with impunity.— Thoreau.

Let men laugh when you sacrifice desire to duty, if they will. You have time and eternity to rejoice in.— Theodore Parker.

I see nothing worth living for but the divine virtue which endures and surrenders all things for truth, duty, and mankind.—Channing.

Be content with doing calmly the little which depends upon yourself, and let all else be to you as if it were not.—Fénelon.

Can man or woman choose duties? No more than they can choose their birthplace, or their father and mother.—George Eliot.

All duties are matter of conscience, with this restriction that a superior obligation suspends the force of an inferior one.—L'Estrange.

Thy sum of duty let two words contain
(O may they graven in thy heart remain!)
Be humble and be just.   —Prior.

Duty speaks with the lawful authority of many voices; pleasure has no strength except in the longing desire of the hungry unit.—Edith Simcox.

Of an accountable creature, duty is the concern of every moment, since he is every moment pleasing or displeasing God.—Robert Hall.

I think myself obliged, whatever my private apprehensions may be of the success, to do my duty, and leave events to their Disposer.—Robert Boyle.

The thing which must be, must be for the best; God helps us do our duty and not shrink.—Lytton.

Let us hear the conclusion of the whole matter: Fear God and keep His commandments, for this is the whole duty of man.—Bible.

He who is false to present duty breaks a thread in the loom, and will find the flaw when he may have forgotten its cause.—Henry Ward Beecher.

Let us have faith that right makes might, and in that faith let us, to the end, dare to do our duty as we understand it.—Abraham Lincoln.

Never to tire, never to grow cold; to be patient, sympathetic, tender; to look for the budding flower and the opening heart; to hope always; like God, to love always—this is duty.—Amiel.

The gospel chargeth us with piety towards God, and justice and charity to men, and temperance and chastity in reference to ourselves.—Tillotson.

If doing what ought to be done be made the first business, and success a secondary consideration—is not this the way to exalt virtue?—Confucius.

To hallow'd duty
Here with a loyal and heroic heart,
Bind we our lives. —Mrs. Osgood.

Man owes two solemn debts—one to society, and one to nature. It is only when he pays the second that he covers the first.—Douglas Jerrold.

I hate to see a thing done by halves; if it be right, do it boldly; if it be wrong, leave it undone.—Gilpin.

Duty, though set about by thorns, may still be made a staff supporting even while it tortures. Cast it away, and, like the prophet's wand, it changes to a snake.—D. Jerrold.

I slept and dreamed that life was Beauty;
I woke, and found that life was Duty—
Was thy dream then a shadowy lie?
—Ellen Sturgis Hooper.

The great point is to renounce your own wisdom by simplicity of walk, and to be ready to give up the favor, esteem, and approbation of every one, whenever the path in which God leads you passes that way.—Fénelon.

It is not the profession of religion which creates the obligation for the performance of duty; for that existed before any such profession was made. The profession of religion only recognizes the obligation.—Albert Barnes.

Duties are ours; events are God's. This removes an infinite burden from the shoulders of a miserable, tempted, dying creature. On this consideration only, can he securely lay down his head, and close his eyes.—Richard Cecil.

O thou sculptor, painter, poet,
Take this lesson to thy heart;
That is best which lieth nearest;
Shape from that thy work of art.
—Longfellow.

Put thou thy trust in God;
In duty's path go on;
Fix on His word thy steadfast eye;
So shall thy work be done.
—Martin Luther.

When faith and hope fail, as they do sometimes, we must trust charity, which is love in action. We must speculate no more on our duty, but simply do it. When we have done it, however blindly, perhaps heaven will show us the reason why.—D. M. Craik.

If the duties before us be not noble, let us ennoble them by doing them in a noble spirit; we become reconciled to life if we live in the spirit of Him who reconciled the life of God with the lowly duties of servants.—F. W. Robertson.

Do to-day's duty, fight to-day's temptation; and do not weaken and distract yourself by looking forward to things which you cannot see, and could not understand if you saw them.—Charles Kingsley.

Every mission constitutes a pledge of duty. Every man is bound to consecrate his every faculty to its fulfillment. He will derive his rule of action from the profound conviction of that duty.—William Lloyd Garrison.

There is little pleasure in the world that is true and sincere besides the pleasure of doing our duty and doing good. I am sure no other is comparable to this.—Tillotson.

The path of duty lies in what is near, and men seek for it in what is remote; the work of duty lies in what is easy, and men seek for it in what is difficult.—Mencius.

Thet tells the story! Thet's wut we shall git
By tryin' squirtguns on the burnin' Pit;
For the day never comes when it'll du
To kick off dooty like a worn-out shoe.
—Lowell.

However dear you hold your patrimony, your honor, or even your life, you should be willing to sacrifice all to duty, if you are called upon to do so.—Silvio Pellico.

And rank for her meant duty, various
Yet equal in its worth, done worthily.
Command was service; humblest service done
By willing and discerning souls was glory.
—George Eliot.

So nigh is grandeur to our dust,
So near is God to man.
When Duty whispers low, Thou must,
The youth replies, I can.
—Emerson.

Duty reaches down the ages in its effects, and into eternity; and when the man goes about it resolutely, it seems to me now as though his footsteps were echoing beyond the stars, though only heard faintly in the atmosphere of this world.—William Mountford.

A judge's duty is to grant justice, but his practice is to delay it; even those judges who know their duty adhere to the general practice.—La Bruyère.

It is a happy thing for us that this is really all we have to concern ourselves about—what to do next. No man can do the second thing. He can do the first.—George MacDonald.

Thus is man made equal to every event. He can face danger for the right. A poor, tender, painful body, he can run into flame or bullets or pestilence, with duty for his guide.—Emerson.

Every man has obligations which belong to his station. Duties extend beyond obligations, and direct the affections, desires, and intentions, as well as the actions.—Whewell.

Rugged strength and radiant beauty—
These were one in nature's plan;
Humble toil and heavenward duty—
These will form the perfect man.
—Mrs. Hale.

And I read the moral—A brave endeavor
To do thy duty, whate'er its worth,
Is better than life with love forever,
And love is the sweetest thing on earth.
—James J. Roche.

I believe that we are conforming to the divine order and the will of Providence when we are doing even indifferent things that belong to our condition.—Fénelon.

Whoso neglects a thing which he suspects he ought to do, because it seems to him too small a thing, is deceiving himself; it is not too little, but too great for him, that he doeth it not.—E. B. Pusey.

The sense of duty is the fountain of human rights. In other words, the same inward principle which teaches the former bears witness to the latter. Duties and rights must stand and fall together.—William Ellery Channing.

In all ordinary cases we see intuitively at first view what is our duty, what is the honest part. In these cases doubt and deliberation is of itself dishonesty; as it was in Balaam's case upon the second message.—Bishop Butler.

Be not diverted from your duty by any idle reflections the silly world may make upon you, for their censures are not in your power, and consequently should not be any part of your concern.—Epictetus.

Let a man begin in earnest with "I ought," and he will end, by God's grace, if he persevere, with "I will." Let him force himself to abound in all small offices of kindliness, attention, affectionateness, and all these for God's sake. By and by he will feel them become the habit of his soul.— F. W. Robertson.

Attention is our first duty whenever we want to know what is our second duty. There is no such cause of confusion and worry about what we ought to do, and how to do it, as our unwillingness to hear what God would tell us on that very point.—H. Clay Trumbull.

The great object of the Christian is duty; his predominant desire to obey God. When he can please the world consistently with these, he will do so; otherwise it is enough for him that God commands, and enough for them that he cannot disobey.—Gardiner Spring.

Go to your duty, every man, and trust yourself to Christ; for He will give you all supply just as fast as you need it. You will have just as much power as you believe you can have. Be a Christian; throw yourself upon God's work; and get the ability you want in it.—Horace Bushnell.

Let him who gropes painfully in darkness or uncertain light, and prays vehemently that the dawn may ripen into day, lay this precept well to heart: "Do the duty which lies nearest to thee," which thou knowest to be a duty! Thy second duty will already have become clearer.—Carlyle.

Submission to duty and God gives the highest energy. He, who has done the greatest work on earth, said that He came down from heaven, not to do His own will, but the will of Him who sent Him. Whoever allies himself with God is armed with all the forces of the invisible world.—Clarke.

Christian obligation cannot be made to accord with a law of expediency. The Christian's maxims are, "Do right because you are bound to do right." "Do right though the heavens fall." There is a world of difference between "You had better" and "You are bound to."—Francis L. Patton.

The secret consciousness
Of duty well performed; the public voice
Of praise that honors virtue, and rewards it;
All these are yours.   —Francis.

To check the erring and reprove;
Thou who art victory and law,
When empty terrors overawe,
Give unto me, made lowly wise,
The spirit of self-sacrifice.
                        —Wordsworth.

Do daily and hourly your duty; do it patiently and thoroughly. Do it as it presents itself; do it at the moment, and let it be its own reward. Never mind whether it is known and acknowledged or not, but do not fail to do it.—Aughey.

We are apt to mistake our vocation by looking out of the way for occasions to exercise great and rare virtues, and by stepping over the ordinary ones that lie directly in the road before us.—Hannah More.

Reverence the highest, have patience with the lowest. Let this day's performance of the meanest duty be thy religion. Are the stars too distant, pick up the pebble that lies at thy feet and from it learn the all.— Margaret Fuller.

The people of this country have shown by the highest proofs human nature can give that wherever the path of duty and honor may lead, however steep and rugged it may be, they are ready to walk in it.— James A. Garfield.

Duty itself is supreme delight when love is the inducement and labor. By such a principle the ignorant are enlightened, the hard-hearted softened, the disobedient reformed, and the faithful encouraged.—Hosea Ballou.

The idea of duty—that recognition of something to be lived for beyond the mere satisfaction of self—is to the moral life what the addition of a great central ganglion is to animal life.—George Eliot.

There is generally no such thing as duty to the people who do it. They simply take life as it comes, meeting, not shirking its demands, whether pleasant or unpleasant; and that is pretty much all there is of it.—Gail Hamilton.

Those who do it always would as soon think of being conceited of eating their dinner as of doing their duty. What honest boy would pride himself on not picking a pocket? A thief who was trying to reform would.—George MacDonald.

High hearts are never long without hearing some new call, some distant clarion of God, even in their dreams; and soon they are observed to break up the camp of ease, and start on some fresh march of faithful service.—James Martineau.

There is no mean work save that which is sordidly selfish; there is no irreligious work save that which is morally wrong; while in every sphere of life "the post of honor is the post of duty."—Chapin.

We require from buildings, as from men, two kinds of goodness; first, the doing their practical duty well; then that they be graceful and pleasing in doing it; which last is itself another form of duty.—Ruskin.

The consideration that human happiness and moral duty are inseparably connected will always continue to prompt me to promote the progress of the former by inculcating the practice of the latter.—Washington.

Commonplace though it may appear, this doing of one's duty embodies the highest ideal of life and character. There may be nothing heroic about it; but the common lot of men is not heroic.—Samuel Smiles.

Duty is a power which rises with us in the morning, and goes to rest with us at night. It is coextensive with the action of our intelligence. It is the shadow which cleaves to us, go where we will, and which only leaves us when we leave the light of life.—Gladstone.

No man living in deliberate violation of his duty, in willful disobedience to God's commands, as taught by conscience, can possibly make progress in acquaintance with the Supreme Being. Vain are all acts of worship in church or in secret, vain are religious reading and conversation, without this instant fidelity.—W. E. Channing.

Men should soon make up their minds to be forgotten, and look about them, or within them, for some higher motive in what they do than the approbation of men, which is fame, namely, their duty; that they should be constantly and quietly at work, each in his sphere, regardless of effects, and leaving their fame to take care of itself.—Longfellow.

My noble father,
I do perceive here a divided duty;
To you, I am bound for life and education;
My life and education both do learn me
How to respect you; you are the lord of duty;
I am hitherto your daughter: But here's my husband.   —Shakespeare.

Both love of mankind, and respect for their rights are duties; the former however is only a conditional, the latter an unconditional, purely imperative duty, which he must be perfectly certain not to have transgressed who would give himself up to the secret emotions arising from benevolence.—Kant.

Speak, Lord, our souls are hushed to hear what Thou hast to say to us. Great is the stake, overwhelming may be the risks—most glorious are the opportunities. Speak, Lord, and show us what our duty is—how high, how difficult, yet how happy, how blessed—show us what our duty is, and, O great God and Father, give us strength to do it.—Dean Stanley.

No man's spirits were ever hurt by doing his duty; on the contrary, one good action, one temptation resisted and overcome, one sacrifice of desire or interest, purely for conscience' sake, will prove a cordial for weak and low spirits, far beyond what either indulgence or diversion or company can do for them.—Paley.

It is an impressive truth that sometimes in the very lowest forms of duty, less than which would rank a man as a villain, there is, nevertheless, the sublimest ascent of self-sacrifice. To do less would class you as an object of eternal scorn, to do so much presumes the grandeur of heroism.—De Quincey.

The duty of man is not a wilderness of turnpike gates, through which he is to pass by tickets from one to the other. It is plain and simple, and consists but of two points—his duty to God, which every man must feel; and, with respect to his neighbor, to do as he would be done by.—Thomas Paine.

As soon as we lay ourselves entirely at His feet, we have enough light given us to guide our own steps; as the foot-soldier, who hears nothing of the councils that determine the course of the great battle he is in, hears plainly enough the word of command which he must himself obey.—George Eliot.

The everyday cares and duties, which men call drudgery, are the weights and counterpoises of the clock of time, giving its pendulum a true vibration and its hands a regular motion; and when they cease to hang upon its wheels, the pendulum no longer swings, the hands no longer move, the clock stands still.—Longfellow.

In the sacred fact of obligation you touch the immutable, and lay hold, as it were, on the eternities. At the very center of your being, there is a fixed element, and that of a kind or degree essentially sovereign. A standard is set up in your very thought, by which a great part of your questions are determined, and about which your otherwise random thoughts may settle into order and law.—Horace Bushnell.

Is there no reconciliation of some ancient quarrel, no payment of some long outstanding debt, no courtesy or love or honor to be rendered to those to whom it has long been due; no charitable, humble, kind, useful deed, by which you can promote the glory of God, or good will among men, or peace upon earth? If there be any such, I beseech you, in God's name, in Christ's name, go and do it.—Dean Stanley.

Let us do our duty in our shop or our kitchen, the market, the street, the office, the school, the home, just as faithfully as if we stood in the front rank of some great battle, and we knew that victory for mankind depended upon our bravery, strength, and skill. When we do that the humblest of us will be serving in that great army which achieves the welfare of the world.—Theodore Parker.

Take your duty, and be strong in it, as God will make you strong. The harder it is, the stronger in fact you will be. Understand, also, that the great question here is, not what you will get, but what you will become. The greatest wealth you can ever get will be in yourself. Take your burdens and troubles and losses and wrongs, if come they must and will, as your opportunity, knowing that God has girded you for greater things than these.—Horace Bushnell.

The moment you can make a very simple discovery, viz., that obligation to God is your privilege, and is not imposed as a burden, your experience will teach you many things—that duty is liberty, that repentance is a release from sorrow, that sacrifice is gain, that humility is dignity, that the truth from which you hide is a healing element that bathes your disordered life, and that even the penalties and terrors of God are the artillery

only of protection to His realm.—
Horace Bushnell.

The things of the world are ever
rising and falling, and in perpetual
change; and this change must be according to the will of God, as He has
bestowed upon man neither the wisdom nor the power to enable him to
check it. The great lesson in these
things is, that man must strengthen
himself doubly at such times to fulfill
his duty and to do what is right, and
must seek his happiness and inward
peace from objects which cannot be
taken away from him.—Wilhelm von
Humboldt.

I cannot but take notice of the wonderful love of God to mankind, who, in
order to encourage obedience to His
laws, has annexed a present as well as
a future reward to a good life; and has
so interwoven our duty and our happiness together that, while we are discharging our obligations to the one,
we are at the same time making the
best provision for the other.—Melmoth.

There is no evil that we cannot
either face or fly from but the consciousness of duty disregarded. A
sense of duty pursues us ever. It is
omnipresent, like the Deity. If we
take to ourselves the wings of the
morning, and dwell in the utmost
parts of the seas, duty performed,
or duty violated, is still with us, for
our happiness or our misery. If we
say the darkness shall cover us, in the
darkness as in the light our obligations are yet with us. We cannot
escape their power, nor fly from their
presence. They are with us in this
life, will be with us at its close, and
in that scene of inconceivable solemnity which lies yet further onward
we shall still find ourselves surrounded by the consciousness of duty,
to pain us wherever it has been vio-

lated, and to console us so far as God
may have given us grace to perform
it.—Webster.

Not infrequently are Christians
heard to speak of duties as crosses to
be borne; and I am convinced that
some among them regard their performance as a complete compliance
with the law of self-denial. It is a
cross to pray, to speak, to commend
Christ to others, to attend church, to
frequent the social meetings, and, indeed, to do anything of a distinctly
religious nature. By the force of
their will and with the aid of sundry
admonitions they bring themselves up
to the discharge of those obligations,
but, on the whole, they feel that it
should entitle them to a place in "the
noble army of martyrs." I am sorry
to dissipate the comfortable illusion;
but I am compelled to assure them
that they totally misapprehend the
doctrine of our Lord. He said that it
was His meat and drink to do the
will of His Father; and He never
once refers to duty in any other way
than as a delight. The cross was
something distinct from it.—George C.
Lorimer.

Feeble are we? Yes, without God
we are nothing. But what, by faith,
every man may be, God requires him
to be. This is the only Christian idea
of duty. Measure obligation by inherent ability! No, my brethren,
Christian obligation has a very different measure. It is measured by the
power that God will give us, measured by the gifts and possible incre-
ments of faith. And what a reckoning will it be for many of us, when
Christ summons us to answer before
Him under the law, not for what we
are, but for what we might have been.
—Horace Bushnell.

Dwarf

A dwarf on a giant's shoulders sees
further of the two.—Herbert.

E

Eagle

Other birds fight in flocks, but the eagle fights his battles alone.

King of the peak and glacier,
  King of the cold, white scalps,
He lifts his head at that close tread,
  The eagle of the Alps.
—Victor Hugo.

Bird of the broad and sweeping wing,
  Thy home is high in heaven,
Where wide the storms their banners fling,
  And the tempest clouds are driven.
—Percival.

Around, around, in ceaseless circles wheel-
    ing,
With clangs of wings and scream, the
    Eagle sailed
Incessantly.   —Shelley.

So the struck eagle, stretched upon the
    plain,
No more through rolling clouds to soar
    again,
Viewed his own feather on the fatal dart,
And winged the shaft that quivered in his
    heart.   —Byron.

Tho' he inherit
Nor the pride, nor ample pinion,
  That the Theban eagle bear,
Sailing with supreme dominion
  Thro' the azure deep of air.
—Gray.

That eagle's fate and mine are one,
  Which, on the shaft that made him die,
Espied a feather of his own,
  Wherewith he wont to soar so high.
—E. Waller.

Shall eagles not be eagles? wrens be wrens?
If all the world were falcons, what of that?
The wonder of the eagle were the less,
But he not less the eagle.   —Tennyson.

He clasps the crag with hooked hands;
Close to the sun in lonely lands,
Ring'd with the azure world, he stands.
The wrinkled sea beneath him crawls:
He watches from his mountain walls,
And like a thunderbolt he falls.
—Tennyson.

Ear

The ear is the road to the heart.—
Voltaire.

One ear it heard, at the other out it
went.—Chaucer.

Make not my ear a stranger to thy
thoughts.—Addison.

Sir J. Davies calls the ear the
wicket of the soul.—G. A. Sala.

A side intelligencer.—Lamb.

The ear in man and beast is an
evidence of blood and high breeding.
—N. P. Willis.

Give every man thine ear, but few
thy voice; take each man's censure,
but reserve thy judgment.—Shakespeare.

Eyes and ears, two traded pilots
'twixt the dangerous shores of will
and judgment.—Shakespeare.

Early Rising

Prevent your day at morning.—
Ben Jonson.

Thus we improve the pleasures of the day,
While tasteless mortals sleep their time
  away.   —Mrs. Centlivre.

When one begins to turn in bed, it
is time to get up.—Wellington.

The early morning has gold in its mouth.—Franklin.

———

I rise with the lark.—Anonymous.

———

Awake before the sun is risen, I call for my pen and papers and desk. —Smart.

———

Few ever lived to a great age, and fewer still ever became distinguished, who were not in the habit of early rising.—Dr. John Todd.

———

Next to temperance, a quiet conscience, a cheerful mind and active habits, I place early rising as a means of health and happiness.—Flint.

———

I would have inscribed on the curtains of your bed, and the walls of your chamber: "If you do not rise early, you can make progress in nothing."—Chatham.

———

He that from childhood has made rising betimes familiar to him will not waste the best part of his life in drowsiness.—Locke.

———

The famous Apollonius being very early at Vespasian's gate, and finding him stirring, from thence conjectured that he was worthy to govern an empire, and said to his companion, "This man surely will be emperor; he is so early."—Caussin.

———

The difference between rising at five and seven o'clock in the morning, for the space of forty years, supposing a man to go to bed at the same hour at night, is nearly equivalent to ten additional years to a man's life.—Doddridge.

———

Early rising not only gives us more life in the same number of our years, but adds likewise to their number; and not only enables us to enjoy more of existence in the same measure of time, but increases also the measure. —Colton.

———

No man can promise himself even fifty years of life, but any man may, if he please, live in the proportion of fifty years in forty—let him rise early.

that he may have the day before him, and let him make the most of the day, by determining to expend it on two sorts of acquaintance only—those by whom something may be got, and those from whom something may be learnt.—Colton.

———

Six, or at most seven, hours' sleep is, for a constancy, as much as you or anybody else can want; more is only laziness and dozing, and is, I am persuaded, both unwholesome and stupefying.—Chesterfield.

———

Whoever has tasted the breath of morning knows that the most invigorating and most delightful hours of the day are commonly spent in bed; though it is the evident intention of nature that we should enjoy and profit by them.—Southey.

———

O, there is a charm
Which morning has, that gives the brow
    of age
A smack of earth, and makes the lip of
    youth
Shed perfume exquisite. Expect it not,
Ye who till noon upon a down bed lie,
Indulging feverous sleep.   —Hurdis.

———

With charwomen such early hours agree,
    And sweeps, that earn betimes their bit
        and sup;
But I'm no climbing boy, and need not be,
    All up—all up!
So here I'll lie, my morning calls deferring,
    Till something nearer to the stroke of
        noon;
A man that's fond precociously of stirring,
    Must be a spoon.   —Thomas Hood.

———

Is there aught in sleep can charm the wise,
To lie in dead oblivion, losing half
The fleeting moments of too short a life;
Total extinction of the enlighten'd soul?
Wilder'd and tossing thro' distemper'd
    dreams?
Who would in such a gloomy state remain
Longer than nature craves; when ev'ry
    muse
And every blooming pleasure wait without,
To bless the wildly devious morning walk?
    —Thomson.

———

When you find an unwillingness to rise early in the morning, endeavor to rouse your faculties, and act up to your kind, and consider that you have to do the business of a man; and that action is both beneficial and the end of your being.—Antoninus.

Earnestness

Earnestness is the devotion of all the faculties.—C. N. Bovee.

Earnestness alone makes life eternity.—Carlyle.

Time and pains will do anything.—F. W. Robertson.

Intense people are usually narrow-minded.—Madame de Sartory.

Earnestness and sincerity are synonymous.—Kant.

Earnestness is the salt of eloquence.—Victor Hugo.

The generous warmth that prompts to worthy deeds.—Gifford.

Earnestness is enthusiasm tempered by reason.—Pascal.

His heart was in his work, and the heart giveth grace unto every art.—Longfellow.

There is no substitute for thorough-going, ardent, and sincere earnestness.—Dickens.

A man in earnest finds means, or, if he cannot find, creates them.—William Ellery Channing.

My God, help me always resolutely to strive, and, through life and death, to force my way unto Thee.—Christian Scriver.

The earnestness of life is the only passport to the satisfaction of life.—Theodore Parker.

Earnestness is needed in this world as much as any virtue.—James Ellis.

Earnestness is the best gift of mental power, and deficiency of heart is the cause of many men never becoming great.—Bulwer.

A man is relieved and gay when he has put his heart into his work and done his best; but what he has said or done otherwise shall give no peace.—Emerson.

Vigor is contagious; and whatever makes us either think or feel strongly adds to our power and enlarges our field of action.—Emerson.

The most precious wine is produced upon the sides of volcanoes. Now bold and inspiring ideals are only born of a clear head that stands over a glowing heart.—Horace Mann.

Child of earth and earthly sorrows—child of God and immortal hopes—arise from thy sadness, gird up the loins of thy mind, and with unfaltering energy press toward thy rest and reward on high.—E. L. Magoon.

Up, then, with speed, and work;
Fling ease and self away—
This is no time for thee to sleep—
Up, watch, and work, and pray!
—Horatius Bonar.

The shortest and surest way to prove a work possible is strenuously to set about it; and no wonder if that proves it possible that for the most part makes it so.—South.

Earnestness commands the respect of mankind. A wavering, vascillating, dead-and-alive Christian does not get the respect of the church or the world.—John Hall.

A man without earnestness is a mournful and perplexing spectacle. But it is a consolation to believe, as we must of such a one, that he is the most effectual and compulsive of all schools.—Sterling.

I look upon enthusiasm in all other points but that of religion to be a very necessary turn of mind; as, indeed, it is a vein which nature seems to have marked with more or less strength in the tempers of most men.—Fitzosborne.

He who would do some great thing in this short life, must apply himself to the work with such a concentration of his forces as to the idle spectators, who live only to amuse themselves, looks like insanity.—John Foster.

Without earnestness no man is ever great, or does really great things. He may be the cleverest of men; he may be brilliant, entertaining, popular; but he will want weight. No soul-moving picture was ever painted that had not in it depth of shadow.—Peter Bayne.

Do you wish to become rich? You may become rich, that is, if you desire it in no half way, but thoroughly. A miser sacrifices all to his single passion; hoards farthings and dies possessed of wealth. Do you wish to master any science or accomplishment? Give yourself to it and it lies beneath your feet. Time and pains will do anything. This world is given as the prize for the men in earnest; and that which is true of this world is truer still of the world to come.—F. W. Robertson.

Earnestness is the cause of patience; it gives endurance, overcomes pain, strengthens weakness, braves dangers, sustains hope, makes light of difficulties, and lessens the sense of weariness in overcoming them.—Bovee.

Earth

The rugged, all-nourishing earth.—Sophocles.

The flowers are but earth vivified.—Lamartine.

Earth, air, and ocean, glorious three.—R. Montgomery.

Earth, ocean, air, beloved brotherhood.—Shelley.

The earth, that's nature's mother, is her tomb.—Shakespeare.

This goodly frame, the earth, seems to me a sterile promontory.—Shakespeare.

I believe this earth on which we stand is but the vestibule to glorious mansions through which a moving crowd forever press.—Joanna Baillie.

Once every atom of this ground lived, breathed, and felt like me!—James Montgomery.

We are pilgrims, not settlers; this earth is our inn, not our home.—J. H. Vincent.

Air, earth, and seas, obey'd th' Almighty nod,
And with a general fear confess'd the God.
—Dryden.

Speak no harsh words of earth; she is our mother, and few of us her sons who have not added a wrinkle to her brow.—Alexander Smith.

Nought so vile that on the earth doth live, but to the earth some special good doth give.—Shakespeare.

Where is the dust that has not been alive?
The spade, the plough, disturb our ancestors;
From human mould we reap our daily bread.
—Young.

This poor world, the object of so much insane attachment, we are about to leave; it is but misery, vanity, and folly; a phantom—the very fashion of which "passeth away."—Fénelon.

Earth, thou great footstool of our God
Who reigns on high; thou fruitful source
Of all our raiment, life and food,
Our house, our parent, and our nurse.
—Watts.

Friend, hast thou considered the "rugged, all-nourishing earth," as Sophocles well names her; how she feeds the sparrow on the housetop, much more her darling man?—Carlyle.

Lean not on earth; it will pierce thee to the heart; a broken reed at best; but oft a spear, on its sharp point Peace bleeds and Hope expires.—Young.

Let the mantle of worldly enjoyments hang loose about you, that it may be easily dropped when death comes to carry you into another world.—T. Boston.

The earth, though in comparison of heaven so small, nor glistering, may of solid good contain more plenty than the sun, that barren shines.—Milton.

I speak of that learning which makes us acquainted with the boundless extent of nature, and the universe, and which even while we remain in this world, discovers to us both heaven, earth, and sea.—Cicero.

The earth is bright,
And I am earthly, so I love it well;
Though heaven is holier, and full of light
Yet I am frail, and with frail things would dwell.   —Mrs. Judson.

Our earthly possessions will indeed perish in the final wreck of all things; but let the ship perish, let all we have sink in the deep, if we may come "safe to land." From these storms and billows—these dangerous seas—these tempestuous voyages—may we all be brought at last safe to heaven.—Albert Barnes.

The cloud-capped towers, the gorgeous palaces,
The solemn temples, the great globe itself,
Yea, all which it inherit, shall dissolve,
And, like this unsubstantial pageant faded,
Leave not a rack behind. —Shakespeare.

Transiency is stamped on all our possessions, occupations, and delights. We have the hunger for eternity in our souls, the thought of eternity in our hearts, the destination for eternity written on our inmost being, and the need to ally ourselves with eternity proclaimed by the most short-lived trifles of time. Either these things will be the blessing or the curse of our lives. Which do you mean that they shall be for you?—Alexander Maclaren.

Thou sure and firm-set earth,
Hear not my steps, which way they walk, for fear
The very stones prate of my whereabout.
—Shakespeare.

It is this earth that, like a kind mother, receives us at our birth, and sustains us when born; it is this alone, of all the elements around us, that is never found an enemy of man. —Pliny.

The waters deluge man with rain, oppress him with hail, and drown him with inundations; the air rushes in storms, prepares the tempest, or lights up the volcano; but the earth, gentle and indulgent, ever subservient to the wants of man, spreads his walks with flowers and his table with plenty; returns with interest every good committed to her care, and though she produces the poison, she still supplies the antidote; though constantly teased more to furnish the luxuries of man than his necessities, yet, even to the last, she continues her kind indulgence, and when life is over she piously covers his remains in her bosom.—Pliny.

The common growth of Mother Earth
Suffices me—her tears, her mirth,
Her humblest mirth and tears.
—Wordsworth.

Diseased nature oftentimes breaks forth
In strange eruptions; oft the teeming earth
Is with a kind of colic pinch'd and vex'd
By the imprisoning of unruly wind
Within her womb; which, for enlargement striving,
Shakes the old beldame earth, and topples down
Steeples and moss-grown towers.
—Shakespeare.

Earth fills her lap with pleasures of her own;
Yearnings she hath in her own natural kind,
And, even with something of a mother's mind,
And no unworthy aim,
The homely nurse doth all she can
To make her foster child, her inmate man,
Forget the glories he hath known
And that imperial palace whence he came.
—Wordsworth.

Ease

A life of ease is a difficult pursuit. —Cowper.

Indulge, and to thy genius freely give,
For not to live at ease is not to live.
—Persius.

Ease leads to habit, as success to ease.
He lives by rule who lives himself to please
—Crabbe.

He lives at ease that freely lives.— Barbour.

Easter

Hail, day of days! in peals of praise
Throughout all ages owned,
When Christ, our God, hell's empire trod,
And high o'er heaven was throned.
—Fortunatus.

Ye heavens, how sang they in your courts,
How sang the angelic choir that day,
When from His tomb the imprisoned God,
Like the strong sunrise, broke away?
—Frederick William Faber, D. D.

Christ is our Passover!
And we will keep the feast
With the new leaven,
The bread of heaven:
All welcome, even the least!
—A. R. Thompson, D. D.

"Christ the Lord is risen to-day,"
Sons of men and angels say.
Raise your joys and triumphs high;
Sing, ye heavens, and earth reply.
—Charles Wesley.

Jesus lives, to Him the Throne
Over all the world is given,
May we go where He is gone,
Rest and reign with Him in heaven.
Alleluia! —C. F. Gillert.

Yes, He is ris'n who is the First and Last;
Who was and is; who liveth and was
dead;
Beyond the reach of death He now has
pass'd,
Of the one glorious Church the glorious
Head. —Horatius Bonar, D. D.

O Risen Christ! O Easter Flower!
How dear Thy Grace has grown!
From east to west, with loving power,
Make all the world Thine own.
—Phillips Brooks.

Awake, thou wintry earth—
Fling off thy sadness!
Fair vernal flowers, laugh forth
Your ancient gladness!
Christ is risen.
—Thomas Blackburn.

Come, ye saints, look here and wonder,
See the place where Jesus lay;
He has burst His bands asunder;
He has borne our sins away;
Joyful tidings,
Yes, the Lord has risen to-day.
—Thomas Kelly.

God expects from men something
more at such times, and that it were
much to be wished for the credit of
their religion as well as the satisfaction of their conscience that their
Easter devotions would in some measure come up to their Easter dress.—
South.

Rise, heart! thy Lord is risen. Sing His
praise
Without delays.
Who takes thee by the hand, that thou
likewise
With Him mayst rise—
That as His death condemned thee to dust,
His life may make thee gold, and much
more just. —Herbert.

The fasts are done; the Aves said;
The moon has filled her horn;
And in the solemn night I watch
Before the Easter morn.
So pure, so still the starry heaven,
So hushed the brooding air,
I could hear the sweep of an angel's wings
If one should earthward fare.
—Edna Dean Proctor.

Ring, snow-white bells, your purest praise
To glorify this Easter day,
And let our risen Saviour's joy
Your voiceless, fragrant breath employ—
Fill every valley with perfume
And lighten death's appalling gloom,
Teach ye our troubled hearts the way
To trust our Saviour every day.
—W. J. R. Taylor.

Christ hath arisen! O mountain peaks,
attest—
Witness, resounding glen and torrent wave!
The immortal courage in the human breast
Sprung from that victory—tell how oft the
brave
To camp 'midst rock and cave,
Nerved by those words, their struggling
faith have borne,
Planting the cross on high above the clouds
of morn! —Mrs. Hemans.

Sing aloud, children! sing to the glorious
King
Of Redemption, who sits on the throne,
For the seraphim high veil their faces, and
cry,
And the angels are praising the Son.
With His raiment blood-dyed, and with
wounds in His side,
He returns like a chief from the war,
When His champion blow hath laid death
and hell low,
And hath driven destruction afar.
—A. R. Thompson, D. D.

Our faith in God asks of Him a
risen Redeemer, and the faith is answered in a Saviour raised from the
dead.—Bishop Fallows.

But now is Christ risen from the dead, and become the first fruits of them that slept.—Bible.

Immortality is the glorious discovery of Christianity.—Channing.

The resurrection of Jesus Christ is a certainty. If any fact, not merely of Christianity, but of history, stands on an impregnable foundation, this does.—E. P. Goodwin, D. D.

Tomb, thou shalt not hold Him longer;
Death is strong, but life is stronger;
Stronger than the dark, the light;
Stronger than the wrong, the right;
Faith and hope triumphant say,
"Christ will rise on Easter day!"
—Phillips Brooks.

Up and down our lives obedient
Walk, dear Christ, with footsteps radiant,
Till those garden lives shall be
Fair with duties done for Thee;
And our thankful spirits say,
"Christ arose on Easter Day."
—Phillips Brooks, D. D.

The fact of resurrection is not extraordinary; it is in accord with what we who believe at all believe to be the uniform law of life—that death does not touch it. The witnesses to the resurrection of Christ were unprejudiced, unexpectant, incredulous, and their honesty is not doubted even by skeptical criticism.—Spurgeon.

Had Christ not risen we could not believe Him to be what He declared Himself when He "made Himself equal with God." But He has risen in the confirmation of all His claims. By it alone, but by it thoroughly, is He manifested as the very Son of God, who has come into the world to reconcile the world to Himself. It is the fundamental fact in the Christian's unwavering confidence in "all the words of this life."—Benj. B. Warfield, D. D.

From the empty grave of Jesus the enemies of the cross turn away in unconcealable dismay. Those whom the force of no logic can convince, and whose hearts are steeled against the appeal of almighty love from the cross itself, quail before the irresistible power of this simple fact. Christ has risen from the dead! After two thousand years of the most determined assault upon the evidence which demonstrates it, that fact stands. And so long as it stands Christianity, too, must stand as the one supernatural religion.—Benj. B. Warfield, D. D.

This Easter-time brings us the assurance that when He comes and shall descend from heaven with a shout, with the voice of the archangel and with the trump of God, believers who sleep in Christ and those then living will be caught up together to meet Him in the air, and all will be, as in the twinkling of an eye, transformed and transfigured and possessed of bodies as perfect and as glorious as His own, and in these glorious and resplendent bodies we shall reign and rejoice forever.—E. P. Goodwin, D. D.

Had He not emerged from the tomb all our hopes, all our salvation would be lying dead with Him unto this day. But as we see Him issue from the grave we see ourselves issue with Him in newness of life. Now we know that His shoulders were strong enough to bear the burden that was laid upon them, and that He is able to save to the uttermost all that come unto God through Him. The resurrection of Christ is thus the indispensable evidence of His completed work, His accomplished redemption.—Benj. B. Warfield.

All Christian worship is a witness of the resurrection of Him who liveth for ever and ever. Because He lives, "now abideth faith, hope, charity."—Lyman Abbott.

In every grave on earth's green sward is a tiny seed of the resurrection life of Jesus Christ, and that seed cannot perish. It will germinate when the warm south wind of Christ's return brings back the spring-tide to this cold sin-cursed earth of ours; and then they that are in their graves, and we who shall lie down in ours, will feel in our mortal bodies the power of His resurrection, and will come forth to life immortal.—Dr. David Gregg.

In Christ's resurrection, therefore, the Christian man sees the earnest and pledge of his own resurrection; and by it he is enheartened as he lays away the bodies of those dear to him, not sorrowing "as the rest that have no hope," but with hearts swelling with glad anticipations of the day when they shall rise to meet their Lord. "For if we believe that Jesus died and rose again, even so them also that are fallen asleep in Jesus will He bring with Him."—Benj. B. Warfield, D. D.

A happy and a glorious Easter will this one be to all of us who get a new vision of the risen Christ, and prostrate ourselves in humble adoration at His feet, and cry out: "Rabboni! Rabboni!" Then shall we set our hearts, lifted into a new atmosphere, on things above, and reach an actual higher life. We shall know more of what it is to live by Christ, in Christ, for Christ, and with Christ, till we reach the marvelous light around the throne in glory.—Theo. L. Cuyler, D. D.

We can no longer speak of a bourne from which no traveler e'er returns. The middle wall of partition has been broken down and the boundary become but an invisible line by the resurrection of Christ. That He who died has been raised again and ever lives in the form of a complete humanity is the fundamental fact in the revelation of the Christian doctrine of immortality.—Benj. B. Warfield, D. D.

It was for the glory that was set before Him that Christ endured the humiliation and suffering of the cross. Let us keep our eyes fixed steadily on the crown immortal, and then our sacrifices and services, and sufferings for Christ's cause, will seem light and trival in comparison. * * * The seal of the Sanhedrim, a regiment of soldiers from the town, a floor of rock, a roof of rock, a wall of rock, a niche of rock, cannot keep Christ in the crypt. Though you pile upon us all the boulders of the mountains, you cannot keep us down. The door of the tomb will be lifted from its hinges and flung flat in the dust.—Talmage.

Over all earth's scarred and graveridged surface it kindled the light of this great hope: These moldering ashes may live again in human form. By the testimony of the senses Jesus is alive from the dead, and by the emptiness of Joseph's sepulcher, by Mary's risen Son, the resurrection is not incredible. Bereaved hearts may wrap themselves around with its sweet hope; human graves may be made vocal with its promise! the dying race of man come unto victory through faith.—S. S. Mitchell, D. D.

Jesus has redeemed not only our souls, but our bodies. When the Lord shall deliver His captive people out of the land of the enemy He will not leave a bone of one of them in the adversary's power. The dominion of death shall be utterly broken.—Spurgeon.

Ring, joyous bells of Easter,
   Death hath not conquered Life;
Victorious is our risen Lord,
   And finished all His strife,
From Calvary's mount of darkness,
   Lo! starry lilies bloom;
For by the cross we conquer
   And fearless face the tomb.
          —Mary E. Sangster.

For forty centuries, in one unbroken column, the race of man had been marching into the shadows. And of all the millions who had descended into the shadowed valley, not one had ever returned. No dead human form through all the centuries had risen up into a post-mortem life. There was in all Earth's area not one empty grave. No human heart believed, no human voice declared that there was such a grave—a grave robbed by the power of a victor stronger than man's great enemy, death. It was therefore a new and wonderful message which the Apostle communicated, when unto the dying race of man he lifted up his voice in the words: "One human form has risen from the dead; one grave of earth is empty; the man Christ Jesus who was dead, is alive again."—S. S. Mitchell, D. D.

This, then, is the doctrine of the resurrection. We do not believe—at least I do not—that law has been rudely violated in one extraordinary and unparalleled episode. We believe that a universal law of life, overmastering death, and always superior to it, has had once a visible witness.—Spurgeon.

If you have no share in the living Lord may God have mercy upon you! If you have no share in Christ's rising from the dead then you will not be raised up in the likeness of His glorified body. If you do not attain to that resurrection from among the dead then you must abide in death.—Spurgeon.

Whoever, therefore, is a true believer has of necessity an indefeasible hope, an absolute certainty of salvation. He shares the resurrection of Christ. His sins are as absolutely buried out of God's sight as the body of Christ was buried in the tomb from the light of day. They can no more touch and spoil his hope than they can touch and condemn the risen Lord. All true children of God are now, because of His resurrection, wholly and forever justified, assured absolutely that they are now heirs of God and joint heirs with Jesus Christ, and waiting only for the day of full and final deliverance and glorification. E. P. Goodwin, D. D.

We have often asserted, and we affirm it yet again, that no fact in history is better attested than the resurrection of Jesus Christ from the dead. It must not be denied, by any who are willing to pay the slightest respect to the testimony of their fellow-men, that Jesus, who died upon the cross, and was buried in the tomb of Joseph of Arimathea, did literally rise again from the dead.—Spurgeon.

A bare seed is the former. Look into the wheat bin. There lie the bare seeds—the natural bodies—but no artist would think of sitting down before them. Now turn your eyes upon the field of living grain as the winds of summer billow its surface. What

beauty—what a glory! The bare grains have risen from death in a body of living green, matchless in the splendor of a new and a higher material body. So is the resurrection of the human form. It is sown corruptible —it is raised incorruptible; it is sown in weakness—it is raised in power; a low, inferior, imperfect body is sown —one of glorious perfection rises up from this, as from a seed. There is a natural body and there is a spiritual body, and the former comes first—is the seed of the latter? As we have borne the image of the earthly, so also shall we bear the image of the heavenly.—S. S. Mitchell, D. D.

We Christians do not believe that Jesus Christ was the only one that ever rose from the dead. We believe that every death-bed is a resurrection; that from every grave the stone is rolled away.—Spurgeon.

No one has ever yet succeeded in resolving the narrative of this event into figure or myth, and failures in this direction go to prove that the evidence on which the event rests is unimpeachable. And if it is trustworthy, then Christianity rests on a sure foundation, and our faith is in no sense vain, but warrantable and precious.—Geo. C. Lorimer, D. D.

Let patriotism have its high days and freedom its monuments, and let the triumphs of navigators and generals be annually observed; but surely, beyond all these, a season that stands for as much to the race as Easter does may well be remembered each year with songs and flowers and with every mark of gratitude and of loftiest jubilation.—Rev. Geo. C. Lorimer, D. D.

It longs for existence that it may have life. Life and immortality are brought to light by the higher and holy nature of the risen Christ, who shows the meaning and possibilities of life, and awakens in all responsive natures a desire to live. Every Christian life becomes thus a witness of the resurrection. Its very possibility in a world of evil is due to a living Saviour. "Because I live, ye shall live also."—Bishop Hendrix.

See the land, her Easter keeping,
  Rises as her Maker rose;
Seeds so long in darkness sleeping
  Burst at last from winter snows.
Earth with heaven above rejoices;
  Fields and garlands hail the spring;
Shaughs and woodlands ring with voices
  While the wild birds build and sing.
      —Charles Kingsley.

Christ is risen from the dead, and thus His own words have been justified. Christ is risen from the dead, and thus God has given Him the sign of His Messianic mission. The final and absolute seal of genuineness has been put on all His claims, and the indelible stamp of a divine authority upon all His teachings. The resurrection spans and binds the sacred Scriptures from Genesis to Revelation. Christ is risen from the dead, and every promise of God is yea and amen in Him.—Bishop Fallows.

Was it not most meet that a woman should first see the risen Saviour? She was first in the transgression; let her be first in the justification. In you garden she was first to work our wo; let her in that other garden be the first to see Him who works our weal. She takes first the apple of that bitter tree which brings us all our sorrow; let her be the first to see the Mighty Gardener, who has planted a tree which brings forth fruit unto everlasting life.—Spurgeon.

Let all the jubilant sounds of earth swing up in one resonant wave of triumphant song. Let us robe ourselves in the sunny gladness of a hope so bright—the hope that defies death, and reaches across all the breadth of graves, and clasps the hand of an immortal friend, and says through any hour of sorrow, "It doth not yet appear what we shall be: but we know that, when He shall appear, we shall be like Him"—waking or sleeping, for, waking or sleeping, we are the Lord's; and while it thus chants its faith, hears, rising slow and sweet, and with an olden pathos, out of the deeps of ancient days, the quenchless faith of a twilight child of God: "I

know that my Redeemer liveth: * * * and though after my skin worms destroy this body, yet in my flesh shall I see God."—Rev. I. M. Haldemann.

Christendom never came from an unbroken grave. It would have been buried in that grave, as Judas thought it was going to be, and as the Jews thought it was going to be, except there had been a resurrection from the dead. Then you can explain Christendom, churches, and literatures, if Christ rose again; but otherwise they cannot be explained at all. Our whole civilization rests on the broken Cross of the Master, and it is incredible that a civilization like this, in a world advancing steadily for eighteen centuries, has been founded on a lie.—Richard S. Storrs, D. D.

We do not strike out one part or another part of the prophecy on record; we have the whole compacted together by this mighty keystone in the arch, the resurrection of the Son of God and the glorious manifestation given by Him as the divine representative and Son in the world. Then the world is beautiful; it is not a place of graves; it is a place of graves that are to be opened. It is not the city of the dead. They who are dead to human view are living unto God. It is a portal of paradise instead of a place of graves, and there is light upon it every Easter morning such as never was before on sea or shore until the Master had risen from the grave.—Richard S. Storrs, D. D.

We greatly need the cheer of this precious Easter truth. We make too little of the place our Lord has gone to prepare for us. We rob ourselves greatly when we try to reduce heaven to a mere state of ecstatic feeling. We need the cheer which comes of having the eye of faith fixed on the better country and the city that hath the foundations. Such a certainty of an inheritance that is real and that cannot fade away goes far to mitigate the pangs which come of the fires and floods and disasters and frauds which so often despoil God's people of their earthly possessions; for we know that the things seen are temporal, but the things not seen are eternal, and they are only a few heart-beats away.—E. P. Goodwin, D. D.

He who burst the bars of death was thereby declared to be the Son of God with power. Since the resurrection morning there has never been—there could not be—the slightest question as to His final rulership of the world. Death was conquered, Satan was conquered, and He proclaimed the wearer of the name above every name. His final triumph was hence merely a question of the fullness of time. And He is now seated at the right hand of the Father, from henceforth expecting till His enemies are made His footstool. This Easter morning certifies us of that approaching day, and with, as it were, the foregleams of its glory on our faces and the stirrings of its mighty joy in our hearts, bids us watch and pray and look for the coming of the King.—E. P. Goodwin, D. D.

Preach the defeat of death and the triumph over the grave as historic facts; preach it as the great middle truth, as the potent truth out of which all others of our faith flow forth; keep it ever lifted up as the justification of all our best endeavors; preach it as the one great thing that rails off the children of God from the children of death; hold it out as the beacon across all the dark waters of time's tumult; throw it out in the face of human fears, and tell it increasingly with joy.—Rev. I. M. Haldemann.

Remember there is no man can say that Jesus is the Lord but by the Holy Ghost; so no man can profess, to any purpose, faith in Christ's resurrection but by the Holy Ghost. "It is the Spirit that beareth witness" now, as nineteen centuries ago, by that influence on the will of man which leaves the intellect at liberty to do justice to the evidence before it. Pray that most blessed Spirit so to teach your hearts and wills that you may, at least, have no reason for wishing the resurrection to be untrue.

Pray Him for His gracious assistance that you may recover or may strengthen the great grace of faith and have your part in the blessed promise of the apostle: "If thou shalt confess with thy mouth the Lord Jesus, and shalt believe in thy heart that God hath raised Him from the dead, thou shalt be saved."—Canon Liddon, D. D.

Thine, O death, was the furrow: we cast therein the precious seed. Now let us wait and see what God shall bring forth for us. A single leaf falls—the bud at its axil will shoot forth many leaves. The husbandman bargains with the year to give back a hundred grains for the one buried. Shall God be less generous? Yet, when we sow, our hearts think that beauty is gone out, that all is lost. But when God shall bring again to our eyes the hundredfold beauty and sweetness of that which we planted, how shall we shame over that dim faith that, having eyes, saw not, and ears, heard not, though all heaven and all the earth appeared, and spake, to comfort those who mourn!—Henry Ward Beecher.

There can, I apprehend, my dear brethren, be no sort of doubt that, if an ordinary historical occurrence, such as the death of Julius Cæsar, is attested as clearly as the resurrection of our Lord—not, we will suppose, more clearly nor less—as having taken place nineteen centuries ago, all the world would believe it as a matter of course. Nay, more: if an extraordinary occurrence traversing the usual operations of God in nature were similarly tested, it would be easily believed if only it stood alone as an isolated wonder connected with no religious claims, implying no religious duties, appealing only to the bare understanding, and having no bearing, however remote, upon the will. The reason why the resurrection was not always believed upon the evidence of those who were witness to it was because to believe means for a consistent and thoughtful man to believe in and accept practically a great deal else. To believe the resurrection is to believe implicitly in the Christian faith.—Canon Liddon, D. D.

He (Death) carries a black flag, and he takes no prisoners. He digs a trench across the hemispheres and fills it with the carcasses of nations. Fifty times would the world have been depopulated had not God kept making new generations. Fifty times the world would have swung lifeless through the air—no man on the mountain, no man on the sea—an abandoned ship plowing through immensity. Again and again has He done this work with all generations. He is a monarch as well as a conqueror; His palace a sepulcher; His fountains the falling tears of a world. Blessed be God! in the light of this Easter morning I see the prophecy that His scepter shall be broken and His palace shall be demolished. The hour is coming when all who are in their graves shall come forth. Christ risen, we shall rise. Jesus is "the first-fruits of them that slept."

Day of the Crucified Lord's Resurrection;
  Day that the Lord by His triumph hath
    made;
Day of Redemption's seal of perfection;
  Day of the Crown of His power dis-
    played;
Beautiful Easter, dazzling bright;
Sun-Day that filleth all Sundays with light!
Queen of all festivals; glad culmination
  Of the bright feasts that encircle the
    year;
Glimpsing the Life, in a transfiguration,
  That shall at length in its glory appear.
Beautiful Easter; day in its height;
Sun-Day that filleth all Sundays with light!
He who redeemeth, consoleth, forgiveth;
  Who His own body raised up from the
    dead,
Holdeth all evil in bondage and liveth,
  Source of all blessing, our Life and our
    Head.
It is His Glory that maketh thee bright,
Sun-Day that filleth all Sundays with light!
    —Harriet McEwen Kimball.

Most of all, when the very anniversary comes and we are carried back to the cross and to the sepulcher from which the Master came, should this note of triumph be in our hearts or on our lips: songs of triumphant praise should sound from organ and voice. When we go home, it should be with a feeling that the world is consecrated,

the sepulcher has been broken, and that life is lovelier than ever, and duty more beautiful, and death not terrible. So we should walk with an elastic step, with a light shining over our faces and in our eyes, and with music on our lips as we go to our homes; and if any one ask, Whence came this new expression? Whence came this sweeter and more victorious tone? we should be able to say to them, It is natural, for to-day I have walked with the risen Christ; to-day I have walked as conqueror of the Cross, with Him who conquered it; to-day I have walked near the gates which He entered who broke the bars of the sepulcher and ascended in glory to heaven.—Richard S. Storrs, D. D.

Eating

We must eat to live, not live to eat.
—Fielding.

He was a bold man that first ate an oyster.—Swift.

The proof of the pudding is in the eating.—Cervantes.

Strive mightily, but eat and drink as friends.—Shakespeare.

Unquiet meals make ill digestions.
—Shakespeare.

Feast to-day makes fast to-morrow.
—Plautus.

Appetite comes with eating.—Rabelais.

Go to your banquet then, but use delight
So as to rise still with an appetite.
    —Herrick.

Sit down and feed, and welcome to our table.—Shakespeare.

Tell me what you eat, and I will tell you what you are.—Brillat Savarin.

I want every peasant to have a chicken in his pot on Sundays.—Henry IV. of France.

To abstain that we may enjoy is the epicureanism of reason.—Rousseau.

A warmed-up dinner was never worth much.—Boileau.

They say fingers were made before forks, and hands before knives.—Swift.

With eager feeding food doth choke the feeder.—Shakespeare.

Now good digestion wait on appetite,
And health on both.   —Shakespeare.

They are as sick that surfeit with too much, as they that starve with nothing.——Shakespeare.

Famish'd people must be slowly nurst,
And fed by spoonfuls, else they always burst.   —Byron.

A stomach that is seldom empty despises common food.—Horace.

A surfeit of the sweetest things
The deepest loathing to the stomach brings.
     —Shakespeare.

For a man seldom thinks with more earnestness of anything than he does of his dinner.—Samuel Johnson.

My soul tasted that heavenly food, which gives new appetite while it satiates.—Dante.

One solid dish his weekday meal affords,
An added pudding solemniz'd the Lord's.
     —Pope.

Bad men live that they may eat and drink, whereas good men eat and drink that they may live.—Socrates.

O hour, of all hours, the most bless'd upon earth,
The blessed hour of our dinners!
     —Lord Lytton.

The turnpike road to people's hearts I find
Lies through their mouths, or I mistake mankind.   —Dr. Wolcot.

For the sake of health, medicines are taken by weight and measure; so ought food to be, or by some similar rule.—Skelton.

For I look upon it, that he who does not mind his belly will hardly mind anything else.—Samuel Johnson.

Your supper is like the Hidalgo's dinner; very little meat, and a great deal of table-cloth.—Longfellow.

The difference between a rich man and a poor man is this—the former eats when he pleases, and the latter when he can get it.—Sir Walter Raleigh.

Some hae meat and canna eat,
And some wad eat that want it;
But we hae meat, and we can eat;
Sae let the Lord be thankit.
     —Burns.

"Here, dearest Eve," he exclaims, "here is food." "Well," answered she, with the germ of a housewife stirring within her, "we have been so busy to-day that a picked-up dinner must serve."—Nath. Hawthorne.

All human history attests
That happiness for man—the hungry sinner—
Since Eve ate apples, much depends on dinner.   —Byron.

Yet shall you have to rectify your palate,
An olive, capers, or some better salad
Ushering the mutton; with a short-legged hen,
If we can get her, full of eggs, and then,
Limons, and wine for sauce: to these a coney
Is not to be despaired of for our money;
And though fowl now be scarce, yet there are clerks,
The sky not falling, think we may have larks.   —Ben Jonson.

"Good well-dress'd turtle beats them hol-low—
It almost makes me wish, I vow,
To have two stomachs, like a cow!"
And, lo! as with the cud, an inward thrill
Upheaved his waistcoat and disturb'd his frill,
His mouth was oozing, and he work'd his jaw—
"I almost think that I could eat one raw."
     —Hood.

The chief pleasure (in eating) does not consist in costly seasoning, or exquisite flavor, but in yourself. Do you seek sauce by sweating.—Horace.

A woman asked a coachman, "Are you full inside"? Upon which Lamb put his head through the window and said: "I am quite full inside; that last piece of pudding at Mr. Gillman's did the business for me."—Charles Lamb.

Man is a carnivorous production,
And must have meals, at least one meal
  a day;
He cannot live, like woodcocks, upon suc-
  tion,
But, like the shark and tiger, must have
  prey;
Although his anatomical construction
  Bears vegetables, in a grumbling way,
Your laboring people think beyond all ques-
  tion,
Beef, veal, and mutton better for digestion.
      —Byron.

Oh, better no doubt is a dinner of herbs,
When season'd by love, which no rancor
  disturbs
And sweeten'd by all that is sweetest in
  life
Than turbot, bisque, ortolans, eaten in
  strife!
But if, out of humor, and hungry, alone
A man should sit down to dinner, each one
Of the dishes of which the cook chooses to
  spoil
With a horrible mixture of garlic and oil,
The chances are ten against one, I must
  own,
He gets up as ill-tempered as when he sat
  down.   —Lord Lytton.

We may live without poetry, music and art;
We may live without conscience, and live
  without heart;
We may live without friends; we may live
  without books;
But civilized man cannot live without cooks.
He may live without books—what is knowl-
  edge but grieving?
He may live without hope—what is hope but
  deceiving?
He may live without love—what is passion
  but pining?
But where is the man that can live without
  dining?   —Lord Lytton.

Their best and most wholesome feeding is upon one dish and no more and the same plaine and simple; for surely this hudling of many meats one upon another of divers tastes is pestiferous. But sundrie sauces are more dangerous than that.—Pliny.

Eccentricity

Eccentricity is developed monoma-nia.—Bayard Taylor.

Who affects useless singularities has surely a little mind.—Lavater.

Even beauty cannot always palliate eccentricity.—Balzac.

Men are of necessity so mad, that not to be mad were madness in another form.—Pascal.

Often extraordinary excellence, not being rightly conceived, does rather offend than please.—Sir P. Sidney.

Oddities and singularities of behavior may attend genius; but when they do, they are its misfortunes and blemishes. The man of true genius will be ashamed of them, or at least will never affect to be distinguished by them.—Sir W. Temple.

Eccentricity has always abounded when and where strength of character has abounded; and the amount of eccentricity in a society has been proportional to the amount of genius, mental vigor, and moral courage it contained. That so few now dare to be eccentric, marks the chief danger of the time.—John Stuart Mill.

Echo

Echo is the voice of a reflection in a mirror.—Hawthorne.

The babbling gossip of the air.—Shakespeare.

That tuneful nymph, the babbling Echo.—Ovid.

The old echoes are long in dying.—Charles H. Parkhurst.

Lost Echo sits amid the voiceless mountains,
And feeds her grief.   —Shelley.

Echo waits with art and care
And will the faults of song repair.
      —Emerson.

The invisible and loquacious maiden of the mountain passes.—Horace Smith.

And when the echoes had ceased, like a sense of pain was the silence.—Longfellow.

The Jews of old called an echo "the daughter of the voice."—Bathkeel.

The shadow of a sound,—a voice
without a mouth, and words without
a tongue.—Paul Chatfield.

———

I heard * * *
* * * the great echo flap
And buffet round the hills from bluff to
bluff.   —Tennyson.

———

So plain is the distinction of our words,
That many have supposed it a spirit
That answers.   —Webster.

———

Let echo, too, perform her part,
Prolonging every note with art;
And in a low expiring strain,
Play all the comfort o'er again.
                         —Addison.

———

And a million horrible bellowing echoes
broke
From the red-ribb'd hollow behind the
wood,
And thunder'd up into heaven.
                         —Tennyson.

———

Hark! how the gentle echo from her cell
Talks through the cliffs, and murmuring
o'er the stream,
Repeats the accent—we shall part no more.
                         —Akenside.

———

Sweetest Echo, sweetest nymph, that liv'st
unseen
Within thy airy shell,
By slow Meander's margent green,
And in the violet-embroidered vale.
                         —Milton.

———

O love, they die, in yon rich sky,
They faint on hill or field or river:
Our echoes roll from soul to soul,
And grow forever and forever.
Blow, bugle, blow, set the wild echoes
flying,
And answer, echoes, answer, dying, dying,
dying.   —Tennyson.

How sweet the answer Echo makes
To music at night,
When, roused by lute or horn, she wakes,
And far away, o'er lawns and lakes,
Goes answering light.
                         —Moore.

———

Where we find echoes, we generally find emptiness and hollowness:
it is the contrary with the echoes of
the heart.—J. F. Boyes.

Economy

Economy is a savings-bank, into
which men drop pennies, and get dollars in return.—H. W. Shaw.

Economy is a great revenue.—Cicero.

———

Economy, the poor man's mint.—
Tupper.

———

Ere fancy you consult, consult your
purse.—Franklin.

———

A creative economy is the fuel of
magnificence.—Emerson.

———

Let heaven-eyed Prudence battle
with Desire.—J. T. Fields.

———

The back door robs the house.—
George Herbert.

———

To make three guineas do the work
of five.—Burns.

———

Beware of little expenses; a small
leak will sink a great ship.—Franklin.

———

Economy is half the battle of life;
it is not so hard to earn money as to
spend it well.—Spurgeon.

———

It would be well had we more
misers than we have among us.—
Goldsmith.

———

There can be no economy where
there is no efficiency.—Beaconsfield.

———

If you know how to spend less than
you get you have the philosopher's
stone.—Franklin.

———

The injury of prodigality leads to
this, that he who will not economize
will have to agonize.—Confucius.

———

A penny saved is two pence clear,
A pin a day's a groat a year.
                         —Franklin.

———

Where there is a question of economy, I prefer privation.—Madame
Swetchine.

———

Not to be covetous is money, not to
be a purchaser is a revenue.—Cicero.

———

Take care to be an economist in
prosperity; there is no fear of your
being one in adversity.—Zimmermann.

Economy is an excellent lure to betray people into expense.—Zimmermann.

Frugality is founded on the principle that all riches have limits.—Burke.

There is no gain so certain as that which arises from sparing what you have.—Publius Syrus.

To balance fortune by a just expense,
Join with Economy, Magnificence.
—Pope.

Be saving, but not at the cost of all liberality. Have the soul of a king and the hand of a wise economist.—Joubert.

There are but two ways of paying debt: increase of industry in raising income, increase of thrift in laying out.—Carlyle.

No man is rich whose expenditure exceeds his means; and no one is poor whose incomings exceed his outgoings.—Haliburton.

I can get no remedy against this consumption of the purse; borrowing only lingers and lingers it out, but the disease is incurable.—Shakespeare.

The man who will live above his present circumstances is in great danger of living, in a little, much beneath them.—Addison.

As much wisdom may be expended on a private economy as on an empire, and as much wisdom may be drawn from it.—Emerson.

Men live best upon small means. Nature has provided for all, if they only knew how to use her gifts.—Claudianus.

The world abhors closeness, and all but admires extravagance; yet a slack hand shows weakness, a tight hand strength.—Charles Buxton.

He that, when he should not, spends too much, shall, when he would not, have too little to spend.—Feltham.

Economy is the parent of integrity, of liberty, and of ease, and the beauteous sister of temperance, of cheerfulness and health.—Dr. Johnson.

A man may, if he knows not how to save as he gets, keep his nose all his life to the grindstone and die not worth a groat at last.—Benjamin Franklin.

I knew once a very covetous, sordid fellow, who used to say, Take care of the pence; for the pounds will take care of themselves.—Lord Chesterfield.

The regard one shows economy is like that we show an old aunt who is to leave us something at last.—Shenstone.

With parsimony a little is sufficient; and without it nothing is sufficient; whereas frugality makes a poor man rich.—Seneca.

He who is taught to live upon little owes more to his father's wisdom than he that has a great deal left him does to his father's care.—William Penn.

Sense can support herself handsomely in most countries on some eighteen pence a day; but for fantasy, planets and solar systems, will not suffice.—Macaulay.

Certainly, if a man will but keep of an even hand, his ordinary expenses ought to be but to the half of his receipts; and if he thinks to wax rich, but to the third part.—Bacon.

The prospect of penury in age is so gloomy and terrifying that every man who looks before him must resolve to avoid it; and it must be avoided generally by the science of sparing.—Dr. Johnson.

Proportion and propriety are among the best secrets of domestic wisdom; and there is no surer test of integrity than a well-proportioned expenditure.—Hannah More.

Gain may be temporary and uncertain; but ever while you live expense is constant and certain; and it is easier to build two chimneys than to keep one in fuel.—Franklin.

Qualities not regulated run into their opposites. Economy before competence is meanness after it. Therefore economy is for the poor; the rich may dispense with it.—Bovee.

Nature is avariciously frugal; in matter it allows no atom to elude its grasp; in mind, no thought or feeling to perish. It gathers up the fragments that nothing be lost.—Rev. Dr. Thomas.

Let us learn the meaning of economy. Economy is a high human office,—a sacrament when its aim is grand, when it is the prudence of simple tastes, when it is practised for freedom or for love or devotion.—Emerson.

As boys should be educated with temperance, so the first greatest lesson that should be taught them is to admire frugality. It is by the exercise of this virtue alone they can ever expect to be useful members of society.—Goldsmith.

The man who will live above his present circumstances is in great danger of living in a little time much beneath them, or, as the Italian proverb says: "The man who lives by hope will die by despair."—Addison.

Economy is integrity and profuseness is a cruel and crafty demon, that gradually involves her followers in dependence and debts; that is, fetters them with irons that enter into their souls.—Hawkesworth.

Men talk in raptures of youth and beauty, wit and sprightliness; but after seven years of union not one of them is to be compared to good family management, which is seen at every meal, and felt every hour in the husband's purse.—Witherspoon.

Sound economy is a sound understanding brought into action; it is calculation realized; it is the doctrine of

proportion reduced to practice; it is foreseeing contingencies, and providing against them.—Hannah More.

Expense, and great expense, may be an essential part in true economy. If parsimony were to be considered as one of the kinds of that virtue, there is, however, another and a higher economy. Economy is a distinctive virtue, and consists not in saving, but in selection.—Burke.

All to whom want is terrible, upon whatever principle, ought to think themselves obliged to learn the sage maxims of our parsimonious ancestors, and attain the salutary arts of contracting expense; for without economy none can be rich, and with it few can be poor.—Johnson.

It is no small commendation to manage a little well. He is a good waggoner that can turn in a little room. To live well in abundance is the praise to the estate, is the praise not of the person. I will study more how to give a good account of my little, than how to make it more.—Bishop Hall.

He regarded nothing to be cheap that was superfluous, for what one does not need is dear at a penny; and it was better to possess fields, where the plough goes and cattle feed, than fine gardens that require much watering and sweeping.—Plutarch.

Let honesty and industry be thy constant companions and spend one penny less than thy clear gains; then shall thy hide-bound pocket soon begin to thrive and will never again cry with the empty belly-ache; neither will creditors insult thee, nor want oppress, nor hunger bite, nor nakedness freeze thee.—Franklin.

The mere power of saving what is already in our hands must be of easy acquisition to every mind; and as the example of Lord Bacon may show that the highest intellect cannot safely neglect it, a thousand instances every day prove that the humblest may practise it with success.—Dr. Johnson.

Those individuals who save money are better workmen; if they do not the work better, they behave better and are more respectable; and I would sooner have in my trade a hundred men who save money than two hundred who would spend every shilling they get. In proportion as individuals save a little money their morals are much better; they husband that little, and there is a superior tone given to their morals, and they behave better for knowing that they have a little stake in society.

Education

Education is the cheap defence of nations.—Burke.

Just education forms the man.—Gay.

A boy is better unborn than untaught.—Gascoigne.

The secret of education lies in respecting the pupil.—Emerson.

Love is the greatest of educators.—Mrs. Osgood.

Capacity without education is deplorable.—Saadi.

To form a brave man, educate boldly.—Richter.

Hew the block off, and get out the man.—Pope.

Teach the children! It is painting in fresco.—Emerson.

By education most have been misled.—Dryden.

I carry my satchel still.—Michael Angelo.

We are taught words, not ideas.—Beaconsfield.

Education is only second to nature.—Horace Bushnell.

The best and most important part of every man's education is that which he gives himself.—Gibbon.

Education should be as broad as man.—Emerson.

Education is the apprenticeship of life.—Willmott.

We should ask, not who is the most learned, but who is the best learned.—Lady Montagu.

There are many things which we can afford to forget which it is yet well to learn.—Holmes.

To breed up the son to common sense is evermore the parent's least expense.—Dryden.

Each excellent thing, once well learned, serves for a measure of all other knowledge.—Sir P. Sidney.

Schoolhouses are the republican line of fortifications.—Horace Mann.

'Tis education forms the common mind, Just as the twig is bent, the tree's inclined.
—Pope.

Man must either make provision of sense to understand, or of a halter to hang himself.—Antisthenes.

In this country every one gets a mouthful of education, but scarcely any one a full meal.—Theodore Parker.

Capacity without education is deplorable, and education without capacity is thrown away.—Saadi.

Observation more than books, experience rather than persons, are the prime educators.—A. Bronson Alcott.

The world is only saved by the breath of the school children.—Talmud.

The best education is to be had at a price, as well as the best broadcloth.—Anthony Trollope.

We shall one day learn to supersede politics by education.—Emerson.

Whose school-hours are all the days and nights of our existence.—Carlyle.

Learned women are ridiculed because they put to shame unlearned men.—George Sand.

The education of life perfects the thinking mind, but depraves the frivolous.—Mme. de Staël.

The acquirements of science may be termed the armor of the mind.—Colton.

Man forms and educates the world, but woman educates man.—Julie Burow.

Education alone can conduct us to that enjoyment which is at once best in quality and infinite in quantity.—Horace Mann.

No woman is educated who is not equal to the successful management of a family.—Burnap.

Education may work wonders as well in warping the genius of individuals as in seconding it.—A. Bronson Alcott.

Education is a capital to the poor man, and an interest to the rich man.—Horace Mann.

Men must be taught as if you taught them not,
And things unknown proposed as things forgot.
—Pope.

Reading maketh a full man, conference a ready man, and writing an exact man.—Bacon.

Education is only like good culture,—it changes the size, but not the sort.—Henry Ward Beecher.

The worst education, which teaches self-denial, is better than the best which teaches everything else and not that.—John Sterling.

What sculpture is to a block of marble, education is to an human soul.—Addison.

We speak of educating our children. Do we know that our children also educate us?—Mrs. Sigourney.

No inheritance can supply the want of a virtuous education.—Thomas Wilson.

Every fresh acquirement is another remedy against affliction and time.—Willmott.

Education is our only political safety. Outside of this ark all is deluge.—Horace Mann.

The wisest man may always learn something from the humblest peasant.—J. Petit-Senn.

The self-educated are marked by stubborn peculiarities.—Isaac Disraeli.

Learning by study must be won
'Twas ne'er entail'd from sire to son.
—Gay.

Delightful task! to rear the tender thought, to teach the young idea how to shoot.—Thomson.

The best education in the world is that got by struggling to get a living.—Wendell Phillips.

Public instruction should be the first object of government.—Napoleon.

A college education shows a man how little other people know.—Haliburton.

The best that we can do for one another is to exchange our thoughts freely; and that, after all, is about all.—Froude.

Education is the only interest worthy the deep, controlling anxiety of the thoughtful man.—Wendell Phillips.

Histories make men wise: poets, witty; the mathematics, subtle; natural philosophy, deep; moral, grave; logic and rhetoric, able to contend.—Bacon.

Education must bring the practice as nearly as possible to the theory. As the children now are, so will the sovereigns soon be.—Horace Mann.

A complete and generous education fits a man to perform justly, skilfully and magnanimously all the offices of peace and war.—Milton.

Next in importance to freedom and justice is popular education, without which neither justice nor freedom can be permanently maintained.—James A. Garfield.

He is to be educated because he is a man, and not because he is to make shoes, nails, and pins.—Channing.

Education begins the gentleman, but reading, good company, and education must finish him.—Locke.

The pains we take in books or arts which treat of things remote from the necessaries of life is a busy idleness.—Fuller.

In exalting the faculties of the soul, we annihilate, in a great degree, the delusion of the senses.—Aimé-Martin.

I think I should know how to educate a boy, but not a girl; I should be in danger of making her too learned.—Niebuhr.

On the diffusion of education among the people rests the preservation and perpetuation of our free institutions.—Webster.

Prussia is great because her people are intelligent. They know the alphabet. The alphabet is conquering the world.—G. W. Curtis.

The true purpose of education is to cherish and unfold the seed of immortality already sown within us.—Mrs. Jameson.

Restraint of discipline, emulation, examples of virtue and of justice, form the education of the world.—Burke.

I have hope that society may be reformed, when I see how much education may be reformed.—Leibnitz.

It is not the mediocrity of women's education which makes their weakness; it is their weakness which necessarily causes their mediocrity.—De Maistre.

The opening of the first grammar-school was the opening of the first trench against monopoly in Church and State.—Lowell.

Nothing so good as a university education, nor worse than a university without its education.—Bulwer-Lytton.

All of us who are worth anything, spend our manhood in unlearning the follies, or expiating the mistakes of our youth.—Shelley.

Women, like men, must be educated with a view to action, or their studies cannot be called education.—Harriet Martineau.

When you introduce into our schools a spirit of emulation, you have present the keenest spur admissible to the youthful intellect.—Horace Mann.

Modern education too often covers the fingers with rings, and at the same time cuts the sinews at the wrist.—Earl of Sterling.

The reason why education is usually so poor among women of fashion is, that it is not needed for the life which they elect to lead.—Julia Ward Howe.

Only the refined and delicate pleasures that spring from research and education can build up barriers between different ranks.—Mme. de Staël.

Do not then train boys to learning by force and harshness; but direct them to it by what amuses their minds.—Plato.

Finally, education alone can conduct us to that enjoyment which is, at once, best in quality and infinite in quantity.—Horace Mann.

No education deserves the name unless it develops thought, unless it pierces down to the mysterious spiritual principle of mind, and starts that into activity and growth.—E. P. Whipple.

The fruit of liberal education is not learning, but the capacity and desire to learn; not knowledge, but power. —C. W. Eliot.

Do not ask if a man has been through college. Ask if a college has been through him; if he is a walking university.—Chapin.

To be thoroughly imbued with the liberal arts refines the manners, and makes men to be mild and gentle in their conduct.—Ovid.

As the fertilest ground must be manured, so must the highest flying wit have a Dædalus to guide him.—Sir P. Sidney.

Unless the people can be kept in total darkness, it is the wisest way for the advocates of truth to give them full light.—Whately.

Education, however indispensable in a cultivated age, produces nothing on the side of genius. When education ends, genius often begins.—Isaac Disraeli.

To pour the fresh instruction o'er the mind,
To breathe the enliv'ning spirit, and to fix
The generous purpose in the glowing breast.
—Thomson.

God hath blessed you with a good name: to be a well-favored man is the gift of fortune, but to write and read comes by nature.—Shakespeare.

A free school
For th' education of young gentlemen,
To study how to drink and take tobacco.
—Randolph.

The best system of education is that which draws its chief support from the voluntary effort of the community, from the individual efforts of citizens, and from those burdens of taxation which they voluntarily impose upon themselves.—Garfield.

Education is the constraining and directing of youth towards that right reason, which the law affirms, and which the experience of the best of our elders has agreed to be truly right. —Plato.

The awakening of our best sympathies, the cultivation of our best and purest tastes, strengthening the desire to be useful and good, and directing youthful ambition to unselfish ends,— such are the objects of true education.—J. T. Headley.

Jails and state prisons are the complement of schools; so many less as you have of the latter, so many more you must have of the former.—Horace Mann.

Education commences at the mother's knee, and every word spoken within the hearing of little children tends toward the formation of character. Let parents bear this ever in mind.— Hosea Ballou.

But it was in making education not only common to all, but in some sense compulsory on all, that the destiny of the free republics of America was practically settled.—Lowell.

Enflamed with the study of learning, and the admiration of virtue; stirred up with high hopes of living to be brave men, and worthy patriots, dear to God, and famous to all ages. —Milton.

He can write and read and cast accompt.
O monstrous!
We took him setting of boys' copies.
Here's a villain!   —Shakespeare.

Girls, like the priestesses of old, should be educated only in sacred places, and never hear, nor much less see, what is rude, immoral, or violent. —Richter.

Wherever is found what is called a paternal government, was found a State education. It had been discovered that the best way to insure implicit obedience was to commence tyranny in the nursery.—Beaconsfield.

They who provide much wealth for their children, but neglect to improve them in virtue, do like those who feed their horses high, but never train them to the manage.—Socrates.

Were it not better for a man in a fair room to set up one great light, or branching candlestick of lights, than to go about with a rushlight into every dark corner.—Bacon.

A journalist is a grumbler, a censurer, a giver of advice, a regent of sovereigns, a tutor of nations. Four hostile newspapers are more to be feared than a thousand bayonets.—Napoleon.

Slavery is but half abolished, emancipation is but half completed, while millions of freemen with votes in their hands are left without education.—Robert C. Winthrop.

An acquaintance with the muses, in the education of youth, contributes not a little to soften manners. It gives a delicate turn to the imagination and a polish to the mind.—Richardson.

Education keeps the key of life; and a liberal education insures the first conditions of freedom,—namely, adequate knowledge and accustomed thought.—Julia Ward Howe.

Very few men are wise by their own counsel, or learned by their own teaching; for he that was only taught by himself had a fool to his master.—Ben Jonson.

'Tis pleasing to be school'd in a strange tongue
By female lips and eyes—that is, I mean,
When both the teacher, and the taught are young,
They smile so when one's right; and when one's wrong
They smile still more.　　—Byron.

The fruits of the earth do not more obviously require labor and cultivation to prepare them for our use and subsistence than our faculties demand instruction.—Barrow.

A true teacher should penetrate to whatever is vital in his pupil, and de-

velop that by the light and heat of his own intelligence.—E. P. Whipple.

It is wonderful what a difference learning makes upon people even in the common intercourse of life, which does not appear to be much connected with it.—Dr. Johnson.

If Nature be not improved by instruction, it is blind; if instruction be not assisted by Nature, it is maimed; and if exercise fail of the assistance of both, it is imperfect.—Plutarch.

Oh ye, who teach th' ingenuous youth of nations—
Holland, France, England, Germany, or Spain—
I pray ye flog them upon all occasions;
It mends their morals; never mind the pain.　　—Byron.

A little learning is a dangerous thing,
Drink deep, or taste not the Pierian spring,
There shallow draughts intoxicate the brain,
And drinking largely sobers us again.
　　—Pope.

The greatest defect of common education is, that we are in the habit of putting pleasure all on one side, and weariness on the other; all weariness in study, all pleasure in idleness.—Fénelon.

How can man be intelligent, happy, or useful, without the culture and discipline of education? It is this that unlocks the prison-house of his mind, and releases the captive.—Rev. Dr. Humphrey.

An intelligent class can scarce ever be, as a class, vicious; never, as a class, indolent. The excited mental activity operates as a counterpoise to the stimulus of sense and appetite.—Edward Everett.

As an apple is not in any proper sense an apple until it is ripe, so a human being is not in any proper sense a human being until he is educated.—Horace Mann.

It depends on education (that holder of the keys which the Almighty hath put into our hands) to open the gates which lead to virtue or to vice, to happiness or misery.—Jane Porter.

All who have meditated on the art of governing mankind have been convinced that the fate of empires depends on the education of youth.—Aristotle.

Education is a better safeguard of liberty than a standing army. If we retrench the wages of the schoolmaster, we must raise those of the recruiting sergeant.—Edward Everett.

I consider that it is on instruction and education that the future security and direction of the destiny of every nation chiefly and fundamentally rests.—Kossuth.

A good education is generally considered as reflecting no small credit on its possessor; but in the majority of cases it reflects credit on the wise solicitude of his parents or guardians, rather than on himself.—James Cotter Morison.

The most important part of education is right training in the nursery. The soul of the child in his play should be trained to that sort of excellence in which, when he grows to manhood, he will have to be perfected.—Plato.

The essential difference between a good and a bad education is this, that the former draws on the child to learn by making it sweet to him, the latter drives the child to learn, by making it sour to him if he does not.—Charles Buxton.

I consider a human soul without education like marble in the quarry, which shows none of its inherent beauties until the skill of the polisher fetches out the colors and makes the surface shine.—Addison.

Bonaparte asked Mme. de Staël in what manner he could best promote the happiness of France. Her reply is full of political wisdom. She said, "Instruct the mothers of the French people."—Daniel Webster.

School is no place of education for any children whatever till their minds are well put in action. This is the work which has to be done at home, and which may be done in all homes where the mother is a sensible woman.—Harriet Martineau.

We are inclined to think that the study of the classics is, on the whole, advantageous to public morals, by inspiring an elegance of sentiments and an elevation of soul which we should in vain seek for elsewhere.—Robert Hall.

The young boys that went to Athens, the first year, were wise men; the second year, philosophers, lovers of wisdom; the third year, mere orators; and the fourth but plebeians, and understood nothing but their own ignorance.—Mendemus.

I have no sympathy whatever with those who would grudge our workmen and our common people the very highest acquisitions which their taste or their time or their inclination would lead them to realize.—Chalmers.

The greatest of all warriors that went to the siege of Troy had not the pre-eminence because Nature had given him strength and he carried the largest bow, but because self-discipline had taught him how to bend it.—Daniel Webster.

The most distinguished professional men bear witness, with an overwhelming authority, in favor of a course of education in which to train the mind shall be the first object, and to stock it, the second.—Gladstone.

If you suffer your people to be ill educated, and their manners to be corrupted from their infancy, and then punish them for those crimes to which their first education disposed them—you first make thieves and then punish them.—Sir Thomas More.

Into what boundless life does education admit us. Every truth gained through it expands a moment of time into illimitable being—positively enlarges our existence, and endows us with qualities which time cannot weaken or destroy.—Chapin.

That there should one man die ignorant who had capacity for knowledge, this I call a tragedy, were it to happen more than twenty times in a minute, as by some computations it does.—Carlyle.

The true order of learning should be first, what is necessary; second, what is useful, and third, what is ornamental. To reverse this arrangement is like beginning to build at the top of the edifice.—Mrs. Sigourney.

Promote as an object of primary importance institutions for the general diffusion of knowledge. In proportion as the structure of a government gives force to public opinion, it should be enlightened.—Washington.

Education is the leading human souls to what is best, and making what is best out of them; and these two objects are always attainable together, and by the same means. The training which makes men happiest in themselves also makes them most serviceable to others.—Ruskin.

The different steps and degrees of education may be compared to the artificer's operations upon marble; it is one thing to dig it out of the quarry, and another to square it, to give it gloss and lustre, call forth every beautiful spot and vein, shape it into a column, or animate it into a statue.—Thomas Gray.

The aim of education should be to teach us rather how to think than what to think,—rather to improve our minds, so as to enable us to think for ourselves, than to load the memory with the thoughts of other men.—Beattie.

Upon the education of the people of this country the fate of this country depends. There is no period in the history of the world in which I believe it has been more important that the disposition and mind of the people

should be considered by the State than it is at present.—Disraeli.

We shall one day learn to supersede politics by education. What we call our root-and-branch reforms of slavery, war, gambling, intemperance, is only medicating the symptoms. We must begin higher up, namely, in education.—Emerson.

A father inquires whether his boy can construe Homer, if he understands Horace, and can taste Virgil; but how seldom does he ask, or examine, or think whether he can restrain his passions,—whether he is grateful, generous, humane, compassionate, just and benevolent.—Lady Hervey.

It was the German schoolhouse which destroyed Napoleon III. France, since then, is making monster cannon and drilling soldiers still, but she is also building schoolhouses. As long as war is possible, anything that makes better soldiers people want.—Beecher.

I believe that our experience instructs us that the secret of education lies in respecting the pupil. It is not for you to choose what he shall know and what he shall do. It is chosen and foreordained, and he only holds the key to his own secret.—Emerson.

Could we know by what strange circumstances a man's genius became prepared for practical success, we should discover that the most serviceable items in his education were never entered in the bills which his father paid for.—Bulwer-Lytton.

Any who says (with Mandeville in his treatise against charity schools), "If a horse knew as much as a man, I should not like to be his rider," ought to add, "If a man knew as little as a horse, I should not like to trust him to ride."—Whately.

Virtue and talents, though allowed their due consideration, yet are not enough to procure a man a welcome wherever he comes. Nobody contents himself with rough diamonds, or wears them so. When polished and set, then they give a lustre.—Locke.

Education is all paint: it does not alter the nature of the wood that is under it, it only improves its appearance a little. Why I dislike education so much is that it makes all people alike, until you have examined into them; and it is sometimes so long before you get to see under the varnish!—Lady Hester Stanhope.

I am always for getting a boy forward in his learning, for that is sure good. I would let him at first read any English book which happens to engage his attention; because you have done a great deal when you have brought him to have entertainment from a book. He'll get better books afterwards.—Dr. Johnson.

The education of the present race of females is not very favorable to domestic happiness. For my own part, I call education, not that which smothers a woman with accomplishments, but that which tends to consolidate a firm and regular system of character; that which tends to form a friend, a companion, and a wife.—Hannah More.

What we do not call education is more precious than that which we call so. We form no guess, at the time of receiving a thought, of its comparative value. And education often waste its efforts in attempts to thwart and balk this natural magnetism, which is sure to select what belongs to it.—Emerson.

The real object of education is to give children resources that will endure as long as life endures; habits that time will ameliorate, not destroy; occupation that will render sickness tolerable, solitude pleasant, age venerable, life more dignified and useful, and death less terrible.—Sydney Smith.

I shall detain you no longer in the demonstration of what we should not do, but straight conduct ye to a hillside, where I will point ye out the right path of a virtuous and noble education; laborious indeed at the first ascent, but else so smooth, so green, so full of goodly prospect, and melodious sounds on every side, that the harp of Orpheus was not more charming.—Milton.

We know that the gifts which men have do not come from the schools. If a man is a plain, literal, factual man, you can make a great deal more of him in his own line by education than without education, just as you can make a great deal more of a potato if you cultivate it than if you do not; but no cultivation in this world will ever make an apple out of a potato.—Beecher.

Knowledge does not comprise all which is contained in the large term of education. The feelings are to be disciplined, the passions are to be restrained; true and worthy motives are to be inspired; a profound religious feeling is to be instilled, and pure morality inculcated under all circumstances. All this is comprised in education.—Webster.

Whatever expands the affections, or enlarges the sphere of our sympathies, whatever makes us feel our relation to the universe, "and all that it inherits," in time and in eternity, to the great and beneficent Cause of all, must unquestionably refine our nature, and elevate us in the scale of being.—Channing.

When a king asked Euclid, the mathematician, whether he could not explain his art to him in a more compendious manner, he was answered, that there was no royal way to geometry. Other things may be seized by might, or purchased with money; but knowledge is to be gained only by study, and study to be prosecuted only in retirement.—Johnson.

Education is either from nature, from man, or from things; the developing of our faculties and organs is the education of nature; that of man is the application we learn to make of this very developing; and that of things is the experience we acquire in regard to the different objects by which we are affected. All that we have not at our birth, and that we stand in need of at the years of maturity, is the gift of education.—Rousseau.

———

Begin the education of the heart, **n**ot with the cultivation of noble propensities, but with the cutting away of those that are evil. When once the noxious herbs are withered and rooted out, then the more noble plants, strong in themselves, will shoot upwards. The virtuous heart, like the body, becomes strong and healthy more by labor than nourishment.—Richter.

———

If we work upon marble, it will perish; if we work upon brass, time will efface it; if we rear temples, they will crumble into dust; but if we work upon immortal minds, if we imbue them with principles, with the just fear of God and love of our fellowmen, we engrave on those tablets something which will brighten to all eternity.—Daniel Webster.

———

And say to mothers what a holy charge
Is theirs—with what a kingly power their
    love
Might rule the fountains of the new-born
    mind;
Warn them to wake at early dawn, and sow
Good seed before the world has sown its
    tares.   —Mrs. Sigourney.

———

There is, between the sexes, a law of incessant reciprocal action, of which God avails himself in the constitution of the family, when He permits brothers and sisters to nestle about the same hearthstone. Its ministration is essential to the best educational results. Our own educational institutions should rest upon this divine basis.—Caroline H. Dall.

———

Curiosity is as much the parent of attention as attention is of memory; therefore the first business of a teacher—first not only in point of time, but of importance—should be to excite not merely a general curiosity

on the subject of the study, but a particular curiosity on particular points in that subject. To teach one who has no curiosity to learn, is to sow a field without ploughing it.—Whately.

———

I too acknowledge the all-but omnipotence of early culture and nurture; hereby we have either a doddered dwarf-bush, or a high-towering, wide-shadowing tree! either a sick yellow cabbage, or an edible luxuriant green one. Of a truth, it is the duty of all men, especially of all philosophers, to note down with accuracy the characteristic circumstances of their education,— what furthered, what hindered, what in any way modified it.—Carlyle.

———

A statue lies hid in a block of marble, and the art of the statuary only clears away the superfluous matter and removes the rubbish. The figure is in the stone; the sculptor only finds it. What sculpture is to a block of marble, education is to a human soul. The philosopher, the saint, or the hero,—the wise, the good, or the great man,—very often lies hid and concealed in a plebeian, which a proper education might have disinterred, and have brought to light.—Addison.

———

It is not scholarship alone, but scholarship impregnated with religion, that tells on the great mass of society. We have no faith in the efficacy of mechanics' institutes, or even of primary and elementary schools, for building up a virtuous and well-conditioned peasantry so long as they stand dissevered from the lessons of Christian piety. Unless your cask is perfectly clean, whatever you pour into it turns sour.—Horace.

———

Minds that are stupid and incapable of science are in the order of nature to be regarded as monsters and other extraordinary phenomena; minds of this sort are rare. Hence I conclude that there are great resources to be found in children, which are suffered to vanish with their years. It is evident, therefore, that it is not of nature, but of our own negligence, we ought to complain.—Quintilian.

All that a university or final highest school can do for us is still but what the first school began doing—teach us to read. We learn to read in various languages, in various sciences; we learn the alphabet and letters of all manner of books. But the place where we are to get knowledge, even theoretic knowledge, is the books themselves. It depends on what we read, after all manner of professors have done their best for us. The true university of these days is a collection of books.—Carlyle.

Thalwell thought it very unfair to influence a child's mind by inculcating any opinions before it had come to years of discretion to choose for itself. I showed him my garden, and told him it was a botanical garden. "How so?" said he; "it is covered with weeds." "O," I replied, "that is only because it has not yet come to its age of discretion and choice. The weeds, you see, have taken the liberty to grow, and thought it unfair in me to prejudice the soil towards roses and strawberries."—Coleridge.

Every man has two educations—that which is given to him, and the other, that which he gives to himself. Of the two kinds, the latter is by far the most valuable. Indeed, all that is most worthy in a man, he must work out and conquer for himself. It is that constitutes our real and best nourishment. What we are merely taught seldom nourishes the mind like that which we teach ourselves.—Richter.

Man is an animal, formidable both from his passions and his reason; his passions often urging him to great evils, and his reason furnishing means to achieve them. To train this animal, and make him amenable to order; to inure him to a sense of justice and virtue; to withhold him from ill courses by fear, and encourage him in his duty by hopes; in short, to fashion and model him for society, hath been the aim of civil and religious institutions; and, in all times, the endeavor of good and wise men. The aptest method for attaining this end hath been always judged a proper education.—Bishop Berkeley.

There have been periods when the country heard with dismay that "the soldier was abroad." That is not the case now. Let the soldier be abroad; in the present age he can do nothing. There is another person abroad—a less important person in the eyes of some, an insignificant person, whose labors have tended to produce this state of things. The schoolmaster is abroad! And I trust more to him, armed with his primer, than I do to the soldier in full military array, for upholding and extending the liberties of his country.—Brougham.

Egotism

Egotism is the tongue of vanity.—Chamfort.

The egotist is next door to a fanatic.—Samuel Smiles.

The unfortunate are always egotistical.—Beaconsfield.

The pest of society is egotists.—Emerson.

Love is an egotism of two.—Antoine de la Salle.

The egotism of woman is always for two.—Mme. de Staël.

It is never permissible to say, I say.—Mme. Necker.

Let the degree of egotism be the measure of confidence.—Lavater.

Avoid making yourself the subject of conversation.—Bruyère.

And though all cry down self, none means his own self in a literal sense.—Butler.

He who discommendeth others obliquely commendeth himself.—Sir T. Browne.

Be your character what it will, it will be known; and nobody will take it upon your word.—Chesterfield.

Discourse ought to be as a field, without coming home to any man.—Bacon.

Do you wish men to speak well of you? Then never speak well of yourself.—Pascal.

Here is the egotist's code: everything for himself, nothing for others.—Sanial-Dubay.

The more you speak of yourself, the more you are likely to lie.—Zimmermann.

We would rather speak ill of ourselves than not to talk of ourselves at all.—Rochefoucauld.

Men are egotists, and not all tolerant of one man's selfhood; they do not always deem the affinities elective.—Stedman.

The more anyone speaks of himself the less he likes to hear another talked of.—Lavater.

The personal pronoun "I" should be the coat of arms of some individuals.—Rivarol.

Christian piety annihilates the egotism of the heart; worldly politeness veils and represses it.—Pascal.

To speak highly of one with whom we are intimate is a species of egotism. Our modesty as well as our jealousy teaches us caution on this subject.—Hazlitt.

There is a serious and resolute egotism that makes a man interesting to his friends and formidable to his opponents.—Whipple.

When all is summed up, a man never speaks of himself without loss; his accusations of himself are always believed, his praises never.—Montaigne.

We often boast that we are never bored, but yet we are so conceited that we do not perceive how often we bore others.—La Rochefoucauld.

We never could clearly understand how it is that egotism, so unpopular in conversation, should be so popular in writing.—Macaulay.

Seldom do we talk of ourselves with success. If I condemn myself, more is believed than is expressed; if I praise myself, much less.—Henry Home.

The reason why lovers are never weary of one another is this—they are always talking of themselves.—Rochefoucauld.

What hypocrites we seem to be whenever we talk of ourselves! Our words sound so humble, while our hearts are so proud.—Hare.

I shall never apologize to you for egotism. I think very few men writing to their friends have enough of it.—Sydney Smith.

If the egotist is weak, his egotism is worthless. If the egotist is strong, acute, full of distinctive character, his egotism is precious, and remains a possession of the race.—Alexander Smith.

Byron owed the vast influence which he exercised over his contemporaries at least as much to his gloomy egotism as to the real power of his poetry.—Macaulay.

He who thinks he can find in himself the means of doing without others is much mistaken; but he who thinks that others cannot do without him is still more mistaken.—La Rochefoucauld.

It is natural to man to regard himself as the object of the creation, and to think of all things in relation to himself, and the degree in which they can serve and be useful to him.—Goethe.

It is a false principle that because we are entirely occupied with ourselves, we must equally occupy the thoughts of others. The contrary inference is the fair one.—Hazlitt.

The passages in which Milton has alluded to his own circumstances are perhaps read more frequently, and with more interest, than any other lines in his poems.—Macaulay.

It is a hard and nice subject for a man to speak of himself: it grates his own heart to say anything of disparagement, and the reader's ear to hear anything of praise from him.—Cowley.

An egotist will always speak of himself, either in praise or in censure, but a modest man ever shuns making himself the subject of his conversation.—La Bruyère.

Every man, like Narcissus, becomes enamored of the reflection of himself, only choosing a substance instead of a shadow. This love for any particular woman is self-love at second hand, vanity reflected, compound egotism.—Horace Smith.

All the walks of literature are infested with mendicants for fame, who attempt to excite our interest by exhibiting all the distortions of their intellects and stripping the covering from all the putrid sores of their feelings.—Macaulay.

There is scarce any man who cannot persuade himself of his own merit. Has he common sense, he prefers it to genius; has he some diminutive virtues, he prefers them to great talents.—Sewall.

The awkwardness and embarrassment which all feel on beginning to write, when they themselves are the theme, ought to serve as a hint to authors that self is a subject they ought very rarely to descant upon.—Colton.

Egotism is more like an offense than a crime; though it is allowable to speak of yourself, provided nothing is advanced in favor; but I cannot help suspecting that those who abuse themselves are, in reality, angling for approbation.—Zimmermann.

Only by the supernatural is a man strong—only by confiding in the divinity which stirs within us. Nothing is so weak as an egotist—nothing is mightier than we, when we are vehicles of a truth before which the state and the individual are alike ephemeral.—Emerson.

Five, or six, or ten people shall be made temporarily wretched because one person, unconsciously perhaps, yet supremely egotistic and selfish, has never learned to control his disposition and bridle his tongue.—Aughey.

Every real master of speaking or writing uses his personality as he would any other serviceable material; the very moment a speaker or writer begins to use it, not for his main purpose, but for vanity's sake, as all weak people are sure to do, hearers and readers feel the difference in a moment.—Holmes.

We like so much to talk of ourselves that we are never weary of those private interviews with a lover during the course of whole years, and for the same reason the devout like to spend much time with their confessor; it is the pleasure of talking of themselves, even though it be to talk ill.—Mme. de Sévigné.

There are dull and bright, sacred and profane, coarse and fine egotists. It is a disease that, like influenza, falls on all constitutions. In the distemper known to physicians as *chorea*, the patient sometimes turns round, and continues to spin slowly in one spot. Is egotism a metaphysical varioloid of this malady?—Emerson.

Egotism erects its center in itself: love places it out of itself in the axis of the universal whole. Love aims at unity, egotism at solitude. Love is the citizen ruler of a flourishing republic, egotism is a despot in a devastated creation. Egotism sows for gratitude, love for the ungrateful. Love gives, egotism lends; and love does this before the throne of judicial truth, indifferent if for the enjoyment of the following moment, or with the view to a martyr's crown—indifferent whether the reward is in this life or in the next.—Schiller.

Speech of a man's self ought to be seldom and well chosen. I knew one was wont to say in scorn, "He must needs be a wise man, he speaks so much of himself." There is but one case wherein a man may commend himself with good grace, and that is in commending virtue in another, especially if it be a virtue whereunto himself pretendeth.—Bacon.

Election Day

Free and just political institutions are absolutely essential to the progress and development both of the individual and of the race.—Rev. Hugh Price Hughes.

In every movement that Christianity makes to eradicate the corrupt practices of men in political and in social life Christ is setting up His kingdom on the earth.—Rev. Bernard Paine.

The trouble is not in our institutions, imperfect as they doubtless are. The crying necessity for reform springs from the fact that while our institutions are representative theoretically, our public officials are not so, actually.—Fulton McMahon.

Long may a ballot pure proclaim
 The nation's righteous, sovereign will,
Their highest thought and loftiest aim
 Their own high mission to fulfill.
Thus shall the ballot prove a guide
 To point the way that should be trod,
And prove to them no less, beside,
 The people's voice the voice of God.
    —V. G. Haesdarth.

The men needed for all our offices are men to whom righteousness, temperance and judgment are obligations which they feel called upon to fulfill—not men who, like Felix, tremble, self-convicted, when these are urged upon them. A candidate for office should be as white in principle and in practice as his title indicates or suggests that he is.—Homiletic Review.

Profligacy in taking office is so extreme that we have no doubt public men may be found who for half a century would postpone all remedies for a pestilence, if the preservation of their places depended upon the propagation of the virus.—Selected.

A faithful setting forth of Christian duty at the polls, not to vote for this or that man, but to vote conscientiously as before God, and to make the use of the franchise a solemn duty to be prayerfully performed, is a part of the minister's function, when he is teaching his people how to live on earth as representatives of God's truth.—Howard Crosby, D. D.

Let the ministry hold high and fast the standard of Christ's cross, which means pardon and renewal to every sinner that repents and trusts in His atoning sacrifice. Let this be the first and main work of the Christian ministry, and from this, as a source, let the life of both minister and people be fitted to discharge the personal duties which belong to them both as men and citizens. So will the ministry best work to purify our politics and to serve the state.—Howard Crosby, D. D.

Municipal government is corrupt simply because corrupt and corruptible men are elected to office. Corrupt men are elected to office because office "pays," and corruptible men yield because they make money by yielding. If municipal governments had no profitable contracts to award, if school boards had no text-books to select, we should have no "municipal problem."—Forum.

It must recognize and hold up before men the moral character of this corruption of the ballot. Bribery is a sin. It is condemned in the laws of Moses: "And thou shalt take no gift; for a gift blindeth the wise, and perverteth the words of the righteous." These words are as true to-day as when they were written.—Rev. Bernard Paine.

Politics is the only serious subject that men think themselves qualified to act upon without any previous education or instruction whatever. If it happened to be astronomy, or botany, or medicine, or law, he would never be allowed to work in any of these arts, or to take a decisive part in the history of any one of these sciences without having, at least, acquired the A B C of it; but the awful fact of politics is that we do not take the trouble seriously to understand the political situation.—Rev. Hugh Price Hughes.

I have seen the sea lashed into fury and tossed into spray, and its grandeur moves the soul of the dullest man; but I remember that it is not the billows, but the calm level of the sea, from which all heights and depths are measured. When the storm has passed and the hour of calm settles on the ocean, when the sunlight bathes its smooth surface, then the astronomer and surveyor take the level from which to measure all terrestial heights and depths. Gentlemen of the convention, your present temper may not mark the healthful pulse of our people when our enthusiasm has passed. When the emotions of this hour have subsided, we shall find that calm level of public opinion below the storm, from which the thoughts of a mighty people are to be measured, and by which their final action will be determined.—James A. Garfield.

Parties are an essential part of representative governments, and can be effective only by organization; but when organization degenerates into a brutal machinery that stifles intelligence and true patriotism, the republic is moribund. As the perfunctory and bigoted exercise of the suffrage has gradually extinguished much of the manhood of American citizenship, so the restoration of intelligence, conscience and individual independence in this prime duty will be the sole effective means of curing many existing evils and preventing others that might be equally dangerous.—Silas W. Burt.

The large use of money, both before and after election, in the political campaigns of the present day, is a phase of modern public life that represents one of the great changes in our political methods since our forefathers established and practiced the principles laid down in the constitution. The constitution, as we know, was based on the pure democratic idea of government, in which all power and initiative should proceed from the people themselves. Gradually we have substituted for this, which we might call the spontaneous expression of the people, a mechanism by which, instead of the people's instructing their delegates, the presumption is that the delegates are going to instruct the people. In other words, we have absolutely inverted the original idea that lay at the basis of our political fabric.—Silas W. Burt.

One of the most iniquitous forms of taking from an American citizen his right to a free ballot is through intimidation. This is not bribery; it is oppression. It is oppression in a free land. It is practiced by both parties, sometimes through corporations and capitalists, and sometimes by threats of violence at the polls. The evidence is spread before the nation that it is practiced at elections in various states at the South for the suppression of the colored voters.—Rev. Bernard Paine.

You cannot help being a politician. You cannot live for an hour without being a politician. But what a man generally means when he says that he is not a politician I am afraid is this —that he has been all his life enjoying his political privileges and grossly neglecting his political duties; and in that sense the observation is scarcely to his credit. As a matter of fact, politics, properly understood, is simply Science of Life—the doctrine of the way in which I am to do my duty to my neighbor, which is an essential part of true religion. It is nothing in the world except religion applied to human society; in fact, it is the practical recognition of the Second Table of the Law of God.—Rev. Hugh Price Hughes.

Now, I do implore those who are listening to me to realize the gravity of all these questions. There is nothing that you do in all your life for which you are more accountable to God, or which is more serious, than the vote which many of you are going to give at the approaching general election (1892). I dare say you have already made up your mind which party you are going to vote for, but I confess I have some suspicion that, even in an unusually intelligent audience like this, if I brought some of you up to this platform and elicited from you for whom you were going to vote, and then were permitted to cross examine you as to why you were going to give that vote, the answers which you would give would not satisfy yourselves or the audience.—Rev. Hugh Prices Hughes.

It is because politics, as I have already said, have been confounded with party politics; have often been contemptible and wicked beyond description; and, indeed, when not carried so far as that, there are a great many persons who positively cannot discuss politics without losing their temper. And this is so well known that the subject is tabooed to a very great extent in polite society, so-called, so that if you go to a dinner party the one thing of which you must not speak is politics, and the place that might reasonably be occupied by noble and instructive conversation about the science and art of life, and human progress, is occupied by inane, and worse than inane, gossip.—Rev. Hugh Price Hughes.

It is difficult to estimate the cost of a great presidential campaign. There is no doubt but what it might be measured by millions of dollars, apart from the loss involved in the general destruction of business. It has been said that frequent elections have their value in keeping alive public interest in public affairs, and in educating the people upon the great questions that are to be solved. But when we recollect that a great part of the expenses of the campaign are spent in badges, torchlight processions and other appeals to the imagination and sensation rather than to reason, it seems probable that a very large part of this expenditure is practically valueless, so far as the education of the people is concerned, and is really spent to pervert their intelligence.—Silas W. Burt.

Electricity

Striking the electric chain wherewith we are darkly bound.—Byron.

Too like the lightning, which doth cease to be
Ere one can say "it lightens."
—Shakespeare.

The earth is rocking, the skies are riven—
Jove in a passion, in god-like fashion,
Is breaking the crystal urns of heaven.
—Robert Buchanan.

For the poplars showed
The white of their leaves, the amber grain
Shrunk in the wind—and the lightning now
Is tangled in tremulous skeins of rain.
—T. B. Aldrich.

Stretches, for leagues and leagues, the Wire,
A hidden path for a Child of Fire—
Over its silent spaces sent,
Swifter than Ariel ever went,
From continent to continent.
—Wm. Henry Burleigh.

Swift as a shadow, short as any dream;
Brief as the lightning in the collied night,
That, in a spleen, unfolds both heaven and earth,
And ere a man hath power to say "Behold!"
The jaws of darkness do devour it up.
—Shakespeare.

Is it a fact—or have I dreamt it—that by means of electricity the world of matter has become a great nerve, vibrating thousands of miles in a breathless point of time? Rather, the round globe is a vast head, a brain, instinct with intelligence; or shall we say it is itself a thought, nothing but thought, and no longer the substance which we dreamed it.—Nathaniel Hawthorne.

Elegance

Elegance is not an ornament worthy of man.—Seneca.

Elegance is exquisite polish.—Mme. Necker.

Many a woman will pass for elegant in a ballroom, or even at a court drawing room, whose want of true breeding would become evident in a chosen company.—Julia Ward Howe.

Neither refinement nor delicacy is indispensable to produce elegance.—Lavater.

Elegance of manner is the outgrowth of refined and exalted sense.—Chesterfield.

When the mind loses its feeling for elegance, it grows corrupt and groveling, and seeks in the crowd what ought to be found at home.—Landor.

The wisest woman you talk with is ignorant of something that you know; but an elegant woman never forgets her elegance.—O. W. Holmes.

Elegance is something more than ease; it is more than a freedom from awkwardness or restraint. It implies, I conceive, a precision, a polish, a sparkling, spirited yet delicate.—Hazlitt.

Taste and elegance, though they are reckoned only among the smaller and secondary morals, yet are of no mean importance in the regulations of life. A moral taste is not of force to turn vice into virtue; but it recommends virtue with something like the blandishments of pleasure, and it infinitely abates the evils of vice.—Burke.

Elephant

The elephant hath joints, but none for courtesy; his legs are legs for necessity, not for flexure.—Shakespeare.

Th' unwieldy elephant,
To make them mirth, us'd all his might, and wreathed
His lithe proboscis. —Milton.

Eloquence

The poetry of speech.—Byron.

Eloquence is the language of Nature.—Colton.

Eloquence is to the sublime what the whole is to its part.—La Bruyère.

Eloquence is the poetry of prose.—Bryant.

Silence is more eloquent than words.—Carlyle.

The glorious burst of winged words! —Tupper.

Thoughts that breathe and words that burn.—Gray.

Eloquence is vehement simplicity.—Burleigh.

Eloquence the soul, song charms the senses.—Milton.

Continued eloquence wearies.—Pascal.

Action is eloquence.—Shakespeare.

Brevity is a great praise of eloquence.—Cicero.

Words sweetly placed and modestly directed.—Shakespeare.

True eloquence scorns eloquence.—Pascal.

Silence that spoke, and eloquence of eyes.—Pope.

There is no eloquence which does not agitate the soul.—Landor.

Eloquence must be grounded on the plainest narrative.—Emerson.

Great eloquence we cannot get, except from human genius.—Thomas Starr King.

That besotting intoxication which verbal magic brings upon the mind.—South.

Ev'ry word he speaks is a syren's note
To draw the careless hearer.
—Beaumont.

Silence that wins, where eloquence is vain.—William Hayley.

Eloquence shows the power and possibility of man.—Emerson.

Honesty is one part of eloquence. We persuade others by being in earnest ourselves.—Hazlitt.

The art of clothing the thought in apt, significant and sounding words.—Dryden.

Her tears her only eloquence.—Rogers.

There was speech in their dumbness, language in their very gesture.—Shakespeare.

Eloquence is the power to translate a truth into language perfectly intelligible to the person to whom you speak.—Emerson.

True eloquence consists in saying all that is necessary, and nothing but what is necessary. — La Rochefoucauld.

Verily, O man, with truth for thy theme, eloquence shall throne thee with archangels.—Tupper.

In an easy cause any man may be eloquent.—Ovid.

Your Words are like the notes of dying swans,
Too sweet to last!   —Dryden.

False eloquence is exaggeration, true eloquence is emphasis.—W. R. Alger.

He has oratory who ravishes his hearers while he forgets himself.—Lavater.

Those who would make us feel must feel themselves.—Churchill.

Eloquence is the appropriate organ of the highest personal energy.—Emerson.

It is but poor eloquence which only shows that the orator can talk.—Sir Joshua Reynolds.

Eloquence is in the assembly, not in the speaker.—William Pitt.

Manner, as much as matter, constitutes eloquence.—François Delsarte.

Eloquence, when in its highest pitch, leaves little room for reason or reflection.—Hume.

Pour the full tide of eloquence along,
Serenely pure, and yet divinely strong.
                              —Pope.

Words are like leaves, and where they most abound,
Much fruit of sense beneath is rarely found.   —Pope.

O! as a bee upon the flower, I hang
Upon the honey of thy eloquent tongue.
                              —Bulwer.

Were we as eloquent as angels, we should please some more by listening than by talking.—Colton.

There is no talent so pernicious as eloquence to those who have it under command.—Addison.

But for your words, they rob the Hybla bees, and leave them honeyless.—Shakespeare.

Eloquence dwells quite as much in the hearts of the hearers as on the lips of the orator.—Lamartine.

Such was the force of his eloquence. to make the hearers more concerned than he that spake.—Denham.

Here rills of oily eloquence in soft
Meanders lubricate the course they take.
                              —Cowper.

Men are more eloquent than women made; but women are more powerful to persuade.—Thomas Randolph.

As the grace of man is in the mind, so the beauty of the mind is eloquence.—Cicero.

The manner of your speaking is full as important as the matter, as more people have ears to be tickled than understandings to judge. — Chesterfield.

The nature of our constitution makes eloquence more useful and more necessary in this country than in any other in Europe.—Chesterfield.

There is as much eloquence in the tone of the voice, in the eyes, and in the air of a speaker as in his choice of words.—Rochefoucauld.

Every tongue that speaks But Romeo's name speaks heavenly eloquence. —Shakespeare.

Many are ambitious of saying grand things, that is, of being grandiloquent. Eloquence is speaking out * * * a quality few esteem, and fewer aim at.—Hare.

It is of eloquence as of a flame; it requires matter to feed it, motion to excite it, and it brightens as it burns. —Tacitus.

An orator of past times declared that his calling was to make small things appear to be grand.—Montaigne.

There should be in eloquence that which is pleasing and that which is real; but that which is pleasing should itself be real.—Pascal.

Talking and eloquence are not the same: to speak and to speak well are two things. A fool may talk, but a wise man speaks.—Ben Jonson.

Eloquence is the child of knowledge. When a mind is full, like a wholesome river, it is also clear.—Beaconsfield.

Copiousness of words is always false eloquence, though it will ever impose on some sort of understandings.—Montagu.

Eloquence may be found in conversation and all kinds of writings; 'tis rarely where we seek it, and sometimes where 'tis least expected.—La Bruyère.

Profane eloquence is transferred from the bar, where it formerly reigned, to the pulpit, where it never ought to come.—Bruyère.

O Eloquence! thou violated fair, how thou art wooed and won to either bed of right or wrong!—Havard.

Eloquence is a painting of thought; and thus, those who, after having painted it, still add to it, make a picture instead of a portrait.—Pascal.

He is an eloquent man who can speak of low things acutely, and of great things with dignity, and of moderate things with temper.—Cicero.

His tongue dropped manna, and could make the worse appear the better reason, to perplex and dash maturest counsels.—Milton.

When he spoke, what tender words he us'd! So softly, that like flakes of feather'd snow, They melted as they fell. —Dryden.

Go on, spare no invectives, but open the spout of your eloquence, and see with what a calm, connubial resignation I will both hear and bow to the chastisement.—Colley Cibber.

Say she be mute and will not speak a word; Then I'll commend her volubility, And say she uttereth piercing eloquence. —Shakespeare.

No man can make a speech alone. It is the great human power that strikes up from a thousand minds that acts upon him, and makes the speech. —James A. Garfield.

Eloquence is an engine invented to manage and wield at will the fierce democracy, and, like medicine to the sick, is only employed in the paroxysms of a disordered state.—Montaigne.

The spell is thine that reaches The heart, and makes the wisest head its sport; And there's one rare, strange virtue in thy speeches, The secret of their mastery—they are short. —Halleck.

No man ever did or ever will become truly eloquent without being a constant reader of the Bible, and an admirer of the purity and sublimity of its language.—Fisher Ames.

The art of saying well what one thinks is different from the faculty of thinking. The latter may be very deep and lofty and far-reaching, while the former is altogether wanting.—Joubert.

Great is the power of Eloquence; but never is it so great as when it pleads along with nature, and the culprit is a child strayed from his duty, and returned to it again with tears.—Sterne.

Her words were like a stream of honey
  fleeting,
The which doth softly trickle from the
  hive,
Able to melt the hearer's heart unweeting,
And eke to make the dead again alive.
        —Spenser.

In oratory affectation must be avoided; it being better for a man by a native and clear eloquence to express himself than by those words which may smell either of the lamp or inkhorn.—Lord Herbert.

Power above powers! O heavenly eloquence! that, with the strong reign of commanding words, dost manage, guide and master the high eminence of men's affections!—Daniel.

The art of declamation has been sinking in value from the moment that speakers were foolish enough to publish, and hearers wise enough to read.—Colton.

A cold-blooded learned man might, for anything I know, compose in his closet an eloquent book; but in public discourse, arising out of sudden occasions, he could by no possibility be eloquent.—Erskine.

And when she spake,
Sweete words, like dropping honey, she did
  shed;
And 'twixt the perles and rubies softly
  brake
A silver sound, that heavenly musicke
  seem'd to make.   —Spenser.

The pleasure of eloquence is in greatest part owing often to the stimulus of the occasion which produces it —to the magic of sympathy, which exalts the feeling of each by radiating on him the feeling of all.—Emerson.

Eloquence is relative. One can no more pronounce on the eloquence of any composition than the wholesomeness of a medicine, without knowing for whom it is intended.—Whately.

God gave you that gifted tongue of yours, and set it between your teeth, to make known your true meaning to us, not to be rattled like a muffin man's bell.—Carlyle.

True eloquence, indeed, does not consist in speech. It cannot be brought from far. Labor and learning may toil for it, but they will toil in vain. Words and phrases may be marshaled in every way, but they cannot compass it. It must exist in the man, in the subject, and in the occasion.—Webster.

I have often heard it said, and I believe it to be true, that even the most eloquent man living, and however deeply impressed with the subject, could scarcely find utterance if he were to be standing up alone, and speaking only against a dead wall.—Erskine.

Eloquence, when at its highest pitch, leaves little room for reason or reflection, but addresses itself entirely to the fancy or the affections, captivates the willing hearers, and subdues their understanding. Happily, this pitch it seldom attains.—Hume.

Eloquence, to produce her full effect, should start from the head of the orator, as Pallas from the brain of Jove, completely armed and equipped. Diffidence, therefore, which is so able a mentor to the writer, would prove a dangerous counsellor for the orator.—Colton.

Fine declamation does not consist in flowery periods, delicate allusions or musical cadences, but in a plain, open, loose style, where the periods are long and obvious, where the same thought is often exhibited in several points of view.—Goldsmith.

We may put too high a premium on speech from platform and pulpit, at the bar and in the legislative hall, and pay dear for the whistle of our endless harangues. England, and especially Germany, are less loquacious, and attend more to business. We let the eagle, and perhaps too often the peacock, scream.—Bartol.

By eloquence I understand those appeals to our moral perceptions that produce emotion as soon as they are uttered. * * * This is the very enthusiasm that is the parent of poetry. Let the same man go to his closet and clothe in numbers conceptions full of the same fire and spirit, and they will be poetry.—Bryant.

His words seem'd oracles
That pierc'd their bosoms; and each man would turn
And gaze in wonder on his neighbour's face,
That with the like dumb wonder answer'd him.
You could have heard
The beating of your pulses while he spoke.
—George Croly.

Extemporaneous and oral harangues will always have this advantage over those that are read from a manuscript: every burst of eloquence or spark of genius they may contain, however studied they may have been beforehand, will appear to the audience to be the effect of the sudden inspiration of talent.—Colton.

Pow'r above pow'rs! O heavenly eloquence!
That with the strong rein of commanding words,
Dost manage, guide, and master th' eminence
Of men's affections, more than all their swords!
—Daniel.

How often in the halls of legislation does eloquence unmask corruption, expose intrigue, and overthrow tyranny! In the cause of mercy it is omnipotent. It is bold in the consciousness of its superiority, fearless and unyielding in the purity of its motives. All opposition it destroys; all power it defies.—Henry Melville.

This is that eloquence the ancients represented as lightning, bearing down every opposer; this the power which has turned whole assemblies into astonishment, admiration and awe—that is described by the torrent, the flame, and every other instance of irresistible impetuosity.—Goldsmith.

Eloquence is the language of nature, and cannot be learned in the schools; the passions are powerful pleaders, and their very silence, like that of Garrick, goes directly to the soul, but rhetoric is the creature of art, which he who feels least will most excel in.; it is the quackery of eloquence, and deals in nostrums, not in cures.—Colton.

His eloquent tongue so well seconds his fertile invention that no one speaks better when suddenly called forth. His attention never languishes; his mind is always before his words; his memory has all its stock so turned into ready money that, without hesitation or delay, it supplies whatever the occasion may require.—Erasmus.

The charm of eloquence—the skill
To wake each secret string,
And from the bosom's chords at will
Life's mournful music bring;
The o'ermast'ring strength of mind, which sways
The haughty and the free,
Whose might earth's mightiest ones obey
This charm was given to thee.
—Mrs. Embury.

Method, we are aware, is an essential ingredient in every discourse designed for the instruction of mankind; but it ought never to force itself on the attention as an object—never appear to be an end instead of an instrument; or beget a suspicion of the sentiments being introduced for the sake of the method, not the method for the sentiments.—Robert Hall.

Whene'er he speaks, Heaven, how the list'ning throng
Dwell on the melting music of his tongue!
His arguments are emblems of his mien,
Mild but not faint, and forcing, though serene:
And when the power of eloquence he'd try,
Here lightning strikes you, there soft breezes sigh.
—Garth.

The clear conception, outrunning the deductions of logic, the high purpose, the dauntless spirit, speaking on the tongue, beaming from the eye, informing every feature, and urging the whole man onward, right onward, to his object—this is eloquence, or rather it is something greater and higher than all eloquence—it is action, noble, sublime, godlike action.—Webster.

A just and reasonable modesty does not only recommend eloquence, but sets off every great talent which a man can be possessed of. It heightens all the virtues which it accompanies; like the shades of paintings, it raises and rounds every figure, and makes the colors more beautiful, though not so glowing as they would be without it.—Addison.

There's a charm in deliv'ry, a magical art,
That thrills like a kiss from the lip to the heart;
'T is the glance—the expression—the well-chosen word—
By whose magic the depths of the spirit are stirr'd.
The lip's soft persuasion—its musical tone:
Oh! such were the charms of that eloquent one! —Mrs. Welby.

In eloquence, the great triumphs of the art are when the orator is lifted above himself; when consciously he makes himself the mere tongue of the occasion and the hour, and says what cannot but be said. Hence the term "abandonment," to describe the self-surrender of the orator. Not his will, but the principle on which he is horsed, the great connection and crisis of events, thunder in the ear of the crowd.—Emerson.

His eloquence is classic in its style,
Not brilliant with explosive coruscations
Of heterogeneous thoughts, at random caught,
And scatter'd like a shower of shooting stars,
That end in darkness: no;—his noble mind
Is clear, and full, and stately, and serene.
His earnest and undazzled eye he keeps
Fix'd on the sun of Truth, and breathes his words
As easily as eagles cleave the air;
And never pauses till the height is won;
And all who listen follow where he leads.
—Mrs. Hale.

The receipt to make a speaker, and an applauded one too, is short and easy. Take common sense *quantum*

sufficit; add a little application to the rules and orders of the House [of Commons], throw obvious thoughts in a new light, and make up the whole with a large quantity of purity, correctness and elegancy of style. Take it for granted that by far the greatest part of mankind neither analyze nor search to the bottom; they are incapable of penetrating deeper than the surface.—Chesterfield.

Gentlemen, do you know what is the finest speech that I ever in my life heard or read? It is the address of Garibaldi to his Roman soldiers, when he told them: "Soldiers, what I have to offer you is fatigue, danger, struggle and death; the chill of the cold night in the free air, and heat under the burning sun; no lodgings, no munitions, no provisions, but forced marches, dangerous watchposts and the continual struggle with the bayonet against batteries;—those who love freedom and their country may follow me." That is the most glorious speech I ever heard in my life.—Kossuth.

Emancipation Day

A freeman contending for liberty on his own ground is superior to any slavish mercenary on earth.—Washington.

They who refuse education to a black man would turn the South into a vast poorhouse, and labor into a pendulum, necessity vibrating between povery and indolence.—Henry Ward Beecher.

The very best thing we can do for the black man, or for the white, is to strive with all our might to promote and secure the establishment of his inalienable rights.—John Swinton.

I do order and declare that all persons held as slaves, within said designated States and parts of States, are, and henceforth shall be, free; and that the Executive Government of the United States, including the military and navy authorities thereof, will recognize and maintain the freedom of said persons. And I hereby enjoin upon the people so declared to be free to abstain from all violence; and I recommend to them that in all cases, when allowed, they labor faithfully for reasonable wages.—Abraham Lincoln's Proclamation.

But, inasmuch as the Almighty has created His children of various hues, I plead again, that if one of these children be cast in an image of pearl, another in the image of ebony, another in the image of bronze, if their work be meritorious, then should they receive social and public recognition for their work's sake. Those works demonstrate beyond all cavil that the souls enshrined within those caskets emanate from the same divine source and partake of the same indefinable essence of infinitude.—Rev. J. A. Brockett.

To-day Massachusetts, and the whole of the American republic, from the border of Maine to the Pacific slopes, and from the Lakes to the Gulf, stand upon the immutable and everlasting principles of equal and exact justice. The days of unrequited labor are numbered with the past. Fugitive slave laws are only remembered as relics of that barbarism which John Wesley pronounced "the sum of all villainies," and whose knowledge of its blighting effects was matured by his travels in Georgia and the Carolinas.—Horace Mann.

The black man will not be faded out by miscegenation. The fate of the Indian, and the supposed fate of all weaker races in the presence of the stronger, will not be the fortune of the American negro. He has his great defense already in his hand. He is the peer at the ballot-box and in the courts of his white fellow-citizen. For the present, through his ignorance, he is made his tool, or is wronged out of his rights. He may make merchandise of his right of suffrage for a while; but it is his, and every year he will come to have a higher conception of its significance.—North American Review.

The only written theology of the negro is found in the plantation melodies; what are they but the plaintive

strains of weeping faith which came from hearts in vital union with God? He has an absolute faith in a personal Saviour who, only, has power on earth to forgive sin, and in a Holy Spirit upon whom he relies as the witness with his spirit that he is a child of God.—P. P. Hood.

The old South rested everything on slavery and agriculture, unconscious that these could neither give nor maintain healthy growth. The new South presents a perfect democracy, the oligarchs leading into the popular movement—a social system compact and closely knitted, less splendid on the surface, but stronger at the core—a hundred farms for every plantation, fifty homes for every palace, and a diversified industry that meets the complex needs of this complex age.—H. W. Grady.

When I recall the negro as I knew him during the existence of slavery, in the Carolinas, in the States of the Gulf, and in those along the Mississippi—when I behold the improvement that has been brought about in his being and condition since his liberation—I feel bound to say that he is doing as well as could be expected, and to express the opinion that he will do yet better under a larger liberty. He has been transformed within a generation, and the work of transformation will go on steadily, if it be not impeded.—John Swinton.

The new South is enamored of her new work. Her soul is stirred with the breath of a new life. The light of a grander day is falling fair on her face. She is thrilling, sir, with the consciousness of growing power and prosperity. As she stands full-statured and equal among the peoples of the earth, breathing the keen air and looking out upon an expanding horizon, she understands that her emancipation came because in the inscrutable wisdom of God her honest purpose was crossed and her brave armies were beaten.—H. W. Grady.

There is a good day coming for the South. Through darkness and tears and blood she has sought it. It has been an unconscious Via Dolorosa. But, in the end, it will be worth all it has cost. Her institutions before were deadly. She nourished death in her bosom. The greater her secular prosperity the more sure was her ruin. Every year of delay but made the change more terrible. Now, by an earthquake, the evil is shaken down. Her own historians in a better day shall write that from that day the sword cut off the cancer she began to find her health.—Henry Ward Beecher.

During the darkest days of slavery on every plantation there were Christian negroes who could be trusted anywhere and with anything, so much so that when the war came their masters felt free to go to the front and leave their treasures, their wives, their daughters and helpless children in the absolute care and protection of these negroes, and their trust was not betrayed. To-day you will find in these black belts the most honorable marriages, and the tie in many cases sacredly kept, churches disciplining members for immoralities, and ministers, ignorant men, giving their trumpet no uncertain sound upon these great principles.—P. P. Hood.

The white children have been brought up on dusky bosoms and love them. It is caste that alone creates an offense, and this is unchristian and must die out, as will every other indignity to humanity and to God. The black man, wearing his unfaded and God-given badge of race, equally cultivated, equally rich and self-possessed, will live beside his white neighbor and enjoy the opportunities and bounties of a common heaven equally with his Saxon fellow-citizen, both alike unconscious of the different livery each one wears. This condition of things is seen in all portions of Europe and will, ere long, be witnessed on American soil.—North American Review.

On January 1, 1863, went forth the decree of emancipation, the proclamation of which startled the world with its just magnanimity and challenged the admiration of an onlooking uni-

verse. Five millions of people, helpless, worse than poor because of their ignorance, made the air resonant with their songs of praise. Along the dusty turnpikes men, women, and children journeyed with joy—but where? The world's history does not furnish a parallel case. But with undaunted courage they faced the world, wrested from the field its stores, and, under the star of nominal liberty, they are marching on to-day to a higher destiny and to an exalted plane of heroic endeavor undreamed of by their liberator.—Rev. J. A. Brockett.

To liberty and enfranchisement is as far as law can carry the negro. The rest must be left to conscience and common sense. It should be left to those among whom his lot is cast, with whom he is indissolubly connected and whose prosperity depends upon their possessing his intelligent sympathy and confidence. Faith has been kept with him in spite of calumnious assertions to the contrary, by those who assume to speak for us or by frank opponents. Faith will be kept with him in the future, if the South holds her reason and integrity.—H. W. Grady.

No land ever, even in war, did so brave and bold a thing as to take from the plantation a million black men who could not read the Constitution or the spelling-book, and who could hardly tell one hand from the other, and permit them to vote, in the sublime faith that liberty, which makes a man competent to vote, would render him fit to discharge the duties of the voter. And I beg to say, as I am bound to say, that when this one million unwashed black men came to vote, though much disturbance occurred—as much disturbance always occurs upon great changes—they proved themselves worthy of the trust that had been confided to them.—Henry Ward Beecher.

Through fire and blood freedom and citizenship came to us. The conflict was waged for the preservation of the Union, but back of all of that were the prayers, the tears, and the heart throbs of the millions in the bonds of chattel slavery. We stand to-day in the presence of the American people, and with uncovered heads before the statue of Abraham Lincoln to celebrate the emancipation from slavery in the District of Columbia. This occasion should be a suggestive one to us. We should realize that awful grandeur in the responsibility of American citizenship, and we should read our duty on the starry firmament of the old flag. This is our country, our home. We know no cause but the American cause; no flag but the American flag! Let others appeal to England and the nations of the earth, but our appeal is to the American people and to their sense of fair play.— Jesse Lawson.

But, as the storm-dipping eagle nurtures her eaglets amid the thunder-scarred crags and peaks of the loftiest mountains, and teaches them to float with joy on the lightning-torn bosom of the blackest storm, so had the Almighty, while the storms of war's horrors were marshaling their forces of awful wrath, raised up the man of liberty amid the majestic forests of a western home. Like ancient Israel, the prayers, tears, and groans of mothers and sisters had gone up a pitiful memorial to God. And when the thunders of cannon, on land and sea, began to shock the continent with their fearful din, forth came the choice of God—the man of liberty— Abraham Lincoln. Notwithstanding that various official mistakes were made in the commencement of his administration, never has there a greater man graced the American soil, nor the whole circumference of God's footstool, than Abraham Lincoln.—Rev. J. A. Brockett.

Let this day be to us as sacred as was the night of the Passover to ancient Israel. Let the anthems of your praise ring out with joyous liberty until the glad sound shall be caught up by the hoary heights of the western mountains, "Lincoln and freedom!" By the mountains let the electric words be hurled down to the embattled hills—thence, down to the lowlands, through the shaded aisles of dark-

plumed forests, until the skies shall catch the glad sound—"Lincoln, beyond the stars, and freedom inseparable now and forever." Thus, hurled from glory to glory, and from age to age, shall these words pass on until the unsightly piece of ebony, quarried from the depths of slavery's pit, shall prove a priceless jewel gleaming in the diadem of humanity.—A. M. E. Review.

During the war, when he knew that his liberty was the gage, when he knew the battle was to decide whether he should or should not be free, although the country for hundreds of miles was stripped bare of able-bodied white men, and though property and the lives of the women and children were at the mercy of the slave, there never was an instance of arson, or assassination, or rapine, or conspiracy, and there never was an uprising. They stood still, conscious of their power, and said, "We will see what God will do for us." Such a history has no parallel. And since they began to vote, I beg leave to say, in closing this subject, that they have voted just as wisely and patriotically as their late masters did before the emancipation.—Henry Ward Beecher.

Emigration

The emigrant's way o'er the western desert
  is mark'd by
Camp-fires long consum'd and bones that
  bleach in the sunshine.—Longfellow.

Beheld the duteous son, the sire decayed,
The modest matron, and the blushing maid,
Forc'd from their homes, a melancholy
  train,
To traverse climes beyond the western
  main. —Goldsmith.

Let us depart! the universal sun
Confines not to one land his blessed beams;
Nor is man rooted, like a tree, whose seed
The winds on some ungenial soil have cast
There, where it cannot prosper.
          —Southey.

Down where yon anch'ring vessel spreads
  the sail,
That, idly waiting, flaps with every gale,
Downward they move, a melancholy band,
Pass from the shore and darken all the
  strand. —Goldsmith.

Good heav'n! what sorrows gloom'd that
   parting day,
That call'd them from their native walks
   away,
When the poor exiles, ev'ry pleasure past,
Hung round the bow'rs, and fondly look'd
   their last,
And took a long farewell, and wish'd in
   vain,
For seats like these beyond the western
   main,
And shudd'ring still to face the distant
   deep,
Return'd and wept, and still return'd to
   weep.   —Goldsmith.

I hear the tread of pioneers
Of nations yet to be,
The first low wash of waves where soon
Shall roll a human sea.   —Whittier.

Eminence

He who surpasses or subdues mankind,
Must look down on the hate of those below.
       —Byron.

It is a folly for an eminent man to
think of escaping censure, and a weakness to be affected with it. All the
illustrious persons of antiquity, and
indeed of every age in the world, have
passed through this fiery persecution.
—Addison.

Emotion

Emotion is always new.—Victor
Hugo.

The feelings, like flowers and butterflies, last longer the later they are delayed.—Richter.

It is our kindest and tenderest emotion which we screen from the world.
—Richter.

The heart that is soonest awake to
the flowers is always the first to be
touched by the thorns.—Moore.

Women are ever the dupes or the
victims of their extreme sensitiveness.—Balzac.

Women endowed with remarkable
sensibilities enjoy much; but they
also suffer much.—Anna Cora Mowatt.

All loving emotions, like plants,
shoot up most rapidly in the tempestuous atmosphere of life.—Richter.

Women are more susceptible to pain
than to pleasure.—Montaigne.

Emotion turning back on itself, and
not leading on to thought or action, is
the element of madness.—John Sterling.

The reason that women are so much
more sociable than men is because
they act more from the heart than
the intellect.—Lamartine.

In love we never think of moral
qualities, and scarcely of intellectual
ones. Temperament and manners
alone, with beauty, excite love.—
Hazlitt.

How many women are born too
finely organized in sense and soul for
the highway they must walk with
feet unshod.—O. W. Holmes.

At certain periods of life, we live
years of emotion in a few weeks, and
look back on those times as on great
gaps between the old life and the new.
—Thackeray.

Emotion is the atmosphere in which
thought is steeped, that which lends
to thought its tone or temperature,
that to which thought is often indebted
for half its power.—Hugh R. Haweis.

Natural emotion is the soul of
poetry, as melody is of music; the
same faults are engendered by over-
study of either art; there is a lack of
sincerity, of irresistible impulse in both
the poet and the composer.—Stedman.

Emotion, whether of ridicule, anger, or sorrow,—whether raised at a
puppet show, a funeral, or a battle,—
is your grandest of levellers. The
man who would be always superior
should be always apathetic.—Bulwer-Lytton.

Emotion has no value in the Christian system, save as it stands connected with right conduct as the cause
of it. Emotion is the bud, not the
flower, and never is it of value until
it expands into a flower.—Murray.

There are three orders of emotions,
—those of pleasure, which refer to the
senses; those of harmony, which refer
to the mind; and those of happiness,
which are the natural result of a
union between harmony and pleasure.
—Chapone.

We are but shadows: we are not endowed with real life, and all that
seems most real about us is but the
thinnest substance of a dream,—till
the heart be touched. That touch
creates us—then we begin to be—
thereby we are beings of reality and
inheritors of eternity.—Hawthorne.

Empire

Nations and empires flourish and decay,
By turns command, and in their turns
  obey.   —Ovid.

Extended empire, like expanded gold
Exchanges solid strength for feeble splendor.   —Johnson.

Westward the course of empire takes its
  way,
The four first acts already past,
A fifth shall close the drama with the day;
Time's noblest offspring is the last.
        —Bishop Berkeley.

Employment

Indolence is stagnation; employment is life.—Seneca.

The rust rots the steel which use
preserves.—Lytton.

The hand of little employment hath
the daintier sense.—Shakespeare.

The man who falls in love will find
plenty of occupation.—Ovid.

The devil does not tempt people
whom he finds suitably employed.—
Jeremy Taylor.

Be always employed about some
rational thing, that the devil find thee
not idle.—Jerome.

Employment is nature's physician,
and is essential to human happiness.
—Galen.

The great principle of human satisfaction is engagement.—Paley.

Employment and ennui are simply
incompatible.—Madame Deluzy.

The devil never tempted a man
whom he found judiciously employed.
—Spurgeon.

Give us employment in place of
ennui; for we must have one or the
other.—Mme. De Salm.

The wise prove, and the foolish
confess, by their conduct, that a life
of employment is the only life worth
leading.—Paley.

Employment, which Galen calls
"nature's physician," is so essential
to human happiness, that indolence
is justly considered as the mother of
misery.—Burton.

Women are in this respect more fortunate than men, that most of their
employments are of such a nature
that they can at the same time be
thinking of quite different things.—
Wilhelm von Humboldt.

At present, the most valuable gift
which can be bestowed upon women
is something to do which they can do
well and worthily, and thereby maintain themselves.—James A. Garfield.

A vast deal of human sympathy
runs along the electric line of needle-
work, stretching from the throne to
the wicker chair of the humble seamstress.—Hawthorne.

Life will frequently languish, even
in the hands of the busy, if they have
not some employment subsidiary to
that which forms their main pursuit.
—Blair.

Cares are employments; and without employ
The soul is on a rack; the rack of rest,
To souls most adverse; action all their
  joy.   —Young.

People cry out, and deplore the unre-
munerative employment of woman.
The true want is the other way.
Women really trained, and capable
of good work, can command any wages
or salaries.—Gail Hamilton.

Employment gives health, sobriety, and morals. Constant employment and well-paid labor produce, in a country like ours, general prosperity, content, and cheerfulness. Thus happy have we seen the country.—Daniel Webster.

Nothing can hide from me the conviction that an immortal soul needs for its sustenance something more than visiting, and gardening, and novel-reading, and crochet-needle, and the occasional manufacture of sponge cake.—T. W. Higginson.

Let us candidly confess our indebtedness to the needle. How many hours of sorrow has it softened, how many bitter irritations calmed, how many confused thoughts reduced to order, how many life-plans sketched in purple!—Caroline H. Dall.

The question of woman's work in its economic aspect is really one not so much now of woman's rights as of woman's mights. Pretty much anything she wants to do, a resolute girl may now do.—R. Herbert Newton.

What kind of work would be done if Hercules took to spinning wool in safe places, while Omphales turned out to do battle with monsters, in his stead? What kind of men should we have as the result of the exchange?—E. Lynn Linton.

We have employment assigned to us for every circumstance in life. When we are alone, we have our thoughts to watch; in the family, our tempers; and in company, our tongues.—Hannah More.

Laziness begat wearisomeness, and this put men in quest of diversions, play and company, on which however it is a constant attendant; he who works hard, has enough to do with himself otherwise.—La Bruyère.

Exert your talents, and distinguish yourself, and don't think of retiring from the world until the world will be sorry that you retire. I hate a fellow whom pride or cowardice or laziness drives into a corner, and who does nothing when he is there but sit and growl. Let him come out, as I do, and bark.—Dr. Johnson.

Emulation

Emulation and imitation are of twin birth.—Charles Buxton.

There is emulation even in vice.—Eugene Sue.

'T is no shame to follow the better precedent.—Ben Jonson.

Emulation admires and strives to imitate great actions; envy is only moved to malice.—Balzac.

My heart laments that virtue cannot live out of the teeth of emulation.—Shakespeare.

An envious fever of pale and bloodless emulation.—Shakespeare.

Emulation embalms the dead; envy, the vampire, blasts the living.—Fuseli.

Those fair ideas to my aid I'll call, and emulate my great original.—Dryden.

Envy, to which the ignoble mind's a slave, is emulation in the learned or brave.—Pope.

Emulation is a handsome passion; it is enterprising, but just withal.—Jeremy Collier.

Where there is emulation, there will be vanity; where there is vanity, there will be folly.—Johnson.

Terror has its inspiration, as well as competition.—Beaconsfield.

Emulation is active virtue; envy is brooding malice.—Ouida.

There is a long and wearisome step between admiration and imitation.—Richter.

Emulation is a noble and just passion, full of appreciation.—Schiller.

It is scarce possible at once to admire and excel an author, as water rises no higher than the reservoir it falls from.—Bacon.

Unsuccessful emulation is too apt to sink into envy, which of all sins has not even the excuse to offer of temporary gratification.—Sydney Dobell.

Keeps mankind sweet by action; without that
The world would be a filthy settled mud.
—Crown.

Emulation looks out for merits, that she may exert herself by a victory; envy spies out blemishes, that she may have another by a defeat.—Colton.

Emulation hath a thousand sons, that one by one pursue; if you give way, or edge aside from the direct forthright, like to an entered tide, they all rush by, and leave you hindmost.—Shakespeare.

When emulation leads us to strive for self-elevation by merit alone, and not by belittling another, then it is one of the grandest possible incentives to action.—Dr. Johnson.

Does the man live who has not felt this spur to action, in a more or less generous spirit? Emulation lives so near to envy that it is sometimes difficult to establish the boundary-lines.—Henry Giles.

God grant that we may contend with other churches, as the vine with the olive, which of us shall bear the best fruit; but not as the briar with the thistle, which of us will be the most unprofitable.—Bacon.

Worldly ambition is founded on pride or envy, but emulation, or laudable ambition, is actually founded in humility; for it evidently implies that we have a low opinion of our present attainments, and think it necessary to be advanced.—Bishop Hall.

Emulation has been termed a spur to virtue, and assumes to be a spur of gold. But it is a spur composed of baser materials, and if tried in the furnace will be found to want that fixedness which is the characteristic of gold. He that pursues virtue, only to surpass others, is not far from wishing others less forward than himself; and he that rejoices too much at his own perfections will be too little grieved at the defects of other men.—Colton.

Emulation is a handsome passion; it is enterprising, but just withal. It keeps a man within the terms of honor, and makes the contest for glory just and generous. He strives to excel, but it is by raising himself, not by depressing others.—Jeremy Collier.

Emulation is grief arising from seeing one's self exceeded or excelled by his concurrent, together with hope to equal or exceed him in time to come, by his own ability. But envy is the same grief joined with pleasure conceived in the imagination of some ill-fortune that may befall him.—Thomas Hobbes.

Give me the boy who rouses when he is praised, who profits when he is encouraged and who cries when he is defeated. Such a boy will be fired by ambition; he will be stung by reproach, and aminated by preference; never shall I apprehend any bad consequences from idleness in such a boy.—Quintilian.

It is averse to talent to be consorted and trained up with inferior minds or inferior companions, however high they may rank. The foal of the racer neither finds out his speed, nor calls out his powers, if pastured out with the common herd, that are destined for the collar and the yoke.—Colton.

Emulation, even in brutes, is sensitively "nervous." See the tremor of the thoroughbred racer before he starts. The dray-horse does not tremble, but he does not emulate. It is not his work to run a race. Says Marcus Antoninus, "It is all one to a stone whether it be thrown upward or downward." Yet the emulation of a

man of genius is seldom with his contemporaries, that is, inwardly in his
mind, although outwardly in his act
it would seem so. The competitors
with whom his secret ambition seems
to vie are the dead.—Bulwer-Lytton.

Encouragement

Correction does much, but encouragement does more. Encouragement
after censure is as the sun after a
shower.—Goethe.

More hearts pine away in secret
anguish for the want of kindness from
those who should be their comforters
than for any other calamity in life.—
Young.

It may be proper for all to remember that they ought not to raise expectations which it is not in their
power to satisfy; and that it is more
pleasing to see smoke brightening into
flame than flame sinking into smoke.
—Johnson.

Faint not; the miles to heaven are
but few and short.—Rutherford.

End

Every hour has its end.—Scott.

Deed done is well begun.—Dante.

The end must justify the means.—
Prior.

Let the end try the man.—Shakespeare.

All's well that ends well, still the
finis is the crown.—Shakespeare.

I am the last of my race. My name
ends with me.—Schiller.

We ought to consider the end in
everything.—La Fontaine.

The end crowns all;
And that old common arbitrator, time,
Will one day end it. —Shakespeare.

By the same means we do not always arrive at the same ends.—St.
Real.

Endurance

Still achieving, still pursuing, learn
to labor and to wait.—Longfellow.

Endurance is the crowning quality.
—Lowell.

He conquers who endures.—Persius.

Endurance is patience concentrated.
—Carlyle.

Patience and time conquer all
things—Corneille.

Prolonged endurance tames the bold.
—Byron.

Things may serve long, but not
serve ever.—Shakespeare.

The bird that flutters least is longest on the wing.—Cowper.

The burden becomes light that is
shared by love.—Ovid.

By bravely enduring it, an evil
which cannot be avoided is overcome.
—Old Proverb.

Through suffering and sorrow thou
hast passed, to show us what a woman
true can be.—Lowell.

The seal of suffering impressed upon
our destiny announces in clear characters our high calling.—De Gerando.

I have often had occasion to remark
the fortitude with which women sustain the most overwhelming reverses
of fortune.—Washington Irving.

The greater the difficulty the more
glory in surmounting it. Skilful pilots
gain their reputation from storms and
tempests.—Epicurus.

To endure is the first thing a child
ought to learn, and that which he
will have most need to know.—Rousseau.

There is nothing in the world so
much admired as a man who knows
how to bear unhappiness with courage.—Seneca.

There was never yet philosopher
that could endure the toothache patiently, however they have writ the

style of gods, and make a pish at chance and sufferance.—Shakespeare.

Wounds and hardships provoke our courage, and when our fortunes are at the lowest, our wits and minds are commonly at the best.—Charron.

Endurance is the prerogative of woman, enabling the gentlest to suffer what would cause terror to manhood.—Wieland.

Not in the achievement, but in the endurance of the human soul, does it show its divine grandeur and its alliance with the infinite God.—Chapin.

'Tis not now who's stout and bold?
But who bears hunger best, and cold?
And he's approv'd the most deserving,
Who longest can hold out at starving.
—Butler.

To the disgrace of men it is seen that there are women both more wise to judge what evil is expected, and more constant to bear it when it happens.—Sir P. Sidney.

Women are so gentle, so affectionate, so true in sorrow, so untired and untiring! but the leaf withers not sooner, and tropic light fades not more abruptly.—Barry Cornwall.

Our strength often increases in proportion to the obstacles which are imposed upon it; it is thus that we enter upon the most perilous plans after having had the shame of failing in more simple ones.—Rapin.

Whenever evil befalls us, we ought to ask ourselves, after the first suffering, how we can turn it into good. So shall we take occasion, from one bitter root, to raise perhaps many flowers.—Leigh Hunt.

Allowing everything that can be claimed for the superior patience and self-command of women, still the main solution of their enduring pain better than men is their having less physical sensibility.—Moore.

The women of the poorer classes make sacrifices, and run risks, and bear privations, and exercise patience and kindness to a degree that the world never knows of, and would scarcely believe even if it did know.—Samuel Smiles.

As in labor, the more one doth exercise, the more one is enabled to do, strength growing upon work; so, with the use of suffering, men's minds get the habit of suffering, and all fears and terrors are to them but as a summons to battle, whereof they know beforehand they shall come off victorious.—Sir P. Sidney.

There is a sort of natural instinct of human dignity in the heart of man which steels his very nerves not to bend beneath the heavy blows of a great adversity. The palm-tree grows best beneath a ponderous weight, even so the character of man. There is no merit in it, it is a law of psychology. The petty pangs of small daily cares have often bent the character of men, but great misfortunes seldom. There is less danger in this than in great good luck.—Kossuth.

"Blessed is the man that endureth temptation, for when he is tried he shall receive the crown of life, which the Lord hath promised to them that love Him." It is a verse of climbing power. It begins with man, it ends with God. It begins with earth, it ends with heaven. It begins with struggle, it ends with a crown. Blessed is the man that endureth, stands up under it, resists, conquers. "Blessed," for it means new wisdom, new strength, new joy,—"the crown of life."—Maltbie Babcock.

Enemies

Our enemies are our outward consciences.—Shakespeare.

None but yourself who are your greatest foe.—Longfellow.

There is no little enemy.—Franklin.

The man who has no enemies has no following.—Donn Piatt.

True wisdom, in general, consists in energetic determination.—Napoleon.

A man who makes no enemies is never a positive force.—Simon Cameron.

A man selects his enemies, his friends make themselves, and from these friends he is apt to suffer.—Donn Piatt.

My nearest
And dearest enemy.
—Thomas Middleton.

A merely fallen enemy may rise again, but the reconciled one is truly vanquished.—Schiller.

A man's enemies have no power to harm him, if he is true to himself and loyal to God.—John B. Gough.

That is a most wretched fortune which is without an enemy.—Publius Syrus.

Did a person but know the value of an enemy, he would purchase him with pure gold.—Abbé de Raunci.

If you want enemies excel others; if you want friends let others excel you.—Colton.

Make no enemies; he is insignificant indeed that can do thee no harm.—Colton.

It is better to break off a thousand friendships, than to endure the sight of a single enemy.—Saadi.

There's not so much danger in a known foe as a suspected friend.—Nabb.

The relief of enemies has a tendency to unite mankind in fraternal affection.—Johnson.

A malicious enemy is better than a clumsy friend.—Madame Swetchine.

A friend exaggerates a man's virtues; an enemy inflames his crimes.—Addison.

Inflict not on an enemy every injury in your power, for he may afterwards become your friend.—Saadi.

Our enemies come nearer the truth in the opinions they form of us than we do in our opinion of ourselves.—La Rochefoucauld.

An enemy despised is the most dangerous of all enemies.—Publius Syrus.

It is the enemy whom we do not suspect who is the most dangerous.—Rojas.

Let our friends perish, provided that our enemies fall at the same time.—Cicero.

The body of a dead enemy always smells sweet.—Vespasian.

'Tis death to me to be at enmity;
I hate it, and desire all good men's love.
—Shakespeare.

Though all things do to harm him what they can,
No greater en'my to himself than man.
Earl of Stirling.

'Tis ill to trust a reconciled foe;
Be still in readiness, you do not know
How soon he may assault us.
Webster and Rowley.

If we could read the secret history of our enemies we should find in each man's life sorrow and suffering enough to disarm all hostility.—Longfellow.

I am persuaded that he who is capable of being a bitter enemy can never possess the necessary virtues that constitute a true friend.—Fitzosborne.

It is from our enemies that we often gain excellent maxims, and are frequently surprised into reason by their mistakes.—Thomas Paine.

Discover the opinion of your enemies, which is commonly the truest; for they will give you no quarter, and allow nothing to complaisance.—Dryden.

Whosoever formeth an intimacy with the enemies of his friends, does so to injure the latter. O wise man! wash your hands of that friend who associates with your enemies.—Saadi.

I have adopted the Roman sentiment, that it is more honorable to save a citizen than to kill an enemy.—Dr. Johnson.

It would be a rarity worth seeing could any one show us such a thing as a perfectly reconciled enemy.—South.

The world is large when its weary leagues
　　two loving hearts divide;
But the world is small when your enemy is
　　loose on the other side.
　　　　　　—John Boyle O'Reilly.

It is better to decide a difference between enemies than friends, for one of our friends will certainly become an enemy and one of our enemies a friend.—Bias.

The fine and noble way to kill a foe
Is not to kill him; you with kindness may
So change him, that he shall cease to be so;
Then he's slain.
　　　　　　—Aleyn.

Avoid that which an enemy tells you to do; for if you follow his advice, you will smite your knees with the hand of sorrow. If he shows you a road straight as an arrow, turn from it and go the other way.—Saadi.

Who can look down upon the grave even of an enemy, and not feel a compunctious throb, that he should ever have warred with the poor handful of earth that lies mouldering before him!—Washington Irving.

A certain excess of animal spirits with thoughtless good-humor will often make more enemies than the most deliberate spite and ill-nature, which is on its guard, and strikes with caution and safety.—Hazlitt.

A Christian should not discover that he has enemies by any other way than by doing more good to them than to others. "If thine enemy hunger, feed him; if he thirst, give him drink."—Bishop Wilson.

Let us carefully observe those good qualities wherein our enemies excel us; and endeavor to excel them, by avoiding what is faulty, and imitating what is excellent in them.—Plutarch.

Some men are more beholden to their bitterest enemies than to friends who appear to be sweetness itself. The former frequently tell the truth, but the latter never.—Cato.

It is with many enterprises as with striking fire; we do not meet with success except by reiterated efforts, and often at the instant when we despaired of success.—Madame de Maintenon.

Lands, intersected by a narrow frith,
Abhor each other. Mountains interpos'd
Make enemies of nations, who had else,
Like kindred drops, been mingled into one.
　　　　　　—Cowper.

We pray for our enemies; we seek to persuade those who hate us without cause to live conformably to the goodly precepts of Christ, that they may become partakers with us of the joyful hope of blessings from God, the Lord of all.—Justin Martyr.

Never disregard what your enemies say. They may be severe, they may be prejudiced, they may be determined to see only in one direction, but still in that direction they see clearly. They do not speak all the truth, but they generally speak the truth from one point of view; so far as that goes, attend to them.—B. R. Haydon.

I do defy him, and I spit at him;
Call him a slanderous coward and a villain:
Which to maintain I would allow him odds,
And meet him, were I tied to run afoot
Even to the frozen ridges of the Alps.
　　　　　　—Shakespeare.

Be assured those will be thy worst enemies, not to whom thou hast done evil, but who have done evil to thee. And those will be thy best friends, not to whom thou hast done good, but who have done good to thee.—Lavater.

Plutarch has written an essay on the benefits which a man may receive from his enemies; and, among the good fruits of enmity, mentions this in particular, that by the reproaches which it casts upon us, we see the worst side of ourselves.—Addison.

Everybody has enemies. To have an enemy is quite another thing. One must be somebody in order to have an enemy. One must be a force before he can be resisted by another force.—Madame Swetchine.

When you see discord amongst the troops of your enemy, be of good courage; but if they are united, then be upon your guard. When you see contention amongst your enemies, go and sit at ease with your friends; but when you see them of one mind, string your bow, and place stones upon the ramparts.—Saadi.

Men of sense often learn from their enemies. Prudence is the best safeguard. This principle cannot be learned from a friend, but an enemy extorts it immediately. It is from their foes, not their friends, that cities learn the lesson of building high walls and ships of war. And this lesson saves their children, their homes, and their properties.—Aristophanes.

Energy

Energy and persistence conquer all things.—Franklin.

He alone has energy that cannot be deprived of it.—Lavater.

Women love energy and grand results.—Bulwer-Lytton.

Thought and action are the redeeming features of our lives.—Zimmermann.

Energy, even like the biblical grain of mustard-seed, will remove mountains.—Hosea Ballou.

It is unreasonable for us to look for as great a degree of energy in a woman as in a man; energy is quite as much of a physical as a mental product.—Voltaire.

Energy will do anything that can be done in this world; and no talents, no circumstances, no opportunities, will make a two-legged animal a man without it.—Goethe.

We should act with as much energy as those who expect everything from themselves; and we should pray with as much earnestness as those who expect everything from God.—Colton.

The shortest and surest way to prove a work possible is strenuously to set about it; and no wonder if that proves it possible that for the most part makes it so.—South.

Is there one whom difficulties dishearten—who bends to the storm? He will do little. Is there one who will conquer? That kind of man never fails.—Hunter.

Strong impulses are but another name for energy. Energy may be turned to bad uses; but more good may always be made of an energetic nature, than of an indolent and impassive one.—John Stuart Mill.

He who would do some great thing in this short life must apply himself to the work with such a concentration of his forces as, to idle spectators, who live only to amuse themselves, looks like insanity.—Foster.

No conjunction can possibly occur, however fearful, however tremendous it may appear, from which a man by his own energy may not extricate himself, as a mariner by the rattling of his cannon can dissipate the impending waterspout.—Beaconsfield.

England

The land of scholars, and the nurse of arms.—Goldsmith.

The storehouse of the world.—Dr. Young.

England is safe, if true within itself.—Shakespeare.

England! my country, great and free!
Heart of the world, I leap to thee!
　　　　　　　　—Bailey.

Rule, Britannia, rule the waves;
Britons never will be slaves.
　　　　　　　　—Thomson.

It was always yet the trick of our English nation, if they have a good

thing, to make it too common.—
Shakespeare.

Most brilliant star upon the crest of Time
Is England. England!
—Alexander Smith.

This England never did, nor never shall,
Lie at the proud foot of a conqueror.
—Shakespeare.

O England!—model to thy inward greatness,
Like little body with a mighty heart.
—Shakespeare.

Be England what she will,
With all her faults, she is my country still.
—Churchill.

May he be suffocate,
That dims the honour of this warlike isle!
—Shakespeare.

England, of all countries in the world,
Most blind to thine own good.
—Randolph.

Without one friend, above all foes,
Britannia gives the world repose.
—Cowper.

This land of such dear souls, this dear, dear
land,
Dear for her reputation through the world.
—Shakespeare.

The Continent will not suffer England to be the workshop of the world.
—Earl of Beaconsfield.

The noblest prospect which a
Scotchman ever sees is the high-road
that leads him to England.—Sam'l
Johnson.

England, bound in with the triumphant sea,
Whose rocky shore beats back the envious
siege
Of watery Neptune. —Shakespeare.

Come the three corners of the world in
arms,
And we shall shock them. Naught shall
make us rue,
If England to itself do rest but true.
—Shakespeare.

'T is liberty crowns Britannia's Isle,
And makes her barren rocks and her bleak
mountains smile. —Addison.

The people of England are the most
enthusiastic in the world. There are
others more excitable, but there are
none so enthusiastic.—Earl of Beaconsfield.

Hail, land of bowmen! seed of those who
scorn'd
To stoop the neck to wide imperial Rome:
O dearest half of Albion sea-walled.
—Albania.

Set in this stormy Northern sea,
Queen of these restless fields of tide,
England! what shall men say of thee,
Before whose feet the worlds divide?
—Oscar Wilde.

His home! the Western giant smiles,
And turns the spotty globe to find it;—
This little speck the British Isles?
'Tis but a freckle,—never mind it.
—O. W. Holmes.

Poor England! thou art a devoted deer,
Beset with every ill but that of fear.
The nations hunt; all mock thee for a prey;
They swarm around thee, and thou stand'st
at bay. —Cowper.

England, a happy land we know,
Where follies naturally grow,
Where without culture they arise,
And tow'r above the common size.
—Churchill.

Be Britain still to Britain true,
Amang oursels united;
For never but by British hands,
Maun British wrangs be righted.
—Burns.

Britain, the queen of isles, our fair possession
Secur'd by nature, laughs at foreign force;
Her ships her bulwark, and the sea her
dike,
Sees plenty in her lap, and braves the
world. —Havard.

Oh, when shall Britain, conscious of her
claim,
Stand emulous of Greek and Roman fame?
In living medals see her wars enroll'd,
And vanquished realms supply recording
gold? —Pope.

This precious stone set in the silver sea,
Which serves it in the office of a wall,
Or as a moat defensive to a house,
Against the envy of less happier lands;
This blessed plot, this earth, this realm, this
England. —Shakespeare.

The ocean is the grand vehicle of
trade, and the uniter of distant nations. To us it is peculiarly kind, not

only as it wafts into our ports the harvests of every climate, and renders our island the centre of traffic, but also as it secures us from foreign invasions by a sort of impregnable intrenchment. —Harvey.

For of old time, since first the rushing flood,
Urg'd by Almighty Pow'r, this favour'd isle
Turn'd flashing from the continent aside,
Indented shore to shore responsive still,
Its guardian she. —Thomson.

This royal throne of kings, this scepter'd isle,
This earth of majesty, this seat of Mars,
This other Eden, demi-paradise,
This fortress built by nature for herself
Against infection and the hand of war;
This happy breed of men, this little world,
This precious stone set in the silver sea.
    —Shakespeare.

There is no land like England,
 Whate'er the light of day be;
There are no hearts like English hearts,
 Such hearts of oak as they be;
There is no land like England,
 Whate'er the light of day be:
There are no men like Englishmen,
 So tall and bold as they be!
And these will strike for England,
 And man and maid be free
To foil and spoil the tyrant
 Beneath the greenwood tree.
    —Tennyson.

O native isle! fair freedom's happiest seat!
At thought of thee, my bounding pulses beat;
At thought of thee my heart impatient burns;
And all my country to my soul returns.
When shall I see those fields, whose plenteous grain
No pow'r can ravish from th' industrious swain?
When kiss, with pious love, the sacred earth
That gave a Burleigh or a Russell birth?
When—in the shade of laws that long have stood,
Propt by their care or strengthen'd by their blood,—
Of fearless independence wisely vain,
The proudest slave of Bourbon's race disdain. —Lord Littleton.

England is a domestic country. Here the home is revered and the hearth sacred. The nation is 'represented by a family,—the Royal family, —and if that family is educated with a sense of responsibility and a senti-ment of public duty, it is difficult to exaggerate the salutary influence it may exercise over a nation.—Beaconsfield.

Island of bliss! amid the subject seas,
That thunder round thy rocky coasts, set up,
At once the wonder, terror and delight
Of distant nations: whose remotest shores
Can soon be shaken by thy naval arm;
Not to be shook thyself, but all assaults
Baffling, as thy hoar cliffs the loud sea-wave. —Thomson.

England, our Mother's Mother! Come, and see
A greater England here! O come, and be
At home with us, your children, for there runs
The same blood in our veins as in your sons;
The same deep-seated love of Liberty
Beats in our hearts. We speak the same good tongue:
Familiar with all songs your bards have sung:
Those large men, Milton, Shakespeare, both are ours. —R. H. Stoddard.

There learned arts do flourish in great honour
 And poets's wits are had in peerless price;
Religion hath lay power, to rest upon her,
 Advancing virtue, and suppressing vice.
For end all good, all grace there freely grows,
 Had people grace it gratefully to use:
For God His gifts there plenteously bestows,
 But graceless men them greatly do abuse.
    —Spenser.

A power which has dotted over the surface of the whole globe with her possessions and military posts, whose morning drum-beat, following the sun, and keeping company with the hours, circles the earth with one continuous and unbroken strain of the martial airs of England.—Daniel Webster.

Enjoyment

He scatters enjoyment who can enjoy much.—Lavater.

They most enjoy the world who least admire.—Young.

Be merry if you are wise.—Martial.

Enjoy the present day, trusting very little to the morrow.—Horace.

The enjoyments of this life are not equal to its evils, even if equal in number.—Pliny.

Sleep, riches, and health are only truly enjoyed after they have been interrupted.—Richter.

And 'tis my faith that every flower
Enjoys the air it breathes.
—Wordsworth.

Who can enjoy alone?
Or all enjoying what contentment find?
—Milton.

A day of such serene enjoyment spent,
Were worth an age of splendid discontent.
—James Montgomery.

The less you can enjoy, the poorer, the scantier yourself,—the more you can enjoy, the richer, the more vigorous.—Lavater.

Temper your enjoyments with prudence, lest there be written upon your heart that fearful word "satiety."—Quarles.

Whether with Reason, or with Instinct blest,
Know, all enjoy that pow'r which suits them best. —Pope.

Heaven forbids, it is true, certain gratifications, but there are ways and means of compounding such matters.—Molière.

Pound St. Paul's Church into atoms, and consider any single atom; it is, to be sure, good for nothing; but put all these atoms together, and you have St. Paul's Church. So it is with human felicity, which is made up of many ingredients, each of which may be shown to be very insignificant.—Dr. Johnson.

All solitary enjoyments, quickly pall, or become painful, so that, perhaps, no more insufferable misery can be conceived than that which must follow incommunicable privileges. Only imagine a human being condemned to perpetual youth while all around him decay and die. O, how sincerely would he call upon death for deliverance!—Archbishop Sharp.

You were made for enjoyment, and the world was filled with things which you will enjoy, unless you are too proud to be pleased by them, or too grasping to care for what you cannot turn to other account than mere delight.—Ruskin.

Providence has fixed the limits of human enjoyment by immovable boundaries, and has set different gratifications at such a distance from each other, that no art or power can bring them together. This great law it is the business of every rational being to understand, that life may not pass away in an attempt to make contradictions consistent, to combine opposite qualities, and to unite things which the nature of their being must always keep asunder.—Johnson.

How small of all that human hearts endure,
That part which laws or kings can cause or cure!
Still to ourselves in every place consigned,
Our own felicity we make or find.
With secret course, which no loud storms annoy,
Glides the smooth current of domestic joy.
—Goldsmith.

We are all children in our strife to seize
Each petty pleasure, as it lures the sight,
And like the tall tree swaying in the breeze,
Our lofty wishes stoop their tow'ring flight,
Till when the prize is won it seems no more
Than gather'd shells from ocean's countless store,
And ever those who would enjoyment gain
Must find it in the purpose they pursue.
—Mrs. Hale.

Ye men of gloom and austerity, who paint the face of Infinite Benevolence with an eternal frown, read in the everlasting book, wide open to your view, the lesson it would teach. Its pictures are not in black and sombre hues, but bright and glowing tints; its music—save when ye drown it—is not in sighs and groans, but songs and cheerful sounds. Listen to the million voices in the summer air, and find one dismal as your own.—Dickens.

Ennui

Ennui was born one day of uniformity.—Motte.

___

The curse of the great is ennui.—Bulwer-Lytton.

___

A scholar has no ennui.—Richter.

___

A French word for an English malady.—Chatfield.

___

I am wrapped in dismal thinking.—Shakespeare.

___

Ennui shortens life, and bereaves the day of its light.—Emerson.

___

Ennui is an expressive word invented in France.—Bancroft.

___

Ennui is the rust of the mind born of idleness. It is unused tools that corrode.—Mme. de Girardin.

___

We are amused through the intellect, but it is the heart that saves us from ennui.—Madame Swetchine.

___

Ennui is the desire of activity without the fit means of gratifying the desire.—Bancroft.

___

Ennui, the parent of expensive and ruinous vices.—Ninon de Lenclos.

___

That which renders life burdensome to us generally arises from the abuse of it.—Rousseau.

___

I do pity unlearned gentlemen on a rainy day.—Lord Falkland.

___

Ennui is a growth of English root, though nameless in our language.—Byron.

___

You cannot give me an instance of any man who is permitted to lay out his own time contriving not to have tedious hours.—Dr. Johnson.

___

It is only those who never think at all, or else who have accustomed themselves to brood invariably on abstract ideas, that ever feel ennui.—Hazlitt.

The gloomy and the resentful are always found among those who have nothing to do or who do nothing.—Dr. Johnson.

___

Social life is filled with doubts and vain aspirings; solitude, when the imagination is dethroned, is turned to weariness and ennui.—Miss L. E. Landon.

___

As the gout seems privileged to attack the bodies of the wealthy, so ennui seems to exert a similar prerogative over their minds.—Colton.

___

Ennui, perhaps, has made more gamblers than avarice, more drunkards than thirst, and perhaps as many suicides as despair.—Colton.

___

I am tired of looking on what is,
One might as well see beauty never more,
As look upon it with an empty eye.
I would this world were over. I am tired.
     —Bailey.

___

Alas! I have nor hope nor health,
  Nor peace within nor calm around,
Nor that content surpassing wealth
  The sage in meditation found.
     —Shelley.

___

For Ennui is a growth of English root,
Though nameless in our language:—we retort
The fact for words, and let the French translate
That awful Yawn which Sleep cannot abate.
     —Byron.

___

I have also seen the world, and after long experience have discovered that ennui is our greatest enemy, and remunerative labor our most lasting friend.—Möser.

___

This ennui, for which we Saxons had no name,—this word of France, has got a terrific significance. It shortens life, and bereaves the day of its light.—Emerson.

___

Ambition itself is not so reckless of human life as ennui; clemency is a favorite attribute of the former; but ennui has the taste of a cannibal.—Bancroft.

___

There is nothing so insupportable to man as to be in entire repose, without passion, occupation, amusement, or application. Then it is that he feels his own nothingness, isolation, insignificance, dependent nature, powerlessness, emptiness. Immediately there issue from his soul ennui, sadness, chagrin, vexation, despair.—Pascal.

The victims of ennui paralyze all the grosser feelings by excess, and torpify all the finer by disuse and inactivity. Disgusted with this world, and indifferent about another, they at last lay violent hands upon themselves, and assume no small credit for the *sang froid* with which they meet death. But, alas! such beings can scarcely be said to die, for they have never truly lived.—Colton.

They are mockery all—these skies, these
   skies,
Their untroubled depth of blue—
They are mockery all—those eyes, those
   eyes,
  Which seem so warm and true;
Each tranquil star in the one that lies,
Each meteor glance that at random flies
  The other's lashes through!
They are mockery all, these flowers of
   spring,
  Which her airs so softly woo—
And the love to which we would madly
   cling,
  Ay, it is mockery too!
The winds are false which the perfume
   stir,
  And the looks deceive to which we sue;
And love but leads to the sepulchre,
  Which flowers spring to strew.
         —Hoffman.

Ennui, wretchedness, melancholy, groans, and sighs are the offering which these unhappy Methodists make to a Deity, who has covered the earth with gay colors, and scented it with rich perfumes; and shown us, by the plan and order of His works, that He has given to man something better than a bare existence, and scattered over His creation a thousand superfluous joys, which are totally unnecessary to the mere support of life.—Sydney Smith.

Enterprise

What passes in the world for talent or dexterity or enterprise is often only a want of moral principle. We may succeed where others fail, not from a greater share of invention, but from not being nice in the choice of expedients.—Hazlitt.

On the neck of the young man sparkles no gem so gracious as enterprise.—Hafiz.

Providence has hidden a charm in difficult undertakings which is appreciated only by those who dare to grapple with them.—Madame Swetchine.

How slow the time
To the warm soul, that in the very instant
It forms, would execute a great design.
         Thomson.

The method of the enterprising is to plan with audacity and execute with vigor; to sketch out a map of possibilities, and then to treat them as probabilities.—Bovee.

The fact is, that to do anything in this world worth doing, we must not stand back shivering and thinking of the cold and danger, but jump in and scramble through as well as we can.—Sydney Smith.

Before thy undertaking of any design, weigh the glory of thy action with the danger of the attempt; if the glory outweigh the danger, it is cowardice to neglect it; if the danger exceed the glory, it is rashness to attempt it; if the balances stand poised, let thy own genius cast them.—Quarles.

Enthusiasm

Enthusiasm is the breath of genius—Beaconsfield.

Enthusiasts soon understand each other.—Washington Irving.

Enthusiasm is the fever of reason.—Victor Hugo.

Enthusiasm begets enthusiasm.—Longfellow.

Enthusiasm goes out.—Emerson.

Every great and commanding movement in the annals of the world is the triumph of enthusiasm.—Emerson.

Enthusiasm is the intoxication of earnestness.—Lamartine.

Nothing great was ever achieved without enthusiasm.—Emerson.

Religion is among the most powerful causes of enthusiasm.—Burke.

Great dejection often follows great enthusiasm.—Joseph Roux.

Every production of genius must be the production of enthusiasm.—Beaconsfield.

No wild enthusiast ever yet could rest,
Till half mankind were like himself possess'd.   —Cowper.

For virtue's self may too much zeal be had:
The worst of madmen is a saint run mad.
                              —Pope.

The most enthusiastic man in a cause is rarely chosen as a leader.—Arthur Helps.

In things pertaining to enthusiasm no man is sane who does not know how to be insane on proper occasions.—Henry Ward Beecher.

Alas! how enthusiasm decreases as experience increases!—Mme. Louise Colet.

Enthusiasm imparts itself magnetically and fuses all into one happy and harmonious unity of feeling and sentiment.—A. Bronson Alcott.

And rash enthusiasm in good society
Were nothing but a moral inebriety.
                              —Byron.

The best thing which we derive from history is the enthusiasm that it raises in us.—Goethe.

Opposition may inflame the enthusiast, but never converts him.—Schiller.

Be not afraid of enthusiasm; you need it; you can do nothing effectually without it.—Guizot.

The sense of this word among the Greeks affords the noblest definition of it: enthusiasm signifies God in us.—Mme. de Staël.

There is a melancholy which accompanies all enthusiasm.—Shaftesbury.

All noble enthusiasms pass through a feverish stage and grow wiser and more serene.—Channing.

Enthusiasm gives life to what is invisible, and interest to what has no immediate action on our comfort in this world.—Mme de Staël.

Enthusiasm is the height of man; it is the passing from the human to the divine.—Emerson.

Enthusiasm is always connected with the senses.—Kant.

Enlist the interests of stern Morality and religious Enthusiasm in the cause of Political Liberty, as in the time of the old Puritans, and it will be irresistible.—S. T. Coleridge.

Depend upon it, my younger brethren, the bright, self-sacrificing enthusiasms of early manhood are among the most precious things in the whole course of human life.—H. P. Liddon.

Enthusiasm is grave, inward, self-controlled; mere excitement, outward, fantastic, hysterical, and passing in a moment from tears to laughter.—Sterling.

Enthusiasm is the leaping lightning, not to be measured by the horse-power of the understanding.—Emerson.

When once enthusiasm has been turned into ridicule, everything is undone except money and power.—Mme. de Staël.

There is not a more melancholy object than a man who has his head turned with religious enthusiasm.—Addison.

Nothing is so contagious as enthusiasm; it moves stones, it charms brutes. Enthusiasm is the genius of sincerity, and truth accomplishes no victories without it.—Lytton.

Enthusiasm is that temper of the mind in which the imagination has got the better of the judgment.—Warburton.

Let us recognize the beauty and power of true enthusiasm; and whatever we may do to enlighten ourselves and others, guard against checking or chilling a single earnest sentiment.—Tuckerman.

The same reason makes a man a religious enthusiast that makes a man an enthusiast in any other way, an uncomfortable mind in an uncomfortable body.—Hazlitt.

That youthful fervor, which is sometimes called enthusiasm, but which is a heat of imagination subsequently discovered to be inconsistent with the experience of actual life.—Beaconsfield.

Ridicule has ever been the most powerful enemy of enthusiasm, and properly the only antagonist that can be opposed to it with success.—Goldsmith.

Enthusiasm is the element of success in everything. It is the light that leads and the strength that lifts men on and up in the great struggles of scientific pursuits and of professional labor. It robs endurance of difficulty, and makes a pleasure of duty.—Bishop Doane.

Those who have arrived at any very eminent degree of excellence in the practice of an art or profession have commonly been actuated by a species of enthusiasm in their pursuit of it. They have kept one object in view amidst all the vicissitudes of time and fortune.—John Knox.

Without enthusiasm, the adventurer could never kindle that fire in his followers which is so necessary to consolidate their mutual interests; for no one can heartily deceive numbers who is not first of all deceived himself.—Warburton.

Let us beware of losing our enthusiasms. Let us ever glory in something, and strive to retain our admiration for all that would ennoble, and our interest in all that would enrich and beautify our life.—Phillips Brooks.

The fire of true enthusiasm is like the fires of Baku, which no water can ever quench, and which burn steadily on from night to day, and year to year, because their well-spring is eternal.—Ouida.

The enthusiast has been compared to a man walking in a fog; everything immediately around him, or in contact with him, appears sufficiently clear and luminous; but beyond the little circle of which he himself is the centre, all is mist and error and confusion.—Colton.

Conscience is doubtless sufficient to conduct the coldest character into the road of virtue; but enthusiasm is to conscience what honor is to duty; there is in us a superfluity of soul, which it is sweet to consecrate to the beautiful when the good has been accomplished.—Mme. de Staël.

Enthusiasm begets enthusiasm, eloquence produces conviction for the moment; but it is only by truth to Nature and the everlasting institutions of mankind that those abiding influences are won that enlarge from generation to generation.—Lowell.

Enthusiasm is an evil much less to be dreaded than superstition. Superstition is the disease of nations; enthusiasm that of individuals: the former grows inveterate by time; the latter is cured by it.—Robert Hall.

A mother should give her children a superabundance of enthusiasm; that after they have lost all they are sure to lose on mixing with the world, enough may still remain to prompt and support them through great actions. A cloak should be of three-pile, to keep its gloss in wear.—Hare.

Enthusiasm is that secret and harmonious spirit which hovers over the production of genius, throwing the reader of a book, or the spectator of a statue, into the very ideal presence whence these works have really originated. A great work always leaves us in a state of musing.—Isaac Disraeli.

I look upon enthusiasm, in all other points but that of religion, to be a very necessary turn of mind; as indeed it is a vein which nature seems to have marked with more or less strength, in the tempers of most men. No matter what the object is, whether business, pleasures or the fine arts: whoever pursues them to any purpose must do so *con amore*.—Melmoth.

Enthusiasm is a virtue rarely to be met with in seasons of calm and unruffled prosperity. Enthusiasm flourishes in adversity, kindles in the hour of danger, and awakens to deeds of renown. The terrors of persecution only serve to quicken the energy of its purposes. It swells in proud integrity, and, great in the purity of its cause, it can scatter defiance amidst hosts of enemies.—Dr. Chalmers.

It is impossible to combat enthusiasm with reason; for though it makes a show of resistance, it soon eludes the pressure, refers you to distinctions not to be understood, and feelings which it cannot explain. A man who would endeavor to fix an enthusiast by argument might as well attempt to spread quicksilver with his finger.—Goldsmith.

I gaze upon the thousand stars
  That fill the midnight sky;
And wish, so passionately wish,
  A light like theirs on high.
I have such eagerness of hope
  To benefit my kind;
I feel as if immortal power
  Were given to my mind.
      —Miss Landon.

Enthusiasm is always connected with the senses, whatever be the object that excites it. The true strength of virtue is serenity of mind, combined with a deliberate and steadfast determination to execute her laws. That is the healthful condition of the moral life; on the other hand, enthusiasm, even when excited by representations

of goodness, is a brilliant but feverish glow which leaves only exhaustion and languor behind.—Kant.

They wrong man greatly who say he is to be seduced by ease. Difficulty, abnegation, martyrdom, death, are the allurements that act on the heart of man. Kindle the inner genial life of him, you have a flame that burns up all lower considerations. Not happiness, but something higher; one sees this even in the frivolous classes, with their "point of honor" and the like. Not by flattering our appetites—no, by awakening the heroic that slumbers in every heart can any religious gain follow.—Carlyle.

In the whole range of human vision nothing is more attractive than to see a young man full of promise and of hope, bending all his energies in the direction of truth and duty and God, his soul pervaded with the loftiest enthusiasm, and his life consecrated to the noblest ends. To be such a young man is to rival the noblest and best of men in heroic valor and Christian chivalry. Nay, to be such a young man is to be like Christ, the highest type, the most illustrious example of enthusiasm the world has ever seen.— J. McC. Holmes.

Envy

Envy—the rottenness of the bones. —Proverbs.

Envy, the attendant of the empty mind.—Pindar.

Envy is a kind of praise.—Gay.

Envy is the antagonist of the fortunate.—Epictetus.

Envy is not to be conquered but by death.—Horace.

Envy feeds only on the living.— Ovid.

It was well said that envy keeps no holidays.—Bacon.

Envy pierces more in the restriction of praises than in the exaggeration of its criticisms.—Achilles Poincelot.

Envy, like flame, soars upwards.—Livy.

All envy is proportionate to desire.—Dr. Johnson.

Envy is more irreconcilable than hatred.—La Rochefoucauld.

The man that makes a character makes foes.—Young.

Envy sets the strongest seal on desert.—Ben Jonson.

The envious will die, but envy never.—Molière.

Better it is to be envied than pitied.—Herodotus.

Nothing can allay the rage of biting envy.—Claudianus.

As rust corrupts iron, so envy corrupts man.—Antisthenes.

How bitter a thing it is to look into happiness through another man's eyes!—Shakespeare.

Envy is like a fly that passes all a body's sounder parts, and dwells upon the sores.—Chapman.

Those who raise envy will easily incur censure.—Churchill.

Men that make envy and crooked malice nourishment, dare bite the best.—Shakespeare.

How can we explain the perpetuity of envy—a vice which yields no return?—Balzac.

The hate which we all bear with the most Christian patience is the hate of those who envy us.—Colton.

Envy lies between two beings equal in nature, though unequal in circumstances.—Jeremy Collier.

That incessant envy wherewith the common rate of mankind pursues all superior natures to their own.—Swift.

An envious man waxeth lean with the fatness of his neighbors.—Socrates.

For envy, to small minds, is flattery.—Young.

He who surpasses or subdues mankind must look down on the hate of those below.—Byron.

There is not a passion so strongly rooted in the human heart as envy.—Sheridan.

Envy, like flame, blackens that which is above it, and which it cannot reach.—J. Petit-Senn.

Such men as he be never at heart's ease whiles they behold a greater than themselves.—Shakespeare.

Envy will merit as its shade pursue,
But like a shadow proves the substance true.
    —Pope.

Envy, to which th' ignoble mind's a slave,
Is emulation in the learn'd or brave.
    —Pope.

Base Envy withers at another's joy,
And hates that excellence it cannot reach.
    —Thomson.

Envy not greatness: for thou mak'st thereby
Thyself the worse, and so the distance
   greater.   —Herbert.

But, oh! what mighty magician can assuage,
A woman's envy?   —Geo. Granville.

It is the practice of the multitude to bark at eminent men, as little dogs do at strangers.—Seneca.

A weak mind is ambitious of envy, a strong one of respect. — E. Wigglesworth.

Thy danger chiefly lies in acting well;
No crime's so great as daring to excel.
    —Churchill.

To all apparent beauties blind,
Each blemish strikes an envious mind.
    —Gay.

No metal can—no, not the hangman's axe—bear half the keenness of thy sharp envy.—Shakespeare.

The truest mark of being born with great qualities is being born without envy.—La Rochefoucauld.

Envy is blind, and has no other quality but that of detracting from virtue. —Livy.

The hen of our neighbor appears to us a goose, says the Oriental proverb. —Mme. Deluzy.

The Sicilian tyrants never devised a greater punishment than envy.—Juvenal.

When men are full of envy they disparage everything, whether it be good or bad.—Tacitus.

Envy is but the smoke of low estate,
Ascending still against the fortunate.
               —Lord Brooke.

Envy lurks at the bottom of the human heart, like a viper in its hole.— Balzac.

As a moth gnaws a garment, so doth envy consume a man.—St. Chrysostom.

Envy makes us see what will serve to accuse others, and not perceive what may justify them.—Bishop Wilson.

In short, virtue cannot live where envy reigns, nor liberality subsist with niggardliness.—Cervantes.

Stones and sticks are thrown only at fruit-bearing trees.—Saadi.

For something in the envy of the small
Still loves the vast democracy of death!
               —Lytton.

When we envy another, we make their virtue our vice.—Boileau.

Just so far as we are pleased at finding faults, are we displeased at finding perfection.—Lavater.

We ought to be guarded against every appearance of envy, as a passion that always implies inferiority wherever it resides.—Pliny.

Envy assails the noblest; the winds howl around the highest peaks.—Ovid.

We often glory in the most criminal passion; but that of envy is so shameful that we dare not even own it.— Rochefoucauld.

We are all clever enough at envying a famous man while he is yet alive.— Mimnermus.

Envy is a passion so full of cowardice and shame that nobody ever had the confidence to own it.—Rochester.

If we did but know how little some enjoy of the great things that they possess, there would not be much envy in the world.—Young.

Envy, like a cold prison, benumbs and stupefies; and, conscious of its own impotence, folds its arms in despair.—Jeremy Collier.

Envy is a littleness of soul, which cannot see beyond a certain point, and if it does not occupy the whole space, feels itself excluded.—Hazlitt.

There is but one man who can believe himself free from envy; and it is he who has never examined his own heart.—Helvetius.

Save those who fill the highest stations, I know of none more unfortunate than those who envy them.—Mme. de Maintenon.

Emulation looks out for merits, that she may exalt herself by a victory; envy spies out blemishes, that she may lower another by defeat.—Colton.

Envy, among other ingredients, has a mixture of the love of justice in it. We are more angry at undeserved than at deserved good fortune.—Hazlitt.

Many men profess to hate another, but no man owns envy, as being an enmity or displeasure for no cause but goodness or felicity.—Jeremy Taylor.

'Tis the beginning of hell in this life, and a passion not to be excused. Every other sin hath some pleasure annexed to it, or will admit of an excuse: envy alone wants both.—Burton.

There is a time in every man's education when he arrives at the conviction that envy is ignorance.—Emerson.

Envy sets the stronger seal on desert; if he have no enemies, I should esteem his fortune most wretched.—Ben Jonson.

He that would live clear of envy must lay his finger on his mouth, and keep his hand out of the ink-pot.—L'Estrange.

Envy, my son, wears herself away, and droops like a lamb under the influence of the evil eye.—Sannazaro.

Of all hostile feelings, envy is perhaps the hardest to be subdued, because hardly any one owns it even to himself, but looks out for one pretext after another to justify his hostility.—Whately.

It is because we have but a small portion of enjoyment ourselves that we feel so little pleasure in the good fortune of others. Is it possible for the happy to be envious?—W. B. Clulow.

Envy, if surrounded on all sides by the brightness of another's prosperity, like the scorpion confined within a circle of fire, will sting itself to death.—Colton.

They say that love and tears are learned without any master; and I may say that there is no great need of studying at the court to learn envy and revenge.—N. Caussin.

Newton found that a star, examined through a glass tarnished by smoke, was diminished into a speck of light. But no smoke ever breathed so thick a mist as envy or detraction.—Willmott.

Mankind are so ready to bestow their admiration on the dead, because the latter do not hear it, or because it gives no pleasure to the objects of it.

Even fame is the offspring of envy.—Hazlitt.

Envy is the deformed and distorted offspring of egotism; and when we reflect on the strange and disproportioned character of the parent, we cannot wonder at the perversity and waywardness of the child.—Hazlitt.

Lo! ill-rejoicing envy, wing'd with lies,
Scattering calumnious rumours as she flies,
The steps of miserable men pursue,
With haggard aspect, blasting to the view.
—Elton.

The praise of the envious is far less creditable than their censure; they praise only that which they can surpass, but that which surpasses them they censure.—Colton.

With that malignant envy, which turns pale,
And sickens, even if a friend prevail,
Which merit and success pursues with hate,
And damns the worth it cannot imitate.
—Churchill.

Envy, eldest born of hell, embru'd
Her hands in blood, and taught the sons of men
To make a death which nature never made,
And God abhorr'd. —Dr. Porteus.

Envy is of all others the most ungratifying and disconsolate passion. There is power for ambition, pleasure for luxury, and pelf even for covetousness; but envy gets no reward but vexation.—Jeremy Collier.

There is some good in public envy, whereas in private there is none; for public envy is as an ostracism that eclipseth men when they grow too great; and therefore it is a bridle also to great ones to keep within bounds.—Bacon.

Other passions have objects to flatter them, and seem to content and satisfy them for a while; there is power in ambition, pleasure in luxury, and pelf in covetousness; but envy can gain nothing but vexation.—Montaigne.

Whoever feels pain in hearing a good character of his neighbor will feel a pleasure in the reverse; and those who despair to rise in distinction by their virtues are happy if others can be depressed to a level with themselves.—Rev. John Barker.

———

A man that hath no virtue in himself ever envieth virtue in others; for men's minds will either feed upon their own good or upon others' evil; and who wanteth the one will prey upon the other.—Bacon.

———

Men of noble birth are noted to be envious towards new men when they rise; for the distance is all told, and it is like a deceit of the eye, that when others come on they think themselves going back.—Bacon.

———

In our road through life we may happen to meet with a man casting a stone reverentially to enlarge the cairn of another which stone he has carried in his bosom to sling against that very other's head.—Landor.

———

Envy may justly be called "the gall of bitterness and bond of iniquity;" it is the most acid fruit that grows on the stock of sin, a fluid so subtle that nothing but the fire of divine love can purge it from the soul.—Hosea Ballou.

———

Envy, like the worm, never runs but to the fairest fruit; like a cunning bloodhound, it singles out the fattest deer in the flock. Abraham's riches were the Philistines' envy; and Jacob's blessing bred Esau's hatred.—J. Beaumont.

Envy is a weed that grows in all soils and climates, and is no less luxuriant in the country than in the court; is not confined to any rank of men or extent of fortune, but rages in the breasts of all degrees.—Lord Clarendon.

To pooh-pooh what we are never likely to possess is wonderfully easy. The confirmed celibate is loudest in his denunciations of matrimony. In Æsôp, it is the tailless fox that advocates the disuse of tails. It is the grapes we cannot reach that we call sour.—Æneas Sage.

———

If envy, like anger, did not burn itself in its own fire, and consume and destroy those persons it possesses, before it can destroy those it wishes worst to, it would set the whole world on fire, and leave the most excellent persons the most miserable. — Lord Clarendon.

———

Envy ought in strict truth to have no place whatever allowed it in the heart of man; for the goods of this present world are so vile and low that they are beneath it, and those of the future world are so vast and exalted that they are above it.—Colton.

———

Envy is an ill-natured vice, and is made up of meanness and malice. It wishes the force of goodness to be strained, and the measure of happiness abated. It laments over prosperity, and sickens at the sight of health. It oftentimes wants spirit as well as good nature.—Jeremy Collier.

I don't believe that there is a human creature in his senses, arrived to maturity, that at some time or other has not been carried away by this passion (sc. envy) in good earnest; and yet I never met with any one who dared own he was guilty of it but in jest.—Mandeville.

———

We are often infinitely mistaken, and take the falsest measures, when we envy the happiness of rich and great men; we know not the inward canker that eats out all their joy and delight, and makes them really much more miserable than ourselves.—Bishop Hall.

———

If our credit be so well built, so firm, that it is not easy to be shaken by calumny or insinuation, envy then commends us, and extols us beyond reason to those upon whom we depend, till they grow jealous, and so blow us up when they cannot throw us down. —Clarendon.

———

To our betters we can reconcile ourselves, if you please—respecting them sincerely, laughing at their jokes, making allowance for their stupidities, meekly suffering their insolence; but we can't pardon our equals going beyond us.—Thackeray.

———

We had rather do anything than acknowledge the merit of another if we can help it We cannot bear a superior or an equal. Hence ridicule is sure to prevail over truth, for the malice of mankind, thrown into the scale, gives the casting weight.—Hazlitt.

As the rays of the sun, notwithstanding their velocity, injure not the eye, by reason of their minuteness, so the attacks of envy, notwithstanding their number, ought not to wound our virtue by reason of their insignificance. —Colton.

Do not envy the violet the dew-drop or glitter of a sunbeam; do not envy the bee the plant from which he draws some sweets. Do not envy man the little goods he possesses; for the earth is for him the plant from which he obtains some sweets, and his mind is the dew-drop which the world colors for an instant.—Leopold Schefer.

Surely, if we considered detraction to be bred of envy, nested only in deficient minds, we should find that the applauding of virtue would win us far more honor than the seeking slyly to disparage it. That would show we loved what we commended, while this tells the world we grudge at what we want in ourselves.—Feltham.

An envious man waxeth lean with the fatness of his neighbors. Envy is the daughter of pride, the author of murder and revenge, the beginner of secret sedition and the perpetual tormentor of virtue. Envy is the filthy slime of the soul; a venom, a poison, or quicksilver which consumeth the flesh and drieth up the marrow of the bones. —Socrates.

To be an object of hatred and aversion to their contemporaries has been the usual fate of all those whose merit has raised them above the common level. The man who submits to the shafts of envy for the sake of noble objects pursues a judicious course for his own lasting fame. Hatred dies with its object, while merit soon breaks forth in full splendor, and his glory is handed down to posterity in never-dying strains.—Thucydides.

To diminish envy, let us consider not what others possess, but what they enjoy; mere riches may be the gift of lucky accident or blind chance, but happiness must be the result of prudent preference and rational design; the highest happiness then can have no other foundation than the deepest wisdom; and the happiest fool is only as happy as he knows how to be.— Colton.

Envy is the most universal passion. We only pride ourselves on the qualities we possess, or think we possess; but we envy the pretensions we have, and those which we have not, and do not even wish for. We envy the greatest qualities and every trifling advantage. We envy the most ridiculous appearance or affectation of superiority. We envy folly and conceit; nay, we go so far as to envy whatever confers distinction of notoriety, even vice and infamy.—Hazlitt.

When any person of really eminent virtue becomes the object of envy, the clamor and abuse by which he is assailed is but the sign and accompaniment of his success in doing service to the public. And if he is a truly wise man, he will take no more notice of it than the moon does of the howling of the dogs. Her only answer to them is to shine on.—Whately.

And next to him malicious Envy rode
Upon a ravenous wolfe, and still did chaw
Between his cankered teeth a venomous tode,
That all the poison ran about his jaw;
But inwardly he chawed his own maw
At neighbour's wealth that made him ever sad
For death it was when any good he saw;
And wept, that cause of weeping none he had;
And when he heard of harme he waxed wondrous glad.   —Spenser.

The envious man is in pain upon all occasions which ought to give him pleasure. The relish of his life is inverted; and the objects which administer the highest satisfaction to those who are exempt from this passion give the quickest pangs to persons who are subject to it. All the perfections of their fellow creatures are odious,

Youth, beauty, valor and wisdom are provocations of their displeasure. What a wretched and apostate state is this! to be offended with excellence, and to hate a man because we approve him!—Steele.

Epigram

Diaulus, lately a doctor, is now an undertaker; what he does as an undertaker, he used to do also as a doctor.—Martial.

The book which you are reading aloud is mine, Fidentinus; but, while you read it so badly, it begins to be yours.—Martial.

You see those fish before you, a beautiful example of the sculpture of Phidias; give them water, and they will swim.—Martial.

You wonder that Marius' ear smells unpleasantly. You are the cause of this, Nestor; you whisper into it.—Martial.

Fannius, as he was fleeing from the enemy, put himself to death. Is not this, I ask, madness—to die for fear of dying?—Martial.

You complain, Velox, that the epigrams which I write are long. You yourself write nothing; your attempts are shorter.—Martial.

He who prefers to give Linus the half of what he wishes to borrow, rather than to lend him the whole, prefers to lose only the half.—Martial.

Though I often salute you, you never salute me first; I shall therefore, Pontilianus, salute you with an eternal farewell.—Martial.

You were constantly, Matho, a guest at my villa at Tivoli. Now you buy it—I have deceived you; I have merely sold you what was already your own.—Martial.

Since your legs, Phœbus, resemble the horns of the moon, you might bathe your feet in a cornucopia.—Martial.

Philo swears that he has never dined at home, and it is so; he does not dine at all, except when invited out.—Martial.

Thais has black, Læcania white teeth; what is the reason? Thais has her own, Læcania bought ones.—Martial.

Lycoris has buried all the female friends she had, Fabianus; would she were the friend of my wife.—Martial.

A crafty innkeeper at Ravenna lately cheated me. I asked him for wine and water; he sold me pure wine.—Martial.

When your crowd of attendants so loudly applaud you, Pomponius, it is not you, but your banquet, that is eloquent.—Martial.

See how the mountain goat hangs from the summit of the cliff; you would expect it to fall; it is merely showing its contempt for the dogs.—Martial.

You admire, Vacerra, only the poets of old, and praise only those who are dead. Pardon me, I beseech you, Vacerra, if I think death too high a price to pay for your praise.—Martial.

If your slave commits a fault, do not smash his teeth with your fists; give him some of the (hard) biscuit which famous Rhodes has sent you.—Martial.

You are pretty—we know it; and young—it is true; and rich—who can deny it? But when you praise yourself extravagantly, Fabulla, you appear neither rich, nor pretty, nor young.—Martial.

If I remember right, Ælia, you had four teeth; a cough displaced two, another two more. You can now cough without anxiety all the day long. A third cough can find nothing to do in your mouth.—Martial.

When you try to conceal your wrinkles, Polla, with paste made from heans, you deceive yourself, not me. Let a defeat, which is possibly but small, appear undisguised. A fault concealed is presumed to be great.—Martial.

If you wish, Faustinus, a bath of boiling water to be reduced in temperature—a bath, such as scarcely Julianus could enter—ask the rhetorician Sabinæus to bathe himself in it. He would freeze the warm baths of Nero.—Martial.

Why do I not kiss you, Philænis? you are bald. Why do I not kiss you, Philænis? you are carrotty. Why do I not kiss you, Philænis? you are one-eyed. He who kisses you, Philænus, sins against nature.—Martial.

Do you wonder for what reason, Theodorus, notwithstanding your frequent requests and importunities, I have never presented you with my works? I have an excellent reason; it is lest you should present me with yours.—Martial.

I have not a farthing in the house; one thing only remains for me to do, Regulus, and that is to sell the presents which I have received from you; are you inclined to buy them?—Martial.

Do you ask what sort of a maid I desire or dislike, Flaccus? I dislike one too easy and one too coy. The just mean, which lies between the two extremes, is what I approve; I like neither that which tortures nor that which cloys.—Martial.

In whatever place you meet me, Postumus, you cry out immediately, and your very first words are, "How do you do?" You say this, even if you meet me ten times in one single hour; you, Postumus, have nothing, I suppose, to do.—Martial.

Report says that you, Fidentinus, recite my compositions in public as if they were your own. If you allow them to be called mine, I will send you my verses gratis; if you wish them

to be called yours, pray buy them, that they may be mine no longer.—Martial.

I commend you, Postumus, for kissing me with only half your lip; you may, however, if you please, withhold even the half of this half. Are you inclined to grant me a boon still greater, and even inexpressible? Keep this whole half entirely to yourself, Postumus.—Martial.

I could do without your face, and your neck, and your hands, and your limbs, and your bosom, and other of your charms. Indeed, not to fatigue myself with enumerating each of them, I could do without you, Chloe, altogether.—Martial.

You often ask me, Priscus, what sort of person I should be, if I were to become suddenly rich and powerful. Who can determine what would be his future conduct? Tell me, if you were to become a lion, what sort of a lion would you be?—Martial.

All your female friends are either old or ugly; nay, more ugly than old women usually are. These you lead about in your train, and drag with you to feasts, porticos and theaters. Thus, Fabulla, you seem handsome, thus you seem young.—Martial.

You utter all sorts of falsehoods, Pontilianus; I assent to them. You recite bad verses; I praise them. You sing; I do the same. You drink, Pontilianus; I drink also. You are rude; I pretend not to perceive it. You wish to play at chess; I allow myself to be beaten. There is one thing only which you do without me, and I hold my tongue on the subject. Yet you never make me the slightest present. "When I die," say you, "I shall remember you handsomely." I do not look for anything; but die.—Martial.

What are the precise characteristics of an epigram it is not easy to define. It differs from a joke, in the fact that the wit of the latter dies in the words, and cannot therefore be conveyed in another language; while an epigram is a wit of ideas, and hence is translatable. Like aphorisms, songs and sonnets, it is occupied with some single point, small and manageable; but whilst a song conveys a sentiment, a sonnet, a poetical, and an aphorism a moral reflection, an epigram expresses a contrast.—Wm. Matthews.

Do you ask why I am unwilling to marry a rich wife? It is because I am unwilling to be taken to husband by my wife. The mistress of the house should be subordinate to her husband, for in no other way, Priscus, will the wife and husband be on an equality.—Martial.

Epiphany (See Missions)

The Bartholdi Statue of Liberty enlightening the world. It is the gospel which enlightens the world, and, placed on the church for a pedestal, holds up Jesus to let all on the stormy sea of life see the light of the world and safely reach the desired haven.—Peloubet.

The festival of the Epiphany must be deemed of very high importance by a believing and thoughtful Christian. It does not merely commemorate one of the most beautiful incidents of our Lord's infant life, it asserts one of the most fundamental and vital features of Christianity: the great distinction, in fact, between Christianity and Judaism. The Jewish revelation of God contained within itself the secret and the reason of its vanishing by absorption into the brighter light which should succeed it.—Canon Liddon.

The Light of the world is not put out. Now have death and the grave been converted into the great testimonies for life and immortality. Now may each man, who has the sentence of Adam upon him, know that he is a kinsman of the Son of God. Now may he follow Him; and so, when the darkness is thickest around him and within, not walk in it, but see the Light of Life.—F. D. Maurice.

There is no figure more common in scripture, and none more beautiful, than that by which Christ is likened unto light. Incomprehensible in its nature, itself the first visible, and that by which all things are seen, light represents to us Christ, Whose generation none can declare, but Who must shine upon us ere we can know aught aright, whether of things Divine or human.—H. Melville.

Thou whose almighty Word
Chaos and darkness heard,
 And took their flight,
Hear us, we humbly pray;
And where the gospel's day
Sheds not its glorious ray,
 Let there be light.
Thou, who didst come to bring
On Thy redeeming wing
 Healing and sight—
Health to the sick in mind,
Sight to the inly blind—
Oh, now to all mankind,
 Let there be light.
   —John Marriott.

Epitaph

Peas to his Hashes.—Epitaph on a London Cook.

Satire does not look pretty upon a tombstone.—Charles Lamb.

Here lies one whose name was writ in water.—Engraved on Keats' Tombstone.

It is so soon that I am done for,
I wonder what I was begun for!
—Epitaph in Cheltenham Churchyard.

Shrine of the mighty! can it be,
That this is all remains of thee?
   —Byron.

Grave-stones tell truth scarce forty years. Generations pass while families last not three oaks. —Sir Thomas Browne.

If you would see his monument look around.—Inscription on the tomb of Sir Christopher Wrenn, St. Paul's, London.

Of Manners gentle, of Affections mild;
In Wit a man; Simplicity, a child.
   —Pope.

Nature and Nature's laws lay hid in night.
God said "Let Newton be"! and all was
 light.   —Pope.

Let there be no inscription upon my tomb; let no man write my epitaph;

no man can write my epitaph.—Robert Emmet.

And many a holy text around she strews
That teach the rustic moralist to die.
—Gray.

Life is a jest, and all things show it,
I thought so once, but now I know it.
—Gay.

Here lies Anne Mann; she lived an
Old maid and died an old Mann.
—Bath Abbey.

I conceive disgust at these impertinent and misbecoming familiarities inscribed upon your ordinary tombstone.
—Charles Lamb.

Nobles and heralds, by your leave,
Here lies what once was Matthew Prior
The son of Adam and of Eve:
Can Bourbon or Nassau claim higher?
—Prior.

These are two friends whose lives were undivided;
So let their memory be, now they have glided.
Under the grave; let not their bones be parted,
For their two hearts in life were single-hearted. —Shelley.

To this sad shrine, whoe'er thou art! draw near,
Here lies the friend most lov'd, the son most dear;
Who ne'er knew joy but friendship might divide,
Or gave his father grief but when he died.
—Pope.

By foreign hands thy dying eyes were closed,
By foreign hands thy decent limbs composed,
By foreign hands thy humble grave adorned,
By strangers honored, and by strangers mourned. —Pope.

Beneath these green trees rising to the skies,
The planter of them, Isaac Greentrees, lies;
The time shall come when these green trees shall fall,
And Isaac Greentrees rise above them all.
—Epitaph at Harrow, England.

After your death you were better have a bad epitaph than their ill report while you lived.—Shakespeare.

The turf has drank a
Widow's tear;
Three of her husbands
Slumber here.
—Epitaph at Staffordshire.

Traveller, let your step be light,
So that sleep these eyes may close,
For poor Scarron, till to-night,
Ne'er was able e'en to doze.
—Scarron, Epitaph written by himself.

Johnny Carnegie lies here
Descendit of Adam and Eve,
Gif only can gang hieher,
I'se willing give him leve.
—Epitaph in an old Scottish Churchyard.

Emigravit, is the inscription on the tombstone where he lies;
Dead he is not, but departed,—for the artist never dies.
—Longfellow, Nuremberg.

The hand of him here torpid lies,
That drew th' essential form of grace,
Here closed in death th' attentive eyes
That saw the manners in the face.
—Sam'l Johnson, Epitaph for Hogarth.

Here lies Nolly Goldsmith, for shortness called Noll,
Who wrote like an angel, and talked like poor Poll. —David Garrick.

If e'er she knew an evil thought
She spoke no evil word:
Peace to the gentle! She hath sought
The bosom of her Lord.
—Ebenezer Elliot.

Thou third great Canning, stand among our best
And noblest, now thy long day's work hath ceased,
Here silent in our minster of the West
Who wert the voice of England in the East.
—Tennyson, Epitaph on Lord Stratford.

Here she lies a pretty bud,
Lately made of flesh and blood;
Who, as soon fell fast asleep,
As her little eyes did peep.
Give her strewings, but not stir
The earth, that lightly covers her.
—Herrick.

Ere sin could blight or sorrow fade,
Death came with friendly care;
The opening bud to Heaven conveyed,
And bade it blossom there.
—Coleridge, Epitaph on an Infant.

Here lie the remains of James Pady, Brickmaker, in hope that his clay will be remoulded in a workmanlike manner, far superior to his former perishable materials.—Epitaph from Addiscombe Churchyard, England.

Underneath this stone doth lie
As much beauty as could die;
Which in life did harbor give
To more virtue than doth live.
If at all she had a fault,
Leave it buried in this vault.
—Ben Jonson.

Man's life is like unto a winter's day,
Some break their fast and so depart away,
Others stay dinner then depart full fed;
The longest age but sups and goes to bed.
Oh, reader, then behold and see,
As we are now so must you 'be.
—Bishop Henshaw.

Underneath this crust
Lies the mouldering dust
Of Eleanor Batchelor Shoven,
Well versed in the arts
Of pies, custards and tarts,
And the lucrative trade of the oven.
When she lived long enough,
She made her last puff,
A puff by her husband much praised.
And now she doth lie
And make a dirt pie,
In hopes that her crust may be raised.
—Epitaph on a Yorkshire Cook, England.

And here the precious dust is laid;
Whose purely temper'd clay was made
So fine that it the guest betray'd.
Else the soule grew so fast within,
It broke the outward shell of sinne
And so was hatch'd a cherubin.
—Thos. Carew.

From his cradle
He was a scholar, and a ripe, and good one;
Exceeding wise, fair spoken, and persuading;
Lofty and sour to them that lov'd him not,
But to those men that sought him, sweet as summer:
*   *   *   *   *
And to add greater honors to his age
Than man could give, he died fearing God.
—Shakespeare.

I came at morn—'twas spring, I smiled,
The fields with green were clad;
I walked abroad at noon,—and lo!
'Twas summer,—I was glad;
I sate me down; 'twas autumn eve,
And I with sadness wept;
I laid me down at night, and then
'Twas winter,—and I slept.
—Mary Pyper.

The body of Benjamin Franklin, Printer (like the cover of an old book, its contents torn out and stript of its lettering and gilding), lies here, food for worms; but the work shall not be lost, for it will (as he believed) appear once more in a new and more elegant edition, revised and corrected by the author.—Benjamin Franklin.

Full many a life he saved
With his undaunted crew;
He put his trust in Providence,
And cared not how it blew.
—Epitaph in Deal Churchyard, England.

Here rests his head, upon the lap of earth,
A youth to fortune and to fame unknown;
Fair Science frown'd not on his humble birth,
And Melancholy mark'd him for her own.
Large was his bounty, and his soul sincere;
Heav'n did a recompense as largely send:
He gave to Mis'ry (all he had) a tear,
He gain'd from Heav'n ('twas all he wish'd)
    a friend,
No farther seek his merits to disclose,
Or draw his frailties from their dread abode;
There they alike in trembling hope repose,
The bosom of his Father and his God.
—Gray.

Equality

Mortals are equal; their mask differs.—Voltaire.

We are not all equal, nor can we be so.—Goethe.

Equality is no rule in Love's grammar.—Beaumont and Fletcher.

Bliss is the same, in subject or in king.—Pope.

Liberty, equality and fraternity.—The Motto of France.

An equal has no power over an equal.—Law Maxim.

All men are equal before the natural law.—Law Maxim.

The sun shines even on the wicked.—Seneca.

Liberty and equality—lovely and sacred words!—Mazzini.

So let them ease their hearts with prate of equal rights, which man never knew.—Byron.

All men are equal; it is not birth, but virtue alone, that makes the difference.—Voltaire.

All things whatsoever ye would that men should do to you, do ye even so to them.—Bible.

Children of wealth or want, to each is given
One spot of green, and all the blue of
heaven! —O. W. Holmes.

Some must follow, and some command, though all are made of clay!—Longfellow.

Men are made by nature unequal. It is vain, therefore, to treat them as if they were equal.—Froude.

Mean and mighty, rotting
Together, have one dust.
—Shakespeare.

She in beauty, education, blood,
Holds hand with any princess of the world.
—Shakespeare.

Equality of two domestic powers
Breeds scrupulous faction.
—Shakespeare.

Golden lads and girls all must, as chimney-sweepers, come to dust.—Shakespeare.

In the gates of eternity, the black hand and the white hand hold each other with an equal clasp.—Mrs. Stowe.

Man cannot degrade woman without himself falling into degradation; he cannot elevate her without at the same time elevating himself. — Alexander Walker.

It is untrue that equality is a law of nature. Nature has no equality; its sovereign law is subordination and dependence.—Vauvenargues.

The tallest and the smallest among us are so alike diminutive and pitifully base, it is a meanness to calculate the difference.—Thackeray.

Thersites's body is as good as Ajax's when neither are alive.—Shakespeare.

When we leave this world, and are laid in the earth, the prince walks as narrow a path as the day-laborer.—Cervantes.

Spoons and skimmers you can be undistinguishably together; but vases and statues require each a pedestal for itself.—Emerson.

As if the ray which travels from the sun would reach me sooner than the man who blacks my boots.—Thackeray.

The circle of life is cut up into segments. All lines are equal if they are drawn from the centre and touch the circumference.—Bulwer-Lytton.

Sir, your levellers wish to level down as far as themselves; but they cannot bear levelling up to themselves.—Samuel Johnson.

The foolish and vulgar are always accustomed to value equally the good and the bad.—Yriarte.

Kings and their subjects, masters and slaves, find a common level in two places—at the foot of the cross, and in the grave.—Colton.

Who can in reason then or right assume monarchy over such as live by right his equals, if in power or splendor less, in freedom equal?—Milton.

Equality is the share of every one at their advent upon earth, and equality is also theirs when placed beneath it.—Ninon de Lenclos.

Consider man, weigh well thy frame; the king, the beggar, are the same; dust formed us all.—Gay.

The woman's cause is man's. They rise or sink together; dwarfed or godlike, bond or free: if she be small, slight-natured, miserable, how shall men grow?—Tennyson.

There are some races more cultured and advanced and ennobled by education than others; but there are no races nobler than others. All are equally destined for freedom.—Alexander von Humboldt.

We hold these truths to be self-evident: that all men are created equal; that they are endowed by their Creator with inalienable rights; that among these are life, liberty and the pursuit of happiness.—Thomas Jefferson.

Equality is the life of conversation; and he is as much out who assumes to himself any part above another, as he who considers himself below the rest of the society.—Steele.

My equal he will be again
Down in that cold oblivious gloom,
Where all the prostrate ranks of men
Crowd without fellowship, the tomb.
—J. Montgomery.

Equal nature fashion'd us
All in one mould.   *   *   *
All's but the outward gloss
And politic form that does distinguish us.
—Massinger.

All men are by nature equal, made all of the same earth by one Workman; and however we deceive ourselves, as dear unto God is the poor peasant as the mighty prince.—Plato.

Whatever difference there may appear to be in men's fortunes, there is still a certain compensation of good and ill in all, that makes them equal.—Charron.

Come forward, some great marshal, and organize equality in society, and your rod shall swallow up all the juggling old court gold-sticks. — Thackeray.

For my part, it is not the mystery of the incarnation which I discover in religion, but the mystery of social order, which associates with heaven that idea of equality which prevents the rich from destroying the poor.—Napoleon I.

So far is it from being true that men are naturally equal, that no two people can be half an hour together but one shall acquire an evident superiority over the other.—Johnson.

A leveller has long ago been set down as a ridiculous and chimerical being, who, if he could finish his work to-day, would have to begin it again to-morrow.—Colton.

Your worm is your only emperor for diet: we fat all creatures else to fat us, and we fat ourselves for maggots. Your fat king and your lean beggar is but variable service, two dishes, but to one table: that's the end.—Shakespeare.

The mind of the thinker and the student is driven to admit, though it be awe-struck by apparent injustice, that this inequality is the work of God. Make all men equal to-day, and God has so created them that they shall be all unequal to-morrow.—Anthony Trollope.

It is a commonly observed fact that the enslavement of women is invariably associated with a low type of social life, and that, conversely, her elevation towards an equality with man uniformly accompanies progress.—Herbert Spencer.

All the religions known in the world are founded, so far as they relate to man or the unity of man, as being all of one degree. Whether in heaven or in hell, or in whatever state man may be supposed to exist hereafter, the good and the bad are the only distinctions.—Thomas Paine.

The trickling rain doth fall
Upon us one and all;
The south-wind kisses
The saucy milk-maid's cheek,
The nun's, demure and meek,
Nor any misses. —E. C. Stedman.

The equal right of all men to the use of land is as clear as their equal right to breathe the air—it is a right proclaimed by the fact of their existence. For we cannot suppose that some men have a right to be in this world, and others no right.—Henry George.

Equality is one of the most consummate scoundrels that ever crept from the brain of a political juggler—a fellow who thrusts his hand into the pocket of honest industry or enterprising talent, and squanders their hard-earned profits on profligate idleness or indolent stupidity.—Paulding.

We are foolish, and without excuse foolish, in speaking of the superiority of one sex to the other, as if they could be compared in similar things! Each has what the other has not; each completes the other; they are in nothing alike; and the happiness and perfection of both depend on each asking and receiving from the other what the other only can give.—Ruskin.

Equality is deemed by many a mere speculative chimera, which can never be reduced to practice. But if the abuse is inevitable, does it follow that we ought not to try at least to mitigate it? It is precisely because the force of things tends always to destroy equality that the force of the legislature must always tend to maintain it.—Rousseau.

The king is but a man, as I am; the violet smells to him as it doth to me; the element shows to him as it doth to me; all his senses have but human conditions; his ceremonies laid by, in his nakedness he appears but a man; and though his affections are higher mounted than ours, yet, when they stoop, they stoop with the like wing. —Shakespeare.

As soon the dust of a wretch whom thou wouldest not, as of a prince whom thou couldest not look upon, will trouble thine eyes if the wind blow it thither; and when a whirlwind hath blown the dust of the churchyard into the church, and the man sweeps out the dust of the church into the churchyard, who will undertake to sift those dusts again, and to pronounce, "This is the patrician, this is the noble flower, and this the yeoman, this the plebeian bran?"—Rev. Dr. Donne.

Equanimity

Equanimity is the gem in virtue's chaplet, and St. Sweetness the loveliest in her calendar.—Alcott.

In this thing one man is superior to another, that he is better able to bear adversity and prosperity.—Philemon.

Equity

A good judge decides fairly, preferring equity to strict law.—Law Maxim.

In all things, but particularly in the law, there is equity.—Law Maxim.

All things whatsoever ye would that men should do unto you, do ye even so to them.—Bible.

Equity is a roguish thing: for law we have a measure, know what to trust to; equity is according to the conscience of him that is chancellor, and as that is larger or narrower, so is equity. 'Tis all one as if they should make the standard for the measure we cal' a foot a chancellor's foot; what an uncertain measure would this be! One chancellor has a long foot, another a short foot, a third an indifferent foot. 'Tis the same in the chancellor's conscience.—Selden.

Equivocation

There is no possible excuse for a guarded lie. Enthusiastic and impulsive people will sometimes falsify thoughtlessly, but equivocation is malice prepense.—Hosea Ballou.

To doubt the Equivocation of the fiend,
That lies like truth: Fear not, till Birnam wood
Do come to Dunsinane. —Shakespeare.

A sudden lie may be sometimes only manslaughter upon truth; but by a carefully constructed equivocation, truth always is with malice afore-thought deliberately murdered.—Morley.

But yet,—
I do not like but yet, it does allay
The good precedence; fye upon but yet;
But yet is as a gaoler to bring forth
Some monstrous malefactor.
—Shakespeare.

Faith, here's an equivocator, that could swear in both the scales against either scale; who committed treason enough for God's sake, yet could not equivocate to heaven.—Shakespeare.

Error

Error is worse than ignorance.—Bailey.

Every error is truth abused.—Bossuet.

A man's errors are what make him amiable.—Goethe.

Error is frail.—Zoroaster.

Error is always more busy than truth.—Hosea Ballou.

Error is but the shadow of the truth.—Stillingfleet.

Error is ever talkative.—Goldsmith.

Honest error is to be pitied, not ridiculed.—Lord Chesterfield.

Dark error's other hidden side is truth.—Victor Hugo.

The cautious seldom err.—Confucius.

Man on the dubious waves of error toss'd.—Cowper.

The smallest errors are always the best.—Molière.

Men err from selfishness, women because they are weak.—Mme. de Staël.

While man's desires and aspirations stir,
He can not choose but err.   —Goethe.

Verily, there is nothing so true that the damps of error hath not warp'd it.—Tupper.

An error is the more dangerous in proportion to the degree of truth which it contains.—Amiel.

Error will slip through a crack, while truth will stick in a doorway.—H. W. Shaw.

If the wise erred not, it would go hard with the fools.—George Herbert.

Shall Error in the round of time
Still father Truth?   —Tennyson.

Errors, like straws, upon the surface flow;
He who would search for pearls must dive below.   —Dryden.

Great errors seldom originate but with men of great minds.—Petrarch.

Find earth where grows no weed, and you may find a heart wherein no error grows.—Knowles.

There are few, very few, that will own themselves in a mistake.—Swift.

In all science error precedes the truth, and it is better it should go first than last.—Horace Walpole.

Spurn not a seeming error, but dig below its surface for the truth.—Tupper.

There are some errors so sweet that we repent them only to bring them to memory.—J. Petit-Senn.

An error gracefully acknowledged is a victory won.—Caroline L. Gascoigne.

For to err in opinion, though it be not the part of wise men, is at least human.—Plutarch.

The error of our eye directs our mind:
What error leads must err.
     —Shakespeare.

Our follies and errors are the soiled steps to the Grecian temple of our perfection.—Richter.

Sometimes we may learn more from a man's errors than from his virtues.—Longfellow.

Mistake, error, is the discipline through which we advance.—Channing.

There are men who never err, because they never propose anything rational.—Goethe.

To stumble twice against the same stone is a proverbial disgrace.—Cicero.

From the errors of others, a wise man corrects his own.—Syrus.

The progress of rivers to the ocean is not so rapid as that of man to error.—Voltaire.

Weeds are omnipresent; errors are to be found in the heart of the most lovable.—George Sand.

No tempting form of error is without some latent charm derived from truth.—Keith.

Error's monstrous shapes from earth are driven
They fade, they fly—but truth survives the flight.   —Bryant.

Truth is a good dog; but beware of barking too close to the heels of an error, lest you get your brains kicked out.—Coleridge.

Error is sometimes so nearly allied to truth that it blends with it as imperceptibly as the colors of the rainbow fade into each other.—W. B. Clulow.

There will be mistakes in divinity while men preach, and errors in governments while men govern.—Sir Dudley Carlton.

How full of error is the judgment of mankind! They wonder at results when they are ignorant of the reasons.—Metastasio.

There is in some minds a nucleus of error which attracts and assimilates everything to itself.—Voltaire.

One deviates to the right, another to the left; the error is the same with all, but it deceives them in different ways.—Horace.

Our understandings are always liable to error. Nature and certainty is very hard to come at; and infallibility is mere vanity and pretense.—Marcus Antoninus.

There is scarcely any popular tenet more erroneous than that which holds that when time is slow, life is dull.—Beaconsfield.

Error, when she retraces her steps, has farther to go before she can arrive at truth than ignorance.—Colton.

By Hercules! I prefer to err with Plato, whom I know how much you value, than to be right in the company of such men.—Cicero.

Knowledge being to be had only of visible and certain truth, error is not a fault of our knowledge, but a mistake of our judgment, giving assent to that which is not true.—John Locke.

It is much easier to meet with error than to find truth; error is on the surface, and can be more easily met with; truth is hid in great depths, the way to seek does not appear to all the world.—Goethe.

How happy he who can still hope to lift himself from this sea of error! What we know not, that we are anxious to possess, and cannot use what we know.—Goethe.

All errors spring up in the neighborhood of some truth; they grow round about it, and, for the most part, derive their strength from such contiguity.—Rev. T. Binney.

My principal method for defeating error and heresy is by establishing the truth. One purposes to fill a bushel with tares, but if I can fill it first with wheat, I may defy his attempts.—Newton.

There are errors which no wise man will treat with rudeness while there is a probability that they may be the refraction of some great truth still below the horizon.—Coleridge.

Consciousness of error is, to a certain extent, a consciousness of understanding; and correction of error is the plainest proof of energy and mastery.—Landor.

For the first time, the best may err, art may persuade, and novelty spread out its charms. The first fault is the child of simplicity; but every other the offspring of guilt.—Goldsmith.

The more secure we feel against our liability to any error to which, in fact, we are liable, the greater must be our danger of falling into it.—Whately.

Error is always more busy than ignorance. Ignorance is a blank sheet on which we may write; but error is a scribbled one from which we must first erase.—Colton.

Those things which now seem frivolous and
slight,
Will be of serious consequence to you,
When they have made you once ridiculous.
—Roscommon.

It is only an error of judgment to make a mistake, but it argues an infirmity of character to adhere to it when discovered. Or, as the Chinese better say, "The glory is not in never falling, but in rising every time you fall."—Bovee.

He who only tastes his error will long dwell with it, will take delight in it as in a singular felicity; while he who drains it to the dregs will, if he be not crazy, find it to be what it is.—Goethe.

O hateful Error, Melancholy's child!
Why dost thou show to the apt thoughts of
men
The things that are not? O Error, soon
conceiv'd,
Thou never com'st unto a happy birth,
But kill'st the mother that engender'd thee.
—Shakespeare.

Truth only is prolific. Error, sterile in itself, produces only by means of the portion of truth which it contains. It may have offspring, but the life which it gives, like that of the hybrid races, cannot be transmitted.—Madame Swetchine.

Error is a hardy plant; it flourisheth in
every soil;
In the heart of the wise and good, alike
with the wicked and foolish;
For there is no error so crooked, but it hath
in it some lines of truth. —Tupper.

Errors to be dangerous must have a great deal of truth mingled with them; it is only from this alliance that they can ever obtain an extensive circulation; from pure extravagance, and genuine, unmingled falsehood, the world never has, and never can sustain any mischief.—Sydney Smith.

If a crooked stick is before you, you need not explain how crooked it is. Lay a straight one down by the side of it, and the work is well done. Preach the truth, and error will stand abashed in its presence.—Spurgeon.

Error soon passes away, unless upheld by restraint on thought. History tells us (and the lesson is invaluable) that the physical force which has put down free inquiry has been the main bulwark of the superstitions and illusions of past ages.—Channing.

The more readily we admit the possibility of our own cherished convictions being mixed with error, the more vital and helpful whatever is right in them will become; and no error is so conclusively fatal as the idea that God will not allow us to err, though He has allowed all other men to do so.—Ruskin.

The blindness of bigotry, the madness of ambition, and the miscalculations of diplomacy seek their victims principally amongst the innocent and the unoffending. The cottage is sure to suffer for every error of the court, the cabinet, or the camp. When error sits in the seat of power and of authority, and is generated in high places, it may be compared to that torrent which originates indeed in the mountain, but commits its devastation in the vale.—Colton.

The little I have seen of the world teaches me to look upon the errors of others in sorrow, not in anger. When I take the history of one poor heart that has sinned and suffered, and represent to myself the struggles and temptations it has passed through, the brief pulsations of joy, the feverish inquietude of hope and fear, the pressure of want, the desertion of friends, I would fain leave the erring soul of my fellowman with Him from whose hand it came.—Longfellow.

Esteem

Esteem all things that are good.—Tibullus.

Esteem never makes ingrates.—Rochefoucauld.

I will never pretend esteem for a man whose principles I detest.—Gustavus III. of Sweden.

We should esteem a person according to his actions, not his nationality.—Varenes.

To be loved, we should merit but little esteem; all superiority attracts awe and aversion.—Helvetius.

Prefer not the esteem of men to the approbation of God.—Jortin.

It is common to esteem most what is most unknown.—Tacitus.

Our esteem is apt to be given where we know the least.—Michelet.

Esteem cannot be where there is no confidence, and there can be no confidence where there is no respect.—Henry Giles.

Esteem incites friendship, but not love; the former is the twin brother of Reverence; the latter is the child of Equality.—Lamartine.

Many men and many women enjoy popular esteem, not because they are known, but because they are not.—Chamfort.

No man can have much kindness for him by whom he does not believe himself esteemed, and nothing so evidently proves esteem as imitation.—Johnson.

Esteem has more engaging charms than friendship, and even love. It captivates hearts better, and never makes ingrates.—Rochefoucauld.

As love without esteem is volatile and capricious, so esteem without love is languid and cold.—Dr. Johnson.

There is no rapture in the love which is prompted by esteem; such affection is lasting, not passionate.—Victor Hugo.

Under the assumption of profound esteem, the flatterer wears an outward expression of fidelity, as foreign to his heart as the smile upon the face of the dead.—E. L. Magoon.

By virtue, integrity, perseverance and true modesty it is possible for all men to win the esteem of their fellow beings.—C. N. Douglas.

There is graciousness and a kind of urbanity in beginning with men by esteem and confidence. It proves, at least, that we have long lived in good company with others and with ourselves.—Joubert.

We have so exalted a notion of the human soul that we cannot bear to be despised by it, or even not to be esteemed by it. Man, in fact, places all his happiness in this esteem.—Pascal.

We esteem in the world those who do not merit our esteem, and neglect persons of true worth; but the world is like the ocean—the pearl is in its depths, the seaweed swims.—G. P. Morris.

The chief ingredients in the composition of those qualities that gain esteem and praise are good nature, truth, good sense, and good breeding.—Addison.

The esteem of wise and good men is the greatest of all temporal encouragements to virtue; and it is a mark of an abandoned spirit to have no regard to it.—Burke.

We acquire the love of people who, being in our proximity, are presumed to know us; and we receive reputation or celebrity, from such as are not personally acquainted with us. Merit secures to us the regard of our honest neighbors, and good fortune that of the public. Esteem is the harvest of a whole life spent in usefulness; but reputation is often bestowed upon a chance action, and depends' most on success.—G. A. Sala.

Local esteem is far more conducive to happiness than general reputation. The latter may be compared to the fixed stars which glimmer so remotely as to afford little light and no warmth. The former is like the sun, each day shedding his prolific and cheering beams.—W. B. Clulow.

Estrangement

There is not so agonizing a feeling in the whole catalogue of human suffering, as the first conviction that the heart of the being whom we most tenderly love is estranged from us.—Bulwer.

Eternity

Eternity, thou pleasing, dreadful thought!—Addison.

Eternity forbids thee to forget.—Byron.

God has given to us eternal life; and this life is in His Son.

Who can speak of eternity without a solecism, or think thereof without an ecstasy?—Sir T. Browne.

All that live must die, passing through nature to eternity.—Shakespeare.

Let me dream that love goes with us to the shore unknown.—Mrs. Hemans.

This narrow isthmus 'twixt two boundless seas.—Moore.

That golden key,
That opes the palace of eternity.
—Milton.

If we stretch our thoughts as far as they can reach, eternity is still before us.—J. Edmondson.

Can eternity belong to me, poor pensioner on the bounties of an hour?—Young.

The thought of eternity consoles for the shortness of life.—Malesherbes.

Beyond is all abyss, eternity, whose end no eye can reach.—Milton.

What a sublime doctrine it is, that goodness cherished now is eternal life already entered on!—W. E. Channing.

But felt through all this fleshly dresse
Bright shootes of everlastingnesse.
—Henry Vaughan.

All great men find eternity affirmed in the very promise of their faculties.—Emerson.

Eternity looks grander and kinder if Time grow meaner and more hostile.—Carlyle.

"Time restores all things." Wrong! Time restores many things, but eternity restores all.—Joseph Roux.

The youth of the soul is everlasting, and eternity is youth.—Richter.

Darkness, that here surrounds our purblind understanding, will vanish at the dawning of eternal day.—Boyle.

Yes, I live in God, and shall eternally. It is His hand upholds me now; and death will be but an uplifting of me into His bosom.—Wm. Mountford.

If people would but provide for eternity with the same solicitude and real care as they do for this life, they could not fail of heaven.—Tillotson.

Eternity doth wear upon her face the veil of time. They only see the veil, and thus they know not what they stand so near!—Alexander Smith.

O, if we could tear aside the veil, and see but for one hour what it signifies to be a soul in the power of an endless life, what a revelation would it be!—Horace Bushnell.

This is eternal life; a life of everlasting love, showing itself in everlasting good works; and whosoever lives that life, he lives the life of God, and hath eternal life.—Charles Kingsley.

Eternal life does not depend upon our perfection; but because it does depend upon the grace of Christ and the love of the Spirit, that love shall prompt us to emulate perfection.—William Adams.

Sure there is none but fears a future state;
And when the most obdurate swear they do not,
Their trembling hearts belie their boasting tongues. —Dryden.

In time there is no present,
In eternity no future,
In eternity no past. —Tennyson.

'Tis the divinity that stirs within us;
'Tis Heaven itself that points out an hereafter,
And intimates eternity to man.
—Addison.

Eternity! How know we but we stand
On the precipitous and crumbling verge
Of Time e'en now, Eternity below?
—Abraham Coles.

Nothing is eternal but that which is done for God and others. That which is done for self dies.—Aughey.

Eternity has no gray hairs! The flowers fade, the heart withers, man grows old and dies, the world lies down in the sepulchre of ages, but time writes no wrinkles on the brow of eternity.—Bishop Heber.

Oh! in that future let us think
To hold each heart the heart that shares;
With them the immortal waters drink,
And, soul in soul, grow deathless theirs!
—Byron.

The more we can be raised above the petty vexations and pleasures of this world into the eternal life to come, the more shall we be prepared to enter into that eternal life whenever God shall please to call us hence.—Dean Stanley.

O, that a man might know
The end of this day's business, ere it come,
But it sufficeth that the day will end;
And then the end is known.
—Shakespeare.

Yes, what I am to be everlastingly, I am growing to be now—now in this present time so little thought of, this time which the sun rises and sets in, and the clock strikes in, and I wake and sleep in.—Wm. Mountford.

Eternity is the divine treasure-house and hope is the window, by means of which mortals are permitted to see, as through a glass darkly, the things which God is preparing.—Mountford.

Too curious man! why dost thou seek to know
Events, which, good or ill, foreknown, are woe!
Th' all-seeing power, that made thee mortal, gave
Thee every thing a mortal state should have. —Dryden.

It is a high, solemn, almost awful thought for every individual man, that his earthly influence, which has a commencement, will never, through all ages, have an end.—Aughey.

He that will often put eternity and the world before him, and who will dare to look steadfastly at both of them, will find that the more often he contemplates them, the former will grow greater, and the latter less.—Colton.

If there remains an eternity to us after the short revolution of time we so swiftly run over here, 'tis clear that all the happiness that can be imagined in this fleeting state is not valuable in respect of the future.—Locke.

Certainly the highest and dearest concerns of a temporal life are infinitely less valuable than those of an eternal; and consequently ought, without any demur at all, to be sacrificed to them, whenever they come in competition.—South.

There is, I know not how, in the minds of men, a certain presage, as it were, of a future existence; and this takes the deepest root, and is most discoverable, in the greatest geniuses and most exalted souls.—Cicero.

Sow the seeds of life—humbleness, pure-heartedness, love; and in the long eternity which lies before the soul, every minutest grain will come up again with an increase of thirty, sixty, or a hundredfold.—F. W. Robertson.

In the life to come, at the first ray of its light our true characters, purified but preserving their identity, will more fully expand, and the result of the infinite diversity will be a complete unity.—Madame de Gasparin.

Eternity invests every state, whether of bliss or of suffering, with a mysterious and awful importance, entirely its own. It gives that weight and moment to whatever it attaches, compared to which all interests that know a period fade into absolute insignificance.—Robert Hall.

"What is eternity?" was a question once asked at the deaf and dumb institution at Paris, and the beautiful and striking answer was given by one of the pupils, "The lifetime of the Almighty."—John Bate.

Eternity, thou pleasing dreadful Thought!
Thro' what variety of untry'd beings,
Thro' what new scenes and changes must
   we pass?
The wide, the unbounded Prospect lies be-
   fore me;
But shadows, clouds, and darkness rest
   upon it.   —Addison.

None can comprehend eternity but the eternal God. Eternity is an ocean, whereof we shall never see the shore; it is a deep, where we can find no bottom; a labyrinth from whence we cannot extricate ourselves and where we shall ever lose the door.—Boston.

Eternity is a negative idea clothed with a positive name. It supposes in that to which it is applied a present existence, and is the negation of a beginning or of an end of that existence.—Paley.

Consider and act with reference to the true ends of existence. This world is but the vestibule of an immortal life. Every action of our lives touches on some chord that will vibrate in eternity.—Chapin.

Upon laying a weight in one of the scales, inscribed eternity. though I

threw in that of time, prosperity, affliction, wealth, and poverty, which seemed very ponderous, they were not able to stir the opposite balance.—Addison.

When at eve, at the bounding of the landscape, the heavens appear to recline so slowly on the earth, imagination pictures beyond the horizon an asylum of hope—a native land of love; and nature seems silently to repeat that man is immortal.—Madame de Staël.

The time will come when every change shall
   cease,
This quick revolving wheel shall rest in
   peace:
No summer then shall glow, nor winter
   freeze;
Nothing shall be to come, and nothing past,
But an eternal now shall ever last.
       —Petrarch.

It is only Jesus Christ who has thrown light on life and immortality through the gospel; and because He has done so, and has enabled us by His atoning death and intercession to make the most of this discovery, His gospel is, for all who will, a power of God unto salvation.—H. P. Liddon.

Every natural longing has its natural satisfaction. If we thirst, God has created liquid to gratify thirst. If we are susceptible of attachment, there are beings to gratify that love. If we thirst for life and love eternal, it is likely there are an eternal life and an eternal love to satisfy that craving.—F. W. Robertson.

Life everywhere is in vast and endless variety. So it is with life eternal, that gift of God, constituting, in its length and breadth and height and depth, the reward of the righteous. The penitent, dying thief is not going into heaven like the triumphant, dying Paul.—Herrick Johnson.

Let us be adventurers for another world. It is at least a fair and noble chance; and there is nothing in this worth our thoughts or our passions. If we should be disappointed, we are still no worse than the rest of our fellow-mortals; and if we succeed in our expectations we are eternally happy.—Burnet.

Eternity, thou awful Gulph of Time,
This wide creation on thy surface floats.
Of life—of death—what is, or what shall be,
I nothing know. The world is all a dream,
The consciousness of something that exists,
Yet is not what it seems. Then what am I?
Death must unfold the mystery! —Dowe.

The disappointed man turns his thoughts toward a state of existence where his wiser desires may be fixed with the certainty of faith; the successful man feels that the objects which he has ardently pursued fail to satisfy the cravings of an immortal spirit; the wicked man turneth away from his wickedness, that he may save his soul alive.—Southey.

You reap what you sow—not something else, but that. An act of love makes the soul more loving. A deed of humbleness deepens humbleness. The thing reaped is the very thing sown, multiplied a hundred fold. You have sown a seed of life, you reap life everlasting.—F. W. Robertson.

Our imagination so magnifies this present existence, by the power of continual reflection on it, and so attenuates eternity, by not thinking of it at all, that we reduce an eternity to nothingness, and expand a mere nothing to an eternity; and this habit is so inveterately rooted in us that all the force of reason cannot induce us to lay it aside.—Pascal.

The vaulted void of purple sky
 That everywhere extends,
That stretches from the dazzled eye,
 In space that never ends;
A morning whose uprisen sun
 No setting e'er shall see;
A day that comes without a noon
 Such is eternity. —Clare.

Beyond the grave! As the vision rises how this side dwindles into nothing—a speck—a moment—and its glory and pomp shrink into the trinkets and baubles that amuse an infant for a day. Only those things, in the glory of this light, which lay hold of

immortality, seem to have any value.—Bishop R. S. Foster.

Those spacious regions where our fancies roam,
Pain'd by the past, expecting ills to come,
In some dread moment, by the fates assign'd,
Shall pass away, nor leave a rack behind;
And Time's revolving wheels shall lose at last
The speed that spins the future and the past:
And, sovereign of an undisputed throne,
Awful eternity shall reign alone.
 —Petrarch.

The longest time that man may live,
The lapse of generations of his race,
The continent entire of time itself,
Bears not proportion to Eternity;
Huge as a fraction of a grain of dew
Co-measured with the broad, unbounded ocean!
There is the time of man—his proper time,
Looking at which this life is but a gust,
A puff of breath, that's scarely felt ere gone! —Sheridan Knowles.

Alas! what is man? whether he be deprived of that light which is from on high, or whether he discard it; a frail and trembling creature, standing on time, that bleak and narrow isthmus between two eternities, he sees nothing but impenetrable darkness on the one hand, and doubt, distrust, and conjecture still more perplexing on the other. Most gladly would he take an observation as to whence he has come, or whither he is going. Alas, he has not the means; his telescope is too dim, his compass too wavering, his plummet too short. Nor is that little spot, his present state, one whit more intelligible, since it may prove a quicksand that may sink in a moment from his feet; it can afford him no certain reckoning as to that immeasurable ocean that he may have traversed, or that still more formidable one that he must.—Colton.

Yes, my brethren, Christ will reign—must reign. O what a grand, glorious destiny awaits us who are saved! I stand in the presence of a scheme that I have neither power to comprehend nor to delineate. I tell you, when the end shall come, and God

Almighty shall gather into His kingdom the souls and bodies of men saved upon the earth, they will reach the pinnacle of eternal life in all its splendor! Happy, happy will be the day when you and I, by God's grace, stand in full proportion on the granite platform of an eternal, happy immortality. —Bishop Daggett.

Ethics

Ethics, as has been well said, are the finest fruits of humanity, but they are not its roots.—Miss Mulock.

Ethics may be defined as the obligations of morality.—Kossuth.

Ethics is the doctrine of manners, or science of philosophy, which teaches men their duty and the springs and principles of human conduct.—Maunder.

Art itself is essentially ethical; because every true work of art must have a beauty or grandeur of some kind, and beauty and grandeur cannot be comprehended by the beholder except through the moral sentiment. The eye is only a witness; it is not a judge. The mind judges what the eye reports to it; therefore, whatever elevates the moral sentiment to the contemplation of beauty and grandeur is in itself ethical.—Bulwer-Lytton.

The modern Gamaliel should teach ethics. Ethics is the science of human duty. Arithmetic tells man how to count his money; ethics how he should acquire it, whether by honesty or fraud. Geography is a map of the world; ethics is a beautiful map of duty. This ethics is not Christianity, it is not even religion; but it is the sister of religion, because the path of duty is in full harmony, as to quality and direction, with the path of God.—Professor Swing.

Etiquette

Etiquette is the invention of wise men to keep fools at a distance.—Steele.

What are these wondrous civilizing arts, this Roman polish, and this smooth behavior that render man thus tractable and tame?—Addison.

Trifles themselves are elegant in him.—Pope.

Etiquette has no regard for moral qualities.—Douglas Jerrold.

Starch makes the gentleman, etiquette the lady.—Brummel.

There was a general whisper, toss, and
  wiggle,
But etiquette forbade them all to giggle.
            —Byron.

Etiquette is the ceremonial code of polite life, more voluminous and minute in each portion of society according to its rank.—J. R. MacCulloch.

There's nothing in the world like etiquette
In kingly chambers, or imperial halls,
As also at the race and county balls.
            —Byron.

O form! how oft dost thou with thy case, thy habit, wrench awe from fools, and tie the wiser souls to thy false seeming!—Shakespeare.

We show wisdom by a decent conformity to social etiquette; it is excess of neatness or display that creates dandyism in men, and coquetry in women.—Robert Adam.

A man may with more impunity be guilty of an actual breach, either of real good breeding or good morals, than appear ignorant of the most minute points of fashionable etiquette.—Scott.

Evasion

Evasion is unworthy of us, and is always the intimate of equivocation.—Balzac.

Evasions are the common shelter of the hard-hearted, the false and impotent when called upon to assist; the really great alone plan instantaneous help, even when their looks or words presage difficulties.—Lavater.

Evening

Every evening brings us nearer God.—Luther.

At shut of evening flowers.—Milton.

The pale child, Eve, leading her mother, Night.—Alexander Smith.

Dewy evening's soft and sacred lull.—Paul H. Hayne.

O precious evenings! all too swiftly sped!—Longfellow.

Vast and deep the mountain shadows grew.—Rogers.

Hath not thy heart within thee burned,
At evening's calm and holy hour?
    —S. G. Bulfinch.

To me at least was never evening yet
But seemed far beautifuller than its day.
    —Robert Browning.

Now came still evening on, and twilight
    gray,
Had in her sober livery all things clad.
    —Milton.

Fairest of all that earth beholds, the hues
That live among the clouds, and flush the
    air,
Lingering and deepening at the hour of
    dews.   —Bryant.

How dear to me the hour when daylight
    dies,
And sunbeams melt along the silent sea,
For then sweet dreams of other days arise,
And memory breathes her vesper sigh to
    thee.   —Moore.

Meek-eyed Eve, her cheek yet warm with blushes, slow retires through the Hesperian gardens of the west, and shuts the gates of day.—Mrs. Barbauld.

One by one the flowers close,
Lily and dewy rose
Shutting their tender petals from the moon.
    —Christina G. Rossetti.

Now to the main the burning sun descends,
And sacred night her gloomy veil extends.
The western sun now shot a feeble ray
And faintly scatter'd the remains of day.
    —Addison.

Women have in their natures something akin to owls and fireflies. While men grow stupid and sleepy towards evening, they become brighter and more open-eyed, and show a propensity to flit and sparkle under the light of chandeliers.—Abba Goold Woolson.

Sober Evening takes her wonted station in the middle air, a thousand shadows at her beck.—Thomson.

The summer day has clos'd—the sun is set:
Well have they done their office, those
    bright hours,
The latest of whose train goes softly out
In the red west.   —Bryant.

It was an evening bright and still
As ever blush'd on wave or bower,
Smiling from heaven, as if nought ill
Could happen in so sweet an hour.
    —Moore.

The day is done, and the darkness
Falls from the wings of Night,
As a feather is wafted downward
From an eagle in his flight.
    —Longfellow.

And the night shall be filled with music,
And the cares that infest the day
Shall fold their tents like the Arabs,
And as silently steal away.
    —Longfellow.

Day, like a weary pilgrim, had reached the western gate of heaven, and Evening stooped down to unloose the latchets of his sandal shoon.—Longfellow.

The west with second pomp is bright
Though in the east the dusk is thickening,
Twilight's first star breaks forth in white,
Into night's gold each moment quicken-
    ing.   —Street.

    Evening came.
The setting sun stretched his celestial rods
    of light
Across the level landscape, and, like the
    Hebrews
In Egypt, smote the rivers, brooks, and
    ponds,
And they became as blood.
    —Longfellow.

O how grandly cometh Even,
Sitting on the mountain summit,
Purple-vestured, grave, and silent,
Watching o'er the dewy valleys,
    Like a good king near his end.
    —D. M. Mulock.

Night steals on: and the day takes its farewell, like the words of a departing friend, or the last tone of hallowed music in a minster's aisles, heard when it floats along the shade

of elms, in the still place of graves.—
Percival.

The sun is set; the swallows are asleep;
The bats are flitting fast in the gray air;
The slow soft toads out of damp corners
   creep;
And evening's breath, wandering here and
   there
Over the quivering surface of the stream,
Wakes not one ripple from its silent dream.
           —Shelley.

Now stir the fire, and close the shutters
   fast,
Let fall the curtains, wheel the sofa round,
And while the bubbling and loud-hissing urn
Throws up a steamy column, and the cups
That cheer but not inebriate, wait on each,
So let us welcome peaceful evening in.
           —Cowper.

When day is done, and clouds are low,
  And flowers are honey-dew,
And Hesper's lamp begins to glow
  Along the western blue;
And homeward wing the turtle-doves,
Then comes the hour the poet loves.
           —George Croly.

Silence hath set her finger with deep touch
Upon creation's brow. Like a young bride
  the moon
Lifts up night's curtains, and with countenance mild
Smiles on the beauteous earth, her sleeping
  child.   —Bigg.

    A paler shadow strews
Its mantle o'er the mountains; parting day
Dies like a dolphin, whom each pang im-
  bues
With a new colour as it gasps away
The last still loveliest 'till—'tis gone—and
  all is grey.   —Byron.

An eve intensely beautiful; an eve
Calm as the slumber of a lovely girl
Dreaming of hope. The rich autumnal
  woods,
With their innumerable shades and colour-
  ings,
Are like a silent instrument at rest:
A silent instrument—whereon the wind
Hath long forgot to play. —Houseman.

Evening is the delight of virtuous
age; it seems an emblem of the tranquil close of busy life—serene, placid,
and mild, with the impress of its great
Creator stamped upon it; it spreads
its quiet wings over the grave, and
seems to promise that all shall be peace
beyond it.—Bulwer-Lytton.

The curfew tolls the knell of parting day;
The lowing herd winds slowly o'er the lea;
The ploughman homeward plods his weary
  way,
And leaves the world to darkness and to me.
Now fades the glimmering landscape on the
  sight,
And all the air a solemn stillness holds,
Save where the beetle wheels his droning
  flight,
And drowsy tinklings lull the distant folds.
           —Gray.

Come to the sunset tree!
  The day is past and gone;
The woodman's axe lies free,
  And the reaper's work is done;
The twilight star to heaven,
  And the summer dew to flowers,
And rest to us is given
  By the cool, soft evening hours.
           —Mrs. Hemans.

Come, evening, once again, season of peace;
Return, sweet evening, and continue long!
Methinks I see thee in the streaky west,
With matron step, slow moving, while the
  night
Treads on thy sweeping train; one hand
  employ'd
In letting fall the curtain of repose
On bird and beast, the other charged for
  man
With sweet oblivion of the cares of day.
           —Cowper.

Sweet was the sound, when oft, at even-
  ing's close,
Up yonder hill the village murmur rose;
There as I passed, with careless steps and
  slow,
The mingling notes came soften'd from
  below;
The swain responsive as the milkmaid sung,
The sober herd that low'd to meet their
  young;
The noisy geese that gabbled o'er the pool,
The playful children just let loose from
  school;
The watch-dog's voice that bay'd the whis-
  pering wind,
And the loud laugh that spoke the vacant
  mind;
These all in sweet confusion sought the
  shade,
And fill'd each pause the nightingale had
  made.   —Goldsmith.

Each evening we should meditate
upon the fact that one more day is
gone from the list that make up the
sum of our years. We have one day
less for the seeking and finding Christ;
for cultivating the spirit of holiness
in our hearts, for blessing society,
building up the church, gathering sin-

ners to the Savior, and promoting the glory of God. By so much the time is shortened that separates us from the grave, the judgment and the eternal destiny.

It is the hour when from the boughs
  The nightingale's high note is heard;
It is the hour when lovers' vows
  Seem sweet in every whispered word;
And gentle winds, and waters near,
Make music to the lonely ear.
Each flower the dews have lightly wet,
And in the sky the stars are met,
And on the wave is deeper blue,
And on the leaf a browner hue,
And in the heaven that clear obscure,
So softly dark, and darkly pure.
Which follows the decline of day,
As twilight melts beneath the moon away.
                              —Byron.

Ave Maria! blessed be the hour!
The time, the clime, the spot where I so oft
Have felt that moment in its fullest power
Sink o'er the earth so beautiful and soft,
While swung the deep bell in the distant
    tower,
Or the faint dying day-hymn stole aloft,
And not a breath crept through the rosy air,
And yet the forest leaves seem'd stirr'd with
    prayer.
Soft hour! which makes the wish and melts
    the heart
Of those who sail the seas, on the first day;
When they from their sweet friends are
    torn apart;
Or fills with love the pilgrim on his way,
As the far bell of vesper makes him start,
Seeming to weep the dying day's decay;
Is this a fancy which our reason scorns?
Ah! surely nothing dies but something
    mourns!   —Byron.

Events

Coming events cast their shadows before.—Campbell.

Certain signs precede certain events. —Cicero.

Events of great consequence often spring from trifling circumstances.— Livy.

In the great inconstancy and crowd of events nothing is certain except the past.—Seneca.

What wonderful things are events! The least are of greater importance than the most sublime and comprehensive speculations.—Beaconsfield.

Great events have sent before them their announcements.—Calderon.

Events of all sorts creep or fly exactly as God pleases.—Cowper.

Man reconciles himself to almost any event, however trying, if it happens in the ordinary course of nature. It is the extraordinary alone that he rebels against. There is a moral idea associated with this feeling; for the extraordinary appears to be something like an injustice of heaven.—Humboldt.

Evidence

Facts are stubborn things.—Smollett.

One eye-witness is of more weight than ten hearsays.—Plautus.

Some circumstantial evidence is very strong, as when you find a trout in the milk.—Thoreau.

I do not know what arguments mean in reference to any expression of a thought. I delight in telling what I think; but if you ask me how I dare say so, or why it is so, I am the most helpless of men.—Emerson.

It is not true that a man can believe or disbelieve what he will. But it is certain that an active desire to find any proposition true will unconsciously tend to that result, by dismissing importunate suggestions which run counter to the belief, and welcoming those which favor it. The psychological law, that we only see what interests us, and only assimilate what is adapted to our condition, causes the mind to select its evidence.—G. H. Lewes.

Evil

Of two evils, the less is always to be chosen.—Thomas à Kempis.

From seeming evil still educing good. Thomson.

And out of good still to find means of evil.—Milton.

A bad heart, bad designs.—Terence.

Better one thorn pluck'd out than all remain.—Horace.

None are all evil.—Byron.

I have wrought great use out of evil tools.—Bulwer-Lytton.

Ill deeds are doubled with an evil word.—Shakespeare.

Evil events from evil causes spring.—Aristophanes.

Evil then results from imperfection.—Bailey.

Men's evil manners live in brass; their virtues we write in water.—Shakespeare.

Evil often triumphs, but never conquers.—Joseph Roux.

An evil life is one kind of death.—Ovid.

All things can corrupt perverse minds.—Ovid.

The best known evil is the most tolerable.—Livy.

Desperate evils generally make men safe.—Seneca.

No evil is great if it is the last.—Nepos.

Evil is in antagonism with the entire creation.—Zschokke.

Evil comes not amiss if it comes alone.—Cervantes.

Evil is fittest to consort with evil.—Livy.

By the very constitution of our nature moral evil is its own curse.—Chalmers.

There is some soul of goodness in things evil, would men observingly distil it out.—Shakespeare.

We cannot do evil to others without doing it to ourselves.—Desmahis.

Evil, be thou my good.—Milton.

The evil that men do lives after them; the good is oft interred with their bones.—Shakespeare.

Be deaf to the quarrelsome, blind to the scorner and dumb to the inquisitive.—Aughey.

Still we love
The evil we do, until we suffer it.
    —Johnson.

An evil at its birth is easily crushed, but it grows and strengthens by endurance.—Cicero.

Inasmuch as ill deeds spring up as a spontaneous crop, they are easy to learn.—Cervantes.

Nought is so vile that on the earth doth live,
But to the earth some special good doth give. —Shakespeare.

The doing an evil to avoid an evil cannot be good.—Coleridge.

This is the curse of every evil deed, that, propagating still, it brings forth evil.—Coleridge.

Evils, like poisons, have their uses, and there are diseases which no other remedy can reach.—Thomas Paine.

Three sparks—pride, envy, and avarice—have been kindled in all hearts.—Dante.

Evil is limited. One cannot form
A scheme for universal evil.
    —Bailey.

The fear of one evil often leads us into a worse.—Boileau.

The first lesson of history is the good of evil.—Emerson.

Only evil grows of itself, while for goodness we want effort and courage.—Amiel.

Evil report, like the Italian stiletto, is an assassin's weapon, worthy only of the bravo.—Madame de Maintenon.

Evil and good are everywhere, like shadow and substance; inseparable (for men) yet not hostile, only opposed.—Carlyle.

It is too late to be on our guard when we are in the midst of evils.—Seneca.

As sure as God is good, so surely there is no such thing as necessary evil.—Southey.

There is no evil in human affairs that has not some good mingled with it.—Guicciardini.

Evil is merely privative, not absolute: it is like cold, which is the privation of heat.—Emerson.

The way to wickedness is always through wickedness.—Seneca.

Evil is wrought by want of thought
As well as want of heart.
—Thos. Hood.

There is no evil in the world without a remedy.—Sannazaro.

He who does evil that good may come, pays a toll to the devil to let him into heaven.—J. C. and A. W. Hare.

Physical evils destroy themselves, or they destroy us.—Rousseau.

There is nothing evil but what is within us; the rest is either natural or accidental.—Sir P. Sidney.

Every evil in the bud is easily crushed: as it grows older it becomes stronger.—Cicero.

If there be no enemy, no fight; if no fight, no victory; if no victory, no crown.—Savonarola.

Not one false man but doth uncountable evil.—Carlyle.

Wherever the speech is corrupted the mind is also.—Seneca.

Of the origin of evil no universal solution has been discovered.—Paley.

An evil intention perverts the best actions, and makes them sins.—Addison.

Bad conduct soils the finest ornament more than filth.—Plautus.

Life is not the supreme good, but the supreme evil is to realize one's guilt.—Schiller.

An evil-speaker differs from an evil-doer only in the want of opportunity.—Quintilian.

What has this unfeeling age of ours left untried, what wickedness has it shunned?—Horace.

There are thousands hacking at the branches of evil to one who is striking at the root.—Thoreau.

It is some compensation for great evils that they enforce great lessons.—Bovee.

He who is in evil is also in the punishment of evil.—Swedenborg.

So far as any one shuns evil, so far he does good.—Swedenborg.

The very curse of an evil deed is that it must always continue to engender evil.—Schiller.

Never throw mud. You may miss your mark; but you must have dirty hands.—Joseph Parker.

Slander is a poison which extinguishes charity, both in the slanderer and in the persons who listen to it.—St. Bernard.

If there is any person to whom you feel a dislike, that is the person of whom you ought never to speak.—Richard Cecil.

Nothing is to be esteemed evil which God and nature have fixed with eternal sanction.—Jeremy Taylor.

He who will fight the devil at his own weapon, must not wonder if he finds him an overmatch.—South.

To overcome evil with good is good, to resist evil with evil is evil.—Mohammed.

There are only two bad things in this world, sin and bile.—Hannah More.

The cardinal method with faults is to overgrow them and choke them out with virtues.—John Bascom.

If you do what you should not, you must bear what you would not.—Franklin.

In the history of man it has been very generally the case that when evils have grown insufferable they have touched the point of cure.—Chapin.

Multitudes think they like to do evil; yet no man ever really enjoyed doing evil since God made the world.—Ruskin.

If thou wishest to get rid of thy evil propensities, thou must keep far from evil companions.—Seneca.

To escape from evil we must be made as far as possible like God; and the resemblance consists in becoming just and holy and wise.—Plato.

After some account of good, evil will be known by consequence, as being only a privation, or absence of good.—South.

Evil into the mind of god or man may come and go, so unapproved, and leave no spot or blame behind.—Milton.

There is evil in every human heart, which may remain latent, perhaps, through the whole of life; but circumstances may rouse it to activity.—Hawthorne.

The sins we do, people behold with optics,
Which shew them ten times more than common vices,
And often multiply them. —Fletcher.

If we will rightly estimate what we call good and evil, we shall find it lies much in comparison.—Locke.

A man has no more right to say an uncivil thing than to act one; no more right to say a rude thing to another than to knock him down.—Johnson.

A good word is an easy obligation; but not to speak ill requires only our silence, which costs us nothing.—Tillotson.

Evil springs up, and flowers, and bears no seed,
And feeds the green earth with its swift decay,
Leaving it richer for the growth of truth.
—James Russell Lowell.

Many have puzzled themselves about the origin of evil; I observe that there is evil, and that there is a way to escape it, and with this I begin and end.—John Newton.

There are times when it would seem as if God fished with a line, and the devil with a net.—Madame Swetchine.

Nothing can work me damage except myself. The harm that I sustain I carry about with me, and never am a real sufferer but by my own fault.—St. Bernard.

Philosophy triumphs easily over past and future evils, but present evils triumph over philosophy.—Rochefoucauld.

Where evil may be done, it is right to ponder; where only suffered, know the shortest pause is much too long.—Hannah More.

The dread of evil is a much more forcible principle of human actions than the prospect of good.—Locke.

No propagation or multiplication is more rapid that that of evil, unless it be checked; no growth more certain.—Colton.

Nor all that heralds rake from coffin'd clay,
Nor florid prose, nor honied lies of rhyme,
Can blazon evil deeds, or consecrate a crime.
—Byron.

Is the scrupulous attention I am paying to the government of my tongue at all proportioned to that tremendous truth revealed through St. James, that if I do not bridle my tongue, all my religion is vain?—F. W. Faber.

There is this of good in real evils, they deliver us while they last from the petty despotism of all that were imaginary.—Colton.

As there is much beast and some devil in man, so is there some angel and some God in him. The beast and the devil may be conquered, but in this life never destroyed.—Coleridge.

Evil, once manfully fronted, ceases to be evil; there is generous battle-hope in place of dead, passive misery; the evil itself has become a kind of good.—Carlyle.

It is a proof of our natural bias to evil, that gain is slower and harder than loss in all things good; but in all things bad getting is quicker and easier than getting rid of.—Hare.

If evil is inevitable, how are the wicked accountable? Nay, why do we call men wicked at all? Evil is inevitable, but it is also remediable.—Horace Mann.

Never let man imagine that he can pursue a good end by evil means, without sinning against his own soul! Any other issue is doubtful; the evil effect on himself is certain.—Southey.

With every exertion, the best of men can do but a moderate amount of good; but it seems in the power of the most contemptible individual to do incalculable mischief.—Washington Irving.

Evil is a far more cunning and persevering propagandist than good, for it has no inward strength, and is driven to seek countenance and sympathy.—Lowell.

We sometimes learn more from the sight of evil than from an example of good; and it is well to accustom ourselves to profit by the evil which is so common, while that which is good is so rare.—Pascal.

The aphorism "Whatever is, is right," would be as final as it is lazy, did it not include the troublesome consequence that nothing that ever was, was wrong.—Charles Dickens.

To great evils we submit; we resent little provocations. I have before now been disappointed of a hundred-pound job and lost half a crown at rackets on the same day, and been more mortified at the latter than the former.—Hazlitt.

Evils in the journey of life are like the hills which alarm travelers upon their road; they both appear great at a distance, but when we approach them we find that they are far less insurmountable than we had conceived.—Colton.

Every evil to which we do not succumb is a benefactor. As the Sandwich islander believes that the strength and valor of the enemy he kills passes into himself, so we gain the strength of the temptations we resist.—Emerson.

The truly virtuous do not easily credit evil that is told them of their neighbors; for if others may do amiss then may these also speak amiss. Man is frail, and prone to evil, and therefore may soon fail in words.—Jeremy Taylor.

Even in evil, that dark cloud which hangs over the creation, we discern rays of light and hope, and gradually come to see in suffering and temptation proofs and instruments of the sublimest purposes of wisdom and love.—Channing.

No man, perhaps, is so wicked as to commit evil for its own sake. Evil is generally committed under the hope of some advantage the pursuit of virtue seldom obtains. Yet the most successful result of the most virtuous heroism is never without its alloy.—B. R. Haydon.

Imaginary evils soon become real ones by indulging our reflections on them; as he who in a melancholy fancy sees something like a face on the wall or the wainscot can, by two or three touches with a lead pencil, make it look visible, and agreeing with what he fancied.—Swift.

Evil is easily discovered; there is an infinite variety; good is almost unique. But some kinds of evil are almost as difficult to discover as that which we call good; and often particular evil of this class passes for good. It needs even a certain greatness of soul to attain to this, as to that which is good. —Pascal.

All evil, in fact the very existence of evil, is inexplicable until we refer to the paternity of God. It hangs a huge blot in the universe until the orb of divine love rises behind it. In that apposition we detect its meaning. It appears to us but a finite shadow as it passes across the disk of infinite light.—Chapin.

All animals are more happy than man. Look, for instance, on yonder ass; all allow him to be miserable; his evils, however, are not brought on by himself and his own fault; he feels only those which nature has inflicted. We, on the contrary, besides our necessary ills, draw upon ourselves a multitude of others.—Menander.

When will talkers refrain from evil speaking? When listeners refrain from evil hearing. At present there are many so credulous of evil, they will receive suspicions and impressions against persons whom they don't know, from a person whom they do know— an authority good for nothing.—Hare.

The best antidote against evils of all kinds, against the evil thoughts that haunt the soul, against the needless perplexities which distract the conscience, is to keep hold of the good we have. Impure thoughts will not stand against pure words and prayers and deeds. Little doubts will not avail against great certainties. Fix your affections on things above, and then you will less and less be troubled by the cares, the temptations, the troubles of things on earth.—Dean Stanley.

That which the French proverb hath of sickness is true of all evils, that they come on horseback, and go away on foot; we have often seen a sudden fall or one meal's surfeit hath stuck by many to their graves; whereas pleasures come like oxen, slow and heavily, and go away like post-horses, upon the spur.—Bishop Hall.

Evils * * * can never pass away; for there must always remain something which is antagonistic to good. Having no place among the Gods in heaven, of necessity they hover around the earthly nature and this mortal sphere. Wherefore we ought to fly away from earth to heaven as quickly as we can; and to fly away is to become like God, as far as this is possible; and to become like Him is to become holy and just and wise.— Plato.

The truest definition of evil is that which represents it as something contrary to nature; evil is evil because it is unnatural; a vine which should bear olive-berries, an eye to which blue seems yellow, would be diseased; an unnatural mother, an unnatural son, an unnatural act, are the strongest terms of condemnation.—F. W. Robertson.

It is not good to speak evil of all whom we know bad; it is worse to judge evil of any who may prove good. To speak ill upon knowledge shows a want of charity; to speak ill upon suspicion shows a want of honesty. I will not speak so bad as I know of many; I will not speak worse than I know of any. To know evil of others and not speak it, is sometimes discretion; to speak evil of others and not know it, is always dishonesty. He may be evil himself who speaks good of others upon knowledge, but he can never be good himself who speaks evil of others upon suspicion.—Arthur Warwick.

We are neither obstinately nor wilfully to oppose evils, nor truckle under them for want of courage, but that we are naturally to give way to them, according to their condition and our own, we ought to grant free passage to diseases; and I find they stay less with me who let them alone. And I have lost those which are reputed the most tenacious and obstinate of their own defervescence, without any help or art, and contrary to their rules. Let us a little permit nature to take her own way; she better understands her own affairs than we.—Montaigne.

Keep clear of personalities in conversation. Talk of things, objects, thoughts. The smallest minds occupy themselves with persons. Do not needlessly report ill of others. As far as possible, dwell on the good side of human beings. There are family boards where a constant process of depreciating, assigning motives, and cutting up character goes forward. They are not pleasant places. One who is healthy does not wish to dine at a dissecting table. There is evil enough in man, God knows. But it is not the mission of every young man and woman to detail and report it all. Keep the atmosphere as pure as possible, and fragrant with gentleness and charity.—John Hall.

Evolution

Let the great world spin forever down the ringing grooves of change.—Tennyson.

Evolution ever climbing after some ideal
good
And Reversion ever dragging Evolution in
the mud.   —Tennyson.

The expression often used by Mr. Herbert Spencer of the Survival of the Fittest is more accurate, and is sometimes equally convenient.—Charles Darwin.

Is there evil but on earth? Or pain in
every peopled sphere?
Well, be grateful for the sounding watchword "Evolution" here. —Tennyson.

The tree of human history, as it has grown from age to age, has been but

the unfolding of a single germ—but the development of Christ and Him crucified.—J. McC. Holmes.

Observe constantly that all things take place by change, and accustom thyself to consider that the nature of the universe loves nothing so much as to change the things which are, and to make new things like them.—Marcus Aurelius.

Till o'er the wreck, emerging from the
storm,
Immortal Nature lifts her changeful form:
Mounts from her funeral pyre on wings of
flame,
And soars and shines, another and the same.
—Erasmus Darwin.

This survival of the fittest, which I have here sought to express in mechanical terms, is that which Mr. Darwin has called "natural selection, or the preservation of favored races in the struggle for life."—Herbert Spencer.

The Lord let the house of a brute to the
soul of a man,
And the man said, "Am I your debtor"?
And the Lord—"Not yet: but make it as
clean as you can,
And then I will let you a better."
—Tennyson.

As ages roll on there is doubtless a progression in human nature. The intellectual comes to rule the physical, and the moral claims to subordinate both. It is no longer strength of body that prevails, but strength of mind; while the law of God proclaims itself superior to both.—James McCosh.

All true development tends ever to God. Its objective aim is the restoration by the second Adam of the Divine image forfeited by the first; and, incidentally, it transmutes grief into gladness and sighs into songs. But it is always a development in Christ, since it is only "in the unity of the faith and the knowledge of the Son of God" that any of our race can come "unto a perfect man."—J. McC. Holmes.

God has been always working, evolving, in His quiet power, from the seeming, the real, from the false, the true

Not for nothing blazed the martyr's fires—not for nothing toiled brave sufferers up successive hills of shame. God's purpose doth not languish. The torture and the trial of the past have been the stern ploughers in His service who never suspended their husbandry, and who have made long their furrows. Into those furrows the imperishable seed hath fallen. The heedless world hath trodden it in; tears and blood have watered it; the patient sun hath warmed and cheered it to its ripening; and it shall be ready soon.—Wm. M. Punshon.

Exaggeration

We weaken what we exaggerate.—La Harpe.

There is no greater sin than to be *trop prononcé.*—Beaconsfield.

Exaggeration is a blood relation to falsehood and nearly as blamable.—Hosea Ballou.

Exaggeration misleads the credulous and offends the perceptive.—Eliza Cook.

There would be few enterprises of great labor or hazard undertaken if we had not the power of magnifying the advantages which we persuade ourselves to expect from them.—Dr. Johnson.

Never believe extraordinary characters which you hear of people. Depend upon it, they are exaggerated. You do not see one man shoot a great deal higher than another.—Dr. Johnson.

Examination

Examinations are formidable even to the best prepared, for the greatest fool may ask more than the wisest man can answer.

Example

Example is more forcible than precept. People look at my six days in the week to see what I mean on the seventh.—Rev. R. Cecil.

Examples hasten deeds to good effects.—Mirror for Magistrates.

Much more profitable and gracious is doctrine by example than by rule.—Spenser.

A true life is at once interpreter and proof of the gospel.—Whittier.

The best teachers of humanity are the lives of great men.—C. H. Fowler.

Example is more efficacious than precept.—Johnson.

We can do, more good by being good than in any other way.—Rowland Hill.

Children have more need of models than of critics.—Joubert.

Allured to brighter worlds, and led the way.—Goldsmith.

Content to follow when we lead the way.—Homer.

Advice may be wrong, but examples prove themselves.—H. W. Shaw.

Ill patterns are sure to be followed more than good rules.—Locke.

People seldom improve when they have no other model but themselves to copy after.—Goldsmith.

No reproof or denunciation is so potent as the silent influence of a good example.—Hosea Ballou.

Man is an imitative creature, and whoever is foremost leads the herd.—Schiller.

I am satisfied that we are less convinced by what we hear than by what we see.—Herodotus.

No man is so insignificant as to be sure his example can do no hurt.—Lord Clarendon.

How far that little candle throws his beams! So shines a good deed in a naughty world.
—Shakespeare.

None preaches better than the ant, and she says nothing.—Franklin.

Example 646 **Example**

Example is contagious behavior.—Charles Reade.

By his life alone,
Gracious and sweet, the better way was shown. —Whittier.

Thieves for their robbery have authority, when judges steal themselves.—Shakespeare.

The road by precepts is tedious, by example, short and efficacious.—Seneca.

Children will imitate their fathers in their vices, seldom in their repentance.—Spurgeon.

We live in an age that hath more need of good example than precepts.—George Herbert.

Example is a dangerous lure; where the wasp got through the gnat sticks fast.—La Fontaine.

There are follies which are caught like contagious diseases.—Rochefoucauld.

Other men are lenses through which we read our own minds.—Emerson.

Example acquires tenfold authority when it speaks from the grave.—Wendell Phillips.

Example is the school of mankind, and they will learn at no other.—Burke.

Every man is bound to tolerate the act of which he himself has set the example.—Phædrus.

He who should teach men to die, would at the same time teach them to live.—Montaigne.

I do not give you to posterity as a pattern to imitate, but as an example to deter.—Junius.

Why doth one man's yawning make another yawn?—Burton.

It is a world of mischief that may be done by a single example of avarice

or luxury. One voluptuous palate makes many more.—Seneca.

First find the man in yourself if you will inspire manliness in others.—A. Bronson Alcott.

Example is a motive of very prevailing force on the actions of men.—Rogers.

They asked Lucman the fabulist, From whom did you learn manners? He answered, From the unmannerly.—Saadi.

"Not the cry, but the flight of a wild duck," says a Chinese author, "leads the flock to fly and follow."—Richter.

Examples would indeed be excellent things were not people so modest that none will set, and so vain that none will follow them.—Hare.

My advice is to consult the lives of other men, as we would a looking-glass, and from thence fetch examples for our own imitation.—Terence.

Alexander received more bravery of mind by the pattern of Achilles than by hearing the definition of fortitude.—Sir P. Sidney.

He was indeed the glass
Wherein the noble youth did dress themselves. —Shakespeare.

This noble ensample to his sheepe he gaf,—
That firste he wroughte and afterwarde he taughte. —Chaucer.

Happy thou that learnest from another's griefs, not to subject thyself to the same.—Tibullus.

I shall tread in the footsteps of my illustrious predecessor.—Martin Van Buren, Complimenting Gen. Jackson.

It is well to learn from the misfortunes of others what should be avoided.—Syrus.

Preaching is of much avail, but practice is far more effective. A godly life is the strongest argument that you can offer to the skeptic.—Hosea Ballou.

Example 647 **Example**

Whence do you derive the power and privilege of a parent, when you, though an old man, do worse things (than your child) ?—Juvenal.

The people are fashioned according to the example of their kings; and edicts are of less power than the life of the ruler.—Claudianus.

A man improves more by reading the story of a person eminent for prudence and virtue, than by the finest rules and precepts of morality.—Addison.

There is a transcendent power in example. We reform others unconsciously when we walk uprightly.—Madame Swetchine.

So work the honey-bees—creatures that, by a rule in nature, teach the art of order to a peopled kingdom.—Shakespeare.

What you learn from bad habits and in bad society you will never forget, and it will be a lasting pang to you.—John B. Gough.

The corruption of the positively wicked is often less sad and fatal to society than the irregularities of a virtuous man who yields and falls.—Desmahis.

Be a pattern to others, and then all will go well; for as a whole city is infected by the licentious passions and vices of great men, so it is likewise reformed by their moderation.—Cicero.

Examples of vicious courses practiced in a domestic circle corrupt more readily and more deeply when we behold them in persons in authority.—Juvenal.

It is certain that either wise bearing or ignorant carriage is caught, as men take disease, one of another; therefore let men take heed of their company.—Shakespeare.

No man or woman of the humblest sort can really be strong, gentle, pure, and good, without the world being the better for it, without somebody being

helped and comforted by the very existence of that goodness.—Phillips Brooks.

There are bad examples which are worse than crimes; and more states have perished from the violation of morality than from the violation of law.—Montesquieu.

Men trust rather to their eyes than to their ears; the effect of precepts is therefore slow and tedious, whilst that of examples is summary and effectual.—Seneca.

Men judge things more fully by the eye than by the ear; consequently a minister's practice is as much regarded, if not more, than his sermons.—Bridges.

Precept is instruction written in the sand, the tide flows over it and the record is gone. Example is graven on the rock, and the lesson is not soon lost.—Channing.

Lives of great men all remind us
We can make our lives sublime,
And, departing, leave behind us
Footprints on the sands of time.
—Longfellow.

These taught us how to live; and (oh, too high
The price for knowledge!) taught us how to die. —Thomas Tickell.

We are more speedily and fatally corrupted by domestic examples of vice, and particularly when they are impressed on our minds as from authority.—Horace.

Nothing enlarges the gulf of atheism more than the wide passage which lies between the faith and lives of men pretending to teach Christianity.—Stillingfleet.

A wise and good man will turn examples of all sorts to his own advantage. The good he will make his patterns, and strive to equal or excel them. The bad he will by all means avoid.—Thomas à Kempis.

When we see men of worth, we should think of becoming like them;

Example   648   **Example**

when we see men of a contrary character, we should turn inward and examine ourselves.—Confucius.

The common people do not judge of vice or virtue by morality or immorality, so much as by the stamp that is set upon it by men of figure.—L'Estrange.

It is a well-known psychological fact that the conscience of children is formed by the influences that surround them; and that their notions of good and evil are the result of the moral atmosphere they breathe.—Richter.

The pulpit only "teaches" to be honest; the market-place "trains" to overreaching and fraud; and teaching has not a tithe of the efficiency of training. Christ never wrote a tract, but He went about doing good.—Horace Mann.

Whatever parent gives his children good instruction, and sets them at the same time a bad example, may be considered as bringing them food in one hand and poison in the other.—Balguy.

Tarquin and Cæsar had each his Brutus—Charles the First his Cromwell—and George the Third—("Treason!" shouted the speaker)—may profit by their example. If this be treason, make the most of it.—Patrick Henry.

As a neighboring funeral terrifies sick misers, and fear obliges them to have some regard for themselves; so, the disgrace of others will often deter tender minds from vice.—Horace.

Think not, Sultan, that in the sequestered vale alone dwells virtue, and her sweet companion, with attentive eye, mild, affable benevolence! No, the first great gift we can bestow on others is a good example.—Sir Charles Morell.

Be more prudent for your children than perhaps you have been for yourself. When they, too, are parents they will imitate you, and each of you will have prepared happy generations, who will transmit, together with your memory, the worship of your wisdom.—La Beaume.

Nothing is so contagious as example; never was there any considerable good or ill done that does not produce its like. We imitate good actions through emulation, and bad ones through a malignity in our nature, which shame conceals, and example sets at liberty.—Rochefoucauld.

For as the light
Not only serves to show, but render us
Mutually profitable; so our lives,
In acts exemplary, not only win
Ourselves good names, but do to others give
Matter for virtuous deeds, by which we live
—Chapman.

Example has more followers than reason. We unconsciously imitate what pleases us, and insensibly approximate to the characters we most admire. In this way, a generous habit of thought and of action carries with it an incalculable influence.—Bovee.

Example comes in by the eyes and ears, and slips insensibly into the heart, and so into the outward practice, by a kind of secret charm, transforming men's minds and manners into his own likeness.—Waterland.

I question if Epicurus and Hume have done mankind a greater service by the looseness of their doctrines than by the purity of their lives. Of such men we may more justly exlaim, than of Cæsar, "Confound their virtues, they've undone the world!"—Colton.

The efficacy of good examples in the formation of public opinion is incalculable. Though men justify their conduct by reasons, and sometimes bring the very rules of virtue to the touchstone of abstraction, yet they principally act from example.—Robert Hall.

So admirably hath God disposed of the ways of men, that even the sight of vice in others is like a warning arrow shot for us to take heed. We should correct our own faults by seeing how uncomely they appear in others; who will not abhor a choleric passion, and a saucy pride in himself, that sees how ridiculous and contemptible they render those who are infested with them?—J. Beaumont.

The character, the counsels and example of our Washington * * * they will guide us through the doubts and difficulties that beset us; they will guide our children and our children's children in the paths of prosperity and peace, while America shall hold her place in the family of nations.—Edward Everett.

If thou desire to see thy child virtuous, let him not see his father's vices; thou canst not rebuke that in children that they behold practiced in thee; till reason be ripe, examples direct more than precepts; such as thy behavior is before they children's faces, such commonly is theirs behind their parents' backs.—Quarles.

Though "the words of the wise be as nails fastened by the masters of the assemblies," yet sure their examples are the hammer to drive them in to take the deeper hold. A father that whipped his son for swearing, and swore himself whilst he whipped him, did more harm by his example than good by his correction.—Fuller.

Excellence

To excel is to live.—Beranger.

.There is no excellence uncoupled with difficulties.—Ovid.

The variation of excellence among men is rather in degree than in kind. —Bancroft.

It is the witness still of excellency to put a strange face on his own perfection.—Shakespeare.

If you want enemies, excel others; if you want friends, let others excel you.—Colton.

When a man appreciates only eating and sleeping, what excellence has he over the reptiles?—Saadi.

The more we sympathize with excellence, the more we go out of self,

the more we love, the broader and deeper is our personality.—Chapin.

A man that is desirous to excel should endeavor it in those things that are in themselves most excellent.— Epictetus.

Those who attain any excellence commonly spend life in one common pursuit; for excellence is not often gained upon easier terms.—Johnson.

He who excels in his art so as to carry it to the utmost height of perfection of which it is capable may be said in some measure to go beyond it: his transcendent productions admit of no appellations.—La Bruyère.

Born to excel, and to command!
As by transcendent beauty to attract
All eyes, so by pre-eminence of soul
To rule all hearts.   —Congreve.

What is excellent,
As God lives, is permanent;
Hearts are dust, hearts' loves remain,
Heart's love will meet thee again.
—Emerson.

There is a moral excellence attainable by all who have the will to strive after it; but there is an intellectual and physical superiority which is above the reach of our wishes, and is granted to a few only.—Crabb.

Human excellence, parted from God, is like a fable flower, which, according to Rabbis, Eve plucked when passing out of paradise—severed from its native root, it is only the touching memorial of a lost Eden; sad, while charming — beautiful, but dead.—C. Stanford.

Excellence is never granted to man, but as the reward of labor. It argues, indeed, no small strength of mind to persevere in the habits of industry, without the pleasure of perceiving those advantages which, like the hands of a clock, whilst they make hourly approaches to their point, yet proceed so slowly as to escape observation.—Sir Joshua Reynolds.

The desire of excellence is the necessary attribute of those who excel. We work little for a thing unless we

Wish for it. But we cannot of ourselves estimate the degree of our success in what we strive for; that task is left to others. With the desire for excellence comes, therefore, the desire for approbation. And this distinguishes intellectual excellence from moral excellence; for the latter has no necessity of human tribunal; it is more inclined to shrink from the public than to invite the public to be its judge.—Bulwer-Lytton.

Excelsior

By steps we may ascend to God.—Milton.

———

Fearless minds climb soonest unto crowns.—Shakespeare.

———

O sacred hunger of ambitious minds! Spenser.

———

Too low they build who build beneath the stars.—Young.

———

The movement of the species is upward, irresistibly upward.—Bancroft.

———

Man can only learn to rise from the consideration of that which he cannot surmount.—Richter.

———

The little done vanishes from the sight of man, who looks forward to what is still to do.—Goethe.

———

Whilst we converse with what is above us, we do not grow old, but grow young.—Emerson.

———

Lifted up so high I disdained subjection, and thought one step higher would set me highest.—Milton.

———

It is but a base, ignoble mind that mounts no higher than a bird can soar.—Shakespeare.

———

Lift thyself up, look around, and see something higher and brighter than earth, earthworms, and earthly darkness.—Richter.

———

Our natures are like oil; compound us with anything, yet still we strive to swim upon the top.—Beaumont and Fletcher.

What we truly and earnestly aspire to be, that in some sense we are. The mere aspiration, by changing the frame of the mind, for the moment realizes itself.—Mrs. Jameson.

———

Who shoots at the midday sun, though he be sure he shall never hit the mark, yet as sure he is that he shall shoot higher than he who aims but at a bush.—Sir P. Sidney.

———

Besides the pleasure derived from acquired knowledge, there lurks in the mind of man, and tinged with a shade of sadness, an unsatisfactory longing for something beyond the present, a striving towards regions yet unknown and unopened.—Wilhelm von Humboldt.

———

Darwin remarks that we are less dazzled by the light at waking, if we have been dreaming of visible objects. Happy are those who have here dreamt of a higher vision! They will the sooner be able to endure the glories of the world to come.—Novalis.

———

Bright and illustrious illusions! Who can blame, who laugh at the boy, who not admire and commend him, for that desire of a fame outlasting the Pyramids by which he insensibly learns to live in a life beyond the present, and nourish dreams of a good unattainable by the senses?—Bulwer-Lytton.

———

It is not to taste sweet things, but to do noble and true things, and vindicate himself under God's heaven as a God-made man, that the poorest son of Adam dimly longs. Show him the way of doing that, the dullest day-drudge kindles into a hero. They wrong man greatly who say he is to be seduced by ease. Difficulty, abnegation, martyrdom, death, are the allurements that act on the heart of man. Kindle the inner genial life of him, you have a flame that burns up all lower considerations.—Carlyle.

Exceptions

The exceptions of the scrupulous put one in mind of some general pardons where everything is forgiven except crimes.—Fielding.

Excess

Excess always carries its own retribution.—Ouida.

Allow not nature more than nature needs.—Shakespeare.

Excess weakens the spirits.—Confucius.

Excess of power intoxicates.—Mme. de Rémusat.

All is wholesome in the absence of excess.—Molière.

The ass bears the load, but not the overload.—Cervantes.

A surfeit or the sweetest things
The deepest loathing to the stomach brings.
—Shakespeare.

Let pleasure be ever so innocent, the excess is always criminal.—St. Evremond.

Every morsel to a satisfied hunger is only a new labor to a tired digestion.—South.

Of what delights are we deprived by our excesses!—Joubert.

Every inordinate cup is unblessed, and the ingredient is a devil.—Shakespeare.

To gild refined gold, to paint the lily, is wasteful and ridiculous excess.—Shakespeare.

They are sick that surfeit with too much, as they that starve with nothing.—Shakespeare.

He does nothing who endeavors to do more than is allowed to humanity.—Johnson.

The excesses of our youth are drafts upon our old age, payable with interest, about thirty years after date.—Colton.

As surfeit is the father of much fast, so every scope by the immoderate use turns to restraint.—Shakespeare.

Let us teach ourselves that honorable step, not to outdo discretion.—Shakespeare.

The body oppressed by excesses bears down the mind, and depresses to the earth any portion of the divine spirit we had been endowed with.—Horace.

There can be no excess to love, none to knowledge, none to beauty, when these attributes are considered in the purest sense.—Emerson.

Excessive liberty and excessive servitude are equally dangerous, and produce nearly the same effect.—Zoroaster.

The eye that gazes upon the sun sees not the orb it looks upon, confounded by the excess of its brightness.—Metastasio.

We cannot employ the mind to advantage when we are filled with excessive food and drink.—Cicero.

Most persons are disposed to expend more than they can afford, and to indulge more than they can endure.—Mme. de Puisieux.

The excess of the voluptuary, like the austerities of the recluse, triumphs in the suffrage of perverted reason.—Dr. Parr.

Violent delights have violent ends, and in their triumph die; like fire and powder, which as they kiss consume.—Shakespeare.

In the history of man it has been very generally the case that when evils have grown insufferable they have touched the point of cure.—Chapin.

To regard the excesses of the passions as maladies has so salutary an effect that this idea renders all moral sermons useless.—Boiste.

The misfortune is that when man has found honey, he enters upon the feast with an appetite so voracious that he usually destroys his own delight by excess and satiety.—Knox.

Too much of a good thing.—Shakespeare.

As frost, raised to its utmost intensity, produces the sensation of fire, so any good quality, overwrought and pushed to excess, turns into its own contrary.—William Matthews.

He who indulges his sense in any excesses renders himself obnoxious to his own reason; and, to gratify the brute in him, displeases the man, and sets his two natures at variance.—Walter Scott.

The desire of power in excess caused angels to fall; the desire of knowledge in excess caused man to fall; but in charity is no excess, neither can man nor angels come into danger by it.—Bacon.

If a man get a fever, or a pain in the head with overdrinking, we are subject to curse the wine, when we should rather impute it to ourselves for the excess.—Erasmus.

Pleasures bring effeminacy, and effeminacy foreruns ruin; such conquests, without blood or sweat, sufficiently do revenge themselves upon their intemperate conquerors.—Quarles.

The body, too, with yesterday's excess
Burden'd and tired shall the pure soul depress;
Weigh down this portion of celestial birth,
The breath of God, and fix it to the earth.
—Francis.

Even in evil, that dark cloud which hangs over the creation, we discern rays of light and hope, and gradually come to see in suffering and temptation proofs and instruments of the sublimest purposes of wisdom and love.—Channing.

In its primary signification, all vice, that is, all excess, brings on its own punishment, even here. By certain fixed, settled and established laws of Him who is the God of nature, excess of every kind destroys that constitution which temperance would preserve. The debauchee offers up his body a "living sacrifice to sin."—Colton.

The greatest miracle that the Almighty could perform would be to make a bad man happy, even in heaven; he must unparadise that blessed place to accomplish it. In its primary signification, all vice—that is, all excess—brings its own punishment even here.—Colton.

It is a common thing to screw up justice to the pitch of an injury. A man may be over-righteous, and why not over-grateful, too? There is a mischievous excess that borders so close upon ingratitude that it is no easy matter to distinguish the one from the other; but, in regard that there is good-will in the bottom of it, however distempered; for it is effectually but kindness out of the wits.—Seneca.

There is no unmixed good in human affairs; the best principles, if pushed to excess, degenerate into fatal vices. Generosity is nearly allied to extravagance; charity itself may lead to ruin; the sternness of justice is but one step removed from the severity of oppression. It is the same in the political world; the tranquillity of despotism resembles the stagnation of the Dead Sea; the fever of innovation the tempests of the ocean. It would seem as if, at particular periods, from causes inscrutable to human wisdom, a universal frenzy seizes mankind; reason experience, prudence, are alike blind ed; and the very classes who are to perish in the storm are the first to raise its fury.—Sir A. Alison.

Excitement

He used to raise a storm in a tea pot.—Cicero.

Women of the world crave excitement.—Chamfort.

Excitement is the drunkenness of the spirits. Only calm waters reflect heaven in their bosom.—Marguerite de Valois.

Excitement is not enjoyment; in calmness lies true pleasure. The most precious wines are sipped, not bolted at a swallow.—Victor Hugo.

Excuse

An excuse is worse and more terrible than a lie; for an excuse is a lie guarded.—Pope.

Men think they may justly do that for which they have a precedent.—Cicero.

Oftentimes, excusing of a fault
Doth make the fault the worse by the excuse;
As patches, set upon a little breach,
Discredit more in hiding of the fault,
Than did the fault before it was so patched.
—Shakespeare.

An excuse for sin is a statement of the circumstances under which a man did wrong. When we say, "I could not help it; circumstances were too much for me," do our hearts believe it to be true? We say, "My temperament, my inherited appetite, business exigencies, irresistible pressure," as though we were compelled to do wrong. The first man in the long line of apologetic succession said, "The woman tempted me, but did not say, "and made me eat." Whatever he might wish implied, he could only say, "And I did eat." No unconsenting soul can be made to sin, and so sin is inexcusable.

Execution

See they suffer death;
But in their deaths remember they are men;
Strain not the laws to make their tortures grievous. —Addison.

I have seen
When, after execution, judgment hath
Repented o'er his doom.
—Shakespeare.

Exercise

Let exercise alternate with rest.—Pythagoras.

It is exercise alone that supports the spirits, and keeps the mind in vigor.—Cicero.

A man must often exercise or fast or take physic, or be sick.—Sir W. Temple.

Exercise is the chief source of improvement in all our faculties.—Blair.

Vigorous exercise will often fortify a feeble constitution.—Mrs. Sigourney.

You will never live to my age without you keep yourself in breath with exercise.—Sir P. Sidney.

I take the true definition of exercise to be labor without weariness.—Johnson.

Such is the constitution of man that labor may be said to be its own reward.—Dr. Johnson.

The wise. for cure on exercise depend: God never made His work for man to mend.—Dryden.

Often try what weight you can support,
And what your shoulders are too weak to bear. —Roscommon.

Take a walk to refresh yourself with the open air, which inspired fresh doth exceedingly recreate the lungs, heart and vital spirits.—Harvey.

Weariness
Can snore upon the flint, when resty sloth
Finds the down pillow hard.
—Shakespeare.

There are many troubles which you cannot cure by the Bible and the hymn-book, but which you can cure by a good perspiration and a breath of fresh air.—Beecher.

By looking into physical causes our minds are opened and enlarged; and in this pursuit, whether we take or whether we lose the game, the chase is certainly of service.—Burke.

No body's healthful without exercise:
Just wars are exercises of a state;
Virtue 's in motion, and contends to rise,
With generous ascents above a mate.
—Aleyn.

In those vernal seasons of the year when the air is soft and pleasant, it were an injury and sullenness against nature not to go out and see her riches and partake of her rejoicings with heaven and earth.—Milton.

Labor or exercise ferments the humors, casts them into their proper channels, throws off redundances, and helps nature in those secret distributions without which the body cannot subsist in its vigor nor the soul act with cheerfulness.—Addison.

Exertion

With every exertion, the best of men can do but a moderate amount of good; but it seems in the power of the most contemptible individual to do incalculable mischief.—Washington Irving.

Exile

What exile from himself can flee.— Byron.

Beloved country! banish'd from thy shore,
A stranger in this prison-house of clay,
The exil'd spirit weeps and sighs for thee!
Heavenward the bright perfections I adore
direct.   —Longfellow.

An exile, ill in heart and frame,—
A wanderer, weary of the way;—
A stranger, without love's sweet claim
On any heart, go where I may!
                    —Mrs. Osgood.

"Farewell, my Spain! a long farewell!" he
cried.
"Perhaps I may revisit thee no more,
But die, as many an exiled heart hath died,
Of its own thirst to see again thy shore."
                    —Byron.

Even now, as, wandering upon Erie's shore,
I hear Niagara's distant cataract roar,
I sigh for England—oh! these weary feet
Have many a mile to journey, ere we meet.
                    —Moore.

There came to the beach a poor Exile of
Erin;
The dew on his thin robe was heavy and
chill!
For his country he sighed, when at twilight
repairing,
To wander alone by the wind-beaten hill.
                    —Campbell.

Home, kindred, friends, and country—these
Are ties with which we never part;
From clime to clime, o'er land and seas,
We bear them with us in our heart:
But, oh! 't is hard to feel resign'd,
When these must all be left behind!
                    —J. Montgomery.

Exile is terrible to those who have, as it were, a circumscribed habitation; but not to those who look upon the whole globe but as one city.—Cicero.

Oh! when shall I visit the land of my birth,
The loveliest land on the face of the earth?
When shall I those scenes of affection ex-
plore,
Our forests, our fountains,
Our hamlets, our mountains,
With the pride of our mountains, the maid
I adore?
Oh! when shall I dance on the daisy-white
mead,
In the shade of an elm, to the sound of the
reed?   —Montgomery.

But me, not destined such delights to share,
My prime of life in wandering spent and
care;
Impell'd, with steps unceasing, to pursue
Some fleeting good, that mocks me with the
view
That, like the circle bounding earth and
skies,
Allures from far, yet, as I follow, flies;
My fortune leads to traverse realms alone,
And find no spot of all the world my own.
                    —Goldsmith.

Expectation

Expectation ends only in heaven.— St. Kentijern.

'T is expectation makes a blessing dear.—Pope.

To-day for thee, and to-morrow for me.—Cervantes.

Everything comes if a man will only wait.—Benj. Disraeli.

With what a heavy and retarding weight Does expectation load the wing of time.
                    —Mason.

Every beginning is cheerful; the threshold is the place of expectation.— Goethe.

Those who live on expectation are sure to be disappointed.—Joachim Murat.

The gratitude of place expectants is a lively sense of future favors.—Sir Robert Walpole.

Great expectations are better than a poor possession.—Cervantes.

We anticipate our own happiness, and eat out the heart and sweetness of worldly pleasures by delightful forethought of them.—Tillotson.

They that marry ancient people merely in expectation to bury them, hang themselves in hope that one will come and cut the halter.—Fuller.

Oft Expectation fails, and most oft there Where most it promises.
—Shakespeare.

'Tis Expectation makes a blessing dear; Heaven were not heaven, if we knew what it were. —Sir J. Suckling.

He who will lose a present good for one in expectation hath some wit, but a small store of wisdom.—Bias.

Expectation whirls me round. The imaginary relish is so sweet That it enchants my sense.
—Shakespeare.

Oh! how impatience gains upon the soul When the long-promis'd hour of joy draws near!
How slow the tardy moments seem to roll! What spectres rise of inconsistent fear!
—Mrs. Tighe.

So tedious is this day, As is the night before some festival To an impatient child, that hath new robes, And may not wear them.
—Shakespeare.

How slow This old moon wanes! she lingers my desires,
Like to a stepdame, or a dowager, Long withering out a young man's revenue.
—Shakespeare.

How the time Loiters in expectation! Then the mind Drags ⸜he dead burden of a hundred years In one short moment's space. The nimble heart
Beats with impatient throbs,—sick of delay, And pants to be at ease. —Havard.

Although I enter not, Yet round about the spot Ofttimes I hover; And near the sacred gate, With longing eyes I wait, Expectant of her.
—Thackeray.

The great source of pleasure is variety. Uniformity must tire at last, though it be uniformity of excellence. We love to expect, and when expectation is disappointed or gratified, we want to be again expecting.—Johnson.

Uncertainty and expectation are joys of life. Security is an insipid thing; and the overtaking and possessing of a wish discovers the folly of the chase.—Congreve.

Expediency

Expediency is the science of exigencies.—Kossuth.

Expediency often silences justice.—Seneca.

Expediency is a law of nature. The camel is a wonderful animal, but the desert made the camel.—Beaconsfield.

It is not expedient or wise to examine our friends too closely; few persons are raised in our esteem by a close examination.—Rochefoucauld.

Nothing but the right can ever be expedient, since that can never be true expediency which would sacrifice a great good to a less.—Whately.

Experience

Experience is the extract of suffering.—Arthur Helps.

Experience is retrospect knowledge.—Hosea Ballou.

The bitter past, more welcome is the sweet.—Shakespeare.

Alas, could experience be bought for gold!—Mme. Deluzy.

Experience converts us to ourselves when books fail us.—A. Bronson Alcott.

Years teach us more than books.—Auerbach.

Believe one who has tried it.—Virgil.

The finest poetry was first experience.—Emerson.

Great men never require experience.—Beaconsfield.

God sends experience to paint men's portraits.—Henry Ward Beecher.

Experience makes us wise.—Hazlitt.

All is but lip wisdom which wants experience.—Sir P. Sidney.

Making all futures fruits of all the past.—Edwin Arnold.

Experience is our only teacher both in war and peace.—Landor.

Only so much do I know, as I have lived.—Emerson.

Long-travelled in the ways of men. —Young.

Who heeds not experience, trust him not.—John Boyle O'Reilly.

He jests at scars, that never felt a wound.—Shakespeare.

Experience is the teacher of fools.— Livy.

Experience wounded is the school where man learns piercing wisdom out of smart.—Lord Brooke.

Experience does take dreadfully high school-wages, but he teaches like no other.—Carlyle.

Men may rise on stepping-stones
Of their dead selves to higher things.
　　　　　—Tennyson.

Our ancestors have travelled the iron age; the golden is before us.— Bernardin de St. Pierre.

Experience is by industry achieved,
And perfected by the swift course of time.
　　　　　—Shakespeare.

Experience is always sowing the seed of one thing after another.— Manilius.

What we gain by experience is not worth that we lose in illusion.—J. Petit-Senn.

What is every year of a wise man's life but a censure or critic on the past? —Pope.

One thorn of experience is worth a whole wilderness of warning.—Lowell.

Theories are very thin and unsubstantial; experience only is tangible.— Hosea Ballou.

What! wouldst thou have a serpent sting thee twice?—Shakespeare.

It is the nature of experience to come to us only when too late for use. —Mme. de Rieux.

Experience teaches slowly, and at the cost of mistakes.—Froude.

Experience is the only prophecy of wise men.—Lamartine.

History should be to the political economist a wellspring of experience and wisdom.—Gibbon.

Is there any one so wise as to learn by the experience of others?—Voltaire.

We gain justice, judgment, with years, or else years are in vain.— Owen Meredith.

To Truth's house there is a single door, which is experience.—Bayard Taylor.

Experience is a jewel, and it had need be so, for it is often purchased at an infinite rate.—Shakespeare.

To some purpose is that man wise who gains his wisdom at another's expense.—Plautus.

Experience join'd with common sense,
To mortals is a providence.　—Green.

Oh, who can tell, save he whose heart hath tried?　　　—Byron.

A sadder and a wiser man,
He rose the morrow morn.
　　　　　—Coleridge.

　　　　　He teaches best,
Who feels the hearts of all men in his breast,
And knows their strength or weakness through his own.　—Bayard Taylor.

I have but one lamp by which my feet are guided, and that is the lamp of experience.—Patrick Henry.

Experience is no more transferable in morals than in art.—Froude.

In almost everything, experience is more valuable than precept.—Quintilian.

Nobody will use other people's experience, nor have any of his own till it is too late to use it.—Hawthorne.

Each succeeding day is the scholar of that which preceded.—Publius Syrus.

Experience is the name men give to their follies or their sorrows.—Alfred de Musset.

Experience, that chill touchstone whose sad proof reduces all things from their hue.—Byron.

The ever-burning lamp of accumulated wisdom.—G. W. Curtis.

That experience which does not make us better makes us worse.—J. Petit-Senn.

I had rather have a fool to make me merry than experience to make me sad.—Shakespeare.

We are often prophets to others only because we are our own historians.—Mme. Swetchine.

Experience is a keen knife that hurts while it extracts the cataract that blinds.—De Finod.

A man who does not learn to live while he is getting a living is a poorer man after his wealth is won than he was before.—J. G. Holland.

To most men, experience is like the stern lights of a ship, which illumine only the track it has passed.—Coleridge.

Everything is worth seeing once, and the more one sees the less one either wonders or admires.—Chesterfield.

To have a true idea of man or of life, one must have stood himself on the brink of suicide, or on the door-sill of insanity, at least once.—Taine.

Experience is a grindstone; and it is lucky for us if we can get brightened by it, and not ground.—H. W. Shaw.

I scarcely exceed the middle age of man; yet between infancy and maturity I have seen ten revolutions!—Lamartine.

Ah! the youngest heart has the same waves within it as the oldest, but without the plummet which can measure their depths.—Richter.

I think there are stores laid up in our human nature that our understandings can make no complete inventory of.—George Eliot.

Would they could sell us experience, though at diamond prices, but then no one would use the article second-hand!—Balzac.

Experience is the common schoolhouse of fools and ill men. Men of wit and honesty be otherwise instructed.—Erasmus.

The experience of others adds to our knowledge, but not to our wisdom; that is dearer-bought.—Hosea Ballou.

The only faith that wears well and holds its color in all weathers is that which is woven of conviction, and set with the sharp mordant of experience.—Lowell.

To wilful men,
The injuries that they themselves procure
Must be their school-masters.—Shakespeare.

Experience is a safe light to walk by, and he is not a rash man who expects to succeed in future from the same means which have secured it in times past.—Wendell Phillips.

Experience only can teach men not to prefer what strikes them for the present moment, to what will have much greater weight with them hereafter.—Lord Chesterfield.

The head learns new things, but the heart forevermore practices old experiences. Therefore our life is but a new form of the way men have lived from the beginning.—Henry Ward Beecher.

Too high an appreciation of our own talents is the chief cause why experience preaches to us all in vain.—Colton.

'Tis greatly wise to talk with our past hours,
And ask them what report they bore to heaven.   —Young.

Conflicts bring experience; and experience brings that growth in grace which is not to be attained by any other means.—Spurgeon.

Oft have I thought—jabber as he will, how learned soever, man knows nothing but what he has learned from experience!—Wieland.

This is one of the sad conditions of life, that experience is not transmissible. No man will learn from the suffering of another; he must suffer himself.—Aughey.

Taught by experience to know my own blindness, shall I speak as if I could not err, and as if others might not in some disputed points be more enlightened than myself?—Channing.

I learn several great truths; as that it is impossible to see into the ways of futurity, that punishment always attends the villain, that love is the fond soother of the human breast.—Goldsmith.

It may serve as a comfort to us in all our calamities and afflictions that he that loses anything and gets wisdom by it is a gainer by the loss.—L'Estrange.

Experience unveils too late the snares laid for youth; it is the white frost which discovers the spider's web when the flies are no longer there to be caught.—J. Petit-Senn.

The petty cares, the minute anxieties, the infinite littles which go to make up the sum of human experience, like the invisible granules of

powder, give the last and highest polish to a character.—William Matthews.

Every man's experience of to-day is that he was a fool yesterday and the day before yesterday. To-morrow he will most likely be of exactly the same opinion.—Charles Mackay.

In all instances where our experience of the past has been extensive and uniform, our judgment concerning the future amounts to moral certainty. —Beattie.

Experience, next, to thee I owe,
Best guide; not following thee, I had remain'd
In ignorance; thou open'st wisdom's way,
And giv'st access, though secret she retire.
                                    —Milton.

What matters it that a soldier has a sword of dazzling finish, of the keenest edge, and finest temper, if he has never learned the art of fence.—William Matthews.

All reasoning is retrospect; it consists in the application of facts and principles previously known. This will show the very great importance of knowledge, especially of that kind called experience.—J. Foster.

Thou shalt know by experience how salt the savor is of other's bread, and how sad a path it is to climb and descend another's stairs.—Dante.

Learn the lesson of your own pain—learn to seek God, not in any single event of past history, but in your own soul—in the constant verifications of experience, in the life of Christian love.—Mrs. Humphry Ward.

There are many arts among men, the knowledge of which is acquired bit by bit by experience. For it is experience that causeth our life to move forward by the skill we acquire, while want of experience subjects us to the effects of chance.—Plato.

He hazardeth much who depends for his learning on experience. An unhappy master, he that is only made wise by many shipwrecks; a miserable merchant, that is neither rich nor wise till he has been bankrupt. By experience we find out a short way by a long wandering.—Roger Ascham.

Experience keeps a dear school, but fools will learn in no other, and scarcely in that; for it is true, we may give advice, but we cannot give conduct. Remember this; they that will not be counseled cannot be helped. If you do not hear reason she will rap you over your knuckles.—Franklin.

What man would be wise, let him drink of the river
  That bears on his bosom the record of time;
A message to him every wave can deliver
  To teach him to creep till he knows how to climb.   —John Boyle O'Reilly.

Not only the individual experience slowly acquired, but the accumulated experience of the race, organized in language, condensed in instruments and axioms, and in what may be called the inherited intuitions—these form the multiple unity which is expressed in the abstract term "experience."—G. H. Lewes.

Experience: in that all our knowledge is founded; and from that it ultimately derives itself. Our observation employed either about external or sensible objects or about the internal operations of our minds, perceived and reflected on by ourselves, is that which supplies our understandings with all the materials of thinking.—John Locke.

Each successive generation plunges into the abyss of passion, without the slightest regard to the fatal effects which such conduct has produced upon their predecessors; and lament, when too late, the rashness with which they slighted the advice of experience, and stifled the voice of reason.—Steele.

Young men are as apt to think themselves wise enough, as drunken men are to think themselves sober enough. They look upon spirit to be a much better thing than experience; which

they call coldness. They are but half mistaken; for though spirit without experience is dangerous, experience without spirit is languid and ineffective.—Chesterfield.

Just as a tested and rugged virtue of the moral hero is worth more than the lovely, tender, untried innocence of the child, so is the massive strength of a soul that has conquered truth for itself worth more than the soft peach-bloom faith of a soul that takes truth on trust.—F. E. Abbot.

Behold, we live through all things,—famine, thirst,
Bereavement, pain; all grief and misery,
All woe and sorrow; life inflicts its worst
  On soul and body,—but we cannot die,
Though we be sick, and tired, and faint, and worn,—
Lo, all things can be borne!
    —Elizabeth Akers Allen.

If I might venture to appeal to what is so much out of fashion at Paris, I mean to experience, I should tell you that in my course I have known and, according to my measure, have co-operated with great men; and I have never yet seen any plan which has not been mended by the observations of those who were much inferior in understanding to the person who took the lead in the business.—Burke.

        I know
The past and thence I will essay to glean
A warning for the future, so that man
May profit by his errors, and derive
Experience from his folly;
For, when the power of imparting joy
Is equal to the will, the human soul
  Requires no other heaven.
       —Shelley.

Man little knows what calamities are beyond his patience to bear till he tries them; as in ascending the heights of ambition, which look bright from below, every step we rise shows us some new and gloomy prospect of hidden disappointment; so in our descent from the summits of pleasure, though the vale of misery below may appear, at first, dark and gloomy, yet the busy mind, still attentive to its own amusement, finds, as we descend, something to flatter and to please. Still as we approach, the darkest objects appear to brighten, and the mortal eye becomes adapted to its gloomy situation. —Goldsmith.

No man was ever endowed with a judgment so correct and judicious, in regulating his life, but that circumstances, time and experience would teach him something new, and apprize him that of those things with which he thought himself the best acquainted he knew nothing; and that those ideas which in theory appeared the most advantageous were found, when brought into practice, to be altogether inapplicable.—Terence.

Expression

There's a language in her eye, her cheek, her lip,
Nay, her foot speaks; her wanton spirits look out
At every joint and motive of her body.
—Shakespeare.

But true expression, like th' unchanging sun,
Clears and improves whate'er it shines upon;
It gilds all objects, but it alters none.
—Pope.

Extenuation

Oftentimes excusing of a fault doth make the fault the worse by the excuse; as patches, set upon a little breach, discredit more in hiding of the fault than did the fault before it was so patched.—Shakespeare.

Extravagance

Extravagance is its own destroyer. —Zeno.

Extravagance is the rich man's pitfall.—Tupper.

Wisdom seldom consorts with extravagance.—Mendemus.

Dreading that climax of all human ills,
The inflammation of his weekly bills.
—Byron.

The man who builds, and wants wherewith to pay,
Provides a home from which to run away.
—Young.

There is hope in extravagance, there is none in routine.—Emerson.

Expense of time is the most costly of all expenses.—Theophrastus.

If extravagance were a fault, it would not have a place in the festivals of the gods.—Aristippus.

A large retinue upon a small income, like a large cascade upon a small stream, tends to discover its tenuity.— Shenstone.

That is suitable to a man in point of ornamental expense, not which he can afford to have, but which he can afford to lose.—Whately.

He who is extravagant will quickly become poor; and poverty will enforce dependence, and invite corruption.— Dr. Johnson.

Prodigality is indeed the vice of a weak nature, as avarice is of a strong one; it comes of a weak craving for those blandishments of the world which are easily to be had for money—Henry Taylor.

Profuseness is a cruel and crafty demon, that gradually involves her followers in dependence and debt; that is, fetters them with irons that enter into their souls.—Dr. Johnson.

We sacrifice to dress, till household joys
And comforts cease. Dress drains our cellar dry,
And keeps our larder lean; puts out our fires,
And introduces hunger, frost and woe,
Where peace and hospitality might reign.
—Cowper.

Mansions once
Knew their own masters, and laborious hinds,
That had surviv'd the father, serv'd the son.
Now the legitimate and rightful lord
Is but a transient guest, newly arrived,
And soon to be supplanted. He that saw
His patrimonial timber cast its leaf,
Sells the last scantling, and transfers the price
To some shrewd sharper ere it buds again.
Estates are landscapes, gazed upon awhile,
Then advertised and auctioneer'd away.
—Cowper.

The passion of acquiring riches in order to support a vain expense corrupts the purest souls.—Fénelon.

When parents put gold into the hands of youth, when they should put a rod under their girdle—when instead of awe they make them past grace, and leave them rich executors of goods, and poor executors of godliness, then it is no marvel that the son being left rich by his father's will, becomes reckless by his own will.—John Lyly.

Extremes

Extremes meet.—Mercier.

Perfect reason avoids all extremes. —Molière.

No violent extreme endures.—Carlyle.

There is danger in all extremes.— James Ellis.

Extremity is the trier of spirits.— Shakespeare.

Women are ever in extremes; they are either better or worse than men.— Bruyère.

Extremes are vicious, and proceed from men; compensation is just, and proceeds from God.—Bruyère.

Men are as much blinded by the extremes of misery, as by the extremes of prosperity.—Burke.

Extremes are ever neighbors; 'tis a step from one to the other.—Sheridan Knowles.

Extremes in nature equal good produce,
Extremes in man concur to general use.
—Pope.

Thus each extreme to equal danger tends,
Plenty, as well as Want, can separate friends.
—Cowley.

Avoid Extremes; and shun the fault of such
Who still are pleas'd too little or too much.
—Pope.

Shun equally a sombre air and vivacious sallies.—Marcus Antoninus.

Mistrust the man who finds everything good, the man who finds everything evil, and still more, the man who is indifferent to everything.—Lavater.

In everything the middle course is best; all things in excess bring trouble.—Plautus.

Our age knows nothing but reactions, and leaps from one extreme to another.—Niebuhr.

Extreme views are never just; something always turns up which disturbs the calculations formed upon their data.—Beaconsfield.

Those edges soonest turn, that are most keen;
A sober moderation stands secure,
No violent extremes endure. —Aleyn.

All extremes are error. The reverse of error is not truth, but error still. Truth lies between these extremes.— Cecil.

That extremes beget extremes is an apothegm built on the most profound observation of the human mind.— Colton.

There is a mean in all things. Even virtue itself hath its stated limits; which not being strictly observed it ceases to be virtue.—Horace.

Extremes are for us as if they were not, and as if we were not in regard to them; they escape from us, or we from them.—Pascal.

We must remember how apt man is to extremes—rushing from credulity and weakness to suspicion and distrust.—Bulwer-Lytton.

Like to the time o' the year between the extremes
Of hot and cold, he was nor sad nor merry.
—Shakespeare.

Cruel men are the greatest lovers of mercy, avaricious men of generosity, and proud men of humility; that is to say, in others, not in themselves.— Colton.

Everything runs to excess; every good quality is noxious, if unmixed; and, to carry the danger to the edge of ruin, nature causes each man's peculiarity to superabound.—Emerson.

It is a hard but good law of fate, that as every evil, so every excessive power, wears itself out.—Herder.

Too austere a philosophy makes few wise men; too rigorous politics, few good subjects; too hard a religion, few religious persons whose devotion is of long continuance.—St. Evremond.

The greatest flood has the soonest ebb; the sorest tempest the most sudden calm; the hottest love the coldest end; and from the deepest desire oftentimes ensues the deadliest hate.—Socrates.

Extremes, though contrary, have the like effect; extreme heat mortifies, like extreme cold; extreme love breeds satiety, as well as extreme hatred.—Chapman.

Pleasure and pain, though directly opposite, are yet so contrived by nature as to be constant companions; and it is a fact that the same motions and muscles of the face are employed both in laughing and crying.—Charron.

As great enmities spring from great friendships, and mortal distempers from vigorous health, so do the most surprising and the wildest frenzies from the high and lively agitations of our souls.—Montaigne.

He that had never seen a river imagined the first he met with to be the sea; and the greatest things that have fallen within our knowledge we conclude the extremes that nature makes of the kind.—Montaigne.

Both in individuals and in masses violent excitement is always followed by remission, and often by reaction. We are all inclined to depreciate whatever we have overpraised, and, on the other hand, to show undue indulgence where we have shown undue rigor.—Macaulay.

Extremes are dangerous: a middle estate is safest; as a middle temper of the sea, between a still calm and a violent tempest, is most helpful to convey the mariner to his haven.—Swinnock,

We feel neither extreme heat nor extreme cold; qualities that are in excess are so much at variance with our feelings that they are impalpable: we do not feel them, though we suffer from their effects.—Pascal.

Extremes touch: he who wants no favors from Fortune may be said to have obtained the very greatest that she can bestow, in realizing an independence which no changes can diminish.—Chatfield.

Our senses will not admit anything extreme. Too much noise confuses us, too much light dazzles us, too great distance or nearness prevents vision, too great prolixity or brevity weakens an argument, too much pleasure gives pain, too much accordance annoys.—Pascal.

So near are the boundaries of panegyric and invective, that a worn-out sinner is sometimes found to make the best declaimer against sin. The same high-seasoned descriptions which in his unregenerate state served to inflame his appetites, in his new province of a moralist will serve him (a little turned) to expose the enormity of those appetites in other men.—Lamb.

'T is in worldly accidents,
As in the world itself, where things most
    distant
Meet one another: Thus the east and west,
Upon the globe a mathematical point
Only divides: Thus happiness and misery,
And all extremes, are still contiguous.
                                —Denham.

Let wealth come in by comely thrift,
And not by any sordid shift;
    'T is haste
    Makes waste;
Extremes have still their fault.
Who gripes too hard the dry and slipp'ry
    sand,
Holds none at all, or little, in his hand.
                                —Herrick.

Extreme old age is childhood; extreme wisdom is ignorance, for so it may be called, since the man whom the oracle pronounced the wisest of men professed that he knew nothing; yea, push a coward to the extreme and he will show courage; oppress a man to the last, and he will rise above oppression.—J. Beaumont.

Eyes

These lovely lamps, these windows of the soul.—Du Bartas.

The eyes are the amulets of the mind.—W. R. Alger.

Her eyes are homes of silent prayer.—Tennyson.

The eye sees what it brings the power to see.—Carlyle.

Glances are the first billets-doux of love.—Ninon de Lenclos.

Eyes that droop like summer flowers.—Miss L. E. Landon.

Soul-deep eyes of darkest night.—Joaquin Miller.

Women read each other at a single glance.—Rivarol.

In one soft look what language lies!—Dibdin.

She has an eye that could speak, though her tongue were silent.—Aaron Hill.

Hell trembles at a heaven-directed eye.—Bishop Ken.

In woman's eye the unanswerable tear.—Byron.

Disdain and scorn ride sparkling in her eyes.—Shakespeare.

A lover's eyes will gaze an eagle blind.—Shakespeare.

Sweet, silent rhetoric of persuading eyes.—Sir W. Davenant.

My eyes make pictures, when they are shut.—Coleridge.

The eyes are the pioneers that first announce the soft tale of love.—Propertius.

Like a star glancing out from the blue of the sky!—Whittier.

The eyes of women are Promethean fires.—Shakespeare.

An eye like Mars, to threaten or command.—Shakespeare.

Men of cold passions have quick eyes.—Hawthorne.

Those blue violets, her eyes.—Heine.

I prize the soul that slumbers in a quiet eye.—Eliza Cook.

Heart on her lip and soul within her eyes.—Byron.

Eyes bright, with many tears behind them.—Carlyle.

Flaw-seeing eyes, like needle points.—Lowell.

Stabbed with a white wench's black eye.—Shakespeare.

He travels with his eyes.—Dr. Walter Harte.

Large, musing eyes, neither joyous nor sorry.—Mrs. Browning.

Ah! the soft starlight of virgin eyes.—Balzac.

What a soul, twenty fathom deep, in her eyes!—Leigh Hunt.

Such eyes as may have looked from heaven, but never were raised to it before!—Moore.

Love, anger, pride and avarice all visibly move in those little orbs.—Addison.

A wanton eye is a messenger of an unchaste heart.—St. Augustine.

Love looketh from the eye, and kindleth love by looking.—Tupper.

Faster than his tongue did make offense, his eye did heal it up.—Shakespeare.

Drink to me only with thine eyes, and I will pledge with mine.—Ben Jonson.

For brilliancy, no gem compares with the eyes of a beautiful woman.—Dr. J. V. C. Smith.

The heart's hushed secret in the soft dark eye.—L. E. Landon.

Sometimes from her eyes I did receive fair speechless messages.—Shakespeare.

Eyes not down-dropped nor over-bright, but fed with the clear-pointed flame of chastity.—Tennyson.

What an eye she has! methinks it sounds a parley of provocation.—Shakespeare.

Who has a daring eye tells down-right truths and downright lies.—Lavater.

The eye strays not while under the guidance of reason.—Publius Syrus.

And eyes disclosed what eyes alone could tell.—Dwight.

Where is any author in the world teaches such beauty as a woman's eye? Shakespeare.

Tell me, sweet eyes, from what divinest star did ye drink in your liquid melancholy?—Bulwer-Lytton.

Persuasive, yet denying eyes, all eloquent with language of their own.—Locke.

Windows, white and azure-laced with blue of heaven's own tinct.—Shakespeare.

Eyes that displace the neighbor diamond, and outface that sunshine by their own sweet grace.—Crashaw.

The curious questioning eye, that plucks the heart of every mystery.—Grenville Mellen.

Our eyes when gazing on sinful objects are out of their calling and God's keeping.—Fuller.

The eye of the master will do more work than both his hands.—Franklin.

A withered hermit, fivescore winters worn, might shake off fifty, looking in her eye.—Shakespeare.

We credit most our sight; one eye doth please
Our trust far more than ten ear witnesses.
—Herrick.

His eye was blue and calm, as is the sky
In the serenest noon. —Willis.

A heaven of dreams in her large lotus eyes, darkly divine.—Gerald Massey.

'Tis sweet to know there is an eye will mark our coming, and look brighter when we come.—Byron.

Pure vestal thoughts in the translucent fane of her still spirit.—Tennyson.

The flash of his keen black eyes
Forerunning the thunder.
—Longfellow.

Those laughing orbs, that borrow from azure skies the light they wear.—Frances S. Osgood.

Within her tender eye
The heaven of April, with its changing light.
—Longfellow.

Where did you get your eyes so blue?
Out of the sky as I came through.
—Geo. MacDonald.

And thy deep eyes, amid the gloom,
Shine like jewels in a shroud.
—Longfellow.

Eyes so transparent,
That through them one sees the soul.
—Theophile Gautier.

Her eye in silence hath a speech which eye best understands.—Southwell.

And violets, transform'd to eyes,
Inshrined a soul within their blue.
—Moore.

Alack, there lies more peril in thine eye
Than twenty of their swords.
—Shakespeare.

A suppressed resolve will betray itself in the eyes.—George Eliot.

There is no end of affection taken in at the eyes only.—Steele.

Bright as the sun her eyes the gazers strike, And, like the sun, they shine on all alike.
—Pope.

The harvest of a quiet eye, That broods and sleeps on his own heart.
—Wordsworth.

Blue eyes shimmer with angel glances, Like spring violets over the lea.
—Constance F. Woolson.

With eyes that look'd into the very soul—
* * * * * * *
Bright—and as black and burning as a coal.
—Byron.

The eyes of other people are the eyes that ruin us.—Franklin.

His eyes have all the seeming of a demon's that is dreaming.—Poe.

The eye sees not itself But by reflection, by some other things.
—Shakespeare.

Folded eyes see brighter colors than the open ever do.—Mrs. Browning.

Her eye in heaven Would through the airy region stream so bright, That birds would sing, and think it were not night.
—Shakespeare.

The eyes are the windows of a woman's heart; you may enter that way!
—Eugene Sue.

A lamp is lit in woman's eye, that souls, else lost on earth, remember angels by.—N. P. Willis.

Eyes and ears, two trade pilots 'twixt the dangerous shores of will and judgment.—Shakespeare.

Thine eyes are springs in whose serene And silent waters heaven is seen.
William Cullen Bryant.—

Her deep blue eyes smile constantly, as if they had by fitness won the secret of a happy dream she does not care to speak.—Mrs. Browning.

The eye of Paul Pry often finds more than he wished to find.—Lessing.

The eyes, being in the highest part, have the office of sentinels.—Cicero.

This little member can behold the earth, and in a moment view things as high as heaven.—Charnock.

But her's, which through the crystal tears gave light, Shone like the moon in water seen by night.
—Shakespeare.

Eyes raised toward heaven are always beautiful, whatever they be.—Joubert.

Beautiful eyes in the face of a handsome woman are like eloquence to speech.—Bulwer-Lytton.

His eyebrow dark, and eye of fire, showed spirit proud, and prompt to ire.—Sir Walter Scott.

Women's glances express what they dare not speak.—Alphonse Karr.

In her eyes a thought Grew sweeter and sweeter, deepening like the dawn,— A mystical forewarning. —T. B. Aldrich.

True eyes, too pure and too honest in aught to disguise the sweet soul shining through them.—Owen Meredith.

In those sunk eyes the grief of years I trace, And sorrow seems acquainted with that face.
—Ickell.

Dear eyes!—do not my heart forsake, Shine, like the stars within the lake,— Shine, and the darksome shadows break.
—Augustine J. H. Dugane.

Deep brown eyes running over with glee; Blue eyes are pale, and gray eyes are sober; Bonnie brown eyes are the eyes for me.
—Constance F. Woolson.

O lovely eyes of azure, Clear as the waters of a brook that run Limpid and laughing in the summer sun!
—Longfellow.

Eyes of most unholy blue!—Moore.

I dislike an eye that twinkles like a star. Those only are beautiful which, like the planets, have a steady, lambent light—are luminous, but not sparkling.—Longfellow.

Gradual as the snow, at heaven's breath, melts off and shows the azure flowers beneath, her lids unclosed, and the bright eyes were seen.—Moore.

All the gazers on the skies read not in fair heaven's story expresser truth or truer glory than they might in her bright eyes.—Ben Jonson.

Where such radiant lights have shone, no wonder if her cheeks be grown sunburnt with lustre of their own.—John Cleaveland.

The eye is the inlet to the soul, and it is well to beware of him whose visual organs avoid your honest regard.—Hosea Ballou.

The balls of sight are so formed that one man's eyes are spectacles to another to read his heart with.—Johnson.

When there is love in the heart there are rainbows in the eyes, which cover every black cloud with gorgeous hues.—Beecher.

One of the most wonderful things in nature is a glance; it transcends speech; it is the bodily symbol of identity.—Emerson.

There is a lore simple and sure, that asks no discipline of weary years—the language of the soul, told through the eye.—Mrs. Sigourney.

The eyes have a property in things and territories not named in any title-deeds, and are the owners of our choicest possessions.—Alcott.

Eyes will not see when the heart wishes them to be blind. Desire conceals truth as darkness does the earth.—Seneca.

Those eyes, soft and capricious as a cloudless sky, whose azure depth their color emulates, must needs be conversant with upward looks—prayer's voiceless service.—Wordsworth.

Since your eyes are so sharpe, that you cannot onely looke through a milstone, but cleane through the minde.—Lyly.

The eyes of a man are of no use without the observing power. Telescopes and microscopes are cunning contrivances, but they cannot see of themselves.—Paxton Hood.

Her eyes, like marigolds, had sheathed their light, and, canopied in darkness, sweetly lay, till they might open to adorn the day.—Shakespeare.

Beneath her drooping lashes slept a world of eloquent meaning; passionate but pure, dreamy, subdued, but, oh, how beautiful!—Mrs. Osgood.

　　　　　　　　With eyes
Of microscopic power, that could discern
The population of a dew-drop.
　　　　　　—James Montgomery.

There are whole veins of diamonds in thine eyes,
Might furnish crowns for all the Queens of earth.　　　　　　—Bailey.

Guns, swords, batteries, armies and ships of war are set in motion by man for the subjugation of an enemy. Women bring conquerors to their feet with the magic of their eyes.—Dr. J. V. C. Smith.

Speech is a laggard and a sloth; but the eyes shoot out electric fluid that condenses all the elements of sentiment and passion in one single emanation.—Horace Smith.

When a man speaks the truth in the spirit of truth, his eye is as clear as the heavens. When he has base ends, and speaks falsely, the eye is muddy, and sometimes asquint.—Emerson.

Satan turned Eve's eye to the apple, Achan's eye to the wedge of gold, Ahab's eye to Naboth's vineyard, and then what work did he make with them!—Rev. J. Alleine.

Lovers are angry, reconciled, entreat, thank, appoint, and finally speak all things, by their eyes.—Montaigne.

Men are born with two eyes, but with one tongue, in order that they should see. twice as much as they say. —Colton.

The learned compute that seven hundred and seven millions of millions of vibrations have penetrated the eye before the eye can distinguish the tints of a violet.—Bulwer-Lytton.

How blue were Ariadne's eyes
When, from the sea's horizon line,
At eve, she raised them on the skies!
My Psyche, bluer far are thine.
—Aubrey De Vere.

There are eyes half defiant,
Half meek and compliant;
Black eyes, with a wondrous, witching charm
To bring us good or to work us harm.
—Phœbe Cary.

O, the eye's light is a noble gift of heaven! All beings live from light; each fair created thing, the very plants, turn with a joyful transport to the light.—Schiller.

Crows pick out the eyes of the dead when they are no longer of any use. But flatterers destroy the souls of the living by blinding their eyes.—Maximus.

Little eyes must be good-tempered or they are ruined. They have no other resource. But this will beautify them enough. They are made for laughing, and should do their duty.—Leigh Hunt.

People forget that it is the eye which makes the horizon, and the rounding mind's eye which makes this or that man a type or representative of humanity with the name of hero or saint.—Emerson.

Some eyes threaten like a loaded and levelled pistol, and others are as insulting as hissing or kicking; some have no more expression than blueberries, while others are as deep as a well which you can fall into.—Emerson.

Somebody once observed—and the observation did him credit, whoever he was—that the dearest things in the world were neighbors' eyes, for they cost everybody more than anything else contributing to housekeeping.—Albert Smith.

Those laughing orbs, that borrow
From azure skies the light they wear,
Are like heaven—no sorrow
Can float o'er hues so fair.
—Mrs. Osgood.

And then her look—Oh, where's the heart so wise
Could, unbewilder'd, meet those matchless eyes?
Quick, restless, strange, but exquisite withal,
Like those of angels. —Moore.

Why was the sight to such a tender ball as the eye confined, so obvious and so easy to be quenched, and not, as feeling, through all parts diffused, that she might look at will through every pore?—Milton.

The eye observes only what the mind, the heart, and the imagination are gifted to see; and sight must be reinforced by insight before souls can be discerned as well as manners, ideas as well as objects, realities and relations as well as appearances and accidental connections.—Whipple.

If I could write the beauty of your eyes,
And in fresh numbers number all your graces,
The age to come would say, "This poet lies;
Such heavenly touches ne'er touch'd earthly faces."
—Shakespeare.

Men with gray eyes are generally keen, energetic, and at first cold; but you may depend upon their sympathy with real sorrow. Search the ranks of our benevolent men and you will agree with me.—Dr. Leask.

A woman with a hazel eye never elopes from her husband, never chats scandal, never finds fault, never talks too much nor too little—always is an entertaining, intellectual, agreeable and lovely creature.—Frederic Saunders.

Thou tell'st me there is murder in my eye: 'tis pretty, sure, and very probable that eyes—that are the frailest and softest things, who shut their coward gates on atomies—should be called tyrants, butchers, murderers!—Shakespeare.

The eye is continually influenced by what it cannot detect; nay, it is not going too far to say that it is most influenced by what it detects least. Let the painter define, if he can, the variations of lines on which depend the change of expression in the human countenance.—Ruskin.

None but those who have loved can be supposed to understand the oratory of the eye, the mute eloquence of a look, or the conversational powers of the face. Love's sweetest meanings are unspoken; the full heart knows no rhetoric of words, and resorts to the pantomime of sighs and glances.—Bovee.

The eye is the window of the soul, the mouth the door. The intellect, the will, are seen in the eye; the emotions, sensibilities, and affections, in the mouth. The animals look for man's intentions right into his eyes. Even a rat, when you hunt him and bring him to bay, looks you in the eye.—Hiram Powers.

Ahab cast a covetous eye at Naboth's vineyard, David a lustful eye at Bathsheba. The eye is the pulse of the soul; as physicians judge of the heart by the pulse, so we by the eye; a rolling eye, a roving heart. The good eye keeps minute time, and strikes when it should; the lustful, crochet-time, and so puts all out of tune.—Rev. T. Adams.

Dark eyes—eternal soul of pride!
  Deep life in all that's true!
  *   *   *   *   *
Away, away to other skies!
  Away o'er seas and sands!
Such eyes as those were never made
  To shine in other lands.   —Leland.

The eye speaks with an eloquence and truthfulness surpassing speech. It is the window out of which the winged thoughts often fly unwittingly. It is the tiny magic mirror on whose crystal surface the moods of feeling fitfully play, like the sunlight and shadow on a still stream.—Tuckerman.

Thine eyes are like the deep, blue, boundless heaven
Contracted to two circles underneath
Their long, fine lashes; dark, far, measureless,
Orb within orb, and line through line inwoven.   —Shelley.

I never saw an eye so bright,
  And yet so soft as hers;
It sometimes swam in liquid light,
  And sometimes swam in tears;
It seem'd a beauty set apart
  For softness and for signs.
          —Mrs. Welby.

That fine part of our construction, the eye, seems as much the receptacle and seat of our passions as the mind itself; and at least it is the outward portal to introduce them to the house within, or rather the common thoroughfare to let our affections pass in and out.—Addison.

The intelligence of affection is carried on by the eye only; good-breeding has made the tongue falsify the heart, and act a part of continued restraint, while nature has preserved the eyes to herself, that she may not be disguised or misrepresented.—Addison.

What a curious workmanship is that of the eye, which is in the body, as the sun in the world; set in the head as in a watch-tower, having the softest nerves for receiving the greater multitude of spirits necessary for the act of vision!—Charnock.

It is wonderful indeed to consider how many objects the eye is fitted to take in at once, and successively in an instant, and at the same time to make a judgment of their position, figure, and color. It watches against our dangers, guides our steps, and lets in all the visible objects, whose beauty and variety instruct and delight.—Steele.

We lose in depth of expression when we go to inferior animals for comparisons with human beauty. Homer calls Juno ox-eyed; and the epithet suits well with the eyes of that goddess, because she may be supposed, with all her beauty, to want a certain humanity. Her large eyes look at you with a royal indifference.—Leigh Hunt.

Whatever of goodness emanates from the soul, gathers its soft halo in the eyes; and if the heart be a lurking-place of crime, the eyes are sure to betray the secret. A beautiful eye makes silence eloquent, a kind eye makes contradiction assent, an enraged eye makes beauty a deformity; so you see, forsooth, the little organ plays no inconsiderable, if not a dominant, part. —Frederick Saunders.

Say, what other metre is it
Than the meeting of the eyes?
Nature poureth into nature
Through the channels of that feature
Riding on the ray of sight,
Fleeter far than whirlwinds go,
Or for service, or delight,
Hearts to hearts their meaning show.
—Emerson.

If the eye were so acute as to rival the finest microscope, and to discern the smallest hair upon the leg of a gnat, it would be a curse, and not a blessing to us; it would make all things appear rugged and deformed; the most finely polished crystal would be uneven and rough; the sight of our own selves would affright us; the smoothest skin would be beset all over with rugged scales and bristly hair.—Bentley.

Her eye (I am very fond of handsome eyes),
Was large and dark, suppressing half its fire
Until she spoke, then through its soft disguise
Flash'd an expression more of pride than ire,
And love than either; and there would arise,
A something in them which was not desire,
But would have been, perhaps, but for the soul,
Which struggled through and chasten'd down the whole.   —Byron.

Large eyes were admired in Greece, where they still prevail. They are the finest of all when they have the internal look, which is not common.

The stag or antelope eye of the Orientals is beautiful and lamping, but is accused of looking skittish and indifferent. "The epithet of 'stag-eyed,'" says Lady Wortley Montagu, speaking of a Turkish love-song, "pleases me extremely; and I think it a very lively image of the fire and indifference in his mistress' eye."—Leigh Hunt.

A gray eye is a sly eye,
    And roguish is a brown eye,—
Turn full upon me thy eye,—
    Ah, how its wavelets drown one!
A blue eye is a true eye;
    Mysterious is a dark one,
Which flashes like a spark-sun!
    A black eye is the best one.
            —W. R. Alger.

Long while I sought to what I might compare
Those powerful eyes, which light my dark spirit;
Yet found I nought on earth, to which I dare
Resemble th' image of their goodly light.
Not to the sun, for they do shine by night;
Nor to the moon, for they are changed never;
Nor to the stars, for they have purer sight;
Nor to the fire, for they consume not ever;
Nor to the lightning, for they still persever;
Nor to the diamond, for they are more tender;
Nor unto crystal, for nought may they sever;
Nor unto glass, such baseness might offend her;
Then to the Maker's self the likest be;
Whose light doth lighten all that here we see.   —Spenser.

A pair of bright eyes with a dozen glances suffice to subdue a man; to enslave him, and inflame; to make him even forget; they dazzle him so that the past becomes straightway dim to him; and he so prizes them that he would give all his life to possess them. What is the fond love of dearest friends compared to his treasure? Is memory as strong as expectancy, fruition as hunger, gratitude as desire?—Thackeray.

A beautiful eye makes silence eloquent, a kind eye makes contradiction an assent, an enraged eye makes beauty deformed. This little member gives life to every other part about us; and I believe the story of Argus implies no more than that the eye is in every part; that is to say, every other part would be mutilated were not its force represented more by the eye than even by itself.—Addison.

Those eyes that were so bright, love,
　Have now a dimmer shine;
But what they've lost in light, love,
　Is what they gave to mine.
And still those orbs reflect, love,
　The beams of former hours,
That ripen'd all my joys, love,
　And tinted all my flowers.　—Hood.

Eyes are bold as lions, roving, running, leaping, here and there, far and near. They speak all languages; they wait for no introduction; they are no Englishmen; ask no leave of age or rank; they respect neither poverty nor riches, neither learning nor power, nor virtue, nor sex, but intrude, and come again, and go through and through you in a moment of time. What inundation of life and thought is discharged from one soul into another through them!—Emerson.

F

Fable

History is but a fable agreed upon.—Napoleon I.

Fiction or fable allures to instruction.—Franklin.

A certain class of novels may with propriety be called fables.—Whately.

As we are poetical in our natures, so we delight in fable.—Hazlitt.

There should always be some foundation of fact for the most airy fabric; and pure invention is but the talent of a deceiver.—Byron.

Willmott has very tersely said that embellished truths are the illuminated alphabet of larger children.—Horace Mann.

Fables take off from the severity of instruction, and enforce it at the same time that they conceal it.—Addison.

All the fairy tales of Aladdin, or the invisible Gyges, or the talisman that opens kings' palaces, or the enchanted halls underground or in the sea, are only fictions to indicate the one miracle of intellectual enlargement.—Emerson.

The difference between a parable and an apologue is that the former, being drawn from human life, requires probability in the narration, whereas the apologue, being taken from inanimate things or the inferior animals, is not confined strictly to probability. The fables of Æsop are apologues.—Fleming.

Face

The countenance is the portrait of the soul.—Cicero.

The magic of a face.—Thomas Carew.

Thy face the index of a feeling mind. —Crabbe.

Features, the great soul's apparent seat.—Bryant.

Human face divine.—Milton.

The worst of faces still is human. —Lavater.

He had a face like a benediction.— Cervantes.

A face without a heart.—Shakespeare.

Trust not too much to an enchanting face.—Virgil.

Sea of upturned faces.—Sir W. Scott.

Her face, all red and white, like the inside of a shoulder of mutton.— Foote.

An unforgiving eye, and a damned disinheriting countenance.—R. B. Sheridan.

Those faces which have charmed us most escape us the soonest.—Walter Scott.

A February face, so full of frost, of storm and cloudiness.—Shakespeare.

671.

In youth, the artless index of the mind.—Horace Mann.

A face like nestling luxury of flowers.—Gerald Massey.

God has given you one face, and you make yourselves another.—Shakespeare.

Expression alone can invest beauty with supreme and lasting command over the eye.—Fuseli.

A countenance more in sorrow than in anger.—Shakespeare.

The mind, the music breathing from her face.—Byron.

In thy face I see the map of honor, truth, and loyalty.—Shakespeare.

If to her share some female errors fall
Look on her face, and you'll forget 'em all.
—Pope.

Her face is like the Milky Way i' the sky,—
A meeting of gentle lights without a name.
—Sir John Suckling.

A face with gladness overspread!
Soft smiles, by human kindness bred!
—Wordsworth.

That same face of yours looks like the title-page to a whole volume of roguery.—Colley Cibber.

Truth makes the face of that person shine who speaks and owns it.—South.

These faces in the mirrors
Are but the shadows and phantoms of myself.
—Longfellow.

Two similar faces, neither of which alone causes laughter, use laughter when they are together, by their resemblance.—Pascal.

All men's faces are true, whatsome'er their hands are.
—Shakespeare.

There's no art
To find the mind's construction in the face.
—Shakespeare.

A good face is the best letter of recommendation.—Queen Elizabeth.

Her cheek like apples which the sun had ruddied.—Spenser.

His face was of that doubtful kind,
That wins the eye but not the mind.
—Scott.

A cheerful face is nearly as good for an invalid as healthy weather.—Franklin.

Your face, my Thane, is as a book, where men
May read strange matters. —Shakespeare.

A sweet expression is the highest type of female loveliness.—Dr. J. V. C. Smith.

The countenance is more eloquent than the tongue.—Lavater.

Some women's faces are, in their brightness, a prophecy; and some, in their sadness, a history.—Dickens.

A beloved face cannot grow ugly, because, not flesh and complexion, but expression, created love.—Richter.

Though men can cover crimes with bold, stern looks, poor women's faces are their own faults' books.—Shakespeare.

Her angel's face,
As the great eye of heaven, shyned bright,
And made a sunshine in the shady place.
—Spenser.

For my soul prays, Sweet,
Still to your face in Heaven,
Heaven in your face, Sweet.
—Francis Thompson.

And to his eye
There was but one beloved face on earth,
And that was shining on him. —Byron.

The light upon her face
Shines from the windows of another world.
Saints only have such faces.
—Longfellow.

It is the common wonder of all men how among so many millions of faces there should be none alike.—Sir Thomas Browne.

The loveliest faces are to be seen by moonlight, when one sees half with the eye and half with the fancy.—Bovee.

Fire burns only when we are near it, but a beautiful face burns and inflames, though at a distance.—Xenophon.

Where the mouth is sweet and the eyes intelligent, there is always the look of beauty, with a right heart.—Leigh Hunt.

A face which is always serene possesses a mysterious and powerful attraction: sad hearts come to it as to the sun to warm themselves again.—Joseph Roux.

And her face so fair
Stirr'd with her dream, as rose-leaves with the air. —Byron.

Thou hast a grim appearance, and thy face
Bears a command in it; tho' thy tackle's torn,
Thou showest a noble vessel.
—Shakespeare.

A noble soul spreads even over a face in which the architectonic beauty is wanting an irresistible grace, and often even triumphs over the natural disfavor.—Schiller.

There is in every human countenance either a history or a prophecy, which must sadden, or at least soften, every reflecting observer.—Coleridge.

Look in the face of the person to whom you are speaking, if you wish to know his real sentiments; for he can command his words more easily than his countenance.—Chesterfield.

What furniture can give such finish to a room as a tender woman's face? And is there any harmony of tints that has such stirring of delight as the sweet modulation of her voice?—George Eliot.

There are women who do not let their husbands see their faces until they are married. Not to keep you in suspense, I mean that part of the sex who paint.—Steele.

Not the entrance of a cathedral, not the sound of a passing bell, not the furs of a magistrate, nor the sables of a funeral, were fraught with half the solemnity of face!—Shenstone.

The face of a woman, whatever be the force or extent of her mind, whatever be the importance of the object she pursues, is always an obstacle or a reason in the story of her life.—Mme. de Staël.

Contending Passions jostle and displace
And tilt and tourney mostly in the Face:
 * * * * * *
Unmatched by Art, upon this wondrous scroll
Portrayed are all the secrets of the soul.
—Abraham Coles.

Her face betokened all things dear and good,
The light of somewhat yet to come was there
Asleep, and waiting for the opening day,
When childish thoughts, like flowers, would drift away. —Jean Ingelow.

What a man is lies as certainly upon his countenance as in his heart, though none of his acquaintances may be able to read it. The very intercourse with him may have rendered it more difficult.—George MacDonald.

Faces are as legible as books, only with these circumstances to recommend them to our perusal, that they are read in much less time, and are much less likely to deceive us.—Lavater.

Nature cuts queer capers with men's phizzes at times, and confounds all the deductions of philosophy. Character does not put all its goods, sometimes not any of them, in its shop-window.—Wm. Matthews.

There remains in the faces of women who are naturally serene and peaceful, and of those rendered so by religion, an after-spring, and, later, an after-summer, the reflex of their most beautiful bloom.—Richter.

True beauty is in the mind; and the expression of the features depends more upon the moral nature than most persons are accustomed to think.—Frederic Saunders.

Her closed lips were delicate as the tinted penciling of veins upon a flower; and on her cheek the timid blood had faintly melted through, like something that was half afraid of light.—Willis.

We are all sculptors and painters, and our material is our own flesh and blood and bones. Any nobleness begins at once to refine a man's features, any meanness or sensuality to imbrute them.—Thoreau.

A face that had a story to tell. How different faces are in this particular! Some of them speak not. They are books in which not a line is written, save perhaps a date.—Longfellow.

The countenance may be rightly defined as the title-page which heralds the contents of the human volume, but, like other title-pages, it sometimes puzzles, often misleads, and often says nothing to the purpose.—Wm. Matthews.

Doubtless the human face is the grandest of all mysteries; yet fixed on canvas it can hardly tell of more than one sensation; no struggle, no successive contrasts accessible to dramatic art, can painting give, as neither time nor motion exists for her.—Madame de Staël.

Read o'er the volume of young Paris' face,
And find delight writ there with beauty's pen;
Examine every several lineament,
 * * * * * *
And what obscur'd in this fair volume lies,
Find written in the margin of his eyes.
—Shakespeare.

A girl of eighteen imagines the feelings behind the face that has moved her with its sympathetic youth as easily as primitive people imagined the humors of the gods in fair weather. What is she to believe in if not in this vision woven from within?—George Eliot.

On his bold visage middle age
Had slightly press'd its signet sage,
Yet had not quenched the open truth
And fiery vehemence of youth;
Forward and frolic glee was there,
The will to do, the soul to dare.
—Scott.

There are faces so fluid with expression, so flushed and rippled by the play of thought, that we can hardly find what the mere features really are. When the delicious beauty of lineament loses its power, it is because a more delicious beauty has appeared, that an interior and durable form has been disclosed.—Emerson.

Her face had a wonderful fascination in it. It was such a calm, quiet face, with the light of a rising soul shining so peacefully through it. At times it wore an expression of seriousness, of sorrow even; and then seemed to make the very air bright with what the Italian poets so beautifully call the "lampeggiar dell' angelico riso,"—the lightning of the angelic smile.—Longfellow.

Alas! how few of nature's faces there are to gladden us with their beauty! The cares and sorrows and hungerings of the world change them as they change hearts; and it is only when those passions sleep, and have lost their hold forever, that the troubled clouds pass off, and leave heaven's surface clear.—Dickens.

Nature has laid out all her art in beautifying the face; she has touched it with vermilion, planted in it a double row of ivory, made it the seat of smiles and blushes, lighted it up and enlivened it with the brightness of the eyes, hung it on each side with curious organs of sense, given it airs and graces that cannot be described, and surrounded it with such a flowing shade of hair as sets all its beauties in the most agreeable light.—Addison.

In vain we fondly strive to trace
The soul's reflection in the face;
In vain we dwell on lines and crosses,
Crooked mouths and short proboscis;
Boobies have looked as wise and bright
As Plato and the Stagyrite
And many a sage and learned skull
Has peeped through windows dark and dull.
—Moore.

No human face is exactly the same in its lines on each side, no leaf perfect in its lobes, no branch in its symmetry. All admit irregularity as they imply change; and to banish imperfection is to destroy expression, to check exertion, to paralyze vitality. All things are literally better, lovelier, and more beloved for the imperfections which have been divinely appointed, that the law of human life may be effort, and the law of human judgment mercy.—Ruskin.

As the language of the face is universal, so is it very comprehensive. No laconism can reach it. It is the short-hand of the mind, and crowds a great deal in a little room. A man may look a sentence as soon as speak a word. The strokes are small, but so masterly drawn that you may easily collect the image and proportions of what they resemble.—Jeremy Collier.

Now and then one sees a face which has kept its smile pure and undefiled. It is a woman's face usually; often a face which has trace of great sorrow all over it, till the smile breaks. Such a smile transfigures: such a smile, if the artful but knew it, is the greatest weapon a face can have.—Helen Hunt.

Quite the ugliest face I ever saw was that of a woman whom the world called beautiful. Through its silver veil the evil and ungentle passions looked out, hideous and hateful. On the other hand, there are faces which the multitude, at first glance, pronounce homely, unattractive, and such as "Nature fashions by the gross," which I always recognize with a warm heart-thrill. Not for the world would I have one feature changed; they please me as they are; they are hallowed by kind memories, and are beautiful through their associations.—Whittier.

Faction

So false is faction, and so smooth a liar,
As that it never had a side entire.
—Daniel.

Seldom is faction's ire in haughty minds
Extinguish'd but by death: it oft like fire
Suppress'd, breaks forth again, and blazes
higher.   —May.

Avoid the politic, the factious fool,
The busy, buzzing, talking harden'd knave;
The quaint smooth rogue that sins against
his reason,
Calls saucy loud sedition public zeal,
And mutiny the dictates of his spirit.
—Otway.

Facts

Facts are stubborn things.—Elliot.

Facts are plain spoken; hopes and figures are its aversion.—Addison.

Every fact that is learned becomes a key to other facts—E. L. Youmans.

But facts are chiels that winna ding,
An' downa be disputed.   —Burns.

There is nothing I know of so sublime as a fact.—George Canning.

Some people have a peculiar faculty for denying facts.—G. D. Prentice.

One fact is better than one hundred analogies.

From principles is derived probability; but truth, or certainty, is obtained only from facts.

In matters of fact, they say there is some credit to be given to the testimony of men, but not in matters of judgment.—Hooker.

Facts are to the mind the same thing as food to the body. On the due digestion of facts depends the strength and wisdom of the one, just as vigour and health depend on the other. The wisest in council, the ablest in debate, and the most agreeable in the commerce of life, is that man who has assimilated to his understanding greatest number of facts.—Burke.

Fail — Failure

A first failure is often a blessing.—A. L. Brown.

It is the empiric who never fails.—Willmott.

Half the failures in life come from pulling one's horse when he is leaping.—Thomas Hood.

But screw your courage to the sticking place and we'll not fail.—Shakespeare.

Failure is more frequently from want of energy than want of capital.—Daniel Webster.

There is not a fiercer hell than failure in a great object.—Keats.

A failure establishes only this, that our determination to succeed was not strong enough.—Bovee.

Now a' is done that men can do
And a' is done in vain.   —Burns.

To fail at all is to fail utterly.—Lowell.

He only is exempt from failures who makes no efforts.—Whately.

What is failure except feebleness? And what is it to miss one's mark except to aim widely and weakly?—Ouida.

Wherever there is failure, there is some giddiness, some superstition about luck, some step omitted, which Nature never pardons.—Emerson

Failures always overtake those who have the power to do, without the will to act, and who need that essential quality in life, energy.—James Ellis.

In the lexicon of youth, which fate reserves
For a bright manhood, there is no such word
As—fail.   —Lytton.

Although strength should fail, the effort will deserve praise. In great enterprises the attempt is enough.—Propertius.

Many men and women spend their lives in unsuccessful attempts to spin the flax God sends them upon a wheel they can never use.—J. G. Holland.

Complaints are vain; we will try to do better another time. To-morrow and to-morrow. A few designs and a few failures, and the time of designing is past.—Johnson.

He who bears failure with patience is as much of a philosopher as he who succeeds; for to put up with the world needs as much wisdom as to control it.—Aughey.

Every failure is a step to success: every detection of what is false directs us toward what is true; every trial exhausts some tempting form of error.

Not only so, but scarcely any attempt is entirely a failure; scarcely any theory, the result of steady thought, is altogether false; no tempting form of error is without some latent charm derived from truth.—Whewell.

Albeit failure in any cause produces a correspondent misery in the soul, yet it is, in a sense, the highway to success, inasmuch as every discovery of what is false leads us to seek earnestly after what is true, and every fresh experience points out some form of error which we shall afterward carefully eschew.—Keats.

What keeps persons down in the world, besides lack of capacity, is not a philosophical contempt of riches or honors, but thoughtlessness and improvidence, a love of sluggish torpor, and of present gratification. It is not from preferring virtue to wealth—the goods of the mind to those of fortune —that they take no thought for the morrow; but from want of forethought and stern self-command. The restless, ambitious man too often directs these qualities to an unworthy object; the contented man is generally deficient in the qualities themselves. The one is a stream that flows too often in a wrong channel, and needs to have its course altered, the other is a stagnant pool.—Wm. Matthews.

Fairies

Moonshine revellers.—Shakespeare.

Fairies use flowers for their charactery.—Shakespeare.

On the tawny sands and shelves trip the pert fairies and the dapper elves.—Milton.

Be secret and discreet; the fairy favors are lost when not concealed.—Dryden.

Wherever is love and loyalty, great purposes and lofty souls, even though in a hovel or a mine, there is fairyland.—Kingsley.

In this state she gallops, night by night, o'er ladies' lips, who straight on kisses dream.—Shakespeare.

Their little minim forms arrayed in
all the tricksy pomp of fairy pride.—
Drake.

This is the fairy land; O spite of spites,
We talk with goblins, owls, and elvish
   sprites.   —Shakespeare.

Then take me on your knee, mother;
   And listen, mother of mine.
A hundred fairies danced last night,
   And the harpers they were nine.
      —Mary Howitt.

    In silence sad,
Trip we after the night's shade;
We the globe can compass soon,
Swifter than the wand'ring moon.
      —Shakespeare.

But light as any wind that blows
So fleetly did she stir,
The flower, she touch'd on, dipt and rose,
   And turned to look at her.
      —Tennyson.

O, then, I see Queen Mab hath been with
   you.
She is the fairies' midwife, and she comes
In shape no bigger than an agate-stone
On the forefinger of an alderman.
      —Shakespeare.

Sometimes she driveth o'er a soldier's neck,
And then dreams he of cutting foreign
   throats,
Of breaches, ambuscadoes, Spanish blades,
Of healths five fathoms deep; and then
   anon
Drums in his ear, at which he starts, and
   wakes,
And, being thus frighted, swears a prayer
   or two,
And sleeps again.   —Shakespeare.

Bright Eyes, Light Eyes! Daughter of a
   Fay!
I had not been a married wife a twelve-
   month and a day,
I had not nursed my little one a month
   upon my knee,
When down among the blue bell banks rose
   elfins three times three:
They griped me by the raven hair, I could
   not cry for fear,
They put a hempen rope around my waist
   and dragged me here;
They made me sit and give thee suck as
   mortal mothers can,
Bright Eyes, Light Eyes! strange and weak
   and wan!   —Robert Buchanan.

The maskers come late, and I think
will stay, like fairies, till the cock
crow them away.—Donne.

The dances ended, all the fairy train
For pinks and daisies search'd the flow'ry
   plain.   —Pope.

Where the bee sucks, there suck I;
In a cowslip's bell I lie;
There I couch when owls do cry.
On the bat's back I do fly.
      —Shakespeare.

Their harps are of the amber shade,
   That hides the blush of waking day,
And every gleamy string is made
   Of silvery moonshine's lengthen'd ray.
      —Drake.

Her mantle was the purple roll'd
   At twilight in the west afar;
'Twas tied with threads of dawning gold,
   And button'd with a sparkling star.
      —Drake.

      Oft fairy elves,
Whose midnight revels by a forest side,
Or fountain, some belated peasant sees,
Or dreams he sees, while o'erhead the moon
Sits arbitress, and nearer to the earth
Wheels her pale course, they on their mirth
   and dance
Intent, with jocund music charm his ear;
At once with joy and fear his heart re-
   bounds.   —Milton.

The palace of the sylphid queen—
Its spiral columns, gleaming bright,
Were streamers of the northern light;
Its curtain's light and lovely flush
Was of the morning's rosy blush;
And the ceiling fair, that rose aboon,
The white and feathery fleece of noon.
      —Drake.

Did you ever hear
Of the frolic fairies dear?
They're a blessed little race,
Peeping up in fancy's face,
In the valley, on the hill,
By the fountain and the rill;
Laughing out between the leaves
That the loving summer weaves.
      —Mrs. Osgood.

He put his acorn-helmet on;
It was plum'd of the silk of the thistle-
   down;
The corselet plate, that guarded his breast,
Was once the wild bees' golden vest;
His cloak, of a thousand mingled dyes,
Was form'd of the wings of butterflies;
His shield was the shell of a lady-bug queen,
Studs of gold on a ground of green;
And the quivering lance which he brand-
   ish'd bright,
Was the sting of a wasp he had slain in
   fight.   —Drake.

About this spring of ancient fame say true,
The dapper elves their moonlight sports re-
  new;
Their pigmy king and little fairy queen
In circling dances gamboll'd on the green,
With tuneful sprites a merry concert made,
And airy music warbled through the shade.
—Pope.

To pass their lives on fountains and on flowers, and never know the weight of human hours.—Byron.

Faith

Faith is the force of life.—Tolstoi.

Faith is the continuation of reason. —William Adams.

Though he slay me, yet will I trust in him.—Job xiii. 15.

Faith is the heroism of intellect.— Charles H. Parkhurst.

Faith is a higher faculty than reason.—Bailey.

Faith is not reason's labor, but repose.—Young.

Faith lights us through the dark to Deity.—Sir W. Davenant.

Faith is necessary to victory.—Hazlitt.

Faith creates the virtues in which it believes.—Mme. de Sévigné.

Faith loves to lean on time's destroying arm.—Holmes.

Faith is deferential incredulity.— Voltaire.

On argument alone my faith is built. —Young.

Youth without faith is a day without sun.—Ouida.

Faith is the substance of things hoped for, the evidence of things not seen.—Bible.

The power of faith will often shine forth the most when the character is naturally weak.—Hare.

A perfect faith would lift us absolutely above fear.—George MacDonald.

Our life must answer for our faith. —Thomas Wilson.

Faith is obedience, not compliance. —George MacDonald.

The principal part of faith is patience.—George MacDonald.

Faith is love taking the form of aspiration.—William Ellery Channing.

Faith is nothing but spiritualized imagination.—Henry Ward Beecher.

There are no tricks in plain simple faith.—Shakespeare.

Faith builds a bridge from this world to the next.—Dr. Young.

This is faith: it is nothing more than obedience.—Voltaire.

O welcome, pure-eyed Faith, white-handed Hope.
Thou hovering angel, girt with golden wings.
—Milton.

Faith in a better than that which appears is no less required by art than by religion.—John Sterling.

Faith always implies the disbelief of a lesser fact in favor of a greater.— Holmes.

Faith is the subtle chain that binds us to the Infinite.—Mrs. E. Oakes Smith.

Faith is the root of works. A root that produceth nothing is dead.— Thomas Wilson.

He wears his faith but as the fashion of his hat; it ever changes with the next block.—Shakespeare.

The great world's altar-stairs
That slope thro' darkness up to God.
Tennyson.

As the flower is before the fruit, so is faith before good works.—Whately.

Faith, amid the disorders of a sinful life, is like the lamp burning in an ancient tomb.—Madame Swetchine.

Man is not made to question, but adore.—Young.

Faith needs her daily bread.—Georgiana M. Craik.

Faith is the flame that lifts the sacrifice to heaven.—J. Montgomery.

Let us fear the worst, but work with faith; the best will always take care of itself.—Victor Hugo.

The faith which you keep must be a faith that demands obedience, and you can keep it only by obeying it.—Phillips Brooks.

Without faith a man can do nothing. But faith can stifle all science.—Amiel.

No cloud can overshadow a true Christian but his faith will discern a rainbow in it.—Bishop Horne.

It is impossible to be a hero in anything unless one is first a hero in faith.—Jacobi.

For modes of faith let graceless zealots fight;
His can't be wrong whose life is in the right.—Pope.

There lives more faith in honest doubt,
Believe me, than in half the creeds.
—Tennyson.

The saddest thing that can befall a soul
Is when it loses faith in God and woman.
—Alexander Smith.

"Patience!" * * * "have faith and thy prayer will be answered!"—Longfellow.

But Faith, fanatic Faith, once wedded fast
To some dear falsehood, hugs it to the last.
—Moore.

Faith is the pencil of the soul
That pictures heavenly things.
—Burbidge.

Faith is the soul going out of itself for all its wants.—Boston.

The faith of immortality gives to every mind that cherishes it a certain firmness of texture.—Wilberforce.

A lively faith will bear aloft the mind, and leave the luggage of good works behind.—Dryden.

Not prayer without faith, nor faith without prayer, but prayer in faith, is the cost of spiritual gifts and graces.—H. Clay Trumbull.

None live so easily, so pleasantly, as those that live by faith.—Matthew Henry.

Faith is among men what gravity is among planets and suns.—Charles H. Parkhurst.

Faith converses with the angels, and antedates the hymns of glory.—Jeremy Taylor.

The highest order that was ever instituted on earth is the order of faith.—Henry Ward Beecher.

Heaven alone, not earth, is destined to witness the repose of faith.—Moses Harvey.

Faith makes the discords of the present the harmonies of the future.—Robert Collyer.

It was Lazarus' faith, not his poverty, which brought him into Abraham's bosom.—Trench.

Pin thy faith to no man's sleeve. Hast thou not two eyes of thy own?—Carlyle.

Systems exercise the mind; but faith enlightens and guides it.—Voltaire.

All I have seen teaches me to trust the Creator for all I have not seen.—Emerson.

A maxim in law has more weight in the world than an article of faith.—Swift.

Faith makes us, and not we it; and faith makes its own forms.—Emerson.

The steps of faith fall on the seeming void, and find the rock beneath.—Whittier.

For mysterious things of faith, rely on the proponent, Heaven's authority.—Dryden.

In affairs of this world men are saved, not by faith, but by the want of it.—Fielding.

When faith is lost, when honor dies, the man is dead.—Whittier.

Faith is the champion of grace, and love the nurse; but humility is the beauty of grace.—Thomas Brooks.

Let us have faith that right makes might; and in that faith, let us, to the end, dare to do our duty as we understand it.—Abraham Lincoln.

Faith, though it hath sometimes a trembling hand, it must not have a withered hand, but must stretch.—Watson.

Religion is the true Philosophy!
Faith is the last great link 'twixt God and man. —Bigg.

When the soul grants what reason makes her see,
That is true faith, what's more 's credulity. —Sir F. Fane.

One in whom persuasion and belief
Had ripened into faith, and faith become
A passionate intuition. —Wordsworth.

All the scholastic scaffolding falls, as a ruined edifice, before one single word —faith.—Napoleon I.

The Americans have no faith, they rely on the power of a dollar; they are deaf to sentiment.—Emerson.

Christians are directed to have faith in Christ, as the effectual means of obtaining the change they desire.—Franklin.

If you have any faith, give me, for heaven's sake, a share of it! Your doubts you may keep to yourself, for I have a plenty of my own.—Goethe.

Faith is the key that unlocks the cabinet of God's treasures; the king's messenger from the celestial world, to bring all the supplies we need out of the fullness that there is in Christ.—J. Stephens.

Our Lord does not praise the centurion for his amiable care of his servants, nor for his generosity to the Jews, nor for his public spirit, nor for his humility, but for his faith.—William Adams.

Have you not observed that faith is generally strongest in those whose character may be called the weakest?—Mme. de Staël.

Faith is letting down our nets into the untransparent deeps, at the Divine command, not knowing what we shall take.—Faber.

Faith is necessary to explain anything, and to reconcile the foreknowledge of God with human evil.—Wordsworth.

Love is a bodily shape; and Christian works are no more than animate faith and love, as flowers are the animate springtide.—Longfellow.

The inventory of my faith for this lower world is soon made out. I believe in Him who made it.—Mme. Swetchine.

Lay not the plummet to the line; religion hath no landmarks; no human keenness can discern the subtle shades of faith.—Tupper.

Strike from mankind the principle of faith, and men would have no more history than a flock of sheep.—Bulwer-Lytton.

Faith draws the poison from every grief, takes the sting from every loss, and quenches the fire of every pain; and only faith can do it.—J. G. Holland.

I wonder many times that ever a child of God should have a sad heart, considering what the Lord is preparing for him.—Rutherford.

Youth, beauty, wit may recommend you to men, but only faith in Jesus Christ can recommend you to God.—Aughey.

The person who has a firm trust in the Supreme Being is powerful in his power, wise by his wisdom, happy by his happiness.—Addison.

Life grows dark as we go on, till only one clear light is left shining on it, and that is faith.—Mme. Swetchine.

Faith is an humble, self-denying grace; it makes the Christian nothing in himself, and all in God.—Leighton.

I'll ne'er distrust my God for cloth and bread while lilies flourish and the raven's fed.—Quarles.

Were it not for an unquestioning faith, human progress would be an intolerable burden.—Aughey.

All sects, as far as reason will help them, gladly use it; when it fails them, they cry out it is a matter of faith, and above reason.—Locke.

That faith which is required of us is then perfect when it produces in us a fiduciary assent to whatever the Gospel has revealed.—William Wake.

Which to believe of her must be a faith that reason without miracle shall never plant in me.—Shakespeare.

Those who have obtained the farthest insight into Nature have been, in all ages, firm believers in God.—Whewell.

Faith is to believe what we do not see; and the reward of this faith is to see what we believe.—St. Augustine.

Faith, like light, should ever be simple and unbending; while love, like warmth, should beam forth on every side, and bend to every necessity of our brethren.—Martin Luther.

Faith and works are necessary to our spiritual life as Christians, as soul and body are to our natural life as men; for faith is the soul of religion, and works the body.—Colton.

Faith, in order to be genuine and of any real value, must be the offspring of that divine love which Jesus manifested when He prayed for His enemies on the cross.—Hosea Ballou.

As a weak limb grows stronger by exercise, so will your faith be strengthened by the very efforts you make in stretching it out toward things unseen.—Aughey.

There never was found in any age of the world, either philosopher or sect, or law or discipline, which did so highly exalt the public good as the Christian faith.—Bacon.

Faith affirms many things, respecting which the senses are silent, but nothing that they deny. It is superior, but never opposed to their testimony.—Pascal.

Faith is mind at its best, its bravest, and its fiercest. Faith is thought become poetry, and absorbing into itself the soul's great passions. Faith is intellect carried up to its transfiguration.—Chas. H. Parkhurst.

In our age faith and charity are found, but they are found apart. We tolerate everybody, because we doubt everything; or else we tolerate nobody, because we believe something.—Mrs. E. B. Browning.

There is one inevitable criterion of judgment touching religious faith in doctrinal matters. Can you reduce it to practice? If not, have none of it.—Hosea Ballou.

A firm faith is the best theology; a good life is the best philosophy; a clear conscience the best law; honesty the best policy, and temperance the best physic.—Aughey.

It is by faith that poetry, as well as devotion, soars above this dull earth; that imagination breaks through its clouds, breathes a purer air, and lives in a softer light.—Henry Giles.

Faith may rise into miracles of might, as some few wise men have shown; faith may sink into credulities of weakness, as the mass of fools have witnessed.—Tupper.

Faith is the key that unlocks the cabinet of God's treasures; the king's messenger from the celestial world, to bring all the supplies we need out of the fullness that there is in Christ.—J. Stephens.

Faith builds a bridge across the gulf of death,
To break the shock blind nature cannot shun,
And lands Thought smoothly on the further shore.   —Young.

Given a man full of faith, you will have a man tenacious in purpose, absorbed in one grand object, simple in his motives, in whom selfishness has been driven out by the power of a mightier love, and indolence stirred into unwearied energy. — Alexander Maclaren.

The only faith that wears well and holds its color in all weathers is that which is woven of conviction and set with the sharp mordant of experience.—Lowell.

The childlike faith that asks not sight, waits not for wonder or for sign, believes, because it loves, aright, shall see things greater, things divine.—Keble.

Not that God doth require nothing unto happiness at the hands of men saving only a naked belief, but that without belief all other things are as nothing.—Hooker.

We cannot live on probabilities. The faith in which we can live bravely and die in peace must be a certainty, so far as it professes to be a faith at all, or it is nothing.—Froude.

Let none henceforth seek needless cause to approve the faith they own; when earnestly they seek such proof, conclude they then begin to fail.—Milton.

Faith must be not only living, but lively, too; it must be brightened and stirred up by a particular exercise of those virtues specifically requisite to a due performance of duty.—South.

Faith in God, faith in man, faith in work: this is the short formula in which we may sum up the teachings of the founders of New England—a creed ample enough for this life and the next.—Lowell.

The faith to which the Scriptures attach such momentous consequences and ascribe such glorious exploits is a practical habit, which, like every other, is strengthened and increased by continual exercise.—Robert Hall.

The highest historical probability can be adduced in support of the proposition that, if it were possible to annihilate the Bible, and with it all its influences, we should destroy with it the whole spiritual system of the moral world.—Edward Everett.

We should act with as much energy as those who expect everything from themselves; and we should pray with as much earnestness as those who expect everything from God.—Colton.

Works without faith are like a fish without water, it wants the element it should live in. A building without a basis cannot stand; faith is the foundation, and every good action is as a stone laid.—Feltham.

Men seldom think deeply on subjects in which they have no choice of opinion: they are fearful of encountering obstacles to their faith—as in religion—and so are content with the surface.—Sheridan.

The great desire of this age is for a doctrine which may serve to condense our knowledge, guide our researches, and shape our lives, so that conduct may really be the consequence of belief.—G. H. Lewes.

Faith is the revealer of knowledge; it is the office of reason to defend that knowledge and to preserve it pure. Independent knowledge—the knowledge that comes not through faith—whether it be of things earthly or things heavenly, never can be ours.—Sunday School Times.

Faith is a homely, private capital; as there are public savings-banks and poor funds, out of which in times of want we can relieve the necessities of individuals, so here the faithful take their coin in peace.—Goethe.

Faith without works is like a bird without wings; though she may hop with her companions on earth, yet she will never fly with them to heaven; but when both are joined together, then doth the soul mount up to her eternal rest.—J. Beaumont.

In your intercourse with sects, the sublime and abstruse doctrines of Christian belief belong to the Church; but the faith of the individual, centred in his heart, is, or may be, collateral to them. Faith is subjective.—Coleridge.

Faith is the very heroism and enterprise of intellect. Faith is not a passivity, but a faculty. Faith is power, the material of effect. Faith is a kind of winged intellect. The great workmen of history have been men who believed like giants.—Charles H. Parkhurst.

Faith without evidence is, properly, not faith, but prejudice or presumption; faith beyond evidence is superstition, and faith contrary to evidence is either insanity or willful perversity of mind.—Aughey.

What we believe we must believe wholly and without reserve; wherefore the only perfect and satisfying object of faith is God. A faith that sets bounds to itself, that will believe so much and no more, that will trust thus far and no farther, is none.

Through this dark and stormy night
Faith beholds a feeble light
  Up the blackness streaking;
Knowing God's own time is best,
In a patient hope I rest
  For the full day-breaking!
          —Whittier.

Never yet did there exist a full faith in the Divine word which did not expand the intellect, while it purified the heart; which did not multiply the aims and objects of the understanding, while it fixed and simplified those of the desires and feelings.—S. T. Coleridge.

And we shall be made truly wise if we be made content; content, too, not only with what we can understand, but content with what we do not understand—the habit of mind which theologians call—and rightly—faith in God.—Charles Kingsley.

If faith produce no works, I see
That faith is not a living tree,
Thus faith and works together grow;
No separate life they e'er can know:
They're soul and body, hand and heart:
What God hath joined, let no man part.
          —Hannah More.

Ye children of promise, who are awaiting your call to glory, take possession of the inheritance that now is yours. By faith take the promises. Live upon them, not upon emotions. Remember, feeling is not faith. Faith grasps and clings to the promises. Faith says, "I am certain, not because feeling testifies to it, but because God says it."—Mandeville.

When my reason is afloat, my faith cannot long remain in suspense, and I believe in God as firmly as in any other truth whatever; in short, a thousand motives draw me to the consolatory side, and add the weight of hope to the equilibrium of reason.—Rousseau.

All the strength and force of man comes from his faith in things unseen. He who believes is strong; he who doubts is weak. Strong convictions precede great actions. The man strongly possessed of an idea is the master of all who are uncertain or wavering. Clear, deep, living convictions rule the world.—James Freeman Clarke.

Flatter not thyself in thy faith to God, if thou wantest charity for thy neighbor; and think not thou hast charity for thy neighbor if thou wantest faith to God. Where they are not both together, they are both wanting; they are both dead if once divided.—Quarles.

Faith is a practical habit, which, like every other, is strengthened and increased by continual exercise. It is nourished by meditation, by prayer, and the devout perusal of the Scriptures; and the light which it diffuses becomes stronger and clearer by an uninterrupted converse with its object, and a faithful compliance with its dictates.—Robert Hall.

Faith is the inspiration of nobleness, it is the strength of integrity; it is the life of love, and is everlasting growth for it; it is courage of soul, and bridges over for our crossing the gulf between worldliness and heavenly-mindedness; and it is the sense of the unseen, without which we could not feel God nor hope for heaven.—Wm. Mountford.

True faith nor biddeth nor abideth form,
The bended knee, the eye uplift, is all
Which men need render; all which God can bear.
What to the faith are forms?   A passing speck,
A crow upon the sky.   —Bailey.

It is sufficiently humiliating to our nature to reflect that our knowledge is but as the rivulet, our ignorance as the sea. On points of the highest interest, the moment we quit the light of revelation we shall find that Platonism itself is intimately connected with Pyrrhonism, and the deepest inquiry with the darkest doubt.—Colton.

Never yet did there exist a full faith in the Divine Word (by whom light as well as immortality was brought into the world) which did not expand the intellect, while it purified the heart—which did not multiply the aims and objects of the understanding, while it fixed and simplified those of the desires and passions.—Coleridge.

If thy faith have no doubts, thou has just cause to doubt thy faith; and if thy doubts have no hope, thou hast just reason to fear despair; when therefore thy doubts shall exercise thy faith, keep thy hopes firm to qualify thy doubts; so shall thy faith be secured from doubts; so shall thy doubts be preserved from despair.—Quarles.

Faith is the backbone of the social and the foundation of the commercial fabric; remove faith between man and man, and society and commerce fall to pieces. There is not a happy home on earth but stands on faith; our heads are pillowed on it, we sleep at night in its arms with greater security for the safety of our lives, peace, and prosperity than bolts and bars can give.—Thomas Guthrie.

Mahomet made the people believe that he would call a hill to him, and from the top of it offer up his prayers for the observers of his law. The people assembled; Mahomet called the hill to come to him, again and again, and when the hill stood still, he was never awhit abashed, but said, if the hill will not come to Mahomet, Mahomet will go to the hill.—Bacon.

Judge not man by his outward manifestation of faith; for some there are who tremblingly reach out shaking hands to the guidance of faith; others who stoutly venture in the dark their human confidence, their leader, which they mistake for faith; some whose hope totters upon crutches; others who stalk into futurity upon stilts. The difference is chiefly constitutional with them.—Lamb.

The light of genius is sometimes so resplendent as to make a man walk through life, amid glory and acclamation; but it burns very dimly and low when carried into "the valley of the shadow of death." But faith is like the evening star, shining into our souls the more brightly, the deeper is the night of death in which they sink.—Mountford.

There are three means of believing —by inspiration, by reason, and by custom. Christianity, which is the only rational institution, does yet admit none for its sons who do not believe by inspiration. Nor does it injure reason or custom, or debar them of their proper force; on the contrary, it directs us to open our minds by the proofs of the former, and to confirm our minds by the authority of the latter.—Pascal.

There is a grand fearlessness in faith. He who in his heart of hearts reverences the good, the true, the holy —that is, reverences God—does not tremble at the apparent success of attacks upon the outworks of faith.

They may shake those who rest on those outworks—they do not move him whose soul reposes on the truth itself. He needs no prop or crutches to support his faith. Founded on a Rock, Faith can afford to gaze undismayed at the approaches of Infidelity.—F. W. Robertson.

He had great faith in loaves of bread
For hungry people, young and old,
And hope inspired; kind words he said
To those he sheltered from the cold.
In words he did not put his trust;
His faith in words he never writ;
He loved to share his cup and crust
With all mankind who needed it.
He put his trust in Heaven and he
Worked well with hand and head;
And what he gave in charity
Sweetened his sleep and daily bread.

Faith in Christ

O, for a living faith in a living Redeemer!—Richard Fuller.

There are three acts of faith, assent, acceptance and assurance.—John Flavel.

There can be no faith so feeble that Christ does not respond to it.—Alexander Maclaren.

When you have given yourself to Christ, leave yourself there, and go about your work as a child in His household.—C. S. Robinson.

That is faith, cleaving to Christ, twining round Him with all the tendrils of our heart, as the vine does round its support.—Alexander Maclaren.

Faith refers to Christ. Holiness depends on faith. Heaven depends on holiness.—Alexander Maclaren.

This is faith, receiving the truth of Christ; first knowing it to be true, and then acting upon that belief.—C. H. Spurgeon.

Faith is the act of trust by which one being, a sinner, commits himself to another being, a Saviour.—Horace Bushnell.

We have nothing to do but to receive, resting absolutely upon the

merit, power, and love of our Redeemer.—William James.

The true confidence which is faith in Christ, and the true diffidence which is utter distrust of myself — are identical.—Alexander Maclaren.

Faith is a simple trust in a personal Redeemer. The simpler our trust in Christ for all things, the surer our peace.—William Adams.

We shall never recover the true apostolic energy, and be endued with power from on high, as the first disciples were, till we recover the lost faith.—Horace Bushnell.

No man's salvation depends on his believing that he believes; but it does depend on his seeing and receiving Jesus Christ as his Saviour.—M. R. Vincent.

Faith does not first ask what the bread is made of, but eats it. It does not analyze the components of the living stream, but with joy draws water from the "wells of salvation."—J. R. Macduff.

I have taken my good deeds and bad deeds, and thrown them together into a heap, and fled from them both to Christ, and in Him I have peace.—David Dickson.

The righteousness which is by faith in Christ is a loving heart and a loving life, which every man will long to lead who believes really in Jesus Christ.—Charles Kingsley.

Faith in Christ is not an exercise of the understanding merely; it is an affection of the heart. "With the heart man believeth." To those who believe Christ is precious.—Gardiner Spring.

We are not saved by nations or by churches or by families, but as individuals, through a personal interest in a personal Saviour.—John James.

Child of God, if you would have your thought of God something beyond a cold feeling of His presence, let faith appropriate Christ.—F. W. Robertson.

Faith is the bond of union, the instrument of justification, the spring of spiritual peace and joy, the means of spiritual peace and subsistence.—John Flavel.

Saving faith is confidence in Jesus; a direct, confidential transaction with Him.—Richard Fuller.

Faith in Jesus Christ is a saving grace, whereby we receive and rest upon Him alone for salvation, as He is offered to us in the gospel.—Westminster Catechism.

Faith is the gift of God, wrought by the Holy Spirit through the means of grace, in the heart of every penitent and seeking sinner; who faithfully uses them.—Evangelical Lutheran Catechism.

We must not think that faith itself is the soul's rest; it is only the means of it. We cannot find rest in any work or duty of our own, but we may find it in Christ, whom faith apprehends for justification and salvation.—John Flavel.

Nothing but Christian faith gives to the furthest future the solidity and definiteness which it must have if it is to be a breakwater for us against the fluctuating sea of present cares and thoughts.—Alexander Maclaren.

These poor people had never heard the distinctions between intellectual faith, historic faith, and saving faith; but they did as they were taught,—reached out their dirty hands to take Christ, and attended to the washing of their hands afterwards.—W. H. Daniels.

True faith, by a mighty effort of the will, fixes its gaze on our Divine Helper, and there finds it possible and wise to lose its fears. It is madness to say, "I will not be afraid:" it is wisdom and peace to say, "I will trust and not be afraid."—Alexander Maclaren.

Faith is the vital artery of the soul. When we begin to believe, we begin to love. Faith grafts the soul into Christ, as the scion into the stock, and fetches all its nutriment from the blessed Vine.—Watson.

Faith then, in its relation to salvation, is that confidence by which we accept it as a free gift from the Saviour, and is the only possible way in which the gift of God could be appropriated.—Mark Hopkins.

The soul is the life of the body, faith is the life of the soul, and Christ is the life of faith. Justification by faith in Christ's righteousness is the golden chain which binds the Christian world in one body.—Aughey.

We believe that the very beginning and end of salvation and the sum of Christianity, consists of faith in Christ, who by His blood alone, and not by any works of ours, has put away sin, and destroyed the power of death.—Martin Luther.

The act of faith, which separates us from all men, unites us for the first time in real brotherhood; and they who, one by one, come to Jesus and meet Him alone, next find that they are come to the city of God "and to an innumerable company."—Alexander Maclaren.

Oh, my soul! why art thou so often disquieted within thee? How is it that thou hast so little faith? Wilt thou never learn that Jesus has even the least of His little boats always under His watchful eye, and all the winds and the waves obey Him?—T. L. Cuyler.

Logically, faith comes first, and love next; but in life they will spring up together in the soul; the interval which separates them is impalpable, and in every act of trust, love is present; and fundamental to every emotion of love to Christ is trust in Christ.—Alexander Maclaren.

Faith, considered as a habit, is no more precious than other gracious habits are; but considered as an instrument to receive Christ and His righteousness, it excels them all; and this instrumentality of faith is noted in the phrases, "by faith," and "through faith."—John Flavel.

Faith is trusting Jesus to lead us and going where He leads. What avails it to me to analyze Saratoga water, and to believe in its virtues? I must drink the water if I want its purifying power. And the soul that has not actually drunk of Christ can never be purged from sin.—T. L. Cuyler.

Faith has a saving connection with Christ. Christ is on the shore, so to speak, holding the rope, and as we lay hold of it with the hand of our confidence, He pulls us to shore; but all good works having no connection with Christ are drifted along down the gulf of fell despair.—C. H. Spurgeon.

The first thing in faith is knowledge. What we know we must also agree unto. What we agree unto we must rest upon alone for salvation. It will not save me to know that Christ is a Saviour; but it will save me to trust Him to be my Saviour.—C. H. Spurgeon.

Faith that trusts on Jesus alone for salvation, and not on your respectable life, and the obedience that follows Him, are the indispensable steps to salvation. You admit that you have not taken these decisive steps. Then, however near you are, you are not in Christ.—T. L. Cuyler.

Faith is the nail which fastens the soul to Christ; and love is that grace that drives the nail to the head. Faith takes hold of Him, and love helps to keep the grip. Christ dwells in the heart by faith, and He burns in the heart by love, like a fire melting the breast. Faith casts the knot, and love draws it fast.—Erskine.

Relying on the atonement which Christ has made, and desiring to be saved in no other way, I commit myself into Thy hands, O God, my Father! Take me, and do with me as Thou seest to be for Thy glory. I consecrate myself forever to Thy service, and trust for acceptance in the merits of Thy Son.—Samuel Irenæus Prime.

Faith is a Christian's right eye, without which he cannot look for Christ; right hand, without which he cannot do for Christ; it is his tongue, without which he cannot speak for Christ; it is his vital spirit, without which he cannot act for Christ.—Thomas Brooks.

To trust God, as seen in the face of His Son, and to believe that He loves us, that is faith, that is what we must do to be saved. And to love God, as seen in the face of His Son, and to seek to testify our love by our whole life,—that is Christian duty; that is all we have to do.—A. H. Boyd.

Faith from its essential nature implies the fallen state of man, while it recognizes the principles of the covenant of grace. It is itself the condition of that covenant. It is a grace which is alike distinguished from the love of angels and the faith of devils. It is peculiar to the returning sinner. None but a lost sinner needs it; none but a humbled sinner relishes it.—Gardiner Spring.

It appears to me that, even within the recollection of living men, the Christian faith has come to be less and less regarded as a commanding and mighty power from heaven, a voice of authority, a law of holy life, but more and more as an easy going guide to future enjoyment, to a universal happiness and an indiscriminate salvation.—Bishop Huntington.

If we bear an inward enmity to all sins because they are offensive to God, if we can say that it is the desire of our souls to love Christ above all things, and to be eternal debtors to free grace, reigning through His righteousness, then we may warrantably conclude, that our faith, however weak, is yet of a saving nature.—Fisher's Catechism.

If you feel sincerely sorry on account of your sins, and believe that Christ is able and willing to forgive you, the work is done. You may trust with all the confidence of a child who confesses his fault, and casts himself into his father's arms. This is faith; a simple trust in the power and willingness of the Father to forgive, for the sake of what Christ the Son has done.—Samuel Irenæus Prime.

Seek for a fresh invoice of grace. Unbelief can scoff or growl; faith is the nightingale that sings in the darkest hour. Faith can draw honey out of the rock and oil out of the flint. With Christ in possession and heaven in reversion, it marches to the time of the One-hundred-and-third Psalm over the roughest road, and against the most cutting blast.—T. L. Cuyler.

Here then is man's duty. It is to receive that free and full salvation that Christ has provided. It is to stretch forth the hand of faith, and with it take the proffered salvation. It is to cling to the cross as the only hope of everlasting life. Will you do it? Weary, working, plodding one, will you, ceasing all this vain attempt to save yourself, receive Christ, and Christ alone as your Saviour?—Henry Darling.

I expect eternal life, not as a reward of merit, but a pure act of bounty. Detesting myself in every view I can take, I fly to the righteousness and atonement of my great Redeemer for pardon and salvation; this is my only consolation and hope. "Enter not into judgment, O Lord, with Thy servant; for in Thy sight shall no flesh be justified."—Elizabeth Rowe.

If faith, then, new birth; if new birth, then sonship; if sonship, then "an heir of God, and a joint-heir with Christ." But if you have not got your foot upon the lowest round of the ladder, you will never come within sight of the blessed face of Him who stands at the top of it, and who looks down to you at this moment, saying to you, "My child, wilt thou not at this time cry unto me, 'Abba, Father?'"—Alexander Maclaren.

This saving faith is the perceiving, believing, and resting upon a fact— the atoning death of Jesus Christ. The failure to understand this is one fruitful cause of the confusion in many minds about this subject. For not unfrequently persons are looking into their own hearts, and trying to discover whether they have faith or not, instead of looking away from themselves altogether at the object of faith.—M. R. Vincent.

True faith is not only a certain knowledge, whereby I hold for truth all that God has revealed to us in His word, but also an assured confidence, which the Holy Ghost works by the gospel, in my heart; that not only to others but to me also, remission of sin, everlasting righteousness, and salvation are freely given by God merely of grace, only for the sake of Christ's merits.—Heidelberg Catechism.

Faith is reliance upon the sacrificial death of Christ for salvation and everlasting life. It is the act of the heart by which we heartily welcome Him into our souls. Faith is the primal grace. Faith is the cardinal grace. By holiness we are made like Christ; by faith we are made one with Christ; and being in Christ, we have peace.—Elihu Noble.

Faith—saving faith—whatever other definition may be framed—is best described as that act of the soul by which the whole man is given over to the guardianship of the Mediator. He who thus resigns himself to Jesus avouches two things: first, his belief that he needs a protector; secondly, his belief that Christ is just that protector which his necessities require.—Henry Melvill.

When a miner looks at the rope that is to lower him into the deep mine, he may coolly say, "I have faith in that rope as well made and strong." But when he lays hold of it, and swings down by it into the tremendous chasm, then he is believing on the rope. Then he is trusting himself to the rope. It is not a mere opinion— it is an act. The miner lets go of every thing else, and bears his whole weight on those well braided strands of hemp. Now that is faith.—T. L. Cuyler.

Faith is not the lazy notion that a man may with careless confidence throw his burden upon the Saviour and trouble himself no further, a pillow upon which he lulls his conscience to sleep, till he drops into perdition; but a living and vigorous principle, working by love, and inseparably connected with true repentance as its motive and with holy obedience as its fruits.

———

Above all things I entreat you to preserve your faith in Christ. It is my wealth in poverty, my joy in sorrow, my peace amid tumult. For all the evil I have committed, my gracious pardon; and for every effort, my exceeding great reward. I have found it to be so. I can smile with pity at the infidel whose vanity makes him dream that I should barter such a blessing for the few subtleties from the school of the cold-blooded sophists. —S. T. Coleridge.

———

Faith has in it the recognition of the certainty and the justice of a judgment that is coming down crashing on every human head; and then from the midst of these fears and sorrows and the tempest of that great darkness there rises up in the night of terrors the shining of one perhaps pale, quivering, distant, but divinely given hope, " My Saviour! My Saviour! He is righteous; He has died; He lives! I will stay no longer; I will cast myself upon Him! "—Alexander Maclaren.

———

If God made no response except to perfect faith, who could hope for help? But God has regard for beginnings, and His eye perceives greatness in the germ. The hand of the woman in the crowd trembled as it was stretched toward Jesus, and the faith back of it was superstitiously reverent, trusting in the virtue of the robe, rather than in the One who wore it; yet the genuineness of that faith, feeble though it was, triumphed in God's loving sight. Real trust is real power, though the heart and hand be feeble.—Maltbie Babcock.

———

When there is a clear reception of truth as revealed, declared, or testified to, the soul believes in that truth. There is here the idea of transfer. The truth has been received through or from an accredited witness. " It is revealed from faith to faith." When the soul, conscious of weakness or want, looks to, trusts in, or waits upon. another for help and strength,

this is resting on, relying on, acting faith on, that other for the desired blessing. And when the soul believes or acts faith into another, there is an entire self-surrender to the authority and sovereign will of that other to rule. There is here the idea of the soul going out to rest on the power, and to be subordinate to, the authority of another. Thus the Israelites " were all baptized unto or into Moses in the cloud and in the sea."—John James.

———

The natural homage which such a creature as Man bears to an infinitely wise and good God, is a firm Reliance on Him for the blessings and conveniences of life, and an habitual Trust in Him for deliverance out of all such dangers and difficulties as may befall us. The man who always lives in this disposition of mind, when he reflects upon his own weakness and imperfection, comforts himself with the contemplation of those Divine attributes which are employed for his safety and welfare. He finds his want of foresight made up by the omniscience of Him who is his support. He is not sensible of his own want of strength when he knows that his Helper is Almighty. In short, the person who has a firm Trust on the Supreme Being, is powerful in his power, wise by his wisdom, happy by his happiness.—Addison.

Faith in God

Large asking and large expectation on our part honor God.—A. L. Stone.

———

Orthodoxy can be learnt from others; living faith must be a matter of personal experience.—Büchsel.

———

Faith is letting down our nets into the transparent deeps at the Divine command, not knowing what we shall draw.—Fénelon.

———

An active faith can give thanks for a promise even though it be not yet performed, knowing that God's bonds are as good as ready money.—Matthew Henry.

———

If our faith in God is not the veriest sham, it demands, and will produce, the abandonment sometimes, the subordination always, of external helps and material good.—Alexander Maclaren.

The person who has a firm trust in the Supreme Being is powerful in his power, wise by his wisdom, happy by his happiness.—Addison.

God does not give us ready money. He issues promissory notes, and then pays them when faith presents them at the throne. Each one of us has a check-book.—T. L. Cuyler.

He that buildeth his nest upon a Divine promise shall find it abide and remain until he shall fly away to the land where promises are lost in fulfillments.—C. H. Spurgeon.

Let us aspire towards this living confidence, that it is the will of God to unfold and exalt without end the spirit that entrusts itself to Him in well-doing as to a faithful Creator.—W. E. Channing.

If we had strength and faith enough to trust ourselves entirely to God, and follow Him simply wherever He should lead us, we should have no need of any great effort of mind to reach perfection.—Fenelon.

I envy no quality of the mind or intellect in others; not genuis, power, wit, nor fancy; but, if I could choose what would be most delightful, and, I believe, most useful to me, I should prefer a firm religious belief to every other blessing.—Sir Humphry Davy.

Serve God, and God will take care of you. Submit to His will, trust in His grace, and resign yourself into His hands with the assurance that the Lord is well pleased with those "that hope in His mercy." — Gardiner Spring.

You cannot be too active as regards your own efforts; you cannot be too dependent as regards Divine grace. Do every thing as if God did nothing; depend upon God as if He did everything.—John Angel James.

The soul seeks God by faith, not by the reasonings of the mind and labored efforts, but by the drawings of love; to which inclinations God responds, and instructs the soul, which co-operates actively. God then puts the soul in a passive state where He accomplishes all, causing great progress, first by way of enjoyment, then by privation, and finally by pure love. Mme. Guyon.

Faith is a grasping of Almighty power;
The hand of man laid on the arm of God;—
The grand and blessed hour in which the
    things impossible, O Lord, through Thee.
Become the possible, O Lord, through Thee.
        —A. E. Hamilton.

The last decisive energy of a rational courage which confides in the Supreme Power is very sublime. It makes a man who intrepidly dares every thing that can oppose or attack him within the sphere of mortality—who will press toward his object while death is impending over him—who would retain his purpose unshaken amidst the ruins of the world.—Bishop R. S. Foster.

So for us, the condition and preparation on and by which we are sheltered by that great hand, is the faith that asks, and the asking of faith. We must forsake the earthly props, but we must also believingly desire to be upheld by the heavenly arms. We make God responsible for our safety when we abandon other defense, and commit ourselves to Him. —Alexander Maclaren.

God cannot lie; and if, fleeing for refuge, you have run to the hope set before you in the gospel — if, nestling in some invitation or promise of God's changeless word, you are resolved that Death and the Judgment shall find you there, you are safe. The way to honor God is to trust His truth, and hidden in His word you are also hidden in His love. Rest there. —James Hamilton.

Faith, then, generically, is confidence in a personal being. Specifically, religious faith is confidence in God, in every respect and office in which He reveals Himself. As that love of which God is the object is religious love, so that confidence in Him as a Father, a Moral Governor, a Redeemer, a Sanctifier, in all the modes of His manifestation, by which we believe whatever He says because He says it, and commit ourselves and all our interests cheerfully and entirely into His hands, is religious faith.—Mark Hopkins.

In reviewing the most mysterious doctrines of revelation, the ultimate appeal is to reason, not to determine whether she could have discovered these truths; not to declare whether, considered in themselves, they appear probable; but to decide whether it is not more reasonable to believe what God speaks than to confide in our own crude and feeble conceptions. No doctrine can be a proper object of our faith, which is not more reasonable to believe than to reject.—Alexander.

Entireness, illimitableness is indispensable to Faith. What we believe, we must believe wholly and without reserve; wherefore the only perfect and satisfying object of Faith is God. A Faith that sets bounds to itself, that will believe so much and no more, that will trust thus far and no further, is none.

There is a power in the soul, quite separate from the intellect, which sweeps away or recognizes the marvelous, by which God is felt. Faith stands serenely far above the reach of the atheism of science. It does not rest on the wonderful, but on the eternal wisdom and goodness of God. The revelation of the Son was to proclaim a Father, not a mystery. No science can sweep away the everlasting love which the heart feels, and which the intellect does not even pretend to judge or recognize.—F. W. Robertson.

Never more than to-day were needed the men of calm and resolute faith. Brothers, to your knees and to your ranks! To your knees in humblest supplication; to your ranks in steadfast bravery which no foe can cause to quail. Stand forth in courage and in gentleness for the truth which you believe to be allied to Freedom and Progress and God. Be so strong that you are not afraid to be just. Cherish a tender humanity and a catholic heart. Then take your

stand, calm and moveless as the stars. —Wm. M. Punshon.

Falsity

Splendidly mendacious.—Horace.

False in one thing, false in everything.—Law Maxim.

Had she been true,
If Heaven would make me such another world
Of one entire and perfect chrysolite,
I'd not have sold her for it.
—Shakespeare.

As false
As air, as water, as wind, as sandy earth;
As fox to lamb; as wolf to heifer's calf;
Pard to the hind, or stepdame to her son.
—Shakespeare.

He who is false to his fellow-man is also false to his Maker.—Stahl.

False as the adulterate promises of favorites in power when poor men court them.—Otway.

False-dealing travels a short road, and surely detected.—William Penn.

Stealing her soul with many vows of faith; And ne'er a true one. —Shakespeare.

False as stairs of sand.—Shakespeare.

To be true is manly, chivalrous, Christian; to be false is mean, cowardly, devilish.—Carlyle.

He seemed for dignity composed and high exploit; but all was false and hollow.—Milton.

It is far better to be deceived than undeceived by those whom we tenderly love.—Rochefoucauld.

So the false spider, when her nets are spread, deep ambushed in her silent den does lie.—Dryden.

Falsehood

Falsehood is cowardice.—Hosea Ballou.

Falsehood is so easy, truth so difficult.—George Eliot.

Falsehood is for a season.—Landor.

Falsehood always endeavors to copy the mien and attitude of truth.—Dr. Johnson.

Falsehood and death are synonymous.—Bancroft.

Past all shame, so past all truth.—Shakespeare.

O, what a goodly outside falsehood hath!—Shakespeare.

A lie never lives to be old.—Sophocles.

The crime of cowards.—Dr. Johnson.

False as the fowler's artful snare.—Smollett.

This shows that liars ought to have good memories.—Algernon Sidney.

And, after all, what is a lie? 'Tis but
The truth in masquerade. —Byron.

Who dares think one thing, and another tell,
My heart detests him as the gates of hell.
—Homer.

Falsehood and fraud shoot up in every soil
The product of all climes. Addison.

For my part, if a lie may do thee grace, I'll gild it with the happiest terms I have.—Shakespeare.

Let a man be ne'er so wise, he may be caught with sober lies.—Swift.

False modesty is the most decent of all falsehoods.—Chamfort.

Falsehoods which we spurn to-day were the truths of long ago.—Whittier.

And none speaks false, when there is none
to hear. —Beattie.

Cottages have them (falsehood and dissimulation) as well as courts, only with worse manners.—Lord Chesterfield.

For no falsehood can endure touch of celestial temper, but returns of force to its own likeness.—Milton.

There is no such thing as white lies: a lie is as black as a coal-pit, and twice as foul.—Beecher.

The dull flat falsehood serves for policy, and in the cunning, truth's itself a lie.—Pope.

Where fraud and falsehood invade society, the band presently breaks.—South.

These lies are like the father that begets them; gross as a mountain, open, palpable.—Shakespeare.

Sin has many tools, but a lie is the handle which fits them all.—O. W. Holmes.

Money and man a mutual falsehood show,
Men make false money,—money makes men
so. —Aleyn.

Dissembling profiteth nothing; a feigned countenance, and slightly forged externally, deceiveth but very few.—Seneca.

It is not without good reason said, that he who has not a good memory should never take upon him the trade of lying.—Montaigne.

Falsehood is often rocked by truth; but she soon outgrows her cradle and discards her nurse.—Colton.

It is more from carelessness about truth than from intentional lying that there is so much falsehood in the world.—Johnson.

Falsehood, like the dry-rot, flourishes the more in proportion as air and light are excluded.—Whately.

Every lie, great or small, is the brink of a precipice, the depth of which nothing but omniscience can fathom.—Reade.

I have seldom known any one who deserted truth in trifles that could be trusted in matters of importance.—Paley.

Falsehoods not only disagree with truths, but usually quarrel among themselves.—Daniel Webster.

Falsehood avails itself of haste and uncertainty.—Tacitus.

Large offers and sturdy rejections are among the most common topics of falsehood.—Johnson.

Wisdom and truth, the offspring of the sky, are immortal; while cunning and deception, the meteors of the earth, after glittering for a moment, must pass away.—Robert Hall.

To lapse in fulness is sorer than to lie for need; and falsehood is worse in kings than beggars.—Shakespeare.

A liar would be brave toward God, while he is a coward toward men; for a lie faces God, and shrinks from man.—Montaigne.

The first great requisite is absolute sincerity. Falsehood and disguise are miseries and misery-makers. — Coleridge.

If an ingenuous detestation of falsehood be but carefully and early instilled, that is the true and genuine method to obviate dishonesty.—Locke.

Every breach of veracity indicates some latent vice or some criminal intention, which the individual is ashamed to avow.—Dugald Stewart.

To tell a falsehood is like the cut of a sabre; for though the wound may heal, the scar of it will remain.—Saadi.

Dissimulation in youth is the forerunner of perfidy in old age; its first appearance is the fatal omen of growing depravity and future shame.—Blair.

Lie not, neither to thyself nor men nor God. Let mouth and heart be one—beat and speak together, and make both felt in action. It is for cowards to lie.—George Herbert.

A lie should be trampled on and extinguished wherever found. I am for fumigating the atmosphere when I suspect that falsehood, like pestilence, breathes around me.—Carlyle.

Not the least misfortune in a prominent falsehood is the fact that tradition is apt to repeat it for truth.—Hosea Ballou.

The gain of lying is nothing else but not to be trusted of any, nor to be believed when we speak the truth.—Sir Walter Raleigh.

He who tells a lie is not sensible how great a task he undertakes; for he must be forced to invent twenty more to maintain that one.—Pope.

A few men are sufficient to broach falsehoods, which are afterwards innocently diffused by successive relaters.—Johnson.

Falsehood, like poison, will generally be rejected when administered alone; but when blended with wholesome ingredients, may be swallowed unperceived.—Whately.

Falsehood is susceptible of an infinity of combinations, but truth has only one mode of being.—Rousseau.

Dissimulation is but a faint kind of policy or wisdom; for it asketh a strong wit and a strong heart to know when to tell truth, and to do it.—Bacon.

There is often seen this anomaly in women, especially in those of childish natures,—that they possess at once great promptness and unskilfulness in falsehood.—Daudet.

Round dealing is the honor of man's nature; and a mixture of falsehood is like alloy in gold and silver, which may make the metal work the better, but it embaseth it.—Bacon.

Woe to falsehood! it affords no relief to the breast, like truth; it gives us no comfort, pains him who forges it, and like an arrow directed by a god flies back and wounds the archer.—Goethe.

When a man has once forfeited the reputation of his integrity, he is set fast, and nothing will then serve his turn, neither truth nor falsehood.—Tillotson.

Nothing gives such a blow to friendship as the detecting another in an untruth. It strikes at the root of our confidence ever after.—Hazlitt.

Although the Devil be the father of lies, he seems, like other great inventors, to have lost much of his reputation by the continual improvements that have been made upon him.—Swift.

If there were no falsehood in the world, there would be no doubt; if there were no doubt, there would be no inquiry; if no inquiry, no wisdom, no knowledge, no genius.—Landor.

Habitual liars invent falsehoods not to gain any end or even to deceive their hearers, but to amuse themselves. It is partly practice and partly habit. It requires an effort in them to speak truth.—Hazlitt.

Start a lie and a truth together, like hare and hound: the lie will run fast and smooth, and no man will ever turn it aside; but at the truth most hands will fling a stone, and so hinder it for sport's sake, if they can. —Ouida.

What wit so sharp is found in age or youth,
That can distinguish truth from treachery?
Falsehood puts on the face of simple truth,
And masks i' th' habit of plain honesty,
When she in heart intends most villany.
—Mirror for Magistrates.

Falsehood is fire in stubble; it likewise turns all the light stuff around it into its own substance for a moment, one crackling blazing moment, and then dies; and all its converts are scattered in the wind, without place or evidence of their existence, as viewless as the wind which scatters them. —Coleridge.

That a lie which is half a truth is ever the
  blackest of lies;
That a lie which is all a lie may be met and
  fought with outright—
But a lie which is part a truth is a harder
  matter to fight.   —Tennyson.

Figures themselves, in their symmetrical and inexorable order, have their mistakes like words and speeches. An hour of pleasure and an hour of pain

are alike only on the dial in their numerical arrangement. Outside the dial they lie sixty times.—Méry.

Falsehood is difficult to be maintained. When the materials of a building are solid blocks of stone, very rude architecture will suffice; but a structure of rotten materials needs the most careful adjustment to make it stand at all.—Whately.

Falsehood is never so successful as when she baits her hook with truth, and no opinions so fatally mislead us as those that are not wholly wrong, as no watches so effectually deceive the wearer as those that are sometimes right.—Colton.

There is a set of harmless liars, frequently to be met with in company, who deal much in the marvellous. Their usual intention is to please and entertain; but as men are most delighted with what they conceive to be the truth, these people mistake the means of pleasing, and incur universal blame.—Hume.

How false are men, both in their heads and
  hearts;
And there is falsehood in all trades and arts.
Lawyers deceive their clients by false law;
Priests, by false gods, keep all the world in
  awe.
For their false tongues such flatt'ring knaves
  are rais'd,
For their false wit, scribblers by fools are
  prais'd.   —Crown.

Let falsehood be a stranger to thy lips;
Shame on the policy that first began
To tamper with the heart to hide its thoughts!
And doubly shame on that inglorious tongue,
That sold its honesty and told a lie.
—Havard.

Whatever convenience may be thought to be in falsehood and dissimulation, it is soon over; but the inconvenience of it is perpetual, because it brings a man under everlasting jealousy and suspicion, so that he is not believed when he speaks the truth, nor trusted when perhaps he means honestly.—Tillotson.

Falsehood, like a drawing in perspective, will not bear to be examined in every point of view, because it is a good imitation of truth, as a perspective is of the reality, only in one. But truth, like that reality of which the perspective is the representation, will bear to be scrutinized in all points of view, and though examined under every situation, is one and the same.—Colton.

Fame

Fame is the perfume of heroic deeds. —Socrates.

The breath of popular applause.— Herrick.

Fame,—a flower upon a dead man's heart.—Motherwell.

A woman's fame is the tomb of her happiness.—L. E. Landon.

The greatest can but blaze and pass away.—Pope.

Fame,—next grandest word to God! —Alexander Smith.

To many fame comes too late.— Camoens.

She comes unlooked for if she comes at all.—Pope.

Fame is no plant that grows on mortal soil.—Milton.

With fame, in just proportion, envy grows.—Young.

Raised by fortune to a ridiculous visibility.—Grattan.

Fame! that common crier.—J. Q. Adams.

Grant me honest fame or grant me none.—Pope.

Short is my date, but deathless my renown.—Homer.

Deathless laurel is the victor's due. —Dryden.

He lives in fame, that died in virtue's cause.—Shakespeare.

Fame sometimes hath created something of nothing.—Thomas Fuller.

I awoke one morning and found myself famous.—Byron.

Fame, the sovereign deity of proud ambition.—Sheridan.

To myself alone do I owe my fame. —Corneille.

Song forbids victorious deeds to die. —Schiller.

I would give all my fame for a pot of ale and safety.—Shakespeare.

Let fame, that all hunt after in their lives, Live register'd upon our brazen tombs.
—Shakespeare.

Fame is the thirst of youth.—Byron.

And yet, after all, what is posthumous fame? Altogether vanity.— Antoninus.

Even the best things are not equal to their fame.—Thoreau.

Celebrity sells dearly what we think she gives.—Emile Souvestre.

Money will buy money's worth; but the thing men call fame, what is it?— Carlyle.

Fame has eagle wings, and yet she mounts not so high as man's desires.— Beaconsfield.

Fame is but the breath of the people, and that often unwholesome.— Rousseau.

Fame must necessarily be the portion of but few.—Robert Hall.

None despise fame more heartily than those who have no possible claim to it.—J. Petit-Senn.

How idle a boast, after all, is the immortality of a name!—Washington Irving.

Many have lived on a pedestal who will never have a statue when dead.— Béranger.

Fame can never make us lie down contentedly on a death-bed.—Pope.

What is the end of fame? it is but to fill a certain portion of uncertain paper.—Byron.

Who despises fame will soon renounce the virtues that deserve it.—Mallet.

Never get a reputation for a small perfection if you are trying for fame in a loftier area.—Bulwer-Lytton.

If fame is only to come after death, I am in no hurry for it.—Martial.

The way to fame is like the way to heaven, through much tribulation.—Steele.

A few words upon a tombstone, and the truth of those not to be depended on.—Bovee.

No true and permanent fame can be founded, except in labors which promote the happiness of mankind.—Charles Sumner.

The love of fame is the last weakness which even the wise resign.—Tacitus.

The love of fame gives an immense stimulus.—Ovid.

What is fame? a fancied life in others' breath.—Pope.

He that will sell his fame will also sell the public interest.—Solon.

To have fame follow us is well, but it is not a desirable avant-courier.—Balzac.

Rash combat oft immortalizes man. If he should fall, he is renowned in song.—Goethe.

What a heavy burden is a name that has become too soon famous!—Voltaire.

Though fame is smoke, its fumes are frankincense to human thoughts.—Byron.

Better than fame is still the wish for fame, the constant training for a glorious strife.—Bulwer-Lytton.

It often happens that those of whom we speak least on earth are best known in heaven.—N. Caussin.

Unlike the sun, intellectual luminaries shine brightest after they set.—Colton.

Celebrity is the chastisement of merit and the punishment of talent.—Chamfort.

Fame is the shame of immortality, and is itself a shadow.—Young.

No one would ever meet death in defence of his country without the hope of immortality.—Cicero.

Fame comes only when deserved, and then is as inevitable as destiny, for it is destiny.—Longfellow.

What shall I do to be forever known,
And make the age to come my own?
     —Cowley.

Seven cities warr'd for Homer being dead,
Who living had no roofe to shroud his
  head.   —Thos. Heywood.

He shines in the second rank, who is eclipsed in the first.—Voltaire.

She is best who is least spoken of among men, whether for good or evil.—Pericles.

Many actions calculated to procure fame are not conducive to ultimate happiness.—Addison.

I have learned to prize the quiet, lightning deed, not the applauding thunder at its heels that men call fame.—A. Smith.

Men have a solicitude about fame; and the greater share they have of it, the more afraid they are of losing it.—Johnson.

The temple of fame stands upon the grave; the flame that burns upon its altars is kindled from the ashes of dead men.—Hazlitt.

The fame of great men ought always to be estimated by the means used to acquire it.—La Rochefoucauld.

Naked glory is the true and honorable recompense of gallant actions.—Le Sage.

He that would have his virtue published, is not the servant of virtue, but glory.—Ben Jonson.

The love of letters is the forlorn hope of the man of letters. His ruling passion is the love of fame.—Hazlitt.

Let humble Allen, with an awkward shame,
Do good by stealth, and blush to find it
Fame.   —Pope.

I'll make thee glorious by my pen
And famous by my sword.
                    —Marquis of Montrose.

Fame lulls the fever of the soul, and makes
Us feel that we have grasp'd an immortality.   —Joaquin Miller.

Fame! it is the flower of a day, that dies when the next sun rises.—Ouida.

Men's evil manners live in brass; their virtues we write in water.—Shakespeare.

Only the actions of the just smell sweet and blossom in the dust.—James Shirley.

Death makes no conquest of this conqueror;
For now he lives in Fame, though not in
life.   —Shakespeare.

The drying up a single tear has more
Of honest fame than shedding seas of gore.
                             —Byron.

Mere family never made a man great. Thought and deed, not pedigree, are the passports to enduring fame.—Skobeleff.

Avoid shame, but do not seek glory: nothing so expensive as glory.—Sydney Smith.

What rage for fame attends both great and
    small!
Better be d—n'd than mentioned not at all.
                        —John Wolcott.

An enduring fame is one stamped by the judgment of the future,—that future which dispels illusions, and smashes idols into dust.—Gladstone.

The way to fame is like the way to heaven—through much tribulation.—Sterne.

No true and permanent Fame can be founded except in labors which promote the happiness of mankind.—Charles Sumner.

Ah! who can tell how hard it is to climb
The steep where Fame's proud temple shines
    afar?   —Beattie.

Sloth views the towers of fame with envious
    eyes,
Desirous still, still impotent to rise.
                          —Shenstone.

Go where glory waits thee;
But while fame elates thee,
Oh! still remember me.   —Moore.

In fame's temple there is always a niche to be found for rich dunces, importunate scoundrels, or successful butchers of the human race.—Zimmermann.

It deserves with characters of brass,
A forted residence, 'gainst the tooth of time
And razure of oblivion. —Shakespeare.

He left a name at which the world grew
    pale,
To point a moral, or adorn a tale.
                        —Dr. Johnson.

If you would not be forgotten as soon as you are dead, either write things worth reading or do things worth writing.—Franklin.

Men's fame is like their hair, which grows after they are dead, and with just as little use to them.—George Villiers.

Of all the rewards of virtue, . . . the most splendid is fame, for it is fame alone that can offer us the memory of posterity.—Cicero.

He who would acquire fame must not show himself afraid of censure. The dread of censure is the death of genius.—Simms.

As the pearl ripens in the obscurity of its shell, so ripens in the tomb all the fame that is truly precious.—Landor.

Men think highly of those who rise rapidly in the world; whereas nothing rises quicker than dust, straw, and feathers.—Hare.

Fame and admiration weigh not a feather in the scale against friendship and love, for the heart languishes all the same.—George Sand.

The thirst after fame is greater than that after virtue; for who embraces virtue if you take away its rewards?—Juvenal.

It is pleasing to be pointed at with the finger and to have it said, "There goes the man."—Persius.

What is fame? The advantage of being known by people of whom you yourself know nothing, and for whom you care as little.—Stanislaus.

Time magnifies everything after death; a man's fame is increased as it passes from mouth to mouth after his burial.—Propertius.

The splendors that belong unto the fame of earth are but a wind, that in the same direction lasts not long.—Dante.

Fame is the echo of actions, resounding them to the world, save that the echo repeats only the last part; but fame relates all, and often more than all.—Thomas Fuller.

The aspiring youth that fired the Ephesian dome outlives in fame the pious fool that raised it.—Colley Cibber.

Fame, they tell you, is air; but without air there is no life for any; without fame there is none for the best.—Landor.

Fame usually comes to those who are thinking about something else,—very rarely to those who say to themselves, "Go to, now let us be a celebrated individual!"—Holmes.

Your fame is as the grass, whose hue comes and goes, and His might withers it by whose power it sprang from the lap of the earth.—Dante.

Fame, we may understand, is no sure test of merit, but only a probability of such: it is an accident, not a property of a man.—Carlyle.

Were not this desire of fame very strong, the difficulty of obtaining it, and the danger of losing it when obtained, would be sufficient to deter a man from so vain a pursuit.—Addison.

Then shall our names
Familiar in his mouth as household words,
  *   *   *   *   *
Be in their flowing cups freshly remembered.
      —Shakespeare.

Scarcely two hundred years back can Fame recollect articulately at all; and there she but maunders and mumbles.—Carlyle.

If parts allure thee, think how Bacon shined,
The wisest, brightest, meanest of mankind;
Or, ravished with the whistling of a name,
See Cromwell, damned to everlasting fame!
      —Pope.

What of them is left, to tell
  Where they lie, and how they fell?
Not a stone on their turf, nor a bone in their graves:
But they live in the Verse that immortally saves.
      —Byron.

And glory long has made the sages smile;
  'Tis something, nothing, words, illusion, wind—
Depending more upon the historian's style
Than on the name a person leaves behind.
      —Byron.

Of all the possessions of this life fame is the noblest; when the body has sunk into the dust the great name still lives.—Schiller.

Fame may be compared to a scold: the best way to silence her is to let her alone, and she will at last be out of breath in blowing her own trumpet.—Fuller.

Of all the phantoms fleeting in the mist
Of time, though meagre all and ghostly thin;
Most unsubstantial, unessential shade
Was earthly fame.   —Pollok.

Be not liquorish after fame, found by experience to carry a trumpet, that doth for the most part congregate more enemies than friends.—Osborn.

Sound, sound the clarion, fill the fife!
To all the sensual world proclaim,
One crowded hour of glorious life
Is worth an age without a name.
—Scott.

Fame, as a river, is narrowest where it is bred, and broadest afar off; so exemplary writers depend not upon the gratitude of the world.—Sir W. Davenant.

The love of fame is a passion natural and universal, which no man, however high or mean, however wise or ignorant, was yet able to despise.—Dr. Johnson.

None of the projects or designs which exercise the mind of man are equally subject to obstructions and disappointments with the pursuit of fame.—Dr. Johnson.

In the career of female fame, there are few prizes to be obtained which can vie with the obscure state of a beloved wife or a happy mother.—Jane Porter.

The Duke of Wellington brought to the post of first minister immortal fame; a quality of success which would almost seem to include all others.—Benj. Disraeli.

Fame is a shuttlecock. If it be struck only at one end of a room it will soon fall to the floor. To keep it up, it must be struck at both ends.—Johnson.

Fame is not won on downy plumes nor under canopies; the man who consumes his days without obtaining it leaves such mark of himself on earth as smoke in air or foam on water.—Dante.

The fame which bids fair to live the longest resembles that which Horace attributes to Marcellus, whose progress he compares to the silent, imperceptible growth of• a tree.—W. B. Clulow.

When Fame stands by us all alone, she is an angel clad in light and strength; but when Love touches her she drops her sword, and fades away, ghostlike and ashamed.—Ouida.

Fame is an undertaker that pays but little attention to the living, but bedizens the dead, furnishes out their funerals, and follows them to the grave.—Colton.

Fame is the inheritance not of the dead, but of the living. It is we who look back with lofty pride to the great names of antiquity, who drink of that flood of glory as of a river, and refresh our wings in it for future flight.—Hazlitt.

Valor and power may gain a lasting memory, but where are they when the brave and mighty are departed? Their effects may remain, but they live not in them any more than the fire in the work of the potter.—Hartley Coleridge.

The only pleasure of fame is that it proves the way to pleasure; and the more intellectual our pleasure, the better for the pleasure and for us too.—Byron.

There is no employment in the world so laborious as that of making to one's self a great name; life ends before one has scarcely made the first rough draught of his work.—Bruyère.

It is more reasonable to wish for reputation while it may be enjoyed, as Anacreon calls upon his companions to give him for present use the wine and garlands which they propose to bestow upon his tomb.—Dr. Johnson.

Our admiration of a famous man lessens upon our nearer acquaintance with him; and we seldom hear of a celebrated person without a catalogue of some notorious weaknesses and infirmities.—Addison.

It is not without reason that fame is awarded only after death. The cloud-dust of notoriety which follows and envelops the men who drive with the wind bewilders contemporary judgment.—Lowell.

Fame confers a rank above that of gentleman and of kings. As soon as she issues her patent of nobility, it matters not a straw whether the recipient be the son of a Bourbon or of a tallow-chandler.—Bulwer-Lytton.

The desire of posthumous fame and the dread of posthumous reproach and execration are feelings from the influence of which scarcely any man is perfectly free, and which in many men are powerful and constant motives of action.—Macaulay.

If opinion hath lighted the lamp of thy name, endeavor to encourage it with thy own oil, lest it go out and stink; the chronical disease of popularity is shame; if thou be once up, beware; from fame to infamy is a beaten road.—Quarles.

Fame is a good so wholly foreign to our natures that we have no faculty in the soul adapted to it, nor any organ in the body to relish it; an object of desire placed out of the possibility of fruition.—Addison.

Those who despise fame seldom deserve it. We are apt to undervalue the purchase we cannot reach, to conceal our poverty the better. It is a spark which kindles upon the best fuel, and burns brightest in the bravest breast.—Jeremy Collier.

Fame often rests at first upon something accidental, and often, too, is swept away, or for a time removed; but neither genius nor glory is conferred at once, nor do they glimmer and fall, like drops in a grotto, at a shout.—Landor.

Common fame is the only liar that deserveth to have some respect still reserved to it; though she telleth many an untruth, she often hits right, and most especially when she speaketh ill of men.—Saville.

It is the penalty of fame that a man must ever keep rising. "Get a reputation and then go to bed," is the absurdest of all maxims. "Keep up a reputation or go to bed," would be nearer the truth.—Chapin.

Among the writers of all ages, some deserve fame, and have it; others neither have nor deserve it; some have it, not deserving it; others, though deserving it, yet totally miss it, or have it not equal to their deserts.—Milton.

Time has a doomsday book, upon whose pages he is continually recording illustrious names. But as often as a new name is written there, an old one disappears. Only a few stand in illuminated characters never to be effaced.—Longfellow.

The best-concerted schemes men lay for fame.
Die fast away; only themselves die faster.
The far-fam'd sculptor, and the laurell'd bard,
Those bold insurancers of deathless fame,
Supply their little feeble aids in vain.
      —Blair.

What a wretched thing is all fame! A renown of the highest sort endures, say, for two thousand years. And then? Why, then, a fathomless eternity swallows it. Work for eternity: not the meagre rhetorical eternity of the periodical critics, but for the real eternity, wherein dwelleth the Divine.—Carlyle.

How idle a boast, after all, is the immortality of a name! Time is ever silently turning over his pages; we are too much engrossed by the story of the present to think of the character and anecdotes that gave interest to the past; and each age is a volume thrown aside and forgotten.—Washington Irving.

Thy fanes, thy temple, to the surface bow,
Commingling slowly with heroic earth,
Broke by the share of every rustic plough:
So perish monuments of mortal Birth,
To perish all in turn, save well-recorded Worth.
      —Byron.

Fame has no necessary conjunction with praise; it may exist without the breath of a word; it is a recognition of excellence which must be felt, but need not be spoken. Even the envious must feel it,—feel it, and hate in silence.—Washington Allston.

The love of fame is too high and delicate a feeling in the mind to be mixed up with realities,—it is a solitary abstraction. * * A name "fast anchored in the deep abyss of time" is like a star twinkling in the firmament, cold, silent, distant, but eternal and sublime; and our transmitting one to posterity is as if we should con-

template our translation to the skies.
—Hazlitt.

Fame is a revenue payable only to
our ghosts; and to deny ourselves all
present satisfaction, or to expose ourselves to so much hazard for this, were
as great madness as to starve ourselves, or fight desperately for food,
to be laid on our tombs after our
death.—Mackenzie.

Fame is like a river, that bareth up
things light and swollen, and drowns
things weighty and solid; but if persons of quality and judgment concur,
then it filleth all round about, and will
not easily away; for the odors of oint-
ments are more durable than those of
flowers.—Bacon.

Popular glory is a perfect coquette;
her lovers must toil, feel every inquietude, indulge every caprice, and
perhaps at last be jilted into the bargain. True glory, on the other hand,
resembles a woman of sense; her admirers must play no tricks. They feel
no great anxiety, for they are sure in
the end of being rewarded in proportion to their merit.—Goldsmith.

An earthly immortality belongs to a
great and good character. History
embalms it; it lives in its moral influence, in its authority, in its example,
in the memory of the words and deeds
in which it was manifested; and as
every age adds to the illustrations of
its efficacy, it may chance to be the
best understood by a remote posterity.
—Edward Everett.

To some characters, fame is like an
intoxicating cup placed to the lips,—
they do well to turn away from it who
fear it will turn their heads. But to
others fame is "love disguised," the
love that answers to love in its widest,
most exalted sense.—Mrs. Jameson.

Posthumous fame is a plant of
tardy growth, for our body must be the
seed of it; or we may liken it to a
torch, which nothing but the last spark
of life can light up; or we may compare it to the trumpet of the archangel, for it is blown over the dead;
but unlike that awful blast, it is of

earth, not of heaven, and can neither
rouse nor raise us.—Colton.

It is a very indiscreet and troublesome ambition which cares so much
about fame; about what the world
says of us; to be always looking in the
faces of others for approval; to be always anxious about the effect of what
we do or say; to be always shouting,
to hear the echoes of our own voices.—
Longfellow.

What so foolish as the chase of fame?
How vain the prize! how impotent our aim!
For what are men who grasp at praise sub-
    lime,
But bubbles on the rapid stream of time,
That rise and fall, that swell, and are no
    more,
Born and forgot, ten thousand in an hour.
    —Young.

Reputation being essentially contemporaneous, is always at the mercy of
the Envious and the Ignorant. But
Fame, whose very birth is posthumous, and which is only known to exist
by the echo of its footsteps through
congenial minds, can neither be increased nor diminished by any degree
of wilfulness.—Mrs. Jameson.

A man who cannot win fame in his
own age will have a very small chance
of winning it from posterity. True,
there are some half-dozen exceptions
to this truth among millions of
myriads that attest it; but what man
of common sense would invest any
large amount of hope in so unpromis-
ing a lottery?—Bulwer-Lytton.

After upwards of two thousand
years Epicurus has been exonerated
from the reproach that the doctrines
of his philosophy recommended the
pleasures of sensuality and voluptuousness as the chief good. Calumny may
rest on genius a considerable part of a
world's duration; what then is the
value of fame?—W. B. Clulow.

Happy indeed the poet of whom, like
Orpheus, nothing is known but an
immortal name! Happy next, perhaps, the poet of whom, like Homer,
nothing is known but the immortal
works. The more the merely human
part of the poet remains a mystery,

the more willing is the reverence given to his divine mission.—Bulwer-Lytton.

The triumphs of the warrior are bounded by the narrow theater of his own age, but those of a Scott or a Shakespeare will be renewed with greater luster in ages yet unborn, when the victorious chieftain shall be forgotten, or shall live only in the song of the minstrel and the page of the chronicler.—Prescott.

Milton neither 'aspired to present fame, nor even expected it; but (to use his own words) his high ambition was "to leave something so written to after ages, that they should not willingly let it die." And Cato finely observed, he would much rather that posterity should inquire why no statues were erected to him, than why they were.—Colton.

To be read by bare inscriptions, like many in Grüter,—to hope for eternity by enigmatical epithets or first letters of our names—to be studied by antiquarians who we were, and have new names given us like many of the mummies, are cold consolation unto the students of perpetuity, even by everlasting languages.—T. Hughes.

Live for something! Do good and leave behind you a monument of virtue that the storm of time can never destroy. Write your name in kindness, love, and mercy on the hearts of the thousands you come in contact with, year by year, and you will never be forgotten. Your name, your deeds, will be as legible on the hearts you leave behind, as the stars on the brow of evening. Good deeds will shine as the stars of heaven.—Chalmers.

Vain empty words
Of honour, glory, and immortal fame,
Can these recall the spirit from its place,
Or re-inspire the breathless clay with life?
What tho' your fame with all its thousand
    trumpets,
Sound o'er the sepulchres, will that awake
The sleeping dead.   —Sewell.

One might feel indignant at the injustice which deals out what is called fame with so unequal a hand, were it not for the reflection that men who are competent to add to the intel-

lectual wealth of the world, and enlarge the domain of knowledge, have learned to take popular applause at its true value, and to find in the faithful discharge of honorable duty a satisfaction which is its own reward.—George S. Hillard.

Of present fame think little and of future less; the praises that we receive after we are buried, like the posies that are strewn over our grave, may be gratifying to the living, but they are nothing to the dead: the dead are gone either to a place where they hear them not, or where, if they do, they will despise them.—Colton.

Fame is the spur that the clear spirit doth
    raise
(That last infirmity of noble mind)
To scorn delights and live laborious days;
But the fair guerdon when we hope to find,
And think to burst out into sudden blaze,
Comes the blind Fury with the abhorred
    shears,
And slits the thin-spun life.   —Milton.

A man's heart must be very frivolous if the possession of fame rewards the labor to attain it. For the worst of reputation is that it is not palpable or present,—we do not feel or see or taste it. People praise us behind our backs, but we hear them not; few before our faces, and who is not suspicious of the truth of such praise?—Bulwer-Lytton.

Lives of great men all remind us
  We can make our lives sublime,
And departing, leave behind us
  Footprints on the sands of time;—
Footprints, that perhaps another,
  Sailing o'er life's solemn main,
A forlorn and shipwreck'd brother,
  Seeing, shall take heart again.
    —Longfellow.

The highest greatness, surviving time and stone, is that which proceeds from the soul of man. Monarchs and cabinets, generals and admirals, with the pomp of court and the circumstance of war, in the lapse of time disappear from sight; but the pioneers of truth, though poor and lowly, especially those whose example elevates human nature, and teaches the rights of man, so that "a government of the people, by the people, for the people, may not perish from the earth;" such a harbinger can never be forgotten, and their renown spreads co-extensive with the cause they served so well.—Charles Sumner.

To be rich, to be famous? do these profit a year hence, when other names sound louder than yours, when you lie hidden away under ground, along with the idle titles engraven on your coffin? But only true love lives after you, follows your memory with secret blessings or pervades you, and intercedes for you. *Non omnis moriar*, if, dying, I yet live in a tender heart or two; nor am lost and hopeless, living, if a sainted departed soul still loves and prays for me.—Thackeray.

Familiarity

Be thou familiar, but by no means vulgar.—Shakespeare.

All objects lose by too familiar a view.—Dryden.

Familiarity and satiety are twins. —Mme. Deluzy.

Make not thy friends too cheap to thee, nor thyself to thy friend.— Fuller.

The confidant of my vices is my master, though he were my valet.— Goethe.

Beauty soons grows familiar to the lover, fades in his eyes, and palls upon the sense.—Addison.

Though familiarity may not breed contempt, it takes off the edge of admiration.—Hazlitt.

A woman who throws herself at a man's head will soon find her place at his feet.—Louis Desnoyers.

Familiarity is a magician that is cruel to beauty, but kind to ugliness. —Ouida.

Familiarity is the most destructive of all iconoclasts.—Mme. de Genlis.

The ways suited to confidence are familiar to me, but not those that are suited to familiarity.—Joubert.

Familiarities are the aphides that imperceptibly suck out the juice intended for the germ of love.—Landor.

Be not too familiar with thy servants; at first it may beget love, but in the end it will breed contempt.— Fuller.

Familiarity is a suspension of almost all the laws of civility, which libertinism has introduced into society under the notion of ease.—Rochefoucauld.

Familiarity so dulls the edge of perception as to make us least acquainted with things forming part of our daily life.—Julia Ward Howe.

The living together for three long, rainy days in the country has done more to dispel love than all the perfidies in love that have ever been committed.—Arthur Helps.

An idol may be undeified by many accidental causes. Marriage, in particular, is a kind of counter apotheosis, as a deification inverted. When a man becomes familiar with his goddess she quickly sinks into a woman. —Addison.

A man does not wonder at what he sees frequently, even though he be ignorant of the reason. If anything happens which he has not seen before, he calls it a prodigy.—Cicero.

The man that hails you Tom or Jack,
And proves by thumps upon your back
How he esteems your merit,
Is such a friend that one had need
Be very much his friend indeed
To pardon or to bear it.   —Cowper.

Famine
Famine ends famine.—Ben Jonson.

This famine has a sharp and meagre face;
'Tis death in an undress of skin and bone,
Where age and youth, their landmark, ta'en away,
Look all one common sorrow. —Dryden.

Fanaticism
Fanaticism is governed by imagination rather than judgment.—Mrs. Stowe.

The child of false zeal.—Chapin.

The false fire of an overheated mind.—Cowper.

Reason is not compatible with zeal run mad.—South.

A fanatic, either religious or political, is the subject of strong delusions. —Whately.

The downright fanatic is nearer to the heart of things than the cool and slippery disputant.—Chapin.

If you see one cold and vehement at the same time, set him down for a fanatic.—Lavater.

That can never be reasoned down which was not reasoned up.—Fisher Ames.

Fanaticism is the child of false zeal and of superstition, the father of intolerance and of persecution.—J. W. Fletcher.

Fanaticism is such an overwhelming impression of the ideas relating to the future world as disqualifies for the duties of life.—Robert Hall.

The blind fanaticism of one foolish honest man may cause more evil than the united efforts of twenty rogues.— Baron de Grimm.

What is fanaticism to-day is the fashionable creed to-morrow, and trite as the multiplication table a week after.—Wendell Phillips.

An uncontrolled imagination may become as surely intoxicated by over-indulgence as a toper may do bodily with strong drink.—Haliburton.

Fanaticism, to which men are so much inclined, has always served not only to render them more brutalized but more wicked.—Voltaire.

Though fanaticism drinks at many founts, its predisposing cause is mostly the subject of an invisible futurity.— Atterbury.

There is such a delusion as evinces itself in cool vehemence; and it is the most dangerous of all expressions of fanaticism.—W. B. Clulow.

Earnestness is good; it means business. But fanaticism overdoes, and is consequently reactionary.—Spurgeon.

E. P. Whipple calls fanaticism "religion caricatured," which is a full definition in a word.—James Parton.

There is no doubt that religious fanatics have done more to prejudice the cause they affect to advocate than have its opponents.—Hosea Ballou.

Painful and corporeal punishments should never be applied to fanaticism; for, being founded on pride, it glories in persecution.—Beccaria.

Fanaticism is a fire, which heats the mind indeed, but heats without purifying. It stimulates and ferments all the passions; but it rectifies none of them.—Warburton.

To conquer fanaticism, you must tolerate it; the shuttlecock of religious difference soon falls to the ground when there are no battledoors to beat it backward and forward.— Chatfield.

Of all things, wisdom is the most terrified with epidemical fanaticism, because, of all enemies, it is that against which she is the least able to furnish any kind of resource.—Burke.

Fanaticism, or, to call it by its milder name, enthusiasm, is only powerful and active so long as it is aggressive. Establish it firmly in power, and it becomes conservatism, whether it will or no.—Lowell.

Fanaticism is an inflamed state of the passions; and nothing that is violent will last long. The vicissitudes of the world and the business of life are admirably adapted to abate the excesses of religious enthusiasm.— Robert Hall.

Everybody knows that fanaticism is religion caricatured; bears, indeed, about the same relation to it that a monkey bears to a man; yet, with many, contempt of fanaticism is received as a sure sign of hostility to religion.—Whipple.

There is no cruelty so inexorable and unrelenting as that which proceeds from a bigoted and presumptuous supposition of doing service to God. The victim of the fanatical persecutor will find that the stronger the motives he can urge for mercy are, the weaker will be his chance for obtaining it, for the merit of his destruction will be supposed to rise in value in proportion as it is effected at the expense of every feeling both of justice and of humanity.—Colton.

Fancy

Fancy light from fancy caught.—Tennyson.

Every fancy you consult, consult your purse.—Franklin.

Fancy tortures more people than does reality.—Ouida.

In maiden meditation, fancy free.—Shakespeare.

Fancy, like the finger of a clock,
Runs the great circuit, and is still at home.
—Cowper.

All power of fancy over reason is a degree of insanity.—Dr. Johnson.

False fancy brings real misery.—Schiller.

Fancy sets the value on the gifts of fortune.—Rochefoucauld.

Do not let fancy outrun your means. —Franklin.

Fancy and pride seeks things at vast expense.—Young.

Who does not know the bent of woman's fancy?—Spenser.

Ever let the fancy roam; pleasure never is at home.—Keats.

Mine eyes he closed, but open left the cell of Fancy, my immortal sight. —Milton.

The devious paths where wanton fancy leads.—Rowe.

Fancy brings us as many vain hopes as idle fears.—Humboldt.

All impediments in fancy's course are motives of more fancy.—Shakespeare.

Pacing through the forest,
Chewing the cud of sweet and bitter fancy.
—Shakespeare.

Woe to the youth whom fancy gains
Winning from reason's hand the reins.
—Scott.

Two meanings have our lightest fantasies,
One of the flesh, and of the spirit one.
—James Russell Lowell.

So full of shapes is fancy,
That it alone is high fantastical.
—Shakespeare.

When at the close of each sad, sorrowing day,
Fancy restores what vengeance snatch'd away.
—Pope.

A fretful fancy is constantly flinging its possessor into gratuitous tophets.—W. R. Alger.

Fancy borrows much from memory, and so looks back to the past.—Ruffini.

Fancy runs most furiously when a guilty conscience drives it.—Fuller.

Nothing is so atrocious as fancy without taste.—Goethe.

She's all my fancy painted her,
She's lovely, she's divine.
—Wm. Mee.

The earth hath bubbles, as the water has.
And these are of them. —Shakespeare.

Fancy is imagination in her youth and adolescence. Fancy is always excursive; imagination, not seldom, is sedate.—Landor.

Bright-eyed fancy, hovering o'er,
Scatters from her pictured urn,
Thoughts that breathe, and words that burn.
—Gray.

'Tis not necessity, but opinion, that makes men miserable; and when we come to be fancy-sick, there's no cure.—L'Estrange.

Why will any man be so impertinently officious as to tell me all this is only fancy? If it is a dream, let me enjoy it.—Addison.

In the loss of an object we do not proportion our grief to the real value it bears, but to the value our fancies set upon it.—Addison.

Fancy and humour, early and constantly indulged in, may expect an old age overrun with follies.—Watts.

Fancy is a fairy, that can hear
Ever, the melody of nature's voice,
And see all lovely visions that she will.
—Mrs. Osgood.

Sentiment is intellectualized emotion, emotion precipitated, as it were, in pretty crystals by the fancy.—Lowell.

Tell me where is fancy bred,
Or in the heart, or in the head?
How begot, how nourished?
—Shakespeare.

The mere reality of life would be inconceivably poor without the charm of fancy, which brings in its bosom, no doubt, as many vain fears as idle hopes, but lends much oftener to the illusions it calls up a gay flattering hue than one which inspires terror.—Wilhelm von Humboldt.

Fancy restrained may be compared to a fountain, which plays highest by diminishing the aperture.—Goldsmith.

Our fancies are more giddy and unfirm, more longing, wavering, sooner lost and won, than women's are.—Shakespeare.

Fancy rules over two thirds of the universe, the past and the future, while reality is confined to the present.—Richter.

Every fancy that we would substitute for a reality is, if we saw aright, and saw the whole, not only false, but every way less beautiful and excellent than that which we sacrifice to it.—Sterling.

It is the fancy, not the reason of things, that makes us so uneasy. It is not the place, nor the condition, but the mind alone, that can make anybody happy or miserable.—L'Estrange.

If ever (as that ever may be near) you meet in some fresh cheek the power of fancy, then shall you know the wounds invisible that love's keen arrows make.—Shakespeare.

Fancy, when once brought into religion, knows not where to stop. It is like one of those fiends in old stories which any one could raise, but which, when raised, could never be kept within the magic circle.—Whately.

When my way is too rough for my feet, or too steep for my strength, I get off it to some smooth velvet path which fancy has scattered over with rosebuds of delights; and, having taken a few turns in it, come back strengthened and refreshed.—Sterne.

That queen of error, whom we call fancy and opinion, is the more deceitful because she does not always deceive. She would be the infallible rule of truth if she were the infallible rule of falsehood; but being only most frequently in error, she gives no evidence of her real quality, for she marks with the same character both that which is true and that which is false.—Pascal.

A confused mass of thoughts, tumbling over one another in the dark; when the fancy was yet in its first work, moving the sleeping images of things towards the light, there to be distinguished and then either chosen or rejected by the judgment.—Dryden.

Fancy has an extensive influence in morals. Some of the most powerful and dangerous feelings in nature, as those of ambition and envy, derive their principal nourishment from a cause apparently so trivial. Its effect on the common affairs of life is greater than might be supposed.

Naked reality would scarcely keep the world in motion.—W. B. Clulow.

The difference is as great between
The optics seeing as the objects seen.
All manners take a tincture from our own;
Or come discolor'd through our passions shown;
Or fancy's beam enlarges, multiplies,
Contracts, inverts, and gives ten thousand dyes.   —Pope.

Most marvellous and enviable is that fecundity of fancy which can adorn whatever it touches, which can invest naked fact and dry reasoning with unlooked-for beauty, make flowerets bloom even on the brow of the precipice, and, when nothing better can be had, can turn the very substance of rock itself into moss and lichens. This faculty is incomparably the most important for the vivid and attractive exhibition of truth to the minds of men.—Fuller.

Fancy, an animal faculty, is very different from imagination, which is intellectual. The former is passive; but the latter is active and creative. Children, the weak minded, and the timid, are full of fancy. Men and women of intellect, of great intellect, are alone possessed of great imagination.—Joubert.

Farewell

The bitter word which closed all earthly friendships, and finished every feast of love,—farewell.—Pollok.

Farewell! "But not for ever."—Cowper.

Sweets to the sweet; farewell!—Shakespeare.

Farewell, happy fields,
Where joy forever dwells; hail, horrors!
    —Milton.

So sweetly she bade me adieu,
I thought that she bade me return.
    —Shenstone.

To all, to each, a fair good-night,
And pleasing dreams, and slumbers light.
    —Scott.

Fare thee well! and if for ever,
Still for ever, fare thee well.
    —Byron.

Farewell! if ever fondest prayer
For other's weal availed on high,
Mine will not all be lost in air
But waft thy name beyond the sky.
    —Byron.

Farewell the tranquil mind! farewell content!
Farewell the plumed troops, and the big wars
That make ambition virtue.
    —Shakespeare.

Fare thee well;
The elements be kind to thee, and make
Thy spirits all of comfort! —Shakespeare.

Farewell! a word that must be, and hath been—
A sound which makes us linger;—yet—farewell.
    —Byron.

Farewell!
For in that word,—that fatal word,—howe'er
We promise—hope—believe,—there breathes despair.
    —Byron.

One kind kiss before we part,
Drop a tear, and bid adieu;
Though we sever, my fond heart
Till we meet shall pant for you.
    —Robert Dodsley.

'Twere vain to speak, to weep, to sigh;
Oh, more than tears of blood can tell
When wrung from guilt's expiring eye,
Are in the word farewell—farewell.
    —Byron.

The happy never say, and never hear said, farewell.—Landor.

Where thou art gone, adieus and farewells are a sound unknown.—Cowper.

Gude nicht, and joy be wi' you a'.
—Lady Nairne.

Give me your hand first; fare you well.—Shakespeare.

"Adieu," she cries, and waved her lily hand.—Gay.

Farewell, and stand fast.—Shakespeare.

So, farewell hope, and with hope farewell fear,
Farewell remorse: all good to me is lost.
    —Milton.

Here's a sigh to those who love me,
And a smile to those who hate;
And, whatever sky's above me,
Here's a heart for ev'ry fate.—Byron.

One struggle more, and I am free
From pangs that rend my heart in twain;
One last long sigh to love and thee,
Then back to busy life again.   —Byron.

Then fare thee well, deceitful maid,
'Twere vain and fruitless to regret thee;
Nor hope nor memory yield their aid,
But time may teach me to forget thee.
—Byron.

Let's not unman each other—part at once;
All farewells should be sudden, when for-
ever,
Else they make an eternity of moments,
And clog the last sad sands of life with
tears.   —Byron.

Farewell the plumed troop, and the big
wars,
That make ambition virtue! O, farewell!
Farewell the neighing steed, and the shrill
trump,
The spirit-stirring drum, the ear-piercing
fife.   —Shakespeare.

Farewell, a long farewell, to all my great-
ness!
This is the state of man; To-day he puts
forth
The tender leaves of hope; to-morrow blos-
soms
And bears his blushing honors thick upon
him:
The third day comes a frost, a killing frost;
And—when he thinks, good easy man, full
surely
His greatness is a-ripening,—nips his root,
And then he falls as I do.   —Shakespeare.

Farming

Farming is a most senseless pursuit, a mere laboring in a circle. You
sow that you may reap, and then you
reap that you may sow. Nothing ever
comes of it.—Stobæus.

Let us never forget that the cultivation of the earth is the most important labor of man. Man may be
civilized in some degree without great
progress in manufactures and with little commerce with his distant neighbors. But without the cultivation of
the earth, he is, in all countries, a
savage. Until he gives up the chase,
and fixes himself in some place, and
seeks a living from the earth. he is a
roaming barbarian. When tillage begins, other arts follow. The farmers,
therefore, are the founders of civilization.—Daniel Webster.

Fashion

Fashion is aristocratic-autocratic.—
J. G. Holland.

The fashion wears out more apparel
than the man.—Shakespeare.

Fashionability is a kind of elevated
vulgarity.—George Darley.

Fashion is the bastard of vanity,
dressed by art.—Fuseli.

As soon as fashion is universal, it
is out of date.—Marie Ebner-Eschenbach.

Lie ten nights awake carving the
fashion of a new doublet.—Shakespeare.

He is only fantastical that is not
in fashion.—Burton.

Ridiculous modes, invented by ignorance, and adopted by folly.—Smollett.

Fashion is only the attempt to realize art in living forms and social
intercourse.—O. W. Holmes.

Every generation laughs at the old
fashions, but follows religiously the
new.—Thoreau.

Fashion,—a word which knaves and
fools may use, their knavery and folly
to excuse.—Churchill.

Silks, velvets, calicoes, and the
whole lexicon of female fopperies.—
Swift.

While fashion's brightest arts decoy, the heart, distrusting, asks if this
be joy.—Goldsmith.

A woman would be in despair if
Nature had formed her as fashion
makes her appear.—Mlle. de l'Espi-
nasse.

Fashion seldom interferes with nature without diminishing her grace and
efficiency.—Tuckerman.

A fashionable woman is always in
love—with herself.—La Rochefoucauld.

Fashion is the veriest goddess of semblance and of shade.—Colton.

The glass of fashion and the mould of form,
The observ'd of all observers.
—Shakespeare.

Fashion is, for the most part, nothing but the ostentation of riches.—Locke.

Women cherish fashion because it rejuvenates them, or at least renews them.—Madame de Preizeux.

Fashion is a potency in art, making it hard to judge between the temporary and the lasting.—Stedman.

Change of fashions is the tax which industry imposes on the vanity of the rich.—Chamfort.

Be not the first by whom the new is tried,
Nor yet the last to lay the old aside.
—Pope.

The secret of fashion is to surprise and never to disappoint.—Bulwer-Lytton.

Though wrong the mode, comply;
more sense is shown in wearing others' follies than our own.—Young.

Fashion's smile has given wit to dullness and grace to deformity, and has brought everything into vogue, by turns, except virtue.—Colton.

New customs, though they be never so ridiculous,—nay, let them be unmanly,—yet are followed.—Shakespeare.

There would not be so much harm in the giddy following the fashions, if somehow the wise could always set them.—Bovee.

Nothing is thought rare which is not new, and followed; yet we know that what was worn some twenty years ago comes into grace again.—Beaumont and Fletcher.

Fashion is gentility running away from vulgarity, and afraid of being overtaken by it. It is a sign the two things are not far asunder.—Hazlitt.

As good be out of the World as out of the Fashion.—Colley Cibber.

Be neither too early in the fashion, nor too long out of it; nor at any time in the extremes of it.—Lavater.

Fashion is the science of appearances, and it inspires one with the desire to seem rather than to be—Chapin.

He alone is a man who can resist the genius of the age, the tone of fashion with vigorous simplicity and modest courage.—Lavater.

Ladies of fashion starve their happiness to feed their vanity, and their love to feed their pride.—Colton.

It is the rule of rules, and the general law of all laws, that every person should observe those of the place where he is.—Montaigne.

Where doth the world thrust forth a vanity (so it be new, there is no respect how vile) that is not quickly buzzed into the ears?—Shakespeare.

Those who seem to lead the public taste are, in general, merely outrunning it in the direction which it is spontaneously pursuing.—Macaulay.

As the eye becomes blinded by fashion to positive deformity, so, through social conventionalism, the conscience becomes blinded to positive immorality.—Mrs. Jameson.

The coat of the buffalo never pinches under the arm, never puckers at the shoulders; it is always the same, yet never old fashioned nor out of date.—Theodore Parker.

We laugh heartily to see a whole flock of sheep jump because one did so. Might not one imagine that superior beings do the same, and for exactly the same reason?—Greville.

When I would go a-visiting, I find that I go off the fashionable street,—not being inclined to change my dress, —to where man meets man, and not polished shoe meets shoe.—Thoreau.

One would not object to the prevalent notion that whatever is fashionable is right, if our rulers of the mode would contrive that whatever is right should be fashionable.—Chatfield.

Custom is the law of one description of fools and fashion of another; but the two parties often clash; for precedent is the legislator of the first, and novelty of the last.—Colton.

And as the French we conquer'd once,
Now give us laws for pantaloons,
The length of breeches and the gathers,
Port-cannons, periwigs, and feathers.
　　　　　　　　—Butler.

Thus grows up fashion, an equivocal semblance, the most puissant, the most fantastic and frivolous, the most feared and followed, and which morals and violence assault in vain.—Emerson.

Fashion is a great restraint upon your persons of taste and fancy; who would otherwise in the most trifling instances be able to distinguish themselves from the vulgar.—Shenstone.

We are taught to clothe our minds, as we do our bodies, after the fashion in vogue; and it is accounted fantastical, or something worse, not to do so.—Locke.

Our dress still varying, nor to forms confined,
Shifts like the sands, the sport of every wind.　　　　—Propertius.

Seest thou not, I say, what a deformed thief this fashion is, how giddily he turns about all the hot bloods between fourteen and five-and-thirty?—Shakespeare.

The Empress of France had but to change the position of a ribbon to set all the ribbons in Christendom to rustling. A single word from her convulsed the whalebone market of the world.—J. G. Holland.

Fashion builds her temple in the capital of some mighty empire, and having selected four or five hundred of the silliest people it contains, she dubs them with the magnificent and imposing title of "the world."—Colton.

Fashion being the art of those who must purchase notice at some cheaper rate than that of being beautiful, loves to do rash and extravagant things. She must be forever new, or she becomes insipid.—Lowell.

Fashion is the veriest goddess of semblance and of shade; to be happy is of far less consequence to her worshippers than to appear so; even pleasure itself they sacrifice to parade, and enjoyment to ostentation.—Colton.

Fashion is a tyrant from which nothing frees us. We must suit ourselves to its fantastic tastes. But being compelled to live under its foolish laws, the wise man is never the first to follow, nor the last to keep it.—Pascal.

I'll be at charges for a looking-glass,
And entertain some score or two of tailors,
To study fashions to adorn my body:
Since I am crept in favour with myself,
I will maintain it with some little cost.
　　　　　　—Shakespeare.

Fashion is the abortive issue of vain ostentation and exclusive egotism: it is haughty, trifling, affected, servile, despotic, mean and ambitious, precise and fantastical, all in a breath,—tied to no rule, and bound to conform to every whim of the moment.—Hazlitt.

Avoid singularity. There may often be less vanity in following the new modes than in adhering to the old ones. It is true that the foolish invent them, but the wise may conform to, instead of contradicting, them.—Joubert.

I have seen many men and women of fashion die, and I never saw one of them die well. The trappings off, there they lay on the tumbled pillow, and there were just two things that bothered them, a wasted life and a coming eternity.—Aughey.

Fashion is an odd jumble of contradictions, of sympathies and antipathies. It exists only by its being participated among a certain number of persons, and its essence is destroyed by being communicated to a greater number. * * * Fashion constantly begins and ends in the two things it abhors most,—singularity and vulgarity.—Hazlitt.

The mere leader of fashion has no genuine claim to supremacy; at least, no abiding assurance of it. He has embroidered his title upon his waistcoat, and carries his worth in his watch chain; and, if he is allowed any real precedence for this it is almost a moral swindle,—a way of obtaining goods under false pretences.—Chapin.

· I have been told by persons of experience in matters of taste, that the fashions follow a law of gradation, and are never arbitrary. The new mode is always only a step onward in the same direction as the last mode; and a cultivated eye is prepared for and predicts the new fashion.—Emerson.

We ought always to conform to the manners of the greater number, and so behave as not to draw attention to ourselves. Excess either way shocks, and every man truly wise ought to attend to this in his dress as well as language, never to be affected in anything, and follow without being in too great haste the changes of fashion.—Molière.

Manners have been somewhat cynically defined to be a contrivance of wise men to keep fools at a distance. Fashion is shrewd to detect those who do not belong to her train, and seldom wastes her attentions. Society is very swift in its instincts, and if you do not belong to it, resists and sneers at you, or quietly drops you.—Emerson.

Something clearly is wrong with fashionable women. They accept the thinnest gilt, the poorest pinchbeck, for gold. They care more for a dreary social pre-eminence than for home or children. They find in extravagance of living and a vulgar costliness of dress their only expression of vague desire for the beauty and elegance of life.—Mrs. L. G. Calhoun.

Fashion is not public opinion, or the result of embodiment of public opinion. It may be that public opinion will condemn the shape of a bonnet, as it may venture to do always, and with the certainty of being right nine times in ten: but fashion will place it upon the head of every woman in America; and, were it literally a crown of thorns, she would smile contentedly beneath the imposition.—J. G. Holland.

Mark yonder pomp of costly fashion,
　Round the wealthy bride;
But when compar'd with real passion
　Poor is all that pride,—
What are their showy treasures?
　What are their noisy pleasures?
The gay, gaudy glare of vanity and art—
　The polish'd jewels blaze
　May draw the wond'ring gaze,
But never, never can come near the worthy
　heart.　　　　—Burns.

　Fashion, leader of a chatt'ring train,
Whom man for his own hurt permits to
　reign
Who shifts and changes all things but his
　shape,
And would degrade her vot'ry to an ape,
The fruitful parent of abuse and wrong,
Holds a usurp'd dominion o'er his tongue,
There sits and prompts him with his own
　disgrace,
Prescribes the theme, the tone, and the
　grimace,
And when accomplish'd in her wayward
　school,
Calls gentleman whom she has made a fool.
　　　　　—Cowper.

Beauty too often sacrifices to fashion. The spirit of fashion is not the beautiful, but the wilful; not the graceful, but the fantastic; not the superior in the abstract, but the superior in the worst of all concretes,—the vulgar. The high point of taste and elegance is to be sought for, not in the most fashionable circles, but in the best-bred, and such as can dispense with the eternal necessity of never being twice the same.—Leigh Hunt.

Without depth of thought or earnestness of feeling or strength of purpose, living an unreal life, sacrificing substance to show, substituting the fictitious for the natural, mistaking a crowd for society, finding its chief pleasure in ridicule, and exhausting its ingenuity in expedients for killing time, fashion is among the last influences under which a human being who respects himself, or who comprehends the great end of life, would desire to be placed.—Channing.

Fastidiousness

Fastidiousness is the envelope of indelicacy.—Haliburton.

Fastidiousness is only another word for egotism; and all men who know not where to look for truth save in the narrow well of self will find their own image at the bottom, and mistake it for what they are seeking.—Lowell.

Fate

The die is cast.—The exclamation of Cæsar as he crossed the Rubicon.—Suetonius.

Fate is unpenetrated causes.—Emerson.

Fate hath no voice but the heart's impulse.—Schiller.

No one becomes guilty by fate.—Seneca.

The heart is its own fate.—Bailey.

To bear is to conquer our fate.—Campbell.

From no place can you exclude the fates.—Martial.

Yet who shall shut out fate?—Edwin Arnold.

The compulsion of fate is bitter.—Wieland.

He must needs go that the devil drives.—George Peele.

We bear each one our own destiny.—Virgil.

For rarely man escapes his destiny.—Ariosto.

Fulfil thy fate! Be—do—bear—and thank God.—Bailey.

Fair or foul the lot apportioned life on earth, we bear alike.—Robert Browning.

Fate is character.—William Winter.

We can only obey our own polarity.—Emerson.

This day we fashion destiny, our web of fate we spin.—Whittier.

Heaven from all creatures hides the book of fate.—Pope.

When fate summons, monarchs must obey.—Dryden.

Wherever the fates lead us let us follow.—Virgil.

Man blindly works the will of fate.—Wieland.

Things are where things are, and, as fate
has willed,
So shall they be fulfilled.
—Robert Browning.

A man's power is hooped in by a necessity, which, by many experiments, he touches on every side until he learns its arc.—Emerson.

And out of darkness came the hands
That reach thro' nature, moulding men.
—Tennyson.

What fates impose, that men must needs
abide;
It boots not to resist both wind and tide.
—Shakespeare.

Those whom God to ruin has design'd,
He fits for fate, and first destroys their
mind.
—Dryden.

With equal pace, impartial fate,
Knocks at the palace and the cottage gate.
—Horace.

But, O vain boast!
Who can control his fate?
—Shakespeare.

Necessity and chance
Approach not me, and what I will is fate.
—Milton.

Fate holds the strings, and men like chil-
dren, move
But as they're led; success is from above
—Lord Lansdowne.

Jove lifts the golden balances that show
The fates of mortal men, and things below.
—Homer.

All things are in fate, yet all things are not decreed by fate.—Plato.

One common fate we both must prove;
You die with envy, I with love.   —Gay.

'Tis writ on Paradise's gate,
"Woe to the dupe that yields to Fate!"
    —Hafiz.

Must helpless man, in ignorance sedate,
Roll darkling down the torrent of his fate?
    —Sam'l Johnson.

But blind to former as to future fate,
What mortal knows his pre-existent state?
    —Pope.

Whither the fates lead virtue will follow without fear.—Lucan.

Many have reached their fate while dreading fate.—Seneca.

The fates glide with linked hands over life.—Richter.

They only fall that strive to move, or lose that care to keep.—Owen Meredith.

We are led on, like little children, by a way we know not.—George Eliot.

We make our fortunes, and we call them fate.—Beaconsfield.

There is no good in arguing with the inevitable.—Lowell.

There is a divinity that shapes our ends, rough-hew them how we will.—Shakespeare.

Fate and the dooming gods are deaf to tears.—Dryden.

If you believe in fate to your harm, believe it, at least, for your good.—Emerson.

The slippery tops of human state, the gilded pinnacles of fate.—Cowley.

Men are the sport of circumstances, when circumstances seem the sport of men.—Byron.

The fates lead the willing, and drag the unwilling.—Seneca.

It is often a comfort in misfortune to know our own fate.—Quintus Curtius Rufus.

Man, be he who he may, experiences a last piece of good fortune and a last day.—Goethe.

Every soul has a landscape that changes with the wind that sweeps the sky, with the clouds that return after its rain.—George MacDonald.

Struggle against it as thou wilt, yet heaven's ways are heaven's ways.—Lessing.

What should be spoken here, where our fate,
Hid within an auger-hole, may rush, and seize us?   —Shakespeare.

Alas, by what rude fate
Our lives, like ships at sea, an instant meet,
Then part forever on their courses fleet.
    —E. C. Stedman.

And sing to those that hold the vital shears;
And turn the adamantine spindle round,
On which the fate of gods and men is wound.
    —Milton.

"Whosoever quarrels with his fate, does not understand it," says 'Bettine; and among all her inspired sayings, she spoke none wiser.—Mrs. L. M. Child.

Fate whirls on the bark, and the rough gale sweeps from the rising tide the lazy calm of thought.—Bulwer-Lytton.

God overrules all mutinous accidents, brings them under His laws of fate, and makes them all serviceable to His purpose.—Marcus Antoninus.

Fate is the friend of the good, the guide of the wise, the tyrant of the foolish, the enemy of the bad.—W. R. Alger.

Fate with impartial hand turns out the doom of high and low; her capacious urn is constantly shaking names of all mankind.—Horace.

Who is it needs such flawless shafts as fate? What archer of his arrows is so choice, or hits the white so surely?—Lowell.

Fates! we will know your pleasures: that we shall die, we know; 'tis but the time, and drawing days

out, that men stand upon.—Shakespeare.

Though fear should lend him pinions like the wind, yet swifter fate
will seize him from behind.—Swift.

Stern fate and time will have their
victims; and the best die first, leaving
the bad still strong, though past their
prime.—Ebenezer Elliott.

No power or virtue of man could
ever have deserved that what has
been fated should not have taken
place.—Ammianus Marcellinus.

Our wills and fates do so contrary run
That our devices still are overthrown;
Our thoughts are ours, their ends none of
    our own. —Shakespeare.

When fate has allowed to any man
more than one great gift, accident or
necessity seems usually to contrive
that one shall encumber and impede
the other.—Swinburne.

The glories of our blood and state
    Are shadows, not substantial things;
There is no armour against fate;
    Death lays his icy hand on kings.
        —Shirley.

Lucky he who has been educated to
bear his fate, whatsoever it may be,
by an early example of uprightness,
and a childish training in honor.—
Thackeray.

All are architects of Fate,
    Working in these walls of Time;
Some with massive deeds and great,
    Some with ornaments of rhyme.
        —Longfellow.

Fate steals along with silent tread,
Found oftenest in what least we dread;
Frowns in the storm with angry brow,
But in the sunshine strikes the blow.
        —Cowper.

A strict belief in fate is the worst
of slavery, imposing upon our necks
an everlasting lord and tyrant, whom
we are to stand in awe of night and
day.—Epicurus.

Our life is determined for us; and
it makes the mind very free when we
give up wishing, and only think of
bearing what is laid upon us and

---

doing what is given us to do.—George
Eliot.

A man's fate is his own temper;
and according to that will be his opinion as to the particular manner in
which the course of events is regulated. A consistent man believes in
destiny, a capricious man in chance.—
Beaconsfield.

            Man, tho' limited
By fate, may vainly think his actions free,
While all he does, was at his hour of birth,
Or by his gods, or potent stars ordain'd.
            —Rowe.

Ships that pass in the night, and speak
    each other in passing,
Only a signal shown and a distant voice in
    the darkness;
So on the ocean of life we pass and speak
    one another,
Only a look and a voice, then darkness again
    and a silence.
            —Longfellow.

A few seem favourites of fate,
    In pleasure's lap caress'd;
Yet, think not all the rich and great
    Are likewise truly blest. —Burns.

Alas, what stay is there in human state,
Or who can shun inevitable fate?
The doom was written, the decree was past,
Ere the foundations of the world were cast.
            —Dryden.

We defy augury; there is a special
providence in the fall of a sparrow.
If it be now, 'tis not to come; if it be
not to come, it will be now; if it be
not now, yet it will come: the readiness is all.—Shakespeare.

Sometimes an hour of Fate's serenest
    weather
    Strikes through our changeful sky its
        coming beams;
Somewhere above us, in elusive ether,
    Waits the fulfillment of our dearest
    dreams.   —Bayard Taylor.

Let those deplore their doom,
Whose hope still grovels in this dark so-
    journ;
But lofty souls, who look beyond the tomb,
Can smile at Fate, and wonder how they
    mourn.   —Beattie.

Whatever may happen to thee, it
was prepared for thee from all eternity; and the implication of causes
was from eternity spinning the thread

of thy being and of that which is incident to it.—Marcus Antoninus.

It is an awful thing to get a glimpse, as one sometimes does, when the time is past, of some little, little wheel which works the whole mighty machinery of fate, and see how our destinies turn on a minute's delay or advance.—Thackeray.

As fate is inexorable, and not to be moved either with tears or reproaches, an excess of sorrow is as foolish as profuse laughter; while, on the other hand, not to mourn at all is insensibility.—Seneca.

It was a smart reply that Augustus made to one that ministered this comfort of the fatality of things: this was so far from giving any ease to his mind, that it was the very thing that troubled him.—Tillotson.

O beautiful, awful Summer day,
What hast thou given, what taken away?
Life and death, and love and hate,
Homes made happy or desolate,
Hearts made sad or gay. —Longfellow.

Ask me no more; thy fate and mine are
        seal'd;
I strove against the stream and all in vain:
Let the great river take me to the main:
No more, dear love, for at a touch I yield;
        Ask me no more.
        —Tennyson.

'Tis the best use of fate to teach a fatal courage. Go face the fire at sea, or the cholera in your friend's house, or the burglar in your own, or what danger lies in the way of duty, knowing you are guarded by the cherubim of destiny.—Emerson.

Success, the mark no mortal wit,
Or surest hand, can always hit;
For whatsoe'er we perpetrate,
We do but row—w'are steer'd by fate,
Which in success oft disinherits,
For spurious causes, noblest merits.
        —Butler.

The Stoics held a fatality, and a fixed, unalterable course of events; but they held also that they fell out by a necessity emergent from and inherent in the things themselves, which God Himself could not alter.—South.

The wrath peculiar to ardent natures rudely awakened by the sudden annihilation of a hope—dream, if you will—in which the choicest happinesses were thought to be certainly in reach. In such cases nothing intermediate will carry off the passion,—the quarrel is with fate. * * * It were well in such quarrels if fate were something tangible, to be despatched with a look or a blow, or a speaking personage with whom high words were possible; then the unhappy mortal would not always end the affair by punishing himself.—Lew Wallace.

Father

Oh, who would be a father!—Holcroft.

No one ever knew his own father.—Buckley.

It is a wise father that knows his own child.—Shakespeare.

The child is father of the man.—Wordsworth.

Father of all! in every age
    In every clime adored,
By saint, by savage, and by sage,
    Jehovah, Jove, or Lord. —Pope.

To you your father should be as a god;
One that compos'd your beauties; yea, and
    one,
To whom you are but as a form in wax,
By him imprinted, and within his power
To leave the figure, or disfigure it.
        —Shakespeare.

Fathers that wear rags do make their children blind:
But fathers that bear bags shall see their children kind. —Shakespeare.

Faults

Best men oft are moulded out of faults.—Shakespeare.

Condemn the fault, but not the actor.—Shakespeare.

Faults are beauties in a lover's eye. —Theocritus.

A fault finds its own authors.—Law Maxim.

Is she not a wilderness of faults and follies?—Sheridan.

Bad men excuse their faults, good men will leave them.—Ben Jonson.

Unless you bear with the faults of a friend, you betray your own.—Syrus.

He who overlooks a fault, invites the commission of another.—Syrus.

The greatest of faults, I should say, is to be conscious of none.—Carlyle.

The first fault is the child of simplicity, but every other the offspring of guilt.—Goldsmith.

All his faults are such that one loves him still the better for them.—Goldsmith.

Had we not faults of our own we should take less pleasure in observing those of others.—Rochefoucauld.

Why do we discover faults so much more readily than perfections?—Madame de Sévigné.

We are often more agreeable through our faults than through our good qualities.—Rochefoucauld.

It is not so much the being exempt from faults, as the having overcome them, that is an advantage to us.—Alexander Pope.

Every one fault seeming monstrous till his fellow-fault came to match it.—Shakespeare.

If the best man's faults were written on his forehead, he would draw his hat over his eyes.—Gray.

We easily forget those faults which are known only to ourselves.—La Rochefoucauld.

The faults of our neighbours with freedom we blame,
But tax not ourselves, though we practise the same.   —Cunningham.

Excusing of a fault
Doth make the fault worse by the excuse.
                —Shakespeare.

Only those faults which we encounter in ourselves are insufferable to us in others.—Madame Swetchine.

Why beholdest thou the mote that is in thy brother's eye, but perceivest not the beam that is in thine own eye?—Bible.

No man is born without faults, he is best who has the fewest.—Horace.

A woman will confess her faults sooner than her follies.—Alfred Bougeart.

The great fault in women is to desire to be like men.—De Maistre.

'Tis a meaner part of sense to find a fault than taste an excellence.—Rochester.

It requires less character to discover the faults of others than to tolerate them.—J. Petit-Senn.

He shall be immortal who liveth till he be stoned by one without fault.—Fuller.

Just as you are pleased at finding faults, you are displeased at finding perfections.—Lavater.

Women will sometimes confess their sins, but I never knew one to confess her faults.—Haliburton.

God Himself allows certain faults; and often we say, "I have deserved to err; I have deserved to be ignorant." Mme. Swetchine.

It is a shrewd device to pretend we have some one unimportant fault,—it overshadows so many serious defects.—Mme. Deluzy.

Most of their faults women owe to us, whilst we are indebted to them for the most of our better qualities.—Lemesles.

It is well that there is no one without a fault, for he would not have a friend in the world. He would seem to belong to a different species.—Hazlitt.

We need not be much concerned about those faults which we have the courage to own.—Rochefoucauld.

Every man has a bag hanging before him, in which he puts his neighbor's faults, and another behind him in which he stows his own.—Knight's Shakespeare.

Relative to getting rid of it, a fault is serious or not in proportion to the depth of its root rather than the amount of its foliage.—George MacDonald.

What sort of faults may we retain, nay, even cherish in ourselves? Those faults which are rather pleasant than offensive to others.—Goethe.

A woman's faults, be they never so small, cast a shadow which all her virtues cannot dispel.—Achilles Poincelot.

While we are indifferent to our good qualities, we keep on deceiving ourselves in regard to our faults, until we at last come to look upon them as virtues.—Heine.

There are some faults which, when well managed, make a greater figure than virtue itself.—Rochefoucauld.

The ability to find fault is believed, by some people, to be a sure sign of great wisdom, when, in most cases, it only indicates narrowness of mind and ill nature.—Aughey.

None, none descends into himself, to find
The secret imperfections of his mind:
But every one is eagle-ey'd to see
Another's faults, and his deformity.
—Dryden.

Then gently scan your brother man,
Still gentler, sister woman;
Tho' they may gang a kennin' wrang;
To step aside is human! —Burns.

Men still had faults, and men will have them still;
He that hath none, and lives as angels do,
Must be an angel. —Wentworth Dillon.

O wad some pow'r the giftie gie us
To see ourselves as others see us!
It wad frae mony a blunder free us,
And foolish notion. —Burns.

I like her, with all her faults; nay, like her for her faults. Her follies are so natural, or so artful, that they become her; and those affections which in another woman would be odious serve but to make her more agreeable. —Congreve.

Moral epochs have their course as well as the seasons. We can no more hold them fast than we can hold sun, moon, and stars. Our faults perpetually return upon us; and herein lies the subtlest difficulty of self-knowledge.—Goethe.

To acknowledge our faults when we are blamed, is modesty; to discover them to one's friends in ingenuousness, is confidence; but to preach them to all the world, if one does not take care, is pride.—Confucius.

He who exhibits no faults is a fool or a hypocrite, whom we should mistrust. There are faults so intimately connected with fine qualities that they indicate them, and we do well not to correct them.—Joubert.

It is not so much the being exempt from faults as the having overcome them that is an advantage to us; it being with the follies of the mind as with weeds of a field, which, if destroyed and consumed upon the place where they grow, enrich and improve it more than if none had ever sprung there.—Swift.

If we were faultless, we should not be so much annoyed by the defects of those with whom we associate. If we were to acknowledge honestly that we have not virtue enough to bear patiently with our neighbor's weaknesses, we should show our own imperfection, and this alarms our vanity.—Fénelon.

Do you wish to find out a person's weak points? Note the failings he has the quickest eye for in others. They may not be the very failings he is himself conscious of; but they will be their next door neighbors. No man keeps such a jealous lookout as a rival.—J. C. and A. W. Hare.

As there are some faults that have been termed faults on the right side, so there are some errors that might be denominated errors on the safe side.

Thus we seldom regret having been too mild, too cautious, or too humble; but we often repent having been too violent, too precipitate, or too proud.—Colton.

Favor

To accept a favor is to sell one's freedom.—Syrus.

That man is worthless who knows how to receive a favor, but not how to return one.—Plautus.

No free man will ask as favor, what he cannot claim as reward.—Terence.

He only confers favors generously who appears, when they are once conferred, to remember them no more.—Johnson.

Favor exalts a man above his equals, but his dismissal from that favor places him below them.—La Bruyère.

A favor tardily bestowed is no favor; for a favor quickly granted is a more agreeable favor.—Ausonius.

For however often a man may receive an obligation from you, if you refuse a request, all former favors are effaced by this one denial.—Pliny the Younger.

'Tis ever thus when favours are denied;
All had been granted but the thing we beg:
And still some great unlikely substitute—
Your life, your soul, your all of earthly good—
Is proffer'd, in the room of one small boon.
—Joanna Baillie.

Poor wretches, that depend
On greatness' favor, dream as I have done;
Wake, and find nothing. But, alas, I swerve.
Many dream not to find, neither deserve,
And yet are steep'd in favors.
—Shakespeare.

'Tis the curse of service;
Preferment goes by letter, and affection,
And not by old gradation, where each second
Stood heir to the first. —Shakespeare.

Fear

The concessions of the weak are the concessions of fear.—Burke.

Fear not; for I am with thee.—Bible.

Nothing is to be feared but fear.—Bacon.

Fear is the mother of safety.—Burke.

Fear has many eyes.—Cervantes.

Fear always springs from ignorance.—Emerson.

Fear is the mother of foresight.—Henry Taylor.

Fear is the tax that conscience pays to guilt.—Sewell.

Fear naturally quickens the flight of guilt.—Johnson.

Fear is the parent of cruelty.—Froude.

Fear in the world first created the gods.—Statius.

The fear of the Lord is the beginning of wisdom.—Bible.

Of all base passions fear is most accurs'd.—Shakespeare.

No one loves the man whom he fears.—Aristotle.

Fear is faithlessness.—George MacDonald.

Fear makes men believe the worst.—Quintus Curtius Rufus.

In time we hate that which we often fear—Shakespeare.

To grief there is a limit; not so to fear.—Bacon.

In extreme danger fear feels no pity.—Cæsar.

Fear loves the idea of danger.—Joubert.

Fear makes us feel our humanity.—Beaconsfield.

Fear is cruel and mean.—Emerson.

By daring, great fears are often concealed.—Lucan.

Noiseless as fear in a wide wilderness.—Keats.

'Tis time to fear when tyrants seem to kiss.—Pericles.

Fain would I climb, yet fear I to fall.—Sir Walter Raleigh.

Fear though blind is swift and strong.—Dr. Mackay.

He has but one great fear that fears to do wrong.—Bovee.

Fear is the proof of a degenerate mind.—Virgil.

Hang those that talk of fear.—Shakespeare.

Fear is not a lasting teacher of duty.—Cicero.

Less base the fear of death than fear of life.—Young.

Fearless as the strong-winged eagle.—Ossian.

Whistling to keep myself from being afraid.—Dryden.

Fear is the white lipp'd sire
Of subterfuge and treachery.
—Mrs. Sigourney.

Desponding fear, of feeble fancies full,
Weak and unmanly, loosens ev'ry power.
—Thomson.

There is not such a word
Spoke of in Scotland, as this term of fear.
—Shakespeare.

Those linen cheeks of thine
Are counsellors to fear.   —Shakespeare.

When our actions do not,
Our fears do make us traitors.
—Shakespeare.

Fear not the proud and the haughty; fear rather him who fears God.—Saadi.

We Germans fear God, but nothing else in the world.—Prince Bismarck.

Of all faults the greatest is the excess of impious terror, dishonoring divine grace.—Metastasio.

Present fears are less than horrible imaginings.—Shakespeare.

Fear is a dagger with which hypocrisy assassinates the soul.—R. G. Ingersoll.

Mutual fear is a principal link in the chain of mutual love.—Thomas Paine.

There is no fear in love, but perfect love casteth out fear, because fear hath torment.—Bible.

The Fear of God is freedom, joy, and peace;
And makes all ills that vex us here to cease.
—Waller.

In politics, what begins in fear usually ends in folly.—Coleridge.

Fear is far more painful to cowardice than death to true courage.—Sir Philip Sidney.

The Lord is my light and my salvation; whom shall I fear——Bible.

It is only the fear of God that can deliver us from the fear of man.—Witherspoon.

You are uneasy, * * * you never sailed with me before, I see.—Andrew Jackson.

We are not apt to fear for the fearless, when we are companions in their danger.—George Eliot.

Stared in her eyes and chalk'd her face.—Tennyson.

Fear invites danger; concealed cowards insult known ones.—Chesterfield.

Speechless with wonder and half dead with fear.—Addison.

No one but a poltroon will boast that he never was afraid.—Marshal Lannes.

If you will fear nothing, think that all things are to be feared.—Seneca.

Every one wishes that the man whom he fears would perish.—Ovid.

An immense, misshapen, marvelous monster, whose eye is out.—Virgil.

The absent danger greater still appears; less fears he who is near the thing he fears.—Daniel.

Fear, either as a principle or a motive, is the beginning of all evil.—Mrs. Jameson.

Whom we fear more than love, we are not far from hating.—Richardson.

The only inheritance I have received from my ancestors is a soul incapable of fear.—Julian.

When the truth cannot be clearly made out, what is false is increased through fear.—Quintus Curtius Rufus.

Even the bravest men are frightened by sudden terrors.—Tacitus.

From the moment fear begins I have ceased to fear.—Schiller.

Fear on guilt attends, and deeds of darkness;
The virtuous breast ne'er knows it.
—Havard.

Fear is implanted in us as a preservative from evil.—Dr. Johnson.

I rather tell thee what is to be feared than what I fear; for always I am Cæsar.—Shakespeare.

The miser acquires, yet fears to use his gains.—Horace.

To die without fear of death is to be desired.—Seneca.

Why, what should be the fear? I do not set my life at a pin's fee; and, for my soul, what can it do to that, being a thing immortal.—Shakespeare.

A certain degree of fear produces the same effects as rashness.—Cardinal de Retz.

Apprehensions are greater in proportion as things are unknown.—Livy.

He must necessarily fear many, whom many fear.—Seneca.

Or in the night, imagining some fear,
How easy is a bush suppos'd a bear!
—Shakespeare.

Nothing routs us but the villainy of our fears.—Shakespeare.

We must expect everything and fear everything from time and from men.—Vauvenargues.

There is this paradox in fear: he is most likely to inspire it in others who has none himself!—Colton.

From a distance it is something; and nearby it is nothing.—La Fontaine.

Oh! that fear
When the heart longs to know, what it is
death to hear.
—Croly.

The direct foe of courage is the fear itself, not the object of it; and the man who can overcome his own terror is a hero, and more.—George MacDonald.

The wounded limb shrinks from the slightest touch; and a slight shadow alarms the nervous.—Ovid.

To fear the foe, since fear oppresseth strength,
Gives in your weakness strength unto your foe.
—Shakespeare.

The dove, O hawk, that has once been wounded by thy talons, is frightened by the least movement of a wing.—Ovid.

There is a courageous wisdom; there is also a false, reptile prudence, the result not of caution, but of fear.—Burke.

Fear is that passion which hath the greatest power over us, and by which God and His laws take the surest hold of us.—Tillotson.

Nothing so demoralizes the forces of the soul as fear. Only as we realize the presence of the Lord does fear give place to faith.—Sarah Smiley.

What can that man fear who takes care to please a Being that is able to crush all his adversaries?—Addison.

We often pretend to fear what we really despise, and more often to despise what we really fear.—Colton.

I feel my sinews slackened with the fright, and a cold sweat trills down all over my limbs, as if I were dissolving into water.—Dryden.

Fearfulness, contrary to all other vices, maketh a man think the better of another, the worse of himself.—Sir P. Sidney.

Fear sometimes adds wings to the heels, and sometimes nails them to the ground, and fetters them from moving.—Montaigne.

In how large a proportion of creatures is existence composed of one ruling passion, the most agonizing of all sensations—fear.—Bulwer-Lytton.

There is great beauty in going through life fearlessly. Half our fears are baseless, the other half discreditable.—Bovee.

Good men have the fewest fears. He has but one great fear who fears to do wrong; he has a thousand who has overcome it.—Bovee.

And being thus frighted swears a prayer or two,
And sleeps again.   —Shakespeare.

Imagination frames events unknown,
In wild, fantastic shapes of hideous ruin,
And what it fears creates.
        —Hannah More.

We must be afraid of neither poverty nor exile nor imprisonment; of fear itself only should we be afraid.—Epictetus.

Nothing is so rash as fear; and the counsels of pusillanimity very rarely put off, whilst they are always sure to aggravate, the evils from which they would fly.—Burke.

The thing in the world I am most afraid of is fear, and with good reason; that passion alone, in the trouble of it, exceeding all other accidents.—Montaigne.

Fear hath the common fault of a justice of peace, and is apt to conclude hastily from every slight circumstance, without examining the evidence on both sides.—Fielding.

O, fear not in a world like this,
  And thou shalt know ere long,—
Know how sublime a thing it is
  To suffer and be strong.
        —Longfellow.

Shun fear, it is the ague of the soul! a passion man created for himself—for sure that cramp of nature could not dwell in the warm realms of glory.—Aaron Hill.

There is nothing so ingenious as fear; it is even more ingenious than hatred, especially when its concern is with the preservation of money.—Bayle St. John.

The fear o' hell's the hangman's whip
  To haud the wretch in order;
But where ye feel your honor grip,
  Let that aye be your border.
        —Burns.

A man should always allow his fears to rise to their highest possible pitch, and then some consolation or other will suddenly fall, like a warm rain-drop, upon his heart.—Richter.

Many never think on God but in extremity of fear; and then, perplexity not suffering them to be idle, they think and do as it were in a frenzy.—Hooker.

We are ashamed of our fear; for we know that a righteous man would not suspect danger nor incur any. Wherever a man feels fear, there is an avenger.—Thoreau.

All fear is in itself painful, and, when it conduces not to safety, is painful without use. Every consideration, therefore, by which groundless terrors may be removed adds something to human happiness.—Johnson.

Fear guides more to their duty than gratitude; for one man who is virtuous from the love of virtue, from the obligation he thinks he lies under to the Giver of all, there are ten thousand who are good only from their apprehension of punishment.—Goldsmith.

Must I consume my life—this little life,
In guarding against all may make it less?
It is not worth so much!—it were to die
Before my hour, to live in dread of death.
            —Byron.

What are fears but voices airy?
  Whispering harm where harm is not,
And deluding the unwary
  Till the fatal bolt is shot!
            —Wordsworth.

The dreadful fear of hell is to be driven out, which disturbs the life of man and renders it miserable, overcasting all things with the blackness of darkness, and leaving no pure, unalloyed pleasure.—Lucretius.

In every mind where there is a strong tendency to fear there is a strong capacity to hate. Those who dwell in fear dwell next door to hate; and I think it is the cowardice of women which makes them such intense haters.—Mrs. Jameson.

God planted fear in the soul as truly as He planted hope or courage. Fear is a kind of bell, or gong, which rings the mind into quick life and avoidance upon the approach of danger. It is the soul's signal for rallying.—Beecher.

Fear nothing but what thy industry may prevent; be confident of nothing but what fortune cannot defeat; it is no less folly to fear what is impossible to be avoided than to be secure when there is a possibility to be deprived.—Quarles.

In morals, what begins in fear usually ends in wickedness; in religion, what begins in fear usually ends in fanaticism. Fear, either as a principle or a motive, is the beginning of all evil.—Mrs. Jameson.

They who cannot be induced to fear for love will never be enforced to love for fear. Love opens the heart, fear shuts it; that encourages, this compels; and victory meets encouragement, but flees compulsion.—Quarles.

Timidity is a disease of the mind, obstinate and fatal; for a man once persuaded that any impediment is insuperable has given it, with respect to himself, that strength and weight which it had not before.—Dr. Johnson.

                        Things done well,
And with a care, exempt themselves from
    fear;
Things done without example, in their issue
Are to be feared.   —Shakespeare.

The wretch that fears to drown, will break
    through flames;
Or, in his dread of flames, will plunge in
    waves.
When eagles are in view, the screaming
    doves
Will cower beneath the feet of man for
    safety.   —Cibber.

Were a man's sorrows and disquietudes summed up at the end of his life, it would generally be found that he had suffered more from the apprehension of such evils as never happened to him than from those evils which had really befallen him.—Addison.

Many men affect to despise fear, and in preaching resent any appeal to it; but not to fear when there is occasion is as great a weakness as to fear unduly without reason. God implanted fear in the soul as truly as He implanted hope or courage.—Aughey.

Man begins life helpless. The babe is in paroxysms of fear the moment its nurse leaves it alone, and it comes so slowly to any power of self-protection that mothers say the salvation of the life and health of a young child is a perpetual miracle.—Emerson.

Fear is implanted in us as a preservative from evil; but its duty, like that of other passions, is not to overbear reason, but to assist it; nor should it be suffered to tyrannize in the imagination, to raise phantoms of horror, or to beset life with supernumerary distresses.—Johnson.

Fear accomplishes much in love. The husband of the Middle Ages was loved by his wife for his very severity. The bride of William the Conqueror, having been beaten by him, recognized him by this token for her lord and husband.—Michelet.

Thou shalt be punish'd for thus frighting me.
For I am sick and capable of fears;
Oppress'd with wrongs, and therefore full of fears;
A widow, husbandless, subject to fears;
A woman, naturally born to fears;
And though thou now confess, thou did'st but jest,
With my vex'd spirits I cannot take a truce,
But they will quake and tremble all this day.   —Shakespeare.

Fear never was a friend to the love of God or man, to duty or conscience, truth, probity, or honor. It therefore can never make a good subject, a good citizen, or a good soldier, and, least of all, a good Christian; except the devils, who believe and tremble, are to be accounted good Christians.—Henry Brooke.

The passion of fear (as a modern philosopher informs me) determines the spirits of the muscles of the knees, which are instantly ready to perform their motion, by taking up the legs with incomparable celerity, in order to remove the body out of harm's way.—Shaftesbury.

The weakness we lament, ourselves create.
Instructed from our infant years to court,
With counterfeited fears, the aid of man,
We learn to shudder at the rustling breeze,
Start at the light, and tremble in the dark,
Till affectation, rip'ning to belief
And folly, frighted at our own chimeras,
Habitual cowardice usurps the soul.
          —Johnson.

I saw a delicate flower had grown up two feet high, between the horses' path and the wheel-track. An inch more to the right or left had sealed its fate, or an inch higher; and yet it lived to flourish as much as if it had a thousand acres of untrodden space around it, and never knew the danger it incurred. It did not borrow trouble, nor invite an evil fate by apprehending it.—Thoreau.

Such as are in immediate fear of losing their estates, of banishment, or of slavery, live in perpetual anguish, and lose all appetite and repose; whereas such as are actually poor

slaves and exiles oftentimes live as merrily as men in a better condition; and so many people who, impatient of the perpetual alarms of fear, have hanged and drowned themselves give us sufficiently to understand that it is more importunate and insupportable than death itself.—Montaigne.

I could a tale unfold whose lightest word
Would harrow up thy soul, freeze thy young blood,
Make thy two eyes, like stars, start from their spheres,
Thy knotted and combined locks to part
And each particular hair to stand on end,
Like quills upon the fretful porpentine.
          —Shakespeare.

There is a virtuous fear which is the effect of faith; and there is a vicious fear, which is the product of doubt. The former leads to hope, as relying on God, in whom we believe; the latter inclines to despair, as not relying on God, in whom we do not believe. Persons of the one character fear to lose God; persons of the other character fear to find Him.—Pascal.

When the sun sets, shadows that show'd at noon
But small, appear most long and terrible:
So when we think fate hovers o'er our heads,
Our apprehensions shoot beyond all bounds;
Owls, ravens, crickets, seem the watch of death:
Nature's worst vermin scare her godlike sons.
Echoes, the very leaving of a voice,
Grow babbling ghosts, and call us to our graves.
Each mole-hill thought swells to a huge Olympus,
While we, fantastic dreamers, heave and puff,
And sweat with an imagination's weight.
          —Lee.

Feasting

The feast of reason and the flow of soul.—Pope.

The turnpike road to people's hearts, I find,
Lies through their mouths, or I mistake mankind.   —Peter Pindar.

Their various cares in one great point combine
The business of their lives, that is—to dine.
          —Young.

It is not the quantity of the meat, but the cheerfulness of the guests,

which makes the feast; at the feast of
the Centaurs they ate with one hand,
and had their drawn swords in the
other; where there is no peace, there
can be no feast.—Clarendon.

The latter end of a fray, and the beginning
    of a feast,
Fits a dull fighter, and a keen guest.
          —Shakespeare.

Blest be those feasts with simple plenty
    crown'd,
Where all the ruddy family around
Laugh at the jests or pranks that never fail,
Or sigh with pity at some mournful tale.
          —Goldsmith.

But 'twas a public feast, and public day,
Quite full, right dull, guests hot, and dishes
    cold,
Great plenty, much formality, small cheer,
And everybody out of their own sphere.
      Of all appeals,—although
I grant the power of pathos, and of gold,
Of beauty, flattery, threats, a shilling,—no
    Methods more sure at moments to take
    hold,
Of the best feelings of mankind, which
    grow
    More tender, as we every day behold,
Than that all-softening, overpow'ring knell,
The tocsin of the soul—the Dinner Bell.
          —Byron.

Features

Features—the great soul's apparent
seat.—Bryant.

Feeling

A fellow-feeling makes one wondrous
kind.—Garrick.

Feeling comes before reflection—
Hugh R. Haweis.

I would help others, out of a fellow-
feeling.—Burton.

The feelings, like flowers and butterflies, last longer the later they are delayed.—Richter.

Life is a comedy to him who thinks,
and tragedy to him who feels.—Horace
Walpole.

Though there is nothing more dangerous, yet there is nothing more ordinary, than for weak saints to make
their sense and feeling the judge of
their condition. We must strive to
walk by faith.—Thomas Brooks.

Every human feeling is greater and
larger than the exciting cause.—Coleridge.

Some feelings are to mortals given
with less of earth in them than
heaven.—Sir Walter Scott.

A man deep wounded may feel too
much pain to feel much anger.—
George Eliot.

What unknown seas of feeling lie in
man, and will from time to time break
through!—Carlyle.

He best shall paint them who shall
feel them most.—Pope.

Feeling in the young precedes philosophy, and often acts with a more certain aim.—Wm. Carleton.

But spite of all the criticising elves,
Those who would make us feel, must feel
    themselves.   —Churchill.

The head best leaves to the heart
what the heart alone divines.—A.
Bronson Alcott.

He thought as a sage, though he felt
as a man.—Beattie.

The heart that is soonest awake to
the flowers is always the first to be
touched by the thorns.—Moore.

Fine feelings, without vigor of reason, are in the situation of the extreme
feather of a peacock's tail—dragging in
the mud.—Foster.

Our feelings were given us to excite
to action, and when they end in themselves, they are impressed to no one
good purpose that I know of.—Bishop
Sandford.

Feelings come and go like light
troops following the victory of the
present; but principles, like troops of
the line, are undisturbed, and stand
fast.—Richter.

Some people carry their hearts in
their heads; very many carry their
heads in their hearts. The difficulty
is to keep them apart, and yet both
actively working together.—Anon.

My friends, does God invite you? If He does, why don't you accept the invitation? If you want to come, just come along, and don't be talking about feeling. Do you think Lazarus had any feeling when Christ called him out of the sepulchre?—D. L. Moody.

The soul of music slumbers in the shell,
Till wak'd and kindled by the master's spell,
And feeling hearts—touch them but lightly
    —pour
A thousand melodies unheard before.
    —Rogers.

Feeling is deep and still; and the word that
    floats on the surface
Is as the tossing buoy, that betrays where
    the anchor is hidden. —Longfellow.

The wealth of rich feelings—the deep—the
    pure;
With strength to meet sorrow, and faith to
    endure.   —Frances S. Osgood.

Tears never yet saved a soul. Hell is full of weepers weeping over lost opportunities, perhaps over the rejection of an offered Saviour. Your Bible does not say, "Weep, and be saved." It says, "Believe, and be saved." Faith is better than feeling.—T. L. Cuyler.

"Verily I say unto you, he that heareth My word and believeth on Him that sent Me, hath everlasting life, and shall not come into condemnation, but is passed from death unto life." My friend, that is worth more than all the feeling you can have in a lifetime.—D. L. Moody.

A word, a look, which at one time would make no impression, at another time wounds the heart; and like a shaft flying with the wind pierces deep, which, with its own natural force, would scarce have reached the object aimed at.—Sterne.

The heart of man is older than his head. The first-born is sensitive, but blind—his younger brother has a cold, but all-comprehensive glance. The blind must consent to be led by the clear-sighted if he would avoid falling.—Ziegler.

The last, best fruit which comes to perfection, even in the kindliest soul, is tenderness toward the hard, forbearance toward the unforbearing, warmth of heart toward the cold, philanthropy toward the misanthropic.—Richter.

It is far more easy not to feel, than always to feel rightly, and not to act, than always to act well. For he that is determined to admire only that which is beautiful imposes a much harder task upon himself than he that, being determined not to see that which is the contrary, effects it by simply shutting his eyes.—Colton.

Some feelings are quite untranslatable; no language has yet been found for them. They gleam upon us beautifully through the dim twilight of fancy, and yet when we bring them close to us, and hold them up to the light of reason, lose their beauty all at once, as glow worms which gleam with such a spiritual light in the shadows of evening, when brought in where the candles are lighted, are found to be only worms like so many others.—Longfellow.

Feelings are like chemicals — the more you analyze them the worse they smell. So it is best not to stir them up very much, only enough to convince one's self that they are offensively wrong, and then look away as far as possible, out of one's self, for a purifying power; and that we know can only come from Him who holds our hearts in His hands, and can turn us whither He will.—Charles Kingsley.

Felicity

True felicity consists of its own consciousness.—Rivarol.

Felicity is in possession, happiness in anticipation.—Racine.

True happiness resides in things not seen.—Young.

Since every man that lives is born to die, and none can boast sincere felicity, with equal minds what happens let us bear.—Dryden.

The world produces for every pint of honey a gallon of gall, for every dram of pleasure a pound of pain, for every inch of mirth an ell of moan; and as the ivy twines around the oak, so does misery and misfortune encompass the happy man. Felicity, pure and unalloyed felicity, is not a plant of earthly growth; her gardens are the skies.—Robert Burton.

Festivity

Oh, leave the gay and festive scenes,
The halls of dazzling light.
—H. S. Vandyke.

Venice once was dear,
The pleasant place of all festivity,
The rival of the earth, the masque of Italy.
—Byron.

We keep the day. With festal cheer,
With books and music, surely we
Will drink to him, whate'er he be,
And sing the songs he loved to hear.
—Tennyson.

There was a sound of revelry by night,
And Belgium's capital had gather'd then
Her Beauty and her Chivalry, and bright
The lamps shone o'er fair women and
brave men. —Byron.

The music, and the banquet, and the wine—
The garlands, the rose odors, and the flow-
ers,
The sparkling eyes, and flashing ornaments—
The white arms and the raven hair—the
braids,
And bracelets; swan-like bosoms, and the
necklace,
An India in itself, yet dazzling not.
—Byron.

Fickleness

Fickleness has always befriended the beautiful.—Propertius.

Change amuses the mind, but rarely profits.—Goethe.

Stand firm, don't flutter!—Franklin.

Frailty, thy name is woman!—Shakespeare.

Woman is a miracle of divine contradictions.—Michelet.

The irresolute man flecks from one egg to another, so hatches nothing.—Feltham.

Love is not love which alters where it alteration finds.—Shakespeare.

Was ever feather so lightly blown to and fro as this multitude.—Shakespeare.

Men love little and often, women much and rarely.—Basta.

He wears his faith but as the fashion of his hat; it ever changes with the next block.—Shakespeare.

Ladies, like variegated tulips, show
'Tis to their changes half their charms we
owe. —Pope.

There are three things a wise man will not trust—the wind, the sunshine of an April day, and woman's plighted faith.—Southey.

It will be found that they are the weakest winded and the hardest hearted men that most love change.—Ruskin.

There is in all of us an impediment to perfect happiness; namely, weariness of the things which we possess, and a desire for the things which we have not.—Mme. de Rieux.

Sigh no more, ladies, sigh no more,
Men were deceivers ever,
One foot in sea and one on shore;
To one thing constant never.
—Shakespeare.

He cast off his friends, as a huntsman his
pack,
For he knew when he pleased he could
whistle them back. —Goldsmith.

We are all of us, in this world, more or less like St. January, whom the inhabitants of Naples worship one day, and pelt with baked apples the next.—Mme. Swetchine.

Oh! the tender ties,
Close twisted with the fibres of the heart!
Which broken, break them, and drain off the
soul
Of human joy, and make it pain to live.
—Young.

The hearts of all his people shall revolt from him, and kiss the lips of unacquainted change.—Shakespeare.

To be longing for this thing to-day and for that thing to-morrow; to change likings for loathings, and to stand wishing and hankering at a venture—how is it possible for any man to be at rest in this fluctuant, wandering humor and opinion?—L'Estrange.

Papillia, wedded to her amorous spark,
Sighs for the shades—"How charming is a
    park?"
A park is purchas'd, but the fair he sees
All bath'd in tears—"O odious, odious
    trees!"   —Pope.

It carries too great an imputation of ignorance, lightness or folly for men to quit and renounce their former tenets presently upon the offer of an argument which they cannot immediately answer.—Locke.

It is plain there is not in nature a point of stability to be found; everything either ascends or declines; when wars are ended abroad, sedition begins at home; and when men are freed from fighting for necessity, they quarrel through ambition.—Sir Walter Raleigh.

A man so various that he seem'd to be,
Not one, but all mankind's epitome.
Stiff in opinions, always in the wrong;
Was everything by starts, and nothing long;
But, in the course of one revolving moon,
Was chymist, fiddler, statesman and buffoon.
                            —Dryden.

Who o'er the herd would wish to reign,
Fantastic, fickle, fierce, and vain?
Vain as the leaf upon the stream,
And fickle as a changeful dream;
Fantastic as a woman's mood,
And fierce as Frenzy's fever'd blood—
Thou many-headed monster thing,
Oh, who would wish to be thy king?
                            —Scott.

Fiction

Fiction is the microscope of truth.—Lamartine.

Truth, severe by fairy fiction drest.—Gray.

Parent of golden dreams—romance!—Byron.

The greater portion of our lives is thrown away in fiction; it is only in maturer years that we awake to the stern realities of life.—James Ellis.

Tales that have the rime of age.—Longfellow.

An old novel has a history of its own.—Alexander Smith.

Every novel is a debtor to Homer.—Emerson.

Novels are to love as fairy tales to dreams.—Coleridge.

Wondrous strong are the spells of fiction.—Longfellow.

I have often maintained that fiction may be much more instructive than real history.—John Foster.

Man is a poetical animal, and delights in fiction.—Hazlitt.

Truth and fiction are so aptly mixed that all seems uniform and of a piece.—Roscommon.

More strange than true, I never may believe
These antique fables, nor these fairy toys.
                            —Shakespeare.

Unbind the charms that in slight fables lie, and teach that truth is truest poesy.—Cowley.

No author ever drew a character consistent to human nature but what he was forced to ascribe it to many inconsistencies.—Bulwer-Lytton.

In employing fiction to make truth clear and goodness attractive, we are only following the example which every Christian ought to propose to himself.—Macaulay.

Those who relish the study of character may profit by the reading of good works of fiction, the product of well-established authors.—Whately.

Fiction may be said to be the caricature of history.—Bulwer-Lytton.

Who would with care some happy fiction frame, so mimics truth it looks the very same.—Granville.

Fiction is most powerful when it contains most truth; and there is little truth we get so true as that which we find in fiction.—J. G. Holland.

If you would understand your own age, read the works of fiction produced in it. People in disguise speak freely. —Arthur Helps.

He cometh to you with a tale which holdeth children from play, and old men from the chimney-corner.—Sir P. Sidney.

When fiction rises pleasing to the eye,
Men will believe, because they love the lie;
But truth herself, if clouded with a frown,
Must have some solemn proof to pass her down.
—Churchill.

Fiction is no longer a mere amusement; but transcendent genius, accommodating itself to the character of the age, has seized upon this province of literature, and turned fiction from a toy into a mighty engine.—Channing.

Fiction is of the essence of poetry as well as of painting; there is a resemblance in one of human bodies, things, and actions which are not real, and in the other of a true story by fiction.—Dryden.

Every fiction since Homer has taught friendship, patriotism, generosity, contempt of death. These are the highest virtues; and the fictions which taught them were therefore of the highest, though not of unmixed, utility. —Sir J. Mackintosh.

Addison acknowledged that he would rather inform than divert his reader; but he recollected that a man must be familiar with wisdom before he willingly enters on Seneca and Epictetus. Fiction allures him to the severe task by a gayer preface. Embellished truths are the illuminated alphabet of larger children.—Willmott.

The most influential books, and the truest in their influence, are works of fiction. * * * They repeat, they re-arrange, they clarify the lessons of life; they disengage us from ourselves, they constrain us to the acquaintance of others; and they show us the web of experience, but with a singular

change—that monstrous, consuming ego of ours being, nonce, struck out.— Robert Louis Stevenson.

Fidelity

Fidelity is the sister of justice.— Horace.

To God, thy country, and thy friend be true.—Vaughan.

Faithful found among the faithless. —Milton.

The root of all steadfastness is in consecration to God.—Alexander Maclaren.

Trust reposed in noble natures obliges them the more.—Dryden.

With strength to meet sorrow, and faith to endure.—Mrs. Osgood.

Prosperity asks for fidelity; adversity exacts it.—Seneca.

Ever keep thy promise, cost what it may; this it is to be "true as steel."— Charles Reade.

She is as constant as the stars
That never vary, and more chaste than they.
—Proctor.

The fidelity of barbarians depends on fortune.—Livy.

Through perils both of wind and limb,
Through thick and thin she follow'd him.
—Butler.

Flesh of flesh,
Bone of my bone, thou art, and from thy state
Mine never shall be parted, bliss or woe.
—Milton.

True as the needle to the pole,
Or as the dial to the sun.
—Barton Booth.

But faithfulness can feed on suffering,
And knows no disappointment.
—George Eliot.

Fidelity bought with money is overcome by money.—Seneca.

No man can mortgage his injustice as a pawn for his fidelity.—Burke.

It is more difficult for a man to be faithful to his mistress when he is favored than when he is ill treated by her.—Rochefoucauld.

Master, go on, and I will follow thee
To the last gasp, with truth and loyalty.
—Shakespeare.

Years have not seen, Time shall not see
The hour that tears my soul from thee.
—Byron.

Unkindness may do much;
And his unkindness may defeat my life,
But never taint my love. —Shakespeare.

To be true to each other, let 'appen what
   maäy
Till the end o' the daäy
An the last loäd hoäm. —Tennyson.

Then come the wild weather, come sleet or
   come snow,
We will stand by each other, however it
   blow. —Simon Dach.

I am constant as the Northern Star,
of whose true-fixed and resting quality there is no fellow in the firmament.
—Shakespeare.

His words are bonds, his oaths are oracles;
His love sincere, his thoughts immaculate;
His tears pure messengers sent from his
   heart;
His heart as far from fraud as heaven from
   earth. —Shakespeare.

Full many a miserable year hath past—
She knows him as one dead, or worse than
   dead,
And many a change her varied life hath
   known,
But her heart none. —Maturin.

Confirm'd then I resolve,
Adam shall share with me in bliss or woe:
So dear I love him, that with him all deaths
I could endure, without him live no life.
—Milton.

Nothing is more noble, nothing more venerable than fidelity. Faithfulness and truth are the most sacred excellences and endowments of the human mind.—Cicero.

Let it be ours to be self-reliant amidst hosts of the vacillating—real in a generation of triflers—true amongst a multitude of shams; when tempted to swerve from principle, sturdy as an oak in its maintenance; when solicited by the enticement of sinners, firm as a rock in our denial.—Wm. M. Punshon.

Within her heart was his image,
Cloth'd in the beauty of love and youth, as
   last she beheld him,
Only more beautiful made by his death-like
   silence and absence. —Longfellow.

For me—I have no lingering wish to rove;
For though I worship all things fair and
   free,
Of outward grace, of soul nobility,
Happier than thou, I find them all in one,
And I would worship at thy shrine alone.
—Miss Lynch.

He who is faithful over a few things is a lord of cities. It does not matter whether you preach in Westminster Abbey or teach a ragged class, so you be faithful. The faithfulness is all.—George MacDonald.

Be but faithful, that is all;
Go right on, and close behind thee
There shall follow still and find thee
Help, sure help.
—Arthur Hugh Clough.

No grace is more necessary to the Christian worker than fidelity: the humble grace that marches on in sunshine and storm, when no banners are waving, and there is no music to cheer the weary feet.—S. J. Nicholls.

Come, rest in this bosom, my own stricken
   deer!
Tho' the herd hath fled from thee, thy home
   is still here;
Here is still the smile that no cloud can
   o'ercast,
And the heart and the hand all thy own
   to the Last! —Moore.

Where is honor,
Innate and precept-strengthen'd, 'tis the
   rock
Of faith connubial: where it is not—where
Light thoughts are lurking, or the vanities
Of worldly pleasure rankle in the heart,
Or sensual throbs convulse it. —Byron.

Oh! it irradiates all our days with lofty beauty, and it makes them all hallowed and divine, when we feel that not the apparent greatness, not the prominence nor noise with which it is done, nor the external consequences which flow from it, but the motive from which it flowed, determines the worth of our deed in God's eyes. Faithfulness is faithfulness, on whatsoever scale it be set forth.—Alexander Maclaren.

It goes a great way towards making a man faithful to let him understand that you think him so, and he that does but so much as suspect that I will deceive him gives me a sort of right to cozen him.—Seneca.

He who, being bold
For life to come, is false to the past sweet
Of mortal life, hath killed the world above.
For why to live again if not to meet?
And why to meet if not to meet in love?
And why in love if not in that dear love
of old?   —Sydney Dobell.

Yes!—still I love thee: Time, who sets
His signet on my brow,
And dims my sunken eye, forgets,
The heart he could not bow;—
Where love, that cannot perish, grows
For one, Alas! that little knows
How love may sometimes last;
Like sunshine wasting in the skies
When clouds are overcast.
                    —Rufus Dawes.

Believe me, if all those endearing young charms,
Which I gaze on so foldly to-day,
Were to change by to-morrow, and fleet in my arms,
Like fairy-gifts fading away!
Thou would'st still be ador'd, as this moment thou art,
Let thy loveliness fade as it will,
And, around the dear ruin, each wish of my heart
Would entwine itself verdantly still!
                    —Moore.

I durst, my lord, to wager she is honest,
Lay down my soul at stake: if you think other,
Remove your thought; it doth abuse your bosom.
If any wretch hath put this in your head,
Let heaven requite it with the serpent's curse!
For, if she be not honest, chaste, and true,
There's no man happy: the purest of their wives
Is foul as slander.   —Shakespeare.

There is a third silent party to all our bargains. The nature and soul of things takes on itself the guaranty of the fulfillment of every contract, so

that honest service cannot come to loss. If you serve an ungrateful master, serve him the more. Put God in your debt. Every stroke shall be repaid. The longer the payment is withholden, the better for you; for compound interest on compound interest is the rate and usage of this exchequer.—Emerson.

Pure as the snow the summer sun—
Never at noon hath look'd upon—
Deep, as is the diamond wave,
Hidden in the desert cave—
Changeless, as the greenest leaves
Of the wreath the cypress weaves—
Hopeless, often, when most fond—
Without hope or fear beyond
Its own pale fidelity—
And this woman's love can be.
                    —Miss Landon.

Chain me with roaring bears;
Or shut me nightly in a charnel-house,
O'er-covered quite with dead men's rattling bones,
With reeky shanks and yellow chapless skulls;
Or bid me go into a new-made grave,
And hide me with a dead man in his shroud;
Things that, to hear them told, have made me tremble;
And I will do it without Fear or Doubt,
To live an unstain'd Wife of my sweet Love.   —Shakespeare.

They said her cheek of youth was beautiful
Till withering sorrow blanch'd the bright rose there;
But grief did lay his icy finger on it,
And chill'd it to a cold and joyless statue.
Methought she caroll'd blithely in her youth,
As the couched nestling trills his vesper lay;
But song and smile, beauty and melody,
And youth and happiness are gone from her,
Perchance—even as she is—he would not scorn her,
If he could know her—for, for him she's chang'd,
She is much alter'd—but her heart—her heart!   —Maturin.

Give us a man, young or old, high or low, on whom we know we can thoroughly depend, who will stand firm when others fail: the friend faithful and true, the adviser honest and fearless, the adversary just and chivalrous —in such a one there is a fragment of the Rock of Ages.—Dean Stanley.

Fighting

Fight the good fight.—Bible.

I'll fight till from my bones my flesh be hacked.—Shakespeare.

The combat deepens. On, ye brave,
Who rush to glory, or the grave!
—Campbell.

Those who in quarrels interpose,
Must often wipe a bloody nose.
—Gay.

For those that fly may fight again,
Which he can never do that's slain.
—Butler.

He who fights and runs away,
May live to fight another day;
But he who is in battle slain
Can never rise and fight again.
—Goldsmith.

Fiend

Satan—the impersonation of that mixture of the bestial, the malignant, the impious, and the hopeless, which constitute the fiend—the enemy of all that is human and divine.—Mrs. Jameson.

Finis

My pen is at the bottom of a page,
Which being finished, here the story ends;
'Tis to be wish'd it had been sooner done,
But stories somehow lengthen when begun.
—Byron.

Finesse

Sure never to o'ershoot, but just to hit.—Pope.

Finesse is the best adaptation of means to circumstances.—Macaulay.

Grant graciously what you cannot refuse safely, and conciliate those you cannot conquer.—Colton.

The moment one begins to solder right and wrong together, one's conscience becomes like a piece of plated goods.—Mrs. Jameson.

A man who knows the world will not only make the most of everything he does know, but of many things he does not know, and will gain more credit by his adroit mode of hiding his ignorance than the pedant by his awkward attempt to exhibit his erudition.—Colton.

"There is no difficulty," says the steward of Molière's miser, "in giving a fine dinner with plenty of money; the really great cook is he who can set out a banquet with no money at all." Macaulay.

Fire

From small fires comes oft no small mishap.—George Herbert.

From little spark may burst a mighty flame.—Dante.

Fire that's closest kept burns most of all.—Shakespeare.

A spark neglected makes a mighty fire.—Herrick.

The most tangible of all visible mysteries—fire.—Leigh Hunt.

Behold, how great a matter a little fire kindleth.—Bible.

The fire i' the flint
Shows not till it be struck.
—Shakespeare.

A little fire is quickly trodden out;
Which, being suffer'd, rivers cannot quench.
—Shakespeare.

And where two raging fires meet together
They do consume the thing that feeds their fury.
—Shakespeare.

Your own property is concerned when your neighbor's house is on fire.—Horace.

What is more useful than fire? Yet if any one prepares to burn a house, it is with fire that he arms his daring hands.—Ovid.

Be of good comfort, Master Ridley, play the man! We shall this day light such a candle, by God's grace, in England, as I trust shall never be put out.—Latimer.

Firmness

Stubbornness is not firmness.—Schiller.

Stand firm and immovable as an anvil when it is beaten upon.—St. Ignatius.

It is only dislocated minds whose movements are spasmodic.—Willmott.

It is firmness that makes the gods on our side.—Voltaire.

The greatest firmness is the greatest mercy.—Longfellow.

Firmness is great; persistency is greater.—Ninon de Lenclos.

I am here, here I remain.—Marshal MacMahon.

When firmness is sufficient, rashness is unnecessary.—Napoleon.

He who is firm in will molds the world to himself.—Goethe.

That which is called firmness in a king is called obstinacy in a donkey.—Lord Erskine.

You will hardly conquer; but conquer you must.—Ovid.

Be steadfast as a tower, that doth not bend its stately summit to the tempest's shock.—Dante.

I know no real worth but that tranquil firmness which seeks dangers by duty, and braves them without rashness.—Stanislaus.

Cowards are scared with threatenings; boys are whipped into confession; but a steady mind acts of itself, ne'er asks the body counsel.—Otway.

There is a natural firmness in some minds, which cannot be unlocked by trifles, but which, when unlocked, discovers a cabinet of fortitude.—Thomas Paine.

Firmness of purpose is one of the most necessary sinews of character and one of the best instruments of success. Without it, genius wastes its efforts in a maze of inconsistencies.—Chesterfield.

Rely on principles; walk erect and free, not trusting to bulk of body, like a wrestler, for one should not be un-conquerable in the sense that an ass is. Who then is unconquerable? He whom the inevitable cannot overcome —Epictetus.

That profound firmness which enables a man to regard difficulties but as evils to be surmounted, no matter what shape they may assume.—Colton.

Firmness, both in sufferance and exertion, is a character which I would wish to possess. I have always despised the whining yelp of complaint, and the cowardly, feeble resolve.—Burns.

The aged oak upon the steep stands more firm and secure if assailed by angry winds; for if the winter bares its head, the more strongly it strikes its roots into the ground, acquiring strength as it loses beauty.—Metastasio.

It is only persons of firmness that car have real gentleness; those who appear gentle are in general only of a weak character, which easily changes into asperity.—Rochefoucauld.

I said to Sorrow's awful storm,
  That beat against my breast,
Rage on—thou may'st destroy this form,
  And lay it low at rest;
But still the spirit that now brooks
  Thy tempest raging high,
Undaunted on its fury looks
  With steadfast eye. —Mrs. Stoddard.

Fish

It is unseasonable and unwholesome in all months that have not an R in their names to eat an oyster.—Butler.

Master, I marvel how the fishes live in the sea.
Why, as men do a-land: the great ones eat up the little ones.—Pericles.

Our plenteous streams a various race supply,
The bright-eye perch with fins of Tyrian dye,
The silver eel, in shining volumes roll'd,
The yellow carp, in scales bedropp'd with gold,
Swift trouts, diversified with crimson stains,
And pikes, the tyrants of the wat'ry plains.
          —Pope.

They say fish should swim thrice * * * first it should swim in the sea (do you mind me?), then it should swim in butter, and at last, sirrah, it should swim in good claret.—Swift.

"Will you walk a little faster?" said a whiting to a snail,
"There's a porpoise close behind us, and he's treading on my tail!
See how eagerly the lobsters and the turtles all advance:
They are waiting on the shingle—will you come and join the dance?"
—Lewis Carroll.

O scaly, slippery, wet, swift, staring wights,
What is 't ye do? what life lead? eh, dull goggles?
How do ye vary your vile days and nights?
How pass your Sundays? Are ye still but joggles
In ceaseless wash? Still nought but gapes and bites,
And drinks, and stares, diversified with boggles. —Leigh Hunt.

Fitness

When James and John asked Jesus for the best places in His kingdom, they were told in His gentle, gracious way that the main point was not wanting the best places, but being worth them. It is a question of preparation —"For whom they are prepared" is only another way of saying for those who are prepared. We are so used to favoritism in public life that we turn every way for enough influence to get ourselves appointed. But perfect governments are officered, not by official favorites, but by qualified men. "God is no respecter of persons." He does not look twice at a man's petition and signatures. It is wholly a question of personal fitness. Let us put the emphasis of our life, then, in the right place. It is not wanting something, but being worth something. God has plenty of time in which to make discoveries, but we have none too much time in which to become worth discovering. We should care, not so much about being recognized as about being worth recognition. The real values of life are spiritual and eternal, and the fit man will some day succeed the favorite.—Maltbie Babcock.

Flag

The flag of our union forever!—George P. Morris.

A star for every state, and a state for every star.—Robert C. Winthrop.

The meteor flag of England.—Campbell.

This token serveth for a flag of truce Betwixt ourselves and all our followers.
—Shakespeare.

Under spread ensigns moving nigh, in slow But firm battalion. —Milton.

When Freedom from her mountain height Unfurled her standard to the air.
—Joseph Rodman Drake.

If any one attempts to haul down the American flag, shoot him on the spot.—John A. Dix.

Bastard Freedom waves
Her fustian flag in mockery over slaves.
—Moore.

Who forthwith from the glittering staff unfurl'd
Th' imperial ensign, which full high advanc'd
Shone like a meteor streaming to the wind.
—Milton.

Ay, tear her tattered ensign down!
Long has it waved on high,
And many an eye has danced to see
That banner in the sky.
—Oliver Wendell Holmes.

Let it rise! let it rise, till it meet the sun in his coming; let the earliest light of the morning gild it, and the parting day linger and play on its summit.—Daniel Webster.

Flag of the free heart's hope and home!
By angel hands to valor given,
Thy stars have lit the welkin dome,
And all thy hues were born in heaven.
—Joseph Rodman Drake.

Ye mariners of England!
That guard our native seas;
Whose flag has braved a thousand years,
The battle and the breeze.—Campbell.

Nail to the mast her holy flag,
Set every threadbare sail,
And give her to the God of storms,
The lightning and the gale.
—O. W. Holmes.

"A song for our banner?"—The watchword recall
Which gave the republic her station;
"United we stand—divided we fall!"
It made and preserves us a nation!
—George P. Morris.

Praise the Power that hath made and preserved us a nation!
Then conquer we must when our cause it
is just.
And this be our motto, "In God is our
trust!"
And the star-spangled banner in triumph
shall wave
O'er the land of the free and the home of
the brave. —F. S. Key.

Fling out, fling out, with cheer and shout,
To all the winds Our Country's Banner!
Be every bar, and every star,
Displayed in full and glorious manner!
Blow, zephyrs, blow, keep the dear ensign
flying!
Blow, zephyrs, sweetly mournful, sighing,
sighing, sighing! —Abraham Coles.

Banner of England, not for a season,
O banner of Britain, has thou
Floated in conquering battle or flapt to the
battle-cry!
Never with mightier glory than when we
had rear'd thee on high,
Flying at top of the roofs in the ghastly
siege of Lucknow—
Shot thro' the staff or the halyard, but ever
we raised thee anew,
And ever upon the topmost roof our ban-
ner of England blew. —Tennyson.

Flattery

All-potent flattery, universal lord!—
Pope.

Flatterers are the worst kind of enemies.—Tacitus.

Flatterers are the bosom enemies of
princes.—South.

Oh, flatter me; for love delights in
praises.—Shakespeare.

Knavery and flattery are blood relations.—Abraham Lincoln.

Flattery is the handmaid of the
vices.—Cicero.

Self-love is the greatest of flatterers.
—La Rochefoucauld.

Flattery, the dangerous nurse of
vice.—Daniel.

No man flatters the woman he truly
loves.—Tuckerman.

He that is much flattered soon
learns to flatter himself.—Johnson.

Parent of wicked, bane of honest
deeds.—Prior.

The lie that flatters I abhor the
most.—Cowper.

A flatterer is the shadow of a fool.
—Sir Thomas Overbury.

Imitation is the sincerest of flattery.
—Colton.

It is easy to flatter; it is harder to
praise.—Richter.

If you mean to profit, learn to
praise.—Churchill.

See how they beg an alms of flattery!—Young.

Lay not that flattering unction to
your soul.—Shakespeare.

Just praise is only a debt, but flattery is a present.—Johnson.

Flattery labors under the odious
charge of servility.—Tacitus.

Nothing is so great an instance of
ill-manners as flattery.—Swift.

The most subtle flattery that a
woman can receive is by actions, not
by words.—Mme. Necker.

Those are generally good at flattering who are good for nothing else.—
South.

When flatterers meet the devil goes
to dinner.—De Foe.

Of all wild beasts preserve me from a
tyrant;
Of all tame—a flatterer. —Johnson.

Flattery corrupts both the receiver
and the giver; and adulation is not
of more service to the people than to
kings.—Burke.

The firmest purpose of a woman's
heart to well-timed, artful flattery may
yield.—Lillo.

He that loves to be flattered is
worthy o' the flatterer.—Shakespeare.

Meddle not with him that flattereth with his lips.—Bible.

Flattery is like a painted armor; only for show.—Socrates.

The most dangerous of all flattery is the inferiority of those about us.—Mme. Swetchine.

A man who flatters a woman hopes either to find her a fool or to make her one.—Richardson.

People flatter us because they can depend upon our credulity.—Tacitus.

But when I tell him he hates flatterers,
He says he does, being then most flattered.
—Shakespeare.

No visor does become black villainy so well as soft and tender flattery.—Shakespeare.

A man finds no sweeter voice in all the world than that which chants his praise.—Fontenelle.

O that men's ears should be to counsel deaf, but not to flattery!—Shakespeare.

Gallantry of mind consists in saying flattering things in an agreeable manner.—La Rochefoucauld.

Sirs, adulation is a fatal thing—
Rank poison for a subject, or a king.
—Dr. Wolcot.

Men are like stone jugs—you may lug them where you like by the ears.—Johnson.

When the world frowns, we can face it; but let it smile, and we are undone.—Bulwer-Lytton.

Flattery is a sort of bad money, to which our vanity gives currency.—La Rochefoucauld.

A fool flatters himself, a wise man flatters the fool.—Bulwer-Lytton.

If we would not flatter ourselves, the flattery of others could not harm us.—Rochefoucauld.

Not kings alone—the people, too, have their flatterers.—Mirabeau.

The most skillful flattery is to let a person talk on, and be a listener.—Addison.

Alas! the praise given to the ear
Ne'er was nor ne'er can be sincere.
—Miss Landon.

If any man flatters me, I'll flatter him again, though he were my best friend.—Franklin.

Flattery, which was formerly a vice, is now grown into a custom.—Publius Syrus.

Flattery is like base coin; it impoverishes him who receives it.—Madame Voillez.

There is no flattery so adroit or effectual as that of implicit assent.—Hazlitt.

This barren verbiage current among men,
Light coin, the tinsel clink of compliment.
—Tennyson.

Who flatters is of all mankind the lowest,
Save he who courts the flattery.
—Hannah More.

He does me double wrong, that wounds me with the flatteries of his tongue.—Shakespeare.

If we never flattered ourselves we should have but scant pleasure.—La Rochefoucauld.

It is better to fall among crows than flatterers; for those devour the dead only, these the living.—Antisthenes.

The flatterer easily insinuates himself into the closet, while honest merit stands shivering in the hall or antechamber.—Jane Porter.

You play the spaniel,
And think with wagging of your tongue to win me. —Shakespeare.

Applause is of too coarse a nature to be swallowed in the gross, though the extract or tincture be ever so agreeable.—Shenstone.

Flatterers are but the shadows of princes' bodies; the least thick cloud makes them invisible.—John Webster.

Though flattery blossoms like friendship, yet there is a vast difference in the fruit.—Socrates.

O flatt'ry!
How soon thy smooth insinuating oil
Supples the toughest fool!   —Fenton.

We sometimes think we hate flattery, when we only hate the manner in which we have been flattered.—Rochefoucauld.

Flattery is no more than what raises in a man's mind an idea of a preference which he has not.—Burke.

There is nothing which so poisons princes as flattery, nor anything whereby wicked men more easily obtain credit and favor with them.—Montaigne.

It hath been well said that the arch-flatterer, with whom all the petty flatterers have intelligence, is a man's self.—Bacon.

People generally despise where they flatter, and cringe to those they would gladly overtop; so that truth and ceremony are two things.—Marcus Antonius.

Give me flattery—flattery, the food of courts, that I may rock him, and lull him in the down of his desires.—Beaumont.

The love of flattery in most men proceeds from the mean opinion they have of themselves; in women, from the contrary.—Swift.

Among all the diseases of the mind, there is not one more epidemical or more pernicious than the love of flattery.—Steele.

The rich man despises those who flatter him too much, and hates those who do not flatter him at all.—Talleyrand.

The art of flatterers is to take advantage of the foibles of the great, to foster their errors, and never to give advice which may annoy.—Molière.

Flattery is often a traffic of mutual meanness, where although both parties intend deception, neither are deceived.—Colton.

Beware of flattery, 'tis a weed
Which oft offends the very idol—vice,
Whose shrine it would perfume.
—Fenton.

There is not one of us that would not be worse than kings, if so continually corrupted as they are with a sort of vermin called flatterers.—Montaigne.

No flattery, boy! an honest man cannot live by it; it is a little, sneaking art, which knaves use to cajole and soften fools withal.—Otway.

Very ugly or very beautiful women should be flattered on their understanding, and mediocre ones on their beauty.—Chesterfield.

His nature is too noble for the world; he would not flatter Neptune for his trident, or Jove for his power to thunder.—Shakespeare.

Because all men are apt to flatter themselves, to entertain the addition of other men's praises is most perilous.—Sir Walter Raleigh.

Commend a fool for his wit and a knave for his honesty, and they will receive you into their bosoms.—Fielding.

It is possible to be below flattery as well as above it. One who trusts nobody will not trust sycophants. One who does not value real glory will not value its counterfeit.—Macaulay.

We must define flattery and praise; they are distinct. Trajan was encouraged to virtue by the panegyric of Pliny; Tiberius became obstinate in vice from the flattery of his senators.—Louis the Sixteenth.

If you had told Sycorax that her son Caliban was as handsome as Apollo, she would have been pleased, witch as she was.—Thackeray.

Some indeed there are, who profess to despise all flattery, but even these are, nevertheless, to be flattered, by being told that they do despise it.—Colton.

Ah! when the means are gone, that buy this praise,
The breath is gone whereof this praise is made. —Shakespeare.

If you tell a woman she is beautiful, whisper it softly, for if the devil hears, he will echo it many times.—F. A. Durivage.

Women swallow at one mouthful the lie that flatters, and drink drop by drop the truth that is bitter.—Diderot.

Flatterers of every age resemble those African tribes of which the credulous Pliny speaks, who made men, animals, and even plants perish, while fascinating them with praises.—Richter.

Adroit observers will find that some who affect to dislike flattery may yet be flattered, indirectly by a well-seasoned abuse and ridicule of their rivals.—Colton.

Flattery is an ensnaring quality, and leaves a very dangerous impression. It swells a man's imagination, entertains his vanity, and drives him to a doting upon his own person.—Jeremy Collier.

There is no detraction worse than to overpraise a man, for if his worth proves short of what report doth speak of him, his own actions are ever giving the lie to his honor.—Feltham.

Flattery pleases very generally. In the first place, the flatterer may think what he says to be true, but, in the second place, whether he thinks so or not, he certainly thinks those whom he flatters of consequence enough to be flattered.—Johnson.

An ingenuous mind feels in unmerited praise the bitterest reproof. If you reject it, you are unhappy; if you accept it, you are undone.—Landor.

At the throng'd levee bends the venal tribe:
With fair but faithless smiles each varnish'd o'er,
Each smooth as those that mutually deceive. —Thomson.

I would give worlds, could I believe
One-half that is profess'd me;
Affection! could I think it Thee,
When Flattery has caress'd me. —Miss Landon.

Of praise a mere glutton, he swallow'd what came,
And the puff of a dunce he mistook it for fame;
Till his relish grown callous, almost to disease,
Who pepper'd the highest was surest to please. —Goldsmith.

For praise too dearly lov'd, or warmly sought,
Enfeebles all internal strength of thought;
And the weak soul within itself unblest,
Leans for all pleasure on another's breast. —Goldsmith.

Should the poor be flattered? No; let the candied tongue lick absurd pomp, and crook the pregnant hinges of the knee where thrift may follow fawning.—Shakespeare.

'Tis an old maxim in the schools,
That flattery's the food of fools,
Yet now and then you men of wit
Will condescend to take a bit. —Swift.

Of folly, vice, disease, men proud we see,
And (stranger still!) of blockhead's flattery,
Whose praise defames; as if a fool should mean,
By spitting on your face, to make it clean. —Young.

Fine speeches are the instruments of fools or knaves, who use them when they want good sense; but honesty needs no disguise or ornament.—Otway.

---

* * * for ne'er
Was flattery lost on Poet's ear;
A simple race! they waste their toil
For the vain tribute of a smile.—Scott.

The mischief of flattery is, not that it persuades any man that he is what he is not, but that it suppresses the influence of honest ambition by raising an opinion that honor may be gained without the toil of merit.—Johnson.

There is no tongue that flatters like a lover's; and yet, in the exaggeration of his feelings, flattery seems to him commonplace. Strange and prodigal exuberance, which soon exhausts itself by flowing!—Bulwer-Lytton.

First we flatter ourselves; and then the flattery of others is sure of success. It awakens our self-love within —a party who is ever ready to revolt from our better judgment, and join the enemy without.—Steele.

Christian! thou knowest thou carriest gunpowder about thee. Desire them that carry fire to keep at a distance. It is a dangerous crisis when a proud heart meets with flattering lips.—Flavel.

Take care how you listen to the voice of the flatterer, who, in return for his little stock, expects to derive from you considerable advantage. If one day you do not comply with his wishes, he imputes to you two hundred defects instead of perfections.—Saadi.

Let the passion of flattery be ever so inordinate, the supply can keep pace with the demand, and in the world's great market, in which wit and folly drive their bargains with each other, there are traders of all sorts.—Cumberland.

Flattery, though a base coin, is the necessary pocket money at court; where, by custom and consent, it has obtained such a currency that it is no longer a fraudulent, but a legal payment.—Chesterfield.

Flatterers are the worst kind of traitors, for they will strengthen thy imperfections, encourage thee in all evils, correct thee in nothing, but so shadow and paint thy follies and vices as thou shalt never, by their will, discover good from evil, or vice from virtue.—Sir Walter Raleigh.

A flatterer is said to be a beast that biteth smiling. But it is hard to know them from friends, they are so obsequious and full of protestations; for as a wolf resembles a dog, so doth a flatterer a friend.—Sir Walter Raleigh.

Praise not people to their faces, to the end that they may pay thee in the same coin. This is so thin a cobweb that it may with little difficulty be seen through; it is rarely strong enough to catch flies of any considerable magnitude.—Fuller.

Know thyself, thy evil as thy good, and flattery shall not harm thee; yea, her speech shall be a warning, a humbling, and a guide. For wherein thou lackest most, there chiefly will the sycophant commend thee.—Tupper.

By God, I cannot flatter: I do defy
The tongues of soothers; but a braver place
In my heart's love, hath no man than yourself;
Nay, task me to my word; approve me,
lord.   —Shakespeare.

Delicious essence! how refreshing art thou to nature! how strongly are all its powers and all its weaknesses on thy side! how sweetly dost thou mix with the blood, and help it through the most difficult and tortuous passages to the heart!—Sterne.

It requires but little acquaintance with the heart to know that woman's first wish is to be handsome; and that, consequently, the readiest method of obtaining her kindness is to praise her beauty.—Johnson.

Blinded as they are to their true character by self-love, every man is his own first and chiefest flatterer, prepared, therefore, to welcome the flatterer from the outside, who only comes confirming the verdict of the flatterer within.—Plutarch.

Nature has hardly formed a woman ugly enough to be insensible to flattery upon her person: if her face is so shocking that she must in some degree be conscious of it, her figure and her air, she trusts, make ample amends for it.—Chesterfield.

To be flattered is grateful, even when we know that our praises are not believed by those who pronounce them; for they prove at least our power, and show that our favor is valued, since it is purchased by the meanness of falsehood.—Johnson.

Parent of wicked, bane of honest deeds,
Pernicious flattery! thy malignant seeds,
In an ill hour, and by a fatal hand,
Sadly diffus'd o'er virtue's gleby land,
With rising pride amidst the corn appear,
And choke the hopes and harvest of the
year. —Prior.

It is scarcely credible to what degree discernment may be dazzled by the mist of pride, and wisdom infatuated by the intoxication of flattery; or how low the genius may descend by successive gradations of servility, and how swiftly it may fall down the precipice of falsehood.—Johnson.

Allow no man to be so free with you as to praise you to your face. Your vanity by this means will want its food. At the same time your passion for esteem will be more fully gratified; men will praise you in their actions; where you now receive one compliment, you will then receive twenty civilities.—Steele.

We must be careful how we flatter fools too little, or wise men too much; for the flatterer must act the very reverse of the physician, and administer the strongest dose only to the weakest patient.—Colton.

Take no repulse, whatever she doth say;
For, "get you gone," she doth not mean,
"away."
Flatter and praise, commend, extol their
graces;
Though ne'er so black, say they have
angels' faces.
That man that hath a tongue, I say, is no
man,
If with his tongue he cannot win a woman.
—Shakespeare.

We must suit the flattery to the mind and taste of the recipient. We do not put essences into hogsheads, nor porter into phials. Delicate minds may be disgusted by compliments that would please a grosser intellect; as some fine ladies who would be shocked at the idea of a dram will not refuse a liqueur.—Colton.

In order that all men may be taught to speak truth, it is necessary that all likewise should learn to hear it; for no species of falsehood is more frequent than flattery, to which the cow-

ard is betrayed by fear, the dependent by interest, and the friend by tenderness. Those who are neither servile nor timorous are yet desirous to bestow pleasure; and while unjust demands of praise continue to be made, there will always be some whom hope, fear, or kindness will dispose to pay them.—Johnson.

Flirting

Flirtation is the tomb of virtue.—
Mme. Roland.

Who is it can read a woman?—
Shakespeare.

Alas, the transports beauty can inspire!—Bovee.

One expresses well only the love he does not feel.—Alphonse Karr.

It is the same in love as in war; a fortress that parleys is half taken.—
Marguerite de Valois.

Cupid makes it his sport to pull the warrior's plum.—Sir P. Sidney.

Flirtation is a circulating library, in which we seldom ask twice for the same volume.—N. P. Willis.

Do you know a young and beautiful woman who is not ready to flirt—just a little?—J. Petit-Senn.

There are women who fly their falcons at any game, little birds and all.
—George MacDonald.

As the excitement of the game increases, prudence is sure to diminish.
—Bulwer-Lytton.

That soul-subduing sentiment, harshly called flirtation, which is the spell of a country house.—Beaconsfield.

Flirtation and coquetry are so nearly allied as to be identical; both are the art of successful and pleasing deception.—Mme. Louise Colet.

Admiration is natural; and it has been said there are many lovable women, but no perfect ones.—Laténa.

Novelty is to love like bloom to fruit; it gives a luster which is easily effaced, but never returns.—Rochefoucauld.

There are few young women in existence who have not the power of fascinating, if they choose to exert it.—Beaconsfield.

From a grave thinking mouser she was grown
The gayest flirt that coach'd it round the town.   —Pitt.

There are some women who are flirts upon principle; they consider it their duty to make themselves as pleasing as possible to every one.—Rivarol.

How happy could I be with either,
Were t'other dear charmer away!
But, while ye thus tease me together,
To neither a word will I say.   —Gay.

Never wedding, ever wooing,
Still a love-lorn heart pursuing,
Read you not the wrong you're doing,
In my cheek's pale hue?
All my life with sorrow strewing,
Wed, or cease to woo.   —Campbell.

I assisted at the birth of that most significant word flirtation, which dropped from the most beautiful mouth in the world, and which has since received the sanction of our most accurate laureate in one of his comedies.—Chesterfield.

Flowers

The bright consummate flower.—Milton.

Flowers are love's truest language.—Park Benjamin.

Prophets of fragrance, beauty, joy, and song.—Ebenezer Elliott.

Wee, modest, crimson-tipped flower.—Burns.

Flowers preach to us if we will hear.—Christina G. Rossetti.

How like they are to human things!—Longfellow.

Ye pretty daughters of the earth and sun.—Sir Walter Raleigh.

The amen! of nature is always a flower.—Holmes.

They speak of hope to the fainting heart.—Mrs. Hemans.

Where flowers degenerate man cannot live.—Napoleon.

The flower of sweetest smell is shy and lowly.—Wordsworth.

Flowers are like the pleasures of the world.—Shakespeare.

That queen of secrecy, the violet.—Keats.

These stars of earth, these golden flowers.—Longfellow.

There spring the wild-flowers—fair as can be.—Eliza Cook.

The flowers are gone when the fruits appear to ripen.—Pope.

Flora peering in April's front.—Shakespeare.

A snow of blossoms, and a wild of flowers.—Tickell.

Hope's gentle gem, the sweet forget-me-not.—Coleridge.

Beautiful objects of the wild-bee's love.—Nicoll.

Sweet flowers are slow, and weeds make haste.—Shakespeare.

The moss-clad violet, fragrant and concealed like hidden charity.—J. F. Hollings.

The plants look up to heaven, from whence they have their nourishment.—Shakespeare.

Flowers are sent to do God's work in unrevealed paths, and to diffuse influence by channels that we hardly suspect.—Henry Ward Beecher.

There's rosemary, that's for remembrance; * * * and there is pansies, that's for thoughts.—Shakespeare.

Flowers are the sweetest things that God ever made and forgot to put a soul into.—Beecher.

But the rose leaves herself upon the brier
For winds to kiss and grateful bees to feed.
—Keats.

The daisy is fair, the day-lily rare,
The bud o' the rose as sweet as it's bonnie.
—Hogg.

Roses, and pinks, and violets, to adorn
The shrine of Flora in her early May.
—Keats.

Flowers are words
Which even a babe may understand.
—Bishop Coxe.

To me the meanest flower that blows can give
Thoughts that do often lie too deep for tears. —Wordsworth.

Hope smiled when your nativity was cast,
Children of Summer! —Wordsworth.

Full many a flower is born to blush unseen, and waste its sweetness on the desert air.—Gray.

Look how the blue-eyed violets glance love to one another!—T. B. Read.

Ye living flowers, that skirt the eternal frost!—Coleridge.

The milk-white lilies that lean from the fragrant hedge.—Alice Cary.

Fade, flowers, fade! Nature will have it so; 'tis but what we in our autumn do.—Waller.

With fragrant breath the lilies woo me now, and softly speaks the sweet-voiced mignonette.—Julia C. R. Dorr.

The sweet forget-me-nots that grow for happy lovers.—Tennyson.

The daisies' eyes are a-twinkle with happy tears of dew.—Fitz-Hugh Ludlow.

Sweet flowers alone can say what passion fears revealing.—Moore.

Flowers, leaves, fruit, are the air-woven children of light.—Moleschott.

Foster the beautiful, and every hour thou callest new flowers to birth.—Schiller.

The buttercups across the field made sunshine rifts of splendor.—Miss Mulock.

And the spring arose on the garden fair like the spirit of Love felt everywhere.—Shelley.

Like saintly vestals, pale in prayer, their pure breath sanctifies the air.—Julia C. R. Dorr.

Flowers may beckon towards us, but they speak toward heaven and God.—Henry Ward Beecher.

The opening and the folding flowers, that laugh to the summer's day.—Mrs. Hemans.

He who does not love flowers has lost all love and fear of God.—Ludwig Tieck.

These children of the meadows, born
Of sunshine and of showers!
—Whittier.

Flowers spring up unsown and die ungathered.—Bryant.

Floral apostles! that in dewy splendor weep without woe, and blush without a crime.—Horace Smith.

I always think the flowers can see us, and know what we are thinking about.—George Eliot.

The gentle race of flowers
Are lying in their lowly beds.
—William Cullen Bryant.

Emblems of our own great resurrection, emblems of the bright and better land.—Longfellow.

In eastern lands they talk in flowers, and they tell in a garland their loves and cares.—Percival.

Lovely flowers are smiles of God's goodness.—Wilberforce.

I do love violets; they tell the history of woman's love.—L. E. Landon.

Happy are they who can create a rose tree or erect a honeysuckle.—Gray.

How the universal heart of man blesses flowers! They are wreathed round the cradle, the marriage altar, and the tomb.—Mrs. L. M. Child.

The snowdrop and primrose our woodlands adorn,
And violets bathe in the wet o' the morn.
—Burns.

The breath of flowers is far sweeter in the air (where it comes and goes like the warbling of music) than in the hand.—Bacon.

It is with flowers as with moral qualities; the bright are sometimes poisonous: but, I believe, never the sweet.—Hare.

Who that has loved knows not the tender tale which flowers reveal, when lips are coy to tell?—Bulwer-Lytton.

E'en the rough rocks with tender myrtle bloom, and trodden weeds send out a rich perfume.—Addison.

Flowers are the beautiful hieroglyphics of nature, with which she indicates how much she loves us.—Goethe.

If thou wouldest attain to thy highest, go look upon a flower; what that does willessly, that do thou willingly.—Schiller.

The daffodil is our door-side queen; she pushes up the sward already, to spot with sunshine the early green.—Bryant.

May-flowers blooming around him.
Fragrant, filling the air with a strange and wonderful sweetness. —Longfellow.

I regard them, as Charles the Emperor did Florence, that they are too pleasant to be looked upon except on holidays.—Izaak Walton.

Most gladly would I give the blood-stained laurel for the first violet which March brings us, the fragrant pledge of the new-fledged year.—Schiller.

There is not the least flower but seems to hold up its head and to look pleasantly, in the secret sense of the goodness of its Heavenly Maker.—South.

A passion for flowers is, I really think, the only one which long sickness leaves untouched with its chilling influence.—Mrs. Hemans.

The Omnipotent has sown His name on the heavens in glittering stars; but upon earth He planteth His name by tender flowers.—Richter.

Leaves are the Greek, flowers the Italian, phase of the spirit of beauty that reveals itself through the flora of the globe.—T. Starr King.

I think I am quite wicked with roses. I like to gather them, and smell them till they have no scent left.—George Eliot.

As timid violets lade the ambient air
With their heart's richest fragrance, unaware
The fragrance whispers that the flower is there. —Anna Katharine Green.

Sweet flower, thou tellest how hearts as pure and tender as thy leaf, as low and humble as thy stem, will surely know the joy that peace imparts.—Percival.

The harebells nod as she passes by,
The violet lifts its tender eye,
The ferns bend her steps to greet,
And the mosses creep to her dancing feet.
—Julia C. R. Dorr.

And all the meadows, wide unrolled,
Were green and silver, green and gold,
Where buttercups and daisies spun
Their shining tissues in the sun.
—Julia C. R. Dorr.

Spake full well, in language quaint and olden,
One who dwelleth by the castled Rhine,
When he called the flowers, so blue and golden,
Stars, that in earth's firmament do shine.
—Longfellow.

Your voiceless lips, O flowers, are living preachers—each cup a pulpit, and each leaf a book.—Horace Smith.

The herb feeds upon the juice of a good soil, and drinks in the dew of heaven as eagerly, and thrives by it as effectually, as the stalled ox that tastes everything that he eats or drinks.—South.

I know a bank where the wild thyme blows,
Where oxlips and the nodding violet grows;
Quite over-canopied with luscious wood-
bine,
With sweet musk-roses, and with eglantine.
—Shakespeare.

Flowers never emit so sweet and strong a fragrance as before a storm. Beauteous soul! when a storm approaches thee, be as fragrant as a sweet-smelling flower.—Richter.

Gorgeous flowerets in the sunlight shining,
Blossoms flaunting in the eye of day,
Tremulous leaves, with soft and silver
lining,
Buds that open only to decay.
—Longfellow.

The purple heath and golden broom
On moory mountains catch the gale,
O'er lawns the lily sheds perfume,
The violet in the vale.
—Montgomery.

Not a flower but shows some touch, in freckle, streak, or stain, of His unrivaled pencil. He inspires their balmy odors, and imparts their hues.—Cowper.

The rose is fragrant, but it fades in time:
The violet sweet, but quickly past the
prime:
White lilies hang their heads, and soon
decay,
And white snow in minutes melts away.
—Dryden.

What a pity flowers can utter no sound! A singing rose, a whispering violet, a murmuring honeysuckle—oh, what a rare and exquisite miracle would these be!—Beecher.

Flowers and fruits are always fit presents—flowers, because they are a proud assertion that a ray of beauty outvalues all the utilities of the world.—Emerson.

Yellow japanned buttercups and star-disked dandelions—just as we see them lying in the grass, like sparks that have leaped from the kindling sun of summer.—O. W. Holmes.

Underneath large blue-bells tented
Where the daisies are rose-scented,
And the rose herself has got
Perfume which on earth is not.
—Keats.

Now blooms the lily by the bank,
The primrose down the brae;
The hawthorn's budding in the glen,
And milkwhite is the slae. —Burns.

To analyze the charms of flowers is like dissecting music; it is one of those things which it is far better to enjoy than to attempt to understand.—Tuckerman.

What a desolate place would be a world without a flower! It would be a face without a smile, a feast without a welcome. Are not flowers the stars of the earth, and are not our stars the flowers of heaven?—Mrs. Balfour.

They speak of hope to the fainting heart,
With a voice of promise they come and
part,
They sleep in dust through the wintry
hours,
They break forth in glory—bring flowers,
bright flowers! —Mrs. Hemans.

A love-tint flushes the wind-flower's cheek,
Rich melodies gush from the violet's beak,
On the rifts of the rock, the wild colum-
bines grow,
Their heavy honey-cups bending low.
—Sarah Helen Whitman.

Learn, O student, the true wisdom. See yon bush aflame with roses, like the burning bush of Moses. Listen, and thou shalt hear, if thy soul be not deaf, how from out it, soft and clear, speaks to thee the Lord Almighty.—Hafiz.

Flowers are the bright remembrances of youth; they waft us back, with their bland odorous breath, the joyous hours that only young life knows, ere we have learnt that this fair earth hides graves.—Countess of Blessington.

There is to the poetical sense a ravishing prophecy and winsome intimation in flowers that now and then, from the influence of mood or circumstance, reasserts itself like the reminiscence of childhood, or the spell of love.—Tuckerman.

As for marigolds, poppies, hollyhocks, and valorous sunflowers, we shall never have a garden without them, both for their own sake and for the sake of old-fashioned folks, who used to love them.—Beecher.

Doubtless botany has its value; but the flowers knew how to preach divinity before men knew how to dissect and botanize them; they are apt to stop preaching, though, so soon as we begin to dissect and botanize them. —H. N. Hudson.

The instinctive and universal taste of mankind selects flowers for the expression of its finest sympathies, their beauty and their fleetingness serving to make them the most fitting symbols of those delicate sentiments for which language itself seems almost too gross a medium.—Hillard.

The loveliest flowers the closest cling to
    earth,
And they first feel the sun: so violets blue;
So the soft star-like primrose—drenched in
    dew—
The happiest of spring's happy, fragrant
    birth.   —Keble.

They know the time to go!
    The fairy clocks strike their inaudible
      hour
In field and woodland, and each punctual flower
Bows at the signal an obedient head
    And hastes to bed.
        —Susan Coolidge.

Flowers are Love's truest language; they
    betray,
Like the divining rods of Magi old,
Where precious wealth lies buried, not of
    gold,
But love—strong love, that never can decay!
        —Park Benjamin.

Flowers have an expression of countenance as much as men or animals. Some seem to smile; some have a sad expression; some are pensive and diffident; others again are plain, honest and upright, like the broad-faced sunflower and hollyhock.—Henry Ward Beecher.

With roses musky-breathed,
  And drooping daffodilly,
  And silver-leaved lily,
And ivy darkly-wreathed,
I wove a crown before her,
For her I love so dearly.
      —Tennyson.

Flowers belong to Fairyland: the flowers and the birds and the butterflies are all that the world has kept of its golden age—the only perfectly beautiful things on earth—joyous, innocent, half divine—useless, say they who are wiser than God.—Ouida.

To cultivate a garden is to walk with God, to go hand in hand with nature in some of her most beautiful processes, to learn something of her choicest secrets, and to have a more intelligent interest awakened in the beautiful order of her works elsewhere.—Bovee.

There is to me a daintiness about early flowers that touches me like poetry. They blow out with such a simple loveliness among the common herbs of pastures, and breathe their lives so unobtrusively, like hearts whose beatings are too gentle for the world.—Willis.

Every rose is an autograph from the hand of the Almighty God on this world about us. He has inscribed His thoughts in these marvelous hieroglyphics which sense and science have been these many thousand years seeking to understand.—Theodore Parker.

Flowers should deck the brow of the youthful bride, for they are in themselves a lovely type of marriage. They should twine round the tomb, for their perpetually renewed beauty is a symbol of the resurrection. They should festoon the altar, for their fragrance and their beauty ascend in perpetual worship before the Most High.—Mrs. L. M. Child.

"If flowers have souls," said Undine, "the bees, whose nurses they are, must seem to them darling children at

the breast. I once fancied a paradise for the spirits of departed flowers."
"They go," answered I, "not into paradise, but into a middle state; the souls of lilies enter into maidens' foreheads, those of hyacinths and forget-me-nots dwell in their eyes, and those of roses in their lips."—Richter.

The little flower which sprung up through the hard pavement of poor Picciola's prison was beautiful from contrast with the dreary sterility which surrounded it. So here amid rough walls, are there fresh tokens of nature. And O, the beautiful lessons which flowers teach to children, especially in the city! The child's mind can grasp with ease the delicate suggestions of flowers.—Chapin.

Yet, no—not words, for they
But half can tell love's feeling;
Sweet flowers alone can say
What passion fears revealing:
A once bright rose's wither'd leaf,
A tow'ring lily broken—
Oh, these may paint a grief
No words could e'er have spoken.
—Moore.

Daffodils,
That come before the swallow dares, and take
The winds of March with beauty; violets dim,
But sweeter than the lids of Juno's eyes,
Or Cytherea's breath; pale primroses,
That die unmarried ere they can behold
Bright Phœbus in his strength—a malady
Most incident to maids; bold oxlips and
The crown-imperial; lilies of all kinds,
The flower-de-luce being one!
—Shakespeare.

I remember, I remember
The roses, red and white,
The violets, and the lily-cups,
Those flowers made of light!
The lilacs, where the robin built,
And where my brother set
The laburnum on his birthday—
The tree is living yet. —Hood.

Often a nosegay of wild flowers, which was to us, as village children, a grove of pleasure, has in after years of manhood, and in the town, given us by its old perfume, an indescribable transport back into godlike childhood; and how, like a flower goddess, it has raised us into the first embracing Aurora clouds of our first dim feelings!—Richter.

Sweet is the rose, but grows upon a brere;
Sweet is the juniper, but sharp his bough;
Sweet is the eglantine, but sticketh nere;
Sweet is the firbloome, but its braunches rough;
Sweet is the cypress, but its rynd is tough;
Sweet is the nut, but bitter is his pill;
Sweet is the broome-flowre, but yet sowre enough;
And sweet is moly, but his root is ill.
—Spenser.

Here eglantine embalm'd the air,
Hawthorne and hazel mingled there;
The primrose pale, and violet flower,
Found in each cliff a narrow bower;
Fox-glove and nightshade, side by side,
Emblems of punishment and pride,
Group'd their dark hues with every stain
The weather-beaten crags retain.—Scott.

There bloomed the strawberry of the wilderness;
The trembling eyebright showed her sapphire blue,
The thyme her purple, like the blush of Even;
And if the breath of some to no caress
Invited, forth they peeped so fair to view,
All kinds alike seemed favorites of heaven.
—Wordsworth.

Sweet letters of the angel tongue,
I've loved ye long and well,
And never have failed in your fragrance sweet
To find some secret spell—
A charm that has bound me with witching power,
For mine is the old belief,
That midst your sweets and midst your bloom,
There's a soul in every leaf!
—M. M. Ballou.

He bore a simple wild-flower wreath:
Narcissus, and the sweet brier rose;
Vervain, and flexile thyme, that breathe
Rich fragrance; modest heath, that glows
With purple bells; the amaranth bright,
That no decay, nor fading knows,
Like true love's holiest, rarest light;
And every purest flower, that blows
In that sweet time, which Love most blesses,
When spring on summer's confines presses. —Thomas Love Peacock.

He must have an artist's eye for color and form who can arrange a hundred flowers as tastefully, in any other way, as by strolling through a garden, and picking here one and there one, and adding them to the bouquet

In the accidental order in which they chance to come. Thus we see every summer day the fair lady coming in from the breezy side hill with gorgeous colors and most witching effects. If only she could be changed to alabaster, was ever a finer show of flowers in so fine a vase? But instead of allowing the flowers to remain as they were gathered, they are laid upon the table, divided, rearranged on some principle of taste, I know not what, but never again have that charming naturalness and grace which they first had.—Beecher.

The foxglove, with its stately bell
Of purple, shall adorn thy dells;
The wallflower, on each rifted rock,
From liberal blossoms shall breathe down,
(Gold blossoms frecked with iron-brown,)
Its fragrance; while the hollyhock,
The pink, and the carnation vie
With lupin and with lavender,
To decorate the fading year;
And larkspurs, many-hued, shall drive
Gloom from the groves, where red leaves lie,
And Nature seems but half alive.
        —D. M. Moir.

The windflower and the violet, they perished long ago,
And the brier-rose and the orchis died amid the summer glow;
But on the hills the golden-rod, and the aster in the wood,
And the yellow sunflower by the brook, in autumn beauty stood,
Till fell the frost from the clear cold heaven, as falls the plague on men,
And the brightness of their smile was gone, from upland glade and glen.
        —Bryant.

Foe

He makes no friend who never made a foe.—Tennyson.

Cursed be the verse, how well soe'er it flow,
That tends to make one worthy man my foe.   —Pope.

Alike reserved to blame, or to commend,
A timorous foe and a suspicious friend.
        —Pope.

A foe to God was ne'er true friend to man,
Some sinister intent taints all he does.
        —Young.

Fool — Folly

Fools are not mad folks.—Shakespeare.

None but a fool is always right.—Hare.

Fools rush in where angels fear to tread.—Pope.

A fool at forty is a fool indeed.—Young.

To the fool-king belongs the world.—Schiller.

No creature smarts so little as a fool.—Pope.

A fool's bolt is soon shot.—Shakespeare.

A rogue is a roundabout fool.—Coleridge.

It needs brains to be a real fool.—George MacDonald.

The wise man knows himself to be a fool.—Shakespeare.

Better a witty fool, than a foolish wit.—Shakespeare.

Fools are apt to imitate only the defects of their betters.—Swift.

Men may live fools, but fools they cannot die.—Young.

A fool may now and then be right by chance.—Cowper.

The fool doth think he is wise.—Shakespeare.

Even the fool is wise after the event.—Homer.

A fool with judges, amongst fools a judge.—Cowper.

Fool beckons fool, and dunce awakens dunce.—Churchill.

Levity of behavior, always a weakness, is far more unbecoming in a woman than a man.—William Penn.

Fools are my theme, let satire be my song.—Byron.

Too many giddy, foolish hours are gone.—Rowe.

Fortune makes folly her peculiar care.—Churchill.

Folly loves the martyrdom of fame. —Byron.

Old fools are more foolish than young ones.—Rochefoucauld.

Mingle a little folly with your wisdom.—Horace.

Who lives without folly is not so wise as he thinks.—La Rochefoucauld.

Fools, to talking ever prone
Are sure to make their follies known.
—Gay.

A man may be as much a fool from the want of sensibility as the want of sense.—Mrs. Jameson.

Women, like men, may be persuaded to confess their faults; but their follies, never.—Alfred de Musset.

'Tis my maxim, he's a fool that marries; but he's a greater that does not marry a fool.—Wycherly.

O noble fool!
A worthy fool! Motley's the only wear.
—Shakespeare.

Thou little thinkest what a little foolery governs the whole world.—John Selden.

Leave such to trifle with more grace and ease,
Whom Folly pleases, and whose Follies please. —Pope.

Young men think old men are fools; but old men know young men are fools.—George Chapman.

There are well-dressed follies, as there are well-clothed fools.—Chamfort.

No one should so act as to take advantage of another's folly.—Cicero.

If thou hast never been a fool, be sure thou wilt never be a wise man.— Thackeray.

By outward show let's not be cheated;
An ass should like an ass be treated.
—Gay.

People are never so near playing the fool as when they think themselves wise.—Lady Montagu.

Every man's follies are the caricature resemblances of his wisdom.— John Sterling.

Ever since Adam fools have been in the majority.—Casimir Delavigne.

It is the peculiar quality of a fool to perceive the faults of others, and to forget his own.—Cicero.

If the advice of a fool for once happens to be good, it requires a wise man to carry it out.—Lessing.

I am always afraid of a fool. One cannot be sure that he is not a knave as well.—Hazlitt.

A man of wit would often be much embarrassed without the company of fools.—Rochefoucauld.

Generally nature hangs out a sign of simplicity in the face of a fool.— Thomas Fuller.

Of all thieves, fools are the worst; they rob you of time and temper.— Goethe.

Surely he is not a fool that hath unwise thoughts, but he that utters them. —Bishop Hall.

Tricks and treachery are the practice of fools that have not wit enough to be honest.—Benjamin Franklin.

There are follies as catching as contagious disorders.—La Rochefoucauld.

A learned fool is more foolish than an ignorant fool.—Molière.

He must be a thorough fool who can learn nothing from his own folly.—J. C. and A. W. Hare.

It would be easier to endow a fool with intellect than to persuade him that he had none.—Babinet.

A fool is often as dangerous to deal with as a knave, and always more incorrigible.—Colton.

What shadows we are, and what shadows we pursue!—Burke.

If you wish to avoid seeing a fool you must first break your looking-glass.—Rabelais.

The instruction of the foolish is a waste of knowledge; soap cannot wash charcoal white.—Kabir.

What matter though the scorn of fools be given,
If the path follow'd lead us on to heaven!
—Mrs. Hale.

I am a fool, I know it; and yet, God help me, I'm poor enough to be a wit.—Congreve.

A fool cannot look, nor stand, nor walk like a man of sense.—La Bruyère.

Men are so necessarily fools that it would be being a fool in a higher strain of folly, not to be a fool.—Pascal.

All men are fools, and with every effort they differ only in the degree.—Boileau.

He who provides for this life, but takes no care for eternity, is wise for a moment, but a fool forever.—Tillotson.

As riches and honor forsake a man, we discover him to be a fool, but nobody could find it out in his prosperity.—La Bruyère.

Oh, brother wearers of motley, are there not moments when one grows sick of grinning and trembling and the jingling of cap and bells?—Thackeray.

How can you make a fool perceive that he is a fool? Such a personage can no more see his own folly than he can see his own ears.—Thackeray.

Fools with bookish knowledge are children with edged weapons; they hurt themselves, and put others in pain.—Zimmermann.

There are certain people fated to be fools; they not only commit follies by choice, but are even constrained to do so by fortune.—Rochefoucauld.

A fool who has a flash of wit creates astonishment and scandal, like hack-horses setting out to gallop.—Chamfort.

After a man has sown his wild oats in the years of his youth, he has still every year to get over a few weeks and days of folly.—Richter.

He is one of those wise philanthropists who, in a time of famine, would vote for nothing but a supply of tooth-picks.—Douglas Jerrold.

People have no right to make fools of themselves, unless they have no relations to blush for them.—Haliburton.

Fools and sensible men are equally innocuous. It is in the half fools and the half wise that the greatest danger lies.—Goethe.

Well, thus we play the fools with the time, and the spirits of the wise sit in the clouds and mock us.—Shakespeare.

Fools are very often united in the strictest intimacies, as the lighter kinds of woods are the most closely glued together.—Shenstone.

There is nothing which one regards so much with an eye of mirth and pity as innocence when it has in it a dash of folly.—Addison.

Women are charged with a fondness for nonsense and frivolity. Did not Talleyrand say, "I find nonsense singularly refreshing"?—Alfred de Musset.

The multitude of fools is a protection to the wise.—St. Augustine.

You pity a man who is lame or blind, but you never pity him for being a fool, which is often a much greater misfortune.—Sydney Smith.

Though thou shouldst bray a fool in a mortar among wheat with a pestle, yet will not his foolishness depart from him.—Bible.

Folly is like the growth of weeds, always luxurious and spontaneous; wisdom, like flowers, requires cultivation.—Hosea Ballou.

The compliments of the season to my worthy masters, and a merry first of April to us all. We have all a speck of the motley.—Lamb.

The greatest of fools is he who imposes on himself, and in his greatest concern thinks certainly he knows that which he has least studied, and of which he is most profoundly ignorant. —Shaftesbury.

The imputation of being a fool is a thing which mankind, of all others, is the most impatient of, it being a blot upon the prime and specific perfection of human nature.—South.

To succeed in the world, it is much more necessary to possess the penetration to discover who is a fool than to discover who is a clever man.— Cato.

There is in human nature generally more of the fool than of the wise; and therefore those faculties by which the foolish part of men's minds are taken are more potent.—Bacon.

Men of all ages have the same inclinations, over which reason exercises no control. Thus, wherever men are found, there are follies, ay, and the same follies.—La Fontaine.

Men are so completely fools by necessity that he is but a fool in a higher strain of folly who does not confess his foolishness.—Pascal.

Some old men, by continually praising the time of their youth, would almost persuade us that there were no fools in those days; but unluckily they are left themselves for examples. —Pope.

If a traveler does not meet with one who is his better or his equal, let him firmly keep to his solitary journey; there is no companionship with a fool. —Max Müller.

To pardon those absurdities in ourselves which we cannot suffer in others is neither better nor worse than to be more willing to be fools ourselves than to have others so.—Pope.

I have play'd the fool, the gross fool, to
  believe
The bosom of a friend will hold a secret
Mine own could not retain.
               —Massinger.

The right to be a cussed fool
  Is safe from all devices human,
It's common (ez a gin'l rule)
  To every critter born of woman.
               —Lowell.

A rational reaction against irrational excesses and vagaries of skepticism may * * * readily degenerate into the rival folly of credulity. —Gladstone.

Nothing exceeds in ridicule, no doubt,
A fool in fashion, but a fool that's out;
His passion for absurdity's so strong,
He cannot bear a rival in the wrong.
               —Young.

'Tis not by guilt the onward sweep
Of truth and right, O Lord, we stay;
'Tis by our follies that so long
We hold the earth from heaven away.
               —Sill.

Always win fools first. They talk much, and what they have once uttered they will stick to; whereas there is always time, up to the last moment, to bring before a wise man arguments that may entirely change his opinion. —Helps.

Men, when their actions succeed not as they would, are always ready to impute the blame thereof to heaven, so as to excuse their own follies.—Spenser.

A fool and a wise man are alike both in the starting-place—their birth, and at the post—their death; only they differ in the race of their lives.—Fuller.

Folly consists in the drawing of false conclusions from just principles, by which it is distinguished from madness, which draws just conclusions from false principles.—Locke.

At thirty man suspects himself a fool;
Knows it at forty, and reforms his plan;
At fifty chides his infamous delay,
Pushes his prudent purpose to resolve,
Resolves—and re-resolves; then dies the
　same.　　　　　　　　—Young.

A harmless hilarity and a buoyant cheerfulness are not infrequent concomitants of genius; and we are never more deceived than when we mistake gravity for greatness, solemnity for science, and pomposity for erudition.—Colton.

If men are to be fools, it were better that they were fools in little matters than in great; dullness, turned up with temerity, is a livery all the worse for the facings; and the most tremendous of all things is a magnanimous dunce.—Sydney Smith.

The wise man has his follies no less than the fool; but it has been said that herein lies the difference—the follies of the fool are known to the world, but are hidden from himself; the follies of the wise are known to himself, but hidden from the world.—Colton.

Were I to be angry at men being fools, I could here find ample room for declamation; but, alas! I have been a fool myself; and why should I be angry with them for being something so natural to every child of humanity? —Goldsmith.

For not only is Fortune herself blind, but she generally causes those men to be blind whose interests she has more particularly embraced. Therefore they are often haughty and arrogant; nor is there anything more intolerable than a prosperous fool. And hence we often see that men who were at one time affable and agreeable are completely changed by prosperity, despising their old friends, and clinging to new.—Cicero.

Foot — Feet

Nay, her foot speaks.—Shakespeare.

Feet like sunny gems on our English green.—Tennyson.

The grass stoops not, she treads on it so light.—Shakespeare.

Feet that run on willing errands!—Longfellow.

Footprints on the sands of time.—Longfellow.

Dance on the sands, and yet no footing seen.—Shakespeare.

And the prettiest foot; Oh, if a man could but fasten his eyes to her feet as they steal in and out, and play at bo-peep under her petticoats, Ah! Mr. Trapland?—Congreve.

Steps with a tender foot, light as on air,
The lovely, lordly creature floated on.
　　　　　　　　—Tennyson.

So lightly walks, she not one mark imprints,
Nor brushes off the dews, nor soils the
　tints.　　　　　　—Churchill.

　　　　O happy earth,
Whereon thy innocent feet doe ever tread!
　　　　　　　　—Spenser.

As if the wind, not she, did walk,
Nor pressed a flower, nor bowed a stalk.
　　　　　　　　—Ben Jonson.

There is as much expression in the feet as in the hands.—Chamfort.

A foot more light, a step more true,
Ne'er from the heath-flower dashed the
　dew.　　　　　　—Scott.

Her pretty feet, like snails, did creep
　A little out, and then,
As if they played at bo-peep,
　Did soon draw in again.
　　　　　　—Robert Herrick.

So light a foot will ne'er wear out the everlasting flint.—Shakespeare.

The flower she touched on dipped and rose.—Tennyson.

Her feet beneath her petticoat like little mice stole in and out, as if they feared the light.—Suckling.

Fop — Foppery

Foppery is the egotism of clothes.—Victor Hugo.

A dandy is a clothes-wearing man.—Carlyle.

Nature made every fop to plague his
  brother,
Just as one beauty mortifies another.
          —Pope.

Their methods various, but alike their aim; the sloven and the fopling are the same.—Young.

A fop takes great pains to hang out a sign, by his dress, of what he has within.—Richardson.

Ambiguous things that ape goats in their visage, women in their shape.—Byron.

A coxcomb is ugly all over with affectation of a fine gentleman.—Dr. Johnson.

Nature has sometimes made a fool; but a coxcomb is always of a man's own making.—Addison.

So gentle, yet so brisk, so wondrous sweet,
So fit to prattle at a lady's feet.
          —Churchill.

Foppery, being the chronic condition of women, is not so much noticed as it is when it breaks out on the person of the male bird.—Balzac.

Foppery is never cured; it is the bad stamina of the mind, which, like those of the body, are never rectified; once a coxcomb always a coxcomb.—Johnson.

A beau is one who arranges his curled locks gracefully, who ever smells of balm, and cinnamon; who hums the songs of the Nile, and Cadiz; who throws his sleek arms into various attitudes; who idles away the whole day among the chairs of the ladies, and is ever whispering into some one's ear; who reads little billets-doux from this quarter and that, and writes them in return; who avoids ruffling his dress by contact with his neighbors sleeve, who knows with whom everybody is in love; who flutters from feast to feast, who can recount exactly the pedigree of Hirpinus. What do you tell me? is this a beau, Cotilus? Then a beau, Cotilus, is a very trifling thing.—Martial.

A fop who admires his person in a glass soon enters into a resolution of making his fortune by it, not questioning that every woman who falls in his way will do him as much justice as himself.—Thomas Hughes.

In form so delicate, so soft his skin,
So fair in feature, and so smooth his chin,
Quite to unman him nothing wants but
  this;
Put him in coats, and he's a very miss.
          —Horace.

A six-foot suckling, mincing in its gait,
Affected, peevish, prim and delicate;
Fearful it seemed, tho' of athletic make,
Lest brutal breezes should so roughly shake
Its tender form, and savage motion spread
O'er its pale cheeks, the horrid manly red.
          —Churchill.

The all importance of clothes has sprung up in the intellect of the dandy without effort, like an instinct of genius; he is inspired with clothes, a poet of clothes.—Carlyle.

Forbearance

If thou wouldst be borne with bear with others.—Fuller.

Whosoever shall smite thee on thy right cheek, turn to him the other also. And if any man will sue thee at the law, and take away thy coat, let him have thy cloak also.—Bible.

The kindest and the happiest pair
Will find occasion to forbear;
And something every day they live
To pity and perhaps forgive.—Cowper.

Learn from Jesus to love and to forgive. Let the blood of Jesus, which implores pardon for you in heaven, obtain it from you for your brethren here upon earth.—Valpy.

Be to her virtues very kind;
Be to her faults a little blind.
Let all her ways be unconfin'd,
And clap your padlock on her mind.
—Prior.

It is a noble and a great thing to cover the blemishes and to excuse the failings of a friend; to draw a curtain before his stains, and to display his perfections; to bury his weaknesses in silence, but to proclaim his virtues upon the housetop.—South.

Everything has two handles; the one soft and manageable, the other such as will not endure to be touched. If then your brother do you an injury, do not take it by the hot hard handle, by representing to yourself all the aggravating circumstances of the fact; but look rather on the soft side, and extenuate it as much as is possible, by considering the nearness of the relation, and the long friendship and familiarity between you—obligations to kindness which a single provocation ought not to dissolve. And thus you will take the accident by its manageable handle. —Epictetus.

Force

Right reason is stronger than force. —James A. Garfield.

Gentleness succeeds better than violence.—La Fontaine.

The power that is supported by force alone will have cause often to tremble.—Kossuth.

Force is all-conquering, but its victories are short-lived.—Abraham Lincoln.

That which had no force in the beginning can gain no strength from the lapse of time.—Law Maxim.

Force, force, everywhere force; we ourselves a mysterious force in the center of that. There is not a leaf rotting on the highway but has force in it; how else could it rot?—Carlyle.

It is now as in the days of yore when the sword ruled all things.— Schiller.

Who overcomes by force,
Hath overcome but half his foe.
—Milton.

Force and not opinion is the queen of the world; but it is opinion that uses the force.—Pascal.

Hence it happened that all the armed prophets conquered, all the unarmed perished.—Machiavelli.

Everything is heaving and great events are pending, and it is hard to study Genesis when all is now Revelation.—Dr. M. W. Jacobus.

What otherwise is good and just, if it be aimed at by fraud or violence, becomes evil and unjust.—Law Maxim.

Those glorious days, when man said to man, Let us be brothers, or I will knock you down.—Le Brun.

Forefathers Day

Among the sentiments of most powerful operation upon the human heart, and most highly honorable to the human character, are those of veneration for our forefathers, and of love for our posterity.—John Quincy Adams.

As Mecca is to the Mohammedan and Jerusalem to the Christian, so we make our pilgrimage to-night to Plymouth Rock, hoping that as we lay our tribute upon that hill, we shall gird up our loins to meet the fortunes, the successes, the trials, and the duties that are before us.—Judge Russell.

It was reserved for the first settlers of New England to perform achievements equally arduous, to trample down obstructions equally formidable, to dispel dangers equally terrific, under the single inspiration of conscience. —John Quincy Adams.

No nation since the days of Israel was ever founded with so choice people, selected by the operation of so high and spiritual motives, as those whose vanguard was borne across the sea in the Mayflower. It was truly said of them that "God sifted a whole nation that He might send choice grain into the wilderness."—Rev. H. Wayland.

American history has been too largely written from the English standpoint. Let us divide honors all around and give all of our forefathers their share. England was not the first to lead Europe. It was the Dutch republic that first led Europe.—Judge Russell.

They (the Pilgrims) believed in the existence of right and wrong, and in the infinite supremacy of righteousness. They believed in the intense reality of God and of the unseen and the spiritual; they held that these were the real, and that everything else was the shadow.—Rev. H. Wayland.

Moses and Joshua and Samuel were Puritans in their reverent regard for rigorous righteousness.—Judge Russell.

Poor, but independent, not frilled and powdered, but armed mightily with the sword of the Spirit, and with purpose of freedom pulsating at the very centers of their hearts—these were the men whom God had chosen for the settlement of this land. For a hundred years He had kept the new world waiting until they should be ready to possess it.—Rev. D. J. Burrell, D. D.

Guizot, when he was in exile, asked Mr. Lowell, when he was our minister in London, how long the American union would exist, and Lowell said to him: "It will exist so long as the men of America hold to the fundamental principles of their fathers." Central in these fundamental principles is the determination of fathers and of children that in each day of life the world shall be a better world; that is, in each day of life a man shall live to the glory of God.—Edward Everett Hale.

Why is it that the states lying side by side are not quarreling together as they always do in feudal institutions

or in European history? The difference is that the feudal institutions die within fifteen minutes after the immigrant lands in America. The word feudal is a good one, because it describes the eternal war which exists between the men who are educated in that complicated social system of top, bottom, and middle. The feudal system perishes as soon as every man understands that he is his brother's keeper, and in the company of men who know that they live together for the greater glory of God.—Edward Everett Hale.

The theocratic state which the Puritans founded in Massachusetts was not suited to our present civilization, with its representatives of all nations and creeds. But it contained the springs of life which purify our civilization and the seeds of that free government of which our liberty under law is the fairest fruit.—Congregationalist.

But the closer we study their lives, and the better we know their deeds, the more profound is our admiration and the greater our reverence for the Pilgrim fathers. Between the drafting of their immortal charter of liberty in the cabin of the Mayflower and the fruition of their principles in the power and majesty of the republic of the United States of to-day is but a span in the records of the world, and yet it is the most important and beneficent chapter in history. To be able to claim descent from them, either by birth or adoption, is to glory in kinship with God's nobility.—Chauncey Depew.

France lost her Pilgrim element in the expulsion and massacre of the Huguenots, and her noblest political aspirations have lacked the moral strength that comes of a pure and vigorous religious faith. * * * But the men who came hither brought the fundamental conception of man restored as a child of God. Personality was their root idea, the personal soul linked to the personal God; and this was greater than king or parliament, this was greater than church or bishop, and no combination against this could ever crush it.—Rev. Dr. J. P. Thompson.

They believed, and truly, that the strength of Romanism in religion, as well as its despotism in politics, lay in the ignorance of the people; and they sought the freedom which is grander than they knew in the education of all the people, while they sought to inculcate a sense of supreme personal obligation to God. Hence came free churches and free schools, the essential elements of the free state. Hence the Puritan aristocracy, not of birth but of character, because the American republic, with vitality to assimilate the incoming multitudes of all nations.— Rev. D. J. Burrell, D. D.

The Pilgrims were right in affirming the paramount authority of the law of God. If they erred in seeking that authoritative law, and passed over the Sermon on the Mount for the stern Hebraisms of Moses; if they hesitated in view of the largeness of Christian liberty; if they seemed unwilling to accept the sweetness and light of the good tidings—let us not forget that it was the mistake of men who feared more than they dared to hope, whose estimate of the exceeding awfulness of sin caused them to dwell upon God's vengeance rather than His compassion; and whose dread of evil was so great that, in shutting their hearts against it, they sometimes shut out the good.—Whittier.

The great west and the awakening south have felt the influence of the same sturdy endurance, enterprise, and resolute faith that drove the famous little company to brave the unknown dangers of a bleak and hostile country. Plymouth, historic and filled with interest as it is, does not, and cannot, hold the full story of the Pilgrims. That story is written in letters of light over the whole continent; all over the country, wherever they have gone, they have carried with them a respect for law, a reverence for God, education and freedom of worship, and a courage to uphold them, that has made this our great nation the "land of the free and the home of the brave." May Amer-

ica, with her churches, her schools, her civil and religious liberty, her great past and her glorious future be truly and forever the "land of the Pilgrims' pride."—Priscilla Leonard.

But while the Jews repudiated the giving of their religion to the nations, the Puritans have been and continue to be foremost in giving their gospel to mankind. They sought to serve God with all their hearts, and they believed that in making a nation He could use as freemen only those who sought to serve Him both in their spirit and in their way. But when they could no longer carry out their plan for a nation, they set themselves to maintain in the nation they had planted the ethical impulse which brought them to these shores and controlled their lives.—Congregationalist.

They sailed away from Provincetown Bay
  In the fireless light of the sun,
And they came at night to a havened height,
  And the journey at last was done.
With rain and sleet were the tall masts
    iced,
  And frosty and dark was the air,
But they looked from the crystal sails to
    Christ
As they moored in the harbor fair.
    The sky was cold and gray,
  And there were no ancient bells to ring,
  No priests to chant, no choirs to sing,
  No chapel of baron, lord or king,
    That gray, cold winter day.
      —Hezekiah Butterworth.

The revolutions of time furnish no previous example of a nation shooting up to maturity and expanding into greatness with the rapidity which has characterized the growth of the American people. In the luxuriance of youth, and in the vigor of manhood, it is pleasing and instructive to look backwards upon the helpless days of infancy; but in the continual and essential changes of a growing subject the transactions of that early period would soon be obliterated from the memory but for some periodical call of attention to aid the silent records of the historian. Such celebrations arouse and gratify the kindliest emotions of the bosom. They are faithful pledges of the respect we bear to the memory of our ancestors and of the tenderness with which we cherish the rising generation. They introduce the sages and heroes of ages past to the notice and emulation of succeeding times; they are at once testimonials of our gratitude, and schools of virtue to our children.—John Quincy Adams.

Shall we be ashamed because our ancestors were trading colonists; because they bought and sold and exchanged the products of the new world for the riches of the old? Nay, rather let us have a care that they have no cause to be ashamed of us. Let us see to it that amid the broadening of our enterprises and the increase of our wealth, we do not lose those principles of uprightness and strict justice and old-fashioned honor which made the merchants of New York and New England respected and renowned. Above all, let us remember with pride and loyalty that we are Americans.— Rev. H. J. Van Dyke.

Thou who didst steer the little Mayflower to her desired haven, bring America to port! Grant that upon this gathering of the people our dear flag may shine with the light of an evangel, pure as the sweet influences of the Pleiades and firm as the bands of Orion. Thou who dost guide Arcturus, grant that those stars may glow in the coronet of Christ. In the enthusiasm of loyalty to God and serried against the evils and forebodings of the time we will march in the footsteps of a believing ancestry. Let every flagstaff, and belfry, every throbbing dome and thundering cannon, every eloquent orator and voice of multitudes, every prayer of gratitude and every tear of joy, carry the name that is above every name and swear it with a mighty oath: "This God is our God, as He was our fathers' God, and He shall be ours forever and forever."—M. W. Stryker, D. D.

Give a thing time; if it can succeed it is a right thing. Look now at American Saxondom; and at that little fact of the sailing of the Mayflower two hundred years ago * * * ! Were we of open sense as the Greeks were, we had found a poem here; one of nature's own poems, such as she

writes in broad facts over great continents. For it was properly the beginning of America. There were straggling settlers in America before, some material as if a body was there; but the soul of it was first this. * * * They thought the earth would yield them food, if they tilled honestly; the everlasting heaven would stretch there, too, overhead; they should be left in peace to prepare for eternity by living well in this world of time, worshiping in what they thought the true, not the idolatrous, way. * * * Hah! these men, I think, had a work! The weak thing, weaker than a child, becomes strong in one day, if it be a true thing. Puritanism was only despicable, laughable then, but nobody can manage to laugh at it now.—Thomas Carlyle.

Not satisfied with great principles, they were avaricious of great achievements. They subdued forests, organized emigration, marched westward under the star of empire. They achieved Louisburg and Concord and Lexington, and Paul Revere's ride and the Charter Oak and Bennington and Gaspee Point, and Harvard and Yale and Bowdoin and Dartmouth. They preserved the union, annihilated slavery, crushed repudiation, made the promises of the nation equal to gold. They have spoken the word of protest and pleading in behalf of the Chinaman and the Indian and the African, in behalf of a reformed civil service, and of honest elections. And where has there been a battle for God and humanity that they and their sons have not been in it?—Rev. H. Wayland, D. D.

With our sympathy for the wrongdoer we need the old Puritan and Quaker hatred of wrongdoing; with our just tolerance of men and opinions a righteous abhorrence of sin. * * * The true life of a nation is in its personal morality, and no excellence of constitution and laws can avail much if the people lack purity and integrity. Culture, art, refinement, care for our own comfort and that of others are well, but truth, honor, reverence, and fidelity to duty are indispensable. * * * It is well for us if we have learned to listen to the sweet persuasion of the Beatitudes, but there are crises in all lives which require also the emphatic "Thou shalt not" of the decalogue which the founders wrote on the gateposts of their commonwealth. * * * The great struggle through which we have passed (the Civil war) has taught us how much we owe to the men and women of the Plymouth colony—the noblest ancestry that ever a people looked back to with love and reverence.—John G. Whittier.

Laugh at their whims and rigid tenets as we may, they have left us a heritage unequaled in the story of the world. Theirs was a mighty struggle for all that may ennoble man or make him better than his fathers were. The hopes and fears of all the ages centered in that shaky ship bound westward on an unknown and tempestuous sea. The spirit of the free was with that little bark, as each day gave its light, the God of the heroic and the true its pilot, when the night came down on the sea. A wild and stormy ride from shore to shore; a fierce and bitter strife with fire and flood, savage and element, their daily portion as they sail and when they rested on the rocky shore they called at last their home. What wonder that they cradled there at once the offspring of their love and the freedom of their kind; what wonder that from their sturdy loins sprang forth a race of giants, fit warriors for the rights of generations yet to be; what wonder that sires and sons have laughed to scorn the fear of tempest or of tyrant in service of their faith through all the years.—David C. Robinson.

Holland's place in history is not fixed by its institutional greatness, but rather by the diffusiveness of the ideas, the spirit, which constitutes its real life. Its part in the making of America is not seen in the separate institutions, civil, educational, religious, which it transplanted, but in the spirit of its scattered people losing everything like organic union, but thereby carrying into every community and every school and every church the influence of a high ideal of character, a strong sense of human brotherhood, a spirit of conciliation and kindness which is to make it the destiny of Holland to live a still larger life in the America which is to be the strong and helpful neighbor to all the world, hastening the time when all the sons of men shall be the sons of God, and He who "went about doing good" shall be in truth the king of a regenerated humanity, and the whole earth one great neighborhood, where the need of each will be the care of all.—Andrew U. V. Raymond.

But though your forefathers may not have been much, if any, better than yourselves, let us extol them for the fact that they started this country in the right direction. They laid the foundation for American manhood. The foundation must be more solid and firm and unyielding than any other part of the structure. On that Puritanic foundation we can safely build all nationalities. Let us remember that the coming American is to be an admixture of all foreign bloods. In about twenty-five or fifty years the model American will step forth. He will have the strong brain of the German, the polished manners of the French, the artistic taste of the Italian, the stanch heart of the English, the steadfast piety of the Scotch, the lightning wit of the Irish, and when he steps forth, bone, muscle, nerve, brain entwined with the fibers of all the nationalities, the nations will break out in the cry: "Behold the American!" Columbus discovered only the shell of this country. Agassiz came and discovered fossiliferous America. Silliman came and discovered geological America. Audubon came and discovered bird America. Longfellow came and discovered poetic America; and there are a half-dozen other Americas yet to be discovered. — Rev. T. De Witt Talmage, D. D.

A hardy race, worthy to set the pattern of civilization and liberty to the mighty people who to-night affectionately called them "fathers" in blood, in liberty, love and truth. All that nations can owe to founders; all that children can owe to parents; all that truth and self-denial can owe to their especial champions, is laid upon the altar of their memory to-night. Peace to their sacred ashes, those Pilgrim Fathers of our life. Their sacrifices were many and their joys were few. Yet somewhere in the land where faith meets its reward; somewhere in the heaven of the good and pure; somehere within those temples of magnificent justice where is given alike reward for good and punishment for evil done on earth; somewhere beyond the reach of human toil or strife, those Pilgrim ancestors shall be given meed well-fitted to their high deservings; and

Till the sun grows cold and the stars are
  old,
And the leaves of the judgment book unfold,

no man among their sons shall feel within his veins the bounding of their consecrating blood without thanks for every drop that links him to their heroic lives.

The breaking waves dashed high
  On a stern and rock-bound coast,
And the woods against a stormy sky
  Their giant branches tossed.
And the heavy night hung dark
  The hills and waters o'er,
When a band of exiles moored their bark
  On the wild New England shore.
What sought they thus afar?
  Bright jewels of the mine?
The wealth of seas, the spoils of war?
  They sought a faith's pure shrine!
Ay, call it holy ground,
  The soil where first they trod;
They left unstained what there they
  found—
Freedom to worship God.
              —Felicia Dorothea Hemans.

Our fathers brought with them from England two priceless possessions—the common law and King James' Bible—the former a vital organism, not of symmetrical form and graceful outline, but full of the vigorous sap of liberty and drawing its growth from the soil of the popular heart; the latter, apart from its transcendent claims as the revelation of God to man, in a purely intellectual aspect the most precious treasure that any modern nation enjoys, preserving as it does

our noble language at its best point of growth—just between antique ruggedness and modern refinement—embalming immortal truths in words simple, strong, and sweet, that charm the child at the mother's knee, that nerve and calm the soldier in the dread half hour before the shock of battle, that comfort and sustain the soul that is entering upon the valley of the shadow of death. * * * The progress of our country is not traced by the camp, the café, the theater, and the prison, but by the meeting house, the school house, the court house, and the ballot box—all the legitimate fruits of the Bible and the common law.—Hon. George S. Hillard.

Foresight

To fear the worst, oft cures the worst.—Shakespeare.

Look ere thou leap, see ere thou go. —Thomas Tusser.

Human foresight often leaves its proudest possessor only a choice of evils.—Colton.

Those old stories of visions and dreams guiding men have their truth; we are saved by making the future present to ourselves.—George Eliot.

It is only the surprise and newness of the thing which makes that misfortune terrible which by premeditation might be made easy to us. For that which some people make light by sufferance, others do by foresight.—Seneca.

Accustom yourself to submit on all and every occasion, and on the most minute, no less than on the most important circumstances of life, to a small present evil, to obtain a greater distant good. This will give decision, tone, and energy to the mind, which, thus disciplined, will often reap victory from defeat and honor from repulse.—Colton.

That is to be wise to see not merely that which lies before your feet, but to foresee even those things which are in the womb of futurity.—Terence.

Forest

This is the forest primeval.
—Longfellow.

Summer or winter, day or night,
The woods are an ever-new delight;
They give us peace, and they make us
    strong,
Such wonderful balms to them belong:
So, living or dying, I'll take mine ease
Under the trees, under the trees.
—R. H. Stoddard.

Forethought

In life, as in chess, forethought wins.—Charles Buxton.

Forethought we may have, undoubtedly, but not foresight.—Napoleon I.

If a man take no thought about what is distant, he will find sorrow near at hand.—Confucius.

God will not suffer man to have the knowledge of things to come.—St. Augustine.

Whoever fails to turn aside the ills of life by prudent forethought, must submit to fulfill the course of destiny. —Schiller.

To have too much forethought is the part of a wretch; to have too little is the part of a fool.—Cecil.

If I foreknew, foreknowledge had no influence on their fault, which had no less proved certain unforeknown.— Milton.

As a man without forethought scarcely deserves the name of a man, so forethought without reflection is but a metaphorical phrase for the instinct of a beast.—Coleridge.

Forgetfulness

The world forgetting, by the world forgot.—Pope.

Men are men; the best sometimes forget.—Shakespeare.

It is sure the hardest science to forget!—Pope.

Oh, if, in being forgotten, we could only forget.—Lew Wallace.

Forget thyself to marble.—Milton.

And when he is out of sight, quickly also is he out of mind.—Thomas à Kempis.

Quit the world, and the world forgets you.—Beaconsfield.

It is far off; and rather like a dream than an assurance that my remembrance warrants.—Shakespeare.

There is nothing new except what is forgotten.—Mlle. Bertin.

The pyramids themselves, doting with age, have forgotten the names of their founders.—Fuller.

There is no remembrance which time does not obliterate, nor pain which death does not terminate.—Cervantes.

Lethe, the river of oblivion, rolls his watery labyrinth, which whoso drinks forgets both joy and grief.—Milton.

We bury love,
Forgetfulness grows over it like grass;
That is a thing to weep for, not the dead.
—Alexander Smith.

It is sometimes expedient to forget what you know.—Syrus.

When I forget that the stars shine in air—
When I forget that beauty is in stars—
When I forget that love with beauty is—
Will I forget thee: till then all things else.
—Bailey.

Fill with Forgetfulness, fill high! yet stay—
—'Tis from the past we shadow forth the
    land
Where smiles, long lost, again shall light
    our way,
—Though the past haunt me as a spirit—
    yet I ask not to forget!
—Mrs. Hemans.

If e'er I win a parting token,
    'Tis something that has lost its power—
A chain that has been used and broken,
    A ruin'd glove, a faded flower;
Something that makes my pleasure less,
Something that means—forgetfulness.
—Willis.

Some men treat the God of their fathers as they treat their father's friend. They do not deny Him; by no means: they only deny themselves to

Him, when He is good enough to call upon them.—J. C. and A. W. Hare.

Go, forget me—why should sorrow
 O'er that brow a shadow fling?
Go, forget me— and to-morrow
 Brightly smile and sweetly sing.
Smile—though I shall not be near thee;
Sing—though I shall never hear thee.
 —Charles Wolfe.

Forgotten? No, we never do forget;
We let the years go; wash them clean with
 tears,
Leave them to bleach out in the open day,
Or lock them careful by, like dead friends'
 clothes,
Till we shall dare unfold them without
 pain—
But we forget not, never can forget.
 —D. M. Mulock.

There is nothing—no, nothing—innocent or good, that dies and is forgotten; let us hold to that faith or none. An infant, a prattling child, dying in the cradle, will live again in the better thoughts of those that loved it, and play its part through them in the redeeming actions of the world, though its body be burnt to ashes or drowned in the deep sea.—Dickens.

Forgiveness

They who forgive most shall be most forgiven.—Bailey.

When women love us they forgive everything.—Balzac.

A coward never forgives.—Sterne.

Write thy wrongs in ashes.—Sir T. Browne.

Forgive others often, yourself never. —Syrus.

The brave only know how to forgive. —Sterne.

Men are less forgiving than women. —Richardson.

The offender never pardons.—Herbert.

That curse shall be—forgiveness!— Byron.

She hugged the offender and forgave the offense—sex to the last!—Dryden.

Forgive us our trespasses, as we forgive them that trespass against us.— The Lord's Prayer.

We pardon as long as we love.— Rochefoucauld.

To err is human; to forgive, divine. —Pope.

Pardon, not wrath, is God's best attribute.—Bayard Taylor.

I pardon him, as God shall pardon me.—Shakespeare.

God pardons like a mother, who kisses the offense into everlasting forgetfulness.—Beecher.

To forgive a fault in another is more sublime than to be faultless one's self. —George Sand.

Life, that ever needs forgiveness, has, for its first duty, to forgive.— Lytton.

We may forgive those who bore us, we cannot forgive those whom we bore. —La Rochefoucauld.

Never does the human soul appear so strong as when it foregoes revenge, and dares to forgive an injury.—E. H. Chapin.

The mind that too frequently forgives bad actions will at last forget good ones.—Reynolds.

Good, to forgive;
Best to forget!
 —Robert Browning.

As you from crimes would pardon'd be,
Let your indulgence set me free.
 —Shakespeare.

It is right for him who asks forgiveness for his offenses to grant it to others.—Horace.

Young men soon give, and soon forget
 affronts:
Old age is slow in both.   —Addison.

We should always forgive,—the penitent for their sake, the impenitent for our own.—Marie Ebner-Eschenbach.

It is easier to forgive an enemy than a friend.—Mme. Deluzy.

To bear no malice or hatred in my heart.—Church Catechism.

'Tis easier for the generous to forgive, Than for offence to ask it.—Thomson.

We forgive too little, forget too much.—Mme. Swetchine.

The rarer action is in virtue than in vengeance.—Shakespeare.

The truly great man is as apt to forgive as his power is able to revenge.—Sir P. Sidney.

There is no revenge so complete as forgiveness.—H. W. Shaw.

Forgiveness is commendable, but apply not ointment to the wound of an oppressor.—Saadi.

If we can still love those who have made us suffer, we love them all the more.—Mrs. Jameson.

As nice as we are in love, we forgive more faults in that than in friendship.—Henry Horne.

Only a woman will believe in a man who has once been detected in fraud and falsehood.—Dumas, Père.

Never does the human soul appear so strong as when it foregoes revenge, and dares to forgive an injury.—Chapin.

It is easy enough to forgive your enemies if you have not the means to harm them.—Heinrich Heine.

Yes, we ought to forgive our enemies, but not until they are hanged.—Heinrich Heine.

He that cannot forgive others breaks the bridge over which he must pass himself; for every man has need to be forgiven.—Lord Herbert.

Women do not often have it in their power to give like men, but they forgive like Heaven.—Mme. Necker.

Forgiveness to the injured does belong; but they ne'er pardon, who commit the wrong.—Dryden.

The more we know, the better we forgive; Whoe'er feels deeply, feels for all who live. —Mme. de Staël.

It is necessary to repent for years in order to efface a fault in the eyes of men; a single tear suffices with God. —Chateaubriand.

His heart was as great as the world, but there was no room in it to hold the memory of a wrong.—Emerson.

There is a manner of forgiveness so divine that you are ready to embrace the offender for having called it forth. —Lavater.

Receive no satisfaction for premeditated impertinence; forget it, forgive it, but keep him inexorably at a distance who offered it.—Lavater.

'Tis sweet to stammer one letter of the Eternal's language; on earth it is called forgiveness.—Longfellow.

May I tell you why it seems to me a good thing for us to remember wrong that has been done us? That we may forgive it.—Dickens.

God's way of forgiving is thorough and hearty—both to forgive and to forget; and if thine be not so, thou hast no portion of His.—Leighton.

An old Spanish writer says, "To return evil for good is devilish; to return good for good is human; but to return good for evil is godlike."—Whately.

When a man but half forgives his enemy, it is like leaving a bag of rusty nails to interpose between them.—Latimer.

If you bethink yourself of any crime, unreconciled as yet to heaven and grace, solicit for it straight.—Shakespeare.

If thou wouldst find much favor and peace with God and man, be very low in thine own eyes. Forgive thyself little, and others much.—Leighton.

The narrow soul knows not the god-like glory of forgiving.—Rowe.

If ye forgive men their trespasses, your Heavenly Father will also forgive you.—Bible.

He who has not forgiven an enemy has never yet tasted one of the most sublime enjoyments of life.—Lavater.

We read that we ought to forgive our enemies; but we do not read that we ought to forgive our friends.—Cosmus.

Great souls forgive not injuries till time has put their enemies within their power, that they may show forgiveness is their own.—Dryden.

Humanity is never so beautiful as when praying for forgiveness, or else forgiving another.—Richter.

Thou whom avenging pow'rs obey,
Cancel my debt (too great to pay)
Before the sad accounting day.
          —Wentworth Dillon.

God never pardons: the laws of His universe are irrevocable. God always pardons: sense of condemnation is but another word for penitence, and penitence is already new life.—William Smith.

A more glorious victory cannot be gained over another man than this, that when the injury began on his part the kindness should begin on ours.—Tillotson.

More bounteous run rivers when the ice that locked their flow melts into their waters. And when fine natures relent, their kindness is swelled by the thaw.—Bulwer-Lytton.

His great offence is dead,
And deeper than oblivion do we bury
The incensing relics of it.
          —Shakespeare.

The world never forgives our talents, our successes, our friends, nor our pleasures. It only forgives our death. Nay, it does not always pardon that.
—Elizabeth, Queen of Roumania.

A brave man thinks no one his superior who does him an injury: for he has it then in his power to make himself his superior to the other by forgiveness.—Drummond.

Forgive and forget!—why, the world would be lonely,
The garden a wilderness left to deform,
If the flowers but remember'd the chilling winds only,
And the fields gave no verdure for fear of the storm.   —Charles Swain.

To have the power to forgive,
Is empire and prerogative,
And 'tis in crowns a nobler gem,
To grant a pardon than condemn.
          —Butler.

Hath any wronged thee? be bravely revenged; slight it, and the work is begun; forgive it, and it is finished; he is below himself that is not above an injury.—Quarles.

Let us no more contend, nor blame
Each other, blam'd enough elsewhere, but strive
In offices of love, how we may lighten
Each other's burden, in our share of woe.
          —Milton.

It is right that man should love those who have offended him. He will do so when he remembers that all men are his relations, and that it is through ignorance and involuntarily that they sin,—and then we all die so soon.—Marcus Aurelius.

The sun should not set upon our anger, neither should he rise upon our confidence. We should forgive freely, but forget rarely. I will not be revenged, and this I owe to my enemy; but I will remember, and this I owe to myself.—Colton.

When thou forgivest,—the man who has pierced thy heart stands to thee in the relation of the sea-worm that perforates the shell of the mussel which straightway closes the wound with a pearl.—Richter.

It is vain for you to expect, it is impudent for you to ask of God forgiveness on your own behalf, if you refuse to exercise this forgiving temper with respect to others.—Hoadley.

"I can forgive, but I cannot forget," is only another way of saying "I will not forgive." A forgiveness ought to be like a cancelled note, torn in two and burned up, so that it never can be shown against the man.—Beecher.

Of him that hopes to be forgiven it is indispensably required that he forgive. It is, therefore, superfluous to urge any other motive. On this great duty eternity is suspended, and to him that refuses to practise it, the throne of mercy is inaccessible, and the Saviour of the world has been born in vain.—Johnson.

Alas! if my best Friend, who laid down His life for me, were to remember all the instances in which I have neglected Him, and to plead them against me in judgment, where should I hide my guilty head in the day of recompense? I will pray, therefore, for blessings on my friends, even though they cease to be so, and upon my enemies, though they continue such.—Cowper.

The fairest action of our human life
Is scorning to revenge an injury;
For who forgives without a further strife,
His adversary's heart to him doth tie:
And 'tis a firmer conquest, truly said,
To win the heart than overthrow the head.
—Lady Elizabeth Carew.

There is an ugly kind of forgiveness in this world,—a kind of hedgehog forgiveness, shot out like quills. Men take one who has offended, and set him down before the blowpipe of their indignation, and scorch him, and burn his fault into him; and when they have kneaded him sufficiently with their fiery fists, then — they forgive him.—Beecher.

The brave only know how to forgive; it is the most refined and generous pitch of virtue human nature can arrive at. Cowards have done good and kind actions,—cowards have even fought, nay, sometimes even conquered; but a coward never forgave. It is not in his nature; the power of doing it flows only from a strength and greatness of soul, conscious of its own force and security, and above the little temptations of resenting every fruit-less attempt to interrupt its happiness.—Sterne.

The gospel comes to the sinner at once with nothing short of complete forgiveness as the starting point of all his efforts to be holy. It does not say, "Go and sin no more, and I will not condemn thee." It says at once, "Neither do I condemn thee: go and sin no more."—Horatius Bonar.

Behold affronts and indignities which the world thinks it right never to pardon, which the Son of God endures with a divine meekness! Let us cast at the feet of Jesus that false honor, that quick sense of affronts, which exaggerates everything, and pardons nothing, and, above all, that devilish determination in resenting injuries.—Quesnel.

How sure we are of our own forgiveness from God. How certain we are that we are made in His image, when we forgive heartily and out of hand one who has wronged us. Sentimentally we may feel, and lightly we may say, "To err is human, to forgive divine;" but we never taste the nobility and divinity of forgiving till we forgive and know the victory of forgiveness over our sense of being wronged, over mortified pride and wounded sensibilities. Here we are in living touch with Him who treats us as though nothing had happened—who turns His back upon the past, and bids us journey with Him into goodness and gladness, into newness of life.—Maltbie Babcock.

In what a delightful communion with God does that man live who habitually seeketh love! With the same mantle thrown over him from the cross—with the same act of amnesty, by which we hope to be saved—injuries the most provoked, and transgressions the most aggravated, are covered in eternal forgetfulness.—E. L. Magoon.

Formality

Oh, I see thee old and formal, fitted to thy
    petty part,
With a little hoard of maxims preaching
    down a daughter's heart!—Tennyson.

Lord Angelo is precise;
Stands at a guard with envy; scarce confesses
That his blood flows, or that his appetite
Is more to bread than stone.
—Shakespeare.

There are a sort of men, whose visages
Do cream and mantle, like a standing pond;
And do a willful stillness entertain,
With purpose to be dressed in an opinion
Of wisdom, gravity, profound conceit;
As who should say, I am sir Oracle,
And when I ope my lips, let no dog bark!
—Shakespeare.

Fortitude

Learn to labor and to wait.—Longfellow.

Fortitude is a great help in distress. —Plautus.

Fortitude is the guard and support of the other virtues.—Locke.

He who weighs his burdens, can bear them.—Martial.

Bid that welcome which comes to punish us, and we punish it, seeming, to bear it lightly.—Shakespeare.

In struggling with misfortunes lies the true proof of virtue.—Shakespeare.

We men are but poor, weak souls, after all; women beat us out and out in fortitude.—Charles Buxton.

Where true fortitude dwells, loyalty, bounty, friendship and fidelity may be found.—Gay.

The vulgar refuse or crouch beneath their load; the brave bear theirs without repining.—Mallet.

Gird your hearts with silent fortitude,
Suffering, yet hoping all things.
—Mrs. Hemans.

True fortitude is seen in great exploits, that justice warrants and that wisdom guides.—Addison.

Providence has clearly ordained that the only path fit and salutary for man on earth is the path of persevering fortitude—the unremitting struggle of

deliberate self-preparation and humble but active reliance on divine aid.—E. L. Magoon.

The burden which is well borne becomes light.—Ovid.

'Tis easiest dealing with the firmest mind—
More just when it resists, and, when it yields, more kind. —Crabbe.

White men should exhibit the same insensibility to moral tortures that red men do to physical torments.—Théophile Gautier.

Though Fortune's malice overthrow my state,
My mind exceeds the compass of her wheel.
—Shakespeare.

Who fights
With passions and o'ercomes, that man is arm'd
With the best virtue—passive fortitude.
—Webster.

Every man should bear his own grievances rather than detract from the comforts of another.—Cicero.

Fortitude has its extremes as well as the rest of the virtues, and ought, like them, to be always attended by prudence.—Voet.

Brave spirits are a balsam to themselves;
There is a nobleness of mind that heals
Wounds beyond salves. —Cartwright.

There is a strength of quiet endurance as significant of courage as the most daring feats of prowess.—Tuckerman.

The fortitude of a Christian consists in patience, not in enterprises which the poets call heroic, and which are commonly the effects of interest, pride and worldly honor.—Dryden.

Fortitude is not the appetite of formidable things, nor inconsult rashness; but virtue fighting for a truth, derived from knowledge of distinguishing good or bad causes.—Nabb.

The greatest man is he who chooses the right with invincible resolution; who resists the sorest temptations from within and without; who is calmest in storms, and whose reliance on truth, on virtue, on God, is the most unfaltering.—Channing.

We deem those happy who, from the experience of life, have learned to bear its ills, without being overcome by them.—Juvenal.

True fortitude I take to be the quiet possession of a man's self, and an undisturbed doing his duty, whatever evil besets or danger lies in his way.—Locke.

Blessed are those whose blood and judgment are so well commingled that they are not a pipe for Fortune's finger to sound what stop she please.—Shakespeare.

It is true fortitude to stand firm against
All shocks of fate, when cowards faint and die
In fear to suffer more calamity.
—Massinger.

Fortitude is the marshal of thought, the armor of the will, and the fort of reason.—Bacon.

Be not cast down. If ye saw Him who is standing on the shore, holding out His arms to welcome you to land, ye would wade, not only through a sea of wrongs, but through hell itself to be with Him.—Rutherford.

Fortitude implies a firmness and strength of mind that enables us to do and suffer as we ought. It rises upon an opposition, and, like a river, swells the higher for having its course stopped.—Jeremy Collier.

Every man must bear his own burden, and it is a fine thing to see any one trying to do it manfully; carrying his cross bravely, silently, patiently, and in a way which makes you hope that he has taken for his pattern the greatest of all sufferers.—James Hamilton.

The man who is just and resolute will not be moved from his settled purpose, either by the misdirected rage of his fellow citizens, or by the threats of an imperious tyrant.—Horace.

A Christian builds his fortitude on a better foundation than stoicism; he is pleased with everything that happens, because he knows it could not happen unless it first pleased God, and that which pleases Him must be best.—C. C. Colton.

—There is a strength
Deep-bedded in our hearts, of which we reck
But little, till the shafts of heaven have pierced
Its fragile dwelling. Must not earth be rent
Before her gems are found?
—Mrs. Hemans.

Bear your burden manfully. Boys at school, young men who have exchanged boyish liberty for serious business—all who have got a task to do, a work to finish—bear the burden till God gives the signal for repose—till the work is done, and the holiday is fairly earned.—James Hamilton.

It is sufficient to have a simple heart in order to escape the harshness of the age, in order not to fly from the unfortunate; but it is to have some understanding of the imperishable law, to seek them in the forgetfulness against which they dare not complain, to prefer them in their ruin, to admire them in their struggles.—Sénancour.

Existence may be borne, and the deep root
Of life and sufferance make its firm abode
In bare and desolate bosoms: mute
The camel labors with the heaviest load,
And the wolf dies in silence: Not bestow'd
In vain should such examples be; if they,
Things of ignoble or of savage mood,
Endure and shrink not, we of nobler clay
May temper it to bear—it is but for a day.
—Byron.

My sole resources in the path I trod,
Were these—my bark—my sword—my love
—my God.
The last I left in youth—He leaves me now—
And man but works His will to lay me low.
I have no thought to mock His throne with prayer,
Wrung from the coward crouching of despair;
It is enough—I breathe—and I can bear.
—Byron.

Fortune

Fortune favors the bold.—Cicero.

Fortune, not wisdom, human life doth sway.—Cicero.

Fortune favors fools.—Anonymous.

That strumpet — Fortune.—Shakespeare.

Every man is the architect of his own fortune.—Sallust.

Lucky men are favorites of Heaven. —Dryden.

O 'Fortune, Fortune! all men call thee fickle.—Shakespeare.

Lucky people are her favorites.— Mme. de Genlis.

Fortune is not content to do a man one ill turn.—Bacon.

A good man's fortune may grow out at heels.—Shakespeare.

Ill fortune seldom comes alone.— Dryden.

No man has perpetual good fortune. —Plautus.

Fortune makes him fool, whom she makes her darling.—Bacon.

The bitter dregs of Fortune's cup to drain.—Homer.

The mould of a man's.fortune is in his own hands.—Bacon.

It is the fortunate who should extol fortune.—Goethe.

The prudent man really frames his own fortunes for himself.—Plautus.

A just fortune awaits the deserving. —Statius.

The less we deserve good fortune, the more we hope for it.—Molière.

When Fortune means to men most good, She looks upon them with a threatening eye. —Shakespeare.

The good or the bad fortune of men depends not less upon their own dispositions than upon fortune.—La Rochefoucauld.

Some are born great, some achieve greatness, and some have greatness thrust upon them.—Shakespeare.

Man's fortune is usually changed at once; life is changeable.—Plautus.

Fortune never seems so blind as to those upon whom she confers no favors.—La Rochefoucauld.

Blind fortune pursues inconsiderate rashness.—La Fontaine.

Men are seldom blessed with good fortune and good sense at the same time.—Livy.

Fortune is gentle to the lowly, and heaven strikes the humble with a light hand.—Seneca.

It is doubtful what fortune to-morrow will bring.—Lucretius.

The least reliance can be placed even on the most exalted fortune.— Livy.

Fortune! There is no fortune; all is trial, or punishment, or recompense, or foresight.—Voltaire.

The moderation of fortunate people comes from the calm which good fortune gives to their tempers. — La Rochefoucauld.

If fortune favors you do not be elated; if she frowns do not despond.— Ausonius.

It is fortune, not wisdom, that rules man's life.—Cicero.

The most wretched fortune is safe; for there is no fear of anything worse. —Ovid.

We treat fortune like a mistress— the more she yields, the more we demand.—Mme. Roland.

Fortune molds and circumscribes human affairs as she pleases.—Plautus.

Fortune gives too much to many, enough to none.—Martial.

They make their fortune who are stout and wise.—Tasso.

Men may second fortune, but they cannot thwart her.—Machiavelli.

Fortune does not change men; it only unmasks them.—Mme. Riccoboni.

We make our fortunes, and we call them "fate."—Beaconsfield.

We rise to fortune by successive steps; we descend by only one.—Stanislaus.

We are sure to get the better of fortune if we do but grapple with her.—Seneca.

We do not know what is really good or bad fortune.—Rousseau.

We do not commonly find men of superior sense amongst those of the highest fortune.—Juvenal.

Fortune brings in some boats that are not steered.—Shakespeare.

Many fortunes, like rivers, have a pure source, but grow muddy as they grow large.—J. Petit-Senn.

Those who lament for fortune do not often lament for themselves.—Voltaire.

Fortune is like a market, where many times if you wait a little the price will fall.—Bacon.

Our probity is not less at the mercy of fortune than our property.—Rochefoucauld.

Fortune is the rod of the weak and the staff of the brave.—Lowell.

Fortune is merry,
And in this mood will give us anything.
—Shakespeare.

The good, we do it; the evil, that is fortune; man is always right, and destiny always wrong.—La Fontaine.

Fortune dreads the brave, and is only terrible to the coward.—Seneca.

Whatever fortune has raised to a height, she has raised only that it may fall.—Seneca.

Fortune is like a coquette; if you don't run after her, she will run after you.—H. W. Shaw.

Ill-fortune never crushed that man whom good fortune deceived not.—Ben Jonson.

Fortune is but a synonymous word for nature and necessity.—Bentley.

Fickle Fortune reigns, and, undiscerning, scatters crowns and chains.—Pope.

Fortune, that arrant whore,
Ne'er turns the key to the poor.
—Shakespeare.

Fortune turns everything to the advantage of her favorites.—Rochefoucauld.

Let not one look of Fortune cast you down; she were not Fortune if she did not frown.—Earl of Orrery.

Fortune is like glass; when she shines, she is broken.—Syrus.

Fortune cannot take away what she did not give.—Seneca.

How Fortune piles her sports when she begins to practise them!—Ben Jonson.

Many dream not to find, neither deserve, and yet are steeped in favors.—Shakespeare.

For fortune's wheel is on the turn,
And some go up and some go down.
—Mary F. Tucker.

Receive the gifts of fortune without pride, and part with them without reluctance.—Antoninus.

Dame Nature gave him comeliness and health; and Fortune, for a passport, gave him wealth.—Walter Harte.

If a man look sharply and attentively, he shall see Fortune, for, though she be blind, yet she is not invisible.—Bacon.

Fortune makes quick dispatch, and in a day May strip you bare as beggary itself.
—Cumberland.

Fortune in men has some small difference made,
One flaunts in rags, one flutters in brocade.
—Pope.

Who thinks that Fortune cannot change her mind,
Prepares a dreadful jest for all mankind.
—Pope.

Fortune's unjust; she ruins oft the brave, and him who should be victor, makes the slave.—Dryden.

Let fortune do her worst, whatever she makes us lose, so long as she never makes us lose our honesty and our independence.—Pope.

It is a madness to make fortune the mistress of events, because in herself she is nothing, but is ruled by prudence.—Dryden.

Men have made of fortune an all-powerful goddess, in order that she may be made responsible for all their blunders.—Mme. de Staël.

Fortune confounds the wise,
And when they least expect it turns the dice. —Dryden.

The Spaniards have a saying that there is no man whom Fortune does not visit at least once in his life.—Ik Marvel.

Since you will buckle fortune on my back,
To bear her burden whe'r I will or no,
I must have patience to endure the load.
—Shakespeare.

The power of fortune is confessed only by the miserable; for the happy impute all their successes to prudence and merit.—Swift.

Fortune, to show us her power in all things, and to abate our presumption, seeing she could not make fools wise, has made them fortunate.—Montaigne.

If fortune wishes to make a man estimable she gives him virtues; if she wishes to make him esteemed she gives him success.—Joubert.

Fortune, like a coy mistress, loves to yield her favors, though she makes us wrest them from her.—Bovee.

The old saying is expressed with depth and significance: "On the pinnacle of fortune man does not long stand firm."—Goethe.

Dame Fortune, like most others of the female sex, is generally most indulgent to the nimble-mettled blockheads.—Otway.

Good and bad fortune are found severally to visit those who have the most of the one or the other.—Rochefoucauld.

It is a law of the gods which is never broken, to sell somewhat dearly the great benefits which they confer on us.—Corneille.

Fortune rules in all things, and advances and depresses things more out of her own will than right and justice.—Sallust.

Fortune, my friend, I've often thought
Is weak, if Art assist her not:
So equally all Arts are vain,
If Fortune help them not again.—Sheridan.

The wheel of fortune turns incessantly round, and who can say within himself, I shall to-day be uppermost?—Confucius.

Fortune is ever seen accompanying industry, and is as often trundling in a wheelbarrow as lolling in a coach and six.—Goldsmith.

It is a madness to make fortune the mistress of events, because in herself she is nothing, but is ruled by prudence.—Dryden.

The bad fortune of the good turns their faces up to heaven; and the good fortune of the bad bows their heads down to the earth.—Saadi.

There are some men who are fortune's favorites, and who, like cats, light forever on their legs.—Colton.

The fortunate circumstances of our lives are generally found at last to be of our own producing.—Goldsmith.

Though Fortune's malice overthrow my state, my mind exceeds the compass of her wheel.—Shakespeare.

A broken fortune is like a falling column; the lower it sinks, the greater weight it has to sustain.—Ovid.

Fortune's wings are made of Time's feathers, which stay not whilst one may measure them.—Lilly.

O Fortune, that enviest the brave, what unequal rewards thou bestowest on the righteous!—Seneca.

Fortunes made in no time are like shirts made in no time; it's ten to one if they hang long together.—Douglas Jerrold.

I am amazed how men can call her blind, when, by the company she keeps, she seems so very discriminating.—Goldsmith.

There is nothing which continues longer than a moderate fortune; nothing of which one sees sooner the end than a large fortune.—Bruyère.

He whom fortune has never deceived rarely considers the uncertainty of human events.—Livy.

If a man's fortune does not fit him, it is like the shoe in the story; if too large it trips him up, if too small it pinches him.—Horace.

Luck affects everything; let your hook always be cast; in the stream where you least expect it, there will be a fish.—Ovid.

We should manage our fortune as we do our health—enjoy it when good, be patient when it is bad, and never apply violent remedies except in an extreme necessity.—La Rochefoucauld.

As long as you are fortunate you will have many friends, but if the times become cloudy you will be alone.—Ovid.

Vicissitudes of fortune, which spare neither man nor the proudest of his works, which bury empires and cities in a common grave.—Gibbon.

Let fortune empty her whole quiver on me.
I have a soul that, like an ample shield,
Can take in all, and verge enough for more.
—Dryden.

Adverse fortune seldom spares men of the noblest virtues. No one can with safety expose himself often to dangers. The man who has often escaped is at last caught.—Seneca.

Happy the man who can endure the highest and the lowest fortune. He, who has endured such vicissitudes with equanimity, has deprived misfortune of its power.—Seneca.

Golden palaces break man's rest, and purple robes cause watchful nights.
Oh, if the breasts of the rich could be seen into, what terrors high fortune places within! —Seneca.

But assuredly fortune rules in all things; she raises to eminence or buries in oblivion everything from caprice rather than from well-regulated principle.—Sallust.

Whereas they have sacrificed to themselves, they become sacrificers to the inconstancy of fortune, whose wings they thought, by their self-wisdom, to have pinioned.—Bacon.

Many have been ruined by their fortunes; many have escaped ruin by the want of fortune. To obtain it, the great have become little, and the little great.—Zimmermann.

There is some help for all the defects of fortune; for if a man cannot attain to the length of his wishes, he may have his remedy by cutting of them shorter.—Cowley.

It is often the easiest move that completes the game. Fortune is like the lady whom a lover carried off from all his rivals by putting an additional lace upon his liveries.—Bulwer-Lytton.

All our advantages are those of fortune; birth, wealth, health, beauty, are her accidents; and when we cry out against fate, it were well we should remember fortune can take naught save what she gave.—Byron.

It cannot be denied but outward accidents conduce much to fortune's favor,—opportunity, death of others, occasion fitting virtue; but chiefly the mould of a man's fortune is in his own hands.—Bacon.

I have heard Cardinal Imperiali say: "There is no man whom fortune does not visit once in his life; but when she does not find him ready to receive her, she walks in at the door, and flies out at the window."—Montesquieu.

What real good does an addition to a fortune already sufficient procure? Not any. Could the great man, by having his fortune increased, increase also his appetites, then precedence might be attended with real amusement.—Goldsmith.

To be thrown on one's own resources is to be cast on the very lap of fortune; for our faculties undergo a development, and display an energy, of which they were previously unsusceptible.—Franklin.

The fortunate man is he who, born poor or nobody, works gradually up to wealth and consideration, and, having got them, dies before he finds they were not worth so much trouble.—Charles Reade.

The good things of life are not to be had singly, but come to us with a mixture,—like a schoolboy's holiday, with a task affixed to the tail of it.—Lamb.

A fortunate shepherd is nursed in a rude cradle in some wild forest, and, if fortune smile, has risen to empire. That other, swathed in purple by the throne, has at last, if fortune frown, gone to feed the herd.—Metastasio.

Fortune is said to be blind, but her favorites never are. Ambition has the eye of the eagle, prudence that of the lynx; the first looks through the air, the last along the ground.—Bulwer-Lytton.

So is Hope
Changed for Despair—one laid upon the shelf,
We take the other. Under heaven's high cope
Fortune is god—all you endure and do
Depends on circumstance as much as you.
—Shelley.

Oft, what seems
A trifle, a mere nothing, by itself,
In some nice situation, turns the scale
Of fate, and rules the most important actions.
—Thomson.

If fortune has fairly sat on a man, he takes it for granted that life consists in being sat upon; but to be coddled on Fortune's knee, and then have his ears boxed,—that is aggravating.—Charles Buxton.

A man is thirty years old before he has any settled thoughts of his fortune; it is not completed before fifty. He falls to building in his old age, and dies by the time his house is in a condition to be painted and glazed.—Bruyère.

Alas! the joys that fortune brings
Are trifling, and decay,
And those who prize the trifling things,
More trifling still than they.
—Goldsmith.

Fortune, like other females, prefers a lover to a master, and submits with impatience to control; but he that wooes her with opportunity and importunity will seldom court her in vain.—Colton.

So quickly sometimes has the wheel turned round that many a man has lived to enjoy the benefit of that charity which his own piety projected.—Sterne.

The heavens do not send good haps in handfuls; but let us pick out our good by little, and with care, from out much bad, that still our little world may know its king.—Sir P. Sidney.

Fortune has rarely condescended to be the companion of Genius; others find a hundred by-roads to her palace; there is but one open, and that a very indifferent one, for men of letters.—Disraeli.

It is we that are blind, not fortune; because our eye is too dim to discern the mystery of her effects, we foolishly paint her blind, and hoodwink the providence of the Almighty.—Sir Thomas Browne.

In human life there is a constant change of fortune; and it is unreasonable to expect an exemption from the common fate. Life itself decays, and all things are daily changing.—Plutarch.

The old Scythians painted blind fortune's powerful hands with wings, to show her gifts come swift and suddenly, which, if her favorite be not swift to take, he loses them forever.—Chapman.

This is most true, and all history bears testimony to it, that men may second fortune, but they cannot thwart her,—they may weave her web, but they cannot break it.—Machiavelli.

It is with fortune as with fantastical mistresses,—she makes sport with those that are ready to die for her, and throws herself at the feet of others that despise her.—J. Beaumont.

The way of fortune is like the milky way in the sky, which is a meeting or knot of a number of small stars, not seen asunder, but giving light together; so are there a number of little and scarce discerned virtues, or rather faculties and customs, that make men fortunate.—Bacon.

Fortune does us neither good nor hurt; she only presents us the matter, and the seed, which our soul, more powerfully than she, turns and applies as she best pleases; being the sole cause and sovereign mistress of her own happy or unhappy condition.—Montaigne.

Fortune is painted blind in order to show her impartiality; but when she cheers the needy with hope, and depresses the wealthy with distrust, methinks she confers the richest boon on the poorest man, and injures those on whom she bestows her favors.—Chatfield.

Will fortune never come with both hands full,
But write her fair words still in foulest letters?
She either gives a stomach, and no food—
Such as are the poor in health; or else a feast,
And takes away the stomach—such are the rich,
That have abundance, and enjoy it not.
                              —Shakespeare.

Fortune made up of toys and impudence,
That common judge that has not common sense,
But fond of business insolently dares
Pretend to rule, yet spoils the world's affairs.   —Buckingham.

Fortune, the great commandress of the world,
Hath divers ways t' enrich her followers:
To some she honor gives without deserving;
To other some, deserving without honor;
Some, wit—some, wealth—and some, wit without wealth;
Some, wealth without wit—some, nor wit nor wealth.   —Chapman.

It has been remarked that almost every character which has excited either attention or pity has owed part of its success to merit, and part to a happy concurrence of circumstances in its favor. Had Cæsar or Cromwell exchanged countries, the one might have been a sergeant and the other an exciseman.—Goldsmith.

What men usually say of misfortunes, that they never come alone, may with equal truth be said of good fortune; nay, of other circumstances which gather round us in a harmonious way, whether it arise from a kind of fatality, or that man has the power of attracting to himself things that are mutually related.—Goethe.

The Europeans are themselves blind who describe fortune without sight. No first-rate beauty ever had finer eyes, or saw more clearly. They who have no other trade but seeking their fortune need never hope to find her; coquette-like, she flies from her close pursuers, and at last fixes on the plodding mechanic who stays at home and minds his business.—Goldsmith.

To catch Dame Fortune's golden smile,
  Assiduous wait upon her;
And gather gear by every wile
  That's justified by honor.
Not for to hide it in a hedge,
  Nor for a train attendant;
But for the glorious privilege
  Of being independent.   —Burns.

In losing fortune many a lucky elf
  Has found himself.
As all our moral bitters are design'd
  To brace the mind,
And renovate its healthy tone, the wise
Their sorest trials hail as blessings in disguise.   —Horace Smith.

Fortunes are made, if I the facts may state—
Though poor myself, I know the fortunate:
First, there's a knowledge of the way from whence
Good fortune comes—and this is sterling sense:
Then perseverance, never to decline
The chase of riches till the prey is thine;
And firmness never to be drawn away
By any passion from that noble prey—
By love, ambition, study, travel, fame,
Or the vain hope that lives upon a name.
                      —Crabbe.

Frailty

Man is frail, and prone to evil.—Jeremy Taylor.

Man with frailty is allied by birth.—Bishop Lowth.

Frailty, thy name is woman!—Shakespeare.

Fine by defect, and delicately weak.—Pope.

Love has a tide.—Helen Hunt.

Great for good, or great for evil.—Burns.

Unthought-of frailties cheat us in the wise.—Pope.

The French have a significant saying, that a woman who buys her complexion will sell it.—Tuckerman.

A woman filled with faith in the one she loves is the creation of a novelist's imagination.—Balzac.

Universal love is a glove without fingers, which fits all hands alike, and none closely.—Richter.

What is man's love? His vows are broke even while his parting kiss is warm.—Halleck.

All men are frail; but thou shouldst reckon none so frail as thyself.—Thomas à Kempis.

This is the porcelain clay of human kind.—Dryden.

Alas! our frailty is the cause, not we;
For, such as we are made of, such we be.
                      —Shakespeare.

Court a mistress, she denies you; let her alone, she will court you.—Ben Jonson.

Sometimes we are devils to ourselves,
When we will tempt the frailty of our powers,
Presuming on their changeful potency.
                      —Shakespeare.

Weep no more, lady, weep no more,
  Thy sorrow is in vain;
For violets plucked, the sweetest showers
  Will ne'er make grow again.   —Percy.

The summer's flower is to the summer sweet,
Though to itself it only live and die;
But if that flower with base infection meet,
The basest weed outbraves its dignity:
For sweetest things turn sourest by their deeds;
Lilies that fester smell far worse than weeds.   —Shakespeare.

When lovely woman stoops to folly,
And finds too late that men betray,
What charm can soothe her melancholy,
What art can wash her guilt away?—
The only art her guilt to cover,
To hide her shame from every eye,
To give repentance to her lover,
And wring his bosom—is to die.
                      —Goldsmith.

When with care we have raised an imaginary treasure of happiness, we find at last that the materials of the structure are frail and perishing, and the foundation itself is laid in the sand.—Rogers.

Glass antique! 'twixt thee and Nell
Draw we here a parallel.
She, like thee, was forced to bear
All reflections, foul or fair.
  Thou art deep and bright within—
Depths as bright belong'd to Gwynne;
Thou art very frail as well,
Frail as flesh is—so was Nell.
      —L. Blanchard.

France

A monarchy tempered by songs.—Chamfort.

Decayed in thy glory and sunk in thy worth.—Byron.

France is a dog-hole, and it no more merits the tread of a man's foot.—Shakespeare.

Studious to please, and ready to submit; the supple Gaul was born a parasite.—Johnson.

Gay, sprightly land of mirth and social ease,
Pleased with thyself. whom all the world
  can please.   —Goldsmith.

'Tis better using France than trusting
  France;
Let us be back'd with God, and with the
  seas,
Which He hath given for fence impreg-
  nable,
And with their helps only defend ourselves;
In them, and in ourselves, our safety lies.
      —Shakespeare.

Frankness

He speaks home; you may relish him more in the soldier than in the scholar.—Shakespeare.

He that openly tells his friends all that he thinks of them, must expect that they will secretly tell his enemies much that they do not think of him.—Colton.

It is wrong to believe that frank sentiments and the candor of the mind are the exclusive share of the young; they ornament oftentimes old age, upon which they seem to spread a chaste reflection of the modest graces of their younger days, where they shine with the same brightness as those flowers which are often seen peeping, fresh and laughing, from among ruins.—Poincelot.

Fraud

The first and worst of all frauds is to cheat one's self.—Bailey.

His heart as far from fraud as heaven from earth.—Shakespeare.

Some cursed fraud
Of enemy hath beguiled thee, yet unknown,
And me with thee hath ruined.—Milton.

So glistered the dire Snake, and into fraud
Led Eve, our credulous mother, to the Tree
Of Prohibition, root of all our woe.
      —Milton.

Though fraud in all other actions be odious, yet in matters of war it is laudable and glorious, and he who overcomes his enemies by stratagem is as much to be praised as he who overcomes them by force.—Machiavelli.

Freedom

The cause of freedom is the cause of God.—Bowles.

Freedom is only in the land of dreams.—Schiller.

The man is free who is protected from injury.—Daniel Webster.

Freedom is a new religion, the religion of our time.—Heine.

Free soil, free men, free speech, Fremont.—Republican Rallying Cry, 1856.

Freedom is not caprice, but room to enlarge.—C. A. Bartol.

Void of freedom, what would virtue be?—Lamartine.

A bird in a cage is not half a bird.—Beecher.

Knowledge is essential to freedom.—William Ellery Channing.

O freedom, first delight of human kind!—Dryden.

The cry of the soul is for freedom. It longs for liberty, from the date of its first conscious moments.—J. G. Holland.

Is it worth the name of freedom to be at liberty to play the fool?—Locke.

Merely to breathe freely does not mean to live.—Goethe.

Freedom's soil hath only place
For a free and fearless race!
　　　　　　　　—Whittier.

Is any man free except the one who can pass his life as he pleases?—Persius.

Man is created free, and is free, even though born in chains.—Schiller.

Liberty is given by nature even to mute animals.—Tacitus.

That is true liberty which bears a pure and firm breast.—Ennius.

Oh, only a free soul will never grow old!
　　　　—Jean Paul Richter.

In giving freedom to the slave we assure freedom to the free—honorable alike in what we give and what we preserve.—Abraham Lincoln.

Slow are the steps of freedom, but her feet turn never backward.—Lowell.

All special charters of freedom must be abrogated where the universal law of freedom is to flourish.—Heine.

The greatest glory of a free-born people,
Is to transmit that freedom to their children.　　　　　—Havard.

The recovery of freedom is so splendid a thing that we must not shun even death when seeking to recover it.—Cicero.

I intend no modification of my oft-expressed wish that all men everywhere could be free.—Abraham Lincoln.

Nations grow corrupt, love bondage more than liberty; bondage with ease than strenuous liberty.—Milton.

Countries are well cultivated, not as they are fertile, but as they are free.—Montesquieu.

Hope for a season bade the world farewell, and Freedom shrieked as Kosciusko fell.—Campbell.

The whole freedom of man consists either in spiritual or civil liberty.—Milton.

Personal liberty is the paramount essential to human dignity and human happiness.—Bulwer-Lytton.

And ne'er shall the sons of Columbia be slaves,
While the earth bears a plant, or the sea rolls its waves.　—Robert Treat Paine.

The man who seeks freedom for anything but freedom's self is made to be a slave.—De Tocqueville.

No, Freedom has a thousand charms to show,
That slaves, howe'er contented, never know.　　　　　—Cowper.

A day, an hour of virtuous liberty,
Is worth a whole eternity of bondage.
　　　　　　　—Addison.

The only freedom worth possessing is that which gives enlargement to a people's energy, intellect and virtues.—Channing.

As freedom is the only safeguard of governments, so are order and moderation generally necessary to preserve freedom.—Macaulay.

For Freedom's battle once begun,
Bequeath'd by bleeding sire to son,
Though baffled oft is ever won.
　　　　　　　—Byron.

Service cannot be expected from a friend in service; let him be a freeman who wishes to be my master.—Martial.

And lo! the fullness of the time has come,
And over all the exile's western home,
From sea to sea the flowers of freedom bloom!　　　　　—Whittier.

Freedom and slavery, the one is the name of virtue, and the other of vice.

and both are acts of the will.—Epictetus.

We must be free or die, who speak the tongue
That Shakespeare spake; the faith and morals hold
Which Milton held. —Wordsworth.

'Tis liberty alone that gives the flowers
Of fleeting life their luster and perfume,
And we are weeds without it.—Cowper.

There are two freedoms—the false, where a man is free to do what he likes; the true, where a man is free to do what he ought.—Charles Kingsley.

We do not know of how much a man is capable if he has the will, and to what point he will raise himself if he feels free.—J. von Müller.

Freedom is the ferment of freedom. The moistened sponge drinks up water greedily; the dry one sheds it.—Holmes.

Know ye not who would be free themselves must strike the blow? by their right arms the conquest must be wrought?—Byron.

In a free country there is much clamor, with little suffering; in a despotic state there is little complaint, with much grievance.—Carnot.

To prove that the Americans ought not to be free, we are obliged to deprecate the value of freedom itself.—Burke.

Men are qualified for civil liberty in exact proportion to their disposition to put moral chains upon their own appetites.—Burke.

Freedom may come quickly in robes of peace, or after ages of conflict and war; but come it will, and abide it will, so long as the principles by which it was acquired are held sacred.—Edward Everett.

By the laws of God, of nature, of nations, and of your country you are and ought to be as free a people as your brethren in England.—Swift.

I always had an aversion to your apostles of freedom; each but sought for himself freedom to do what he liked.—Goethe.

I am as free as nature first made man,
Ere the base laws of servitude began,
When wild in woods the noble savage ran.
—Dryden.

Freedom in a democracy is the glory of the state, and, therefore, in a democracy only will the freeman of nature deign to dwell.—Plato.

Freedom needs all her poets; it is they
Who give her aspirations wings,
And to the wiser law of music sway
Her wild imaginings. —Lowell.

My angel—his name is Freedom—
Choose him to be your king;
He shall cut pathways east and west,
And fend you with his wing.
—Emerson.

When Freedom from her mountain height
Unfurled her standard to the air,
She tore the azure robe of night,
And set the stars of glory there.
—Joseph Rodman Drake.

How does the meadow flower its bloom unfold?
Because the lovely little flower is free
Down to its root, and in that freedom, bold. —Wordsworth.

Better to dwell in freedom's hall,
With a cold damp floor and mouldering wall,
Than bow the head and bend the knee
In the proudest palace of slaverie.
—Moore.

To have freedom is only to have that which is absolutely necessary to enable us to be what we ought to be, and to possess what we ought to possess.—Rahel.

The cause of freedom is identified with the destinies of humanity, and in whatever part of the world it gains ground by and by, it will be a common gain to all those who desire it.—Kossuth.

Blandishments will not fascinate us, nor will threats of a "halter" intimidate. For, under God, we are determind that, wheresoever, whensoever, or howsoever we shall be called to make our exit, we will die freemen.—Josiah Quincy.

———

That man is deceived who thinks it slavery to live under an excellent prince. Never does liberty appear in a more gracious form than under a pious king.—Claudianus.

———

Easier were it
To hurl the rooted mountain from its base,
Than force the yoke of slavery upon men
Determin'd to be free.   —Southey.

———

He was the freeman whom the truth made free;
Who first of all, the bands of Satan broke;
Who broke the bands of sin, and for his soul,
In spite of fools consulted seriously.
                                —Pollok.

———

Whatever natural right men may have to freedom and independency, it is manifest that some men have a natural ascendency over others.—Lord Greville.

———

Oh, Liberty! thou goddess heavenly bright!
Profuse of bliss, and pregnant with delight!
Eternal pleasures in thy presence reign,
And smiling plenty leads thy wanton train.
                                —Addison.

———

In the long vista of the years to roll,
Let me not see my country's honor fade;
Oh! let me see our land retain its soul!
Her pride in Freedom, and not Freedom's shade.   —Keats.

———

The only freedom which deserves the name is that of pursuing our own good in our own way, so long as we do not attempt to deprive others of theirs, or impede their efforts to obtain it.—John Stuart Mill.

———

Progress, the growth of power, is the end and boon of liberty; and, without this, a people may have the name, but want the substance and spirit of freedom.—Channing.

———

England may as well dam up the waters of the Nile with bulrushes as to fetter the step of freedom, more proud and firm in this youthful land than where she treads the sequestered glens of Scotland, or couches herself among the magnificent mountains of Switzerland.—Lydia Maria Child.

———

The water-lily, in the midst of waters, opens its leaves and expands its petals, at the first pattering of the shower, and rejoices in the rain-drops with a quicker sympathy than the packed shrubs in the sandy desert.—Coleridge.

———

Yes! to this thought I hold with firm persistence;
The last result of wisdom stamps it true;
He only earns his freedom and existence
Who daily conquers them anew.
                                —Goethe.

———

Here the free spirit of mankind, at length,
Throws its last fetters off; and who shall place
A limit to the giant's unchained strength,
Or curb his swiftness in the forward race?   —Bryant.

———

Freedom is alone the unoriginated birthright of man; it belongs to him by force of his humanity, and is in dependence on the will and coaction of every other, in so far as this consists with every other person's freedom.—Kant.

———

The moment men obtain perfect freedom, that moment they erect a stage for the manifestation of their faults. The strong characters begin to go wrong by excess of energy; the weak by remissness of action.—Goethe.

———

The mountains look on Marathon,
And Marathon looks on the sea;
And musing there an hour alone
I dream'd that Greece might still be free.
For standing on the Persians' grave
I could not deem myself a slave.
                                —Byron.

———

Many politicians are in the habit of laying it down as a self-evident proposition that no people ought to be free till they are fit to use their freedom. The maxim is worthy of the fool in the old story who resolved not to go into the water till he had learned to swim.—Macaulay.

———

The sea, as well as the air, is a free and common thing to all; and a particular nation cannot pretend to have the right to the exclusion of all others, without violating the rights of nature and public usage.—Queen Elizabeth.

In a free country every man thinks he has a concern in all public matters,—that he has a right to form and a right to deliver an opinion on them. This it is that fills countries with men of ability in all stations.—Burke.

We grant no dukedoms to the few,
We hold like rights and shall;
Equal on Sunday in the pew,
On Monday in the mall.
For what avail the plough or sail,
Or land, or life, if freedom fail?
—Emerson.

When freedom, on her natal day,
Within her war-rock'd cradle lay,
An iron race around her stood,
Baptiz'd her infant brow in blood,
And through the storm that round her swept,
Their constant ward and watching kept.
—Whittier.

Oh; not yet
May'st thou unbrace thy corslet, nor lay by
Thy sword, nor yet, O Freedom! close thy lids
In slumber; for thine enemy never sleeps.
And thou must watch and combat, till the day
Of the new earth and heaven.—Bryant.

Stranger, new flowers in our vales are seen,
With a dazzling eye, and a lovely green.—
They scent the breath of the dewy morn:
They feed no worm, and they hide no thorn,
But revel and glow in our balmy air;
They are flowers which Freedom hath planted there.   —Mrs. Sigourney.

In the beauty of the lilies Christ was born across the sea,
With a glory in His bosom that transfigures you and me;
As He died to make men holy, let us die to make men free,
While God is marching on.
—Julia Ward Howe.

The slave will be free. Democracy in America will yet be a glorious reality; and when the top-stone of that temple of freedom which our fathers left unfinished shall be brought forth with shoutings and cries of grace unto it, when our now drooping Liberty lifts up her head and prospers, happy will he be who can say, with John Milton, "Among those who have something more than wished her welfare,

I, too, have my charter and freehold of rejoicing to me and my heirs."—Whittier.

Stone walls do not a prison make,
Nor iron bars a cage;
Minds innocent and quiet take
That for an hermitage;
If I have freedom in my love,
And in my soul am free,
Angels alone that soar above,
Enjoy such liberty.
—Richard Lovelace.

Who then is free?—the wise, who well maintains
An empire o'er himself; whom neither chains,
Nor want, nor death, with slavish fear inspire;
Who boldly answers to his warm desire;
Who can ambition's vainest gifts despise;
Firm in himself, who on himself relies;
Polish'd and round, who runs his proper course,
And breaks misfortune with superior force.
—Horace.

Oh, Freedom! thou art not, as poets dream,
A fair young girl, with light and delicate limbs,
And wavy tresses gushing from the cap
With which the Roman master crowned his slave
When he took off the gyves. A bearded man
Armed to the teeth, art thou; one mailèd hand
Grasps the broad shield, and one the sword; thy brow,
Glorious in beauty though it be, is scarred
With tokens of old wars.
—William Cullen Bryant.

They never fail who die
In a great cause: the block may soak their gore,
Their heads may sodden in the sun; their limbs
Be strung to city gates and castle walls;—
But still their spirit walks abroad. Though years
Elapse, and others share as dark a doom,
They but augment the deep and sweeping thoughts
Which overpower all others, and conduct
The world at last to freedom.   —Byron.

The man who stands upon his own soil, who feels, by the laws of the land in which he lives,—by the laws of civilized nations,—he is the rightful and exclusive owner of the land which he tills, is, by the constitution of our nature, under a wholesome influence, not easily imbibed from any other source.—Edward Everett.

We hail the return of the day of thy birth,
Fair Columbia! washed by the waves of
    two oceans—
Where men from the farthest dominions of
    'earth
    Rear altars to Freedom, and pay their de-
    votions;
Where our fathers in fight, nobly strove for
    the Right,
Struck down their fierce foemen or put
    them to flight;
Through the long lapse of ages, that so
    there might be
An asylum for all in the Land of the Free.
    —Abraham Coles.

Freedom all winged expands,
Nor perches in a narrow place;
Her broad van seeks unplanted lands;
She loves a poor and virtuous race.
Clinging to a colder zone
Whose dark sky sheds the snow-flake down,
The snow-flake is her banner's star,
Her stripes the boreal streamers are.
Long she loved the Northman well;
Now the iron age is done,
She will not refuse to dwell
With the offspring of the Sun.
    —Emerson.

What art thou Freedom? Oh, could slaves
Answer from their living graves
This demand, tyrants would flee
Like a dim dream's imagery!
Thou art Justice—ne'er for gold
May thy righteous laws be sold,
As laws are in England: thou
Shield'st alike high and low.
Thou art Peace—never by thee
Would blood and treasure wasted be
As tyrants wasted them when all
Leagued to quench thy flame in Gaul!
Thou art love: the rich have kist
Thy feet and like him following Christ
Given their substance to be free
And through the world have followed thee.
    —Shelley.

Oh, joy to the world! the hour is come,
  When the nations to freedom awake,
When the royalists stand agape and dumb,
  And monarchs with terror shake!
Over the walls of majesty
  "Upharsin" is writ in words of fire,
And the eyes of the bondsman, wherever
    they be
Are lit with wild desire.
Soon shall the thrones that blot the world,
Like the Orleans, into the dust be hurl'd,
And the word roll on like a hurricane's
    breath,
Till the farthest slave hears what it saith—
    Arise, arise, be free!
      —T. Buchanan Read.

There is what I call the American idea. * * * This idea demands, as the proximate organization thereof, a democracy; that is, a government of all the people, by all the people, for all the people; of course, a government of the principles of eternal justice, the unchanging law of God: for shortness' sake I will call it the idea of freedom.—Theodore Parker.

Free Speech

There is tonic in the things that men do not love to hear; and there is damnation in the things that wicked men love to hear. Free speech is to a great people what winds are to oceans and malarial regions, which waft away the elements of disease, and bring new elements of health. And where free speech is stopped miasma is bred, and death comes fast. —Beecher.

Fretting

Most men call fretting a minor fault, a foible, and not a vice. There is no vice except drunkenness which can so utterly destroy the peace, the happiness of a home.—Mrs. H. F. Jackson.

However nervous, depressed, and despairing may be the tone of any one, the Lord leaves him no excuse for fretting; for there is enough in God's promise to overbalance all these natural difficulties. In the measure in which the Christian enjoys his privileges, rises above the things that are seen, hides himself in the refuge provided for him, will he be able to voice the confession of Paul, and say, "None of these things move me."— S. H. Tyng, Jr.

Friendless

Deserted at his utmost need,
By those his former bounty fed;
On the bare earth exposed he lies,
With not a friend to close his eyes.
    —Dryden.

Friends

A friend may well be reckoned the masterpiece of nature.—Emerson.

A true friend is one soul in two bodies.—Aristotle.

Oblige a friend.—Stobæus.

Of friends, however humble, scorn not one.—Wordsworth.

Friends are ourselves.—John Donne.

Have no friends not equal to yourself.—Confucius.

The way to gain a friend is to be one.—Michelet.

Make friends of the wise.—Stobæus.

Make friends of equals.—Stobæus.

The greatest medicine is a true friend.—Sir W. Temple.

My friends! There are no friends! —Aristotle.

A friend to everybody is a friend to nobody.—Spanish Proverb.

A true friend is forever a friend.— George MacDonald.

He who reckons ten friends has not one.—Malesherbes.

Men make the best friends.—La Bruyère.

The wretched have no friends.— Dryden.

Amongst true friends there is no fear of losing anything.—Jeremy Taylor.

A friend must not be injured, even in jest.—Syrus.

It is a friendly heart that has plenty of friends.—Thackeray.

Save, oh! save me from the candid friend.—George Canning.

A man dies as often as he loses his friends.—Bacon.

To lose a friend is the greatest of all losses.—Syrus.

A friend is worth all hazards we can run.—Young.

Friends are to incite one another to God's works.—William Ellery Channing.

Be slow in choosing a friend, slower in changing.—Benjamin Franklin.

For his friend is another self.— Aristotle.

A book is a friend that never deceives.—Guilbert De Pixérécourt.

Virtuous men alone possess friends. —Voltaire.

He who hath many friends, hath none.—Aristotle.

Oh, be my friend, and teach me to be thine!—Emerson.

To God, thy country, and thy friend be true.—Vaughan.

Women, like princes, find few real friends.—Lord Lyttleton.

Nature teaches beasts to know their friends.—Shakespeare.

Friend more divine than all divinities.—George Eliot.

Kiss and be friends.—Farquhar.

True friends have no solitary joy or sorrow.—William Ellery Channing.

A constant friend is a thing rare and hard to find.—Plutarch.

No friend's a friend till he shall prove a friend.—Beaumont and Fletcher.

Have friends, not for the sake of receiving, but of giving.—Joseph Roux.

Thine own friend, and thy father's friend, forsake not.—Bible.

Keep thy friend under thy own life's key.—Shakespeare.

A man cannot be said to succeed in this life who does not satisfy one friend.—Henry D. Thoreau.

Between friends, frequent reproofs make the friendship distant.—Confucius.

My joy in friends, those sacred people, is my consolation.—Emerson.

A friend should bear his friend's infirmities.—Shakespeare.

Be kind to my remains; and O defend
Against your judgment, your departed
　friend.　　　　　—Dryden.

I have loved my friends as I do virtue, my soul, my God.—Sir Thomas Browne.

Where you have friends you should not go to inns.—George Eliot.

I have myself to respect, but to myself I am not amiable; but my friend is my amiableness personified.—Henry D. Thoreau.

Defend me from my friends; I can defend myself from my enemies.—The French Ana.

The fallying out of faithful frends is the renuyng of love.—Richard Edwards.

A foe to God was ne'er true friend to man,
Some sinister intent taints all he does.
　　　　　—Young.

'Tis thus that on the choice of friends
Our good or evil name depends.
　　　　　—Gay.

Nothing makes the earth seem so spacious as to have friends at a distance; they make the latitudes and longitudes.—Henry D. Thoreau.

We have been friends together
In sunshine and in shade.
　—Caroline E. S. Norton.

Eternal blessings crown my earliest friend,
And round his dwelling guardian saints attend.　　　　　—Goldsmith.

Old friends are best. King James used to call for his old shoes. They were easiest for his feet.—John Selden.

May I never sit on a tribunal where my friends shall not find more favor from me than strangers.—Themistocles.

Friendship is the ideal; friends are the reality; reality always remains far apart from the ideal.—Joseph Roux.

Nothing endears so much a friend as sorrow for his death. The pleasure of his company has not so powerful an influence.—Hume.

A day for toil, an hour for sport,
But for a friend is life too short.
　　　　　—Emerson.

Two persons will not be friends long if they cannot forgive each other little failings.—La Bruyère.

It is good to have friends at court.—Charles Lamb.

A friend should be like money, tried before being required, not found faulty in our need.—Plutarch.

Know this, that he that is a friend of himself is a friend to all men.—Seneca.

Animals are such agreeable friends—they ask no questions. They pass no criticisms.—George Eliot.

My designs and labors
And aspirations are my only friends.
　　　　　—Longfellow.

He is a friend who, in dubious circumstances, aids in deeds when deeds are necessary.—Plautus.

The wound is for you, but the pain is for me.—Charles IX.

For to cast away a virtuous friend, I call as bad as to cast away one's own life, which one loves best.—Sophocles.

'Tis something to be willing to commend;
But my best praise is, that I am your
　friend.　　　　　—Southerne.

When our friends are present we ought to treat them well; and when they are absent, to speak of them well.—Epictetus.

Our most intimate friend is not he to whom we show the worst, but the best of our nature.—Hawthorne.

Choose a good disagreeable friend, if you be wise—a surly, steady, economical, rigid fellow.—Thackeray.

Friends are rare, for the good reason that men are not common.—Joseph Roux.

A friend that you have to buy won't be worth what you pay for him, no matter what that may be.—George D. Prentice.

There are three faithful friends—an old wife, an old dog, and ready money.—Benjamin Franklin.

He that will lose his friend for a jest deserves to die a beggar by the bargain.—Thomas Fuller.

He will never have true friends who is afraid of making enemies.—Hazlitt.

If we are long absent from our friends, we forget them; if we are constantly with them, we despise them. —Hazlitt.

It is better to make friends than adversaries of a conquered race.—B. R. Haydon.

Promises may get friends, but it is performance that must nurse and keep them.—Owen Feltham.

Take the advice of a faithful friend, and submit thy inventions to his censure.—Thomas Fuller.

It is virtue which should determine us in the choice of our friends, without inquiring into their good or evil fortune.—La Bruyère.

Poor is the friendless master of a world:
A world in purchase for a friend is gain.
    —Dr. Young.

There is nothing more friendly than a friend in need.—Plautus.

A faithful friend is the true image of the Deity.—Napoleon.

Chance makes our parents, but choice makes our friends.—Delille.

Friends I have made, whom envy must commend,
But not one foe whom I would wish a friend.   —Churchill.

A friend loveth at all times; and a brother is born for adversity.—Bible.

The ornaments of a home are the friends who frequent it.—Emerson.

No better relation than a prudent and faithful friend.—Franklin.

O friend! O best of friends! Thy absence more
Than the impending night darkens the landscape o'er.   —Longfellow.

Those who want friends to open themselves unto are cannibals of their own hearts.—Bacon.

From the loss of our friends teach us how to enjoy and improve those who remain.—William Ellery Channing.

Trust not yourself; but your defects to know,
Make use of ev'ry friend—and ev'ry foe.
    —Pope.

The difficulty is not so great to die for a friend as to find a friend worth dying for.—Henry Home.

Nothing shows one who his friends are like prosperity and ripe fruit.—C. D. Warner.

A friend gives himself to his beloved, and the higher his excellence the richer the gift.—William Ellery Channing.

He who has ceased to enjoy his friend's superiority has ceased to love him.—Madame Swetchine.

We want but two or three friends, but these we cannot do without, and they serve us in every thought we think.—Emerson.

Purchase no friends by gifts; when thou ceasest to give such will cease to love.—Fuller.

Summer friends vanish when the cask is drained to the dregs.—Horatius.

In prosperity it is very easy to find a friend; but in adversity it is the most difficult of all things.—Epictetus.

There have been fewer friends on earth than kings.—Cowley.

Friends, those relations that one makes for one's self.—Deschamps.

Every friend is to the other a sun, and a sunflower also. He attracts and follows.—Richter.

True friends appear less moved than counterfeit.—Roscommon.

Talking with a friend is nothing else but thinking aloud.—Addison.

We want our friend as a man of talent, less because he has talent than because he is our friend.—Joseph Roux.

The genius of life is friendly to the noble, and, in the dark, brings them friends from far.—Emerson.

Some dire misfortune to portend, no enemy can match a friend.—Swift.

Chide a friend in private and praise him in public.—Solon.

Our friends interpret the world and ourselves to us, if we take them tenderly and truly.—A. Bronson Alcott.

Costly followers are not to be liked, lest while a man maketh his train longer, he make his wings shorter.—Bacon.

Friends are much better tried in bad fortune than in good.—Aristotle.

There is no man so friendless but what he can find a friend sincere enough to tell him disagreeable truths.—Bulwer-Lytton.

Friends are the thermometers by which we may judge the temperature of our fortunes.—Lady Blessington.

Friends are the leaders of the bosom, being more ourselves than we are, and we complement our affections in theirs.—A. Bronson Alcott.

The beloved friend does not fill one part of the soul, but, penetrating the whole, becomes connected with all feeling.—William Ellery Channing.

He casts off his friends, as a huntsman his pack,
For he knew, when he pleased, he could whistle them back.   —Goldsmith.

A faithful friend is better than gold —a medicine for misery, an only possession.—Burton.

The loss of a friend is like that of a limb. Time may heal the anguish of the wound, but the loss cannot be repaired.—Southey.

False friends are like our shadow, keeping close to us while we walk in the sunshine, but leaving us the instant we cross into the shade.—Bovee.

Whatever the number of a man's friends, there will be times in his life when he has one too few.—Bulwer-Lytton.

Very pleasant hast thou been unto me; thy love to me was wonderful, passing the love of women.—Bible.

He is happy that hath a true friend at his need; but he is more truly happy that hath no need of his friend.—Warwick.

Friends are often chosen for similitude of manners, and therefore each palliates the other's failings because they are his own.—Dr. Johnson.

We must love our friends as true amateurs love paintings; they have their eyes perpetually fixed on the fine parts, and see no others.—Mme. d'Epinay.

Friends should be weighed, not told; who boasts to have won a multitude of friends has never had one.—Coleridge.

Nothing is more dangerous than a friend without discretion; even a prudent enemy is preferable.—La Fontaine.

We never know the true value of friends. While they live we are too sensitive of their faults: when we have lost them we only see their virtues.—J. C. and A. W. Hare.

Thou dost conspire against thy friend, Iago, if thou but think'st him wronged, and mak'st his ear a stranger to thy thoughts.—Shakespeare.

Among real friends there is no rivalry or jealousy of one another, but they are satisfied and contented alike whether they are equal or one of them is superior.—Plutarch.

Sometimes we lose friends for whose loss our regret is greater than our grief, and others for whom our grief is greater than our regret.—La Rochefoucauld.

It is hard to dispraise those who are dispraised by others. He is little short of a hero who perseveres in thinking well of a friend who has become a butt for slander, and a by-word.—Hazlitt.

'Twas sung, how they were lovely in their lives,
And in their deaths had not divided been.
—Campbell.

"Necessarius," the friend, the man who is necessary. * * * A deep word, an ingenious word, a touching word. When will it be French?—Joseph Roux.

Sweet is the memory of distant friends!
Like the mellow rays of the departing sun,
It falls tenderly, yet sadly, on the heart.
—Washington Irving.

The man abandoned by his friends, one after another, without just cause, will acquire the reputation of being hard to please, changeable, ungrateful, unsociable.—Joseph Roux.

Take heed of a speedy professing friend; love is never lasting which flames before it burns.—Feltham.

When we exaggerate the tenderness of our friends towards us, it is often less from gratitude than from a desire to exhibit our own merit.—La Rochefoucauld.

The poor make no new friends;
But oh, they love the better still
The few our Father sends.
—Lady Dufferin.

One faithful friend is enough for a man's self; 'tis much to meet with such an one, yet we can't have too many for the sake of others.—De La Bruyère.

He that doth a base thing in zeal for his friend burns the golden thread that ties their hearts together.—Jeremy Taylor.

Alas! to-day I would give everything
To see a friend's face, or hear a voice
That had the slightest tone of comfort in it.
—Longfellow.

Real friends are our greatest joy and our greatest sorrow. It were almost to be wished that all true and faithful friends should expire on the same day.—Fénelon.

True friends visit us in prosperity only when invited, but in adversity they come without invitation.—Theophrastus.

To wail friends lost
Is not by much so wholesome—profitable,
As to rejoice at friends but newly found.
—Shakespeare.

Real friendship is a slow grower; and never thrives unless engrafted upon a stock of known and reciprocal merit.—Chesterfield.

It is easy to say how we love new friends, and what we think of them, but words can never trace out all the fibers that knit us to the old.—George Eliot.

Then came your new friend: you began to change—
I saw it and grieved.   —Tennyson.

They who dare to ask anything of a friend, by their very request seem to imply that they would do anything for the sake of that friend.—Cicero.

The place where two friends first met is sacred to them all through their friendship, all the more sacred as their friendship deepens and grows old.—Phillips Brooks.

As you grow ready for it, somewhere or other you will find what is needful for you in a book or a friend.—George MacDonald.

As we sail through life towards death,
Bound unto the same port—heaven—
Friend, what years could us divide?
—D. M. Mulock.

Friends are like melons. Shall I tell you why?
To find one good, you must a hundred try.
—Claude Mermet.

'Tis sweet, as year by year we lose
Friends out of sight, in faith to muse
How grows in Paradise our store.
—Keble.

Give, and you may keep your friend if you lose your money; lend, and the chances are that you lose your friend if ever you get back your money.—Bulwer-Lytton.

The friends thou hast, and their adoption tried, grapple them to thy soul with hooks of steel.—Shakespeare.

All are friends in heaven, all faithful friends,
And many friendships in the days of Time
Begun, are lasting there and growing still.
—Pollok.

When our friends die, in proportion as we loved them, we die with them—we go with them. We are not wholly of the earth.—William Ellery Channing.

Our very best friends have a tincture of jealousy even in their friendship; and when they hear us praised by others, will ascribe it to sinister and interested motives if they can.—Colton.

For men may prove and use their friends, as the poet expresses it, *usque ad aras*, meaning that a friend should not be required to act contrary to the law of God.—Cervantes.

The attempt to make one false impression on the mind of a friend respecting ourselves is of the nature of perfidy. Sincerity should be observed most scrupulously.—William Ellery Channing.

The friend asks no return but that his friend will religiously accept and wear, and not disgrace, his apotheosis of him.—Thoreau.

Friends are as companions on a journey, who ought to aid each other to persevere in the road to a happier life.—Pythagoras.

Friends should not be chosen to flatter. The quality we should prize is that rectitude which will shrink from no truth. Intimacies which increase vanity destroy friendship.—William Ellery Channing.

I consider beyond all wealth, honor, or even health, is the attachment due to noble souls; because to become one with the good, generous, and true, is to be, in a manner, good, generous, and true yourself.—Dr. Arnold.

A true friend embraces our objects as his own. We feel another mind bent on the same end, enjoying it, ensuring it, reflecting it, and delighting in our devotion to it.—William Ellery Channing.

Wise were the kings who never chose a friend till with full cups they had unmasked his soul, and seen the bottom of his deepest thoughts.—Horace.

The qualities of your friends will be those of your enemies; cold friends, cold enemies—half friends, half enemies—fervid enemies, warm friends.—Lavater.

First on thy friend deliberate with thyself;
Pause, ponder, sift; not eager in the choice;
Nor jealous of the chosen; fixing, fix;—
Judge before friendship, then confide till death.
—Young.

A female friend, amiable, clever, and devoted, is a possession more valuable than parks and palaces; and without such a muse, few men can succeed in life, none be contented.—Beaconsfield.

A true friend is distinguished in the crisis of hazard and necessity; when the gallantry of his aid may show the worth of his soul and the loyalty of his heart.—Ennius.

The lightsome countenance of a friend giveth such an inward decking to the house where it lodgeth, as proudest palaces have cause to envy the gilding.—Sir Philip Sidney.

To act the part of a true friend requires more conscientious feeling than to fill with credit and complacency any other station or capacity in social life.—Sarah Ellis.

The generality of friends puts us out of conceit with friendship; just as the generality of religious people puts us out of conceit with religion.—Rochefoucauld.

No receipt openeth the heart but a true friend, to whom you may impart griefs, joys, fears, hopes, suspicions, counsels, and whatsoever lieth upon the heart to oppress it, in a kind of civil shrift or confession.—Bacon.

A friend is he who sets his heart upon us, is happy with us and delights in us; does for us what we want, is willing and fully engaged to do all he can for us, on whom we can rely in all cases.—William Ellery Channing.

A true friend will appear such in leaving us to act according to our intimate conviction,—will cherish this nobleness of sentiment, will never wish to substitute his power for our own.—William Ellery Channing.

Other blessings may be taken away, but if we have acquired a good friend by goodness, we have a blessing which improves in value when others fail. It is even heightened by sufferings.—William Ellery Channing.

The flatterer's object is to please in everything he does; whereas the true friend always does what is right, and so often gives pleasure, often pain, not wishing the latter, but not shunning it either, if he deems it best.—Plutarch.

We cannot enjoy a friend here. If we are to meet it is beyond the grave. How much of our soul a friend takes with him! We half die in him.—William Ellery Channing.

When true friends meet in adverse hour,
'Tis like a sunbeam through a shower;
A watery ray an instant seen,
The darkly closing clouds between.
—Scott.

So also it is good not always to make a friend of the person who is expert in twining himself around us; but, after testing them, to attach ourselves to those who are worthy of our affection and likely to be serviceable to us.—Plutarch.

Give thy friend counsel wisely and charitably, but leave him to his liberty whether he will follow thee or no; and be not angry if thy counsel be rejected, for advice is no empire, and he is not my friend that will be my judge whether I will or no.—Jeremy Taylor.

Ah! were I sever'd from thy side,
Where were thy friend and who my guide?
Years have not seen, Time shall not see
The hour that tears my soul from thee.
—Byron.

It's an overcome sooth fo' age an' youth,
  And it brooks wi' nae denial,
That the dearest friends are the auldest
  friends,
And the young are just on trial.
—Robert Louis Stevenson.

But oh! if grief thy steps attend,
  If want, if sickness be thy lot,
And thou require a soothing friend,
  Forget me not! forget me not!
—Mrs. Opie.

At death our friends and relatives either draw nearer to us and are found out, or depart farther from us and are forgotten. Friends are as often brought nearer together as separated by death.—Henry D. Thoreau.

Self-love increases or diminishes for us the good qualities of our friends, in proportion to the satisfaction we feel with them; and we judge of their merit by the manner in which they act towards us.—La Rochefoucauld.

A friend whom you have been gaining during your whole life, you ought not to be displeased with in a moment. A stone is many years becoming a ruby; take care that you do not destroy it in an instant against another stone.—Saadi.

Yes, we must ever be friends; and of all
  who offer you friendship
Let me be ever the first, the truest, the
  nearest and dearest! —Longfellow.

Dear is my friend—yet from my foe, as
  from my friend, comes good:
My friend shows what I can do, and my
  foe what I should. —Schiller.

The most I can do for my friend is simply to be his friend. I have no wealth to bestow on him. If he knows that I am happy in loving him, he will want no other reward. Is not friendship divine in this?—Henry D. Thoreau.

Experience has taught me that the only friends we can call our own, who can have no change, are those over whom the grave has closed; the seal of death is the only seal of friendship. —Byron.

I would not enter on my list of friends,
(Though graced with polished manners and
  fine sense,
Yet wanting sensibility) the man
Who needlessly sets foot upon a worm.
          —Cowper.

His gain is loss; for he that wrongs his
  friend
Wrongs himself more, and ever bears about
A silent court of justice in his breast,
Himself a judge and jury, and himself
The prisoner at the bar, ever condemned.
          —Tennyson.

I have friends in Spirit Land—
Not shadows in a shadowy band,
Not others but themselves are they,
And still I think of them the same
As when the Master's summons came.
          —Whittier.

When I choose my friend, I will not stay till I have received a kindness; but I will choose such a one that can do me many if I need them; but I mean such kindnesses which make me wiser, and which make me better.—Jeremy Taylor.

This communicating of a man's self to his friend works two contrary effects, for it redoubleth joys, and cutteth griefs in halves; for there is no man that imparteth his joys to his friend but he enjoyeth the more; and no man that imparteth his griefs to his friend, but he grieveth the less.— Bacon.

It is better to decide between our enemies than our friends; for one of our friends will most likely become our enemy; but on the other hand, one of your enemies will probably become your friend.—Bias.

Generally speaking, among sensible persons, it would seem that a rich man deems that friend a sincere one who does not want to borrow his money; while, among the less favored with fortune's gifts, the sincere friend is generally esteemed to be the individual who is ready to lend it.—Disraeli.

"Wal'r, my boy," replied the captain; "in the proverbs of Solomon you will find the following words: 'May we never want a friend in need, nor a bottle to give him!' When found, make a note of."—Dickens.

Now when men either are unnatural or irreligious they will not be friends; when they are neither excellent nor useful, they are not worthy to be friends; when they are strangers or unknown, they cannot be friends actually and practically; but yet, as any man hath anything of the good, contrary to those evils, so he can have and must have his share of friendship. —Jeremy Taylor.

A slender acquaintance with the world must convince every man that actions, not words, are the true criterion of the attachment of friends;

and that the most liberal professions of good-will are very far from being the surest marks of it.—George Washington.

Let no man choose him for his friend whom it shall be possible for him ever after to hate; for though the society may justly be interrupted, yet love is an immortal thing, and I will never despise him whom I could once think worthy of my love.—Jeremy Taylor.

It is a mere and miserable solitude to want true friends, without which the world is but a wilderness; and even in this scene also of solitude, whosoever in the frame of his nature and affections is unfit for friendship he taketh it of the beast, and not from humanity.—Bacon.

The man that hails you Tom or Jack,
And proves by thumps upon your back
   How he esteems your merit,
Is such a friend, that one had need
Be very much his friend indeed
   To pardon or to bear it.
          —Cowper.

In all thy humors, whether grave or mellow,
Thou'rt such a touchy, testy, pleasant fellow,
Hast so much wit and mirth, and spleen about thee,
That there's no living with thee, nor without thee.   —Addison.

If we take the freedom to put a friend under our microscope, we thereby insulate him from many of his true relations, magnify his peculiarities, inevitably tear him into parts, and, of course, patch him very clumsily together again. What wonder, then, should we be frightened by the aspect of a monster.—Hawthorne.

Nobody who is afraid of laughing, and heartily too at his friend, can be said to have a true and thorough love for him; and, on the other hand, it would portray a sorry want of faith to distrust a friend because he laughs at you. Few men, I believe, are much worth loving in whom there is not something well worth laughing at.—J. C. and A. W. Hare.

Deliberate long before thou consecrate a friend, and when thy impartial justice concludes him worthy of thy bosom, receive him joyfully, and entertain him wisely; impart thy secrets boldly, and mingle thy thoughts with his: he is thy very self; and use him so; if thou firmly think him faithful, thou makest him so.—Quarles.

The sun is a hundred thousand leagues away, and the water-roses that open to the light of day are in the pool; the moon, friend of the night-blooming lotus, is two hundred thousand leagues distant. Friendship knows no separation that divides it in space.—Vikramacharita.

We learn our virtues from the bosom friends who love us; our faults from the enemy who hates us. We cannot easily discover our real form from a friend. He is a mirror on which the warmth of our breath impedes the clearness of the reflection.—Richter.

Choose your friend wisely,
   Test your friend well;
True friends, like rarest gems,
   Prove hard to tell.
Winter him, summer him,
   Know your friend well.
          —Unknown.

True friends are the whole world to one another; and he that is a friend to himself is also a friend to mankind. Even in my studies the greatest delight I take is of imparting it to others; for there is no relish to me in the possessing of anything without a partner.—Seneca.

Friends are discovered rather than made; there are people who are in their own nature friends, only they don't know each other; but certain things, like poetry, music, and paintings are like the Freemason's sign,— they reveal the initiated to each other. —Mrs. Stowe.

The noblest part of a friend is an honest boldness in the notifying of errors. He that tells me of a fault, aiming at my good, I must think him wise and faithful—wise in spying that which I see not; faithful in a plain admonishment, not tainted with flattery.—Feltham.

We ought to give our friend pain if it will benefit him, but not to the extent of breaking off our friendship; but just as we make use of some biting medicine that will save and preserve the life of the patient. And so the friend, like a musician, in bringing about an improvement to what is good and expedient, sometimes slackens the chords, sometimes tightens them, and is often pleasant, but always useful.—Plutarch.

However we may flatter ourselves to the contrary, our friends think no higher of us than the world do. They see us with the jaundiced or distrustful eyes of others. They may know better, but their feelings are governed by popular prejudice. Nay, they are more shy of us (when under a cloud) than even strangers; for we involve them in a common disgrace, or compel them to embroil themselves in continual quarrels and disputes in our defence.—Hazlitt.

Make not a bosom friend of a melancholy soul; he'll be sure to aggravate thy adversity and lessen thy prosperity. He goes always heavily loaded, and thou must bear half. He is never in a good humor, and may easily get into a bad one, and fall out with thee.—Fuller.

With regard to the choice of friends, there is little to say; for a friend is never chosen. A secret sympathy, the attraction of a thousand nameless qualities, a charm in the expression of the countenance, even in the voice or manner, a similarity of circumstances,—these are the things that begin attachment.—Mrs. Barbauld.

If thy friends be of better quality than thyself, thou mayest be sure of two things: the first, that they will be more careful to keep thy counsel, because they have more to lose than thou hast: the second, they will esteem thee for thyself, and not for that which thou dost possess.—Sir Walter Raleigh.

Few of us have been so exceptionally unfortunate as not to find, in our own age, some experienced friend who has helped us by precious counsel, never to be forgotten. We cannot render it in kind, but perhaps in the fulness of time it may become our noblest duty to aid another as we have ourselves been aided, and to transmit to him an invaluable treasure, the tradition of the intellectual life.—Hamerton.

Our friends should be our incentives to right, but not only our guiding, but our prophetic, stars. To love by right is much, to love by faith is more; both are the entire love, without which heart, mind, and soul cannot be alike satisfied. We love and ought to love one another, not merely for the absolute worth of each, but on account of a mutual fitness of temporary character.—Margaret Fuller Ossoli.

Thou may'st be sure that he that will in private tell thee of thy faults, is thy friend, for he adventures thy dislike, and doth hazard thy hatred; for there are few men that can endure it, every man for the most part delighting in self-praise, which is one of the most universal follies that bewitcheth mankind.—Sir Walter Raleigh.

There is no treasure the which may be
  compared unto a faithful friend;
Gold soone decayeth, and worldly wealth
  consumeth, and wasteth in the winde;
But love once planted in a perfect and pure
  minde endureth weale and woe;
The frownes of fortune, come they never so
  unkinde, cannot the same overthrowe.
      —Roxburghe Ballads.

The way is short, O friend,
That reaches out before us;
God's tender heavens above us bend,
His love is smiling o'er us;
A little while is ours
For sorrow or for laughter;
I'll lay the hand you love in yours
On the shore of the Hereafter.
      —Mary Clemmer.

No man can expect to find a friend without faults; nor can he propose himself to be so to another. Without reciprocal mildness and temperance there can be no continuance of friendship. Every man will. have

something to do for his friend, and
something to bear with in him. The
sober man only can do the first; and
for the latter, patience is requisite.
It is better for a man to depend
on himself, than to be annoyed with
either a madman or a fool.—Owen
Feltham.

What shall I do, my friend,
When you are gone forever?
My heart its eager need will send
Through the years to find you never,
And how will it be with you,
In the weary world, I wonder,
Will you love me with a love as true,
When our paths lie far asunder?
　　　　　　　—Mary Clemmer.

O friend, my bosom said,
Through thee alone the sky is arched.
Through thee the rose is red;
All things through thee take nobler form,
And look beyond the earth,
The mill-round of our fate appears
A sun-path in thy worth.
Me too thy nobleness has taught
To master my despair;
The fountains of my hidden life
Are through thy friendship fair.
　　　　　　　—Emerson.

Old friends are the great blessings
of one's latter years. Half a word
conveys one's meaning. They have
memory of the same events, and have
the same mode of thinking. I have
young relations that may grow upon
me, for my nature is affectionate,
but can they grow old friends? My
age forbids that. Still less can they
grow companions. Is it friendship to
explain half one says? One must
relate the history of one's memory
and ideas; and what is that to the
young but old stories?—Horace Walpole.

Friendship

Friendship is the wine of life.—
Young.

Friendship is communion.—Aristotle.

Friendship is a sheltering tree.—
Coleridge.

Friendship requires deeds.—Richter.

Preserve friendship.—Stobæus.

Friendship? two bodies and one soul.
—Joseph Roux.

Friendship is the marriage of the
soul.—Voltaire.

Friendship is full of dregs.—Shakespeare.

Friendship is love without its flowers or veil.—Hare.

Friendship is infinitely better than
kindness.—Cicero.

Friendship is stronger than kindred.—Publius Syrus.

Friendship buys friendship.—Emerson.

Friendship is love without his
wings!—Byron.

Rare as is true love, true friendship is rarer.—La Fontaine.

Faith in friendship is the noblest
part.—Earl of Orrery.

We call friendship the love of the
Dark Ages.—Madame de Salm.

Female friendships are of rapid
growth.—Beaconsfield.

Make yourself necessary to somebody.—Emerson.

Is mutual service the bond of friendship?—William Ellery Channing.

Sudden friendships rarely live to
ripeness.—Mlle. de Scudéri.

Love and friendship exclude each
other.—De La Bruyère.

No friendship can excuse a sin.—
Jeremy Taylor.

The youth is better than the old age
of friendship.—Hazlitt.

Poor is the friendless master of
a world.—Young.

The most violent friendships soonest wear themselves out.—Hazlitt.

To friendship every burden's light.
—Gay.

Hold friendship in regard.—Stobæus.

Friendship is but a name. I love no one.—Napoleon I.

Virtue is presupposed in friendship.
—Landor.

There is flattery in friendship.—Shakespeare.

Friendship is constant in all other things, save in the office and affairs of love.—Shakespeare.

Kindred weaknesses induce friendships as often as kindred virtues.—Bovee.

Women bestow on friendship only what they borrow from love.—Chamfort.

Friendship is given us by nature, not to favor vice, but to aid virtue.
—Cicero.

Dread more the blunderer's friendship than the calumniator's enmity.—Lavater.

Friendship is the shadow of the evening, which strengthens with the setting sun of life.—La Fontaine.

Be slow to fall into friendship; but when thou art in continue firm and constant.—Socrates.

That friendship will not continue to the end that is begun for an end.
—Quarles.

Let friendship creep gently to a height; if it rush to it, it may soon run itself out of breath.—Fuller.

Honest men esteem and value nothing so much in this world as a real friend. Such a one is, as it were, another self.—Pilpay.

Friendship is a disinterested commerce between equals.—Goldsmith.

The friendships of the world are oft confederacies in vice, or leagues of pleasure.—Addison.

The vulgar herd estimate friendship by its advantages.—Ovid.

To desire the same things and to reject the same things, constitutes true friendship.—Sallust.

Friendship is a cadence of divine melody melting through the heart.—Mildmay.

Do not allow grass to grow on the road of friendship.—Madame Geoffrin.

The ideal of friendship is to feel as one while remaining two.—Madame Swetchine.

He who has not the weakness of friendship has not the strength.—Joubert.

Neither is life long enough for friendship. That is a serious and majestic affair.—Emerson.

Friendship should be in the singular; it can be no more plural than love.—Ninon de Lenclos.

Friendship needs to be rooted in respect, but love can live upon itself alone.—Ouida.

It is true that friendship often ends in love, but love in friendship never.
—Colton.

Friendship always benefits, while love sometimes injures.—Seneca.

In friendship we find nothing false or insincere; everything is straightforward, and springs from the heart.
—Cicero.

I think there is nothing more lovely than the love of two beautiful women who are not envious of each other's charms.—Beaconsfield.

Friendship is an order of nobility; from its revelations we come more worthily into nature.—Emerson.

Friendship is made fast by interwoven benefits.—Sir P. Sidney.

He removes the greatest ornament of friendship who takes away from it respect.—Cicero.

Friendship is the gift of the gods, and the most precious boon to man.—Earl of Beaconsfield.

The essence of friendship is entireness, a total magnanimity and trust.—Emerson.

Friendship should be surrounded with ceremonies and respects, and not crushed into corners.—Emerson.

The corpse of friendship is not worth embalming.—Hazlitt.

A sudden thought strikes me, let us swear eternal friendship.—Canning.

The highest friendship must always lead us to the highest pleasure.—Fielding.

Sincerity, truth, faithfulness, come into the very essence of friendship.—William Ellery Channing.

What is commonly called friendship even is only a little more honor among rogues.—Thoreau.

We inspire friendship in men when we have contracted friendship with the gods.—Thoreau.

Friendship has a power
To soothe affliction in her darkest hour.
—H. K. White.

Friendship is a plant that loves the sun, thrives ill under clouds.—A. Bronson Alcott.

Friendship with a man is friendship with his virtue, and does not admit of assumptions of superiority.—Mencius.

In friendship your heart is like a bell struck every time your friend is in trouble.—Henry Ward Beecher.

True friendship is like sound health, the value of it is seldom known until it be lost.—Colton.

Friendship is cemented by interest, vanity, or the want of amusement; it seldom implies esteem, or even mutual regard.—Hazlitt.

Friendship is the most pleasant of all things, and nothing more glads the heart of man.—Plutarch.

There are no rules for friendship. It must be left to itself; we cannot force it any more than love.—Hazlitt.

Friendship that possesses the whole soul, and there rules and sways with an absolute sovereignty, can admit of no rival.—Montaigne.

O friendship! thou divinest alchemist, that man should ever profane thee!—Douglas Jerrold.

Friendship is a traffic wherein self-love always proposes to be the gainer.—Rochefoucauld.

Friendship requires a steady, constant, and unchangeable character, a person that is uniform in his intimacy.—Plutarch.

Friendship * * * is a long time in forming, it is of slow growth, through many trials and months of familiarity.—La Bruyère.

Friendship is the greatest honesty and ingenuity in the world.—Jeremy Taylor.

Interest, ambition, fortune, time, temper, love, all kill friendship.—Joseph Roux.

I love a friendship that flatters itself in the sharpness and vigor of its communications.—Montaigne.

The vital air of friendship is composed of confidence. Friendship perishes in proportion as this air diminishes.—Joseph Roux.

Other men are lenses through which we read our own minds.—Emerson.

The dearest thing in nature is not comparable to the dearest thing of friendship.—Jeremy Taylor.

'Tis thus that on the choice of friends Our good or evil name depends.—Gay.

To have the same desires and the same aversion is assuredly a firm bond of friendship.—Sallust.

Be slow to fall into friendship; but when thou art in continue firm and constant.—Socrates.

Literary friendship is a sympathy not of manners, but of feelings.—Isaac Disraeli.

Friendships begin with liking or gratitude—roots that can be pulled up.—George Eliot.

Pure friendship is something which men of an inferior intellect can never taste.—De La Bruyère.

Great souls by instinct to each other turn, Demand alliance, and in friendship burn.
—Addison.

As often as I come back to his door, his love met me on the threshold, and his noble serenity gave me comfort and peace.—William Winter.

Ceremony and great professing renders friendships as much suspected as it does religion.—Wycherley.

It is said that friendship between women is only a suspension of hostilities.—Rivarol.

In the forming of female friendships beauty seldom recommends one woman to another.—Fielding.

A true and noble friendship shrinks not at the greatest of trials.—Jeremy Taylor.

Friendship between two women is always a plot against another one.—Alphonse Karr.

The light of friendship is like the light of phosphorus,—seen plainest when all around is dark.—Crowell.

Life is to be fortified by many friendships. To love, and to be loved, is the greatest happiness of existence.—Sydney Smith.

True friendship's laws are by this rule express'd,
Welcome the coming, speed the parting guest.   —Homer.

"There is nothing that is meritorious but virtue and friendship; and indeed friendship itself is only a part of virtue."—Pope.

The friendship between me and you I will not compare to a chain; for that the rains might rust, or the falling tree might break.—Bancroft.

Some friendships are made by nature, some by contract, some by interest, and some by souls.—Jeremy Taylor.

A summer friendship, whose flattering leaves, that shadowed us in our prosperity, with the least gust drop off in the autumn of adversity.—Massinger.

We cannot expect the deepest friendship unless we are willing to pay the price, a self-sacrificing love.—Peloubet.

If we would build on a sure foundation in friendship, we must love our friends for their sake rather than our own.—Charlotte Brontë.

In the opinion of the world marriage ends all, as it does in a comedy. The truth is precisely the reverse; it begins all.—Mme. Swetchine.

Friendship, like love, is self-forgetful. The only inequality it knows is one that exalts the object, and humbles self.—Henry Giles.

Friendship throws a greater luster on prosperity, while it lightens adversity by sharing in its griefs and anxieties.—Cicero.

Friendship consists properly in mutual offices, and a generous strife in alternate acts of kindness.—South.

Friendship is the only thing in the world concerning the usefulness of which all mankind are agreed.—Cicero.

A friendship that makes the least noise is very often the most useful; for which reason I should prefer a prudent friend to a zealous one.—Addison.

To what gods is sacrificed that rarest and sweetest thing upon earth, friendship? To vanity and to interest.—Malesherbes.

I would give more for the private esteem and love of one than for the public praise of ten thousand.—W. R. Alger.

Friendship is too pure a pleasure for a mind cankered with ambition, or the lust of power and grandeur.—Junius.

He who cannot feel friendship is alike incapable of love. Let a woman beware of the man who owns that he loves no one but herself.—Talleyrand.

As the yellow gold is tried in fire, so the faith of friendship must be seen in adversity.—Ovid.

We only need to be as true to others as we are to ourselves, that there may be grounds enough for friendship.—Thoreau.

Friendship improves happiness and abates misery, by the doubling of our joy and the dividing of our grief.—Cicero.

There is no friendship between those associated in power; he who rules will always be impatient of an associate.—Lucan.

Nature loves nothing solitary, and always reaches out to something, as a support, which ever in the sincerest friend is most delightful.—Cicero.

Friendship is seldom lasting, but between equals, or where superiority is reduced by some equivalent advantage.—Johnson.

Love and esteem are the first principles of friendship, which always is imperfect where either of these two is wanting.—Budgell.

We should remember that it is quite as much a part of friendship to be delicate in its demands as to be ample in its performances.—J. F. Boyes.

Friendship is like those ancient altars where the unhappy, and even the guilty, found a sure asylum.—Madame Swetchine.

Friendship is the medicine for all misfortune; but ingratitude dries up the fountain of all goodness.—Richelieu.

The services which cement friendship are reciprocal services. A feeling of dependence is scarcely compatible with friendship.—William Smith.

A friendship formed in childhood, in youth,—by happy accident at any stage of rising manhood,—becomes the genius that rules the rest of life.—A. Bronson Alcott.

The most familiar and intimate habitudes, connections, friendships, require a degree of good-breeding both to preserve and cement them.—Lord Chesterfield.

Friendship is to be purchased only by friendship. A man may have authority over others, but he can never have their heart but by giving his own.—Thomas Wilson.

Friendship's said to be a plant of tedious growth, its root composed of tender fibers, nice in their taste, cautious in spreading.—Vanbrugh.

Nature and religion are the bands of friendship, excellence and usefulness are its great endearments.—Jeremy Taylor.

The friendship I have conceived will not be impaired by absence; but it may be no unpleasing circumstance to brighten the chain by a renewal of the covenant.—George Washington.

We are most of us very lonely in this world; you who have any who love you, cling to them and thank God.—Thackeray.

The feeling of friendship is like that of being comfortably filled with roast beef; love, like being enlivened with champagne.—Johnson.

There is a magic in the memory of schoolboy friendships; it softens the heart, and even affects the nervous system of those who have no hearts.—Beaconsfield.

Whosoever in the frame of his nature and affections is unfit for friendship, he taketh it of the beast, and not from humanity.—Bacon.

I hate the prostitution of the name of friendship to signify modish and worldly alliances.—Emerson.

Friendship heightens all our affections. We receive all the ardor of our friend in addition to our own. The communication of minds gives to each the fervor of each.—William Ellery Channing.

That friendship only is, indeed, genuine when two friends, without speaking a word to each other, can, nevertheless, find happiness in being together.—George Ebers.

Fix yourself upon the wealthy. In a word, take this for a golden rule through life: Never, never have a friend that is poorer than yourself.—Douglas Jerrold.

Thou learnest no secret until thou knowest friendship, since to the unsound no heavenly knowledge enters.—Hafiz.

The firmest friendships have been formed in mutual adversity; as iron is most strongly united by the fiercest flame.—Colton.

If a man does not make new acquaintances as he advances through life, he will soon find himself left alone. A man, sir, should keep his friendship in constant repair.—Johnson.

Friendships are the purer and the more ardent, the nearer they come to the presence of God, the Sun not only of righteousness but of love.—Landor.

A good man is the best friend, and therefore soonest to be chosen, longer to be retained, and, indeed, never to be parted with, unless he cease to be that for which he was chosen.—Jeremy Taylor.

No friendship is so cordial or so delicious as that of girl for girl; no hatred so intense and immovable as that of woman for woman.—Landor.

To find by experience that friendships are mortal, is the hard but inevitable lot of fallible and imperfect men.—Dr. Parr.

Friendship, peculiar boon of Heaven,
  The noble mind's delight and pride,
To men and angels only given,
  To all the lower world denied.
            —Sam'l Johnson.

          Hand
Grasps hand, eye lights eye in good
  friendship,
And great hearts expand,
And grow one in the sense of this world's
  life.   —Robert Browning.

Friendship's an abstract of this noble
  flame,
'Tis love refin'd, and purged from all its
  dross,
'Tis next to angel's love, if not the same,
  As strong in passion is, though not so
  gross.   Catherine Philips.

O friendship, equal-poised control,
  O heart, with kindliest motion warm,
  O sacred essence, other form,
O solemn ghost, O crowned soul!
            —Tennyson.

Friendship, gift of heaven, delight of great souls; friendship which kings, so distinguished for ingratitude, are unhappy enough not to know.—Voltaire.

Charity commands us, where we know no ill, to think well of all;

but friendship that always goes a step higher, gives a man a peculiar right and claim to the good opinion of his friend.—South.

And what is friendship but a name,
  A charm that lulls to sleep;
A shade that follows wealth or fame,
And leaves the wretch to weep?
      —Goldsmith.

In friendship we only see those faults which may be prejudicial to our friends. In love we see no faults but those by which we suffer ourselves.—De La Bruyère.

As the shadow in early morning, is friendship with the wicked; it dwindles hour by hour. But friendship with the good increases, like the evening shadows, till the sun of life sets.—Herder.

If two men are united, the wants of neither are any greater, in some respects, than they would be were they alone, and their strength is superior to the strength of two separate men.—Sénancour.

We value the devotedness of friendship rather as an oblation to vanity than as a free interchange of hearts; an endearing contract of sympathy, mutual forbearance, and respect!—Jane Porter.

False friendship, like the ivy, decays and ruins the walls it embraces; but true friendship gives new life and animation to the object it supports.—Robert Burton.

He who disguises tyranny, protection, or even benefits under the air and name of friendship reminds me of the guilty priest who poisoned the sacramental bread.—Chamfort.

Should auld acquaintance be forgot,
  And never brought to mind?
Should auld acquaintance be forgot,
  And days o' lang syne?   —Burns.

Friendship hath the skill and observation of the best physician, the diligence and vigilance of the best nurse, and the tenderness and patience of the best mother.—Clarendon.

Thou mayest be sure that he who will in private tell thee of thy faults is thy friend, for he adventures thy dislike and doth hazard thy hatred.—Sir Walter Raleigh.

Friendship, mysterious cement of the soul,
Sweetener of life, and solder of society,
I owe thee much: thou hast deserv'd from me
Far, far beyond what I can ever pay.
      —Blair.

Although a friend may remain faithful in misfortune, yet none but the very best and loftiest will remain faithful to us after our errors and our sins.—F. W. Farrar.

What is friendship in virtuous minds but the concentration of benevolent emotions heightened by respect, and increased by exercise on one or more objects?—Robert Hall.

Friendship is made up of esteem and pleasure; pity is composed of sorrow and contempt: the mind may for some time fluctuate between them, but it can never entertain both at once.—Goldsmith.

A generous friendship no cold medium knows,
Burns with one love, with one resentment glows;
One should our interests and our passions be,
My friend must hate the man that injures me.   —Pope.

I account that one of the greatest demonstrations of real friendship, that a friend can really endeavor to have his friend advanced in honor, in reputation, in the opinion of wit or learning, before himself.—Jeremy Taylor.

What is more notorious than that wherever a pecuniary interest appears upon the scene, friendship retires? Whether you take money from me, or whether you give it, the transaction is alike fatal to our old bond of amity.—William Smith.

The soil of friendship is worn out with constant use. Habit may still attach us to each other, but we feel ourselves fettered by it. Old friends might be compared to old married people without the tie of children.—Hazlitt.

A woman's friendship borders more closely on love than man's. Men affect each other in the reflection of noble or friendly acts; whilst women ask fewer proofs and more signs and expressions of attachment.—Coleridge.

It seems to me that a truly lovable woman is thereby unfitted for friendship, and that a woman fitted for friendship is but little fitted for love. —Alexander Walker.

I have too deeply read mankind to be amused with friendship; it is a name invented merely to betray credulity; it is intercourse of interest, not of souls.—Havard.

There is this important difference between love and friendship: while the former delights in extremes and opposites, the latter demands equalities.—Mme. de Maintenon.

Friendship is a calm and sedate affection, conducted by reason and cemented by habit; springing from long acquaintance and mutual obligations, without jealousies or fears, and without those feverish fits of heat and cold, which cause such an agreeable torment in the amorous passion. —Hume.

There is a power in love to divine another's destiny better than that other can, and by heroic encouragements, hold him to his task. What has friendship so signal as its sublime attraction to whatever virtue is in us?—Emerson.

True friendship cannot be among many. For since our faculties are of a finite energy, it is impossible our love can be very intense when divided among many. No, the rays must be contracted to make them burn.—John Norris.

We love everything on our own account; we even follow our own taste and inclination when we prefer our friends to ourselves; and yet it is this preference alone that constitutes true and perfect friendship.—Rochefoucauld.

What is commonly called friendship is no more than a partnership; a reciprocal regard for one another's interests, and an exchange of good offices; in a word, a mere traffic, wherein self-love always proposes to be a gainer.—Rochefoucauld.

These hearts which suck up friendship like water, and yield it again with the first touch, might as well expect to squeeze a sponge and find it hold its moisture, as to retain affections which they are forever dashing from them.—Jane Porter.

As friendship must be founded on mutual esteem, it cannot long exist among the vicious; for we soon find ill company to be like a dog, which dirts those the most whom he loves the best.—Chatfield.

Character is so largely affected by associations that we cannot afford to be indifferent as to who and what our friends are. They write their names in our albums, but they do more, they help make us what we are. Be therefore careful in selecting them; and when wisely selected, never sacrifice them.—M. Hulburd.

O friendship! thou fond soother of the human breast, to thee we fly in every calamity; to thee the wretched seek for succor; on thee the care-tired son of misery fondly relies; from thy kind assistance the unfortunate always hopes relief, and may be sure of—disappointment.—Goldsmith.

In your friendships and in your enmities let your confidence and your hostilities have certain bounds; make not the former dangerous, nor the latter irreconcilable. There are strange vicissitudes in business.—Chesterfield.

It is hard to believe long together that anything is "worth while," unless there is some eye to kindle in common with our own, some brief word uttered now and then to imply that what is infinitely precious to us is precious alike to another mind. —George Eliot.

We hate some persons because we do not know them; and we will not know them because we hate them. The friendships that succeed to such aversions are usually firm; for those qualities must be sterling that could not only gain our hearts, but conquer our prejudices.—Colton.

The friendship between great men is rarely intimate or permanent. It is a Boswell that most appreciates a Johnson. Genius has no brother, no co-mate; the love it inspires is that of a pupil or a son.—Bulwer-Lytton.

Old books, old wine, old nankin blue—
 All things, in short, to which belong
The charm, the grace that Time makes strong,
 All these I prize, but (entre nous)
Old friends are best.
                              —Austin Dobson.

Friendship, like love, is but a name,
Unless to one you stint the flame.
The child, whom many fathers share,
Hath seldom known a father's care.
'Tis thus in friendships; who depend
On many, rarely find a friend.   —Gay.

It may be worth noticing as a curious circumstance, when persons past forty before they were at all acquainted form together a very close intimacy of friendship. For grafts of old wood to take, there must be a wonderful congeniality between the trees.—Whately.

Once let friendship be given that is born of God, nor time nor circumstance can change it to a lessening; it must be mutual growth, increasing trust, widening faith, enduring patience, forgiving love, unselfish ambition,—an affection built before the throne, that will bear the test of time and trial.—Allan Throckmorton.

Friendship is the unspeakable joy and blessing that result to two or more individuals who from constitution sympathize. Such natures are liable to no mistakes, but will know each other through thick and thin. Between two by nature alike and fitted to sympathize, there is no veil, and there can be no obstacle. Who are the estranged? Two friends explaining.—Thoreau.

Friendship, like love, is destroyed by long absence, though it may be increased by short intermissions. What we have missed long enough to want it, we value more when it is regained; but that which has been lost till it is forgotten will be found at last with little gladness, and with still less if a substitute has supplied the place.— Johnson.

Of all intellectual friendships, none are so beautiful as those which subsist between old and ripe men and their younger brethren in science or literature or art. It is by these private friendships, even more than by public performance, that the tradition of sound thinking and great doing is perpetuated from age to age.— Hamerton.

There are three friendships which are advantageous, and three which are injurious. Friendship with the upright; friendship with the sincere; and friendship with the man of much observation: these are advantageous. Friendship with the man of specious airs; friendship with the insinuatingly soft; and friendship with the glib-tongued: these are injurious.—Confucius.

Perfect friendship puts us under the necessity of being virtuous. As it can only be preserved among estimable persons, it forces us to resemble them. You find in friendship the surety of good counsel, the emulation of good example, sympathy in our griefs, succor in our distress.—Madame de Lambert.

Friendship is the alloy of our sorrows, the ease of our passions, the discharge of our oppressions, the sanctuary to our calamities, the counsellor of our doubts, the clarity of our minds, the emission of our thoughts, the exercise and improvement of what we meditate. And although I love my friend because he is worthy, yet he is not worthy if he can do no good. —Jeremy Taylor.

When I see leaves drop from their trees in the beginning of autumn, just such, think I, is the friendship of the world. Whilst the sap of maintenance lasts my friends swarm in abundance; but in the winter of my need they leave me naked.—Warwick.

The friendship of high and sanctified spirits loses nothing by death but its alloy; failings disappear, and the virtues of those whose "faces we shall behold no more" appear greater and more sacred when beheld through the shades of the sepulchre.—Robert Hall.

The most elevated and pure souls cannot hear, even from the lips of the most contemptible men, these words, "friendship," "sensibility," "virtue," without immediately attaching to them all the grandeur of which their heart is susceptible.—Richter.

Let me take up your metaphor. Friendship is a vase, which, when it is flawed by heat or violence or accident, may as well be broken at once; it can never be trusted after. The more graceful and ornamental it was, the more clearly do we discern the hopelessness of restoring it to its former state. Coarse stones, if they are fractured, may be cemented again; precious stones, never.—Landor.

With a clear sky, a bright sun, and a gentle breeze, you will have friends in plenty; but let fortune frown, and the firmament be overcast, and then your friends will prove like the strings of the lute, of which you will tighten ten before you find one that will bear the stretch and keep the pitch. —Gotthold.

The highest compact we can make with our fellow is,—let there be truth between us two forevermore. * * * It is sublime to feel and say of another, I need never meet, or speak, or write to him; we need not reinforce

ourselves or send tokens of remembrance; I rely on him as on myself; if he did thus or thus, I know it was right.—Emerson.

Thy presence sweet
Still through long years of vigil I may share,
For if from that enchanted spirit-land
Thy healthful thought into my soul may shine
(E'en though thy voice be still, and cold thy hand,)
To lift my life and make it pure as thine;
Then, though thy place on earth a void must be,
Beloved friend, thou art not dead to me.
—H. H. Boyesen.

Come back! ye friendships long departed!
That like o'erflowing streamlets started,
And now are dwindled, one by one,
To stony channels in the sun!
Come back! ye friends, whose lives are ended,
Come back, with all that light attended,
Which seemed to darken and decay
When ye arose and went away!
—Longfellow.

Fast as the rolling seasons bring
The hour of fate to those we love,
Each pearl that leaves the broken string
Is set in Friendship's crown above.
As narrower grows the earthly chain,
The circle widens in the sky;
These are our treasures that remain,
But those are stars that beam on high.
—O. W. Holmes.

How were friendship possible? In mutual devotedness to the good and true; otherwise impossible, except as armed neutrality or hollow commercial league. A man, be the heavens ever praised, is sufficient for himself; yet were ten men, united in love, capable of being and of doing what ten thousand singly would fail in. Infinite is the help man can yield to man. —Carlyle.

People young, and raw, and self-natured, think it an easy thing to gain love, and reckon their own friendship a sure price of any man's; but when experience shall have shown them the hardness of most hearts, the hollowness of others, and the baseness and ingratitude of almost all, they will then find that a true friend is the gift of God, and that He only who made hearts can unite them.—South.

A wound in the friendship of young persons, as in the bark of young trees, may be so grown over as to leave no scar. The case is very different in regard to old persons and old timber. The reason of this may be accountable from the decline of the social passions, and the prevalence of spleen, suspicion, and rancor towards the latter part of life.—Shenstone.

Rejoice, and men will seek you;
　Grieve, and they turn and go,
They want full measure of all your pleasure,
　But they do not need your woe.
Be glad, and your friends are many;
　Be sad, and you lose them all,—
There are none to decline your nectar'd wine,
　But alone you must drink life's gall.
　　　　　　—Ella Wheeler Wilcox.

When the first time of love is over, there comes a something better still. Then comes that other love; that faithful friendship which never changes, and which will accompany you with its calm light through the whole of life. It is only needful to place yourself so that it may come, and then it comes of itself. And then everything turns and changes itself to the best.—Fredrika Bremer.

Such is friendship, that through it we love places and seasons; for as bright bodies emit rays to a distance, and flowers drop their sweet leaves on the ground around them, so friends impart favor even to the places where they dwell. With friends even poverty is pleasant. Words cannot express the joy which a friend imparts; they only can know who have experienced. A friend is dearer than the light of heaven, for it would be better for us that the sun were exhausted than that we should be without friends.—St. Chrysostom.

There are many moments in friendship, as in love, when silence is beyond words. The faults of our friend may be clear to us, but it is well to seem to shut our eyes to them. Friendship is usually treated by the majority of mankind as a tough and everlasting thing which will survive all manner of bad treatment. But

this is an exceedingly great and foolish error; it may die in an hour of a single unwise word; its conditions of existence are that it should be dealt with delicately and tenderly, being as it is a sensitive plant and not a roadside thistle. We must not expect our friend to be above humanity.—Ouida.

Frivolity

Frivolity, under whatever form it appears, takes from attention its strength, from thought its originality, from feeling its earnestness.—Madame de Staël.

Alas! that Christians should stand at the door of eternity having more work upon their hands than their time is sufficient for, and yet be filling their heads and hearts with trifles. —John Flavel.

Frost

All the panes are hung with frost
Wild wizard-work of silver lace.
　　　　　　—T. B. Aldrich.

What miracle of weird transforming
Is this wild work of frost and light,
This glimpse of glory infinite!
　　　　　　—Whittier.

Come see the north-wind's masonry.
Out of an unseen quarry evermore
Furnished with tile, the fierce artificer
Curves his white bastions with projected
　roof
Round every windward stake, or tree, or
　door.　　　　　—Emerson.

These winter nights, against my window-
　pane
Nature with busy pencil draws designs
Of ferns and blossoms and fine spray of
　pines,
Oak-leaf and acorn and fantastic vines,
Which she will make when summer comes
　again—
Quaint arabesques in argent, flat and cold,
Like curious Chinese etchings.
　　　　　　—T. B. Aldrich.

He comes,—he comes,—the Frost Spirit
　comes!—from the frozen Labrador,—
From the icy bridge of the Northern seas,
　which the white bear wanders o'er,—
Where the fisherman's sail is stiff with ice,
　and the luckless forms below
In the sunless cold of the lingering night
　into marble statues grow!
　　　　　　—Whittier.

Frugality

By sowing frugality we reap liberty, a golden harvest.—Agesilaus.

The world has not yet learned the riches of frugality.—Cicero.

Frugality is founded upon the principle, that all riches have limits.—Burke.

Frugality may be termed the daughter of prudence, the sister of temperance, and the parent of liberty.—Dr. Johnson.

Frugality, when all is spent, comes too late.—Seneca.

He will always be a slave, who does not know how to live upon a little.—Horace.

He seldom lives frugally who lives by chance. Hope is always liberal, and they that trust her promises make little scruple of revelling to-day on the profits of to-morrow.—Johnson.

He that spareth in everything is an inexcusable niggard. He that spareth in nothing is an inexcusable madman. The mean is to spare in what is least necessary, and to lay out more liberally in what is most required in our several circumstances.—Lord Halifax.

Frugality is good if liberality be joined with it. The first is leaving off superfluous expenses; the last is bestowing them to the benefit of others that need. The first without the last begets covetousness; the last without the first begets prodigality.—William Penn.

Fruit

The ripest fruit first falls.—Shakespeare.

Fruits that blossom first will first be ripe.—Shakespeare.

The ripest peach is highest on the tree.—James Whitcomb Riley.

The juicy pear
Lies, in a soft profusion, scattered round.
—Thompson.

As touching peaches in general, the very name in Latine whereby they are called Persica, doth evidently show that they were brought out of Persia first.—Pliny.

But the fruit that can fall without shaking,
Indeed is too mellow for me.
—Lady Montagu.

Oh, happy are the apples when the south winds blow.—Wm. Wallace Harney.

The strawberry grows underneath the nettle
And wholesome berries thrive and ripen best
Neighbour'd by fruit of baser quality.
—Shakespeare.

To satisfy the sharp desire I had
Of tasting those fair apples, I resolv'd
Not to defer; hunger and thirst at once
Powerful persuaders, quicken'd at the scent
Of that alluring fruit, urged me so keen.
—Milton.

Superfluous branches
We lop away, that bearing boughs may live.
—Shakespeare.

O,—fruit loved of boyhood!—the old days recalling,
When wood-grapes were purpling and brown nuts were falling!
When wild, ugly faces were carved in its skin,
Glaring out through the dark with a candle within!
When we laughed round the corn-heap, with hearts all in tune,
Our chair a broad pumpkin,—our lantern the moon,
Telling tales of the fairy who travelled like steam
In a pumpkin-shell coach, with two rats for her team!
—Whittier.

After the conquest of Afric, Greece, the lesser Asia, and Syria were brought into Italy all the sorts of their Mala, which we interpret apples, and might signify no more at first; but were afterwards applied to many other foreign fruits.—Sir Wm. Temple.

The flowers of life are but visionary. How many pass away and leave no trace behind! How few yield any fruit,—and the fruit itself, how rarely does it ripen! And yet there are flowers enough; and is it not strange, my friend, that we should suffer the little that does really ripen to rot, decay, and perish unenjoyed?—Goethe.

Nothing great is produced suddenly, since not even the grape or the fig is. If you say to me now that you want a fig, I will answer to you that it requires time: let it flower first, then put forth fruit, and then ripen. —Epictetus.

Fun

To a young heart everything is fun. —Dickens.

Next to the virtue, the fun in this world is what we can least spare.— Agnes Strickland.

Fun is a sugar-coated physic.—H. W. Shaw.

Fun has no limits. It is like the human race and face; there is a family likeness among all the species, but they all differ.—Haliburton.

There is nothing like fun, is there? I haven't any myself, and I do like it in others. Oh, we need it!—we need all the counterweights we can muster to balance the sad relations of life. God has made sunny spots in the heart: why should we exclude the light from them?—Haliburton.

Funeral

It is but waste to bury them preciously.—Chaucer.

The nodding plume,
Which makes poor man's humiliation proud;
Boast of our ruin! triumph of our dust!
—Dr. Young.

Groans and convulsions, and discolour'd faces,
Friends weeping round us, blacks, and obsequies,
Make death a dreadful thing; the pomp of death
Is far more terrible than death itself.
—Nat. Lee.

The only kind office performed for us by our friends of which we never complain is our funeral; and the only thing which we most want, happens to be the only thing we never purchase—our coffin.—Colton.

Of all
The fools who flock'd to swell or see the show,
Who car'd about the corpse? The funeral
Made the attraction, and the black the woe;
There throbb'd not there a thought which pierc'd the pall.   —Byron.

Why is the hearse with scutcheons blazon'd round,
And with the nodding plume of ostrich crown'd?
The dead know it not, nor profit gain;
It only serves to prove the living vain,
How short is life; how frail is human trust!
Is all this pomp for laying dust to dust?
—Gay.

But see! the well-plumed hearse comes nodding on, stately and slow;
But tell us, why this waste?
Why this ado in earthing up a carcass
That's fallen into disgrace, and in the nostrils smells horrible?   —Blair.

What though no friends in sable weeds appear,
Grieve for an hour, perhaps, then mourn a year?
And bear about the mockery of woe
To midnight dances, and the public show!
—Pope.

Thus, day by day, and month by month, we pass'd;
It pleas'd the Lord to take my spouse at last.
I tore my gown, I soil'd my locks with dust,
And beat my breasts—as wretched widows must.
Before my face my handkerchief I spread,
To hide the flood of tears I did—not shed.
—Pope.

Fuss

A paroxysm of nervous effervescence.—Douglas Jerrold.

Fuss is the froth of business.— Hood.

Fuss is half-sister to hurry, and neither of them can do anything without getting in their own way.— H. W. Shaw.

Future — Futurity

The best preparation for the future is the present well seen to, the last duty done.—George MacDonald.

Futurity is the great concern of mankind.—Burke.

The future is purchased by the present.—Johnson.

Belief in a future life is the appetite of reason.—Landor.

You can never plan the future by the past.—Burke.

But there's a gude time coming.—Scott.

It is easy to see, hard to foresee.—Franklin.

The curtain of the future is always drawn.—John Bigelow.

Oh, could we lift the future's sable shroud.—Bailey.

The glories of the possible are ours.—Bayard Taylor.

Coming events cast their shadows before.—Campbell.

The present is great with the future.—Leibnitz.

Boast not thyself of to-morrow; for thou knowest not what a day may bring forth.—Bible.

The mind that is anxious about the future is miserable.—Seneca.

A wise God shrouds the future in obscure darkness.—Horace.

Trust no future, howe'er pleasant!
Let the dead Past bury its dead!
—Longfellow.

No one sees what is before his feet: we all gaze at the stars.—Cicero.

Man must have some fears, hopes, and cares, for the coming morrow.—Schiller.

O Death, O Beyond,
Thou art sweet, thou art strange!
Mrs. Browning.

We know what we are, but know not what we may be.—Shakespeare.

It is vain to be always looking toward the future and never acting toward it.—J. F. Boyes.

If there was no future life, our souls would not thirst for it.—Richter.

We are always looking into the future, but we see only the past.—Madame Swetchine.

Locked up from mortal eye in shady leaves of destiny.—Crashaw.

Another life, if it were not better than this, would be less a promise than a threat.—J. Petit-Senn.

We always live prospectively, never retrospectively, and there is no abiding moment.—Jacobi.

When all else is lost, the future still remains.—Bovee.

Who knows whether the gods will add to-morrow to the present hour?—Horace.

O heaven! that one might read the book of fate, and see the revolution of the times.—Shakespeare.

Age and sorrow have the gift of reading the future by the sad past.—Rev. J. Farrar.

Ay, but to die, and go we know not where;
To lie in cold obstruction and to rot.
—Shakespeare.

The great world's altar-stairs
That slope thro' darkness up to God.
—Tennyson.

It may be we shall touch the Happy Isles,
And see the great Achilles, whom we knew.
—Tennyson.

It is heaven itself that points out an hereafter, and intimates eternity to man.—Addison.

After us the deluge.—Mme. Pompadour.

The earth with its scarred face is the symbol of the past; the air and heaven, of futurity.—Coleridge.

The veil which covers the face of futurity is woven by the hand of mercy.—Bulwer-Lytton.

There is no hope—the future will but turn
The old sand in the falling glass of time.
—R. H. Stoddard.

The state of that man's mind who feels too intense an interest as to future events, must be most deplorable.—Seneca.

The future does not come from before to meet us, but comes streaming up from behind over our heads.—Rahel.

It ever is the marked propensity of restless and aspiring minds to look into the stretch of dark futurity.—Joanna Baillie.

There is no divining-rod whose dip shall tell us at twenty what we shall most relish at thirty.—N. P. Willis.

How narrow our souls become when absorbed in any present good or ill! it is only the thought of the future that makes them great.—Richter.

No soul is bad enough for a fixed "hell," or good enough for a fixed "heaven," however useful the words may be as pointing to opposite states.—Hugh R. Haweis.

Sure there is none but fears a future state
And when the most obdurate swear they
    do not,
Their trembling hearts belie their boasting
    tongues.   —Dryden.

Oh, blindness to the future! kindly giv'n,
That each may fill the circle marked by
    Heaven.   —Pope.

We may believe that we shall know each other's forms hereafter; and in the bright fields of the better land call the lost dead to us.—Willis.

There was a wise man in the East whose constant prayer was that he might see to-day with the eyes of to-morrow.—Alfred Mercier.

Nothing can be reckoned good or bad to us in this life, any further than it indisposes us for the enjoyment of another.—Atterbury.

It has been well observed that we should treat futurity as an aged friend from whom we expect a rich legacy.—Colton.

Cease to inquire what the future has in store, and to take as a gift whatever the day brings forth.—Horace.

The spirit of man, which God inspired, cannot together perish with this corporeal clod.—Milton.

Whatever improvement we make in ourselves, we are thereby sure to meliorate our future condition.—Paley.

Everything that looks to the future elevates human nature; for never is life so low or so little as when occupied with the present.—Landor.

May you live unenvied, and pass many pleasant years unknown to fame; and also have congenial friends.—Ovid.

God will not suffer man to have the knowledge of things to come; for if he had prescience of his prosperity, he would be careless; and, understanding of his adversity, he would be senseless.—St. Augustine.

Trust no future, howe'er pleasant;
    Let the dead past bury its dead;
Act,—act in the living present,
    Heart within and God o'erhead!
          —Longfellow.

When the world dissolves,
And every creature shall be purified,
All places shall be hell that are not
    heaven.   —Marlowe.

O if this were seen!
The happiest youth—viewing his progress
    through
What perils past, what crosses to ensue—
Would shut the book, and sit him down and
    die.   —Shakespeare.

The golden age is not in the past, but in the future; not in the origin of human experience, but in its consummate flower; not opening in Eden, but out from Gethsemane.—Chapin.

There is, I know not how, in the minds of men, a certain presage, as it were, of a future existence, and this takes the deepest root, and is most discoverable, in the greatest geniuses and most exalted souls.—Cicero.

Beyond this vale of tears
There is a life above,
Unmeasured by the flight of years;
And all that life is love.
—Montgomery.

Dear Land to which Desire forever flees;
Time doth no present to our grasp allow,
Say in the fixed Eternal shall we seize
At last the fleeting Now?
—Bulwer-Lytton.

The year goes wrong, and tares grow strong.
Hope starves without a crumb;
But God's time is our harvest time,
And that is sure to come.
—Lewis J. Bates.

But ask not bodies (doomed to die),
To what abode they go;
Since knowledge is but sorrow's spy,
It is not safe to know.   —Davenant.

What a world were this
How unendurable its weight, if they
Whom Death hath sundered did not meet again!   —Southey.

We bewail our friends as if there were no better futurity yonder, and bewail ourselves as if there were no better futurity here; for all our passions are born atheists and infidels.—Richter.

Look not mournfully into the past,—it comes not back again; wisely improve the present,—it is thine; go forth to meet the shadowy future without fear, and with a manly heart.—Longfellow.

My mind can take no hold on the present world, nor rest in it a moment, but my whole nature rushes onward with irresistible force towards a future and better state of being.—Fichte.

There is something beyond the grave; death does not put an end to everything, the dark shade escapes from the consumed pile.—Propertius.

The things of another world being distant, operate but faintly upon us: to remedy this inconvenience, we must frequently revolve their certainty and importance.—Atterbury.

Some day Love shall claim his own,
Some day Right ascend his throne,
Some day hidden Truth be known;
Some day—some sweet day.
—Lewis J. Bates.

A. N. hopes in the next world for his felicity to live with Raphael, Mozart, and Goethe. But how can they be happy if they must live with him?—Auerbach.

We live in the future. Even the happiness of the present is made up mostly of that delightful discontent which the hope of better things inspires.—J. G. Holland.

The present is never the mark of our designs. We use both past and present as our means and instruments, but the future only as our object and aim.—Pascal.

The search of our future being is but a needless, anxious, and uncertain haste to be knowing, sooner than we can, what, without all this solicitude, we shall know a little later.—Pope.

Ah Christ, that it were possible
For one short hour to see
The souls we loved, that they might tell us
What and where they be.   —Tennyson.

What after all remains, when life is sped,
And man is gathered to the silent dead?
Home to the narrow house, the long, long sleep,
Where pain is stilled, and sorrow doth not weep.   —William Winter.

O, that a man might know
The end of this day's business, ere it come!
But it sufficeth that the day will end,
And then the end is known.
—Shakespeare.

To me there is something thrilling and exalting in the thought that we are drifting forward into a splendid mystery,—into something that no mortal eye has yet seen, no intelligence has yet declared.—Chapin.

There's nae sorrow there, John,
There's neither cauld nor care, John,
The day is aye fair,
In the land o' the leal.
—Lady Nairne.

O heavens! that one might read the book of fate,
And see the revolutions of the times
Make mountains level, and the continent,
(Weary of solid firmness,) melt itself
Into the sea. —Shakespeare.

If you can look into the seeds of time,
And say which grain will grow, and which will not;
Speak then to me, who neither beg nor fear
Your favors nor your hate.
—Shakespeare.

What cities, as great as this, have * * * promised themselves immortality! posterity can hardly trace the situation of some. The sorrowful traveler wanders over the awful ruins of others.—Goldsmith.

For tho' from out our bourne of Time and Place
The flood may bear me far,
I hope to see my Pilot face to face
When I have crossed the bar.
—Tennyson.

Divine wisdom, intending to detain us some time on earth, has done well to cover with a veil the prospect of life to come; for if our sight could clearly distinguish the opposite bank, who would remain on this tempestuous coast?—Madame de Staël.

It is one of God's blessings that we cannot foreknow the hour of our death; for a time fixed, even beyond the possibility of living, would trouble us more than doth this uncertainty.—James the Sixth.

The future is lighted for us with the radiant colors of hope. Strife and sorrow shall disappear. Peace and love shall reign supreme. The dream of poets, the lesson of priest and prophet, the inspiration of the great musician, is confirmed in the light of modern knowledge.—John Fiske.

One might as well attempt to calculate mathematically the contingent forms of the tinkling bits of glass in a kaleidoscope as to look through the tube of the future and foretell its pattern.—Beecher.

The dread of something after death,
The undiscover'd country, from whose bourn
No traveller returns, puzzles the will;
And makes us rather bear those ills we have,
Than fly to others that we know not of.
—Shakespeare.

Why will any man be so impertinently officious as to tell me all prospect of a future state is only fancy and delusion? Is there any merit in being the messenger of ill news? If it is a dream, let me enjoy it, since it makes me both the happier and better man.—Addison.

The grand difficulty is to feel the reality of both worlds, so as to give each its due place in our thoughts and feelings, to keep our mind's eye and our heart's eye ever fixed on the land of promise, without looking away from the road along which we are to travel toward it.—Hare.

The dead carry our thoughts to another and a nobler existence. They teach us, and especially by all the strange and seemingly untoward circumstances of their departure from this life, that they and we shall live in a future state forever.—Orville Dewey.

We are born for a higher destiny than that of earth; there is a realm where the rainbow never fades, where the stars will be spread before us like islands that slumber on the ocean,—and where the beings that pass before us like shadows will stay in our presence forever.—Bulwer-Lytton.

We are lead to the belief of a future state, not only by the weaknesses, by the hopes and fears of human nature, but by the noblest and best principles which belong to it,—by the love of virtue, and by the abhorrence of vice and injustice.—Adam Smith.

Futurity is impregnable to mortal ken : no prayer pierces through heaven's adamantine walls. Whether the birds fly right or left, whatever be the aspect of the stars, the book of nature is a maze, dreams are a lie, and every sign a falsehood.—Schiller.

While a man is stringing a harp, he tries the strings, not for music, but for construction. When it is finished it shall be played for melodies. God is fashioning the human heart for future joy. He only sounds a string here and there to see how far His work has progressed.—Beecher.

Since we stay not here, being people but of a day's abode, and our age is like that of a fly, and contemporary with that of a gourd, we must look somewhere else for an abiding city, a place in another country, to fix our house in, whose walls and foundation is God, where we must rest, or else be restless forever.—Jeremy Taylor.

God keeps a niche
In Heaven, to hold our idols; and albeit
He brake them to our faces, and denied
That our close kisses should impair their
   white,—
I know we shall behold them raised complete,
The dust swept from their beauty, glorified,
New Memnons singing in the great Godlight.   —E. B. Browning.

If that marvellous microcosm, man, with all the costly cargo of his faculties and powers, were indeed a rich argosy, fitted out and freighted only for shipwreck and destruction, who amongst us that tolerate the present only from the hope of the future, who that have any aspirings of a high and intellectual nature about them, could be brought to submit to the disgusting mortifications of the voyage?—Colton.

The future is always fairyland to the young. Life is like a beautiful and winding lane, on either side bright flowers, and beautiful butterflies and tempting fruits, which we scarcely pause to admire and to taste, so eager are we to hasten to an opening which we imagine will be more beautiful still. But by degrees, as we advance, the trees grow bleak ; the flowers and butterflies fail, the fruits disappear, and we find we have arrived—to reach a desert waste.—G. A. Sala.

There's a good time coming, boys;
  A good time coming:
We may not live to see the day,
But earth shall glisten in the ray
  Of the good time coming.
Cannon-balls may aid the truth,
  But thought's a weapon stronger;
We'll win our battle by its aid,
  Wait a little longer.
      —Chas. Mackay.

Is there a rarer being,
Is there a fairer sphere
Where the strong are not unseeing,
And the harvests are not sere;
Where, ere the seasons dwindle
They yield their due return;
Where the lamps of knowledge kindle
While the flames of youth still burn?
      —E. C. Stedman.

It is the "where I am" that makes heaven. The life after death might become through its very endlessness a burden to our spirits, if it were not to be filled with the infinite variety and freshness of God's love. Some have shrunk from its very infinitude, because they have not realized what God's love can make of it. Human love helps us to understand this. When we have come to love any one with all our power of affection, then there is no monotony or weariness in the days and hours we spend with them.—
—Maltbie Babcock.

G

Gaiety

Gaiety is often the reckless ripple over depths of despair.
—Chapin.

Gaiety is the soul's health; sadness is its poison.—Stanislaus.

Gaiety pleases more when we are assured that it does not cover carelessness.—Mme. de Staël.

Some people are commended for a giddy kind of good-humor, which is as much a virtue as drunkenness.—Pope.

Leaves seem light and useless, and idle and wavering, and changeable—they even dance; yet God has made them part of the oak. In so doing, He has given us a lesson, not to deny the stout-heartedness within because we see the lightsomeness without.—Leigh Hunt.

Gaiety is to good-humor as animal perfumes to vegetable fragrance. The one overpowers weak spirits, the other recreates and revives them. Gaiety seldom fails to give some pain; good-humor boasts no faculties which every one does not believe in his own power, and pleases principally by not offending.—Johnson.

Is there anything in life so lovely and poetical as the laugh and merriment of a young girl, who, still in harmony with all her powers, sports with you in luxuriant freedom, and in her mirthfulness neither despises nor dislikes? Her gravity is seldom as innocent as her playfulness; still less that haughty discontent which converts the youthful Psyche into a dull, thick, buzzing, wing-drooping night-moth.—Richter.

Gain

For me to live is Christ, to die is gain.—Bible.

An evil gain equals a loss.—Syrus.

The elegant simplicity of the three per cents.—Lord Eldon.

A captive fetter'd at the oar of gain.—Falconer.

He who seeks for gain must be at some expense.—Plautus.

Counts his sure gains, and hurries back for more.—Montgomery.

Everywhere in life, the true question is not what we gain, but what we do.—Carlyle.

From others' slips some profit from one's self to gain.—Terence.

Little pains
In a due hour employ'd great profit yields.
—John Philips.

Men that hazard all
Do it in hope of fair advantages:
A golden mind stoops not to shows of dross.
—Shakespeare.

That, sir, which serves and seeks for gain,
And follows but for form,
Will pack, when it begins to rain,
And leave thee in a storm.
—Shakespeare.

Keep thy shop, and thy shop will keep thee. Light gains make heavy purses. 'Tis good to be merry and wise.—George Chapman.

As to pay, sir, I beg leave to assure the Congress that as no pecuniary consideration could have tempted me to accept this arduous employment at the expense of my domestic ease and happiness, I do not wish to make any profit from it.—George Washington.

Gallantry

A gallant man is above ill words.—Selden.

Love is the smallest part of gallantry.—Rochefoucauld.

The gallantry of the mind consists in agreeable flattery.—Rochefoucauld.

Gallantry thrives most in the atmosphere of the court.—Mme. Necker.

Conscience has no more to do with gallantry than it has with politics.—Sheridan.

Gallantry, though a fashionable crime, is a very detestable one; and the wretch who pilfers from us in the hour of distress is an innocent character compared to the plunderer who wantonly robs us of happiness and reputation.—Rev. H. Kelley.

Gallantry to women (the sure road to their favor) is nothing but the appearance of extreme devotion to all their wants and wishes, a delight in their satisfaction, and a confidence in yourself as being able to contribute towards it. The slightest indifference with regard to them, or distrust of yourself is equally fatal.—Hazlitt.

Gambling

It is lost at dice, what ancient honor won.—Shakespeare.

Keep flax from fire, youth from gaming.—Franklin.

A heavy tax placed upon fools.—Castelar.

Games of chance are traps to catch schoolboy novices and gaping country squires, who begin with a guinea and end with a mortgage.—Cumberland.

European lotteries are the tax on fools.—Count Cavour.

The gambler is a moral suicide.—Colton.

Oh, this pernicious vice of gaming! —Ed. Moore.

Could fools to keep their own contrive, On what, on whom could gamesters thrive? —Gay.

Curst is the wretch enslaved to such a vice, Who ventures life and soul upon the dice. —Horace.

Lookers-on many times see more than gamesters.—Bacon.

The most patient man in loss, the most coldest that ever turned up ace. —Shakespeare.

It is the child of avarice, the brother of iniquity, and the father of mischief.—Washington.

The gambler is more wicked as he is a greater proficient in his art.—Syrus.

What more than madness reigns, when one short sitting many hundreds drains.—Sir J. Davies.

There is but one good throw upon the dice, which is to throw them away. —Chatfield.

What honest man would not rather be the sufferer than the defrauder?—Richardson.

A mode of transferring property without producing any intermediate good.—Dr. Johnson.

Cards were at first for benefits designed, Sent to amuse, not to enslave the mind. —David Garrick.

Gambling with cards, or dice, or stocks, is all one thing—it is getting money without giving an equivalent for it.—Henry Ward Beecher.

Gaming finds a man a cully, and leaves him a knave.—T. Hughes.

A gamester, as such, is the cool, calculating, essential spirit of concentrated, avaricious selfishness.—Henry Ward Beecher.

The deal, the shuffle, and the cut.—Swift.

Gaming is the child of avarice, but the parent of prodigality.—Colton.

Our Quixote bard sets out a monster taming.
Arm'd at all points to fight that hydra, gaming.   —David Garrick.

A gamester, the greater master he is in his art, the worse man he is.—Bacon.

Bets at first were fool-traps, where the wise like spiders lay in ambush for the flies.—Dryden.

Play not for gain, but sport. Who plays for more
Than he can lose with pleasure, stakes his heart;
Perhaps his wife's too, and whom she hath bore.   —Herbert.

All gaming, since it implies a desire to profit at the expense of another, involves a breach of the tenth commandment.—Whately.

Gaming is the destruction of all decorum; the prince forgets at it his dignity, and the lady her modesty.—Marchioness d'Alembert.

Look round, the wrecks of play behold,
Estates dismember'd, mortgag'd, sold!
Their owners now to jails confin'd,
Show equal poverty of mind.   —Gay.

The gamester, if he die a martyr to his profession, is doubly ruined. He adds his soul to every other loss, and by the act of suicide, renounces earth to forfeit heaven.—Colton.

It is possible that a wise and good man may be prevailed on to game; but it is impossible that a professed gamester should be a wise and good man.—Lavater.

By gaming we lose both our time and treasure—two things most precious to the life of man.—Feltham.

Ay, rail at gaming—'tis a rich topic, and affords noble declamation. Go, preach against it in the city—you'll find a congregation in every tavern.—Ed. Moore.

Some play for gain; to pass time others play
For nothing; both play the fool, I say:
Nor time nor coin I'll lose, or idly spend;
Who gets by play, proves loser in the end.   —Heath.

Whose game was empires, and whose stakes were thrones;
Whose table earth, whose dice were human bones.   —Byron.

A night of fretful passion may consume
All that thou hast of beauty's gentle bloom;
And one distemper'd hour of sordid fear
Print on thy brow the wrinkles of a year.   —Sheridan.

I look upon every man as a suicide from the moment he takes the dice-box desperately in his hand; and all that follows in his fatal career from that time is only sharpening the dagger before he strikes it to his heart.—Cumberland.

It is well for gamesters that they are so numerous as to make a society of themselves; for it would be a strange abuse of terms to rank those among society at large, whose profession it is to prey upon all who compose it.—Cumberland.

The coldness of a losing gamester lessens the pleasure of the winner. I would no more play with a man that slighted his ill fortune than I would make love to a woman who undervalued the loss of her reputation.—Congreve.

Sports and gaming, whether pursued from a desire of gain or love of pleasure, are as ruinous to the temper and disposition of the party addicted to them, as they are to his fame and fortune.—Burton.

Gaming has been resorted to by the affluent as a refuge from ennui. It is a mental dram, and may succeed for a moment; but, like all other stimuli, it produces indirect debility.—Colton.

That reproach of modern times, that gulf of time and fortune, the passion for gaming, which is so often the refuge of the idle sons of pleasure and often, alas! the last resource of the ruined.—Blair.

I'll tell thee what it says; it calls me villain, a treacherous husband, a cruel father, a false brother; one lost to nature and her charities; or to say all in one short word, it calls me—gamester.—Ed. Moore.

The exercises I wholly condemn are dicing and carding, especially if you play for any great sum of money, or spend any time in them, or use to come to meetings in dicing-houses, where cheaters meet and cozen young gentlemen out of all their money.—Lord Herbert.

Gambling houses are temples where the most sordid and turbulent passions contend; there no spectator can be indifferent. A card or a small square of ivory interests more than the loss of an empire, or the ruin of an unoffending group of infants, and their nearest relatives.—Zimmermann.

Gaming is a kind of tacit confession that the company engaged therein do in general exceed the bounds of their respective fortunes, and therefore they cast lots to determine upon whom the ruin shall at present fall, that the rest may be saved a little longer.—Blackstone.

Be assured that, although men of eminent genius have been guilty of all other vices, none worthy of more than a secondary name has ever been a gamester. Either an excess of avarice or a deficiency of what, in physics, is called excitability, is the cause of it; neither of which can exist in the same bosom with genius, with patriotism, or with virtue.—Landor.

There is nothing that wears out a fine lace like the vigils of the card table, and those cutting passions which naturally attend them. Hollow eyes, haggard looks and pale complexions are the natural indications.—Steele.

Gaming is a vice the more dangerous as it is deceitful; and, contrary to every other species of luxury, flatters its votaries with the hopes of increasing their wealth; so that avarice itself is so far from securing us against its temptations that it often betrays the more thoughtless and giddy part of mankind into them.—Fielding.

An assembly of the states, a court of justice, shows nothing so serious and grave as a table of gamesters playing very high; a melancholy solicitude clouds their looks; envy and rancor agitate their minds while the meeting lasts, without regard to friendship, alliances, birth or distinctions.—Bruyère.

If thy desire to raise thy fortunes encourage thy delights to the casts of fortune, be wise betimes, lest thou repent too late; what thou gettest, thou gainest by abused providence; what thou losest, thou losest by abused patience; what thou winnest is prodigally spent; what thou losest is prodigally lost; it is an evil trade that prodigality drives; and a bad voyage where the pilot is blind.—Quarles.

This is a vice which is productive of every possible evil, equally injurious to the morals and health of its votaries. It is the child of avarice, the brother of iniquity, and the father of mischief. It has been the ruin of many worthy families, the loss of many a man's honor, and the cause of suicide. To all those who enter the lists, it is equally fascinating. The successful gamester pushes his good fortune, till it is overtaken by a reverse. The losing gamester, in hopes of retrieving past misfortunes, goes on from bad to worse, till, grown desperate, he pushes at everything and loses his all. In a word, few gain by this abominable practice, while thousands are injured.—George Washington.

Games

As to cards and dice, I think the safest and best way is never to learn to play upon them, and so to be incapacitated for those dangerous temptations and encroaching wasters of time.—Locke.

Let the world have their May games, wakes, and whatever sports and recreations please them, provided they be followed with discretion.—Robert Burton.

Games lubricate the body and the mind.—Franklin.

Games are good or bad as to their nature; all may be perverted.—Dr. Johnson.

It is wonderful to see persons of sense passing away a dozen hours together in shuffling and dividing a pack of cards.—Addison.

The games of the ancient Greeks were, in their original institutions, religious solemnities.—Brande.

Garden

God the first garden made, and the first city, Cain.—Cowley.

And add to these retired Leisure,
That in trim gardens takes his pleasure.
—Milton.

The garden lies,
A league of grass, wash'd by a slow broad stream.
—Tennyson.

My garden is a forest ledge
Which older forests bound;
The banks slope down to the blue lake-edge,
Then plunge to depths profound!
—Emerson.

A little garden square and wall'd;
And in it throve an ancient evergreen,
A yew-tree, and all round it ran a walk
Of shingle, and a walk divided it.
—Tennyson.

His gardens next your admiration call,
On every side you look, behold the wall!
No pleasing intricacies intervene,
No artful wildness to perplex the scene;
Grove nods at grove, each alley has a brother,
And half the platform just reflects the other.
The suffering eye inverted nature sees,
Trees cut to statues, statues thick as trees;
With here a fountain, never to be play'd,
And there a summer-house that knows no shade.
—Pope.

A garden, sir, wherein all rain-bowed flowers were heaped together.—Charles Kingsley.

The splash and stir
Of fountains spouted up and showering down
In meshes of the jasmine and the rose:
And all about us peal'd the nightingale,
Rapt in her song, and careless of the snare.
—Tennyson.

An album is a garden, not for show
Planted, but use; where wholesome herbs should grow.　—Charles Lamb.

Who loves a garden loves a greenhouse, too.—Cowper.

Generosity

Generosity is only benevolence in practice.—Bishop Ken.

Generosity is more charitable than wealth.—Joseph Roux.

One can love any man that is generous.—Leigh Hunt.

Generosity is the flower of justice.—Hawthorne.

Bounty, being free itself, thinks all others so.—Shakespeare.

Our generosity never should exceed our abilities.—Cicero.

The secret pleasure of a generous act is the great mind's great bribe.—Dryden.

It is not enough to help the feeble up, but to support him after.—Shakespeare.

In this world, it is not what we take up, but what we give up, that makes us rich.—Beecher.

A giving hand, though foul, shall have fair praise.—Shakespeare.

Some are unwisely liberal; and more delight to give presents than to pay debts.—Sir P. Sidney.

Almost always the most indigent are the most generous.—Stanislaus.

If there be any truer measure of a man than by what he does, it must be by what he gives.—South.

To give awkwardly is churlishness. The most difficult part is to give, then why not add a smile?—La Bruyère.

Generosity, wrong placed, becometh a vice; a princely mind will undo a private family.—Fuller.

The truly generous is the truly wise; And he who loves not others, lives unblest. —Horace.

Bounty always receives part of its value from the manner it is bestowed. —Dr. Johnson.

A man who suddenly becomes generous may please fools, but he will not deceive the wise.—Phædrus.

Many men have been capable of doing a wise thing, more a cunning thing, but very few a generous thing.—Alexander Pope.

Generosity, to be perfect, should always be accompanied by a dash of humor.—Marie Ebner-Eschenbach.

Generosity is the accompaniment of high birth; pity and gratitude are its attendants.—Corneille.

For his bounty, there was no winter in it; an autumn 'twas that grew the more by reaping.—Shakespeare.

What seems generosity is often disguised ambition, that despises small to run after greater interests.—Rochefoucauld.

How much easier it is to be generous than just! Men are sometimes bountiful who are not honest.—Junius.

In giving, a man receives more than he gives; and the more is in proportion to the worth of the thing given.—George MacDonald.

O the world is but a word; were it all yours to give it in a breath, how quickly were it gone!—Shakespeare.

Men of the noblest dispositions think themselves happiest when others share their happiness with them.—Duncan.

The generous who is always just, and the just who is always generous, may, unannounced, approach the throne of heaven.—Lavater.

When you give, take to yourself no credit for generosity, unless you deny yourself something in order that you may give.—Henry Taylor.

To be generous, guiltless, and of a free disposition is to take those things for bird-bolts that you deem cannon-bullets.—Shakespeare.

No one ever sowed the grain of generosity who gathered not up the harvest of the desire of his heart.—Saadi.

Wherever I find a great deal of gratitude in a poor man, I take it for granted there would be as much generosity if he were a rich man.—Pope.

Let us proportion our alms to our ability, lest we provoke God to proportion His blessings to our alms.—Beveridge.

They that do an act that does deserve requital pay first themselves the stock of such content.—Sir Robert Howard.

Any one may do a casual act of good-nature; but a continuation of them shows it a part of the temperament.—Sterne.

There were in him candor and generosity, which, unless tempered by due moderation, lead to ruin.—Tacitus.

There is a greatness in being generous, and there is only simple justice in satisfying creditors. Generosity is the part of the soul raised above the vulgar.—Goldsmith.

He who gives what he would as readily throw away gives without generosity; for the essence of generosity is in self-sacrifice.—Henry Taylor.

It is a pleasure appropriate to man for him to save a fellow-man, and gratitude is acquired in no better way. —Ovid.

All my experience of the world teaches me that in ninety-nine cases out of a hundred the safe side and the just side of a question is the generous side and the merciful side.—Mrs. Jameson.

True generosity is a duty as indispensably necessary as those imposed upon us by the law. It is a rule imposed upon us by reason, which should be the sovereign law of a rational being.—Goldsmith.

Generosity, when once set going, knows not how to stop; as the more familiar we are with the lovely form, the more enamored we become of her charms.—Pliny the Younger.

God blesses still the generous thought
  And still the fitting word He speeds,
And truth, at His requiring taught,
  He quickens into deeds.   —Whittier.

It is good to be unselfish and generous; but don't carry that too far. It will not do to give yourself to be melted down for the benefit of the tallow-trade; you must know where to find yourself.—George Eliot.

A friend to everybody is often a friend to nobody, or else in his simplicity he robs his family to help strangers, and becomes brother to a beggar. There is wisdom in generosity, as in everything else.—Spurgeon.

He that gives all, though but little, gives much; because God looks not to the quantity of the gift, but to the quality of the givers; he that desires to give more than he can hath equaled his gift to his desire, and hath given more than he hath.—Quarles.

The reputation of generosity is to be purchased pretty cheap; it does not depend so much upon a man's general expense, as it does upon his giving handsomely where it is proper to give at all. A man, for instance, who should give a servant four shillings would pass for covetous, while he who gave him a crown would be reckoned generous; so that the difference of those two opposite characters turns upon one shilling.—Chesterfield.

One great reason why men practice generosity so little in the world is their finding so little there. Generosity is catching; and if so many men escape it, it is in a great degree from the same reason the countrymen escape the smallpox,—because they meet no one to give it to them.—Greville.

There is a story of some mountains of salt in Cumana, which never diminished, though carried away in much abundance by merchants; but when once they were monopolized to the benefit of a private purse, then the salt decreased, till afterward all were allowed to take of it, when it had a new access and increase. The truth of this story may be uncertain, but the application is true; he that envies others the use of his gifts decays then, but he thrives most that is most diffusive.—Spencer.

Genius

Genius is only great patience.—Buffon.

Genius is universal.—David Dudley Field.

Genius does not herd with genius.—O. W. Holmes.

Genius is independent of situation.—Churchill.

Genius involves both envy and calumny.—Pope.

Genius speaks only to genius.—Stanislaus.

A happy genius is the gift of nature.—Dryden.

No enemy is so terrible as a man of genius.—Disraeli.

Genius is intensity.—Balzac.

Genius, even, as it is the greatest good, is the greatest harm.—Emerson.

Genius can never despise labor.—Abel Stevens.

Genius, like humanity, rusts for want of use.—Hazlitt.

Genius has no brother.—Bulwer-Lytton.

Genius must be born, and never can be taught.—Dryden.

The faculty of growth.—Coleridge.

Genius points the way; talent pursues it.—Marie Ebner-Eschenbach.

Genius is ever a riddle to itself.—Richter.

All great men are in some degree inspired.—Cicero.

One genius has made many clever artists.—Martial.

Genius is clairvoyant.—Abel Stevens.

The freemasonry of genius.—Moses Harvey.

To do what is impossible for talent is the mark of genius.—Amiel.

Genius is that in whose power a man is.—Lowell.

Genius only leaves behind it the monuments of its strength.—Hazlitt.

Genius can only breathe freely in an atmosphere of freedom.—John Stuart Mill.

Great geniuses have the shortest biographies.—Emerson.

The lamp of genius burns quicker than the lamp of life.—Schiller.

The honors of genius are eternal.—Propertius.

We measure genius by quality, not by quantity.—Wendell Phillips.

Courage of soul is necessary for the triumphs of genius.—Mme. de Staël.

No age is shut against great genius.—Seneca.

Genius is mainly an affair of energy.—Matthew Arnold.

Genius is always more suggestive than expressive.—Abel Stevens.

Talent should minister to genius.—Robert Browning.

Patience is a necessary ingredient of genius.—Beaconsfield.

Genius, in one respect, is like gold—numbers of persons are constantly writing about both, who have neither.—Colton.

A woman must be a genius to create a good husband.—Balzac.

Taste consists in the power of judging; genius in the power of executing.—Blair.

There are no laws by which we can write Iliads.—Ruskin.

Genius is not a single power, but a combination of great powers.—Whipple.

Genius does what it must; and talent does what it can.—Owen Meredith.

The path of genius is not less obstructed with disappointment than that of ambition.—Voltaire.

One science only will one genius fit, so vast is art, so narrow human wit.—Pope.

Genius of the highest kind implies an unusual intensity of the modifying power.—Coleridge.

There is no great genius free from some tincture of madness.—Seneca.

Genius, thou gift of Heaven! thou light divine!—Crabbe.

The proportion of genius to the vulgar is like one to a million.—Lavater.

Nature is the master of talent; genius is the master of nature.—J. G. Holland.

Genius is the highest type of reason —talent the highest type of the understanding.—Hickok.

Genius, the Pythian of the beautiful, leaves its large truths a riddle to the dull.—Bulwer-Lytton.

Genius is an immense capacity for taking trouble.—Carlyle.

Genius is the gold in the mine, talent is the miner who works and brings it out.—Lady Blessington.

The first and last thing which is required of genius is the love of truth. —Goethe.

Genius always gives its best at first, prudence at last.—Lavater.

The life of great geniuses is nothing but a sublime storm.—George Sand.

I know no such thing as genius— genius is nothing but labor and diligence.—Hogarth.

Philosophy becomes poetry, and science imagination, in the enthusiasm of genius.—Isaac Disraeli.

Genius unexerted is no more genius than a bushel of acorns is a forest of oaks.—Beecher.

Many men of genius must arise before a particular man of genius can appear.—Isaac Disraeli.

Fortune has rarely condescended to be the companion of genius.—Isaac Disraeli.

Genius in poverty is never feared, because nature, though liberal in her gifts in one instance, is forgetful in another.—B. R. Haydon.

Every man who observes vigilantly and resolves steadfastly, grows unconsciously into genius.—Bulwer-Lytton.

A man of genius is inexhaustible only in proportion as he is always renourishing his genius.—Bulwer-Lytton.

He alone can claim this name, who writes
With fancy high, and bold and daring
  Flights.   —Horace.

Intelligence is to genius as the whole is in proportion to its part.— De La Bruyère.

Genius is essentially creative; it bears the stamp of the individual who possesses it.—Mme. de Staël.

Wit is the god of moments, but Genius is the god of ages.—La Bruyère.

Steady work turns genius to a loom. —George Eliot.

It is the privilege of genius that to it life never grows commonplace as to the rest of us.—Lowell.

Genius—the free and harmonious play of all the faculties of a human being.—Alcott.

Genius does not care much for a set of explicit regulations, but that does not mean that genius is lawless.— Charles H. Parkhurst.

Many a genius has been slow of growth. Oaks that flourish for a thousand years do not spring up into beauty like a reed.—George Henry Lewes.

The scorn of genius is the most arrogant and the most boundless of all scorn.—Ouida.

Genius is inconsiderate, self-relying, and, like unconscious beauty, without any intention to please.—Isaac Mayer Wise.

Genius is subject to the same laws which regulate the production of cotton and molasses.—Macaulay.

Of the three requisitions of genius, the first is soul, and the second, soul, and the third, soul.—E. P. Whipple.

Genius finds its own road and carries its own lamp.—Willmott.

Heaven and earth, advantages and obstacles, conspire to educate genius.—Fuseli.

Genius may be almost defined as the faculty of acquiring poverty.—Whipple.

Genius is the power of carrying the feelings of childhood into the powers of manhood.—Coleridge.

Genius makes its observations in shorthand; talent writes them out at length.—Bovee.

The miracles of genius always rest on profound convictions which refuse to be analyzed.—Emerson.

How often we see the greatest genius buried in obscurity!—Plautus.

Genius may at times want the spur, but it stands as often in need of the curb.—Longinus.

There is genius as well in virtue as in intellect. 'Tis the doctrine of faith over works.—Emerson.

That genius is feeble which cannot hold its own before the masterpieces of the world.—T. W. Higginson.

Genius is always impatient of its harness; its wild blood makes it hard to train.—-Holmes.

The gifts of genius are far greater than the givers themselves venture to suppose.—Moses Harvey.

Genius is lonely without the surrounding presence of a people to inspire it.—T. W. Higginson.

Men of genius are often dull and inert in society, as the blazing meteor when it descends to the earth is only a stone.—Longfellow.

A man of genius may sometimes suffer a miserable sterility; but at other times he will feel himself the magician of thought.—John Foster.

Genius cannot escape the taint of its time more than a child the influence of its begetting.—Ouida.

Refined taste forms a good critic; but genius is further necessary to form the poet or the orator.—Blair.

There is none but he whose being I do fear; and, under him, my genius is rebuked, as it is said Antony's was by Cæsar.—Shakespeare.

It is in the heart that God has placed the genius of women, because the works of this genius are all works of love.—Lamartine.

Genius is rarely found without some mixture of eccentricity, as the strength of spirit is proved by the bubbles on its surface.—Mrs. Balfour.

His genius quite obscured the brightest ray
Of human thought, as Sol's effulgent beams
At morn's approach, extinguished all the
stars.　　　　　—R. Wynne.

The finest flowers of genius have grown in an atmosphere where those of Nature are prone to droop, and difficult to bring to maturity.—Dr. Guthrie.

The greatest genius is never so great as when it is chastised and subdued by the highest reason.—Colton.

Talent, lying in the understanding, is often inherent; genius, being the action of reason and imagination, rarely or never.—Coleridge.

There is hardly a more common error than that of taking the man who has but one talent for a genius.—Arthur Helps.

Some have the temperament and tastes of genius, without its creative power. They feel acutely, but express tamely.—Bulwer.

The true characteristic of genius—without despising rules, it knows when and how to break them.—Channing.

Genius has its fatality. Must we not see in its works a manifestation of the will of Providence?—Arsène Houssaye.

When a true genius appears in the world you may know him by this sign, that the dunces are all in confederacy against him.—Swift.

Genius, like a torch, shines less in the broad daylight of the present than in the night of the past.—J. Petit-Senn.

Talent wears well, genius wears itself out; talent drives a brougham in fact; genius, a sun-chariot in fancy.—Ouida.

Not oft near home does genius brightly shine,
No more than precious stones while in the mine.   —Omar Khayyam.

Genius and its rewards are briefly told:
A liberal nature and a niggard doom,
A difficult journey to a splendid tomb.
          —Forster.

Genius inspires this thirst for fame: there is no blessing undesired by those to whom Heaven gave the means of winning it.—Mme. de Staël.

To think and to feel, constitute the two grand divisions of men of genius —the men of reasoning and the men of imagination.—Isaac Disraeli.

Men of humor are always in some degree men of genius; wits are rarely so, although a man of genius may, amongst other gifts, possess wit, as Shakespeare.—Coleridge.

Men of genius are rarely much annoyed by the company of vulgar people, because they have a power of looking at such persons as objects of amusement of another race altogether.—Coleridge.

Latent genius is but a presumption. Everything that can be, is bound to come into being, and what never comes into being is nothing.—Amiel.

It is the habit of party in England to ask the alliance of a man of genius, but to follow the guidance of a man of character.—Lord John Russell.

The very thrills of genius are disorganizing. The body is never quite acclimated to its atmosphere, but how often succumbs and goes into a decline.—Henry D. Thoreau.

Eccentricity is not a proof of genius, and even an artist should remember that originality consists not only in doing things differently, but also in "doing things better."—Stedman.

This is the highest miracle of genius, that things which are not should be as though they were, that the imaginations of one mind should become the personal recollections of another. —Macaulay.

There is no work of genius which has not been the delight of mankind, no word of genius to which the human heart and soul have not, sooner or later, responded.—Lowell.

Many have genius, but, wanting art, are forever dumb. The two must go together to form the great poet, painter, or sculptor.—Longfellow.

It is good sense applied with diligence to what was at first a mere accident, and which by great application grew to be called, by the generality of mankind, a particular genius.—Johnson.

This is the method of genius, to ripen fruit for the crowd by those rays of whose heat they complain.— Margaret Fuller.

The greatest geniuses have always attributed everything to God, as if conscious of being possessed of a spark of His divinity.—B. R. Haydon.

Men of genius are often considered superstitious, but the fact is, the fineness of their nerve renders them more alive to the supernatural than ordinary men.—B. R. Haydon.

Genius is only as rich as it is generous. If it hoards, it impoverishes itself. What the banker sighs for, the meanest clown may have—leisure and a quiet mind.—Henry D. Thoreau.

So far from genius discarding law, rather is it the supreme joy of genius to re-enact the eternal and unwritten law in the chamber of its own intellect.—Charles H. Parkhurst.

Rising genius always shoots forth its rays from among clouds and vapors, but these will gradually roll away and disappear as it ascends to its steady and meridian lustre.—Washington Irving.

Men of genius do not excel in any profession because they labor in it, but they labor in it because they excel.—Hazlitt.

Unpretending mediocrity is good, and genius is glorious; but the weak flavor of genius in a person essentially common is detestable.—Holmes.

Genius, that power which constitutes a poet; that quality without which judgment is cold and knowledge is inert; that energy which collects, combines, amplifies and animates.—Johnson.

There never appear more than five or six men of genius in an age, but if they were united the world could not stand before them.—Swift.

With the offspring of genius, the law of parturition is reversed; the throes are in the conception, the pleasure in the birth.—Colton.

A nation does wisely, if not well, in starving her men of genius. Fatten them, and they are done for.—Charles Buxton.

Without a genius, learning soars in vain;
And, without learning, genius sinks again;
Their force united, crowns the sprightly
     reign.   —Elphinston.

Every age might perhaps produce one or two geniuses, if they were not sunk under the censure and obloquy of plodding, servile, imitating pedants.—Swift.

Genius grafted on womanhood is like to overgrow it and break its stem, as you may see a grafted fruit-tree

spreading over the stock which cannot keep pace with its evolutions.—Holmes.

But the sublime, when it is introduced at a seasonable moment, has often carried all before it with the rapidity of lightning, and shown at a glance the mighty power of genius.—Longinus.

Genius is allied to a warm and inflammable constitution; delicacy of taste, to calmness and sedateness. Hence it is common to find genius in one who is a prey to every passion.—Lord Kames.

To be endowed with strength by nature, to be actuated by the powers of the mind, and to have a certain spirit almost divine infused into you.—Cicero.

Who in the same given time can produce more than many others, has vigor; who can produce more and better, has talents; who can produce what none else can, has genius.—Lavater.

Genius, without religion, is only a lamp on the outer gate of a palace. It may serve to cast a gleam of light on those that are without while the inhabitant sits in darkness.—Hannah More.

Genius is supposed to be a power of producing excellences which are out of the reach of the rules of art: a power which no precepts can teach, and which no industry can acquire.—Sir J. Reynolds.

Genius, with all its pride in its own strength, is but a dependent quality, and cannot put forth its whole powers nor claim all its honors without an amount of aid from the talents and labors of others which it is difficult to calculate.—Bryant.

As what we call genius arises out of the disproportionate power and size of a certain faculty, so the great difficulty lies in harmonizing with it the rest of the character.—Mrs. Jameson.

The drafts which true genius draws upon posterity, although they may not always be honored so soon as they are due, are sure to be paid with compound interest in the end.—Colton.

And genius hath electric power,
Which earth can never tame;
Bright suns may scorch, and dark clouds
  lower—
Its flash is still the same.
        —Lydia M. Child.

The highest genius never flowers in satire, but culminates in sympathy with that which is best in human nature, and appeals to it.—Chapin.

Genius is intensity of life; an overflowing vitality which floods and fertilizes a continent or a hemisphere of being; which makes a nature manysided and whole, while most men remain partial and fragmentary.—Hamilton W. Mabie.

There are two kinds of genius. The first and highest may be said to speak out of the eternal to the present, and must compel its age to understand it; the second understands its age, and tells it what it wishes to be told.—Lowell.

Men of the greatest genius are not always the most prodigal of their encomiums. But then it is when their range of power is confined, and they have in fact little perception, except of their own particular kind of excellence.—Hazlitt.

Genius is nothing more than our common faculties refined to a greater intensity. There are no astonishing ways of doing astonishing things. All astonishing things are done by ordinary materials.—B. R. Haydon.

Obey thy genius, for a minister it is unto the throne of fate. Draw to thy soul, and centralize the rays which are around of the Divinity.—Bailey.

The productions of a great genius, with many lapses and inadvertences, are infinitely preferable to the works of an inferior kind of author which are scrupulously exact, and conform-able to all the rules of correct writing.—Addison.

The effusions of genius, or rather the manifestations of what is called talent, are often the effects of distempered nerves and complexional spleen, as pearls are morbid secretions.—Robert Walsh.

The light of genius is sometimes so resplendent as to make a man walk through life amid glory and acclamation; but it burns very dimly and low when carried into "the valley of the shadow of death."—Mountford.

Genius does not seem to derive any great support from syllogisms. Its carriage is free; its manner has a touch of inspiration. We see it come, but we never see it walk.—Count de Maistre.

It is interesting to notice how some minds seem almost to create themselves, springing up under every disadvantage, and working their solitary but irresistible way through a thousand obstacles.—Washington Irving.

The effusions of genius are entitled to admiration rather than applause, as they are chiefly the effect of natural endowment, and sometimes appear to be almost involuntary.—W. B. Clulow.

Genius never grows old—young today, mature yesterday, vigorous tomorrow, always immortal. It is peculiar to no sex or condition, and is the divine gift to woman no less than to man.—Juan Lewis.

We declare to you that the earth has exhausted its contingent of master spirits. Now for decadence and general closing. We must make up our minds to it. We shall have no more men of genius.—Victor Hugo.

As diamond cuts diamond, and one hone smooths a second, all the parts of intellect are whetstones to each other; and genius, which is but the result of their mutual sharpening, is character, too.—C. A. Bartol.

Genius is to other gifts what the carbuncle is to the precious stones. It sends forth its own light, whereas other stones only reflect borrowed light.—A. Schopenhauer.

Some very dull and sad people have genius though the world may not count it as such; a genius for love, or for patience, or for prayer, maybe. We know the divine spark is here and there in the world: who shall say under what manifestations, or humble disguise!—Anne Isabella Thackeray.

Genius, indeed, melts many ages into one, and thus effects something permanent, yet still with a similarity of office to that of the more ephemeral writer. A work of genius is but the newspaper of a century, or perchance of a hundred centuries.—Hawthorne.

High original genius is always ridiculed on its first appearance; most of all by those who have won themselves the highest reputation in working on the established lines. Genius only commands recognition when it has created the taste which is to appreciate it.—Froude.

All the means of action, the shapeless masses—the materials—lie everywhere about us. What we need is the celestial fire to change the flint into transparent crystal, bright and clear. That fire is genius!—Longfellow.

The light of genius never sets, but sheds itself upon other faces, in different hues of splendor. Homer glows in the softened beauty of Virgil, and Spenser revives in the decorated learning of Gray.—Willmott.

The richest genius, like the most fertile soil, when uncultivated, shoots up into the rankest weeds; and instead of vines and olives for the pleasure and use of man, produces to its slothful owner the most abundant crop of poisons.—Hume.

The wild force of genius has often been fated by Nature to be finally overcome by quiet strength. The volcano sends up its red bolt with terrific force, as if it would strike the stars; but the calm, resistless hand of gravitation seizes it and brings it to the earth.—Bayne.

Was genius ever ungrateful? Mere talents are dry leaves, tossed up and down by gusts of passion, and scattered and swept away; but Genius lies on the bosom of Memory, and Gratitude at her feet.—Landor.

The whole genius of an author consists in describing well, and delineating character well. Homer, Plato, Virgil, Horace only excel other writers by their expressions and images; we must indicate what is true if we mean to write naturally, forcibly and delicately.—La Bruyère.

Genius, without work, is certainly a dumb oracle; and it is unquestionably true that the men of the highest genius have invariably been found to be amongst the most plodding, hardworking, and intent men—their chief characteristic apparently consisting simply in their power of laboring more intensely and effectively than others.—Samuel Smiles.

The very greatest genius, after all, is not the greatest thing in the world, any more than the greatest city in the world is the country or the sky. It is the concentration of some of its greatest powers, but it is not the greatest diffusion of its might. It is not the habit of its success, the stability of its sereneness.—Leigh Hunt.

Genius is not a single power, but a combination of great powers. It reasons, but it is not reasoning; it judges, but it is not judgment; it imagines, but it is not imagination; it feels deeply and fiercely, but it is not passion. It is neither, because it is all.—Whipple.

All are to be men of genius in their degree,—rivulets or rivers, it does not matter, so that the souls be clear and pure; not dead walls encompassing dead heaps of things, known and numbered, but running waters in the sweet wilderness of things unnumbered and unknown, conscious only of the living banks, on which they partly refresh and partly reflect the flowers, and so pass on.—Ruskin.

Neither can we admit that definition of genius that some would propose— "a power to accomplish all that we undertake;" for we might multiply examples to prove that this definition of genius contains more than the thing defined. Cicero failed in poetry, Pope in painting, Addison in oratory; yet it would be harsh to deny genius to these men.—Colton.

When the great Kepler had at length discovered the harmonic laws that regulate the motions of the heavenly bodies, he exclaimed: "Whether my discoveries will be read by posterity or by my contemporaries is a matter that concerns them more than me. I may well be contented to wait one century for a reader, when God Himself, during so many thousand years, has waited for an observer like myself."—Macaulay.

What we call genius may, perhaps, in more strict propriety, be described as the spirit of discovery. Genius is the very eye of intellect and the wing of thought. It is always in advance of its time. It is the pioneer for the generation which it precedes. For this reason it is called a seer—and hence its songs have been prophecies. —Simms.

As well might a lovely woman look daily in her mirror, yet not be aware of her beauty, as a great soul be unconscious of the powers with which Heaven has gifted him; not so much for himself, as to enlighten others—a messenger from God Himself, with a high and glorious mission to perform. Woe unto him who abuses that mission!—Chambers.

There is nothing so remote from vanity as true genius. It is almost as natural for those who · are endowed with the highest powers of the human mind to produce the miracles of art, as for other men to breathe or move. Correggio, who is said to have produced some of his divinest works almost without having seen a picture,

probably did not know that he had done anything extraordinary.—Hazlitt.

Genius! thou gift of Heav'n! thou Light divine!
Amid what dangers art thou doom'd to shine!
Oft will the body's weakness check thy force,
Oft damp thy Vigour, and impede thy course;
And trembling nerves compel thee to restrain
Thy noble efforts, to contend with pain;
Or Want (sad guest!) will in thy presence come,
And breathe around her melancholy gloom:
To Life's low cares will thy proud thought confine,
And make her sufferings, her impatience, thine.　　　　—Crabbe.

The whole difference between a man of genius and other men, it has been said a thousand times, and most truly, is that the first remains in great part a child, seeing with the large eyes of children, in perpetual wonder, not conscious of much knowledge—conscious, rather, of infinite ignorance—and yet infinite power; a fountain of eternal admiration, delight, and creative force within him meeting the ocean of visible and governable things around him. —Ruskin.

The only difference between a genius and one of common capacity is that the former anticipates and explores what the latter accidentally hits upon. But even the man of genius himself more frequently employs the advantages that chance presents to him. It is the lapidary that gives value to the diamond, which the peasant has dug up without knowing its worth.—Abbé Raynal.

Nature seems to delight in disappointing the assiduities of art, with which it would rear dulness to maturity, and to glory in the vigor and luxuriance of her chance productions. She scatters the seeds of genius to the winds, and though some may perish among the stony places of the world, and some may be choked by the thorns and brambles of early adversity, yet others will now and then strike root even in the clefts of the rock, struggle bravely up into sunshine, and spread over their sterile birthplace all the beauties of vegetation.—Washington Irving.

Gentility

How weak a thing is gentility, if it wants virtue.—Fuller.

There cannot be a surer proof of low origin, or of an innate meanness of disposition, than to be always talking and thinking of being genteel.—Hazlitt.

I would have you not stand so much on your gentility, which is an airy and mere borrowed thing from dead men's dust and bones; and none of yours except 'you make and hold it.—Ben Jonson.

Gentleman

He is gentle that doth gentle deeds.—Chaucer.

The gentleman is a Christian product.—George H. Calvert.

An affable and courteous gentleman.—Shakespeare.

The prince of darkness is a gentleman.—Marlowe.

His tribe were God Almighty's gentlemen.—Dryden.

Since every Jack became a gentleman,
There's many a gentle person made a Jack.
   —Shakespeare.

To make a fine gentleman, several trades are required, but chiefly a barber.—Goldsmith.

When Adam dolve and Eva span
Who was then the gentleman?
   —Pegge.

The look of a gentleman is little else than the reflection of the looks of the world.—Hazlitt.

Education begins the gentleman, but reading, good company, and reflection must finish him.—Locke.

He is the best gentleman who is the son of his own deserts.—Victor Hugo.

The gentleman is solid mahogany; the fashionable man is only veneer.—J. G. Holland.

He whom we call a gentleman is no longer the man of Nature.—Diderot.

There is no man that can teach us to be gentlemen better than Joseph Addison.—Thackeray.

He that bears himself like a gentleman, is
Worth to have been born a gentleman.
   —Chapman.

Gentleman is a term which does not apply to any station, but to the mind and the feelings in every station.—Talfourd.

Repose and cheerfulness are the badge of the gentleman—repose in energy.—Emerson.

In a word, to be a fine gentleman is to be a generous and brave man.—Steele.

The gentle minde by gentle deeds is knowne;
For a man by nothing is so well bewrayed
As by his manners. —Spenser.

It is difficult to believe that a true gentleman will ever become a gamester, a libertine, or a sot.—Chapin.

Tho' modest, on his unembarrass'd brow
Nature had written—"Gentleman."
   —Byron.

Oh! St. Patrick was a gentleman,
Who came of decent people.
   —Henry Bennett.

The taste of beauty and the relish of what is decent, just, and amiable perfects the character of the gentleman and the philosopher.—Shaftesbury.

A gentleman is always a gentleman; but the butterflies of society differ as much in their moods as does that insect in its colors.—Mme. Dufresnoy.

My master hath been an honorable gentleman; tricks he hath had in him which gentlemen have.—Shakespeare.

Religion is the most gentlemanly thing in the world. It alone will gentilize, if unmixed with cant.—Coleridge.

The grand old name of gentleman
Defam'd by every charlatan
And soil'd with all ignoble use.
—Tennyson.

We sometimes meet an original gentleman, who, if manners had not existed, would have invented them.—Emerson.

He had then the grace, too rare in every clime,
Of being, without alloy of fop or beau,
A finish'd gentleman from top to toe.
—Byron.

We are gentlemen,
That neither in our hearts, nor outward eyes,
Envy the great, nor do the low despise.
—Shakespeare.

Propriety of manners and consideration for others are the two main characteristics of a gentleman.—Beaconsfield.

Men of courage, men of sense, and men of letters are frequent; but a true gentleman is what one seldom sees.—Steele.

A gentleman is one who understands and shows every mark of deference to the claims of self-love in others, and exacts it in return from them.—Hazlitt.

God knows that all sorts of gentlemen knock at the door; but whenever used in strictness and with any emphasis, the name will be found to point at original energy.—Emerson.

Perhaps propriety is as near a word as any to denote the manners of the gentleman; elegance is necessary to the fine gentleman; dignity is proper to noblemen, and majesty to kings.—Hazlitt.

The flowering of civilization is the finished man, the man of sense, of grace, of accomplishment, of social power—the gentleman.—Emerson.

A gentleman has ease without familiarity, is respectful without meanness; genteel without affectation, insinuating without seeming art.—Chesterfield.

The best of men
That e'er wore earth about him was a sufferer;
A soft, meek, patient, humble, tranquil spirit.
The first true gentleman that ever breathed.
—T. Dekker.

Measure not thy carriage by any man's eye,
Thy speech by no man's ear; but be resolute
And confident in doing and saying;
And this is the grace of a right gentleman.
—Chapman.

"I am a gentleman." I'll be sworn thou art;
Thy tongue, thy face, thy limbs, actions and spirit,
Do give thee five-fold blazon.
—Shakespeare.

Of the offspring of the gentilman Jafeth, came Habraham, Moyses, Aron and the profettys; and also the kyng of the right line of Mary, of whom that gentilman Jhesus was borne.—Juliana Berners.

A sweeter and a lovelier gentleman,
Fram'd in the prodigality of nature,
Young, valiant, wise, and, no doubt right royal;
The spacious world cannot again afford.
—Shakespeare.

That man will never be a perfect gentleman who lives only with gentlemen. To be a man of the world we must view that world in every grade and in every perspective.—Bulwer-Lytton.

The expression of a gentleman's face is not so much that of refinement, as of flexibility, not of sensibility and enthusiasm as of indifference; it argues presence of mind rather than enlargement of ideas.—Hazlitt.

He that can enjoy the intimacy of the great, and on no occasion disgust them by familiarity, or disgrace himself by servility, proves that he is as perfect a gentleman by nature, as his companions are by rank.—Colton.

To be a gentleman does not depend upon the tailor or the toilet. Good clothes are not good habits. A gentleman is just a gentle-man—no more, no less: a diamond polished, that was first a diamond in the rough.—Bishop Doane.

We may daily discover crowds acquire sufficient wealth to buy gentility, but very few that possess the virtues which ennoble human nature, and (in the best sense of the word) constitute a gentleman.—Shenstone.

A gentleman's first characteristic is that fineness of structure in the body which renders it capable of the most delicate sensation; and of structure in the mind which renders it capable of the most delicate sympathies: one may say simply "fineness of nature."—Ruskin.

Our manners, our civilization, and all the good things connected with manners and civilization, have, in this European world of ours, depended for ages upon two principles: I mean the spirit of a gentleman, and the spirit of religion.—Burke.

Self-command is often thought a characteristic of high breeding. * * * A true gentleman has no need of self-command; he simply feels rightly in all directions on all occasions, and, desiring to express only so much of his feeling as it is right to express, does not need to command himself.—Ruskin.

His qualities depend, not upon fashion or manners, but upon moral worth; not on personal possessions, but on personal qualities. The Psalmist briefly describes him as one "that walketh uprightly, and worketh righteousness, and speaketh the truth in his heart."—Samuel Smiles.

He is like to be mistaken who makes choice of a covetous man for a friend, or relieth upon the reed of narrow and poltroon friendship. Pitiful things are only to be found in the cottages of such breasts; but bright thoughts, clear deeds, constancy, fidelity, bounty and generous honesty are the gems of noble minds, wherein (to derogate from none) the true, heroic English gentleman hath no peer.—Sir Thomas Browne.

He is a noble gentleman; withal
Happy in 's endeavours: the gen'ral voice
Sounds him for courtesy, behaviour, language,
And ev'ry fair demeanour, an example:
Titles of honour add not to his worth;
Who is himself an honour to his title.
—John Ford.

The true gentleman is extracted from ancient and worshipful parentage. When a pepin is planted on a pepin-stock, the fruit growing thence is called a renate, a most delicious apple, as both by sire and dame well descended. Thus his blood must needs be well purified who is genteelly born on both sides.—Fuller.

His years are young, but his experience old;
His head unmellow'd, but his judgment ripe;
And in a word (for far behind his worth
Come all the praises that I now bestow)
He is complete in feature and in mind,
With all good grace to grace a gentleman.
—Shakespeare.

The taste of beauty, and the relish of what is decent, just and amiable, perfects the character of the gentleman and the philosopher. And the study of such a taste or relish will, as we suppose, be ever the great employment and concern of him who covets as well to be wise and good, as agreeable and polite.—Shaftesbury.

There are some spirits nobly just, unwarp'd by pelf or pride,
Great in the calm, but greater still when dash'd by adverse tide;—
They hold the rank no king can give, no station can disgrace;
Nature puts forth her gentleman, and monarchs must give place.
—Eliza Cook.

What is it to be a gentleman? Is it to be honest, to be gentle, to be generous, to be brave, to be wise, and, possessing all these qualities, to exercise them in the most graceful outward manner? Ought a gentleman to be a loyal son, a true husband, an honest father? Ought his life to be decent, his bills to be paid, his taste to be high and elegant, his aims in life lofty and noble?—Thackeray.

But nature, with a matchless hand, sends forth her nobly born,
And laughs the paltry attributes of wealth and rank to scorn;
She moulds with care a spirit rare, half human, half divine,
And cries, exulting, "Who can make a gentleman like mine?"
—Eliza Cook.

A gentleman is a rarer thing than some of us think for. Which of us can point out many such in his circle—men whose aims are generous, whose truth is constant and elevated; who can look the world honestly in the face, with an equal manly sympathy for the great and the small? We all know a hundred whose coats are well made, and a score who have excellent manners; but of gentlemen how many? Let us take a little scrap of paper and each make out his list.—Thackeray.

After all, there is such a thing as looking like a gentleman. There are men whose class no dirt or rags can hide, any more than they could Ulysses. I have seen such men in plenty among workmen, too; but, on the whole, the gentleman—by whom I do not mean just now the rich—have the superiority in that point. But not, please God, forever. Give us the same air, water, exercise, education, good society, and you will see whether this "haggardness," this "coarseness" (etc., for the list is too long to specify), be an accident, or a property, of the man of the people.—Charles Kingsley.

A Christian is God Almighty's gentleman; a gentleman, in the vulgar, superficial way of understanding the word, is the devil's christian. But to throw aside these polished and too current counterfeits for something valuable and sterling, the real gentleman should be gentle in everything, at least in everything that depends on himself—in carriage, temper, constructions, aims, desires. He ought, therefore, to be mild, calm, quiet, even, temperate—not hasty in judgment, not exorbitant in ambition, not overbearing, not proud, not rapacious, not oppressive; for these things are contrary to gentleness. Many such gentlemen are to be found, I trust; and many more would be were the true meaning of the name borne in mind and duly inculcated.—Hare.

Gentleness

Gentleness is the outgrowth of benignity.—Hannah More.

The gentleness of all the gods go with thee.—Shakespeare.

Let gentleness thy strong enforcement be.—Shakespeare.

Gentleness and affability conquer at last.—Terence.

We must be gentle now we are gentlemen.—Shakespeare.

Sweet speaking oft a currish heart reclaims.—Sir P. Sidney.

Let mildness ever attend thy tongue.—Theogius.

The mildest manners and the gentlest heart.—Homer.

The power of gentleness is irresistible.—H. Martyn.

Gentleness! more powerful than Hercules.—Ninon de Lenclos.

A woman's strength is most potent when robed in gentleness.—Lamartine.

Your gentleness shall force, more than your force move us to gentleness.—Shakespeare.

Gentleness and repose are paramount to everything else in woman.—Montaigne.

With all women gentleness is the most persuasive and powerful argument.—Théophile Gautier.

The human heart becomes softened by hearing of instances of gentleness and consideration.—Plutarch.

In the husband, wisdom; in the wife, gentleness.—George Herbert.

Gentleness in the gait is what simplicity is in the dress. Violent gestures or quick movements inspire involuntary disrespect.—Balzac.

Those that do teach young babes
Do it with gentle means and easy tasks.
—Shakespeare.

They are as gentle
As zephyrs blowing below the violet.
—Shakespeare.

Better make penitents by gentleness than hypocrites by severity.—St. Francis de Sales.

Gentleness corrects whatever is offensive in our manners.—Blair.

We do not believe, or we forget, that "the Holy Ghost came down, not in shape of a vulture, but in the form of a dove."—Emerson.

A man never so beautifully shows his own strength as when he respects a woman's softness.—Douglas Jerrold.

Fearless gentleness is the most beautiful of feminine attractions, born of modesty and love.—Mrs. Balfour.

It is only people who possess firmness who can possess true gentleness. In those who appear gentle, it is generally only weakness, which is readily converted into harshness.—La Rochefoucauld.

Power can do by gentleness that which violence fails to accomplish; and calmness best enforces the imperial mandate.—Claudianus.

What thou wilt, thou rather shalt enforce it with thy smile, than hew to it with thy sword.—Shakespeare.

If you would fall into any extreme, let it be on the side of gentleness. The human mind is so constructed that it resists rigor, and yields to softness.—St. Francis de Sales.

Gentleness, which belongs to virtue, is to be carefully distinguished from the mean spirit of cowards and the fawning assent of sycophants.—Blair.

The golden beams of truth and the silken cords of love, twisted together, will draw men on with a sweet violence, whether they will or not.—Cudworth.

In families well ordered, there is always one firm, sweet temper, which controls without seeming to dictate. The Greeks represented Persuasion as crowned.—Bulwer-Lytton.

Gentleness is far more successful in all its enterprises than violence; indeed, violence generally frustrates its own purpose, while gentleness scarcely ever fails.—Locke.

Experience has caused it to be remarked that in the country where the laws are gentle, the minds of the citizens are struck by it, as it is elsewhere by the most severe.—Catherine the Second.

With regard to manner, be careful to speak in a soft, tender, kind and loving way. Even when you have occasion to rebuke, be careful to do it with manifest kindness. The effect will be incalculably better.—Hosea Ballou.

A crystal river
Diaphanous because it travels slowly,
Soft is the music that would charm forever;
The flower of sweetest smell is shy and lowly. —Wordsworth.

True gentleness is founded on a sense of what we owe to Him who made us, and to the common nature which we all share. It arises from reflection on our own failings and wants, and from just views of the condition and the duty of man. It is native feeling heightened and improved by principle.—Blair.

If we were to form an image of dignity in a man, we should give him wisdom and valor, as being essential to the character of manhood. In the like manner, if you describe a right woman, in a laudable sense, she should have gentle softness, tender fear, and all those parts of life which distinguish her from the other sex, with some subordination to it, but such an inferiority as makes her still more lovely.—Steele.

The best and simplest cosmetic for women is constant gentleness and sympathy for the noblest interests of her fellow-creatures. This preserves and gives to her features an indelibly gay, fresh, and agreeable expression. If women would but realize that harshness makes them ugly, it would prove the best means of conversion.—Auerbach.

An accent very low
In blandishment, but a most silver flow
Of subtle-pacèd counsel in distress,
Right to the heart and brain, though undiscried,
Winning its way with extreme gentleness
Through all the outworks of suspicion's
  pride.   —Tennyson.

Gesture

The natural language of gesture is God's language. We did not invent it. Surely natural language is the language of nature; and these gestures which make us hang the head, and give us the erect attitude, are proclamations made, not by the will of man, but by the will of that Power which has co-ordinated all things, and given them harmony with each other, and never causes an instinct to utter a lie. —Joseph Cook.

Ghosts

For spirits, freed from mortal laws, with
  ease
Assume what sexes and what shapes they
  please.   —Pope.

Thou canst not say, I did it: never shake
Thy gory locks at me.   —Shakespeare.

It was about to speak, when the cock
  crew,
And then it started like a guilty thing
Upon a fearful summons.
          —Shakespeare.

Many ghosts, and forms of fright,
Have started from their graves to-night;
They have driven sleep from mine eyes
  away.   —Longfellow.

But, soft: behold! lo, where it comes again!
I'll cross it, though it blast me.—Stay,
  illusion!
If thou hast any sound, or use a voice,
Speak to me.   —Shakespeare.

I can call up spirits from the vasty deep.—
——Why so can I, or so can any man;
But will they come, when you do call for
  them?   —Shakespeare.

Avaunt! and quit my sight! Let the earth
  hide thee!
Thy bones are marrowless, thy blood is
  cold;
Thou hast no speculation in those eyes,
Which thou dost glare with!
          —Shakespeare.

Some have mistaken blocks and posts,
For spectres, apparitions, ghosts,
With saucer-eyes and horns; and some
Have heard the devil beat a drum.
          —Butler.

I am thy father's spirit;
Doom'd for a certain term to walk the
  night
And, for the day, confin'd to fast in fires,
Till the foul crimes, done in my days of
  nature,
Are burnt and purg'd away.
          —Shakespeare.

They gather round, and wonder at the tale
Of horrid apparition, tall and ghostly,
That walks at dead of night, or takes his
  stand
O'er some new-open'd grave, and (strange
  to tell),
Evanishes at crowing of the cock.
          —Blair.

Angels and ministers of grace, defend us!—
Be thou a spirit of health, or goblin damn'd,
Bring with thee airs from heaven, or blasts
  from hell,
Be thy intents wicked or charitable,
Thou comest in such questionable shape
That I will speak to thee.
          —Shakespeare.

O, answer me:
Let me not burst in ignorance! but tell,
Why thy canoniz'd bones, hearsed in death,
Have burst their cerements! why the sepulchre,
Wherein we saw thee quietly in-urn'd,
Hath op'd his ponderous and marble jaws,
To cast thee up again?   —Shakespeare.

Gibbet

The gibbet is a species of flattery to the human race. Three or four persons are hung from time to time for the sake of making the rest believe that they are virtuous.—Sanial-Dubay.

Gifts

The more we give to others, the more we are increased.—Lao-Tze.

He gives twice who gives quickly.—Syrus.

When you give, give with joy and smiling.—Joubert.

Riches, understanding, beauty, are fair gifts of God.—Luther.

For the will and not the gift makes the giver.—Lessing.

We like the gift when we the giver prize.—Sheffield.

For to give is the business of the rich.—Goethe.

Giving requires good sense.—Ovid.

God hands gifts to some, whispers them to others.—W. R. Alger.

Who gives a trifle meanly is meaner than the trifle.—Lavater.

Of gifts, there seems none more becoming to offer a friend than a beautiful book.—Amos Bronson Alcott.

That which is given with pride and ostentation is rather an ambition than a bounty.—Seneca.

Rich gifts wax poor when givers prove unkind.—Shakespeare.

Gifts are as gold that adorns the temple; grace is like the temple that sanctifies the gold.—Burkitt.

There is no grace in a benefit that sticks to the fingers.—Seneca.

Gifts come from above in their own peculiar forms.—Goethe.

For whatever man has, is in reality only a gift.—Wieland.

The gift derives its value from the rank of the giver.—Ovid.

Those gifts are ever the most acceptable which the giver makes precious.—Ovid.

Give freely to him that deserveth well, and asketh nothing: and that is a way of giving to thyself.—Fuller.

The manner of giving shows the character of the giver more than the gift itself.—Lavater.

He who loves with purity considers not the gift of the lover, but the love of the giver.—Thomas à Kempis.

While you look at what is given, look also at the giver.—Seneca.

Wear this for me,—one out of suits with fortune,
That could give more, but that her hand lacks means. —Shakespeare.

Saints themselves will sometimes be,
Of gifts that cost them nothing, free.
—Butler.

The greatest grace of a gift, perhaps, is that it anticipates and admits of no return.—Longfellow.

One must be poor to know the luxury of giving.—George Eliot.

The heart of the giver makes the gift dear and precious.—Luther.

Take gifts with a sigh; most men give to be paid.—Boyle O'Reilly.

How can that gift leave a trace which has left no void?—Mme. Swetchine.

You gave with them words of so sweet breath composed, as made the things more rich.—Shakespeare.

That alone belongs to you which you have bestowed.—Vemuna.

Whoever makes great presents, expects great presents in return.—Martial.

Every gift which is given, even though it be small, is in reality great, if it be given with affection.—Pindar.

It is a proof of boorishness to confer a favor with a bad grace; it is the act of giving that is hard and painful. How little does a smile cost?—Bruyère.

Gifts, they weigh like mountains on a sensitive heart. To me they are

oftener punishments than pleasures.—
Mme. Fee.

The making presents to a lady one
addresses is like throwing armor into
an enemy's camp, with a resolution to
recover it.—Shenstone.

He was one of those men, moreover,
who possess almost every gift except
the gift of the power to use them.—
Charles Kingsley.

Posthumous charities are the very
essence of selfishness, when bequeathed
by those who, when alive, would part
with nothing.—Colton.

Gifts are like fish-hooks; for who
is not aware that the greedy char is
deceived by the fly which he swallows?
—Martial.

It is a cold, lifeless business, when
you go to the shops to buy something,
which does not represent your life and
talent, but a goldsmith's.—Emerson.

Your gift is princely, but it comes too late,
And falls like sunbeams on a blasted blos-
    som.   —Suckling.

The gift, to be true, must be the
flowing of the giver unto me, correspondent to my flowing unto him.—
Emerson.

Win her with gifts, if she respect not
    words:
Dumb jewels often, in their silent kind,
More than quick words, do move a woman's
    mind.   —Shakespeare.

She gave me eyes, she gave me ears;
And humble cares, and delicate fears;
A heart, the fountain of sweet tears;
And love, and thought, and joy.
        —Wordsworth.

A gift—its kind, its value and appearance; the silence or the pomp that
attends it; the style in which it
reaches you—may decide the dignity
or vulgarity of the giver.—Lavater.

Liberty is of more value than any
gifts; and to receive gifts is to lose it.
Be assured that men most commonly
seek to oblige thee only that they may
engage thee to serve them.—Saadi.

Gifts are the greatest usury, because
a two-fold retribution is an urged effect that a noble mind prompts us to;
and it is said we pay the most for
what is given us.—J. Beaumont.

If we will take the good we find,
asking no questions, we shall have
heaping measures. The great gifts are
not got by analysis. Everything good
is on the highway.—Emerson.

When thou makest presents, let
them be of such things as will last
long; to the end they may be in some
sort immortal, and may frequently refresh the memory of the receiver.—
Fuller.

Nature makes us buy her presents
at the price of so many sufferings that
it is doubtful whether she deserves
most the name of parent or step-
mother.—Pliny the Elder.

She prizes not such trifles as these are:
The gifts she looks from me are pack'd and
    lock'd
Up in my heart, which I have given al-
    ready,
But not deliver'd.   —Shakespeare.

He ne'er consider'd it as loath
To look a gift-horse in the mouth,
And very wisely would lay forth
No more upon it than 'twas worth.
        —Butler.

Policy counselleth a gift, given wisely and
    in season;
And policy afterwards approveth it, for
    great is the influence of gifts.
        —Tupper.

I never cast a flower away,
    A gift of one who car'd for me;
A flower—a faded flower,
    But it was done reluctantly.
        —L. E. Landon.

Favors, and especially pecuniary
ones, are generally fatal to friendship;
for our pride will ever prompt us to
lower the value of the gift by diminishing that of the donor.—Chatfield.

The only gift is a portion of thyself. * * * Therefore the poet
brings his poem; the shepherd, his
lamb; the farmer, corn; the miner, a
gem; the sailor, coral and shells; the

painter, his picture; the girl, a handkerchief of her own sewing.—Emerson.

People do not care to give alms without some security for their money; and a wooden leg or a withered arm is a sort of draft upon heaven for those who choose to have their money placed to account there.—Mackenzie.

In giving, a man receives more than he gives; and the more is in proportion to the worth of the thing given.—George MacDonald.

We are as answerable for what we give as for what we receive; nay, the misplacing of a benefit is worse than the not receiving of it; for the one is another person's fault, but the other is mine.—Seneca.

No man esteems anything that comes to him by chance; but when it is governed by reason, it brings credit both to the giver and receiver; whereas those favors are in some sort scandalous that make a man ashamed of his patron.—Seneca.

God's love gives in such a way that it flows from a Father's heart, the well-spring of all good. The heart of the giver makes the gift dear and precious; as among ourselves we say of even a trifling gift, "It comes from a hand we love," and look not so much at the gift as at the heart.—Luther.

He gives not best that gives most; but he gives most who gives best. If then I cannot give bountifully, yet I will give freely; and what I want in my hand, supply by my heart. He gives well that gives willingly.—Arthur Warwick.

Those Spaniards in Mexico who were chased of the Indians tell us what to do with our goods in our extremity. They being to pass over a river in their flight, as many as cast away their gold swam over safe; but some, more covetous, keeping their gold, were either drowned with it, or overtaken and slain by the savages:

you have received, now learn to give.—Bacon.

It passes in the world for greatness of mind, to be perpetually giving and loading people with bounties; but it is one thing to know how to give and another thing not to know how to keep. Give me a heart that is easy and open, but I will have no holes in it; let it be bountiful with judgment, but I will have nothing run out of it I know not how.—Seneca.

The secret of giving affectionately is great and rare; it requires address to do it well; otherwise we lose instead of deriving benefit from it. This man gives lavishly in a way that obliges no one; the manner of giving is worth more than the gift. Another loses intentionally at a game, thus disguising his present; another forgets a jewel, which would have been refused as a gift. A generous booby seems to be giving alms to his mistress when he is making a present.—Corneille.

Some men give so that you are angry every time you ask them to contribute. They give so that their gold and silver shoot you like a bullet. Other persons give with such beauty that you remember it as long as you live; and you say, "It is a pleasure to go to such men." There are some men that give as springs do: whether you go to them or not, they are always full; and your part is merely to put your dish under the ever-flowing stream. Others give just as a pump does where the well is dry, and the pump leaks.—Beecher.

Gipsies

There are men and women who are in life as the wild river and the nightowl, as the blasted tree and the wind over ancient graves.—Charles G. Leland.

Gipsies, who every ill can cure,
Except the ill of being poor,
Who charms 'gainst love and agues sell,
Who can in hen-roost set a spell,
Prepar'd by arts, to them best known
To catch all feet except their own,
Who, as to fortune, can unlock it,
As easily as pick a pocket.
—Churchill.

Girlhood

A lovely girl is above all rank.—Charles Buxton.

The blushing beauty of a modest maid.—Dryden.

Girls we love for what they are; young men for what they promise to be.—Goethe.

The inward fragrance of a young girl's heart is what crystallizes into love.—Richter.

When one is five-and-twenty, one has not chalk-stones at one's finger-ends that the touch of a handsome girl should be entirely indifferent.—George Eliot.

The girl of the period sets up to be natural, and is only rude; mistakes insolence for innocence; says everything that comes first to her lips, and thinks she is gay when she is only giddy.—Beaconsfield.

One must always regret that law of growth which renders necessary that kittens should spoil into demure cats, and bright, joyous school-girls develop into the spiritless, crystallized beings denominated young ladies. — Abba Goold Woolson.

She was in the lovely bloom and spring-time of womanhood; at the age when, if ever angels be for God's good purpose enthroned in mortal form, they may be, without impiety, supposed to abide in such as hers.—Dickens.

We love a girl for very different qualities than understanding. We love her for her beauty, her youth, her mirth, her confidingness, her character, with its faults, caprices and God knows what other inexpressible charms; but we do not love her understanding.—Goethe.

The presence of a young girl is like the presence of a flower; the one gives its perfume to all that approach it, the other her grace to all that surround her.—Louis Desnoyers.

Gladness

True gladness doth not always speak; joy, bred and born but in the tongue, is weak.—Ben Jonson.

Nations and men are only the best when they are the gladdest, and deserve heaven when they enjoy it.—Richter.

For from the crushed flowers of gladness on the road of life a sweet perfume is wafted over to the present hour, as marching armies often send out from heaths the fragrance of trampled plants.—Richter.

Gloom

He who is only just is stern; he who is only wise lives in gloom.—Voltaire.

Gloom and sadness are poison to us, and the origin of hysterics. You are right in thinking that this disease is in the imagination; you have defined it perfectly; it is vexation which causes it to spring up, and fear that supports it.—Madame de Sévigné.

Glory

Glory is priceless.—Lytton.

True glory is a flame lighted at the skies.—Horace Mann.

Glory is the fair child of peril.—Smollett.

Glory grows guilty of detested crimes.—Shakespeare.

No flowery road leads to glory.—La Fontaine.

The paths of glory lead but to the grave.—Gray.

Alas! how difficult it is to retain glory!—Syrus.

Glory paid to our ashes comes too late.—Martial.

For what is glory but the blaze of fame?—Milton.

The glory dies not, and the grief is past.—Brydges.

We rise in glory as we sink in pride.—Young.

His glory now lies buried in the dust.—Quarles.

Nothing is so expensive as glory.—Sydney Smith.

This goin' ware glory waits ye haint one agreeable feetur.—Lowell.

A field of glory is a field for all.—Pope.

Great is the glory, for the strife is hard!—Wordsworth.

Like madness is the glory of this life.—Shakespeare.

So may a glory from defect arise.—Robert Browning.

Fame points the course, and glory leads the way.—Pye.

Glory, the casual gift of thoughtless crowds!
Glory, the bribe of avaricious virtue!
—Johnson.

Rising glory occasions the greatest envy, as kindling fire the greatest smoke.—Spenser.

Our greatest glory consists not in never falling, but in rising every time we fall.—Goldsmith.

Glory is a poison, good to be taken in small doses.—Balzac.

The love of glory can only create a great hero; the contempt of it creates a great man.—Talleyrand.

Glory built
On selfish principles, is shame and guilt.
—Cowper.

Glory follows virtue as if it were its shadow.—Cicero.

Unless what we do is useful, our glory is vain.—Phædrus.

Glory long has made the sages smile; 'tis something, nothing, words, illusion, wind.—Byron.

I am climbing a difficult road; but the glory gives me strength.—Propertius.

Glories, like glow-worms, afar off shine bright;
But look'd too near, have neither heat nor light.   —Webster.

The smoke of glory is not worth the smoke of a pipe.—George Sand.

Glory can be for a woman but the brilliant morning of happiness.—Mme. de Staël.

The sweetness of glory is so great that, join it to what we will, even to death, we love it.—Pascal.

Men are guided less by conscience than by glory; and yet the shortest way to glory is to be guided by conscience.—Henry Home.

As to be perfectly just is an attribute of the Divine nature, to be so to the utmost of our abilities is the glory of man.—Addison.

Glory fills the world with virtue, and, like a beneficent sun, covers the whole earth with flowers and with fruits.—Vauvenargues.

The glory of a people and of an age is always the work of a small number of great men, and disappears with them.—Baron de Grimm.

Real glory springs from the quiet conquest of ourselves; and without that the conqueror is nought but the first slave.—Thomson.

True glory takes root, and even spreads; all false pretenses, like flowers, fall to the ground; nor can any counterfeit last long.—Cicero.

Let us not disdain glory too much —nothing is finer except virtue. The height of happiness would be to unite both in this life.—Chateaubriand.

Glory is safe when it is deserved; it is not so with popularity; one lasts like a mosaic, the other is effaced like a crayon drawing.—Boufflers.

The pure soul shall mount on native
wings, . . . and cut a path into the
heaven of glory.—Blake.

'Twas glory once to be a Roman;
She makes it glory, now, to be a man.
—Bayard Taylor.

Glory drags all men along, low as
well as high, bound captive at the
wheels of her glittering car.—Horace.

Glory darts her soul-pervading ray
on thrones and cottages, regardless
still of all the artificial nice distinctions vain human customs make.—
Hannah More.

The shortest way to arrive at glory
should be to do that for conscience
which we do for glory.—Montaigne.

Our glories float between the earth and
heaven
Like clouds which seem pavilions of the
sun,
And are the playthings of the casual wind.
—Bulwer-Lytton.

To a father who loves his children
victory has no charms. When the
heart speaks, glory itself is an illusion.
Napoleon I.

Glory is a shroud that posterity
often tears from the shoulders of those
who wore it when living—Béranger.

Glory is like a circle in the water,
Which never ceaseth to enlarge itself
Till, by broad spreading it disperse to
nought. —Shakespeare.

The road to glory would cease to be
arduous if it were trite and trodden;
and great minds must be ready not
only to take opportunities but to make
them.—Colton.

Those great actions whose luster
dazzles us are represented by politicians as the effects of deep design;
whereas they are commonly the effects
of caprice and passion.—Rochefoucauld.

I have ventured like little wanton
boys that swim on bladders, this many
summers in a sea of glory, but far beyond my depth: my high-blown pride
at length broke under me.—Shakespeare.

Sound, sound the clarion, fill the fife!
To all the sensual world proclaim,
One crowded hour of glorious life
Is worth an age without a name.
—Scott.

True glory consists in doing what
deserves to be written, in writing
what deserves to be read, and in so
living as to make the world happier
and better for our living in it.—Pliny.

There are two things which ought
to teach us to think but meanly of
human glory; the very best have had
their calumniators, the very worst
their panegyrists.—Colton.

Ye sons of France, awake to glory!
Hark! Hark! what myriads bid you rise!
Your children, wives, and grandsires hoary,
Behold their tears and hear their cries!
—Rouget de l'Isle.

Is death more cruel from a private
dagger than in the field from murder-
ing swords of thousands? Or does
the number slain make slaughter glorious?—Cibber.

Glory relaxes often and debilitates
the mind; censure stimulates and contracts—both to an extreme. Simple
fame is, perhaps, the proper medium.
—Shenstone.

Gashed with honourable scars,
Low in Glory's lap they lie;
Though they fell, they fell like stars,
Streaming splendour through the sky.
Montgomery.

He that first likened glory to a
shadow did better than he was aware
of. They are both of them things ex-
cellently vain. Glory also, like a
shadow, goes sometimes before the
body, and sometimes in length infinitely exceeds it.—Montaigne.

There is but one thing necessary to
keep the possession of true glory,
which is to hear the opposers of it
with patience, and preserve the virtue
by which it was acquired.—Steele.

Glory is sometimes a low courtesan
who on the road entices many who did

not think of her. They are astonished
to obtain favors without having done
anything to deserve them.—Prince de
Ligne.

Who is it that does not voluntarily
exchange his health, his repose, and
his very life for reputation and glory?
The most useless, frivolous, and false
coin that passes current among us.—
Montaigne.

Individuals may wear for a time
the glory of our institutions, but they
carry it not to the grave with them.
Like raindrops from heaven, they may
pass through the circle of the shining
bow and add to its luster; but when
they have sunk in the earth again, the
proud arch still spans the sky and
shines gloriously on.—James A. Garfield.

The shortest way to arrive at glory
should be to do that for conscience
which we do for glory. And the virtue of Alexander appears to me with
much less vigor in his theater than
that of Socrates in his mean and obscure employment. I can easily conceive Socrates in the place of Alexander, but Alexander in that of Socrates I cannot.—Montaigne.

Wood burns because it has the
proper stuff for that purpose in it;
and a man becomes renowned because
he has the necessary stuff in him.
Renown is not to be sought, and all
pursuit of it is vain. A person may,
indeed, by skillful conduct and various
artificial means, make a sort of name
for himself; but if the inner jewel is
wanting, all is vanity, and will not
last a day.—Goethe.

What is glory? what is fame?
  The echo of a long-lost name;
A breath, an idle hour's brief talk;
The shadow of an arrant naught;
A flower that blossoms for a day,
  Dying next morrow;
A stream that hurries on its way,
  Singing of sorrow.—Motherwell.

Those who start for human glory,
like the mettled hounds of Actæon,
must pursue the game not only where
there is a path, but where there is

none. They must be able to simulate
and dissimulate; to leap and to creep;
to conquer the earth like Cæsar, or to
fall down and kiss it like Brutus; to
throw their sword like Brennus into
the trembling scale, or, like Nelson, to
snatch the laurels from the doubtful
hand of Victory, while she is hesitating where to bestow them.—Colton.

The muffled drum's sad roll has beat
  The soldier's last tattoo;
No more on Life's parade shall meet
  The brave and fallen few.
On Fame's eternal camping-ground
  Their silent tents are spread,
And Glory guards, with solemn round
  The bivouac of the dead.
              —Theodore O'Hara.

Gluttony

He is a very valiant trencher-man.
—Shakespeare.

Born merely for the purpose of digestion.—Bruyère.

Hunger makes everything sweet.—
Antiphanes.

Reason should direct and appetite
obey.—Cicero.

The turnpike road to people's
hearts, I find, lies through their
mouths.—Dr. John Wolcott.

Such, whose sole bliss is eating, who
can give but that one brutal reason
why they live.—Juvenal.

I am a great eater of beef, and I
believe that does harm to my wit.—
Shakespeare.

Their various cares in one great point com-
    bine,
The business of their lives—that is, to dine.
              —Young.

As for me, give me turtle or give
me death. What is life without
turtle? nothing. What is turtle without life? nothinger still.—Artemus
Ward.

I have come to the conclusion that
mankind consume twice too much food.
—Sydney Smith.

The belly has no ears.—Plutarch.

Whose god is their belly and whose glory is their shame.—Bible.

Fat paunches have lean pates; and dainty bits
Make rich the ribs, but bankrupt quite the wits. —Shakespeare.

The pleasures of the palate deal with us like Egyptian thieves who strangle those whom they embrace.—Seneca.

As houses well stored with provisions are likely to be full of mice, so the bodies of those that eat much are full of diseases.—Diogenes.

Gluttony and drunkenness have two evils attendant on them; they make the carcass smart, as well as the pocket.—Marcus Antoninus.

Why, at this rate, a fellow that has but a groat in his pocket may have a stomach capable of a ten-shilling ordinary.—Congreve.

Let me have men about me that are fat; sleek-headed men, and such as sleep o' nights; yonder Cassius has a lean and hungry look; he thinks too much; such men are dangerous.—Shakespeare.

He was a kind and thankful toad, whose heart dilated in proportion as his skin was filled with good cheer; and whose spirits rose with eating, as some men's do with drink.—Washington Irving.

Swinish gluttony never looks to heaven amidst its gorgeous feast; but with besotted, base ingratitude, cravens and blasphemes his feeder.—Milton.

He that prolongs his meals, and sacrifices his time as well as his other conveniences, to his luxury, how quickly does he outset his pleasure!—South.

Gluttony is the source of all our infirmities, and the fountain of all our diseases. As a lamp is choked by a superabundance of oil, a fire extinguished by excess of fuel, so is the natural health of the body destroyed by intemperate diet.—Burton.

And by his side rode loathsome gluttony,
Deform'd creature, on a filthy swine;
His belly was up-blown with luxury,
And eke with fatness swollen were his eyne. —Spenser.

But for the cravings of the belly not a bird would have fallen into the snare; nay, nay, the fowler would not have spread his net. The belly is chains to the hands and fetters to the feet. He who is a slave to his belly seldom worships God.—Saadi.

Some men find happiness in gluttony and in drunkenness, but no delicate viands can touch their taste with the thrill of pleasure, and what generosity there is in wine steadily refuses to impart its glow to their shriveled hearts.—Whipple.

Some men are born to feast, and not to fight;
Whose sluggish minds, e'en in fair honor's field,
Still on their dinner turn—
Let such pot-boiling varlets stay at home,
And wield a flesh-hook rather than a sword. —Joanna Baillie.

When I behold a fashionable table set out in all its magnificence, I fancy that I see gouts and dropsies, fevers and lethargies, with other innumerable distempers lying in ambuscade among the dishes. Nature delights in the most plain and simple diet. Every animal but man keeps to one dish. Herbs are the food of this species, fish of that, and flesh of a third. Man falls upon everything that comes in his way; not the smallest fruit or excrescence of the earth, scarce a berry or a mushroom can escape him.—Addison.

God

For God is love.—Bible.

God's glory is His goodness.—Henry Ward Beecher.

There is a God within us.—Ovid.

I am athirst for God, the living God.—Jean Ingelow.

God alone is true; God alone is great; alone is God.—Laboulaye.

God, from a beautiful necessity, is love.—Tupper.

Thou Great First Cause, least understood.—Pope.

O Thou above all gods supreme.—Klopstock.

God is the one great employer, thinker, planner, supervisor.—Henry Ward Beecher.

His steps are beauty, and His presence light.—Montgomery.

God is truth, and light His shadow.—Plato.

God's will is the very perfection of all reason.—Edward Payson.

Space is the statue of God.—Joubert.

Where God is, all agree.—Vaughan.

God is the only sure foundation on which the mind can rest.—S. Irenæus Prime.

Fear that man who fears not God.—Abdl-el-Kader.

The rolling year is full of Thee.—Thomson.

All but God is changing day by day.—Charles Kingsley.

We love Him, because He first loved us.—Bible.

His eye is upon every hour of my existence.—Chalmers.

Nothing with God can be accidental.—Longfellow.

The divine essence itself is love and wisdom.—Swedenborg.

The Eternal Being is forever if He is at all.—Pascal.

Nothing reveals character more than self-sacrifice. So the highest knowledge we have of God is through the gift of His Son.—William Harris.

God is able to do more than man can understand.—Thomas à Kempis.

Can we outrun the heavens?—Shakespeare.

Acquaint thyself with God, if thou wouldst taste His works.—Cowper.

God never made His work for man to mend.—Dryden.

Think of God oftener than you breathe.—Epictetus.

God tempers the wind to the shorn lamb.—Laurence Sterne.

These are Thy glorious works, Parent of good.—Milton.

God deceiveth thee not.—Thomas à Kempis.

A foe to God was never true friend to man.—Young.

History is the revelation of Providence.—Kossuth.

By night an atheist half believes a God.—Young.

Let us think less of men and more of God.—Bailey.

There is a God to punish and avenge.—Schiller.

A God all mercy is a God unjust.—Young.

I believe the promises of God enough to venture an eternity on them.—Watts.

As a man is, so is his God; therefore God was so often an object of mockery.—Goethe.

He who knows what it is to enjoy God will dread His loss; he who has seen His face will fear to see His back.—Richard Alleine.

God said, "Let us make man in our image." Man said, "Let us make God in our image."—Douglas Jerrold,

A God alone can comprehend a God. —Dr. Young.

One on God's side is a majority.—Wendell Phillips.

God's in His Heaven—
All's right with the world!
—Robert Browning.

God enters by a private door into every individual.—Emerson.

Of what I call God,
And fools call Nature.
—Robert Browning.

Naught but God
Can satisfy the soul. —Bailey.

All are but parts of one stupendous whole,
Whose body nature is, and God the soul.
—Pope.

God shall be my hope,
My stay, my guide and lantern to my feet.
—Shakespeare.

To attain the height and depth of Thy eternal ways, all human thoughts come short.—Milton.

He mounts the storm and walks upon the wind.—Pope.

God is as great in minuteness as He is in magnitude.—Colton.

Philosophers call God "the great unknown." "The great mis-known" would be more correct.—Joseph Roux.

God often visits us, but most of the time we are not at home.—Joseph Roux.

Give me Thy light, and fix my eyes on Thee!—Boethius.

Heaven is above all yet; there sits a Judge that no king can corrupt.—Shakespeare.

There is no God but God, the living, the self-subsisting.—Koran.

And God said, Let there be light, and there was light.—Bible.

God's power never produces what His goodness cannot embrace.—South.

'Tis heaven alone that is given away,
'Tis only God may be had for the asking.
—Lowell.

It is folly to seek the approbation of any being besides the Supreme.—Addison.

God governs the world, and we have only to do our duty wisely, and leave the issue to Him.—John Jay.

The perfect love of God knoweth no difference between the poor and the rich.—Pacuvius.

God alone is entirely exempt from all want: of human virtues, that which needs least is the most absolute and divine.—Plutarch.

Thy attributes, how endearing! how parental! all loving, all forgiving.—Hosea Ballou.

The angel of the Lord encampeth round about them that fear Him.—Bible.

Happy the man who sees a God employ'd
In all the good and ill that chequer life!
—Cowper.

God is absolutely good; and so, assuredly, the cause of all that is good.—Sir Walter Raleigh.

Men sunk in the greatest darkness imaginable retain some sense and awe of the Deity.—Tillotson.

Lo, the poor Indian! whose untutored mind
Sees God in clouds, or hears Him in the wind. —Pope.

He that doth the ravens feed,
Yea, providently caters for the sparrow.
—Shakespeare.

There's a Divinity that shapes our ends,
Rough-hew them as we will.
—Shakespeare.

If God were not a necessary being of Himself, He might almost seem to be made for the use and benefit of men.—John Tillotson.

How did the atheist get his idea of that God whom he denies?—Coleridge.

If God did not exist, it would be necessary to invent Him.—Voltaire.

O Thou, whose certain eye foresees
The fix'd event of fate's remote decrees.
—Homer.

God is a perfect poet,
Who in His person acts His own creations.
—Robert Browning.

I fear God, and next to God I chiefly fear him who fears Him not.—Saadi.

At whose sight all the stars
Hide their diminished heads.—Milton.

God had sifted three kingdoms to find the wheat for this planting.—Longfellow.

There is no creature so small and abject. that it representeth not the goodness of God.—Thomas à Kempis.

'Tis hard to find God, but to comprehend Him, as He is, is labour without end.
—Herrick.

As long as we work on God's line, He will aid us. When we attempt to work on our own lines, He rebukes us with failure.—T. L. Cuyler.

God's justice and love are one. Infinite justice must be infinite love. Justice is but another sign of love.—F. W. Robertson.

Can we be unsafe where God has placed us, and where He watches over us as a parent a child that he loves?—Fénelon.

The great soul that sits on the throne of the universe is not, never was, and never will be, in a hurry.—J. G. Holland.

The presence of God calms the soul, and gives it quiet and repose.—Fénelon.

The God of merely traditional believers is the great Absentee of the universe.—W. R. Alger.

God is all love; it is He who made everything, and He loves everything that He has made.—Henry Brooke.

God wishes to exhaust all means of kindness before His hand takes hold on justice.—Henry Ward Beecher.

We know God easily, provided we do not constrain ourselves to define Him.—Joubert.

God is a being who gives everything but punishment in over measure.—Henry Ward Beecher.

Thou awakest us to delight in Thy praise; for Thou madest us for Thyself, and our heart is restless until it repose in Thee.—Augustine.

The vision of the Divine Presence ever takes the form which our circumstances most require.—Alexander Maclaren.

God never makes us sensible of our weakness except to give us of His strength.—Fénelon.

However wickedness outstrips men, it has no wings to fly from God.—Shakespeare.

God's truth is too sacred to be expounded to superficial worldliness in its transient fit of earnestness.—F. W. Robertson.

Born of God, attach thyself to Him, as a plant to its root, that ye may not be withered.—Demophilus.

God is like us to this extent, that whatever in us is good is like God.—Henry Ward Beecher.

God's sovereignty is not in His right hand; God's sovereignty is not in His intellect; God's sovereignty is in His love.—Henry Ward Beecher.

O, there is naught on earth worth being known but God and our own souls!—Bailey.

We must be in some way like God in order that we may see God as He is.—Chapin.

I believe not only in "special providences," but in the whole universe as one infinite complexity of "special providences."—Charles Kingsley.

To be struck with His power, it is only necessary to open our eyes.—Burke.

Under whose feet (subjected to His grace),
Sit nature, fortune, motion, time, and place.
—Tasso.

To attain the height and depth of Thy eternal ways, all human thoughts come short.—Milton.

There is no god but God!—to prayer—lo! God is great!—Byron.

Sometimes Providences, like Hebrew letters, must be read backwards.—John Flavel.

But, oh, Thou bounteous Giver of all good, Thou art, of all Thy gifts, Thyself the crown!—Cowper.

Everyone is in a small way the image of God.—Manilius.

God can change the lowest to the highest, abase the proud, and raise the humble.—Horace.

Nothing is so high and above all danger that is not below and in the power of God.—Ovid.

There is indeed a God that hears and sees whate'er we do.—Plautus.

God is a shower to the heart burned up with grief; God is a sun to the face deluged with tears.—Joseph Roux.

My God, my Father, and my Friend,
Do not forsake me in the end.
—Wentworth Dillon.

To Him no high, no low, no great, no small;
He fills, He bounds, connects and equals all!
—Pope.

The very impossibility in which I find myself to prove that God is not, discloses to me His existence.—La Bruyère.

God's mercy is a holy mercy, which knows how to pardon sin, not to protect it; it is a sanctuary for the penitent, not for the presumptuous.—Bishop Reynolds.

And now we beseech of Thee that we may have every day some such sense of God's mercy and of the power of God above us, as we have of the fullness of the light of heaven before us.—H. W. Beecher.

It is as easy for God to supply thy greatest as thy smallest wants, even as it was within His power to form a system or an atom, to create a blazing sun as to kindle the fire-fly's lamp.—Thomas Guthrie.

Our God is a household God, as well as a heavenly one. He has an altar in every man's dwelling; let men look to it when they rend it lightly, and pour out its ashes.—Ruskin.

If God be infinitely holy, just, and good, He must take delight in those creatures that resemble Him most in these perfections.—Atterbury.

Such was God's original love for man, that He was willing to stoop to any sacrifice to save him; and the gift of a Saviour was the mere expression of that love.—Albert Barnes.

The love of God ought continually to predominate in the mind, and give to every act of duty grace and animation.—Beattie.

It is highly convenient to believe in the infinite mercy of God when you feel the need of mercy, but remember also His infinite justice.—B. R. Haydon.

Mistrusts sometimes come over one's mind of the justice of God. But let a real misery come again, and to whom do we fly? To whom do we instinctively and immediately look up? —B. R. Haydon.

There is nothing left to us but to see how we may be approved of Him, and how we may roll the weight of our weak souls in well-doing upon Him, who is God omnipotent.—Rutherford.

To love God, which was a thing far excelling all the cunning that is possible for us in this life to obtain.—Sir Thomas More.

Not a flower
But shows some touch, in freckle, streak, or stain,
Of His unrivall'd pencil.   —Cowper.

Thou sovereign power, whose secret will controls the inward bent and motion of our souls.—Prior.

Be He nowhere else, God is in all that liberates and lifts, in all that humbles, sweetens, and consoles.—Lowell.

There is no worm of the earth, no spire of grass, no leaf, no twig, wherein we see not the footsteps of a Deity.—Robert Hall.

Remember that there is nothing in God but what is godlike; and that He is either not at all, or truly and perfectly good.—Shaftesbury.

To escape from evil, we must be made as far as possible like God; and this resemblance consists in becoming just and holy and wise.—Plato.

The Providence that watches over the affairs of men works out of their mistakes, at times, a healthier issue than could have been accomplished by their wisest forethought.—J. A. Froude.

It is a most unhappy state to be at a distance with God; man needs no greatei infelicity than to be left to himself.—Feltham.

The Omnipotent has sown His name on the heavens in glittering stars, but upon earth He planteth His name by tender flowers.—Richter.

As the soul is the life of the body, so God is the life of the soul. As therefore the body perishes when the soul leaves it, so the soul dies when God departs from it.—St. Augustine.

Let us always remember that God has never promised to supply our wishes, but only our wants, and these only as they arise from day to day.—Alexander Dickson.

Contemplation of human nature doth by a necessary connection and chain of causes carry us up to the Deity.—Sir M. Hale.

When God reveals His march through Nature's night
His steps are beauty, and His presence light.   —Montgomery.

All things that are on earth shall wholly pass away,
Except the love of God, which shall live and last for aye.   —Bryant.

The very impossibility in which I find myself to prove that God is not discovers to me His existence.—Bruyère.

When we have broken our god of tradition, and ceased from our god of rhetoric, then may God fire the heart with His presence.—Emerson.

Take comfort, and recollect however little you and I may know, God knows; He knows Himself and you and me and all things; and His mercy is over all His works.—Charles Kingsley.

The moral perfections of the Deity, the more attentively we consider, the more perfectly still shall we know them.—Addison.

God, who oft descends to visit men
Unseen, and through their habitations walks
To mark their doings.   —Milton.

One sole God;
One sole ruler,—His Law;
One sole interpreter of that law—Humanity.   —Mazzini.

Yet forget not that "the whole world is a phylactery, and everything we see an item of the wisdom, power, or goodness of God"—Sir Thomas Browne.

When we attempt to define and describe God, both language and thought desert us, and we are as helpless as fools and savages.—Emerson.

As a countenance is made beautiful by the soul's shining through it, so the world is beautiful by the shining through it of a God.—Jacobi.

The glorious Author of the universe,
Who reins the winds, gives the vast ocean
    bounds,
And circumscribes the floating worlds their
    rounds!   —Gay.

God has been pleased to prescribe limits to His own power, and to work His ends within these limits.—Paley.

What can 'scape the eye
Of God, all-seeing, or deceive His heart,
Omniscient!   —Milton.

The glory of Him who hung His masonry pendent on nought, when the world He created.—Longfellow.

I sought Thee at a distance, and did not know that Thou wast near. I sought Thee abroad, and behold, Thou wast within me.—St. Augustine.

There is nothing so small but that we may honor God by asking His guidance of it, or insult Him by taking it into our own hands.—John Ruskin.

If thou art fighting against thy sins so is God. On thy side is God who made all, and Christ who died for all, and the Holy Spirit who alone gives wisdom, purity, and nobleness.—Charles Kingsley.

If I make the seven oceans ink, if I make the trees my pen, if I make the earth my paper, the glory of God cannot be written.—Kabir.

As the sensation of hunger presupposes food to satisfy it, so the sense of dependence on God presupposes His existence and character.—O. B. Frothingham.

Who can know heaven except by its gifts? and who can find out God unless the man who is himself an emanation from God?—Manilius.

When the Master of the universe has points to carry in His government

He impresses His will in the structure of minds.—Emerson.

But who with filial confidence inspired,
Can lift to heaven an unpresumptuous eye.
And smiling say, my Father made them all.
                                      —Cowper.

God should be the object of all our desires, the end of all our actions, the principle of all our affections, and the governing power of our whole souls.—Massillon.

We are never less alone than when we are in the society of a single, faithful friend; never less deserted than when we are carried in the arms of the All-Powerful.—Fénelon.

It is a great truth, "God reigns," and therefore grace reigns through righteousness unto eternal life, by Jesus Christ our Lord; and, therefore, no sinner on earth need ever despair.—Ichabod Spencer.

God's commandments are the iron door into Himself. To keep them is to have it opened and His great heart of love revealed.—Samuel Willoughby Duffield.

Forgetful youth! but know, the Power
    above
With ease can save each object of His love;
Wide as His will, extends His boundless
    grace.   —Homer.

It is one of my favorite thoughts that God manifests Himself to men in all the wise, good, humble, generous, great, and magnanimous men.—Lavater.

I know by myself how incomprehensible God is, seeing I cannot comprehend the parts of my own being.—St. Bernard.

We cannot think too oft there is a never, never-sleeping Eye, which reads the heart, and registers our thoughts.—Bacon.

In all God's providences, it is good to compare His word and His works together; for we shall find a beautiful harmony between them, and that they mutually illustrate each other.—Matthew Henry.

God governs in the affairs of men; and if a sparrow cannot fall to the ground without His notice, neither can a kingdom rise without His aid.—Benjamin Franklin.

Tell me how it is that in this room there are three candles and but one light, and I will explain to you the mode of the Divine existence.—John Wesley.

God works in a mysterious way in grace as well as in nature, concealing His operations under an imperceptible succession of events, and thus keeps us always in the darkness of faith.—Fénelon.

Not a sorrow, not a burden, not a temptation, not a bereavement, not a disappointment, not a care, not a groan or tear, but has its antidote in God's rich and inexhaustible resources.—George C. Lorimer.

Converting grace puts God on the throne, and the world at His footstool; Christ in the heart, and the world under His feet.—Joseph Alleine.

Though man sits still, and takes his ease,
  God is at work on man;
No means, no moment unemploy'd,
  To bless him, if He can.   —Young.

A Deity believed, is joy begun;
A Deity adored, is joy advanced;
A Deity beloved, is joy matured.
Each branch of piety delight inspires.
                                    —Young.

  I know not where His islands lift
    Their fronded palms in air;
  I only know I cannot drift
    Beyond His love and care.
                            —Whittier.

The God of metaphysics is but an idea. But the God of religion, the Maker of heaven and earth, the sovereign Judge of actions and thoughts, is a power.—Joubert.

God is the light which, never seen itself, makes all things visible, and clothes itself in colors. Thine eye

feels not its ray, but thine heart feels its warmth.—Richter.

The sun and every vassal star,
  All space, beyond the soar of angel's
    wings,
Wait on His word: and yet He stays His
    car
  For every sigh a contrite suppliant
    brings.   —Keble.

By tracing Heaven His footsteps may be
    found:
Behold! how awfully He walks the round!
God is abroad, and wondrous in His ways
The rise of empires, and their fall surveys.
                                    —Dryden.

A voice is in the wind I do not know;
A meaning on the face of the high hills
Whose utterance I cannot comprehend.
A something is behind them: that is God.
                          —George MacDonald.

God is everywhere! the God who framed
Mankind to be one mighty family,
Himself our Father, and the world our
    home.   —Coleridge.

Praise to our Father-God,
  High praise in solemn lay,
Alike for what His hand hath given,
  And what it takes away.
                          —Mrs. Sigourney.

Amid so much war and contest and variety of opinion, you will find one consenting conviction in every land, that there is one God, the King and Father of all.—Maximus Tyrius.

He made little, too little of sacraments and priests, because God was so intensely real to him. What should he do with lenses who stood thus full in the torrent of the sunshine.—Phillips Brooks.

To God belongeth the east and the west; therefore, whithersoever ye turn yourselves to pray, there is the word of God; for God is omnipresent and omniscient.—Koran.

They that deny a God destroy man's nobility; for certainly man is like the beasts in his body; and if he is not like God in his spirit, he is an ignoble creature.—Bacon.

I can understand the things that afflict mankind, but I often marvel at those which console. An atom may wound, but God alone can heal.—Mme. Swetchine.

From God derived, to God by nature joined,
We act the dictates of His mighty mind:
And though the priests are mute and temples still,
God never wants a voice to speak His will.
—Rowe.

He who bridles the fury of the billows knows also to put a stop to the secret plans of the wicked. Submitting with respect to His holy will, I fear God, and have no other fear.—Racine.

He hath made the earth by His power, He hath established the world by His wisdom, and hath stretched out the heavens by His discretion.—Bible.

The slender capacity of man's heart cannot comprehend, much less utter, that unsearchable depth and burning zeal of God's love towards us.—Luther.

If we look closely at this earth, where God seems so utterly forgotten, we shall find that it is He, after all, who commands the most fidelity and the most love.—Madame Swetchine.

Since therefore all things are ordered in subserviency to the good of man, they are so ordered by Him that made both man and them.—Charnock.

Give God the margin of eternity to justify Himself in, and the more we live and know of our own souls and of spiritual experience generally, the more we shall be convinced that we have to do with one who is good and just.—Hugh R. Haweis.

God, so to speak, is myriad-minded. We cannot look, therefore, to put ourselves in accord with His plans any more than one man can run a line for a railroad which it requires a small army to survey.—Samuel Willoughby Duffield.

Kircher lays it down as a certain principle, that there never was any

people so rude which did not acknowledge and worship one supreme Deity.—Stillingfleet.

God is not dumb that He should speak no more; if thou hast wanderings in the wilderness and find'st no Sinai, 'tis thy soul is poor.—Lowell.

He who can imagine the universe fortuitous or self-created is not a subject for argument, provided he has the power of thinking or even the faculty of seeing.—MacCulloch.

When we would think of God, how many things we find which turn us away from Him, and tempt us to think otherwise. All this is evil, yet it is innate.—Pascal.

Be an observer of providence; for God is showing you ever, by the way in which He leads you, whither He means to lead. Study your trials, your talents, the world's wants, and stand ready to serve God now, in whatever He brings to your hand.—Horace Bushnell.

My bark is wafted to the strand
  By breath Divine;
And on the helm there rests a hand
  Other than mine.   —Dean Alford.

I need Thy presence every passing hour;
What, but Thy grace, can foil the tempter's
  power?
Who, like Thyself, my guide and stay can
  be?
Through cloud and sunshine, oh, abide with
  me!   —H. F. Lyte.

What must be the knowledge of Him, from whom all created minds have derived both their power of knowledge, and the innumerable objects of their knowledge! What must be the wisdom of Him, from whom all things derive their wisdom!—Timothy Dwight.

Chance and change are busy ever;
  Man decays, and ages move;
But His mercy waneth never;
  God is wisdom, God is love.
    —Bowring.

We never know through what Divine mysteries of compensation the great Father of the universe may be carrying out His sublime plan; but those three words, "God is love," ought to contain, to every doubting soul, the solution of all things.—D. M. Craik.

God is kind; but within the limits of inexorable law. He is good; but you can take no liberties with Him; for back of His pity and kindness is the righteousness that is so exact, and that must be satisfied to the uttermost farthing.—J. R. Paxton.

God's highest gifts—talent, beauty, feeling, imagination, power—they carry with them the possibility of the highest heaven and the lowest hell. Be sure that it is by that which is highest in you that you may be lost.—F. W. Robertson.

O God, our help in ages past,
  Our hope for years to come,
Be Thou our guard while troubles last,
  And our eternal home!   —Watts.

God's treasury where He keeps His children's gifts will be like many a mother's store of relics of her children, full of things of no value to others, but precious in His eyes for the love's sake that was in them.—Fénelon.

The mystery of the universe, and the meaning of God's world, are shrouded in hopeless obscurity, until we learn to feel that all laws suppose a lawgiver, and that all working involves a Divine energy.—Alexander Maclaren.

God hides nothing. His very work from the beginning is revelation—a casting aside of veil after veil, a showing unto men of truth after truth. On and on from fact Divine He advances, until at length in His Son Jesus He unveils His very face.—George MacDonald.

The man who forgets the wonders and mercies of the Lord is without any excuse; for we are continually surrounded with objects which may serve to bring the power and goodness of God strikingly to mind.—Slade.

Think not thy love to God merits God's love to thee; His acceptance of thy duty crowns His own gifts in thee; man's love to God is nothing but a faint reflection of God's love to man.—Quarles.

How calmly may we commit ourselves to the hands of Him who bears up the world—of Him who has created, and who provides for the joys even of insects, as carefully as if He were their father.—Richter.

It takes something of a poet to apprehend and get into the depth, the lusciousness, the spiritual life of a great poem. And so we must be in some way like God in order that we may see God as He is.—Chapin.

Is there any other seat of the Divinity than the earth, sea, air, the heavens, and virtuous minds? why do we seek God elsewhere? He is whatever you see; He is wherever you move.—Lucan.

There are regions beyond the most nebulous outskirts of matter; but no regions beyond the Divine goodness. We may conceive of tracts where there are no worlds, but not of any where there is no God of mercy.—J. W. Alexander.

Since, in possessing You, we possess all if we had nothing else, and in not possessing You we have nothing if we had all the rest, oh, my God! I will love You that I may possess You upon earth; and I will possess You that I may love You one day in heaven.—Joseph Roux.

A secret sense of God's goodness is by no means enough. Men should make solemn and outward expressions of it, when they receive His creatures for their support; a service and homage not only due to Him, but profitable to themselves.—Dean Stanhope.

There never was a man of solid understanding, whose apprehensions are sober, and by a pensive inspection advised, but that he hath found by an irresistible necessity one true God and everlasting being.—**Sir Walter** Raleigh.

Of what consequence is it that anything should be concealed from man? Nothing is hidden from God; He is present in our minds and comes into the midst of our thoughts. Comes, do I say?—as if He were ever absent!— Seneca.

If you wish to behold God, you may see Him in every object around; search in your breast, and you will find Him there. And if you do not yet perceive where He dwells, confute me, if you can, and say where He is not.—Metastasio.

With God is terrible majesty. Touching the Almighty we cannot find Him out. He is excellent in power and in judgment, and in plenty of justice. He will not afflict. Men do therefore fear Him.—Bible.

Though, in debating with regard to theories, it be lawful to say whether this or that is consistent with the Divine attributes, yet, when we find that God has actually done any thing, all question about its justice, wisdom, and benevolence is forever out of place.—Nehemiah Adams.

Who best
Bear His mild yoke, they serve Him best:
  His state
Is kingly; thousands at His bidding speed,
And post o'er land and ocean without rest.
        —Milton.

The kingdom of God which is within us consists in our willing whatever God wills, always, in everything, and without reservation; and thus His kingdom comes; for His will is then done as it is in heaven, since we will nothing but what is dictated by His sovereign pleasure.—Fénelon.

Whatever may be the mysteries of life and death, there is one mystery which the cross of Christ reveals to us, and that is the infinite and absolute goodness of God. Let all the rest remain a mystery so long as the mystery of the cross of Christ gives us faith for all the rest.—Charles Kingsley.

It were better to have no opinion of God at all than such an opinion as is unworthy of Him; for the one is unbelief, and the other is contumely; and certainly superstition is the reproach of the Deity.—Bacon.

Dear Lord, our God and Saviour! for Thy gifts
The world were poor in thanks, though every soul
Were to do nought but breathe them, every blade
Of grass, and every atomie of earth
To utter it like dew.   —Bailey.

It never frightened a Puritan when you bade him stand still and listen to the speech of God. His closet and his church were full of the reverberations of the awful, gracious, beautiful voice for which he listened.—Phillips Brooks.

If you were to spend a month feeding on the precious promises of God, you would not be going about with your heads hanging down like bulrushes, complaining how poor you are; but you would lift up your heads with confidence, and proclaim the riches of His grace because you could not help it.—D. L. Moody.

God is everywhere present by His power. He rolls the orbs of heaven with His hand; He fixes the earth with His foot; He guides all creatures with His eye, and refreshes them with His influence; He makes the powers of hell to shake with His terrors, and binds the devils with His word.—Jeremy Taylor.

We are not to consider the world as a body of God: He is an uniform being, devoid of organs, members, or parts; and they are His creatures, subordinate to Him, and subservient to His will.—Newton.

Because I believe in a God of absolute and unbounded love, therefore I believe in a loving anger of His which will and must devour and destroy all which is decayed, monstrous, abortive in His universe till all enemies shall be put under His feet, and God shall be all in all.—Charles Kingsley.

So long as the word "God" endures in a language will it direct the eyes of men upwards. It is with the Eternal as with the sun, which, if but its smallest part can shine uneclipsed, prolongs the day, and gives its rounded image in the dark chamber.—Richter.

In all thy actions think God sees thee; and in all His actions labor to see Him; that will make thee fear Him; this will move thee to love Him; the fear of God is the beginning of knowledge, and the knowledge of God is the perfection of love.—Quarles.

Thou art, O God, the life and light
Of all this wondrous world we see;
Its glow by day, its smile by night,
Are but reflections caught from Thee!
Where'er we turn thy glories shine,
And all things fair and bright are thine!
—Moore.

Ah, my friends, we must look out and around to see what God is like. It is when we persist in turning our eyes inward and prying curiously over our own imperfections, that we learn to make God after our own image, and fancy that our own darkness and hardness of heart are the patterns of His light and love.—Charles Kingsley.

Whenever I think of God I can only conceive of Him as a Being infinitely great and infinitely good. This last quality of the divine nature inspires me with such confidence and joy that I could have written even a *miserere* in *tempo allegro*.—Haydn.

We worship unity in trinity, and trinity in union; neither confounding the person nor dividing the substance. There is one person of the Father, another of the Son, and another of the Holy Ghost; but the Godhead of the Father, and of the Son, and of the Holy Ghost, is all one; the glory equal, the majesty co-eternal.—Tertullian.

The hand of God never tires, nor are its movements aimless. It makes all things subservient to its designs, and, at every turn, disappoints the calculations of man, causing the most insignificant events to expand to the mightiest consequences, while those that have the appearance of mountains vanish into nothing.—John Lanahan.

Thine, O Lord, is the greatness, and the power, and the glory, and the victory, and the majesty; for all that is in the heaven and in the earth, is Thine; Thine is the kingdom, O Lord, and Thou art exalted as head above all.—Bible.

Nothing is more ancient than God, for He was never created; nothing more beautiful than the world, it is the work of that same God; nothing more active than thought, for it flies over the whole universe; nothing stronger than necessity, for all must submit to it.—Thales.

God's truth and faithfulness "are a great deep." They resemble the ocean itself; always there—vast, fathomless, sublime, the same in its majesty, its inexhaustible fullness, yesterday, today, and forever; the same in calm and storm, by day and by night; changeless while generations come and pass; everlasting while ages are rolling away.—Richard Fuller.

The wisdom of the Lord is infinite as are also His glory and His power. Ye heavens, sing His praises; sun, moon, and planets, glorify Him in your ineffable language! Praise Him, celestial harmonies, and all ye who can comprehend them! And thou, my soul, praise thy Creator! It is by Him and in Him that all exist.—Kepler.

While earthly objects are exhausted by familiarity the thought of God becomes to the devout man continually brighter, richer, vaster; derives fresh luster from all that he observes of nature and Providence, and attracts to itself all the glories of the universe.—Channing.

However dark our lot may be, there is light enough on the other side of the cloud, in that pure empyrean where God dwells, to irradiate every darkness of this world; light enough to clear every difficult question, remove every ground of obscurity, conquer every atheistic suspicion, silence every hard judgment, light enough to satisfy, nay, to ravish the mind forever.—Horace Bushnell.

When my reason is afloat, my faith cannot long remain in suspense, and I believe in God as firmly as in any other truth whatever; in short, a thousand motives draw me to the consolatory side, and add the weight of hope to the equilibrium of reason.—Rousseau.

God! sing, ye meadow-streams, with gladsome voice!
Ye pine-groves, with your soft and soul-like sounds!
And they too have a voice, yon piles of snow,
And in their perilous fall shall thunder, God!
                                    —Coleridge.

The Christian will sometimes be brought to walk in a solitary path. God seems to cut away his props, that He may reduce him to Himself. His religion is to be felt as a personal, particular, appropriate possession. He is to feel that, as there is but one Jehovah to bless, so there seems to him as though there were but one penitent in the universe to be blessed by Him.—Richard Cecil.

There is a God! the sky His presence shares,
His hand upheaves the billows in their mirth,
Destroys the mighty, yet the humble spares
And with contentment crowns the thought of worth.   —Charlotte Cushman.

Day and night, and every moment, there are voices about us. All the hours speak as they pass; and in every event there is a message to us; and all our circumstances talk with us; but it is in Divine language, that worldliness misunderstands, that selfishness is frightened at, and that only the children of God hear rightly and happily.—Wm. Mountford.

O Thou, above all gods supreme! who broughtest the world out of darkness, and gavest man a heart to feel! By whatsoever name Thou art addressed—God, Father, or Jehovah; the God of Romulus or of Abraham—not the God of one man, but the Father and Judge of all!—Klopstock.

Every created thing glorifies God in its place by fulfilling His will, and the great purposes of His providence; but man alone can give tongue to every creature, and pronounce for all a general orthodoxy.—Kirby.

God shows us in Himself, strange as it may seem, not only authoritative perfection, but even the perfection of obedience—an obedience to His own laws; and in the cumbrous movement of those unwieldiest of his creatures we are reminded, even in His divine essence, of that attribute of uprightness in the human creature "that sweareth to his own hurt and changeth not."—Ruskin.

"God saw everything that He had made, and behold it was very good." * * * Wheresoever I turn my eyes, behold the memorials of His greatness! of His goodness! * * * What the world contains of good is from His free and unrequited mercy; what it presents of real evil arises from ourselves.—Bishop Blomfield.

                         Thy great name
In all its awful brevity, hath nought
Unholy breeding it, but doth bless
Rather the tongue that uses it; for me,
I ask no higher office than to fling
My spirit at Thy feet, and cry Thy name,
God! through eternity.   —Bailey.

There is a beauty in the name appropriated by the Saxon nations to the Deity, unequalled, except by His most venerated Hebrew appellation. They call him "God," which is literally "The Good." The same word thus signifying the Deity, and His most endearing quality.—Turner.

We find in God all the excellences of light, truth, wisdom, greatness, goodness and life. Light gives joy and gladness; truth gives satisfaction; wisdom gives learning and instruction; greatness excites admiration; goodness produces love and gratitude; life gives immortality and insures enjoyment.—Jones of Nayland.

If we can keep our minds calm on the subject of the "Eternity of God," if reason does not totter on her seat at the contemplation of underived existence, it will be strange if any other mystery relating to God should disturb us. He who can bring his reason to bow reverently at the idea of a Being who had no beginning, is well prepared to receive any communication of His will.—Nehemiah Adams.

At last I heard a voice upon the slope
Cry to the summit, "Is there any hope?"
To which an answer pealed from that high
    land,
But in a tongue no man could understand;
And on the glimmering limit far with-
    drawn,
God made Himself an awful rose of dawn.
                            —Tennyson.

Not a step can we take in any direction without perceiving the most extraordinary traces of design; and the skill everywhere conspicuous is calculated in so vast a proportion of instances to promote the happiness of living creatures, and especially of ourselves, that we feel no hesitation in concluding that, if we knew the whole scheme of Providence, every part would appear to be in harmony with a plan of absolute benevolence.—Lord Brougham.

Was it possible that Napoleon should win the battle of Waterloo? We answer, No! Why? Because of Wellington? Because of Blucher? No! Because of God! For Bonaparte to conquer at Waterloo was not the law of the nineteenth century. It was time that this vast man should fall. He had been impeached before the Infinite! He had vexed God! Waterloo was not a battle. It was the change of front of the universe!—Victor Hugo.

God is not to be worshiped with sacrifices and blood; for what pleasure can He have in the slaughter of the innocent? but with a pure mind, a good and honest purpose. Temples are not to be built for Him with stones piled on high; God is to be consecrated in the breast of each.—Seneca.

The moral government of God is a movement in a line onwards towards some grand consummation, in which the principles, indeed, are ever the same, but the developments are always new—in which, therefore, no experience of the past can indicate with certainty what new openings of truth, what new manifestations of goodness, what new phases of the moral heaven may appear.—Mark Hopkins.

Many people have their own God; and He is much what the French may mean when they talk of Le bon Dieu —very indulgent, rather weak, near at hand when we want anything, but far away, out of sight, when we have a mind to do wrong. Such a God is as much an idol as if He were an image of stone.—Hare.

Whoever studies Divine providence, whether it be in relation to the events that concern us, our families, the cities and nations to which we belong; whoever studies the rise and fall of nations and empires, whoever looks at the clashing of armies, will perceive that these are only parts of one grand movement. God is marching on to the accomplishment of an appointed end; namely, the subjugation of the world to Himself.—J. M. Reid.

All is of God. If He but wave His hand,
    The mists collect, the rains fall thick
        and loud;
Till, with a smile of light on sea and land,
    Lo! He looks back from the departing
        cloud.
Angels of life and death alike are His;
    Without His leave they pass no threshold
        o'er;
Who, then, would wish or dare, believing
        this,
Against His messengers to shut the door?
                        —Longfellow.

A source of cheerfulness to a good mind is the consideration of that Being on whom we have our dependence, and in whom, though we behold Him as yet but in the first faint discoveries of His perfections, we see everything that we can imagine as great, glorious, or amiable. We find ourselves everywhere upheld by His goodness and surrounded by an immensity of love and mercy.—Addison.

God is alpha and omega in the great world; endeavor to make Him so in the little world; make Him thy evening epilogue and thy morning prologue; practice to make Him thy last thought at night when thou sleepest, and thy first thought in the morning when thou awakest; so shall thy fancy be sanctified in the night, and thy understanding rectified in the day; so shall thy rest be peaceful, thy labors prosperous, thy life pious, and thy death glorious.—Quarles.

Of old hast Thou laid the foundation of the earth: and the heavens are the work of Thy hands. They shall perish, but Thou shalt endure; yea all of them shall wax old like a garment: as a vesture shalt Thou change them, and they shall be changed, but thou art the same, and thy years shall have no end.—Bible.

———

Thou, my all!
My theme! my inspiration! and my crown!
My strength in age; my rise in low estate!
My soul's ambition, pleasure, wealth!—my world!
My light in darkness! and my life in death!
My boast through time! bliss through eternity!
Eternity, too short to speak Thy praise!
Or fathom Thy profound of love to man!
—Young.

———

Do you feel that you have lost your way in life? Then God Himself will show you your way. Are you utterly helpless, worn out, body and soul? Then God's eternal love is ready and willing to help you up, and revive you. Are you wearied with doubts and terrors? Then God's eternal light is ready to show you your way; God's eternal peace ready to give you peace. Do you feel yourself full of sins and faults? Then take heart; for God's unchangeable will is, to take away those sins, and purge you from those faults.—Charles Kingsley.

It is impossible for the mind which is not totally destitute of piety to behold the sublime, the awful, the amazing works of creation and providence —the heavens with their luminaries, the mountains, the ocean, the storm, the earthquake, the volcano, the circuit of the seasons, and the revolutions of empires—without marking in them all the mighty hand of God, and feeling strong emotions of reverence toward the Author of these stupendous works.—Timothy Dwight.

———

What an immense workman is God! in miniature as well as in the great. With the one hand, perhaps, He is making a ring of one hundred thousand miles in diameter, to revolve round a planet like Saturn, and with the other is forming a tooth in the ray of the feather of a humming-bird, or a point in the claw of the foot of a microscopic insect. When He works in miniature, everything is gilded, polished, and perfect, but whatever is made by human art, as a needle, etc., when viewed by a microscope, appears rough, and coarse, and bungling.— Bishop Law.

———

The same Being that fashioned the insect, whose existence is only discerned by a microscope, and gave that invisible speck a system of ducts and other organs to perform its vital functions, created the enormous mass of the planet thirteen hundred times larger than our earth, and launched it in its course round the sun, and the comet, wheeling with a velocity that would carry it round our globe in less than two minutes of time, and yet revolving through so prodigious a space that it takes near six centuries to encircle the sun!—Lord Brougham.

———

God Himself—His thoughts, His will, His love, His judgments are men's home. To think His thoughts, to choose His will, to judge His judgments, and thus to know that He is in us, with us, is to be at home. And to pass through the valley of the shadow of death is the way home, but only thus, that as all changes have hitherto led us nearer to this home, the knowledge of God, so this greatest of all outward changes—for it is but an outward change—will surely usher us into a region where there will be fresh possibilities of drawing nigh in heart, soul, and mind to the Father of us all.—George MacDonald.

———

Running like a gulf-stream through the sea of times comes the affirmation that God has manifested Himself to man, and the best men have affirmed it most persistently. Wherever this affirmation has made its way, the icebergs of skepticism have disappeared, the temperature of virtue has risen, and the sweet fruits of charity have ripened. If the belief be false, then a lie has blessed the world, and the soul is so organized that it reaches its highest state of development in an atmosphere of deception; for it is a fact that man is purest and woman most virtuous where belief in God's manifestations is most intense and real.—O. P. Gifford.

As Phidias contrived his mechanism so that his memory could never be obliterated without the destruction of his work, so the great name of God is interwoven in the texture of all that He has made. His goodness blooms in every flower; His glory beams in every star. There is a God! The sun speaks it in his splendor by day, and the moon in her radiance by night. There is a God! Inanimate nature, from the pebble upon the beach, to the orb that shines in the vaulted sky, declares it; and animate existence, from the tiniest insect, to Gabriel before the throne. The earth is full of Him. His majesty commands the cherubim; His temple is all space; His arm is around all worlds.—Joseph Dare.

We have a friend and protector, from whom, if we do not ourselves depart from Him, nor power nor spirit can separate us. In His strength let us proceed on our journey, through the storms, and troubles, and dangers of the world. However they may rage and swell, though the mountains shake at the tempests, our rock will not be moved: we have one friend who will never forsake us; one refuge, where we may rest in peace and stand in our lot at the end of the days. That same is He who liveth, and was dead; who is alive forevermore; and hath the keys of hell and of death.—Bishop Heber.

As a man exhibits himself in physical forms and actions, so there is one other Spirit, a great, wide, mighty, in-

finite, eternal Spirit back there in the depths of space, and in the present, and in the future, and in the abysses of space, who at His will wrestles into existence great globes, and keeps them in their position. He builds them, and places on them these mysterious forms of earth which are signals hung out over these abysses to tell coming spirits who He is, what He is, what He does, how high is His throne, and how vast is His power from eternity to eternity, from infinity to infinity through all ages of all time; He is holding forth to men and angels these external tokens of His almighty power, of His infinite skill, and of His everlasting love.—Bishop R. S. Foster.

Guide me, O Thou great Jehovah,
  Pilgrim through this barren land;
I am weak, but Thou are mighty;
  Hold me with Thy powerful hand;
  Bread of heaven!
Feed me till I want no more.
                              —W. Williams.

Lead, kindly Light! amid the encircling gloom,
        Lead Thou me on;
The night is dark, and I am far from home,
        Lead Thou me on;
Keep Thou my feet; I do not ask to see
The distant scene; one step enough for me.
                              —John H. Newman.

Godliness

Godliness is practical religion.—Dewey.

Truthfulness is godliness.—Beecher.

All flows out from the Deity, and all must be absorbed in Him again.—Zoroaster.

The form of godliness may exist with secret and with open wickedness, but the power of godliness cannot.—Phillips Brooks.

Godliness is profitable unto all things, having promise of the life that now is, and of that which is to come.—Bible.

Gods (The)

Man is certainly stark mad; he cannot make a flea, and yet he will be making gods by dozens.—Montaigne

The gods play games with men as balls.—Plautus.

The gods my protectors.—Horace.

Who hearkens to the gods, the gods give ear.—Homer.

I would the gods had made thee poetical.—Shakespeare.

Speak of the gods as they are.—Bias.

The matchless Ganymede, divinely fair.—Homer.

The world is the mighty temple of the gods.—Seneca.

As flies to wanton boys, are we to the gods;
They kill us for their sport.
　　　　　—Shakespeare.

Jove weighs affairs of earth in dubious scales,
And the good suffers while the bad prevails.　　　　　—Homer.

Shakes his ambrosial curls, and gives the nod,
The stamp of fate, and sanction of the god.
　　　　　—Homer.

The gods are just, and of our pleasant vices
Make instruments to plague us.
　　　　　—Shakespeare.

Some thoughtlessly proclaim the Muses nine:
A tenth is Sappho, maid divine.
　　　　　—Greek Anthology.

The more we deny ourselves, the more the gods supply our wants.—Horace.

Cease to think that the decrees of the gods can be changed by prayers.—Virgil.

Ye immortal gods! where in the world are we?—Cicero.

For the gods, instead of what is most pleasing, will give what is most proper. Man is dearer to them than he is to himself.—Juvenal.

The gods and their tranquil abodes appear, which no winds disturb, nor clouds bedew with showers, nor does the white snow, hardened by frost, annoy them; the heaven, always pure, is without clouds, and smiles with pleasant light diffused.—Lucretius.

In the elder days of Art,
　Builders wrought with greatest care
Each minute and unseen part;
　For the gods see everywhere.
　　　　　—Longfellow.

　　　　　As sweet and musical
As bright Apollo's lute, strung with his hair;
And when Love speaks, the voice of all the gods
Makes heaven drowsy with the harmony.
　　　　　—Shakespeare.

Say, Bacchus, why so placid? What can there be
In commune held by Pallas and by thee?
Her pleasure is in darts and battles; thine
In joyous feasts and draughts of rosy wine.
　　　　　—Greek Anthology.

With ravish'd ears
The monarch hears,
Assumes the god,
Affects to nod,
And seems to shake the spheres.
　　　　　—Dryden.

　　　　　The gods
Grow angry with your patience. 'Tis their care
And must be yours, that guilty men escape not:
As crimes do grow, justice should rouse itself.　　　　　—Ben Jonson.

　　　　　The son of Saturn gave
The nod with his dark brows. The ambrosial curls
Upon the Sovereign One's immortal head
Were shaken, and with them the mighty mount,
Olympus trembled.　　　　　—Homer.

High in the home of the summers, the seats of the happy immortals,
Shrouded in knee-deep blaze, unapproachable; there ever youthful
Hebé, Harmonié, and the daughter of Jove, Aphrodité,
Whirled in the white-linked dance, with the gold-crowned Hours and Graces.
　　　　　—Charles Kingsley.

When a man is laboring under the pain of any distemper, it is then that he recollects there are gods, and that he himself is but a man; no mortal is then the object of his envy, his admiration, or his contempt, and having no malice to gratify, the tales of slander excite not his attention.—Pliny the Younger.

———

Janus am I; oldest of potentates!
Forward I look and backward and below
I count—as god of avenues and gates—
The years that through my portals come and
    go.
I block the roads and drift the fields with
    snow,
I chase the wild-fowl from the frozen fen;
My frosts congeal the rivers in their flow,
My fires light up the hearths and hearts of
    men.   —Longfellow.

———

Creator Venus, genial power of love,
The bliss of men below, and gods above!
Beneath the sliding sun thou runn'st thy
    race,
Dost fairest shine, and best become thy
    place;
For thee the winds their eastern blasts for-
    bear,
Thy mouth reveals the spring, and opens all
    the year;
Thee, goddess, thee, the storms of winter
    fly,
Earth smiles with flowers renewing, laughs
    the sky.   —Dryden.

Gold

All that glitters is not gold.—Shakespeare.

———

Gold all is not that doth golden seem.—Spenser.

———

All is not golde that outward sheweth bright.—Lydgate.

———

Gold—what can it not do, and undo?—Shakespeare.

———

A mask of gold hides all deformities.—Decker.

———

Gold—the picklock that never fails.—Massinger.

———

Can pocket states, or fetch or carry kings.—Pope.

———

Bright and yellow, hard and cold.—Hood.

———

There is no place invincible, wherein an ass loaden with gold may not enter.—Collett.

———

Saint-seducing gold.—Shakespeare.

Poison is drunk out of golden cups.—Seneca.

———

Thou more than stone of the philosopher!—Byron.

———

The dangers gather as the treasures rise.—Dr. Johnson.

———

If all were rich, gold would be penniless.—Bailey.

———

For gold in phisik is a cordial;
Therefore he lovede gold in special.
    —Chaucer.

———

For gold the merchant ploughs the main,
The farmer ploughs the manor. —Burns.

———

The plague of gold strikes far and near.—Mrs. Browning.

———

Accursed thirst for gold! what dost thou not compel mortals to do?—Virgil.

———

Judges and senates have been bought for
    gold;
Esteem and love were never to be sold.
    —Pope.

———

How quickly nature falls to revolt when gold becomes her object!—Shakespeare.

———

How few, like Daniel, have God and gold together!—George Villiers.

———

Gold adulterates one thing only—the human heart.—Marguerite de Valois.

———

Gold is a living god, and rules in scorn all earthly things but virtue.—Shelley.

———

Gold is the fool's curtain, which hides all his defects from the world.—Feltham.

———

Foul-cankering rust the hidden treasure
    frets;
But gold, that's put to use, more gold be-
    gets.   —Shakespeare.

———

And mammon wins his way where seraphs might despair.—Byron.

———

It is much better to have your gold in the hand than in the heart.—Fuller.

As the touchstone tries gold, so gold tries men.—Chilo.

Gold hath no lustre of its own.
It shines by temperate use alone.
—Francis.

Gold is, in its last analysis, the sweat of the poor and the blood of the brave.—Joseph Napoleon.

No, let the monarch's bags and coffers hold
The flattering mighty, nay, all-mighty gold.
—John Wolcott.

Thou true magnetic pole, to which all hearts point duly north, like trembling needles!—Byron.

For gold the hireling judge distorts the laws.—Dr. Johnson.

Because its blessings are abused, must gold be censured, cursed, accused?—Gay.

Gold can gild a rotten stick, and dirt sully an ingot.—Sir P. Sidney.

O, I cry your mercy;
There is my purse, to cure that blow of thine. —Shakespeare.

What nature wants, commodious gold bestows;
'Tis thus we cut the bread another sows.
—Pope.

Though authority be a stubborn bear, yet he is oft led by the nose with gold.—Shakespeare.

O cursed lust of gold! when for thy sake
The fool throws up his interest in both worlds. —Blair.

The lust of gold succeeds the rage of conquest;
The lust of gold, unfeeling and remorseless!
The last corruption of degenerate man.
—Sam'l Johnson.

Gold glitters most where virtue shines no more, as stars from absent suns have leave to shine.—Young.

Midas longed for gold. He got gold, so that whatever he touched became gold; and he, with his long ears, was little the better for it.—Carlyle.

Gold, like the sun, which melts wax and hardens clay, expands great souls and contracts bad hearts.—Rivarol.

Gold is a wonderful clearer of the understanding; it dissipates every doubt and scruple in an instant.—Addison.

Commerce has set the mark of selfishness, the signet of its all-enslaving power, upon a shining ore and called it gold.—Shelley.

Because my blessings are abus'd,
Must I be censur'd, curs'd, accus'd?
Even virtue's self by knaves is made
A cloak to carry on the trade. —Gay.

O what a world of vile ill-favored faults looks handsome in three hundred pounds a year!—Shakespeare.

Gold loves to make its way through guards, and breaks through barriers of stone more easily than the lightning's bolt.—Horace.

It is observed of gold, by an old epigrammatist, "that to have it is to be in fear, and to want it, to be in sorrow."—Johnson.

Can gold calm passion, or make reason shine?
Can we dig peace, or wisdom, from the mine?
Wisdom to gold prefer; for 'tis much less
To make our fortune, than our happiness.
—Young.

Gold is the strength, the sinews of the world;
The health, the soul, the beauty most divine;
A mask of gold hides all deformities;
Gold is heaven's physic, life's restorative.
—Decker.

Stronger than thunder's winged force
All-powerful gold can speed its course;
Through watchful guards its passage make,
And loves through solid walls do break.
—Francis.

Gold begets in brethren hate;
Gold in families debate;
Gold does friendship separate;
Gold does civil wars create.
—Abraham Cowley.

It is gold which buys admittance: and it is gold which makes the true man killed, and saves the thief; nay, sometimes hangs both thief and true man; what can it not do and undo?—Shakespeare.

_____

Gold is Cæsar's treasure, man is God's; thy gold hath Cæsar's image, and thou hast God's: give, therefore, those things unto Cæsar which are Cæsar's, and unto God which are God's.—Quarles.

_____

Abundance is a blessing to the wise;
The use of riches in discretion lies:
Learn this, ye men of wealth—a heavy purse
In a fool's pocket is a heavy curse.
—Cumberland.

_____

There are two metals, one of which is omnipotent in the cabinet, and the other in the camp—gold and iron. He that knows how to apply them both may indeed attain the highest station.—Colton.

_____

You know the Ark of Israel and the calf of Belial were both made of gold. Religion has never yet changed the metal of her one adoration.—Ouida.

_____

There is thy gold, worse poison to men's souls,
Doing more murders in this loathsome world,
Than these poor compounds that thou mayst not sell.
I sell thee poison, thou hast sold me none.
—Shakespeare.

_____

I know not whether there exists such a thing as a coin stamped with a pair of pinions; but I wish this were the device which monarchs put upon their dollars and ducats, to show that riches make to themselves wings, and fly away.—Gotthold.

_____

Gold! gold! in all ages the curse of mankind,
Thy fetters are forged for the soul and the mind.
The limbs may be free as the wings of a bird,
And the mind be the slave of a look and a word.
To gain thee men barter eternity's crown,
Yield honour, affection, and lasting renown.
—Park Benjamin.

_____

By gold all good faith has been banished; by gold our rights are abused: the law itself is influenced by gold, and soon there will be an end of every modest restraint.—Propertius.

_____

How quickly nature falls into revolt
When gold becomes her object!
For this the foolish over-careful fathers
Have broke their sleep with thoughts, their brains with care,
Their bones with industry:
For this they have engrossed and pil'd up
The canker'd heaps of strange-achieved gold;
For this they have been thoughtful to invest
Their sons with arts and martial exercises.
—Shakespeare.

_____

Oh, bane of man! seducing cheat!
Can man, weak man, thy power defeat?
Gold banish'd honor from the mind,
And only left the name behind;
Gold sow'd the world with ev'ry ill,
Gold taught the murderer's sword to kill;
'Twas gold instructed coward hearts
In treachery's more pernicious arts.
—Gay.

_____

Thus, when the villain crams his chest,
Gold is the canker of the breast;
'Tis avarice, insolence, and pride,
And every shocking vice beside:—
But when to virtuous hands 'tis given,
It blesses, like the dews of heaven:
Like heaven, it hears the orphans' cries,
And wipes the tears from widows' eyes.
—Gay.

_____

O thou sweet king-killer, and dear divorce
Twixt natural son and sire! thou bright defiler
Of hymen's purest bed! thou valiant Mars!
Thou ever young, fresh, lov'd, and delicate wooer,
Whose blush doth thaw the consecrated snow
That lies on Dian's lip! thou visible god,
That solder'st close impossibilities,
And mak'st them kiss! and speak'st with every tongue,
To every purpose!   —Shakespeare.

_____

Why lose we life in anxious cares,
To lay in hoards for future years?
Can these, when tortur'd by disease,
Cheer our sick hearts, or purchase ease?
Can these prolong one gasp of breath,
Or calm the troubled hour of death?
—Gay.

_____

Those who worship gold in a world so corrupt as this we live in have at least one thing to plead in defense of their idolatry—the power of their idol. It is true that, like other idols, it can neither move, see, hear, feel nor understand; but, unlike other idols, it has often communicated all these powers to those who had them not, and annihilated them in those who had. This idol can boast of two peculiarities; it is worshipped in all climates, without a single temple, and by all classes, without a single hypocrite.—Colton.

Commerce has set the mark of selfishness,
The signet of its all-enslaving power
Upon a shining ore, and called it gold;
Before whose image bow the vulgar great,
The vainly rich, the miserable proud,
The mob of peasants, nobles, priests, and
 kings,
And with blind feelings reverence the
 power
That grinds them to the dust of misery.
But in the temple of their hireling hearts
Gold is a living god, and rules in scorn
All earthly things but virtue.—Shelley.

 Give him gold enough, and marry him to a puppet, or an aglet-baby; or an old trot with ne'er a tooth in her head, though she have as many diseases as two and fifty horses; why, nothing comes amiss, so money comes withal.—Shakespeare.

Goldenrod

   I know the lands are lit
With all the autumn blaze of Goldenrod.
   —Helen Hunt Jackson.

Still the Goldenrod of the roadside clod
   Is of all, the best!
   —Simeon Tucker Clark.

Welcome, dear Goldenrod, once more,
 Thou mimic, flowering elm!
I always think that summer's store
Hangs from thy laden stem.
   —Horace H. Scudder.

Graceful, tossing plume of glowing gold,
 Waving lonely on the rocky ledge;
Leaning seaward, lovely to behold,
 Clinging to the high cliff's ragged edge.
   —Celia Thaxter.

Nature lies disheveled, pale,
 With her feverish lips apart—
Day by day the pulses fail,
 Nearer to her bounding heart;
Yet that slackened grasp doth hold
Store of pure and genuine gold;
Quick thou comest, strong and free,
Type of all the wealth to be—
   Goldenrod!
   —Elaine Goodale.

Because its myriad glimmering plumes
 Like a great army's stir and wave;
Because its golden billows blooms,
 The poor man's barren walks to lave:
Because its sun-shaped blossoms show
 How souls receive the light of God,
And unto earth give back that glow—
 I thank Him for the Goldenrod.
   —Lucy Larcom.

I lie amid the Goldenrod,
 I love to see it lean and nod;
I love to feel the grassy sod
Whose kindly breast will hold me last,
Whose patient arms will fold me fast!—
Fold me from sunshine and from song,
Fold me from sorrow and from wrong:
Through gleaming gates of Goldenrod
I'll pass into the rest of God.
   —Mary Clemmer.

Golf

 Your play needs no excuse.—Shakespeare.

 What subtle hole is this?—Shakespeare.

 The harder match'd, the greater victory.—Shakespeare.

 Strike, brave boys, and take your turns.—Shakespeare.

      So they
 Doubly redoubled strokes.
    —Shakespeare.

Where will I get a little page,
Where will I get a caddie?
   · —Thistle of Scotland.

 Don't drive at a fellow-creature, so long as there is a reasonable chance of hitting him.—W. E. Norris.

When driving ceases, may we still be able
To play the shorts, putt and be comfortable.   —G. F. Carnegie.

Welcome, grave stranger, to our green retreats,
Where health with exercise and freedom meets.   —Scott.

 Either a wise man will not go into bunkers, or, being in, he will endure such things as befall him with patience.—A. Lang.

 We want a boy extremely for this function.—Beaumont and Fletcher.

Time-honored golf! I heard it whispered
once
That he who could not play was held a
dunce
On old Olympus, when it teemed with
gods.   —G. F. Carnegie.

One only thought can enter every head;
The thought of golf, to wit—and that en-
gages
Men of all sizes, tempers, ranks and ages.
    —G. F. Carnegie.

And we've leeved it every hour,
But say not at all we will loft our ball
And hauff the hole in fower.
Then dormy hame we can sing through the
round,
And die like golfers keen,
We've played fu' weel the short game and
lang,
The game on the golfing-green.
    —Thomas Dykes.

Good-Breeding

Good-breeding is surface Christianity.—Holmes.

Virtue itself often offends when
coupled with bad manners.—Middleton.

A man's good-breeding is the best
security against another's bad manners.—Chesterfield.

One may know a man that never
conversed in the world, by his excess of good-breeding.—Addison.

Good-breeding shows itself most
where to an ordinary eye it appears
the least.—Addison.

Good qualities are the substantial
riches of the mind; but it is good
breeding that sets them off to advantage.—Locke.

The scholar without good breeding is a pedant; the philosopher, a
cynic; the soldier, a brute; and every
man disagreeable.—Chesterfield.

There are few defects in our nature so glaring as not to be veiled
from observation by politeness and
good-breeding.—Stanislaus.

As ceremony is the invention of
wise men to keep fools at a distance,
so good-breeding is an expedient to
make fools and wise men equals.—
Steele.

Good-breeding is as necessary a quality in conversation, to accomplish all
the rest, as grace in motion and
dancing.—Sir Wm. Temple.

Good manners is the art of making
those people easy with whom we converse. Whoever makes the fewest
persons uneasy is the best bred in
the company.—Swift.

It is not wit merely, but temper,
which must form the well-bred man.
In the same manner it is not a head
merely, but a heart and resolution,
which must complete the real philosopher.—Shaftesbury.

Good-breeding carries along with it
a dignity that is respected by the
most petulant. Ill-breeding invites
and authorizes the familiarity of the
most timid.—Chesterfield.

The highest point of good-breeding,
if any one can hit it, is to show a
very nice regard to your own dignity,
and with that in your heart, to express your value for the man above
you.—Steele.

Good-breeding is the art of showing men, by external signs, the internal regard we have for them. It
arises from good sense, improved by
conversing with good company.—Cato.

A man endowed with great perfections, without good-breeding, is like
one who has his pockets full of gold,
but always wants change for his ordinary occasions.—Steele.

One principal object of good-breeding is to suit our behaviour to the
three several degrees of men,—our superiors, our equals, and those below
us.—Swift.

Good-breeding is the result of much
good sense, some good-nature, and a
little self-denial for the sake of others,
and with a view to obtain the same
indulgence from them.—Chesterfield.

Perhaps the summary of good-breeding may be reduced to this rule. "Behave unto all men as you would they should behave unto you." This will most certainly oblige us to treat all mankind with the utmost civility and respect, there being nothing that we desire more than to be treated so by them.—Fielding.

Some young people do not sufficiently understand the advantages of natural charms, and how much they would gain by trusting to them entirely. They weaken these gifts of heaven, so rare and fragile, by affected manners and an awkward imitation. Their tones and their gait are borrowed: they study their attitudes before the glass until they have lost all trace of natural manner, and, with all their pains, they please but little.—Bruyère.

We see a world of pains taken and the best years of life spent in collecting a set of thoughts in a college for the conduct of life, and after all the man so qualified shall hesitate in his speech to a good suit of clothes, and want common sense before an agreeable woman. Hence it is that wisdom, valour, justice and learning cannot keep a man in countenance that is possessed with these excellencies, if he wants that inferior art of life and behaviour called good-breeding. —Steele.

There is no society or conversation to be kept up in the world without good-nature, or something which must bear its appearance, and supply its place. For this reason mankind have been forced to invent a kind of artificial humanity, which is what we express by the word "good-breeding." For, if we examine thoroughly the idea of what we call so, we shall find it to be nothing else but an imitation and mimicry of good-nature, or, in other terms, affability, complaisance, and easiness of temper reduced into an art.—Addison.

Good-By

Why should we hesitate to say "good-by" to each other? Are we not Pagans, to think that a word has power over God's quiet purposes, and that saying "good-by" smells of death? Must men die intestate because they think that making their wills is cutting out their shrouds? If we were old Romans, who thought "vale!" meant "forever," we might be shy of such a word, but "good-by," even if it should be for the last time on earth, is only the difference between "good-night" and "good-morning." Say it, then, like a Christian, and, if it still comes hesitatingly, stretch it out into the loveliest of wishes, "God be with you."—Maltbie Babcock.

Good Friday

Who His own self bare our sins in His own body on the tree, that we, being dead to sins, should live unto righteousness.—Bible.

In the cross of Christ I glory,
  Towering o'er the wrecks of time,
All the light of sacred story
  Gathers round its head sublime.

Death is the justification of all the ways of the Christian, the last end of all his sacrifices, the touch of the Great Master which completes the picture.—Mme. Swetchine.

The cross was two pieces of dead wood; and a helpless, unresisting Man was nailed to it; yet it was mightier than the world, and triumphed, and will ever triumph over it.—Hare.

Exalt the Cross! God has hung the destiny of the race upon it. Other things we may do in the realm of ethics, and on the lines of philanthropic reforms; but our main duty converges into setting that one glorious beacon of salvation, Calvary's Cross, before the gaze of every immortal soul.—Theo. L. Cuyler, D. D.

When God's children pass under the shadow of the cross of Calvary, they know that through that shadow lies their passage to the great white throne. For them Gethsemane is as paradise. God fills it with sacred presences; its solemn silence is broken by the music of tender promises, its awful darkness softened and brightened by the sunlight of Heavenly faces and the music of angel wings. —Dear Farrar.

We see that brow bruised; we hear that dying groan; and while the priests scoff and the devils rave, and the lightnings of God's wrath are twisted into a wreath for that bloody mount, you and I will join the cry, the supplication, of the penitent malefactor, "Lord, remember me when thou comest into thy kingdom."—T. DeWitt Talmage, D. D.

The mob that hounded Christ from Jerusalem to "the place of a skull" has never been dispersed, but is augmenting yet, as many of the learned men of the world and great men of the world come out from their studies and their laboratories and their palaces, and cry, "Away with this man! Away with him!" The most bitter hostility which many of the learned men of this day exercise in any direction they exercise against Jesus Christ the Son of God, the Saviour of the world.— T. DeWitt Talmage, D. D.

Christ took hold of the work of the world's saving in a larger way than it is possible for us to do, and therefore the burden of His undertaking came upon Him in a heavier, wider, and more crushing way than it can come upon us; and therefore, while it overwhelmed Him in sorrow, our smaller mission and lighter task can with entire propriety leave us buoyant and gladsome.—Chas. A. Parkhurst, D. D.

The essence of that by which Jesus overcame the world was not suffering, but obedience. Yes, men may puzzle themselves and their hearers over the question where the power of the life of Jesus and the death of Jesus lay; but the soul of the Christian always knows that it lay in the obedience of Christ. He was determined at every sacrifice to do His Father's will. Let us remember that; and the power of Christ's sacrifice may enter into us, and some little share of the redemption of the world may come

through us, as the great work came through Him.—Phillips Brooks.

By the cross we, too, are crucified with Christ; but alive in Christ. We are no more rebels, but servants; no more servants, but sons! "Let it be counted folly," says Hooker, "or fury, or frenzy, or whatever else; it is our wisdom and our comfort. We care for no knowledge in the world but this, that man hath sinned, and that God hath suffered; that God has made Himself the Son of Man, and that men are made the righteousness of God."—Dean Farrar.

All His life long Christ was the light of the world, but the very noon-tide hour of His glory was that hour when the shadow of eclipse lay over all the land, and He hung on the Cross dying in the dark. At His eventide "it was light," and "He endured the Cross, despising the shame"·: and, lo! the shame flashed up into the very brightness of glory, and the very ignominy and the suffering were the jewels of His crown.—Anglican and American Pulpit Library.

We may say that on the first Good Friday afternoon was completed that great act by which light conquered darkness and goodness conquered sin. That is the wonder of our Saviour's crucifixion. There have been victories all over the world, but wherever we look for the victor we expect to find him with his heel upon the neck of the vanquished. The wonder of Good Friday is that the victor lies vanquished by the vanquished one. We have to look deeper into the very heart and essence of things before we can see how real the victory is that thus hides itself under the guise of defeat.—Phillips Brooks.

And thus He had lived, and thus the world rewarded Him! For lies and baseness, for selfish greed and destructive ambition, for guilty wealth and mean compliance, the world has a diadem; for perfect holiness it has the cross! The darkness quenched the Light, His own disowned Him. They had repaid by hatred that life of love; envy, malice, slander, calumny, false witness, had done its work. Jesus had been excommunicated, hunted as a fugitive, with a price upon His head, buffeted, insulted, spit upon mocked, scourged, crowned with thorns—thus had the world shown its gratitude to its Redeemer; and the end was here! After thirty hours of sleepless agony Jesus was hanging upon the cross. Infinite malignity! Could there be any greater proof of man's ruin than the fact that this was the sole reward which was requited to immeasurable love?—Dean Farrar.

———

Bound upon th' accursed tree,
Dread and awful, who is He?
By the prayer for them that slew—
"Lord, they know not what they do!"
By the spoiled and empty grave;
By the souls He died to save;
By the conquest He hath won;
By the saints before His throne;
By the rainbow round His brow;
Son of God, 'tis Thou! 'tis Thou!
—Henry Hart Millman.

———

Yet once more that cross moves closer, and yet more intensely and eagerly He who hangs upon it seems to speak to us, and the burden of His words is: "I bring to you that which is highest and best for time and eternity; I bring to you the assurance that there is no grief and no sorrow that is not always in the Father's sight and may not be turned into blessing. I bring to you a power by which evil thoughts and tendencies may be destroyed. I bring to you whose memories are full of sad and bad recollections the assurance that no life can have been so wicked, no past so foul, no strength so far gone, as to cut off from the love of God and His willingness to save." Are you willing to hear that voice and to respond to its invitation?—Amory H. Bradford, D. D.

———

So shall we join the disciples of our Lord, keeping faith in Him in spite of the crucifixion, and making ready, by our loyalty to Him in the days of His darkness, for the time when we shall enter into His triumph in the days of His light. And the beauty of it is that the same method runs throughout the disciples' work which ran through His work. Christ's method is repeating itself in the work of His disciples for ever and ever. As He who first gained the great victory overcame by undergoing the power of evil, shall we be surprised if that is the sort of victory that God calls upon us to gain? It is the victory which it is always the best to gain which makes the richest victory for any soul.—Phillips Brooks.

———

We cannot have the heart that Christ had and not in the same degree have His suffering. We may be sound in our doctrinal position, fight doctrinal heresy as though it were an exhalation from the under-world, be instant in our attendance upon the means of grace, statedly participate in the service memorial of our Lord's dying love, but a loving heart is what makes out the major part of the whole Christian matter—a heart, therefore, that feels others' burdens and griefs as though they were its own; and one cannot have such a heart in the midst of this world and not have an aching heart. It is aside from the mark to say that that makes of the Christian religion a gloomy religion. The gloom is not in the religion, the gloom is in the world, and sorrow of spirit like that of our Lord is simply the way tender-heartedness like that of our Lord is certain to be affected when the shadow of the world's suffering falls upon it.—Chas. H. Parkhurst, D. D.

———

Nothing is further from the way in which Christ's apostles and Christ Himself teach us to regard the cross than the morbid, effeminate, gloating luxury of self-stimulated emotion. The unnatural self-torture of the flagellant, the hysterics of the convulsionary, the iron courage of the mistaken penitents, are manifestly out of place in contemplating that cross, which is the symbol of sin defeated, of sorrow transmuted, of effort victorious, which is the pledge of God's peace with man, and man's peace with God, which is the comfort of the penitent, which is the inspiration of the philanthropist, which is the symbol of divine charity on fields of slaughter, which was the banner in the van of every battle which good has waged with ill! The cross does not mean whipping, anguish, morbid wailing, morose despair; it means joy, it means peace, it means exultation, it means the atonement, it means the redemption, it means the liberty of humanity, it means the advance of holiness, it means the remission of sins!—Dean Farrar.

There is a green hill far away,
  Without a city wall,
Where the dear Lord was crucified,
  Who died to save us all.
We may not know, we cannot tell
  What pains He had to bear;
But we believe it was for us
  He hung and suffered there.
He died that we might be forgiven,
  He died to make us good,
That we might go at last to heaven,
  Saved by His precious blood.
                    —Mrs. C. F. Alexander.

A more sympathetic consideration of the personal element in the sufferings of our Lord, the meditation upon the sorrows of the Messiah, would prove a source of spiritual quickening not only to those who are accustomed to live in the region of philosophic thought, but also to those who are in the midst of evangelistic work. The following of Christ down into the valley of humiliation and death, the study, day by day, of the last days of His earthly life, the reverent watch by the cross, the waiting for the resurrection—these are spiritual exercises which cannot fail to give warmth and reality to the Christian faith. The majority of Christian believers, without reference to sect, now observe Easter. By the "logic of events" no less than by spiritual sympathy, Passion week deserves its place in the calendar of the private Christian; and the more remote the thoughts which it suggests may be to his ordinary religious thinking, the more helpful they may be to the spirit of devotion. —Christian Age.

Good-Humor

Affability, mildness, tenderness, and a word which I would fain bring back to its original signification of virtue,—I mean good-nature,—are of daily use: they are the bread of mankind and staff of life.—Dryden.

The sunshine of the mind.—Bulwer Lytton.

Good-humor is the clear blue sky of the soul.—Frederic Saunders.

Good-humor makes all things tolerable.—Beecher.

Good-humor is always a success.— Lavater.

Good-nature is stronger than tomahawks.—Emerson.

Good-humor is goodness and wisdom combined.—Owen Meredith.

Good-humor is the health of the soul, sadness its poison.—Stanislaus.

The good-humor of a man elated with success often displays itself towards enemies.—Macaulay.

Good-humor will even go so far as often to supply the lack of wit.— Fielding.

Good-humor is allied to generosity, ill-humor to meanness.—Greville.

Men naturally warm and heady are transported with the greatest flush of good-nature.—Addison.

Learn good-humor, never to oppose without just reason; abate some degree of pride and moroseness.—Dr. Watts.

Gayety is to good-humor as perfumes to vegetable fragrance: the one overpowers weak spirits; the other recreates and revives them.—Dr. Johnson.

Good-humor, gay spirits, are the liberators, the sure cure for spleen and melancholy. Deeper than tears, these irradiate the tophets with their glad heavens. Go laugh, vent the pits, transmuting imps into angels by the alchemy of smiles. The satans flee at the sight of these redeemers.—Alcott.

It is also important to guard against mistaking for good-nature what is properly good-humor,—a cheerful flow of spirits and easy temper not readily annoyed, which is compatible with great selfishness.—Whately.

People are not aware of the very great force which pleasantry in company has upon all those with whom a man of that talent converses.—Steele.

A cheerful temper, joined with innocence, will make beauty attractive, knowledge delightful, and wit good-natured.—Addison.

Good-humor is a state between gayety and unconcern,—the act or emanation of a mind at leisure to regard the gratification of another.—Dr. Johnson.

When good-natured people leave us we look forward with extra pleasure to their return.—H. W. Shaw.

Good-humor will sometimes conquer ill-humor, but ill-humor will conquer it oftener; and for this plain reason, good-humor must operate on generosity, ill-humor on meanness.—Greville.

Good sense and good-nature are never separated, though the ignorant world has thought otherwise. Good-nature, by which I mean beneficence and candor, is the product of right reason.—Dryden.

Good Intention

Many a good intention dies from inattention. If, through carelessness or indolence, or selfishness, a good intention is not put into effect, we have lost an opportunity, demoralized ourselves, and stolen from the pile of possible good. To be born and not fed, is to perish. To launch a ship and neglect it is to lose it. To have a talent and bury it, is to be a "wicked and slothful servant." For in the end we shall be judged, not alone by what we have done, but by what we could have done.—Maltbie Babcock.

Good-Nature

Good-nature is one of the richest fruits of true Christianity.—Henry Ward Beecher.

All other knowledge is hurtful to him who has not the science of honesty and good-nature.—Montaigne.

Nothing can constitute good-breeding that has not good-nature for its foundation.—Bulwer-Lytton.

Good-nature is the very air of a good mind, the sign of a large and generous soul, and the peculiar soil in which virtue prospers.—Goodman.

Good-nature is the beauty of the mind, and like personal beauty, wins almost without anything else,—sometimes, indeed, in spite of positive deficiencies.—Hanway.

Honest good-humor is the oil and wine of a merry meeting, and there is no jovial companionship equal to that where the jokes are rather small and the laughter abundant.—Washington Irving.

Good sense and good-nature are never separated, though the ignorant world has thought otherwise. Good-nature, by which I mean beneficence and candor, is the product of right reason.—Dryden.

That inexhaustible good-nature which is the most precious gift of Heaven, spreading itself like oil over the troubled sea of thought, and keeping the mind smooth and equable in the roughest weather.—Washington Irving.

Good-nature is more agreeable in conversation than wit, and gives a certain air to the countenance which is more amiable than beauty. It shows virtue in the fairest light; takes off in some measure from the deformity of vice; and makes even folly and impertinence supportable.—Addison.

Good-nature is worth more than knowledge, more than money, more than honor, to the persons who possess it, and certainly to everybody who dwells with them, in so far as mere happiness is concerned.—Henry Ward Beecher.

There are persons of that general philanthropy and easy tempers, which the world in contempt generally calls good-natured, who seem to be sent into the world with the same design with which men put little fish into a pike pond, in order only to be devoured by that voracious water-hero.—Fielding.

'Tis good nature only wins the heart;
It moulds the body to an easy grace
And brightens every feature of the face;
It smoothes th' unpolish'd tongue with eloquence
And adds persuasion to the finest sense.
—Stillingfleet.

Good-nature is that benevolent and amiable temper of mind which disposes us to feel the misfortunes and enjoy the happiness of others, and, consequently, pushes us on to promote the latter and prevent the former; and that without any abstract contemplation on the beauty of virtue, and without the allurements or terrors of religion.—Fielding.

Goodness

Goodness is beauty in its best estate.—Marlowe.

'Tis only noble to be good.—Tennyson.

O goodness! that shall evil turn to good.—Milton.

Seek for good, but expect evil.—Cervantes.

Nothing rarer than real goodness.—Rochefoucauld.

If you wish to be good, first believe that you are bad.—Epictetus.

How goodness heightens beauty!—Hannah More.

The true and good resemble gold.—Jacobi.

And learn the luxury of doing good.—Goldsmith.

Evil and good are God's right hand and left.—Bailey.

Do good by stealth, and blush to find it fame.—Pope.

How near to good is what is fair!—Ben Jonson.

Sin writes histories, goodness is silent.—Goethe.

The soul is strong that trusts in goodness.—Massinger.

That good diffused may more abundant grow.—Cowper.

Goodness admits of no excess, but error.—Bacon.

Goodness thinks no ill where no ill seems.—Milton.

Man should be ever better than he seems.—Sir Aubrey de Vere.

Virtue is bold and goodness never fearful.—Shakespeare.

He is good that does good to others.—La Bruyère.

Doing good is the only certainly happy action of a man's life.—Sir P. Sidney.

There is some soul of goodness in things evil, would men observingly distil it out.—Shakespeare.

Good deeds ring clear through heaven, like a bell.—Richter.

Scream as we may at the bad, the good prevails.—Bartol.

My heart contains of good, wise, just, the perfect shape.—Milton.

All are of the race of God, and have in themselves good.—Bailey.

Heaven prepares good men with crosses; but no ill can happen to a good man.—Ben Jonson.

A real man is he whose goodness is a part of himself.—Mencius.

Great hearts alone understand how much glory there is in being good.—Michelet.

Good, the more communicated, the more abundant grows.—Milton.

Real goodness does not attach itself merely to this life; it points to another world.—Daniel Webster.

There is a warp of evil woven in the woof of good.—Manilius.

Be not simply good; be good for something.—Thoreau.

Goodness is the only investment that never fails.—Thoreau.

He who believes in goodness has the essence of all faith. He is a man "of cheerful yesterdays and confident to-morrows."—J. F. Clarke.

Great hearts alone understand how much glory there is in being good.—Michelet.

Every day should be distinguished by at least one particular act of love.—Lavater.

When what is good comes of age, and is likely to live, there is reason for rejoicing.—George Eliot.

He is a truly good man who desires always to bear the inspection of good men.—La Rochefoucauld.

The good are better made by ill,
As odors crushed are sweeter still.
              —S. Rogers.

Forever all goodness will be most charming; forever all wickedness will be most odious.—Thomas Sprat.

What is good only because it pleases cannot be pronounced good till it has been found to please.—Johnson.

Men have less lively perception of good than of evil.—Livy.

A charmed life old goodness hath; the tares may perish, but the grain is not for death.—Whittier.

Whatever any one does or says, I must be good.—Aurelius Antoninus.

Few persons have courage enough to seem as good as they really are.—Hare.

A good man enlarges the term of his own existence.—Martial.

His daily prayer, far better understood in acts than words, was simply doing good.—Whittier.

You are not very good if you are not better than your best friends imagine you to be.—Lavater.

If for anything he loved greatness, it was because therein he might exercise his goodness.—Sir P. Sidney.

How far that little candle throws his beams! so shines a good deed in a naughty world.—Shakespeare.

She has more goodness in her little finger than he has in his whole body.—Swift.

Only the actions of the just
Smell sweet, and blossom in their dust.
              —Shirley.

What is beautiful is good, and who is good will soon also be beautiful.—Sappho.

Happy were men if they but understood
There is no safety but in doing good.
              —John Fountain.

It is only great souls that know how much glory there is in being good.—Sophocles.

Goodness consists not in the outward things we do, but in the inward thing we are. To be is the great thing.—E. H. Chapin.

He that does good for good's sake seeks neither praise nor reward, though sure of both at last.—William Penn.

Doing good,
Disinterested good, is not our trade.
—Cowper.

Look around the habitable world, how few Know their own good, or knowing it, pursue. —Dryden.

Your goodness must have some edge to it, else it is none.—Emerson.

No good book, or good thing of any sort, shows its best face at first.—Carlyle.

Real excellence, indeed, is most recognized when most openly looked into. —Plutarch.

Goodness does not more certainly make men happy than happiness makes them good.—Landor.

How indestructibly the good grows, and propagates itself, even among the weedy entanglements of evil.—Carlyle.

We may be as good as we please, if we please to be good.—Barrow.

It is not goodness to be better than the very worst.—Seneca.

Experience makes us see a wonderful difference between devotion and goodness.—Pascal.

He whose goodness is part of himself, is what is called a real man.—Mencius.

Good men are the stars, the planets of the ages wherein they live, and illustrate the times.—Ben Jonson.

Everything good in a man thrives best when properly recognized.—J. G. Holland.

There was never law or sect or opinion did so much magnify goodness as the Christian religion doth.—Bacon.

Whatever makes men good Christians, makes them good citizens.—Daniel Webster.

'Tis a kind of good deed to say well, And yet words are no deeds.
—Shakespeare.

Who does the best his circumstance allows, Does well, acts nobly; angels could no more. —Young.

Hard was their lodging, homely was their food,
For all their luxury was doing good.
—Garth.

A good man is kinder to his enemy than bad men are to their friends. —Bishop Hall.

He who loves goodness harbors angels, reveres reverence, and lives with God.—Emerson.

Never be afraid of what is good; the good is always the road to what is true.—Hamerton.

There is in the soul a taste for the good, just as there is in the body an appetite for enjoyment.—Joubert.

He that loveth God will do diligence to please God by his works, and abandon himself, with all his might, well for to do.—Chaucer.

The fragrance of the flower is never borne against the breeze; but the fragrance of human virtues diffuses itself everywhere.—Ramayana.

True goodness is like the glow-worm in this, that it shines most when no eyes except those of heaven are upon it.—J. C. Hare.

Nothing that man ever invents will absolve him from the universal necessity of being good as God is good, righteous as God is righteous, and holy as God is holy.—Charles Kingsley.

As the greatest liar tells more truths than falsehoods, so may it be said of the worst man, that he does more good than evil.—Dr. Johnson.

As I know more of mankind, I expect less of them, and am ready now to call a man a good man upon easier terms than I was formerly.—Dr. Johnson.

A good man doubles the length of his existence; to have lived so as to look back with pleasure on our past existence is to live twice.—Martial.

What a sublime doctrine it is, that goodness cherished now is eternal life already entered on!—Channing.

He that is a good man is three-quarters of his way towards the being a good Christian, wheresoever he lives, or whatsoever he is called.—South.

Experience has convinced me that there is a thousand times more goodness, wisdom, and love in the world than men imagine.—Gehler.

There is no odor so bad as that which arises from goodness tainted. It is human, it is divine carrion.—Thoreau.

Little men build up great ones, but the snow colossus soon melts; the good stand under the eye of God, and therefore stand.—Landor.

The soil out of which such men as he are made is good to be born on, good to live on, good to die for and to be buried in.—Lowell.

Who soweth good seed shall surely reap;
The year grows rich as it groweth old,
And life's latest sands are its sands of
   gold.   —Julia C. R. Dorr.

A good deed is never lost; he who sows courtesy reaps friendship, and he who plants kindness gathers love.—Basil.

The good, alas! are few: they are scarcely as many as the gates of Thebes or the mouths of the Nile.—Juvenal.

It is all a mistake that we cannot be good and manly without being scrupulously and studiously good. There is too much mechanism about our virtue.—Charles H. Parkhurst.

A good man will avoid the spot of any sin. The very aspersion is grievous, which makes him choose his way in his life, as he would in his journey.—Ben Jonson.

Abash'd the devil stood,
And felt how awful goodness is, and saw
Virtue in her shape how lovely.—Milton.

Who is a good man? He who keeps the decrees of the fathers, and both human and divine laws.—Horace.

This is a proof of a well-trained mind, to rejoice in what is good and to grieve at the opposite.—Cicero.

And so it happens oft in many instances; more good is done without our knowledge than by us intended.—Plautus.

There is no man so good who, were he to submit all his thoughts and actions to the law, would not deserve hanging ten times in his life.—Montaigne.

It is of unspeakable advantage to possess our minds with an habitual good intention, and to aim all our thoughts, words, and actions at some laudable end.—Addison.

He that does good to another man does also good to himself, not only in the consequence, but in the very act of doing it; for the consciousness of well-doing is an ample reward.—Seneca.

Be good, my child, and let who will be
   clever;
Do noble deeds, not dream them all day
   long;
And so make life, death, and that vast forever
One grand, sweet song.
          —Charles Kingsley.

Whatever any one does or says, I must be good; just as if the emerald were always saying this: "Whatever any one does or says, I must still be emerald, and keep my color."—Marcus Aurelius.

Goodness and love mould the form into their own image, and cause the joy and beauty of love to shine forth from every part of the face.—Swedenborg.

A glass is good, and a lass is good.
And a pipe to smoke in cold weather;
The world is good, and the people are good,
    And we're all good fellows together.
            —John O'Keefe.

The scent of flowers does not travel against the wind; but the odor of good people travels even against the wind: a good man pervades every place.—Max Müller.

A bad man is like an earthen vessel,—easy to break, and hard to mend. A good man is like a golden vessel,—hard to break, and easy to mend.—Hitopadesa.

While tenderness of feeling and susceptibility to generous emotions are accidents of temperament, goodness is an achievement of the will and a quality of the life.—Lowell.

Howe'er it be, it seems to me,
'Tis only noble to be good,
Kind hearts are more than coronets,
And simple faith than Norman blood.
            —Tennyson.

Nothing good bursts forth all at once. The lightning may dart out of a black cloud; but the day sends his bright heralds before him, to prepare the world for his coming.—Hare.

A more glorious victory cannot be gained over another man than this, that when the injury began on his part, the kindness should begin on ours.—Tillotson.

That which is good to be done, cannot be done too soon; and if it is neglected to be done early, it will frequently happen that it will not be done at all.—Bishop Mant.

In the heraldry of heaven goodness precedes greatness; so on earth it is more powerful. The lowly and the lovely may frequently do more in their own limited sphere than the gifted.—Bishop Horne.

There are people whose good qualities shine brightest in the darkness, like the ray of a diamond; but there are others whose virtues are only brought out by the light, like the colors of a silk.—Justin McCarthy.

O, if the good deeds of human creatures could be traced to their source, how beautiful would even death appear; for how much charity, mercy, and purified affection would be seen to have growth in dusty graves!—Dickens.

Our whole life is startlingly moral. There is never an instant's truce between virtue and vice. Goodness is the only investment that never fails.—Thoreau.

The hand that hath made you fair hath made you good. The goodness that is cheap in beauty makes beauty brief in goodness; but grace, being the soul of your complexion, should keep the body of it ever fair.—Shakespeare.

God whose gifts in gracious flood
    Unto all who seek are sent,
Only asks you to be good
    And is content.   —Victor Hugo.

Who is only good that others may know it, and that he may be the better esteemed when 'tis known, who will do well but upon condition that his virtue may be known to men, is one from whom much service is not to be expected.—Montaigne.

Goodness is generous and diffusive; it is largeness of mind, and sweetness of temper,—balsam in the blood, and justice sublimated to a richer spirit.—Jeremy Collier.

A good disposition I far prefer to gold; for gold is the gift of fortune; goodness of disposition is the gift of nature. I prefer much rather to be called good than fortunate.—Plautus.

Let no man think lightly of good, saying in his heart, It will not benefit me. Even by the falling of water-drops a water-pot is filled; the wise man becomes full of good, even if he gather it little by little.—Buddha.

"Good and stupid," is a common saying. I have found that only the judicious are really good. Only clever men know what is good for others; and at the first appearance of disadvantage to himself, the stupid man deserts.—Auerbach.

To love the public, to study universal good, and to promote the interest of the whole world, as far as lies within our power, is the height of goodness, and makes that temper which we call divine.—Shaftesbury.

God's livery is a very plain one; but its wearers have good reason to be content. If it have not so much gold-lace about it as Satan's, it keeps out foul weather better, and is besides a great deal cheaper.—Lowell.

None
But such as are good men can give good things,
And that which is not good, is not delicious
To a well-governed and wise appetite.
—Milton.

We may have an excellent ear for music, without being able to perform in any kind; we may judge well of poetry, without being poets, or possessing the least of a poetic vein; but we can have no tolerable notion of goodness without being tolerably good.—Shaftesbury.

What is good-looking, as Horace Smith remarks, but looking good? Be good, be womanly, be gentle, generous in your sympathies, heedful of the well-being of all around you; and, my word for it, you will not lack kind words of admiration.—Whittier.

Some good we all can do; and if we do all that is in our power, however little that power may be, we have performed our part, and may be as near perfection as those whose influence extends over kingdoms, and whose good actions are felt and applauded by thousands.—Bowdler.

Goodness I call the habit, and goodness of nature the inclination. This of all the virtues and dignities of the mind, is the greatest, being the character of the Deity; and without it man is a busy, mischievous, wretched thing.—Bacon.

No good thing is ever lost. Nothing dies, not even life which gives up one form only to resume another. No good action, no good example dies. It lives forever in our race. While the frame moulders and disappears, the deed leaves an indelible stamp, and molds the very thought and will of future generations.—Samuel Smiles.

Whatever mitigates the woes or increases the happiness of others is a just criterion of goodness; and whatever injures society at large, or any individual in it, is a criterion of iniquity. One should not quarrel with a dog without a reason sufficient to vindicate one through all the courts of morality.—Goldsmith.

Goodness answers to the theological virtue charity, and admits no excess but error. The desire of power in excess caused the angels to fall; the desire of knowledge in excess caused man to fall. But in charity there is no excess; neither can angel or man come in danger by it.—Bacon.

How many people would like to be good, if only they might be good without taking trouble about it! They do not like goodness well enough to hunger and thirst after it, or to sell all that they have that they may buy it; they will not batter at the gate of the kingdom of heaven; but they look with pleasure on this or that aerial castle of righteousness, and think it would be rather nice to live in it.—George MacDonald.

Goodness does not more certainly make men happy, than happiness makes them good. We must distinguish between felicity and prosperity; for prosperity leads often to ambition, and ambition to disappointment; the course is then over, the wheel turns round but once; while the reaction of goodness and happiness is perpetual.—Landor.

It is pleasant to be virtuous and good, because that is to excel many others; it is pleasant to grow better, because that is to excel ourselves; it is pleasant to mortify and subdue our lusts, because that is victory; it is pleasant to command our appetites and passions, and to keep them in due order within the bounds of reason and religion, because this is empire.—Tillotson.

We cannot rekindle the morning beams of childhood; we cannot recall the noontide glory of youth; we cannot bring back the perfect day of maturity; we cannot fix the evening rays of age in the shadowy horizon; but we can cherish that goodness which is the sweetness of childhood, the joy of youth, the strength of maturity, the honor of old age, and the bliss of saints.—Henry Giles.

One of the almost numberless advantages of goodness is, that it blinds its possessor to many of those faults in others which could not fail to be detected by the morally defective. A consciousness of unworthiness renders people extremely quick-sighted in discerning the vices of their neighbors; as persons can easily discover in others the symptoms of those diseases beneath which they themselves have suffered.—Godfrey.

Why is it that the bad side of life seems so much more conspicuous than the good? Is it because predominance of evil makes it more common, or that we being evil see it more readily, or that the abnormal, by its nature, stands out excrescent and disfiguring? Whatever the answer, it should be the ambition of every lover of goodness to make much of goodness, to sound its praises, to flavor his words with its appreciation. Part of hating evil is ignoring it, neglecting it. Thinking of things of good report and

speaking of them strengthens good. Shutting our mouths as well as our ears against the bruit of evil, in the scorn of silence, weakens its hold upon us. What the redeemed of the Lord say should strengthen the side of the Lord of the redeemed.—Maltie Babcock.

Live for something. Do good, and leave behind you a monument of virtue that the storm of time can never destroy. Write your name, in kindness, love, and mercy, on the hearts of thousands you come in contact with year by year; you will never be forgotten. No, your name, your deeds, will be as legible on the hearts you leave behind as the stars on the brow of evening. Good deeds will shine as the stars of heaven.—Chalmers.

Natural good is so intimately connected with moral good, and natural evil with moral evil, that I am as certain as if I heard a voice from heaven proclaim it, that God is on the side of virtue. He has learnt much, and has not lived in vain, who has practically discovered that most strict and necessary connection, that does and will ever exist between vice and misery, and virtue and happiness.—Colton.

There shall never be one lost good! What
    was shall live as before;
The evil is null, is nought, is silence im-
    plying sound;
What was good shall be good, with, for
    evil, so much good more;
On the earth the broken arcs; in the
    heaven a perfect round.
                    —Robert Browning.

For ever and ever, my darling, yes—
    Goodness and love are undying;
Only the troubles and cares of earth
    Are winged from the first for flying.
    Our way we plough
        In the furrow "now;"
But after the tilling and growing the sheaf;
Soil for the root, but the sun for the leaf—
    And God keepeth watch forever.
                    —Mary Mapes Dodge.

Goodness conditions usefulness. A grimy hand may do a gracious deed, but a bad heart cannot. What a man says and what a man is must stand together,—must con-sist. His life can ruin his lips or fill them with power. It is what men see that gives value to what we say. Paul had the right order, "Take heed unto thyself, and unto the doctrine." Being comes before saying or doing. Well may we pray, "Search me, O God! Reveal me to myself. Cleanse me from secret faults, that those who are acquainted with me, who know my down-sittings and my uprisings, may not see in me the evil way that gives the lie to my words."—Maltbie Babcock.

———

Men live a moral life, either from regard to the Divine Being, or from regard to the opinion of the people in the world; and when a moral life is practised out of regard to the Divine Being, it is a spiritual life. Both appear alike in their outward form; but in their inward, they are completely different. The one saves a man, but the other does not; for he that leads a moral life out of regard to the Divine Being is led by him, but he who does so from regard to the opinion of people in the world is led by himself.—Swedenborg.

Good-Night

Good night! good night! parting is such
    sweet sorrow,
That I shall say good night, till it be
    morrow.   —Shakespeare.

———

To all, to each, a fair good night,
And pleasing dreams, and slumbers light.
        —Scott.

———

      At once, good night—
Stand not upon the order of your going,
But go at once.   —Shakespeare.

———

Look, the world's comforter, with weary
    gait,
His day's hot task hath ended in the west:
The owl, night's herald, shrieks—'tis very
    late;
The sheep are gone to fold, birds to their
    nest;
And coal-black clouds, that shadow heaven's
    light,
Do summon us to part, and bid good night.
      —Shakespeare.

Good-Taste

Good taste is the modesty of the mind; that is why it cannot be either imitated or acquired.—Madame de Girardin.

Gospel

It is the grand endeavor of the gospel to communicate God to men.—Horace Bushnell.

———

The true disciple should aim to live for the gospel, rather than to die for it.—Saadi.

———

Lincoln did but pour the soul of the nation into the monumental act of universal liberty; and that soul was inspired by the gospel.—Edward Thomson.

———

The gospel breathes the spirit of love. Love is the fulfilling of its precepts, the pledge of its joys, and the evidence of its power.—Gardiner Spring.

———

Take Christ out of the gospel, and you take its very heart out. He has not only originated a system, but He has put Himself into it, as its very life and soul and power.—Herrick Johnson.

———

The main object of the gospel is to establish two principles—the corruption of nature, and the redemption by Jesus Christ.—Pascal.

———

God writes the gospel, not in the Bible alone, but on trees and flowers and clouds and stars.—Luther.

———

The gospel is the fulfillment of all hopes, the perfection of all philosophy, the interpretation of all revelation, the key to all the seeming contradictions of the physical and moral world.—Max Müller.

———

No one who has not examined patiently and honestly the other religions of the world can know what Christianity really is, or can join with such truth and sincerity in the words of St. Paul, "I am not ashamed of the gospel of Christ."—Max Müller.

———

O, marvelous power of the Divine seed, which overpowers the strong man armed, softens obdurate hearts, and changes into divine men those who were brutalized in sin, and removed to an infinite distance from God.—John Wycliffe.

I thank God that the gospel is to be preached to every creature. There is no man so far gone, but the grace of God can reach him; no man so desperate or black, but He can forgive him.—D. L. Moody.

The sweetness of the gospel lies mostly in pronouns, as me, my, thy. "Who loved me, and gave Himself for me." "Christ Jesus my Lord." "Son, be of good cheer, thy sins are forgiven thee."—Martin Luther.

I am not ashamed of the gospel of Christ; for it is the power of God unto salvation to every one that believeth; to the Jew first, and also to the Greek.—Bible.

The gospel's glorious hope,
Its rule of purity, its eye of prayer,
Its feet of firmness on temptation's steep,
Its bark that fails not, 'mid the storm of
death.   —Mrs. Sigourney.

Assertion of truths known and felt, promulgation of truth from the high platform of truth itself, declaration of faith by the mouth of moral conviction—this is the New Testament method, and the true one.—J. G. Holland.

The gospel comes to the sinner at once, with nothing short of complete forgiveness as the starting-point of all his efforts to be holy. It does not say, "Go and sin no more, and I will not condemn thee"; it says at once, "Neither do I condemn thee; go and sin no more."—Rev. Dr. Bonar.

Just as in the Father's house there are many mansions, so to suit the various moods and divers cases of anxious souls, there are many chambers and compartments in the gospel citadel; but the very lowest and simplest, if you can only reach it, is salvation. The nearest to the level, but still cleft in the Rock, is called "The Faithful Saying;" and above its doorway you read, "Jesus Christ came into the world to save sinners."—James Hamilton.

The idea of preaching the gospel to all nations alike, regardless of nationality, of internal divisions as to rank and color, complexion and religion, constituted the beginning of a new era in history. You cannot preach the gospel in its purity over the world, without proclaiming the doctrine of civil and religious liberty, —without overthrowing the barriers reared between nations and clans and classes of men,—without ultimately undermining the thrones of despots, and breaking off the shackles of slavery,—without making men everywhere free.—Albert Barnes.

Gossip

Gossip, like ennui, is born of idleness.—Ninon de Lenclos.

A long-tongued, babbling gossip.—Shakespeare.

There are male as well as female gossips.—Colton.

How much an ill word may empoison liking!—Shakespeare.

Old maids sweeten their tea with scandal.—H. W. Shaw.

Foul whisperings are abroad.—Shakespeare.

Everybody says it, and what everybody says must be true.—James Fenimore Cooper.

A knavish speech sleeps in a foolish ear.—Shakespeare.

It is not virtuous women who are so ready to report suspicion of their sisters.—Mme. de Krudener.

Let the greater part of the news thou hearest be the least part of what thou believest.—Quarles.

The subtle sauce of malice is often indulged in by maidens of uncertain age, over their tea.—Rivarol.

Most women indulge in idle gossip, which is the henchman of rumor and scandal.—Octave Feuillet.

Female gossips are generally actuated by active ignorance.—Rochefoucauld.

Love and scandal are the best sweeteners of tea.—Fielding.

Not only is the world informed of everything about you, but of a great deal more.—Thackeray.

Old gossips are usually young flirts gone to seed.—J. L. Basford.

We are disgusted by gossip; yet it is of importance to keep the angels in their proprieties.—Emerson.

Tale-bearers, as I said before, are just as bad as the tale-makers.—Sheridan.

Our globe discovers its hidden virtues, not only in heroes and arch-angels, but in gossips and nurses.—Emerson.

Half the gossip of society would perish if the books that are truly worth reading were but read.—George Dawson.

Too many individuals are like Shakespeare's definition of "echo,"—babbling gossips of the air.—H. W. Shaw.

It is only before those who are glad to hear it, and anxious to spread it, that we find it easy to speak ill of others.—J. Petit-Senn.

He's gone, and who knows how may he report
Thy words by adding fuel to the flame?
—Milton.

In fact, there's nothing makes me so much grieve,
As that abominable tittle-tattle,
Which is the cud eschew'd by human cattle.
—Byron.

Truth is not exciting enough to those who depend on the characters and lives of their neighbors for all their amusement.—Bancroft.

Gossip is a sort of smoke that comes from the dirty tobacco-pipes of those who diffuse it; it proves nothing but the bad taste of the smoker.—George Eliot.

It is among uneducated women that we may look for the most confirmed gossips. Goethe tells us there is nothing more frightful than bustling ignorance.—Chamfort.

For my part, I can compare her (a gossip) to nothing but the sun; for, like him, she knows no rest, nor ever sets in one place but to rise in another.—Dryden.

Such as are still observing upon others are like those who are always abroad at other men's houses, reforming everything there while their own runs to ruin.—Pope.

As to people saying a few idle words about us, we must not mind that, any more than the old church-steeple minds the rooks cawing about it.—George Eliot.

Skill'd by a touch to deepen scandal's tints,
With all the high mendacity of hints,
While mingling truth with falsehood, sneers with smiles,
A thread of candor with a web of wiles.
—Byron.

News-hunters have great leisure, with little thought; much petty ambition to be considered intelligent, without any other pretension than being able to communicate what they have just learned.—Zimmermann.

I will not say it is not Christian to make beads of others' faults, and tell them over every day; I say it is infernal. If you want to know how the Devil feels, you do know, if you are such an one.—Beecher.

I take it as a matter not to be disputed, that if all knew what each said of the other, there would not be four friends in the world. This seems proved by the quarrels and disputes caused by the disclosures which are occasionally made.—Pascal.

Gossip is always a personal confession either of malice or imbecility, and the young should not only shun it, but by the most thorough culture relieve themselves from all temptation to indulge in it. It is a low, frivolous, and too often a dirty business. There are country neighborhoods in which it rages like a pest. Churches are split in pieces by it. Neighbors are made enemies by it for life. In many persons it degenerates into a chronic disease, which is practically incurable. Let the young cure it while they may.—J. G. Holland.

Government

Fortune and caprice govern the world.—Rochefoucauld.

As the government is, such will be the man.—Plato.

Government has been a fossil: it should be a plant.—Emerson.

Those who think must govern those who toil.—Goldsmith.

The end of government is the happiness of the people.—Macaulay.

The duties of government are paternal.—Gladstone.

States are great engines moving slowly.—Bacon.

The right divine of kings to govern wrong.—Pope.

Republics end with luxury: monarchies with poverty.—Montesquieu.

A hated government does not last long.—Seneca.

Influence is not government.—George Washington.

I am the state.—Attributed to Louis XIV.

Governments have their origin in the moral identity of men.—Emerson.

Our domestic affections are the most salutary basis of all good government.—Beaconsfield.

Resolv'd to ruin or to rule the state.—Dryden.

'Tis government that makes them seem divine.—Shakespeare.

Let them obey who know how to rule.—Shakespeare.

Ambassadors are the eye and ear of states.—Guicciardini.

For forms of government let fools contest;
Whate'er is best administer'd is best.
    —Pope.

The essence of a free government consists in an effectual control of rivalries.—John Adams.

The principal foundation of all states are good laws and good arms.—Machiavelli.

Whatever government is not a government of laws is a despotism, let it be called what it may.—Daniel Webster.

If the prince of a State love benevolence, he will have no opponent in all the empire.—Mencius.

All free governments are party governments.—Garfield.

Government is an art above the attainment of an ordinary genius.—South.

A wise man neither suffers himself to be governed, nor attempts to govern others.—La Bruyère.

All governments are, to a certain extent, a treaty with the Devil.—Jacobi.

All men would be masters of others, and no man is lord of himself.—Goethe.

All free governments are managed by the combined wisdom and folly of the people.—James A. Garfield.

If I wished to punish a province, I would have it governed by philosophers.—Frederick the Great.

The government will take the fairest of names, but the worst of realities—mob rule.—Polybius.

Government is a contrivance of human wisdom to provide for human wants.—Burke.

It is better for a city to be governed by a good man than by good laws.—Aristotle.

All your strength is in your union, All your danger is in discord.
—Longfellow.

The people's government, made for the people, made by the people, and answerable to the people.—Daniel Webster.

Which is the best government? That which teaches self-government. —Goethe.

To govern men, you must either excel them in their accomplishments, or despise them.—Beaconsfield.

The trappings of a monarchy would set up an ordinary commonwealth.—Sam'l Johnson.

Anticipate the difficult by managing the easy.—Lao-Tze.

Government, like dress, is the badge of lost innocence.—Thomas Paine.

Virtue alone is not sufficient for the exercise of government; laws alone carry themselves into practice.—Mencius.

Institutions may crumble and governments fall, but it is only that they may renew a better youth.—George Bancroft.

A conservative government is an organized hypocrisy.—Benj. Disraeli.

We are more heavily taxed by our idleness, pride and folly than we are **taxed by government.**—Franklin.

Ill can he rule the great that cannot reach the small.—Spenser.

A thousand years scarce serve to form a state;
An hour may lay it in the dust.—Byron.

For where's the state beneath the Firmament,
That doth excell the Bees for Government?
—Du Bartas.

Though the people support the government the government should not support the people.—Grover Cleveland.

I have considered the pension list of the republic a roll of honor.— Grover Cleveland.

Let men say, we be men of good government; being governed, as the sea is, by our noble and chaste mistress the moon, under whose countenance we steal.—Shakespeare.

Power is detested, and miserable is the life of him who wishes rather to be feared than to be loved.—Nepos.

It may pass for a maxim in State, that the administration cannot be placed in too few hands, nor the legislature in too many.—Swift.

Government arrogates to itself that it alone forms men. * * * Everybody knows that government never began anything. It is the whole world that thinks and governs.—Wendell Phillips.

Governments exist to protect the rights of minorities. The loved and the rich need no protection,—they have many friends and few enemies. —Wendell Phillips.

How, in one house,
Should many people, under two commands,
Hold amity? 'Tis hard; almost impossible.
—Shakespeare.

The deterioration of a government begins almost always by the decay of its principles.—Montesquieu.

A house divided against itself cannot stand. I believe this government cannot endure permanently half-slave and half-free.—Abraham Lincoln.

Oh, it were better to be a poor fisherman than to meddle with the government of men!—Danton.

The freedom of a government does not depend upon the quality of its laws, but upon the power that has the right to create them.—Thaddeus Stevens.

When a government is arrived to that degree of corruption as to be incapable of reforming itself, it would not lose much by being new moulded. —Montesquieu.

The aggregate happiness of society, which is best promoted by the practice of a virtuous policy, is, or ought to be, the end of all government.— George Washington.

All free governments, whatever their name, are in reality governments by public opinion; and it is on the quality of this public opinion that their prosperity depends.—Lowell.

All good government must begin at home. It is useless to make good laws for bad people; what is wanted is this, to subdue the tyranny of the human heart.—Hugh R. Haweis.

All government is an evil, but, of the two forms of that evil, democracy or monarchy, the sounder is monarchy; the more able to do its will, democracy.—B. R. Haydon.

The best government is not that which renders men the happiest, but that which renders the greatest number happy.—Duclos.

The proper function of a government is to make it easy for people to do good, and difficult for them to do evil.—Gladstone.

No government, any more than an individual, will long be respected without being truly respectable.—Madison.

Few consider how much we are indebted to government, because few can represent how wretched mankind would be without it.—Atterbury.

Men who prefer any load of infamy, however great, to any pressure of taxation, however light.—Sydney Smith.

And having looked to government for bread, on the very first scarcity they will turn and bite the hand that fed them.—Burke.

This shall be thy work: to impose conditions of peace, to spare the lowly and to overthrow the proud.—Virgil.

Nothing appears more surprising to those who consider human affairs with a philosophical eye, than the easiness with which the many are governed by the few.—Hume.

In a change of government, the poor seldom change anything except the name of their master.—Phædrus.

A government for protecting the coarser interests of the body, business and bread only, is but a carcass, and soon falls, by its own corruption, to decay.—A. Bronson Alcott.

Nothing will ruin the country if the people themselves will undertake its safety; and nothing can save it if they leave that safety in any hands but their own.—Daniel Webster.

The culminating point of administration is to know well how much power, great or small, we ought to use in all circumstances.—Montesquieu.

The government of man should be the monarchy of reason: it is too often the democracy of passions or the anarchy of humors.—Benjamin Whichcote.

Monarch, thou wishest to cover thyself with glory; be the first to submit to the laws of thy empire.—Bias,

Right is the royal ruler alone; and he who rules with least restraint comes nearest to empire.—Alcott.

Self-government by the whole people is the teleologic idea. The republican form of government is the noblest

*and the best, as it is the latest.—
Henry Ward Beecher.

A mercantile democracy may govern
long and widely; a mercantile aristocracy cannot stand.—Landor.

Government is the greatest combination for forces known to human society. It can command more men and
raise more money than any and all
other agencies combined.—David Dudley Field.

Society is well governed when the
people obey the magistrates, and the
magistrates the laws.—Solon.

There is no part of government
which cannot better suffer derange-
ment than the ballot. If you strike
the ballot with disease, it is heart
disease.—Henry Ward Beecher.

If any ask me what a free government is, I answer that, for any particular purpose, it is what the people
think so.—Burke.

Power exercised with violence has
seldom been of long duration, but temper and moderation generally produce
permanence in all things.—Seneca. .

All government, all exercise of
power, no matter in what form, which
is not based in love and directed by
knowledge, is a tyranny.—Mrs. Jameson.

Our government is built upon the
vote. But votes that are purchasable
are quicksands, and a government built
on them stands upon corruption and
revolution.—Henry Ward Beecher.

All government, indeed every human
benefit and enjoyment, every virtue,
every prudent act, is founded on compromise and barter.—Burke.

The surest way of governing, both
in a private family and a kingdom, is
for a husband and a prince sometimes
to drop their prerogative.—Hughes.

The very idea of the power and the
right of the people to establish govern-

ment presupposes the duty of every individual to obey the established government.—Washington.

The science of government is only a
science of combinations, of applica-
tions, and of exceptions, according to
times, places and circumstances.—
Rousseau.

No government can be free that does
not allow all iis citizens to participate
in the formation and execution of her
laws. There are degrees of tyranny;
but every other government is a despotism.—Thaddeus Stevens.

Every governmental institution has
been a standing testimony to the harmonic destiny of society, a standing
proof that the life of man is destined
for peace and amity, instead of disorder and contention.—Henry James.

A government founded on impartial
liberty, where all have a voice and a
vote, irrespective of color or of sex—
what is there to hinder such a government from standing firm.—Fred.
Douglass.

The history of governments through
the ages is a history red, nay, lurid.
Law represents the effort of men to
organize society; governments, the efforts of selfishness to overthrow liberty.—Henry Ward Beecher.

No man undertakes a trade he has
not learned, even the meanest; yet
every one thinks himself sufficiently
qualified for the hardest of all trades—
that of government.—Socrates.

The administration of government,
like a guardianship, ought to be directed to the good of those who confer, and
not of those who receive the trust.—
Cicero.

A republican government in a hundred points is weaker than an auto-
cratic government; but in this one
point it is the strongest that ever existed—it has educated a race of men
that are men.—Henry Ward Beecher.

In politics it is almost a triviality to
say that public opinion now rules the

world. The only power deserving the name is that of masses and of governments while they make themselves the organ of the tendencies and instincts of masses.—John Stuart Mill.

When Tarquin the Proud was asked what was the best mode of governing a conquered city, he replied only by beating down with his staff all the tallest poppies in his garden.—Livy.

The aggregate happiness of society, which is best promoted by the practice of a virtuous policy, is or ought to be the end of all government.—Washington.

In the government of men, a great deal may be done by severity, more by love, but most of all by clear discernment and impartial justice, which pays no respect to persons.—Goethe.

Government owes its birth to the necessity of preventing and repressing the injuries which the associated individuals had to fear from one another. —Abbé Raynal.

Society cannot exist unless a controlling power upon will and appetite be placed somewhere; and the less of it there is within, the more there must be without.—Burke.

When any of the four pillars of government are mainly shaken or weakened—which are religion, justice, counsel and treasure—men need to pray for fair weather.—Bacon.

What makes a governor justly despised is viciousness and ill morals. Virtue must tip the preacher's tongue and the ruler's sceptre with authority. —South.

A statesman, we are told, should follow public opinion. Doubtless, as a coachman follows his horses; having firm hold on the reins and guiding them.—Hare.

Hereditary right should be kept sacred, not from any inalienable right in a particular family, but to avoid the consequences that usually attend the ambition of competitors.—Swift.

If friends to a government forbear their assistance, they put it in the power of a few desperate men to ruin the welfare of those who are superior to them in strength and interest.—Addison.

Government mitigates the inequality of power, and makes an innocent man, though of the lowest rank, a match for the mightiest of his fellow-subjects.— Addison.

Not stones, nor wood, nor the art of artisans make a state; but where men are who know how to take care of themselves, these are cities and walls. —Alcæus.

It is a great error, in my opinion, to believe that a government is more firm or assured when it is supported by force, than when founded on affection. —Terence.

* * * The manners of women are the surest criterion by which to determine whether a republican government is practicable in a nation or not. —John Adams.

Government is a trust, and the officers of the government are trustees; and both the trust and the trustees are created for the benefit of the people.— Henry Clay.

In the early ages men ruled by strength; now they rule by brain, and so long as there is only one man in the world who can think and plan, he will stand head and shoulders above him who cannot.—Beecher.

For government, through high and low and lower,
Put into parts, doth keep in one consent,
Congreeing in a full and natural close,
Like music.   —Shakespeare.

The surest way to prevent seditions (if the times do bear it) is to take away the matter of them; for if there be fuel prepared it is hard to tell whence the spark shall come that shall set it on fire.—Bacon.

They that govern most make least noise. You see when they row in a barge, they that do drudgery work, slash, and puff, and sweat; but he that governs sits quietly at the stern, and scarce is seen to stir.—Selden.

In all government there must of necessity be both the law and the sword; laws without arms would give us not liberty but licentiousness, and arms without laws would produce not subjection but slavery.—Colton.

The moment you abate anything from the full rights of men each to govern himself, and suffer any artificial positive limitation upon those rights, from that moment the whole organization of government becomes a consideration of convenience.—Burke.

When we have run through all forms of government, without partiality to that we were born under, we are at a loss with which to side; they are all a compound of good and evil. It is therefore most reasonable and safe to value that of our own country above all others, and to submit to it.—La Bruyère.

The people of the United States very deliberately framed their government with the view of remaining the masters of it, and not of being mastered by it; and they are not yet willing to abdicate in favor of any, even the most audacious conspirator against their sovereignty.—John Bigelow.

Government is only a necessary evil, like other go-carts and crutches. Our need of it shows exactly how far we are still children. All governing overmuch kills the self-help and energy of the governed.—Wendell Phillips.

The constitution of England is not a paper constitution. It is an aggregate of institutions, many of them founded merely upon prescription, some of them fortified by muniments, but all of them the fruit and experience of an ancient and illustrious people.—Beaconsfield.

The government of a nation itself is usually found to be but the reflex of the individuals composing it. The government that is head of the people will be inevitably dragged down to their level, as the government that is behind them will in the long run be dragged up.—Samuel Smiles.

One of the most important, but one of the most difficult things to a powerful mind is to be its own master; a pond may lay quiet in a plain, but a lake wants mountains to compass and hold it in.—Addison.

A monarchy is like a man-of-war— bad shots between wind and water hurt it exceedingly; there is danger of capsizing. But democracy is a raft. You cannot easily overturn it. It is a wet place, but it is a pretty safe one.— Joseph Cook.

When any one person or body of men seize into their hands the power in the last resort, there is properly no longer a government, but what Aristotle and his followers call the abuse and corruption of one.—Swift.

A power has arisen up in the government greater than the people themselves, consisting of many and various and powerful interests, combined into one mass, and held together by the cohesive power of the vast surplus in the banks.—John C. Calhoun.

It seems to me a great truth that human things cannot stand on selfishness, mechanical utilities, economies and law courts; that if there be not a religious element in the relations of men, such relations are miserable, and doomed to ruin.—Carlyle.

Forms of government become established of themselves. They shape themselves, they are not created. We may give them strength and consistency, but we cannot call them into being. Let us rest assured that the form of government can never be a matter of choice: it is almost always a matter of necessity.—Joubert.

Freedom of men under government is to have a standing rule to live by, common to every one of that society, and made by the legislative power vested in it; a liberty to follow my own will in all things, when the rule prescribes not, and not to be subject to the inconstant, uncertain, unknown, arbitrary will of another man.—John Locke.

I look upon parliamentary government as the noblest government in the world, and certainly one most suited to England. But without the discipline of political connection, animated by the principle of private honor, I feel certain that a popular assembly would sink before the power or the corruption of a minister.—Beaconsfield.

Beneath a free government there is nothing but the intelligence of the people to keep the people's peace. Order must be preserved, not by a military police or regiments of horse-guards, but by the spontaneous concert of a well-informed population, resolved that the rights which have been rescued from despotism shall not be subverted by anarchy.—Edward Everett.

The wonder is not that the world is so easily governed, but that so small a number of persons will suffice for the purpose. There are dead weights in political and legislative bodies as in clocks, and hundreds answer as pulleys who would never do for politicians.—Simms.

Government began in tyranny and force, began in the feudalism of the soldier and bigotry of the priest; and the ideas of justice and humanity have been fighting their way, like a thunderstorm, against the organized selfishness of human nature.—Wendell Phillips.

Nothing is more deceptive or more dangerous than the pretence of a desire to simplify government. The simplest governments are despotisms; the next simplest, limited monarchies; but all republics, all governments of law, must impose numerous limitations and qualifications of authority, and give many positive and many qualified rights.—Daniel Webster.

Refined policy ever has been the parent of confusion, and ever will be so as long as the world endures. Plain good intention, which is as easily discovered at the first view as fraud is surely detected at last, is of no mean force in the government of mankind.—Burke.

Well, will anybody deny now that the government at Washington, as regards its own people, is the strongest government in the world at this hour? And for this simple reason, that it is based on the will, and the good will, of an instructed people.—John Bright.

It is among the evils, and perhaps not the smallest, of democratical governments, that the people must feel before they will see. When this happens they are roused to action. Hence it is that those kinds of government are so slow.—Washington.

There is no slight danger from general ignorance; and the only choice which Providence has graciously left to a vicious government is either to fall by the people, if they are suffered to become enlightened, or with them, if they are kept enslaved and ignorant.—Coleridge.

An established government has an infinite advantage by that very circumstance of its being established—the bulk of mankind being governed by authority, not reason, and never attributing authority to anything that has not the recommendation of antiquity.—Hume.

It is necessary for a Senator to be thoroughly acquainted with the constitution; and this is a knowledge of the most extensive nature; a matter of science, of diligence, of reflection, without which no Senator can possibly be fit for his office.—Cicero.

Of all the difficulties in a state, the temper of a true government most felicifies and perpetuates it; too sudden alterations distemper it. Had Nero tuned his kingdom as he did his harp, his harmony had been more honorable, and his reign more prosperous.—Quarles.

A government which takes in the consent of the greatest number of the people may justly be said to have the broadest bottom; and if it be terminate ed in the authority of one single person it may be said to have the narrowest top; and so makes the finest pyramid. —Sir Wm. Temple.

When my eyes shall be turned to behold, for the last time, the sun in heaven, may I not see him shining on the broken and dishonored fragments of a once glorious Union; on States dissevered, discordant, belligerent; on a land rent with civil feuds, or drenched, it may be, in fraternal blood!—Daniel Webster.

Each petty hand
Can steer a ship becalm'd; but he that will
Govern and carry her to her ends, must know
His tides, his currents, how to shift his sails;
What she will bear in foul, what in fair weathers;
Where her springs are, her leaks, and how to stop 'em;
What strands, what shelves, what rocks do threaten her.   —Ben Jonson.

And the first thing I would do in my government, I would have nobody to control me, I would be absolute; and who but I: now, he that is absolute, can do what he likes; he that can do what he likes, can take his pleasure; he that can take his pleasure, can be content; and he that can be content has no more to desire; so the matter's over.—Cervantes.

Who's in or out, who moves this grand machine,
Nor stirs my curiosity nor spleen.
Secrets of state no more I wish to know
Than secret movements of a puppet show:
Let but the puppets move, I've my desire,
Unseen the hand which guides the master wire.   —Churchill.

There is what I call the American idea. * * * This idea demands, as the proximate organization thereof, a democracy—that is, a government of all the people, by all the people, for all the people; of course, a government of the principles of eternal justice, the unchanging law of God; for shortness' sake I will call it the idea of Freedom. —Theodore Parker.

We must judge of a form of government by its general tendency, not by happy accidents. Every form of gov-

ernment has its happy accidents. Despotism has its happy accidents. Yet we are not disposed to abolish all constitutional checks, to place an absolute master over us, and to take our chances whether he may be a Caligula or a Marcus Aurelius.—Macaulay.

But I say to you, and to our whole country, and to all the crowned heads and aristocratic powers and feudal systems that exist, that it is to self-government—the great principle of popular representation and administration —the system that lets in all to participate in the counsels that are to assign the good or evil to all—that we may owe what we are and what we hope to be.—Daniel Webster.

The schoolboy whips his taxed top, the beardless youth manages his taxed horse, with a taxed bridle, on a taxed road; and the dying Englishman, pouring his medicine, which has paid seven per cent., flings himself back on his chintz bed, which has paid twenty-two per cent., and expires in the arms of an apothecary who has paid a license of a hundred pounds for the privilege of putting him to death.—Sydney Smith.

Our government has been tried in peace, and it has been tried in war, and has proved itself fit for both. It has been assailed from without, and it has successfully resisted the shock; it has been disturbed within, and it has effectually quieted the disturbance. It can stand trial, it can stand assail, it can stand adversity, it can stand everything but the marring of its own beauty and the weakening of its own strength. It can stand everything but the effects of our own rashness and our own folly. It can stand everything but disorganization, disunion and nullification.—Daniel Webster.

There be three sorts of government —monarchical, aristocratical, democratical; and they are apt to fall three several ways into ruin—the first, by tyranny; the second, by ambition; the last, by tumults. A commonwealth grounded upon any one of these is not of long continuance; but, wisely mingled, each guards the other and makes that government exact.—Quarles.

Grace

Grace is the outcome of inward harmony.—Marie Ebner-Eschenbach.

She moves a goddess, and she looks a queen.—Pope.

Beauty and grace command the world.—Park Benjamin.

Beauty loses its relish; the graces never.—Henry Horne.

Graceful to sight and elegant to thought.—Young.

And snatch a grace beyond the reach of art.—Pope.

Natural graces, that extinguish art. —Shakespeare.

Every natural action is graceful.— Emerson.

Her step is music, and her voice is song.—Bailey.

Grace is to the body what good sense is to the mind.—La Rochefoucauld.

Let grace and goodness be the principle loadstone of thy affections.—Dryden.

Grace has been defined, the outward expression of the inward harmony of the soul.—Hazlitt.

Every natural movement is graceful. Did you ever watch a kitten at play?— Anna Cora Mowatt.

The mother grace of all the graces is Christian good-will.—Beecher.

That caressing and exquisite grace—never bold,
Ever present—which just a few women possess.   —Owen Meredith.

There is no such way to attain to greater measures of grace, as for a man to live up to that little grace he has.— Thomas Brooks.

Grace is the beauty of form under the influence of freedom.—Schiller.

He does it with a better grace, but I do it more natural.—Shakespeare.

See where she comes, apparell'd like the spring;
Graces her subjects.   —Shakespeare.

When once our grace we have forgot,
Nothing goes right.   —Shakespeare.

There's language in her eye, her cheek, her lip,
Nay, her foot speaks.   —Shakespeare.

Take time enough—all other graces
Will soon fill up their proper places.
                —Byron.

Grace imitates modesty, as politeness imitates kindness.—Joubert.

A pleasing figure is a perpetual letter of recommendation.—Bacon.

Beauty, devoid of grace, is a mere hook without the bait.—Talleyrand.

God appoints our graces to be nurses to other men's weaknesses.—Beecher.

To some kind of men their graces serve them but as enemies.—Shakespeare.

Whatever is graceful is virtuous, and whatever is virtuous is graceful.— Cicero.

That word "grace" in an ungracious mouth is but profane.—Shakespeare.

In effective womanly beauty form is more than face, and manner more than either.—Thackeray.

Till all grace be in one woman, one woman shall not come in my grace.— Shakespeare.

Grace was in all her steps, heaven in her eye, in every gesture dignity and love.—Milton.

As prodigal of all dear grace as Nature was in making graces dear.— Shakespeare.

Her walk was like no mortal thing, but shaped after an angel's.—Petrarch,

The light of love, the purity of grace, the mind, the music, breathing in her face.—Byron.

With countenance demure, and modest grace.—Spenser.

Grace comes often clad in the dusky robe of desolation.—Beaumont.

A beautiful form is the finest of the fine arts.—Emerson.

The loveliest hair is nothing, if the wearer is incapable of a grace.—Leigh Hunt.

God giveth true grace to but a chosen few, however many aspire to it. —Dewey.

The king-becoming graces—devotion, patience, courage, fortitude.—Shakespeare.

Oh, mickle is the powerful grace that lies in plants, herbs, stones and their qualities!—Shakespeare.

It is the very nature of grace to make a man strive to be most eminent in that particular grace which is most opposed to his bosom sin.—Thomas Brooks.

Strength is natural, but grace is the growth of habit. This charming quality requires practice if it is to become lasting.—Joubert.

The grace will carry us, if we do not willfully betray our succors, victoriously through all difficulties.—Henry Hammond.

The grace of the spirit comes only from heaven, and lights up the whole bodily presence.—Spurgeon.

Grace is in garments, in movements, in manners; beauty in the nude, and in forms. This is true of bodies; but when we speak of feelings, beauty is in their spirituality, and grace in their moderation.—Joubert.

There are true graces, which, as Homer feigns, are linked and tied hand in hand, because it is by their influence that human hearts are so firmly united to each other.—Robert Burton.

The most divine light only shineth on those minds which are purged from all worldly dross and human uncleanliness.—Sir Walter Raleigh.

All actions and attitudes of children are graceful because they are the luxuriant and immediate offspring of the moment—divested of affectation and free from all pretence.—Fuseli.

An inborn grace that nothing lacked
Of culture or appliance—
The warmth of genial courtesy,
The calm of self-reliance.
—Whittier.

'Cause grace and virtue are within
Prohibited degrees of kin;
And therefore no true saint allows
They should be suffer'd to espouse.
—Butler.

She was the pride of her familiar sphere—the daily joy of all who on her gracefulness might gaze, and in the light and music of her way have a companion's portion.—Willis.

Let grace and goodness be the principal loadstone of thy affections. For love, which hath ends, will have an end; whereas that which is founded on true virtue will always continue.— Dryden.

True grace is natural, not artificial, because, however strenuously you strive to gain it, when it is gained it never gives the impression of effort or straining for effect.—F. D. Huntington.

Every man of any education would rather be called a rascal than accused of deficiency in the graces.—Dr. Johnson.

Every degree of recession from the state of grace Christ first put us in is a recession from our hopes.—Jeremy Taylor.

Her grace of motion and of look, the smooth and swimming majesty of step and tread, the symmetry of form and feature, set the soul afloat, even like delicious airs of flute and harp.—Milman.

The feminine graces of Madame de Sévigné's genius are exquisitely charming; but the philosophy and eloquence of Madame de Staël are above the distinction of sex.—Sir J. Mackintosh.

> For several virtues
> Have I lik'd several women; never any
> With so full soul, but some defect in her
> Did quarrel with the noblest grace she ow'd,
> And put it to the foil. —Shakespeare.

Riches may enable us to confer favors; but to confer them with propriety and with grace requires a something that riches cannot give. Even trifles may be so bestowed as to cease to be trifles.—Colton.

Gracefulness cannot subsist without ease; delicacy is not debility; nor must a woman be sick in order to please. Infirmity and sickness may excite our pity, but desire and pleasure require the bloom and vigor of health.—Rousseau.

> Graceful, when it pleased him, smooth and still
> As the mute swan that floats adown the stream,
> And on the waters of th' unruffled lake,
> Anchors her quiet beauty.—Wordsworth.

Grace is a quality different from beauty, though nearly allied to it, which is never observed without affecting us with emotions of peculiar delight, and which it is, perhaps, the first object of the arts of sculpture and painting to study and to present.—Sir A. Alison.

Grace can never properly be said to exist without beauty; for it is only in the elegant proportions of beautiful forms that can be found that harmonious variety of line and motion which is the essence and charm of grace.—Winckelmann.

It is graceful in a man to think and to speak with propriety, to act with deliberation, and in every occurrence of life to find out and persevere in the truth. On the other hand, to be imposed upon, to mistake, to falter, and to be deceived, is as ungraceful as to rave or to be insane.—Cicero.

Know you not, master, to some kind of men their graces serve them but as enemies? No more do yours; your virtues, gentle master, are sanctified and holy traitors to you. Oh, what a world is this, when what is comely envenoms him that bears it!—Shakespeare.

Virtue, without the graces, is like a rich diamond unpolished—it hardly looks better than a common pebble; but when the hand of the master rubs off the roughness, and forms the sides into a thousand brilliant surfaces, it is then that we acknowledge its worth, admire its beauty, and long to wear it in our bosoms.—Jane Porter.

Grace in women has more effect than beauty. We sometimes see a certain fine self-possession, an habitual voluptuousness of character, which reposes on its own sensations, and derives pleasure from all around it, that is more irresistible than any other attraction. There is an air of languid enjoyment in such persons, "in their eyes, in their arms, and their hands, and their face," which robs us of ourselves, and draws us by a secret sympathy towards them.—Hazlitt.

Grace is in a great measure a natural gift; elegance implies cultivation, or something of more artificial character. A rustic, uneducated girl may be graceful, but an elegant woman must be accomplished and well trained. It is the same with things as with persons; we talk of a graceful tree, but of an elegant house or other building. Animals may be graceful, but they cannot be elegant. The movements of a kitten or a young fawn are full of grace; but to call them "elegant" animals would be absurd.—Whately.

Grammar

Grammar, which knows how to lord it over kings, and with high hand makes them obey its laws.—Molière.

Grandeur

Grandeur and beauty are so very opposite that you often diminish the one as you increase the other. Vanity is most akin to the latter, simplicity to the former.—Shenstone.

Grant's Birthday

I desire the good-will of all, whether hitherto my friends or not.—Gen. Grant's Easter Message, during his sickness, 1885.

I propose to fight it out on this line if it takes all summer.—Gen. Grant, in the Wilderness, May 11, 1864.

The government has educated me for the army. What I am, I owe to my country. I have served her through one war, and, live or die, will serve her through this.—Gen. Grant, at the outbreak of the Civil War, 1861.

No theory of my own will ever stand in the way of my executing, in good faith, any order I may receive from those in authority over me.—Gen. Grant to Secretary Chase, 1863.

Although a soldier by education and profession, I have never felt any sort of fondness for war, and I have never advocated it, except as a means of peace.—Gen. Grant.

There have been many Presidents of the United States and the roll will be indefinitely extended. We have had a number of brilliant soldiers, but only one great general.—Chauncey M. Depew.

His love of justice was equaled only by his delight in compassion, and neither was sacrificed to the other. His self-advancement was subordinated to the public good. His integrity was never questioned; his honesty was above suspicion; his private life and public career were at once reputable to himself and honorable to his country. —Rev. J. P. Newman.

His soul was the home of hope, sustained and cheered by the certainties of his mind and the power of his faith. He was the mathematical genius of a great general, rather than of a great soldier. By this endowment he proved himself equal to the unexpected, and that with the precision of a seer.—Rev. J. P. Newman.

Grant was not a creator of circumstances; had not opportunities sought him, the world would have been ignorant of the gifts God stored in him.—Rev. H. W. Bolton.

The free school is the promoter of that intelligence which is to preserve us as a free nation. If we are to have another contest in the near future of our national existence, I predict that the dividing line will not be Mason and Dixon's, but between patriotism and intelligence on one side, and superstition, ambition, and ignorance on the other.—Gen. Grant.

His tour around the world exhibited another phase of his character—a simplicity and modesty as extraordinary as it is unparalleled. Received by kings and emperors with all the honors of a king, fêted and banqueted by princes and lords, and eulogized by the most distinguished men of the world, he exhibited no pride, no elation, receiving ovations that might well have turned the head of the strongest man with manners and bearing as simple and unostentatious as when a farmer in the west.—J. T. Headley.

The preparations of this wonderful man rarely excited applause of the people, because the workings of his masterful mind were hidden beneath the silence of his lips; but when the supreme moment came, there came also an intellectual elevation, an uplifting of the whole being, a transformation of the silent, thoughtful general, which surprised his foes and astonished his friends. He culminated at the crisis; he was at his best when most needed; he responded in an emergency.—Rev. J. P. Newman.

Out of his great character came the purest motives, as effect follows cause. He abandoned himself to his life mission with the hope of no other reward than the consciousness of duty done. Duty to his conscience, his country, and his God was his standard of successful manhood. With him, true greatness was that in great actions our only care should be to perform well our part and let glory follow virtue. He placed his fame in the service of the state. He was never tempted by false glory. He never acted for effect. He acted because he could not help it. His action was spontaneous. Ambition could not corrupt his patriotism; calumnies could not lessen it.—Rev. J. P. Newman.

As a great soldier leading our armies to victory, he first attracts the eyes of the world. His courage, though lofty and steadfast, was not of that fiery, chivalric kind which dazzles the public. He was not borne up in action by the enthusiasm and pride of the warrior; but apparently unconscious of danger, made battle a business which was to be performed with a clear head and steady nerves. His coolness in deadly peril was wonderful. What was once said of Marshal Ney applies forcibly to him; "In battle he could literally shut up his mind to the one object he had in view." The overthrow of the enemy absorbed every thought within him, and he had none to give to danger or death.—J. T. Headley.

But the supreme will, despotic authority, and the relentless pursuit of an enemy indispensable in a great commander, disappeared when he laid down the sword and became chief magistrate of the union. Not a trace of the military man remained, and his whole thoughts were on peace and the supremacy of law. To the foeman of former days he held out both hands in token of peace, and amid the clamors of excited men and the demands of vindictive passion, he remained unmoved, and breathed the very spirit of kindness and generosity, and exhibited a patriotism that put to shame the partisan zeal of those who constituted themselves his advisers.—J. T. Headley.

Our unconquerable hero has gone forward, until at last he has been called to mingle in the Court of the Most High, and when the roll has been called for the last time, when the last reveille has been sounded, when the last battle has been fought, the honored name of Ulysses S. Grant will be found on the unchanging pages of history as one whom God raised up for a special work; and history will show how nobly was that work done, how fearlessly were our armies led to victory by the greatest military leader of modern times. A leader who battled not for the advancement of his own interests—not that he might be at the head of an empire, but prompted by his love of right, he fought that the millions in bondage should be slaves no more, and for the triumph of right and the preservation of the union.—Rev. H. W. Bolton.

A brilliant soldier, a calm and just ruler, a true patriot, an humble Christian, he yielded up his spirit without a sigh into the hands of his Maker. That character will shine brighter with time, and his memory grow dearer with each successive generation.—J. T. Headley.

Gratitude

Thankfulness is the tune of angels —Spenser.

Gratitude is the memory of the heart.—Massieu.

The still small voice of gratitude.—Gray.

If I only have will to be grateful, I am so.—Seneca.

Th' unwilling gratitude of base mankind!—Pope.

Is no return due from a grateful breast?—Dryden.

Thanks, the exchequer of the poor. —Shakespeare.

Gratitude is a species of justice.—Johnson.

Gratitude is expensive.—Gibbon.

Gratitude is a soil on which joy thrives.—Auerbach.

Small service is true service while it lasts.—Wordsworth.

The debt immense of endless gratitude.—Milton.

To receive honestly is the best thanks for a good thing.—George Mac-Donald.

No metaphysician ever felt the deficiency of language so much as the grateful.—Colton.

O Lord, that lends me life, lend me a heart replete with thankfulness.—Shakespeare.

A single grateful thought towards heaven is the most perfect prayer.—Lessing.

The gratitude of place-expectants is a lively sense of future favors.—Sir Robert Walpole.

It is a species of agreeable servitude, to be under an obligation to those we esteem.—Queen Christina.

Beggar that I am, I am even poor in thanks, but I thank you.—Shakespeare.

Gratitude is a duty none can be excused from, because it is always at our own disposal.—Charron.

He enjoys much who is thankful for little. A grateful mind is a great mind.—Secker.

A grateful mind
By owing owes not, but still pays, at once
Indebted and discharg'd. —Milton.

The heaviest debt is that of gratitude,
When 'tis not in our power to repay it.
—Dr. Thomas Franklin.

Thanks are justly due for things got without purchase.—Ovid.

We seldom find people ungrateful so long as we are in a condition to render them service.—Rochefoucauld.

Gratitude is a duty which ought to be paid, but which none have a right to expect.—Rousseau.

Ingratitude calls forth reproaches as gratitude brings renewed kindnesses. —Mme. de Sévigné.

The gratitude of most men is but a secret desire of receiving greater benefits.—La Rochefoucauld.

It is the will to be grateful which constitutes gratitude.—Joseph Cook.

Gratitude is the fruit of great cultivation; you do not find it among gross people.—Dr. Johnson.

Next to ingratitude, the most painful thing to bear is gratitude.—Henry Ward Beecher.

A thankful man owes a courtesy ever; the unthankful but when he needs it.—Ben Jonson.

Every acknowledgment of gratitude is a circumstance of humiliation.—Goldsmith.

My soul, o'erfraught with gratitude, rejects the aid of language. Lord, behold my heart.—Hannah More.

Thou that hast given so much to me, give one thing more—a grateful heart.—George Herbert.

What can I pay thee for this noble usage but grateful praise? So heaven itself is paid.—Rowe.

A thankful heart is not only the greatest virtue, but the parent of all the other virtues.—Cicero.

The feeling of gratitude has all the ardor of a passion in noble hearts.—Achilles Poincelot.

It is not best to refine gratitude; it evaporates in the process of subtilization.—Nicole.

He who receives a good turn should never forget it; he who does one should never remember it.—Charron.

So long as we stand in need of a benefit, there is nothing dearer to us; nor anything cheaper when we have received it.—L'Estrange.

Justice is often pale and melancholy; but Gratitude, her daughter, is constantly in the flow of spirits and the bloom of loveliness.—Landor.

Gratitude is the fairest blossom which springs from the soul; and the heart of man knoweth none more fragrant.—Hosea Ballou.

Gratitude is a nice touch of beauty added last of all to the countenance, giving a classic beauty, an angelic loveliness, to the character.—Theodore Parker.

Indeed, you thanked me; but a nobler gratitude rose in her soul, for from that hour she loved me.—Otway.

He that has nature in him must be grateful; it is the Creator's primary great law, that links the chain of beings to each other.—Madden.

The grateful person, being still the most severe exactor of himself, not only confesses, but proclaims his debt. —South.

Gratitude is the virtue most deified and most deserted. It is the ornament of rhetoric and the libel of practical life.—J. W. Forney.

It is a dangerous experiment to call in gratitude as an ally to love. Love is a debt which inclination always pays, obligation never.—Pascal.

Those who make us happy are always thankful to us for being so. Their gratitude is the reward of their own benefits.—Madame Swetchine.

O call not to my mind what you have done! It sets a debt of that account before me, which shows me poor and bankrupt even in hopes!—Congreve.

There is a selfishness even in gratitude, when it is too profuse; to be over-thankful for one favor is in effect to lay out for another.—Cumberland.

From David learn to give thanks in everything. Every furrow in the book of Psalms is sown with seeds of thanksgiving.—Jeremy Taylor.

If gratitude is due from children to their earthly parents, how much more is the gratitude of the great family of man due to our Father in heaven!—Hosea Ballou.

The reason for misreckoning in expected returns of gratitude is that the pride of the giver and receiver can never agree about the value of the obligation.—Rochefoucauld.

There is as much greatness of mind in the owning of a good turn as in the doing of it; and we must no more force a requital out of season than be wanting in it.—Seneca.

He who has a soul wholly devoid of gratitude should set his soul to learn of his body; for all the parts of that minister to one another.—South.

What I have done is worthy of nothing but silence and forgetfulness, but what God has done for me is worthy of everlasting and thankful memory.—Bishop Hall.

Look over the whole creation, and you shall see that the band, or cement, that holds together all the parts of this great and glorious fabric is gratitude.—South.

There is not a more pleasing exercise of the mind than gratitude. It is accompanied with such an inward satisfaction that the duty is sufficiently rewarded by the performance.—Addison.

There are minds so impatient of inferiority that their gratitude is a species of revenge; and they return benefits, not because recompense is a pleasure, but because obligation is a pain.—Johnson.

Wherever I find a great deal of gratitude in a poor man I take it for granted there would be as much generosity if he were a rich man.—Pope.

God is pleased with no music below so much as the thanksgiving songs of relieved widows and supported orphans; of rejoicing, comforted, and thankful persons.—Jeremy Taylor.

Gratitude is a virtue which, according to the general apprehension of mankind, approaches more nearly than almost any other social virtue to justice.—Dr. Parr.

The law of the pleasure in having done anything for another is, that the one almost immediately forgets having given, and the other remembers eternally having received.—Seneca.

Gratitude is like the good faith of traders—it maintains commerce; and we often pay, not because it is just to discharge our debts, but that we may more readily find people to trust us.—Rochefoucauld.

Almost everyone takes pleasure in repaying trifling obligations, very many feel gratitude for those that are moderate; but there is scarcely anyone who is not ungrateful for those that are weighty.—Rochefoucauld.

Epicurus says "gratitude is a virtue that has commonly profit annexed to it." And where is the virtue, say I, that has not? But still the virtue is to be valued for itself, and not for the profit that attends it.—Seneca.

I thank my Heavenly Father for every manifestation of human love, I thank Him for all experiences, be they sweet or bitter, which help me to forgive all things, and to enfold the whole world with a blessing.—Mrs. L. M. Child.

I've heard of hearts unkind, kind deeds
  With coldness still returning;
Alas! the gratitude of men
  Hath often left me mourning.
      —Wordsworth.

Do not let the empty cup be your first teacher of the blessings you had when it was full. Do not let a hard place here and there in the bed destroy your rest. Seek, as a plain duty, to cultivate a buoyant, joyous

sense of the crowded kindnesses of God in your daily life.—Alexander Maclaren.

We can set our deeds to the music of a grateful heart, and seek to round our lives into a hymn—the melody of which will be recognized by all who come in contact with us, and the power of which shall not be evanescent, like the voice of the singer, but perennial, like the music of the spheres.—Wm. M. Taylor.

Every acknowledgment of gratitude is a circumstance of humiliation; and some are found to submit to frequent mortifications of this kind, proclaiming what obligations they owe, merely because they think it in some measure cancels the debt.—Goldsmith.

When gratitude o'erflows the swelling heart, and breathes in free and uncorrupted praise for benefits received, propitious heaven takes such acknowledgment as fragrant incense, and doubles all its blessings.—Lillo.

It is a very high mind to which gratitude is not a painful sensation. If you wish to please, you will find it wiser to receive, solicit even, favors, than accord them; for the vanity of the obligor is always flattered, that of the obligee rarely.—Bulwer-Lytton.

Now it was well said, whoever said it, "That he who hath the loan of money has not repaid it, and he who has repaid has not the loan; but he who has acknowledged a kindness has it still, and he who has a feeling of it has requited it."—Cicero.

Among the many acts of gratitude we owe to God, it may be accounted one to study and contemplate the perfections and beauties of His work of creation. Every new discovery must necessarily raise in us a fresh sense of the greatness, wisdom, and power of God.—Jonathan Edwards.

How grateful are we—how touched a frank and generous heart is for a kind word extended to us in our pain! The pressure of a tender hand nerves a man for an operation, and cheers him for the dreadful interview with the surgeon.—Thackeray.

As gratitude is a necessary and a glorious, so also is it an obvious, a cheap, and an easy virtue—so obvious that wherever there is life there is place for it, so cheap that the covetous man may be grateful without expense, and so easy that the sluggard may be so likewise without labor.—Seneca.

As flowers carry dewdrops, trembling on the edges of the petals, and ready to fall at the first waft of wind or brush of bird, so the heart should carry its beaded words of thanksgiving; and at the first breath of heavenly flavor, let down the shower, perfumed with the heart's gratitude.—Beecher.

Thus love is the most easy and agreeable, and gratitude the most humiliating, affection of the mind. We never reflect on the man we love without exulting in our choice, while he who has bound us to him by benefits alone rises to our ideas as a person to whom we have in some measure forfeited our freedom.—Goldsmith.

If gratitude, when exerted towards another, naturally produces a very pleasing sensation in the mind of a grateful man, it exalts the soul into rapture when it is employed on this great object of gratitude to the beneficent Being who has given us everything we already possess, and from whom we expect everything we yet hope for.—Addison.

Let but the commons hear this testament—
Which, pardon me, I do not mean to read—
And they would go and kiss dead Cæsar's wounds
And dip their napkins in his sacred blood,
Yea, beg a hair of him for memory,
And, dying, mention it within their wills,
Bequeathing it as a rich legacy
Unto their issue.   —Shakespeare.

Did you ever think of the reason why the Psalms of David have come, like winged angels, down across all the realms and ages—why they make the key-note of grateful piety in every Christian's soul, wherever he lives? Why? Because they are so full of gratitude. "Oh, that men would praise the Lord for His goodness and for His wonderful works to the children of men!"—A. A. Willets.

Grave

Dark lattice! letting in eternal day!
—Young.

The cradle of transformation.—Mazzini.

The lone couch of his everlasting sleep.—Shelley.

The temple of silence and reconciliation.—Macaulay.

The grave where even the great find rest.—Pope.

Gilded tombs do worms infold.—Shakespeare.

Hark! from the tombs a doleful sound.—Watts.

To that dark inn, the Grave!—Scott.

Never the grave gives back what it has won!—Schiller.

Gravestones tell truth scarce forty years.—Sir Thomas Browne.

Lie lightly on my ashes, gentle earth!—Beaumont and Fletcher.

My heart is its own grave!—Miss L. E. Landon.

How populous, how vital is the grave!—Young.

The grave has a door on its inner side.—Alexander Maclaren.

Who's a prince or beggar in the grave?—Otway.

Death ends our woes, and the kind grave shuts up the mournful scene.—Dryden.

The reconciling grave.—Southern.

Let's talk of graves, of worms, and epitaphs.—Shakespeare.

Grass grows at last above all graves. —Julia C. R. Dorr.

The graves of those we have loved and lost distress and console us.—Arsène Houssaye.

Where blended lie the oppressor and the oppressed.—Pope.

And so sepulchred in such pomp dost lie;
That kings for such a tomb would wish to
die. 	—Milton.

They bore him barefac'd on the bier;
* 	* 	* 	* 	* 	*
And in his grave rain'd many a tear.
	—Shakespeare.

Graves they say are warmed by glory;
Foolish words and empty story.
	—Heine.

	Perhaps the early grave
Which men weep over may be meant to
save. 	—Byron.

Our father's dust is left alone
And silent under other snows.
	—Tennyson.

Kings have no such couch as thine,
As the green that folds thy grave.
	—Tennyson.

Each in his narrow cell forever laid, the rude forefathers of the hamlet sleep.—Gray.

A grave, wherever found, preaches a short and pithy sermon to the soul. —Hawthorne.

That unfathomed, boundless sea, the silent grave!—Longfellow.

How peaceful and how powerful is the grave!—Byron.

Earth's highest station ends in— Here he lies.—Young.

The earth opens impartially her bosom to receive the beggar and the prince.—Horace.

The grave is a common treasury, to which we must all be taken.—Burke.

He spake well who said that graves are the footprints of angels.—Longfellow.

We must be patient; but I cannot choose but weep, to think they should lay him i' the cold ground.—Shakespeare.

Tombs are the clothes of the dead; a grave is but a plain suit, and a rich monument is one embroidered.—Thomas Fuller.

I would rather sleep in the southern corner of a little country churchyard than in the tomb of the Capulets. —Burke.

Lay her i' the earth; and from her fair and unpolluted flesh may violets spring.—Shakespeare.

Death lies on her like an untimely frost upon the sweetest flower of all the field.—Shakespeare.

All that tread the globe are but a handful to the tribes that slumber in its bosom.—Bryant.

This is the field and acre of our God; this is the place where human harvests grow.—Longfellow.

The grave, where sets the orb of being,
	sets
To rise, ascend, and culminate above
Eternity's horizon evermore.
	—Abraham Coles.

	The sepulchre,
Wherein we saw thee quietly inurn'd,
Hath op'd his ponderous and marble jaws.
	—Shakespeare.

Let's choose executors and talk of wills:
And yet not so, for what can we bequeath
Save our deposed bodies to the ground?
	—Shakespeare.

Fond fool! six feet shall serve for all thy store, and he that cares for most shall find no more.—Bishop Hall.

Oh, how a small portion of earth will hold us when we are dead, who ambitiously seek after the whole world while we are living!—Philip, King of Macedon.

If thou hast no inferiors, have patience awhile, and thou shalt have no superiors. The grave requires no marshal.—Quarles.

O heart, and mind, and thoughts! what thing do you
Hope to inherit in the grave below?
—Shelley.

From its peaceful bosom spring none but fond regrets and tender recollections.—Washington Irving.

The reconciling grave swallows distinction first, that made us foes; there all lie down in peace together.—Southern.

We go to the grave of a friend saying, "A man is dead;" but angels throng about him, saying, "A man is born."—Beecher.

An angel's arm can't snatch me from the grave—legions of angels can't confine me there!—Young.

The grave —'dread thing! — men shiver when thou art named; Nature, appalled, shakes off her wonted firmness.—Blair.

However bright the comedy before, the last act is always stained with blood. The earth is laid upon our head, and there it lies forever.—Pascal.

The earth doth not cover our beloved, but heaven hath received him; let us tarry for awhile, and we shall be in his company.—St. Basil.

One destin'd period men in common have,
The great, the base, the coward, and the brave,
All food alike for worms, companions in the grave. —Lansdowne.

Who can look down upon the grave of an enemy, and not feel a compunctious throb that he should have warred with the poor handful of dust that lies mouldering before him?—Washington Irving.

That gloomy outside, like a rusty chest, contains the shining treasures of a soul resolved and brave.—Dryden.

The grave is a very small hillock, but we can see farther from it, when standing on it, than from the highest mountain in all the world.—A. Tholuck.

Without settled principle and practical virtue, life is a desert; without Christian piety, the contemplation of the grave is terrible.—Sir William Knighton.

It is a port where the storms of life never beat, and the forms that have been tossed on its chafing waves lie quiet forevermore.—Chapin.

Under ground
Precedency's a jest; vassal and lord,
Grossly familiar, side by side consume.
—Blair.

Sustained and soothed by an unfaltering trust, approach thy grave like one that wraps the drapery of his couch about him, and lies down to pleasant dreams.—Bryant.

There is a calm for those who weep,
A rest for weary pilgrims found,
They softly lie and sweetly sleep
Low in the ground. —Montgomery.

Then to the grave I turned me to see what therein lay;
'Twas the garment of the Christian, worn out and thrown away.
—Krummacher.

The grave is heaven's golden gate,
And rich and poor around it wait;
O Shepherdess of England's fold,
Behold this gate of pearl and gold!
—William Blake.

But the grandsire's chair is empty,
The cottage is dark and still;
There's a nameless grave on the battlefield,
And a new one under the hill.
—Wm. Winter.

Oh! let not tears embalm my tomb,
None but the dews by twilight given!
Oh! let not sighs disturb the gloom,
None but the whispering winds of heaven.
—Moore.

The grave is a crucible where memory is purified; we only remember a dead friend by those qualities which make him regretted.—J. Petit-Senn.

The grave is, I suspect, the sole commonwealth which attains that dead flat of social equality that life in its every principle so heartily abhors.—Bulwer-Lytton.

As a tract of country narrowed in the distance expands itself when we approach, thus the way to our near grave appears to us as long as it did formerly when we were far off.—Richter.

The disciples found angels at the grave of Him they loved; and we should always find them too, but that our eyes are too full of tears for seeing.—Beecher.

Here may thy storme-bett vessell safely ryde;
This is the port of rest from troublous toyle,
The worlde's sweet inn from paine and wearisome turmoyle. —Spenser.

Men cannot benefit those that are with them as they can benefit those that come after them; and of all the pulpits from which human voice is ever sent forth, there is none from which it reaches so far as from the grave.—Ruskin.

Graves, the dashes in the punctuation of our lives. To the Christian they are but the place at which he gathers breath for a nobler sentence. To Christ, the grave was but the hyphen between man and God, for He was God-man.—Duffield.

The most magnificent and costly dome,
Is but an upper chamber to a tomb;
No spot on earth but has supplied a grave,
And human skulls the spacious ocean pave.
—Young.

Art is long, and Time is fleeting,
And our hearts, though stout and brave,
Still, like muffled drums, are beating
Funeral marches to the grave.
—Longfellow.

We adorn graves with flowers and redolent plants, just emblems of the life of man, which has been compared in the Holy Scriptures to those fading beauties whose roots, being buried in dishonor, rise again in glory.—Evelyn.

There the wicked cease from troubling; and there the weary be at rest. There the prisoners rest together; they hear not the voice of the oppressor. The small and great are there; and the servant is free from his master.—Bible.

Yet shall thy grave with rising flow'rs be dressed,
And the green turf lie lightly on thy breast;
There shall the morn her earliest tears bestow,
There the first roses of the year shall blow.
—Pope.

The grave is a sacred workshop of nature! a chamber for the figure of the body; death and life dwell here together as man and wife. They are one body, they are in union; God has joined them together, and what God hath joined together let no man put asunder.—Hippel.

There is a voice from the tomb sweeter than song. There is a remembrance of the dead to which we turn even from the charms of the living. Oh, the grave! the grave! It buries every error, covers every defect, extinguishes every resentment. From its peaceful bosom spring none but fond regrets and tender recollections.—Washington Irving.

Our lives are rivers gliding free
To that unfathom'd, boundless sea,
The silent grave!
Thither all earthly pomp and boast
Roll, to be swallow'd up and lost
In one dark wave. —Longfellow.

Here the o'erloaded slave flings down his burden
From his gall'd shoulders; and, when the cruel tyrant,
With all his guards and tools of power about him,
Is meditating new, unheard-of hardships,
Mocks his short arm, and, quick as thought, escapes
Where tyrants vex not, and the weary rest. —Blair.

For ages the world has been waiting and watching; millions, with broken hearts, have hovered around the yawning abyss; but no echo has come back from the engulfing gloom—silence, oblivion, covers all. If indeed they survive; if they went away whole and victorious, they give us no signals. We wait for years, but no messages come from the far-away shore to which they have gone.—Bishop R. S. Foster.

What is the grave?

'Tis a cool, shady harbor, where the Christian
Wayworn and weary with life's rugged road,
Forgetting all life's sorrows, joys, and pains,
Lays his poor body down to rest—
Sleeps on—and wakes in heaven.

Mine be the breezy hill that skirts the down;
Where a green grassy turf is all I crave,
With here and there a violet bestrown,
Fast by a brook or fountain's murmuring wave;
And many an evening sun shine sweetly on my grave!   —Beattie.

Here all the mighty troublers of the earth,
Who swam to sov'reign rule through seas of blood;
Th' oppressive, sturdy, man-destroying villains,
Who ravag'd kingdoms, and laid empires waste,
And in a cruel wantonness of power
Thinn'd states of half their people, and gave up
To want the rest; now, like a storm that's spent,
Lie hush'd.   —Blair.

I see their scattered gravestones gleaming white
Through the pale dusk of the impending night.
O'er all alike the imperial sunset throws
Its golden lilies mingled with the rose;
We give to each a tender thought and pass
Out of the graveyards with their tangled grass.   —Longfellow.

Where is the house for all the living found?
Go ask the deaf, the dumb, the dead;
All answer, without voice or sound,
Each resting in his bed;
Look down and see,
Beneath thy feet,
A place for thee;
—There all the living meet.
    —James Montgomery.

Always the idea of unbroken quiet broods around the grave. It is a port where the storms of life never beat, and the forms that have been tossed on its chafing waves lie quiet forever-more. There the child nestles as peacefully as ever it lay in its mother's arms, and the workman's hands lie still by his side, and the thinker's brain is pillowed in silent mystery, and the poor girl's broken heart is steeped in a balm that extracts its secret woe, and is in the keeping of a charity that covers all blame.—Chapin.

I like that ancient Saxon phrase which calls
The burial ground, God's Acre! It is just;
It consecrates each grave within its walls,
And breathes a benison o'er the sleeping dust.
    * * * * *
Into its furrows shall we all be cast,
In the sure faith, that we shall rise again
At the great harvest, when the archangel's blast
Shall winnow, like a fan, the chaff and grain.   —Longfellow.

Build me a shrine, and I could kneel
To rural Gods, or prostrate fall;
Did I not see, did I not feel,
That one Great Spirit governs all.
O heaven, permit that I may lie
Where o'er my corse green branches wave;
And those who from life's tumults fly
With kindred feelings press my grave.
    —Bloomfield.

There are slave-drivers quietly whipped underground,
There bookbinders, done up in boards, are fast bound,
There card-players wait till the last trump be played,
There all the choice spirits get finally laid,
There the babe's that unborn is supplied with a berth,
There men without legs get their six feet of earth,
There lawyers repose, each wrapped up in his case,
There seekers of office are sure of a place,
There defendant and plaintiff get equally cast,
There shoemakers quietly stick to the last.
    —Lowell.

When the dusk of evening had come on, and not a sound disturbed the sacred stillness of the place,—when the bright moon poured in her light on tomb and monument, on pillar, wall, and arch, and most of all (it seemed to them) upon her quiet grave,—in that calm time, when all outward things and inward thoughts teem with assurances of immortality, and worldly hopes and fears are humbled in the dust before them,—then, with tranquil and submissive hearts they turned away, and left the child with God.—Dickens.

Even such is time, that takes on trust
Our youth, our joys, our all we have,
And pays us but with age and dust,
Who in the dark and silent grave,
When we have wandered all our ways,
Shuts up the story of our days!
But from this earth, this grave, this dust,
My God shall raise me up, I trust!
—Sir Walter Raleigh.

The solitary, silent, solemn scene,
Where Cæsars, heroes, peasants, hermits lie,
Blended in dust together; where the slave
Rests from his labors; where th' insulting proud
Resigns his powers; the miser drops his hoard:
Where human folly sleeps. —Dyer.

Beneath those rugged elms, that yew-tree's shade,
Where heaves the turf in many a mouldering heap,
Each in his narrow cell forever laid,
The rude forefathers of the hamlet sleep.
The breezy call of incense-breathing morn,
The swallow twittering from the straw-built shed,
The cock's shrill clarion, or the echoing horn,
No more shall rouse them from their lowly bed.
For them no more the blazing hearth shall burn,
Or busy housewife ply her evening care;
No children run to lisp their sire's return,
Or climb his knees the envied kiss to share. —Gray.

Gravity

Gravity is a kind of quackery.—Mme. de Motteville.

Gravity is more suggestive than convincing.—Douglas Jerrold.

Too much gravity argues a shallow mind.—Lavater.

Gravity is the ballast of the soul.—Fuller.

There is a gravity which is not austere nor captious, which belongs not to melancholy nor dwells in contraction of heart; but arises from tenderness and hangs upon reflection.—Landor.

The body's wisdom to conceal the mind.—Young.

Piety enjoins no man to be dull.—South.

Gravity is the best cloak for sin in all countries.—Fielding.

Gravity is a mysterious carriage of the body invented to cover the defects of the mind.—Rochefoucauld.

Gravity is only the bark of wisdom, but it preserves it.—Confucius.

Is there anything so grave and serious as an ass?—Montaigne.

There is gravity in wisdom, but no particular wisdom in gravity.—H. W. Shaw.

Men of gravity are intellectual stammerers, whose thoughts move slowly.—Hazlitt.

To how many blockheads of my time has a cold and taciturn demeanor procured the credit of prudence and capacity!—Montaigne.

Gravity is of the very essence of imposture; it does not only mistake other things, but is apt perpetually almost to mistake itself.—Shaftesbury.

A grave aspect to a grave character is of much more consequence than the world is generally aware of; a barber may make you laugh, but a surgeon ought rather to make you cry.—Fielding.

I think it is the most beautiful and humane thing in the world, so to mingle gravity with pleasure that the one may not sink into melancholy, nor the other rise up into wantonness.—Pliny the Elder.

There is a false gravity that is a very ill symptom; and it may be said, that as rivers, which run very slowly, have always the most mud at the bottom: so a solid stiffness in the constant course of a man's life, is a sign of a thick bed of mud at the bottom of his brain.—Saville.

Yorick sometimes, in his wild way of talking, would say that gravity was an arrant scoundrel, and, he would add, of the most dangerous kind, too, because a sly one; and that he verily believed more honest well-meaning people were bubbled out of their goods and money by it in one twelvemonth than by pocket-picking and shop-lifting in seven.—Sterne.

The very essence of gravity was design, and, consequently, deceit; it was a taught trick to gain credit of the world for more sense and knowledge than a man was worth; and that with all its pretensions it was no better, but often worse, than what a French wit had long ago defined it—a mysterious carriage of the body to cover the defects of the mind.—Sterne.

Greatness

All great men are partially inspired. —Cicero.

Greatness knows itself.—Shakespeare.

The most useful is the greatest.— Theodore Parker.

Great men are sincere.—Emerson.

Greatness is its own torment.— Theodore Parker.

The world knows nothing of its greatest men.—Henry Taylor.

Great souls are harmonious.— Joseph Roux.

All great men come out of the middle classes.—Emerson.

Greatness appeals to the future.— Emerson.

Great is not great to the greater.— Sir P. Sidney.

The first step to greatness is to be honest.—Johnson.

Every great man is a unique.—Emerson.

In a great soul everything is great. —Pascal.

Great men should not have great faults.—La Rochefoucauld.

Are not great men the models of nations?—Owen Meredith.

Reproach is a concomitant of greatness.—South.

The civilities of the great are never thrown away.—Johnson.

For he that once is good, is ever great.—Ben Jonson.

To be great is to be misunderstood. —Emerson.

Great men are never sufficiently shown but in struggles.—Burke.

Nothing is great but the inexhaustible wealth of nature.—Emerson.

A great mind becomes a great fortune.—Seneca.

No man ever yet became great by imitation.—Johnson.

A great man is one who affects the mind of his generation.—Beaconsfield.

A great man is made so for others. —Thomas Wilson.

None think the great unhappy but the great.—Young.

Greatness, as we daily see it, is unsociable.—Landor.

The great man is the man who does a thing for the first time.—Alexander Smith.

There is but one method, and that is hard labor.—Sydney Smith.

A man in pursuit of greatness feels no little wants.—Emerson.

No really great man ever thought himself so.—Hazlitt.

That man is great who can use the brains of others to carry on his work. —Donn Piatt.

The greatest man is he who chooses right with the most invincible resolution.—Seneca.

The great are only great because we are on our knees. Let us rise up.— Prud'homme.

The tomb is the pedestal of greatness. I make a distinction between God's great and the king's great.— Landor.

It is the prerogative of great men only to have great defects.—Rochefoucauld.

That man is great who rises to the emergencies of the occasion, and becomes master of the situation.—Donn Piatt.

Oh! greatness! thou art but a flattering dream,
A wat'ry bubble, lighter than the air.
—Tracy.

A great man is made up of qualities that meet or make great occasions.—Lowell.

It is not by his faults, but by his excellences, that we must measure a great man.—George Henry Lewes.

To be great one must be positive, and gain strength through foes.—Donn Piatt.

Everything great is not always good, but all good things are great.—Demosthenes.

What your heart thinks great is great. The soul's emphasis is always right.—Emerson.

In all the world there is nothing so remarkable as a great man, nothing so rare, nothing which so well repays study.—Theodore Parker.

It is to be lamented that great characters are seldom without a blot.— Washington.

Great souls attract sorrow as mountains do storms.—Richter.

No great thought, no great object, satisfies the mind at first view, nor at the last.—Abel Stevens.

Nothing is more simple than greatness; indeed, to be simple is to be great.—Emerson.

Great truths are portions of the soul of man;
Great souls are the portions of eternity.
—Lowell.

No sadder proof can be given by a man of his own littleness than disbelief in great men.—Carlyle.

Great men are rarely isolated mountain-peaks; they are the summits of ranges.—T. W. Higginson.

In order to do great things, it is necessary to live as if one was never to die.—Vauvenargues.

Greatness, once fallen out with fortune, must fall out with men too.— Shakespeare.

We have not the love of greatness, but the love of the love of greatness. —Carlyle.

Nothing can make a man truly great but being truly good and partaking of God's holiness.—Matthew Henry.

It is, alas! the poor prerogative of greatness, to be wretched and unpitied. —Congreve.

A great man knows the value of greatness; he dares not hazard it, he will not squander it.—Landor.

What millions died that Cæsar might be great!—Campbell.

Great souls are always loyally submissive, reverent to what is over them: only small mean souls are otherwise.—Carlyle.

The difference between Socrates and Jesus Christ? The great Conscious; the immeasurably great Unconscious. —Carlyle.

Greatness lies, not in being strong, but in the right using of strength.—Beecher.

Not that the heavens the little can make great,
But many a man has lived an age too late.
—R. H. Stoddard.

He is great who is what he is from nature, and who never reminds us of others.—Emerson.

It is the curse of greatness
To be its own destruction.
—Nabb.

When greatness descends from its lofty pedestal, it assumes human dimensions.—Mme. Louise Colet.

True greatness is sovereign wisdom. We are never deceived by our virtues.—Lamartine.

Since we cannot attain to greatness, let us revenge ourselves by railing at it.—Montaigne.

It is the age that forms the man, not the man that forms the age.—Macaulay.

The age does not believe in great men, because it does not possess any.—Beaconsfield.

Great men stand like solitary towers in the city of God.—Longfellow.

It is not in the nature of true greatness to be exclusive and arrogant.—Beecher.

The great man is to be the servant of mankind, not they of him.—Theodore Parker.

Great men are among the best gifts which God bestows upon a people.—George S. Hillard.

Some are born great, some achieve greatness, and some have greatness thrust upon 'em.—Shakespeare.

A solemn and religious regard to spiritual and eternal things is an indispensable element of all true greatness.—Daniel Webster.

Rightly to be great is not to stir without great argument.—Shakespeare.

The great would not think themselves demigods if the little did not worship them.—Boiste.

Great men lose somewhat of their greatness by being near us; ordinary men gain much.—Landor.

Distinction is an eminence that is attained but too frequently at the expense of a fireside.—Simms.

That man lives greatly, whatever his fate or fame, who greatly dies.—Young.

Greatness, thou gaudy torment of our souls,
The wise man's fetter, and the rage of fools.
—Otway.

Great men are they who see that spiritual is stronger than any material force, that thoughts rule the world.—Emerson.

They that stand high have many blasts to shake them; and if they fall, they dash themselves to pieces.—Shakespeare.

There was never yet a truly great man that was not at the same time truly virtuous.—Benjamin Franklin.

Copiousness and simplicity, variety and unity, constitute real greatness of character.—Lavater.

Great men are more distinguished by range and extent than by originality.—Emerson.

Great men do not content us. It is their solitude, not their force, that makes them conspicuous.—Emerson.

Heaven knows, I had no such intent;
But that necessity so bow'd the state,
That I and greatness were compell'd to kiss.
—Shakespeare.

Greatness is not a teachable nor gainable thing, but the expression of the mind of a God-made great man.—Ruskin.

The use of great men is to serve the little men, to take care of the human race, and act as practical interpreters of justice and truth.—Theodore Parker.

Great souls are not those who have fewer passions and more virtues than the common, but those only who have greater designs.—La Rochefoucauld.

In life, we shall find many men that are great, and some men that are good, but very few men that are both great and good.—Colton.

Earthly greatness is a nice thing, and requires so much chariness in the managing, as the contentment of it cannot requite.—Hall.

The great are only great because we carry them on our shoulders; when we throw them off they sprawl on the ground.—Montandré.

There is a better thing than the great man who is always speaking, and that is the great man who only speaks when he has a great word to say.—William Winter.

It is, in a great measure, by raising up and endowing great minds that God secures the advance of human affairs, and the accomplishment of His own plans on earth.—Albert Barnes.

A really great man is known by three signs—generosity in the design, humanity in the execution, and moderation in success.—Bismarck.

He who comes up to his own idea of greatness must always have had a very low standard of it in his mind.—Hazlitt.

A great man, I take it, is a man so inspired and permeated with the ideas of God and the Christly spirit as to be too magnanimous for vengeance, and too unselfish to seek his own ends.—David Thomas.

The truly great rest in the knowledge of their own deserts, nor seek the conformation of the world.—Alexander Smith.

A solid and substantial greatness of soul looks down with neglect on the censures and applauses of the multitude.—Addison.

Like the air-invested heron, great persons should conduct themselves; and the higher they be, the less they should show.—Sir P. Sidney.

By a certain fate, great acts, and great eloquence have most commonly gone hand in hand, equalling and honoring each other in the same ages.—Milton.

No great intellectual thing was ever done by great effort; a great thing can only be done by a great man, and he does it without effort.—Ruskin.

The greatness of action includes immoral as well as moral greatness—Cortes and Napoleon, as well as Luther and Washington.—Whipple.

Great names stand not alone for great deeds; they stand also for great virtues, and, doing them worship, we elevate ourselves.—Henry Giles.

Greatness, in any period and under any circumstances, has always been rare. It is of elemental birth, and is independent alike of its time and its circumstances.—William Winter.

The world cannot do without great men, but great men are very troublesome to the world.—Goethe.

Avoid greatness; in a cottage there may be found more real happiness than kings or their favorites enjoy in palaces.—Horace.

Nature never sends a great man into the planet, without confiding the secret to another soul.—Emerson.

Great abilities, when employed as God directs, do but make the owners of them greater and more painful servants to their neighbors.—Swift.

Great warriors, like great earthquakes, are principally remembered for the mischief they have done.—Bovee.

Great minds do indeed react on the society which has made them what they are; but they only pay with interest what they have received.—Macaulay.

Philosophy may raise us above grandeur, but nothing can elevate us above the ennui which accompanies it. —Mme. de Maintenon.

If it is a pleasure to be envied and shot at, to be maligned standing and to be despised falling, then it is a pleasure to be great.—South.

The great men of the earth are but the marking-stones on the road of humanity; they are the priests of its religion.—Mazzini.

O, be sick, great greatness, and bid thy ceremony give thee cure! Thinkest thou the fiery fever will go out with titles blown from adulation?—Shakespeare.

Those people who are always improving never become great. Greatness is an eminence, the ascent to which is steep and lofty, and which a man must seize on at once by natural boldness and vigor, and not by patient, wary steps.—Hazlitt.

For as much as to understand and to be mighty are great qualities, the higher that they be, they are so much the less to be esteemed if goodness also abound not in the possessor.—Sir P. Sidney.

Be substantially great in thyself, and more than thou appearest unto others; and let the world be deceived in thee, as they are in the lights of heaven.—Sir Thomas Browne.

He only is great who has the habits of greatness; who, after performing what none in ten thousand could accomplish, passes on like Samson, and "tells neither father nor mother of it." —Lavater.

This is the part of a great man, after he has maturely weighed all circumstances, to punish the guilty, to spare the many, and in every state of

fortune not to depart from an upright, virtuous conduct.—Cicero.

There never was a great truth but it was reverenced; never a great institution, nor a great man, that did not, sooner or later, receive the reverence of mankind.—Theodore Parker.

There is something on earth greater than arbitrary power. The thunder, the lightning, and the earthquake are terrific, but the judgment of the people is more.—Daniel Webster.

The truly strong and sound mind is the mind that can embrace equally great things and small. I would have a man great in great things, and elegant in little things.—Johnson.

Speaking generally, no man appears great to his contemporaries, for the same reason that no man is great to his servants—both know too much of him.—Colton.

There is no man so great as not to have some littleness more predominant than all his greatness. Our virtues are the dupes, and often only the plaything of our follies.—Bulwer-Lytton.

A contemplation of God's works, a generous concern for the good of mankind, and the unfeigned exercise of humility only, denominate men great and glorious.—Addison.

Why, man, he doth bestride the narrow world
Like a Colossus; and we petty men
Walk under his huge legs, and peep about
To find ourselves dishonorable graves.
—Shakespeare.

Great men may jest with saints: 'tis wit in them,
But in the less, foul profanation.
*　*　*　*　*
That in the captain's but a choleric word,
Which in the soldier is flat blasphemy.
—Shakespeare.

He is truly great that is great in charity. He is truly great that is little in himself, and maketh no account of any height of honor. And he is truly learned that doeth the will of God, and forsaketh his own will,—Thomas à Kempis.

Great men, great events, great epochs, it has been said, grow as we recede from them; and the rate at which they grow in the estimation of men is in some sort a measure of their greatness.—Principal Shairp.

Great is Youth—equally great is Old Age—
  great are Day and Night.
Great is Wealth—great is Poverty—great
  is Expression—great is Silence.
    —Walt Whitman.

Man's unhappiness, as I construe, comes of his greatness; it is because there is an Infinite in him, which with all his cunning he cannot quite bury under the Finite.—Carlyle.

He fought a thousand glorious wars,
  And more than half the world was his,
And somewhere, now, in yonder stars,
  Can tell, mayhap, what greatness is.
    —Thackeray.

The gifts of Nature and accomplishments of art are valuable but as they are exerted in the interests of virtue or governed by the rules of honor.—Steele.

Great men are always exceptional men; and greatness itself is but comparative. Indeed, the range of most men in life is so limited that very few have the opportunity of being great.—Samuel Smiles.

Greatness is the aggregation of minuteness; nor can its sublimity be felt truthfully by any mind unaccustomed to the affectionate watching of what is least.—Ruskin.

A king or a prince becomes by accident a part of history. A poet or an artist becomes by nature and necessity a part of universal humanity.—Mrs. Jameson.

No man has come to true greatness who has not felt in some degree that his life belongs to his race, and that what God gives him He gives him for mankind.—Phillips Brooks.

Great people and champions are special gifts of God, whom He gives and preserves; they do their work, and achieve great actions, not with vain imaginations, or cold and sleepy cogitations, but by motion of God.—Martin Luther.

Such is the destiny of great men that their superior genius always exposes them to be the butt of the envenomed darts of calumny and envy.—Voltaire.

It appears to be among the laws of nature, that the mighty of intellect should be pursued and carped by the little, as the solitary flight of one great bird is followed by the twittering petulance of many smaller.—Landor.

The truly great consider, first, how they may gain the approbation of God, and, secondly, that of their own consciences; having done this, they would then willingly conciliate the good opinion of their fellow-men.—Colton.

We observe with confidence that the truly strong mind, view it as intellect or morality, or under any other aspect, is nowise the mind acquainted with its strength; that here the sign of health is unconsciousness.—Carlyle.

As the stars are the glory of the sky, so great men are the glory of their country, yea, of the whole earth. The hearts of great men are the stars of earth; and doubtless when one looks down from above upon our planet, these hearts are seen to send forth a silvery light just like the stars of heaven.—Heine.

Since, by your greatness, you
Are nearer heaven in place; be nearer it
In goodness: rich men should transcend the
    poor,
As clouds the earth; rais'd by the comfort of
The sun, to water dry and barren grounds.
    —Tourneur.

Great men need to be lifted upon the shoulders of the whole world, in order to conceive their great ideas or perform their great deeds. That is, there must be an atmosphere of greatness round about them. A hero cannot be a hero unless in an heroic world.—Hawthorne.

Worthy deeds are not often destitute of worthy relaters; as, by a certain fate, great acts and great eloquence have most commonly gone hand in hand, equalling and honoring each other in the same age.—Milton.

Some men who know that they are great are so very haughty withal and insufferable that their acquaintance discover their greatness only by the tax of humility which they are obliged to pay as the price of their friendship. —Colton.

Subtract from a great man all that he owes to opportunity and all that he owes to chance, all that he has gained by the wisdom of his friends and by the folly of his enemies, and our Brobdignag will often become a Liliputian. —Colton.

True greatness, first of all, is a thing of the heart. It is all alive with robust and generous sympathies. It is neither behind its age, nor too far before it. It is up with its age, and ahead of it only just so far as to be able to lead its march. It cannot slumber, for activity is a necessity of its existence. It is no reservoir, but a fountain.—Roswell D. Hitchcock.

That man is great, and he alone,
Who serves a greatness not his own,
  For neither praise nor pelf:
Content to know and be unknown:
  Whole in himself.   —Lord Lytton.

The great make us feel, first of all, the indifference of circumstances. They call into activity the higher perceptions, and subdue the low habits of comfort and luxury; but the higher perceptions find their objects everywhere; only the low habits need palaces and banquets.—Emerson.

He who does the most good is the greatest man. Power, authority, dignity, honors, wealth and station—these are so far valuable as they put it into the hands of men to be more exemplary and more useful than they could be in an obscure and private life. But then these are means conducting to an end, and that end is goodness.— Bishop Jortin.

He only is great at heart who floods the world with a great affection. He only is great of mind who stirs the world with great thoughts. He only is great of will who does something to shape the world to a great career. And he is greatest who does the most of all these things and does them best.— Roswell D. Hitchcock.

Nay, then, farewell!
I have touch'd the highest point of all
  my greatness;
And from that full meridian of my glory,
I haste now to my setting. I shall fall
Like a bright exhalation in the evening,
And no man see me more.
                          —Shakespeare.

The great men of earth are the shadow men, who, having lived and died, now live again and forever through their undying thoughts. Thus living, though their footfalls are heard no more, their voices are louder than the thunder, and unceasing as the flow of tides or air.—Beecher.

The greatest men have not always the best heads; many indiscretions may be pardoned to a brilliant and ardent imagination. The prudence and discretion of a cold heart are not worth half so much as the follies of an ardent mind.—Baron de Grimm.

The reason why great men meet with so little pity or attachment in adversity would seem to be this: the friends of a great man were made by his fortunes, his enemies by himself; and revenge is a much more punctual paymaster than gratitude.—Colton.

I will not go so far as to say, with a living poet, that the world knows nothing of its greatest men; but there are forms of greatness, or at least of excellence, which "die and make no sign"; there are martyrs that miss the palm, but not the stake; heroes without the laurel, and conquerors without the triumph.—G. A. Sala.

He that makes himself famous by his eloquence, justice or arms illustrates his extraction, let it be never so mean; and gives inestimable reputation to his parents. We should never have heard of Sophroniscus, but for his son,

Socrates; nor of Ariosto and Gryllus, if it had not been for Xenophon and Plato.—Seneca.

———

He alone is worthy of the appellation who either does great things, or teaches how they may be done, or describes them with a suitable majesty when they have been done; but those only are great things which tend to render life more happy, which increase the innocent enjoyments and comforts of existence, or which pave the way to a state of future bliss more permanent and more pure.—Milton.

———

The greatest man is he who chooses the right with invincible resolution, who resists the sorest temptations from within and without, who bears the heaviest burdens cheerfully, who is calmest in storms and most fearless under menace and frowns, whose reliance on truth, on virtue, on God, is most unfaltering. I believe this greatness to be most common among the multitude, whose names are never heard.—Channing.

———

Persons in great stations have seldom their true character drawn till several years after their death. Their personal friendships and enmities must cease, and the parties they were engaged in be at an end, before their faults or their virtues can have justice done them. When writers have the least opportunities of knowing the truth, they are in the best disposition to tell it.—Addison.

———

Those who have read history with discrimination know the fallacy of those panegyrics and invectives which represent individuals as effecting great moral and intellectual revolutions, subverting established systems, and imprinting a new character on their age. The difference between one man and another is by no means so great as the superstitious crowd suppose.—Macaulay.

———

Few footprints of the great remain in the sand before the ever-flowing tide. Long ago it washed out Homer's. Curiosity follows him in vain; Greece and Asia perplex us with a rival Strat-ford-upon-Avon. The rank of Aristophanes is only conjectured from his gift to two poor players in Athens. The age made no sign when Shakespeare, its noblest son, passed away.—Willmott.

———

He who ascends to mountain-tops shall find
Their loftiest peaks most wrapt in clouds of snow;
He who surpasses or subdues mankind,
Must look down on the hate of those below.
Tho' high above the sun of glory glow,
And far beneath the earth and ocean spread,
Round him are icy rocks, and loudly blow
Contending tempests on his naked head.
—Byron.

———

I do not hesitate to say that the road to eminence and power, from an obscure condition, ought not to be made too easy, nor a thing too much of course. If rare merit be the rarest of all things, it ought to pass through some sort of probation. The temple of honor ought to be seated on an eminence. If it be open through virtue, let it be remembered, too, that virtue is never tried but by some difficulty and some struggle.—Burke.

———

A great man is a gift, in some measure a revelation of God. A great man, living for high ends, is the divinest thing that can be seen on earth. The value and interest of history are derived chiefly from the lives and services of the eminent men whom it commemorates. Indeed, without these, there would be no such thing as history, and the progress of a nation would be little worth recording, as the march of a trading caravan across a desert.—George S. Hillard.

———

If the title of a great man ought to be reserved for him who cannot be charged with an indiscretion or a vice, who spent his life in establishing the independence, the glory and durable prosperity of his country; who succeeded in all that he undertook, and whose successes were never won at the expense of honor, justice, integrity, or by the sacrifice of a single principle— this title will not be denied to Washington.—Sparks.

The mightier man, the mightier is the
  thing
That makes him honor'd, or begets him
  Hate:
For greatest Scandal waits on greatest
  state.
The Moon being clouded presently is
  miss'd,
But little Stars may hide them when they
  list.
The crow may clothe his coal-black wings
  in mire,
And unperceived fly with the filth away;
But if the like the snow-white swan desire,
The stain upon his silver down will stay.
Poor grooms are sightless night, Kings
  glorious day.
Gnats are unnoted whereso'er they fly,
But eagles gazed upon with every eye.
  —Shakespeare.

Great men are not the mere products
of the times in which they live, the
epitome of their age, the creations of
those formative currents of thought
that are traversing the masses. Great
men are the gifts of kind heaven to our
poor world; instruments by which the
Highest One works out His designs;
light-radiators to give guidance and
blessing to the travellers of time.
Though far above us, they are felt to
be our brothers; and their elevation
shows us what vast possibilities are
wrapped up in our common humanity.
They beckon us up the gleaming
heights to whose summits they have
climbed. Their deeds are the woof of
this world's history.—Moses Harvey.

Greece

Clime of the unforgotten brave!
Whose land, from plain to mountain-cave,
Was Freedom's home, or Glory's grave;
Shrine of the mighty! can it be,
That this is all remains of thee?
  —Byron.

The isles of Greece, the isles of Greece!
  Where burning Sappho loved and sung,
Where grew the arts of war and peace—
  Where Delos rose, and Phœbus sprung!
Eternal summer gilds them yet,
But all, except their sun, is set.
  —Byron.

Greeting

As ships meet at sea a moment together, when words of greeting must
be spoken, and then away upon the
deep, so men meet in this world; and
I think we should cross no man's path
without hailing him, and if he needs
giving him supplies,—Beecher.

Grief

No grief reaches the dead.—Sallust.

Grief has its time.—Johnson.

Grief alone can teach us what is
man.—Bulwer-Lytton.

Grief, like a tree, has tears for its
fruit.—Philemon.

The only cure for grief is action.—
George Henry Lewes.

Griefs assured are felt before they
come.—Dryden.

There is a solemn luxury in grief.—
Wm. Mason.

My grief lies onward and my joy
behind.—Shakespeare.

Grief knits two hearts in closer
bonds.—Lamartine.

None can cure their harms by wailing them.—Shakespeare.

The indulgence in grief is a blunder.
—Beaconsfield.

Every one can master a grief but he
that has it.—Shakespeare.

I will instruct my sorrow to be
proud.—Shakespeare.

She grieves sincerely who grieves
unseen.—Martial.

Grief still treads upon the heels of
pleasure.—Congreve.

No grief is so acute but time ameli-
orates it.—Cicero.

He who is resolute conquers grief.—
Goethe.

Trembling lips, tuned to such grief
that they say bright words sadly.—
Sydney Dobell.

Grief is a stone that bears one down
but two bear it lightly.—W. Hauff.

Grief is crowned with consolation.
—Shakespeare.

Great griefs medicine the less.—
Shakespeare.

Grief is a species of idleness.—
Johnson.

Grief best is pleased with grief's society.—Shakespeare.

When remedies are past, the griefs are ended.—Shakespeare.

The flood of grief decreaseth when it can swell no longer.—Bacon.

Honest plain words best pierce the ear of grief.—Shakespeare.

In rising sighs and falling tears.—Addison.

That eating canker grief, with wasteful spite, preys on the rosy bloom of youth and beauty.—Rowe.

Well has it been said that there is no grief like the grief which does not speak.—Longfellow.

'Tis long ere time can mitigate your grief;
To wisdom fly, she quickly brings relief.
—Grotius.

No future hour can rend my heart like this,
Save that which breaks it. —Maturin.

You may my glories and my state depose,
But not my griefs; still am I king of those.
—Shakespeare.

He gave a deep sigh; I saw the iron enter into his soul.—Sterne.

A malady
Preys on my heart that med'cine cannot reach. —Maturin.

He grieves more than is necesary who grieves before it is necessary.—Seneca.

Some Grief shows much of Love;
But much of Grief shows still some want of Wit. —Shakespeare.

Never morning wore to evening but some heart did break.—Tennyson.

It is dangerous to abandon one's self to the luxury of grief: it deprives one of courage, and even of the wish for recovery.—Amiel.

Half of the ills we hoard within our hearts,
Are ills because we hoard them.
—Proctor.

Some weep in perfect justice to the dead,
As conscious all their love is in arrear.
—Young.

What's gone, and what's past help,
Should be past grief. —Shakespeare.

Light griefs are plaintive, but great ones are dumb.—Seneca.

What need a man forestall his date of grief,
And run to meet what he would most avoid? —Milton.

Weep I cannot;
But my heart bleeds.
—Shakespeare.

We hear the rain fall, but not the snow. Bitter grief is loud, calm grief is silent.—Auerbach.

. They truly mourn that mourn without a witness.—Byron.

It is folly to tear one's hair in sorrow, as if grief could be assuaged by baldness.—Cicero.

Dr. Holmes says, both wittily and truly, that crying widows are easiest consoled.—H. W. Shaw.

Why must we first weep before we can love so deep that our hearts ache'
—Richter.

It will appear how impertinent that grief was which served no end of life.
—Jeremy Taylor.

Grief has been compared to a hydra; for every one that dies, two are born.
—Calderon.

No greater grief than to remember days of joy when misery is at hand.—
Dante.

A little bitter mingled in our cup leaves no relish of the sweet.—Locke.

Whose lenient sorrows find relief, whose joys are chastened by their grief.—Sir Walter Scott.

What's the newest grief? Each minute tunes a new one.—Shakespeare.

Heavy hearts, like heavy clouds in the sky, are best relieved by the letting of water.—Rivarol.

Cease to lament for that thou canst not help; and study help for that which thou lamentest.—Shakespeare.

Woman's grief is like a summer's shower—short as it is violent.—Joubert.

Alas! the breast that inly bleeds has nought to fear from outward blow.—Byron.

The violence of either grief or joy, their own enactures with themselves destroy.—Shakespeare.

The only thing that grief has taught me is to know how shallow it is.—Emerson.

A plague of sighing and grief! it blows a man up like a bladder.—Shakespeare.

The sickness of the heart is most easily got rid of by complaining and soothing confidence.—Goethe.

I grieve that grief can teach me nothing, nor carry me one step into real nature.—Emerson.

The grief that does not speak whispers the overfraught heart and bids it break.—Shakespeare.

Grief hallows hearts, even while it ages heads.—Bailey.

I am not mad; I would to heaven I were! For then, 'tis like I should forget myself: O, if I could, what grief should I forget! —Shakespeare.

Grief is the culture of the soul, it is the true fertilizer.—Mme. de Girardin.

Grief is the agony of an instant: the indulgence of grief the blunder of a life.—Beaconsfield.

A heavier task could not have been impos'd, Than I to speak my griefs unspeakable. —Shakespeare.

Grief hath two tongues; and never woman yet Could rule them both without ten women's wit. —Shakespeare.

Winter is come and gone, But grief returns with the revolving year. —Shelley.

Oft have I heard that grief softens the mind And makes it fearful and degenerate. —Shakespeare.

Grief is a tattered tent Where through God's light doth shine. —Lucy Larcom.

Who fails to grieve when just occasion calls, Or grieves too much, deserves not to be blest: Inhuman, or effeminate, his heart. —Young.

Like the lily, That once was mistress of the field, and flourished, I'll hang my head, and perish. —Shakespeare.

Nothing speaks our grief so well as to speak nothing.—Crashaw.

That grief is the most durable which flows inward, and buries its streams with its fountain, in the depths of the heart.—Jane Porter.

If our inward griefs were seen written on our brow, how many would be pitied who are now envied!—Metastasio.

Excess of grief for the deceased is madness; for it is an injury to the living, and the dead know it not.—Xenophon.

O the things unseen, untold, undreamt of, which like shadows pass hourly over that mysterious world, a mind to ruin struck by grief!—Mrs. Hemans.

Heaven deprives me of a wife who never caused me any other grief than that of her death.—Louis XIV.

How beautiful is sorrow when it is dressed by virgin innocence! it makes felicity in others seem deformed.—Sir W. Davenant.

Grief knits two hearts in closer bonds than happiness ever can; and common sufferings are far stronger links than common joys.—Lamartine.

Great grief makes sacred those upon whom its hand is laid. Joy may elevate, ambition glorify, but sorrow alone can consecrate.—Horace Greeley.

Grief, which disposes gentle natures to retirement, and to inaction, and to meditation, only makes restless spirits more restless.—Macaulay.

While grief is fresh, every attempt to divert only irritates. You must wait till grief be digested, and then amusement will dissipate the remains of it.—Johnson.

The more tender our spirits are made by religion, the more ready we are to let in grief.—Jeremy Taylor.

Grief is so far from retrieving a loss that it makes it greater; but the way to lessen it is by a comparison with others' losses.—Wycherley.

The truth is, we pamper little griefs into great ones, and bear great ones as well as we can.—Hazlitt.

In the loss of an object we do not proportion our grief to its real value, but to the value our fancies set upon it.—Addison.

Give to a wounded heart seclusion; consolation nor reason ever effected anything in such a case.—Balzac.

Sorrow, like a heavy ringing bell, once set on ringing, with its own weight goes; then little strength rings out the doleful knell.—Shakespeare.

Grief is only the memory of widowed affection. The more intense the delight in the presence of the object, the more poignant must be the impression of the absence.—James Martineau.

Each substance of a grief hath twenty shadows,
Which show like grief itself, but are not so:
For sorrow's eye glazed with blinding tears,
Divides one thing entire to many objects.
—Shakespeare.

Why, let the stricken deer go weep,
The heart ungalled play;
For some must watch, while some must sleep;
Thus runs the world away.
—Shakespeare.

The wither'd frame, the ruin'd mind,
The wreck by passion left behind,
A shrivell'd scroll, a scatter'd leaf,
Sear'd by the autumn blast of grief!
—Byron.

Good is that darkening of our lives,
Which only God can brighten;
But better still that hopeless load,
Which none but God can lighten.
—Frederick William Faber.

Upon her face there was the tint of grief,
The settled shadow of an inward strife,
And an unquiet drooping of the eye,
As if its lid were charged with unshed tears.   —Byron.

We know there oft is found an avarice in grief; and the wan eye of sorrow loves to gaze upon its secret hoard of treasured woes, and pine in solitude.—William Mason.

All the joys of earth will not assuage our thirst for happiness; while a single grief suffices to shroud life in a sombre veil, and smite it with nothingness at all points.—Mme. Swetchine.

The man who has learned to triumph over sorrow wears his miseries as though they were sacred fillets upon his brow; and nothing is so entirely admirable as a man bravely wretched. —Seneca.

, O, grief hath changed me since you saw me last; and careful hours, with Time's deformed hand, have written strange defeatures in my face!— Shakespeare.

O brothers! let us leave the shame and sin
Of taking vainly, in a plaintive mood,
The holy name of grief!—holy herein,
That, by the grief of One, came all our
  good.   —Mrs. Browning.

The business of life summons us away from useless grief, and calls us to the exercise of those virtues of which we are lamenting our deprivation.—Dr. Johnson.

'Tis better to be lowly born,
And range with humble livers in content,
Than to be perk'd up in a glistering grief,
And wear a golden sorrow.—Shakespeare.

What an argument in favor of social connections is the observation that by communicating our grief we have less, and by communicating our pleasure we have more.—Greville.

Alas! I have not words to tell my grief;
To vent my sorrow would be some relief;
Light sufferings give us leisure to complain;
We groan, we cannot speak, in greater
  pain.   —Dryden.

Be free from grief not through insensibility like the irrational animals, nor through want of thought like the foolish, but like a man of virtue by having reason as the consolation of grief.—Epictetus.

In youth, grief comes with a rush and overflow, but it dries up, too, like the torrent. In the winter of life it remains a miserable pool, resisting all evaporation.—Madame Swetchine.

Oh! call my brother back to me!
I cannot play alone;
The summer comes with flower and bee—
  Where is my brother gone?
                  —Mrs. Hemans.

Of permanent griefs there are none, for they are but clouds. The swifter they move through the sky, the more follow after them; and even the immovable ones are absorbed by the other, and become smaller till they vanish.—Richter.

Grief or misfortune seems to be indispensable to the development of intelligence, energy, and virtue. The proofs to which the people are submitted, as with individuals, are necessary then to draw them from their lethargy, to disclose their character.— Fearon.

Grief is a flower as delicate and prompt to fade as happiness. Still, it does not wholly die. Like the magic rose, dried and unrecognizable, a warm air breathed on it will suffice to renew its bloom.—Mme. de Gasparin.

What is grief? It is an obscure labyrinth into which God leads man, that he may be experienced in life, that he may remember his faults and abjure them, that he may appreciate the calm which virtue gives.—Leopold Scheffer.

The person who grieves suffers his passion to grow upon him; he indulges it, he loves it; but this never happens in the case of actual pain, which no man ever willingly endured for any considerable time.—Burke.

Grief, like night, is salutary. It cools down the soul by putting out its feverish fires; and if it oppresses her, it also compresses her energies. The load once gone, she will go forth with greater buoyancy to new pleasures.— Dr. Pulsford.

We may deserve grief; but why should women be unhappy?—except that we know heaven chastens those whom it loves best, being pleased by repeated trials to make these pure spirits more pure.—Thackeray.

Why destroy present happiness by a distant misery, which may never come at all, or you may never live to see it? For every substantial grief has twenty shadows, and most of them shadows of your own making.—Sydney Smith.

Griefs are like the beings that endure them—the little ones are the most clamorous and noisy; those of older growth and greater magnitude are generally tranquil, and sometimes silent. —Chatfield.

He that hath so many causes of joy, and so great, is very much in love with sorrow and peevishness, who loses all these pleasures, and chooses to sit down on his little handful of thorns.—Jeremy Taylor.

Grief fills the room up of my absent child,
Lies in his bed, walks up and down with
    me;
Puts on his pretty looks, repeats his words,
Remembers me of all his gracious parts,
Stuffs out his vacant garment with his
    form.   — Shakespeare.

Grief! thou art classed amongst the depressing passions. And true it is that thou humblest to the dust, but also thou exaltest to the clouds. Thou shakest us with ague, but also thou steadiest like frost. Thou sickenest the heart, but also thou healest its infirmities.—De Quincey.

            Sweet source of virtue,
O sacred sorrow! he who knows not thee,
Knows not the best emotions of the heart,
Those tender tears that harmonize the
    soul,
The sigh that charms, the pang that gives
    delight,   —Thomson.

Long thus he chew'd the cud of inward
    griefe,
And did consume his gall with anguish
    sore;
Still when he mused on his late mischiefe,
Then still the smart thereof increased more,
And seemed more grievous than it was be-
    fore,   —Spenser.

As warmth makes even glaciers trickle, and opens streams in the ribs of frozen mountains, so the heart knows the full flow and life of its grief only when it begins to melt and pass away.—Beecher.

I am not prone to weeping as our sex commonly are; the want of which vain dew perchance shall dry your pities; but I have that honorable grief lodged here which burns worse than tears drown.—Shakespeare.

As a fresh wound shrinks from the hand of the surgeon, then gradually submits to and even calls for it; so a mind under the first impression of a misfortune shuns and rejects all comfort, but at length, if touched with tenderness, calmly and willingly resigns itself.—Pliny the Younger.

Oppress'd with grief, oppress'd with care,
A burden more than I can bear,
I sit me down and sigh;
O, life! thou art a galling load,
Along a rough, a weary road,
To wretches such as I.   —Burns.

There is yet a silent agony in which the mind appears to disdain all external help, and broods over its distresses with gloomy reserve. This is the most dangerous state of mind; accidents or friendships may lessen the louder kinds of grief, but all remedies for this must be had from within, and there despair too often finds the most deadly enemy. —Goldsmith.

There are moods in which we court suffering, in the hope that here, at least, we shall find reality, sharp peaks and edges of truth. But it turns out to be scene-painting and counterfeit. The only thing grief has taught me is to know how shallow it is.—Emerson.

Those great and stormy passions do so spend the whole stock of grief that they presently admit a comfort and contrary affection; while a sorrow that is even and temperate goes on to its period with expectation and the distance of a just time.—Jeremy Taylor.

Grotesque

The noble grotesque involves the true appreciation of beauty.—Ruskin.

The true grotesque being the expression of the repose or play of a serious mind, there is a false grotesque opposed to it, which is the result of the full exertion of a frivolous one.— Ruskin.

Wherever the human mind is healthy and vigorous in all its proportions, great in imagination and emotion no less than in intellect, and not overborne by an undue or hardened pre-eminence of the mere reasoning faculties, there the grotesque will exist in full energy.—Ruskin.

I believe that there is no test of greatness in periods, nations or men more sure than the development, among them or in them, of a noble grotesque, and no test of comparative smallness or limitation, of one kind or another, more sure than the absence of grotesque invention, or incapability of understanding it.—Ruskin.

Growth

The lofty oak from a small acorn grows.—Lewis Duncombe.

Gardener, for telling me these news of woe,
Pray God the plants thou graft'st may
never grow.   —Shakespeare.

'Tis thus the mercury of man is fix'd,
Strong grows the virtue with his nature
   mix'd.   —Pope.

In a narrow circle the mind contracts.
Man grows with his expanded needs.
        —Schiller.

Our pleasures and our discontents.
Are rounds by which we may ascend.
        —Longfellow.

He builded better than he knew—
The conscious stone to beauty grew.
        —Emerson.

And so all growth that is not towards God
Is growing to decay.
        —George MacDonald.

Then bless thy secret growth, nor catch
At noise, but thrive unseen and dumb;
Keep clean, be as fruit, earn life, and
   watch
Till the white-wing'd reapers come.
        —Henry Vaughan.

"Ay," quoth my uncle Gloucester,
"Small herbs have grace, great weeds do
   grow apace:"
And since, methinks, I would not grow so
   fast,
Because sweet flowers are slow, and weeds
   make haste.   —Shakespeare.

Arts and sciences are not cast in a mould, but are found and perfected by degrees, by often handling and polish-ing, as bears leisurely lick their cubs into shape.—Montaigne.

Grows with his growth, and strengthens with his strength.—Pope.

Man seems the only growth that dwindles here.—Goldsmith.

What? Was man made a wheel-work to
   wind up,
And be discharged, and straight wound up
   anew?
No! grown, his growth lasts; taught, he
   ne'er forgets;
May learn a thousand things, not twice the
   same.   —Robert Browning.

It is not growing like a tree
In bulk, doth make man better be;
Or standing long an oak, three hundred
   year
To fall a log at last, dry, bald, and sere·
   A lily of a day
   Is fairer far in May,
Although it fall and die that night—
It was the plant and flower of Light.
        —Ben Jonson.

Jock, when ye hae naething else to do, ye may be aye sticking in a tree; it will be growing, Jock, when ye're sleeping.—Scott.

Grumbling

It's a great comfort to some people to groan over their imaginary ills.—Thackeray.

Grumblers deserve to be operated upon surgically; their trouble is usually chronic.—Douglas Jerrold.

Complaint is the largest tribute Heaven receives.—Swift.

Those who complain most are most to be complained of.—Matthew Henry.

I pity the man who can travel from Dan to Beersheba, and cry, it is all barren.—Sterne.

Every one must see daily instances of people who complain from a mere habit of complaining.—Graves.

The very large, very respectable, and very knowing class of misanthropes who rejoice in the name of grumblers,—persons who are so sure that the world is going to ruin, that they resent every attempt to comfort them as an insult to their sagacity, and accordingly seek their chief consolation in being inconsolable, their chief pleasure in being displeased.—Whipple.

When a man is full of the Holy Ghost, he is the very last man to be complaining of other people.—D. L. Moody.

From mad dogs and grumbling professors may we all be delivered; and may we never take the complaint from either of them!—Spurgeon.

There is an unfortunate disposition in a man to attend much more to the faults of his companions which offend him, than to their perfections which please him.—Greville.

No talent, no self-denial, no brains, no character, is required to set up in the grumbling business; but those who are moved by a genuine desire to do good have little time for murmuring or complaint.—Robert West.

Guest

A pretty woman is a welcome guest. —Byron.

Unbidden guests
Are often welcomest when they are gone.
   —Shakespeare.

Here's our chief guest.
If he had been forgotten,
It had been as a gap in our great feast.
   —Shakespeare.

For I, who holds sage Homer's rule the best,
Welcome the coming, speed the going guest.   —Pope.

See, your guests approach:
Address yourself to entertain them sprightly,
And let's be red with mirth.
   —Shakespeare.

Some steam process should be invented for arranging guests when they are above five hundred.—Beaconsfield.

The first day a man is a guest, the second a burden, the third a pest.—Laboulaye.

You must come home with me and be my guest;
You will give joy to me, and I will do
All that is in my power to honor you.
   —Shelley.

For whom he means to make an often guest,
One dish shall serve; and welcome make the rest.   —Joseph Hall.

Guilt

Be sure your sin will find you out. —Bible.

The ghostly consciousness of wrong. —Carlyle.

Guilt's a terrible thing.—Ben Jonson.

Guilt is a spiritual Rubicon.—Jane Porter.

The mind of guilt is full of scorpions.—Shakespeare.

No one becomes guilty by fate.— Seneca.

Let the galled jade wince.—Shakespeare.

He who flees from trial confesses his guilt.—Syrus.

Guilt soon learns to lie.—Miss Braddon.

Guilt has very quick ears to an accusation.—Fielding.

My hands are guilty, but my heart is free.—Dryden.

And then it started like a guilty thing
Upon a fearful summons.—Shakespeare.

The guilt being great, the fear doth still exceed.—Shakespeare.

A land of levity is a land of guilt. —Young.

Guilt is ever at a loss, and confusion waits upon it.—Congreve.

Guilt is a timorous thing ere perpetration; despair alone makes guilty men be bold.—Coleridge.

Thus conscience does make cowards of us all.—Shakespeare.

Wickedness consists in the very hesitation about an act, even though it be not perpetrated.—Cicero.

A wicked conscience mouldeth goblins swift as frenzy thoughts.—Shakespeare.

There are no greater prudes than those women who have some secret to hide.—George Sand.

The sin lessens in human estimation only as the guilt increases.—Schiller.

He that commits a sin shall find the pressing guilt lie heavy on his mind.—Creech.

Guiltiness will speak, though tongues were out of use.—Shakespeare.

All the perfumes of Arabia will not sweeten this little hand.—Shakespeare.

From the body of one guilty deed a thousand ghostly fears and haunting thoughts proceed.—Wordsworth.

It is easy to defend the innocent; but who is eloquent enough to defend the guilty?—Publius Syrus.

One fault begets another; one crime renders another necessary.—Southey.

The guilty mind debases the great image that it wears, and levels us with brutes.—Havard.

Beside one deed of guilt, how blest is guiltless woe!—Bulwer-Lytton.

Thou need'st not answer; thy confession speaks,
Already redd'ning in thy guilty cheeks.
—Byron.

Men's minds are too ingenious in palliating guilt in themselves.—Livy.

Alas! how difficult it is to prevent the countenance from betraying guilt.—Ovid.

How guilt, once harbor'd in the conscious breast,
Intimidates the brave, degrades the great!
Dr. Johnson.

All fear, but fear of heaven, betrays a guilt,
And guilt is villainy. —N. Lee.

Let guilty men remember, their black deeds
Do lean on crutches made of slender reeds.
—John Webster.

I esteem death a trifle, if not caused by guilt.—Plautus.

He is not guilty who is not guilty of his own free will.—Seneca.

Life is not the supreme good; but of all earthly ills the chief is guilt.—Schiller.

I'll haunt thee like a wicked conscience still.—Shakespeare.

The guilt being great, the fear doth still exceed.—Shakespeare.

God hath yoked to guilt her pale tormentor,—misery.—Bryant.

The greatest incitement to guilt is the hope of sinning with impunity.—Cicero.

They whose guilt within their bosoms lie imagine every eye beholds their blame.—Shakespeare.

If one know them they are in the terrors of the shadow of death.—Bible.

Where, where for shelter shall the guilty fly,
When consternation turns the good man pale? —Young.

Guilt is the source of sorrow; 'tis the fiend,
The avenging fiend, that follows us behind
With whips and stings. —Rowe.

Let wickedness escape as it may at the bar, it never fails of doing justice upon itself: for every guilty person is his own hangman.—Seneca.

Our sins, like to our shadows, when our day was in its glory, scarce appeared; toward our evening, how great and monstrous!—Suckling.

Thoughts cannot form themselves in words so horrid
As can express my guilt. —Dryden.

Guilt alone, like brain-sick frenzy in its feverish mood, fills the light air with visionary terrors, and shapeless forms of fear.—Junius.

O, she is fallen
Into a pit of ink, that the wide sea
Hath drops too few to wash her clean again. —Shakespeare.

Every man bears something within him that, if it were publicly announced, would excite feelings of aversion.—Goethe.

Action and care will in time wear down the strongest frame; but guilt and melancholy are poisons of quick despatch.—Thomas Paine.

Let no man trust the first false step of guilt; it hangs upon a precipice, whose steep descent in last perdition ends.—Young.

All good men and women should be on their guard to avoid guilt, and even the suspicion of it.—Plautus.

To what gulfs
A single deviation from the track
Of human duties leads! —Byron.

It is base to filch a purse, daring to embezzle a million, but it is great beyond measure to steal a crown. The sin lessens as the guilt increases.—Schiller.

When guilt is in its blush of infancy, it trembles in a tenderness of shame; and the first eye that pierces through the veil that hides the secret brings it to the face.—Southern.

Guilt has always its horrors and solicitudes; and, to make it yet more shameful and detestable, it is doomed often to stand in awe of those to whom nothing could give influence or weight but their power of betraying.—Johnson.

Fraud and falsehood are his weak and treacherous allies; and he lurks trembling in the dark, dreading every ray of light, lest it should discover him, and give him up to shame and punishment.—Fielding.

He who is conscious of secret and dark designs, which, if known, would blast him, is perpetually shrinking and dodging from public observation, and is afraid of all around him, and much more of all above him.—Wirt.

Guilt was never a rational thing; it distorts all the faculties of the human mind, it perverts them, it leaves a man no longer in the free use of his reason, it puts him into confusion.—Burke.

He swears, but he is sick at heart;
He laughs, but he turns deadly pale;
His restless eye and sudden start—
These tell the dreadful tale
That will be told: it needs no words from thee
Thou self-sold slave to guilt and misery.
—Dana.

Think not that guilt requires the burning torches of the furies to agitate and torment it. Their own frauds, their crimes, their remembrances of the past, their terrors of the future,—these are the domestic furies that are ever present to the mind of the impious.—Robert Hall.

Guilt is a poor, helpless, dependent being. Without the alliance of able, diligent, and let me add, fortunate fraud, it is inevitably undone. If the guilty culprit be obstinately silent, it forms a deadly presumption against him: if he speaks, talking tends only to his discovery, and his very defence often furnishes the materials for his conviction.—Junius.

Guilt, though it may attain temporal splendor, can never confer real happiness; the evil consequences of our crimes long survive their commission, and, like the ghosts of the murdered, forever haunt the steps of the malefactor; while the paths of virtue, though seldom those of worldly greatness, are always those of pleasantness and peace.—Sir Walter Scott.

What we call real estate—the solid ground to build a house on—is the broad foundation on which nearly all the guilt of this world rests.—Nathaniel Hawthorne.

They who once engage in iniquitous designs miserably deceive themselves when they think that they will go so far and no farther; one fault begets another, one crime renders another necessary; and thus they are impelled continually downward into a depth of guilt, which at the commencement of their career they would have died rather than have incurred.—Southey.

There is no man so good, that so squares all his thoughts and actions to the laws, that he is not faulty enough to deserve hanging ten times in his life. Nay, and such a one, too, as it were great pity to make away, and very unjust to punish. And such a one there may be, as has no way offended the laws, who nevertheless would not deserve the character of a virtuous man, and that philosophy would justly condemn to be whipped; so unequal and perplexed is this relation.—Montaigne.

H

Habit

Habit is ten times nature.—Wellington.

Habit, if not resisted, soon becomes necessity.—St. Augustine.

Habit is the nursery of errors.—Victor Hugo.

Habit is necessary to give power.—Hazlitt.

Habit is the most imperious of all masters.—Goethe.

Habit is stronger than nature.—Quintus Curtius Rufus.

Habit is, as it were, a second nature.—Cicero.

Nothing is stronger than habit.—Ovid.

How use doth breed a habit in a man!—Shakespeare.

Pursuits become habits.—Ovid.

The power of habit is very strong.—Syrus.

A large part of Christian virtue consists in right habits.—Paley.

Beware of fixing habits in a child.—Robert Hall.

All habits gather by unseen degrees.—Dryden.

Habit is a cable. We weave a thread of it every day, and at last we cannot break it.—Horace Mann.

Our second mother, habit, is also a good mother.—Auerbach.

In the great majority of things habit is a greater plague than ever afflicted Egypt.—John Foster.

The chain of habit coils itself around the heart like a serpent, to gnaw and stifle it.—Hazlitt.

Ill habits gather by unseen degrees,—as brooks make rivers, rivers run to seas.—Dryden.

For use almost can change the stamp of nature.—Shakespeare.

Man yields to custom as he bows to fate,—in all things ruled, mind, body, and estate.—Crabbe.

Unless the habit leads to happiness the best habit is to contract none.—Zimmermann.

Habit is altogether too arbitrary a master for me to submit to.—Lavater.

It is easy to assume a habit; but when you try to cast it off, it will take skin and all.—H. W. Shaw.

Habits are soon assumed; but when we strive to strip them off, 'tis being flayed alive.—Cowper.

It is almost as difficult to make a man unlearn his errors as his knowledge.—Colton.

The chains of habit are generally too small to be felt till they are too strong to be broken.—Johnson.

Habit is the deepest law of human nature.—Carlyle.

Habit, to which all of us are more or less slaves.—La Fontaine.

Every base occupation makes one sharp in its practice and dull in every other.—Sir P. Sidney.

How many unjust and wicked things are done from mere habit.—Terence.

Habit gives endurance, and fatigue is the best night cap.—Kincaid.

Small habits well pursued, betimes,
May reach the dignity of crimes.
     —Hannah More.

I will be a slave to no habit; therefore farewell tobacco.—Hosea Ballou.

To learn new habits is everything, for it is to reach the substance of life. Life is but a tissue of habits.—Amiel.

Long customs are not easily broken; he that attempts to change the course of his own life very often labors in vain.—Johnson.

Nothing really pleasant or unpleasant subsists by nature, but all things become so by habit.—Epictetus.

Lord Tenterden, the celebrated judge, expired with these words on his lips, "Gentlemen of the jury, you will now consider your verdict."—Lord Campbell.

If an idiot were to tell you the same story every day for a year, you would end by believing him.—Burke.

Are we not like the actor of old times, who wore his mask so long his face took its likeness?—L. E. Landon.

Vicious habits are so odious and degrading that they transform the individual who practices them into an incarnate demon.—Cicero.

Habits, soft and pliant at first, are like some coral stones, which are easily cut when first quarried, but soon become hard as adamant.—Spurgeon.

That beneficent harness of routine, which enables silly men to live respectably and happy men to live calmly. —George Eliot.

Habit will reconcile us to everything but change, and even to change if it recur not too quickly.—Colton.

I have often found a small stream at its fountain-head, that, when followed up, carried away the camel with his load.—Saadi.

Habits are the daughters of action; but they nurse their mothers, and give birth to daughters after her image, more lovely and prosperous.—Jeremy Taylor.

Acts of virtue ripen into habits; and the goodly and permanent result is the formation or establishment of a virtuous character.—Chalmers.

A single bad habit will mar an otherwise faultless character, as an ink-drop soileth the pure white page.—Hosea Ballou.

Habits are like the wrinkles on a man's brow; if you will smooth out the one, I will smooth out the other. —H. W. Shaw.

Marriage should combat without respite or mercy that monster which devours everything,—habit.—Balzac.

To things which you bear with impatience you should accustom yourself, and, by habit you will bear them well. —Seneca.

Habit with him was all the test of truth;
"It must be right: I've done it from my youth."   —Crabbe.

My very chains and I grew friends,
So much a long communion tends
To make us what we are; even I
Regain'd my freedom with a sigh.
     —Byron.

Habit and imitation—there is nothing more perennial in us than these two. They are the source of all working, and all apprenticeship, of all practice, and all learning, in this world,—Thomas Carlyle.

If thou dost still retain the same ill habits, the same follies, too, still thou art bound to vice, and still a slave.—Dryden.

The law of the harvest is to reap more than you sow. Sow an act, and you reap a habit; sow a habit, and you reap a character; sow a character, and you reap a destiny.—G. D. Boardman.

It must be conceded that, after affection, habit has its peculiar value. It is a little stream which flows softly, but freshens everything along its course.—Madame Swetchine.

Habits, though in their commencement like the filmy line of the spider, trembling at every breeze, may in the end prove as links of tempered steel, binding a deathless being to eternal felicity or woe.—Mrs. Sigourney.

The will that yields the first time with some reluctance does so the second time with less hesitation, and the third time with none at all, until presently the habit is adopted.—Henry Giles.

For the honest people, relations increase with the years. For the vicious, inconveniences increase. Inconstancy is the defect of vice; the influence of habit is one of the qualities of virtue.—Madame Necker.

The habit of virtue cannot be formed in a closet. Habits are formed by acts of reason in a persevering struggle through temptation.—Gilpin.

I perceive that the things that we do are silly; but what can one do? According to men's habits and dispositions, so one must yield to them.—Terence.

Habit in most cases hardens and encrusts by taking away the keener edge of our sensations: but does it not in others quicken and refine, by giving a mechanical facility and by engrafting an acquired sense?—Hazlitt.

Habits are formed, not at one stroke, but gradually and insensibly; so that, unless vigilant care be employed, a great change may come over the character without our being conscious of any.—Whately.

A young man ought to cross his own rules, to awake his vigor, and to keep it from growing faint and rusty. And there is no course of life so weak and sottish as that which is carried on by rule and discipline.—Montaigne.

Make sobriety a habit, and intemperance will be hateful; make prudence a habit, and reckless profligacy will be as contrary to the nature of the child, grown or adult, as the most atrocious crimes are to any of us.—Brougham.

To be perpetually longing and impatiently desirous of anything, so that a man cannot abstain from it, is to lose a man's liberty, and to become a servant of meat and drink, or smoke.—Jeremy Taylor.

Habit is the approximation of the animal system to the organic. It is a confession of failure in the highest function of being, which involves a perpetual self-determination, in full view of all existing circumstances.—Holmes.

I will govern my life and my thoughts as if the whole world were to see the one and to read the other; for what does it signify to make anything a secret to my neighbor, when to God (who is the searcher of our hearts) all our privacies are open?—Seneca.

Vicious habits are so great a stain to human nature, and so odious in themselves, that every person actuated by right reason would avoid them, though he were sure they would be always concealed both from God and man, and had no future punishment entailed upon them.—Cicero.

Habit, if wisely and skillfully formed, becomes truly a second nature, as the common saying is; but unskillfully and unmethodically directed, it will be, as it were, the ape of Nature, which imitates nothing to the life, but only clumsily and awkwardly.—Bacon.

I trust everything, under God, to habit, upon which, in all ages, the lawgiver, as well as the schoolmaster, has mainly placed his reliance,—habit, which makes everything easy, and casts all difficulties upon the deviation from the wonted course.—Lord Brougham.

———

Like flakes of snow that fall unperceived upon the earth, the seemingly unimportant events of life succeed one another. As the snow gathers together, so are our habits formed. No single flake that is added to the pile produces a sensible change; no single action creates, however it may exhibit, a man's character.—Jeremy Taylor.

———

And it is a singular truth that, though a man may shake off national habits, accent, manner of thinking, style of dress,—though he may become perfectly identified with another nation, and speak its language well, perhaps better than his own,—yet never can he succeed in changing his handwriting to a foreign style.—Disraeli.

———

Habit hath so vast a prevalence over the human mind that there is scarce anything too strange or too strong to be asserted of it. The story of the miser who, from long accustoming to cheat others, came at last to cheat himself, and with great delight and triumph picked his own pocket of a guinea to convey to his hoard, is not impossible or improbable.—Fielding.

———

Give a child the habit of sacredly regarding the truth—of carefully respecting the property of others—of scrupulously abstaining from all acts of improvidence which can involve him in distress, and he will just as likely think of rushing into the element in which he cannot breathe, as of lying or cheating or stealing.—Lord Brougham.

———

Centres, or centre-pieces of wood, are put by builders under an arch of stone while it is in the process of construction till the key-stone is put in. Just such is the use Satan makes of pleasures to construct evil habits upon; the pleasure lasts till the habit is fully formed; but that done the habit may stand eternal. The pleasures are sent for firewood, and the hell begins in this life.—Coleridge.

———

If we look back upon the usual course of our feelings, we shall find that we are more influenced by the frequent recurrence of objects than by their weight and importance; and that habit has more force in forming our characters than our opinions have. The mind naturally takes its tone and complexion from what it habitually contemplates.—Robert Hall.

———

A tendency to resume the same mode of action at stated times is peculiarly the characteristic of the nervous system; and on this account regularity is of great consequence in exercising the moral and intellectual power. All nervous diseases have a marked tendency to observe regular periods; and the natural inclination to sleep at the approach of night is another instance of the same fact.—Dr. Combe.

Hair

Gray hairs are death's blossoms.—Schiller.

———

When you see fair hair, be pitiful.—George Eliot.

———

The ungrown glories of his beamy hair.—Addison.

———

Sweet girl graduates, in their golden hair.—Tennyson.

———

Robed in the long night of her deep hair.—Tennyson.

———

Thy fair hair my heart enchained.—Sir Philip Sidney.

———

Fair tresses man's imperial race ensnare.—Pope.

———

Her luxuriant hair,—it was like the sweep of a swift wing in visions!—Willis.

———

The robe which curious Nature weaves to hang upon the head.—Decker.

———

How ill white hairs become a fool and jester!—Shakespeare.

Comb down his hair; look, look! it stands upright.—Shakespeare.

And her st ..ny locks
Hang on her temples like a golden fleece.
—Shakespeare.

Golden hair, like sunlight streaming
On the marble of her shoulder.
—J. G. Saxe.

I pray thee let me and my fellow have
A hair of the dog that bit us last night.
—John Heywood.

Make false hair, and thatch your poor thin roofs with burthens of the dead.—Shakespeare.

Loose his beard and hoary hair streamed, like a meteor, to the troubled air.—Gray.

For deadly fear can time outgo, and blanch at once the hair.—Sir Walter Scott.

There seems a life in hair, though it be dead.—Leigh Hunt.

Her hair down-gushing in an armful flows,
And floods her ivory neck, and glitters as she goes.   —Allan Cunningham.

Whose every little ringlet thrilled, as if with soul and passion filled!—Moore.

The hoary head is a crown of glory if it be found in the way of righteousness.—Bible.

A large head of hair adds beauty to a good face, and terror to an ugly one.—Lycurgus.

The glittering tresses which, now shaken loose,
Shower'd gold.   —Owen Meredith.

His hair is of a good color,—an excellent color; your chestnut was ever the only color.—Shakespeare.

By common consent gray hairs are a crown of glory; the only object of respect that can never excite envy.—Bancroft.

Long, glorious locks, which drop upon thy cheek like gold-hued cloud-flakes on the rosy morn.—Bailey.

Give me a look, give me a face that makes simplicity a grace—robes loosely flowing, hair as free!—Ben Jonson.

Dear, dead women, with such hair, too—what's become of all the gold
Used to hang and brush their bosoms?
—Robert Browning.

Her hair was not more sunny than her heart, though like a natural golden coronet it circled her dear head with careless art.—Lowell.

The hair is the finest ornament women have. Of old, virgins used to wear it loose, except when they were in mourning.—Luther.

The redundant locks, robustious to no purpose, clustering down—vast monument of strength.—Milton.

An angel face! its sunny "wealth of hair,"
In radiant ripples, bathed the graceful throat
And dimpled shoulders.—Mrs. Osgood.

Her cap of velvet could not hold
The tresses of her hair of gold,
That flowed and floated like the stream,
And fell in masses down her neck.
—Longfellow.

Her hair is bound with myrtle leaves,
(Green leaves upon her golden hair!)
Green grasses through the yellow sheaves
Of autumn corn are not more fair.
—Oscar Wilde.

Come, let me pluck that silver hair
Which 'mid thy clustering curls I see;
The withering type of time or care
Has nothing, sure, to do with thee.
—Alaric Alex Watts.

Ah, thy beautiful hair! so was it once braided for me, for me;
Now for death is it crowned, only for death, lover and lord of thee,
—Swinburne.

A large bare forehead gives a woman a masculine and defying look. The word "effrontery" comes from it. The hair should be brought over such a forehead as vines are trailed over a wall.—Leigh Hunt.

Her golden locks she roundly did uptie in braided trammels, that no looser hairs did out of order stray about her dainty ears.—Spenser.

Her head was bare, but for her native ornament of hair, which in a simple knot was tied above—sweet negligence, unheeded bait of love!—Dryden.

Her long loose yellow locks lyke golden wyre,
Sprinckled with perle, and perling flowres atweene,
Doe lyke a golden mantle her attyre.
—Spenser.

A silver line, that from the brow to the crown,
And in the middle, parts the braided hair,
Just serves to show how delicate a soil
The golden harvest grows in.
—Wordsworth.

Her hair
In ringlets rather dark than fair,
Does down her ivory bosom roll,
And hiding half adorns the whole.
—Prior.

Her locks are plighted like the fleece of wool
That Jason and his Grecian mates achiev'd,
As pure as gold, yet not from gold deriv'd;
As full of sweets as sweet of sweets is full.
—Robert Greene.

Beware of her fair hair, for she excels
All women in the magic of her locks;
And when she winds them round a young man's neck,
She will not ever set him free again.
—Goethe.

Gray hair is beautiful in itself, and so softening to the complexion and so picturesque in its effect that many a woman who has been plain in her youth is, by its beneficent influence, transformed into a handsome woman.
—Miss Oakey.

It was brown with a golden gloss, Janette,
It was finer than silk of the floss, my pet;
'Twas a beautiful mist falling down to your wrist,
'Twas a thing to be braided, and jewelled, and kissed—
'Twas the loveliest hair in the world, my pet. —Chas. G. Halpine.

God doth bestow that garment, when we die, that, like a soft and silken canopy, is still spread over us. In spite of death, our hair grows in the grave; and that alone looks fresh when all our other beauty's gone.—Decker.

Look on beauty, and you shall see 'tis purchased by the weight; which therein works a miracle in Nature, making them lightest that wear most of it: so are those crispèd snaky golden locks which make such wanton gambols with the wind upon supposed fairness, often known to be the dowry of a second head, the skull that bred them in the sepulchre.—Shakespeare.

This nymph, to the destruction of mankind,
Nourish'd two locks, which graceful hung behind
In equal curls, and well conspir'd to deck,
With shining ringlets, the smooth ivory neck.
Love in these labyrinths his slaves detains,
And mighty hearts are held in slender chains,
With hairy springes we the birds betray,
Slight lines of hair surprise the finny prey.
—Pope.

Bind up those tresses. O, what love I note
In the fair multitude of those her hairs!
Where but by chance a silver drop hath fallen,
Even to that drop ten thousand wiry friends
Do glue themselves in sociable grief,
Like true, inseparable, faithful loves,
Sticking together in calamity.
—Shakespeare.

Hair is the most delicate and lasting of our materials, and survives us, like love. It is so light, so gentle, so escaping from the idea of death, that, with a lock of hair belonging to a child or friend, we may almost look up to heaven and compare notes with the angelic nature,—may almost say, " I have a piece of thee here not unworthy of thy being now."—Leigh Hunt.

Hand

The mind's only perfect vassal.—Tuckerman.

The hand that gives, gathers.—Eugene Sue.

As expressive as the face.—N. P. Willis.

The white wonder of Juliet's hands.—Shakespeare.

There is no better sign of a brave mind than a hard hand.—Shakespeare.

He who beholds her hand forgets her face.—Mrs. Brooks.

A dazzling white hand, veined cerulean.—Massey.

His noble hand did win what he did spend.—Shakespeare.

My hands are clean, but my heart has somewhat of impurity.—Euripides.

The wise hand does not all the tongue dictates.—Cervantes.

His hand will be against every man, and every man's hand against him.—Bible.

I love a hand that meets mine own
With grasp that causes some sensation.
—Mrs. Osgood.

For through the south the custom still commands
The gentleman to kiss the lady's hands.
—Byron.

Even to the delicacy of their hand
There was resemblance such as true blood wears. —Byron.

Women carry a beautiful hand with them to the grave, when a beautiful face has long ago vanished.—Beaconsfield.

Without the bed her other fair hand was,
On the green coverlet; whose perfect white
Show'd like an April daisy on the grass,
With pearly sweat, resembling dew of night. —Shakespeare.

Her hand, in whose comparison all whites are ink writing their own reproach, to whose soft seizure the cygnet's down is harsh, and spirit of sense hard as the palm of ploughman! —Shakespeare.

Venerable to me is the hard hand,—crooked, coarse,—wherein, notwithstanding, lies a cunning virtue, indispensably royal as of the sceptre of the planet.—Carlyle.

Neither the naked hand nor the understanding, left to itself, can do much; the work is accomplished by instruments and helps, of which the need is not less for the understanding than the hand.—Bacon.

Other parts of the body assist the speaker, but these speak themselves. By them we ask, we promise, we invoke, we dismiss, we threaten, we entreat, we deprecate; we express fear, joy, grief, our doubts, our assent, our penitence; we show moderation, profusion; we mark number and time.—Quintilian.

I take thy hand, this hand,
As soft as dove's down, and as white as it;
Or Ethiopian's tooth, or the fann'd snow,
That's bolted by the northern blast twice o'er. —Shakespeare.

The Greeks adored their gods by the simple compliment of kissing their hands; and the Romans were treated as atheists if they would not perform the same act when they entered a temple. This custom, however, as a religious ceremony declined with paganism, but was continued as a salutation by inferiors to their superiors, or as a token of esteem among friends.—Disraeli.

Lavater told Goethe that, on a certain occasion when he held the velvet bag in the church as collector of the offerings, he tried to observe only the hands; and he satisfied himself that in every individual the shape of the hand and of the fingers, the action and sentiment in dropping the gift into the bag, were distinctly different and individually characteristic.—Mrs. Jameson.

'Twas a hand
White, delicate, dimpled, warm, languid, and bland.
The hand of a woman is often, in youth,
Somewhat rough, somewhat red, somewhat graceless, in truth;
Does its beauty refine, as its pulses grow calm,
Or as sorrow has crossed the life line in the palm? —Lord Lytton.

There is a hand that has no heart in it, there is a claw or paw, a flipper or fin, a bit of wet cloth to take hold of, a piece of unbaked dough on the cook's trencher, a cold clammy thing we recoil from, or greedy clutch with the heat of sin, which we drop as a burning coal.

What a scale from the talon to the horn of plenty, is this human palm-leaf! Sometimes it is what a knife-shaped, thin-bladed tool we dare not grasp, or like a poisonous thing we shake off, or unclean member, which, white as it may look, we feel polluted by!—C. A. Bartol.

Happiness

The soul's calm sunshine.—Pope.

Happiness is an exotic of celestial birth.—Sheridan.

Happiness is the natural flower of duty.—Phillips Brooks.

Happiness is reflective, like the light of heaven.—Washington Irving.

There is no man but may make his paradise.—Beaumont and Fletcher.

Happiness is a rare cosmetic.—G. J. W. Melville.

Every one speaks of it, few know it.—Mme. Roland.

The saddest birds a season find to sing.—Southwell.

He who is good is happy.—Habbington.

There are no rules for felicity.—Victor Hugo.

True wisdom is the price of happiness.—Young.

Happiness is unrepented pleasure.—Socrates.

Happiness is a good that Nature sells us.—Voltaire.

Happiness is not perfected until it is shared.—Jane Porter.

Happiness is no laughing matter.—Whately.

They live too long who happiness outlive.—Dryden.

The best happiness will be to escape the worst misery.—George Eliot.

Man is the artificer of his own happiness.—Henry D. Thoreau.

Happiness is an equivalent for all troublesome things.—Epictetus.

Be happy, but be so by piety.—Mme. de Staël.

Happiness seems made to be shared.—Corneille.

Happiness may have but one night, as glory but one day.—Alfred de Musset.

The rays of happiness, like those of light, are colorless when unbroken.—Longfellow.

None are happy but by anticipation of change.—Dr. Johnson.

Happiness lies, first of all, in health.—George William Curtis.

There is in man a higher than love of happiness; he can do without happiness, and instead thereof find blessedness.—Carlyle.

What happiness is there which is not purchased with more or less of pain?—Mrs. Oliphant.

Happiness is where we find it, but very rarely where we seek it.—J. Petit-Senn.

That happiness does still the longest thrive where joys and griefs have turns alternative.—Herrick.

There comes forever something between us and what we deem our happiness.—Byron.

All who joy would win
Must share it—happiness was born a twin.
—Byron.

True happiness ne'er entered at an eye;
True happiness resides in things unseen.
—Young

Happiness—a good bank account, a good cook, and a good digestion.—Rousseau.

One cannot be fully happy until after his sixtieth year.—Bonstetten.

Fortitude, justice, and candor are very necessary instruments of happiness, but they require time and exertion.—Sydney Smith.

Those who seek for something more than happiness in this world must not complain if happiness is not their portion.—Froude.

Happiness without peace is temporal; peace along with happiness is eternal.—Aughey.

We are never happy: we can only remember that we were so once.—Alexander Smith.

So long as you do not quarrel with sin, you will never be a truly happy man.—J. C. Ryle.

Happiness does away with ugliness, and even makes the beauty of beauty.—Amiel.

The happiest women, like the happiest nations, have no history.—George Eliot.

To be happy is not the purpose for which you are placed in this world.—Froude.

            To be strong
Is to be happy!   —Longfellow.

We are no longer happy so soon as we wish to be happier.—Landor.

Nothing is more idle than to inquire after happiness, which nature has kindly placed within our reach.—Johnson.

Happiness never lays its finger on its pulse. If we attempt to steal a glimpse of its features it disappears.—Alexander Smith.

Beware what earth calls happiness; beware all joys but joys that never can expire.—Young.

The happiness or unhappiness of men depends no less upon their dispositions than their fortunes.—La Rochefoucauld.

When we reflect on the shortness and uncertainty of life, how despicable seem all our pursuits of happiness.—Hume.

It is no happiness to live long, nor unhappiness to die soon; happy is he that hath lived long enough to die well.—Quarles.

How bitter a thing it is to look into happiness through another man's eyes!—Shakespeare.

Happiness is not the end of duty, it is a constituent of it. It is in it and of it; not an equivalent, but an element.—Henry Giles.

Happiness is always the inaccessible castle which sinks in ruin when we set foot on it.—Arsène Houssaye.

Our happiness in this world depends on the affections we are enabled to inspire.—Duchesse de Praslin.

Human happiness depends mainly upon the improvement of small opportunities.—J. L. Basford.

No one can be said to be happy until he is dead.—Solon.

Happiness is neither within us nor without us, it is the union of ourselves with God.—Pascal.

To be happy is not the purpose of our being, but to deserve happiness.—Fichte.

Real happiness is cheap enough, yet how dearly we pay for its counterfeit!—Hosea Ballou.

The sunshine of life is made up of very little beams, that are bright all the time.—Aikin.

If we cannot live so as to be happy, let us at least live so as to deserve happiness.—Fichte.

We are never so happy, nor so unhappy, as we suppose ourselves to be.—La Rochefoucauld.

Happiness grows at our own firesides, and is not to be picked in strangers' gardens.—Douglas Jerrold

He who has no wish to be happier is the happiest of men.—W. R. Alger.

There must be some mixture of happiness in everything but sin.—Mrs. Sigourney.

The highest happiness, the purest joys of life, wear out at last.—Goethe.

Happiness is no other than soundness and perfection of mind.—Antoninus.

I have enjoyed earthly happiness,
I have lived and loved.—Schiller.

Domestic happiness, thou only bliss
Of paradise that hast survived the fall!
—Cowper.

He that upon a true principle lives, without any disquiet of thought, may be said to be happy.—L'Estrange.

Nature has granted to all to be happy, if we did but know how to use her benefits.—Claudian.

True happiness (if understood)
Consists alone in doing good.
—Thomson.

Beware what earth calls happiness; beware all joys but joys that never can expire.—Young.

In my opinion it is the happy living, and not, as Antisthenes said, the happy dying, in which human happiness consists.—Montaigne.

Happiness is a sunbeam, which may pass through a thousand bosoms without losing a particle of its original ray. —Sir P. Sidney.

The happiness of the tender heart is increased by what it can take away from the wretchedness of others.—J. Petit-Senn.

Happiness and virtue react upon each other—the best are not only the happiest, but the happiest are usually the best.—Lytton.

The happiness of the human race in this world does not consist in our being devoid of passions, but in our learning to command them.—From the French.

I earn that I eat, get that I wear; owe no man hate, envy no man's happiness; glad of other men's good, content with my harm.—Shakespeare.

Happiness and misery are the names of two extremes, the utmost bounds whereof we know not.—Locke.

Hunting after happiness is like hunting after a lost sheep in the wilderness—when you find it, the chances are that it is a skeleton.—H. W. Shaw.

Happiness is that single and glorious thing which is the very light and sun of the whole animated universe; and where she is not it were better that nothing should be.—Colton.

Happiness is only to be found in a recurrence to the principles of human nature; and these will prompt very simple measures.—Beaconsfield.

It is quite easy for stupid people to be happy; they believe in fables, and they trot on in a beaten track like a horse on a tramway.—Ouida.

The nearest we can come to perfect happiness is to cheat ourselves with the belief that we have got it.—H. W. Shaw.

A sound mind in a sound body is a short but full description of a happy state in this world.—Locke.

Happiness is in taste and not in things; and it is by having what we love that we are happy, not by having what others find agreeable.—Rochefoucauld.

The body is like a piano, and happiness is like music. It is needful to have the instrument in good order.—Beecher.

You traverse the world in search of happiness, which is within the reach of every man; a contented mind confers it on all.—Horace.

Happiness has no limits, because God has neither bottom nor bounds, and because happiness is nothing but the conquest of God through love.—Amiel.

That state of life is most happy where superfluities are not required and necessaries are not wanting.—Plutarch.

It is ever thus with happiness;
It is the gay to-morrow of the mind,
That never comes. —Proctor.

Degrees of happiness vary according to the degrees of virtue, and consequently, that life which is most virtuous is most happy.—Norris.

Happiness is the fine and gentle rain which penetrates the soul, but which afterwards gushes forth in springs of tears.—Maurice de Guérin.

Wouldst thou ever roam abroad? See, what is good lies by thy side. Only learn to catch happiness, for happiness is ever by you.—Goethe.

We take greater pains to persuade others that we are happy than in endeavoring to think so ourselves.—Confucius.

Brethren, happiness is not our being's end and aim. The Christian's aim is perfection, not happiness; and every one of the sons of God must have something of that spirit which marked his Master.—F. W. Robertson.

Terrestrial happiness is of short duration. The brightness of the flame is wasting its fuel; the fragrant flower is passing away in its own odors.—Dr. Johnson.

The great blessings of mankind are within us, and within our reach, but we shut our eyes, and, like people in the dark, we fall foul upon the very thing we search for, without finding it. —Seneca.

If the chief part of human happiness arises from the consciousness of being beloved, as I believe it does, these sudden changes of fortune seldom contribute much to happiness.—Adam Smith.

All mankind are happier for having been happy; so that, if you make them happy now, you make them happy

twenty years hence by the memory of it.—Sydney Smith.

So endless and exorbitant are the desires of men that they will grasp at all, and can form no scheme of perfect happiness with less.—Swift.

Happy! Who is happy? Was there not a serpent in Paradise itself? And if Eve had been perfectly happy beforehand, would she have listened to the tempter?—Thackeray.

The common course of things is in favor of happiness; happiness is the rule, misery the exception. Were the order reversed, our attention would be called to examples of health and competency, instead of disease and want.—Paley.

It is a great truth, wonderful as it is undeniable, that all our happiness—temporal, spiritual and eternal—consists in one thing; namely, in resigning ourselves to God, and in leaving ourselves with Him, to do with us and in us just as He pleases.—Madame Guyon.

True happiness is of a retired nature, and an enemy to pomp and noise. It arises, in the first place, from the enjoyment of one's self, and, in the next, from the friendship and conversation of a few select friends.—Addison.

Happiness is a roadside flower growing on the highways of usefulness; plucked, it shall wither in thy hand; passed by, it is fragrance to thy spirit. Trample the thyme beneath thy feet; be useful, be happy.—Tupper.

The sweetest bird builds near the ground,
The loveliest flower springs low;
And we must stoop for happiness
If we its worth would know.—Swain.

When we are not too anxious about happiness and unhappiness, but devote ourselves to the strict and unsparing performance of duty, then happiness comes of itself—nay, even springs from the midst of a life of troubles and anxieties and privations.—Humboldt.

Alas! if the principles of contentment are not within us—the height of station and worldly grandeur will as soon add a cubit to a man's stature as to his happiness.—Sterne.

Happiness in this world, when it comes, comes incidentally. Make it the object of pursuit, and it leads us a wild-goose chase, and is never attained. —Hawthorne.

There is a gentle element, and man may breathe it with a calm, unruffled soul, and drink its living waters, till his heart is pure; and this is human happiness.—Willis.

Happiness and comfort stream immediately from God himself, as light issues from the sun; and sometimes looks and darts itself into the meanest corners, while it forbears to visit the largest and the noblest rooms.—Aughey.

The most happy women within their homes are those who have married sensible men. The latter suffer themselves to be governed with so much the more pleasure, as they are always masters of themselves.—Prince de Ligne.

In the soul, when the supreme faculties move regularly, the inferior passions and faculties following, there arises a serenity infinitely beyond the highest quintessence of worldly delight. —South.

There is something more awful in happiness than in sorrow—the latter being earthly and finite, the former composed of the substance and texture of eternity, so that spirits still embodied may well tremble at it.—Hawthorne.

To be happy is not only to be freed from the pains and diseases of the body, but from anxiety and vexation of spirit; not only to enjoy the pleasures of sense, but peace of conscience and tranquillity of mind.—Tillotson.

Priestly was the first (unless it was Beccaria) who taught my lips to pronounce this sacred truth—that the greatest happiness of the greatest number is the foundation of morals and legislation.—Bentham.

Youth is too tumultuous for felicity; old age too insecure for happiness. The period most favorable to enjoyment, in a vigorous, fortunate, and generous life, is that between forty and sixty. Life culminates at sixty.— Bovee.

So scanty is our present allowance of happiness that in many situations life could scarcely be supported if hope were not allowed to relieve the present hour by pleasures borrowed from the future.—Johnson.

Without strong affection, and humanity of heart, and gratitude to that Being whose code is mercy, and whose great attribute is benevolence to all things that breathe, true happiness can never be attained.—Dickens.

It is something to look upon enjoyment, so that it be free and wild, and in the face of Nature, though it be but the enjoyment of an idiot. It is something to know that Heaven has left the capacity of gladness in such a creature's breast.—Dickens.

If solid happiness we prize,
Within our breast this jewel lies,
  And they are fools who roam;
The world has nothing to bestow,
From our own selves our bliss must flow,
  And that dear hut—our home.
      —Nathaniel Cotton.

I have lived to know that the great secret of human happiness is this: Never suffer your energies to stagnate. The old adage of "too many irons in the fire," conveys an untruth—you cannot have too many—poker, tongs— and all, keep them going.—Adam Clark.

The haunts of happiness are varied and rather unaccountable, but I have more often seen her among little children, and home firesides, and in country houses, than anywhere else—at least, I think so.—Sydney Smith.

Perfect happiness, 1 believe, was never intended by the Deity to be the lot of one of His creatures in this world; but that He has very much put in our power the nearness of our approaches to it, is what I have steadfastly believed.—Jefferson.

It's no' in books, it's no' in lear,
　To make us truly blest;
If happiness has not her seat
　And center in the breast,
We may be wise, or rich, or great,
　But never can be blest. —Burns.

The utmost we can hope for in this world is contentment; if we aim at anything higher, we shall meet with nothing but grief and disappointment. A man should direct all his studies and endeavors at making himself easy now and happy hereafter.—Addison.

The happiness of life is made up of minute fractions—the little, soon-forgotten charities of a kiss, a smile, a kind look, a heartfelt compliment in the disguise of a playful raillery, and the countless other infinitesimals of pleasant thought and feeling.—Coleridge.

I opened the doors of my heart.
　　　And behold,
There was music within and a song,
And echoes did feed on the sweetness, repeating it long.
I opened the doors of my heart. And behold,
There was music that played itself out in æolian notes:
Then was heard, as a far-away bell at long intervals tolled. —Jean Ingelow.

God loves to see His creatures happy; our lawful delight is His; they know not God that think to please Him with making themselves miserable. The idolaters thought it a fit service for Baal to cut and lance themselves; never any holy man looked for thanks from the true God by wronging himself.—Bishop Hall.

Hume's doctrine was that the circumstances vary, the amount of happiness does not; that the beggar cracking fleas in the sunshine under a hedge, and the duke rolling by in his chariot, the girl equipped for her first ball, and

the orator returning triumphant from the debate, had different means, but the same quantity of pleasant excitement. —Emerson.

Every human soul has the germ of some flowers within; and they would open, if they could only find sunshine and free air to expand in. I always told you that not having enough of sunshine was what ailed the world. Make people happy, and there will not be half the quarreling, or a tenth part of the wickedness there is.—Mrs. Child.

The happiness of life consists, like the day, not in single flashes of light, but in one continuous mild serenity. The most beautiful period of the heart's existence is in this calm, equable light, even although it be only moonshine or twilight. Now the mind alone can obtain for us this heavenly cheerfulness and peace.—Richter.

Happiness no more depends on station, rank, or any local or adventitious circumstances in individuals than a man's life is connected with the color of his garment. The mind is the seat of happiness, and to make it so in reality, nothing is necessary but the balm of gospel peace and the saving knowledge of the Son of God.—

Happiness is much more equally divided than some of us imagine. One man shall possess most of the materials, but little of the thing; another may possess much of the thing, but very few of the materials. In this particular view of it, happiness has been beautifully compared to the man in the desert—he that gathered much had nothing over, and he that gathered little had no lack.—Colton.

No mockery in this world ever sounds to me so hollow as that of being told to cultivate happiness. Happiness is not a potato, to be planted in a mould and tilled with manure. Happiness is a glory shining far down upon us from heaven. She is a divine dew, which the soul feels dropping upon it from the amaranth bloom

and golden fruitage of paradise.—
Charlotte Brontë.

Harlot

'Tis the strumpet's plague
To beguile many, and be beguiled by one.
—Shaftesbury.

She weaves the winding-sheets of souls,
and lays
Them in the urn of everlasting death.
—Pollok.

Harmony

Variety is the condition of harmony.
—James Freeman Clarke.

From harmony, from heavenly harmony,
This universal frame began:
From harmony to harmony
Through all the compass of the notes it
ran,
The diapason closing full in Man.
—Dryden.

Harmonious words render ordinary
ideas acceptable; less ordinary, pleasant; novel and ingenious ones, delightful. As pictures and statues, and living beauty, too, show better by music-
light, so is poetry irradiated, vivified,
glorified, and raised into immortal life
by harmony.—Landor.

Harvest

Nature's bank-dividends.—Haliburton.

And thus of all my harvest-hope I have
Nought reaped but a weedye crop of care.
—Spenser.

To glean the broken ears after the man
That the main harvest reaps.
—Shakespeare.

Our rural ancestors, with little blest,
Patient of labor when the end was rest,
Indulg'd the day that hous'd their annual
grain,
With feasts, and offerings, and a thankful
strain. —Pope.

Fancy with prophetic glance
Sees the teeming months advance;
The field, the forest, green and gay;
The dappled slope, the tedded hay;
Sees the reddening orchard blow,
The harvest wave, the vintage flow.
—Warton.

Think, oh, grateful, think!
How good the God of Harvest is to you;
Who pours abundance o'er your flowing
fields. —Thomson.

The plump swain at evening bringing home four months' sunshine bound
in sheaves.—Lowell.

The feast is such as earth, the general
mother,
Pours from her fairest bosom, when she
smiles,
In the embrace of autumn. —Shelley.

For now, the corn house filled, the harvest
home,
Th' invited neighbors to the husking come;
A frolic scene, where work and mirth and
play
Unite their charms to cheer the hours
away. —Joel Barlow.

The harvest treasures all
Now gather'd in, beyond the rage of
storms,
Sure to the swain; the circling fence shut
up;
And instant winter's utmost rage defy'd.
While loose to festive joy, the country
round
Laughs with the loud sincerity of mirth,
Shook to the wind their cares.
—Thomson.

Glowing scene!
Nature's long holiday! luxuriant—rich,
In her proud progeny, she smiling marks
Their graces, now mature, and wonder
fraught!
Hail! season exquisite!—and hail ye sons
Of rural toil!—ye blooming daughters! ye
Who, in the lap of hardy labor rear'd,
Enjoy the mind unspotted.
—Mary Robinson.

Harvest Home

Be thou diligent to know the state of thy
flocks,
And look well to thy herds:
For riches are not forever;
And doth the crown endure unto all gen-
erations?
The hay is carried, and the tender grass
showeth itself,
And the herbs of the mountain are gath-
ered in.
The lambs are for thy clothing,
And the goats are the price of the field:
And there will be goat's milk enough for
thy food,
For the food of thy household;
And maintenance for thy maidens.
—Bible.

The husbandman is close to the heart
of nature, lives in touch with God, and
so, more than many, shares His deep
content, His tranquillity, and builds up
a character of hardy independence, of

kindly considerateness for His servants, and of helpful ministry to the poor.—John Clifford, D. D.

As clouds and rain, crashing thunder storms, and the chill airs of many a night all contribute to the wealth and ripeness and glory of harvest, so do pain and sorrow and death ripen the human soul for the "harvest home" of eternal rest.—Presbyterian Witness.

Believe in God, believe in nature, and do your duty; and the farm life, with its regular round of duties, its simple loves, its high thoughts, its wise economies, its immediate touch of earth, its charming gossip, its pleasant human interests, and its many windows through which we may catch sight of the face of God, will yield us all we need for a simple, manly, godly life.—John Clifford, D. D.

The farmer is ever a man of faith. Were he not a firm believer in what he has not seen he would not turn a furrow or sow a grain. Why should he believe in a morrow, in a coming summer or autumn; in springtime or harvest, in growth or ripening? It is all of faith, whether we will or no. The harvest is God's testimony that He is the rewarder of them that diligently work with Him.—Presbyterian Witness.

So the seed was sown and the harvest came; and though four thousand times the tender grain has sprung up from the soil, that pledge has never once been violated. The harvest fields form the tawny ocean which flows uninterruptedly from the diluvian age to this. And this is evident: that it is to the covenant faithfulness of God that we are indebted for the harvests of each year. Let that stand as the one first great condition of the harvest.—Illustrated Christian Weekly.

Growth is completed. The fields are at rest, and their green is bordered with russet and gold. The apple-trees are laden with fruit worthy of Eden and reminding one of the forfeited home of the fallen race. Paradise is not wholly gone; rich morsels of pre-cious fruitage still reward the man of well-directed toil. Its flowers bloom for us in summer; its fruits ripen for us in these luscious September days; its fragrance still lingers on the soft wings of the breeze that dances lightly over the fields which the Lord. hath blest.—Presbyterian Witness.

On earth we sang harvest-songs as the wheat came into the barn and the barracks were filled; you know there is no such time on a farm as when they get the crops in; and so in heaven it will be a harvest-song on the part of those who on earth sowed in tears and reaped in joy. Angels shout all through the heavens, and multitudes come down the hills crying, "Harvest-home! harvest-home!"—T. De Witt Talmage.

Do not despise your work. Do it well. Be a whole man to it while you are at it. Israel's great men did not think it beneath them to inspect their flocks. The patriarchs were shepherds and cultivators of the soil. Job was a shepherd. Moses was a shepherd. David looked well after his flocks. Gideon was accosted by God when he was threshing wheat. A great and noble life does not depend on rank or place, but on purpose, faith, love, character and service.—John Clifford, D. D.

The year's food only is grown in the year. Each year the world depends for subsistence upon something freshly given it which it cannot provide for itself. As the harvest approaches the wolf is at the door. Nothing stands between us and starvation but the harvest covenant of the ever-faithful God "seed-time and harvest shall not cease." Away, then, with our fancied independence! Our breath is in our nostrils. Back again to old-time simple dependence on the covenant-keeping God—back to the arms of our Father! We pray in the line of the harvest covenant when we say, "Give us this day our daily bread."—Illustrated Christian Weekly.

When the season has become pronounced and settled there is a ripeness in everything. The leaves die and the fruit falls; they die and drop because they have run their course. They tell of completeness and perfection as well as of decay. We are thoughtful, but yet not sad. Autumn wears no weeds in coming to the goal. Her robes of red and gold are put on—a sort of royal attire. It is the crowning of the year.—Zion's Herald.

So the life of agricultural industry has better guaranties than the crowns of kings. Husbandry is more secure than the treasures of the great. Nature is exhaustlessly reproductive. Let men have free access to and free use of it, and its cultivation will be a sure source of support for the family and a source of progress for the nation. "He that tilleth his land shall have plenty of bread." Mother Earth cares for her children. The landscape of the farm is full of divine feeling and rich in suggestions that inspire calm and quicken industry. It throbs with the tender heart of God. It is alive. In its simple and steady processes it reveals the Father's care for His children.—John Clifford, D. D.

The "harvest home" we sing with cheer,
Now that abundance crowns the year;
The God of harvests now we praise,
To Him our thanks a tribute raise;
For He our anxious care relieves
While reapers home come bringing sheaves,
Till filled are cellars, barns, and bin,
With harvests which are gathered in.
—J. Byington Smith.

Place what value we will on the productiveness of nature, on the regularity, constancy, of the seasons, these things are worthless of themselves. The fact is, man's food will not come to him of itself. It is a peculiarity of all the cereals that they are never found growing wild; they cannot spring up spontaneously. Further, and curiously, they cannot prolong their existence without the care of man; they are never self-sown. A neglected field of wheat or corn may in the first year produce a few scattered stalks of half-filled ears; but soon even these disappear, and a few summers will suffice to obliterate every trace of grain. Thus

undoubtedly is the sentence executed, "In the sweat of thy face shalt thou eat bread." Life depends on labor—here we have the other condition of the harvest. Man may sow and man may water, but God alone gives the increase. But equally true is it that unless man plants and plows and reaps, seed-time and harvest avail him nothing.—Presbyterian Witness.

In language so clear that the unlearned and the young can understand, the Saviour, in the parable of the wheat and the tares, shows that all along the journey of life mankind are sowing seed of some kind, which at the end of life is going to produce a harvest, the sure outcome of the kind of seed sown. Nature is inflexible in certain results, founded and fixed by the great Creator of nature and her laws. What the farmer sows he will be sure to reap. Never yet since the world began have men gathered grapes from a bush of thorn, or figs from a tuft of thistles. And every one throughout Christendom who is old enough and intelligent enough to read the Bible must know and understand that he occupies the place of a sower who will ultimately reap whatever is sown in the heart as to religious or irreligious belief, as to faith in Christ as a Redeemer, or as to indifference concerning the final condition of the soul.—Christian at Work.

Haste

Haste is of the devil.—Koran.

All haste implies weakness.—George MacDonald.

Hurry is only admissible in catching flies.—Haliburton.

Haste is always ungraceful.—Lady Blessington.

Hurry and cunning are the two apprentices of despatch and skill; but neither of them ever learns his master's trade.—Colton.

Manners require time, as nothing is more vulgar than haste.—Emerson.

Raw Haste, half-sister to Delay.—Tennyson.

Wisely, and slow; they stumble that run fast.—Shakespeare.

Men love in haste, but they detest at leisure.—Byron.

The more haste, ever the worst speed.—Churchill.

Haste is needful in a desperate case.—Shakespeare.

Error is ever the sequence of haste.—Wellington.

Farewell; and let your haste commend your duty.—Shakespeare.

Modern wisdom plucks me from over-credulous haste.—Shakespeare.

Haste trips up its own heels, fetters and stops itself.—Seneca.

Celerity is never more admired
Than by the negligent. —Shakespeare.

Stand not upon the order of your going,
But go at once. —Shakespeare.

Hasten slowly, and without losing heart put your work twenty times upon the anvil.—Boileau.

It is of no use running; to set out betimes is the main point.—La Fontaine.

Though I am always in haste, I am never in a hurry.—John Wesley.

He tires betimes that spurs too fast betimes;
With eager feeding food doth choke the feeder. —Shakespeare.

Haste and rashness are storms and tempests, breaking and wrecking business; but nimbleness is a full, fair wind, blowing it with speed to haven.—Fuller.

Sir Amyas Pawlet, when he saw too much haste made in any matter, was wont to say, "Stay awhile, that we may make an end the sooner."—Bacon.

Fraud and deceit are ever in a hurry. Take time for all things. Great haste makes great waste.—Franklin.

Whoever is in a hurry shows that the thing he is about is too big for him. Haste and hurry are very different things.—Chesterfield.

We are in hot haste to set the world right and to order all affairs; the Lord hath the leisure of conscious power and unerring wisdom, and it will be well for us to learn to wait.—Spurgeon.

Haste turns usually upon a matter of ten minutes too late, and may be avoided by a habit like that of Lord Nelson, to which he ascribed his success in life, of being ten minutes too early.—Bovee.

Hate — Hatred

The madness of the heart.—Byron.

Hatred is self-punishment.—Hosea Ballou.

The heart gnawing on itself.—Mme. du Deffand.

Hatred is blind as well as love.—Plutarch.

People hate, as they love, unreasonably.—Thackeray.

Hatred is stronger than friendship.—Rochefoucauld.

Men love in haste, but they detest at leisure.—Byron.

Take care that no one hates you justly.—Syrus.

I do hate him as I hate the devil.—Ben Jonson.

I like a good hater.—Samuel Johnson.

Men hate those to whom they have to lie.—Victor Hugo.

No man hates him at whom he can laugh.—Dr. Johnson.

Hatred is blind, as well as love.—Plutarch.

Hatred is a settled anger.—Cicero.

There are no eyes so sharp as the eyes of hatred.—George S. Hillard.

When our hatred is too keen it places us beneath those we hate.—La Rochefoucauld.

The hatred of persons related to each other is the most violent.—Tacitus.

He, who would free from malice pass his days,
Must live obscure, and never merit praise.
　　　　　　　　　　—Gay.

Offend her, and she knows not to forgive;
Oblige her, and she'll hate you while you live.　　　　—Pope.

Hate furroweth the brow, and a man may frown till he hateth.—Tupper.

Heaven has no rage like love to hatred turn'd,
Nor hell a fury like a woman scorn'd.
　　　　　　　　　—Congreve.

It is the nature of the human disposition to hate him whom you have injured.—Tacitus.

Better is a dinner of herbs where love is than a stalled ox and hatred therewith.—Bible.

Hatred is active, and envy passive disgust; there is but one step from envy to hate.—Goethe.

Hate no one—hate their vices, not themselves.—Brainard.

The passion of hatred is so durable and so inveterate that the surest prognostic of death in a sick man is a wish for reconciliation.—Bruyère.

Plutarch says very finely that a man should not allow himself to hate even his enemies.—Addison.

Hatred is keener than friendship, less keen than love.—Vauvenargues.

The greatest hatred, like the greatest virtue and the worst dogs, is quiet.—Richter.

The hatred we bear our enemies injures their happiness less than our own.—J. Petit-Senn.

Never can true reconcilement grow
Where wounds of deadly hate have pierc'd so deep.　　　　　—Milton.

Life is too short to spare an hour of it in the indulgence of this evil passion.—Lamartine.

There are glances of hatred that stab and raise no cry of murder.—George Eliot.

Hate is like fire; it makes even light rubbish deadly.—George Eliot.

Hatred itself may be a praiseworthy emotion if provoked in us by a lively love of good.—Joubert.

Hate belongs with sin. If we do a wrong, we hate either the thing or God, or ourselves, or somebody else.—Duffield.

The hate which we all bear with the most Christian patience is the hate of those who envy us.—Colton.

Hatred does not cease by hatred at any time; hatred ceases by love; this is an old rule.—Buddha.

There is no faculty of the human soul so persistent and universal as that of hatred.—Henry Ward Beecher.

Hatred is the vice of narrow souls; they feed it with all their littlenesses, and make it the pretext of base tyrannies.—Balzac.

We hate some persons because we do not know them; and we will not know them because we hate them.—Colton.

I will tell you what to hate. Hate hypocrisy, hate cant, hate indolence, oppression, injustice; hate Pharisaism; hate them as Christ hated them—with a deep, living, godlike hatred.—F. W. Robertson.

To be deprived of the person we love is a happiness in comparison to living with one we hate.—La Bruyère.

Were one to ask me in which direction I think man strongest, I should say, his capacity to hate.—Beecher.

National hatred is something peculiar. You will always find it strongest and most violent in the lowest degree of culture.—Goethe.

To harbor hatred and animosity in the soul makes one irritable, gloomy, and prematurely old.—Auerbach.

A woman's head is always influenced by her heart; but a man's heart is always influenced by his head.—Lady Blessington.

Hatred is nearly always honest—rarely, if ever, assumed. So much cannot be said for love.—Ninon de Lenclos.

How apt nature is, even in those who profess an eminence in holiness, to raise and maintain animosities against those whose calling or person they pretend to find cause to dislike!—Bishop Hall.

We are told to walk noiselessly through the world, that we may waken neither hatred nor envy; but, alas! what can we do when they never sleep! —J. Petit-Senn.

All men naturally hate one another. I hold it a fact, that if men knew exactly what one says of the other, there would not be four friends in the world. —Pascal.

If you hate your enemies, you will contract such a vicious habit of mind, as by degrees will break out upon those who are your friends, or those who are indifferent to you.—Plutarch.

Hannah More said to Horace Walpole: "If I wanted to punish an enemy, it should be by fastening on him the trouble of constantly hating somebody."—John Bate.

They did not know how hate can burn
In hearts once changed from soft to stern;
Nor all the false and fatal zeal
The convert of revenge can feel.—Byron.

　　　　Had I power, I should
Pour the sweet milk of concord into hell.
Uproar the universal peace, confound
All unity on earth.　　—Shakespeare.

There was a laughing devil in his sneer,
That rais'd emotions both of rage and fear;
And where his frown of hatred darkly fell,
Hope withering fled, and mercy sigh'd
　　farewell.　　　　—Byron.

Love is rarely a hypocrite; but hate —how detect and how guard against it! It lurks where you least expect it; it is created by causes that you can the least foresee; and civilization multiplies its varieties, whilst it favors its disguise.—Bulwer-Lytton.

I see thou art implacable, more deaf
To pray'rs than winds and seas. Yet winds
　　to seas
Are reconcil'd at length, and sea to shore:
Thy anger, unappeasable, still rages
Eternal tempest never to be calm'd.
　　　　　　　　—Milton.

Hate is of all things the mightiest divider, nay, is division itself. To couple hatred, therefore, though wedlock try all her golden links, and borrow to her aid all the iron manacles and fetters of law, it does but seek to twist a rope of sand.—Milton.

Hawthorn

The hawthorn trees blow in the dew of the morning.—Burns.

And every shepherd tells his tale
Under the hawthorn in the dale.
　　　　　　　　—Milton.

Yet, all beneath the unrivall'd rose,
The lowly daisy sweetly blows;
Tho' large the forest's monarch throws
　　His army shade,
Yet green the juicy hawthorn grows,
　　Adown the glade.
　　　　　　　　—Burns.

Then sing by turns, by turns the Muses
sing;
Now hawthorns blossom.   —Pope.

Head

The head has the most beautiful appearance, as well as the highest station, in a human figure.—Addison.

Their heads sometimes so little, that there is no room for wit; sometimes so long, that there is no wit for so much room.—T. Fuller.

After all, the head only reproduces what the heart creates; and so we give the mocking-bird credit when he imitates the loving murmurs of the dove. —G. J. W. Melville.

Some people carry their hearts in their heads; very many carry their heads in their hearts. The difficulty is to keep them apart, yet both actively working together.—Hare.

Health

Health is the vital principle of bliss. —Thomson.

For life is not to live, but to be well.—Martial.

Health consists with temperance alone.—Pope.

Health and cheerfulness make beauty.—Cervantes.

Thou chiefest good,
Bestow'd by heaven, but seldom understood.   —Lucan.

Be sober and temperate, and you will be healthy.—B. Franklin.

Preserving the health by too strict a regimen is a wearisome malady.— La Rochefoucauld.

He who has health has hope, and he who has hope has everything.— Arabian Proverb.

Christ's gospel could never have been delivered by one who was diseased.—John McC. Holmes.

Physic, for the most part, is nothing else but the substitute of exercise and temperance.—Addison.

What a searching preacher of self-command is the varying phenomenon of health!—Emerson.

From labor health, from health contentment springs.—Beattie.

Health lies in labor, and there is no royal road to it but through toil.— Wendell Phillips.

Gold that buys health can never be ill spent.
Nor hours laid out in harmless merriment.   —John Webster.

Health and cheerfulness mutually beget each other.—Addison.

Health and good humor are to the human body like sunshine to vegetation.—Massillon.

In these days half our diseases come from neglect of the body in overwork of the brain.—Lytton.

There is no health; physicians say that we, at best, enjoy but neutrality. —Donne.

Health is the second blessing that we mortals are capable of: a blessing that money cannot buy.—Izaak Walton.

The only way for a rich man to be healthy is, by exercise and abstinence. to live as if he was poor.—Sir W. Temple.

A sound mind in a sound body, if the former be the glory of the latter, the latter is indispensable to the former.—Edwards.

Health is the greatest of all possessions, and it is a maxim with me that a hale cobbler is a better man than a sick king.—Bickerstaff.

The fate of a nation has often depended on the good or bad digestion of a prime minister.—Voltaire.

Gardening, or husbandry, and working in wood, are healthy recreations.—Locke.

The surest road to health, say what they will,
Is never to suppose we shall be ill.
—Churchill.

Health is the soul that animates all enjoyments of life, which fade and are tasteless, if not dead, without it.—Sir W. Temple.

In health there is liberty. Health is the first of all liberties, and happiness gives us the energy which is the basis of health.—Amiel.

Look to your health; and if you have it, praise God, and value it next to a good conscience.—Izaak Walton.

Reason's whole pleasure, all the joys of sense, lie in three words—health, peace, and competence.—Pope.

The root of sanctity is sanity. A man must be healthy before he can be holy. We bathe first, and then perfume.—Mme. Swetchine.

The requirements of health, and the style of female attire which custom enjoins are in direct antagonism to each other.—Abba Goold Woolson.

Infirmity and sickness may excite our pity; but desire and pleasure require the bloom and vigor of health.—Rousseau.

Health is so necessary to all the duties as well as pleasures of life that the crime of squandering it is equal to the folly.—Dr. Johnson.

Physic is of little use to a temperate person, for a man's own observation on what he finds does him good, and what hurts him is the best physic to preserve health.—Bacon.

In the present day, and especially among women, one would almost suppose that health was a state of unnatural existence.—Beaconsfield.

People who are always taking care of their health are like misers, who are hoarding a treasure which they have never spirit enough to enjoy.—Sterne.

The common ingredients of health and long life are:
Great temp'rance, open air,
Easy labor, little care.   —Sir P. Sidney.

One means very effectual for the preservation of health is a quiet and cheerful mind, not afflicted with violent passions or distracted with immoderate cares.—John Ray.

Nor love, nor honor, wealth, nor power,
Can give the heart a cheerful hour
When health is lost. Be timely wise;
With health all taste of pleasure flies.
—Gay.

Refuse to be ill. Never tell people you are ill; never own it to yourself. Illness is one of those things which a man should resist on principle at the onset.—Lytton.

In our natural body every part has a necessary sympathy with every other; and all together form, by their harmonious conspiration, a healthy whole.—Sir W. Hamilton.

The healthy know not of their health, but only the sick: this is the physician's aphorism, and applicable in a far wider sense than he gives it.—Carlyle.

He who overlooks a healthy spot for the site of his house is mad and ought to be handed over to the care of his relations and friends.—Varro.

The first wealth is health. Sickness is poor-spirited, and cannot serve any one; it must husband its resources to live. But health or fullness answers its own ends, and has to spare, runs over, and inundates the neighborhoods and creeks of other men's necessities.—Emerson.

Anguish of mind has driven thousands to suicide; anguish of body, none. This proves that the health of the mind is of far more consequence to our happiness than the health of the body, although both are deserving of much more attention than either of them receives.—Colton.

O blessed health! thou art above all gold and treasure; 'tis thou who enlargest the soul, and openest all its powers to receive instruction, and to relish virtue. He that has thee has little more to wish for, and he that is so wretched as to want thee, wants everything with thee.—Sterne.

Every man that has felt pain knows how little all other comforts can gladden him to whom health is denied. Yet who is there does not sometimes hazard it for the enjoyment of an hour?—Dr. Johnson.

Adam knew no disease so long as temperance from the forbidden fruit secured him. Nature was his physician; and innocence and abstinence would have kept him healthful to immortality.—South.

The morbid states of health, the irritableness of disposition arising from unstrung nerves, the impatience, the crossness, the fault-finding of men, who, full of morbid influences, are unhappy themselves, and throw the cloud of their troubles like a dark shadow upon others, teach us what eminent duty there is in health.—Beecher.

There are three wicks you know to the lamp of a man's life: brain, blood, and breath. Press the brain a little, its light goes out, followed by both the others. Stop the heart a minute, and out go all three of the wicks. Choke the air out of the lungs, and presently the fluid ceases to supply the other centers of flame, and all is soon stagnation, cold, and darkness.—O. W. Holmes.

Be it remembered that man subsists upon the air more than upon his meat and drink; but no one can exist for an hour without a copious supply of air. The atmosphere which some breathe is contaminated and adulterated, and

with its vital principles so diminished that it cannot fully decarbonize the blood, nor fully excite the nervous system.—Thackeray.

There is this difference between those two temporal blessings, health and money: Money is the most envied, but the least enjoyed; health is the most enjoyed, but the least envied: and this superiority of the latter is still more obvious when we reflect that the poorest man would not part with health for money, but that the richest would gladly part with all their money for heath.—Colton.

Men that look no further than their outsides, think health an appurtenance unto life, and quarrel with their constitutions for being sick; but I that have examined the parts of man, and know upon what tender filaments that fabric hangs, do wonder that we are not always so; and considering the thousand doors that lead to death, do thank my God that we can die but once.—Sir Thomas Browne.

Health is certainly more valuable than money; because it is by health that money is procured; but thousands and millions are of small avail to alleviate the protracted tortures of the gout, to repair the broken organs of sense, or resuscitate the powers of digestion. Poverty is, indeed, an evil from which we naturally fly, but let us not run from one enemy to another, nor take shelter in the arms of sickness.—Johnson.

Hearing

None so deaf as those that will not hear.—Mathew Henry.

Friends, Romans, countrymen, lend me your ears.—Shakespeare.

This is the slowest, yet the daintiest sense;
For ev'n the ears of such as have no skill,
Perceive a discord, and conceive offence;
And knowing not what's good, yet find the
  ill.   —Sir John Davies.

Hear me for my cause, and be silent that you may hear.—Shakespeare.

Where more is meant than meets the ear.—Milton.

Where did you get that pearly ear?
God spoke and it came out to hear.
—George MacDonald.

     I was all ear,
And took in strains that might create a soul
Under the ribs of death. —Milton.

Within a bony, labyrinthean cave,
Reached by the pulse of the aërial wave,
This sibyl, sweet, and mystic sense is found,
Muse, that presides o'er all the powers of sound. —Abraham Coles.

These wickets of the soul are plac'd so high,
Because all sounds do highly move aloft;
And that they may not pierce too violently,
They are delay'd with turns and twinings oft.
For should the voice directly strike the brain,
It would astonish and confuse it much;
Therefore these plaits and folds the sound restrain.
That it the organ may more gently touch.
—Sir John Davies.

Heart

The precious porcelain of human clay.—Byron.

A loving heart is the truest wisdom.—Dickens.

The heart does not lie.—Alfieri.

The more heart, the more sorrow.—Mme. Necker.

Hearts are stronger than swords.—Wendell Phillips.

Alas! there is no instinct like the heart!—Byron.

All offences come from the heart.—Shakespeare.

Home-keeping hearts are happiest.—Longfellow.

The less heart, the more comfort.—Ninon de Lenclos.

Tears may be dried up, but the heart never.—Marguerite de Valois.

A heart to pity, and a hand to bless.—Churchill.

The heart will break, yet broken live on.—Byron.

O heart! love is thy bane and thy antidote.—George Sand.

Worse than a bloody hand is a hard heart.—Shelley.

The ear is the avenue to the heart.—Voltaire.

Better to have the poet's heart than brain.—George MacDonald.

A good heart is worth gold.—Shakespeare.

The head is ever the dupe of the heart.—La Rochefoucauld.

The heart echoes the words of love.—Mme. de Krudener.

The full heart knows no rhetoric of words.—Bovee.

Leap hearts to lips, and in our kisses meet.—John Fletcher.

That hideous sight—a naked human heart.—Young.

I have a heart with room for every joy.—Bailey.

Love is the pass-key to the heart.—Mme. Necker.

The heart is the best logician.—Wendell Phillips.

For his heart was in his work, and the heart
Giveth grace unto every art.
—Longfellow.

There is an evening twilight of the heart,
When its wild passion-waves are lulled to rest. —Fitz-Greene Halleck.

Some hearts are hidden, some have not a heart.—Crabbe.

A heart to resolve, a head to contrive, and a hand to execute.—Gibbon.

A wise man's heart is at his right hand; but a fool's heart is at his left. —Bible.

Maid of Athens, ere we part,
Give, oh, give me back my heart!
—Byron.

Oh, the heart is a free and a fetterless thing—
A wave of the ocean, a bird on the wing.
—Julia Pardoe.

The heart aye's the part aye
That makes us right or wrang.
—Burns.

Never morning wore
To evening but some heart did break.
—Tennyson.

A temple of the Holy Ghost, and yet
Of lodging fiends. —Pollok.

A noble heart, like the sun, showeth its greatest countenance in its lowest estate.—Sir P. Sidney.

None but God can satisfy the longings of an immortal soul; that as the heart was made for Him, so He only can fill it.—Trench.

Do you think that any one can move the heart but He that made it?—John Lyly.

When the heart speaks, glory itself is an illusion.—Napoleon.

The human heart has a sigh lonelier than the cry of the bittern.—W. R. Alger.

Mind is the partial side of men; the heart is everything.—Rivarol.

As the heart is, so is love to the heart. It partakes of its strength or weakness, its health or disease.—Longfellow.

His heart was one of those which most enamours us—wax to receive, and marble to retain.—Byron.

The heart is always young only in the recollection of those whom it has loved in youth.—Arsène Houssaye.

The heart must glow before the tongue can gild.—W. R. Alger.

The heart is deceitful above all things, and desperately wicked; who can know it?—Bible.

The wrinkles of the heart are more indelible than those of the brow.—Madame Deluzy.

Memory, wit, fancy, acuteness, cannot grow young again in old age; but the heart can.—Richter.

If wrong our hearts, our heads are right in vain.—Young.

What the heart has once owned and had, it shall never lose.—Beecher.

In aught that tries the heart, how few withstand the proof.—Byron.

A good heart will, at all times, betray the best head in the world.—Fielding.

I will wear my heart upon my sleeve
For daws to peck at; I am not what I am.
—Shakespeare.

Be persuaded that your only treasures are those which you carry in your heart.—Demophilus.

The human heart is like heaven; the more angels the more room.—Fredrika Bremer.

To try to conceal our own heart is a bad means to read that of others.—Rousseau.

Of all the paths that lead to a woman's heart, pity is the straightest.—Beaumont.

There is in the heart of woman such a deep well of love that no age can freeze it.—Bulwer-Lytton.

A man's own heart must ever be given to gain that of another.—Goldsmith.

All who know their own minds know not their own hearts.—Rochefoucauld.

Keep thy heart with all diligence, for out of it are the issues of life.—Bible.

Out of the abundance of the heart the mouth speaketh.—Bible.

The heart is an astrologer that always divines the truth.—Calderon.

Where there is room in the heart, there is always room in the house.—Moore.

The heart of a good man is the sanctuary of God in this world.—Mme. Necker.

The heart of woman never grows old; when it has ceased to love, it has ceased to live.—Rochepèdre.

The nervous fluid in man is consumed by the brain; in women, by the heart.—Stendhal.

All things but one you can restore; the heart you get returns no more.—Waller.

It is a wonderful subduer—this need of love, this hunger of the heart.—George Eliot.

Look not to a woman's head for her brains, but rather to her heart.—Haliburton.

The heart that has once been bathed in love's pure fountain retains the pulse of youth forever.—Landor.

A woman's heart is as intricate as a raveled skein of silk.—Dumas, Père.

Alas! that we must dwell—my heart and I—so far asunder.—Christina G. Rossetti.

The heart is a small thing, but desireth great matters. It is not sufficient for a kite's dinner, yet the whole world is not sufficient for it.—Victor Hugo.

The heart is like an instrument whose strings steal nobler music from life's many frets.—Gerald Massey.

The very gnarliest and hardest of hearts has some musical strings in it; but they are tuned differently in every one of us.—Lowell.

A millstone and the human heart are
  driven ever round,
If they have nothing else to grind, they
  must themselves be ground.
          —Longfellow.

A woman too often reasons from her heart; hence two-thirds of her mistakes and her troubles.—Bulwer-Lytton.

A woman's heart is just like a lithographer's stone; what is once written upon it cannot be rubbed out. —Thackeray.

When the heart is still agitated by the remains of a passion, we are more ready to receive a new one than when we are entirely cured.—Rochefoucauld.

The poor too often turn away unheard,
From hearts that shut against them with
  a sound
That will be heard in heaven.
          —Longfellow.

The heart of a girl is like a convent: the holier the cloister, the more charitable the door.—Bulwer-Lytton.

The heart of a woman is never so full of affection that there does not remain a little corner for flattery and love.—Marivaux.

To judge human character rightly, a man may sometimes have very small experience, provided he has a very large heart.—Bulwer-Lytton.

Some people's hearts are shrunk in them, like dried nuts. You can hear 'em rattle as they walk.—Douglas Jerrold.

When a young man complains that a young lady has no heart, it is pretty certain that she has his.—G. D. Prentice.

The heart is like the tree that gives balm for the wounds of man only when the iron has pierced it.—Chateaubriand.

Every man must, in a measure, be alone in the world. No heart was ever cast in the same mould as that which we bear within us.—Berne.

What sad faces one always sees in the asylums for orphans! It is more fatal to neglect the heart than the head.—Theodore Parker.

Nothing is less in our power than the heart, and, far from commanding it, we are forced to obey it.—Rousseau.

The heart of a wise man should resemble a mirror, which reflects every object without being sullied by any.—Confucius.

The heart is like a musical instrument of many strings, all the chords of which require putting in harmony.—Saadi.

My heart resembles the ocean; has storm, and ebb and flow; and many a beautiful pearl lies hid in its depths below.—Heinrich Heine.

And when once the young heart of a
  maiden is stolen,
The maiden herself will steal after it soon.
  —Moore.

Something the heart must have to cherish,
  Must love, and joy, and sorrow learn;
Something with passion clasp, or perish,
  And in itself to ashes burn.
  —Longfellow.

Wealth and want equally harden the human heart, as frost and fire are both alien to the human flesh. Famine and gluttony alike drive nature away from the heart of man.—Theodore Parker.

The heart must be at rest before the mind, like a quiet lake under an unclouded summer evening, can reflect the solemn starlight and the splendid mysteries of heaven.—Macdonald Clarke.

When the heart of man is serene and tranquil, he wants to enjoy nothing but himself; every movement, even cor-poreal movement, shakes the brimming nectar cup too rudely.—Richter.

A human heart is a skein of such imperceptibly and subtly interwoven threads that even the owner of it is often himself at a loss how to unravel it.—Ruffini.

A human heart can never grow old, if it takes a lively interest in the pairing of birds, the reproduction of flowers, and the changing tints of autumn leaves.—Mrs. L. M. Child.

A good heart is the sun and moon, or, rather, the sun, and not the moon; for it shines bright and never changes, but keeps its course truly.—Shakespeare.

The heart never grows better by age, I fear rather worse; always harder. A young liar will be an old one; and a young knave will only be a greater knave as he grows older.—Chesterfield.

Many flowers open to the sun, but only one follows him constantly. Heart, be thou the sunflower, not only open to receive God's blessing, but constant in looking to Him.—Richter.

There are treasures laid up in the heart—treasures of charity, piety, temperance, and soberness. These treasures a man takes with him beyond death, when he leaves this world.—Buddhist Scriptures.

What we call the heart is a nervous sensation, like shyness, which gradually disappears in society. It is fervent in the nursery, strong in the domestic circle, tumultuous at school.—Beaconsfield.

There is strength deep bedded in our hearts, of which we reck but little till the shafts of heaven have pierced its fragile dwelling. Must not earth be rent before her gems are found?—Mrs. Hemans.

The human heart is often the victim of the sensations of the moment; success intoxicates it to presumption, and disappointment dejects and terrifies it. —Volney.

Oh, no! my heart can never be
Again in lightest hopes the same;
The love that lingers there for thee
Hath more of ashes than of flame.
—Miss Landon.

The flush of youth soon passes from the face,
The spells of fancy from the mind depart;
The form may lose its symmetry, its grace,
But time can claim no victory o'er the heart.
—Mrs. Dinnies.

The human heart is like a millstone in a mill: when you put wheat under it, it turns and grinds and bruises the wheat to flour; if you put no wheat, it still grinds on, but then 'tis itself it grinds and wears away.—Martin Luther.

Men, as well as women, are oftener led by their hearts than their understandings. The way to the heart is through the senses; please their eyes and ears, and the work is half done.— Chesterfield.

The heart, when broken, is like sweet gums and spices when beaten; for as such cast their fragrant scent into the nostrils of men, so the heart, when broken, casts its sweet smell into the nostrils of God.—Bunyan.

Oh, if the loving, closed heart of a good woman should open before a man, how much controlled tenderness, how many veiled sacrifices and dumb virtues, would be seen reposing there!— Richter.

A loving heart carries with it, under every parallel of latitude, the warmth and light of the tropics. It plants its Eden in the wilderness and solitary place, and sows with flowers the gray desolation of rock and mosses.—Whittier.

When a woman's heart is touched, when it is moved by love, then the electric spark is communicated and the fire of inspiration kindled; but even

then she desires no more than to suffer or to die for what she loves.—Countess Hahn-Hahn.

There are no little events with the heart. It magnifies everything; it places in the same scale the fall of an empire and the dropping of a woman's glove; and almost always the glove weighs more than the empire.—Balzac.

Nothing affects the heart like that which is purely from itself, and of its own nature; such as the beauty of sentiments, the grace of actions, the turn of characters, and the proportions and features of a human mind.—Shaftesbury.

In thy heart there is a holy spot,
As 'mid the waste an isle of fount and palm,
Forever green!—the world's breath enters not,
The passion-tempest may not break its calm,
'Tis thine, all thine.
—Mrs. Hemans.

If you should take the human heart and listen to it, it would be like listening to a sea-shell; you would hear in it the hollow murmur of the infinite ocean to which it belongs, from which it draws its profoundest inspiration, and for which it yearns.—Chapin.

How mighty is the human heart, with all its complicated energies; this living source of all that moves the world! this temple of liberty, this kingdom of heaven, this altar of God, this throne of goodness, so beautiful in holiness, so generous in love!—Henry Giles.

There are chords in the human heart —strange, varying strings—which are only struck by accident; which will remain mute and senseless to appeals the most passionate and earnest, and respond at last to the slightest casual touch.—Dickens.

Intellect alone, however exalted, without strong feelings—without even, irritable sensibility—would be only like an immense magazine of powder, if there were no such element as fire in the natural world. It is the heart which is the spring and fountain of all eloquence.—Lord Erskine.

The heart is like the sky, a part of heaven,
But changes, night and day, too, like the
   sky;
Now o'er it clouds and thunder must be
   driven,
And darkness and destruction as on high;
But when it hath been scorch'd and pierc'd
   and riven,
Its storms expire in water-drops; the eye
Pours forth, at last, the heart's blood
   turn'd to tears.   —Byron.

What a proof of the Divine tenderness is there in the human heart itself, which is the organ and receptacle of so many sympathies! When we consider how exquisite are those conditions by which it is even made capable of so much suffering—the capabilities of a child's heart, of a mother's heart, —what must be the nature of Him who fashioned its depths, and strung its chords.—Chapin.

The wisdom of the Creator is in nothing seen more gloriously than the heart. It was necessary that it should be made capable of working forever without the cessation of a moment, without the least degree of weariness. It is so made; and the power of the Creator, in so constructing it, can in nothing be exceeded but by His wisdom.—Hope.

Who made the heart, 'tis He alone,
   Decidedly can try us,
He knows each chord—its various tone
   Each spring its various bias:
Then at the balance let's be mute,
   We never can adjust it;
What's done we partly may compute,
   But know not what's resisted.
   —Burns.

Heat

Hither rolls the storm of heat;
I feel its finer billows beat
Like a sea which me infolds;
Heat with viewless fingers moulds,
Swells, and mellows, and matures,
Paints, and flavors, and allures,
Bird and brier inly warms,
Still enriches and transforms,
Gives the reed and lily length,
Adds to oak and oxen strength,
Transforming what it doth infold,
Life out of death, new out of old.
   —Emerson.

Heaven

Heaven—it is God's throne. The earth—it is His footstool.—Bible.

Heaven, the treasury of everlasting joy!—Shakespeare.

The redeemed shall walk there.—Bible.

There remaineth therefore a rest to the people of God.—Bible.

I cannot be content with less than heaven.—Bailey.

There's nothing true but heaven.—Moore.

Beyond the clouds and beyond the tomb.—Mrs. Hemans.

All places shall be hell that are not heaven.—Marlowe.

Heaven, the widow's champion and defence.—Shakespeare.

There is another, and a better world. —August Von Kotzebue.

Heaven means to be one with God. —Confucius.

The love of heaven makes one heavenly.—Shakespeare.

Infinite in degree, and endless in duration.—Franklin.

Earth has no sorrow that heaven cannot heal.—Moore.

Nothing is farther than earth from heaven; nothing is nearer than heaven to earth.—Hare.

Heaven does not make holiness, but holiness makes heaven.—Phillips Brooks.

Think of heaven with hearty purposes and peremptory designs to get thither.—Jeremy Taylor.

As much of heaven is visible as we have eyes to see.—William Winter.

One should go to sleep as homesick passengers do, saying, "Perhaps in the morning we shall see the shore."—H. W. Beecher.

Every Christian that goes before us from this world is a ransomed spirit waiting to welcome us in heaven.—Jonathan Edwards.

No fountain so small but that heaven may be imaged in its bosom.—Hawthorne.

Dreams cannot picture a world so fair; sorrow and death may not enter there.—Mrs. Hemans.

In a better world we will find our young years and our old friends.—J. Petit-Senn.

Heaven will be inherited by every man who has heaven in his soul.—Henry Ward Beecher.

There is but one way to heaven for the learned and the unlearned.—Jeremy Taylor.

The heaven of poetry and romance still lies around us and within us.—Longfellow.

Heaven is a place of restless activity, the abode of never-tiring thought.—Beecher.

The ascent from earth to heaven is not easy.—Seneca.

There I'll rest, as after much turmoil a blessed soul doth in Elysium.—Shakespeare.

Heaven's above all; and there be souls that must be saved, and there be souls that must not be saved.—Shakespeare.

I change my place, but not my company. While here I have sometimes walked with God, and now I go to rest with Him.—Dr. Preston.

Perfect purity, fullness of joy, everlasting freedom, perfect rest, health and fruition, complete security, substantial and eternal good.—Hannah More.

The net of heaven is very wide in its meshes, and yet it misses nothing.—Lao-Tze.

Think how completely all the griefs of this mortal life will be compensated by one age, for instance, of the felicities beyond the grave.—John Foster.

In short, heaven is not to be looked upon only as the reward, but as the natural effect, of a religious life.—Addison.

They had finished her own crown in glory, and she couldn't stay away from the coronation.—Gray.

While resignation gently slopes the way;
And, all his prospects brightening to the last,
His heaven commences ere the world be past.   —Goldsmith.

Heaven is endless longing, accompanied with an endless fruition—a longing which is blessedness, a longing which is life.—Alexander Maclaren.

Do we not hear voices, gentle and great, and some of them like the voices of departed friends—do we not hear them saying to us, "Come up hither?"—Wm. Mountford.

The joy of heaven will begin as soon as we attain the character of heaven, and do its duties.—Theodore Parker.

Heaven
Is as the Book of God before thee set,
Wherein to read His wondrous works.
      —Milton.

An everlasting tranquility is, in my imagination, the highest possible felicity, because I know of no felicity on earth higher than that which a peaceful mind and contented heart afford.—Zimmermann.

He who seldom thinks of heaven is not likely to get thither; as the only way to hit the mark is to keep the eye fixed upon it.—Bishop Horne.

The loves that meet in paradise shall cast out fear; and paradise hath room for you and me and all.—Christina G. Rossetti.

Heaven's gates are not so highly arched as princes' palaces; they that enter there must go upon their knees. —Daniel Webster.

It is impossible to have a lively hope in another life, and yet be deeply immersed in the enjoyments of this.— Atterbury.

The generous who is always just, and the just who is always generous, may, unannounced, approach the throne of heaven.—Lavater.

Heaven hath many tongues to talk of it, more eyes to behold it, but few hearts that rightly affect it.—Bishop Hall.

If the way of heaven be narrow, it is not long; and if the gate be straight, it opens into endless life.—Bishop Beveridge.

Ah, what without a heaven would be even love!—a perpetual terror of the separation that must one day come. —Bulwer-Lytton.

I must confess, as the experience of my own soul, that the expectation of loving my friends in heaven principally kindles my love to them while on earth.—Richard Baxter.

And so upon this wise I prayed—
Great Spirit, give to me
A heaven not so large as yours
But large enough for me.
                    —Emily Dickinson.

Love lent me wings; my path was like a stair;
A lamp unto my feet, that sun was given;
And death was safety and great joy to find;
But dying now, I shall not climb to Heaven.   —Michael Angelo.

The joys of heaven are not the joys of passive contemplation, of dreamy remembrance, of perfect repose; but they are described thus: "They rest not day nor night." "His servants serve Him, and see His face."—Alexander Maclaren.

Our souls, piercing through the impurity of flesh, behold the highest heaven, and thence bring knowledge to contemplate the ever-during glory and termless joy.—Sir Walter Raleigh.

We should carry up our affections to the mansions prepared for us above, where eternity is the measure, felicity the state, angels the company, the Lamb the light, and God the inheritance and portion of His people forever.—Jeremy Taylor.

Heaven is the day of which grace is the dawn; the rich, ripe fruit of which grace is the lovely flower; the inner shrine of that most glorious temple to which grace forms the approach and outer court.—Rev. Dr. Guthrie.

If our Creator has so bountifully provided for our existence here, which is but momentary, and for our temporal wants, which will soon be forgotten, how much more must He have done for our enjoyment in the everlasting world!—Hosea Ballou.

We are born for a higher destiny than earth; there is a realm where the rainbow never fades, where the stars will be spread before us like islands that slumber on the ocean, and where the beings that pass before us like shadows will stay in our presence forever.—Bulwer-Lytton.

There are times in the history of men and nations, when they stand so near the vale that separates mortals from the immortals, time from eternity, and men from their God, that they can almost hear the beatings, and feel the pulsations of the heart of the Infinite.—James A. Garfield.

As we look up into these glorious culminations, how grand life becomes! To be forever with the Lord, and forever changing into His likeness, and still more, forever deepening in the companionship of His thought and bliss, "from glory to glory"—could we desire more?—Bishop R. S. Foster.

What, after all, is heaven, but a transition from dim guesses and blind struggling with a mysterious and adverse fate to the fullness of all wisdom—from ignorance, in a word, to knowledge, but knowledge of what order?—Bulwer-Lytton.

We see but dimly through the mists and
   vapors;
Amid these earthly damps,
What seem to us but sad, funereal tapers
May be heaven's distant lamps.
   —Longfellow.

It doth not yet appear what we shall be. We lie here in our nest, unfledged and weak, guessing dimly at our future, and scarce believing what even now appears. But the power is in us, and that power is finally to be revealed. And what a revelation will that be!—Horace Bushnell.

The joys of heaven are without example, above experience, and beyond imagination—for which the whole creation wants a comparison ; we, an apprehension ; and even the Word of God, a revelation.—Bishop Norris.

Christ and His cross are not separable in this life, howbeit Christ and His cross part at heaven's door, for there is no house-room for crosses in heaven. One tear, one sigh, one sad heart, one fear, one loss, one thought of trouble cannot find lodging there.—Rutherford.

A sea before
The Throne is spread;—its pure still glass
Pictures all earth-scenes as they pass.
   We, on its shore,
Share, in the bosom of our rest,
God's knowledge, and are blest.
   —Cardinal Newman.

After the fever of life—after wearinesses, sicknesses, fightings and despondings, languor and fretfulness, struggling and failing, struggling and succeeding—after all the changes and chances of this troubled and unhealthy

state, at length comes death—at length the white throne of God—at length the beatific vision.—Newman.

Heaven is not to sweep our truths away, but only to turn them till we see their glory, to open them till we see their truth, and to unveil our eyes till for the first time we shall really see them.—Phillips Brooks.

Heaven is attracting to itself whatever is congenial to its nature, is enriching itself by the spoils of earth, and collecting within its capacious bosom whatever is pure, permanent and divine.—Robert Hall.

Heaven, the perfection of all that can
Be said, of thought, riches, delight or harmony,
Health, beauty; and all those not subject to
The waste of time, but in their height
   eternal.   —Shirley.

Some people think black is the color of heaven, and that the more they can make their faces look like midnight, the more evidence they have of grace. But God, who made the sun and the flowers, never sent me to proclaim to you such a lie as that.—Beecher.

Perhaps God does with His heavenly garden as we do with our own. He may chiefly stock it from nurseries, and select for transplanting what is yet in its young and tender age—flowers before they have bloomed, and trees ere they begin to bear.—Rev. Dr. Guthrie.

The poets fabulously fancied that the giants scaled heaven by heaping mountain upon mountain. What was their fancy is the gospel truth. If you would get to heaven you must climb thither by putting Mount Sion upon Mount Sinai.—Bishop Hopkins.

What delight will it afford to renew the sweet counsel we have taken together, to recount the toils, the combats, and the labor of the way, and to approach, not the house, but the throne of God, in company, in order to join in the symphonies of heavenly voices, and lose ourselves amidst the splendors and fruitions of the beatific vision.—Robert Hall.

In our father's house it will not be the pearl gate or the streets of gold that will make us happy. But oh, how transcendently glad shall we be when we see our Lord. Perhaps in that "upper room," also, He may show us His hands and His side, and we may cry out with happy Thomas, "My Lord and my God!"—T. L. Cuyler.

There is a world above,
  Where parting is unknown;
A whole eternity of love,
  Form'd for the good alone;
And faith beholds the dying here
Translated to that happier sphere.
  —Montgomery.

Death must obliterate all memories and affections and ideas and laws, or the awakening in the next world will be amid the welcomes, and loves and raptures of those who left us with tearful farewells, and with dying promises that they would wait to welcome us when we should arrive. And so they do. Not sorrowfully, not anxiously, but lovingly, they wait to bid us welcome.—Bishop R. S. Foster.

O, land of rest, how near thou art! O, judgment-seat of Jesus, how thin are the clouds that veil Thee! Through the rifts of cloudland shine rays from this righteous crown. It is "laid up" for him whose hope can never be satisfied with less than the presence of the King.—Stephen H. Tyng, Jr.

It may be that at this moment every battlement of heaven is alive with the redeemed. There is a sainted mother watching for her daughter. Have you no response to that long hushed voice which has prayed for you so often? And for you, young man, are there no voices there that have prayed for you? And are there none whom you promised once to meet again, if not on earth, in heaven?—D. L. Moody.

No wearisome days, no sorrowful nights; no hunger or thirst; no anxiety or fears; no envies, no jealousies, no breaches of friendship, no sad separations, no distrusts or forebodings, no self-reproaches, no enmities, no bitter regrets, no tears, no heartaches; "And there shall be no more death, neither sorrow, nor crying, neither shall there be any more pain; for the former things are passed away."—Bishop R. S. Foster.

Look how the floor of Heaven
Is thick inlaid with patines of bright gold;
There's not the smallest orb which thou
    behold'st
But in his motion like an angel sings,
Still quiring to the young-eyed cherubims:
Such harmony is in immortal souls;
But, whilst this muddy vesture of decay
Doth grossly close it in, we cannot hear it.
  —Shakespeare.

If I am allowed to give a metaphorical allusion to the future state of the blessed, I should imagine it by the orange-grove in that sheltered glen on which the sun is now beginning to shine, and of which the trees are, at the same time, loaded with sweet golden fruit and balmy silver flowers. Such objects may well portray a state in which hope and fruition become one eternal feeling.—Sir H. Davy.

If one could look a while through the chinks of heaven's door, and see the beauty and bliss of paradise; if he could but lay his ear to heaven, and hear the ravishing music of those seraphic spirits, and the anthems of praise which they sing, how would his soul be exhilarated and transported with joy.—Watson.

The song
Of Heaven is ever new; for daily thus,
And nightly, new discoveries are made
Of God's unbounded wisdom, power, and
    love,
Which give the understanding larger room,
And swell the hymn with ever-growing
    praise.
  —Pollok.

They are kings and priests unto God. They wear crowns that flash in the everlasting light. They wear robes that are spotlessly white. They wave victorious palms. They sing anthems of such exceeding sweetness as no earthly choirs ever approach. They stand before the throne. They fly on ministries of love. They muse on the top of Mount Zion. They meditate on the banks of the river of life. They are rapturous with ecstasies of love. God wipes away all tears from their eyes.—Bishop R. S. Foster.

And then, the quiet of the green, inland valleys of our Father's land, where no tempest comes any more, nor the loud winds are ever heard, nor the salt sea is ever seen; but perpetual calm and blessedness; all mystery gone, and all rebellion hushed and silenced, and all unrest at an end forever! "No more sea;" but, instead of that wild and yeasty chaos of turbulent waters, there shall be the river that makes glad the city of God, the river of water of life, that proceeds "out of the throne of God and of the Lamb." —Alexander Maclaren.

Blessed is the pilgrim, who in every place, and at all times of this his banishment in the body, calling upon the holy name of Jesus, calleth to mind his native heavenly land, where his blessed Master, the King of saints and angels, waiteth to receive him. Blessed is the pilgrim who seeketh not an abiding place unto himself in this world; but longeth to be dissolved, and be with Christ in heaven.—Thos. à Kempis.

There is a land where everlasting suns
Shed everlasting brightness; where the soul
Drinks from the living streams of love that roll
By God's high throne! myriads of glorious ones
Bring their accepted offering. Oh! how blest
To look from this dark prison to that shrine,
To inhale one breath of Paradise divine,
And enter into that eternal rest
Which waits the sons of God.
—Bowring.

And looking back upon "the sea that brought us thither," we shall behold its waters flashing in the light of that everlasting morning, and hear them breaking into music upon the eternal shore. And then, brethren, when all

the weary night-watchers on the stormy ocean of life are gathered together around Him who watched with them from His throne on the bordering mountains of eternity, where the day shines forever—then He will seat them at His table in His kingdom, and none will need to ask, "Who art Thou?" or "Where am I?" "for all shall know it is the Lord," and the full, perfect, unchangeable vision of His blessed face will be heaven.—Alexander Maclaren.

Rejoice, oh! grieving heart,
The hours fly past;
With each some sorrow dies,
With each some shadow flies,
Until at last
The red dawn in the east
Bids weary night depart,
And pain is past.
—A. A. Proctor.

What tranquillity will there be in heaven! Who can express the fullness and blessedness of this peace! What a calm is this! How sweet and holy and joyous! What a haven of rest to enter, after having passed through the storms and tempests of this world, in which pride and selfishness and envy and malice and scorn and contempt and contention and vice are as waves of a restless ocean, always rolling, and often dashed about in violence and fury! What a Canaan of rest to come to, after going through this waste and howling wilderness, full of snares and pitfalls and poisonous serpents, where no rest could be found.—Jonathan Edwards.

Yes, thank God! there is rest—many an interval of saddest, sweetest rest—even here, when it seems as if evening breezes from that other land, laden with fragrance, played upon the cheeks, and lulled the heart. There are times, even on the stormy sea, when a gentle whisper breathes softly as of heaven, and sends into the soul a dream of ecstasy which can never again wholly die, even amidst the jar and whirl of daily life. How such whispers make the blood stop and the flesh creep with a sense of mysterious communion! How singularly such moments are the epochs of life—the few points that stand out prominently in the recollection after the flood of years has buried all the rest, as all the low shore disappears, leaving only a few rock points visible at high tide.—F. W. Robertson.

Beyond the smiling and the weeping,
　I shall be soon;
Beyond the waking and the sleeping,
Beyond the sowing and the reaping,
　I shall be soon!
Love, rest, and home—
Sweet hope! Lord, tarry not, but come!
　　　　—Horatius Bonar.

Heavens (The)

　　But the day is spent;
And stars are kindling in the firmament,
To us how silent—though like ours, per-
　chance,
Busy and full of life and circumstance.
　　　　—Rogers.

　　　Heaven's ebon vault,
Studded with stars unutterably bright,
Thro' which the moon's unclouded gran-
　deur rolls,
Seems like a canopy which love has spread
To curtain her sleeping world.
　　　　—Shelley.

This prospect vast, what is it?—weigh'd
　aright,
'Tis nature's system of divinity,
And every student of the night inspires.
'Tis elder scripture, writ by God's own
　hand:
Scripture authentic! uncorrupt by man.
　　　　—Young.

The blue, deep, glorious heavens!—I lift
　mine eye,
　And bless thee, O my God! that I have
　met
And own'd thine image in the majesty
　Of their calm temple still! that never yet
There hath thy face been shrouded from
　my sight
By noontide blaze, or sweeping storm of
　night!
　I bless thee, O my God!
　　　　—Mrs. Hemans.

Ye stars! which are the poetry of heaven;
If in your bright leaves we would read
　the fate
Of men and empires—'t is to be forgiven,
That in our aspirations to be great,
Our destinies o'erleap their mortal state,
And claim a kindred with you; for ye are
A beauty and a mystery, and create
In us such love and reverence from afar,
That fortune, fame, power, life, have
　nam'd themselves a star.　—Byron.

One sun by day, by night ten thousand
　shine;
And light us deep into the deity;
How boundless in magnificence and might!
O what a confluence of ethereal fires,
From urns unnumber'd, down the steep of
　heaven,
Streams to a point, and centres in my
　sight!
Nor tarries there; I feel it at my heart:
My heart, at once, it humbles, and exalts;
Lays it in dust, and calls it to the skies.
　　　　—Young.

Heirs

"Yet doth he live!" exclaims th' impa-
　tient heir,
And sighs for sables which he must not
　wear.　　　　—Byron.

To heirs unknown descends th' unguarded
　store,
Or wanders, heaven-directed, to the poor.
　　　　—Pope.

What madness is it for a man to starve himself to enrich his heir, and so turn a friend into an enemy! For his joy at your death will be proportioned to what you leave him.—Seneca.

He who sees his heir in his own child, carries his eye over hopes and possessions lying far beyond his gravestone, viewing his life, even here, as a period but closed with a comma. He who sees, his heir in another man's child sees the full stop at the end of the sentence.—Bulwer-Lytton.

An heiress, remaining unmarried, is a prey to all manner of extortion and imposition, and with the best intentions, becomes—through a bounty—a corruption to her neighborhood and a curse to the poor; or, if experience shall put her on her guard, she will lead a life of suspicion and resistance, to the injury of her own mind and nature.—Jeremy Taylor.

Hell

Hell is the wrath of God—His hate of sin.—Bailey.

Hell is truth seen too late.—H. G. Adams.

Hell is both sides of the tomb, and a devil may be respectable and wear good clothes.—Charles H. Parkhurst.

Hell is more bearable than nothingness.—Bailey.

Hell is full of good meanings and wishings.—Herbert.

Divines and dying men may talk of hell,
But in my heart her several torments dwell.
—Shakespeare.

Long is the way
And hard, that out of hell leads up to light. —Milton.

Hell is no other but a soundless pit,
Where no one beame of comfort peeps in it. —Herrick.

That's the greatest torture souls feel in hell,
In hell, that they must live, and cannot die. —John Webster.

Self-love and the love of the world constitute hell.—Swedenborg.

I think the devil will not have me damned, lest the oil that's in me should set hell on fire.—Shakespeare.

Hell is paved with good intentions. —Samuel Johnson.

Hell, their fit habitation, fraught with fire
Unquenchable, the house of woe and pain.
—Milton.

Eternal torments, baths of boiling sulphur,
Vicissitude of fires, and then of frosts.
—Dryden.

Hell is empty,
And all the devils are here.—Shakespeare.

There is nothing that keeps wicked men at any one moment out of hell but the mere pleasure of God.—Jonathan Edwards.

The mind is its own place, and in itself
Can make a heaven of hell, a hell of heaven. —Milton.

Hell's court is built deep in a gloomy vale,
High walled with strong damnation, moated round
With flaming brimstone.
—Dr. Joseph Beaumont.

Many might go to heaven with half the labor they go to hell, if they would venture their industry the right way. —Ben Jonson.

No hell will frighten men away from sin; no dread of prospective misery; only goodness can cast hell out of any man, and set up the kingdom of heaven within.—Hugh R. Haweis.

Myself am hell;
And in the lowest deep a lower deep,
Still threat'ning to devour me, opens wide;
To which the hell I suffer seems a heaven.
—Milton.

There is in hell a place stone-built throughout,
Called Malebolge, of an iron hue,
Like to the wall that circles it about.
—Dante.

We spirits have just such natures
We had for all the world, when human creatures;
And, therefore, I, that was an actress here,
Play all my tricks in hell, a goblin there.
—Dryden.

Nay, then, what flames are these that leap and swell
As 'twere to show, where earth's foundations crack,
The secrets of the sepulchres of hell
On Dante's track? —Swinburne.

The place thou saw'st was hell, the groans thou heard'st
The wailings of the damn'd, of those who would
Not be redeem'd. —Pollok.

Ev'n thus in hell, wander the restless damn'd:
From scorching flames to chilling frosts they run;
Then from their frosts to fires return again,
And only prove variety of pain.
—Rowe.

A dungeon horrible, on all sides round,
As one great furnace, flamed; yet from those flames
No light, but rather darkness visible
Serv'd only to discover sights of woe,
Regions of sorrow, doleful shades, where peace
And rest can never dwell, hope never comes
That comes to all; but torture without end.
—Milton.

In the utmost solitudes of nature, the existence of hell seems to me as legibly declared by a thousand spiritual utterances as that of heaven.—Ruskin.

What will you do in a world where the Holy Spirit never strives; where every soul is fully left to its own depravity; and where there is no leisure for repentance, if there were even the desire, but where there is too much present pain to admit repentance; where they gnaw their tongues with pain, and blaspheme the God of heaven?—James Hamilton.

Hell has no limits, nor is circumscribed
In one self place; but where we are is hell
And where hell is, there must we ever be;
And to be short, when all the world dissolves,
And every creature shall be purified,
All places shall be hell that are not
heaven.   —Marlowe.

A dark
Illimitable ocean, without bound,
Without dimension; where length, breadth,
and highth,
And time, and place, are lost; where eldest Night
And Chaos—ancestors of Nature, hold
Eternal anarchy, amidst the noise
Of endless wars, and by confusion stand.
    —Milton.

A universe of death
Where all life dies, death lives, and nature breeds
Perverse, all monstrous, all prodigious things
Abominable, unutterable, and worse
Than fables yet have feign'd, or fear conceived.   —Milton.

Hell is a city much like London—
A populous and a smoky city;
There are all sorts of people undone,
And there is little or no fun done;
Small justice shown, and still less pity.
   *   *   *   *   *
Lawyers—judges—old hobnobbers
Are there—bailiffs—chancellors—
Bishops—great and little robbers—
Rhymesters—pamphleteers—stock-jobbers—
Men of glory in the wars.   —Shelley.

The Lamb is, indeed, the emblem of love; but what so terrible as the wrath of the Lamb? The depth of the mercy despised is the measure of the punishment of him that despiseth. No more fearful words than those of the Saviour. The threatenings of the law were temporal, those of the gospel are eternal. It is Christ who reveals the never-dying worm, the unquenchable fire, and He who contrasts with the eternal joys of the redeemed the everlasting woes of the lost. His loving arms would enfold the whole human race, but not while impenitent or unbelieving; the benefits of His redemption are conditional.—Edward Thomson.

In the throat
Of Hell, before the very vestibule
Of opening Orcus, sit Remorse and Grief,
And pale Disease, and sad Old Age and Fear,
And Hunger that persuades to crime, and Want:
Forms terrible to see. Suffering and Death
Inhabit here, and Death's own brother Sleep;
And the mind's evil lusts and deadly War,
Lie at the threshold, and the iron beds
Of the Eumenides; and Discord wild
Her viper-locks with bloody fillets bound.
    —Virgil.

There is a place in a black and hollow vault,
Where day is never seen; there shines no sun,
But flaming horror of consuming fires;
A lightless sulphur, chok'd with smoky fogs
Of an infected darkness; in this place
Dwell many thousand . thousand sundry sorts
Of never dying deaths; there damn'd souls ·
Roar without pity; there are gluttons fed
With toads and adders; there is burning oil
Pour'd down the drunkard's throat; the usurer
Is forc'd to sup whole draughts of molten gold;
There is the murderer forever stabb'd,
Yet can he never die; there lies the wanton
On racks of burning steel, while in his soul
He feels the torment of his raging lust;
There stand those wretched things,
Who have dream'd out whole years in lawless sheets,
And secret incests, cursing one another.
    —John Ford.

An immortality of pain and tears; an infinity of wretchedness and despair; the blackness of darkness across which conscience will forever shoot her clear and ghastly flashes—like lightning streaming over a desert when midnight and tempest are there; weeping and wailing and gnashing of teeth; long, long eternity, and things that will make eternity seem longer—making each moment seem eternity—

oh, miserable condition of the damned!
—Richard Fuller.

Help

God helps those who help themselves.
—Algernon Sidney.

Light is the task when many share the toil.—Homer.

Heaven's help is better than early rising.—Cervantes.

I would help others, out of a fellow-feeling.—Burton.

In man's most dark extremity
Oft succor dawns from Heaven.
—Scott.

'Tis not enough to help the feeble up,
But to support him after.
—Shakespeare.

I want to help you to grow as beautiful as God meant you to be when He thought of you first.—George MacDonald.

Such help as we can give to each other in this world is a debt to each other; and the man who perceives a superiority or a capacity in a subordinate, and neither confesses nor assists it, is not merely the withholder of kindness, but the committer of injury.—Ruskin.

Heraldry

A court of heraldry sprung up to supply the place of crusade exploits, to grant imaginary shields and trophies to families that never wore real armor, and it is but of late that it has been discovered to have no real jurisdiction.—Shenstone.

We may talk what we please of lilies, and lions rampant, and spread eagles, in fields of d'or or d'argent, but if heraldry were guided by reason, a plough in a field arable would be the most noble and ancient arms.—Cowley.

Herbage

Grass grows at last above all graves.
—Julia C. R. Dorr.

The green grass floweth like a stream
Into the ocean's blue. —Lowell.

How lush and lusty the grass looks! how green!—Shakespeare.

A blade of grass is always a blade of grass, whether in one country or another.—Samuel Johnson.

Heroes

Troops of heroes undistinguished die.—Addison.

No man is a hero to his valet.—Mme. de Cornuel.

Heroes are a mischievous race.—Jeremy Collier.

Yes, Honor decks the turf that wraps their clay.—Byron.

There are heroes in evil as well as in good.—Rochefoucauld.

Heroes as great have died, and yet shall fall.—Homer.

Whoe'er excels in what we prize,
Appears a hero in our eyes.
—Swift.

Worship your heroes from afar; contact withers them.—Mme. Necker.

If hero means sincere man, why may not every one of us be a hero—Carlyle.

Of two heroes, he who esteems his rivals the most is the greatest.—Beaumelle.

We can all be heroes in our virtues, in our homes, in our lives.—James Ellis.

Prodigious actions may as well be done
By weaver's issue, as by prince's son.
—Dryden.

The real heroes of this war are the "great, brave, patient, nameless people."—Whitelaw Reid.

Heroes, it would seem, exist always and a certain worship of them.—Carlyle.

The legacy of heroes—the memory

of a great name, and the inheritance of a great example.—Beaconsfield.

Each man is a hero and an oracle to somebody, and to that person whatever he says has an enhanced value.—Emerson.

Our heroes of the former days deserved and gained their never-fading bays.—Roscommon.

I want a hero: an uncommon wànt,
When every year and month sends forth a
   new one. —Byron.

Hail, Columbia! happy land!
Hail, ye heroes! heaven-born band!
Who fought and bled in Freedom's cause.
   —Joseph Hopkinson.

In analyzing the character of heroes, it is hardly possible to separate altogether the share of fortune from their own.—Hallam.

The gentle breath of peace would leave him on the surface neglected and unmoved. It is only the tempest that lifts him from his place.—Junius.

The idol of to-day pushes the hero of yesterday out of our recollection; and will, in turn, be supplanted by his successor of to-morrow.—Washington Irving.

The heroes of literary history have been no less remarkable for what they have suffered than for what they have achieved.—Johnson.

Heroes are not known by the loftiness of their carriage, as the greatest braggarts are generally the merest cowards.—Rousseau.

Nobody, they say, is a hero to his valet. Of course; for a man must be a hero to understand a hero. The valet, I dare say, has great respect for some person of his own stamp.—Goethe.

The prudent sees only the difficulties, the bold only the advantages, of a great enterprise; the hero sees both, diminishes those, makes these preponderate, and conquers.—Lavater.

Heroes in history seem to us poetic because they are there. But if we should tell the simple truth of some of our neighbors, it would sound like poetry.—G. W. Curtis.

Up rose the hero,—on his piercing eye
Sat observation; on each glance of thought
Decision follow'd, as the thunderbolt
Pursues the flash. —Home.

Place moral heroes in the field, and heroines follow them as brides, but the opposite does not hold true; no heroine can create a hero through love of her, but she may give birth to one.—Richter.

Heroes, notwithstanding the high ideas which, by the means of flatterers, they may entertain of themselves, or the world may conceive of them, have certainly more of mortal than divine about them.—Fielding.

There needs not a great soul to make a hero; there needs a God-created soul which will be true to its origin; that will be a great soul.—Carlyle.

But to the hero, when his sword
Has won the battle for the free,
Thy voice sounds like a prophet's word,
And in its hollow tones are heard
The thanks of millions yet to be.
   —Fitz-Greene Halleck.

The greatest of all heroes is One—whom we do not name here! Let sacred silence meditate that sacred matter; you will find it the ultimate perfection of a principle extant throughout man's whole history on earth.—Carlyle.

A hero is—as though one should say —a man of high achievement, who performs famous exploits—who does things that are heroical, and in all his actions and demeanor is a hero indeed. —H. Brooke.

The heroic soul does not sell its justice and its nobleness. It does not ask to dine nicely and to sleep warm. The essence of greatness is the perception that virtue is enough. Poverty is its ornament. It does not need plenty, and can very well abide its loss.—Emerson.

He who, with strong passions, remains chaste—he who, keenly sensitive, with manly power of indignation in him, can yet restrain himself and forgive—these are strong men, spiritual heroes.—Robertson.

Great men need to be lifted upon the shoulders of the whole world, in order to conceive their great ideas or perform their great deeds; that is, there must be an atmosphere of greatness round about them. A hero cannot be a hero unless in an heroic world.—Hawthorne.

It hath been an ancient custom among them (Hungarians) that none should wear a fether but he who had killed a Turk, to whom onlie yt was lawful to shew the number of his slaine enemys by the number of fethers in his cappe.—Richard Hansard.

It were well if there were fewer heroes; for I scarcely ever heard of any, excepting Hercules, but did more mischief than good. These overgrown mortals commonly use their will with their right hand, and their reason with their left.—Jeremy Collier.

Whoever, with an earnest soul,
Strives for some end from this low world afar,
Still upward travels though he miss the goal,
And strays—but towards a star.
　　　　　　　—Bulwer.

Yet reason frowns in war's unequal game,
Where wasted nations raise a single name;
And mortgag'd states their grandsire's wreaths regret,
From age to age in everlasting debt;
Wreaths which at last the dear-bought right convey
To rust on medals, or on stones decay.
　　　　　　　—Dr. Johnson.

Heroism

Self-trust is the essence of heroism.—Emerson.

In a truly heroic life there is no peradventure. It is always either doing or dying.—Roswell D. Hitchcock.

Heroism—the divine relation which in all times unites a great man to other men.—Carlyle.

The grandest of heroic deeds are those which are performed within four walls and in domestic privacy.—Jean Paul Richter.

There is more heroism in self-denial than in deeds of arms.—Seneca.

Take away ambition and vanity, and where will be your heroes or patriots?—Seneca.

Heroes did not make our liberties: they but reflected and illustrated them.—James A. Garfield.

Mankind is not disposed to look narrowly into the conduct of great victors when their victory is on the right side.—George Eliot.

The world's battlefields have been in the heart chiefly, and there the greatest heroism has been secretly exercised.—Beecher.

The true epic of our times is not "Arms and the Man," but "Tools and the Man"—an infinitely wider kind of epic.—Carlyle.

Heroism is active genius; genius, contemplative heroism. Heroism is the self-devotion of genius manifesting itself in action.—J. C. and A. W. Hare.

A noble life, crowned with heroic death, rises above and outlives the pride and pomp and glory of the mightiest empire of the earth.—Garfield.

Every heroic act measures itself by its contempt of some external good. But it finds its own success at last, and then the prudent also extol.—Emerson.

Those whom the world has delighted to honor have oftener been influenced in their doings by ambition and vanity than by patriotism.—Rochefoucauld.

The greatest obstacle to being heroic is the doubt whether one may not be going to prove one's self a fool; the truest heroism is to resist the doubt, and the profoundest wisdom to know when it ought to be resisted, and when to be obeyed.—Hawthorne.

Heroism works in contradiction to the voice of mankind, and in contradiction, for a time, to the voice of the great and good. Heroism is an obedience to a secret impulse of an individual's character.—Emerson.

Heroism, self-denial, and magnanimity, in all instances where they do not spring from a principle of religion, are but splendid altars on which we sacrifice one kind of self-love to another.—Colton.

A light supper, a good night's sleep, and a fine morning have often made a hero of the same man who, by indigestion, a restless night, and a rainy morning, would have proved a coward.—Chesterfield.

If we must have heroes and wars wherein to make them, there is no war so brilliant as a war with wrong; no hero so fit to be sung as he who has gained the bloodless victory of truth and mercy.—Horace Bushnell.

True heroism is alike positive and progressive. It sees in right the duty which should dominate, and in truth the principle which should prevail. And hence it never falters in the faith that always and everywhere sin must be repressed, and righteousness exalted.—John McC. Holmes.

Enthusiasm springs from the imagination, and self-sacrifice from the heart. Women are, therefore, more naturally heroic than men. All nations have in their annals some of these miracles of patriotism, of which woman is the instrument in the hands of God.—Lamartine.

Heroism is the brilliant triumph of the soul over the flesh; that is to say, over fear: fear of poverty, of suffering, of calumny, of sickness, of isolation, and of death. There is no serious piety without heroism. Heroism is the dazzling and glorious concentration of courage.—Amiel.

Don't aim at any impossible heroisms. Strive rather to be quiet in your own sphere. Don't live in the cloudland of some transcendental heaven; do your best to bring the glory of a real heaven down, and ray it out upon your fellows in this work-day world. Seek to make trade bright with a spotless integrity, and business lustrous with the beauty of holiness.—Wm. M. Punshon.

There is a heroism in crime as well as in virtue. Vice and infamy have their altars and their religion. This makes nothing in their favor, but is a proud compliment to man's nature. Whatever he is or does, he cannot entirely efface the stamp of the divinity on him. Let him strive ever so, he cannot divest himself of his natural sublimity of thought and affection, however he may pervert or deprave it to ill.—Hazlitt.

There is an army of memorable sufferers who suffer inwardly and not outwardly. The world's battlefields have been in the heart chiefly. More heroism has there been displayed in the household and in the closet, I think, than on the most memorable military battlefields of history.—Beecher.

Heroism is no extempore work of transient impulse—a rocket rushing fretfully up to disturb the darkness by which, after a moment's insulting radiance, it is ruthlessly swallowed up, —but a steady fire, which darts forth tongues of flame. It is no sparkling epigram of action, but a luminous epic of character.—Whipple.

We cannot think too highly of our nature, nor too humbly of ourselves. When we see the martyr to virtue, subject as he is to the infirmities of a man, yet suffering the tortures of a demon, and bearing them with the magnanimity of a God, do we not behold a heroism that angels may indeed surpass, but which they cannot imitate, and must admire.—Colton.

Never was there a time, in the history of the world, when moral heroes were more needed. The world waits for such, the providence of God has commanded science to labor and prepare the way for such. For them she is laying her iron tracks, and stretching her wires, and bridging the oceans. But where are they? Who shall breathe into our civil and political relations the breath of a higher life? Who shall touch the eyes of a paganized science, and of a pantheistic philosophy, that they may see God? Who shall consecrate to the glory of God the triumphs of science? Who shall bear the life-boat to the stranded and perishing nations.—Mark Hopkins.

Hero-Worship

Society is founded on hero-worship. —Carlyle.

Worship of a hero is transcendent admiration of a great man.—Carlyle.

Hero-worship exists, has existed, and will forever exist, universally, among mankind.—Carlyle.

If silence is ever golden, it must be * * * beside the graves of * * * men, whose lives were more significant than speech, and whose death was a poem, the music of which can never be sung.—Garfield.

Fortunate men! your country lives because you died. Your fame is placed where the breath of calumny can never reach it, where the mistakes of a weary life can never dim its brightness! Coming generations will rise up and call you blessed.—Garfield.

Unmixed praise is not due to any one. It leaves behind a sense of unreality. We can only do justice to a great man by a discriminating criticism. Hero-worship, which paints a faultless monster, whom the world never saw, is like those modern pic-

tures which are a blaze of light without any shadow.—James Freeman Clarke.

Pure hero-worship is healthy. It stimulates the young to deeds of heroism, stirs the old to unselfish efforts, and gives the masses models of mankind that tend to lift humanity above the commonplace meanness of ordinary life.—Donn Piatt.

They summed up and perfected, by one supreme act, the highest virtues of men and citizens. For love of country they accepted death, and thus resolved all doubts, and made immortal their patriotism and their virtue.—Garfield.

These heroes are dead. They died for liberty—they died for us. They are at rest. They sleep in the land they made free, under the flag they rendered stainless, under the solemn pines, the sad hemlocks, the tearful willows, and the embracing vines. They sleep beneath the shadows of the clouds, careless alike of sunshine or of storm, each in the windowless palace of rest. Earth may run red with other wars; they are at peace. In the midst of battle, in the roar of conflict, they found the serenity of death. I have one sentiment for soldiers living and dead: cheers for the living; tears for the dead.—Robert G. Ingersoll.

Historians

To be a really good historian is perhaps the rarest of intellectual distinctions.—Macaulay.

Histories are as perfect as the historian is wise, and is gifted with an eye and a soul.—Carlyle.

Instructed by the antiquary times,
He must, he is, he cannot but be wise.
—Shakespeare.

Every great writer is a writer of history, let him treat on almost any subject he may.—Landor.

It is to me a peculiarly noble work rescuing from oblivion those who deserve immortality, and extending their renown at the same time that we advance our own.—Pliny the Younger.

———

Historians ought to be precise, faithful, and unprejudiced; and neither interest nor fear, hatred nor affection, should make them swerve from the way of truth.—Cervantes.

———

Historians, only things of weight,
Results of persons, or affairs of State,
Briefly, with truth and clearness should relate;
Laconic shortness memory feeds.
—Heath.

———

The historian must be a poet; not to find, but to find again; not to breathe life into beings, into imaginary deeds, but in order to re-animate and revive that which has been; to represent what time and space have placed at a distance from us.—Joseph Roux.

———

The true historical genius, to our thinking, is that which can see the nobler meaning of events that are near him, as the true poet is he who detects the divine in the casual; and we somewhat suspect the depth of his insight into the past, who cannot recognize the godlike of to-day under that disguise in which it always visits us. —Lowell.

———

A perfect historian must possess an imagination sufficiently powerful to make his narrative affecting and picturesque; yet he must control it so absolutely as to content himself with the materials which he finds, and to refrain from supplying deficiencies by additions of his own. He must be a profound and ingenious reasoner; yet he must possess sufficient self-command to abstain from casting his facts in the mould of his hypothesis.— Macaulay.

———

The true historian, therefore, seeking to compose a true picture of the thing acted, must collect facts and combine facts. Methods will differ, styles will differ. Nobody ever does anything like anybody else; but the end in view is generally the same, and the historian's end is truthful narration. Maxims he will have, if he is

wise, never a one; and as for a moral, if he tell his story well, it will need none; if he tell it ill, it will deserve none.—Augustine Birrell.

History

History teaches everything, even the future.—Lamartine.

———

All history is a lie!—Sir Robert Walpole.

———

There is a history in all men's lives. —Shakespeare.

———

History is but the unrolled scroll of prophecy.—James A. Garfield.

———

What is history but a fable agreed upon?—Napoleon I.

———

Truth is liable to be left-handed in history.—Dumas, Père.

———

Sin writes history; goodness is silent.—Goethe.

———

To study history is to study literature.—Willmott.

———

History is the complement of poetry. —Sir J. Stephen.

———

Biography is the only true history.— Carlyle.

———

All history was at first oral.—Dr. Johnson.

———

Her ample page rich with the spoils of time.—Gray.

———

The mystery of history is an insoluble problem.—Henry Ward Beecher.

———

History is a pageant and not a philosopher.—Augustine Birrell.

———

History is only a confused heap of facts.—Lord Chesterfield.

———

History is the revelation of Providence.—Kossuth.

———

History itself is nothing more than legend and romance.—Thomas Wright.

History is clarified experience.—Lowell.

History is, after all, the crystallization of popular beliefs.—Donn Piatt.

History ought to be guided by strict truth; and worthy actions require nothing more.—Pliny the Younger.

History is neither more nor less than biography on a large scale.—Lamartine.

History shows that the majority of men who have done anything great have passed their youth in seclusion.—Heine.

History, which is, indeed, little more than the register of the crimes, follies, and misfortunes of mankind.—Gibbon.

That which history can give us best is the enthusiasm which it raises in our hearts.—Goethe.

The Grecian history is a poem, Latin history a picture, modern history a chronicle.—Chateaubriand.

History casts its shadow far into the land of song.—Longfellow.

History, in whatever way it may be executed, is a great source of pleasure.—Pliny the Younger.

History is little else than a picture of human crimes and misfortunes.—Voltaire.

Anything but history, for history must be false.—Horace Walpole.

They who live in history only seemed to walk the earth again.—Longfellow.

History is the essence of innumerable biographies.—Carlyle.

History is only time furnished with dates and rich with events.—Rivarol.

History is the depository of great actions, the witness of what is past, the example and instructor of the present, and monitor to the future.—Cervantes.

History makes us some amends for the shortness of life.—Skelton.

The historian is a prophet looking backwards.—Schlegel.

History hath triumphed over Time, which besides it, nothing but Eternity hath triumphed over.—Sir Walter Raleigh.

History is but a kind of Newgate calendar, a register of the crimes and miseries that man has inflicted on his fellow-man.—Washington Irving.

History is a mighty drama, enacted upon the theatre of time, with suns for lamps and eternity for a background.—Carlyle.

A Grecian history, perfectly written should be a complete record of the rise and progress of poetry, philosophy, and the arts.—Macaulay.

The impartiality of history is not that of the mirror, which merely reflects objects, but of the judge, who sees, listens, and decides.—Lamartine.

Providence conceals itself in the details of human affairs, but becomes unveiled in the generalities of history.—Lamartine.

History is the witness of the times, the torch of truth, the life of memory, the teacher of life, the messenger of antiquity.—Cicero.

History needs distance, perspective. Facts and events which are too well attested cease, in some sort, to be malleable.—Joubert.

A cultivated reader of history is domesticated in all families; he dines with Pericles, and sups with Titian.—Willmott.

There is no history worthy of attention but that of a free people; the history of a people subjected to despotism is only a collection of anecdotes.—Chamfort.

History is constantly repeating itself, making only such changes of programme as the growth of nations and centuries requires.—Garfield.

History, as it lies at the root of all science, is also the first distinct product of man's spiritual nature; his earliest expression of what can be called thought.—Carlyle.

Not to know what has been transacted in former times is to continue always a child. If no use is made of the labors of past ages, the world must remain always in the infancy of knowledge.—Cicero.

It is when the hour of the conflict is over that history comes to a right understanding of the strife, and is ready to exclaim, "Lo, God is here, and we knew Him not!"—Bancroft.

History, like religion, unites all learning and power, especially ancient history; that is, the history of the nations of the youthful world—Grecian and Roman, Jewish and early Christian.—Richter.

There is nothing that solidifies and strengthens a nation like reading of the nation's own history, whether that history is recorded in books, or embodied in customs, institutions, and monuments.—Joseph Anderson.

What is public history but a register of the successes and disappointments, the vices, the follies, and the quarrels, of those who engage in contention for power?—Paley.

At the bottom there is no perfect history; there is none such conceivable. All past centuries have rotted down, and gone confusedly dumb and quiet.—Carlyle.

Each generation gathers together the imperishable children of the past, and increases them by new sons of

light, alike radiant with immortality.—Bancroft.

History maketh a young man to be old, without either wrinkles or grey hairs, privileging him with the experience of age, without either the infirmities or inconveniences thereof.—Fuller.

The history of the past is a mere puppet-show. A little man comes out and blows a little trumpet, and goes in again. You look for something new, and lo! another little man comes out, and blows another little trumpet, and goes in again. And it is all over.—Longfellow.

The student is to read history actively and not passively; to esteem his own life the text, and books the commentary. Thus compelled, the muse of history will utter oracles as never to those who do not respect themselves.—Emerson.

Truth comes to us from the past, as gold is washed down from the mountains of Sierra Nevada, in minute but precious particles, and intermixed with infinite alloy, the debris of the centuries.—Bovee.

In a word, we may gather out of history a policy no less wise than eternal; by the comparison and application of other men's forepassed miseries with our own like errors and ill deservings.—Sir Walter Raleigh.

We must consider how very little history there is—I mean real, authentic history. That certain kings reigned and certain battles were fought, we can depend upon as true; but all the coloring, all the philosophy, of history is conjecture.—Dr. Johnson.

Facts are the mere dross of history. It is from the abstract truth which interpenetrates them, and lies latent among them, like gold in the ore, that the mass derives its whole value; and the precious particles are generally combined with the baser in such a manner that the separation is a task of the utmost difficulty.—Macaulay.

———

Geologists complain that when they want specimens of the common rocks of a country, they receive curious spars; just so, historians give us the extraordinary events and omit just what we want,—the every-day life of each particular time and country.—Whately.

———

History is a great painter, with the world for canvas, and life for a figure. It exhibits man in his pride, and nature in her magnificence,—Jerusalem bleeding under the Roman, or Lisbon vanishing in flame and earthquake. History must be splendid. Bacon called it the pomp of business. Its march is in high places, and along the pinnacles and points of great affairs. —Willmott.

———

History presents the pleasantest features of poetry and fiction,—the majesty of the epic, the moving accidents of the drama, the surprises and moral of the romance. Wallace is a ruder Hector; Robinson Crusoe is not stranger that Crœsus; the Knights of Ashby never burnish the page of Scott with richer lights of lance and armor than the Carthaginians, winding down the Alps, cast upon Livy.—Willmott.

———

The world's history is a divine poem of which the history of every nation is a canto and every man a word. Its strains have been pealing along down the centuries, and though there have been mingled the discords of warring cannon and dying men, yet to the Christian philosopher and historian —the humble listener—there has been a divine melody running through the song which speaks of hope and halcyon days to come.—James A. Garfield.

Hobbies

Hobbies should be wives, not mistresses. It will not do to have more than one at a time. One hobby leads you out of extravagance; a team of hobbies you cannot drive till you are rich enough to find corn for them

all. Few men are rich enough for that.—Bulwer-Lytton.

Holidays

If all the year were playing holidays,
To sport would be as tedious as to work.
    —Shakespeare.

———

I have a great confidence in the revelations which holidays bring forth.—Beaconsfield.

———

You sunburnt sicklemen, of August weary,
Come hither from the furrow and be merry:
Make holiday; your rye-straw hats put on
And these fresh nymphs encounter every one
In country footing.   —Shakespeare.

———

The holiest of all holidays are those
Kept by ourselves in silence and apart;
The secret anniversaries of the heart,
When the full river of feeling overflows;—
The happy days unclouded to their close;
The sudden joys that out of darkness start
As flames from ashes; swift desires that dart
Like swallows singing down each wind that blows!   —Longfellow.

———

The second day of July, 1776, will be the most memorable epoch in the history of America. I am apt to believe that it will be celebrated by succeeding generations as the great anniversary festival. It ought to be commemorated as the day of deliverance, by solemn acts of devotion to God Almighty. It ought to be solemnized with pomp and parade, with shows, games, sports, guns, bells, bonfires, and illuminations, from one end of this continent to the other, from this time forward forevermore.—John Adams.

Holiness

Holiness is an unselfing of ourselves. —F. W. Faber.

———

The symmetry of the soul.—Philip Henry.

———

Holiness is the architectural plan upon which God buildeth up His living temple.—C. H. Spurgeon.

———

Holiness is happiness; and the more you have of the former, the more you will undoubtedly enjoy of the latter.—John Angel James.

What Christianity in her antagonism with every form of unbelief most needs is holy living.—Christlieb.

The most holy men are always the most humble men; none so humble on earth as those that live highest in heaven.—Aughey.

Remember that holiness is not the way to Christ, but Christ is the way to holiness.—Aughey.

Whoso lives the holiest life
Is fittest far to die.
—Margaret J. Preston.

Seek and possess holiness, and consolation will follow, as assuredly as warmth follows the dispensation of the rays of the sun.—Upham.

Christ came to give us a justifying righteousness, and He also came to make us holy—not chiefly for the purpose of evidencing here our possession of a justifying righteousness—but for the purpose of forming and fitting us for a blessed eternity.—Chalmers.

If it be heaven toward which we journey, it will be holiness in which we delight; for if we cannot now rejoice in having God for our portion, where is our meetness for a world in which God is to be all in all forever and forever?—Henry Melvill.

It must be a prospect pleasing to God Himself to see His creation forever beautifying in His eyes, and drawing nearer Him by greater degrees of resemblance.—Addison.

The inquirer after holiness should associate with those whose intelligence will instruct him; whose example will guide him; whose conversation will inspire him; whose cautions will warn him.—John Angel James.

Blessed is the memory of those who have kept themselves unspotted from the world. Yet more blessed and more

dear the memory of those who have kept themselves unspotted in the world.—Mrs. Jameson.

Holiness consists of three things—separation from sin, dedication to God, transformation into Christ's image. It is in vain that we talk about the last, unless we know something experimentally about the first.—Aughey.

If it be the characteristic of a worldly man that he desecrates what is holy, it should be of the Christian to consecrate what is secular, and to recognize a present and presiding divinity in all things.—Chalmers.

The narrow way, the way of holiness, not only leads to life, but it is life. Walking there, serene are our days, peaceful our nights, happy—high above the disorders and miseries of a wretched world—shall be our hourly communion with God; happy—full of assurance, of calm and sacred triumph, shall be our dying hour.—Richard Fuller.

But all his mind is bent to holiness,
To number Ave-Maries on his beads;
His champions are the prophets and apostles,
His weapons only saws of sacred writ,
His study is his tilt-yard, and his loves
Are brazen images of canonized saints.
—Shakespeare.

Holiness is religious principle put into motion. It is the love of God sent forth into circulation, on the feet, and with the hands of love to men. It is faith gone to work. It is charity coined into actions, and devotion breathing benedictions on human suffering, while it goes up in intercession to the Father of all piety.—F. D. Huntington.

I make it my constant prayer that God would most graciously be pleased to dispose us all to do justice, to love mercy, and to demean ourselves with that charity, humility, and pacific temper of mind, which were the characteristics of the Divine Author of our blessed religion; without a humble imitation of whose example in these things, we can never hope to be a happy nation.—George Washington.

Everything holy is before what is unholy; guilt presupposes innocence, not the reverse; angels, but not fallen ones, were created. Hence man does not properly rise to the highest, but first sinks gradually down from it, and then afterwards rises again; a child can never be considered too innocent and good.—Richter.

It is of things heavenly and universal declaration, working in them whose hearts God inspireth with the due consideration thereof, and habit or disposition of mind whereby they are made fit vessels both for the receipt and delivery of whatsoever spiritual perfection.—Hooker.

He who the sword of heaven will bear
Should be as holy as severe;
Pattern in himself to know,
Grace to stand, and virtue go;
More nor less to others paying
Than by self-offences weighing.
Shame to him whose cruel striking
Kills for faults of his own liking!
　　　　　　　—Shakespeare.

Holy Spirit

A religion without the Holy Ghost, though it had all the ordinances and all the doctrines of the New Testament, would certainly not be Christianity.—William Arthur.

There is no reason to believe that the Holy Spirit ever leaves awakened sinners, only as they leave the truth of God for some error or sin.—Ichabod Spencer.

You will find that for a smoking flax there is no specific like heaven's oxygen; for a faint and flickering piety there is no cure comparable to the one without which all our own exertions are but an effort to light a lamp in a vacuum—the breath of the Holy Spirit.—James Hamilton.

Whatever the Holy Spirit prompts a true Christian to do for the glory of God, He allures him to do in a modest way, and with a disposition of indescribable tenderness.—C. S. Robinson.

The work of the Spirit is to impart life, to implant hope, to give liberty, to testify of Christ, to guide us into all truth, to teach us all things, to comfort the believer, and to convict the world of sin.—D. L. Moody.

Culture is good, genius is brilliant, civilization is a blessing, education is a great privilege; but we may be educated villains. The thing that we want most of all is the precious gift of the Holy Ghost.—John Hall.

The believing man hath the Holy Ghost; and where the Holy Ghost dwelleth, He will not suffer a man to be idle, but stirreth him up to all exercises of piety and godliness, and of true religion, to the love of God, to the patient suffering of afflictions, to prayer, to thanksgiving, and the exercise of charity towards all men. —Martin Luther.

I firmly believe that the moment our hearts are emptied of pride and selfishness and ambition and self-seeking and every thing that is contrary to God's law, the Holy Ghost will come and fill every corner of our hearts; but if we are full of pride and conceit and ambition and self-seeking and pleasure and the world, there is no room for the Spirit of God; and I believe many a man is praying to God to fill him when he is full already with something else.— D. L. Moody.

Home

Home is the grandest of all institutions.—Spurgeon.

Home is the chief school of human virtues.—Channing.

Home is the seminary of all other institutions.—Chapin.

Home—the nursery of the Infinite. William Ellery Channing.

Our home is still home, be it ever so homely.—Charles Dibdin.

A happy home is the single spot of rest which a man has upon this earth for the cultivation of his noblest sensibilities.—F. W. Robertson.

Home makes the man.—Samuel Smiles.

Home interprets heaven. Home is heaven for beginners.—Charles H. Parkhurst.

The sweetest type of heaven is home. —J. G. Holland.

Home, in one form or another, is the great object of life.—J. G. Holland.

There is no sanctuary of virtue like home.—Edward Everett.

Home-keeping youth have ever homely wits.—Shakespeare.

The strength of a nation, especially of a republican nation, is in the intelligent and well-ordered homes of the people.—Mrs. Sigourney.

His home, the spot of earth supremely blest,
A dearer, sweeter spot than all the rest.
—Montgomery.

Just the wee cot—the cricket's chirr—
Love and the smiling face of her.
—James Whitcomb Riley.

Every one in his own house and God in all of them.—Cervantes.

I value this delicious home-feeling as one of the choicest gifts a parent can bestow.—Washington Irving.

The air of paradise did fan the house, and angels officed all.—Shakespeare.

'Mid pleasures and palaces though we may roam,
Be it ever so humble, there's no place like home. —J. Howard Payne.

He is happiest, be he king or peasant, who finds peace in his home.—Goethe.

Home should be an oratorio of the memory, singing to all our after life melodies and harmonies of old-remembered joy.—Henry Ward Beecher.

Communion is the law of growth, and homes only thrive when they sustain relations with each other.—J. G. Holland.

There is no place more delightful than one's own fireside.—Cicero.

The paternal hearth, the rallying-place of the affections.—Washington Irving.

Home should be the centre of joy, equatorial and tropical.—Beecher.

To Adam Paradise was home. To the good among his descendants home is paradise.—Hare.

The first indication of domestic happiness is the love of one's home.—M. de Montlosier.

The spirit and tone of your home will have great influence on your children. If it is what it ought to be, it will fasten conviction on their minds, however wicked they may become.—Richard Cecil.

A Christian home! What a power it is to the child when he is far away in the cold, tempting world, and voices of sin are filling his ears, and his feet stand on slippery places.—A. E. Kittreage.

The house of every one is to him as his castle and fortress, as well for his defence against injury and violence, as for his repose.—Sir Edward Coke.

No genuine observer can decide otherwise than that the homes of a nation are the bulwarks of personal and national safety and thrift.—J. G. Holland.

There is a magic in that little word, —it is a mystic circle that surrounds comforts and virtues never known beyond its hallowed limits.—Southey.

A man who in the struggles of life has no home to retire to, in fact or in memory, is without life's best rewards and life's best defences.—J. G. Holland.

To be happy at home is the ultimate result of all ambition, the end to which every enterprise and ' labor tends, and of which every desire prompts the prosecution.—Johnson.

When home is ruled according to God's word, angels might be asked to stay a night with us,· and they would not find themselves out of their element.—C. H. Spurgeon.

There is no happiness in life, there is no misery, like that growing out of the dispositions which consecrate or desecrate a home.—Chapin.

Home is the resort
Of love, of joy, of peace and plenty, where,
Supporting and supported, polish'd friends
And dear relations mingle into bliss.
                    —Thomson.

This fond attachment to the well-known place
Whence first we started into life's long race,
Maintains its hold with such unfailing sway,
We feel it e'en in age, and at our latest day.   —Cowper.

'Tis sweet to hear the watch-dog's honest bark
Bay deep-mouthed welcome as we draw near ho˅ne;
'Tis sweet to know there is an eye will mark
Our coming, and look brighter when we come.   —Byron.

Stint yourself, as you think good, in other things; but don't scruple freedom in brightening home. Gay furniture and a brilliant garden are a sight day by day, and make life blither.—Charles Buxton.

A house is never perfectly furnished for enjoyment unless there is a child in it rising three years old, and a kitten rising six weeks.—Southey.

We may build more splendid habitations, fill our rooms with paintings and with sculptures; but we cannot buy with gold the old associations.—Longfellow.

How dear to this heart are the scenes of my childhood,
When fond recollection presents them to view:—
The orchard, the meadow, the deep-tangled wildwood,
And every lov'd spot which my infancy knew.   —Woodworth.

By the fireside still the light is shining,
The children's arms round the parents twining.
From love so sweet, O who would roam?
Be it ever so homely, home is home.
                    —D. M. Mulock.

Peace and rest at length have come,
    All the day's long toil is past;
And each heart is whispering, "Home,
    Home at last!"   —Hood.

Our natural and happiest life is when we lose ourselves in the exquisite absorption of home, the delicious retirement of dependent love.—Miss Mulock.

To make a happy fireside clime
        To weans and wife,
That's the true pathos and sublime
        Of human life.   —Burns.

The little smiling cottage! where at eve
He meets his rosy children at the door,
Prattling their welcomes, and his honest wife,
With good brown cake and bacon slice, intent
To cheer his hunger after labor hard.
                    —Dyer.

There's a strange something, which without a brain
Fools feel, and which e'en wise men can't explain,
Planted in man, to bind him to that earth,
In dearest ties, from whence he drew his birth.   —Churchill.

Breathes there the man with soul so dead,
Who never to himself hath said,
This is my own, my native land!
Whose heart hath ne'er within him burn'd,
As home his foosteps he hath turn'd,
From wandering on a foreign strand!
                    —Scott.

It is a woman, and only a woman, —a woman all by herself, if she likes, and without any man to help her,—who can turn a house into a home.—Frances Power Cobbe.

Keep the home near heaven. Let it face toward the Father's house. Not only let the day begin and end with God, with mercies acknowledged and forgiveness sought, but let it be seen and felt that God is your chiefest joy, His will in all you do the absolute and sufficient reason.—James Hamilton.

I have always felt that the best security for civilization is the dwelling, and that upon properly appointed and becoming dwellings depends more than anything else the improvement of mankind. Such dwellings are the nursery of all domestic virtues, and without a becoming home the exercise of those virtues is impossible.—Beaconsfield.

I never heard my father's or mother's voice once raised in any question with each other; nor saw any angry or even slightly hurt or offended glance in the eyes of either. I never heard a servant scolded, nor even suddenly, passionately, or in any severe manner, blamed; and I never saw a moment's trouble or disorder in any household matter.—John Ruskin.

A house is no home unless it contains food and fire for the mind as well as for the body. For human beings are not so constituted that they can live without expansion. If they do not get it in one way, they must in another, or perish.—Margaret Fuller Ossoli.

The home came from heaven. Modeled on the Father's house and the many mansions, and meant the one to be a training place for the other, the home is one of the gifts of the Lord Jesus—a special creation of Christianity.—James Hamilton.

In the homes of America are born the children of America; and from them go out into American life, American men and women. They go out with the stamp of these homes upon them; and only as these homes are what they should be, will they be what they should be.—J. G. Holland.

It is to Jesus Christ we owe the truth, the tenderness, the purity, the warm affection, the holy aspiration, which go together in that endearing word—home; for it is He who has made obedience so beautiful, and affection so holy; it is He who has brought the Father's home so near, and has taught us that love is of God.—James Hamilton.

If ever household affections and loves are graceful things, they are graceful in the poor. The ties that bind the wealthy and the proud to home may be forged on earth, but those which link the poor man to his humble hearth are of the true metal and bear the stamp of heaven.—Dickens.

The sweetest type of heaven is home—nay, heaven is the home for whose acquisition we are to strive the most strongly. Home, in one form and another, is the great object of life. It stands at the end of every day's labor, and beckons us to its bosom; and life would be cheerless and meaningless, did we not discern across the river that divides us from the life beyond, glimpses of the pleasant mansions prepared for us.—J. G. Holland.

The whitewash'd wall, the nicely sanded floor,
The varnish'd clock that click'd behind the door;
The chest contriv'd a double debt to pay,
A bed by night, a chest of drawers by day.
                                   —Goldsmith.

The poorest man may in his cottage bid defiance to all the force of the Crown. It may be frail, its roof may shake; the wind may blow through it; the storms may enter,—the rain may enter,—but the King of England cannot enter; all his forces dare not cross the threshold of the ruined tenement!—William Pitt.

Are you not surprised to find how independent of money peace of conscience is, and how much happiness can be condensed in the humblest home? A cottage will not hold the bulky furniture and sumptuous accommodations of a mansion; but if God be there, a cottage will hold as much happiness as might stock a palace.—Dr. James Hamilton.

The domestic relations precede, and in our present existence are worth more than all our other social ties. They give the first throb to the heart, and unseal the deep fountains of its love. Home is the chief school of human virtue. Its responsibilities, joys, sorrows, smiles, tears, hopes, and solicitudes form the chief interest of human life.—Channing.

The Cottage Homes of England!
By thousands on her plains,
They are smiling o'er the silvery brooks,
And round the hamlet-fanes;
Through glowing orchards forth they peep,
Each from its nook of leaves;
And fearless there the lowly sleep,
As the birds beneath their eaves.
—Mrs. Hemans.

At night returning, every labour sped,
He sits him down, the monarch of a shed;
Smiles by his cheerful fire, and round surveys
His children's looks, that brighten at the blaze;
While his lov'd partner, boastful of her hoard,
Displays her cleanly platter on the board.
—Goldsmith.

Cling to thy home! If there the meanest shed
Yield thee a hearth and shelter for thy head,
And some poor plot, with vegetables stored,
Be all that Heaven allots thee for thy board,
Unsavory bread, and herbs that scatter'd grow
Wild on the river-brink or mountain-brow;
Yet e'en this cheerless mansion shall provide
More heart's repose than all the world beside. —Leonidas.

Home and heaven are not so far separated as we sometimes think. Nay, they are not separated at all, for they are both in the same great building. Home is the lower story, and is located down here on the ground floor; heaven is above stairs, in the second and third stories; and, as one after another the family is called to come up higher, that which seemed to be such a strange place begins to wear a familiar aspect; and, when at last not one is left below, the home is transferred to heaven, and heaven is home.—Alexander Dickson.

In all my wanderings round this world of care,
In all my griefs—and God has given my share—
I still had hopes my latest hours to crown,
Amidst these humble bowers to lay me down;
To husband out life's taper at the close,
And keep the flame from wasting, by repose:
I still had hopes, for pride attends us still,
Amidst the swains to show my book-learn'd skill,
Around my fire an evening group to draw,
And tell of all I felt, and all I saw;
And as a hare, whom hounds and horns pursue,
Pants to the place from whence at first she flew,
I still had hopes, my long vexations past,
Here to return—and die at home at last.
—Goldsmith.

The pleasant converse of the fireside, the simple songs of home, the words of encouragement as I bend over my school-tasks, the kiss as I lie down to rest, the patient bearing with the freaks of my restless nature, the gentle counsels mingled with reproofs and approvals, the sympathy that meets and assuages every sorrow, and sweetens every little success—all these return to me amid the responsibilities which press upon me now, and I feel as if I had once lived in heaven, and, straying, had lost my way.—J. G. Holland.

Homeliness

Homeliness has this advantage over its enemy, beauty. It is that it is as difficult for an ugly woman to be calumniated as for a pretty woman not to be.—Stahl.

Homer

Like Shakespeare, for all time.—Emerson.

Homer excels all the inventors of other arts in this: that he has swallowed up the honor of those who suc-ceeded him.—Pope.

Milton is the most sublime, and Homer the most picturesque.—Robert Hall.

I can no more believe old Homer blind,
Than those who say the sun hath never
  shin'd;
The age wherein he liv'd was dark, but he
Could not want sight who taught the world
  to see.   —Denham.

Read Homer once, and you can read no
  more,
For all books else appear so mean, so poor;
Verse may seem prose; but still persist to
  read,
And Homer will be all the books you need.
          —Duke of Buckinghamshire.

Honesty

Honesty is the best policy.—Cervantes.

An honest man's the noblest work of God.—Pope.

No legacy is so rich as honesty.—Shakespeare.

Honest minds are pleased with honest things.—Beaumont and Fletcher.

An honest heart possesses a kingdom.—Seneca.

An honest man is respected by all parties.—Hazlitt.

An honest man's word is as good as his bond.—Cervantes.

Honest men are the gentlemen of nature.—Bulwer-Lytton.

An honest man is always a child.—Martial.

The badge of honesty is simplicity.—Novalis.

Honesty needs no disguise or ornament.—Otway.

Honesty needs no pains to set itself off.—Edward Moore.

Honesty is a warrant of far more safety than fame.—Owen Feltham.

Integrity gains strength by use.—Tillotson.

For honesty coupled to beauty, is to have honey a sauce to sugar.—Shakespeare.

An honest man, sir, is able to speak for himself, when a knave is not.—Shakespeare.

"Honesty is the best policy;" but he who acts on that principle is not an honest man.—Whately.

All other knowledge is hurtful to him who has not honesty and good-nature.—Montaigne.

Friends, if we be honest with ourselves, we shall be honest with each other.—George MacDonald.

What is becoming is honest, and whatever is honest must always be becoming.—Cicero.

I like people to be saints; but I want them to be first and superlatively honest men.—Madame Swetchine.

Honesty is good sense, politeness, amiableness,—all in one.—Richardson.

Rich honesty dwells like a miser, in a poor house, as your pearl in your foul oyster.—Shakespeare.

To be honest as this world goes is to be one man picked out of ten thousand.—Shakespeare.

The more honesty a man has, the less he affects the air of a saint.—Lavater.

Be true, and thou shalt fetter time with everlasting chain.—Schiller.

After all, the most natural beauty in the world is honesty and moral truth; for all beauty is truth.—Shaftesbury.

It is necessary in this life,—at first honesty; then usefulness, which follows nearly always, for they cannot be separated.—Palmieri.

There is no terror in your threats; for I am armed so strong in honesty that they pass by me as the idle wind which I respect not.—Shakespeare.

I hope I shall always possess firmness and virtue enough to maintain, what I consider the most enviable of all titles, the character of an "honest man."—George Washington.

A rich man is an honest man, no thanks to him, for he would be a double knave to cheat mankind when he had no need of it.—Daniel De Foe.

Lands mortgaged may return, and more esteem'd,
But honesty once pawn'd, is ne'er redeem'd.
—Middleton.

Money dishonestly acquired is never worth its cost, while a good conscience never costs as much as it is worth.—J. Petit-Senn.

When men cease to be faithful to their God, he who expects to find them so to each other will be much disappointed.—Bishop Horne.

If he does really think that there is no distinction between virtue and vice, why, sir, when he leaves our houses let us count our spoons.—Dr. Johnson.

He who freely praises what he means to purchase, and he who enumerates the faults of what he means to sell, may set up a partnership with honesty.—Lavater.

Honest and courageous people have very little to say about either their courage or their honesty. The sun has no need to boast of his brightness, nor the moon of her effulgence.—Hosea Ballou.

It would be an unspeakable advantage, both to the public and private, if men would consider that great truth, that no man is wise or safe but he that is honest.—Sir Walter Raleigh.

It should seem that indolence itself would incline a person to be honest, as it requires infinitely greater pains and contrivance to be a knave.—Shenstone.

What's the news?
None, my lord, but that the world's grown honest,
Then is doomsday near.
—Shakespeare.

The first step toward greatness is to be honest, says the proverb; but the proverb fails to state the case strong enough. Honesty is not only "the first step toward greatness,"—it is greatness itself.—Bovee.

A prince can mak a belted knight,
A marquis, duke, and a' that;
But an honest man's aboon his might,
Guid faith, he maunna fa' that.
—Burns.

It is much easier to ruin a man of principle than a man of none, for he may be ruined through his scruples. Knavery is supple and can bend; but honesty is firm and upright, and yields not.—Colton.

Nothing really succeeds which is not based on reality; sham, in a large sense, is never successful. In the life of the individual, as in the more comprehensive life of the State, pretension is nothing and power is everything.—Whipple.

Who is the honest man?
He that doth still and strongly good pursue,
To God, his neighbor, and himself most true:
Whom neither force nor fawning can
Unpin, or wrench from giving all their due.
—Herbert.

Nothing more completely baffles one who is full of trick and duplicity himself than straightforward and simple integrity in another. A knave would rather quarrel with a brother-knave than with a fool, but he would rather avoid a quarrel with one honest man than with both.—Colton.

A right mind and generous affection hath more beauty and charms than all other symmetries in the world besides; and a grain of honesty and native worth is of more value than all the adventitious ornaments, estates, or preferments; for the sake of which some of the better sort so oft turn knaves. —Shaftesbury.

It is with honesty in one particular as with wealth,—those that have the thing care less about the credit of it than those who have it not. No poor man can well afford to be thought so, and the less of honesty a finished rogue possesses the less he can afford to be supposed to want it. —Colton.

Put it out of the power of truth to give you an ill character; and if anybody reports you not to be an honest man, let your practice give him the lie; and to make all sure, you should resolve to live no longer than you can live honestly; for it is better to be nothing than a knave.—Marcus Antoninus.

Honesty is not only the deepest policy, but the highest wisdom; since, however difficult it may be for integrity to get on, it is a thousand times more difficult for knavery to get off; and no error is more fatal than that of those who think that Virtue has no other reward because they have heard that she is her own.—Colton.

The man who is so conscious of the rectitude of his intentions as to be willing to open his bosom to the inspection of the world is in possession of one of the strongest pillars of a decided character. The course of such a man will be firm and steady, because he has nothing to fear from the world, and is sure of the approbation and support of heaven.—Wirt.

The root of honesty is an honest intention, the distinct and deliberate purpose to be true, to handle facts as they are, and not as we wish them to be. Facts lend themselves to manipulation. Many a butcher's hand is worth more than its weight in gold. What we want things to be, we come to see them to be; and the tailor pulls the coat and the truth into a perfect fit from his point of view.—Maltbie Babcock.

There is no man but for his own interest hath an obligation to be honest. There may be sometimes temptations to be otherwise; but, all cards cast up, he shall find it the greatest ease, the highest profit, the best pleasure, the most safety, and the noblest fame, to hold the horns of this altar, which, in all assays, can in himself protect him.—Feltham.

An entirely honest man, in the severe sense of the word, exists no more than an entirely dishonest knave; the best and the worst are only approximations to those qualities. Who are those that never contradict themselves? yet honesty never contradicts itself. Who are they that always contradict themselves? yet knavery is mere self-contradiction. Thus the knowledge of man determines not the things themselves, but their proportions, the quantum of congruities and incongruities.—Lavater.

Let honesty be as the breath of thy soul, and never forget to have a penny, when all thy expenses are enumerated and paid: then shalt thou reach the point of happiness and independence shall be thy shield and buckler, thy helmet and crown; then shall thy soul walk upright nor stoop to the silken wretch because he hath riches, nor pocket an abuse because the hand which offers it wears a ring set with diamonds.—Franklin.

Honor

Honor is the moral conscience of the great.—Sir W. Davenant.

Honor lies in honest toil.—Grover Cleveland.

Honor's a lease for life to come.— Samuel Butler.

That chastity of honor which felt a stain like a wound.—Burke.

Probity is true honor.—From the Latin.

Honor, thou strong idol of man's mind.—Sir P. Sidney.

Let us do what honor demands.—Racine.

If I lose mine honor, I lose myself. —Shakespeare.

One honor won is a surety for more. —La Rochefoucauld.

The due of honor in no point omit. —Shakespeare.

What is honorable is also safest.—Livy.

Posts of honor are evermore posts of danger and of care.—J. G. Holland.

Act well your part; there all the honor lies.—Pope.

The strongest passion which I have is honor.—Bailey.

To those whose god is honor, disgrace alone is sin.—J. C. and A. W. Hare.

Purity is the feminine, truth the masculine, of honor.—J. C. and A. W. Hare.

When honor comes to you be ready to
    take it;
But reach not to seize it before it is near.
    —John Boyle O'Reilly.

The noblest spur unto the sons of fame,
Is thirst of honour.   —John Hall.

Honor travels in a strait so narrow,
Where one but goes abreast: keep then
    the path.   —Shakespeare.

If honor calls, where'er she points the way
The sons of honor follow, and obey.
    —Churchill.

We'll shine in more substantial honours,
And to be noble, we'll be good.
    —Thos. Percy.

All is lost save honor.—Francis I.

As the sun breaks through the darkest clouds, so honor peereth in the meanest habit.—Shakespeare.

But if it be a sin to covet honour,
I am the most offending soul alive.
    —Shakespeare.

True, conscious honor is to feel no sin:
He's arm'd .without that's innocent within.
    —Pope.

Better to die ten thousand thousand
    deaths,
Than wound my honor.   —Addison.

Honor is an old-world thing; but it smells sweet to those in whose hand it is strong.—Ouida.

Honors achieved far exceed those that are created.—Solon.

What stronger breastplate than a heart untainted?—Shakespeare.

Hope is a delusion; no hand can grasp a wave or a shadow.—Victor Hugo.

Woman's honor, as nice as ermine, will not bear a soil.—Dryden.

I would not love thee, dear, so much,
Loved I not honour more.   —Lovelace.

Let honor be to us as strong an obligation, as necessity is to others.—Pliny.

Our own heart, and not other men's opinions, forms our true honor.—Coleridge.

When a virtuous man is raised, it brings gladness to his friends, grief to his enemies, and glory to his posterity.—Ben Jonson.

Honor is unstable, and seldom the same; for she feeds upon opinion, and is as fickle as her food.—Colton.

That nation is worthless which does not joyfully stake everything on her honor.—Schiller.

The journey of high honor lies not in smooth ways.—Sir P. Sidney.

When about to commit a base deed, respect thyself, though there is no witness.—Ausonius.

There is no praise in being upright, where no one can, or tries to corrupt you.—Cicero.

The giving riches and honors to a wicked man is like giving strong wine to him that hath a fever.—Plutarch.

Honor is like an island, rugged and without a landing-place; we can nevermore re-enter when we are once outside of it.—Boileau.

Honor is the most capricious in her rewards. She feeds us with air, and often pulls down our house, to build our monument.—Colton.

Discretion and hardy valor are the twins of honor, and, nursed together, make a conqueror; divided, but a talker.—Beaumont and Fletcher.

Honor and fortune exist for him who always recognizes the neighborhood of the great, always feels himself in the presence of high causes.—Emerson.

Unblemished honor is the flower of virtue! the vivifying soul! and he who slights it will leave the other dull and lifeless dross.—Thomson.

Honour is purchas'd by the deeds we do;
* * * honour is not won,
Until some honourable deed be done.
—Marlowe.

The purest treasure mortal times afford
Is—spotless reputation; that away,
Men are but gilded loam, or painted clay.
—Shakespeare.

Honor is like the eye, which cannot suffer the least injury without damage; it is a precious stone, the price of which is lessened by the least flaw.—Bossuet.

Honor is but the reflection of a man's own actions shining bright in the face of all about him, and from thence rebounding upon himself.—South.

Honour, thou blood-stained god! at whose red altar
Sit war and homicide; oh, to what madness
Will insult drive thy votaries.
—Geo. Coleman, Jr.

Honour is like that glassy bubble,
That finds philosophers such trouble,
Whose least part crack'd, the whole does fly
And wits are crack'd to find out why.
—Butler.

To contemn all the wealth and power in the world, where they stand in competition with a man's honor, is rather good sense than greatness of mind.—Steele.

High honor is not only gotten and born by pain and danger, but must be nursed by the like, else it vanisheth as soon as it appears to the world.—Sir P. Sidney.

The Athenians erected a large statue of Æsop, and placed him, though a slave, on a lasting pedestal, to show that the way to honor lies open indifferently to all.—Phædrus.

Honor is unstable, and seldom the same; for she feeds upon opinion, and is as fickle as her food. She builds a lofty structure on the sandy foundation of the esteem of those who are of all beings the most subject to change.—Colton.

What can be more honorable than to have courage enough to execute the commands of reason and conscience,—to maintain the dignity of our nature, and the station assigned us?—Jeremy Collier.

Keep unscathed the good name; keep out of peril the honor without which even your battered old soldier who is hobbling into his grave on half-pay and a wooden leg would not change with Achilles.—Bulwer-Lytton.

The law of honor is a system of rules constructed by people of fashion, and calculated to facilitate their intercourse with one another.—Paley.

The sense of honor is of so fine and delicate a nature, that it is only to be met with in minds which are naturally noble, or in such as have been cultivated by good examples, or a refined education.—Addison.

Set honor in one eye, and death i' the other,
And I will look on both indifferently:
For, let the gods so speed me as I love
The name of honor more than I fear death.   —Shakespeare.

Man is his own star, and the soul that can
Render an honest and a perfect man,
Commands all light, all influence, all fate;
Nothing to him falls early, or too late.
Our acts our angels are, or good or ill,—
Our fatal shadows that walk by us still!
                                —Fletcher.

A life of honor and of worth
Has no eternity on earth,—
    'Tis but a name—
And yet its glory far exceeds
That base and sensual life which leads
    To want and shame.
                    —Longfellow.

                        Honour is
Virtue's allowed ascent: honour that clasps
All perfect justice in her arms; that craves
No more respect than that she gives; that does
Nothing but what she'll suffer.
                        —Massinger.

To be ambitious of true honor, of the true glory and perfection of our natures, is the very principle and incentive of virtue; but to be ambitious of titles, of place, of ceremonial respects and civil pageantry, is as vain and little as the things are which we court.—Sherlock.

Honour's a sacred tie, the law of kings,
The noble mind's distinguishing perfection
That aids and strengthens virtue where it meets her,
And imitates her actions where she is not:
It is not to be sported with.
                        —Addison.

Honor is not a virtue in itself, it is the mail behind which the virtues fight more securely. A man without honor is as maimed in his equipment as an accoutred knight without helmet. Honor is not simply truthfulness; it is truthfulness sparkling with the fire of a suspective personality. It is something more than an ornament even to the loftiest.—George H. Calvert.

No man of honor, as the word is usually understood, did ever pretend that his honor obliged him to be chaste or temperate, to pay his creditors, to be useful to his country, to do good to mankind, to endeavor to be wise or learned, to regard his word, his promise, or his oath.—Swift.

Your honors here may serve you for a time, as it were for an hour, but they will be of no use to you beyond this world. Nobody will have heard a word of your honors in the other life. Your glory, your shame, your ambitions, and all the treasures for which you push hard and sacrifice much will be like wreaths of smoke. For these things, which you mostly seek, and for which you spend your life, only tarry with you while you are on this side of the flood.—Beecher.

Well, 'tis no matter; honor pricks me on. Yea, but how if honor prick me off, when I come on? how then? Can honor set to a leg? no: or an arm? no: or take away the grief of a wound? no: Honor hath no skill in surgery, then? no. What is honor? a word. What is in that word honor? What is that honor? air. A trim reckoning! Who hath it? he that died o' Wednesday. Doth he feel it? no. Doth he hear it? no. 'Tis insensible, then. Yea, to the dead. But will it not live with the living? no. Why? detraction will not suffer it. Therefore, I'll none of it. Honor is a mere scutcheon; and so ends my catechism.—Shakespeare.

Hope

Hope springs eternal in the human breast.—Pope.

Hope is the mother of faith.—Landor.

Thou sick man's health!—Cowley.

Hope deferred maketh the heart sick.
—Bible.

Hope is the ruddy morning of joy.
—Richter.

Hope is brightest when it dawns from fears.—Sir Walter Scott.

That star on life's tremulous ocean.
—Moore.

Hope is a light diet, but very stimulating.—Balzac.

Hope springs exulting on triumphant wing.—Burns.

The sickening pang of hope deferred.
—Scott.

Delusive hope still points to distant good.—Euripides.

Hope is a working-man's dream.—Pliny.

Hope is the poor man's bread.—Thales.

Hope is such a bait, it covers any hook.—Ben Jonson.

Who against hope believed in hope.
—Bible.

He that lives upon hopes will die fasting.—Benjamin Franklin.

Hope is a lover's staff.—Shakespeare.

The mighty hopes that make us men.
—Longfellow.

Where no hope is left, is left no fear.
—Milton.

Hope against hope, and ask till ye receive.—Jas. Montgomery.

Folly ends where genuine hope begins.—Cowper.

Hope, deceitful as she is, serves at least to conduct us through life by an agreeable path.—Rochefoucauld.

Hope! thou nurse of young desire.
—Bickerstaff.

The most wretched have yet hope.—Tupper.

Hope is the most treacherous of all human fancies.—James Fenimore Cooper.

When our hopes break, let our patience hold.—Thomas Fuller.

Where there is no hope there can be no endeavor.—Johnson.

Sire of repentance, child of fond desire!—Cowley.

Hope is love's happiness, but not its life.—Miss L. E. Landon.

He that loses hope may part with anything.—Congreve.

Hope, alas! is our waking dream.—Madame de Girardin.

The greatest architect and the one most needed is hope.—Henry Ward Beecher.

It is to hope, though hope were lost.
—Mrs. Barbauld.

Auspicious Hope! in thy sweet garden grow
Wreaths for each toil, a charm for every woe.   —Campbell.

Be still, sad heart! and cease repining;
Behind the cloud is the sun still shining.
      —H. W. Longfellow.

Things at the worst will cease, or else climb upward
To what they were before.
      —Shakespeare.

While there is life, there's hope, (he cried,)
Then why such haste?—so groan'd and died.   —Gay.

Hope and fear alternate chase
Our course through life's uncertain race.
      —Scott.

Hope ever urges on, and tells us tomorrow will be better.—Tibullus.

Hope is a willing slave; despair is free.—Dawes.

For hope is but the dream of those that wake!—Prior.

The miserable have no other medicine, But only hope.   —Shakespeare.

What can we not endure, When pains are lessen'd by the hope of cure?   —Nabb.

Hope itself is a pain, while it is overmatched by fear.—Sir P. Sidney.

His worth shines forth the brightest who in hope always confides; the abject soul despairs.—Euripides.

Hope! fortune's cheating lottery; when for one prize an hundred blanks there be!—Cowley.

The shadow of human life is traced upon a golden ground of immortal hope.—Hillard.

If thy hope be any thing worth, it will purify thee from thy sins.—Joseph Alleine.

A religious hope does not only bear up the mind under her sufferings but makes her rejoice in them.—Addison.

Hope will make thee young; for Hope and Youth are children of one mother.—Shelley.

The night is past,—joy cometh with the morrow.—Bulwer-Lytton.

Hope is a leaf-joy which may be beaten out to a great extension, like gold.—Bacon.

Hope is an amusement rather than a good, and adapted to none but very tranquil minds.—Dr. Johnson.

Whatever enlarges hope, will also exalt courage.—Johnson.

The hope of all earnest souls must be realized.—Whittier.

No hope so bright but is the beginning of its own fulfilment.—Emerson.

Hope awakens courage. He who can implant courage in the human soul is the best physician.—Von Knebel.

Hope is the pillar that holds up the world. Hope is the dream of a waking man.
            —Pliny.

With a mind not diseased, a holy life is a life of hope; and at the end of it, death is a great act of hope.—Wm. Mountford.

Hope says to us constantly, "Go on, go on," and leads us thus to the grave.—Mme. de Maintenon.

Things which you don't hope happen more frequently than things which you do hope.—Plautus.

A woman's hopes are woven of sunbeams; a shadow annihilates them.—George Eliot.

Take hope from the heart of man, and you make him a beast of prey.—Ouida.

Hope is like the sun, which, as we journey towards it, casts the shadow of our burden behind us.—Samuel Smiles.

A propensity to hope and joy is real riches; one to fear and sorrow, real poverty.—Hume.

However deceitful hope may be, yet she carries us on pleasantly to the end of life.—La Rochefoucauld.

A wise Providence consoles our present afflictions by joys borrowed from the future.—Hosea Ballou.

God puts the excess of hope in one man, in order that it may be a medicine to the man who is despondent.—Henry Ward Beecher.

Hope travels through, nor quits us when we die.—Pope.

The setting of a great hope is like the setting of the sun. The brightness of our life is gone.—Longfellow.

Hope is the best possession. None are completely wretched but those who are without hope; and few are reduced so low as that.—Hazlitt.

Through the sunset of hope,
Like the shapes of a dream,
What paradise islands of glory gleam!
—Shelley.

Hope is like the wing of an angel, soaring up to heaven, and bearing our prayers to the throne of God.—Jeremy Taylor.

Hope is the only good which is common to all men; those who have nothing more possess hope still.—Thales.

Hope animates the wise, and lures the presumptuous and indolent who repose inconsiderately on her promises.—Vauvenargues.

Dear hope! earth's dowry and heav'n's debt,
The entity of things that are not yet
Subtlest, but surest thing. —Crashaw.

Hope proves man deathless. It is the struggle of the soul, breaking loose from what is perishable, and attesting her eternity.—Henry Melvill.

Hope is the virgin of the ideal world, who opens heaven to us in the midst of every tempest.—Arsène Houssaye.

Man is, properly speaking, based upon hope, he has no other possession but hope; this world of his is emphatically the place of hope.—Carlyle.

It is when our budding hopes are nipped beyond recovery by some rough wind, that we are the most disposed to picture to ourselves what flowers it might have borne, if they had flourished.—Dickens.

There are hopes, the bloom of whose beauty would be spoiled by the trammels of description; too lovely, too delicate. too sacred for words, they should only be known through the sympathy of hearts.—Dickens.

Hope is the last lingering light of the human heart. It shines when every other is put out. Extinguish it, and the gloom of affliction becomes the very blackness of darkness—cheerless and impenetrable.—Aughey.

O Hope, sweet flatterer! thy delusive touch
Sheds on afflicted minds the balm of comfort,
Relieves the load of poverty, sustains
The captive, bending with the weight of bonds,
And smooths the pillow of disease and pain. —Glover.

Hope is the best part of our riches. What sufficeth it that we have the wealth of the Indies in our pockets, if we have not the hope of heaven in our souls?—Bovee.

Hope is a pleasant acquaintance, but an unsafe friend. Hope is not the man for your banker, though he may do for a traveling companion.—Haliburton.

"Hast thou hope?" they asked of John Knox, when he lay a-dying. He spoke nothing, but raised his finger and pointed upward, and so died.—Carlyle.

A loving heart encloses within itself an unfading and eternal Eden. Hope is like a bad clock, forever striking the hour of happiness, whether it has come or not.—Richter.

Hope is that pleasure of the mind which every one finds in himself upon the thought of a probable future enjoyment of a thing which is apt to delight him.—Locke.

True hope is swift, and flies with swallow's wings:
Kings it makes gods, and meaner creatures kings. —Shakespeare.

Behind the cloud the starlight lurks,
Through showers the sunbeams fall;
For God, who loveth all His works,
Has left His Hope with all.
—Whittier.

It is necessary to hope, though hope should be always deluded; for hope itself is happiness, and its frustrations, however frequent, are yet less dreadful than its extinction.—Dr. Johnson.

Hope, like the gleaming taper's light,
    Adorns and cheers our way;
And still, as darker grows the night,
    Emits a brighter ray.   —Goldsmith.

Know then, whatever cheerful and serene
Supports the mind, supports the body too:
Hence, the most vital movement mortals
    feel
Is hope, the balm and lifeblood of the soul.
    John Armstrong.

Hope is the mainspring of human action; faith seals our lease of immortality; and charity and love give the passport to the soul's true and lasting happiness.—Street.

A hope unaccompanied with a godly life had better be given up, and the sooner the better; for, if retained, it will prove as a spider's web when God shall take away the soul.—Aughey.

Hope rules a land forever green,
All powers that serve the bright-eyed queen
And confident and gay;
Clouds at her bidding disappear,
Points she to aught?—the bliss draws near
And fancy smooths the way.
    —Wordsworth.

Cease, every joy, to glimmer in my mind,
But leave,—oh! leave the light of Hope
    behind!
What though my winged hours of bliss
    have been,
Like angel-visits, few and far between.
    —Campbell.

Human life has not a surer friend, nor oftentimes a greater enemy, than hope. It is the miserable man's god, which in the hardest gripe of calamity never fails to yield to him beams of comfort. It is the presumptuous man's devil, which leads him a while in a smooth way, and then suddenly breaks his neck.—Owen Feltham.

This comforts me, that the most weather-beaten vessel cannot properly be seized on for a wreck which hath any quick cattle remaining therein. My spirits are not as yet forfeited to despair, having one lively spark of hope in my heart because God is even where He was before.—Fuller.

All which happens in the whole world happens through hope. No husbandman would sow a grain of corn if he did not hope it would spring up and bring forth the ear. How much more are we helped on by hope in the way to eternal life!—Luther.

Hope is a vigorous principle; it is furnished with light and heat to advise and execute; it sets the head and heart to work, and animates a man to do his utmost. And thus, by perpetually pushing and assurance, it puts a difficulty out of countenance, and makes a seeming impossibility give way.—Jeremy Collier.

Hope is our life when first our life grows
    clear,
Hope and delight, scarce crossed by lines
    of fear:
Yet the day comes when fain we would
    not hope—
But forasmuch as we with life must cope,
Struggling with this and that—and who
    knows why?
Hope will not give us up to certainty,
But still must bide with us.
    —Wm. Morris.

The riches of heaven, the honor which cometh from God only, and the pleasures at His right hand, the absence of all evil, the presence and enjoyment of all good, and this good enduring to eternity, never more to be taken from us, never more to be in any, the least degree, diminished, but forever increasing, these are the wreaths which form the contexture of that crown held forth to our hopes.—Bishop Horne.

Never give up! it is wiser and better
Always to hope, than once to despair;
Fling off the load of Doubt's cankering
    fetter,
And break the dark spell of tyrannical
    Care:
Never give up or the burden may sink
    you,—
Providence kindly has mingled the cup;
And in all trials and troubles, bethink you
The watchword of life must be,—never
    give up.   —Tupper.

True hope is based on the energy of character. A strong mind always hopes, and has always cause to hope, because it knows the mutability of human affairs, and how slight a circumstance may change the whole course of events. Such a spirit, too, rests upon itself; it is not confined to partial views or to one particular object. And if at last all should be lost, it has saved itself.—Von Knebel.

Hope is to a man as a bladder to a learning swimmer—it keeps him from sinking in the bosom of the waves, and by that help he may attain the exercise; but yet it many times makes him venture beyond his height, and then if that breaks, or a storm rises, he drowns without recovery. How many would die, did not hope sustain them! How many have died by hoping too much! This wonder we find in Hope, that she is both a flatterer and a true friend.—Feltham.

Used with due abstinence, hope acts as a healthful tonic; intemperately indulged, as an enervating opiate. The visions of future triumph, which at first animate exertion, if dwelt upon too intently, will usurp the place of the stern reality; and noble objects will be contemplated, not for their own inherent worth, but on account of the day-dreams they engender. Thus hope, aided by imagination, makes one man a hero, another a somnambulist, and a - third a lunatic; while it renders them all enthusiasts.—Sir J. Stephen.

Failure will hurt but not hinder us. Disillusion will pain but not dishearten us. Sorrows will shake us but not break us. Hope will set the music ringing and quicken our lagging pace. We need hope for living far more than for dying. Dying is easy work compared with living. Dying is a moment's transition; living, a transaction of years. It is the length of the rope that puts the sag in it. Hope tightens the cords and tunes up the heart-strings. Work well, then; suffer patiently, rejoicing in hope. God knows all, and yet is the God of Hope. And when we have hoped to the end here, He will give us something to look forward to, for all eternity. For "hope abideth."—Maltbie Babcock.

Horse — Horsemanship

A horse! a horse! my kingdom for a horse!—Shakespeare.

And witch the world with noble horsemanship.—Shakespeare.

A good rider on a good horse is as much above himself and others as the world can make him.—Lord Herbert.

I will not change my horse with any that treads but on four pasterns. When I bestride him I soar, I am a hawk; he trots the air; the earth sings when he touches it.—Shakespeare.

My beautiful! my beautiful!
  That standest meekly by
With thy proudly arch'd and glossy neck,
  And dark and fiery eye;—
The stranger hath thy bridle-rein—
  Thy master hath his gold—
Fleet-limb'd and beautiful, farewell!
Thou 'rt sold, my steed—thou 'rt sold!
                —Mrs. Norton.

Oh! not all the pleasure that poets may
    praise,—
Not the wildering waltz in the ball-room's
    blaze,
Nor the chivalrous joust, nor the daring
    race,
Nor the swift regatta, nor merry chase,
Nor the sail high heaving waters o'er,
Nor the rural dance on the moonlight
    shore,—
Can the wild and fearless joy exceed
Of a fearless leap on a fiery steed.
                —Sara J. Clarke.

Gamaun is a dainty steed,
Strong, black, and of a noble breed,
Full of fire, and full of bone,
With all his line of fathers known;
Fine his nose, his nostrils thin,
But blown abroad by the pride within;
His mane is like a river flowing,
And his eyes like embers glowing
In the darkness of the night,
And his pace as swift as light.
                —Barry Cornwall.

Hospitality

Provision is the foundation of hospitality, and thrift the fuel of magnificence.—Sir P. Sidney.

It is not the quantity of the meat, but the cheerfulness of the guests, which makes the feast.—Clarendon.

Hospitality sitting with gladness.—Longfellow.

Hospitality sometimes degenerates into profuseness, and ends in madness and folly.—Atterbury.

Be not forgetful to entertain strangers; for thereby some have entertained angels unawares.—Bible.

There is an emanation from the heart in genuine hospitality which cannot be described, but is immediately felt and puts the stranger at once at his ease.—Washington Irving.

Like many other virtues, hospitality is practiced in its perfection by the poor. If the rich did their share, how would the woes of this world be lightened!—Mrs. Kirkland.

Let not the emphasis of hospitality lie in bed and board; but let truth and love and honor and courtesy flow in all thy deeds.—Emerson.

It is an excellent circumstance that hospitality grows best where it is most needed. In the thick of men it dwindles and disappears, like fruit in the thick of a wood; but where men are planted sparely it blossoms and matures, like apples on a standard or an espalier. It flourishes where the inn and lodging-house cannot exist.—Hugh Miller.

Blest be that spot, where cheerful guests retire
To pause from toil, and trim their evening fire;
Blest that abode, where want and pain repair,
And every stranger finds a ready chair:
Blest be those feasts with simple plenty crown'd,
Where all the ruddy family around
Laugh at the jest or pranks, that never fail,
Or sigh with pity at some mournful tale,
Or press the bashful stranger to his food,
And learn the luxury of doing good.
　　　　　　　—Goldsmith.

Hours

Hours are golden links — God's tokens reaching heaven.—Dickens.

Catch, then, oh! catch the transient hour,
Improve each moment as it flies;
Life's a short summer—man a flower,
He dies—alas! how soon he dies!
　　　　　　　—Dr. Johnson.

House

Houses are like the human beings that inhabit them.—Victor Hugo.

Old houses mended,
Cost little less than new before they're ended.　　—Colley Cibber.

The house of every one is to him as his castle and fortress, as well for his defence against injury and violence as for his repose.—Sir Edward Coke.

My precept to all who build is, that the owner should be an ornament to the house, and not the house to the owner.—Cicero.

A house is never perfectly furnished for enjoyment unless there is a child in it rising three years old, and a kitten rising six weeks.—Southey.

Housekeeping

Nothing lovelier can be found
In woman, than to study household good,
And good works in her husband to promote.　　—Milton.

Human Nature

A rational nature admits of nothing but what is serviceable to the rest of mankind.—Antoninus.

In so complex a thing as human nature, we must consider it is hard to find rules without exception.—George Eliot.

It is the talent of human nature to run from one extreme to another.—Swift.

The scrutiny of human nature on a small scale is one of the most dangerous of employments; the study of it on a large scale is one of the safest and truest.—Isaac Taylor.

If we did not take great pains, and were not at great expense to corrupt our nature, our nature would never corrupt us.—Lord Clarendon.

As there is much beast and some devil in man, so is there some angel and some God in him. The beast and the devil may be conquered, but in this life never wholly destroyed.—Coleridge.

———

Console yourself, dear man and brother; whatever you may be sure of, be sure at least of this, that you are dreadfully like other people. Human nature has a much greater genius for sameness than for originality.—Lowell.

———

Human nature is so weak that the honest men who have no religion make me fret with their perilous virtue, as rope-dancers with their dangerous equilibrium.—De Lévis.

———

A man's nature is best perceived in privateness, for there is no affectation; in passion, for that putteth a man out of his precepts; and in a new case or experiment, for there custom leaveth him.—Bacon.

———

There do remain dispersed in the soil of human nature divers seeds of goodness, of benignity, of ingenuity, which being cherished, excited, and quickened by good culture, do by common experience thrust out flowers very lovely, and yield fruits very pleasant of virtue and goodness.—Mrs. L. M. Child.

———

The fact of our deriving constant pleasure from whatever is a type or semblance of divine attributes, and from nothing but that which is so, is the most glorious of all that can be demonstrated of human nature; it not only sets a great gulf of specific separation between us and the lower animals, but it seems a promise of a communion ultimately deep, close, and conscious, with the Being whose darkened manifestations we here feebly and unthinkingly delight in.—Ruskin.

———

No doubt hard work is a great police agent. If everybody were worked from morning till night, and then carefully locked up, the register of crime might be greatly diminished. But what would become of human nature? Where would be the room for growth in such a system of things? It is

through sorrow and mirth, plenty and need, a variety of passions, circumstances, and temptations, even through sin and misery, that men's natures are developed.—Arthur Helps.

Humanity

Humanity is the Son of God.—Theodore Parker.

———

Humanity is the equity of the heart.—Confucius.

———

The still, sad music of humanity.—Wordsworth.

———

Christianity is the highest perfection of humanity.—Johnson.

———

Humanity always becomes a conqueror.—Sheridan.

———

Every human heart is human.—Longfellow.

———

Poor humanity!—so dependent, so insignificant, and yet so great.—Mme. Swetchine.

———

So much to pardon, so much to pity, so much to admire!—Longfellow.

———

I am a man; I count nothing human foreign to me.—Terence.

———

Our humanity were a poor thing but for the divinity that stirs within us.—Bacon.

———

One sole God; one sole ruler. His law; one sole interpreter of that law—humanity.—Mazzini.

———

The gods are immortal men, and men are mortal gods.—Heraclitus.

———

True men and women are all physicians to make us well.—C. A. Bartol.

———

What a vile and abject thing is man if he do not raise himself above humanity.—Seneca.

———

There is nothing on earth divine beside humanity.—Melanchthon.

———

I am not an Athenian, nor a Greek, but a citizen of the world.—Socrates.

When I touch a human hand, I touch heaven.—Malebranche.

The age of chivalry has gone; the age of humanity has come.—Charles Sumner.

Human life is God's outer church. Its needs and urgencies are priests and pastors.—Henry Ward Beecher.

The ingratitude of the world can never deprive us of the conscious happiness of having acted with humanity ourselves.—Goldsmith.

Love, hope, fear, faith—these make humanity;
These are its sign and note and character.
—Robert Browning.

I love my country better than my family; but I love human nature better than my country.—Fénelon.

Woman, above all other educators, educates humanly. Man is the brain, but woman is the heart, of humanity.—Samuel Smiles.

I never knew a young man remarkable for heroic bravery whose very aspect was not lighted up by gentleness and humanity.—Lord Erskine.

Humanity is about the same the world over; and while the earth has its uniformity, with slight differences in mountain and plain, so its products are very nearly alike.—Donn Piatt.

Humanity has won its suit (in America), so that liberty will nevermore be without an asylum.—Lafayette.

Man is the will, and woman the sentiment. In this ship of humanity, Will is the rudder, and Sentiment the sail; when woman affects to steer, the rudder is only a masked sail.—Emerson.

There is a book into which some of us are happily led to look, and to look again, and never tire of looking. It is the Book of Man. You may open that book whenever and wherever you find another human voice to answer yours, and another human hand to take in your own.—Walter Besant.

No piled-up wealth, no social station, no throne, reaches as high as that spiritual plane upon which every human being stands by virtue of his humanity.—Chapin.

Humanity is the peculiar characteristic of great minds; little vicious minds abound with anger and revenge, and are incapable of feeling the exact pleasure of forgiving their enemies.—Chesterfield.

I own that there is a haughtiness and fierceness in human nature which will cause innumerable broils, place men in what situation you please.—Burke.

What proposition is there respecting human nature which is absolutely and universally true? We know of only one,—and that is not only true, but identical,—that men always act from self-interest.—Macaulay.

Humanity is much more shown in our conduct towards animals, where we are irresponsible except to heaven, than towards our fellow-creatures, where we are restrained by the laws, by public opinion, and fear of retaliation.—Chatfield.

There is but one temple in the world, and that is the body of man. Nothing is holier than this high form. Bending before men is a reverence done to this revelation in the flesh. We touch heaven when we lay our hand on a human body.—Novalis.

True humanity consists not in a squeamish ear; it consists not in starting or shrinking at tales of misery, but in a disposition of heart to relieve it. True humanity appertains rather to the mind than to the nerves, and prompts men to use real and active endeavors to execute the actions which it suggests.—Charles James Fox.

The great duty of God's children is to love one another. This duty on earth takes the name and form of the law of humanity. We are to recognize all men as brethren, no matter where born, or under what sky, or institution or religion they may live. Every man belongs to the race, and owes a duty to mankind. Every nation belongs to the family of nations, and is to desire the good of all. Nations are to love one another. * * * Men cannot vote this out of the universal acclamation. * * * Men cannot, by combining themselves into narrower or larger societies, sever the sacred, blessed bond which joins them to their kind. * * * The law of humanity must reign over the assertion of all human rights.—William Ellery Channing

Humility

Blessed are the meek, for they shall inherit the earth.—Bible.

I believe the first test of a truly great man is his humility.—John Ruskin.

In humility imitate Jesus and Socrates.—Franklin.

The most essential point is lowliness.—Fénelon.

Humbleness is always grace, always dignity.—Lowell.

Modest humility is beauty's crown.—Schiller.

Content thyself to live obscurely good.—Addison.

Love's humility is love's true pride.—Bayard Taylor.

My favored temple is an humble heart.—Bailey.

Do not practise excessive humility.—Dr. John Todd.

Humble things become the humble.—Horace.

Highest when it stoops.—Pollok.

True love is the parent of a noble humility.—William Ellery Channing.

The doctrines of grace humble man without degrading him and exalt him without inflating him.—Charles Hodge.

Heaven's gates are not so highly arched as king's palaces; they that enter there must go upon their knees.—Daniel Webster.

Humility is the altar upon which God wishes that we should offer Him His sacrifices.—La Rochefoucauld.

Humility is the first of the virtues—for other people.—Holmes.

By humility and the fear of the Lord are riches, honor, and life.—Bible.

After crosses and losses, men grow humbler and wiser.—Franklin.

Humility is the solid foundation of all the virtues.—Confucius.

There is nothing so clear-sighted and sensible as a noble mind in a low estate.—Jane Porter.

The street is full of humiliations to the proud.—Emerson.

We cannot think too highly of our nature, nor too humbly of ourselves.—Colton.

Humility, like darkness, reveals the heavenly lights.—Thoreau.

Humility—that low, sweet root from which all heavenly virtues shoot.—Moore.

If man makes himself a worm he must not complain when he is trodden on.—Kant.

The higher a man is in grace, the lower he will be in his own esteem.—Spurgeon.

Humility is eldest-born of Virtue, and claims the birthright at the throne of heaven.—Arthur Murphy.

They that know God will be humble; they that know themselves cannot be proud.—Flavel.

Nothing can be further apart than true humility and servility.—Beecher.

Humanity cannot be degraded by humiliation.—Burke.

'Umble we are, 'umble we have been, 'umble we shall ever be.—Dickens.

The grace that makes every grace amiable is humility.—Richardson.

Humility and resignation are our prime virtues.—Dryden.

It is the cringer to his equal that is chiefly seen bold to his God.—Tupper.

Humility mainly becometh the converse of man with his Maker.—Tupper.

Humility leads to the highest distinction, because it leads to self-improvement.—Sir Benjamin Brodie.

Be very sure that no man will learn anything at all unless he first will learn humility.—Owen Meredith.

Lowliness is the basis of every virtue; and he who goes the lowest builds the safest.—Bailey.

Wellnigh the whole substance of the Christian discipline is humility.—St. Augustine.

I have sounded the very base-string of humility.—Shakespeare.

The fullest and best ears of corn hang lowest toward the ground.—Bishop Reynolds.

The sufficiency of my merit is to know that my merit is not sufficient.—St. Augustine.

Humility is the root, mother, nurse, foundation, and bond of all virtue.—Chrysostom.

It is in vain to gather virtues without humility; for the Spirit of God delighteth to dwell in the hearts of the humble.—Erasmus.

The beloved of the Almighty are the rich who have the humility of the poor, and the poor who have the magnanimity of the rich.—Saadi.

Sense shines with a double lustre when it is set in humility. An able and yet humble man is a jewel worth a kingdom.—William Penn.

May exalting and humanizing thoughts forever accompany me, making me confident without pride, and modest without servility.—Leigh Hunt.

Humility is the Christian's greatest honor; and the higher men climb, the farther they are from heaven.—Burder.

To be humble to our superiors is duty; to our equals, courtesy; to our inferiors, generosity.—Feltham.

True humility—the basis of the Christian system—is the low but deep and firm foundation of all virtues.—Burke.

If thou wouldst find much favor and peace with God and man, be very low in thine own eyes; forgive thyself little, and others much.—Leighton.

The humble soul is like the violet, which grows low, hangs the head downward, and hides itself with its own leaves.—Fredrika Bremer.

Some one called Sir Richard Steele the "vilest of mankind," and he retorted with proud humility, "It would be a glorious world if I were."—Bovee.

"He that humbleth himself shall be exalted." This great law of the kingdom of God is, in the teaching of Christ, inscribed over its entrance-gate.—Thomas Browne.

Shall we speak of the inspiration of a poet or a priest, and not of the heart impelled by love and self-devotion to the lowliest work in the lowliest way of life?—Dickens.

He that places himself neither higher nor lower than he ought to do exercises the truest humility.—Colton.

Whatever obscurities may involve religious tenets, humility and love constitute the essence of true religion; the humble is formed to adore, the loving to associate with eternal love.—Lavater.

———

God's sweet dews and showers of grace slide off the mountains of pride, and fall on the low valleys of humble hearts, and make them pleasant and fertile.—Leighton.

———

The high mountains are barren, but the low valleys are covered over with corn; and accordingly the showers of God's grace fall into lowly hearts and humble souls.—Worthington.

———

Humility is a virtue all preach, none practice, and yet everybody is content to hear. The master thinks it good doctrine for his servant, the laity for the clergy, and the clergy for the laity.—John Selden.

———

Humility is like a tree, whose root when it sets deepest in the earth rises higher, and spreads fairer and stands surer, and lasts longer, and every step of its descent is like a rib of iron.—Jeremy Taylor.

———

The loveliest, sweetest flower that bloomed in paradise, and the first that died, has rarely blossomed since on mortal soil. It is so frail, so delicate, a thing, it is gone if it but look upon itself; and she who ventures to esteem it hers proves by that single thought she has it not.—Mrs. E. Fry.

———

He who sacrifices a whole offering shall be rewarded for a whole offering; he who offers a burnt-offering shall have the reward of a burnt-offering; but he who offers humility to God and man shall be rewarded with a reward as if he had offered all the sacrifices in the world.—The Talmud.

———

If thou desire the love of God and man, be humble; for the proud heart, as it loves none but itself, so it is beloved of none but by itself; the voice of humility is God's music, and the silence of humility is God's rhetoric. Humility enforces where neither virtue nor strength can prevail nor reason.—Quarles.

———

I do not know what I may appear to the world; but to myself I seem to have been only like a boy playing on the sea shore, and diverting myself in now and then finding a smoother pebble or a prettier shell than ordinary, whilst the great ocean of truth lay all undiscovered before me.—Newton.

———

"If you ask what is the first step in the way of truth? I answer humility," saith St. Austin. "If you ask, what is the second? I say humility. If you ask, what is the third? I answer the same—humility." Is it not as the steps of degree in the temple, whereby we descend to the knowledge of ourselves, and ascend to the knowledge of God? Would we attain mercy? humility will help us.—C. Sutton.

———

All the world, all that we are, and all that we have, our bodies and our souls, our actions and our sufferings, our conditions at home, our accidents abroad, our many sins, and our seldom virtues, are as so many arguments to make our souls dwell low in the valley of humility.—Jeremy Taylor.

Humor

Humor is wit and love.—Thackeray.

———

Humor is the pensiveness of wit.—Willmott.

———

The oil and wine of merry meeting.—Washington Irving.

———

Humor is the mistress of tears.—Thackeray.

———

Humor is the harmony of the heart.—Douglas Jerrold.

———

A little nonsense now and then
Is relished by the wisest men.
—Anonymous.

Humor has justly been regarded as the finest perfection of poetic genius.—Carlyle.

———

Whenever you find Humor, you find Pathos close by its side.—Whipple.

The essence of humor is sensibility; warm, tender fellow-feeling with all forms of existence.—Carlyle.

Humor is of a genial quality, and closely allied to pity.—Henry Giles.

Flashes of merriment that were wont to set the table on a roar.—Shakespeare.

Humor, warm and all-embracing as the sunshine, bathes its objects in a genial and abiding light.—E. P. Whipple.

Men of humor are always in some degree men of genius; wits are rarely so, although a man of genius may, amongst other gifts, possess wit, as Shakespeare.—Coleridge.

What an ornament and safeguard is humor! Far better than wit for a poet and writer. It is a genius itself, and so defends from the insanities.—Walter Scott.

Humor is one of the elements of genius—admirable as an adjunct; but as soon as it becomes dominant, only a surrogate for genius.—Goethe.

The genius of the Spanish people is exquisitely subtle, without being at all acute; hence there is so much humor and so little wit in their literature.—Coleridge.

It is not in the power of every one to taste humor, however he may wish it; it is the gift of God! and a true feeler always brings half the entertainment along with him.—Sterne.

True humor springs not more from the head than from the heart; it is not contempt; its essence is love; it issues not in laughter, but in still smiles, which lie far deeper. It is a sort of inverse sublimity, exalting, as it were, into our affections what is below us, while sublimity draws down into our affections what is above us.—Carlyle.

Humor implies a sure conception of the beautiful, the majestic, and the true, by whose light it surveys and shapes their opposites. It is an humane influence, softening with mirth the ragged inequalities of existence, prompting tolerant views of life, bridging over the spaces which separate the lofty from the lowly, the great from the humble.—E. P. Whipple.

Hunger

Hunger is sharper than the sword.—Beaumont and Fletcher.

Cruel as death, and hungry as the grave.—Thomson.

Hunger was the best seasoning for meat.—Cicero.

They that die by famine die by inches.—Matthew Henry.

Famished people must be slowly nursed,
And fed by spoonfuls, else they always burst.　　　　　—Byron.

Hunger is the teacher of the arts, and the bestower of invention.—Persius.

Hunger is the mother of impatience and anger.—Zimmermann.

A hungry people listens not to reason, nor cares for justice, nor is bent by any prayers.—Seneca.

Man is a carnivorous production,
And must have meals, at least one meal a day;
He cannot live, like woodcocks, upon suction,
But, like the shark and tiger, must have prey.
Although his anatomical construction
Bears vegetables, in a grumbling way,
Your laboring people think beyond all question,
Beef, veal, and mutton better for digestion.　　　　　—Byron.

Hunting

Hunting is not a proper employment for a thinking man.—Addison.

Proud Nimrod first the bloody chase began,
A mighty hunter, and his prey was man.　　　　　—Pope.

It is very strange and very melancholy that the paucity of human pleasures should persuade us to call hunting one of them.—Dr. Johnson.

A man who can, in cold blood, hunt and torture a poor, innocent animal, cannot feel much compassion for the distress of his own species.—Frederick the Great.

Hunting is a relic of the barbarous spirit that thirsted formerly for human blood, but is now content with the blood of birds and animals.—Bovee.

Poor Jack,—no matter who,—for when I blame
I pity, and must therefore sink the name,—
Liv'd in his saddle, lov'd the chase, the course,
And always ere he mounted, kiss'd his horse. —Cowper.

The healthy huntsman, with a cheerful horn,
Summons the dogs and greets the dappled Morn.
The jocund thunder wakes the enliven'd hounds,
They rouse from sleep, and answer sounds for sounds. —Gay.

Husband

The lover in the husband may be lost.—Lord Lyttleton.

And to thy husband's will
Thine shall submit; he over thee shall rule.
  —Milton.

I will attend my husband, be his nurse,
Diet his sickness, for it is my office.
  —Shakespeare.

With thee goes
Thy husband, him to follow thou art bound;
Where he abides, think there thy native soil. —Milton.

To all married men, be this a caution,
Which they should duly tender as their life,
Neither to doat too much, nor doubt a wife. —Massinger.

As the husband is, the wife is:
Thou art mated with a clown,
And the grossness of his nature
Will have weight to drag thee down.
  —Tennyson.

The wife, where danger or dishonour lurks,
Safest and seemliest by her husband stays,
Who guards her, or with her the worst endures. —Milton.

A good husband makes a good wife at any time.—Farquhar.

Marry! no, faith; husbands are like lots in
The lottery, you may draw forty blanks
Before you find one that has any prize
In him; a husband generally is a
Careless domineering thing, that grows like
Coral; which as long as it is under water
Is soft and tender; but as soon
As it has got its branch above the waves
Is presently hard, stiff, not to be bow'd.
  —Marston.

Know then,
As women owe a duty—so do men.
Men must be like the branch and bark to trees,
Which doth defend them from tempestuous rage;—
Clothe them in winter, tender them in age,
Or as ewes' love unto their eanlings lives;
Such should be husbands' custom to their wives.
If it appears to them they've stray'd amiss,
They only must rebuke them with a kiss;
Or cluck them as hens' chickens, with kind call,
Cover them under their wing, and pardon all. —Wilkins.

Hypocrisy

Every man is a hypocrite.—Frederick IV.

Trust not him that seems a saint.—Fuller.

Sin is not so sinful as hypocrisy.—Mme. de Maintenon.

Hypocrisy is the homage vice pays to virtue.—La Rochefoucauld.

Saint abroad, and a devil at home.—Bunyan.

Hypocrisy is the necessary burden of villainy.—Johnson.

Hypocrisy is nothing, in fact, but a horrible hopefulness.—Victor Hugo.

No man is a hypocrite in his pleasures.—Johnson.

If Satan ever laughs, it must be at hypocrites; they are the greatest dupes he has.—Colton.

Hypocrites do the devil's drudgery in Christ's livery.—Matthew Henry.

Hypocrisy is oftenest clothed in the garb of religion.—Hosea Ballou.

No task is more difficult than systematic hypocrisy.—Bulwer-Lytton.

Oh, what may man within him hide, though angel on the outward side!—Shakespeare.

To wear long faces, just as if our Maker, The God of goodness, was an undertaker.
—Peter Pindar.

If the world despises hypocrites, what must be the estimate of them in heaven?—Madame Roland.

To live a life which is a perpetual falsehood is to suffer unknown tortures.—Victor Hugo.

It will not do to be saints at meeting and sinners everywhere else.—Henry Ward Beecher.

God has given you one face, and you make yourselves another.—Shakespeare.

The only vice that cannot be forgiven is hypocrisy. The repentance of a hypocrite is itself hypocrisy.—Hazlitt.

There is no vice so simple, but assumes Some mark of virtue on its outward parts.
—Shakespeare.

Hypocrisy, the only evil that walks invisible, except to God alone.—Milton.

Whoever is a hypocrite in his religion mocks God, presenting to Him the outside and reserving the inward for his enemy.—Jeremy Taylor.

Hypocrisy is no cheap vice; nor can our natural temper be masked for many years together.—Burke.

The words of his mouth were smoother than butter, but war was in his heart: his words were softer than oil, yet were they drawn swords.—Bible.

Oh, that deceit should steal such gentle shapes, and with a virtuous vizard hide foul guile!—Shakespeare.

A hypocrite despises those whom he deceives, but has no respect for himself. He would make a dupe of himself, too, if he could.—Hazlitt.

The world's all title-page; there's no contents;
The world's all face; the man who shows his heart
Is hooted for his nudities, and scorn'd.
—Young.

Hypocrisy is folly. It is much easier, safer, and pleasanter to be the thing which a man aims to appear than to keep up the appearance of being what he is not.—Cecil.

When you see a man with a great deal of religion displayed in his shop window, you may depend upon it he keeps a very small stock of it within.—Spurgeon.

He was the mildest manner'd man That ever scuttled ship, or cut a throat!
With such true breeding of a gentleman, You never could divine his real thought.
—Byron.

I know of but one garment which the fashionable social life of this country borrows of Christianity; it is that ample garment of charity which covers a multitude of sins—particularly fashionable sins.—J. G. Holland.

The devil can cite Scripture for his purpose.
An evil soul, producing holy witness, Is like a villain with a smiling cheek;
A goodly apple rotten at the heart;
O, what a goodly outside falsehood hath!
—Shakespeare.

For every man's nature is concealed with many folds of disguise, and covered as it were with various veils. His brows, his eyes, and very often his countenance, are deceitful, and his speech is most commonly a lie.—Cicero.

Hypocrisy itself does great honor, or rather justice, to religion, and tacitly acknowledges it to be an ornament to human nature. The hypocrite would not be at so much pains to put on the appearance of virtue, if he did not know it was the most proper and effectual means to gain the love and esteem of mankind.—Addison.

No man's condition is so base as his;
None more accurs'd than he; for man es-
    teems
Him hateful, 'cause he seems not what he is;
God hates him, 'cause he is not what he
    seems;
What grief is absent, or what mischief can
Be added to the hate of God and man?
    —Quarles.

Surely the mischief of hypocrisy can never be enough inveighed against. When religion is in request, it is the chief malady of the church, and numbers die of it; though because it is a subtle and inward evil, it be little perceived. It is to be feared there are many sick of it, that look well and comely in God's outward worship, and they may pass well in good weather, in times of peace; but days of adversity are days of trial.—Bishop Hall.

Lord love you! when we see what some people do all the week—people who are stanch at church, remember —I can't help thinking there are a good many poor souls who are only Christians at morning and afternoon service.—Dickens.

All live by seeming.
The beggar begs with it, and the gay cour·
    tier
Gains land and title, rank and rule, by
    seeming;
The clergy scorn it not, and the bold
    soldier
Will eke with it his service.—All admit it,
All practise it; and he who is content
With showing what he is, shall have small
    credit
In church, or camp, or state.—So wags
    the world.   —Scott.

I

Ideality

Ideals are the world's masters.—J. G. Holland.

Ideality is the avant-courier of the mind.—Horace Mann.

Our ideals are our better selves.—A. Bronson Alcott.

To have greatly dreamed precludes low ends.—Lowell.

Ideals we do not make. We discover, not invent, them.—Charles H. Parkhurst.

Be true to your own highest convictions.—William Ellery Channing.

Without the ideal, the inexhaustible source of all progress, what would man be?—Mme. de Girardin.

When we idealize the real, we sacrifice to artistic fancy.—Fuseli.

Freedom is only in the land of dreams, and the beautiful only blooms in song.—Schiller.

Ideality consists of the rainbow rays of intellect.—Alfred Mercier.

We build statues of snow, and weep to see them melt.—Walter Scott.

It is the vain endeavor to make ourselves what we are not that has strewn history with so many broken purposes and lives left in the rough.—Lowell.

What we need most is not so much to realize the ideal as to idealize the real.—F. H. Hedge.

Ideal beauty is a fugitive which is never located.—Madame Sévigné.

The ideal itself is but truth clothed in the forms of art.—Octave Feuillet.

The ideal is the flower-garden of the mind, and very apt to run to weeds unless carefully tended.—Mrs. Oliphant.

Every life has its actual blanks, which the ideal must fill up, or which else remain bare and profitless forever.—Julia Ward Howe.

The true ideal is not opposed to the real, nor is it any artificial heightening thereof, but lies in it; and blessed are the eyes that find it.—Lowell.

The ideal is the only absolute real; and it must become the real in the individual life as well, however impossible they may count it who never tried it.—George MacDonald.

God hides some ideal in every human soul. At some time in our life we feel a trembling, fearful longing to do some good thing. Life finds its noblest spring of excellence in this hidden impulse to do our best.—Robert Collyer.

All men need something to poetize and idealize their life a little—something which they value for more than its use, and which is a symbol of their emancipation from the mere materialism and drudgery of daily life.—Theodore Parker.

Most people carry an ideal man and woman in their head, and when the practical relations of the men and women of every day are discussed with reference only to these impossible ideals, we need not marvel at any ridiculous conclusions.—Mary Clemmer.

A large portion of human beings live not so much in themselves as in what they desire to be. They create what is called an ideal character, in an ideal form, whose perfections compensate in some degree for the imperfections of their own.—Whipple.

The situation that has not its duty, its ideal, was never yet occupied by man. Yes, here, in this poor, miserable, hampered, despicable actual, wherein thou even now standest, here or nowhere is thy ideal; work it out therefrom, and, working, believe, live, be free. Fool! the ideal is in thyself. —Carlyle.

Alas! we know that ideals can never be completely embodied in practice. Ideals must ever lie a great way off— and we will thankfully content ourselves with any not intolerable approximation thereto! Let no man, as Schiller says, too querulously "measure by a scale of perfection the meager product of reality" in this poor world of ours.—Carlyle.

Honor to the idealists, whether philosophers or poets. They have improved us by mingling with our daily pursuits great and transcendent conceptions. They have thrown around our sensual life the grandeur of a better, and drawn us up from contacts with the temporal and the selfish to communion with beauty and truth and goodness.—Chapin.

Every man has at times in his mind the ideal of what he should be, but is not. This ideal may be high and complete, or it may be quite low and insufficient; yet, in all men that really seek to improve, it is better than the actual character. Perhaps no one is so satisfied with himself that he never wishes to be wiser, better, and more holy.—Theodore Parker.

Ideas

The very coinage of your brain.— Shakespeare.

Our ideas are transformed sensations.—Condillac.

Every idea must have a visible enfolding.—Victor Hugo.

Ideas in the head set hands about their several tasks.—A. Bronson Alcott.

An idea, like a ghost (according to the common notion of ghosts), must be spoken to a little before it will explain itself.—Dickens.

Ideas are pitiless.—Lamartine.

It is not my periods that I polish, but my ideas.—Joubert.

The persistence of an all-absorbing idea is terrible.—Victor Hugo.

A fixed idea ends in madness or heroism.—Victor Hugo.

Words are daughters of earth, but ideas are sons of heaven.—Dr. Johnson.

Ideas are like beards; men do not have them until they grow up.—Voltaire.

In these days we fight for ideas, and newspapers are our fortresses.— Heinrich Heine.

Our ideas, like pictures, are made up of lights and shadows.—Joubert.

We live in an age in which superfluous ideas abound and essential ideas are lacking.—Joubert.

Our land is not more the recipient of the men of all countries than of their ideas.—Bancroft.

The material universe exists only in the mind.—Jonathan Edwards.

If the ancients left us ideas, to our credit be it spoken that we moderns are building houses for them.—A. Bronson Alcott.

A sublime idea remains the same, from whatever brain or in whatever region it has its birth.—Menzel.

Ideas must work through the brains and the arms of good and brave men, or they are no better than dreams.—Emerson.

Ideas often flash across our minds more complete than we could make them after much labor.—La Rochefoucauld.

Ideas once planted in the brain fructify, and bear their harvest more or less bountiful and rich as they are fertilized by thought.—Bartol.

To have ideas is to gather flowers. To think is to weave them into garlands.—Madame Swetchine.

Great ideas travel slowly, and for a time noiselessly, as the gods whose feet were shod with wool.—James A. Garfield.

Our ideas, like orange-plants, spread out in proportion to the size of the box which imprisons the roots.—Bulwer-Lytton.

One should conquer the world, not to enthrone a man, but an idea; for ideas exist forever.—Beaconsfield.

Time is but the measure of the difficulty of a conception. Pure thought has scarcely any need of time, since it perceives the two ends of an idea almost at the same moment.—Amiel.

To be fossilized is to be stagnant, unprogressive, dead, frozen into a solid. It is only liquid currents of thought that move men and the world. —Wendell Phillips.

Whatsoever the mind perceives of itself, or is the immediate object of perception, thought, or understanding, that I call an idea.—Locke.

Events are only the shells of ideas; and often it is the fluent thought of ages that is crystallized in a moment by the stroke of a pen or the point of a bayonet.—Chapin.

Ideas go booming through the world louder than cannon. Thoughts are mightier than armies. Principles have achieved more victories than horsemen and chariots.—W. M. Paxton.

Ideas are, like matter, infinitely divisible. It is not given to us to get down, so to speak, to their final atoms, but to their molecular groupings the way is never ending, and the progress infinitely delightful and profitable.—Bovee.

Many ideas grow better when transplanted into another mind than in the one where they sprung up. That which was a weed in one intelligence becomes a flower·in the other, and a flower again dwindles down to a mere weed by the same change.—O. W. Holmes.

By what strange law of mind is it that an idea long overlooked, and trodden underfoot as a useless stone, suddenly sparkles out in new light, as a discovered diamond?—Mrs. Stowe.

Idleness

Disciplined inaction.—Mackintosh.

Stagnant satisfaction! — Samuel Smiles.

Idleness is the holiday of fools.—Chesterfield.

Idleness is the sepulchre of a living man.—J. G. Holland.

An idler is a watch that wants both hands.—Cowper.

A poor idle man cannot be an honest man.—Achilles Poincelot.

How sweet and sacred idleness is!—Landor.

Lost time is never found again.—Aughey.

I live an idle burden to the ground.—Homer.

Idleness is paralysis.—Roswell D. Hitchcock.

To do nothing is in every man's power.—Johnson.

Idleness is the key of beggary.—Spurgeon.

An idle man's brain is the devil's workshop.—Bunyan.

The ruin of most men dates from some idle moment.—Hillard.

Idleness is the nurse of naughtiness.—Robert Burton.

Sluggish idleness—the nurse of sin.—Spenser.

Doing nothing with a deal of skill.—Cowper.

In idleness there is perpetual despair.—Carlyle.

Enjoyment stops where indolence begins.—Pollok.

Watch, for the idleness of the soul approaches death.—Demophilus.

Idleness is emptiness: the tree in which the sap is stagnant, remains fruitless.—Hosea Ballou.

Some people have a perfect genius for doing nothing, and doing it assiduously.—Haliburton.

Absence of occupation is not rest,
A mind quite vacant is a mind distress'd.
—Cowper.

I look upon indolence as a sort of suicide.—Chesterfield.

There is really nothing left to a genuine idle man, who possesses any considerable degree of vital power, but sin.—J. G. Holland.

If idleness do not produce vice or malevolence, it commonly produces melancholy.—Sydney Smith.

To be idle is the ultimate purpose of the busy.—Dr. Johnson.

Give time to the Evil One, and you give him all he requires.—Gladstone.

Idleness is both a great sin, and the cause of many more.—South.

As idle as a painted ship
Upon a painted ocean.   —Coleridge.

Every hour of lost time is a chance of future misfortune.—Napoleon I.

Is there anything so wretched as to look at a man of fine abilities doing nothing?—Chapin.

Satan finds some mischief still
For idle hands to do.   —Watts.

I pity the man overwhelmed with the weight of his own leisure.—Voltaire.

Idleness is more an infirmity of the mind than of the body.—Rochefoucauld.

Drones suck not eagles' blood, but rob beehives.—Shakespeare.

Stagnation is something worse than death, it is corruption also.—Simms.

Slothfulness casteth into a deep sleep; and an idle soul shall suffer hunger.—Bible.

Idleness is the stupidity of the body, and stupidity the idleness of the mind.—Seume.

He is not only idle who does nothing, but he is idle who might be better employed.—Socrates.

Idleness is an inlet to disorder, and makes way for licentiousness. People that have nothing to do are quickly tired of their own company.—Jeremy Collier.

Idleness is many gathered miseries in one name.—Richter.

Laziness grows on people; it begins in cobwebs, and ends in iron chains. The more business a man has to do, the more he is able to accomplish; for he learns to economize his time.—Judge Hale.

Idleness travels very slowly, and poverty soon overtakes her.—Hunter.

Indolent people, whatever taste they may have for society, seek eagerly for pleasure, and find nothing. They have an empty head and seared hearts.—Zimmermann.

There is no remedy for time misspent;
No healing for the waste of idleness,
Whose very languor is a punishment
Heavier than active souls can feel or guess. —Sir Aubrey de Vere.

Too much idleness, I have observed, fills up a man's time more completely and leaves him less his own master, than any sort of employment whatsoever.—Burke.

So long as idleness is quite shut out from our lives, all the sins of wantonness, softness, and effeminacy are prevented; and there is but little room for temptation.—Jeremy Taylor.

The idle man stands outside of God's plan, outside of the ordained scheme of things; and the truest self-respect, the noblest independence, and the most genuine dignity, are not to be found there.—J. G. Holland.

Idleness is a constant sin, and labor is a duty. Idleness is the devil's home for temptation, and for unprofitable, distracting musings; while labor profiteth others and ourselves.—Baxter.

If you ask me which is the real hereditary sin of human nature, do you imagine I shall answer pride or luxury or ambition or egotism? No; I shall say indolence. Who conquers indolence will conquer all the rest. Indeed, all good principles must stagnate without mental activity.—Zimmermann.

To be idle and to be poor have always been reproaches; and therefore every man endeavors with his utmost care to hide his poverty from others, and his idleness from himself.—Johnson.

He that embarks in the voyage of life will always wish to advance, rather by the impulse of the wind than the strokes of the oar; and many founder in their passage while they lie waiting for the gale.—Johnson.

Sloth makes all things difficult, but industry all easy; and he that riseth late must trot all day, and shall scarce overtake his business at night; while laziness travels so slowly that poverty soon overtakes him.—Franklin.

What is a man, if his chief good and market of his time be but to sleep and feed? a beast, no more. Sure, he that made us with such large discourse, looking before and after, gave us not that capability and godlike reason to fust in us unused.—Shakespeare.

Rather do what is nothing to the purpose than be idle; that the devil may find thee doing. The bird that sits is easily shot, when fliers scape the fowler. Idleness is the Dead Sea that swallows all the virtues, and the self-made sepulchre of a living man.—Quarles.

Idleness is the grand Pacific Ocean of life, and in that stagnant abyss the most salutary things produce no good, the most noxious no evil. Vice, indeed, abstractedly considered, may be, and often is engendered in idleness; but the moment it becomes efficiently vice, it must quit its cradle and cease to be idle.—Colton.

In such a world as ours the idle man is not so much a biped as a bivalve; and the wealth which breeds idleness, of which the English peerage is an example, and of which we are beginning to abound in specimens in this country, is only a sort of human oyster bed, where heirs and heiresses are planted, to spend a contemptible life of slothfulness in growing plump and succulent for the grave-worms' banquet.—Horace Mann.

Idleness is the badge of the gentry, the bane of body and mind, the nurse of naughtiness, the stepmother of discipline, the chief author of all mischief, one of the seven deadly sins, the cushion upon which the devil chiefly reposes, and a great cause not only of melancholy, but of many other diseases; for the mind is naturally active, and, if it is not occupied about some honest business, it rushes into mischief or sinks into melancholy.—Burton.

Time, with all its celerity, moves slowly on to him whose whole employment is to watch its flight.—Dr. Johnson.

If you are idle, you are on the road to ruin; and there are few stopping-places upon it. It is rather a precipice than a road.—Beecher.

The bees can abide no drones amongst them; but as soon as they begin to be idle, they kill them.—Plato.

Idolatry

The idol is the measure of the worshipper.—Lowell.

'Tis mad idolatry,
To make the service greater than the god.
—Shakespeare.

It is not he who forms idols in gold or marble that makes them gods, but he who kneels before them.—Martial.

Man may content himself with the applause of the world, and the homage paid to his intellect; but woman's heart has holier idols.—George Eliot.

Philosophers and common heathen believed one God, to whom all things were referred; but under this God they worshipped many inferior and subservient gods.—Stillingfleet.

Make no man your idol; for the best man must have faults, and his faults will usually become yours in addition to your own. This is as true in art as in morals.—Washington Allston.

Idolatry is certainly the first-born of folly, the great and leading paradox; nay, the very abridgment and sum total of all absurdities.—South.

This idol gold can boast of two peculiarities: it is worshipped in all climates without a single temple, and by all classes without a single hypocrite.—Colton.

God will put up with a great many things in the human heart, but there is one thing that He will not put up with in it—a second place. He who offers God a second place, offers Him no place.—Ruskin.

Ignorance

O thou monster ignorance!—Shakespeare.

The more one endeavors to sound the depths of his ignorance the deeper the chasm appears.—A. Bronson Alcott.

Ignorance is the mother of fear.—Lord Kames.

The common curse of mankind, folly and ignorance.—Shakespeare.

Ignorance never settles a question.—Beaconsfield.

They most assume, who know the least.—Gay.

The law succors the ignorant.—Law Maxim.

Ignorance is the dominion of absurdity.—Froude.

Ignorance is bold, and knowledge reserved.—Thucydides.

Whoever is ignorant is vulgar.—Cervantes.

There is no calamity like ignorance.—Richter.

Positive in proportion to their ignorance.—Hosea Ballou.

Dull, unfeeling, barren ignorance.—Shakespeare.

What ignorance there is in human minds.—Ovid.

The ignorant classes are the dangerous classes. Ignorance is the womb of monsters.—Henry Ward Beecher.

Detraction is the sworn friend to ignorance.—John Webster.

There is no darkness but ignorance. —Shakespeare.

Ignorance is the wet-nurse of prejudice.—H. W. Shaw.

Nothing is more terrible than active ignorance.—Goethe.

Mr. Kremlin was distinguished for ignorance; for he had only one idea, and that was wrong.—Beaconsfield.

To be ignorant of one's ignorance is the malady of the ignorant.—A. Bronson Alcott.

Ignorance is a dangerous and spiritual poison, which all men ought warily to shun.—Gregory.

Where ignorance is bliss
'Tis folly to be wise.   —Gray.

How wretched are the minds of men, and how blind their understandings. —Lucretius.

From ignorance our comfort flows,
The only wretched are the wise.
                 —Prior.

It is better to be unborn than untaught; for ignorance is the root of misfortune.—Plato.

Ignorance is a prolonged infancy only deprived of its charm.—De Bouffiers.

There is nothing more daring than ignorance.—Menander.

Ignorance is the night of the mind, but a night without moon or star.— Confucius.

Ignorance is the curse of God; knowledge, the wing wherewith we fly to heaven.—Shakespeare.

Ignorant men differ from beasts only in their figure.—Cleanthes.

In friendship, as in love, we are often happier through our ignorance than our knowledge.—Shakespeare.

The truest characters of ignorance are vanity and pride and arrogance.— Samuel Butler.

Well-meant ignorance is a grievous calamity in high places.—Bossuet.

Scholars are frequently to be met with who are ignorant of nothing— saving their own ignorance.—Zimmermann.

A wise man in the company of those who are ignorant has been compared by the sages to a beautiful girl in the company of blind men.—Saadi.

Ignorance is not so damnable as humbug; but when it prescribes pills it may happen to do more harm.— George Eliot.

A man may live long, and die at last in ignorance of many truths, which his mind was capable of knowing, and that with certainty.—Locke.

A man is never astonished or ashamed that he don't know what another does, but he is surprised at the gross ignorance of the other in not knowing what he does.—Haliburton.

Man is arrogant in proportion to his ignorance. Man's natural tendency is to egotism. Man, in his infancy of knowledge, thinks that all creation was formed for him.—Bulwer-Lytton.

Ignorance, when voluntary, is criminal, and a man may be properly charged with that evil which he neglected or refused to learn how to prevent.—Johnson.

Ignorance breeds monsters to fill up all the vacancies of the soul that are unoccupied by the verities of knowledge. He who dethrones the idea of law bids chaos welcome in its stead.— Horace Mann.

Did we but compare the miserable scantiness of our capacities with the vast profundity of things, truth and modesty would teach us wary language.—Glanvill.

So long as thou art ignorant, be not ashamed to learn. Ignorance is the greatest of all infirmities; and when justified, the chiefest of all follies.—Izaak Walton.

Ignorance is mere privation by which nothing can be produced: it is a vacuity in which the soul sits motionless and torpid for want of attraction; and, without knowing why, we always rejoice when we learn, and grieve when we forget.—Johnson.

It is impossible to make people understand their ignorance, for it requires knowledge to perceive it; and, therefore, he that can perceive it hath it not.—Jeremy Taylor.

It is with narrow-souled people as with narrow-necked bottles—the less they have in them the more noise they make in pouring it out.—Pope.

It is thus that we walk through the world like the blind, not knowing whither we are going, regarding as bad what is good, regarding as good what is bad, and ever in entire ignorance.—Madame de Sévigné.

It is with nations as with individuals, those who know the least of others think the highest of themselves; for the whole family of pride and ignorance are incestuous, and mutually beget each other.—Colton.

Do not take the yardstick of your ignorance to measure what the ancients knew, and call everything which you do not know lies. Do not call things untrue because they are marvelous, but give them a fair consideration.—Wendell Phillips.

There is no slight danger from general ignorance; and the only choice which Providence has graciously left to a vicious government, is either to fall by the people, if they are suffered to become enlightened, or with them, if they are kept enslaved and ignorant.—Coleridge.

Without knowledge there can be no sure progress. Vice and barbarism are the inseparable companions of ignorance. Nor is it too much to say that, except in rare instances, the

highest virtue is attained only through intelligence.—Charles Sumner.

Ignorance lies at the bottom of all human knowledge, and the deeper we penetrate the nearer we arrive unto it. For what do we truly know, or what can we clearly affirm, of any one of those important things upon which all our reasonings must of necessity be built—time and space, life and death, matter and mind?—Colton.

There are two sorts of ignorance: we philosophize to escape ignorance; we start from the one, we repose in the other; they are the goals from which and to which we tend; and the pursuit of knowledge is but a course between two ignorances, as human life is only a traveling from grave to grave.—Sir William Hamilton.

Thy ignorance in unrevealed mysteries is the mother of a saving faith, and thy understanding in revealed truths is the mother of a sacred knowledge; understand not therefore that thou mayest believe, but believe that thou mayest understand; understanding is the wages of a lively faith, and faith is the reward of an humble ignorance.—Quarles.

Ill-Nature

Think of a man in a chronic state of anger!—Beecher.

Some natures are so sour and ungrateful that they are never to be obliged.—L'Estrange.

Must I give way and room to your rash choler?—Shakespeare.

By indulging this fretful temper, you alienate those on whose affection much of your comfort depends.—Blair.

Ill-nature is a sort of running sore of the disposition.—H. W. Shaw.

Ill-nature consists of a proneness to do ill turns, attended with a secret joy upon the sight of any mischief that befalls another.—South.

Though I carry always some ill-nature about me, yet it is, I hope, no more than is in this world necessary for a preservative.—Marvell.

You have only to watch other ill-natured people to resolve to be unlike them.—Charles Buxton.

Ill-humor is nothing more than an inward feeling of our own want of merit, a dissatisfaction with ourselves which is always united with an envy that foolish vanity excites.—Goethe.

The world is so full of ill-nature that I have lampoons sent me by people who cannot spell, and satires composed by those who scarce know how to write.—Addison.

They give up all sweets of kindness for the sake of peevishness, petulance, or gloom, and alienate the world by neglect of the common forms of civility, and breach of the established laws of conversation.—Dr. Johnson.

Peevishness may be considered the canker of life, that destroys its vigor and checks its improvement; that creeps on with hourly depredations, and taints and vitiates what it cannot consume.—Dr. Johnson.

Ills

Think of the ills from which you are exempt.—Joubert.

Keep what you've got: the ills that we know are the best.—Plautus.

O, yet we trust that somehow good will be the final goal of ill!—Tennyson.

We satisfied ourselves the other day that there was no real ill in life except severe bodily pain; everything else is the child of the imagination, and depends on our thoughts; all other ills find a remedy, either from time or moderation, or strength of mind.—Madame de Sévigné.

Philosophy easily triumphs over past and future ills; but present ills triumph over philosophy.—Rochefoucauld.

All ills spring from some vice, either in ourselves or others; and even many of our diseases proceed from the same origin. Remove the vices, and the ills follow. You must only take care to remove all the vices. If you remove part, you may render the matter worse. By banishing vicious luxury, without curing sloth and an indifference to others, you only diminish industry in the state, and add nothing to men's charity or their generosity.—Hume.

Common and vulgar people ascribe all ill that they feel to others; people of little wisdom ascribe to themselves; people of much wisdom, to no one.—Epictetus.

Illusion

Illusion is the first of all pleasures.—Voltaire.

In youth we feel richer for every new illusion; in maturer years, for every one we lose.—Mme. Swetchine.

A pleasant illusion is better than a harsh reality.—Bovee.

Women are happier in their illusions than in their most agreeable experiences.—Mme. Dufresnoy.

The loss of our illusions is the only loss from which we never recover.—Ouida.

Illusion and wisdom combined are the charm of life and art.—Joubert.

Time is indeed the theater and seat of illusions; nothing is so ductile and elastic. The mind stretches an hour to a century, and dwarfs an age to an hour.—Emerson.

There is no such thing as real happiness in life. The justest definition that was ever given of it was "a tranquil acquiescence under an agreeable delusion"—I forget where.—Sterne.

When the boys come into my yard for leave to gather horse-chestnuts, I own I enter into nature's game, and affect to grant the permission reluctantly, fearing that any moment they will find out the imposture of that showy chaff. But this tenderness is quite unnecessary; the enchantments are laid on very thick. Their young life is thatched with them. Bare and grim to tears is the lot of the children in the hovel I saw yesterday; yet not the less they hang it round with frippery romance, like the children of the happiest fortune.—Emerson.

Every generous illusion of youth leaves a wrinkle as it departs. Experience is the successive disenchanting of the things of life; it is reason enriched with the heart's spoils.—J. Petit-Senn.

Imagination

Imagination rules the world.—Napoleon I.

Imagination is the eye of the soul. —Joubert.

Imagination is the air of mind.— Bailey.

He waxes desperate with imagination.—Shakespeare.

The imagination never dies.—Stedman.

The incurable ills are the imaginary ills.—Marie Ebner-Eschenbach.

Imagination is the mightiest despot. —Auerbach.

Keep the imagination sane—that is one of the truest conditions of communion with heaven.—Hawthorne.

The imagination is the secret and harrow of civilization. It is the very eye of faith.—Henry Ward Beecher.

This is the very coinage of your brain; This bodiless creation ecstasy.
　　　　　　—Shakespeare.

We are all of us imaginative in some form or other; for images are the brood of desire.—George Eliot.

There comes a period of the imagination to each—a later youth—the power of beauty, the power of looks, of poetry.—Emerson.

Science does not know its debt to imagination. Goethe did not believe that a great naturalist could exist without this faculty.—Emerson.

The imagination is of so delicate a texture that even words wound it.— Hazlitt.

An uncommon degree of imagination constitutes poetical genius.—Dugald Stewart.

He who has imagination without learning has wings but no feet.— Joubert.

There is nothing more fearful than imagination without taste.—Goethe.

Men speak from knowledge, women from imagination.—Rousseau.

Solitude is as needful to the imagination as society is wholesome for the character.—Lowell.

The soul without imagination is what an observatory would be without a telescope.—Beecher.

The lunatic, the lover, and the poet are of imagination all compact.— Shakespeare.

A ray of imagination or of wisdom may enlighten the universe, and glow into remotest centuries.—Bishop Berkeley.

Women have much more heart and much more imagination than men; hence, fancy often allures them.— Lamartine.

Imagination is not thought, neither is fancy reflection; thought paceth like a hoary sage, but imagination hath wings as an eagle.—Tupper.

But what is the imagination? Only an arm or weapon of the interior energy; only the precursor of the reason.—Emerson.

Imagination disposes of everything; it creates beauty, justice, and happiness, which is everything in this world.—Pascal.

Such is the power of imagination, that even a chimerical pleasure in expectation affects us more than a solid pleasure in possession.—Henry Home.

Imagination without culture is crippled and moves slowly; but it can be pure imagination, and rich also, as folk-lore will tell the vainest.—Ouida.

The sound and proper exercise of the imagination may be made to contribute to the cultivation of all that is virtuous and estimable in the human character.—John Abercrombie.

When I could not sleep for cold
I had fire enough in my brain,
And builded with roofs of gold
My beautiful castles in Spain!
—Lowell.

Imagining is in itself the very height and life of poetry, which, by a kind of enthusiasm or extraordinary emotion of the soul, makes it seem to us that we behold those things which the poet paints.—Dryden.

The world of reality has its limits; the world of imagination is boundless. Not being able to enlarge the one, let us contract the other; for it is from their difference alone that all the evils arise which render us really unhappy. —Rousseau.

Men as yet need some help to their imagination. There remains still room for a little illusion. It is better for men, it is better for women, that each somewhat idealize the other. Much is lost when life has lost its atmosphere, and is reduced to naked fact. —Gail Hamilton.

Imagination is that faculty which arouses the passions by the impression of exterior objects; it is influenced by these objects, and consequently it is in affinity with them; it is contagious; its fear or courage flies from imagination to imagination; the same in love, hate, joy, or grief: hence I conclude it to be a most subtle atmosphere.—Lord John Russell.

Imagination, where it is truly creative, is a faculty, and not a quality; it looks before and after, it gives the form that makes all the parts work together harmoniously toward a given

end, its seat is in the higher reason, and it is efficient only as a servant of the will. Imagination, as it is too often misunderstood, is mere fantasy, the image-making power, common to all who have the gift of dreams.— Lowell.

Imagination I understand to be the representation of an individual thought. Imagination is of three kinds: joined with belief of that which is to come; joined with memory of that which is past; and of things present.—Bacon.

A vile imagination, once indulged, gets the key of our minds, and can get in again very easily, whether we will or no, and can so return as to bring seven other spirits with it more wicked than itself; and what may follow no one knows.—Spurgeon.

Imagination is the organ through which the soul within us recognizes a soul without us; the spiritual eye by which the mind perceives and converses with the spiritualities of nature under her material forms; which tends to exalt even the senses into soul by discerning a soul in the objects of sense.—H. N. Hudson.

Fancy can save or kill; it hath clos'd up
Wounds when the balsam could not, and without
The aid of salves:—to think hath been a cure.
For witchcraft then, that's all done by the force
Of mere imagination.   —Cartwright.

In woman the imagination and fancy have such lively play that the homeliest principles assume forms of beauty. In intellectual pursuits she is destined to excel by her fine sensibilities, her nice observations, and exquisite taste; while man is appointed to investigate the laws of abstruse sciences, and perform in literature and art the bolder flights of genius.—F. D. Fulton.

The imagination acquires by custom a certain involuntary, unconscious power of observation and comparison, correcting its own mistakes, and arriving at precision of judgment, just as the outward eye is disciplined to compare, adjust, estimate, measure, the objects reflected on the back of its retina. The imagination is but the faculty of glassing images; and it is with exceeding difficulty, and by the imperative will of the reasoning faculty resolved to mislead it, that it glasses images which have no prototype in truth and nature.—Bulwer-Lytton.

It is the divine attribute of the imagination, that it is irrepressible, unconfinable; that when the real world is shut out, it can create a world for itself, and with a necromantic power can conjure up glorious shapes and forms, and brilliant visions to make solitude populous, and irradiate the gloom of a dungeon.—Washington Irving.

And as imagination bodies forth
The forms of things unknown, the poet's
        pen
Turns them to shape and gives to airy
        nothing
A local habitation and a name.
Such tricks has strong imagination
That if he would but apprehend some joy,
It comprehends some bringer of that joy;
Or in the night imagining some fear,
How easy is a bush supposed a bear?
                        —Shakespeare.

Imitation

Imitation is the sincerest of flattery.—Colton.

Imitators are but a servile kind of cattle.—Dryden.

You may imitate, but never counterfeit.—Balzac.

Even a man's exact imitation of the song of the nightingale displeases us when we discover that it is a mimicry, and not the nightingale.—Kant.

Borrowed wit is the poorest wit.—Lavater.

Man is an imitative creature, and whoever is foremost leads the herd.—Schiller.

I hardly know so true a mark of a little mind as the servile imitation of others.—Lord Greville.

Imitation forms our manners, our opinions, our very lives.—John Weiss.

A good imitation is the most perfect originality.—Voltaire.

We are all easily taught to imitate what is base and depraved.—Juvenal.

Some imitation is involuntary and unconscious.—Willmott.

Human reason borrowed many arts from the instinct of animals.—Dr. Johnson.

He who imitates what is evil always goes beyond the example that is set; on the contrary, he who imitates what is good always falls short.—Guicciardini.

It is certain that either wise bearing or ignorant carriage is caught as men take diseases, one of another.—Shakespeare.

Imitation causes us to leave natural ways to enter into artificial ones; it therefore makes slaves.—Professor Vinet.

Men are so constituted that everybody undertakes what he sees another successful in, whether he has aptitude for it or not.—Goethe.

It is by imitation, far more than by precept, that we learn everything; and what we learn thus, we acquire not only more effectually, but more pleasantly.—Burke.

Imitation pleases, because it affords matter for inquiring into the truth or falsehood of imitation, by comparing its likeness or unlikeness with the original.—Dryden.

For imitation is natural to man from his infancy. Man differs from other animals particularly in this, that he is imitative, and acquires his rudiments of knowledge in this way; besides, the delight in it is universal.—Aristotle.

O imitators, a servile race, how often have your attacks roused my bile and often my laughter!—Horace.

To be as good as our fathers, we must be better. Imitation is not discipleship. When some one sent a cracked plate to China to have a set made, every piece in the new set had a crack in it.—Wendell Phillips.

Since a true knowledge of nature gives us pleasure, a lively imitation of it, either in poetry or painting, must produce a much greater; for both these arts are not only true imitations of nature, but of the best nature.—Dryden.

No single character is ever so great that a nation can afford to form itself upon it. Imitation belittles. This appears in the instance of the Chinese. The Chinese are so many Confucii, in miniature. And so with the Jews. Moses, the lawgiver, is poorly represented by Moses, the old clothesman; or even by Dives, the hanker.—Bovee.

Immigration

If you should turn back from this land to Europe the foreign ministers of the gospel, and the foreign attorneys, and the foreign merchants, and the foreign philanthropists, what a robbery of our pulpits, our court rooms, our storehouses, and our beneficent institutions, and what a putting back of every monetary, merciful, moral, and religious interest of the land! This commingling here of all nationalities under the blessing of God will produce in seventy-five or one hundred years the most magnificent style of man and woman the world ever saw. They will have the wit of one race, the eloquence of another race, the kindness of another, the generosity of another, the æsthetic taste of another, the high moral character of another, and when that man and woman step forth, their brain and nerve and muscle an intertwining of the fibers of all nationalities, nothing but the new electric photographic apparatus, that can see clear through body and mind and soul, can take of them an adequate picture.—T. DeWitt Talmage.

Immodesty

The chariest maid is prodigal enough if she unmask her beauty to the moon. —Shakespeare.

Immodest words admit of no defence For want of decency is want of sense. —Pope.

Immortality

Immortality—twin sister of Eternity.—J. G. Holland.

All men desire to be immortal.— Theodore Parker.

I am conscious of eternal life.— Theodore Parker.

What is human is immortal!—Bulwer-Lytton.

Death from sin no power can separate.—Milton.

A good man never dies.—Callimachus.

I look through the grave into heaven.—Theodore Parker.

Immortality is the glorious discovery of Christianity.—William Ellery Channing.

Work for immortality if you will: then wait for it.—J. G. Holland.

The immortality of the soul is assented to rather than believed, believed rather than lived.—O. A. Brownson.

Immortality
Alone could teach this mortal how to die.
—D. M. Mulock.

And in the wreck of noble lives Something immortal still survives.
—Longfellow.

Let a disciple live as Christ lived, and he will easily believe in living again as Christ does.—Wm. Mountford.

'Tis immortality to die aspiring, As if a man were taken quick to heaven.
—Geo. Chapman.

All men's souls are immortal, but the souls of the righteous are immortal and divine.—Socrates.

The hope of immortality makes heroes of cowards.—Thomas Guthrie.

The seed dies into a new life, and so does man.—George MacDonald.

There is nothing strictly immortal but immortality.—Sir T. Browne.

Cold in the dust this perished heart may lie, but that which warmed it once shall never die.—Campbell.

To destroy the idea of the immortality of the soul is to add death to death.—Mme. de Souza.

The spirit of man, which God inspired, cannot together perish with this corporeal clod.—Milton.

I have been dying for twenty years, now I am going to live.—Jas. Drummond Burns.

Without a belief in personal immortality, religion surely is like an arch resting on one pillar, like a bridge ending in an abyss.—Max Müller.

No one could ever meet death for his country without the hope of immortality.—Cicero.

May we be satisfied with nothing that shall not have in it something of immortality.—H. W. Beecher.

It is our souls which are the everlastingness of God's purpose in this earth.—Wm. Mountford.

Still seems it strange, that thou shouldst
  live for ever?
Is it less strange, that thou shouldst live
  at all?
This is a miracle, and that no more.
        —Young.

Though inland far we be,
Our souls have sight of that immortal sea
Which brought us hither.
        —Wordsworth.

The nearer I approach the end, the plainer I hear around me the immortal symphonies of the worlds which invite me. It is marvelous, yet simple.—Victor Hugo.

Whatsoever that be within us that feels, thinks, desires, and animates, is something celestial, divine, and consequently imperishable.—Aristotle.

Everything is prospective, and man is to live hereafter. That the world

is for his education is the only sane solution of the enigma.—Emerson.

Immortality o'ersweeps all pains, all tears, all time, all fears, and peals, like the eternal thunder of the deep, into my ears this truth: Thou livest forever!—Byron.

Safe from temptation, safe from sin's pollution,
She lives, whom we call dead.
        —Longfellow.

'Tis true; 'tis certain; man though dead
  retains
Part of himself; the immortal mind remains.   —Homer.

I came from God, and I'm going back to God, and I won't have any gaps of death in the middle of my life.—George MacDonald.

We do not believe immortality because we have proved it, but we forever try to prove it because we believe it.—James Martineau.

Ah, Christ, that it were possible
For one short hour to see
The souls we loved, that they might tell us
What and where they be.   —Tennyson.

Men of dissolute lives have little incentive to look forward to the hopes and glories of immortality. A due conception of these would be incompatible with such a life.—Beecher.

After the sleep of death we are to gather up our forces again with the incalculable results of this life, a crown of shame or glory upon our heads, and begin again on a new level of progress.—Hugh R. Haweis.

Press onward through each varying hour;
  Let no weak fears thy course delay;
Immortal being! feel thy power,
  Pursue thy bright and endless way.
        —Andrews Norton.

Faith in the hereafter is as necessary for the intellectual as the moral character; and to the man of letters, as well as to the Christian, the present forms but the slightest portion of his existence.—Southey.

I feel that I was made to complete things. To accomplish only a mass of beginnings and attempts would be to make a total failure of life. Perfection is the heritage with which my Creator has endowed me, and since this short life does not give completeness, I must have immortal life in which to find it.—Bishop R. S. Foster.

I long to believe in immortality. * * * If I am destined to be happy with you here—how short is the longest life. I wish to believe in immortality—I wish to live with you forever.—Keats.

Earthly providence is a travesty of justice on any other theory than that it is a preliminary stage, which is to be followed by rectifications. Either there must be a future, or consummate injustice sits upon the throne of the universe. This is the verdict of humanity in all the ages.—Bishop R. S. Foster.

How gloomy would be the mansions of the dead to him who did not know that he should never die; that what now acts shall continue its agency, and what now thinks shall think on forever!—Johnson.

How can it enter into the thoughts of man, that the soul, which is capable of such immense perfections, and of receiving new improvements to all eternity, shall fall away into nothing almost as soon as it is created?—Addison.

The three states of the caterpillar, larva, and butterfly have, since the time of the Greek poets, been applied to typify the human being,—its terrestrial form, apparent death, and ultimate celestial destination.—Sir H. Davy.

O, what a fate is that of man! As often as I hear of some undeserved wretchedness, my thoughts rest on that world where all will be made straight, and where the labors of the sorrowful will end in joy. O that we could call up in the hearts of the afflicted such thoughts!—Fichte.

Man is so created that as to his internal he cannot die; for he is capable of believing in God, and thus of being conjoined to God by faith and love, and to be conjoined to God is to live to eternity.—Swedenborg.

We are born for a higher destiny than that of earth; there is a realm where the rainbow never fades, where the stars will be spread before us like islands that slumber on the ocean, and where the beings that pass before us like shadows will stay in our presence forever.—Bulwer-Lytton.

No, no! The energy of life may be
Kept on after the grave, but not begun;
And he who flagg'd not in the earthly strife,
From strength to strength advancing—only he
His soul well-knit, and all his battles won,
Mounts, and that hardly, to eternal life.
    —Matthew Arnold.

There may be beings, thinking beings, near or surrounding us, which we do not perceive, which we cannot imagine. We know very little; but, in my opinion, we know enough to hope for the immortality, the individual immortality, of the better part of man.—Sir H. Davy.

It is only our mortal duration that we measure by visible and measurable objects; and there is nothing mournful in the contemplation for one who knows that the Creator made him to be the image of his own eternity, and who feels that in the desire for immortality he has sure proof of his capacity for it.—Southey.

Immortality! We bow before the very term. Immortality! Before it reason staggers, calculation reclines her tired head, and imagination folds her weary pinions. Immortality! It throws open the portals of the vast forever; it puts the crown of deathless destiny upon every human brow; it cries to every uncrowned king of men, "Live forever, crowned for the empire of a deathless destiny!"—George Douglas.

Doth this soul within me, this spirit of thought, and love, and infinite desire, dissolve as well as the body? Has nature, who quenches our bodily thirst, who rests our weariness, and perpetually encourages us to endeavor onwards, prepared no food for this appetite of immortality?—Leigh Hunt.

When I consider the wonderful activity of the mind, so great a memory of what is past, and such a capacity of penetrating into the future: when I behold such a number of arts and sciences, and such a multitude of discoveries thence arising,—I believe and am firmly persuaded that a nature which contains so many things within itself cannot be mortal.—Cicero.

O, listen man!
A voice within us speaks that startling word,
"Man, thou shalt never die!" Celestial voices
Hymn it unto our souls: according harps,
By angel fingers touched, when the mild stars
Of morning sang together, sound forth still
The song of our great immortality.
—Dana.

And now have I finished a work which neither the wrath of Jove, nor fire, nor steel, nor all-consuming time can destroy. Welcome the day which can destroy only my physical man in ending my uncertain life. In my better part I shall be raised to immortality above the lofty stars, and my name shall never die.—Ovid.

It must be so—Plato, thou reasonest well!—
Else whence this pleasing hope, this fond desire,
This longing after immortality?
Or whence this secret dread, and inward horror,
Of falling into nought? Why shrinks the soul
Back on herself, and startles at destruction?
'Tis the divinity that stirs within us;
'Tis heaven itself, that points out an hereafter,
And intimates eternity to man.
The stars shall fade away, the sun himself
Grow dim with age, and nature sink in years,
But thou shalt flourish in immortal youth,
Unhurt amidst the war of elements,
The wreck of matter, and the crash of worlds.   —Addison.

Whence comes the powerful impression that is made upon us by the tomb? Are a few grains of dust deserving of our veneration? Certainly not; we respect the ashes of our ancestors for this reason only—because a secret voice whispers to us that all is not extinguished in them. It is this that confers a sacred character on the funeral ceremony among all the nations of the globe; all are alike persuaded that the sleep, even of the tomb, is not everlasting, and that death is but a glorious transfiguration. —Chateaubriand.

Impatience

Impatience never commanded success.—Chapin.

Impatience dries the blood sooner than age or sorrow.—Chapin.

Whoever is out of patience is out of possession of his soul.—Bacon.

We waste the power in impatience which, if otherwise employed, might remedy the evil.—Willmott.

Adversity borrows its sharpest sting from our impatience.—Bishop Horne.

Nature is methodical, and doeth her work well. Time is never to be hurried.—Emerson.

Impatient people, according to Bacon, are like the bees, and kill themselves in stinging others.—George Eliot.

Oh! how impatience gains upon the soul,
When the long promised hour of joy draws near!
How slow the tardy moments seem to roll!
—Mrs. Tighe.

Impatience turns an ague into a fever, a fever to the plague, fear into despair, anger into rage, loss into madness, and sorrow to amazement.—Jeremy Taylor.

I have not so great a struggle with my vices, great and numerous as they are, as I have with my impatience.—Calvin.

The schoolboy counts the time till the return of the holidays; the minor longs to be of age; the lover is impatient till he is married.—Addison.

Procrastination is hardly more evil than grasping impatience.—Kant.

The beautiful laws of time and space, once dislocated by our inaptitude, are holes and dens. If the hive be disturbed by rash and stupid hands, instead of honey, it will yield us bees. —Emerson.

You are convinced by experience that very few things are brought to a successful issue by impetuous desire, but most by calm and prudent forethought.—Thucydides.

We would willingly, and without remorse, sacrifice not only the present moment, but all the interval (no matter how long) that separates us from any favorite object.—Hazlitt.

Impatience is a quality sudden, eager and insatiable, which grasps at all, and admits of no delay; scorning to wait God's leisure, and attend humbly and dutifully upon the issues of His wise and just Providence.—South.

Such is our impatience, such our hatred of procrastination, in everything but the amendment of our practices and the adornment of our nature, one would imagine we were dragging Time along by force, and not he us.—Landor.

Impenitence

It is not sin that kills the soul, but impenitence.—Bishop Hall.

He that has no present Christ has a future, dark, chaotic, heaving with its destructive ocean; and over it there goes forever—black-pinioned, winging its solitary and hopeless flight, the raven of his anxious thoughts, and finds no place to rest, and comes back again to the desolate ark with its foreboding croak of evil in the present and evil in the future.—Alexander Maclaren.

We pray for those who have ceased to pray. We pray for those that need prayer more than ever, that have fewer and fewer seasons even of thought, that grow hard with years, that are less and less troubled by sin, and that

are more and more irreverent of religion. We pray for the children of Christian parents who sometimes weep at the memory of father and mother, but who never have thought of God.— H. W. Beecher.

Ah, sinner, may the Lord quicken thee! But it is a work that makes the Saviour weep. I think when He comes to call some of you from your death in sin, He comes weeping and sighing for you. There is a stone that is to be rolled away—your bad and evil habits—and when that stone is taken away, a still small voice will not do for you; it must be the loud crashing voice, like the voice of the Lord which breaketh the cedars of Lebanon.—C. H. Spurgeon.

Imperfection

No reckoning made, but sent to my account With all my imperfections on my head. —Shakespeare.

What an absurd thing it is to pass over all the valuable parts of a man, and fix our attention on his infirmities!—Addison.

It is only imperfection that complains of what is imperfect. The more perfect we are, the more gentle and quiet we become towards the defects of others.—Fénelon.

All things are literally better, lovelier, and more beloved for the imperfections which have been divinely appointed, that the law of human life may be Effort, and the law of human judgment Mercy.—Ruskin.

The finer the nature, the more flaws it will show through the clearness of it; and it is a law of this universe, that the best things shall be seldomest seen in their best form.—Ruskin.

Imperfection is in some sort essential to all that we know of life. It is the sign of life in a mortal body, that is to say, of a state of progress and change. Nothing that lives is, or can be rigidly perfect; part of it is decaying, part nascent. The foxglove blossom—a third part bud, a third part past, a third part in full bloom—is a type of the life of this world.—Ruskin.

Imperfection

Where imperfection ceaseth, heaven begins.—Bailey.

Men are more unwilling to have their imperfections known than their crimes.—Chesterfield.

Impertinence

Impertinence will intermeddle in things in which it has no concern, showing a want of breeding, or, more commonly, a spirit of sheer impudence.—Crabbe.

Receive no satisfaction for premeditated impertinence; forget it, forgive it, but keep him inexorably at a distance who offered it.—Lavater.

That man is guilty of impertinence who considers not the circumstances of time, or engrosses the conversation, or makes himself the subject of his discourse, or pays no regard to the company he is in.—Tully.

Imposition

I could hardly feel much confidence in a man who had never been imposed upon.—Hare.

To the generality of men you cannot give a stronger hint for them to impose upon you than by imposing upon yourself.—Fielding.

There are cases in which a man would have been ashamed not to have been imposed on. There is a confidence necessary to human intercourse, and without which men are more injured by their suspicions than they could be by the perfidy of others.—Burke.

Impossibility

Never let me hear that foolish word again.—Mirabeau.

One great difference between a wise man and a fool is: the former only wishes for what he may possibly obtain; the latter desires impossibilities.—Democritus.

Hope not for impossibilities.—Fuller.

Impossible desires are the height of unreason.—Haliburton.

Impossible is a word only to be found in the dictionary of fools.—Napoleon Buonaparte.

To the timid and hesitating everything is impossible because it seems so.—Scott.

Who loves
Believes the impossible.
—Elizabeth B. Browning.

Do not think that what is hard for thee to master is impossible for man; but if a thing is possible and proper to man, deem it attainable by thee,—Marcus Aurelius.

We have more strength than will; and it is often merely for an excuse we say things are impossible,—La Rochefoucauld.

Few things are impossible to diligence and skill.—Sam'l Johnson.

It is not a lucky word, this same impossible; no good comes of those that have it so often in their mouth.—Carlyle.

Nothing is impossible; there are ways which lead to everything; and if we had sufficient will we should always have sufficient means.—Rochefoucauld.

My Lord Anson, at the Admiralty, sends word to Chatham, then confined to his chamber by one of his most violent attacks of the gout, that it is impossible for him to fit out a naval expedition within the period to which he is limited. "Impossible!" cried Chatham, glaring at the messenger; "who talks to me of impossibilities?" Then starting to his feet, and forcing out great drops of agony on his brow with the excruciating torment of the effort, he exclaimed, "Tell Lord Anson that he serves under a minister who treads on impossibilities!"—Whipple.

Imprisonment

Captivity
That comes with honor is true liberty.
—Massinger and Field.

Let them fear bondage who are slaves to fear; the sweetest freedom is an honest heart.—John Ford.

Improvement

Improvement is nature.—Leigh Hunt.

Real improvement is of slow growth only.—Seneca.

Infinite toil would not enable you to sweep away a mist; but by ascending a little, you may often look over it altogether. So it is with our moral improvement: we wrestle fiercely with a vicious habit, which could have no hold upon us if we ascended into a higher moral atmosphere.—Helps.

People seldom improve when they have no other model but themselves to copy after.—Goldsmith.

Look up, and not down; look forward, and not back; look out, and not in; and lend a hand.—E. E. Hale.

The improvement of the mind improves the heart and corrects the understanding.—Agathon.

It is necessary to try to surpass one's self always; this occupation ought to last as long as life.—Queen Christiana.

Slumber not in the tents of your fathers. The world is advancing. Advance with it!—Mazzini.

Let us strive to improve ourselves, for we cannot remain stationary: one either progresses or retrogrades.—Mme. du Deffand.

It seems as if the day was not wholly profane in which we have given heed to some natural object.—Emerson.

Judge of thine improvement, not by what thou speakest or writest, but by the firmness of thy mind, and the government of thy passions and affections.—Fuller.

To hear always, to think always, to learn always, it is thus that we live truly. He who aspires to nothing, who learns nothing, is not worthy of living.—Helps.

Where we cannot invent, we may at least improve: we may give some-what of novelty to that which was old, condensation to that which was diffuse, perspicuity to that which was obscure, and currency to that which was recondite.—Colton.

Improvidence

Buy what thou hast no need of, and ere long thou shalt sell thy necessaries.—Benjamin Franklin.

There are men born under that constellation which maketh them, I know not how, as unapt to enrich themselves as they are ready to impoverish others.—Hooker.

It has always been more difficult for a man to keep than to get; for, in the one case, fortune aids, which often assists injustice; but in the other case, sense is required. Therefore, we often see a person deficient in cleverness rise to wealth; and then, from want of sense, roll head over heels to the bottom.—Count Basil.

Impudence

What! canst thou say all this and never blush?—Shakespeare.

A true and genuine impudence is ever the effect of ignorance, without the least sense of it.—Steele.

There is no better provision for life than impudence and a brazen face.—Menander.

What was said by the Latin poet of labor—that it conquers all things—is much more true when applied to impudence.—Fielding.

He that has but impudence,
To all things has a fair pretence;
And put among his wants but shame,
To all the world may lay his claim.
—Butler.

With that dull, rooted, callous impudence,
Which, dead to shame, and ev'ry nicer sense,
Ne'er blushed, unless, in spreading vice's snares,
She blunder'd on some virtue unawares.
—Churchill.

The way to avoid the imputation of impudence is not to be ashamed of what we do, but never to do what we ought to be ashamed of.—Tully.

Impudence is no virtue; yet able to beggar them all; being for the most part in good plight, when the rest starve, and capable of carrying her followers up to the highest preferments; as useful in a court as armor in a camp.—Sir Thomas Osborne.

Impulse

What persons are by starts they are by nature.—Sterne.

Calculation is of the head; impulse is of the heart; and both are good in their way.—Henry Giles.

All our first movements are good, generous, heroical.—Aimé-Martin.

A warm blundering man does more for the world than a frigid wise man.—Cecil.

Act upon your impulses, but pray that they may be directed by God.—Emerson Tennent.

The affection of young ladies is of as rapid growth as Jack's bean-stalk, and reaches up to the sky in a night.—Thackeray.

Women are far more impulsive than men; this is because they are more influenced by the heart than the head.—Mme. Deluzy.

What reason would grope for in vain, spontaneous impulse ofttimes achieves at a stroke, with light and pleasureful guidance.—Goethe.

Impulse is, after all, the best linguist; its logic, if not conformable to Aristotle, cannot fail to be most convincing.—Thoreau.

Since the generality of persons act from impulse, much more than from principle, men are neither so good nor so bad as we are apt to think them.—Hare.

I venture to suggest that the most developed man is he who has the least reason for not simply obeying his impulses, or that perfect impulses mark the perfect man.—James Hinton.

A true history of human events would show that a far larger proportion of our acts are the results of sudden impulses and accidents than of that reason of which we so much boast.—Cooper.

The Indian who fells the tree that he may gather the fruit, and the Arab who plunders the caravans of commerce are actuated by the same impulse of savage nature, and relinquish for momentary rapine the long and secure possession of the most important blessings.—Gibbon.

On great occasions it is almost always women who have given the strongest proofs of virtue and devotion; the reason is, that with men good and bad qualities are in general the result of calculation, while in women they are impulses springing from the heart.—Montholon.

Incivility

Incivility is the extreme of pride; it is built on the contempt of mankind.—Zimmermann.

A man has no more right to say an uncivil thing, than to act one; no more right to say a rude thing to another, than to knock him down.—Johnson.

Inclination

In this world the inclination to do things is of more importance than the mere power.—Chapin.

Our senses, our appetite, and our passions are our lawful and faithful guides in things that relate solely to this life.—Dr. Johnson.

There is no mind so weak and powerless as not to have its inclinations, and none so guarded as to be without its prepossessions.—Crabbe.

Almost every one has a predominant inclination, to which his other desires and affections submit, and which governs him, though perhaps with some intervals, though the whole course of his life.—Hume.

From the very first instances of perception, some things are grateful and others unwelcome to us; some things

we incline to, and others we fly.—
Locke.

Every one follows the inclinations
of his own nature.—Propertius.

If you have overcome your inclination and not been overcome by it, you
have reason to rejoice.—Plautus.

Inconsistency

Mutability of temper and inconsistency with ourselves is the great weakness of human nature.—Addison.

Woman is a most charming creature, who changes her heart as easily
as she does her gloves.—Balzac.

Only imagine a man acting for one
single day on the supposition that all
his neighbors believe all that they profess, and act up to all that they believe!—Macaulay.

Men talk as if they believed in God,
but they live as if they thought there
was none; their vows and promises
are no more than words, of course.—
L'Estrange.

There are some who affect a want
of affectation, and flatter themselves
that they are above flattery; they are
proud of being thought extremely humble, and would go round the world to
punish those who thought them capable of revenge; they are so satisfied
of the suavity of their own temper
that they would quarrel with their
dearest benefactor only for doubting
it.—Colton.

I have known several persons of
great fame for wisdom in public affairs and councils governed by foolish
servants. I have known great ministers, distinguished for wit and learning, who preferred none but dunces.
I have known men of valor cowards
to their wives. I have known men of
cunning perpetually cheated. I knew
three ministers who would exactly
compute and settle the accounts of a
kingdom, wholly ignorant of their own
economy.—Horace Walpole.

Inconstancy

They are not constant, but are
changing still.—Shakespeare.

Nothing that is not a real crime
makes a man appear so contemptible
and little in the eyes of the world as
inconstancy.—Addison.

Inconstancy falls off ere it begins.
—Shakespeare.

Ladies, like variegated tulips, show
'tis to their changes half their charms
we owe.—Pope.

Inconstancy is the child of satiety.
—Ninon de Lenclos.

Sigh no more, ladies, sigh no more;
Men were deceivers ever;
One foot in sea, and one on shore;
To one thing constant never.
—Shakespeare.

We pardon infidelities, but we do
not forget them.—Madame de Lafayette.

There are three things a wise man will not
  trust,—
The wind, the sunshine of an April day,
And woman's plighted faith.
—Southey.

Or as one nail by strength drives out an-
  other,
So the remembrance of my former love
Is by a newer object quite forgotten.
—Shakespeare.

I hate inconstancy—I loathe, detest,
Abhor, condemn, abjure the mortal made
Of such quicksilver clay that in his breast
No permanent foundation can be laid.
—Byron.

O, swear not by the moon, the inconstant
  moon,
That monthly changes in her circled orb,
Lest that thy love prove likewise variable.
—Shakespeare.

The dream on the pillow,
  That flits with the day,
The leaf of the willow
  A breath wears away;
The dust on the blossom,
  The spray on the sea;
Ay,—ask thine own bosom—
  Are emblems of thee.
—Miss Landon.

Such an act, that blurs the grace
and blush of modesty; calls virtue hypocrite; takes off the rose from the
fair forehead of an innocent love, and
sets a blister there.—Shakespeare.

Clocks will go as they are set; but man, irregular man, is never constant, never certain.—Otway.

Love, like men, dies oftener of excess than of hunger.—Richter.

How long must women wish in vain
A constant love to find?
No art can fickle man retain,
Or fix a roving mind.
Yet fondly we ourselves deceive,
And empty hopes pursue;
Though false to others, we believe
They will to us prove true.
—Thomas Shadwell.

Inconstancy is but a name,
To fright poor lovers from a better choice.
—Joseph Rutter.

Trust not the treason of those smiling looks,
Until ye have their guileful trains well tried;
For they are like but unto golden hooks,
That from the foolish fish their baits do hide:
So she with flattering smiles weak hearts doth guide
Unto her love, and tempt to their decay;
Whom, being caught, she kills with cruel pride,
And feeds at pleasure on the wretched prey. —Spenser.

Incredulity

Incredulity is not wisdom.—Spurgeon.

Incredulity is the wisdom of a fool. —H. W. Shaw.

The incredulous are the most credulous.—Pascal.

The whole trouble is, that we won't let God help us.—George MacDonald.

There lives more faith in honest doubt, believe me, than in half the creeds.—Tennyson.

Incredulity robs us of many pleasures, and gives us nothing in return. —Lowell.

Nothing is so contemptible as that affectation of wisdom, which some display, by universal incredulity.—Goldsmith.

The amplest knowledge has the largest faith. Ignorance is always incredulous. Tell an English cottager that the belfries of Swedish churches are crimson, and his own white steeple furnishes him with a contradiction.— Willmott.

Some men will believe nothing but what they can comprehend; and there are but few things that such are able to comprehend.—St. Evremond.

Of all the signs of a corrupt heart and a feeble head, the tendency of incredulity is the surest. Real philosophy seeks rather to solve than to deny.—Bulwer-Lytton.

Incredulity is not wisdom, but the worst kind of folly. It is folly, because it causes ignorance and mistake, with all the consequents of these; and it is very bad, as being accompanied with disingenuity, obstinacy, rudeness, uncharitableness, and the like bad dispositions; from which credulity itself, the other extreme sort of folly, is exempt.—Barrow.

Indecision

The wavering mind is a base property.—Euripides.

When a man has not a good reason for doing a thing, he has one good reason for letting it alone.—Rev. Thomas Scott.

There is nothing more pitiable in the world than an irresolute man, oscillating between two feelings, who would willingly unite the two, and who does not perceive that nothing can unite them.—Goethe.

In matters of great concern, and which must be done, there is no surer argument of a weak mind than irresolution; to be undetermined where the case is so plain, and the necessity so urgent. To be always intending to live a new life, but never to find time to set about it; this is as if a man should put off eating, and drinking, and sleeping, from one day and night to another, till he is starved and destroyed.—Tillotson.

Independence

Independence now and independence forever.—Daniel Webster.

Independence, like honor, is a rocky island, without a beach.—Napoleon.

For my own private satisfaction, I had rather be master of my own time than wear a diadem.—Bishop Berkeley.

To be truly and really independent is to support ourselves by our own exertions.—Porter.

Can anything be so elegant as to have few wants, and to serve them one's self?—Emerson.

Ourselves are to ourselves the cause of ill;
We may be independent if we will.
　　　　　　　—Churchill.

The king is the least independent man in his dominions; the beggar the most so.—J. C. and A. W. Hare.

All we ask is to be let alone.—Jefferson Davis.

It is not the greatness of a man's means that makes him independent, so much as the smallness of his wants.—Cobbett.

I would rather sit on a pumpkin, and have it all to myself, than to be crowded on a velvet cushion.—Thoreau.

The man is best served who has no occasion to put the hands of others at the end of his own arms.—Rousseau.

Let Fortune do her worst, whatever she makes us lose, as long as she never makes us lose our honesty and our independence.—Pope.

The greatest of all human benefits, that at least without which no other benefit can be truly enjoyed, is independence.—Parke Godwin.

How happy is he born or taught,
　That serveth not another's will;
Whose armor is his honest thought
And simple truth his utmost skill!
　　　　—Sir Henry Wotton.

I never thrust my nose into other men's porridge. It is no bread and butter of mine: Every man for himself and God for us all.—Cervantes.

These two things, contradictory as they may seem, must go together,—manly dependence and manly independence, manly reliance and manly self-reliance.—Wordsworth.

The word "independence" is united to the accessory ideas of dignity and virtue. The word "dependence" is united to the ideas of inferiority and corruption.—Bentham.

Hail! Independence, hail! Heaven's next
　best gift,
To that of life and an immortal soul!
　　　　　　　—Thomson.

We hold these truths to be self-evident: that all men are created equal; that they are endowed by their Creator with certain inalienable rights; that among these are life, liberty, and the pursuit of happiness.—Thomas Jefferson.

　　　　　 * * * but while
I breathe Heaven's air, and Heaven looks
　down on me,
And smiles at my best meanings, I remain
Mistress of mine own self and mine own
　soul.　　　　　　—Tennyson.

Gather gear by ev'ry wile
That's justified by honor;
Not for to hide it in a hedge,
Nor for a train attendant;
But for the glorious privilege
Of being independent.
　　　　　　　—Burns.

Independence Day

From the year 1789 to the year 1860 no nation has ever known a more unbounded prosperity, a fuller space of happiness. In the short space of seventy years, within the turn of a single life, the nation, poor, weak and despised, raised itself to the pinnacle of power and of glory.—Robert C. Winthrop.

God endowed and set us for a sign to testify the worth of men and the hope there is for man. It is not our national prosperity, great as it is, that is the appropriate theme of our most joyful congratulations, but it is our success in demonstrating that men are equal as God's children, which affords a prophecy of better things for the race.—Leonard Bacon, D. D.

The man, woman or child who hangs out an American flag or a piece of tri-color as a mark of appreciation of July the Fourth does a hundred times more than the noisiest citizen who explodes powder from sundown on the 3d to the morning of the 5th of July.—Vermont Watchman.

Our growth is wreathed and entwined with man's well-being and woman's exaltation. It is a poem of happiness conferred, not of suffering endured. This alone makes our career a blessed one among all the people.—John O'Byrne.

The Fourth of July marks an epoch in the world's history. It marks the birth of a free nation, with all that implies—a nation in the existence of which the oppressed of all lands rejoice, and of which every true American is justly proud.—Selected.

Tracing the progress of mankind in the ascending path of civilization, and moral and intellectual culture, our fathers found that the divine ordinance of government, in every stage of the ascent, was adjustable on principles of common reason to the actual condition of a people, and always had for its objects, in the benevolent councils of the divine wisdom, the happiness, the expansion, the security, the elevation of society, and the redemption of man. They sought in vain for any title of authority of man over man, except of superior capacity and higher morality.—Wm. M. Evarts.

We deplore the decadence of the old-fashioned celebration of the Fourth, with its reading of the Declaration of Independence, patriotic music, and stirring addresses, instinct with the true spirit of the day, American—as they should be—in every syllable, but having a new trend in the direction of sound, sensible consideration of the quality of good citizenship, its practical duties and their faithful performance.—Vermont Watchman.

Many of the features of Independence Day are harmless, enjoyable, inspiring. We would not lessen the sports, processions, excursions, outdoor

and indoor entertainments. But the burning of powder, the Chinese firecrackers, the tin horns, and the ill manners that turn the day into a barbaric carnival are as great an enemy to patriotism as they are a libel on the good sense of the people.—Congregationalist.

Is life so dear, or peace so sweet, as to be purchased at the price of chains and slavery? Forbid it, Almighty Powers!—I know not what course others may take; but as for me, give me liberty or give me death!—Patrick Henry.

"Resolved, That these united colonies are, and of right ought to be, free and independent states; that they are absolved from all allegiance to the British crown; and that all political connection between them and the State of Great Britain is, and ought to be, dissolved."—Richard Henry Lee.

If we wish to be free, if we mean to preserve inviolate those inestimable privileges for which we have been so long contending; if we mean not basely to abandon the noble struggle in which we have been so long engaged and which we have pledged ourselves never to abandon until the glorious object of our contest shall be obtained, we must fight; I repeat it, sir, we must fight! An appeal to arms, and to the God of Hosts, is all that is left us!—Patrick Henry.

A century and more has passed, and as the foundations of this government are more firmly settled, as the great structure reared by the fathers now spans the continent from ocean to ocean, and has victoriously established its right to be, political liberty has ceased to be the mere dream of the enthusiast, and has become the every-day fact of the men of thought and action in the world. This was the first step; and we are here to glory in it, and to boast of those ancestors who suffered and toiled and fought to accomplish it.—Judge David J. Brewer.

Grand as have been the achievements of our forefathers under the blessings of Almighty God, there remains a great revolutionary work for us to do; not by dint of arms, not at the sacrifice of fortune, home and life, but with enlightened reason and a pure conscience; we want to do our duty everywhere, and especially at the ballot-box. We no longer want to countenance evil or legalize what will make us blush and cause a net to be spread before our brightest sons and fairest daughters.—Rev. J. W. Loose.

Was it the discipline and skill of the Revolutionists which gave them success? That can hardly be the case as they were not well versed in the tactics of war. We believe that with their loyalty and faithful use of arms in self-defense, they also enjoyed the favor and help of the Almighty, to whom they had appealed for the rectitude of their intentions, and in their greatest extremities sought His aid. They recognized the fact that "the powers that be are ordained of God."—Rev. J. W. Loose.

We shall best honor these men and days of old by signing our own declaration of independence from all those elements of selfishness and sordidness that lead to indifference as to the country's welfare and to an all-absorbing desire for mere personal ease or acquisition.—Princeton Press.

I could not omit to urge on every man to remember that self-government politically can only be successful if it be accompanied by self-government personally; that there must be government somewhere; and that, if the people are indeed to be sovereigns, they must exercise their sovereignty over themselves individually, as well as over themselves in the aggregate—regulating their own lives, resisting their own temptations, subduing their own passions, and voluntarily imposing upon themselves some measure of that restraint and discipline which, under other systems, is supplied from the armories of arbitrary power—the discipline of virtue in the place of the discipline of slavery.—Robert C. Winthrop.

Without Virginia, as we must all acknowledge—without her Patrick Henry among the people, her Lees and Jefferson in the forum, and her Wash-

ington in the field—I will not say that the cause of American liberty and American independence must have been ultimately defeated—no, no, there was no ultimate defeat for that cause in the decrees of the Most High; but it must have been delayed, postponed, perplexed, and to many eyes and hearts rendered seemingly hopeless.—Robert C. Winthrop.

The hand that wrote the Declaration of Independence has long ago palsied in death. For more than sixty years Charles Carroll, the last member of that immortal company who appended their names to that famous document, has been slumbering in his grave, but the Declaration is yet a living fact, and to-day the instrument has as much force and meaning as it had one hundred and —— years ago.— Christian Enquirer.

Standing, as we do to-day, upon the eminence of more than a century's growth, we can look back the way we have come and see more plainly than it ever appeared before that on the little hill just out of Boston the battle of the 17th of June, 1775, changed, indeed, the front of the universe and set liberty so far in advance of tyranny that liberty will never be overtaken again. Children born in America since that day are heirs to all which that victory portended, and the further up the slope of centuries we go the richer will be our inheritance if we are wise and patriotic enough to appreciate, guard and defend the heritage that our fathers won and handed down.—Rev. W. B. Riley.

The dignity of the act is the deliberate, circumspect, open, and serene performance by these men in the clear light of day, and by a concurrent purpose, of a civic duty, which embraced the greatest hazards to themselves and to all the people from whom they held this deputed discretion, but which, to their sober judgments, promised benefits to that people and their posterity, from generation to generation, exceeding these hazards and commensurate with its own fitness.—Wm. M. Evarts.

The bravest and best men of all times have perished in the struggles against tyranny and despotism, and free government has never secured even a feeble existence save at a most fearful cost. The experiment of republican government in our own country is similar to that of all others. Here, however, liberty has won her grandest triumphs. Here freedom is enthroned securely and is the unchallenged boon of every inhabitant. But we contemplate the cost of the victory with mournful and pitying hearts. To secure it the patriots of the Revolution died; to secure it the hosts who fell in the struggle against the Rebellion were sacrificed.—H. E. Havens.

These are reasons why the most should be made of our national festivals in the direct line of keeping alive our national principles, and it is a happy circumstance that our public schools have become awake to the fact, and are making the exercises of the day before each national holiday point especially to that day. It is a happy circumstance, too, that many of our country towns are going back to the "good old way" of celebrating the "Glorious Fourth": the parade and the reading of the Declaration of Independence and the oration by some genius, local or imported. Even the spread-eagleism which generally characterizes such effusions is not without its value in rekindling the fire of patriotism, which is apt to be pretty deeply buried under the ashes of commonplace self-seeking. —New York Evangelist.

In what region of the earth ever so remote from us, in what corner of creation ever so far out of the range of our communication, does not some burden lightened, some bond loosened, some yoke lifted, some labor better remunerated, some new hope for despairing hearts, some new light or new liberty for the benighted or the oppressed, bear witness this day, and trace itself, directly or indirectly, back to the impulse given to the world by the successful establishment and operation of free institutions on this American continent?—Robert C. Winthrop.

"We wish that whoever in all coming time shall turn his eye hither, may behold that the place is not undistinguished where the first great battle of

the Revolution was fought. We wish that this structure may proclaim the magnitude and importance of that event, to every class, in every age. We wish that infancy may learn the purpose of its erection from maternal lips, and that weary and withered age may behold it, and be solaced by the recollections it suggests. We wish that labor may look up here, and be proud, in the midst of its toil. We wish that, in those days of disaster, which, as they come on all nations, must be expected to come on us also, desponding patriotism may turn its eyes hitherward, and be assured that the foundations of our national power still stand strong. We wish that this column, rising toward heaven among the pointed spires of so many temples dedicated to God, may contribute also to produce in all minds a pious feeling of dependence and gratitude. We wish, finally, that the last object on the sight of him who leaves his native shore, and the first to gladden his who revisits it, may be something which shall remind him of the liberty and the glory of his country. Let it rise till it meets the sun in his coming; let the earliest light of the morning gild it, and parting day linger and play on its summit.—Daniel Webster, Dedication Bunker Hill Monument.

Indexes

Time is of more value than type, and the wear and tear of the temper than an extra page of index.—R. H. Busk.

If a book has no index or good table of contents, it is very useful to make one as you are reading it.—Dr. Watts.

I wish you would add an *index rerum*, that when the reader recollects any incident he may easily find it.— Dr. Johnson.

I certainly think that the best book in the world would owe the most to a good index, and the worst book, if it had but a single good thought in it, might be kept alive by it.—Horace Binney.

So essential did I consider an index to be to every book, that I proposed to bring a bill into Parliament to deprive an author who publishes a book without an index of the privilege of copyright, and, moreover, to subject him for his offence to a pecuniary penalty. —Lord Campbell.

Indian Summer

It is the Indian summer. The rising sun blazes through the misty air like a conflagration. A yellowish, smoky haze fills the atmosphere, and a filmy mist lies like a silver lining on the sky. The wind is soft and low. It wafts to us the odor of forest leaves, that hang wilted on the dripping branches, or drop into the stream. Their gorgeous tints are gone, as if the autumnal rains had washed them out. Orange, yellow and scarlet, all are changed to one melancholy russet hue. The birds, too, have taken wing, and have left their roofless dwellings. Not the whistle of a robin, not the twitter of an eaves-dropping swallow, not the carol of one sweet, familiar voice. All gone. Only the dismal cawing of a crow, as he sits and curses that the harvest is over; or the chit-chat of an idle squirrel, the noisy denizen of a hollow tree, the mendicant friar of a large parish, the absolute monarch of a dozen acorns.— Longfellow.

Indifference

The indifference of men, far more than their tyranny, is the torment of women.—Michelet.

Indifference is the invincible grant of the world.—Oudia.

Of all heavy bodies, the heaviest is the woman we have ceased to love.— Lemontey.

Selfish people, with no heart to speak of, have the best time of it.— H. W. Shaw.

How chronic is the unconcern of men and women of the world!—Miss Braddon.

The depreciation of Christianity by indifference is a more insidious and less curable evil than infidelity itself. —Whately.

What is a woman's surest guardian angel? Indifference.—Mme. Deluzy.

Indifferent souls never part. Impassioned souls part, and return to one another, because they can do no better. —Mme. Swetchine.

A lady of fashion will sooner excuse a freedom flowing from admiration than a slight resulting from indifference —Colton.

Affection can withstand very severe storms of vigor, but not a long polar frost of indifference.—Sir Walter Scott.

Mme. Deluzy has said that indifference is a woman's guardian angel,—a remark not only applicable in France, but all over the world.—Anna Cora Mowatt.

Let the world slide, let the world go;
A fig for care, and a fig for woe!
If I can't pay, why I can owe,
And death makes equal the high and low.
—John Heywood.

She commands who is blest with indifference.—Chamfort.

When one becomes indifferent to women, to children, and young people, he may know that he is superannuated, and has withdrawn from whatsoever is sweetest and purest in human existence.—Alcott.

Shall I, wasting in despair,
Die because a woman's fair?
Or make pale my cheeks with care,
'Cause another's rosy are?
Be she fairer than the day,
Or the flow'ry meads in May,
If she be not so to me,
What care I how fair she be?
—Geo. Wither.

Indiscretion

Wicked is not much worse than indiscreet.—Donne.

Indiscretion and wickedness, be it known, are first cousins.—Ninon de Lenclos.

The generality of men expend the early part of their lives in contributing to render the latter part miserable.— La Bruyère.

We waste our best years in distilling the sweetest flowers of life into potions which, after all, do not immortalize, but only intoxicate.—Longfellow.

Three things too much and three too little are pernicious to man : to speak much and know little ; to spend much and have little ; to presume much and be worth little.—Cervantes.

An indiscreet man is more hurtful than an ill-natured one ; for as the latter will only attack his enemies, and those he wishes ill to, the other ,injures indifferently both friends and foes.—Addison.

A man should be careful never to tell tales of himself to his own disadvantage; people may be amused, and laugh at the time, but they will be remembered, and brought up against him upon some subsequent occasion.—Johnson.

Individuality

Every great man is a unique. The Scipionism of Scipio is precisely that part he could not borrow.—Emerson.

Individuals, not stations, ornament society.—Gladstone.

Individuality is everywhere to be spared and respected as the root of everything good.—Richter.

The worth of a state, in the long run, is the worth of the individuals composing it.—J. S. Mill.

Every individual has a place to fill in the world, and is important in some respect, whether he chooses to be so or not.—Hawthorne.

The greatness of an artist or a writer does not depend on what he has in common with other artists and writers, but on what he has peculiar to himself.—Alexander Smith.

Thou art in the end what thou art. Put on wigs with millions of curls, set thy foot upon ell-high rocks. Thou abidest ever—what thou art.—Goethe.

God gave every man individuality of constitution, and a chance for achieving individuality of character. He

puts special instruments into every man's hands by which to make himself and achieve his mission.—J. G. Holland.

Let us shun everything which might tend to efface the primitive lineaments of our individuality. Let us reflect that each one of us is a thought of God.—Mme. Swetchine.

The epoch of individuality is concluded, and it is the duty of reformers to initiate the epoch of association. Collective man is omnipotent upon the earth he treads.—Mazzini.

Not nations, not armies, have advanced the race; but here and there, in the course of ages, an individual has stood up and cast his shadow over the world.—Chapin.

Experience serves to prove that the worth and strength of a state depend far less upon the form of its institutions than upon the character of its men; for the nation is only the aggregate of individual conditions, and civilization itself is but a question of personal improvement.—Samuel Smiles.

We move too much in platoons; we march by sections; we do not live in our vital individuality enough; we are slaves to fashion, in mind and in heart, if not to our passions and appetites.—Chapin.

An institution is the lengthened shadow of one man; as, monachism of the Hermit Anthony, the Reformation of Luther, Quakerism of Fox, Methodism of Wesley, abolition of Clarkson. Scipio, Milton called "the height of Rome ;" and all history resolves itself easily into the biography of a few stout and earnest persons. Let a man, then, know his worth, and keep things under his feet.—Emerson.

Every individual nature has its own beauty. One is struck in every company, at every fireside, with the riches of nature, when he hears so many new tones, all musical, sees in each person original manners, which have a proper and peculiar charm, and reads new expressions of face. He perceives that nature has laid for each the foundations of a divine building, if the soul will build thereon.—Emerson.

Human faculties are common, but that which converges these faculties into my identity separates me from every other man. That other man cannot think my thoughts, he cannot speak my words, he cannot do my works. He cannot have my sins, I cannot have his virtues.—Henry Giles.

Indolence

The paralysis of the soul.—Lavater.

The canker-worm of every gentle breast.—Spenser.

Lives spent in indolence, and therefore sad.—Cowper.

The sluggard is a living insensible. —Zimmermann.

Indolence is the sleep of the mind.— Vauvenargues.

Indolence is the devil's cushion.— Dr. Johnson.

As a sex, women are habitually indolent; and everything tends to make them so.—Mary Wollstonecraft.

A useless life is but an early death. —Goethe.

Nothing is difficult; it is only we who are indolent.—B. R. Haydon.

Indolence and stupidity are first cousins.—Rivarol.

Go to the ant, thou sluggard; consider her ways, and be wise.—Bible.

What is often called indolence is in fact the unconscious consciousness of incapacity.—H. C. Robinson.

The want of occupation is no less the plague of society than of solitude. —Rousseau.

The desire of leisure is much more natural than of business and care.— Sir W. Temple.

We bring forth weeds when our quick minds lie still.—Shakespeare.

Indolence, languid as it is, often masters both passions and virtues.— Rochefoucauld.

Who conquers indolence conquers all other hereditary sins.—Zimmermann.

Thou seest how sloth wastes the sluggish body, as water is corrupted unless it moves.—Ovid.

Never suffer youth to be an excuse for inadequacy, nor age and fame to be an excuse for indolence.—B. R. Haydon.

We have more indolence in the mind than in the body.—Rochefoucauld.

I look upon indolence as a sort of suicide; for the man is effectually destroyed, though the appetite of the brute may survive.—Chesterfield.

It should seem that indolence itself would incline a person to be honest; as it requires infinitely greater pains and contrivance to be a knave.—Shenstone.

Indolence is the worst enemy that the church has to encounter. Men sleep around her altar, stretching themselves on beds of ease, or sit idly with folded hands looking lazily out on fields white for the harvest, but where no sickle rings against the wheat.—Bishop Huntington.

If men were weaned from their sauntering humor, wherein they let a good part of their lives run uselessly away, they would acquire skill in hundreds of things.—Locke.

An idle man has a constant tendency to torpidity. He has adopted the Indian maxim—that it is better to walk than to run, and better to stand than to walk, and better to sit than to stand, and better to lie than to sit. He hugs himself into the notion, that God calls him to be quiet.—Richard Cecil.

If you ask me which is the real hereditary sin of human nature, do you imagine I shall answer pride, or luxury, or ambition, or egotism? No; I shall say indolence. Who conquers indolence will conquer all the rest. Indeed all good principles must stagnate without mental activity.—Zimmermann.

To do nothing is in every man's power; we can never want an opportunity of omitting duties. The lapse to indolence is soft and imperceptible, because it is only a mere cessation of activity; but the return to diligence is difficult, because it implies a change from rest to motion, from a privation to reality.—Dr. Johnson.

Indulgence

A fat kitchen makes a lean will.—Franklin.

Rare indulgence produces greater pleasure.—Juvenal.

Feast to-day makes fast to-morrow.—Plautus.

Indulgence, twin sister of guilt.—Mme. Necker.

Indulgence is lovely in the sinless; toleration, adorable in the pious and believing heart.—Mme. Swetchine.

Had doting Priam checked his son's desire, Troy had been bright with fame, and not with fire.—Shakespeare.

Industry

Hell itself must yield to industry.—Ben Jonson.

Keep your working power at its maximum.—W. R. Alger.

Industry need not wish.—Benjamin Franklin.

Sloth makes all things difficult, but industry all things easy.—Benjamin Franklin.

Few things are impossible to diligence and skill.—Johnson.

Plough deep while sluggards sleep.—Franklin.

Nothing is denied to well-directed labor.—Sir Joshua Reynolds.

Genius begins great works, labor alone finishes them.—Joubert.

Diligence is the mother of good luck.—Franklin.

The laborer is worthy of his hire.—Bible.

In every rank, or great or small,
'Tis industry supports us all.
   —Gay.

The sweat of industry would dry, and die,
But for the end it works to.
   —Shakespeare.

Seest thou a man diligent in his business? he shall stand before kings.—Bible.

The more we do, the more we can do; the more busy we are, the more leisure we have.—Hazlitt.

In this theater of man's life, it is reserved only for God and angels to be lookers-on.—Pythagoras.

One loses all the time which he can employ better.—Rousseau.

Industry has annexed thereto the fairest fruits and the richest rewards.—Barrow.

The end of labor is to gain leisure. It is a great saying.—Aristotle.

That man is but of the lower part of the world that is not brought up to business and affairs.—Feltham.

Earnest, active industry is a living hymn of praise,—a never-failing source of happiness.—Mme. de Wald.

We mistake the gratuitous blessings of heaven for the fruits of our own industry.—L'Estrange.

The great end of all human industry is the attainment of happiness.—Hume.

At the workingman's house, hunger looks in, but dares not enter.—Benjamin Franklin.

Genius is the father of a heavenly line, but the mortal mother, that is industry.—Theodore Parker.

In the ordinary business of life, industry can do anything which genius can do, and very many things which it cannot.—Henry Ward Beecher.

Shortly his fortune shall be lifted higher;
True industry doth kindle honour's fire.
—Shakespeare.

God has so made the mind of man that a peculiar deliciousness resides in the fruits of personal industry.—Wilberforce.

A man who gives his children habits of industry provides for them better than by giving them a fortune.—Whately.

A plodding diligence brings us sooner to our journey's end than a fluttering way of advancing by starts.—L'Estrange.

Application is the price to be paid for mental acquisition. To have the harvest, we must sow the seed.—Bailey.

If you have great talents, industry will improve them; if you have but moderate abilities, industry will supply their deficiencies.—Samuel Smiles.

Industry is a Christian obligation, imposed on our race to develop the noblest energies, and insures the highest reward.—E. L. Magoon.

Honorable industry always travels the same road with enjoyment and duty, and progress is altogether impossible without it.—Samuel Smiles.

Mankind are more indebted to industry than ingenuity; the gods set up their favors at a price, and industry is the purchaser.—Addison.

The bread earned by the sweat of the brow is thrice blessed bread, and it is far sweeter than the tasteless loaf of idleness.—Crowquill.

No man is born into the world whose work is not born with him: there is always work, and tools to work withal, for those who will; and blessed are the horny hands of toil!—Lowell.

The way to wealth is as plain as the way to market. It depends chiefly on two words, industry and frugality;

that is, waste neither time nor money, but make the best use of both.—Franklin.

Well for the drones of the social hive that there are bees of an industrious turn, willing, for an infinitesimal share of the honey, to undertake the labor of its fabrication.—Hood.

I have observed that as long as one lives and bestirs himself, he can always find food and raiment, though it may not be of the choicest description.—Goethe.

Whenever you see want or misery or degradation in this world about you, then be sure either industry has been wanting, or industry has been in error.—Ruskin.

The celebrated Galen said employment was nature's physician. It is indeed so important to happiness that indolence is justly considered the parent of misery.—Colton.

Our remedies oft in ourselves do lie,
Which we ascribe to Heav'n. The fated
  sky
Gives us free scope; only doth backward
  pull
Our slow designs, when we ourselves are
  dull. —Shakespeare.

Everything is sold to skill and labor; and where nature furnishes the materials, they are still rude and unfinished, till industry, ever active and intelligent, refines them from their brute state, and fits them for human use and convenience.—Hume.

Protected industry, careering far,
Detects the cause and cures the rage of
  war,
And sweeps, with forceful arm, to their
  last graves,
Kings from the earth and pirates from the
  waves. —Joel Barlow.

The great high-road of human welfare lies along the old highway of steadfast well-doing; and they who are the most persistent, and work in the true spirit, will invariably be the most successful. Success treads on the heels of every right effort.—Samuel Smiles.

Wherever a ship ploughs the sea, or a plough furrows the field; wherever a mine yields its treasure; wherever a ship or a railroad train carries freight to market; wherever the smoke of the furnace rises, or the clang of the loom resounds; even in the lonely garret where the seamstress plies her busy needle—there is industry.—Garfield.

Industry is not only the instrument of improvement, but the foundation of pleasure. He who is a stranger to it may possess, but cannot enjoy; for it is labor only which gives relish to pleasure. It is the appointed vehicle of every good to man. It is the indispensable condition of possessing a sound mind in a sound body.—Blair.

Why, man of idleness, labor has rocked you in the cradle, and nourished your pampered life; without it, the woven silk and the wool upon your back would be in the shepherd's fold. For the meanest thing that ministers to human want, save the air of heaven, man is indebted to toil; and even the air, in God's wise ordination, is breathed with labor.—Chapin.

There is no art or science that is too difficult for industry to attain to; it is the gift of tongues, and makes a man understood and valued in all countries and by all nations; it is the philosopher's stone, that turns all metals, and even stones, into gold, and suffers not want to break into its dwelling; it is the northwest passage, that brings the merchant's ship as soon to him as he can desire. In a word, it conquers all enemies and makes fortune itself pay contribution.—Clarendon.

Inequality

One-half of the world must sweat and groan that the other half may dream.—Longfellow.

Inevitable (The)

To face the inevitable is to confront something sacred. As long as anything is uncertain, the roads are open in more than one direction, and right and wrong may have many aspects. But let the issue be determined, let the die be cast, and acceptance and adjustment become our immediate duty. Until God's will is known, we may work and wrestle and pray to carry our point, to save the day, to win the prize, spurred only the more by the uncertainty of the result. But let the result be known, however dark and disappointing, and we should view it in the light of God's plan to make us His evident children, and ask what we are to learn, what next we are to do. Chafing, fretting and complaining are more than a waste of time and energy. End that episode with an amen. Refer the inevitable to God, and face the future, not only with knowledge born of new experience, but with the courage born of the faith, that God's will is always best, and sooner or later will seem best to us.

Infancy (See Childhood)

A babe in a house is a well-spring of pleasure.—Tupper.

Of all the joys that brighten suffering earth,
What joy is welcom'd like a new-born child?
—Mrs. Norton.

A young star, who shone
O'er life, too sweet an image for such gloss,
A lovely being scarcely form'd or moulded,
A rose with all its sweetest leaves yet folded.
—Byron.

Joy thou bring'st, but mix'd with trembling;
Anxious hopes and tender fears,
Pleasing hopes and mingled sorrows,
Smiles of transport dashed with tears.
—Cottle.

'Tis aye a solemn thing to me
To look upon a babe that sleeps—
Wearing in its spirit-deeps
The unrevealed mystery
Of its Adam's taint and woe,
Which, when they revealed lie,
Will not let it slumber so.
—Mrs. Browning.

The hour arrives, the moment wish'd and fear'd,
The child is born by many a pang endear'd,
And now the mother's ear has caught his cry;
O grant the cherub to her asking eye!
He comes—she clasps him. To her bosom press'd
He drinks the balm of life, and drops to rest.
—Rogers.

Infatuation

An infatuated man is not only foolish, but wild.—Crabbe.

Passion is the infatuation of the mind.—South.

The evil of infatuation is illustrated by the drunkard.—John B. Gough.

Infatuation is the language of a beautiful eye upon a sensitive heart.—Joseph Bartlett.

Infidelity

The fool hath said in his heart, There is no God.—Bible.

The nurse of infidelity is sensuality.—Cecil.

Now, infidel, I have thee on the hip.—Shakespeare.

What ardently we wish, we soon believe.—Young.

Infidelity, like death, admits of no degrees.—Mme. de Girardin.

Freethinkers are generally those that never think at all.—Laurence Sterne.

No one is so much alone in the universe as a denier of God.—Richter.

An atheist has got one point beyond the devil.—Swift.

There is not a single spot between Christianity and atheism, upon which a man can firmly fix his foot.—Emmons.

I know not any crime so great that a man could contrive to commit as poisoning the sources of eternal truth.—Samuel Johnson.

There never yet was a mother who taught her child to be an infidel.—Henry W. Shaw.

To destroy the ideas of immortality of the soul is to add death to death.—Madame de Souza.

A foe to God was ne'er true friend to man;
Some sinister intent taints all he does.
—Young.

General infidelity is the hardest soil which the propagators of a new religion can have to work upon.—Paley.

They that deny a God destroy a man's nobility.—Bacon.

There is but one thing without honor, smitten with eternal barrenness, inability to do or to be—insincerity, unbelief.—Carlyle.

When once infidelity can persuade men that they shall die like beasts, they will soon be brought to live like beasts also.—South.

What can be more foolish than to think that all this rare fabric of heaven and earth could come by chance when all the skill of art is not able to make an oyster?—Jeremy Taylor.

There is one single fact, which one may oppose to all the wit and argument of infidelity, namely, that no man ever repented of being a Christian on his death-bed.—Hannah More.

They that deny a God, destroy a man's nobility; for certainly man is of kin to the beasts by his body; and if he is not kin to God by his spirit he is a base and ignoble creature.—Bacon.

I would rather dwell in the dim fog of superstition than in air rarefied to nothing by the air-pump of unbelief—in which the panting breast expires, vainly and convulsively gasping for breath.—Richter.

A skeptical young man one day conversing with the celebrated Dr. Parr, observed that he would believe nothing which he could not understand. "Then, young man, your creed will be the shortest of any man's I know."—Helps.

Mere negation, mere Epicurean infidelity, as Lord Bacon most justly observes, has never disturbed the peace of the world. It furnishes no motive for action; it inspires no enthusiasm; it has no missionaries, no crusades, no martyrs.—Macaulay.

Infidelity is one of those coinages—a mass of base money that won't pass current with any heart that loves truly, or any head that thinks correctly. And infidels are poor sad creatures; they carry about them a load of dejection and desolation, not the less heavy that it is invisible. It is the fearful blindness of the soul.—Chalmers.

Infidelity gives nothing in return for what it takes away. What, then, is it worth? Everything valuable has a compensating power. Not a blade of grass that withers, or the ugliest weed that is flung away to rot and die, but reproduces something.—Chalmers.

No men deserve the title of infidels so little as those to whom it has been usually applied; let any of those who renounce Christianity, write fairly down in a book all the absurdities that they believe instead of it, and they will find that it requires more faith to reject Christianity than to embrace it.—Colton.

Infidelity and faith look both through the perspective glass, but at contrary ends. Infidelity looks through the wrong end of the glass; and, therefore, sees those objects near which are afar off, and makes great things little—diminishing the greatest spiritual blessings, and removing far from us threatened evils. Faith looks at the right end, and brings the blessings that are far off in time close to our eye, and multiplies God's mercies, which, in a distance, lost their greatness.—Bishop Hall.

Infinite

The thirst for the infinite proves infinity.—Victor Hugo.

Finite mind cannot comprehend infinity.—Jeremiah Seed.

God has thickly strewn infinity with grandeur.—Alexander Smith.

The finite is annihilated in the presence of infinity, and becomes a simple nothing.—Pascal.

It is only the finite that has wrought and suffered; the infinite lies stretched in smiling repose.—Emerson.

Infinity is the retirement in which perfect love and wisdom only dwell with God. In infinity and eternity the skeptic sees an abyss in which all is

lost. I see in them the residence of Almighty power, in which my reason and my wishes find equally a firm support. Here, holding by the pillars of heaven, I exist—I stand fast.—Miller.

That which we foolishly call vastness is, rightly considered, not more wonderful, not more impressive, than that which we insolently call littleness; and the infinity of God is not mysterious, it is only unfathomable, not concealed, but incomprehensible: it is a clear infinity, the darkness of the pure, unsearchable sea.—Ruskin.

Influence

Men are what their mothers made them.—Emerson.

I am a part of all that I have met.—Tennyson.

Woman's influence embraces the whole of life.—Alexander Walker.

You can only make others better by being good yourself.—Hugh R. Haweis.

Influence is exerted by every human being from the hour of birth to that of death.—Chapin.

It is by women that nature writes on the hearts of men.—Sheridan.

A woman is more influenced by what she divines than by what she is told.—Ninon de Lenclos.

If woman lost us Eden, such as she alone restore it!—Whittier.

We perceive and are affected by changes too subtle to be described.—Thoreau.

He raised a mortal to the skies;
She drew an angel down.
—Dryden.

Not one false man but does uncountable mischief.—Carlyle.

The humblest individual exerts some influence, either for good or evil, upon others.—Beecher.

The serene, silent beauty of a holy life is the most powerful influence in the world, next to the might of the Spirit of God.—C. H. Spurgeon.

Blessed influence of one true loving human soul on another.—George Eliot.

It is a maxim that no man was ever enslaved by influence while he was fit to be free.—Johnson.

Race and temperament go for much in influencing opinion.—Lady Morgan.

He is greatest whose strength carries up the most hearts by the attraction of his own.—Henry Ward Beecher.

Every thought which genius and piety throw into the world alters the world.—Emerson.

No life
Can be pure in its purpose and strong in its strife,
And all life not be purer and stronger thereby.   —Owen Meredith.

The influence of woman will ever be exercised directly in all good or evil. Give her, then, such light as she is capable of receiving.—Lady Morgan.

Nothing more surely cultivates and embellishes a man than association with refined and virtuous women.—Gladstone.

Every man is a missionary, now and forever, for good or for evil, whether he intends or designs it or not.—Chalmers.

No human being can come into this world without increasing or diminishing the sum total of human happiness.—Elihu Burritt.

If I can put one touch of a rosy sunset into the life of any man or woman, I shall feel that I have worked with God.—George MacDonald.

The work an unknown good man has done is like a vein of water flowing hidden underground, secretly making the ground green.—Carlyle.

We must succumb to the general influence of the times. No man can be

of the tenth century, if he would; he must be a man of the nineteenth century.—Macaulay.

Would Shakespeare and Raleigh have done their best, would that galaxy have shone so bright in the heavens had there been no Elizabeth on the throne?—Alcott.

No man or woman of the humblest sort can really be strong, gentle, pure, and good, without somebody being helped and comforted by the very existence of that goodness.—Phillips Brooks.

The career of a great man remains an enduring monument of human energy. The man dies and disappears, but his thoughts and acts survive, and leave an indelible stamp upon his race.—Samuel Smiles.

Such souls,
Whose sudden visitations daze the world,
Vanish like lightning, but they leave behind
A voice that in the distance far away
Wakens the slumbering ages.
          —Sir Henry Taylor.

It is an old saying, and one of fearful and fathomless import, that we are forming characters for eternity. Forming characters! Whose? our own or others? Both—and in that momentous fact lies the peril and responsibility of our existence. Who is sufficient for the thought?—Elihu Burritt.

It is very true that I have said that I considered Napoleon's presence in the field equal to forty thousand men in the balance. This is a very loose way of talking; but the idea is a very different one from that of his presence at a battle being equal to a reinforcement of forty thousand men.—Duke of Wellington.

So when a great man dies,
For years beyond our ken,
The light he leaves behind him lies
Upon the paths of men.
          —Longfellow.

Ingratitude

One ungrateful man does an injury to all who are in suffering.—Syrus.

Ingratitude is treason to mankind.—Thomson.

The wicked are always ungrateful.—Cervantes.

Ingratitude is abhorred by God and man.—L'Estrange.

You love a nothing when you love an ingrate.—Plautus.

He that is ungrateful has no guilt but one; all other crimes may pass for virtues in him.—Young.

How sharper than a serpent's tooth it is
To have a thankless child. —Shakespeare.

To be ungrateful is to be unnatural. The head may be thus guilty, not the heart.—Rivarol.

Brutes leave ingratitude to man.—Colton.

Earth produces nothing worse than an ungrateful man.—Ausonius.

Ingratitude is monstrous; and for the multitude to be ingrateful were to make a monster of the multitude.—Shakespeare.

The animal with long ears, after having drunk, gives a kick to the bucket.—From the Italian.

Ingratitude calls forth reproaches, as gratitude brings fresh kindnesses.—Madame de Sévigné.

He that calls a man ungrateful sums up all the evil that a man can be guilty of.—Swift.

Ingratitude dries up the fountain of all goodness.—Richelieu.

There is something noble in hearing myself ill spoken of when I am doing well.—Alexander the Great.

Flints may be melted—we see it daily—but an ungrateful heart cannot; no, not by the strongest and the noblest flame.—South.

Throw no stones into the well whence you have drunk.—Talmud.

How bitter it is to reap a harvest of evil for good that you have done.—Plautus.

Men may be ungrateful, but the human race is not so.—De Boufflers.

Ingratitude is the abridgment of all baseness,—a fault never found unattended with other viciousness.—Fuller.

He that forgets his friend is ungrateful to him; but he that forgets his Saviour is unmerciful to himself.—Bunyan.

One great cause of our insensibility to the goodness of our Creator is the very extensiveness of His bounty.—Paley.

We seldom find people ungrateful as long as we are in a condition to render them services.—La Rochefoucauld.

Do you know what is more hard to bear than the reverses of fortune? It is the baseness, the hideous ingratitude, of man.—Napoleon.

Ingratitude is always a kind of weakness. I have never seen that clever men have been ungrateful.—Goethe.

Ingratitude never so thoroughly pierces the human breast as when it proceeds from those in whose behalf we have been guilty of transgressions.—Fielding.

The worst of ingratitude lies not in the ossified heart of him who commits it, but we find it in the effect it produces on him against whom it was committed.—Landor.

Man is, beyond dispute, the most excellent of created beings, and the vilest animal is a dog; but the sages agree that a grateful dog is better than an ungrateful man.—Saadi.

I hate ingratitude more in a man
Than lying, vainness, babbling, drunkenness,
Or any taint of vice, whose strong corruption
Inhabits our frail blood. —Shakespeare.

Everybody takes pleasure in returning small obligations; many go so far as to acknowledge moderate ones; but there is hardly any one who does not repay great obligations with ingratitude.—Rochefoucauld.

Ingratitude is a nail which, driven into the tree of courtesy, causes it to wither; it is a broken channel, by which the foundations of the affections are undermined; and a lump of soot, which, falling into the dish of friendship, destroys its scent and flavor.—Basil.

The greatest evils in human society are such as no law can come at; as in the case of ingratitude, where the manner of obligation very often leaves the benefactor without means of demanding justice, though that very circumstance should be the more binding to the person who has received the benefit.—Steele.

Blow, blow, thou winter wind,
Thou art not so unkind
As man's ingratitude;
Thy tooth is not so keen,
Because thou art not seen,
Although thy breath be rude.
—Shakespeare.

So the struck eagle stretch'd upon the plain,
No more through rolling clouds to soar again,
View'd his own feather on the fatal dart,
And wing'd the shaft that quivered in his heart:
Keen were his pangs, but keener far to feel
He nurs'd the pinion which impelled the steel. —Byron.

You may rest upon this as an unfailing truth, that there neither is, nor never was, any person remarkably ungrateful, who was not also insufferably proud. In a word, ingratitude is too base to return a kindness, too proud to regard it, much like the tops of mountains, barren indeed, but yet lofty; they produce nothing; they feed nobody; they clothe nobody; yet are high and stately, and look down upon all the world.—South.

Inheritance
Say not you know another, until you have divided an inheritance with him. —Lavater.

They who provide much wealth for their children, but neglect to improve

them in virtue, do like those who feed their horses high, but never train them to the *ménage.*—Socrates.

Enjoy what thou hast inherited from thy sires if thou wouldst possess it; what we employ not is an oppressive burden; what the moment brings forth, that only can it profit by.—Goethe.

Injuries
No man is hurt but by himself.—Diogenes.

Slight small injuries, and they'll become none at all.—Fuller.

Christianity commands us to pass by injuries; policy, to let them pass by us.—Franklin.

There is no ghost so difficult to lay as the ghost of an injury.—Alexander Smith.

Recompense injury with justice, and recompense kindness with kindness.—Confucius.

Lay silently the injuries you receive upon the altar of oblivion.—Hosea Ballou.

No man ever did a designed injury to another without doing a greater to himself.—Henry Home.

He who has injured thee was either stronger or weaker; if weaker, spare him; if stronger, spare thyself.—Seneca.

Nothing can work me damage except myself; the harm that I sustain I carry about with me, and never am a real sufferer but by my own fault.—St. Bernard.

If men wound you with injuries, meet them with patience: hasty words rankle the wound, soft language dresses it, forgiveness cures it, and oblivion takes away the scar. It is more noble by silence to avoid an injury than by argument to overcome it. —J. Beaumont.

To willful men, the injuries that they themselves procure must be their schoolmasters.—Shakespeare.

As a Christian should do no injuries to others, so he should forgive the injuries that others do to him. It is to be like God, who is a good-giving God, and a sin-forgiving God.—R. Venning.

Injuries accompanied by insults are never forgiven, all men on these occasions are good haters, and lay out their revenge at compound interest.—Colton.

Injustice

Fraud is the ready minister of injustice.—Burke.

The world has no long injustices.—Mme. de Sévigné.

Extremists are seldom just.—Paley.

If thou sustain injustice, console thyself; the true unhappiness is in doing it.—Democritus.

He who commits injustice is ever made more wretched than he who suffers it.—Plato.

The injustice of men subserves the justice of God, and often His mercy.—Mme. Swetchine.

Those who commit injustice bear the greatest burden.—Hosea Ballou.

Did the mass of men know the actual selfishness and injustice of their rulers, not a government would stand a year. The world would foment with revolution.—Theodore Parker.

The greatest of all injustice is that which goes under the name of law; and of all sorts of tyranny the forcing the letter of the law against the equity is the most insupportable.—L'Estrange.

He that acts unjustly
Is the worst rebel to himself; and though
  now
Ambition's trumpet. and the drum of power
May drown the sound, yet conscience will
  one day
Speak loudly to him.   —Havard.

Injustice arises either from precipitation or indolence, or from a mixture of both. The rapid and the slow are seldom just; the unjust wait either not at all, or wait too long.—Lavater.

It is not possible to found a lasting power upon injustice, perjury, and treachery. These may, perhaps, succeed for once, and borrow for awhile, from hope, a gay and flourishing appearance. But time betrays their weakness, and they fall into ruin of themselves. For, as in structures of every kind, the lower parts should have the greatest firmness—so the grounds and principles of actions should be just and true.—Demosthenes.

Ink

A drop of ink may make a million think.—Byron.

The colored slave that waits upon thought.—Mrs. Balfour.

Ink is the transcript of thought.—Lamartine.

The blackest of fluid is used as an agent to enlighten the world.—Douglas Jerrold.

Inn

There is nothing which has yet been contrived by man, by which so much happiness is produced as by a good tavern or inn.—Johnson.

Now spurs the lated traveler apace
To gain the timely inn.   —Shakespeare.

Whoe'er has travel'd life's dull round,
  Where'er his stages may have been,
May sigh to think he still has found
  The warmest welcome, at an inn.
      —Shenstone.

Near yonder thorn, that lifts its head on
  high,
Where once the sign-post caught the passing
  eye,
Low lies that house where nut-brown
  draughts inspired,
Where graybeard mirth and smiling toil retired,
Where village statesmen talk'd with looks
  profound,
And news much older than their ale went
  round.   —Goldsmith.

Innocence

Happy the innocent whose equal thoughts are free from anguish as they are from faults.—Waller.

Unto the pure all things are pure.—Bible.

Innocence is ignorance.—Mme. de Girardin.

The innocent seldom find an uneasy pillow.—Cowper.

Innocence is always unsuspicious.—Haliburton.

They that know no evil will suspect none.—Ben Jonson.

Oh, keep me innocent, make others great.—Written on a Window by Caroline.

Who knows nothing base, fears nothing known.—Owen Meredith.

The most effective coquetry is innocence.—Lamartine.

The first of all virtues is innocence; the next is modesty.—Addison.

He's armed without that's innocent within.—Pope.

There is no courage but in innocence, no constancy but in an honest cause.—Southern.

What can innocence hope for, When such as sit her judges are corrupted!
—Massinger.

The silence often of pure innocence Persuades, when speaking fails.
—Shakespeare.

Innocence is like polished armor; it adorns and it defends.—South.

Innocence and mystery never dwell long together.—Madame Necker.

Let our lives be pure as snow-fields, where our footsteps leave a mark, but not a stain.—Madame Swetchine.

Alas! innocence is but a poor substitute for experience.—Bulwer-Lytton.

Innocence is a flower which withers when touched, but blooms not again, though watered with tears.—Hooper.

Innocence finds not near so much protection as guilt.—Rochefoucauld.

There is a heroic innocence, as well as a heroic courage.—St. Evremond.

We have not the innocence of Eden; but by God's help and Christ's example we may have the victory of Gethsemane.—Chapin.

The innocence that feels no risk and is taught no caution is more vulnerable than guilt, and oftener assailed.—Willis.

To dread no eye and to suspect no tongue is the great prerogative of innocence—an exemption granted only to invariable virtue.—Dr. Johnson.

What a power there is in innocence! whose very helplessness is its safeguard: in whose presence even passion himself stands abashed, and stands worshipper at the very altar he came to despoil.—Moore.

Of all the sights which can soften and humanize the heart of man, there is none that ought so surely to reach it as that of innocent children enjoying the happiness which is their proper and natural portion.—Southey.

Coerced innocence is like an imprisoned lark,—open the door, and it is off forever. The bird that roams through the sky and the groves unrestrained knows how to dodge the hawk and protect itself; but the caged one, the moment it leaves its bars and bolts behind, is pounced upon by the fowler or the vulture.—Haliburton.

I have mark'd
A thousand blushing apparitions start
Into her face; a thousand innocent shames
In angel whiteness bear away those blushes;
And in her eye there hath appear'd a fire,
To burn the errors that these princes hold
Against her maiden truth. —Shakespeare.

O innocence, how glorious and happy a portion art thou to the breast that possesses thee! thou fearest neither the eyes nor the tongues of men. Truth, the most powerful of all things, is thy strongest friend; and the brighter the light is in which thou art displayed, the more it discovers thy transcendent beauties.—Fielding.

Inquisitiveness

Inquisitiveness is an uncomely guest.—Sir P. Sidney.

Few men are raised in our estimation by being too closely examined.—Balzac.

Shun the inquisitive person, for he is also a talker.—Horace.

Our inquisitive disposition is excited by having its gratification deferred.—Pliny the Younger.

An inquisitive man is a creature naturally very vacant of thought itself, and therefore forced to apply itself to foreign assistance.—Steele.

Inquisitive people are the funnels of conversation; they do not take in anything for their own use, but merely to pass it to another.—Steele.

Inquisitiveness or curiosity is a kernel of the forbidden fruit, which still sticketh in the throat of a natural man, and sometimes to the danger of his choking.—Fuller.

In ancient days the most celebrated precept was, "Know thyself;" in modern times it has been supplanted by the more fashionable maxim, "Know thy neighbor, and everything about him."—Johnson.

Shun the inquisitive, for thou wilt be sure to find him leaky; open ears do not keep conscientiously what has been intrusted to them, and a word once spoken flies never to be recalled.—Horace.

Insanity

Every madman thinks all other men mad.—Syrus.

Fetter strong madness in a silken thread.—Shakespeare.

Insanity is not a distinct and separate empire; our ordinary life borders upon it, and we cross the frontier in some part of our nature.—Taine.

Though this be madness, yet there is method in it.—Shakespeare.

I am not mad; I would to heaven I were! For then, 'tis like I should forget myself.
—Shakespeare.

There is a pleasure, sure,
In being mad, which none but madmen know!
—Dryden.

For those whom God to ruin has designed He fits for fate, and first destroys their mind.
—Dryden.

No excellent soul is exempt from a mixture of madness.—Aristotle.

Great wits are sure to madness near allied, and thin partitions do their bounds divide.—Dryden.

He appears mad indeed but to a few, because the majority is infected with the same disease.—Horace.

Oppression makes wise men mad; but the distemper is still the madness of the wise, which is better than the sobriety of fools.—Burke.

All power of fancy over reason is a degree of insanity.—Johnson.

With curious art the brain, too finely wrought, preys on itself, and is destroyed by thought.—Churchill.

The alleged power to charm down insanity, or ferocity in beasts, is a power behind the eye.—Emerson.

We are not ourselves
When nature, being oppress'd, commands the mind
To suffer with the body. —Shakespeare.

Much madness is divinest sense
To a discerning eye;
Much sense the starkest madness,
'Tis the majority
In this, as all, prevails.
Assent, and you are sane;
Demur,—you're straightway dangerous,
And handled with a chain.
—Emily Dickinson.

Ever as before does madness remain, terrific, altogether infernal, boiling up of the nether chaotic deep, through this fair painted vision of creation, which swims thereon, and which we name the real.—Carlyle.

If the raving be not directed to a single object it is mania, properly so called; if to one object, it constitutes monomania.—R. Dunglison.

Insincerity

Nothing is more disgraceful than insincerity.—Cicero.

It is a shameful and unseemly thing to think one thing and to speak another, but how odious to write one thing and to think another.—Seneca.

Insincerity in a man's own heart must make all his enjoyments, all that concerns him, unreal; so that his whole life must seem like a merely dramatic representation.—Hawthorne.

Inspiration

Inspiration and genius—one and the same.—Victor Hugo.

No man was ever great without divine inspiration.—Cicero.

Inspiration must find answering inspiration.—A. Bronson Alcott.

Contagious enthusiasm.—Mrs. Balfour.

Inspiration is solitary, never consecutive.—Lamartine.

Inspiration developed the noblest fantasies of the ancients.—Jules Janin.

He is gifted with genius who knoweth much by natural inspiration.—Pindar.

Do we not all agree to call rapid thought and noble impulse by the name of inspiration?—George Eliot.

Our poesy is as a Gum, which oozes
From whence 'tis nourish'd: The fire i' the flint
Shows not till it be struck; our gentle Flame
Provokes itself, and, like the current, flies
Each bound it chafes. —Shakespeare.

The glow of inspiration warms us; this holy rapture springs from the

seeds of the Divine mind sown in man. —Ovid.

Installation Service

Your employment is that of the Son of God; it makes no great appearance before men, but it will finally arise in majesty to overshadow all created glory.—Robert Hall.

Ever remember you are an ambassador of Christ. You have received a commission from the King of kings to be his representative, and to minister in His name to your fellow men.— Professor Duffield.

But again, may I not presume that I commend myself to you when I say that the essential part of your pastor's power to teach and guide must be derived from your consent and desire to submit to His guidance?—Rev. Alex. McGregor.

I charge you to preach the whole gospel, both sides of the gospel, and the only way of escape through faith in Christ.—Rev. E. O. Bartlett.

The minister of Christ, and all who are associated with him, should make diligent use of all legitimate means to bring to the gospel feast those who are perishing through lack of the bread of life and the water of life.—Professor Duffield.

Be tender, sympathetic, with nothing of arrogance or assumption in your manner or matter; only that earnestness which comes from a hearty faith in the great truths you utter. Contend earnestly for the faith once delivered to the saints, but in a kind spirit and with a mild temper, with entire candor, avoiding all that tends to provoke and irritate, seeking at all times to preserve "the bond of peace." —Rev. E. O. Bartlett.

As such, "salute no man by the way." Esteem no man your superior, or rather, esteem no one as having a superior work to do. Yours is the highest office God has committed to earthen vessels. It is the most important as related to this world or the next; important, because you bear the message of the King of kings and herald the gospel that saves souls.—Rev. E. O. Bartlett.

Speak boldly, with the courage of one whose inspiration and authority come from heaven. Fear no man; be under the dominion of no man or clique of men, for that bringeth a snare. Take counsel with God; and then come into this pulpit unshamed to preach His truth, and His truth only, whether men will hear, or whether they will forbear.—Rev. E. O. Bartlett.

Appropriate a due portion of your time to pastoral work, and cultivate such a personal acquaintance with every member of your charge—the lowliest and the youngest as well as the more prominent—that in their afflictions and temptations, which sooner or later come to all, they will feel that they have in you a sympathizing friend to whom they may tell the heart bitterness "with which a stranger intermeddleth not," assured of your interest, your friendly counsel, and your prayers.—Professor Duffield.

Study the Word. Know it, believe it, and preach it with your whole heart. It is not only the sword that can pierce all adversaries, it is the power that can draw all men. You are to stand in this pulpit not to preach philosophy and teach history, but to tell the everlasting gospel of the Lord Jesus Christ. —Rev. E. O. Bartlett.

The age is intensely practical, and little influenced by formalism or cant or dead orthodoxy or the perfunctory performance of ministerial duty. It appreciates preaching that is direct, unaffected, solemn, sincere; that is adapted to the spiritual wants of men; that presents the profound yet precious truths of our holy religion not in the terminology of the schools, but in the language of familiar speech, and presents them with an earnestness due to a conviction of their vital importance, and an anxious solicitude for the salvation of those addressed.—Professor Duffield.

Instinct

Instinct is intelligence incapable of self-consciousness.—John Sterling.

Instinct is the nose of the mind.—Mme. de Girardin.

We are too good for pure instinct.—Goethe.

Instinct is animal strength.—Daniel Webster.

Instinct is a great matter; I was a coward on instinct.—Shakespeare.

Instinct harmonizes the interior of animals, as religion does the interior of men.—Jacobi.

Brutes find out where their talents lie: a bear will not attempt to fly.—Swift.

And reason raise o'er instinct as you can, in this 'tis God directs, in that 'tis man.—Pope.

Who taught the nations of the field and wood
To shun their poison and to choose their food. —Pope.

The active part of man consists of powerful instincts.—F. W. Newman.

Tell me why the ant midst summer's plenty thinks of winter's want.—Prior.

A goose flies by a chart which the Royal Geographical Society could not mend.—Holmes.

All our first movements are good, generous, heroical; reflection weakens and kills them.—Aimé-Martin.

A bird sings, a child prattles, but it is the same hymn; hymn indistinct, inarticulate, but full of profound meaning.—Victor Hugo.

A good man, through obscurest aspirations, Has still an instinct of the one true way. —Goethe.

Every animal is providentially directed to the use of its proper weapon. —Ray.

The instinct of brutes and insects can be the effect of nothing else than the wisdom and skill of a powerful, ever-living agent.—Newton.

An instinct is a propensity prior to experience and independent of instruction.—Paley.

An instinct is an agent which performs blindly and ignorantly a work of intelligence and knowledge.—Sir W. Hamilton.

By a divine instinct, men's minds mistrust ensuing danger; as, by proof, we see the waters swell before a boisterous storm.—Shakespeare.

Animals in their generation are wiser than the sons of men; but their wisdom is confined to a few particulars, and lies in a very narrow compass.—Addison.

But honest instinct comes a volunteer;
Sure never to o'er-shoot, but just to hit,
While still too wide or short in human wit.
—Pope.

Five thousand years have added no improvement to the hive of the bee, nor to the house of the beaver; but look at the habitations and the achievements of men!—Colton.

An instinct is a blind tendency to some mode of action, independent of any consideration, on the part of the agent, of the end to which the action leads.—Whately.

There is not, in my opinion, anything more mysterious in nature than this instinct in animals, which thus rise above reason and fall infinitely short of it.—Addison.

Learn from the birds what food the thickets yield;
Learn from the beasts the physic of the field;
Thy arts of building from the bee receive;
Learn of the mole to plough, the worm to weave.   —Pope.

To the present impulse of sense, memory, and instinct, all the sagacities of brutes may be reduced; though witty men, by analytical resolution, have chemically extracted an artificial logic out of their actions.—Sir M. Hale.

Beasts, birds, and insects, even to the minutest and meanest of their kind,

act with the unerring providence of instinct; man, the while, who possesses a higher faculty, abuses it, and therefore goes blundering on.—Southey.

Reason shows itself in all occurrences of life; whereas the brute makes no discovery of such a talent, but in what immediately regards his own preservation or the continuance of his species.—Addison.

Instead of judgment, woman has rather a quick perception of what is fitting, owing to the predominance of her instinctive faculties. The quick perception, indeed, bears the stamp of instinct.—Alexander Walker.

Who taught the parrot his "Welcome?" Who taught the raven in a drought to throw pebbles into a hollow tree where she espied water, that the water might rise so as she might come to it? Who taught the bee to sail through such a vast sea of air, and to find the way from a flower in a field to her hive? Who taught the ant to bite every grain of corn that she burieth in her hill, lest it should take root and grow?—Bacon.

How often we feel and know, either pleasurably or painfully, that another is looking on us, before we have ascertained the fact with our own eyes! How often we prophesy truly to ourselves the approach of friend or enemy just before either has really appeared! How strangely and abruptly we become convinced, at a first introduction, that we shall secretly love this person and loathe that, before experience has guided us with a single fact in relation to their characters!—Wilkie Collins.

Instruction

From one learn all.—Virgil.

It is lawful to be taught by an enemy.—Ovid.

The seeds of first instructions are dropp'd into the deepest furrows.—Tupper.

Instruction enlarges the natural powers of the mind.—Horace.

He need not go away from home for instruction.—Terence.

To be instructed in the arts softens the manners and makes men gentle.—Ovid.

Seek to delight, that they may mend mankind.
And, while they captivate, inform the mind.
—Cowper.

Instruction does not prevent waste of time or mistakes; and mistakes themselves are often the best teachers of all.—Froude.

He is wise who can instruct us and assist us in the business of daily virtuous living.—Carlyle.

The wise are instructed by reason, ordinary minds by experience; the stupid by necessity; and brutes by instinct.—Cicero.

The heavens and the earth, the woods and the wayside, teem with instruction and knowledge to the curious and thoughtful.—Hosea Ballou.

We must not contradict, but instruct him that contradicts us; for a madman is not cured by another running mad also.—Antisthenes.

Men must be taught as if you taught them not,
And things unknown propos'd as things forgot.   —Pope.

It is a good divine that follows his
Own instructions; I can easier teach twenty
What were good to be done, than be one
Of the twenty to follow mine own teaching:
The brain may devise laws for the blood;
but
A hot temper leaps o'er a cold decree.
—Shakespeare.

Let us consider how great a commodity of doctrine exists in books; how easily, how secretly, how safely they expose the nakedness of human ignorance without putting it to shame. These are the masters who instruct us without rods and ferules, without hard words and anger, without clothes or money. If you approach them they are not asleep; if investigating you interrogate them, they conceal nothing; if you mistake them they never

grumble; if you are ignorant, they cannot laugh at you.—Richard de Bury.

Insult

Insults admit of no compensation.—Junius.

It is often better not to see an insult than to avenge it.—Seneca.

What wilt thou do to thyself, who hast added insult to injury?—Phædrus.

Even a hare, the weakest of animals, may insult a dead lion.—Æsop.

It is very clear that one way to challenge insults is to submit to them.—Aimé-Martin.

Fate never wounds more deep the generous heart than when a blockhead's insult points the dart.—Dr. Johnson.

Insults are engendered from vulgar minds, like toadstools from a dunghill.—Colton.

I once met a man who had forgiven an injury. I hope some day to meet the man who has forgiven an insult.—Charles Buxton.

He who allows himself to be insulted deserves to be so; and insolence, if unpunished, goes on increasing.—Corneille.

A man who insults the modesty of a woman, as good as tells her that he has seen something in her conduct that warranted his presumption.—Richardson.

Injuries may be atoned for, and forgiven; but insults admit of no compensation. They degrade the mind in its own esteem, and force it to recover its level by revenge.—Junius.

Receive no satisfaction for premeditated impertinence; forget it, forgive it, but keep him inexorably at a distance who offered it.—Lavater.

Injuries accompanied with insults are never forgiven: all men, on these occasions, are good haters, and lay

out their revenge at compound interest.
—Colton.

The way to procure insults is to submit to them. A man meets with no more respect than he exacts.—Hazlitt.

It is only the vulgar who are always fancying themselves insulted. If a man treads on another's toe in good society, do you think it is taken as an insult?—Lady Hester Stanhope.

Thus the greater proportion of mankind are more sensitive to contemptuous language than unjust acts; for they can less easily bear insult than wrong.—Plutarch.

Whatever be the motive of insult, it is always best to overlook it; for folly scarcely can deserve resentment, and malice is punished by neglect.—Johnson.

The slight that can be conveyed in a glance, in a gracious smile, in a wave of the hand, is often the *ne plus ultra* of art. What insult is so keen, or so keenly felt, as the polite insult, which it is impossible to resent.—Julia Kavanagh.

As it is the nature of a kite to devour little birds, so it is the nature of some minds to insult and tyrannize over little people; this being the means which they use to recompense themselves for their extreme servility and condescension to their superiors; for nothing can be more reasonable than that slaves and flatterers should exact the same taxes on all below them which they themselves pay to all above them.—Fielding.

Integrity

Integrity is the evidence of all civil virtues.—Diderot.

Integrity without knowledge is weak and useless.—Johnson.

Follow your honest convictions, and be strong.—Thackeray.

Though a hundred crooked paths may conduct to a temporary success, the one plain and straight path of public and private virtue can alone lead to a pure and lasting fame and the blessings of posterity.—Edward Everett.

Our integrity is never worth so much as when we have parted with our all to keep it.—Colton.

Both wit and understanding are trifles without integrity. The ignorant peasant without fault is greater than the philosopher with many. What is genius or courage without a heart?—Goldsmith.

Give us a man, young or old, high or low, on whom we know we can thoroughly depend—who will stand firm when others fail—the friend faithful and true, the adviser honest and fearless, the adversary just and chivalrous; in such an one there is a fragment of the Rock of Ages—a sign that there has been a prophet amongst us.—Dean Stanley.

Aaron Burr was a more brilliant man than George Washington. If he had been loyal to truth, he would have been an abler man; but that which made George Washington the chief hero in our great republic was the sagacity, not of intellectual genius, but of the moral element in him.—A. E. Dunning.

Intellect

Intellect—brain force.—Schiller.

Thou living ray of intellectual fire.—Falconer.

Light has spread, and even bayonets think.—Kossuth.

The electric force of the brain.—Haliburton.

God has placed no limit to intellect.—Bacon.

Genius is intellect constructive.—Emerson.

Intellect is stronger than cannon.—Theodore Parker.

Intellect really exists in its products; its kingdom is here.—Coleridge.

The starlight of the brain.—N. P. Willis.

The march of intellect.—Southey.

The hand that follows intellect can achieve.—Michael Angelo.

The march of the human mind is slow.—Burke.

Everything connected with intellect is permanent.—William Roscoe.

There is no creature so lonely as the dweller in the intellect.—William Winter.

Mind is the great lever. . . . Thought is the process by which human ends are answered.—Webster.

Intellect is the soul of man, the only immortal part of him.—Carlyle.

Character is higher than intellect. A great soul will be strong to live as well as strong to think.—R. W. Emerson.

If a man empties his purse into his head, no one can take it from him.—Franklin.

A man cannot leave a better legacy to the world than a well-educated family.—Rev. Thomas Scott.

The intellect of the wise is like glass; it admits the light of heaven and reflects it.—Hare.

It is the nature of intellect to strive to improve in intellectual power.—Hosea Ballou.

Works of the intellect are great only by comparison with each other.—Emerson.

In the scale of the destinies, brawn will never weigh so much as brain.—Lowell.

'Tis goodwill makes intelligence.—Emerson.

The brain women never interest us like the heart women; white roses please less than red.—O. W. Holmes.

Intellect annuls fate. So far as a man thinks, he is free.—Emerson.

Nature is good, but intellect is better, as the law-giver is before the law-receiver.—Emerson.

The march of intellect, which licks all the world into shape, has even reached the devil.—Goethe.

The human intellect is the great truth-organ; realities, as they exist, are the subjects of its study; and knowledge is the result of its acquaintance with the things which it investigates.—Moses Harvey.

A man of intellect is lost unless he unites energy of character to intellect. When we have the lantern of Diogenes we must have his staff.—Chamfort.

The intellect has only one failing, which, to be sure, is a very considerable one. It has no conscience.—Lowell.

The intellect of the generality of women serves more to fortify their folly than their reason.—Rochefoucauld.

The term "intellect" includes all those powers by which we acquire, retain, and extend our knowledge; as perception, memory, imagination, judgment, and the like.—William Fleming.

Sensual pleasures are like soap-bubbles, sparkling, evanescent. The pleasures of intellect are calm, beautiful, sublime, ever enduring and climbing upward to the borders of the unseen world.—Aughey.

The intellect of man sits enthroned visibly upon his forehead and in his eye, and the heart of man is written on his countenance; but the soul reveals itself in the voice only.—Longfellow.

The growth of the intellect is spontaneous in every expansion. The mind that grows could not predict the times, the means, the mode of that spontaneity. God enters by a private door into every individual.—Emerson.

The intellect of woman bears the same relationship to that of man as her physical organization; it is inferior in power and different in kind. —Mrs. Jameson.

Glorious indeed is the world of God around us, but more glorious the world of God within us. There lies the Land of Song; there lies the poet's native land.—Longfellow.

Man gains wider dominion by his intellect than by his right arm. The mustard-seed of thought is a pregnant treasury of vast results. Like the germ in the Egyptian tombs, its vitality never perishes; and its fruit will spring up after it has been buried for long ages.—Chapin.

It is only the intellect that can be thoroughly and hideously wicked. It can forget everything in the attainment of its ends. The heart recoils; in its retired places some drops of childhood's dew still linger, defying manhood's fiery noon.—Lowell.

Some men of a secluded and studious life have sent forth from their closet or their cloister rays of intellectual light that have agitated courts and revolutionable kingdoms; like the moon which, though far removed from the ocean, and shining upon it with a serene and sober light, is the chief cause of all those ebbings and flowings which incessantly disturb that restless world of waters.—Colton.

Intelligence

To educate the intelligence is to enlarge the horizon of its desires and wants.—Lowell.

The intelligent have a right over the ignorant; namely, the right of instructing them.—Emerson.

God multiplies intelligence, which communicates itself, like fire, *ad infinitum*. Light a thousand torches at one touch, the flame remains always the same.—Joubert.

Every breeze wafts intelligence from country to country, every wave rolls it, all give it forth, and all in turn receive it. There is a vast commerce of ideas, there are marts and exchanges for intellectual discoveries, and a wonderful fellowship of those individual intelligences which make up the mind and opinion of the age.—Daniel Webster.

It is no proof of a man's understanding to be able to confirm whatever he pleases; but to be able to discern that what is true is true, and that what is false is false, this is the mark and character of intelligence.—Swedenborg.

Intemperance

Intemperance weaves the winding-sheet of souls.—John B. Gough.

Allow not nature more than nature needs.—Shakespeare.

Bacchus has drowned more men than Neptune.—Garibaldi.

Intemperance is a great decayer of beauty.—Junius.

All learned, and all drunk!—Cowper.

The smaller the drink, the clearer the head.—William Penn.

Gloriously drunk, obey the important call.—Cowper.

Purged from drugs of foul intemperance.—Spenser.

Greatness of any kind has no greater foe than a habit of drinking.—Walter Scott.

He that tempts me to drink beyond my measure, civilly invites me to a fever.—Jeremy Taylor.

O, that men should put an enemy in their mouths to steal away their brains!—Shakespeare.

Every inordinate cup is unblessed and the ingredient is a devil.—Shakespeare.

In our world, death deputes intemperance to do the work of age.—Young.

Other vices make their own way; this makes way for all vices. He that

is a drunkard is qualified for all vice.
—Francis Quarles.

Sweet fellowship in shame!
One drunkard loves another of the name.
—Shakespeare.

He calls drunkenness an expression identical with ruin.—Diogenes Laertius.

Drunkenness is nothing but voluntary madness.—Seneca.

A sensual and intemperate youth hands over a worn-out body to old age. —Cicero.

If a man empties his purse into his head, no one can take it from him.— Franklin.

Wine displays every little spot of the soul in its utmost deformity.—Addison.

In the bottle discontent seeks for comfort, cowardice for courage, and bashfulness for confidence.—Dr. Johnson.

He is certainly as guilty of suicide who perishes by a slow, as he who is despatched by an immediate, poison.— Steele.

It is little the sign of a wise or good man, to suffer temperance to be transgressed in order to purchase the repute of a generous entertainer.— Atterbury.

It is not fitting that the evil produced by men should be imputed to things; let those bear the blame who make an ill use of things in themselves good.—Isocrates.

Intemperance is the epitome of every crime, the cause of every kind of misery.—Douglas Jerrold.

All the crimes on earth do not destroy so many of the human race, nor alienate so much property, as drunkenness.—Bacon.

In the flowers that wreathe the sparkling bowl, fell adders hiss, and poisonous serpents roll.—Prior.

Intemperance is a hydra with a hundred heads. She never stalks abroad unaccompanied with impurity, anger, and the most infamous profligacies.— Chrysostom.

I have very poor and unhappy brains for drinking : I could wish courtesy would invent some other custom of entertainment.—Shakespeare.

In what pagan nation was Moloch ever propitiated by such an unbroken and swift-moving procession of victims as are offered to this Moloch of Christendom, intemperance.—Horace Mann.

Shall I, to please another wine-sprung minde,
Lose all mine own? God hath giv'n me a measure
Short of His can and body; must I find
A pain in that, wherein he finds a pleasure.
—Herbert.

Wise men mingle mirth with their cares, as a help either to forget or overcome them; but to resort to intoxication for the ease of one's mind is to cure melancholy by madness.— Charron.

I never drink. I cannot do it, on equal terms with others. It costs them only one day; but me three,—the first in sinning, the second in suffering, and the third in repenting.—Sterne.

The bliss of the drunkard is like the expectation of the dying Atheist who hopes no more than to lie down in the grave with the beasts.—Jane Porter.

The pleasing poison the visage quite transforms of him that drinks, and the inglorious likeness of a beast fixes instead, unmoulding reason's mintage charactered in the face.—Milton.

The body oppressed by excess bears down the mind, and depresses to the earth any portion of the divine spirit we had been endowed with.—Horace.

There is more of turn than of truth in a saying of Seneca, "That drunkenness does not produce but discover faults." Common experience teaches the contrary. Wine throws a man out of himself, and infuses qualities into the mind which she is a stranger to in her sober moments.—Addison.

Ha! see where the wild-blazing Grog-shop appears,
As the red waves of wretchedness swell.
How it burns on the edge of tempestuous years
The horrible Light-House of Hell!
—M'Donald Clarke.

Every apartment devoted to the circulation of the glass, may be regarded as a temple set apart for the performance of human sacrifices. And they ought to be fitted up like the ancient temples in Egypt, in a manner to show the real atrocity of the superstition that is carried on within their walls.—Beddoes.

The habit of using ardent spirits, by men in office, has occasioned more injury to the public and more trouble to me, than all other causes. And were I to commence my administration again, the first question I would ask, respecting a candidate for office would be, "Does he use ardent spirits?"—Jefferson.

Who hath woe? who hath sorrow? who hath contentions? who hath babbling? who hath wounds without cause? who hath redness of eyes? They that tarry long at the wine; they that go to seek mixed wine. Look not thou upon the wine when it is red, when it giveth his color in the cup, when it moveth itself aright; at the last it biteth like a serpent, and stingeth like an adder.—Bible.

If the bones of all those who have fallen as a prey to intemperance could be piled up it would make a vast pyramid. Who will gird himself for the journey and try with me to scale this mountain of the dead—going up miles high on human carcasses to find still other peaks far above, mountain above mountain, white with the bones of drunkards.—Talmage.

Intentions

Purposes, like eggs, unless they be hatched into action, will run into rottenness.—Samuel Smiles.

If religion might be judged of, according to men's intentions, there would scarcely be any idolatry in the world.—Bishop Hall.

Hell is paved with good intentions.—Johnson.

Many good purposes lie in the churchyard.—Philip Henry.

Intercourse

The kindly intercourse will ever prove
A bond of amity and social love.
—Bloomfield.

Intercourse is after all man's best teacher. "Know thyself" is an excellent maxim; but even self-knowledge cannot be perfected in closets and cloisters—nor amid lake scenery, and on the sunny side of the mountains. Men who seldom mix with their fellow-creatures are almost sure to be one-sided—the victims of fixed ideas, that sometimes lead to insanity.—Wm. Matthews.

Interest

Interest makes all seem reason that leads to it.—Dryden.

The virtues and vices are all put in motion by interest.—Rochefoucauld.

The instinct of interest is the universal instinct of mankind.—Charles Macklin.

As the interest of man, so his God; as his God, so he.—Lavater.

Interest blinds some people, and enlightens others.—Rochefoucauld.

Interest speaks all languages, and acts all parts, even that of disinterestedness itself.—Rochefoucauld.

Interest is the spur of the people, but glory that of great souls.—Rousseau.

It is more than possible, that those who have neither character nor honor may be wounded in a very tender part, —their interest.—Junius.

When interest is at variance with conscience, any distinction to make them friends will serve the hollow-hearted.—Henry Home.

How difficult a thing it is to persuade a man to reason against his own interest, though he is convinced that equity is against him.—Dr. John Trusler.

Our interests are grains of opium to our consciences, but they only put it to sleep for a terrible awakening.—J. Petit-Senn.

Interest has the security, though not the virtue of a principle. As the world goes, it is the surest side; for men daily leave both relations and religion to follow it.—William Penn.

Interest makes some people blind and others quick-sighted. We promise according to our hopes, and perform according to our fears. Virtues are lost in interest, as rivers are swallowed up in the sea.—J. Beaumont.

Intolerance

The intolerant man is the real pedant.—Richter.

It were better to be of no church, than to be bitter for any.—William Penn.

The devil loves nothing better than the intolerance of reformers, and dreads nothing so much as their charity and patience.—Lowell.

Some men will not shave on Sunday, and yet they spend all the week in shaving their fellow-men; and many folks think it very wicked to black their boots on Sunday morning, yet they do not hesitate to black their neighbor's reputation on week-days.—Beecher.

It appears an extraordinary thing to me, that since there is such a diabolical spirit in the depravity of human nature, as persecution for difference of opinion in religious tenets, there never happened to be any inquisition, any *auto da fé*, any crusade, among the Pagans.—Sterne.

As no roads are so rough as those that have just been mended, so no sinners are so intolerant as those that have just turned saints.—Colton.

Intrigue

Intrigue is a court distemper.—Mme. Deluzy.

Every woman is at heart a rake.—Pope.

As love increases, prudence diminishes.—Rochefoucauld.

Audacity as against modesty will win the battle over most men.—Mme. Deluzy.

There are many women who never have had one intrigue; but there are few who have had only one.—Rochefoucauld.

There are many women who have never intrigued, and many men who have never gamed; but those who have done either but once are very extraordinary animals.—Colton.

When women oppose themselves to the projects and ambition of men, they excite their lively resentment; if in their youth they meddle with political intrigues, their modesty must suffer.—Mme. de Staël.

If often happens too, both in courts and in cabinets, that there are two things going on together,—a main plot and an under-plot; and he that understands only one of them will, in all probability, be the dupe of both. A mistress may rule a monarch, but some obscure favorite may rule the mistress.—Colton.

Intuition

Intuition is the clear conception of the whole at once. It seldom belongs to man to say without presumption, "I came, I saw, I conquered."—Lavater.

This, therefore, is a law not found in books, but written on the fleshly tablets of the heart, which we have not learned from man, received or read, but which we have caught up from Nature herself, sucked in and imbibed; the knowledge of which we were not taught, but for which we were made; we received it not by education, but by intuition.—Cicero.

Invention

Necessity, mother of invention.—Wycherley.

Invention is totally independent of the will.—B. R. Haydon.

Invention is not so much the result of labor as of judgment.—Roscommon.

Invention is the talent of youth, and judgment of age.—Swift.

Only an inventor knows how to borrow, and every man is or should be an inventor.—Emerson.

Invention is activity of mind, as fire is air in motion; a sharpening of the spiritual sight, to discern hidden aptitudes.—Tupper.

Very learned women are to be found, in the same manner as female warriors; but they are seldom or never inventors.—Voltaire.

The introduction of noble inventions seems to hold by far the most excellent place among human actions.—Bacon.

A tool is but the extension of a man's hand, and a machine is but a complex tool. And he that invents a machine augments the power of a man and the well-being of mankind.—Henry Ward Beecher.

The great inventor is one who has walked forth upon the industrial world, not from universities, but from hovels; not as clad in silks and decked with honors, but as clad in fustian and grimed with soot and oil.—Isaac Taylor.

Th' invention all admir'd, and each, how he
To be th' inventor miss'd; so easy it seem'd,
Once found, which yet unfound most would
   have thought
Impossible.   —Milton.

Invention, strictly speaking, is little more than a new combination of those images which have been previously gathered and deposited in the memory. Nothing can be made of nothing; he who has laid up no material can produce no combinations.—Sir J. Reynolds.

The golden hour of invention must terminate like other hours; and when the man of genius returns to the cares, the duties, the vexations, and the amusements of life, his companions behold him as one of themselves,— the creature of habits and infirmities. —Isaac Disraeli.

It is frivolous to fix pedantically the date of particular inventions. They have all been invented over and over fifty times. Man is the arch machine, of which all these shifts drawn from himself are toy models. He helps himself on each emergency by copying or duplicating his own structure, just so far as the need is.—Emerson.

Founders and senators of states and cities, lawgivers, extirpers of tyrants, fathers of the people, and other eminent persons in civil government, were honored but with titles of worthies or demigods; whereas such as were inventors and authors of new arts, endowments, and commodities towards man's life, were ever consecrated among the gods themselves.—Bacon.

Electric telegraphs, printing, gas,
  Tobacco, balloons, and steam,
Are little events that have come to pass
  Since the days of the old régime.
And, spite of Leprière's dazzling page,
  I'd give—though it might seem bold—
A hundred years of the Golden Age
  For a year of the Age of Gold.
         —Henry S. Leigh.

Investigation

Attempt the end and never stand to doubt;
Nothing so hard but search will find it out.
         —Herrick.

Nothing has such power to broaden the mind as the ability to investigate systematically and truly all that comes under thy observation in life.—Marcus Aurelius.

Irony

Irony is an insult conveyed in the form of a compliment * * * placing its victim naked on a bed of briars and bristles, thinly covered with rose-leaves; adorning his brow with a crown of gold, which burns into his brain; teasing, and fretting, and riddling him through and through with incessant discharges of hot shot from a masked battery; laying bare the most sensitive and shrinking nerves of his mind, and then blandly touching them with ice, or smilingly pricking them with needles.—E. P. Whipple.

Irony is jesting hidden behind gravity.—John Weiss.

Clap an extinguisher upon your irony, if you are unhappily blessed with a vein of it.—Lamb.

Irresolution

Don't stand shivering upon the bank; plunge in at once and have it over.—Haliburton.

We spend our days in deliberating, and we end them without coming to any resolve.—L'Estrange.

Like a man to double business bound,
I stand in pause where I shall first begin,
And both neglect. —Shakespeare.

I am a heavy stone,
Roll'd up a hill by a weak child: I move
A little up, and tumble back again.
—W. Rider.

Not to resolve is to resolve; and many times it breeds as many necesities, and engageth as far in some other sort, as to resolve.—Bacon.

In matters of great concern, and which must be done, there is no surer argument of a weak mind than irresolution.—Tillotson.

Nothing of worth or weight can be achieved with half a mind, with a faint heart, and with a lame endeavor. —Barrow.

Irresolution on the schemes of life which offer themselves to our choice, and inconstancy in pursuing them, are the greatest causes of all our unhappiness.—Addison.

Irresolution and mutability are often the faults of men whose views are wide, and whose imagination is vigorous and excursive.—Dr. Johnson.

Irresolution is a worse vice than rashness. He that shoots best may sometimes miss the mark; but he that shoots not at all can never hit it. Irresolution loosens all the joints of a state; like an ague, it shakes not this nor that limb, but all the body is at once in a fit. The irresolute man is lifted from one place to another; so hatcheth nothing, but addles all his actions.—Feltham.

Italy

Italia! O Italia! thou who hast
The fatal gift of beauty, which became
A funeral dower of present woes and past,
On thy sweet brow is sorrow plough'd by shame,
And annals graved in characters of flame.
—Byron.

Italy, my Italy!
Queen Mary's saying serves for me—
(When fortune's malice
Lost her Calais)—
Open my heart and you will see
Graved inside of it, "Italy."
—Robert Browning.

Fair Italy!
Thou art the garden of the world, the home
Of all Art yields, and Nature can decree,
Even in thy desert, what is like to thee?
Thy very weeds are beautiful, thy waste
More rich than other climes' fertility;
Thy wreck a glory, and thy ruin graced
With an immaculate charm which cannot
be defac'd. —Byron.

Ivy

Oh, a dainty plant is the ivy green,
That creepeth o'er ruins old!
Of right choice food are his meals I ween,
In his cell so lone and cold.
 * * * * * *
Creeping where no life is seen,
A rare old plant is the ivy green.
—Dickens.

For ivy climbs the crumbling hall
To decorate decay. —Bailey.

Oh! how could fancy crown with thee,
In ancient days, the God of Wine,
And bid thee at the banquet be
Companion of the vine?
Ivy! thy home is where each sound
Of revelry hath long been o'er;
Where song and beaker once went round,
But now are known no more.
—Mrs. Hemans.

J

January

Come, ye cold winds, at January's
call,
On whistling wings, and with white
flakes bestrew
The earth.   —Ruskin.

Jealousy

Love's sentinel.—Shakespeare.

Jealousy is not love, but self-love.
—Rochefoucauld.

Jealousy lives upon doubts.—Rochefoucauld.

Jealousy is the paralysis of love.—
Vauvenargues.

He that is not jealous is not in love.
—St. Augustine.

Jealousy is one of love's parasites.
—H. W. Shaw.

What frenzy dictates, jealousy believes.—Gay.

Oft my jealousy shapes faults that
are not.—Shakespeare.

How many fond fools serve mad jealousy!—Shakespeare.

Jealousy is the apprehension of superiority.—Shenstone.

S e l f-h a r m i n g jealousy.—Shakespeare.

Jealousy is sustained as often by
pride as by affection.—Colton.

A jealous man always finds more
than he looks for.—Mlle. de Scudéri.

Jealousy is the forerunner of love,
and often its awakener.—F. Marion
Crawford.

A jealous lover lights his torch
from the firebrand of the fiend.—
Burke.

Anger and jealousy can no more
bear to lose sight of their objects
than love.—George Eliot.

O, what damned minutes tells he
o'er, who dotes, yet doubts; suspects,
yet strongly loves!—Shakespeare.

Jealousy, thou grand counterpoise
for all the transports beauty can inspire!—Young.

Jealousy is the sister of love, as the
devil is the brother of angels.—Boufflers.

There is never jealousy where there
is not strong regard.—Washington
Irving.

'Tis a monster begot upon itself,
born on itself.—Shakespeare.

The jealous is possessed by a "fine
mad devil" and a dull spirit at once.
—Lavater.

Jealousy is an awkward homage
which inferiority renders to merit.—
Madame de Puisieux.

Jealousy is always born with love,
but does not always die with it.—La
Rochefoucauld.

Jealousy lives upon doubt, and comes
to an end or becomes a fury as soon

as it passes from doubt to certainty.
—La Rochefoucauld.

Jealousy, that doats but dooms, and
murders, yet adores.—Sprague.

The venom clamours of a jealous woman
Poison more deadly than a mad-dog's tooth.
—Shakespeare.

O jealousy! thou magnifier of trifles.
—Schiller.

Jealousy—it is a green-eyed monster,
which doth mock the meat it feeds on.
—Shakespeare.

——No greater mischief could be wrought
Than love united to a jealous thought.
—Greene.

Love often reillumes his extinguished flame at the torch of jealousy.—
Lady Blessington.

Trifles, light as air,
Are to the jealous confirmations strong
As proofs of Holy Writ. —Shakespeare.

Jealousy is cruel as the grave: the
coals thereof are coals of fire, which
hath a most vehement flame.—Bible.

No true love there can be without
Its dread penalty—jealousy.
—Lord Lytton.

Yet he was jealous, though he did not show
it,
For jealousy dislikes the world to know it.
—Byron.

The jealous man's disease is of so
malignant a nature that it converts
all it takes into its own nourishment.
—Addison.

Men of strong affections are jealous of their own genius. They fear
lest they should be loved for a quality,
and not for themselves.—Bulwer-Lytton.

People who are jealous, or particularly careful of their own rights and
dignity, always find enough of those
who do not care for either to keep
them continually uncomfortable.—
Barnes.

Men are the cause of women not
loving one another.—La Bruyère.

Jealousy sees things always with
magnifying glasses which make little
things large,—of dwarfs giants, suspicions truths.—Cervantes.

Women detest a jealous man whom
they do not love, but it angers them
when a man they do love is not jealous at times.—Mlle. de Scudéri.

Oh! the pain of pains
Is when the fair one, whom our soul is fond
of,
Gives transport, and receives it from an·
other.   —Young.

Jealousy is never satisfied with anything short of an omniscience that
would detect the subtlest fold of the
heart.—George Eliot.

Ten thousand furies lash my soul with
whips,
At ev'ry look sharp stings transfix my
heart,
And my chill blood thrills cold through
ev'ry vein.   —Darcy.

Jealousy is said to be the offspring
of love. Yet, unless the parent makes
haste to strangle the child, the child
will not rest till it has poisoned the
parent.—J. C. and A. W. Hare.

Foul jealousy! that turnest love divine to joyless dread, and makest the
loving heart with hateful thoughts to
languish and to pine.—Spenser.

Jealousy is a painful passion; yet
without some share of it, the agreeable
affection of love has difficulty to subsist in its full force and violence.—
Hume.

Of all the passions, jealousy is that
which exacts the hardest service and
pays the bitterest wages. Its service
is, to watch the success of our enemy,
to be sure of it.—Colton.

That anxious torture may I never feel,
Which doubtful, watches o'er a wandering
heart.
O, who that bitter torment can reveal,
Or tell the pining anguish of that smart!
—Byron.

To doubt is an injury; to suspect
a friend is breach of friendship; jealousy is a seed sown but in vicious

minds; prone to distrust, because apt to deceive.—Lord Lansdowne.

All the other passions condescend at times to accept the inexorable logic of facts; but jealousy looks facts straight in the face, ignores them utterly, and says that she knows a great deal better than they can tell her.—Helps.

It is with jealousy as with the gout. When such distempers are in the blood, there is never any security against their breaking out, and that often on the slightest occasions, and when least suspected.—Fielding.

Yet is there one more cursed than they all,
That canker-worm, that monster, jealousie,
Which eats the heart and feeds upon the gall,
Turning all love's delight to misery,
Through fear of losing his felicity.
—Spenser.

We are more jealous of frivolous accomplishments with brilliant success, than of the most estimable qualities without. Dr. Johnson envied Garrick, whom he despised, and ridiculed Goldsmith, whom he loved.—Hazlitt.

O jealousy, thou ugliest fiend of hell! thy deadly venom preys on my vitals, turns the healthful hue of my fresh cheek to haggard sallowness, and drinks my spirit up.—Hannah More.

But through the heart
Should jealousy its venom once diffuse
'Tis then delightful misery no more
But agony unmix'd, incessant gall
Corroding every thought, and blasting all
Love's paradise.   —Thomson.

If you are wise, and prize your peace of mind,
Believe me true, nor listen to your jealousy,
Let not that devil which undoes your sex,
That curs'd curiosity seduce you
To hunt for needless secrets, which, neglected,
Shall never hurt your quiet, but once known
Shall sit upon your heart, pinch it with pain,
And banish sweet sleep forever from you.
—Rowe.

Love may exist without jealousy, although this is rare: but jealousy may exist without love, and this is common; for jealousy can feed on that which is bitter no less than on that which is sweet, and is sustained by pride as often as by affection.—Colton.

Jeering

Abstain from dissolute laughter, uncomely jests, loud talking, and jeering.—Jeremy Taylor.

Scoff not at the natural defects of any which are not in their power to amend. Oh, it is cruel to beat a cripple with his own crutches.—Fuller.

Jeer not others upon any occasion If they be foolish, God hath denied them understanding; if they be vicious, you ought to pity, not revile them; if deformed, God framed their bodies, and will you scorn His workmanship? Are you wiser than your Creator? If poor, poverty was designed for a motive to charity, not to contempt; you cannot see what riches they have within.—South.

Jesting

A good jest forever.—Shakespeare.

Jesters do often prove prophets.—Shakespeare.

I do not like this fooling.—Shakespeare.

How ill white hairs become a fool and jester!—Shakespeare.

A jest is a very serious thing.—Churchill.

A jest loses its point when he who makes it is the first to laugh.—Schiller.

No time to break jests when the heartstrings are about to be broken.—Fuller.

A bitter jest, when it comes too near the truth, leaves a sharp sting behind it.—Tacitus.

Judge of a jest when you have done laughing.—Lloyd.

This fellow pecks up wit, as pigeons peace,
And utters it again when Jove doth please;
He is wit's peddler.   —Shakespeare.

Jest with your equals.—Bion.

A jester, a bad character.—Pascal.

If anything is spoken in jest, it is not fair to turn it to earnest.—Plautus.

The jest which is expected is already destroyed.—Johnson.

Wanton jests make fools laugh, and wise men frown.—Fuller.

Jesting, often, only proves a want of intellect.—La Bruyère.

Jests,—brain-fleas that jump about among the slumbering ideas.—Heinrich Heine.

Jesting is frequently an evidence of the poverty of the understanding.—Voltaire.

The fund of sensible discourse is limited; that of jest and badinerie is infinite.—Shenstone.

A joker is near akin to a buffoon; and neither of them is the least related to wit.—Chesterfield.

It is good to jest, but not to make a trade of jesting.—Queen Elizabeth.

Harmless mirth is the best cordial against the consumption of the spirit; wherefore jesting is not unlawful, if it trespasseth not in quantity, quality, or season.—Thomas Fuller.

A jest's prosperity lies in the ear
Of him that hears it, never in the tongue
Of him that makes it.   —Shakespeare.

Of all the griefs that harass the distress'd,
Sure the most bitter is a scornful jest.
Fate never wounds more deep the generous heart,
Than when a blockhead's insult points the dart.   —Dr. Johnson.

Wit loses its respect with the good when seen in company with malice; and to smile at the jest which plants a thorn in another's breast is to become a principal in the mischief.—Sheridan.

As to jest, there ought to be certain things privileged from it,—namely, religion, matters of state, great persons, and man's present business of importance, and any case that deserveth pity.—Bacon.

Beware of biting jests; the more truth they carry with them, the greater wounds they give, the greater smarts they cause, and the greater scars they leave behind them.—Lavater.

He that will lose his friend for a jest deserves to die a beggar by the bargain. Such let thy jests be, that they may not grind the credit of thy friend; and make not jests so long till thou becomest one.—Fuller.

It is dangerous to jest with God, death, or the devil; for the first neither can nor will be mocked; the second mocks all men at one time or another; and the third puts an eternal sarcasm on those that are too familiar with him.—J. Beaumont.

He who never relaxes into sportiveness is a wearisome companion; but beware of him who jests at everything! Such men disparage by some ludicrous association, all objects which are presented to their thoughts, and thereby render themselves incapable of any emotion which can either elevate or soften them; they bring upon their moral being an influence more withering than the blasts of the desert.—Southey.

Jewels

I'll give my jewels for a set of beads.—Shakespeare.

Full many a gem of purest ray serene
The dark unfathom'd caves of ocean bear.   —Gray.

If that a pearl may in a toad's head dwell,
And may be found too in an oyster shell.   —Bunyan.

These gems have life in them: their colors speak,
Say what words fail of.   —George Eliot.

Jewels five-words-long,
That on the stretch'd forefinger of all Time
Sparkle for ever.   —Tennyson.

There is many a rich stone laid up in the bowels of the earth, many a fair pearl laid up in the bosom of the sea,

that never was seen nor never shall
be.—Bishop Hall.

The lively Diamond drinks thy purest rays,
Collected light, compact.   —Thomson.

Some ask'd how pearls did grow, and where,
  Then spoke I to my girle,
To part her lips, and showed them there
  The quarrelets of pearl.   —Herrick.

Jews

The Jews were God's chosen people.
—Chrysostom.

There is no clime which they can
call home.—Hayes.

Sufferance is the badge of all our
tribe.—Shakespeare.

The adherence of the Jews to their
religion makes their testimony un-
questionable.—J. Perles.

To the Jews only, and not to the
Gentiles, was a Saviour promised.—
Elias Hicks.

The great number of the Jews furnishes us with a sufficient cloud of
witnesses that attest the truth of the
Bible.—Addison.

They are a piece of stubborn antiquity, compared with which Stone-
henge is in its nonage. They date beyond the Pyramids.—Lamb.

I am a Jew. Hath not a Jew eyes?
hath not a Jew hands, organs, dimensions, senses, affections, passions?
fed with the same food, hurt with the
same weapons, subject to the same
diseases, healed by the same means,
warmed and cooled by the same winter
and summer, as a Christian is?—
Shakespeare.

The Jews are among the aristocracy
of every land ; if a literature is called
rich in the possession of a few classic
tragedies, what shall we say to a national tragedy lasting for fifteen hundred years, in which the poets and the
actors were also the heroes.—George
Eliot.

Talk what you will of the Jews,—
that they are cursed: they thrive
wherever they come; they are able to

oblige the prince of their country by
lending him money ; none of them beg ;
they keep together ; and as for their
being hated, why, Christians hate one
another as much.—Selden.

Joke (See Jesting)

Jokes are the cayenne of conversation, and the salt of life.—Chatfield.

The next best thing to a very good
joke is a very bad one.—J. C. Hare.

And gentle Dullness ever loves a
joke.—Pope.

It requires a surgical operation to
get a joke well into a Scotch understanding.—Sydney Smith.

Be not affronted at a joke. If one
throw salt at thee, thou wilt receive no
harm, unless thou art raw.—Junius.

Journalism

Journalism has already come to be
the first power in the land.—Samuel
Bowles.

The mob of gentlemen who wrote
with ease.—Pope.

The press is the fourth estate of the
realm.—Carlyle.

      Report me and my cause aright
To the unsatisfied.   —Shakespeare.

Did Charity prevail, the press would prove
A vehicle of virtue, truth, and love.
                        —Cowper.

Four hostile newspapers are more
to be feared than a thousand bayonets.—Napoleon I.

Journalism is an immense power.
that threatens soon to supersede sermons, lectures, and books.—Theodore
Tilton.

The journalist should be on his
guard against publishing what is false
in taste or exceptionable in morals.—
Bryant.

A journal should be neither an echo
nor a pander.—G. W. Curtis.

Newspapers always excite curiosity.
No one ever lays one down without a

feeling of disappointment.—Charles Lamb.

He's gone, and who knows how he may report
Thy words by adding fuel to the flame?
—Milton.

To serve thy generation, this thy fate:
"Written in water," swiftly fades thy name;
But he who loves his kind does, first and late,
A work too great for fame.
—Mary Clemmer.

They consume a considerable quantity of our paper manufacture, employ our artisans in printing, and find business for great numbers of indigent persons.—Addison.

A would-be satirist, a hired buffoon,
A monthly scribbler of some low lampoon,
Condemn'd to drudge, the meanest of the mean,
And furbish falsehoods for a magazine.
—Byron.

Hear, land o' cakes, and brither Scots,
Frae Maidenkirk to Johnny Groat's;
If there's a hole in a' your coats,
I rede you tent it:
A chiel's amang you taking notes,
And, faith, he'll prent it.
—Burns.

Here shall the Press the People's right maintain,
Unawed by influence and unbribed by gain;
Here Patriot Truth her glorious precepts draw,
Pledged to Religion, Liberty, and Law.
—Joseph Story.

Trade hardly deems the busy day begun
Till his keen eye along the sheet has run;
The blooming daughter throws her needle by,
And reads her schoolmate's marriage with a sigh;
While the grave mother puts her glasses on,
And gives a tear to some old crony gone.
The preacher, too, his Sunday theme lays down,
To know what last new folly fills the town;
Lively or sad, life's meanest, mightiest things,
The fate of fighting cocks, or fighting kings.
—Sprague.

The best use of a journal is to print the largest practical amount of important truth,—truth which tends to make mankind wiser, and thus happier.—Horace Greeley.

The News-writer lies down at Night in great Tranquillity, upon a piece of News which corrupts before Morning, and which he is obliged to throw away as soon as he awakes.—De La Bruyère.

Only a newspaper! Quick read, quick lost,
Who sums the treasure that it carries hence?
Torn, trampled under feet, who counts thy cost,
Star-eyed intelligence? —Mary Clemmer.

Joy

Joyousness is Nature's garb of health.—Lamartine.

Joy is the best of wine.—George Eliot.

Without kindness, there can be no true joy.—Carlyle.

Sorrows remembered sweeten present joy.—Pollok.

I wish you all the joy that you can wish.—Shakespeare.

True joy is only hope put out of fear.—Lord Brooke.

Joys are our wings, sorrows are our spurs.—Richter.

Far beneath a soul immortal is a mortal joy.—Young.

A blithe heart makes a blooming visage.—Scotch Proverb.

A thing of beauty is a joy forever.
—Keats.

Joy in one's work is the consummate tool.—Phillips Brooks.

Joy surfeited turns to sorrow.—Alfieri.

He who can conceal his joys is greater than he who can hide his griefs.—Lavater.

In every exalted joy, there mingles a sense of gratitude.—Marie Ebner-Eschenbach.

The cup of joy is heaviest when empty.—Marguerite de Valois.

Profound joy has more of severity than gayety in it.—Montaigne.

Joy softens more hearts than tears.—Mme. de Sartory.

True joy is a serene and sober motion.—Seneca.

Joy never feasts so high as when the first course is of misery.—Suckling.

Joy is more divine than sorrow; for joy is bread, and sorrow is medicine.—Beecher.

Joys too exquisite to last, and yet more exquisite when passed.—Montgomery.

There is a sweet joy that comes to us through sorrow.—Spurgeon.

The joy of a strong nature is as cloudless as its suffering is desolate.—Ouida.

Deep joy is a serene and sober emotion, rarely evinced in open merriment.—Mme. Roland.

How happy are the pessimists! What joy is theirs when they have proved there is no joy.—Marie Ebner-Eschenbach.

Silence is the perfectest herald of joy: I were but little happy if I could say how much.—Shakespeare.

We lose the peace of years when we hunt after the rapture of moments.—Bulwer-Lytton.

Sweets with sweets war not; joy delights in joy.—Shakespeare.

These spiritual joys are dogged by no sad sequels.—Glanvill.

Capacity for joy admits temptation.—Mrs. Browning.

What is joy? A sunbeam between two clouds.—Madame Deluzy.

In this world, full often our joys are only the tender shadows which our sorrows cast.—Beecher.

There is not a joy the world can give like that it takes away.—Byron.

The joy which is caused by truth and noble thoughts shows itself in the words by which they are expressed.—Joubert.

One hour of joy dispels the cares
And sufferings of a thousand years.
—Baptiste.

Joys
Are bubble-like—what makes them,
Bursts them too.   —Bailey.

When the power of imparting joy is equal to the will, the human soul requires no other heaven.—Shelley.

Joy is a flame which association alone can keep alive, and which goes out unless communicated.—Lamartine.

Who partakes in another's joys is a more humane character than he who partakes in his griefs.—Lavater.

Joy is an import; joy is an exchange;
Joy flies monopolists: it calls for two;
Rich fruit! Heaven planted! never pluck'd
    by one.   —Young.

Little joys refresh us constantly, like house-bread, and never bring disgust; and great ones, like sugar-bread, briefly, and then satiety.—Richter.

Trouble is a thing that will come without our call; but true joy will not spring up without ourselves.—Bishop Patrick.

Joy is the mainspring in the whole
Of endless Nature's calm rotation.
Joy moves the dazzling wheels that rol'
In the great Time-piece of Creation.
                        —Schiller.

Here below is not the land of happiness: I know it now; it is only the land of toil, and every joy which comes to us is only to strengthen us for some greater labor that is to succeed.—Fichte.

The very society of joy redoubles it; so that, whilst it lights upon my friend it rebounds upon myself, and the brighter his candle burns the more easily will it light mine.—South.

There are joys which long to be ours. God sends ten thousand truths, which come about us like birds seeking inlet; but we are shut up to them, and so they bring us nothing, but sit and sing awhile upon the roof, and then fly away.—Beecher.

Joy wholly from without, is false, precarious, and short. From without it may be gathered; but, like gathered flowers, though fair, and sweet for a season, it must soon wither, and become offensive. Joy from within is like smelling the rose on the tree; it is more sweet and fair, it is lasting; and, I must add, immortal.—Young.

The joy resulting from the diffusion of blessings to all around us is the purest and sublimest that can ever enter the human mind, and can be conceived only by those who have experienced it. Next to the consolations of divine grace, it is the most sovereign balm to the miseries of life, both in him who is the object of it, and in him who exercises it.—Bishop Porteus.

God is merely tuning the soul, as an instrument, in this life. And these joys of the Christian, are only the notes and chords that are sounded out in the preparation—preludes to the perfect harmony that shall flood the soul—forerunners of the perfected and rapturous joy that shall bless the soul, in that exceeding and eternal weight of glory.—Herrick Johnson.

Real joy seems dissonant from the human character in its present condition; and if it be felt, it must come from a higher region, for the world is shadowed by sorrow; thorns array the ground; the very clouds, while they weep fertility on our mountains, seem also to shed a tear on man's grave who departs, unlike the beauties of summer, to return no more; who fades unlike the sons of the forest, which another summer beholds new clothed, when he is unclothed and forgotten. —Rev. Dr. Andrews.

Many men fail to realize that joy is distinctly moral. It is a fruit of the spiritual life. We have no more right to pray for joy, if we are not doing the things that Jesus said would bring it, than we would have to ask interest in a savings bank in which we had never deposited money. Joy does not happen. It is a flower that springs from roots. It is the inevitable result of certain lines followed and laws obeyed, and so a matter of character. Therefore, we cannot say that joy is like a fine complexion, a distinct addition to the charm of the face, which yet would be structurally perfect without this charm. Joy is a feature, and the face that does not have it is disfigured. The Christian life that is joyless is a discredit to God, and a disgrace to itself.—Maltbie Babcock.

Judaism (See Jews)

There was a twilight before the dawn, and a dawn before the morning, and a morning before the day.— W. E. Gladstone.

Stands midway between Heathenism and Christianity. It rose out of Heathenism as twilight out of night and melted into Christianity as twilight into morning.—Anonymous.

Judge

The cold neutrality of an impartial judge.—Burke.

When a man's life is under debate,
The judge can ne'er too long deliberate.
—Dryden.

A wise judge, by the craft of the law, was never seduced from its purpose.—Southey.

What can innocence hope for,
When such as sit her judges are corrupted?
—Massinger.

It is better that a judge should lean on the side of compassion than severity.—Cervantes.

Heaven is above all yet; there sits a judge,
That no king can corrupt.   —Shakespeare.

The hungry judges soon the sentence sign,
And wretches hang that jurymen may dine.
—Pope.

Let the judges answer to the question of law, and the jurors to the matter of fact.—Law Maxim.

A corrupt judge is not qualified to inquire into the truth.—Horace.

Four things belong to a judge: to hear courteously, to answer wisely, to consider soberly, and to decide impartially.—Socrates.

If judges would make their decisions just, they should behold neither plaintiff, defendant, nor pleader, but only the cause itself.—Livingston.

Judges ought to be more learned than witty, more reverent than plausible, and more advised than confident. Above all things, integrity is their portion and proper virtue.—Bacon.

Judges are but men, and are swayed like other men by vehement prejudices. This is corruption in reality, give it whatever other name you please. —David Dudley Field.

A good judge should never boast of his power, because he can do nothing but what he can do justly: he is not the master, but the minister of the law. Authority without virtue is a very dangerous state.—Thomas Wilson.

                    And then, the justice;
In fair round belly, with good capon lin'd,
With eyes severe, and beard of formal cut,
Full of wise saws and modern instances,
And so he plays his part.   —Shakespeare.

He who the sword of heaven will bear
Should be as holy as severe;
Pattern in himself to know,
Grace to stand, and virtue go;
More nor less to others paying
Than by self-offenses weighing.
Shame to him, whose cruel striking
Kills for faults of his own liking!
                    —Shakespeare.

Judgment

Forbear to judge, for we are sinners all.—Shakespeare.

Wise judges are we of each other! —Richelieu.

When we love, it is the heart that judges.—Joubert.

Judge thyself with a judgment of sincerity, and thou wilt judge others with a judgment of charity.—Mason.

The more one judges, the less one loves.—Balzac.

No man should be judge in his own case.—Law Maxim.

Extreme justice is extreme injustice.—Cicero.

He hurts the good who spares the bad.—Syrus.

For every event is a judgment of God.—Schiller.

Judgment is forced upon us by experience.—Johnson.

Make not thyself the judge of any man.—Longfellow.

One man's word is no man's word; we should quietly hear both sides.— Goethe.

Who upon earth could live were all judged justly?—Byron.

Every one complains of the badness of his memory, but nobody of his judgment.—Rochefoucauld.

'Tis with our judgments as our watches; none
Go just alike, yet each believes his own.
                    —Pope.

The right of private judgment is absolute in every American citizen.— James A. Garfield.

The judgment of a great people is often wiser than the wisest men.— Kossuth.

Judging is balancing an account, and determining on which side the odds lie.—Locke.

I will chide no heathen in the world, but myself, against whom I know most faults.—Shakespeare.

The world is an excellent judge in general, but a very bad one in particular.—Lord Greville.

A judgment is the mental act by which one thing is affirmed or denied of another.—Sir W. Hamilton.

And how his audit stands, who knows, save Heaven?—Shakespeare.

How would you be if He, which is the top of judgment, should but judge you as you are?—Shakespeare.

Men's judgments sway on that side fortune leans.—George Chapman.

Outward judgment often fails, inward justice never.—Theodore Parker.

Hear one side, and you will be in the dark; hear both sides, and all will be clear.—Haliburton.

I can promise to be sincere, but I cannot promise to be impartial.—Goethe.

There are no judgments so harsh as those of the erring, the inexperienced, and the young.—Miss Mulock.

I mistrust the judgment of every man in a case in which his own wishes are concerned.—Wellington.

They, judgment and reason, have been grandjurymen since before Noah was a sailor.—Shakespeare.

Next to sound judgment, diamonds and pearls are the rarest things to be met with.—Bruyère.

O judgment! thou art fled to brutish beasts,
And men have lost their reason!
　　　　　　　—Shakespeare.

We shall be judged, not by what we might have been, but what we have been.—Sewell.

Woe to him, * * * who has no court of appeal against the world's judgment.—Carlyle.

Human judgment is finite, and it ought always to be charitable.—William Winter.

How little do they see what is, who frame
Their hasty judgment upon that which seems.
　　　　　　　—Southey.

If we will measure other people's corn in our own bushel, let us first take it to the Divine standard, and have it sealed.—J. G. Holland.

Judge thyself with a judgment of sincerity, and thou wilt judge others with a judgment of charity.—Mason.

We judge ourselves by what we feel capable of doing, while others judge us by what we have already done.—Longfellow.

The very thing that men think they have got the most of, they have got the least of; and that is judgment.—H. W. Shaw.

How are we justly to determine in a world where there are no innocent ones to judge the guilty?—Madame de Genlis.

Men are not to be judged by their looks, habits, and appearances; but by the character of their lives and conversations, and by their works.—L'Estrange.

The most generous and merciful in judgment upon the faults of others, are always the most free from faults themselves.—Aughey.

Give every man thy ear, but few thy voice;
Take each man's censure, but reserve by
　judgment.　　　　　　—Shakespeare.

We neither know nor judge ourselves; others may judge, but cannot know us. God alone judges and knows us.—Wilkie Collins.

In judging of others, a man laboreth in vain,—often erreth and easily sinneth; but in judging and examining himself, he always laboreth fruitfully.—Thomas à Kempis.

For we must all appear before the judgment-seat of Christ, that every one may receive the things done in his body, according to that he hath done, whether it be good or bad.—Bible.

Rashly, nor ofttimes truly, doth man pass judgment on his brother; for he seeth not the springs of the heart, nor heareth the reasons of the mind.—Tupper.

Fools measure actions after they are done by the event; wise men beforehand, by the rules of reason and right. The former look to the end to judge of the act. Let me look to the act, and leave the end to God.— Bishop Hale.

O, how full of error is the judgment of mankind. They wonder at results when they are ignorant of the reasons. They call it fortune when they know not the cause, and thus worship their own ignorance changed into a deity.—Metastasio.

In forming a judgment, lay your hearts void of fore-taken opinions; else, whatsoever is done or said, will be measured by a wrong rule; like them who have the jaundice, to whom everything appeareth yellow.—Sir P. Sidney.

It is very questionable, in my mind, how far we have the right to judge one of another, since there is born within every man the germs of both virtue and vice. The development of one or the other is contingent upon circumstances.—Ballou.

The judgment may be compared to a clock or watch, where the most ordinary machine is sufficient to tell the hours; but the most elaborate alone can point out the minutes and seconds, and distinguish the smallest differences of time.—Fontenelle.

Foolish men imagine that because judgment for an evil thing is delayed, there is no justice, but an accident alone, here below. Judgment for an evil thing is many times delayed some day or two, some century or two; but it is sure as life, it is sure as death! —Carlyle.

Ev'n not all these, in one rich lot combined,
Can make the happy man, without the mind,
Where judgment sits clear-sighted, and surveys
The chain of reason with unerring gaze.
—Thomson.

It behooves us always to bear in mind, that while actions are always to be judged by the immutable standard of right and wrong, the judgments which we pass upon men must be qualified by considerations of age,

country, station, and other accidental circumstances; and it will then be found that he who is most charitable in his judgment is generally the least unjust.—Southey.

God does not weigh criminality in our scales. We have one absolute, with the seal of authority upon it; and with us an ounce is an ounce, and a pound a pound. God's measure is the heart of the offender,—a balance which varies with every one of us, a balance so delicate that a tear cast in the other side may make the weight of error kick the beam.— Lowell.

Would that our harsh judgments could be restrained, our impatience checked, our selfishness broken down, our passions controlled, our waste of time and life in worthless or unworthy objects corrected, by the thought that there is One in whose hands we are, who cares for us with a parent's love, who will judge us hereafter without the slightest tinge of human infirmity, the All-Merciful and the All-Just.—Dean Stanley.

Judgment Day

Truly at the day of judgment we shall not be examined as to what we have read, but as to what we have done; not as to how well we have spoken, but as to how religiously we have lived.—Thomas à Kempis.

Oh, on that day, that wrathful day,
When man to judgment wakes from clay,
Be Thou, O Christ, the sinner's stay,
Though heaven and earth shall pass away.
—Walter Scott.

We are all approaching that dread tribunal. However diversified our paths, they all converge toward that common centre. The young, with their elastic tread, are striding to the judgment; the old, with their tottering limbs are creeping to the judgment; the rich in their splendid equipages are driving to the judgment; the poor in rags and barefooted are walking to the judgment. The Christian making God's statutes his song, is a pilgrim to the judgment; the sinner, treading upon the mercy of Jesus, and trampling upon His blood, is hastening to the judgment. "We must all appear before the judgment-seat of Christ."—Richard Fuller.

Glorious transformation! glorious translation! I seem already to behold the wondrous scene. The sea and the land have given up their dead! the quickened myriads have been judged according to their works. And now, an innumerable company, out of all nations and tribes and tongues, ascend with the Mediator towards the kingdom of His Father. Can it be that these, who were born children of earth, who were long enemies to God by wicked works, are to enter the bright scenes of paradise? Yes, He who leads them has washed them in His blood; He who leads them has sanctified them by His Spirit.—Henry Melvill.

Meanwhile the globe begins to tremble on its axis; the moon is covered with a bloody veil, the threatening stars hang half detached from the vault of heaven, and the agony of the world commences. Then, all at once, the fatal hour strikes; God suspends the movements of the creation, and the earth has passed away like an exhausted river. Now resounds the trumpet of the angel of judgment; and the cry is heard, "Arise, ye dead!" The sepulchres burst open with a terrific noise, the human race issues all at once from the tomb, and the assembled multitudes fill the valley of Jehoshaphat. Behold, the Son of Man appears in the clouds; the powers of hell ascend from the depths of the abyss to witness the last judgment pronounced upon the ages; the goats are separated from the sheep, the wicked are plunged into the gulf, the just ascend triumphantly to heaven, God returns to His repose, and the reign of eternity commences.—Chateaubriand.

June

And what is so rare as a day in June?
Then, if ever, come perfect days;
Then heaven tries earth if it be in tune,
And over it softly her warm ear lays.
    —Lowell.

It is the month of June,
    The month of leaves and roses,
When pleasant sights salute the eyes
And pleasant scents the noses.
            —N. P. Willis.

June falls asleep upon her bier of flowers;
In vain are dewdrops sprinkled o'er her,
In vain would fond winds fan her back to life,
Her hours are numbered on the floral dial.
        —Lucy Larcom.

July

The summer looks out from her brazen tower,
Through the flashing bars of July.
            —Francis Thompson.

Loud is the summer's busy song
The smallest breeze can find a tongue,
While insects of each tiny size
Grow teasing with their melodies,
Till noon burns with its blistering breath
Around, and day lies still as death.
                —Clare.

The linden, in the fervors of July,
Hums with a louder concert. When the wind
Sweeps the broad forest in its summer prime,
As when some master-hand exulting sweeps
The keys of some great organ, ye give forth
The music of the woodland depths, a hymn
Of gladness and of thanks.   —Bryant.

Jury

Do not your juries give their verdict
As if they felt the cause, not heard it.
                —Butler.

The hungry judges soon the sentence sign,
And wretches hang, that jurymen may dine.
                    —Pope.

The jury, passing on the prisoner's life,
May, in the sworn twelve, have a thief or two
Guiltier than him they try.—Shakespeare.

In my mind he was guilty of no error, he was chargeable with no exaggeration, he was betrayed by his fancy into no metaphor, who once said, that all we see about us, Kings, Lords, and Commons, the whole machinery of the state, all the apparatus of the system, and its varied workings, end in simply bringing twelve good men into a box.—Lord Brougham.

Justice

Heaven's slow but sure redress of human ills.—Owen Meredith.

Justice is truth in action.—Joubert.

Justice is the soul of the universe.
—Omar Khayam.

Justice satisfies everybody, and justice alone.—Emerson.

Justice delayed is justice denied.—Gladstone.

Justice without wisdom is impossible.—Froude.

Delay of justice is injustice.—Landor.

He who is only just is cruel.—Byron.

Justice always whirls in equal measure.—Shakespeare.

Justice is the great end of civil society.—David Dudley Field.

Moderation is the basis of justice.—George MacDonald.

The great soul of this world is just.—Carlyle.

Justice is lame as well as blind among us.—Otway.

The books are balanced in heaven, not here.—H. W. Shaw.

Let us be sacrificers, but no butchers.—Shakespeare.

Let justice be done, though the heavens should fall.—Motto of Emperor Ferdinand I.

Peace, if possible, but justice at any rate.—Wendell Phillips.

The virtue of justice consists in moderation, as regulated by wisdom.—Aristotle.

Justice discards party, friendship, kindred, and is always, therefore, represented as blind.—Addison.

There is no virtue so truly great and godlike as justice.—Addison.

It is impossible to be just if one is not generous.—Joseph Roux.

Every place is safe to him who lives with justice.—Epictetus.

Be just in all thy actions, and if join'd
With those that are not, never change thy
mind.   —Denham.

God's mill grinds slow, but sure.—George Herbert.

The sweet remembrance of the just
Shall flourish when he sleeps in dust.
            —Paraphrase of Psalm cxii. 6.

Above all other things is justice: success is a good thing; wealth is good also; honor is better; but justice excels them all.—David Dudley Field.

Man is unjust, but God is just; and finally justice triumphs.—Longfellow.

The hope of all who suffer,
The dread of all who wrong.
                    —Whittier.

Poise the cause in justice's equal scales,
Whose beam stands sure, whose rightful
    cause prevails.   —Shakespeare.

Whoever fights, whoever falls,
Justice conquers evermore.
                    —Emerson.

No obligation to justice does force a man to be cruel, or to use the sharpest sentence.—Jeremy Taylor.

Justice, being destroyed, will destroy; being preserved, will preserve.—Manu.

Justice is but the distributing to everything according to the requirements of its nature.—Glanvill.

Justice is like the north star, which is fixed, and all the rest revolve about it.—Confucius.

Justice is the bread of the nation; it is always hungry for it.—Chateaubriand.

Pity and forbearance should characterize all acts of justice.—Franklin.

Sound policy is never at variance with substantial justice.—Dr. Parr.

The injustice of men subserves the justice of God, and often His mercy.—Madame Swetchine.

Justice consists in doing no injury to men; decency, in giving them no offence.—Cicero.

All religion and all ethics are summed up in justice.—Conway.

Men are always invoking justice; yet it is justice which should make them tremble.—Mme. Swetchine.

Liberty, equality,—bad principles! The only true principle for humanity is justice, and justice towards the feeble becomes necessarily protection or kindness.—Amiel.

I beseech you,
Wrest once the law to your authority:
To do a great right, do a little wrong.
—Shakespeare.

Justice is the fundamental and almost only virtue of social life, as it embraces all those actions which are useful to society.—Volney.

Justice offers nothing but what may be accepted with honor; and lays claim to nothing in return but what we ought not even to wish to withhold.—Woman's Rights and Duties.

The sentiment of justice is so natural, so universally acquired by all mankind, that it seems to me independent of all law, all party, all religion.—Voltaire.

Justice is the insurance which we have on our lives and property; to which may be added, and obedience is the premium which we pay for it.—William Penn.

Truth is its handmaid, freedom is its child, peace is its companion, safety walks in its steps, victory follows in its train; it is the brightest emanation from the gospel, it is the attribute of God.—Sydney Smith.

God gives manhood but one clew to success,—utter and exact justice; that he guarantees shall be always expediency.—Wendell Phillips.

God's justice, tardy though it prove perchance,
Rests never on the track until it reach
Delinquency.   —Robert Browning.

Thrice is he arm'd that hath his quarrel just,
And he but naked, though lock'd up in steel,
Whose conscience with injustice is corrupted.   —Shakespeare.

Justice is the idea of God, the ideal of man, the rule of conduct writ in the nature of mankind.—Theodore Parker.

Be just and fear not:
Let all the ends thou aim'st at be thy country's,
Thy God's, and truth's.   —Shakespeare.

Justice is the great interest of man on earth. It is the ligament which holds civilized beings and civilized nations together.—Webster.

In matters of equity between man and man, our Saviour has taught us to put my neighbor in place of myself, and myself in place of my neighbor.—Dr. Watts.

Who shall put his finger on the work of justice, and say, "It is there"? Justice is like the kingdom of God: it is not without us as a fact; it is within us as a great yearning.—George Eliot.

At present we can only reason of the divine justice from what we know of justice in man. When we are in other scenes, we may have truer and nobler ideas of it; but while we are in this life, we can only speak from the volume that is laid open before us.—Pope.

Though justice be thy plea, consider this, that in the course of justice none of us should see salvation. We do pray for mercy; and that same prayer doth teach us all to render the deeds of mercy.—Shakespeare.

Ay, justice, who evades her?
  Her scales reach every heart;
The action and the motive,
  She weigheth each apart;
And none who swerve from right or truth
  Can 'scape her penalty.   —Mrs. Hale.

———

Justice is immortal, eternal, and immutable, like God Himself; and the development of law is only then a progress when it is directed towards those principles which like Him, are eternal; and whenever prejudice or error succeeds in establishing in customary law any doctrine contrary to eternal justice.—Kossuth.

———

Justice is passionless and therefore sure;
Guilt for a while may flourish; virtue sink
'Neath the shade of calumny and ill; justice
At last, like the bright sun, shall break majestic forth,
The shield of innocence, the guard of truth.   —J. F. Smith.